Born in New Orleans in 1941, the second daughter of an Irish Catholic family, Anne Rice is the author of the phenomenally successful Vampire Chronicles beginning with *Interview with the Vampire*. She has also written twenty-one other novels, including three books in the Mayfair Witches sequence. After many years in San Francisco, she now lives in California.

Further praise for *Servant of the Bones*

'Rice's writing is wonderfully imaginative and as creepily splendid as a hot-house orchid' *Sunday Times*

'Her work has echoes of the freewheeling, fast-talking style of the eighteenth-century novel . . . lush, baroque prose . . . fantastical plots . . . Rice keeps her nerve and her triumphant sense of prose' *Observer*

'Another tale of destruction, sex and monsters – no-one does this better' *Lancashire Evening Post*

'Maintains your interest right to the end and beyond . . . She has always had a way with a story . . . there's no better woman to keep pages turning . . . as strange, and strangely compelling, as all her other books. *Servant of the Bones* has plenty of Rice hallmarks' *Irish Times*

'Rice at her descriptive best . . . Her imaginative energies are at their strongest' *Kirkus*

'Plenty of Rice's trademarks' *Guardian*

'A real gift for rendering physically changed mood and melancholy atmosphere' *New York Times Book Review*

Servant of the Bones

The Feast of All Saints

Anne Rice

arrow books

Arrow Books
The Random House Group Limited
20 Vauxhall Bridge Road, London SW1V 2SA

www.randomhouse.co.uk

Addresses for companies within The Random House Group Limited
can be found at:
www.randomhouse.co.uk/offices.htm

The Random House Group Limited Reg. No. 954009

A CIP catalogue record for this book
is available from the British Library

ISBN 9780099524748

The Random House Group Limited makes every effort to ensure
that the papers used in its books are made from trees that
have been legally sourced from well-managed and credibly
certified forests. Our paper procurement policy can be found at:
www.randomhouse.co.uk/paper.htm

Printed and bound in Great Britain by
Cox & Wyman Ltd, Reading, Berkshire

SERVANT OF
THE BONES

This book
is
dedicated
to
GOD.

By the rivers of Babylon, there we sat down, yea, we wept, when we remembered Zion.

We hanged our harps upon the willows in the midst thereof.

For there they that carried us away captive required of us a song; and they that wasted us *required of us* mirth, *saying*, Sing us *one* of the songs of Zion.

How shall we sing the Lord's song in a strange land?

If I forget thee, O Jerusalem, let my right hand forget *her cunning*.

If I do not remember thee, let my tongue cleave to the roof of my mouth; if I prefer not Jerusalem above my chief joy.

Remember, O Lord, the children of Edom in the day of Jerusalem; who said, Rase *it*, rase *it*, *even* to the foundation thereof.

O daughter of Babylon, who art to be destroyed; happy *shall he be*, that rewardeth thee as thou hast served us.

Happy *shall he be*, that taketh and dasheth thy little ones against the stones.

Proem

Murdered. Her hair was black and so were her eyes. It happened on Fifth Avenue, the murder, inside a fine clothing store, amid hustle and bustle. Hysteria as she fell . . . perhaps.

Soundlessly I saw it on the television screen. Esther. I knew her. Yes, Esther Belkin. She'd been a student once in my class. Esther. Rich and lovely to behold.

Her father. He was the head of that worldwide temple. New Age platitudes and T-shirts. And the Belkins had all the money human beings could ever want or dream of, and now Esther, sweet Esther, that flower of a girl who had always asked her questions so timidly – was dead.

On the news, 'live,' I think I saw her die. I was reading a book, not paying much attention. The news went on in silence, mingling movie stars and war. It made slow garish flickers on the walls of the room. The silent leap and flare of a television watched by no one. I read on after she died 'live.'

Now and then in the days that followed I thought about her. Some horrors followed her death, having to do with her father and his electronic church. More blood shed.

I never knew her father. His followers had been detritus on street corners.

But I remembered Esther pretty well. She wanted to know everything, one of those kind, humble, ever listening, and sweet, yes, very sweet. I remembered her. Sure. Ironic, that doe of a girl slain and then the tragedy of her father's delusions.

I never tried to understand the whole story.

I forgot about her. I forgot that she'd been murdered. I forgot about her father. I guess I forgot that she'd ever been alive.

There was news and news and news.

It was time to stop teaching for a while.

I went away to write my book. I went up into the

mountains. I went to the snow. I hadn't so much as offered a prayer in Esther Belkin's memory, but I am a historian and not a praying man.

In the mountains, I learnt everything. Her death came after me, vivid and lush with meaning, through the words of another.

Part I

THE BONES OF WOE

Golden are the bones of woe.
Their brilliance has no place to go.
It plunges inward,
Spikes through snow.

Of weeping fathers whom we drink
And mother's milk and final stink
We can dream but cannot think.
Golden bones encrust the brink.

Golden silver copper silk.
Woe is water shocked by milk.
Heart attack, assassin, cancer.
Who would think these bones such dancers.

Golden are the bones of woe.
Skeleton holds skeleton.
Words of ghosts are not to know.
Ignorance is what we learn.

Stan Rice, *Some Lamb* 1975

One

This is Azriel's tale as he told it to me, as he begged me to
bear witness and to record his words. Call me Jonathan as he
did. That was the name he chose on the night he appeared in
my open door and saved my life.

Surely if he hadn't come to seek a scribe, I would have
died before morning.

Let me explain that I am well known in the fields of
history, archaeology, Sumerian scholarship. And Jonathan is
indeed one of the names given me at birth, but you won't
find it on the jackets of my books, which the students study
because they must, or because they love the mysteries of
ancient lore as much as I do.

Azriel knew this – the scholar, the teacher I was – when he
came to me.

Jonathan was a private name for me that we agreed upon
together. He had plucked it from the string of three names on
the copyright pages of my books. And I had answered to it. It
became my name for him during all those hours as he told
his tale – a tale I would never publish under my regular
professorial name, knowing full well, as he did, that this story
would never be accepted alongside my histories.

So I am Jonathan; I am the scribe; I tell the tale as Azriel
told it. It doesn't really matter to him what name I use with
you. It only mattered that one person wrote down what he
had to say. The Book of Azriel was dictated to Jonathan.

He did know who I was; he knew all my works, and had
painstakingly read them before ever coming. He knew my
academic reputation, and something in my style and outlook
had caught his fancy. Perhaps he approved that I had
reached the venerable age of sixty-five, and still wrote and
worked night and day like a young man, with no intentions
of retiring ever from the school where I taught, though I had
now and then to get completely away from it.

So it was no haphazard choice that made him climb the steep forested mountains, in the snow, on foot, carrying only a curled newsmagazine in his hand, his tall form protected by a thick mass of curly black hair that grew long below his shoulders – a true protective mantle for a man's head and neck – and one of those double-tiered and flaring winter coats that only the tall of stature and the romantic of heart can wear with aplomb or the requisite charming indifference.

By the light of the fire, he appeared at once a kind young man, with huge black eyes and thick prominent brows, a small thick nose, and a large cherub's mouth, his hair dappled with snow, the wind blowing his coat wildly about him as it tore through the house, sending my precious papers swirling in all directions.

Now and then this coat became too large for him. His appearance completely changed to match that of the man on the cover of the magazine he'd brought with him.

It was that miracle I saw early on, before I knew who he was, or that I was going to live, that the fever had broken.

Understand I am not insane or even eccentric by nature, and have never been self-destructive. I didn't go to the mountains to die. It had seemed a fine idea to seek out the absolute solitude of my northern house, unconnected to the world by phone, fax, television, or electricity. I had a book to complete which had taken me some ten years, and it was in this self-imposed exile that I meant to finish it.

The house is mine, and was then, as always, well stocked, with plenty of bottled water for drinking, and oil and kerosene for its lamps, candles by the crate, and electric batteries of every conceivable size for the small tape recorder I use and the laptop computers on which I work, and an enormous shed of dried oak for the fires I would need throughout my stay there.

I had the few medical necessaries a man can carry in a metal box. I had the simple food I eat and can cook by fire: rice, hominy, cans upon cans of saltless chicken broth, and also a few barrels of apples which should have lasted me the winter. A sack or two of yams I'd also brought, discovering I

4

could wrap these in foil and roast them in my coal-and-oak fire.

I liked the bright orange color of yams. And please be assured, I was not proud of this diet, or seeking to write a magazine article on it. I'm simply tired of rich food; tired of crowded fashionable New York restaurants and glittering party buffets, and even the often wonderful meals offered me weekly by colleagues at their own tables. I am merely trying to explain. I wanted fuel for the body and the mind.

I brought what I needed so that I might write in peace. There was nothing that peculiar about all this.

The place was already lined in books, its old barn wood walls fully insulated and then shelved to the ceiling. There was a duplicate here of every important text I ever consulted at home, and the few books of poetry I read over and over for ecstasy.

My spare computers, all small and very powerful beyond any understanding I ever hope to acquire of hard drives, bytes, megabytes of memory, or 486 chips, had been delivered earlier, along with a ludicrous supply of diskettes on which to 'back up' or copy my work.

Truth is, I worked mostly by hand, on yellow legal pads. I had cartons of pens, the very fine-point kind, with black ink.

Everything was perfect.

And I should add here that the world I had left behind seemed just a little more mad than usual.

The news was full of a lurid murder trial on the West Coast having to do with a famous athlete accused of slitting his wife's throat, an entertainment par excellence that had galvanized the talk shows, the news shows, and even that vapid, naive, and childlike connection to the world that calls itself E! Entertainment.

In Oklahoma City, a Federal office building had been blown sky high – and not by alien terrorists, it was believed, but by our own Americans, members of the militia movement they were called, who had decided in much the same manner of the hippies of years before that our government was a dangerous enemy. Whereas the hippies and the protesters of the Vietnam War had merely lain on railroad tracks and sung in ranks, these new crewcut militants – filled with fantasies of impending doom – killed our own people. By the hundreds.

Then there were the battles abroad, which had become regular circuses. Not a day went by when one was not reminded of atrocities committed among the Bosnians and the Serbs in the Balkans – a region that had been at war for one reason or another for centuries. I had lost track of who was Moslem, Christian, Russian ally, or friend. The city of Sarajevo had been a familiar word to television-watching Americans for years now. In the streets of Sarajevo people died daily, including men they called United Nations peace keepers.

In African countries, people starved as the result of civil strife and famine. It was a nightly sight as common as a beer commercial to see on television fresh footage of starving African babies, bellies swollen, faces covered with flies.

Jews and Arabs fought in the streets of Jerusalem. Bombs went off; protesters were shot at by armies; and terrorists destroyed innocent people to strengthen their demands.

In the Ukraine, remnants of a fallen Soviet Union made war on mountain folk who had never given in to any foreign power. People died in the snow and cold for reasons that were nearly impossible to explain.

In sum there were dozens of places raging with suffering in which to fight, to die, to film, as the parliaments of the world tried in vain to find answers without bullets. The decade was a feast of wars.

Then there was the death of Esther Belkin, followed by the scandal of the Temple of the Mind. Caches of assault weapons had been found in the Temple's outposts from New Jersey to Libya. Explosives and poisonous gases had been stockpiled in its hospitals. The great mentor of this popular international church – Gregory Belkin – was insane.

Before Gregory Belkin, there had been other madmen with great dreams perhaps but smaller resources. Jim Jones and his People's Temple committing mass suicide in the jungles of Guyana; David Koresh, who believed himself the

Christ, perishing by gun and fire in a Waco, Texas, compound.

A Japanese religious leader had just recently been accused of killing innocent people on the country's public subways.

A church with the lovely name of the Temple Solaire had not so long ago staged a mass suicide coordinated at three different locations in Switzerland and Canada.

A popular talk show host gave directions to his listeners as to how they might assassinate the President of the United States.

A fatal virus had only recently broken out with stunning fury in an African country, then died away, leaving all thinking individuals with a renewed interest in the age-old obsession: that the end of the world might be at hand. Apparently there were more than three kinds of this virus, and numerous others equally as deadly lurking in the rain forests of the world.

A hundred other surreal stories made up each day's news, and each day's inevitable civilized conversation.

So I ran from this, as much as anything else. I ran for the solitude, the whiteness of snow, the brutal indifference of towering trees and tiny winter stars.

It was my own jeep which had brought me up through 'the leather stocking woods,' as it is sometimes still called, in honor of James Fenimore Cooper, to barricade myself for the winter. There was a phone in the jeep by which one could, with perseverance if possible, reach the outside world. I was for tearing it out, but the truth is I'm not very handy and I couldn't get the thing loose without damaging my car.

So you see, I am not a fool, just a scholar. I had a plan. I was prepared for the heavy snow to come, and the winds to whistle in the single metal chimney above the round central hearth. The smell of my books, the oak fire, the snow itself whirling down at times in tiny specks into the flames, these things I love and need now and then. And many a winter before this house had given me exactly what I asked of it.

The night began like any other. The fever took me completely by surprise, and I remember building up the fire in the round pit of a fireplace very high because I did not

7

want to have to tend it. When I drank all the water nearest the bed, I don't know. I couldn't have been fully conscious then. I know that I went to the door, that I myself unbolted it, and then could not get it closed; this much I do recall. I must have been trying to reach the jeep.

Bolting the door was simply impossible. I lay for a long time in the snow itself before I crawled back inside, and away from the mouth of the winter, or so it seemed.

I remember these things because I remember knowing then that I was very much in danger. The long journey back to the bed, the long journey back to the warmth of the fire, utterly exhausted me. Beneath the heap of wool blankets and quilts, I hid from the whirlwind that entered my house. And I knew that if I didn't clear my head, if I didn't recover somehow, the winter would just come inside soon and put to sleep forever the fire, and take me too.

Lying on my back, the quilts up to my chin, I sweated and shivered. I watched the flakes of snow fly beneath the sloping beams of the roof. I watched the raging pyramid of logs as it blazed. I smelled the burnt pot when the soup boiled dry. I saw the snow covering my desk.

I made a plan to rise, then fell asleep. I dreamed those fretful stupid dreams that fever makes, then woke with a start, sat up, fell back, dreamed again. The candles were gone out, but the fire still burned, and snow now filled the room, blanketing my desk, my chair, perhaps the bed itself. I licked snow from my lips once, that I do recall, and it tasted good, and now and then I licked the melted snow I could gather with my hand. My thirst was hellish. Better to dream than to feel it.

It must have been midnight when Azriel came.

Did he choose his hour with a sense of drama? Quite to the contrary. A long way off, walking through snow and wind, he had seen the fire high on the mountain above, sparks flying from the chimney and a light that blinkered through the open door. He had hurried towards these beacons.

Mine was the only house on the land and he knew it. He had learnt that from the casual tactful remarks of those who had told him officially and gently that I could not be reached in the months to come, that I had gone into hiding.

I saw him the very moment he stood in the door. I saw the sheen of his mass of black curling hair and fire in both his eyes. I saw the strength and swiftness with which he closed and locked the door and came directly towards me.

I believe I said, 'I'm going to die.'

'No, you won't, Jonathan,' he answered. He brought the bottle of water at once and lifted my head. I drank and I drank and my fever drank, and I blessed him.

'It's only kindness, Jonathan,' he said with simplicity.

I dozed as he built up the fire again, wiped away the snow, and I have a very distinct and wondrous memory of him gathering my papers from everywhere, with great care, and kneeling by the fire to lay them out so that they might dry and some of the writing might be saved after all.

'This is your work, your precious work,' he said to me when he saw that I was watching him.

He had taken off the big double-mantled coat. He was in shirt sleeves which meant we were safe. I smelled the soup cooking again, the bubbling chicken broth. He brought the soup to me in an earthen bowl – the sort of rustic things I chose for this place – and he said drink the soup, and I did.

Indeed, it was by water and broth that he brought me slowly back. Never once did I have the presence of mind to mention the few medications in the white box of first-aid supplies. He bathed my face with cold water.

He bathed all of me slowly and patiently, turning me gently, and rolling under me the new fresh clean sheets. 'The broth,' he said, 'the broth, no, you must.' And the water. The water he gave me perpetually.

Was there enough for him, he had asked. I had almost laughed.

'Of course, my friend, dear God, take anything you want.'

And he drank the water down in greedy gulps, saying it was all he needed now, that once again the Stairway to Heaven had disappeared and left him stranded.

'My name is Azriel,' he said, sitting by the bed. 'They

called me the Servant of the Bones,' he said, 'but I became a rebel ghost, a bitter and impudent genii.'

He unfurled the magazine for me to see. My head was clear. I sat up, propped by the divine luxury of clean pillows. He looked as unlike a ghost as a man can look, muscular, brimming with life, the dark hair on the backs of his hands and on his arms making him appear all the more strong and vital.

Gregory Belkin's face stared forward from the famous *Time* magazine frame. Gregory Belkin – Esther's father – founder of the Temple of the Mind. The man who would have brought harm to millions.

'I killed that man,' he said.

I turned to look at him, and then it was that I first saw the miracle.

He wanted me to see it. He did it for me.

He had grown smaller in size, though only slightly; his mane of tangled black curls was gone; he had the trimmed hair of a modern businessman; even his large loose shirt was changed for the supremely acceptable and impeccably tailored black suit, and he had become ... before my very eyes ... the figure of Gregory Belkin.

'Yes,' he said. 'It was the way I looked on the day I made my choice, to forfeit my powers forever; to take on real flesh and real suffering. I looked just like Gregory when I shot him.'

Before I could answer, he began to change again, the head to grow larger, the features to become broader, forehead stronger and more distinctive, the cherub mouth of his own to replace the thin line of Belkin's. His fierce eyes grew large beneath the thick eyebrows that tended to dip as he smiled, making the smile and immensity of the eyes seem secretive and seductive.

It was not a happy smile. It had no humor or sweetness in it.

'I thought I would look this way forever,' he said, holding up the magazine for me to see. 'I thought I would die in that form.' He sighed. 'The Temple of the Mind lies in ruins. The people will not die. The women and children will not fall on

10

the road as they breathe the evil gas. But I didn't die. I am Azriel again.'

I took his hand. 'You're a living breathing man,' I said. 'I don't know how you made yourself look like Gregory Belkin.'

'No, not a man – a ghost,' he said, 'a ghost so strong that he can wrap himself in the form he had when he was alive; and now he cannot make it go away. Why did God do this to me? I am not an innocent being; I have sinned. But why can't I die?'

Suddenly a smile came over his face. He was almost a boy, the tangled curls making their dark frame for his low cheeks and the large beautiful cherub mouth.

'Maybe God let me live to save you, Jonathan. Maybe that's all it was. He gave me my old flesh back so I could climb this mountain and tell you all this, and you would have died had I not come here.'

'Perhaps, Azriel,' I said.

'You rest now,' he said. 'Your forehead is cool. I'll wait, and I'll watch, and if you see me, now and then, turn into that man again, it is only that I'm trying to measure each time the difficulty of it. It was never so very hard for me to change my shape – for the sorcerer who called me up from the bones. It was never so hard for me to throw an illusion to trick my master's enemies or those he would rob or cheat.

'But it's hard now to be anything but the young man I was when it started. When I bought their lies. When I became a ghost and not the martyr they promised. Lie still now, Jonathan, sleep. Your eyes are clear and your cheeks have color.'

'Give me more of the broth,' I said.

He did.

'Azriel, I *would* be dead without you.'

'Yes, that much is true, isn't it? But I had my foot on the Ladder to Heaven, I was on it this time, I tell you, when I made this choice, and I thought when it was all over, the Temple destroyed, the Stairway might come down for me again. The Hasidim are pure and innocent. They are good. But battles they must leave to monsters like me.'

'Lord, God,' I said. Gregory Belkin. A lunatic plan. I

remember fragments … 'And there was that beautiful girl,' I said.

He put down the cup of broth, and wiped my face and my hands.

'Her name was Esther.'

'Yes.'

He opened the curled and damp magazine for me. It was now badly creased as it was drying out in the warm room. I saw the famous photograph of Esther Belkin, on Fifth Avenue. I saw her lying on the stretcher just before they had put her into the ambulance, and just before she had died.

Only this time I focused on a figure in this photograph which I had noticed before, yes, in television broadcasts, and in the larger cover photographs of this very scene. But I hadn't until now paid any real attention to the figure. I saw a young man by Esther's stretcher, with his hands raised to his head, as though crying out in grief for her, a young man blurry and indistinct as all the other crowd figures in the famous photograph, except for his heavy beautifully shaped eyebrows and his mane of thick black curly hair.

'That's you,' I said. 'Azriel, that's you there in the photograph.'

He was distracted. He didn't reply. He put his finger on the figure of Esther. 'She died there, Esther, his daughter.'

I explained that I had known her. The Temple was new then, and controversial rather than solid and immense and indefatigable. She had been a good student, serious and modest and alert.

He looked at me for a long time. 'She was a sweet, kind girl, wasn't she?'

'Yes, very much so. Very unlike her stepfather.'

He pointed to his own shape in the picture.

'Yes, the ghost, the Servant of the Bones,' he said. 'I was visible then in my grief. I will never know who called me. Maybe it was only her death, the dark horrible beauty of it. I'll never know. But you see now, you feel now, I have the solid shape of that form which was nothing before but vapor. God has wrapped me in my old flesh; he makes it harder and harder for me to vanish and return; to take to the air and to

12

nothingness and to reassemble. What is to become of me, Jonathan? As I grow stronger and stronger in this seeming human form, I fear I *can't* die. I will never.'

'Azriel, you must tell me everything.'

'Everything? Oh, I want to, Jonathan. I want to.'

Within an hour, I was able to walk about the house without dizziness. He'd found my thick robe for me, and my leather slippers. Within a few more hours I was hungry.

It must have been morning when I fell asleep. And then waking in the later afternoon, I was myself, clearheaded, sharp, and the house was not only safely warmed by the fire, but he had put a few candles around, the thick kind, so that the corners had a dusty soft nonintrusive light.

'Is it all right?' he asked me gently.

I told him to put out a few more. And to light the kerosene lamp on my desk. He did these things with no trouble. A match was no mystery to him, or a cigarette lighter. He raised the wick of the lamp. He put two more of the candles on the stone-top table by the bed.

The room, with its wooden windows bolted shut as tight as its door, was softly, evenly visible. The wind howled in the chimney. Again came the volley of flakes dissolving in the heat. The storm had slackened but the snow still fell. The winter surrounded us.

And no one will come, no one will disturb us, no one will distract us. I stared at him in keen interest. I was happy. Uncommonly happy.

I taught him how to make cowboy coffee by merely throwing the grinds into the pot, and I drank plenty of it, loving the smell of it.

Though he wanted to do it, I mixed up the grits for a good meal, showing him again how it came in little packets, and all one had to do was boil the water on the fire, and then stir the grits to a thick delicious porridge.

He watched me eat it. He said he wanted nothing.

'Why don't you taste it?' I said. I begged.

'Because my body won't take it,' he said. 'It's not human, I told you.'

He stood up and walked slowly to the door. I thought he

13

might open it on the storm and I hunkered my shoulders, ready for the blast. I would not even consider asking him to keep it shut. After all he had done, if he wanted to see the snow, I wouldn't deny him anything.

But he lifted his arms. And without the door being opened, there came a blast of wind and his figure paled, seemed to swirl for a moment, its colors and textures mingled in a vortex and then vanished.

Spellbound, I rose from my place by the fire. I held the bowl to my chest in a desperate childlike gesture.

The wind died away. He was nowhere to be seen, and then, when the wind came again, it was hot: a blast as if from a furnace.

Azriel stood opposite the fire, looking at me. Same white shirt, same black pants. The same dark black hair of his chest thick beneath his open collar.

'Will I never be *nefesh*?' he asked. 'That is, body and soul together.'

I knew the Hebrew word.

I sat him down. He said he could drink water. He said that all ghosts and spirits could drink water, and they drank up the scents of sacrifice and that was why all the ancient talk of libations and of incense, of burnt offerings and of smoke rising from the altars. He drank the water, and it seemed to relax him again.

He sat back in one of my many cracked and broken leather chairs, oblivious to its worn crevices and rips. He put his feet up on the stone hearth, and I saw his shoes were still wet.

I finished my meal, cleared it away, and came back with the picture of Esther. At this round hearth, six people could have sat in a circle. We were near to one another, near enough, him with his back to the desk and beyond it the door, and I with my back to the warmer, smaller, darker corner of the room in my favorite chair, of broken springs and round fat arms, stained from careless wine and coffee.

I looked at her. She was half a page, in this the recurrent story of her death which had been retold only because of Gregory's downfall.

'He killed her, didn't he?' I said. 'It was the first assassination.'

'Yes,' Azriel answered. I marveled that his eyebrows could be so thick, beautiful and brooding, and yet his mouth so gentle as he smiled. There was no double to die in her place. He killed his own stepdaughter.

'That's when I came, you see,' he went on. 'That's when I came out of the darkness as if called by the master sorcerer, only there was none. I appeared fully formed and hurrying down the New York street, only to witness her death, her cruel death, and to kill those who killed her.'

'The three men? The men who stabbed Esther Belkin?'

He didn't answer. I remembered. The men had been stabbed with their own ice picks only a block and a half away from the crime. So thick was the crowd on Fifth Avenue that day that no one even connected the deaths of three street toughs with the slaughter of the beautiful girl inside the fashionable store of Henri Bendel. Only the next day had the ice picks told the story of blood, her blood on three, their blood on the one chosen by someone to do away with them.

'I suppose I thought it was part of his plot, then,' I said. 'She was killed by terrorists, he said, and he had disposed of those henchmen so that he might make the lie bigger and bigger.'

'No, those henchmen were to *get away*, so that he could make the lie of the terrorists bigger and bigger. But I came there, and I killed them.' He looked at me. 'She saw me through the window before she died, the window of the ambulance that came to take her away, and she said my name: "Azriel."'

'Then she called you.'

'No, she was no sorceress; she didn't know the words. She didn't have the Bones. I was the Servant of the Bones.' He fell back in the chair. Quiet, looking at the fire, his eyes fierce and thick with dark curling eyelashes, the bones of his forehead strong as the line of his jaw.

After a long time he cast on me the most bright and innocent boyish smile. 'You're well now, Jonathan. You're cured of your fever.' He laughed.

'Yes,' I said. I lay back enjoying the dry warmth of the room, the smell of burning oak. I drank the coffee until I tasted the grounds in my teeth, then I put the cup on the circular stone hearth. 'Will you let me record what you tell me?' I asked.

The light shone bright in his face again. With a boy's enthusiasm, he leant forward in the chair, his massive hands on his knees. 'Would you do it? Would you write down what I tell you?'

'I have a machine,' I said, 'that will remember every word for us.'

'Oh, yes, I know,' he said. He smiled contentedly and put his head back. 'You mustn't think me an addlebrained spirit, Jonathan. The Servant of the Bones was never that.

'I was made a strong spirit, I was made what the Chaldeans would have called a genii. When brought forth, I knew all that I should know – of the times, of the language, of the ways of the world near and far – all I need to know to serve my Master.'

I begged him to wait. 'Let me turn on our little recorder,' I said.

It felt good to stand up, for my head not to swim, for my chest not to ache, and for most of the blur of the fever to have been banished.

I put down two small machines, as all of us do who have lost a tale through one. I checked their batteries and that the stones were not too warm for them, and I put the tape cassettes inside and then I said, 'Tell me.' I pressed the buttons so that both little ears would be on full alert. 'And let me say first,' I said, speaking for microphones now, 'that you seem a young man to me, no more than twenty. You've a hairy chest and hair on your arms, and it's dark and healthy, and your skin is an olive tone, and the hair of your head is lustrous and I would think the envy of women.'

'They like to touch it,' he said with a sweet and kindly smile.

'And I trust you,' I said for my record. 'I trust you. You saved my life, and I trust you. And I don't know why I should. I myself have seen you change into another man.

16

Later I will think I dreamt it. I've seen you vanish and come back. Later I won't believe it. I want this recorded too, by the scribe. Jonathan. Now we can begin your story, Azriel.

'Forget this room, forget this time. Go to the beginning for me, will you? Tell me what a ghost knows, how a ghost begins, what a ghost remembers of the living but no ...' I stopped, letting the cassettes turn. 'I've made my worst mistake already.'

'And what is that, Jonathan?' he asked.

'You have a tale you want to tell and you should tell it.'

He nodded. 'Kindly teacher,' he said, 'let's draw a little closer. Let's bring our chairs near. Let's bring our little machines closer so that we can talk softly. But I don't mind beginning as you wish. I want to begin that way. I want for it all to be known, at least, to both of us.'

We made the adjustments as he asked, the arms of our chairs touching. I made a movement to clasp his hand and he didn't draw back; his handshake was firm and warm. And when he smiled again, the little dip of his brows made him look almost playful. But it was only the way his face was made – brows that curve down in the middle to make a frown, and then curve gently up and out from the nose. They give a face a look of peering from a secret vantage point, and they make its smile all the more radiant.

He took a drink of the water, a long deep drink.

'Does the fire feel good to you, too?' I asked.

He nodded. 'But it looks ever so much better.'

Then he looked at me. 'There will be times when I'll forget myself. I'll speak to you in Aramaic, or in Hebrew. Sometimes in Persian. I may speak Greek or Latin. You bring me back to English, bring me back to your tongue quickly.'

'I will,' I said, 'but never have I so deeply regretted my own lack of education in languages. The Hebrew I would understand, the Latin too, the Persian never.'

'Don't regret,' he said. 'Perhaps you spent that time looking at the stars or the fall of the snow, or making love. My language should be that of a ghost – the language of you and your people. A genii speaks the language of the Master

17

he must serve and of those among whom he must move to do his Master's bidding. I am Master here. I know that now. I have chosen your language for us. That is sufficient.'

We were ready. If this house had ever been warmer and sweeter, if I had ever enjoyed the company of someone else more than I did then, I didn't recall it. I wanted only to be with him and talk to him, and I had a small, painful feeling in my heart, that when he finished his tale, when somehow or other this closeness between us had come to an end, nothing would ever be the same for me.

Nothing was ever the same afterwards.

He began.

Two

I didn't remember Jerusalem,' he said. 'I wasn't born there. My mother was carried off as a child by Nebuchadnezzar along with our whole family, and our tribe, and I was born a Hebrew in Babylon, in a rich house – full of aunts and uncles and cousins – rich merchants, scribes, sometime prophets, and occasional dancers and singers and pages at court.

'Of course,' he smiled. 'Every day of my life, I wept for Jerusalem.' He smiled. 'I sang the song: "If I forget thee, oh Jerusalem, may my right hand wither." And at night prayers we begged the Lord to return us to our land, and at morning prayers as well.

'But what I'm trying to say is that Babylon was my whole life. At twenty, when my life came to its first – shall we say – great tragedy, I knew the songs and gods of Babylon as well as I knew my Hebrew and the Psalms of David that I copied daily, or the book of Samuel, or whatever other texts we were constantly studying as a family.

'It was a grand life. But before I describe myself further, my circumstances, so to speak, let me just talk of Babylon.

'Let me sing the song of Babylon in a strange land. I am not pleasing in the eyes of the Lord or I wouldn't be here, so I think now I can sing the songs I want, what do you think?'

'I want to hear it,' I said gravely. 'Shape it the way you would. Let the words spill. You don't want to be careful with your language, do you? Are you talking to the Lord God now, or are you simply telling your tale?'

'Good question. I'm talking to you so that you will tell the story for me in my words. Yes. I'll rave and cry and blaspheme when I want. I'll let my words come in a torrent. They always did, you know. Keeping Azriel quiet was a family obsession.'

This was the first time I'd seen him really laugh, and it was a light heartfelt laugh that came up as easily as breath, nothing strangled or self-conscious in it.

He studied me.

'My laugh surprises you, Jonathan?' he asked. 'I believe laughter is one of the common traits of ghosts, spirits, and even powerful spirits like me. Have you been through the scholarly accounts? Ghosts are famous for laughing. Saints laugh. Angels laugh. Laughter is the sound of Heaven, I think. I believe. I don't know.'

'Maybe you feel close to Heaven when you laugh,' I said.

'Maybe so,' he said. His large cherubic mouth was really beautiful. Had it been small it would have given him a baby face. But it wasn't small, and with his thick black eyebrows and the large quick eyes, he looked pretty remarkable.

He seemed to be taking my measure again too, as if he had some capacity to read my thoughts. 'My scholar,' he said to me, 'I've read all your books. Your students love you, don't they? But the old Hasidim are shocked by your biblical studies, I suppose.'

'They ignore me. I don't exist for the Hasidim,' I said, 'but for what it's worth my mother was a Hasid, and so maybe I'll have a little understanding of things that will help us.'

I knew now that I liked him, whatever he had done, liked him for himself in a way – young man of twenty, as he said, and though I was still fairly stunned from the fever, from his appearance, from his tricks, I was actually getting used to him.

He waited a few minutes, obviously ruminating, then began to talk:

'Babylon,' he said. 'Babylon! Give the name of any city which echoes as loud and as long as Babylon. Not even Rome, I tell you. And in those days there was no Rome. The center of the world was Babylon. Babylon had been built by the Gods as their gate. Babylon had been the great city of Hammurabi. The ships of Egypt, the Peoples of the Sea, the people of Dilmun, came to the docks of Babylon. I was a happy child of Babylon.

'I've seen what stands today, in Iraq, going there myself to see the walls restored by the tyrant Saddam Hussein. I've seen the mounds of sand that dot the desert, all of this covering old cities and towns that were Assyrian, Babylonian, Judean.

'And I've walked into the museum in Berlin to weep at the sight of what your archaeologist, Koldewey, has re-created of the mighty Ishtar Gate and the Processional Way.

'Oh, my friend, what it was to walk on that street! What it was to look up at those walls of gleaming glazed blue brick, what it was to pass the golden dragons of Marduk.

'But even if you walked the length and breadth of the old Processional Way, you would have only a taste of what was Babylon. All our streets were straight, many paved in limestone and red breccia. We lived as if in a place made of semiprecious stones. Think of an entire city glazed and enameled in the finest colors, think of gardens everywhere.

'The god Marduk built Babylon with his own hands, they told us, and we believed it. Early on I fell in with Babylonian ways and you know everybody had a god, a personal god he prayed to, and beseeched for this and that, and I chose Marduk. Marduk himself was my personal god.

'You can imagine the uproar when I walked in the house with a small pure-gold statue of Marduk, talking to it, the way the Babylonians did. But then my father just laughed. Typical of my father, my beautiful and innocent father.

'And throwing back his head, my father sang in his beautiful voice, "Yahweh is your God, the God of your Father, your Father's Father, the God of Abraham, Isaac, and Jacob."

'To which one of my somber uncles popped up at once, "And what is that idol in his hands!"

'"A toy!" said my father. "Let him play with it. Azriel, when you get sick of all this superstitious Babylonian stuff, break the statue. Or sell it. You cannot break our god, for our god is not in gold or precious metal. He has no temple. He is above such things."

'I nodded, went into my room, which was large and full of silken pillows and curtains, for reasons I'll get to later, and I lay down and I started just, you know, calling on Marduk to be my guardian.

21

'In this day and age, Americans do it with a guardian angel. I don't know how many Babylonians took it all that seriously either, the Babylonian personal god. You know the old saying, "If you plan ahead a god goes with you." Well, what does that mean?'

'The Babylonians,' I said, 'they were a practical people rather than superstitious, weren't they?'

'Jonathan, they were exactly like Americans today. I have never seen a people so like the ancient Sumerians and Babylonians as the Americans of today.

'Commerce was everything, but everybody went about consulting astrologers, talking about magic, and trying to drive out evil spirits. People had families, ate, drank, tried to achieve success in every way possible, yet carried on all the time about luck. Now Americans don't talk about demons, no, but they rattle on about "negative thinking" and "self-destructive ideas" and "bad self-image." It was a lot the same, Babylon and America, a lot the same.

'I would say that here in America I have found the nearest thing to Babylon in the good sense that I have ever found. We were not slaves to our gods! We were not slaves to each other.

'What was I saying? Marduk, my personal god. I prayed to him all the time. I made offerings, you know, little bits of incense when nobody was watching; I poured out a little honey and wine for him in the shrine I made for him in the deep brick wall of my bedroom. Nobody paid much attention.

'But then Marduk began to answer me. I'm not sure when Marduk first started answering me. I think I was still fairly young. I would say something idly to him, "Look, my little brothers are running rampant and my father just laughs as though he were one of them and I have to do everything here!" and Marduk would laugh. As I said spirits laugh. Then he'd say some gentle thing like "You know your father. He will do what you tell him, Big Brother." His voice was soft, a man's voice. He didn't start actually speaking questions in my ear till I was nearly nine and some of these were simply little riddles and jokes and teasing about Yahweh . . .

'He never got tired of teasing me about Yahweh, the god who preferred to live in a tent, and couldn't manage to lead his people out of a little bitty desert for over forty years. He made me laugh. And though I tried to be most respectful, I became more and more familiar with him, and even a little smart mouthed and ill behaved.

'"Why don't you go tell all this nonsense to Yahweh Himself since you are a god?" I asked him. "Invite him to come down to your fabulous temple all full of cedars from Lebanon and gold." And Marduk would fire off with "What? Talk to your god? Nobody can look at the face of your god and live! What do you want to happen to me? What if he turns into a pillar of fire like he did when he brought you out of Egypt . . . ho, ho, ho . . . and smashes my temple and I end up being carried around in a tent!"

'I didn't truly think about it till I was perhaps eleven years old. That was when I first came to know that not everybody heard from his or her personal god, and also I had learnt this: I didn't have to talk to Marduk to start him off talking to me. He could begin the conversation and sometimes at the most awkward moments. He also had bright ideas in his head. "Let's go down into the potters' district, or let's go to the marketplace," and we would.'

'Azriel, let me stop you,' I said. 'When all this happened, you spoke to the little statue of Marduk or you carried it with you?'

'No, not at all, your personal god was always with you, you know. The idol at home, well, it received the incense, yes, I guess you could say that the god came down into it then to smell the incense. But no, Marduk was just there.

'I did, stupidly enough, imitate the habit of other Babylonians of threatening him sometimes . . . you know, saying, "Look, what kind of god are you that you can't help me find my sister's necklace! You won't get any incense out of me!" That was the way with the Babylonians, you know, to bawl out the god fiercely if things didn't go right. They would yell and scream at their personal gods: "Who worships you like I do! Why don't you grant my wishes! Who else would pour out these libations for you!"'

Azriel laughed again. I was considering this whole question which was not unfamiliar to me as a historian naturally. But I laughed too.

'Times haven't changed that much, I don't really think,' I said. 'Catholics can get very angry with their saints when the saints don't get results. And I think once in Naples, when a local saint refused to work a yearly miracle, people stood up in the church and yelled "You pig of a saint!" But how deep do these convictions go?'

'There's an alliance there,' Azriel answered. 'You know, there are several layers to that alliance. Or shall I say, the alliance is a braid of many strands. And the truth lies in this: the gods need us! Marduk needed . . .' He stopped again. He looked suddenly utterly forlorn. He looked at the fire.

'He needed you?'

'Well, he wanted my company,' said Azriel. 'I can't say he needed me. He had all of Babylon. But these feelings, they are impossibly complex.' He looked at me. 'Where are the bones of your father?' he asked.

'Wherever the Nazis buried them in Poland,' I said, 'or in the wind if they were burnt.'

He looked heart stricken at these words.

'You know I'm speaking of our World War II and the Holocaust, the persecution of the Jews, don't you?'

'Yes, yes, I know so very much about it, only to hear that your father and mother were lost to it, it hurts my heart, and it makes my question pointless. I meant only to point out to you that you probably have superstitions about your parents, that's all, that you wouldn't disturb their bones.'

'I have such superstitions,' I said. 'I have them about photographs of my parents. I won't let anything happen to them, and when I do lose one of them, it's a deep sin to me that I did it, as if I insulted my ancestor and my tribe.'

'Ah,' said Azriel, 'that's what I was talking about. And I want to show you something. Where is my coat?'

He got up from the hearth, found the big double-mantled coat, and took out of the inside pocket a small plastic packet. 'This plastic, you know, I rather love it.'

'Yes,' I said, watching him as he came back to the fire,

sank down on the chair, and opened the packet. 'I dare say all the world loves plastic, but why do you?'

'Because it keeps things clean and pure,' he said looking up at me, and then he handed me a picture of what looked like Gregory Belkin. But it wasn't. This man had the long beard and forelocks and the silk black hat of the Hasidim. I was puzzled.

He didn't explain the picture.

'I was made to destroy,' he said, 'and you remember, don't you, the beautiful Hebrew word before so many of the old Psalms, telling us to sing it to that certain melody: "Do Not Destroy."'

I had to think.

'Come on, Jonathan, you know,' he said.

'Altashheth!' I said. '"Do Not Destroy."'

He smiled and his eyes filled with tears. He put back with shaking hands the picture and he laid the plastic packet aside on the small footstool between our chairs, far enough away from the fire for it not to be hurt, and then he looked again at the flames.

I felt the most sudden overwhelming emotion. I couldn't talk. It wasn't only that we had mentioned my mother and father, killed in Poland by the Nazis. It wasn't only that he had reminded me of the mad plot of Gregory Belkin which had come perilously close to success; it wasn't only his beauty, or that we were together, or that I was speaking with a spirit. I don't know what it was.

I thought of Ivan in *The Brothers Karamazov* and I thought, Is this my dream? I am dying actually, the room's filling with snow, and I'm dying, imagining I'm talking to this beautiful young man with curling black hair, like the carvings on the stones from Mesopotamia in the British Museum, those stately kings never feline like the Pharaohs but with hair that was almost sexual on their faces, dark hair, hair as thick as the hair around their balls must have been. I don't know what was coming over me.

I looked at him. He turned slowly, and just for one moment I knew fear. It was the first time. It was the way he moved his head. He turned towards me, obviously listening

25

to my thoughts, or reading my emotion, or touching my heart, or however one would say it, and then I realized he had done a trick for me.

He was dressed differently. He wore a soft tunic of red velvet, tied loosely at the waist and loose red velvet pants and slippers.

'You're not dreaming, Jonathan Ben Isaac, I'm here.'

The fire gave off an incredible burst of sparks. It gave off sparks as if things had been tossed on it.

I realized that something else about him had changed. He had now his heavy smooth mustache and his beard curling exactly as the beards of kings and soldiers in those old tablets, and I saw why God had given him the large cherubic mouth because it was a mouth you could see in spite of all that hair, a mouth that talked to you, a mouth developed by nature at a time when mouths had to compete with hair.

He started. He reached up. He touched the hair and then he scowled. 'I didn't mean to do that part. I think I shall give up on it. The hair wants to come back.'

'The Lord God wants you to have it?' I asked.

'I don't think so. I don't know!'

'How did you make the clothes change? How do you make yourself disappear?'

'There's little to it. Science will one day be able to control it. Today, science knows all about atoms and neutrinos. All I did was throw off all the tiny particles smaller than atoms which I had drawn to myself, through a magnetic strength you might say, to make my old clothes. They weren't real clothes. They just were clothes made by a ghost. And then to banish them, I said, as the sorcerer would say, "Return until I call to you again." And then I called up new clothes. I said in my heart with the sorcerer's conviction:

'"From the living and the dead, from the raw earth and from that which is forged and refined, woven, and treasured, come to me, tinier than grains of sand, and without sound, unnoticed, hurting no one, at your greatest speed, penetrating whatever barriers surround me that you must and clothe me in red velvet, soft garments the color of rubies. See these clothes in my mind, come."'

He sighed. 'And it was done.'

He sat quiet for a moment. I was so mesmerized by this new red attire, and by the way it seemed to change him somewhat, give him a sort of regal air, that I didn't speak. I pushed another big log into the pyramid of the fire, and threw some more coal on it from the scuttle, all of this without leaving the sanctuary of my rotting and crunched old chair.

Then and only then did I look at him. And at that same moment, when his eyes were utterly remote, I realized he was singing in a very low voice, a voice so low I had to strain to disentangle it from the soft devouring rush of the fire.

He was singing in Hebrew but it wasn't the Hebrew I knew. But I knew enough of it to know what it was: It was the Psalm 'By the Rivers of Babylon.' When he finished, I was awestruck and even more shaken than before.

I wondered if it was snowing in Poland. I wondered if my parents had been buried or cremated. I wondered if he could call together the ashes of my parents, but it seemed a horrible, blasphemous thought.

'That was my point, that we have things about which we are superstitious,' he said. 'When I blunderingly asked about your parents, I meant to say, you believe certain things but you don't believe them. You live in a double frame of mind.'

I reflected.

He looked at me deliberately, eyebrows curving down, though his cherubic mouth smiled. It was a respectful, sincere expression. 'And I can't bring them back to life. I can't do that!' he said.

He looked back at the flames.

'The parents of Gregory Belkin perished in the Holocaust in Europe,' he said. 'And Gregory became a madman. And his brother a holy man, a saint, zaddik. And you became a scholar, and a teacher, with a gentle gift for making students understand.'

'You honor me,' I said softly. There were a thousand little questions buzzing around me like bees. I wasn't going to cheapen things.

27

'Go on, Azriel, please,' I said. 'Tell me what you want to tell me. Tell me what you want me to know.'

'Ah, well, as I indicated we were the rich exiles. You know the story. Nebuchadnezzar came down on Jerusalem and slew the soldiers and littered the streets with bodies, and left behind a Babylonian governor to rule over the peasants who would tend our estates and vineyards and send the produce home to his Court. Customary.

'But rich men, tradesmen, scribes like the men of my family? We weren't slain. He didn't come sharpening his sword on our necks. We were deported to Babylon with everything that we could carry, I might add, wagons of our fine furniture which he allowed us to have, although he had thoroughly looted our temple, and we were given fine houses in which to live so that we might set up shop and serve the markets of Babylon and serve the temple and the Court.

'This happened a thousand times over in those centuries. Even the cruel Assyrians would do the same thing. They'd put to the sword the soldiers and then drag off the man who knew how to write three languages, and the boy who could carve perfectly in ivory, and so it was with us. The Babylonians, they weren't as bad as other enemies might have been. Imagine being dragged back to Egypt. Imagine. Egypt, where people live just to die, and sing night and day of dying, and of being dead, and there was nothing but village after village and field after field.

'No, we didn't have it bad off.

'By eleven years old, I had been to the temple itself, a page, as many a rich Hebrew boy was, and I had seen the great statue of Marduk himself, the god, in his high sanctuary atop the great ziggurat of Etemenanki. I had entered into the inner shrine with the priests, and the strangest thought had occurred to me! This big statue looked more like me than the little one I had which I had always thought bore a distinct resemblance.

'Of course I didn't chirp this out loud. But as I looked up at mighty Marduk, the great gold Marduk, the statue in which the god lived and ruled, and should have been carried each year in the New Year's Procession, the statue smiled.

'I was too clever to say anything to the priests. We were in the process of preparing the inner sanctuary for the woman who would come and spend the night with the god. But the priests noticed something. And they saw me look at Marduk and one of them asked, "What did you say?" and of course I'd said nothing. But Marduk had said, "Well, what do you think of my house, Azriel? I've been so often to yours."

'From that moment, the priests were on to it. Yet things might still have gone differently. I might have had a long human life. I might have had a different path. Sons, daughters. I don't know.

'At the time, I thought it was hilarious and wonderful, and loved Marduk for this little trick. But we continued to ready the chamber, which was truly magnificent in plated gold, and the silken couch where the woman would lie to be taken by the god that night, and then we left, and one of the priests said: "The God smiled on you!"

'I was stiff with fear. I didn't want to answer.

'Rich Hebrew hostages or deportees like us were treated very well, as I said, but I didn't really talk to the priests, you know, as if they were Hebrews. They were the priests of the gods we were forbidden to worship. Besides, I didn't trust them and there were too many of them and some were very stupid and others very sly and smart. I said simply that I had seen the smile too and thought it was sunlight.

'The priest was quaking.

'I forgot about that for years. I don't know why I remember it now, except to say that that might have been the very moment when my fate was sealed.

'Marduk started talking to me all the time then. I'd be in the tablet house, working hard, you know, learning thoroughly every text we possessed in Sumerian so that I could copy it out, read it, even speak it, though by then nobody spoke Sumerian. Ah, I must tell you a funny thing. I heard only recently here in this twentieth century world. I heard it in New York in the days after it was all over, finished with, Gregory Belkin I mean, and I was wandering around trying to make my body take the form of other men – and it kept changing back. I heard this funny thing . . .'

'What?' I asked at once.

'That nobody even now knows where the Sumerians came from! Not even to this day. That they came out of nowhere the Sumerians, with their language which was different from all others, and they built the first cities in our beautiful valleys. Nobody knows more about them even to this day.'

'That's true. Did you know then?'

'No,' he said, 'we knew what was written in the tablets, that Marduk had made people from clay and put life into them. That's all we knew. But to find out two thousand years later that you have no long archaeological or historical record for the origin of the Sumerians – how their language developed and how they migrated into the valley and all of that – it's funny to me.'

'Well, haven't you noticed that nobody now knows where the Jews came from either?' I asked. 'Or are you going to tell me that you knew for a fact in those days, when you were a Babylonian boy, that God called Abraham out of the city of Ur and that Jacob did wrestle with the angel?'

He laughed and shrugged. 'There were so many versions of that story! If you only knew. Of course people wrestled all the time with angels. That was beyond dispute. But what do you have today in the Holy Books? Its remnants! The whole story of Yahweh defeating the Leviathan is gone, gone! And I used to copy that story all the time! But I get ahead of myself. I want to describe things in some order. No, I am not surprised to hear that no one knows where the Jews came from. Because even then there were just too many stories . . .

'Let me tell you about my house. It was in the rich Hebrew quarter. I've explained what exile meant.

'We were to be citizens of quality of a city filled with people of all nations. We were booty, set free to increase and multiply and make wealth. By my time, as you can guess, Nebuchadnezzar had died, and we were ruled by Nabonidus, and he was not in the city and everybody hated him. Just hated him.

'He was thought to be mad, or obsessed. This is told in the book of Daniel though he is given the wrong name. And true, our prophets did go try to drive him crazy with their predictions about how he ought to let us go home. But I don't think they got anywhere with him.

'Nabonidus was driven by secret ideas of his own. Nabonidus was a scholar for one thing, a digger into the mounds, and he was determined to keep Babylon in glory, yes, but he had a mad love for the god Sin. Well, Babylon was Marduk's city. Of course there were many other temples and chapels even in Marduk's temple, but still, for the King to fall crazy in love with another god?

'And then to go running off for ten years, ten years into the desert, leaving behind Belshazzar as the ruler, well, that made everybody hate Nabonidus even more. The whole time that Nabonidus was gone, the New Year's Festival couldn't happen, and this was the biggest festival in Babylon where Marduk takes the hand of the King and walks through the street with him! That couldn't happen with no King. And the priests of Marduk, by the time I came to serious work in the temple and palace, were really despising Nabonidus. And so were many other people too.

'To tell you the truth, I never knew the whole secret of Nabonidus. If we could call him up, you know, as the Witch of Endor called up the dead prophet Samuel, disturbing his sleep, remember, so that Saul the King could talk to him . . . if we could call up Nabonidus he might tell us wondrous things. But that is not my mission now, to become a necromancer or a sorcerer, it's to find the stairway to heaven, and I am done with the fog and the mist in which the lost souls linger begging for someone to call a name.

'Besides, maybe Nabonidus has gone into the light. Maybe he's mounted the stairs. He didn't live his life in cruelty or debauchery but devotion to a god who was not the god of his city, that's all.

'I only saw him once, and that was during the last days of my life, and he was all caught up in the plot of course, and he seemed to me a dead man already, a King whose time had passed, and he seemed also blessed with an indifference to life. All he wanted, on that last day when we met, or that night, was that Babylon would not be sacked. That's what everybody wanted. That's how I lost my soul.

31

'But I'll come to that awful part soon enough.

'I was talking about being alive. I didn't give a damn about Nabonidus. We lived in the rich Hebrew quarter. It was filled with beautiful houses; we made the walls then about six feet thick, which I know sounds mad to you today, but you cannot imagine how effectively it kept our houses cool; they were sprawling affairs, with many anterooms and big dining rooms, and all these rooms surrounded a large central courtyard. My father's house was four stories high and the wooden rooms above were full of cousins and the elderly aunts, and they often didn't come all the way down to the yard, but merely sat in the open courtyard windows taking the breeze.

'The courtyard was Eden. It was like a small portion of the hanging gardens themselves, and the other public gardens all over the city. It was big. We had a fig tree, a willow tree, and two date palms, and flowers of all kinds, grape vines covering the arbor where we could take our evening meal, and fountains that never stopped sending their rivers of sparkling water down into the basins where the fish darted about like living jewels.

'The brickwork was glazed and beautiful, and had many figures in it, having been built by some Akkadian before us, before the Chaldeans came, and it was full of blue and red and yellow and flowers, but there was also plenty of grass in the courtyard, and then the room off it where the ancestors were buried.

'I grew up playing among the date palms and flowers, and I loved it till the day . . . the day I died. I loved lying out there in the late afternoon listening to the water of the fountains, and ignoring everybody who kept telling me I ought to be in the scriptorium copying psalms or some such. I wasn't lazy by nature. I just sort of did what I wanted to do. I got away with things. But I wasn't bad by any stretch; in fact, I was far and away the best scholar of the family, at least as I saw it, and many times, my uncles, though they didn't want to admit it, would bring to me three versions of a Psalm by King David and ask me which I thought was the most nearly correct, and then they'd follow my judgment.

'We had no official gathering place for prayers, of course, because we had such grandiose plans for going home and building the Temple of Solomon all over again; I mean no one was going to throw up any little street-side temple in Babylon. The temple would have to be done according to sacred dimensions, and after I was dead and cursed and had become the Servant of the Bones, the Jews did go home and build that temple. In fact, I know they did, because I saw it once . . . once, as if in a fog, but I saw it.

'In our Babylonian life we gathered at private homes for prayers, and also for the elders among us to read the letters we received from the rebels still hiding on Mount Zion, and also the letters coming from our prophets in Egypt. Jeremiah was imprisoned there for a long time. I don't remember anyone ever reading one of his letters. But I remember a lot of mad writing by Ezekiel. He didn't write it down himself. He walked about talking and predicting and then other people wrote it down.

'But so we prayed, in our homes, to our invisible and all-powerful Yahweh — reminded always that before David promised him a temple, Yahweh and the Ark of the Covenant had been housed only in a tent, and that had its meaning and its value. Lots of the Elders thought the whole temple idea was Babylonian, you know. Go back to the tent.

'On the other hand, our family had for nine generations been rich merchants, city men, living in Nineveh before Jerusalem, I think, and we had little concept of the nomad life or carrying about shrines in tents. The story of Moses didn't make a great deal of sense to us. For instance, how could the people be so lost in the desert for forty years? But, I repeat myself, don't I? . . . What am I saying . . .

'A tent to me was all the silk over my bed, the red-tinged light in which I lay with my hands cupped under my head talking to Marduk about the prayer meetings and listening to his jokes.

'At some of these prayer meetings we had our own prophets, whose books are lost now, who did a great deal of ranting and screaming. I was frequently pointed to, and told

33

that I had found favor in the eyes of Yahweh, though what this meant nobody was certain.

'I guess they all knew in a way that I could see farther than others, look into souls, you know, see like a zaddik, a saint, but I was no saint, only an obstreperous young man.'

He stopped. The sharpness of memory seemed to cut him off and hold him.

'You were happy,' I said. 'By nature, you were happy, truly happy.'

'Oh, yes, I knew it, and so did my friends. In fact, they often teased me about being too happy. Things never seemed all that difficult, you see. Things never seemed dark! Darkness came with death, and the worst darkness for me was right before it, and maybe ... maybe even now. But darkness. Oh, to take on the world of darkness, that is like trying to chart the stars of heaven.

'What was I saying? Things were easy for me. I enjoyed them. For example, to be educated I had to work in the tablet house. I had to get a real Babylonian education. This was wise, this was for the future, this was for trade, this was to be a man of learning. And they beat the daylights out of us if we were late, or didn't learn our lessons, but usually it was easy for me.

'I loved the old Sumerian. I loved writing out the whole stories of Gilgamesh and "In the Beginning" and copying all kinds of records so that fresh tablets could be sent to other cities in Babylonia. I could practically speak Sumerian. I could now sit down and write for you my life in Sumerian –' He stopped. 'No, I couldn't do that. I couldn't because if I could have written my life, I wouldn't have climbed up this snowy mountain to commit it to you ... I can't ... I can't. ... write it in any tongue. Talking lets the pain flow ...'

'That I understand perfectly, and am here to listen. The point is, you know Sumerian, and you can read it, and you can translate it.'

'Yes, yes, yes, and Akkadian, the language that had been used after, and the Persian which was creeping up on us all then, and Greek – I could read that well – and Aramaic which was taking the place of our own Hebrew in daily life, but then I wrote Hebrew too.

'I learnt my lessons. I wrote fast. I had a way of plunging the stylus into the clay that made everybody laugh but my writing was good. Really good. And I also loved to stand up and read out loud, so whenever the teacher took sick, or was called out, or suddenly needed some medicine, otherwise known as beer, I'd stand up and start reading Gilgamesh to everybody in an exaggerated voice, making them laugh.

'You know the old myth of course. And it's important to our story, stupid and crazy as it is. Here is this king Gilgamesh and he is running wild around his city – on some tablets he is a giant, on others he is the size of a man. He behaves like a bull. He has the drums beaten all the time, which makes everybody unhappy. You're not supposed to beat the drums except for certain reasons – to frighten spirits, to call to nuptials, you know.

'Okay, so we have Gilgamesh tearing up the city of Uruk. And what do the gods do, being the Sumerian gods, being about as smart as a bunch of water buffalo – they make an equal for Gilgamesh in a wild man called Enkido, who is covered with hair, lives in the woods, and likes to drink with beasts – oh, it is so important in this world with whom one eats and drinks and what! – anyway, here we have wild Enkido coming down to the stream to drink with the beasts, and he is rendered tame by spending seven days with a temple harlot!

'Stupid, no? The beasts wouldn't have anything to do with him once he knew the harlot. Why? Were the beasts jealous because they didn't get to lie with the harlot? Don't beasts copulate with beasts? Are there no beast harlots? Why does copulating with a woman make a man less of a beast? Well, the whole story of Gilgamesh never made any sense anyway except as a bizarre code. Everything is code, is it not?'

'I think you're right, it's code,' I said, 'but code for what? Keep telling me the story of Gilgamesh. Tell me how your version ended,' I asked. I simply couldn't resist the question. 'You know we have only fragments now, and we don't have the old script that you had.'

'It ended the same way as your modern versions. Gilgamesh couldn't resign himself that Enkido could die. Enkido did die, too, though I don't remember quite why. Gilgamesh acted as if he'd never seen anybody die before, and he went to the immortal who had survived the great flood. The great flood. Your flood. Our flood. Everyone's flood. With us it was Noah and his sons. With them it was an immortal who lived in the land of Dilmun in the sea. He was the great survivor of the flood. And off to see him, to get immortality, goes this genius Gilgamesh. And that ancient one – who would be the Hebrew Noah for our people – says what? 'Gilgamesh, if you can stay awake for seven days and nights, you can be immortal.'

'And what happens? Gilgamesh instantly fell asleep. Instantly! He didn't even wait a day! A night. He keeled over! Smash. Asleep. So that was the end of that plan, except that the immortal widow of the immortal man who had survived the flood took pity on him, and they told Gilgamesh that if he tied stones to his feet and sank down in the sea he could find a plant that, once eaten, gives you eternal youth. Well, I think they were trying to drown the man!

'But our version, as yours, followed Gilgamesh in this expedition. Down he went and he found the plant. Then he comes up again. He goes to sleep. His worst habit apparently, this sleeping . . . and a snake comes and takes the plant. Ah, what utter sadness for Gilgamesh and then comes the old advice to all:

'"Enjoy your life, fill your belly with wine and food, and accept death. The Gods kept immortality for themselves, death is the lot of man." You know, profound philosophical revelations!'

I laughed. 'I like your telling of it. When you would stand up in the tablet house, did you read it with that same fervor?'

'Oh, always!' he said. 'But even then, what did we have? Bits and pieces of something ancient. Uruk had been built thousands of years before. Maybe there was such a real king. Maybe.

'If I have a point in all this right now, let me make it. Madness in kings is common. In fact, I think sanity in kings

36

must be rare. Gilgamesh went crazy. Nabonidus was crazy. You ask me, Pharaoh was crazy in every story I ever heard about him.

'And I understand this. I understand it because I have looked into the face of Cyrus the Persian and into the face of Nabonidus, and I know that kings are alone, utterly alone. I have looked into the face of Gregory Belkin, a king in his own right, and I saw this same isolation and terrible weakness; there is no mother, there is no father, there is no limit to power, and disaster is the portion of kings. I have looked into the face of other kings, but that we will pass over quickly later on, because what I did as the evil Servant of the Bones does not matter now, except that every time I killed a human life, I destroyed a universe, did I not?'

'Perhaps, or you sent the evil flame home to be cleansed in the great fire of God.'

'Ah, that is beautiful,' he said to me.

I was complimented. But did I believe this?

'So, let's go on with my life,' he said. 'I worked at the Court as soon as I left the tablet house, and then my writing and reading were of the utmost importance. I knew all languages. I saw many strange documents and old letters in Sumerian and was useful to the King's regent, Belshazzar. No one much cared for Belshazzar, as I said. He couldn't hold the New Year's Festival, or the priests didn't want him, or Marduk wouldn't do it, who knows, but he wasn't destined to be loved.

'Yet I can't say this made for a bad atmosphere in the palace. It was fairly congenial and of course the correspondence was endless. Letters were pouring in from the outlying territories complaining about the Persians being on the march, or about the Egyptians being on the march, or about the stars as seen by various astrologists predicting very bad or good things for the King.

'I became acquainted in the palace with the wise men who advised the King on everything, and liked listening to them, and realized that when Marduk spoke to me, sometimes the wise men could hear it. And I also came to know that the

37

story of the smile had never been forgotten. Marduk had smiled on Azriel.

'Well, what secrets I had.

'So look. I am walking home. I am nineteen. I have very little time left to live and I don't know it. I said to Marduk, How could the wise men hear it when you talk to me? He said that these men, these wise men, were seers and sorcerers just as were some of our Hebrews, our prophets, our wise men, though nobody wanted much to admit it, and they had the power as I did to hear a spirit.

'He sighed and he said to me in Sumerian that I must take the utmost care. "These men know your powers."'

'I'd never heard Marduk sounded dejected. We had long ago passed the foolish point of me asking him for favors or to play tricks on people, and now we talked more about things all the time, and he frequently said that he could see more clearly through my eyes. I didn't know what this meant, but on this day when he seemed dejected I was worried.

'"My powers!" I said sarcastically. "What powers! You smiled. You are the god!"

'Silence, but I knew he was still there. I could always feel him, like heat; I heard him like breath. You know, the way a blind person knows that someone is there.

'I got to my front door and was ready to go in, and I turned around and for the first time I actually laid eyes on him. I saw Marduk. Not the gold statuette in my room. Not the big statues in the temple. But Marduk, himself.

'He was standing against the far wall, arms folded, one knee bent, just looking at me. It was Marduk. He was completely covered in gold as he was at the shrine but he was alive and his curly hair and beard seemed not made of solid gold as they were on the statue but living gold. His eyes were browner than mine, that is, paler, with more yellow in the irises. He smiled at me.

'"Ah, Azriel," he said. "I knew it would happen. I knew it." And then he came forward and he kissed me on both cheeks. His hands were so smooth. He was my height, and I was right, there was a great resemblance between us, though his eyebrows were set just a bit higher than mine and his

38

forehead was smoother, so he didn't look so mischievous or ferocious by nature as I did.

'I wanted to throw my arms around him. He didn't wait for me to say it. He said, "Do it, but for that moment maybe others will see me too."

'I hugged him as my oldest friend, as the dearest to me in the world next to my father, and it was that night I made the mistake of telling my father that I talked with my god all the time. I should never have done it. I wonder now what would have happened if I had not done that.'

I interrupted. 'Did anyone else see him, to the best of your knowledge?'

'Yes, as a matter of fact, they did. The doorkeeper of our house saw him and all but fainted dead away to see a man all covered in gold paint, and one of my sisters looking down from the lattice above saw him too, and an elder of the Hebrews got a glimpse of him for a moment and came flying at me later that night with his staff, claiming he had seen me with a devil or an angel, and he did not know which.

'That's when my father, my beloved, sweet, good-hearted father said, "It was Marduk, Babylon's god, whom you saw." And maybe that is why . . . that is why, we are here now. My father never meant to hurt me. Never. He never meant to do a cruel thing to anyone in his life! He never meant it! He was . . . he was my little brother.

'Let me explain. I have figured it out. I was the eldest son, born when my father was young, because the deportation from Jerusalem had been hard on our people and they married quickly to have sons.

'But my father was the baby of his family, the little Benjamin beloved by everyone, and somehow or other in our family I fell into being his elder brother, and treating him as such. As eldest son I bossed him about a bit. Or rather, we became . . . we became as friends.

'My father worked hard. But we were close. We drank together. We went to the taverns together. We shared women together. And I told him, drunk that night, how Marduk had talked to me for years, and how now I had seen him, and my personal god was the great god of Babylon himself.

'So foolish to have done it! What good could have come of it! At first he laughed, then he worried, then he became engrossed. Oh, I never should have done it. And Marduk knew this. He was in the tavern but so far from me that he had no visibility, he was vaporous and golden like light, and only I could see him, and he shook his head "no," and turned his back when I told my father. But you know, I loved my father, and I was so happy! And I wanted him to know. I wanted him to know how I had put my arms around the god!

'Stupid!

'Let me return to the background. The foreground is suddenly too hot for me and it hurts me and stings my eyes.

'The family. I was telling you what we were. We were rich merchants and we were scribes of our Sacred Books. All of the Hebrew tribes in Babylon were in one way or another scribes of the Sacred Books and busy making copies for their own families at all times, but with us it was a very large business because we were known for the rapid and accurate copy. And we had a huge library of old texts. I think I told you, we had maybe, I don't know, twenty-five different stories about Joseph and Egypt and Moses and so forth, and it was always a matter of dispute what to include and what not to. We had so many stories of Joseph in Egypt that we decided not to give all of them credit. I wonder what became of all those tablets, all those scrolls. We just didn't think all those stories were true. But maybe we were wrong. Oh, who knows?

'But to return to the fabric of my life. Whenever I left the court of the palace, or the tablet house, or the marketplace, I came right home to work all evening on the Holy Scriptures, with my sisters and my cousins and uncles in the scriptoria of our houses, which were big rooms.

'As I told you, I was never very quiet, and I would sing the psalms out loud as I wrote them, and this irritated my deaf uncle more than anyone. I don't know why. He was deaf! And besides, I have a good voice.'

'Yes, you do.'

'Why should a deaf uncle get so upset? But he knew I was singing the psalms not as I just sang that one for you, but as one would sing, with cymbals, dancing, you know, with a little bit of added dash, shall we say, and he wasn't so happy about it.

'He said that we were to write when we were to write and to sing the Lord's songs at the appropriate time. I shrugged and gave in but I was one for cutting up all the time. But I'm giving the wrong impression. I wasn't really bad . . .'

'I know what kind of man you are, and were then . . .'

'Yes, I think by now you do, and maybe if you thought me bad you would have thrown me out in the snow.'

He looked at me. His eyes weren't ferocious. The brows were low and thick, but the eyes were plenty big enough beneath them to give him a pretty look. And, it seemed to me that he was warmer and more relaxed now than earlier, and I felt drawn to him and wanting to hear everything he said.

But I wondered: Could I throw him out in the snow?

'I've taken many lives,' he said, plucking the thought right from me, 'but I would not hurt you, Jonathan Ben Isaac, you know that. I wouldn't hurt such a man as you. I killed assassins. At least when I came to myself that was my code of honor. That is my code now.

'In my early days as the Servant of the Bones, as the bitter, angry ghost for the powerful sorcerer, I killed the innocent because it was my Master's will and I thought I had to do it, I thought that the man who had called me up could control me, and I did his bidding, until the moment came when I suddenly realized that I did not have to be a slave forever, that maybe though my soul had been taken from my spirit, and my spirit and soul from my flesh, that perhaps I could still be pleasing to God. That somehow all could come and be united once more in one figure! Ah!'

He shook his head.

'But Azriel, maybe it's happened!'

'Oh, Lord God, Jonathan, don't give me consolation. I cannot bear it. Just hear me out. Make sure your tapes record my words. Remember me. Remember what I say . . .'

His confidence broke suddenly. He looked at the fire again.

'My family, my father,' he said. 'My father! How it hurt him what he finally did, and how he looked at me. Do you know what he said about hurting me? He said, "Azriel, who of all my sons loves me as you do? No one else could ever forgive me for this but you!" And he meant it. He meant it, my father, my little brother, looking at me full of tears and sincerity and absolute conviction!

'I'm sorry. I jump ahead. I'll die soon enough. It won't take too many more pages, I don't think.' He shuddered all over. And again the tears stood in his eyes. 'Forgive me, and recall again that for those thousands of years, I didn't remember these things. I was the bitter ghost without memory. And now it has all come back to me and I pour it out to you. I pour it out to you in tears.'

'Continue. Give me your tears, your trust, and your hurt. I won't fail you.'

'Ah, you are the rare thing, Jonathan Ben Isaac,' he said.

'Not really, I'm a teacher and a happy man myself. I have a wife and children who love me. I'm not very special.'

'Ah, but you are a good man who will talk to someone who is evil! That is what is rare. The Rebbe of the Hasidim, he turned his back on me!' He laughed suddenly, a deep bitter laugh. 'He was too good to talk to the Servant of the Bones.'

I smiled. 'We are all Jews, and there are Jews, and there are Jews.'

'Yes, and now Israelis, who would be Maccabees! And there are Hasidim.'

'And other Orthodox, and some "reformed," and so on it goes. Let's go back to your time. You were a big and happy family.'

'Yes, true, and it was regular – I was explaining – it was regular for the rich Hebrews to work at the palace as I said, my father worked there too, and many of my cousins. We were scribes, but also merchants, merchants of jewels, silks, silver, and books. My father's gift in trade was choosing the very finest vessels for the King's table and for the Table of the Gods in Marduk's temple and for Marduk himself.

'Now at the time, the temple was full of chapels, and every day a meal was set out for each deity, including Marduk, so the temple had a huge stock of gold and silver vessels for this. And my father was the one who put aside those vessels not fit.

'I went down with him to the docks all the time to meet the ships coming in from the sea, with the finest new work from Greece or Egypt, and I learned from him how to judge the carving on a goblet, and how to know the heaviest and finest mixture of gold. I learned to know a true ruby or diamond and pearls – pearls, I loved the pearls, we dealt in pearls of all kinds, we didn't call them pearls, you know, we called them eyes of the sea.

'This is how we made our living – in the marketplace and in the temple and in the palace.

'My family had stalls all through the marketplace where they dealt in gems of all kinds, in honey, and in cloth dyed purple and blue, the finest of all silk and linen, and they sold the incense too, though they sold it to idolaters who would burn this incense for Nabu and Ishtar, and for Marduk, of course.

'But it was our living, it was our source of power, it was our way of staying together, of being strong so that one day we could go home. It was as important as the copying of the Sacred Books.'

'It's an old tale,' I said.

'This whole trade, by the way, gave to my own house a sumptuous quality that it might not have had, had we been camel breeders. And that you must understand because the richness around us colored my father's values as much as mine.

'What I mean is, not only did we make money, but the house was always full of merchandise passing through. You know. Here would be a magnificent cedar statue of the goddess Ishtar just come from Dilmun, and my uncle would keep it at home for a week or two, gracing the living room, before the sale was made. The place was full of beautiful

43

footstools, delicate furniture from Egypt, the fine black and red urns and pots of the Greeks, and just about anything portable and ornamental and lovely to behold.'

'You grew up on beauty, didn't you?'

'Yes,' Azriel said. 'I did. I really did. And I grew up, for all my smart talking and carrying on and flirting with Marduk, I grew up with love. My father's love. The love of my brothers. My sisters. The love of my uncles even. Even my deaf uncle. Even once the prophet Azarel said to me, 'Yahweh looks at you with love.' So did the old witch Asenath. Ah, such love.'

He had come to a natural pause. He sat there, resplendent in the red velvet, hair glossy and natural, and the pure skin of his young man's cheeks as soft as a girl's I suppose. I must be getting old. Because young men look to me now as beautiful as girls. Not that I desire them. It's only that life itself is lush.

He was confused. In pain. I hesitated to press him. Then he parted his lips, only to be quiet.

Three

What was it like, roaming in the temple? The palace?' I asked. 'The beautiful house, I can envision. But the palace, was the palace plated in gold? Was the temple?'

He didn't respond.

'Give me pictures, Azriel. Take your time by means of images. The temple, will you tell me what that was like?'

'Yes,' he said. 'It was a house of gems and gold. It was a world of the deep vibrant gleam of the precious, of lovely scents and the sounds of harps, and pipes playing; it was a world for the bare feet to walk on smooth tiles that were themselves cut in the shapes of flowers.' He smiled.

'And,' he said, 'it was a hell of a lot more fun than you might think. Not all that solemn. The two buildings were huge, of course, you know Nebuchadnezzar built the palace to the full glory of the past, or so he thought, and greatly expanded the private gardens; and the temple was the great building known as Esagila, and behind the building itself stood the big ziggurat, Etemenanki, with its stairway to heaven, and then its ramps going up to the very topmost temple of my great and favorite smiling god.

'The temple and the palace were full of locked and sealed doors. Some of these seals had not been broken in a hundred years. And of course, as you probably know, we had contracts made in this way too . . . in that a contract would be written out on a clay tablet, dried, and then enclosed in a clay envelope with the same words on it, which was then dried, so that one could not get to the original tablet inside without breaking the envelope. So if some corrupt individual had made a change on the outer envelope, the sealed inside tablet would tell the truth.

'There was a lot of that at court, people bringing in contracts, breaking open the envelopes, discovering some wily bastard had made a change in the contract, and the

King and his advisors and wise men passing judgment. I never followed out any condemned man to see him executed. As you said, I grew up on beauty.

'In the streets of Babylon I never saw the hungry. I never saw a wretched slave. Babylon was the city people dreamed of living in; everyone was happy in Babylon and under the protection of the King.

'But to return to your question. One could roam in the temple. One could just roam. I could creep in my fine jeweled slippers into the chapels where the other gods were – Nabu and Ishtar and any god or goddess who had been brought from another city for sanctuary.

'You know, that was happening. Cyrus the Persian was on the march most definitely, taking the Greek cities along the coast one after another. And so from all over Babylonia, frightened priests were sending their gods to us for protection, to the great gateway, and we had set up these visiting deities in chapels and these chapels were full of twinkling light.

'This fear for the god, that the enemy would get him, it was very real. Marduk himself had for two hundred years been a prisoner in another city, stolen and taken there, and it had been a great day for Babylon, long before my birth, when Marduk had been recovered and had been brought home.'

'Did he ever tell you about it?' I asked.

'No,' he said. 'But I didn't ask him. We'll come to such things . . .

'As I was saying, I liked roaming about the temple. I took messages to the priests; I waited at table when Belshazzar dined, and I made friends of all the palace crowd, you might say, the eunuchs, the temple slaves, the other pages, and some of the temple prostitutes who were, of course, beautiful women.

'Now all of this work I did in the temple and the palace, there was a Babylonian point to it. The government had a sensible policy. When rich hostages like us, rich deportees, were brought in not only to enhance the culture, young men like me were always picked out to be trained in Babylonian ways. That was so that if or when we were sent back to our own city or some distant province we would be good Babylonians, that is, skilled members of the King's loyal service.

'There were scores of Hebrews at court.

'Nevertheless, I had uncles who went into a fury that my father and I worked at the temple, but my father and I, we would shrug our shoulders and say, 'We don't worship Marduk! We don't eat with the Babylonians. We don't eat the food that the gods have eaten.' And a good deal of the community felt the same way as we did.

'Let me note here, this eating of food. It's still important for the Hebrews. No? You don't eat with heathens. You didn't then. And you didn't eat anything ever that had once been put before an idol. It was a big thing.

'As good Hebrews, we broke bread only with one another, and our hands were always washed carefully with ritual prayer before we took the food, and afterwards there was not one thing in our lives that was not permeated by our desire to praise Yahweh, our Lord God of Hosts.

'But we had to survive in Babylon. We had every intention of returning rich to our homeland. We had to be strong. And that meant what it has always meant to the Hebrews. You must be powerful enough to disperse without being destroyed.'

Again came one of the inevitable pauses. He leant forward and stirred the fire, as people do when they want to think, and want to have the feeling of doing something. Stirring fires can give you that feeling, especially if you aren't drinking anything, clutching your coffee as if that were a fulltime job, the way I was doing.

'You looked then exactly as you look now, didn't you?' I said, though this was a repeat question. It was one of those soft verbal signals: God gave you all the right gifts, young man.

'Yes,' he said. 'I wanted now to be smooth-faced. I think I told you. But it doesn't seem to be in my luck.

'I came as myself this time, and I don't know even to this

moment who called me. Why now? Why has my body come back around me? Why? I don't know.

'In the past when I was called forth by sorcerers, they made me look the way they wanted, and that could be quite horrible. Seldom if ever did they wait, or take a deep breath, to see what I might look like on my own. I would be summoned in a specific form: "Azriel, Servant of the Golden Bones which I hold in my hand, come forth in a blaze of fire and consume my enemies. Make of them cinders." That sort of chant.

'Whatever the case, in answer to your question I looked exactly the same when I died as I do now except for one salient characteristic which had been added to me before my murder, which I will recount later. I am as I died.'

'Your father, why was it a mistake to tell him about Marduk? Why? What did all that mean? What did he do to you, Azriel?'

He shook his head. 'This is the hardest part for me to tell you, Jonathan Ben Isaac, but I have never told anyone, you know. I never told any master. Does God never forget? Will God deny me forever the Stairway to Heaven?'

'Azriel, let me caution you, simply as an older human being, though my soul may be newborn. Don't be so sure of Heaven. Don't be any more sure of the face of our god than Marduk was sure.'

'This means you believe in one and not the other?'

'This means I want to blunt your pain in the telling of what happened. I want to blunt your sense of fatality, and that you are destined for something terrible because of what others have done.'

'Wise of you,' he said. 'And generous in spirit. I am a fool still in so many ways.'

'I see. I understand. Let's go back to Babylon, shall we? Can you explain the plot? What did your father have to do with it in the end?'

'Oh, my father and I, what friends we were! He didn't have a better friend than me, and my best friend was Marduk.

'I was the leader on our drinking jaunts, and it was he . . .

it was only he who could have ever made me do what I did
. . . the thing which made me the Servant of the Bones.

'Strange how it all comes together.' He fell to murmuring.
He was distracted. 'They choose ingredients and they blend
them, because the potion won't work unless you have
everything. The priests alone, they could never have gotten
him to do it. Cyrus the Persian? I trusted him as much as any
tyrant. And old Nabonidus, what was his advice? He was
only there out of some sort of kindness on the part of Cyrus,
and cleverness. Everything with the Persian empire was
cleverness. Perhaps it's so with all empires.'

'Take your time,' I said. 'Catch your breath.'

'Yes . . . let me give you pictures of my family. My mother
died when I was young. She was very sick, and she cried that
she wouldn't live to see Yahweh lift His Face to us again and
take us back to Zion. Her people had all been scribes. She
herself was a scribe and at one time, I heard, had been
something of a prophetess, but this had ceased when she had
sons.

'My father missed her unbearably until the last day I ever
knew him. He had two Gentile women and so did I; in fact,
we shared the same two women most of the time, but this
was not for having children or marriage, this was just for fun.

'And at home in the family my father was a hard worker at
writing down the psalms and trying to get exact the words we
remembered from Jeremiah over which we all argued night
and day. My father seldom if ever led the prayers. But he had
a beautiful voice, and I can still remember him singing the
Lord's praises.

'When we worked in the temple, it was secret between him
and me that we thought all idolaters were completely crazy,
and why not work for them and humor them?

'As I was explaining, we set the meal out for the god
Marduk himself from time to time with the priests. I had
many, many friends among the priests, and you know, it was
like any group of priests; some believed it all, and some
believed nothing. But we drew the veils around the god's
table, and then afterwards we took away the food, which of
course the god Marduk in his own way had actually savored

and fed upon – through fragrance and through the moisture that he could feel – and we helped set up that meal for the members of the royal family, the royal hostages, and the priests and the eunuchs who would eat the god's food, or eat at the King's table.

'But again, as good Hebrews we didn't eat that food ourselves. No, we would never have done that.

'We kept to the laws of Moses in every way that we could. And days ago, when I found myself pitched down into New York, and I began my journey to find the killers of Esther Belkin, when I happened upon the grandfather of Gregory Belkin, the Rebbe in Brooklyn, I saw that many of those Jews, strict as they were, had made a living in the big city of New York in *handel* as we would call it, just as we did in Babylon.

'And I saw also that there were Jews at all levels of devotion, as you yourself said.'

He stopped again. He was not anxious for the pain to come.

'But let me get back to Babylon. Look, I'm dancing in the tavern with my father. All men are dancing there together, you know. No harlots there that night. Just a man's place. And I tell him, "I saw my god with my own eyes. I saw him and I held him to my heart. Father, I am an idolater, but I swear to you, I saw Marduk and Marduk walks with me."

'And there in the far corner, look, Marduk turns his back on me deliberately and he shakes his head.

'And hours later my father and I were still arguing. "You are a wise man, you are a seer, and you have misused your powers," he said. "You should have used them for us."

'"I will, Father, I will use them for us, but tell me, what do you want me to do? Marduk asks nothing of me. What do *you* want me to do?"

'The following day Marduk appeared just a few blocks from the house, vaporous, gold, visible however. He cautioned me: "Don't touch me or we will have a religious spectacle on our hands."

'"Look, are you angry with me for telling my father?" I

asked him straight away. We were walking just like friends, and to have him visible was such a comfort to me.

'"No, I'm not angry with you, Azriel, it's just I don't trust the priests of the temple. There are many, many old and conniving priests, and you never know what they will want of you. Now listen to me. I have some things to tell you before we get deeper into this, before you do, that is, for I am as deep as I can get. Let's go to the public gardens. I like to see you eat and drink."

'We went to his favorite place, a huge public garden right on the Euphrates, down away from all the docks and the shipwrights and the commotion. In fact it was where one of the many canals came in, and it was more on the canal than the river itself which was always busy. This garden was filled with big drooping willow trees, just like in the psalm, you know, and there were a few musicians out there playing their pipes and dancing for trinkets.

'Marduk sat down opposite me and folded his arms. We really did look so much alike that we could have been brothers. It occurred to me that I knew him better than I knew any of my brothers. And by the way, I didn't hate my brothers the way Hebrews are always hating their brothers in the stories. Forget that. I loved my brothers. They were a little tame, when it came to drinking and dancing. I had more fun with my father. But I loved them.'

He stopped. It seemed out of respect for the dead brothers. He was now beyond beautiful in the red velvet, and these pauses brought me back visually to him in a way that was seductive. But then he began to talk again:

'Marduk started in on me right away. "Look, I am going to tell you the truth and you pay attention. I have no memory of my beginnings. I have no memory of slaying Tiamat the great dragon and making the world out of her belly and the sky out of the rest of her. But this does not mean that it didn't happen. I walk most of the time in a fog. I see the spirits of the gods and the roaming spirits of the dead and I listen for prayers and I try to answer them. But this is a dreary place where I live. When I retreat to the temple for the banquet it's a great pleasure because the fog clears. You know what clears it?"

'"No, but I can guess . . . that the priests see you, that powerful seers see you."

'"That is it, Azriel, I can become solid and visible for witches, for sorcerers, for those who have eyes to see, and then I drink up the libations of water, I inhale them and inhale the fragrances of food and this puts me in the mood of life. Then I go into the statue, and I rest in darkness and time means nothing to me, and I listen to Babylon. I listen. I listen. But the myths of the beginning, I don't remember, you see what I'm saying?"

'"Not entirely," I confessed. "Are you telling me that you aren't a god?"

'"No, I am a god and a powerful one. Were I to draw on my will, I could clear this marketplace, this garden now, with a great forceful wind. Easy to do. But what I am saying is that gods don't know everything, and this story of how Marduk became the leader of the gods, how he slew Tiamat, how he built the tower to heaven . . . well, I've either forgotten it, or I am growing weak, and I can't remember. Gods can die. They can fade. Just like Kings. They can sleep and it takes much to wake them up. And when I awake and am fully alert, I love Babylon and Babylon loves me back."

'"Look, my Lord," I said, "you're weary because the New Year's Festival hasn't been held in ten years, because our King Nabonidus has neglected you and your priests. That's all. If we could get the addlebrained old idiot to come home and hold the Festival, you would revive; you would be filled with the life of all of those in Babylon who would see you on the Processional Way."

'"That's a nice idea, Azriel, and there's some truth in it, but I have no love for the New Year's Festival, for residing in the statue and holding hands with the King. I get tempted in the very middle of it, to knock the King down and away from me and right to the gutters of the Processional Way. Don't you see? It's not what they tell you! It's not!"

'He then went silent with a gesture to me to ponder these words and then he said he wanted to try something. These next few moments were to have a crucial influence over my own destiny as a spirit, but I couldn't have known it then.

'"Azriel," he said. "I want you to do this. Look at me, and strip me in your mind of this gold, and see me pink and alive as you are, with my beard black and my eyes brown, and then reach out and touch me with both your hands. Let the god out of the gold. Let's try it."

'I was trembling.

'"Why are you so scared! Nobody will see anyone across from you but a noble in fine dress, that's all."

'"I'm scared because it might work, my Lord," I told him, "and the most troubling thought has come to me. You want to escape, Marduk. You want to get away. And if this works, if my eyes and my touch can render you a visible body, you can escape, can't you?"

'"And why the hell does that frighten a Son of Yahweh!" He took in his breath. "I'm sorry I was angry with you. I love you over all my worshipers and all my subjects. I'm not going to abandon Babylon. I will be here as long as Babylon needs me. I will be here when the sands come to bury us all. And then maybe I will escape. But yes, this would give me freedom. It would teach me that as a god I could slip into a visible human body and walk about. It would teach me something about what I can do, you see? I can make storms, I can heal sometimes though this is very very tricky, and I can make wishes come true because I know things, and I know the demons the people fear are just the restless dead.'

'"This is true?" I asked him. But let me say here that in Babylon getting rid of demons was a big business. I mean men made fortunes getting rid of demons from houses and sick people and so forth. There were rituals and charms for it, and you went to the exorcist and you did what he said. So I wanted to know if there were no demons. But he didn't answer me right away.

'Then he spoke up, "Azriel, *most* of the demons are the restless dead. But there are strong spirits, spirits as strong as gods and some of them are full of hate, and like to hurt. But most of the time they don't bother with making a milkmaid sick or cursing a little house. That's the mischief of the

53

restless dead! And the restless dead need to make mischief so that the fog and the smoke in which they wander will lift."

'I didn't wait any further. I was impressed with his generosity and patience with me – and you must realize how splendid he looked sitting there, covered and permeated with gold, this beautiful noble creature – that I loved him with a beating heart. I loved him with tears. I loved him with laughter.

'I reached out, and as I touched him, I asked that all the gold covering him be stripped and that he have the freedom of a man to walk amongst us. Can you guess what happened.'

'He became visible as real,' I said.

'He did, and I learnt something then about spirits that I was later to use to my advantage and used up till not very long ago. He did. He became visible, a great noble gentleman in festival dress sitting opposite me at the marble table with the wine cup in front of him, and he smiled. There was a stir all around as people saw him, and took notice. I don't think they had seen him materialize as we would say in this day and age. They just noticed him. For he was beautiful.'

'Was it clear that he was Marduk?' I asked.

'No. Without the gold he could have been a King, an ambassador. You know. The statue, you see, it was more stylized, remember. But everybody saw *him*. Even the musicians stopped their piping until he turned his head and gave a gesture for them to go on. And they saw him! And they went on.

'I was frozen with anxiety. "Come on, friend," he said. "I see more clearly than ever, and though this body is light, I like the form of it, and it draws eyes to me which give me power such as the New Year's Procession itself gives. They see me! They don't know who I am but they see. Come on, friend, let's walk, I want to walk up on the walls and through the temple with you, I want to see things clearly now with you. You don't have to take me into your home. Your uncles will all go crazy. Unfortunately, I can hear with this god's ears that they are already gathering the wise men of Judea to talk about you, and that you can see and hear the pagan gods. Come on, let's go, I want to walk."

'He stood up and put his arm around me and we strolled out of the garden. We walked all afternoon. I asked him, "What happens if you don't go back to the temple for the morning feast?"

'"Idiot!" he said laughing. "You know perfectly well what happens. I just smell the food. I don't eat it. They'll lay it down before the statue and take it away and bring it to all the temple personnel who are to eat from the table of God. Nothing is going to happen!"

'We walked all over the quarters of Babylon, along the canals, the river, over the bridges, through different districts and through the marketplace and through the many open gardens and parks. He was staring wildly at things, and now, of course, spirit that I am, I know what it was like for him to see these vivid colors. I understand better what he had endured.

'Suddenly, near the Ishtar Gate, he stopped in his tracks. "Can you see that?" And I did see it; it was the goddess herself. She was glowering at both of us. She was caked with gold and jewels and invisible. In fact I could see through her angry face.

'"Ha, she doesn't like it, what I'm doing, that I escaped!" He stopped and began to worry. He then took on for the first time the look of fear. No, not fear. Apprehension. He became guarded. And I saw why. Many spirits were now around us, looking at him, and envying him and challenging him with their furrowed brows, and gods were there. The god Nabu was there! I saw him. And suddenly I saw the god Shamash. Now all of these were Babylonian gods and they had their own temples and priests. But I could see they were angry at us.

'"Why aren't you afraid of them, Azriel?" Marduk asked me in a confidential breath.

'"Should I be, my Lord? First of all I am with you, and second of all I am Hebrew. They are not my gods."

'This struck him as hilarious and he began to laugh and

laugh. I hadn't heard him laugh since he had become visible. "That's a perfect Hebrew answer," he said.

'"Yes, I think so too," I said. "My Lord, would I offend them if I tried not to see them. Would you offend them if you banished them!"

'"No, I am the great god here." And he did make a decisive and angry and bold gesture, and the spirits turned pale and like smoke, even the angry angry Shamash, and they vanished. But what lingered was the dead, everywhere the restless dead. He opened his arms and he conveyed blessings on them. He began to talk in Sumerian, and he gave blessing after blessing, "Return to your slumber, return to your rest in the Mother Earth, return to the peace of your graves, and to the safety of the memories of you in the hearts and minds of your children."

'And thank God these dead people all went away. Of course he and I were standing there, plainly visible, and attracting much attention, this noble Lord who made extravagant gestures to people nobody could see, and this rich Hebrew overladen with jewelry, standing there like his page, or companion or whatever.

'But the dead did fade. My heart sank. I remembered the ghost of Samuel when he had been called forth by the Witch of Endor for King Saul. He had said, "Why do you disturb my rest?" Oh, but the woe of this rest. I didn't want to be dead. I didn't. I didn't want to be dead. I reached out and clutched his hand. Marduk was of course stronger now, from having been seen for so long by so many. I don't have to tell you the cosmology, it's simple, he would grow stronger and stronger the more he appeared.

'I was confused, however, on every other score. For example. Why did he not let the priests bring him to life in gold and walk in gold, the god himself, about the city? Of course I'd never heard of any god doing that, but then I'd never met a god before Marduk. He read these thoughts for me. He still looked apprehensive.

'"Azriel, first off the priests are not strong enough to make me solid and visible in gold. They cannot move the statue! They cannot make an image of me in gold as you can and then make it walk. They don't have the power. They don't have your gift. And even if they did, what would be my life? An endless New Year's Festival, surrounded by worshipers? I've seen gods fall for this! And in the end they have nothing, they belong to everyone who can touch their garments or their skin or their hair, and they flee into the fog, finally, screaming like the confused dead. No, such a thing I would only do if Babylon needed it of me, and Babylon does not. But Babylon needs something and soon, and you know why."

'"Cyrus the Persian," I said. "He draws closer every day. He'll sack Babylon. And . . . and . . ." I said. "He will either slaughter my people with all the inhabitants or he will maybe let us stay."

'Marduk put his arm around me and we walked bravely through the enormous crowd that had gathered to stare at us and our strange activities, and we went on into another great garden, one of my favorites where the musicians were always playing the harps. In fact, here the Hebrews played their music and the Hebrew men often gathered to dance. I hadn't meant to come to my people directly, but as it turned out it didn't matter. He said quickly,

'"Azriel, I think we took the wrong turn."

'"Why, they won't notice us any more than anyone else. They see me with a rich man. I'm a merchant. I'll say I sold you your beautiful girdle of gold and these jewels."

'He laughed at that, but he made us sit down together and we were once again whispering. "What do you know about the Persians!" he asked me. "What do you know about the cities that Cyrus conquers! What do you know?"

'"Well, I know the lies the Persians spread, that Cyrus brings peace and prosperity and leaves people alone, but I don't believe it. He is a murdering King like any other. He is on the march like Assurbanipal. I don't believe the Persians will peacefully accept the surrender of this city. Who would believe them? Do you?"

'I realized that he was no longer listening to me. He pointed ahead. "This is what I meant," he said, "when I said we took the wrong turn. But they would have found us anyway. Be calm. Say nothing. Give away nothing.'

'I saw what he saw, a great mass of the Hebrew elders storming towards us, clearing back the crowd and thickening it on all sides. And at the head of this crowd was the prophet Enoch in a fury with his white hair streaming in all directions, and he gazed on Marduk, and I knew he saw Marduk, whereas all those around him, uneasy and unsure, and not wanting to provoke a riot, only saw a Noble Man and their slightly crazy Azriel, whom they already knew to be a trouble-maker of a mild, powerful, and obedient sort.

'Marduk looked the prophet in the eye! So did I. He came to a halt not far from us. He was half-naked, as prophets often are. He was covered with ashes and dirt and he carried a staff, and I knew for the first time since I had ever heard of him – he wasn't a favorite of mine – that he was a real prophet because of the way he beheld Marduk with flaming indignation and violent faith.

'"You!" he declared, lifting his staff and pushing it at Marduk. The crowd fell back in fear. I mean, this figure did look like a rich man! But then the most terrible of all things happened. The prophet opened wide his eyes, and said, "Bring to yourself your loot, the gold that your soldiers took from our temple in Jerusalem, clothe yourself with it, you stupid, useless idol, go on, you were made to be metal!'

'And before I could think to act, the gold did come down upon Marduk and enclose him, but he resisted it, and I tried to banish it, and between us we made it a light covering only, and it did not have the deep vitality of the visions I had so long had. But the gold was all over Marduk, and the streets were filled with the sounds of running feet. I looked up at the distant houses that enclosed the garden, and the rooftops were thronged with onlookers.

'My father suddenly pushed his way to the fore, and threw his arm in front of Enoch. "You hurt us with this, don't you see!" he declared, and then he too saw Marduk standing there now dusted with gold, and Enoch hit my father with his staff.

'I was enraged, but my brothers surrounded the prophet, and Marduk took my arm. "Stay with me," he said imploringly in a soft whisper. "Am I all gold?" I explained he

58

was covered over with it, and it was getting thicker but he was not the moving idol that he had seemed to me at first. He merely smiled and he looked up at the people on the rooftops and turned round and round, and people began to scream.

'"Silence," shouted Enoch, stamping the bricks with his staff, his beard shuddering. You should have seen him. He was in his glory. I tell you, prophets are murderous, a murderous breed. "You, Marduk, God of Babylon, are nothing but an impostor sent out from the temple!" he roared.

'Marduk laughed under his breath. "Well, he's giving us a way out, Azriel, what a relief!"

'"Do you want them to believe in you, my Lord? All you need to do is vanish and reappear. I'll help you."

'He gave me a devastating look.

'"I know," I said, "I disappoint you. You don't want to be the god."

'"Who in the hell would want it, Azriel? No, I shouldn't say that. Let me say, who would give up life for it? But there's no time. Your prophet here before us is about to bellow like a bull."

'And Enoch did just that. He raised his powerful voice, though how such a thunder could come from such a scrawny rib cage, it's hard to imagine, and he declared:

'"Babylon, your time is come. You will be humbled. Even as we speak, the anointed one comes, Cyrus the Persian, the scourge whom the Lord God Yahweh has sent to punish you for what you have done to his Chosen people and to lead us back to our own land!"

'Roars came from the Hebrews, roars and prayers and chants and bowing and bowing to the Lord God of Hosts, and the Babylonians looked on in amazement, some of them even laughing, and then Enoch made his prophecy again:

'"Yahweh sends a saviour in the person of Cyrus to save this city ... aye, even you Babylon, you yourself will be delivered out of the hands of mad Nabonidus into the hands of a liberator."

'There was a beat of silence. Only a beat. And then the

roar rose from all – Hebrew, Babylonian, Greek, Persian. The whole crowd cried up for joy. "Yes, yes, the anointed one, Cyrus the Persian, may he liberate us from a mad king who has left the city."

'Hordes began to bow to Marduk, bow at his feet and stretch out their arms and then back away . . .

'"All right, impostor, savor your moment!" cried Enoch. "It is the will of Yahweh that your city be surrendered without bloodshed. But you are no true God. You are an impostor and in the temples there are nought but statues. Statues, I tell you. You and your priests will see us leave in triumph and you will thank us that we have saved Babylon for you!"

'I was truly speechless, no joke. I couldn't figure this out! But Marduk only nodded his head and took the insults of the prophet, and then he turned and threw up his arms. "I'm leaving you now, Azriel, but take care and do nothing until you have my advice! Be on guard against those you love, Azriel. I feel dread, not for Babylon, Babylon shall conquer, but for you. Now comes my moment of pride."

'He then began to blaze with gold light, and I could see by his maddened eyes that it was coming from him, and as the Babylonians and the Jews saw it, he had the strength from them to grow brighter and then he said in a huge voice, more huge than a man's, and rattling the lattices and echoing off the buildings:

'"Get away from me – Enoch and all your tribe. I forgive you your rash words. Your God is faceless and merciless. But I call down the wind now to scatter you all!"

'And the wind came. The wind came with huge ferocity over the rooftops, lifted off the desert and filled with sand. The gold figure of Marduk suddenly grew immense before me, but I knew now this was illusion, for it was paling, and as I stood looking up at him, he exploded into a shower of gold, and the people went completely wild.

'Everyone ran. Panic drove them. What they had seen drove them. What they had heard and, if nothing else, the wind salted with sand drove them.

'Only I stood there, my brothers now rushing to my side,

and the prophet, Enoch, laughing, just laughing and throwing out his arms! Then he bore down on me, shoving my father to one side with his staff. He gave me the evil eye! He looked at me and he said, "You will pay for eating the food of the false gods. You will pay! You will pay." And he spat at me, and reached down for the sand that was gathered and threw it at me. My brothers begged him to stop, but he laughed, and he said, "You will pay."

'I got furious, truly furious. My happy nature left me. I felt the first anger that would soon become common to me after my death. I leant forward and I said,

'"Call on Yahweh to stop this sandstorm, you fool!" and then my brothers literally dragged me away.

'A host of devoted elders rushed out to shelter Enoch and they picked him up and carried him away like a madman thrashing and screaming and gradually, gradually . . . as we ran to the shelter of our own house, the wind died away.'

Four

I was almost sick by the time we reached the house. My brothers were carrying me. And outside the gate, what should we see?

'First were two of the other prophets, the more quiet ones who merely echoed the old words of Jeremiah sent from Egypt, and with them an old woman whom everyone feared and despised. Her name was Asenath, and she was one of our tribe but she was a necromancer, everybody knew, and such things were forbidden, whether the great King Saul had ever called up Samuel with the Witch of Endor or not.

'Also, everybody went to her for help from time to time. So you know, it wasn't so great to see her outside our gate, but she had known my mother and my grandparents, and she wasn't the enemy, just someone with an unsavory reputation who could mix up poisons to kill people and potions to make people fall in love.

'She had straggling hair, very white, and eyes which had turned a perfect brighter blue with age, rather than pale, and a withered long face and a great triumphant expression, and she wore all scarlet, defiant scarlet, silks all over her, as if she were some Egyptian whore or something, and she carried a crooked staff, with a snake on the end of it, not so unlike the staffs of the prophets, and she said to me:

'"Azriel, you come to me. Or you let me in."

'By this time all the household was in the courtyard inside screaming and yelling at her to get away from our house, old witch, and my brothers told her to go, but to my surprise my father said, "Come inside, Asenath, come inside."

'Next I remember lying on my bed, and listening to people talk. My brothers wanted to know how in the hell I had gotten into this, and how could I believe this demon was Marduk when he was obviously a demon, and why had I not told them that I was conversing with other gods! My sisters kept saying, "Oh, leave him alone," and for a moment I thought I saw the ghost of my mother, but this might have been a dream.

'All the uncles and elders were gathered in the long rooms of the scriptoria which flanked the courtyard for half its distance . . . it was quite big, as I told you. And I didn't know where my father was.

'At last, he sent for me, and my brother propped me up, and got me on my feet and took me to him. I didn't like the door through which we passed. This was a small antechamber off the chamber of the ancestors, that is, the little room in which earlier Assyrians and Akkadians of this very house had buried their dead. This little room was part of their old pagan worship and we had never cleaned the paintings of priests and priestesses and ancestors of other people off the walls. Superstition stopped us, and after all, heathens that they were, their bones lay under the floor.

'There were three chairs in the room, simple chairs, you know the kind, of leather and crossed painted legs, but they were our very finest, and also there were three lamp stands, and in each the wick was burning the olive oil brightly, so the room had a splendid but frightening look.

'Old Asenath sat in one chair, and my father in the other, and they were whispering, which they stopped when I came in. I sat down in the free chair, and my brothers left us, and there we were among painted Assyrians, in the flicker of these lamps, in an airless place. I closed my eyes. I opened them. I deliberately tried to see the dead. I tried to see them as I had seen them when Marduk was with me. And for a moment I did. I saw them as wraiths throughout the room, sort of shuffling and mumbling and pointing, and then I shook my head and said, "Be gone."

'Asenath, who had a very young voice for such an old hag, laughed at me.

'"You learnt your imperial ways from the great god Marduk, didn't you?"

'Silence from me.

'Then she said, "What? Won't you own up to your loyalty to your god in your father's presence? It doesn't surprise. You think you are the first Hebrew who has worshipped the Babylonian gods? The hills around Jerusalem are filled with altars where Hebrews still worship pagan gods."

'"Which means what, old woman?" I said, surprised at my own anger and impatience. "Get to the point. What do you have to say to me?"

'"Nothing to you. It's all said to your father. You make your choice. You make it. Ten years since the Festival has been celebrated but many, many more years since the true miracle of the Festival has been brought about. And the old priests; they know how to do it; but they don't know everything; and for this, this which I hold here" – and she drew a cumbersome package out of her garments – "they would give me anything and they will."

'I looked at it. It was an ancient Sumerian clay envelope which meant that the ancient Sumerian tablet was untouched inside. It had never been tampered with. I could see that.

'"What do I want with that? What do I care about the true miracle of the Festival?" I said.

'My father motioned for me to be quiet.

'She put the clay envelope with its secret tablet hidden inside it into my father's hands. "Hide it here with the bones of the Assyrians," she said. She laughed. "And remember what I said, they will give you Jerusalem for it! Do as I say! They've already sent for me. They don't know clearly even how to mix the gold without me. I will help them, but when they demand the tablet of me, it will be safe with you."

'"Who gave you this all-precious tablet, Asenath?" I asked sarcastically, becoming ever more anxious and impatient at this whole thing. I'd never seen my father so serious! I didn't like it.

'"Look at it, scribe, scholar, smart one!" she said. "How old do you think this is?"

'"A thousand kings have reigned since then," I said. "It's as old as Uruk." And really this was the same as saying to you in English, this thing is two thousand years old.

'She nodded. "Given me by the priest they put to death, just to spite them," she said.

'"I want to read the outside," I said.

64

'"No!" she said. "No!" Then she stood up and leaned on her snake staff or whatever the hell she called it, and she said to my father, 'Remember, there are two ways to do this. Two ways. I give you my counsel. Were he my son, I would give them this tablet. I would give it into the hands of the most ambitious. I would give it into the hands of the most dissatisfied and eager to be gone from here, and that is the young priest, Remath. Be clever. You hold your people in your hands.'

'Then she turned and threw out her staff, and lo, the doors opened of themselves and she turned to me and she said, "You are most privileged for I give you my one chance at immortality. Were I to keep it, were I to abide by it, I might rise above this world and the stumbling dead, with the strength of a great spirit."

'"And why don't you?" said I.

'"Because you can save your people. You can save us all. You can take us back to Jerusalem and then, for that you deserve something, yes, you deserve something for that . . . to be an angel or a god."

'I was on my feet, trying to stop her and demand more of her, but she went out directly, scattering the family with wild threats, and strode through the anterooms, and the gate opened for her staff, and on she walked, a blaze of red silk into the street and away.

'I looked at my father. He sat still holding this enveloped tablet and looking at me with large tear-filled eyes. I had never seen his face so frozen. It was as if the muscles of his face didn't know grief or pain or fear well enough to form a face for it. He was at a loss.

'"What the hell is she talking about, Father?" I asked him.

'"Sit down here close to me," he said, the tears spilling now as freely as they might from a woman, and he held my hand.

'"Will you let me read that damned thing?" I asked.

'He didn't respond. He held it close to his chest. And he was thinking. The door lay open and I saw my brothers out there, all peering in and then my sister came and said, "Father, brother, do you want some wine?"

'"There isn't wine in the world enough to get me drunk now," said my father. "Shut the door." My sister did.

'He turned to me suddenly, his lips pursed and then he swallowed and he said, "It was Marduk with you, wasn't it? Or a spirit who claimed that he was Marduk. It was true."

'"Yes, I would say that is precisely the truth, Father. I've talked to him since I was a child. Am I to be punished now for this? What's to happen? What's this about Remath, the priest? You know him? I don't know that I do."

'"You know him," he said. "You just don't remember him. The day that Marduk smiled at you, when you were a boy, Remath was standing in the corner of the banquet chamber. He's young, ambitious, full of hatred of Nabonidus and enough hate of Babylon to want to go away."

'"What's this to me?"

'"I don't know, my son, my beautiful and beloved son. I don't know. All I know is that all Israel is begging for you to do what the priests of Marduk want you to do. As for this enveloped tablet here? I don't know. I just don't know."

'He cried for a long time. I was tempted to snatch the enveloped tablet from him and suddenly I did. I read the Sumerian.

'"To make the Servant of the Bones."

'"What is that, Father?" I said. He turned, his tears disfiguring his face somewhat, and he wiped at his wet beard and lips and he took the tablet back. "Leave that to my judgment," he said in a low voice, and then he stood up and he went along the wall, looking for loose stones, for bricks that might come out, and he found what he wanted, a hiding place, and he put the tablet inside.

'"To make the Servant of the Bones," I repeated. "What can it mean?"

'"We have to go up to the temple, my son, to the Palace. Kings are waiting on us. Deals have been struck. Promises have been exchanged." Then he embraced me and he kissed me slowly all over my face, he kissed my mouth, my forehead, my eyes.

'"When Yahweh told Abraham that he was to bring Isaac

66

and sacrifice him," he said, "you know our great Father Abraham did as he was told."

'"So the tablet and the scrolls tell us, Father, but have you been told by Yahweh that I must be sacrificed? Yahweh has come to you now, along with Enoch and Asenath and all the others? Is that what you expect me to believe? Father, you are grieving for me. I am dead already in your mind. What is this? What, why am I to die? For what? What's wanted, that I personally renounce the god, that I tell the King the god has wished him well, what! If it's a performance I'll do it! But, Father, don't cry for me as if I were dead!"

'"It's a performance," he said, "but it takes a very very strong one to perform it, one with endurance and conviction, and one with a great heart filled with love. Love of his people, love of his tribe, love of our lost Jerusalem and love of the Temple to be built there to honor the Lord. If I thought I could do it, that I could see the performance through to the finish, I would do it. And you can turn on us, you can say no, you can flee.

'"But the priests of Marduk want you, my son, they want you. And so do others even more powerful than they. They want you. And they know you are stronger than your brothers." His voice broke.

'"I see," I said.

'"And you are the only one who could ever forgive me for condemning him to such a fate."

'I was thunderstruck. I just looked at him, at his tearful eyes, and I said, "You know, Father, you are perhaps right, at least insofar as this. I could forgive you anything. Because I know you, and you wouldn't do evil to me, you wouldn't do that."

'"No, I wouldn't. Azriel, do you know what it means to me that you are to be taken from me, you and your future wife and future sons and daughters? Oh, it doesn't matter. Forgive me, son, for what I do. Forgive me. I beg you. Before it begins, before we go to the palace, and hear the lies and look at the map, forgive me."

'He was my father. He was sweet and kind and overcome with grief, terrible grief and pain. It was an easy thing for me to put my arms around him as if he were my little brother and say, "Father, I forgive you."

'"Never forget that, Azriel," he said. "When you are suffering, when the hours are dragging by, when you are in pain, forgive me . . . not just for my sake, son, but for yours!"

'A knock came. Priests were here from the Palace.

'We got up at once, wiped our faces, and then we went into the courtyard.

'Remath was standing there, and as soon as I saw him, I did remember him as my father had said. I had never spoken much with him as he was a real malcontent; I mean he hated Nabonidus beyond belief for not giving Marduk's temple what it should have, but he also hated everybody else. He usually stood around the palace and the temple, doing nothing. But he was clever. I knew that. And he was very restless. He was young and smart.

'He studied us now, his eyes very deep set and seemingly better sculpted in his white skin, and his long thin nose gave him a disdainful look. All the rest was the usual mass of curly black hair . . . and priestly robes very fine, down to his jeweled sandals, and then he drew near my father and he said, "Did Asenath give it to you?"

'"Yes,' said my father. "But that does not mean that I will give it to you."

'"You're stupid not to. Your son goes into the earth otherwise. What good is that?"

'"Don't call me names, you heathen," my father said. "Let's get on with it. Let's go."

'In the anteroom stood other priests waiting for us, and as we went outside, we found that there were brightly adorned litters for us and we were taken to the palace, each alone in his own litter, and I lay back trying to figure this out.

'"Marduk, are you going to help me?" I whispered.

'Marduk answered, "I don't know what to tell you, Azriel. I don't. I can see what is bound to happen. I don't know! I know this, that when it is over, one way or another, I will still be here. I will be walking the streets of Babylon in search of eyes that can see me, and prayers and incense that can arouse me. But where will you be, Azriel?"

68

'"They're going to kill me. Why?"

'"They'll tell you. You'll see it all. But I can assure you of this much. If you refuse to do what they want, they'll kill you anyway. And they'll probably kill your father, because he knows the plot."

'"I see. I should have realized that. They need my cooperation and if I don't give it, well, then it would have been better for me had I never been asked."

'There came only silence from him but I could feel his breath and I knew he was close. He wasn't material, but it didn't matter; we were even closer in the darkness of this litter, being carried with the curtains drawn through Babylon's hollow paved streets.

'"Marduk, can you help me get out of this?" I asked.

'"I have been thinking of that for hours and hours, hours since your prophet spewed out all his filth at me. I have been asking myself, 'Marduk, what can you do?' But you see, Azriel, without your strength, I cannot do what I want to do. I can't. I can be the gold god on his throne and that is all. I can be the standing statue carried in procession. Those objects or encasements they already have. And if I were to run with you . . . if we were to escape, where would we go?"

'A strange sound filled the little curtained compartment. He was weeping. Then suddenly, "Azriel, tell them no! Refuse their filthy designs. Refuse them. Don't do it, not for Israel, not for Abraham, not for Yahweh. Refuse.'

'"And die."

'He didn't answer.

'"Well, either way I shall die, no?"

'"There's a third way," he said.

'"You're speaking of Asenath and the tablet."

'"Yes, but it is terrible, Azriel. It's terrible. And I don't know if there's truth in it. It is older than I am. It is older than Marduk and older than Babylon, that tablet; it came from the city of Uruk. Maybe from before. It is very old. What can I tell you? Know your own mind. Take your chance!"

'"Marduk, don't leave me," I said. "Please."

'"I won't, Azriel, you are the dearest friend of my heart

69

that I have ever had. I won't leave you. Make me appear if you need me to frighten them or stop them. Make me appear and I will try. But I won't leave you, I am your god, your own god, your god, and I'll be with you."

'We had come to the palace. We were being brought in by a private gate, and now we were welcomed out of our little compartments so that we might walk on the grand stairway of gold and glazed brick, through the magnificent veils that separated one giant room from another, and we did, we walked, in silence, my father and I, we walked, following the priest, and they took us into the royal chamber where Belshazzar, listening to cases, made a farce of justice every day, and where his wise men told him hour after hour what the stars were saying to them, and we went beyond that into small and fine apartments that I had never seen.

'I saw that a seal had been broken, an ancient seal, as the doors had been opened. But the servants had come. For everywhere was luxury, fine carpets, pillows, the usual veils, and everywhere the lamps hung from the beams of the ceiling and the oil was sweet and the light was bright.

'A table stood in the middle of the room. Men were seated at it. And behind them stood my uncles, two of them, including the one who was deaf, may he have no name, and the Elders of Israel in Captivity, and Asenath and Enoch the prophet as well.

'Only gradually did I let myself look down at those seated at the table, though we were being placed opposite, the servants hustling to draw back the golden chairs.

'I saw our miserable regent, Belshazzar, and he looked stupid with drink and terrified, and was mumbling to himself something about Marduk, and then I realized I was looking at Nabonidus, old Nabonidus, our true King who had been gone almost half my life. Our true King sat there in his full raiment, though not on a throne, merely at a table, and his big watery eyes were dead and empty already, and he merely smiled at me, and he said, "Pretty, pretty . . . you have chosen one that is so pretty . . . pretty as the god."

'"Pretty enough to be a god!" said a voice, and I looked directly opposite at this fine handsome man, taller than anyone there, thinner in build than any of us, with black curling hair but hair that was cut shorter than ours, and a trimmed mustache and a shorter trimmed beard.

'This was a Persian! The men beside him were Persians. They were in Persian robes, very like our own, but in royal blue, and they were crusted with jewels and gold embroidery, and their fingers were covered with rings, and the goblets before them were our temple goblets!

'These were men from the Persian empire which was conquering us, which was killing us. All the strange predictions of Enoch came back to me and I saw him glaring down at me, with a near impish smile, and Asenath seemed filled with wonder.

'"Sit down, young one," said the tall robust man with the big laughing eyes, the handsomest man, the man who gleamed with power. "I'm Cyrus, and I want you at your ease."

'"Cyrus!" I said. Cyrus was the conqueror.

'The full details of the man's accomplishments were sharpened in my mind. This was Cyrus the Achaemenid King who already ruled half the world. He had united the Medians with the Persians, the man who meant to take Babylon. The man who had scared all the cities around us. This was no longer tavern talk of war. This was Cyrus himself sitting here before us.

'I should have prostrated myself before him but no one was doing anything like that before anyone, and he had said in a clear voice with an excellent command of Aramaic that I was to be at ease.

'Very well. I looked at him directly. After all, I thought, I'm going to die. So what. Why not?

My father took the empty chair beside me.

'"Azriel, my boy, my beautiful boy," said Cyrus. The voice was crisp, full of good humor. "I have been in Babylon for days. There are thousands of my soldiers throughout Babylon. They have come in by many gates over a long time. The priests know. Here, your beloved King – and may the gods keep him well always – Nabonidus himself knows." He gave a generous nod to the suspicious and dying old King.

71

"All your King's regents and his officials know that I am here. Your Elders, you see. Don't feel fear. Feel joy. Your tribe will be rich and they will live forever, and they will go home."

'"Ah, and this depends then on what I do?" I asked.

'I wasn't sure then and am still not today sure why I was so cold and disdainful of him. He was compelling but he was human, and young. And also, no matter what he'd done so far, he was a heathen to me, and he wasn't even Babylonian. So, I was cold to him.

'He gave a silent measuring smile.

'"So it depends then on what I do?" I repeated the question. "Or your will, Lord, has your will already been decided?"

'Cyrus laughed, with crinkling cheerful eyes. He had the vigor of kings all right, and not yet the total madness. He was too young and he'd been drinking up the blood of Asia. He was full of strength. Full of victory. "You speak boldly," he said to me generously. "You look with a bold eye. You are your father's eldest, aren't you?"

'"For the three days required," said one of the priests, "he must be very strong. To be bold is part of it."

'"Put another chair at this table," I said, "with your permission, My Lord King Cyrus, and My Lords, King Nabonidus and Lord Belshazzar. Put it here at the end."

'"Why, for whom?" asked Cyrus politely.

'"For Marduk," I said. "For my god who is with me."

'"Our god is not at the beck and call of you!" roared the High Priest. "He won't come down off the altar for you! You have never seen our god, not really, you are a lying Jew, you are —"

'"Close your mouth, Master," said Remath in a small voice. "He has seen the god and he has spoken with him and the god has smiled at him, and if he invites the god to this chair, the god is most likely to come."

'Cyrus smiled and shook his head. "You know," he said, "this is truly a marvelous city. I am going to love Babylon. I wouldn't hurt a stone of such a place. Ah, Babylon."

'I might have laughed at that, at his wiliness, his disrespect

72

for the elders and the old priests, his ruthlessness and his wit. But I was past laughing. I looked at the light of the lamps and I thought, "I am going to die."

'A hand touched mine. It was vaporous. No one could see it. But it was Marduk. He had taken this chair to my left; invisible, transparent, golden, and vital. My father sat to my right and my father just put his hands up to his face and cried and cried.

'He cried like a child. He cried.

'Cyrus looked with patience and compassion at my father.

'"Let's get on with it," said the High Priest.

'"Yes," said Enoch, "let's get on with it now!"

'"For these men, these elders, these priests, this prophetess, get stools for them to be comfortable," said Cyrus amiably and cheerfully. He smiled at me. "We are all in this together."

'I turned to look at Marduk. "Are we?"

'They all watched me in silence speaking to my invisible god.

'"I can't tell you what to do," said Marduk. "I love you too much to make a mistake, and I have no right answers."

'"Stay then."

'"Throughout," he said.

'The stools and chairs were quickly brought in and the Elders allowed in very casual fashion to sit all about us and this conquering Persian King, this monarch who had driven the Greeks crazy all over the world and now wanted our city and had everything we had but the city.

'Only the priest Remath remained standing, at a distance against a gilded column. The High Priest had told him to leave, but he had ignored this command and apparently been forgotten. He was watching me and my father, and then I realized that he could see Marduk. Not so clearly. But he could see him. Remath moved his position slightly so that he could see all three of us, going to a farther column behind Cyrus where Cyrus's soldiers, by the way, stood poised to become butchers. And there Remath stared at the seemingly empty chair with cold and conniving eyes, and he looked at me.'

Five

'Well, my lord, what do you want of me?' I asked. 'Why am I, a Hebrew scribe, so important so suddenly?'

'"Listen, child," said Cyrus. "I want Babylon without a siege, I want it without a death. I want it the way I have taken the Greek cities when they have been smart enough to let me do it. I don't want ashes behind me and ruins galore! I don't come with a torch, and a bag for loot, a thief. I will not rape your city and deport your populations. On the contrary, I will send home to Jerusalem all of you, with the blessing to build your own temple."

'Enoch now stood up and laid down before us a scroll. I reached for it, and read it. It was a proclamation freeing all the Hebrews to go home. Jerusalem would be under Cyrus's benevolent protection.

'"He is the Messiah," said Enoch to me. And what a change of tone from the old man. Now that Cyrus the Great was talking to me, my own prophet was talking to me. Now, by Messiah he meant "anointed one." Later on the Christians made a big deal of this word, but that's all it meant then. But still, it was a strong word.

'"Add to that proclamation," said Cyrus, "gold, gold beyond your imagining," he said, "and permission to take all that you possess with you, to reclaim your vineyards, your lands, and be loyal to a powerful empire that will let you build your Temple to Yahweh."

'I looked at Marduk. Marduk sighed. "He's speaking the truth, that's all I can tell you. He's going to conquer one way or another."

'"I can trust him, then?" I asked my god.

'Everyone was shocked. "Yes," said Marduk, "but to what degree . . . keep listening. You have something they want, your life, there may be a way, who knows, for you yet to escape with it."

74

'"Ah no," cried Asenath, "God Marduk, you are wrong. There is but one path for him to escape and he should take it for it is better than life itself."

'I realized she could see him, at least partially, and hear his words.

'He turned to her. "Let him be the judge. Death may be better than what you have in store for him."

'Cyrus watched all this in amazement. Then he looked at the priests gathered all around, the High Priest of Marduk, and the wily Remath standing over by the pillar.

'"I need the blessing of your god," said Cyrus, "you are right, you are more than right," he said humbly, but also rather cleverly, since this was just what these priests wanted to hear.

'"You see, Azriel," said Cyrus, "it's this simple. The priesthood is strong. The temple is strong. Your god, if he sits with us, and I must confess I am prepared to worship him, is strong. And they can turn the city of Babylon against me. All the rest of Babylonia, I hold, but this is the jewel, this is the Gate of Heaven."

'"But how could you hold all the rest!" I said. "Our cities are safe and secure. We knew you were coming, but someone is always coming."

'"He's telling you the truth," said Nabonidus, and when he spoke all eyes turned to him. He wasn't addled or stupid. Just very old and tired. "The cities are taken, every one has collapsed into Cyrus's arms. The fire-signal towers have all fallen to him, and the signals being sent are sent by Cyrus's men, to lull Babylon, but the cities are fallen and the signals are false."

'"Look," said Cyrus, "I'll send back to those cities all the gods which have been sent here for refuge. I want your temples to thrive. Don't you see? I want to embrace you! I didn't lay waste Ephesus or Miletus! They are Greek cities still and their philosophers are arguing in the agora. I want Babylonia in my embrace, not her destruction."

'He then turned sharply and stared at the "empty" chair. "But your god Marduk must take my hand," he said, "if I am to conquer this city without fire. And then I shall send home all the gods of Babylonia as I promised."

'Marduk, unseen by him, only listened to him and said nothing. But the High Priest lost his temper. "There is no god in that chair! Our god is neglected by our king and has gone into a deep sleep from which no one can wake him."

'"Look," I said, "why call me into this? What have I to do with it? You have right here in Esagila the statue of Marduk that you need for the procession. You ride with him on the great wagon, and you hold his hand, and he holds your hand and you are King of Babylon. If the priests will let you take the statue, what's it to do with me? Have you heard some rumor, Majesty, that I can control the god or turn him against you? You need a golden idol for your work! It's there, over there in the chapel."

'"No, my son," said Cyrus, "all that might have worked just fine if you had had a procession year after year with the god, and if the people had seen the golden idol, as you call him, and they had cheered him and your King Nabonidus, but those processions were not held, and the precious statue is not going to enter into any procession with me now, even if I wanted it to. What I need is the ceremony as it was done of old."

'A chill passed through me. Marduk looked at me and said, "I know little of what he is talking about, but all spirits see far, and I see horror for you. Don't speak. Just wait."

'Meantime the priests were in a commotion. They had brought in on a bier a great heap of something, which was draped in linen and, now bringing it near to our table, with several torchbearers, they drew away the linen and we all gasped at what we saw.

'It was the processional statue and it was broken, and out of its rotted inside stuck bones which appeared to be those of a man, rotted, too, and half the skull showed where the thick gold-plated enamel had turned to dirt, and the whole mess lay a disgrace and an insult.

'The High Priest glowered at me. He folded his arms. "Did you do this, Hebrew?" he asked. "Did you cause

76

Marduk to leave the statue! To leave this city? Was it you rather than our King here whom we have so accused?"

'I understood a great deal in a moment. I looked at my god who sat staring coldly at the heap of ruin.

'"Are those your bones, my Lord?" I asked Marduk.

'"No," he said, "and I only vaguely remember when they were put there. The spirit of that young one was weak, and I vanquished it and continued my reign. Perhaps it invigorated me that I was to be replaced? *I don't know*, Azriel! Remember, those are the wisest words I have for you. I don't know. Now they mean to put *you* in my place, that much we both know."

'"What do you want, Lord?" I asked Marduk.

'"For you not to be hurt, Azriel," he said. "But do you want to become what I am? Do you want your bones encased three hundred years in that! Until it then crumbles and another young man must be lured for the sacrifice? But let me get to your point." He leaned towards me.

'"I forget how large your heart is, Azriel. You ask for my sake. I can tell you this, I can come and go as I wish. I banished the last replacement with a wave of my arm, and back into the fog he went. For a mortal man to be murdered in this fancy way does not necessarily make him either a god or a strong spirit." He shrugged. "Think of yourself and yourself only. What I am is . . . is what you know." Then the sadness of his face shocked me. "I don't want you to die!" he whispered.

'The High Priest could stand this dialogue no longer. He couldn't see or hear Marduk. He was sputtering with fury. But Asenath was hearing it all and looking from me to the god with great curiosity, and Remath the sly one wouldn't give himself away, but he knew something sat in the empty chair. He knew it. He understood something of what it said also.

'"You're speaking of a statue of gold," my father spoke up. "You can't make a statue of gold without my son?" he asked.

'"The bones are the bones of the god!" declared the High Priest. "This is why our city is as it is, why we need the Persian deliverer. The god is old, the bones are rotten, the statue will not stand, and there must be a new god."

'"But the statue in the High Sanctuary?" my father asked, which was a childish question.

'"That can't be carried through the streets," said the priests. "That's a mere hunk of —"

'"Metal!" said the prophet Enoch with a cruel smile.

'"You are wasting time," said Cyrus. "The ceremony has to be done in the old way," he said, looking at me. "Explain to him, Priests, don't just stand there. Explain. And you, my brave Azriel, what does Marduk say to you?"

'It was old white-haired Asenath who spoke up, stamping the floor first with her serpent staff to let everybody know they had better shut up for her. "The god says he will go or stay as he pleases, that the bones inside the statue do not matter to him, they are not his bones, that's what he says!" Then she looked directly at Marduk, "Well, isn't that what you say, you miserable little god who trembles in the light of Yahweh!"

'The Priests were thoroughly confused. Were they to defend the honor of their Marduk, who wasn't even supposed to be there?

'"Look, my boy," said Cyrus, "become the god. Walk in the procession. You will be delicately covered in gold, though the old formula seems somehow to be . . . missing?" He cast a glance at the High Priest. "You will be alive beneath the covering. You must live long enough to hold my hand, and to raise your other hand to your subjects. And you will live the three days it will take to fight off the forces of chaos, and then return here with me to the Courtyard of Esagila, where I shall be proclaimed King by you. We shall do it faster if we can think of some way to make that acceptable."

'"Alive, covered with gold." I was amazed. "And then?"

'Asenath spoke up. "By then the gold will have hardened and you will be dead. You will see and hear for a while, but you will die inside, and when they see that your eyes are rotting, they will take out your eyes and replace them with jeweled eyes, and the statue of Marduk will be your shroud."

'My father put his face in his hands and then looked up. "I never saw it done in the old way," he said quietly. "But my father's father saw it once, or so he said. And the poison in the gold is what will kill you. You'll die slowly as the gold penetrates, as it reaches your heart and lungs, and then . . . as they say, you will at last be at peace."

'"This," said Asenath, "after you have been carried the full length of the Processional Way, gold and gleaming, raising your hand, even turning your head ever so slightly as the thick coating gets harder and harder."

'"And for this!" said Enoch. "We will return to Jerusalem, all of us, including those in prison, and we will have the means to build the Lord God's Temple again according to the measurement of King Solomon.'

'"I see," I said. "So in the old days, it was a real man! And when the statue finally crumbles . . ."

'"You blaspheme!" said the High Priest. "Those are the bones of Marduk."

'This was too much for Marduk. Invisible or not, he stood up, throwing over the chair, and with a great thrust of his left hand sent the bones swirling in all directions. They shattered and crumbled against the walls. Everyone cowered. Even I lowered my head. Cyrus did not but stared with wild, childlike eyes, and old Nabonidus put his head down on his arm as if he would go to sleep. The prophet Enoch sneered.

'Then Marduk turned to me. He looked hard at me and then at Asenath. "I know your wiles, old woman. But tell him everything! Tell him the full truth of it all. You know the dead. What do they say to you when you call them up? Azriel, do what you want to do for your people and your tribe. I will be here afterwards as I am now, and whether you can see me then and give me strength, and whether I can see you and give you strength, no one knows. Whether I can talk to you, no one can say. Your soul will be tested by this grand procession, this fight with chaos, this courtyard coronation, this torment! But this torment will not necessarily give you spiritual life. And you may fade in the mist with all the other weary and wandering dead. The dead of the whole world, regardless of gods or angels or demons or Yahweh. Do what you will as an honorable man, Azriel. For after it is done, I don't know that even I, strong as I am, will be able to find you or help you."

'Asenath was overcome with excitement. "I would worship you, Marduk, were you not an evil, worthless god. You're clever."

'"What does the god say!" demanded Cyrus.

'Enoch looked at Asenath. "We must tell him now what will happen to him, that is all. Azriel, you resemble the statue of Marduk. Encased with gold, you will fool all of your friends. No one will know that you are not a god, you will seem a man of living gold, and you will feel numbness and some pain, yes, the slow pain as life ebbs, but it's not terrible. Even as you walk the Processional Way, all your people will be preparing to go out of Babylon!"

'"Well, it's simple enough," I said. "Let the entire Hebrew population leave now, and I'll do it." I felt a tightening in my throat. I knew that this was youthful stupidity and that soon horror would come on me that was damn near unbearable.

'"Cannot be done, my son," said Cyrus. "We need your people and we need your prophets. We need them proclaiming Cyrus the Persian is the anointed of your god. We need all the city to roar in one voice, and I will not deceive you, I don't believe in your god, Marduk, and I don't believe that you will become a god if you do this."

'"Tell him all of it!" said Marduk.

'"Not now, and that part doesn't matter," said Asenath. "He may say no to that, you know as well as I do."

'"Azriel," Marduk said turning to me and embracing me. "I love you. I will be with you in the procession. They are speaking the truth. They will let your people go. I can stand this mortal company no longer. Asenath, be kind to the dead whom you call so often for they are desperate to be near to life, you know. Desperate."

'"I know, god of the heathens," she said. "Will you come to me now and talk to me!"

'"Never," screamed the High Priest. Then he quieted down. He looked at two other priests, men I scarcely remember. It was Remath, the sly one, who spoke up. "She is the only one who knows how to mix the gold, remember."

'I laughed. I couldn't stop myself. I laughed.

'"Ah, I see," said Cyrus. "So you turn to the Canaanite

sorceress because your own wise men no longer know the secret."

'My laughter – unshared – finally left me in peace.

'It took great courage for me to turn to my father. He sat as one broken and finished, his eyes wet and his face still. You might have thought I was already buried.

'"You must come too, Father, you and all my brothers."

'"Oh, Azriel –"

'"No, that's the last thing I ask of you, Father. Come. When we are led down the Processional Way let me see your upturned face and the faces of my family. That is, of course, if you believe in these men and you believe in this proclamation."

'"Money has already changed hands," said Cyrus. "Messengers are already on the way to Jerusalem. Your family will be great among the tribe, and you will be remembered for your sacrifice."

'"Like hell, great King," I said. "Hebrews don't remember those who pretend to be Babylonian gods. But I'll do it. I'll do it because my father wants me to do it . . . and I . . . and I forgive him."

'My father looked at me. His eyes said it all, his love, his broken heart. Then he looked at Enoch and Asenath and the Elders of our tribe, who had sat silent all this while, and then he said in the simplest words, "I love you, my son."

'"Father, I want you to know this," I said. "There is another reason why I do this . . . I do it for you, for our people, for Jerusalem, and because I have talked with a god himself. But I do it for one more reason, and that is simple. I wouldn't have anyone else suffer this. I wouldn't wish it on another."

'Surely there was vanity in my words, but no one seemed to think so. Or if they did they forgave it. The Elders rose, they had their Proclamation in their hands. All were satisfied. It was done. Cyrus the Persian was the Messiah.

'"Tomorrow morning, the trumpets sound," said the High Priest. "It will be announced that Marduk has brought Cyrus to liberate us from Nabonidus! The Processional Way is already being prepared. By the time the sun is high everyone will be in the street. The boat waits in the river to take us to the garden house where you will slay the dragon Tiamat, and that, by the way, will be nothing to you. We will return the following day, with you. We will hold you, and do all we can to ease your pain."

'"On the third morning, in the Courtyard, you must have life enough in you to rise and to put the crown on the head of Cyrus. That is all. After that, you may stand, held straight by the gold that kills you, warmed by it, numbed by it, and you may die in it. All the rest, the reading of the poems, the Destinies, all you need do is keep your eyes fixed and open."

'"And if I don't make the three days?"'

'"You will. The others always did. It is after that we may have to ease your death with a little more of the gold perhaps, in your mouth. But it will be painless."

'"I'm sure," I said. "Do you know how I despise you?"

'"I do not care," said the High Priest. "You're a Hebrew. You never loved me. You never loved our god."

'"Oh, but he does!" said Asenath, "that is the pity! But don't fear, Azriel, your sacrifice is so great for Israel that the Lord God of Hosts will forgive you, and your flame will be joined in death with the great fire that He is."

'"I vow it," said Enoch.

'I laughed contemptuously. I looked up, meaning only to look away in disdain, but I could see now that the room was thick with spirits. Like smoke they hovered all around, ghosts. I didn't know what they were or had been, their clothes were gone to such simplicity. Nothing remained except a tunic here or a robe there, sometimes there was not even a real form, only a face looking at me.

'"What is it, son?" asked Cyrus kindly.

'"Nothing. Only I see the lost souls and I hope that I do find rest in the fire of my god. But . . . it's foolish to even think of it."

'"Leave us now, all of you, leave the boy with us," said Remath. "We must groom him and dress him to be the finest Marduk who has ever been carried down the Processional Way, and you, old woman, will keep your promise, and tell us how to mix the gold and how to put the gold on him, on his skin, his hair, his clothes."

'"Go on, Father," I said. "But do let me see you tomorrow. Know that I love you. Know that I forgive you. Make of us a powerful house, Father, make of us a powerful nation." I bent over and kissed him hard on the mouth and on both cheeks and then I looked to King Cyrus.

'After all, he had not dismissed me. But my father left, and the Priests took out old Nabonidus, who had in fact fallen asleep, and the miserable mumbling Belshazzar, who was drunk and confused and seemed ready at any moment to be murdered. I didn't care what happened to either of them. I listened to my father's steps until I couldn't hear them anymore.

'Enoch went out with the Elders, making some big fine speech then, of which I don't remember a single word, except that it sounded like a bad imitation of Samuel.

'Cyrus stared at me. His eyes spoke, they spoke respect, they spoke forgiveness for my rudeness, my lack of servility, my lack of courtesy.

'"There are worse ways to die!" said the High Priest. "You will be surrounded by those who worship you; as your vision dims you will see rose petals fall before you, you will see a king kneel at your feet."

'"We need to take him now," said Remath.

'Cyrus beckoned for me to come to him. I stood up, went round the table and bent down to receive his embrace, and he rose with me, embracing me man to man. "Hold my hand for those three days, my son, hold steady, and I promise you, Israel will live under me forever in peace, as long as there is Cyrus and Persia, and Yahweh will have his temple. You are braver than I am, son, and I consider myself the bravest man in the world, you know. But you are braver. Now go, and tomorrow we will begin our journey together. You have my love, you have my unbounded love, the love of a King who was a King before he came to you and will be a greater King because of you."

'"Thank you, My Lord," I said. "Be good to my people. I am a poor spokesman for my God, but he is powerful."

'"I honor him," said Cyrus, "and all the beliefs and all the gods of those I take under my protection. Good night, child. Good night."

'He turned and his soldiers closed in around him and he walked very straight and calm out of the chamber. No one remained now but me and the priests and Asenath.

'I looked about. The dead had faded. But Marduk had come back and watched with folded arms. Marduk had sent them scurrying perhaps.

'"Parting words for me?" I said.

'"I'll be with you," he said. "I shall use all my power to be with you and ease your pain and help you. As I told you, I remember nothing of any such procession, or birth, or death. And maybe when your flame has gone into the great fire of your god, I will be here still for Babylon. If you love your people so much, maybe I can love my people a little more."

'"Oh, you needn't doubt him, he's a fine demon," said Asenath.

'Marduk glared at her and disappeared.

'The old priest raised his hand as if he would strike her, and she laughed in his face.

'"You can't do this without me, you fool," she said. "And you had better write down everything I tell you. You're a laugh, all of you, you pious priests of Marduk. It's a wonder any of you can even read the prayers!"

Remath came up to her.

'"Remember your promise to me," said Remath under his breath.

'"In time, in the right time," said Asenath, "the Father has the tablet hidden where you will never find it, and when the three days are concluded, when the army has entered through all gates, and when the Hebrews are on the march, I will see that you have its contents."

'"What is this other tablet you speak of?" I asked. "What part does it play?" Of course I knew where it was, where my father had hidden it in our house.

'"A prayer for your soul, son," she said, "that you may see god, and of course you know I'm lying to you." She shook her head. The mirth went out of her, even the hate. "It's an

84

old charm. You can choose then. You'll be dying. It's nothing to worry you now. Just a charm, such as the ancients believed, that's all, nothing else. The rest that we do here is medicine, not magic."

'They led me through the palace and now we broke another ancient seal and entered together a large chamber. Servants moved swiftly past us to place the tables and the lamps. I saw a great cauldron brought in. I saw a brazier for fire that would lie on the floor beneath the cauldron. I felt for the first time total fear. Fear of pain and hurt and burning.

'"If you've lied to me about the pain, tell me the truth, it will make it easier for me."

'"We haven't lied to you about anything!" said the High Priest. "You will stand in the temple of Esagila for centuries and you will receive our libations. Be our god! If you ever saw him, then be him! How did he become what he was, if it wasn't for us?"

'They brought a couch for me, and I lay down on it and shut my eyes. Who knows? Maybe I was home and dreaming. But I wasn't. They began to groom me. I lay there with my eyes closed, turned towards the wall, or towards them, and I felt their hands on me, clipping my hair and my beard, and trimming my nails to the perfect length, and when I had to, I lifted my limbs so that they could undress me and bathe me. And then it was dark. Only the fire beneath the cauldron burned.

'I could hear the old woman reciting the words in Sumerian. It was a formula, a mixture of gold and lead and other herbs and potions, some which I knew and many which only an enchantress might know, but I knew enough to know it would kill anybody.

'I also realized it had in it, this brew, the seeds that people chew to see visions, and a great deal of the potions they drink to make them have wild dreams, and I knew those intoxicants would ease my pain and blur my thoughts. "Who knows? Maybe I'll miss my own death," I thought.

'Remath came to me. His face was very simple and there was no meanness in him. He spoke almost sorrowfully.

'"We won't put on the final garments until dawn," he said.

"They are ready in the other chamber. The gold boils but it will cool, you needn't fear, it will be cool and thick when we apply it to your skin. Now, what can we bring you, lord God, Marduk, what can we bring you to make you happy tonight?" ·

'"I think I want to go to sleep," I said. "I fear that boiling gold."

'"No, it will be cooled," said Asenath. "Remember you must live long days whilst this gold eats into you. It will be cooled. You must be a smiling god as long as you can, and then a god with his hand lifted as long as you can, and then a seeing god as long as you can."

'"Yes, all right, leave me."

'"You don't want to pray to our own god?" asked Asenath.

'"I wouldn't dare," I whispered.

'I turned my back, and closed my eyes. And strangely enough I did sleep.

'They covered me with the softest blanket. That was sweet.

'I slept from sheer exhaustion, as though the ordeal lay behind me rather than ahead. I slept. And what I dreamed I don't know. What does it matter? I do remember being puzzled that I didn't want to see Marduk again; I remember thinking, Why is that, why am I not weeping on his shoulder? But that was just it, I didn't want to weep on anyone's shoulder. I had been dealt the mortal blow. I didn't know what lay ahead. The smoke, the fog, the flame, or power such as his. I couldn't know. And neither could he.

'I think I began to sing the psalm I loved so much of home and then I thought, The hell with it, Jerusalem will be theirs, not mine.

'A vision came to me. I think it was from Ezekiel, whom we were always copying at home, always fighting about, and arguing about . . . it was a vision of a valley of bones, the bones of all the dead, the bones of all mortal men and women and children. And I didn't think of the bones rising, I didn't think of them called to life. I simply saw them, and I thought, 'For that valley, I do this, for that valley, for all of us who are merely human.'

'Was I too proud? I don't know. I was young. I wanted

86

nothing. I slept. And too soon, too soon indeed, came the lamps and the light and the distant shine of the sun on marble floors far from the doors of the chamber.'

Six

'I was dizzy. I think it was the fumes. All night the kettle had cooked its immense blend of golden glaze, such a huge amount of gold and lead and whatever else went into it. The perfume was rich and delicious and I reeled.

'They stood me on my feet.

'I shook myself all over to waken more, to make the lamps stop hurting my eyes. That was sunlight, wasn't it? Asenath was there, and then the priests began to apply the gold. They began at my feet, telling me to stand straight and firm, and they covered my legs all over with the gold, painstakingly, in motions that were almost soothing. It was warm, but it didn't hurt. It held no sting whatsoever. They painted my face slowly. They brought the paint up into my nostrils, and they covered my eyelashes, one by one, and then they took the ringlets of my hair and my beard and one by one made them golden.

'By now I was fully awake.

'"Keep your eyes wide," said Asenath.

'Then they brought all the fine robes of Marduk. Now these were real clothes which were put on the statue every day, but I saw now what they meant to do, not trim them with gold but to coat them, so that indeed I would seem a living statue.

'They dressed me, and this they began to do, painting each fold of the long robe, the long full sleeves, and asking me again and again to raise my arms and to walk as they did their work.

'I stood before a mirror. I saw myself and I looked like the god. I saw the god.

'"You *are* the god!" said a young priest to me. "You are our god and we will serve you forever. Smile on me, Lord God Marduk, please."

'"Do it," said Asenath. "You see, the enamel must not

harden too fast. We can't have it become brittle. And each time it does become too hard, the priests will add more to that place so that you can move the muscle. Smile, open your eyes and close them, that's right, my beautiful boy. That's right. Do you hear that noise?"

'"It sounds like the entire city roaring," I said. I heard the trumpets too, but I didn't speak of that.

'I am dizzy!' I said.

'"We will hold you," said the young priest. "Cyrus himself will hold you, your attendants will hold you. Remember, take his hand, hold his hand. Turn to him often, and kiss him. The little gold from your lips will not harm his skin. You must do it."

'Within seconds we were high on the wagon, and all around me I saw the layers of flowers – every fine flower that can be grown inside or out in Babylonia, and flowers brought in from places far away, the blooms of Egypt and southern islands.

'We were in a war chariot atop this wagon, but the chariot's wheels were fixed, and the attendants stood lower and behind us, and holding me firmly by the waist. And one on the side held me also by the waist. And Cyrus mounted the chariot.

'Screams and cries came from everywhere. The gates had been open all the time. The people flooded in. The Procession had begun. I blinked. I tried to see. I saw the petals flying through the air, pink and red and white, and I smelled the incense rising. I looked down, feeling a stiffness in my neck and I saw all the priesthood and all the women of the temple prostrating themselves on the great tiled floor of the courtyard. The white mules began their slow march forward.

'In a daze I turned and looked at the King! How splendid and beautiful he looked.

'Just as we passed through the gates, there came the loudest shrieks and cries. The Hebrews were on the rooftops. I looked. It was a haze. But I could hear them singing the psalms of Zion. The faces were small and distant.

'The wagon picked up speed, as much speed as a giant

wagon can get, which is not much, but we were rolling steadily, you might say, and I held to the edge of the chariot with one hand, letting my golden fingers curve around it, and then I reached out as if by instinct, for no one told me, and I put my hand into Cyrus's hand and gave him the first kiss.

'The crowd was in ecstasy. Every house along the Processional Way seemed a living thing in itself, with life screaming from its windows and its roof, and life pressed up against its door, and in every side street people sang and waved palms and again and again I heard the Hebrew music. The Hebrew music followed us.

'I don't remember when we crossed the great canal, though I think I did see the dazzle of the water. The attendants were holding me firmly and telling me harshly to be strong.

'"You are my god, Marduk," said Cyrus. "Bear with them, they are fools. Hold my hand, my god. For now, we are King and god and no one can deny it."

'I smiled, and again I bent forward to kiss his cheek and again the screams of joy surged through the crowd. We were approaching the river. We would now be placed in the boat, and taken to the House of the Ordeal with Tiamat, the god's great battle with chaos. And what would that be?

'I was as one so drunk it simply didn't matter. I could feel the gold hardening all over me. And I could feel it caressing me as they said it would. I had anchored my feet fairly well at last and the attendants had their grip, and Cyrus's living hand held warm and tight to mine, and he waved and bowed and shouted a thousand greetings to the eager citizens of Babylon.

'A funny thought came to me as the boat moved up the river. There were crowds on all sides. And I thought, "He thinks this is all for him, Cyrus. And it's really just Babylon. Babylon having a big party or festival like it does so often, but he's never seen the city going crazy with dance and drink, and so he is very impressed. Well, let him enjoy it." Only dimly did I realize, I had not seen my family. They had been there, I was sure, but I had not seen them.

'The House of the Ordeal was splendidly plastered in

silver and emerald and rubies. The pillars were gold and made to look like great lotus blossoms at the top. The middle of the roof was wide open, and all around us were crowded hundreds upon hundreds of noble Babylonians, the rich, great officials from other cities, priests who had come with their gods to Babylon for safety, and also hundreds upon hundreds of Cyrus's court, so like us, yet so different. Taller, leaner, more trim, and more sharp of eye.

'Suddenly I stood alone in the midst of the open court. Everyone had backed away. Remath stood beside me, and on the other side, the young compassionate priest.

'"Lift your arms," said the priest. "Take your sword from the scabbard."

'"Sword, I didn't know I had one."

'"You do," said the young priest eagerly. "Ah, yes, raise it high."

'I scarcely knew whether I obeyed. The world was swimming before me. The nobles were chanting and harps were playing, and then I heard a sound I knew, knew from many spectacles of the past, and from the hunts with my father and brother. I heard the roar of lions, caged lions.

'"Don't fear," said Remath. "These animals are satiated and filled with potions that make them sluggish and they will come one by one as they are released, and they will rise as they have been trained to lick the honey from your lips, which I will put there now, honey and blood, and when they do, you will drive your sword into them."

'I laughed. "And you, where are you going to be?" I asked.

'"Right here, beside you," said the young priest. "This is nothing, Lord God Marduk, these lions want to die for you."

'He lifted a chalice to my lips. "Drink the honey and the blood," he said.

'I did, barely able to feel myself swallowing. I realized suddenly that almost all sensation had left my skin, I was as one in bitter cold night desert wind. But I swallowed and he gave me more until my tongue and lips were coated with blood and honey.

'A terrible excitement ran through the crowd. I could see the fear. The first lion had been released and came towards me. The Persians were backing up against the walls, I think. I could feel the fear, smell it. And I laughed again. "This is so funny," I said. "I'm half-dead and this lion is staggering towards me."

'Suddenly, the lion sprang, and the two priests had to hold me so that the lion's weight didn't throw me backwards. I lifted the sword. I called on the gold enamel to give me strength and I drove the sword into the lion's heart. His hot foul breath blew into my nostrils and his tongue touched my lips, and then he fell over, awkward, dead, and the crowd sang and sang and sang of courage.

'Now the King came to my side, and he too had his sword, and I saw that as the second lion and third lion were released that we were to kill them together. The King's face was as rigid as mine, and he narrowed his eyes at the beast. "They have plenty of life in them, it seems to me," he said.

'"Ah, but you're a King and I'm a god, so let's kill them."

'Behind them the priest cracked the whip which made one lion jump for Cyrus first and he staggered back as he drove the sword and then kicked the animal away from him. The lion rolled on its back roaring, dying. The second beast was in my face. I felt the priest lift my wrist. "Thrust now!" I did. I thrust more than once wanting the thing dead and off me.

'And once again, all sang, and cheered, and I could hear the crowds outside singing and cheering. I saw the lions lifted and carried out. I heard the song of the priest of the slaying by Marduk of the evil Tiamat.

'And from her hide he made the heavens and the earth and the seas . . .' the words rang out in the old Sumerian. And then in Akkadian, and then in Hebrew, and it was like overlapping waves of sound, and I swam in them.

'I stood alone in the court. The priests were painting me with the blood and honey. "They cannot hurt you," said Remath.

'"What?" I asked. But I knew. I could hear them as distinctly as the beasts. It was the bees. And now as a great silken dragon proceeded towards me, tightly sewn with spindly gold ribs and controlled by those who worked it on sticks, I saw it was full of bees. The dragon was wrapped around me, and I was enclosed in a silken tent. Its tail even covered my head. I heard the sound of ripping fabric. The bees were loosed on me and covered my body over. I was filled with loathing. But my feet were frozen in place. And the stings of the bees did not penetrate the gold, and when they came near my eyes I only closed my eyes, and gradually I realized the bees were dying. They were dying from their own sting and from the poison perhaps in the gold. I heaved a great sigh.

'"Keep your eyes open," cried Remath.

'And when all the bees had fallen, and the great silken dragon, now collapsed, had been offered to me to rip with my sword there came the cries again.

'I was being carried up the stairs, to the roof. I could see out over the open fields. I could see the crowds going on and on forever. I lifted my arm with my sword, I lifted it again and again, turning to the east, and the west, and the north, and the south, and lifting it and smiling, and the crowds sang back to me. All the earth sang back to me.

'"It is so very beautiful," I said, "so indescribably beautiful." But there was no one to hear me. The fresh air waked me a little, touching my nostrils and my throat, and cooling my eyes. The priestesses of the temple surrounded me, throwing flowers in the air, and then I knew I was being led away to the royal couch.

'"You can have as many as you want, but I advise you to sleep," said Remath.

'"Yes, good idea. And how do you keep me from dying?"

'"I can hear your heart. You will live long enough to make the journey home. You are stronger than anyone imagined."

'"Then give me a harlot," I said.

'Everyone was upset. "Well?" I said.

'The harlots screamed with delight. I beckoned for them to come. But I couldn't do it with them. I could only take each one in my arms and plant a poison kiss on her grateful upturned sweet little mouth and send her away in swoons, to wipe off the kiss, I hoped, as soon as she could. I laughed deep in my chest with my lips closed.

'Other things were done that night, but I slept. Fire, poetry, dances, things I never saw.

'I slept. I stood, resting back at a tight angle so that I seemed to be supporting myself, and with my eyes open, painted open now with fresh gold, so that I could not close them, but I slept.

'The world seemed a pit of madness. Now and then I woke to see the flames and the dancing figures. Now and then I heard some whisper or sound. Or heard running feet and felt human hands clasp me.

'Once I think I saw the King dancing below. I saw the King dancing with the women in a great strange slow dance, figures turning ceremoniously and then the King threw up his arms and bowed down to me. But nothing was required of me. The smile was fixed on my face now by the hardened gold. And only when I laughed did I feel the flesh tingle.

'At noon, the following day, as we began the procession back into the court of Esagila, I knew for sure I was dying. I could scarcely move at all. The attendants, under the cover of silk scarves and robes, fiercely painted the gold fluid on my knees to keep them flexible, but they didn't want the people to see. And I was not tired so much as stunned, staring at those before me.

'We came now to the gates . . . we went into the courtyard, where the great poem "In the Beginning" would be read, and the actors would begin their pageant. I felt a sadness suddenly, a terrible sadness and confusion. Something was wrong.

'But all of a sudden as if it were the answer to a prayer, the thing was made right. I heard my father singing. I heard him and my brothers:

> "*I will make a man more precious than fine*
> *gold; even a man than the golden*
> *wedge of Ophir.*"

'I struggled to hear it more clearly, their blessed familiar voices:

> "*Thus saith the Lord to his anointed, to*
> *Cyrus, whose right hand I have holden,*
> *to subdue nations before him . . .*"

'"Turn your head to them, Lord God Marduk," said Cyrus. "It is your father, singing with all his heart."

'I turned. I saw nothing but a blur of waving arms, of garlands tossed in the air, of flowers falling, but I heard my father:

> "*I will go before thee, and make the*
> *crooked places straight . . .*
> *And I will give thee the treasures of*
> *darkness, and hidden riches of secret*
> *places, that thou mayest know that I, the*
> *Lord, which call thee by thy name, am*
> *the God of Israel.*"

'The singing went on and on, following us to the gates of the temple. And then came the shouts, "Messiah, Messiah, Messiah!" And Cyrus waved and threw them his kisses, and at last it was time for the coronation.

'We were taken down from the chariot and the wagon, and walked on a bed of flowers up and up the seemingly endless stairway of the great ziggurat Etemenanki, so that the people from far off could see us through the wide gates. I thought I might die before I reached the top; I couldn't look above, only at the golden stairs before me and I thought of the stairway to Heaven which Jacob had seen in his dream with the angels coming and going.

'At last we stood on the summit, the mountain made by and for the god, and I was given the crown. By now it seemed I did not control my limbs at all. I felt nothing. I smiled because it was easiest to smile, and my arms ached suddenly with tiredness as I lifted the big Persian crown of gold and placed it on the head of the Living King.

'"Now may I die," I whispered. Exhaustion overcame me. My knees were in pain, my feet, all of me that could no longer move or stand with any freedom.

'Distinctly I saw the loving eyes of Cyrus, I saw the solemnity in his face, I saw . . . the dedication to Kingship in him. I saw perhaps a little of a King's madness.

'Slyly and cleverly the priests crowded around me and painted me over and over that I might move my limbs, and some vitality came back to me. "Keep your eyes open," Remath said. "Keep your eyes open."

'I did. We were taken down to the courtyard. The banquet lasted for hours. I know the poets came and they sang, and I know that the King dined and all the nobles dined. But I sat rigid staring. My eyes wouldn't close now whatever I did. They had been stupid to add paint. They only softened the lids when they did, I thought to myself, and I looked down at my hands lying on the table, and I thought, "Marduk, I have never once called on you."

'His voice came in my ear. "You have had no need of me, Azriel. But I'm with you."

'Finally it came to an end. Darkness had fallen. It was finished. The King was crowned, Babylonia was Persia, the city was drunk beyond the palace gates and the temple gates, and within these two buildings others drank and sang.

' "Now," said the young priest, "we will carry you up to the shrine. You need walk no more. You need only take your place at your banquet table there, and if you do not die within a few hours we will give you the gold in your mouth."

' "Not quite yet," said Remath. "Follow me and quickly, for we have one more ritual to perform and it must be done properly."

'The young priest was confused. So was I but I didn't care. I didn't give a damn. I didn't care at all. I was slumbering already, and when I saw the vague shapes of the dead hovering about, staring at me in fear, I was pleased. I would have thought they would have come thundering down upon me like an army and dragged me out of my gold clothes and said, "Come stumble through eternity with us!" but they didn't.

'Suddenly I felt an unbearable heat. I saw a huge fire. I thought I heard my father's voice, but I wasn't sure, and then I heard Asenath say,

96

'"It is powerful powerful magic! Do you want him to die! Give it to me!"

'For one brief second I saw my father, and in confusion, he gave over to her the old tablet, in its clay envelope. "Azriel!" he called out. He reached beyond her, towards me.

'I wanted to speak but I was past it. I couldn't do anything.

'The doors were slammed shut on my father and on the world.

'We were in a chamber with a hot, hot fire, the cauldron full of gold boiling, and the air almost impossibly hot. And Asenath then broke the clay envelope of the old tablet. She just smashed the outer clay as if it was nothing, and then she held up the secret tablet to the light of the torch.

'I was standing on my own, too rigid to move, too rigid to fall, staring at them. I wasn't even too horribly afraid of the fire. What were they doing, Remath and the old woman? Where was the High Priest? Hadn't I glimpsed him now and then?

'And then Asenath began to read, but this was not Sumerian, it was Hebrew, old old Canaanite Hebrew.

'". . . and that he should see his own death and that he should see his soul, his tzelem and his spirit and his flesh all boiled together in the bones, to live in the bones, forever, only to be called forth by the Master who knows his name, and calls his name . . .

'"No!" I screamed. "That is not a charm! That is Hebrew. That's a curse. You lying witch."

'The gold covering on me cracked all over as I sprang with all my drunken strength at her, but she backed up like a dancer and Remath had me by the throat. I was as stupefied and weak as those lions who had come against it.

'"You witch, that's a curse," I said.

'"That he shall see all of him that is visible and invisible and all fluids of his body boiled down into the bones, and that he shall be bound to those bones and whoever is Master of those bones, and that he shall not be taken into the darkness of Sheol nor the eternal life of God forever and ever.

'"Marduk!" I screamed.

'I felt myself heaved backwards, and thrown into the boiling gold. I screamed and screamed. It was unthinkable. It was not possible that I could know such pain. It was not possible that such a thing could happen to me, that boiling gold should choke my mouth and cover my eyes!

'And when I thought I would go blank mad, blank mad with horror and pain, with nothing of human thought left, I shot upwards out of the cauldron, free-floating above the body that was slumped and boiling in the pot, with only one open eye above the bubbling gold. The body that had been mine! And I was not in it.

'I was there above, arms outstretched, staring down. And I saw the face of Asenath upturned.

'"Yes, Azriel," she screamed, "watch, watch the gold boil, watch the flesh fall from your bones, watch the bones become the gold, don't take your eyes off it, lest you be drawn back down into agony and death."

'"Marduk," I cried.

'"It's your choice," he said. "Go back down into that cauldron of pain and you die." His voice was broken or sad. I realized that he was below me. He stood looking up.

'And for the first time he looked small to me and simple. Not grand or godly. And Asenath was just an old fool of a woman. And Remath staring at the body sinking into the bubbling pot was jumping up and down and making his hands into fists and cursing and screaming.

'There was no time. There was no decision. Or maybe it was pure cowardice. I could not go down into that pain. I could not be boiled alive. I could not bear that such a thing would happen to any human being. I watched and I watched, and the flesh floated loose in the golden muck and the skull floated to the top, and the pot boiled and boiled and boiled and the room grew denser and denser with steam.

'Asenath was choking. She could not breathe, and she fell forward on her face. Remath stood staring at the pot. And Marduk merely looked up at me with wonder.

'At last the pot was empty save what was left of me. Remath kicked and poked at the fire to put it out. He drew as close as he could to the hot metal and he looked down at the heap of golden bones that lay in the bottom of the pot. The cloth was gone, it had dissolved, the flesh was gone, it had dissolved, the liquid was gone, it had dissolved. Only the bones were left and in this sealed chamber all the fumes and particles of what had been my body. And the bones were all gold.

'"Call it to you, spirit," said Remath. "Call the flesh to you, call it to you now from all the world, call it from the depth of the bones and from the air to which it has tried to flee, call it."

'I moved downwards and stood on my feet. In the thick torturous steam, I saw I had a body. It was vapor. But it was mine, and then it grew denser and denser.

'Marduk took a step backwards, shaking his head.

'"What is it? Why do you do that?" I asked.

'"Oh gods of old, Remath," said Marduk, "what have you and the witch wrought?"

'Remath roared, "You are mine, Servant of the Bones, for I am the Master of the Bones. You will obey me. You will obey."

'Marduk backed up against the wall, staring at me in perfect fear.

'Remath grabbed a heavy bunch of cloth from the couch to protect his hands and with this he managed to throw over the cauldron. The bones spilled out and what did not spill he reached for, hurt by the heat until he had all the bones on the floor.

'"Wake up, old woman!" he screamed. "Wake up! What do I do now!"

'I stood beside him. My body was dense as if it were living. It was pinkish and vivid as his body, but it wasn't real. It didn't feel real. It had no heart, no lungs, no soul, no blood; it had only the shape that my spirit gave to it, down to the last detail.

'"Look, fool," I said, "Asenath is dead. If you want to know what to do, you'd better bring that tablet to me, I am the only one here who can read the old Canaanite words."'

Seven

'Remath did not move. He was far too frightened to move. He even let go of the bones. They lay gleaming on the glazed floor. Scattered, hideous, teeth among them, and the tiny bones of my hands and feet like pebbles.

'Marduk remained still.

'There was a low howling sound gathering round us. I could hear it as if a wind moved through the rest of the palace and temple, slowly, corridor by corridor, alcove by alcove, and then I looked up and saw the dense world of spirits as I had never seen it before.

'The walls and the ceiling of this cell were gone. The whole of the world was the lost mumbling souls staring and pointing and leaping towards me with grasping hands, yet afraid.

'"Get away!" I roared. And at once the entire cloud dispersed, but the howling pierced my ears and hurt me, and when I looked again I saw that Marduk's face was alien to me, and no longer afraid, but neither trusting nor gentle as always before.

'I turned, walking easily and light as a man would walk to the body of the fallen Asenath, and I took from her the tablet. The text wasn't easy for me. It was a form of Hebrew, yes, but a dialect from the time before my time. I stood reading to myself.

'I turned around. The priest had withdrawn to the farthest corner and the god merely stared. I read the words as best I could:

'"And having seen his death, and having seen the fluids of his body, and the flesh and the spirit and soul boiled into the bones, and sealed in the bones in gold forever, let him be called down into the bones, made to enter them, and made to remain in them, until his Master should call him forth."

'"Do it," Remath cried. "Go into the bones."

'I looked down at the tablet. "And once these bones are assembled, they shall forever contain his spirit, passing from one generation to another, to serve the Master by ownership and by power, to do the Master's bidding, and roam only at the Master's will. When the Master shall say, "Come," the Servant of the Bones will appear. When the Master says, "Take on flesh," the Servant of the Bones will take on flesh, and when the Master says, "Return to the bones," the Servant of the Bones will obey him, and when the Master says, "Kill this man for me," the Servant of the Bones shall kill that man, and when the Master says, "Lie quiet and watch, my slave," the Servant of the Bones shall do it. For the Servant and the Bones are now one. And no spirit under heaven can rival the strength of the Servant of the Bones."

'"Well," I said, "that is quite a story."

'"Into the bones," he declared. "Go into the bones." He stood trembling, clenching his fists and bending his knees. "Return to the bones!" he declared. "Lie quiet and watch, my slave!" he declared.

'I did nothing.

'I studied him for a long moment. Nothing changed in me.

'I saw the linen he'd pulled from the couch. There was a sheet, fresh, changed from when I'd last slept here, and I picked it up now, and formed a sack out of it, and into it I put the tablet, and then the bones. I picked up the thigh bone, and the leg bone, and the arm bones, and the skull, my very own skull, still hot and gleaming with gold, and I gathered every tiny fragment of what had been Azriel, the living man, the fool, the idiot. I gathered the teeth, I gathered the bones of the toes. And when I had all of this in a small sack, knotted, I slung it over my shoulder and then I looked at him.

'"Damn you into hell, go into the bones!" he roared.

'I went forward towards him and I put out my right hand and broke his neck. He was dead before he hit his knees. I saw a spirit rise blundering and in terror, gauzy and soon shapeless and then dispersed and gone.

'I looked at Marduk.

101

'"Azriel, what will you do?" he asked. He seemed utterly confounded.

'"What can I do, Lord? What can I do, but find the strongest Magician in Babylon, the one strong enough to help me learn my destiny and my limitations, or shall I simply wander as I am? I am nothing, as you see, nothing, only the semblance of the living. Shall I wander? Look, I am solid and visible, but I am nothing, and all that is left of me is in this sack."

'I didn't wait for his answer. I turned and I left. I turned my back on him as it were. I dismissed him, sadly, I think, and rudely and thoughtlessly and I had a sense of him hovering near me, watching me, as I went on.

'I went through the temple, in the convincing shape of a man, challenged again and again by guards whom I threw off with my right hand. A spear passed through my back. A sword passed through my body. I felt nothing, but merely looked at the perplexed and miserable assailant. I walked on.

'I walked into the palace and I walked towards the chambers of the King. His guards fell on me and I stepped through them, feeling this no more than a shudder and saw them stumble behind me, and then I looked up and saw Marduk watching from afar.

'I went into the King's chamber. Cyrus was in bed with a beautiful harlot, and when he saw me, he leapt up naked from the bed.

'"Do you know me?" I said. "What do you see?"

'"Azriel!" he declared, and then with genuine joy he said, "Azriel, you've cheated death, they've saved you, oh, my son, my son."

'This was so heartfelt and honest that I was stunned. He came towards me but as he put his arms around me he realized I was nothing, only the appearance of something solid, as a shell more or less, or even lighter than that, a bubble on the surface of the water so light it could explode. But it did not. I did not. I merely felt his heavy strong arms around me and then he backed away from me.

'"Yes, I am dead, Lord King," I said. "And all that is left

of me is here in this sack, and covered with gold. Now you must repay me."

'"How, Azriel?" he asked.

'"Who is the greatest sorcerer in all the world? Surely Cyrus knows. Is the strongest and wisest of wise men in Persia? In Ionia? Or is he in Lydia? Tell me where he is. I am a horror. I am a horror! Even Marduk fears me now! Who is the wisest man, Cyrus, to whom you would trust your own damned soul if you stood here as I do!"

'He sank down on the side of the bed. The harlot meantime had covered herself with the sheets and merely stared. Marduk came silently into the room, and though his face was no longer cold with suspicion it lacked the warmth we'd always shared.

'"I know who it is," said Cyrus. "Of all the wizards ever paraded before me, only this man had true power and simplicity of soul."

'"Send me to him. I look human, do I not? I look alive? Send me to him."

'"I will," he said. "He is in Miletus, where he roams the markets daily, purchasing manuscripts from all the world, he is in the great Greek port city, gathering to himself knowledge. He says the purpose of all life is to know and to love."

'"You are saying then that he is a good man?"

'"Don't you want a good man?"

'"I hadn't even thought of it," I said.

'"What about your own people?"

'The question confused me. In one instant I knew a whole list of names and I could smell skin and hair, and then the identity of these beings was gone. "My own people? Do I have people?" I tried desperately to backtrack, to recover my memory. How had I come to this room! I could remember the cauldron. I could remember that woman but what was her name, and the priest I'd slain, the god, the good gentle god who stood there, invisible to the King, who was he?

'"You are Cyrus, King of Persia and Babylonia, King of all the world," I said. I was horrified that I did not know the names of those I loved, for surely I had only moments ago.

And that old woman who had died, I had known her all my life! I turned and looked around the room in confusion. It was filled with offerings, gifts from noble families of all Babylonia. I saw a casket, made of cedar and gold. It wasn't big. I went to it, and opened it.

'The King watched speechless. Inside were plate and goblets.

'"Take them if you wish," said Cyrus, very well masking his fear. "Let me call my Seven Wise Men to me."

'"I want the casket only," said I. I emptied out the contents gently, so as not to dent these precious things and then I held the cedar box and I could smell the cedar beneath the red silk padding that lined it. I tore open the poor linen sack and into this casket I first put the tablet with all its writing, including words I hadn't even read aloud yet, and then I laid down gently my bones.

'I wasn't even finished when the beautiful harlot had come, and she put out a golden silk veil. "Here, to wrap them," she said. "To cushion them." I took it and it wrapped the bones, and she brought me another of deep purple, and I accepted that and wrapped them more securely so that when the casket moved now they wouldn't make any sound. I had scarcely looked at them.

'"Send me into them, Cyrus," I said. "Send me into the bones!"

'Cyrus shook his head.

'Marduk spoke up. "Azriel, go yourself into them and then come out again, do it now or you will never be able to do it, or you will never know. This is the advice of a spirit, Azriel. Cast aside all the particles that make up your form and seek the darkness and if you cannot come out, I will call you forth."

'The King who could neither hear nor see Marduk was confused. Once again he mentioned his Seven Wise Men, and indeed, I could hear men outside the chamber, I could hear their whispering.

'"Don't let them enter, Lord," I said. "Wise men are liars; priests are liars; gods are liars!"

'"I understand you, Azriel," said Cyrus. "You are an angel

104

of might or demon of might. I don't know which, but no ordinary wise man can guide you."

'I looked to Marduk.

'"Go into the bones," he said. "I promise to use all my power to bring you out. See if you can seek refuge there as I do in my statue. You must have refuge!"

'I bowed my head. "Into the bones, until I will myself to return; all of you that are parts of me, you are to remain near and wait for me till I summon you."

'A huge wind caught the bed hangings. The harlot ran to the King and he quietly enfolded her in his arms. And I felt immense and airy – indeed I touched the walls and the ceiling and the four corners of the painted room and then the whirlwind tightened around me, and I felt the intolerable press of the howling, screaming souls. "No, you don't, damn you!" I shouted. "The bones, I have the refuge of my own bones. I go into my bones."

'There was darkness. Perfect darkness and stillness. I drifted. It was the sweetest rest I had ever known. Only I should do something now, should I not? But I couldn't. I couldn't. And then came the voice of Marduk,

'"Servant of the Bones, rise and take form."

'Of course, that was what I had to do, and I did it. It was like a deep intake of breath and then a soundless shout. I found myself again a tolerably perfect replica of Azriel standing beside the open casket and the golden bones. My body shimmered in my own eyes and then grew steady. I felt the cool air as if I had never known it before.

'I looked at Cyrus. I looked at Marduk. I knew now that if I entered into the bones, I didn't have the power to return. But what did it matter? There was velvet sleep. There was the sleep you sleep when you are a boy and lie on the warm grass of a hill and the breeze strokes you, and you have no cares in all the world.

'"Lord King," I said, "I beg you. I will go now back into the bones. Send them in this casket with the tablet to your wise man in Miletus. Do that for me, and if you do betray me, what of it? I won't know. Someone else . . . has betrayed me, but I can't remember who it is . . ."'

'He came forward to kiss me. The kiss was on the lips in the Persian style of kings and equals. I turned and looked at Marduk.

'"Marduk, come with me, I can't remember what is between us except that it was always good."

'"I haven't the power, Azriel," he said calmly. "It's as the Lord King Cyrus says. You are what the Magi call an angel of might or a demon of might. I have no such power. The tender flame of my thoughts is fed by the people of Babylon who believe in me and pray to me. Even in captivity, the devotion of my captors sustained me. I can't go with you. I don't even know how."

'His brow became furrowed. "But why trust any man, even a King?" he asked. "Take the casket yourself and go where you would . . ."

'"No. Look, even now the body quavers. I am newborn and not that strong. I can't. I have to trust in . . . Cytus, King of the Persians, and if he would get rid of me, if he would be as vile to me and as cruel to me as all those whom I loved, if he would do that, I will find a way for vengeance, won't I, great King?"

'"I won't give you cause," said Cyrus. "Turn your hatred from me. It wounds me. I can feel it."

'"So can I," I said. "And it feels divine to hate! To be angry! To destroy!"

'I took a step towards him.

'He didn't move an inch. He stared at me, and I felt myself gently transfixed, unable to do anything really but look into his eyes. I didn't try very hard to oppose him, but I felt his domination, rooted in fearlessness and victory, and I stood still.

'"Trust in me, Azriel, for today you made me King of the World, and I will see that you are taken to the Magus who will teach you all a spirit can be taught."

'"King of the World? Did I do that for you, beautiful man?" I asked. I shook myself all over. Of course, I knew him. I knew the drama. The lion's breath.

'But then I didn't. I knew nothing.

'Marduk spoke up, but by now Marduk was merely a spirit standing there, friendly and good.

'"Azriel, do you know who I am?"

'"A friend, a spirit friend?"

'"What more?"

'I was anguished. "I don't remember," I said. I told him that I could remember the cauldron, murdering that nameless priest and the dead old woman. I knew the King. I knew him. But I couldn't really remember. I caught the sudden scent of roses. I looked down and saw the floor was littered with petals.

'"Give them to him," said Cyrus, pointing to the petals as he spoke to the harlot.

'And the sweet gentle harlot gathered up the petals in handfuls.

'"Put them in the casket for me," I said. "What is this city? Where are we?"

'"Babylon," said Cyrus.

'"And you are sending me to Miletus to a great wizard. I must know and remember his name."

'"He'll call you," said Cyrus.

'I took one last look at them. I walked to the windows which were open to the river and I looked out and I thought, What a beautiful city this is, it is so filled with burning lights tonight, and so much laughter and merriment.

'Without raising my voice, I dissolved my form once more, raging at the souls as they surrounded me and plunged again into the velvet blackness, only this time I could smell the roses, and with the roses there came a memory, a memory of a procession, and people cheering and crying, and waving, and a handsome man singing with a beautiful voice, and petals tossed so high they showered down on us, on our shoulders . . . but the memory faded.

'*I was not to remember these moments, these things, what I have told here for two thousand years.*'

Azriel sat back.

It was almost daylight.

He closed his eyes.

'You have to rest now, Jonathan,' he said, 'or you'll be sick again, and I must sleep, and I fear what will happen. But I'm tired, tired!'

'Where are the bones, Azriel?' I asked.

'That I'll tell you when we wake. I'll tell you everything that happened with Esther, with Gregory and the Temple of the Mind. I'll tell you . . .'

He seemed too weary to continue.

He stood up and then very firmly helped me up from the chair. 'You must drink more broth, Jonathan.'

He gave it to me, from a cup by the hearth, and I drank it, and then he helped me into the small bathroom of the cabin and politely he turned his back as I made water, and then he helped me to bed.

I was shaking badly. My throat was thick, my tongue swollen.

I could see that he was in great anxiety. The telling of the tale had been an ordeal.

He must have read my sympathy. 'I'll never tell it again to anyone else,' he said. 'I don't ever want to say it again, I don't ever want to see the boiling cauldron –' His voice dried up.

He shook his head and his thick hair to wake himself, and then he helped me into the bed. He made me drink more cool water, which was very good.

'Don't fear for me,' I said. 'I'm well. Only a little tired, a little weak.' I took one last deep drink of water then offered the bottle to him and he drank more deeply. And he smiled.

'What can I do for you now?' I asked. 'You're my guest and my protector.'

'Would you let me sleep beside you?' he said. 'As if we were just boys together in the field, so that . . . that . . . so that . . . if the whirlwind comes for me, so that if the souls come, I can reach out and touch your warm hand.'

I nodded. He put me under the covers, and then he climbed in beside me. I turned towards him and he faced away. I put my arm over him. The red velvet robe he wore felt comfortable and thick and warm. I had my arm around him. He went limp, as it were, in the covers, his head deep into the pillow, the big mass of black curls close to my face, and smelling of the clean air outside and the sweet smoke from the fire.

The sunlight was just creeping under the door. And I could tell by its brightness and the warmth of the room that the snowstorm had slacked off. The fire was healthy. The morning was quiet.

I woke once at noon.

I was hot and mumbling and having a horrible dream. He lifted me up and gave me a big drink of cool water. He had put snow in it, and it tasted clean. I drank and drank, and then I lay back down.

He seemed to shimmer, a figure clad in red with deep black eyes. His beard and hair looked silky, and I thought of all the old texts that tell of ointments and oils and perfumes for hair; his hair was worthy of all that, I thought. There came back to me a panorama of the wall carvings I'd seen all over the world.

I saw the great Assyrian carvings in the British Museum. I saw the pictures in books. 'The black-headed people,' that was what the Sumerians had called themselves. And we had come from them, or somehow mingled in them, and I knew now that those strange carvings of bearded kings in robes were nearer to me than European emblems I'd cherished as familiar when in fact they mattered very little at all.

'You slept well?' I asked, but I was already drifting off.

'Yes,' he said. 'You sleep now. I'm going out into the snow to walk. You sleep, you hear me? I'll have your supper for you when you wake.'

Eight

In the very late afternoon I awoke. I could tell again by the light beneath the door that we must have a blue sky and a brightly dying sun.

He wasn't in the house, which was little more than one room. I got up, wrapping my heaviest robe around me, a cashmere robe, and then I looked for him – in the little rooms off the back, the bathroom, the pantry. He wasn't there. I remembered what he said about walking in the snow, but his absence unnerved me.

Then I stared down at the hearth, and I saw the large pot of broth filled with potatoes and carrots he'd put in it, and that meant I hadn't dreamt all this. Someone had come. I also felt very faintly sick. My head wasn't wondrously clear yet, the way it would feel when the illness was completely flown away.

I looked down at my feet. I had on thick wool socks with leather soles. He must have put these on me. I went to the door. I had to find him, find out where he was. I was in terror suddenly that he was gone. Utter terror.

I was in utter terror for a whole series of reasons, and I don't know what they were.

I put on my big boots, and my greatcoat, which is an enormous bulky garment, weighing a ton and made to cover the thickest sweaters, and then I opened the door.

The dying sun was still gleaming on the distant snow of the mountains, but otherwise the light was gone from the sky. The world was gray and white, metallic and growing dim.

I didn't see him anywhere. The air was still and tolerable as it can be in the worst winter, when for a moment there is no wind. Icicles hung from the roof above me. The snow showed no tracks. It looked fresh, and it wasn't impossibly deep.

'Azriel!' I called out to him. Why was I so desperate? Did I

110

fear for him? I knew I did. I feared for him, for me, for my sanity, for my wits, for the security and peace of my entire life . . .

I shut the door, and walked out some distance from the house. The cold began to hurt my face and hands. This was plain stupid and I knew it. The fever would come back. I couldn't stay out here.

I called to him several times, and heard nothing. It was a beautiful snow-laden scene around me in the dusk. The firs wore their snow with dignity, and the evening stars were beginning to shine. The sun had gone. But it was twilight.

I noticed the car some distance away; I had been looking at it all this time, more or less, but had not noticed it because it was all covered with snow. A thought came to me. I hurried to the car, realizing that my feet were already numb, and I opened up the back of it.

There was an old television set there, a portable, the kind they make for fishermen to take on boats. It had a tiny screen, and it was long and with a built-in handle, rather like a giant flashlight. It ran on D-cell batteries. I hadn't used it in years. I picked it up, closed the jeep, and ran back to the house.

As soon as I shut the door, I felt like a traitor to him. I felt as if I wanted to spy upon the world he'd spoken of – the Belkin world, the ugly, ugly world of terrorism and disgusting violence spawned by the Temple of the Mind.

I shouldn't need this, I thought. Well, perhaps it won't even work. I sat down by the fire, took off my boots, and warmed my hands and feet. Stupid, stupid, I thought, but I wasn't shivering. Then I went to the big stash of batteries and I filled up the little television, which I held by its handle, and brought it back so that I could sit in my chair.

Pulling up the aerial, I turned the dial. I had never used this thing here. It had been in the car forever. If I'd remembered it before I had left, I would not have taken it out.

But in a boat I'd used it, fishing five summers ago, and now, as then, it worked. It brought in flashes of black and white, zigzag lines, and then finally a 'news voice,' very distinct, with the authority of a network, summing up the latest events.

I turned up the volume. The picture danced and wiggled and then flipped, but the voice was coming clear. War in the Balkans had taken another terrible turn. Shells heaved into Sarajevo had killed people in a hospital. In Japan, the cult leader had been arrested for conspiracy to commit murder. A murder had happened in a nearby town. It went on and on, the packing of fact into swift crisp sentences . . . the picture was steadying. I saw an anchorwoman, a news face, not distinct, but I could focus now more clearly on the voice.

'. . . horrors of the Temple of the Mind continue. All members in the Bolivian temple are now dead, having set fire to the compound themselves rather than surrender to international agents. Meanwhile, arrests of Gregory Belkin's followers continue in New York.'

I was excited. I picked up the little thing and held it close to look at it. I saw blurry fast coverage of those arrested, handcuffed, and chained.

'. . . enough poisonous gas in New York City alone to have killed the entire population. Meantime, Iranian authorities have confirmed to the United Nations that all members of Belkin's Temple are in custody, however the question of extradition of the Belkin terrorists to the United States will, according to officials, take considerable time. In Cairo, it has been confirmed that all Belkin's followers have surrendered to authorities. All chemicals in their possession have been impounded.'

More pictures, faces, men, shooting, fire, horrid fire reduced to a tiny flash of black and white in my hands. Then the bright face of the newswoman, and a change of tone, as she looked directly in the eyes of the camera and into mine.

'Who was Gregory Belkin? Were there in fact twin brothers, Nathan and Gregory, as those closest to the mogul-cult leader suspect? Two bodies remain, one buried in the Jewish cemetery, the other in the Manhattan morgue. And though the remnants of the Hasidic community in Brooklyn, founded by Belkin's grandfather, refuse to talk to authorities, the coroner's office continues to investigate the two men.'

The woman's face vanished. Azriel appeared. A photograph of him, coarse and remote, but unmistakable.

'Meantime the man accused of the murder of Rachel Belkin, the man who might in fact be deeply involved in the entire conspiracy, is still at large.'

Then came a series of still pictures, obviously gleaned from video surveillance cameras – Azriel beardless and without his mustache walking through the lobby of a building; Azriel in the crowd crying out over the body of Esther Belkin. Azriel in close-up, beardless without his mustache, staring directly in front of him as he went through a door. There was a string of shots, almost too blurry to mean anything, obviously taken from other surveillance cameras, including one of the beardless Azriel walking with Rachel Belkin herself, mother of Esther, wife of Gregory, or so the commentator informed me. Of Rachel, all I saw was a slender body, impossibly high-heel shoes, and mussed hair. But there was Azriel, no doubt.

I was enthralled.

The face of a bald male official, also suffering in freezing weather, probably that of Washington, D.C., appeared suddenly with the reassuring assertion:

'There is no reason at all to fear the Temple or its grandiose schemes. Every single location has been either raided by police, burned during the raid by its own members, or thoroughly cleared, with all members under lock and key. As for the mysterious man, we have no eyewitnesses to him at all after the night of Rachel Belkin's death, and he may very well have perished in the New York Temple along with hundreds of others during the fire that lasted a full twenty-four hours before police could get it under control.'

Another man, even more authoritarian and perhaps angry, took the microphone. 'The Temple is neutralized; the Temple has been stopped; even as we speak, banking connections are being investigated and arrests have already been made in the financial communities of Paris, London, and New York.'

There was a crash of static, of glittering white lights on the little screen. I shook the tiny television. The voice talked again, but this time it was about a terrorist bomb in South

113

America, about drug lords, about trade sanctions against Japan. I put down the little thing. I turned it off. I might have cruised a while for another channel, but I had had enough.

I coughed a couple of times, caught off guard by how deep the cough sounded and by how much it hurt me, and then I tried to remember: Rachel Belkin. Rachel Belkin murdered. That had happened only days after Esther Belkin. Rachel Belkin in Miami. Murdered.

Twins. I remembered the picture Azriel had shown to me – the Hasid with the beard and locks and the silk hat.

From some giant filing system in my mind it came to me that Rachel Belkin had been the socialite wife of Gregory, a conspicuous critic of his Temple, and the only time I had even noticed the woman's name, reputation, or existence is when I'd caught a fragment of the funeral of Esther. And the cameras had followed her mother to a black car, voices clamoring for her opinions. Had Belkin's enemies killed her daughter? Was it a Middle Eastern terrorist plot?

A wave of dizziness came over me. It threatened to get worse. I put down the television and went back to the bed. I lay down. I was tired and thirsty. I covered up, then sat up enough to drink more of the water. I drank it and drank it and drank it and then lay back and I thought.

What seemed real was not the television set and its cryptic reports.

What seemed real was this room, and the way the fire danced, and that he had been here. And what seemed real was the image of the cauldron filled with boiling liquid and the unspeakable, unimaginable idea of being cast into such a thing. Cast into boiling liquid. I closed my eyes.

Then I heard him singing again:

'By the rivers of Babylon, there we sat down, yea, we wept, when we remembered Zion.'

I heard myself singing it.

'Come back, Azriel, come back! Tell me what else happened!' I said, and then I slept.

The sound of the door opening woke me. It was completely dark outside now, and it was deliciously warm in the room. All the chill was gone out of my bones.

I saw a figure standing by the hearth looking down at the flames. I let out a little cry before I could catch myself. Not exactly manly or courageous.

But a steam rose from the figure, or a mist, and the figure appeared to be Gregory Belkin, to have that man's head at least and hair, and then to be shifting back into the massive curls of Azriel, and Azriel's scowl. Another attempt was made. A putrid smell filled the room, as foul as the smell in a morgue. Then it grew faint.

Azriel, restored to himself, was there, with his back to me. He spread out his arms and he said something that was probably Sumerian but I don't know. He called for something, and the something was a sweet fragrance.

I blinked. I could see rose petals in the air. I felt them fall on my face. The morgue smell was gone.

Before the fire, he stretched out his arms again and he changed; it was a pale image of Gregory Belkin; it flickered, and at once his own form swallowed it. And he let down his arms with a sigh.

I climbed out of bed and went to the tape recorder.

'May I turn it on?' I said.

I looked up and saw him in the full light of the fire now, and I realized he was wearing a suit of blue velvet trimmed in an old gold motif around the collar, the ends of the sleeves, and the pant legs. He wore a thick belt of the same color embroidered in gold and his face looked slightly older than it had before.

I stood up and came close to him as politely as I could. What had changed, precisely? Well, his skin was slightly darker, like that of a man who lived in the sun, and his eyes definitely bore more detail, the lids having softened and become less than perfect and perhaps more beautiful. I could see the pores of his skin and the small random hairs, dark, fine, at the edges of his hair.

'What do you see?' he asked.

I sat down, near to the tape recorder. 'Everything is a little bit darker and more detailed,' I said.

He nodded. 'I can no longer summon the shape of Gregory Belkin at will. As for the semblance of anyone else, I cannot hold it very long. I am not a scientist enough to understand it. Someday it will be understood. It will have to do with particles and vibration. It will have to do with things mundane.'

I was in a fury of curiosity.

'Have you tried to take any other form, the form of someone you like perhaps a little more than Gregory Belkin?'

He shook his head. 'I can make myself ugly if I want to frighten you, but I don't want to be ugly. I don't want to frighten anyone. Hate has abandoned me, and it's taken some power with it, I imagine. I can work tricks. Watch this.'

He put his hands up round his neck, and slowly drew them down the embroidered front of his coat, revealing as he did a necklace of engraved gold disks, like ancient coins. The entire house rattled. The fire flared for an instant, and then became smaller.

He picked up the necklace, to demonstrate the solidity and the weight of it, and then he let it drop.

'You have a fear of animals?' he asked me. 'A distaste for wearing their skins? I see no skins here, warm skins, like bearskins.'

'No fear at all,' I said. 'No distaste.'

The temperature of the room rose dramatically, and once again the fire exploded as if someone had fanned it, and I felt myself surrounded by a large dark bearskin blanket, lined in silk. I put my hand up and felt the fur. It was deep and luxurious and made me think of Russian woods, and men in Russian novels who are always dressed in fur. I thought of Jews who used to wear fur hats in Russia, and maybe still do.

I sat up, adjusting the blanket more comfortably around me.

'That's quite wonderful,' I said. I was trembling. So many thoughts were racing in me that I couldn't think what to say first.

He gave a deep sigh and rather dramatically collapsed in his chair.

'This has exhausted you,' I said. 'The changes, the tricks.'

'Yes, somewhat. But I'm not exhausted for talking,

Jonathan. It's that I can only do so much and no more ...
but then ... who knows? What is God doing to me?

'I just thought that this time, after this ordeal was
completed, you know, that the stairway would come ... or
there would be deep sleep. I thought ... so many things.

'And wanted a finish.'

He paused. 'I've learnt something,' he said. 'I've learnt in
these last two days that to tell a story is not what I thought.'

'Explain to me.'

'I thought to talk about the boiling cauldron would send
the pain out of me. It didn't. Unable to hate, to muster
anger, I feel despair.'

He paused.

'I want you to tell me the whole story. You do believe in it.
That's why you came, to tell it all.'

'Well, let's say that I will finish, because ... someone
should know. Someone should record. And out of courtesy
for you because you are gracious and you listen and I think
you want to know.'

'I do. But I must tell you how difficult it was to imagine
such cruelty, to imagine that your own father gave you up to
it. And to imagine a death so contrived. Do you still forgive
your father?'

'Not at the moment,' he said. 'That's what I was talking
about, that telling it did not produce forgiveness. It drew me
close to him, to tell it, to see him.'

'He wasn't as strong as you, on that he was right.'

A silence fell between us. I thought of Rachel Belkin, the
murder of Rachel Belkin, but I said nothing.

'Did you like walking in the snow?' I asked.

He turned to me in surprise and smiled. It was very bright,
and kind.

'Yes, I did, but you haven't eaten your supper which I
warmed for you. No, sit there, I'll get it, and one of your
silver spoons.'

He was good as his word. I ate a bowl of stew, as he
watched with his arms folded.

I put aside the empty plate and at once he took it and then
the spoon. I heard the sound of water running as he washed

them. He brought back to me a small clean bowl of water and a towel, as someone might have done in another country. I didn't need it. But I dipped my fingers, and I used the cloth to wipe my mouth clean, which felt rather comforting, and he took these things away.

It was now that he saw the little boat television set with its built-in handle and tiny screen. I'd probably left it too near the fire. I felt a surge of embarrassment, as though I had spied upon his world while he was gone, as if to verify things he said.

He looked at the thing for a long moment and then away. 'It works? It talked to you?' he asked without enthusiasm.

'News from some local town, network I think, coming through the local channel. The Belkin Temples have been raided, people arrested, the public is being reassured.'

He waited a long time before he answered. Then he said, 'Yes, well, there are some others, perhaps, that they haven't found yet, but the people in them are dead. When you come upon these men with their gun belts, and their vow to kill themselves along with the entire population of a country, it's best just to . . . kill them on the spot.'

'They showed your face,' I said, 'smooth shaven.'

He laughed. 'Which means they'll never find me under all this hair.'

'Especially not if you cut the long part but that would be rather a shame.'

'I don't need to,' he said. 'I can still do the most important thing of all.'

'Which is what?'

'Disappear.'

'Ah! I'm glad to hear it. Do you know they are looking for you? They said something about the murder of Rachel Belkin. I hardly know the name.'

He seemed neither surprised nor insulted nor upset in any way.

'She was Esther's mother. She didn't want to die in Gregory's house. But I'll tell you the strange part. When he looked at her dead body, I think he was grief-stricken. I think he actually loved her. We forget that such men can love.'

118

'Do you want to tell me . . . whether or not you killed her? Or is that something I shouldn't ask?'

'I didn't kill her,' he said simply. 'They know that. They were there. That was early. Why would they bother to look for me anymore?'

'It's all to do with conspiracy, and banks, and plots, and the long tentacles of the Temple. You're a man of mystery.'

'Ah, yes. And as I said, I am one who can, if necessary, disappear.'

'Go to the bones?' I asked.

'Ah, the bones, the golden bones.'

'You ready to tell me?'

'I'm thinking how to do it. There's a little more that I should tell before I come to the moment of Esther Belkin's death. There were masters I did love. I should explain a little more.'

'You won't tell me about all of them?'

'Too many,' he said, 'and some are not worth remembering, and some I can't remember at all. There are two I want to describe to you. The first and the last master whom I ever obeyed. I stopped obedience to any master. I slew when called – not only the man who had called me or the woman, but everyone who had witnessed the calling. I did that for years and years. And then the bones were encased with warnings in Hebrew and German and Polish and no one took the risk to call the Servant of the Bones.

'But I want to tell you about the two – the first and the last masters I obeyed. The others which I do recall we can dismiss with a few words.'

'You look more cheerful now, more rested,' I said.

'I do?' He laughed. 'How is that? Ah, well, I did sleep and I am strong, very strong, there's no doubt of it. And the story has a way of calling me back.'

He sighed.

'I don't know much life in death without pain,' he said. 'But that I deserve, I imagine, being a demon of might. The last Master I obeyed was a Jew in the city of Strasbourg and they burned all the Jews there because they blamed them for the Black Death.'

119

'Ah,' I said. 'That must have been the fourteenth century.'

'The year 1349 of the current era,' he said with a smile. 'I looked it up. They killed the Jews then all over Europe, blaming them for the Black Death.'

'I know. Yes, and there have been many holocausts since.'

'Do you know what Gregory told me? Our beloved Gregory Belkin? When he thought he was my master and that I would help him?'

'I can't guess.'

'He told me that if the Black Death had not come to Europe, Europe would be a desert today. He said that the population had grown rampant; that the trees were being cut down so fast that the entire forests of old Europe were gone by that time. And the forests of Europe we know now date back to the fourteenth century.'

'That's true,' I said. 'I think. Is that how he justified the murder of people?'

'Oh, that was one of just many ways. Gregory was an extraordinary man, really, because he was an honest man.'

'Not mad, to found this worldwide temple and fill it with terrorists?'

'No,' he shook his head. 'Just ruthless and honest. He said to me at one point that there was one man who had utterly changed the history of the world. I thought he would say that that man was Christ or Cyrus the Persian. Or perhaps Mohammed. But he said no. The man who changed the entire world was Alexander the Great. That was his model. Gregory was perfectly sane. He intended to break a giant Gordian knot. He almost succeeded. Almost –'

'How did you stop him? How did it all come about?'

'A fatal flaw in him stopped him,' he said. 'Do you know in the old Persian religion, one legend is that evil came into the world not through sin, or through God, but through a mistake. A ritual mistake?'

'I've heard of it. You're talking of very old myths, fragments of Zoroastrianism.'

'Yes,' he said, 'myths the Medians gave to the Persians and the Persians passed on to the Jews. Not disobedience. Bad judgment. It's almost that way in Genesis, wouldn't you say?

Eve makes a mistake in judgment. A ritual rule is broken. That must be different from sin, don't you think?'

'I don't know. If I knew that, I would be a happier man.' He laughed.

'What undid Gregory was a flaw in judgment,' he said.

'How?'

'He counted on my vanity being as great as his. Or maybe he just misjudged my power, my willingness to intervene . . . No, he thought I would be swept up with his notions; he thought they were irresistible. It was an error in judgment. Had he not told me things, key things right at the appropriate moment, even I could not have stopped his plan. But he had to tell, to boast, to be recognized by me, and to be loved . . . I think, even be loved by me.'

'Did he know what you were? The Servant of the Bones? A spirit?'

'Oh, yes, we came together without any question of credibility, as you would say today. But I'll get to that.'

He sat back. I checked the tape recorders. I removed the small cassettes and replaced them with fresh cassettes, and then made markings on the labels so that I wouldn't confuse myself. I laid both machines back on the hearth.

He was watching me with keen interest and an agreeable look.

Yet he seemed reluctant to begin, or to be finding it difficult, yet yearning to do it.

'Did Cyrus the Persian keep his word to you?' I asked. I had been thinking of this on and off since we'd broken off. 'Did he actually send you to Miletus? I find it hard to believe that Cyrus the Persian would keep his word –'

'You do?' He looked at me and smiled. 'But he kept his word to Israel, as you know. The Jews were allowed to leave Babylon and they went home and they made the Kingdom once again of Judea and they built the Temple of Solomon. You know all this from history. Cyrus kept his word to his conquered peoples and particularly the Jews. Remember, the religion of Cyrus was not so terribly different from our religion. At heart, it was a religion of . . . ethics, wouldn't you say?'

'Yes, and I know that under Persian rule Jerusalem prospered.'

'Oh, indeed, always, for hundreds of years, up until the time of the Romans, actually, when the rebellions started, and then the final defeat of Masada. We speak of these things to remind ourselves. At the time, I knew nothing of what was to come. But even I knew that Cyrus would keep his word, that he would send me on to Miletus. I trusted him from the first moment I ever laid eyes on him. He wasn't a liar. Well, not as much as most men.'

'But if he had his own wise men,' I said, 'why would he let something so powerful . . . I mean, someone so powerful . . . as you slip from his grasp?'

'He was eager to get rid of me!' Azriel said. 'And frankly, so were his wise men! He didn't let me slip from his grasp. Rather he sent me to Zurvan, the most powerful Magus whom he knew. And Zurvan was loyal to Cyrus. Zurvan was rich and lived in Miletus which had fallen to Cyrus and the Persians without even a skirmish as Babylon had. Later on, of course, the Greeks of those Ionian cities, they would rise against the Persians. But at this time, when I stood there, glaring at the great King and begging that he send me to a powerful magician, Miletus was a thriving Greek city under Persian rule.'

He studied me. I started to ask another question but he stopped me.

'You went into the cold, you shouldn't have. You're warm now, and the fever has risen just a little. You need cold water. I'll get it for you. You drink it and then we'll go on.'

He rose from the chair and went to the door. He brought a bottle from near the door. It was very cold, indeed, I could see that, and I was thirsty.

I looked down and saw that he was pouring the water into a silver cup. It wasn't an ancient silver cup. It seemed rather new even, machine-worked perhaps, but it was beautiful, and of course it got cold all over with the water. It was like the Grail, or a chalice or something a Babylonian would drink from. Or perhaps Solomon.

There was another cup just like it in front of the chair.

'How did you make the cups?' I asked.

'Same as I make my garments. I call together all the particles that are required, to come unobtrusively and without disturbance. I am not such a good designer of cups. If my father had designed these cups, they would be gorgeous. I merely told the particles that they were to make ornate cups of the style of this time ... There are many, many more words to it than that, much more energy, but that is the gist.'

I nodded. I was grateful for the explanation.

I drank all the water. He filled it again. I drank. The cup was solid enough. Sterling. I studied it. It had a common Bacchanalian design to it, clustered grapes carved around the rim, and a simple pedestal foot. But it was very fine indeed.

I was holding it in both my hands, lovingly, I suppose, admiring the fluted shape of it, and the deep carving of the grapes, when I heard a faint sound emerge from it, and felt a tiny movement of air beneath my nostrils. I realized that my name was being written on the cup. It was in Hebrew. Jonathan Ben Isaac. The writing went all around and was small and perfect.

I looked at him. He lay back in his chair with his eyes closed. He took a deep breath.

'Memory is everything,' he said softly under his breath. 'Don't you think we can live with the idea that God is not perfect, as long as we are assured that God remembers ... remembers everything ...'

'Knows everything, that's what you mean. We want him to forget our transgressions.'

'Yes, I suppose.'

He poured another cup of water for himself into his goblet, nameless but identical to mine, and he drank it. Again he rested, drifting, staring at the fire, his chest heaving.

I wondered what it would be like to live in a world of figures such as his.

Was that what Esagila had been like? Robed and bearded men dripping with gold ornament, and shining with purpose.

'Do you know,' he asked me, smiling, 'that the old Persians, they thought that ... during the last millennia before the final Resurrection men would gradually turn away from the eating of meat and milk, and even plants, and that they would be sustained only on water? Pure water.'

'And then would come the Resurrection.'

'Yes, the bony world would rise ... the valley of bones would come to life.' He smiled. 'So I think sometimes, when I want to comfort myself that angels of might, demons of might, things such as me ... that we are simply the last stage of humans ... when humans can live on only water. So ... we're not unholy. We are simply very far advanced.'

I smiled. 'There are those who believe our earthly bodies are only one biological stage, that spirits constitute another, that it's all a matter of atoms and particles, as you've said.'

'You pay attention to those people?'

'Of course. I have no fear of death. I hope that my light will rejoin the light of God, but perhaps it won't. But I pay attention, lots of attention to what others believe. This isn't an age of indifference, though it may seem so.'

'Yes, I agree with you,' he said. 'It's a practical, pragmatic time, when decency is the prime virtue – you know, decent clothes, decent shelter, decent food –'

'Yes,' I said.

'But it's also a time of great luxurious spiritual thinking, maybe the only time when such thinking carries no penalty, for after all, one can preach anything and not be dragged away in chains. There is no Inquisition in the heart of anyone.'

'No, there's an Inquisition, alive in the hearts of all fundamentalists of all sects, but they don't in most parts of the world have the power to drag away the prophet or the blasphemer. That's what you've observed.'

'Yes,' he said.

There was a pause.

He sat up, obviously refreshed and willing to talk again. He turned slightly towards me, his left elbow back a bit, his arm outstretched on the arm of the chair. The gold on the blue velvet ran in loops and circles, which no doubt had a venerable history as a pattern, perhaps even a name. It was thick gold thread. It was twinkling in the light of the fire.

He glanced at the tapes. I made the gesture that we were all ears, all of us, the tapes and me.

'Cyrus kept his word,' he said, with a shrug. 'To everyone. He kept his word to my father's family, to the Hebrews of Babylon. Those Hebrews that wanted to, and not all did, by the way, but those that wanted to, went back to Zion and rebuilt the temple and the Persians were never cruel to Palestine. Trouble came only centuries later with the Romans, as we've said. And you know too that many, many Jews stayed in Babylon and they studied there and wrote the Talmud there, and Babylon was a place of great learning until some horrible day in later centuries when it was burnt and then destroyed. But that came much later. I wanted to tell you first of the two masters who taught me everything that would be of use.'

I nodded. He let a silence fall and I didn't disturb it.

I looked into the fire, and for a moment I felt a dizziness, as if the pace of life, my heart, my breath, the world itself, had gradually slowed. The fire was made of wood I hadn't brought here. The fire was full of cedar as well as oak and other wood. It was perfumed and crackling, and for a moment I thought again that perhaps I was dead, that this was some kind of mental stage. I could smell incense, and a feeling of ineffable happiness came over me. I knew I was sick. I had a pain in my chest and my throat, but these things were of no importance at all. I merely felt happy. What if I am dead, I thought.

'You're alive,' he said in a soft, even voice. 'May the Lord God Bless you and Keep you.'

He was watching me. He said nothing.

'What is it, Azriel?' I asked.

'Only that I like you,' he said. 'Forgive me. I knew your books, I loved them, but I didn't know . . . that I would like you. I foresee now what my existence is going to be . . . I see something of what God has planned, but never mind on that. We talk of the past, not God and the future . . .'

Part II

Contrive a poem out of ears.
Tell it
so that its petals unchocolate
like a brain in a jar.
Wax walnut, melting with thought.
Make it a poem almost
lewdly knowledgable
and make its knowledge
ooze, syrup from the punched trunk.
Make it snake up to the molecule whorey
and put its mouth
atomic against the mouth of its core.
Pull on its stem
to expose its foetus. Make it
have children with sleek ginger jaws,
make the dogs moan when it passes,
let it out of its jar,
make it lie with our corpse, our chaos.
Make it hungry, evil, enemy of Death.
Put it on paper. Read it. Make surgery
its sigh, and of such sting
the scorpions call it Jehovah & Who.
Make it now before you crap out.
Contrive it, sperm it, stroke it,
make it efficient, make it fit,
make it more poem than Poem can survive.

Stan Rice, *Some Lamb* 1975

Nine

Now, I begin the story of my two masters and what they taught me. And I assure you that this will be the briefest part of my tale. I am eager to get on to the present. But I want this known and written down by you, if you will be so kind. So . . .

'Zurvan announced himself to me dramatically. As I told you, I had gone into the bones. I was in darkness and sleep. There was an awareness in me, and there always is, but I can't express it in words, this awareness. Perhaps I am like a tablet in my sleep upon which history is being written. But that image is too clumsy and concrete.

'I slept, I knew neither fear nor pain. I certainly didn't feel trapped. I didn't know what I was or where. Then Zurvan called me:

'"Azriel, Servant of the Bones, come to me, invisible, your tzelem only, fly with all your might." I felt I had been sucked up into the sky. I flew towards the voice that called me and as before, I saw the air full of spirits, spirits in all directions, and spirits through which I moved with great determination, trying not to hurt them, yet deeply dismayed by their cries and the look of desperation in their faces.

'Some of these spirits even grabbed onto me and tried to stop me. But I had my command, and I threw them off with wondrous strength, which made me laugh and laugh.

'When I saw the city of Miletus below me, it was midday; the air was clearing of spirits as I neared the earth, or at least I was now moving at a different rate of speed and they weren't visible to me. Miletus lay on its peninsula, the first Ionic or Greek colonial city that I had ever beheld.

'It was beautiful and spacious, containing wondrous open areas and colonnades and all the perfection of Greek art even at that early age. The agora, the palaestra, the temples, the amphitheater . . . it seemed all of it to be like a hand open to catch the summer breeze.

'And on three sides of it was the deep sea, filled with Greek and Phoenician and Egyptian merchant ships, and the harbor swarming with traders and with long lines of slaves in chains.

'The lower I dropped, the more I saw the beauty of it, which of course was not entirely unfamiliar to me in Babylon, but to see a city with so much splendid marble, to see it white and shining and not barricaded against the desert winds, that was the spectacle. It was a city where people went outdoors to talk and walk and gather and do the business of the day, and the heat was not unendurable, and the desert sands did not come.

'Into the house of Zurvan I came immediately and found him sitting at his desk with a letter in his hand.

'He was Persian, maybe I should say Median, black-haired, though with plenty of gray on his head and in his beard, though not too old, and with large blue eyes that looked up at me at once, perceiving my invisible shape perfectly, and then he said,

'"Ah, make yourself flesh; you know how to do it. Do it now!"

'This was exactly the tack to take, I guess, because I took great pride in calling for a body. And I didn't really know any words then other than what had been on the tablet. But I had the body made and well made within seconds, and he sat back laughing with delight, his knee up, looking at me. I suppose I looked as I do now.

'I remember being too astonished by this lovely Greek house with its courtyard and doors open everywhere, and paintings on the wall of slender, big-eyed Greek persons in sinewy flowing garments that made me think of Egypt, but were definitely Ionic, unto themselves.

'He put his foot down on the floor, turned his folded arms, and then stood up. He was dressed in the looser, more naked Greek manner of clothing without fitted sleeves as we always wore, and he wore sandals. He studied me fearlessly as my father might have studied a piece of the silversmith's craft.

'"Where are you fingernails, spirit?" he asked. "Where is the hair on your face? Where are your eyelashes! Be quick! Hereafter you need only say "Bring to me all those details which I require at this moment" and nothing more. Fix an image and you've finished your work. That's it. That's it.'

'He clapped his hands.

'"Now you are plenty complete enough for what you have to do. Sit there. I want to see you move about, walk, talk, lift your arms. Go on, sit down."

'I did. It was a Greek chair, graceful with high arms and no back. Everywhere around me the light seemed glorious and different; outside, the clouds were piled higher. The air was clearer.

'"That's because you are on the shores of the sea," he said. "Do you feel the water in the air, spirit? That will always aid you. That is why the addle-headed ghosts of the dead and the demons like damp places, they need the water, the sound of it, the smell of it, the coolness creeping into them, in whatever form they possess."

'He made a long stroll about the room. Arrogantly I just sat there, showing him no respect. He didn't seem to care.

'A Babylonian or Persian full suit would have been more flattering to him with his thin old legs and feet. But it was too warm.

'I drifted from looking at him. I was marveling at the mosaic floor. Our own floors at home had often been as colorful and as well crafted, but this floor was not full of stiff rosettes or processional figures, but with frolicking dancers and great clusters of grapes for ornament, and there was every kind of inlaid marble around its borders. The designs were fluid and jubilant. I thought of all the Greek vases I had handled in the marketplace, and how I had loved their graceful work. The murals on the walls were equally lovely and lively, and there were the repeated bands of color which utterly delighted my eye.

'He stopped in the middle of the room. "So we admire the beautiful, do we?" I didn't answer him. Then he said: "Speak, I want to hear your voice."

'"And what shall I say?" I answered without rising. "What

131

I want to say? Or what you tell me to say? What my true thoughts are, or some servile nonsense – that I am your spirit-slave!"

'I broke off suddenly. I lost all confidence in myself. I realized I didn't know quite why I was saying these things. I struggled to remember. I had been sent to this man. This man was a great magician. This man was supposed to be a Master of his craft. I was a Servant. Who had made me that?

'"Don't make yourself dissolve with all this petty worry," he said. "You speak well and clearly, that's what I wanted to know, and you think, and you are most powerful. You are perhaps the greatest angel of might I've ever seen, and nothing I've ever conjured has had your strength."

'"Who sent me? It was a King," I said, "But my mind is muddled suddenly, and it's agony not to know."

'"It's the trap of spirits, it's what keeps them weak, it's the hobbling of them provided by God, you might say, so that they don't ever gain strength enough to hurt men and women too much. But you know who sent you. Think! Make yourself come up with the answer. You are going to start remembering things now, you are going to start paying attention. And first, let go of the raging scream in you. I had nothing to do with those who hurt you and killed you. And I suspect there was much bungling to the whole affair, which a weaker spirit than you might never have overcome. But you did overcome it. And the man who sent you? He did as you asked him to do, remember? He did what you asked."

'"Ah, yes, King Cyrus, he did send me to Miletus as I asked." It came clear and it was all the more clear when I tried to let the anger pass from me like so much air out of my lungs. I even felt my lungs. I felt myself breathe.

'"Don't waste your time on that," he said. "Remember the questions I put to you? Your fingernails? Your eyelashes? Details that are visible. You need no inside organs. Your spirit fills up the perfect shell that you are, which no one can tell from a real man. Don't waste your strength making hearts for yourself, or blood or lungs, just to feel human. That's stupid and foolish. Only now and then you'll need to make a little blood flow from your body. That's nothing, but

132

don't go hungering after your human form. You're better now!"

'"Am I?" I asked, still slouching in the chair, ankle on my knee, as this older wiser man put up with my arrogance. "Am I good, or am I something to do evil? You said angel of might. I heard the King use those words. But then he also said demon. Or was it someone else?"

'He stood in the middle of the room, rocking a little, and composed, studying me through narrow eyes.

'"I suspect you will be what you want," he said, "though others may try to make you what they will. You have such hatred in you, Azriel, such hatred."

'"You're right. I do hate. I see a boiling cauldron and I feel terror and then hate."

'"Nobody's ever going to be able to hurt you like that again. And remember, you rose above the cauldron, did you not? Did you feel the scalding gold!"

'I shuddered all over. I gave way to tears. I can't even stand to talk now of it, and I didn't want to talk to him. "I felt it for an instant," I said, "one instant I felt it and what it would mean to remain in it and die in that pain. I felt it . . . I felt it piercing through some covering on me, some thick numbing armor, but where it hurt me . . . was my eyes."

'"Ah, I see. Well, your eyes are fine now. I need the Canaanite tablet that brought you into being. I need the bones."

'"You don't have them here?"

'"Hell, no," he said. "A pack of fools stole them. Desert bandits. They set upon Cyrus's party, slew them for every bit of gold they wore, and went off with the casket. They think the bones are solid gold. Only one Persian lived to reach the nearby village. Messages were sent. Now, you have to go and find the bones and the tablet, the whole casket, and bring it to me."

'"I can do this?"

'"Certainly. You came when I called you. Go back to that place, or to the place from which you came. See, this is the secret of magic, my son. Be specific. Say I wish to return to the very place from which I came. That way, if the bandits

133

have wandered ten miles from where you were when you heard my summons, you'll apprehend them. Now when you reach that place, remain corporeal and kill these thieves if you can. If you are not strong enough to do this, if they combat you with physical weapons which make you stagger, if they hurl charms at you that frighten you – and I warn you there isn't a charm on earth that ought to frighten the Servant of the Bones – then become incorporeal, but take the bones with you, gather them to yourself as though you were a funnel of desert wind, gather them and bring them to me. I will deal with these thieves later. Go, bring the bones to me.'

'"But you do prefer that I kill them?"

'"Desert bandits? Yes, kill them all. Kill them easily with their own weapons. Don't bother with magic. It would be a waste of strength. Grab their swords and cut their heads off. You'll see their spirits for a moment, shout at them to frighten them, believe me you won't have any trouble. Maybe that will soothe your pain. Go on, get the bones for me and the tablet. Hurry."

'I stood up.

'"Do I have to tell you what to say?" he prodded. "Ask that you be returned to the place from which you came, and that all the articles of your present body wait at your beck and call to surround you and make you visible and strong when you reach the location of the bones. You'll love it. Hurry. I estimate this will take you until suppertime. I will be dining when you get back."

'"Can anything happen to me?"

'"You can let them frighten you so that you fail and I can laugh at you," he said with a shrug.

'"Could they have powerful spirits?"

'"Desert bandits, never! Look, you'll enjoy it! Oh, and I forgot to tell you, when you begin your return, of course become invisible. They'll all be dead, you'll hold the casket tightly inside your spirit body, like so much wind surrounding it. I don't want you walking back here in a body with that casket. You have to learn to move things. If anyone sees you, ignore that person because you'll be gone from the sight of that being before he begins to make sense of what he's seen. Hurry."

'I rose to my feet and with an immense roaring in my ears, I re-appeared with the whole shell of the body in a small thick desert house, where a group of bedouins were gathered around a fire.

'At once they leapt to their feet and screamed at the sight of me and drew their swords.

'"You stole the bones, didn't you?" I said. "You killed the King's men."

'I had never felt such pleasure in all my human life; I had never felt such prowess or such utter freedom. I think I gnashed my teeth with happiness. I took a sword from one of them and hacked them all, every one, to pieces, easily cutting off the hands that tried to defend them and slicing some heads from some bodies and kicking their limbs about. I stared at the fire. I dropped the sword and I walked into the fire, and then back out of it. It didn't hurt this body, or its appearance of humanity! I gave out a roar that must have been heard in Hell. I was hysterically happy.

'The place stank of blood and sweat. The death rattle came from one of them, and then he lay still. The door came open, two armed bedouins flew at me, and I grabbed one of them and twisted his head off his neck. The other was now on his knees. But I killed him the same way too – easily. I could hear the noise of the camels outside and shouting.

'But the room was now empty of living beings, and I saw a great heap there covered by rude wool blankets. Throwing them back I discovered the casket of my bones and looked inside. This I have to admit was not a pleasure. It broke the stride of my lusty killing. I looked and saw the bones, and then I sighed and thought, "Ah, well, you knew you were dead. So what?" There was much other treasure there, too. Sacks of it.

'I gathered everything up into the blanket, clutched it with both arms, and said, "Leave me, particles of this body. Allow me to be invisible, swift, and strong as the wind, and keep these precious articles safe in my arms, and take me to my Master in Miletus from whom I was sent."

'The great treasure was like an anchor, a stone, which made my travel slow but delicious. I felt the ascent with exquisite pleasure as I reached the clouds and then came down over the shimmering sea. I was so stunned by the beauty I almost dropped everything, but then I got stern with myself and said, "Go to Zurvan now, idiot! Return to the man who sent you *now*."

'I and the casket landed in the courtyard. Dusk. The sky was filled with a glorious fresh-colored light. The clouds were tinged with it. I was lying there, in manly form, apparently simply by wishing it, and the treasure was there, the casket, now broken from my having crashed, and another box of letters, thrown open.

'Out into the garden came my new Master, who at once started to pick up the letters. "These miserable bastards; all this is from Cyrus to me! I hope you killed them."

'"With great joy," I said. I stood up, lifted the half-broken casket of the bones, and stood ready for any help he would need. He piled my arms with a few soft sacks that apparently held jewels, I wasn't sure, it felt like it, and that was all I'd brought with me, other than the casket and the letters, and he cast aside the blanket.

'To my utter amazement the blanket just drifted off, as if wafted on a draft, and then went over the walls, snarling in the breeze, and disappeared.

'"Some poor hungry person will find it, and do something with it," he said. "Always remember the poor and the hungry when you cast aside what you don't want."

'"Do you really care about the poor and the hungry?" I asked. I followed him. We went back into the great room, which was now lighted by many oil lamps. I noticed for the first time shelves of tablets and lightly built wooden racks for the scrolls which the Greeks preferred. This had all been behind my back when I'd been slouching about before.

'I set down the broken casket on the floor, and opened it. There were the bones, all right.

'He took the letters and the sacks of jewels to his desk, sat down, and at once began to read all the letters, quickly, leaning on his elbows, and only now and then reaching for a grape from a silver disk beside him. He opened the sacks, dumped out great clumps of jewelry, most of it looking Egyptian to me, some of it Greek obviously, and then he went back to reading.

'"Ah," he said, "here is the Canaanite tablet with the ritual that created you. It's in four pieces, but I can put it together." He assembled the four pieces and he made the tablet whole.

'I think I was relieved. I'd forgotten all about it. It had not been in the casket. It was small, thick, covered in tiny cuneiform writing, and seemed perfect, as if it had never been broken.

'He looked up suddenly and then he said, "Don't just stand about. We need to work. Look, lay out all the bones in the form of a man."

'"I will not!" I said. My wrath came up so hot I felt it even in this shell. It didn't make me melt. But it gave me a shimmer of heat which I could almost see. "I will not touch them."

'"All right, suit yourself, sit down and be quiet. Think, try to think of everything you know. Use your mind which is in your spirit, and never was in your body."

'"If we destroy these bones, will I die?" I asked.

'"I said for you to think, not talk," he said. "No, you won't die. You can't die. Do you want to end up a tottering idiot of a spirit mumbling in the wind? You've seen them, haven't you? Or a stupefied angel roaming the fields trying to remember heavenly hymns? You're of this earth now, forever, and you might as well forget any bright ideas of simply dispatching the bones. The bones will keep you together, literally. The bones will give you a badly needed resting place. The bones will keep your spirit formed in a manner that will allow it to use its strength. Listen to what I'm telling you. Don't be a fool."

'"I'm not arguing with you," I said. "Have you finished reading the Canaanite tablet?"

'"Hush up."

'I sighed angrily and sat back. I looked at my fingernails. They were splendid. I felt my hair, thick and the same. What

137

was this like? Being alive in perfect health at a perfect moment of wakefulness and energy, untouched by hunger, fatigue, the remotest discomfort ... a seemingly perfect physical statue. I smacked the floor with my slippered feet. I had on my favorite embroidered robes, naturally, and velvet slippers. The slippers made a good noise.

'Finally he put all the tablets aside and said, "All right, since you are so reluctant to touch your own bones, finicky, cowardly young spirit, I'll do the work for you."

'He came to the center of the room. He dumped all the bones out on the floor. He stood back and he stretched out his hands and then he lowered himself slowly, bending his knees, and out of his mouth came a long series of Persian incantations, murmurings, and I saw from his hands something coming forth, like heat perhaps from a fire, but nothing more visible than that.

'To my amazement the bones assembled themselves in the form of a man laid out for burial, and now he continued his exhortations, and making a whipping gesture with his hand, as though sewing, he brought to him an immense spool of heavy wire, copper, or gold, or what, I couldn't tell, and now with the gesture repeated over and over he made the wire thread the entire skeleton together as if it were beads. He hooked bone to bone with this wire, without ever touching anything, merely making the motions, and he let his hands linger long over the hands and feet of the body which had so many little bones. Then he moved to the ribs and the pelvis, and finally, with a long sweeping gesture of his right hand, he laid out the spine of this skeleton and connected it to the skull. He now had it all threaded together. One could have hung it from a hook to jangle in the wind.

'I saw a skeleton laid there as though in an open grave. I pushed aside all memory of the cauldron, of the pain, and I merely looked at it.

'Meantime he had rushed into another room and now returned with two short little boys, boys about the age of ten, which I realized in an instant were not real, but spirits, barely corporeal. They carried with them another casket, smaller than the first, rectangular, smelling of cedar, yet heavily plated in gold and silver, thick with jewels. He opened this casket. I saw a bed of folded silk. He told the little boys now to take this skeleton and to arrange it as if it were a child in its mother's womb, with its arms drawn up, and its head bent down, and its knees to its chin.

'The little ones obeyed these commands. They both stood up and looked at me with ink-black eyes. The bent-up skeleton just fit into the casket. It hadn't an inch to spare.

'"Go!" he said to the little ones, "and wait for my next command." They didn't want to. "Go!" he roared.

'They ran from the room, and stood peeping at me from the far door.

'I stood up and came towards the casket. It was like an old burial now, one found in the hills, from the ancient times when they buried men like this, in the womb of Mother Earth. I looked down at it.

'He was brooding. "Wax," he said. "I want a great deal of melted wax." He stood up and turned. At once I felt a shock of fear. "What's wrong with you?" he demanded.

'His two servants appeared again, eyeing me cautiously and carrying a big bucket of the melted wax. He took the kettle from them, for that's what it was, more or less, and he poured the wax all around the bones, so that as it hardened before my eyes, it fixed them in place. It was a soft, white fixture for them. And then he told the little ones to go again, get rid of the kettle, and that they could play in the garden for an hour in their bodies if they didn't make noise. They were overjoyed.

'"Are they ghosts?" I asked.

'"They don't know," he said, still staring at the bones now fixed in wax. Obviously the question didn't interest him. He shut the casket. It had strong hinges and a strong lock. He tested this and opened it. "In time," he said, "though I won't wait too long, being as old as I am, I will make a tablet of silver to go with this, containing all that is needed from the Canaanite tablet, but for now, the bones are as they should always be. Go into them and come back out.'

'Naturally I didn't want to do it. I felt a loathing for the bones, and a rebellious temper. But he waited me out like a wise teacher, and I did it, dissolving, feeling the smooth calm darkness, and then being sucked out of it in a whirl of heat and finding myself standing beside him, embodied again.

'"Excellent," he said. "Excellent. Now tell me all you remember of your life."

"Now that request on his part began one of the most unpleasant arguments of my entire immortal existence. I couldn't remember anything of my life. No matter how he badgered me I couldn't remember. I knew I feared a cauldron. I knew I feared heat. I knew I feared bees and the wax had made me think of them. I knew that I had seen Cyrus, King of Persia, and that the favor I had asked of him had not been unreasonable. Other than that? I knew only general things.

'Over and over he demanded I try. Over and over I failed. I wept. Finally I told him to leave me alone, what did he want of me, and he touched me on the shoulder and said, "There, there, don't you see, if you don't remember your life, you can't remember its moral lessons."

'"Well, what if there were none!" I said ominously. "What if all I saw was treachery and lies."

'"That is simply impossible," he said. "But you do remember Cyrus, and you do remember what you did today?"

'All that I could remember – coming to him, all he'd said, being sent to slay the bedouins and enjoying it, and coming back to him and all that had happened since. He threw at me a few random questions about details ... such as what had the fire been made of round which the bedouins camped: camel dung was the answer. Had there been any women? No. Where was the place? I had to think and extract an answer, as I had taken no note, but it came to me to his satisfaction, fifty miles from where the desert begins due east of Miletus.

'"Who is King now?"

'"Cyrus of Persia," I said. He then went into a whole series of questions. I answered them all. Who were the Lydians, the Medians, the Ionians, where was Athens, who was Pharaoh, what was the city where Cyrus had been declared King of the World. I answered and answered and answered.

'He asked practical questions about colors and food and air and warmth and heat. I knew all the answers. I knew everything general, but nothing pertaining to my own life. I knew lots about silver and gold and could tell him that – he was impressed. I looked at the emeralds the King had sent him and told him they were most precious and especially beautiful and which was better than another. I told him the names of flowers in his garden. Then I felt tired.

'A strange thing happened. I began to weep. I began to weep like a child. I couldn't stop myself from it and any sense of being humiliated before him didn't matter to me. Finally I looked up and saw him waiting with his bright, curious, and rather merciless blue eyes.

'"Did you really mean it when you said, always remember the hungry and the poor?" I asked.

'"Yes," he said. "I'm going to tell you the most important things I know now. Listen. I want this repeated back to me whenever I ask you for it. Very well? You call it the lessons of Zurvan and long after I'm dead, you demand of your masters that they tell you what they know, and you keep it in your memory even if it is something stupid, and you'll know when it's stupid. You are a clever, clever spirit."

'"All right, bright-blue-eyed Master," I said angrily. "Tell me all you know."

'He furrowed his brows at the sarcasm and insult. He sat brooding. He put one knee over the other. He looked bony in his tunic. His gray hair came to his shoulders and there broke off, but his face was most alert.

'"Azriel," he said, "I could punish you for your impertinence. I could make you feel pain. I could pitch you into the cauldron you fear so that you do not know that it is not real! I can do that at any time."

'"And if you do, I will climb out of that cauldron and I will rip you limb from limb, magician!"

'"Yes, that's more or less why I haven't done it," he said. "So let me put it to you this way. I want and expect courtesy from you, in return for all that I teach you. I am your Master at your pleasure."

'"Sounds all right," I said.

'"All right. Now this is what I know. Don't ever forget it. As long as you hate, and you roast in a hell of anger, there will be a limit to what you can do. You will be at the mercy of other spirits now and then and magicians. Anger is a confusing force, and hatred is blinding. So. You cripple yourself with this, you see, and that is why I would like to discipline it out of you, but that can't be done.

'"But here are the lessons. Accept what your hatred and anger will allow you to accept. First and foremost, there is one God, and his name does not matter. Yahweh, Ahura-mazda, Zeus, Aten, it does not matter at all. How he is worshipped, how he is served, by what ritual, it doesn't matter at all.

'"There is one purpose to life and one only: to bear witness to and understand as much as possible of the complexity of the world – its beauty, its mysteries, its riddles. The more you understand, the more you look, the greater is your enjoyment of life and your sense of peace. That's all there is to it. Everything else is fun and games. If an activity is not grounded in "to love" or "to learn," it does not have value.

'"Thirdly, be kind. Always, if you have a choice, be kind. Remember the poor, the hungry, and the miserable. Always remember the suffering, and those who need. The greatest creative power you have on earth, whether you are an angel, a spirit, or a man or a woman or a child is to help others . . . the poor, the hungry, the oppressed. To ease pain and give joy are your finest powers. Kindness is a human miracle, so to speak. It's unique to us humans, and our more developed angels or spirits, *to be kind*.

'"Fourth, on the subject of magic. All magic of all lands and all schools is the same. Magic is an attempt to control the unseen spirits, and the spirit within the living, or to bring back the spirits of the dead which still surround the earth. That is all that magic is. Making illusions, doing tricks, bringing wealth, it's all done through spirits, that is, beings without bodies who can more swiftly, unseen, steal, spy, transport, etc. That's all magic. The words differ from country to country, from Ephesus to Delphi, to the northern steppes. But it's all the same. I know all magic that can be known, and I continue my search for more. To learn a new incantation teaches me a new possibility. Now listen to me! It teaches me a new possibility, but it doesn't increase my power, my power increases with understanding and will. All magic is the same. What I'm saying is, you can do most anything whether you know the words or not!

'"Magicians are born for the most part, but some men become magicians . . . incantations school and direct them, but ultimately the words don't count. To God all languages are one. To the spirits all languages are one. Incantations help the weak magician more than the strong. But you can see why, can't you? You are very strong. You can do things without incantations. I've seen that today. So have you. Don't let anyone ever convince you by any incantation that they can have power over you. A magician can have power over you, yes, but don't ever be fooled by mere words. Confront the power if you would resist it. Rouse yourself and make an incantation of your own. Incantations frighten spirits and humans alike. Make a song of strength, a song of might, when you would have your way. Doors will open."

'He snapped his fingers. He waited a moment, then proceeded.

'"Lastly, no one human ever knows what lies beyond true death. Spirits can come very close to knowing; they can see bright stairways to heaven, they can see the fruit trees of paradise, they can talk to the dead in various forms, they can glimpse the light of God, oh, that is forever happening, these glimpses and glimpses of light, but they can't really know what lies beyond true death! No one who really escapes the earth and its earthbound spirits ever comes back. They may appear to you. They may talk to you. But you can't make them come from beyond death. Once they are dead, it is in their hands or God's hands whether they appear here or not. So don't ever believe anyone who tells you he knows all about Heaven. All of the realms of the spirits and angels that

143

will ever be known to you or to me are of the Earth, not beyond Death. You understand?"

'"Yes, I fear I do," I said. "But to love and to learn, why? Why is that the purpose of life? I mean how did it become so, why would one set out to do only those things with such dedication?"

'"You're asking a stupid question," he said. "Doesn't matter why it's that way; it's that way: the purpose of life is to love and to learn." He sighed. "Let's imagine answering the question for others . . . why is it so important to love and to learn? For a cruel, stupid man this would be a sufficient answer: "It is the safest way to live life." For a great man this would be an answer: "It is the most rewarding and illuminating way to live life." For a selfish, blind person, I could say, "It will bring you the greatest peace in the end if you remember the poor, the hungry, the oppressed, if you remember others, if you love, if you learn."' He shrugged. 'To the oppressed themselves, the answer is, "It will alleviate your pain, your terrible pain."'

'"I see," I said. I smiled. I felt a great rush of pleasure. A great sweet rush of pleasure.

'"Ah," he said. "You do understand."

'I started to cry again. "Is there no simple watchword?" I asked.

'"Such as what?"

'"It isn't always so easy to love and to learn; one can make hideous errors, hideous mistakes, hurt others. Is there no watchword! Fox example . . . in Hebrew the word 'Altashheth' – Do Not Destroy." I could barely speak. I was choked with tears. I began to repeat the word over and over again. I said it in one final whisper. "Altashheth."

'He considered, rather solemnly, and then he said, "No. There is no simple watchword. We cannot sing 'Altashheth' until and unless all the world sings the same song."

'"Will that ever happen, that the whole world will sing the same song?"

'"No one knows. Not Medians, not Hebrews, not Egyptians, not Greeks, not warriors from the north countries, no one knows. Remember. I've told you all that can be known.

The rest is chant and rattle and stomp and laughter. Now give me your solemn word that you will serve me and I will give you my solemn word that as long as I live you will never know pain, if it is in my power to prevent it."

'"I give it," I said. "I thank you for your patience. I think in life I was kind once."

'"Why do you keep crying?"

'"Because I don't like to hate or to be angry," I said. "I want to learn and to love."

'"Good enough. You will love and you will learn. Now it's night, I'm old, I'm tired. I want to read until my eyes close, as is my habit. I want you to sleep within the bones until I call you forth. Answer no call but mine. There will be none, most likely, but one never knows what demons are up to, what jealous evil angels may try. Answer only my voice. And then we will begin together. If you are called forth, come to me, wake me up. I'm not worried about you really . . . With your power, you can get me everything I want in this world.'

'"Everything you want? But what do you want? I can't . . ."

'"It's books, mostly, son, don't get so excited," he said. "I have no use for wealth other than the beauty you see around me, which does indeed mean I am rich, but rich enough. I want books from all lands, to be taken to places, to caves in the north, and to the Egyptian cities in the south. You can do this. I'll tell you everything, and by the time I die, you will be strong enough to resist those masters who aren't worthy of your strength. Now go into the bones."

'"I love you, Master," I said.

'"Oh, yes, yes," he said with a wave of his hand, "and I shall love you too, and some day you'll have to watch me die."

'"But do you love me . . . I mean in particular . . . me . . . do you love me?"

'"Yes, angry young spirit, I love you in particular. No more questions before I send you to sleep?"

'"What question would I ask?"

'"The Canaanite tablet by which you were made. You

haven't once asked me to read it to you, or to read it yourself, and obviously you can read."

'"I can read many languages," I said. "I don't want to see it. Ever."

'"Ah, well, I understand. Come into my arms, kiss me, that's it, on the lips as Persians do, on the cheeks as Greeks do, and then leave me until I call you forth again."

'The warmth of his body was good to me, so good, and I rubbed my forehead against his cheek, and then without waiting for a further command, I willed myself into the bones, and into darkness. I felt almost happy.'

Ten

'As I have already mentioned to you, this part of my story – the story pertaining to my two masters – will be the shortest.

'But I must explain fully about Zurvan and what he taught me and what he was. Masters after Zurvan, whether I remember them in particular or not, did not have his strength, I'm convinced of that, but more significantly, they didn't have Zurvan's interest in learning and teaching, and it was this passion of Zurvan, to instruct me, this lack of fear of me, of my independence, which influenced the rest of my existence, even during periods when I could not recall anything about Zurvan, his sharp blue eyes or his ragged white beard.

'In other words, I carried Zurvan's lessons forever, even during the darkest times.

'Zurvan was rich, thanks to Cyrus, and had everything he wanted; and he was true to his word that manuscripts were his primary treasures and I was sent on many errands by him, to detect the hiding places of various manuscripts, sometimes to steal outright, or merely to come back with information which allowed Zurvan to bargain for them. His library was immense and his curiosity insatiable.

'But the very first day I rose, he had far more interesting lessons for me than how I was to travel, invisible, at his command.

'My first waking the following day in his house was a startling affair. I appeared, fully clothed in my finest imitation of flesh, and in Babylonian long-sleeve robes, standing in the study. The sun was just coming in and making a glory of the marble floor. I watched it for some time, and only gradually became conscious of myself, that I was Azriel, and that I was here for some reason and that I was dead.

'I walked through the house, searching for other living creatures. I opened a door on a painted bedroom chamber.

But what struck me was not the beauty of the murals or the arched windows open to the garden, but that a horde of semivisible creatures fled from me, screeching and jumping up and down and then surrounding the figure of Zurvan, who lay on the bed as though asleep.

'These figures were not easy to see, flashing between mere outline and bursts of light, manifesting snarling faces and making little screams so rapidly that it was difficult for me to pick out any one figure or even get some impression of any one shape. They were humanlike but smaller, fainter, weaker, and carrying on like crazed children.

'At last they had clustered themselves entirely around the bed, obviously to guard Zurvan or perhaps to seek his protection. Zurvan opened his eyes. He looked at me for a long moment, then rose with excitement, and glared at me, as if he didn't quite believe what he saw.

'"Surely you remember yesterday, Master, when I came to you. You told me this morning you would call me forth."

'He nodded, and throwing out his arms, he banished the others, until the room lay empty and civilized, a fine Greek bedroom with admirable murals. I stood at the foot of the bed.

'"So what have I done wrong?"

'"You heard me call you in my sleep, that's what you did, and you came, and what this means is your power is even greater than I thought. I was lying here half-awake, merely thinking about you and how to begin, and this was sufficient to call you forth from the bones. The bones, by the way, are there. I didn't touch them. You woke upon hearing yourself the subject of my thoughts."

'He then pointed to the casket, which I saw was on the floor very near to his bed.

'He turned to the side, planted his feet on the floor, and rose, pulling the bedsheet about him like a long toga.

'"But we'll use this strength, we won't try to stifle it for my ends or for the ends of others." He pondered.

'"Go back into the bones," he said, "and when I call you, become flesh and come to me in the agora at noon. I'll be in the tavern. I want you to come to me, fully dressed, solid, having walked the distance from here to there, and having found me by the sheer repetition of my name."

'I did as he said. I sank back into the soft, downy darkness, but this time I took considerable confusion with me, such as why had I waked in the other room, except that it was the room I knew to be his location as of yesterday, and then I slept. I knew the sleep by measures, as one does when one is half-awake, but I suffered nothing but rest.

'When I knew that it was noon – by a series of tiny signals having to do with light and temperature – I found myself standing in the living room again, well formed and dressed. I checked all the particulars. I checked my hands and feet and clothes, and saw that my hair and beard were groomed, and I did this by merely running my hands over my body and wishing for all this to be so.

'A large burnished mirror stood in the room. When I saw myself in it, I was surprised, as I had some superstitious belief that spirits could not be reflected in mirrors. Then a thought occurred to me. I should go to the Master, yes, as told, immediately, but why not call to the others first? See if they were there?

'"Show yourself, you little craven monsters!" I said aloud, and at once I did see the room full of the small spirits all watching me in august fear. This time they were still, and it seemed I saw layers of them, as though their substance easily penetrated the substance of another, and I realized there were tall well-formed human shapes among them, eyeing me with caution, as well as the little imps who seemed no more than faces and limbs. I continued to look and say, "Show yourselves." And soon saw other spirits in the room, spirits that seemed weary and forlorn, like the newly dead perhaps, and one of these spirits lifted his hand to me very slowly and said, "Which way?"

'"I don't know, brother," I said. Looking beyond into the garden, I saw the air full of spirits. I saw them clearly as if they were fixed and could not move. I sensed this was only one way of seeing them. I remembered their attacks in the palace when I'd first been made a spirit, and no sooner did this thought cross my mind than the whole spirit spectacle changed.

'The still and thoughtful dead were invaded from every direction by the angry, whirling, howling spirits I remembered from my first-born minutes. I cried out: "Get back! Get away from me!" I was amazed at the roar which came from me. Most of the enemy fled. But one clung to me, clawing at me, though it made no mark on me and I turned and hit him hard with my fist and cursed at him to return to his safest refuge or I would destroy him! In panic, he disappeared.

'The room was empty and still. I narrowed my eyes. I saw the little spirits waiting. But then I heard a voice very distinctly at my ear; "I told you to come to the agora, to the tavern. Where are you?"

'This was of course Zurvan's voice.

'"Do I have to draw you a map?" asked the voice. "Do you remember my command to you? Start walking towards me. You'll find me, and don't be distracted again by either the living or the dead."

'I felt a crushing anxiety that I had not instantly obeyed him but I did remember his command, I remembered the morning, I made an effort to remember it, then I walked out of the house and into the street.

'This was my first long walk through Miletus, which was a beautiful and open Greek city, filled with marble, and open gathering places, and the fresh air of the coast and the brilliant light of the sea on the clouds. I walked on and on, viewing many things, little shops and stalls and private houses and fountains and small shrines cut in the walls, and then I came to the great open marketplace, surrounded on all sides by the bazaar, and I saw the open tavern, with its bright white awning blowing in the sea breeze, and I saw Zurvan inside, and I came in and stood before him.

'"Sit down," he said. "Tell me why you opened the front door of my house, instead of merely walking through it."

'"I didn't know that I could walk through it. I was flesh. You said come to you in flesh. Are you angry with me? I was distracted by the spirits. I saw the spirits everywhere and I had not seen such a spectacle . . ."

'"Hush, I didn't ask you for all of your thoughts, I merely asked why you didn't walk through the door. Now even when you are most solid, you can walk through the door. You can pass through it, because that which makes you solid is not what makes it solid. You understand? Now, disappear and reappear here. No one will notice. The tavern's half-empty. Go ahead."

'I did this. It was exhilarating, like stretching all my limbs and laughing and then coming back into this solid form.

'He had a much more cheerful expression on his face and now he wanted to hear what I had seen. I told him. Then he asked, "When you were a living man, you saw spirits, didn't you? Answer without thinking or trying to remember."

'"Yes," I said. This was painful and I could recall no details. I didn't want to. I felt a sense of betrayal and hate.

'"I knew it," he said with a sigh. "Cyrus told me this, but he was so vague and diplomatic in his language, it was impossible for me to be sure. Cyrus has some special love for you and sense of obligation to you. Look, we're going to go into the realm of the spirits. That's best, to go so that you know what it is. But listen first:

'"Every magician you will ever know will have a different map of the spirit terrain. He will have a different notion of what spirits are and why they behave the way they do. But essentially, what you will see on any spirit journey is the same."

'"So you want some wine, Master?" I asked. "Your cup is empty."

'"Whatever made you interrupt me with that question?" he asked.

'"You're thirsty," I said. "I know because you are."

'"What am I going to do with you? How am I going to make you pay attention?"

'I turned and gestured for the wine boy, who came at once and filled my Master's cup. He asked me if I wanted anything, treating me with great deference, more deference even than he had shown my Master. I realized it was my ornate clothing, this great Babylonian show of jewels and embroidery and my formal hair and beard.

'"No," I said. I felt sad that I had no money to bestow on him but then I saw several shekels of silver lying on the table. I gave this to him, and he went away.

'When I looked at Zurvan, he was sitting there resting on his elbows merely studying me. "I think I understand it," he said.

'"What in particular?" I asked.

'"You weren't made or born to obey anyone. The whole Canaanite ritual outlined on the tablet —"

'"Must you talk of that disgusting tablet!"

'"Hush! Did you never have an elder in your life, never a teacher, a father, a king? Stop interrupting me. And listen to me. Ye gods, don't you realize, Azriel, you cannot die now! I can teach you what will help you! Don't be so impertinent and stop letting your mind wander. Now! Listen.'

'I nodded. I felt tears spring to my eyes. I felt shame that I'd angered him, and drew a silk napkin out of my robe and blotted my eyes. There was water there I think. Water.

'"Ah, so that's it! I became angry and that makes you obey."

'"Could I leave you if I wished?"

'"Probably so, but you'd be a fool to do it! Now pay attention. What was I saying to you before you decided that I should have a drink of wine?"

'"You said that different magicians would outline the spirit world in different ways, and they would give the spirits different names and attributes."

'He seemed perfectly astonished by this response! I couldn't quite tell why. But it was highly acceptable to him.

'"Yes, precisely. Now do as I say. Look around you. Look in the tavern and into the agora, look out there into the sun. See the spirits. Don't speak to them or accept any invitation or gesture from them. Merely see all that you can. Search the air as if you were searching for things tiny and precious that you must have, but don't move your lips."

'I did as he said. I think I fully expected to see the pesty little demons that infested his house. But these I didn't see, so much as the wandering confused dead. I saw their shades or

152

spirits in the tavern, slumped over the tables, trying to talk to the living, walking about as if searching for something . . .

'"Now look beyond the earthbound dead, the newly dead, and see the older spirits, the spirits that have vitality as spirits," he declared.

'I did and saw again those tall beings with fixed eyes, transparent utterly, but with human shapes and distinct expressions and I saw not only those who looked and pointed at me, and made gestures regarding me, but hordes of others. The whole agora was filled with them. I looked up into the sky and saw more resplendent spirits. I let out a little cry. These resplendent spirits were not disturbed or angry or lost, or seeking, but seemed more to be guardians of the living, to be gods or angels, and I saw them to the very height to which I could see. Their comings and goings were swift. In fact, the entire spirit world was in constant movement, and one could classify the spirits by movement, the shades of the dead being sluggish, the older spirits slow and more human, and these angelic spirits, these joyful ones, rushed at a speed the human eye could not follow.

'I must have made many sounds of pleasure. I was overcome by the beauty of some of these aerial creatures, rising into the sun itself, and then I would see the hunkering shade of a dead person coming towards me, hungry and desperate, and I would flinch and draw back. A contingent of spirits who had noticed me was now drawing the attention of others to me. These were the middle spirits, as I saw it, between the dead and the angels, but even as I looked I saw that they were interpenetrated with savage spirits, who darted back and forth, making horrible faces and gestures at me, as if they would hurt me, shaking their fists and trying to egg me into a battle.

'The vision was becoming impossibly dense. I had lost sight of the awning of the tavern, of the floor of the agora, of the buildings opposite. I was in a terrain that belonged to these beings. I felt something touch me which was alive and warm. It was Zurvan's hand.

'"Become invisible," he said, "and surround me, hold as strong as you can to me and take me with you and up and out of here. I will remain flesh, I have to, but you will surround me, you will cloak me with invisibility and protect me."

'I turned and saw him in brilliant colors of living flesh, and I did as he said, swirling around him, just letting every limb loosen and lengthen until I had him wrapped completely and then I moved out of the cafe, and up into the sky with him, through the thick gang of spirits, and through the startled demonic ones who howled and hissed at us, and tried to grab on to us. I threw them off.

'We went high above the city. I could see it beneath me as I first had, the beautiful peninsula jutting out into the blue sea and the ships at anchor with all their different flags, and men working in a fever, doing seemingly senseless but no doubt routine things.

'"Take me to the mountains," said my Master, "take me to the farthest and highest mountain of the world, the mountain where the Gods came and around which the sun revolves, take me to the mountain called Meru. Take me there."

'We rose up over the desert, over Babylonia, and I saw her cities scattered out like so many flowers, or traps. Traps. They looked like traps. They looked like traps built to make the gods fly down to them . . . the way flowers are traps for bees.

'"Travel north," he said, "to the far north, and wrap me in blankets that I'll be warm and hold me fast. Move with greater speed, until you hear me cry out in pain."

'I obeyed, swaddling him in fine wool, and completely surrounding him and flying ever northward, until nothing lay below us but mountains, mountains capped with snow, and occasional fields, snowy and empty, where flocks grazed and men rode horses, and then it would be mountains again.

'"Mery," he said, "Find it. Meru."

'I set my mind to this completely and was only slowly aware that I couldn't do it. "There is no Meru that I can find," I said.

'"It's as I thought. Let us touch down on the earth, down

there in the valley where the horses are running, let us touch down there."

'We did, and I kept him swathed in blankets and surrounded by my invisibility, and realized that in this state I could press my face right beside his face.

'"It's an old story, an old myth of the great mountain," he said. "It is the mountain which inspires ziggurats and pyramids among the tribes that have only a dim memory of it. It is the mountain that inspired the high temples of all lands. Let me go now, Azriel, make yourself flesh and arm yourself well with weapons against these warriors of the steppes. Don't let them harm me. Kill them if they try."

'I did this, and left him standing, shivering in his blankets. Only a few of the herdsmen had seen us, and they fled at once to the armed men on horseback of whom there were perhaps six, scattered about in some sort of guard. The snow around us was beautiful, but I knew it was cold, I could feel his cold, and I wrapped my fleshly arms around him, commanding myself to be warm and to warm him, and this seemed to give him immediate comfort.

'Meantime the six warriors, stinking worse than their horses, filthy men of the steppes, came riding in a circle around us. My Master called out to them in a language I hadn't heard before, but which was understandable to me, and he asked where was the mountain that was the navel of the world.

'They were taken aback and began to argue, and then all pointed more or less in the same direction, which was north, but no one knew for certain and no one had ever seen it.

'"Become invisible, lift me and take me away from them. Leave them befuddled. They can't harm us, and what they see is no concern of ours."

'Once again we were moving north. The wind was now unbearably cold for him. I didn't think I could protect him any better, I had summoned skins to enclose him and I made my heat as strong as I could but then this began to hurt him. I had gone too far.

'"Meru," he said. "Meru."

'But this gave us no direction, and suddenly he said, "As fast as you can do it, Azriel, take me home."

'There was a great roaring noise as I accelerated, and the landscape virtually vanished in a burst of whiteness, and it seemed that spirits ran at us from all directions, falling back as if blown off their course by our strength. My vision was flooded by the yellow of the desert, and then once again, the city of Miletus was plain to me, and we were in his living room and I picked him up in his blankets and skins and carried him in and laid him on the bed.

'The host of little spirits stood around in awe.

'"Food and drink," he said to them. And they scurried to obey, bringing him a bowl with some broth in it, and a golden goblet of wine. The goblet was Greek and very beautiful, as all Greek things were then, seemingly more graceful and less rigid in form than things Oriental.

'But I feared for Zurvan. He lay there, frozen it seemed, and I lay on top of him, warming him, swirling around him, then hugging him and then finally when he had turned the proper color of a living being, and his eyes were wide and blue, I let go, laying out the covers.

'His flock of little spirits helped him to sit and even brought the spoon to his lips and the cup to his lips.

'I sat at the foot of the bed. I had no need of broth and was proud of it. Released. I was also very strong. After a long time he looked at me.

'"You did well," he said. "You did wondrously well."

'"I never found the mountain."

'He laughed. "And you probably never will, nor I, nor anyone else." He banished all the others, and they fled like slaves, and the room was clean of them. "Every man holds some myth sacred in himself, some old story told to him, which for him had the ring of truth, or maybe just the allure of beauty. So it was with me and the sacred mountain. And so with your power I have journeyed to the very top of the world and seen for myself that Meru is not a place, no more that I thought it was, but a thought, a concept, an ideal."

'He rested, and the curious expression returned to him.

156

Any disappointment or fatigue was swallowed by it. He looked at me and his eyes seemed to fill with delight.

"'What did you learn, Azriel, on your journey? What did you see?'

"'I learned first and foremost that such a thing could be done,' I said. Then I told him all I'd seen, and how the cities looked like traps to lure the gods of Heaven to earth.

'This amused and interested him.

"'They seemed,' I said, 'to have been designed especially to get the attention of the gods, to make the gods cease their ethereal flight and come down, as to the temple of Marduk. The mountain, as you said. They dotted the earth like so many open hands of invitation, or perhaps that is wrong, perhaps they looked like fancy entrances to earth, gateways, ah, that's the word the priest would like, I'm sure, that Babylon is the Gateway of the Gods.'

"'Every city,' he said contemptuously, 'is the gateway of some god.'

"'What were the higher spirits I saw, the ones who looked joyous and ran to and fro, the ones who passed right through the middle spirits, the ones the dead could not see?'

"'As I told you,' he answered, 'every magician will have a different explanation, but you saw what there is to see; you saw a great deal of it. Over time you'll see more, but you saw your own power and how they respected it, you saw that the middle spirits, as you call them, could not hurt you, and the demon spirits are idiots, and you can rout them with a nasty face. You saw.'

"'But what is it all, Master?'

"'It's what I told you yesterday. It's all that we can know on this earth. The joyous ones ascend, the middle ones see, the pale and sorrowful dead become as the middle ones, and whence the demons? Who knows? Were they all humans? No, I think not. Can they possess and confuse men? Oh, yes they can. But you, the Servant of the Bones, can see them in all their weakness, and you have nothing ever to fear from them, remember? Should they block your path, merely shove them aside. Should they come to invade a human under your protection, to penetrate his flesh and enliven him with their own intentions, reach out with your invisible hand and grab the invisible body of the invader and you will find you can lift it up and hurl it away from its human host."

'He gave a great sigh. "I have to rest now, the journey was arduous for me. I'm human. Now, go and walk about the city. Walk in your fleshly body, walk as men do and see as men do. Do not walk through doors or walls, lest you frighten someone, and if the spirits come down to assault you, send them flying with your anger and your fist. If you need me, call out to me. But mostly, you walk now."

'I was delighted at the prospect. I got up and went to the door. His voice called me back.

'"You're the strongest spirit I ever saw or knew," he said. "Look at you, in your splendid blue robes and gold, and with your hair shining as it falls to your shoulders. Look at you. Visible, invisible, an illusion, solid, it's all possible for you. You could be the perfect instrument of evil."

'"I don't want to be!" I said.

'"Remember that, remember that above all things. You were imperfectly made by bumbling idiots. And as the result you are stronger than any magician could have ever wanted, and you have what men have . . ."

'I started to weep. It was that same instantaneous and uncontrollable weeping that had come on me before. "A soul?" I asked. "I have a soul?"

'"I don't know the answer to that question," he said. "I was speaking of something else. You have free will."

'He lay back and closed his eyes. "Bring something back for me which hurts no one."

'"Flowers," I said, "a beautiful gathering of flowers, from this wall and that gate and this garden."

'He laughed. "Yes, and with mortals, be gentle! Don't hurt them. Even if they insult you, thinking you mortal, don't hurt them. Be patient and kind."

'"I will, I vow it," I said.

'And I set out on my way.'

Eleven

'What Zurvan taught me in the next fifteen years was all an extension and elaboration of what was learned in the first three of our days. That I can remember them now clearly for the first time in all these centuries floods me with happiness. I want to tell you the details. Ah, God, that I remember being alive and then not alive, that I can connect one memory to the other, this is . . . this is something more merciful than an answer to prayers.'

I told him I thought I could understand, but I said nothing more because I was eager for him to go on.

'After Zurvan released me to go wandering in the flesh, I didn't return until called, which was midnight or after. I had by then a huge bouquet of extremely delicate flowers, no one the same, and these I put in a vase of water for him and set on his study table.

'He made me recount everything I had seen and done. I described every street in Miletus in which I'd wandered, how I'd been tempted to try to pass through solid objects but stayed with his prohibition, and how I had watched the ships in the harbor for the longest time, and listened to the languages being spoken along the shore. I told him I felt thirst at times, and drank from a fountain not sure of what would happen, and that the water filled my body, not through internal organs which I did not possess, but every fiber of it over all.

'He listened to all this and he said: "What is your estimation of all you saw, or each thing, however you wish to tell me?"

'"Splendid," I said with a shrug. "Temples of incredible beauty. Marble, such marble. The people here are from all nations. I never saw so many Greeks before; I stood listening to a group of Athenians arguing about philosophy, which was very funny to me but I enjoyed watching it, and of course I wandered near the Persian court and was allowed entrance both to the temple and the palace, apparently because of my clothing and demeanor and I wandered in these newly constructed citadels of my old world, and then back out to the temples of the Greek gods, and rather liked their openness and the whiteness, and the whole stamina of the Greek people, which I think is more different from the Babylonians than I ever supposed."

"'But,' he asked, 'is there anything you are burning to tell me, anything that made you angry or sorrowful?'

"'I don't want to disappoint you but I can't think of a thing. Everywhere I beheld splendor. Ah, the colors of the flowers, look at them. Every now and then I'd see the spirits, but all I had to do was close my eyes to them, so to speak, and again there was the bright, living world. I coveted things. I coveted jewelry, and I knew I could steal it in this form. In fact, I did discover one little trick. I could make the jewelry come to me, if I stood close enough and beckoned to it with my whole will. But I gave back what I stole. And I found money in my pockets. I found gold. I don't know how it got there.'

"'I put it there,' he said. 'Anything else? Did you notice or feel anything else?'

"'The Greeks, you know,' I said. 'They are as practical as our people were . . . whoever the hell my people were . . . but they believe in ethics in a way that is not connected to divine worship; it is not merely a question of do not oppress the poor, uphold the weak, and all for the glory of the gods, but some further confirmation of much that is . . . is . . .'

"'Abstract,' he said. 'Invisible and detached from the self-serving.'

"'Yes, precisely. They speak of laws that pertain to behavior in a manner that is not religious, that's it. They don't possess more conscience, however. They can be cruel. Can't all people?'

"'That's enough for now. You've told me what I want to know.'

"'Which is what?' I asked.

"'You don't envy living people.'

160

' "Good heavens, why should I? I've wandered all day and I feel no fatigue, nothing, only a little thirst. No one can harm me. Why would I envy people who are still alive? I feel sorry for them if all that lies ahead is to be a stumbling spirit or a demon. I wish all of them could be born again as I have, but then I know that all I see is, how did you put it, only what is of the earth. Besides . . ."

' "Yes . . ."

' "I don't remember ever being alive. I know you said that I was, or I myself said it, or it seems to be something we both know, and we spoke of that cursed tablet and bungling, but I don't remember being alive. I don't remember aching or being burnt or falling or bleeding. By the way, you are right. I have no need of internal organs. And when I cut myself I can bleed or not bleed as I choose."

' "You realize, of course," he said, "that many of the dead you see hate the living! They hate them."

' "Why?"

' "Because their own existence is shadowy and weak and full of longing for things which they can't have. They cannot be visible, they cannot move objects, they can but buzz like invisible bees through the world."

' "What would happen if I became invisible," I asked, "and I went up with the more joyous creatures, the ones who are so busy and seem to range so high?"

' "Do it and come back safe to me, unless you find Paradise," he said.

' "You think I might?"

' "No, but I would never deny you Paradise or Heaven; would you deny such a thing to anyone?"

'I immediately obeyed, throwing off for the first time the weight of the body and the clothes yet commanding them to be at hand.

'I went out into the courtyard, looked for the spirits and found them surrounding me, thickly, and now that my eyes were focused on them, the demonic among them became ferocious, and I had many a struggle on my hands. Over and over the meandering dead detained me with pathetic questions, questions pertaining to those they'd left behind in the living world.

'And I found these meandering dead were in the higher levels as well as the very low, only they had grown lighter and stronger apparently, or at least they were better off than the shuffling blinded anguished dead that roamed the very earth itself.

'I came into the upper air of the joyous creatures and at once they turned to me, their faces filled with amazement, and with gentle gestures they ordered me down. In an instant I was surrounded by them, many of them having vague yet sparkling shapes, some even wings, and some long, white robes, but to a one, they ordered me down, they pointed, and they gestured, and they urged me as if I were a child blundering into a sanctuary. There was no wrath or contempt in them, they simply pointed downward and told me I must go.

'"No, I won't go," I said, but when I tried to go higher, I saw the way was wholly covered over with them and their bodies, and it seemed for one instant I perceived, far beyond the layers of them, a light shining but it hurt my eyes, and I fell, plummeted, crashed right back down to the earth.

'I lay in some dark place and the demons closed in on me, tearing at my invisible hair and body so that I dissolved and defeated them simply by slipping away and up, and then I made a right arm and a left arm and swept them aside, cursing them in their own tongues until they had fled.

'I tried to get my bearings; was I below the surface of the real earth? I didn't know. I had fallen into an ashy gloom, a fog, through which I could see nothing material. The spirits that fled from me or hovered near me were part of the pollution and density of this place.

'Then striding out of the fog there came a mighty spirit, shaped like a man as I was, smiling at me in cunning fashion, and immediately I sensed danger. He flew at me with both hands, fastening onto my neck, and then the demons closed in again. I fought him furiously, cursing him, and declaring him powerless, rattling off incantations galore to send him hence, and finally throttling him and shaking him until he was screaming for mercy; he lost his human shape; then he flew away, turned into a wisp of a veil as it were, and the demons fled.

'"I have to get back to my Master," I said. I closed my eyes. I called to my Master, and to my body that waited, and my clothes that waited, and then I woke up, sitting in the Greek chair in my Master's study, and he was at his desk, one knee raised with his foot on a foot-stool, tapping his fingers, and watching all.

'"Did you see where I went and what I did?" I asked.

'"Some of it. I saw you rise, but then you could go no higher, the spirits of the upper air wouldn't permit it."

'"No, they wouldn't, but they were kind. Did you see the light, way beyond them?"

'"No, I didn't," he said.

'"That must be the light of Heaven," I said, "and down must come a ladder, a stairway, yes, to the earth, but why not for all the dead, why not for all the muddled and angry?"

'"No one knows. You don't require an answer from me. You can reason it out for yourself. But what makes you so sure there will be a ladder, a stairway for anyone? Is it the promise of the ziggurats, the pyramids? The legend of Mount Meru?"

'I thought a long time before answering. "No," I said. "Though those are proofs of course, no, not proofs but indications. I know because of the faces of the higher spirits . . . as they directed me to go down. There was no meanness in them; no evil; no wrath. They didn't shout like gatekeepers of a palace; they simply made it impossible for me to pass, and over and over they offered by gesture the way I was to go . . . back to the earth."

'He pondered that one in silence. I was too excited to be silent.

'"Did you see that strong one who attacked me," I said, "the one who walked up to me as though he were my height and weight and was smiling, and then flew at me?"

'"No. What happened?"

'"I choked him and shook him and vanquished him and threw him away."

163

'My Master laughed. "Poor foolish spirit."

'"You're speaking to me?"

'"I'm speaking sarcastically of him," he said.

'"But why didn't he talk to me? Why didn't he ask me who I was? Why didn't he greet me as a creature of equal power, you know, engage in some way other than battle?"

'"Azriel, most spirits don't know what they're doing or why," he said. "The longer they drift the less they know. Hate is common to them. He tested his strength against you. Perhaps if he had vanquished you, he would have tried to enslave you among the invisible, but he couldn't do that. He knows nothing else, most likely, but combat, dominance, and submission. Many human beings live in exactly the same way."

'"Oh, yes, I know," I said.

'"Go there, to the pitcher of water," he said. "Drink all of it. You can drink whenever you wish. Water will make your spirit body in any form stronger. That's true of all spirits and ghosts. They love water and crave the damp. Oh, but I told you this. Hurry up. I have something for you to do."

'The water did taste wonderful and I drank an amount which a normal man could never have drunk. When I set down the pitcher, I was ready for his command.

'"I want you to retain your body and walk through the wall into the garden and then back again. You'll feel resistance. Ignore it. You are made of different particles from the wall, and you can pass among the particles of the wall without hurting it. Do it, do it over and over until you can walk through anything solid without hesitation."

'I found this very easy. I walked through doors, I walked through walls three feet thick, I walked through columns. I walked through furniture. Each time I did feel the swirling particles which made up the barrier or the object, but the penetration was not hurtful and it took only will to override any natural instinct to bow or retreat.

'"Are you tired?"

'"No," I said.

'"All right, this is your first real errand for me," he said. "Go to the house of the Greek merchant Lysander in the street of the scribes, steal every manuscript out of his library, and bring them to me. You will take four trips to do it. Do it in the flesh and ignore anyone who sees you, remember that to make the scrolls pass through the wall, you have to put them inside your body, which includes now your robe. You have to envelop them in your spirit. If it is too hard, then go and come by doors. Anyone who strikes you . . . can't hurt you."

'"Do I hurt them?"

'"No. Not unless they have some power to detain you. In general, their daggers and swords will pass right into you and do nothing. But if they take hold of the scrolls, which are material, you may have to knock them away. Do it . . . gently, I suppose. Or . . . as it suits you, depending on how much the person offends you. I leave it to you."

'He lifted his pen and began to write. Then he realized I hadn't moved.

'"So?" he asked.

'"I'm to steal?"

'"Azriel, my conscientious one, my newborn spirit, everything in the house of Lysander is stolen! He obtained it all when the Persians came through Miletus. Most of the library was mine. He is a bad man. You may kill him if you like. Doesn't matter to me. But get going and bring back all those books. Do as I say, and never question me on such matters."

'"Then you will never want for me to rob the poor man, or hurt the afflicted, or frighten the humble and the meek."

'He looked up. "Azriel, we have been over this ground. Your words sound like a variation on one of those pompous inscriptions at the feet of Assyrian Kings."

'"I didn't want to waste your time with lengthier questions," I said.

'"I have no interest in anything but good behavior," he said. "Try to remember my lessons. I love even the pesty familiars I keep here to do my bidding, but Lysander is evil and steals and sells for profit, and cannot even read."

'The chore proved easy enough. I had only to knock about the servants to send them flying and in three journeys back and forth I was able to transport the entire library to my

Master. It was hard, however, with great bundles of scrolls to pass through doors. I couldn't envelop them with my spirit and pass through the particles. But I got better at this as time passed on. Indeed, I learned something he hadn't told me, that I might make my body diffuse and large as I passed through the solid walls and doors, that way better enveloping the scrolls and then contracting again to the normal size of a fleshly man as I walked on with my bundle of goods.

'To be open and fair with him, I did this on my last trip, coming through the wall of his study, with a very large cache of loot, making myself very big and then contracting to lay down the bundle itself.

'He gave me a steady look, and I realized something. All day and night since I had come, I had been amazing him. And he masked it with this look. He showed no fear.

'"I don't feel any fear of you," he said, answering my thoughts, "but you're right; it's not my habit as a magus or a scholar or a man to look startled and to shout."

'"What now, Master?" I asked.

'"Go into the bones, and do not come out until you hear me . . . hear my voice, calling you. That I dream of you or think of you is not enough."

'"I'll try, Master," I said.

'"You'll disappoint me if you disobey; you're too young and strong to run rampant. You'll hurt my soul if you try to come out when I think of you."

'Again I felt the ready tears. "Then I won't do it, Lord," I said.

'I went into the bones. For one moment before my eyes closed I saw the casket itself and that it had been moved to a hiding place, a niche within the wall, but then came the velvet sleep, and the thought, "I love him, and I want to serve him." And that was all.

'The next morning I waked but didn't move. It was a long time, lying in the darkness, feeling nothing of the physical at all, waiting, and then when I heard his voice very distinctly, I answered the call.

'The bright world opened up all around me again. I was seated in the garden, among the flowers, and he was on a couch there, reading, mussed and yawning as if he'd spent the night under the stars.

'"Well, I waited this time," I said.

'"Ah, then you felt yourself wake before I called you?"

'"Yes, but waited, so that you'd be pleased. Some bit of memory came back to me, or has come at this moment, enough to ask a question."

'"Ask. If I can't truly answer I won't make anything up."

'I laughed and laughed at that! I had some firm conviction in my utter forgetfulness that priests and Magi lied ferociously. He nodded in satisfaction at this.

'"Your question?"

'"Do I have a destiny?" I asked.

'"What a strange question. What makes you think anyone has a destiny? We do what we do and we die. I told you. There is but one Creator God and his name does not matter. Our destiny, for all of us, is to love and to gain greater appreciation and understanding of all around us. Why should yours be any different?"

'"Ah, but that's just it. I should have a special destiny, should I not?"

'"The belief in a special destiny is one of the most rampant and harmful delusions on earth. Innocent babes are lifted from the teats of queens and told that they have a special destiny – to rule Athens, or Sparta, or Miletus, or Egypt, or Babylon. What stupidity. But I know what lies behind your question. And you'd better listen now. Go get the Canaanite tablet and don't break it. If you break it, I'll have to put it back together and I'll make you cry."

'"Hmmm. It's easy for you to make me cry, isn't it?"

'"Apparently," he said. "Get the tablet. Hurry. We have a journey ahead of us today. If you can take me to the steppes of the north, to the mountains where the great mountain of the gods is supposed to stand high above all else, then you can take me other places too. I want to go home to Athens. I want to walk in Athens. Go on, powerful spirit. Get the tablet. Hurry. Ignorance is of no use to anyone. Don't be afraid."'

Twelve

'I laid hands on the Canaanite tablet, though it filled me with revulsion and hate. Indeed, I rocked with hate. I was so full of hate that for a moment I couldn't move. His voice called me back, with the command that I was not to break it. The writing was very small, he reminded me, and one chip would hurt the contents, and I must know it all.

'"Why should I?" I asked. I gestured towards the pillows inside the room. Might I bring one out, so that I could sit at his feet without soiling my robes? He nodded.

'I crossed my legs. He was on his couch, one knee up, which seemed his favorite position, and he had the tablet now where he could read it clearly in the sun. This memory is so vivid to me, perhaps because the wall was white and covered in red flowers, and the olive tree was twisted and old, and many-branched as they get, and the green grass sprouting between the marble squares of the garden was soft. I loved to run the palm of my hand over it. I loved to lay the palm of my hand on the marble and feel the sun's heat.

'And of course I remember him with love, in his loose, long, baggy Greek tunic, the gold threads worn off the edging, looking rather scrawny and content and ageless as his blue eyes moved over the tablet, and he drew it close to his face now and then and then moved it far away. I think he must have read every single little word carved on it, in its long narrow columns of cuneiform. I hated it.

'"You escaped into the spirit world at the hands of idiots," he said. "This is an old Canaanite incantation to call up a powerful evil spirit, a servant of evil as powerful as the spirits of evil that might be sent to earth by God. It is to create for a magician a mal'ak, strong as the Mal'ak which Yahweh sent to slay the firstborn of the Egyptians."

'I was stunned. I didn't answer him. I knew many translations of the story of the flight from Egypt and I knew an image of the Mal'ak, the shining angel of the Lord's Wrath.

'"This information was regarded dangerous by the Canaanites and sealed in this tablet, if the date is correct, a thousand years ago. This was black magic, bad magic, magic like that of the Witch of Endor, who brought the spirit Samuel up to speak with King Saul."

'"I know these stories," I said quietly.

'"The magician here would make his own mal'ak which could be as strong as a Satan or fallen angel or evil spirit that had once participated in the power of Yahweh Himself."

'"I understand."

'"The rules are very strict here. The candidate for the mal'ak must be thoroughly evil, opposed to God and all things good, one who had despaired of God in contempt for God's cruelty to man and the injustice He allowed into the world. The candidate for the mal'ak is to be so determined and angry and evil that he would fight God himself if he could or is called upon to do so. He should be able to meet any Angel of the Lord hand to hand and fight him down."

'"You speak of good angels?"

'"Yes, good and bad; you were to be the equal of them and you may be. You are a mal'ak, not an ordinary spirit at all. But as I said, the one who would become this must be evil to the core of his heart, he must have no patience any longer with God and want to serve the rebellious spirit in mankind, that which has refused to accept God's rules. This spirit is not being created to serve a Devil or Demon, but to be one."

'I gasped.

'"You seem rather young to have been so wretchedly evil . . . at least in the form you've chosen on your own, which does seem the perfect emanation of what you were when you were alive. Were you that evil? Did you hate God so much?"

'"No, at least, I don't think I did. If I did, I didn't know."

'"Did you choose to become the Servant of the Bones?"

'"No. I know I did not."

'"More bungling. You weren't evil, you weren't willing, and you did not make a vow to serve whoever would own the bones, did you?"

'"Certainly not!" I tried to remember. It was so difficult now, the past grew bright, then faded, but I could push back to Cyrus's bedchamber, I could remember that Cyrus had sent me here to Zurvan, and I could remember something before that . . . a priest dead on the floor.

'"I killed the one who would be Master," I said. "I killed him and there was death all around me, I was dying when I was made. Only a little flame remained in me. I was to die. The stairway to heaven was to come down perhaps, or I was to go into the light and be part of it. I don't know which happened. But whatever the case, I was not willing to be the Servant of the Bones, I tried to escape . . . I remember running and calling for help, saying this was a Canaanite curse, but I don't remember to whom I appealed. Only afterwards I brought my bones in a sack into the bedchamber of the King."

'"So he's told me. Well, according to this, you should have been an expert on evil and cruelty before you were chosen, and you should have begged for the privilege of eternal life equal to God's angels, and you should have been willing to endure a terrible death. At the moment when the pain became too great for you, your spirit should have separated from the body, and watched the body be boiled down to bones. But only once the pain became too great. Only then. You were to endure the boiling cauldron of gold for as long as you could to perfect your hatred of God that he had made men sentient beings, and then and only then you should have risen free, aware of the power of your triumph over death, and your hatred of God, who made death, and your desire to be the mal'ak who is as strong as Yahweh's cruel heart when he turned it against those whom Saul or David or Joshua would slay.

'"You are to be the avenger of Adam and Eve, that they were foully tricked by your God. What does that say to you?"

'"It was all a blundering affair, as you said. I can't remember being *in* the cauldron, only a terrible, terrible fear of it. I think I escaped my body before the pain came, I think I couldn't endure it, all was confusion, I was surrounded by weak and self-seeking individuals, all grandeur had gone. All majesty had gone. I had done something, something that others wanted me to do, but it seemed tainted, horribly tainted and I'd been confused."

'"And there had been majesty in this tainted act?"

'"Well, I think there had. I can remember a sense of great sacrifice, purpose. I can remember rose petals and a sleepy slow death whose worst pain was knowledge that it was irreversible and would take its time, but not be changed. I don't know why I said majesty. What did Cyrus say of me to you?"

'"Not enough, I don't think. But according to this tablet, you cannot be destroyed. If the bones are destroyed then you are loosed upon the world to take vengeance on everything living, like a pestilence."

'Despair descended on me. It descended on me utterly, a despair that would have been impossible for the spirit I had been only a few hours ago. When I wandered upwards towards those with joyous faces, when I saw the gleam of light, I hadn't known despair! I hadn't known it any more than a child being turned away from a plate of sweets. Now I knew.

'"I want to die," I whispered. "I want to truly die as I was supposed to die, before they did this to me, misguided fools that they were! Before they tried this fearsome magic. Ah, idiots! Ah, God!"

'"Die?" he asked, "and wander among the stupid dead? Become a demon growling among other spirits, become a great foul enemy of all that is good, a bringer of death and torment!"

'"No, just die, die as if in my mother's arms, die as if to lie in my Mother Earth, and if I become light and if there is Heaven so be it, but if not, then simply to die, and to live on in the memory of anything good I ever did for anyone, any good act, any act of kindness and love, and . . ."

'". . . and what?"

'"I was going to say that I wanted to live on in memory for the acts I had done in praise of God, but I don't care about that now. I just want to die. I would rather God would leave

171

me alone." I stood up. I looked down at him. "Did Cyrus tell you who I was in life? How he came to know me?"

'"No, you can go read his letters for yourself. He said only that your strength was too great for any magician but myself, and that he owed you a great debt, that your death had been his doing." He stopped, thinking, pulling on his beard. 'Of course the King of all the world is not going to add to a letter that he was personally frightened of a spirit and wishes to get it as far from him as possible, but there was that, shall we say, tinge to the letter. You know, 'I cannot command this spirit. I dare not. And yet I owe him my Kingdom?"

'"I can't remember his owing me anything. I remember asking to be sent ... I remember ...'

'"Yes?"

'"Being forsaken by all."

'"Well, these fools haven't made a demon. They have made something more like an angel.'

'"Angel of might," I said. "You used those words yourself. Cyrus used them. Marduk used them ..." I stopped. Stumped by the name Marduk, and seeing nothing to surround the name or make it plausible in my speech.

'"Marduk, the god of Babylon?" he asked.

'"Don't mock him, he suffers," I said, amazing myself.

'"You want vengeance on those who did this to you?"

'"I took it. I can't remember anyone else who is not dead. It was the priest's doing, and he ... and the old woman, she died, the witch, the seer. I can't remembered ... I knew only Cyrus could help me and I knew that I had a right to walk into his bedchamber, that I would make him listen to me. No, I don't want vengeance. No. I don't remember anything enough to want it, any more than I hanker after life. I don't. There is something I want ... to die ... to rest, to sleep, to be dead in the sweet-smelling earth ... or to see the light as I become one with it, one tiny spark of the light of God returned to his flame. I want death most ... even more than the light. Just the quiet of death."

'"You want this now," he said. "You didn't want it when you went walking, or roaming the realm of the spirits, or bringing the scrolls for me. Or when you first sat down in this garden and kept touching the grass with your hands."

'"That's because you're a good man," I said.

'"No, that's because *you* are a good man. Or were. And goodness burns as bright in you now as it ever did. Souls without memory are dangerous. You remember . . . but you remember only the good."

'"No, I've told you how much I hate them . . ."

'"Yes, but they're gone, they're receding from you fast. You can't remember their names, or their faces . . . you don't hate them. But you remember good. Last night, you told me you found gold in your pockets. What did you do with it? You didn't say."

'"Well, I gave it to the poor and hungry, a family of them, so they could eat." I reached out and gathered the loose grass that would come up from the cracks between the marble. I looked at the tender green shoots. "You're right. I do remember goodness, or I know it. I know it, and I see it and I feel it . . ."

'"Then I'll teach you everything I can," he said. "We'll travel. We'll go to Athens and then down into Egypt. I have never been deep into Egypt. I want to go. We'll travel by magic. Or sometimes merely in the natural way, because you're a strong guardian, and you must remember everything I teach you . . . your tendency, your weakness, is to veer away from pain by forgetting it, and when I die, you'll feel some pain."

'He fell quiet. I think the lessons were at an end for a little while. He closed his eyes. But I had a further pressing question.

'"Ask it, then, before I go to sleep."

'"These Canaanites, who made this curse. Were they Hebrew?"

'"Not really," he said. "Not Hebrew as you are. Their Yahweh was one of many gods, only the strongest, a war god it seems. They were ancient peoples and they believed in other gods too. Are you glad to hear this?"

'My mind had drifted. "I suppose I am," I said. "Yes, I am. But I belong to no tribe now. My destiny is to belong to

173

the best of Masters, for without them I may forget everything, I may drift ... I may cease to see or hear or feel ... and I won't be dead, merely waiting for the one who calls me forth."

'"I won't live long," he said. "I'll teach you every trick I know that you have the power to do, and how to deceive men with illusions, and how to create spells over them with words and attitudes ... that's all it is ... remember ... words, attitudes ... it's the abstract ... not the particular. You could make a curse of a list of barrels of grain if you said it right, you know? But I'll teach you and you will listen, and when I die ..."

'"Yes ..."

'"We'll see what the wide world teaches you by that time."

'"Don't expect too much of me," I said. I looked at him directly, which I had rarely done in all this time. "You ask me what I remember. I remember killing the bedouins and I liked it very much. Not as much as the flowers, gathering them, you know, but killing ... what is there like it on earth?"

'"You have a point," he said. "You have to learn that to love is better ... to be kind is even better. In killing you crush a universe of beliefs and feelings and generations in that one person whom you kill. But when you do kindness, it's like dropping a pebble in the great ocean and the ripples go on forever and ever, and no wave, not even those as far away as Italy or Egypt, is the same. Kindness actually has considerably more power than killing has. But you'll come to see it. You knew it when you were alive."

'He considered for a moment, and then concluded his advice for the day.

'"You see, it's a matter of how well you can measure these things. When you strike down a man, you don't see the full implications of his death, not then. You feel the blood rush in you, even as a spirit you are formed in the likeness of man. But when you do something good, you can see it often ... you can see it and see it and see it ... and that's what overrides the desire to kill finally. The goodness shines too bright; it's too ... undeniable. When you walked you saw it

174

in people's faces, didn't you? Goodness. No one tried to hurt you. Not even the palace guards. They let you by. Was it your clothing and your demeanor? Or did you smile at them as well? Did your face shine with goodwill? Each time you return to me, you are happy, and your spirit, whatever made it, has a great capacity to love."

'I didn't answer.

'"What is in your head now?" he asked. "Tell me."

'"The bedouins," I said. "What fun it was to kill them," I answered.

'"You're stubborn!" he said.

'He closed his eyes and went to sleep. I sat there watching and gradually I slept too, asleep in my body, listening to the flowers next to my ears, and looking up into the branches of the olive tree now and then to see the birds there, and the distant sounds of the city became a music to me. And when I dreamed, it was of gardens, and light and fruit trees and joyous spirits with faces filled with love.

'Words were woven into my dreams.

'"And I will give thee the treasures of darkness, and hidden riches of secret places, that thou mayest know that I, the Lord, which call *thee* by thy name, *am* the God of Israel . . . I form the light, and I create darkness: I make peace, and create evil . . .' My eyes opened, but then I knew sweeter verses, and sank back into a half sleep of song and willow trees swaying in the breeze.'

Thirteen

'For fifteen years, I traveled with Zurvan. I did his bidding in all things. He was rich, as I've said, and many times he wanted to travel merely as men do, and we went by ship to Egypt, and then back again to Athens and to other cities which he had visited in his youth and had despaired of ever seeing again.

'Almost never did he let on that he was a magician, though now and then he was recognized by one with second sight. And when called upon to heal the sick, he would do what he could. In every place we traveled he bought or had me borrow for him, or even steal, tablets and scrolls of magic, and these he studied and read to me and made me memorize, further reinforcing his conviction that all magic was more or less the same.

'That I can remember these years with crystal clarity is a mercy, because during the time that separated me from his death and the present I have few distinct memories at all. I know there were times after Zurvan's death when I woke with no memory and served my masters out of boredom, and sometimes watched them bring destruction upon themselves and thought it amusing, and even now and then took the bones from them myself to another. But all this is hazy, fog. Meaningless.

'Zurvan was right. My response to pain and to suffering was to forget. And it is the overall tendency of spirits to forget. Flesh and blood, bodily needs, these are what inspire memory in man. And when these are wholly absent, it can be sweet to remember nothing at all.

'During Zurvan's life, he made a better casket for the bones. He made it of very strong wood, plated inside and out with gold, and he made a carved-out space for the bones to rest in their curled position, as that of a child asleep. He had carpenters work on this because, in truth, the work of his

176

spirit familiars was not exact enough for him. Those who know the material world work with greater respect for it, he said.

'On the outside of this casket which was a rectangle just long enough to contain my skeleton, he carved the name of what I was and how I was to be called, and he carved the stern warning that I must never be used for evil, lest that evil descend upon the one who calls. He cautioned against the destruction of my bones, lest all restraint upon me go with it.

'He wrote all this in the form of incantation and sacred poetry in many languages all over the casket.

'He put a Hebrew symbol or letter which means life on the casket.

'It was very good that he did all this early, because his death came quite by surprise. He died in his sleep, and I was called forth only when his house in Syracuse was being raided by petty thieves and people of the village who knew he had no kin and were in no fear for him. And as he had left no demons to guard his body, they sacked the house, found the casket, spoke of the bones, and I awoke.

'I slew everyone present, down to the smallest child who rummaged through Zurvan's clothes. I slew them all. That night, the villagers came to burn the house of the Magus in hopes of dispelling its evil. I was glad of this because I knew that Zurvan, being Greek by birth, though a man of no nation or tribe by choice, wanted his remains to be burnt, and I had arranged them within the house so that they burnt first and fast.

'I journeyed back to Miletus, and then on towards Babylon though I didn't remember why. I grieved for Zurvan. I thought only of Zurvan. I was in pain night and day, invisible, in the flesh, frightened to go into the bones to rest lest I never come out of them, and lugging my skeleton with me through the desert sands.

'At last I came to a city of Babylon but found myself repelled by it and hating it, and walking in pain with every step. I saw nothing that sparked a memory, only a feeling. I left very shortly after I'd come and I went back to Athens, which had been the birthplace of Zurvan. And finding a little house, I made a safe hiding place for the bones far, far beneath it, and then I went into them. And all was blackness.

'Much later I awoke with faint memories of Zurvan, yet remembering all his lessons, but it was another century. And maybe I always remembered his lessons. I think that may be the key to my eventual rebellion, that I remembered his lessons and loathed the perversion of them.

'Whatever the case, I was called forth in Athens. The soldiers of Philip II of Macedon had come down on Athens and beaten the Greeks, and Philip the Barbarian, as they called him, was looting the city, and in the process the bones were unearthed.

'When I came forth it was in the tent of a Macedonian magician, and he was as amazed to lay eyes on me, as I was on him.

'I remember almost nothing of him. What I remember is the vibrant quality of the world, the lure of being solid once more, of tasting water, and of wanting to be a living and breathing thing even if only an imitation. I knew also my great strength, kept this secret from this Master, and only quietly obeyed his largely petty and foolish commands. He was a small magician.

'I was passed by him to another and another. My next distinct memory is only because Gregory Belkin wakened it in me ... that I was in Babylon when Alexander the Great died. How I got there, whom I served, I don't remember. But I remember dressing myself, making my body into that of one of Alexander's soldiers so that I might pass before his bed and see him signal with his hand that he was dying.

'I remember Alexander as he lay on his bed, that he burnt with an aura as bright as that of Cyrus the Persian. Even in dying he was very beautiful and strangely alert. He was observing himself die, and he was not fighting to live. Not desperate to live. It was as if he knew this was to be the end of his life. I don't recall him knowing that a spirit had walked past him, as I was solid and very complete. I do recall going back to my Master of the moment and telling him, Yes, the conqueror of the world was dying, and it seems this Master was old and Greek, too, and that he wept. I recall that I put my arm around him to comfort him.

'I wouldn't remember that much if it weren't for Gregory crying out the name of Alexander with such fury in New York and declaring that Alexander was the only man who had really ever changed the whole world.

'I could struggle now through other masters ... bring up out of the cauldron of memory bits and pieces. But there is no dignity or magic or greatness that calls to me, that makes me long to recount it. I was an errand boy, a spirit sent to spy, to steal, sometimes even to kill. I remember killing. But I don't remember feeling remorse. I don't remember ever serving anyone whom I thought was unspeakably evil. And I do remember that I slew two masters at various times upon waking, because they were evil men.

'But this is hazy, as I said, unclear to me. What I remember next and most vividly, what I remembered only weeks ago when I awoke in the cold clear New York streets to witness the murder of Esther Belkin, what I remembered immediately with any clarity was the last master, Samuel of Strasbourg – named for the prophet, of course.

'Samuel was a leader and a magician among the Jews of Strasbourg. I only remember loving him and his five beautiful daughters, and I remember not the details of the beginning or the middle, but only the last days when the Black Death had come, when the city was in an uproar, and the word came down from the powerful Gentiles that all of us Jews should get out, because the local authorities might not be able to protect us from the mob.

'The last night shines before my eyes. Samuel was the only one left in the house. His five daughters had been smuggled out of Strasbourg to safety, and he and I sat in the main room of his house, a very rich house, I might add, and he made it known to me, that no matter what I said or did, he would not flee the wrath of the mob.

'Many poor Jews could not escape what was about to happen. And Samuel, much to my amazement, had conceived of the notion that someone of his tribe or clan might need him at the end, and that he must remain. He had not always been so self-sacrificing by nature, yet, he had chosen to remain.

'I was frantic, slamming my fists, raging out and coming back to tell him that the entire neighborhood was surrounded, that the entire population of this district would shortly be burned.

'The history of the world was no mystery to me and neither was Samuel; the substance of the man was vivid then and is now; I'd gotten gold for him in abundance; I had spied on his connections in business and banking; I had been the source of his immense and ever increasing wealth. Killing, that was something I had never done for him because he never thought of anything so crude; he was a merchant Jew, a banker Jew, and clever and beloved and respected by the Gentile community for his good rates of interest and his reasonableness when it came to the payment of debt. A kindly man? Yes, but a worldly man, though a bit mystical, and now he sat in this room, as the mob and the fire drew closer, as the city of Strasbourg turned into hell around us, and he quietly refused to leave.

'"There are ways out of this city still, I can take you!" I said. Indeed we both knew of tunnels beneath the house of the Jewish district which led to the world outside the walls. They were old, true, but we knew them. I could have taken him through them. Or upwards, with great power, invisible through the air.

'"Master, what will you do? Let them kill you? Tear you limb from limb? Either the fire will come racing at you from both ends of the street outside, or they will come, to tear off your rings and your robes before they kill you. Master, why are you choosing to die?"

'He had told me twelve times to be quiet and go back into the bones. I wouldn't do it. Finally I said, "I won't let this happen to you. I'll take you from here, you and the bones!"

'"Azriel," he cried. "There is time and you will be still!" He neatly put aside the last of his books, a volume of his cherished Talmud, and his books of the Kabbalah from which had come much of his magic, and then he waited, with his eye on the door.

180

'"Master," I asked. My memory of this is exquisite. "Master what of me? What will happen? Will the bones be found without their casket? Where do I go, Master?"

'Surely I had never asked such a self-serving question. Because the look of surprise on his face was so bright. He broke off his reverie and staring at the door and he looked up at me.

'"Master, when you die, can you take my spirit with you?" I said. "Can you take your loyal servant into the light?"

'"Oh, Azriel," he said in the most despairing voice, "what ever gave you such notions, foolish, foolish spirit. What do you think you are?"

'The tone of his voice infuriated me. The look on his face infuriated me.

'"Master, you're leaving me to the ashes! To the looters!" I cried out. "Can't you clasp my hand as they kill you, if that's what you must have, can't you take my hand and take me with you? Thirty years I've served you, made you rich, made your daughters rich. Master! You're leaving me here. The casket may burn. The bones may burn. What will happen!"

'He looked completely confused. He looked ashamed. At that point the door of the house opened and two very finely dressed Gentile merchant bankers whom I knew came into the room. Both were anxious.

'"We have to hurry, Samuel," they said. "They're starting the fires near the walls. They're killing the Jews everywhere. We cannot help you escape."

'"Did I ask you to?" said Samuel with contempt. "Give me the proof that my daughters are away."

'Anxiously they put a letter in his hand. I saw it was from one of many moneylenders whom he trusted most, who was in Italy and in a safe place, and it confirmed that his daughters had come and described the color of the dress of each and every one, and her hair, and gave the special word from her which her father demanded.

'The Gentiles were terrified.

'"We must hurry, Samuel. If you're determined to die here, keep your word! Where is the casket?"

'At these words I was astonished. Only too quickly did I

181

understand! I had been bartered for the salvation of the five daughters! Neither of these men could see me, but they saw the casket of my bones, which was in plain sight with the books of the Kabbalah, and they went to the casket and opened it and there lay my bones!

'"Master." I said in a secret voice to him. "You can't give me to these men! These men are Gentiles. They aren't magicians. They're not great men."

'Samuel was amazed still, staring at me. "Great? When did I ever tell you I was great or even good, Azriel? When did you ever ask?"

'"In the name of the Lord God of Hosts," I said, "I did for you what was good for you and your family and your elders and your synagogue. Samuel! What do you do to me now?"

'The two Gentiles closed the casket. "Goodbye Samuel," they said as one of them hugged the casket to his breast and they both hurried out the door. I could see the light of the fire. I could smell it. I could hear people screaming.

'"You evil, evil man!" I cursed him. "You think God will forgive you because this fire cleanses you and you've sold me for money, for gold!"

'"For my daughters, Azriel. Spirit, you have found a powerful voice too near the end."

'"The end of what?" But I knew. I could feel already the others calling, those who had their hands on the bones. They were already outside the city gates. And my hatred and contempt was boiling in me. Their calls were a temptation!

'I came at Samuel.

'"No, Spirit!" he declared. "Obey me, go to the bones. Obey as you always have. Leave me to my martyrdom."

'There came the call again. I couldn't hold my form. I was too angry. My body was dissolving. I had in my anger forfeited too much. The voices that called me were strong. They were farther and farther away but nonetheless strong.

'I lunged at Samuel and I threw him out the open door. The street was full of flames. "There's your martyrdom, Rabbi!" I shouted. "I curse you to walk among the undead for all your existence, until God forgives you for what you did to me, leaving me, bartering with me, leading me to love you, and selling me like gold!"

'From both directions terrified people ran to him, people who were suffering their final anguish. "Samuel, Samuel," they called out his name.

'My bitterness broke for an instant when I saw him embrace them. "Samuel," I cried. I came towards him. I was growing weak but I was still visible to him. "Take my hand. Hold the hand of my spirit, please, Samuel, take me with you into death."

'He didn't speak. The crowd surrounded him, sobbing and clinging to him, but I heard his last thought as he rebuffed me as he turned his eyes away. He said as clearly as if aloud,

'"No, Spirit, because if I die with my hand in yours you may take me down into Hell."

'I cursed him.

'*"Not enough grace and goodness for both of us, Master: Master! Leader! Teacher! Rabbi!"*

'The flames engulfed the crowd. I rose upwards through the flame and smoke, and felt the cold night pass through me and I sped towards the sanctuary of the bones. I sped away from smoke and horror and injustice and the screams of the innocent. I went through the dark woods, as a witch to a Sabbath, flying with my arms out, and then I saw the two Gentiles at the door of a small church at a great remove from the city, the casket on the ground between them, and wanting only death and silence; I relaxed into the bones.

'All I learnt of them was that they were weeping for Strasbourg, for the Jews, for Samuel, for the whole tragedy. And that they planned to sell me in Egypt. They were not magicians. I was a marketable prize.

'It didn't seem that mine was a long uninterrupted sleep. I was called, I was taken places, I slew those who called me, and some I can picture, some not. The history of the world was written on the blank and endless tablets of my mind in column after column. I did not think, however; I slept.

'Once a Mameluk in beautiful silk called me forth. It was Cairo, and I chopped him to pieces with his own sword. It took all the wise men of the palace to drive me back into the bones. I remember their beautiful turbans and their frantic cries. They were such a flashy lot, those Moslem soldiers, those strange men who lived all their lives without women, and only to fight and to kill. Why didn't they destroy me? Because of the inscriptions that warned them against a masterless spirit who could seek revenge.

'I recall in Paris a clever satanic magician in a room full of gaslight. The wallpaper was most intriguing to me. A strange black coat hung on a hook. Life almost tempted me. Gaslight and machines; carriages rolling on cobbled streets. But I killed the mysterious man and retreated once more into the bones.

'It was always that way. I slept. I think I remember a winter in Poland. I think I remember an argument between two learned men. But all this is misty and imperfect. They spoke a Hebrew dialect and they had called me, but neither seemed to know I was there. They were good and gentle men. We were in a plain synagogue, and they argued. And then they decided that my bones must be hidden within the wall. Good men. I slept.'

'When I came to life again, it was in the bright winter sunlight only weeks ago, as a trio of assassins made their way through the press on Fifth Avenue to kill Esther Belkin as she came out of her black limousine and entered the store before her – innocent, beautiful, without the slightest sense of death circling her.

'And why was I there? Who had called me? I knew only these assassins meant to kill her, these hideous rustic evil men, drugged and stupid and enchanted with the pleasure of killing her, in all her innocence. I had to stop it. I had to.

'But I was too late. You know what the papers told you.

'Who was this innocent child? She saw me, spoke my name. How had she known me? She had never called me. She had only seen me in the thin realm between life and death where truths are visible which are otherwise veiled.

'Let us linger on this killing. A death such as Esther's deserves a few more words. Or maybe I need to recount my coming into awareness. Maybe I need to describe what it was like to see and breathe again in this mighty city, with towers higher than the mystical mountain of Meru, among thousands of people, good and bad, and without luster, as Esther was being marked for the kill.'

Part III

HOW KEEP DARK AND PATTERN OFF

How keep dark
and pattern that any man suffers
off – at the wall, at where the hat
comes out of the marrow & yawns –
how keep head up the scream
& up the burial where the pattern is born –
how the leagues washing their hearts
& wrung dry only to sponge back up – men
smooching mirrors – blades honing
– tongue & eyelash of Sweet Thing
staggering the shape by the door in the baggy shadow –
how keep dark back?
Or should one bullet-forth, sleek-clothed or naked – pierce
each entity – each clock – sharpened by art
or wine – how
enter the needle, the cloth –
how take the pattern any man suffers
and lose nothing when you
rip it off.

Stan Rice, *Some Lamb* 1975

Fourteen

Follow me now, if you will, into consciousness.

Evals in the bright winter light of day. See how they shine. That's how I first knew them. This was a joke to them because evil was their word for bad, and their names were Eval. Three brothers out of Texas hired to kill the rich girl.

Down the crowded avenue, in a bath of noonday sun they walked, jostling each other, laughing, passing the cigarette, bold and hot for the kill. How they loved to look at themselves in the mirrors of shops, and this was New York, the biggest city in the world, the only city these Evals cared about, except for Las Vegas, where they will go with their earnings after they've 'taken her out,' which in their vernacular meant kill her.

They weren't never going back to Texas. Who knew what jobs 'the man' might have for them? But first they had to kill her dead.

I could feel their easy malice, even as purely as they felt it – Billy Joel Eval in the lead, with the gun in his pocket and also the long sharp pick, such a cruel pick with a rounded blade of steel. And Doby Eval right behind with Hayden Eval 'sucking hind teat,' they taunted him, and all of them had those sharp weapons, long picks made of steel, oh, so ready to kill her but who was she?

There had to be a reason for my seeing this, there had to be a reason that I stood in the city of New York, breathing in the smells of New York as if I were alive, and visible, when I was neither, only knowing what a genii always knows . . . that he has been called again to duty, that once again his eyes and his mind have opened on a blazing and vital world.

You know how rebellious I was, I've told you, how indifferent, how perfectly willing to cut to pieces a despicable master. But what was happening here?

Loathing these rustic monsters was easy enough. I walked

right by them! I saw them up close in their city-drab disguise, in quilted jackets of nylon and ragged cotton pants, machine-made shoes full of nails and hooks for the strings. Billy Joel couldn't wait to see her, couldn't wait to get close to her, and only Hayden held back, scared to tell his brother he didn't like it so much, killing this girl. If only they had known who paid them.

Who had paid them? 'A man through a man through a man,' said Doby Eval, 'as if you can't figure that out?'

Suddenly I felt my feet hit the pavement. But I was too transparent for anyone else to see, gathering slowly, trailing them, coming up so close on them now that they might have looked back and seen me, if anyone could, and I wasn't sure anyone could.

'Who is commanding me?' I whispered. I felt my lips move. The crowd was as thick on this city street as any I'd ever beheld, and the wealth was closing in around me as if this were the marketplace of Babylon on the New Year, or the bazaars of Baghdad or Istanbul.

Through plate glass I saw the faceless white plastic goddesses of fashion in their magnificent fringe and fur, shine of true rubies, magical slippers made of thin steel straps to bind the foot fetchingly.

And all this with no explanation.

Well, you know me well enough by now, the sensualist I am.

Hand me the world in a cup and I'll drink it.

But this killing of the girl, this had to be stopped.

I closed in on them, walked among them, but still they couldn't see me, though I was feeling the shape of my body, the heat of it, the growing density. Yes, I was here all right, this was no garbled hideous phantasm in the wind.

There came the heat of the sidewalk beneath me, and something like the thud of my own feet in leather shoes, just make them plain like theirs. I knew the stench came from the engines in the street, and when I looked up, I saw the towers reaching the noonday clouds, yet lights blazing everywhere, in windows, behind written signs, all fueled by electricity.

What a modern world this was – teeming with the rich –

what a city this was with the humpback dwarf and the cripple lurching past me, both wearing fine clothes and gold, and the screeching woman on the corner, long gone mad, ripped open a blouse of pure silk to show her breasts. Someone pushed her off the curb. Hordes of young men in severe dark suits, each with a tie at the neck of his shirt, walked fast and with purpose, though obviously all disconnected, separate, not even glancing at one another.

The Evals laughed.

'Oh, I'm telling you, this is one hell of a place, this New York, I'm telling you, just look at her, did you see that? Now, you know this broad we're taking out, she's not crazy like that, no way, now you do what I said . . .'

'Do what you said,' cursed the brother Hayden.

I was neck and neck with them, I could smell their sweat and the cheap soap they had used to wash half of it away, and I could smell their guns, but that wasn't the way, the gun, the bullet, the explosion – I tried to learn it all as quickly as I could – they would use the sharp-pointed picks that each carried under his clothes.

'Why do you do this to her?'

I must have spoken aloud, because Billy Joel stopped, right shoulder jerking up, mouth pulled down on the ends as he stared at Hayden, and then told him, 'Will you shut up, you son of a bitch, come on now, I'm telling you we couldn't have gotten out of here any way but this way.'

'Sure and we do her and then we just run, just run, like little kids, just run!' said Hayden, shoving his brother with his left hand in the middle of the back, so the brother Billy Joel said, 'You lay off, look, you son of a bitch, you see it, you see it, Doby, she's in that goddamn car, that's her car, look at that car.'

The three came together, and I fell back, invisible still but totally formed or perhaps I should say conformed to the look of men around me.

I wanted to see her, this girl they meant to kill with their evil picks, as they ambled and danced now, letting the crowd stream past them, nudging each other to stop, there she was! The time had come.

191

Look. See the long black limousine by the curb, and the driver with his white hair opening the door for her?

Esther. Hair a mantle of dark curls, jet-black hair, as black as mine, and her eyes larger, and the whites of them were so shiny they looked as if they were made of pearls, and her long white throat bare to the swell of her breasts beneath a painted coat, a coat painted with the stripes of an animal not to look like the animal itself but to look like the painted stripes of one.

She didn't even notice them, these three common and visible terrors who were going to 'take her out.' The crowd shifted and broke to make an uneven path for her.

'What am I to do?' I whispered. 'Stop this? Why is she to die, for what?' I didn't want to witness it.

She pushed wide the glass doors of the shop and passed inside, with the throng so thick that five people must have followed her before the Evals made their way in, and now they knew they were in trouble.

'Jesus, do we have to do it in here?'

By that Hayden meant that this was a palace of goods, a treasure house of furs and veils, of leathers dyed in all colors, and perfume rising from the glass tables as if from altars.

They didn't look so ordinary in here, these slithering swaggering bucolic men, no, rather like tramps from a waterfront, crawling out from under the rope with the rats to steal what men have dropped, but it was so crowded, even here, shoulder to shoulder, and cheek turned from cheek, as lashes rose and fell to make the eye private. And the noise was loud. No one took the proper notice – three clothed in filth tracking the beautiful woman.

And she the young queen with the dark shining hair and the painted coat came up the steps to the landing, her face innocent and bright as she reached for a long black scarf, a beaded scarf, a lovely twinkling thing, and caught it in her fingers, dangling from the hook, a scarf full of dark stitched flowers and shimmering embroidered designs, lovely, as if meant for her.

'Good afternoon, Miss Belkin.' So the queen had a name,

and the merchants of this time were no less clever than in any other.

But I saw Billy Joel had struck! In that one second, he had pushed against her slender back, Hayden took her from the left, and Doby, as frenzied as Billy Joel, drove his pick from the right, so that the three wounds were made at once, and the life inside her lurched, and the language in her died, but not her heart. Her lungs filled with blood.

Geniuses of the kill, these cheap assassins. They walked right away from her, before she even fell, not even bothering to run, out of the door before she even tottered over the glass case. The scarf was still in her right hand. The woman bent over:

'Miss Belkin?'

I had to follow them. She was falling down dead, leaning over the glass, as if this was just a pain she had to feel and it would pass. She'd be dead in seconds! And I knew the killers, and the merchant lady didn't even know she was dying.

I shot through the front doors. I knew I shoved against the humans to move them out of my way. I felt them. I wasn't going to lose the Evals. I went up.

Over the heads of the crowd, I flew, formed but transparent, nothing anyone would notice, and quickly caught up with them.

The Evals had broken apart. But no one in this next block of shuffling hundreds seemed to notice them; what need was there to hurry? Billy Joel had a smile on his face, bright smile.

They had put three hundred people and ten seconds between them and the murder.

'I will kill you for this!' I heard my voice aloud. I felt the air inside me, swirling, as if I'd made myself solid enough to feed on the fumes that rose from the pavements, from the stalled engines, from the blasting horns, from the swarm of human flesh.

Come to me, garments like those of my enemy, as I am made flesh! I dropped down in front of Billy Joel. Reach for the pick. Get it. Kill him. I saw my fingers close on his wrist. He never clearly saw me, only felt the bone break. As he cried out, his brother turned. I drove the pick into Billy Joel, I took its wooden handle out of his belt and drove it in through his shirt, deep, the way he had driven it into her, only many more times.

Astonished, he spurted blood.

'You die, you filthy dog, you killed that girl, you die.'

Hayden came towards me, right onto the pick, no trouble at all, and I gave him three quick thrusts, including one in the neck. There were people walking by, not turning their heads. Others were looking at the fallen Billy Joel.

Now only Doby was left and Doby had fled, Doby had seen them go down and was running about as fast as a human can run through the obstacle course of the crowd. I reached out, grabbed his shoulder . . .

'Wait a minute, man!' he said to me. I sank the pick into his chest, the same three times, to make it good, and pushed him towards the wall. People stepped out of our way, turning the other way. He slid down to the pavement dead, and a woman cursed as she stepped over his left leg.

Now I understood the genius of their crime in this crowded city. But there was no time to think on it. I had to return to Esther.

My body was formed, I was running, and I had to make my way, like any other human now, solid, back to the glass doors of the palace.

The air was filled with screams. Men ran into the emporium of clothes. I pushed to get close. I could feel my tangled black hair. I could feel my beard. All eyes were on her.

Out she came, laid and covered on a white linen stretcher. I saw her head tumbled to my side, her big glossy eyes, with their pearly whites so pure, her mouth leaking blood like an old fountain. Just a trickle.

Men screamed for others to get back. An old one wailed at the top his lungs, bowing as he saw her. This was her driver, her guard perhaps, the gray-haired man. His face was furrowed, his narrow back bent. He bowed and cried out, he cried out in a dialect of Hebrew. He loved her. I pushed carefully towards her.

A white car came speeding to the spot, printed with red

194

crosses and topped by swirling lights. The sirens were unspeakable. Might as well have been the picks through my ears, but there was no time to worry about my pain. She was still living, breathing, I had to tell her.

Into that car, they carried her, lifted high, like an offering over the crowd . . . Through the back doors she went inside, her eyes looking for something, for someone.

Gathering all my strength, I moved others out of my path. My hands – true and familiar and mine – hit the long glass windowed side of the white car. I looked into the glass. I felt my nose against it. I saw her! Her big sleepy eyes full of dreamy death, I saw her.

And she said aloud, I heard it, a whisper rising like a whiff of smoke.

'The Servant . . . Azriel, the Servant of the Bones!'

The door was open. The men ministering to her bent low.

'What is it, honey? What did you say?'

'Don't make her speak.'

She stared at me through the glass, and she said it again, I saw her lips move. I heard her voice. I heard her thought. 'Azriel,' she whispered. 'The Servant of the Bones!'

'They're dead, my darling!' I cried out. No one around me, pressing as hard as I pressed to see her, cared what I said.

She and I, we looked at each other. Then her soul and spirit blazed for one instant, visible and together, the full shape of her body over her, hair like wings, face expressionless or turned away from the earth forever, who can know, and then she was gone, risen, in a blinding light. I ducked from the light, then tried to see it again. But it was gone.

The body lay an empty sack.

The doors slammed shut.

The siren split my ears again.

The car roared into the stream, forcing other engines out of its path, people shifted and sighed and groaned around me. I stood stock-still on the pavement. Her soul was gone.

I looked up. Knees pushed against my leg. A foot came down hard upon my own. I wore the same kind of dirty string shoe as my enemy. I was almost toppled from the shallow curb.

The car was beyond my sight, and the Evals dead not a hundred feet away, yet no one here in this melee knew, so crowded was it, and I thought – without context, without reason – of what was said about Babylon after Cyrus conquered it, that funny remark which the Greek historian Xenophon had made, or was it Herodotus, that so big was Babylon and so dense with people that it took two whole days before people in the middle of the city knew that it had been taken at all.

Well, not me!

A man said, 'Did you know who that was?' This was English, New York talk, and I turned just as if I were alive and I were going to answer, only there were tears in my eyes. I wanted to say,

'They killed her.' Nothing came out of my mouth but I had a mouth and the man was nodding as if he saw the tears. My God, help me. This man wanted to comfort me. Someone else spoke:

'That was Gregory Belkin's daughter, that's who that was,' the man said, 'That was Esther Belkin.'

'Belkin's daughter –'

'. . . Temple of the Mind.'

'Temple of the Mind of God. Belkin.'

What did these words mean to me?

Master! Where are you? Name yourself or show yourself? Who has called me? Why have I been made to witness this!

'Gregory Belkin's little girl, the Minders –'

Which way?

I began to fade. I felt it swift and terrible as it always is, as surely as if the Master had commanded all the artificial and gathered particles of me, as it is written, *Return now to your place.* Just for a moment, I clung to the storm of matter, commanding it to sheathe me, but my cry was a wail. I stared down at my hands, my feet, such filthy shoes, cloth and string and leather shoes, slippers more than shoes, shoes on the pavement:

'Azriel, stay alive!' came the voice from my mouth.

'Take it easy, son,' said the man beside me. And he looked at me as if he felt sorry for me. He lifted his arm to embrace me. I put my hand up. I saw the tears.

But the wind had come, the wind that comes for all spirits. I was losing my hold.

The man was looking for me and he couldn't find me, and he didn't know why, and thought it was his own confusion.

Then he and all those with him – and the great city – was gone too.

I was nothing now, nothing.

I struggled to see the crowd below, but I couldn't find the spots where the Evals lay dead in their blood still or were being taken away with such care as the queen with her dark hair, the goddess who had died seeing me. She had said it, I heard it, she had said, 'Azriel, the Servant of the Bones.' I had heard her as a spirit hears, though the man in the car with her might not hear something so small and tragic as her whisper.

The wind took me. The wind was filled with the wail of the souls, faces bearing down upon me, hands seeking to grip me, and turning my back on it as always, I let go. I saw the last dim outline of my hands for one instant; I felt the form of arms and legs; I felt the tears on my face. Yes, I felt that. Then I was a goner.

Into the bones, Azriel. I was safe.

So there you have the picture! Masterless, risen, to witness this, to avenge it? Why? The darkness overcame me like a drug. Safe, yes, but I didn't want to be safe; I wanted to find the man who had sent those Evals to kill her.

Fifteen

Time passed.

I felt it more intensely than usual. I knew that I was listening. I was there.

I knew what the world was now, more or less, as always. Bear with me. I knew what men and women knew – those whom I'd seen and touched in the New York street.

The particulars made a moral impression. Emotion gradually accompanied the synthesis of knowledge. Ghosts don't have to interpret. Ghosts don't have to be amazed, or shocked.

But the mind of the ghost, unfettered by flesh, can gather to itself indiscriminately and perhaps infinitely the sum of what is shared or valued by nearby human minds.

Awake once more in the darkness, I grasped the general and the spectacular – that we were nearing the end of the twentieth century of what men call the common era, that fossil fuel and generated electricity were indispensable to the everyday methods of eating, drinking, sleeping, communicating, traveling, building, and fighting, that micromachines of exquisite circuitry could store information in abundance, and that vivid moving pictures in which people appeared and spoke could be transmitted by waves or over tiny delicate fibers more precious than spun glass.

Waves. The air was full of waves. Full of voices speaking both privately and publicly – from telephones, through radios, televisions. The world was as fully surrounded by voices now as it was by air itself.

And the earth was indeed round. Not a mile of it remained uncharted, unowned, or unnamed. No part of it lay beyond communication because the mysterious waves of telephones, radios, and televisions could be bounded off satellites in space and back to earth again at any locale. Sometimes the television pictures and voices were of people and actions taking place at the very moment they were being transmitted: known as live TV.

Chemistry had reached unprecedented heights, achieving through extraction, purification, analysis, and new combinations all manner of new substances, materials, drugs. The very process of combining had been transformed so that there was now physical change, chemical change, chain reaction, chemical reaction, and fusion, to name but a few. Materials had been broken down and made into new materials and the process was without limit.

Science had surpassed the alchemist's dreams.

Diamonds had found their way into the bits of drills, yet people still wore them as ornaments and they commanded millions of dollars, which was, apparently a preferred currency, American dollars, though the world was full of currencies and languages, and people from Hong Kong spoke to people in New York merely by pressing a few buttons. The catalog of synthetic materials and subsequent products had evolved beyond the memory or understanding of the common man so that almost nobody could define for you the ingredients of the nylon shirt he wore, or the plastic calculator in his pocket.

Of course some conclusions – even for me – were inevitable. A car or plane dependent on the combustion of fossil fuel can explode rather than move forward. Bombs can be sent without pilots from one country to another to destroy even the biggest cities with the highest buildings. Hardly anywhere in the world did the sea not taste just a little of gasoline.

New York was very far north of the equator, that was obvious, and one could say it was the capital, in this time, in the Western world.

The Western world. This is where I have found myself. And what is the Western world? Apparently, the Western world was the direct cultural legacy of the Hellenism of Alexander the Great, its concepts of justice and purity infinitely amplified and complicated but never really subverted by Christianity of varying kinds – from crude screaming mystic acceptance of Jesus to dense theological

199

sects which still argue over the nature of the Trinity, that is, whether or not there are three persons in one God. Scarcely a single part of the Western world had not been enriched and invigorated by an immensely creative and relentlessly spiritual Judaism. Jewish scientists, philosophers, doctors, merchants, and musicians were among the most celebrated of the era.

The drive to excel was taken for granted, as it was in Babylon. Even by those in despair.

Natural law and law arrived at by reason had become common values, revealed law and inherited law on the other hand had become suspect and subjected to argument, and all human lives now were 'created equal.' That is, the life of a worker in the fields was as precious as the life of the titular Queen of England or her elected Prime Minister.

Technically, legally, there were no slaves.

Few were certain as to the meaning of life, as few today as there had been in those times when I was alive.

Once in the scriptorium as a human boy I had read in Sumerian the lament: 'Who has ever known the will of heaven?' Any man or woman in the streets of New York today might have spoken the same words.

This Western world, this legacy of Hellenism, infused with ever evolving Judaism and Christianity, had flourished most dramatically in northern climes of the planet both in Europe and in America, harnessing somehow the tenacity and the ferocity of those taller, shaggier, and often fairer dwellers of the woodlands and the steppes, who did not learn to be humans in Eden, but rather in lands where summer was always followed by the brutality of cold and snow.

All the Western world, including its most tropical outposts, lived now as if winter might at any moment descend, isolate, even destroy.

From towns near the northern polar ice cap all the way down to the tip of the jungles of Peru, people thrived in enclaves designed and sustained by machine, microchip, and microbiology, surrounded by surpluses of energy, fuel, finery, and food.

Nobody ever wanted to run out of anything ever again, and this included information.

Storage. Archives. Information banks. Hard disk, floppy disk, backup tape, hard copy – everything worth anything was somehow duplicated in one form or another and stored.

It was basically the same theory that had created the archives of tablets in Babylon which I had once studied. Not difficult to understand.

But in spite of all these dazzling advances, amid which Esther Belkin had somehow drawn me to her like a magnet, and seemed even now to draw my consciousness to her, there existed still 'the Old World.'

Follow the stream into the marshes, into the mountains, into the desert.

'The East' was what they called it, or the Third World, or the Undeveloped Countries, or the Backward Countries, or the Primitive Areas – and it covered continents still where the bedouin in timeless white garments walked his camel through the sandstorm, happy as ever to live amid sun-bright desolation. Only now he might carry with him a battery-operated television set, and a can of a fire-making chemical called Sterno so that when he pitched his tent, he could listen to the Koran read over the television as his food was heated without the use of wood or coal.

In the rice paddies, in the fields of India, in the marshes of Iraq, in the villages the world over, men and women stooped to gather the crop as they had since the dawn of time.

Huge modern urban outposts had arisen amid the millions of Asia, yet the vast majority of tribes, farmers, weavers, vendors, mothers, priests, beggars, and children remained beyond the reach of Western invention, abundance, medicine, and sanitation.

Sanitation was key.

Sanitation involved the chemical purification of human waste and industrial waste, the purification of drinking water and water for bathing – the nullification of filth in all forms and the maintenance of an environment in which one could be born, give birth, grow up, and die – in maximum security

201

against human or industrial or chemical contamination of any kind.

Nothing mattered as much as sanitation. Plagues had vanished from the earth due to sanitation.

In the 'West' sanitation was taken for granted; in the 'East' sanitation was viewed with suspicion, or people were simply too numerous to be made to conform to the inevitable habits required by it.

Disease was rampant in the jungles; in the marshes; in the deep pockets of vast cities or in the wilderness where the peasants, the workers, the fellaheen, still lived as they always had.

Hunger. There was plenty and there was hunger. There was food thrown away in the streets of New York and there were those starving in Asia on television programs. It was a matter of distribution.

Indeed, that there was as much organization amid all of this change was the modern mystery – that so much could happen and that so much could remain the same.

Everywhere were dramatic contrasts which could both confuse and delight the eye. The holy men of India walked naked beside the roaring automobiles in the teeming streets of Calcutta. People in Haiti lay on the ground starving to death as they watched planes fly overhead.

The River Nile flowed into the metropolis of Cairo, where the buildings of steel and glass stand as high as in Manhattan, yet the streets were thronged by men and women in loose, airy cotton robes of white or black, as pure as the garments worn by the Israelites when Pharaoh let the people go.

The pyramids of Giza remained as always, only the air surrounding them was thick with the emission of automobiles, and the modern city crawled almost to their feet.

Within a stone's throw of air-conditioned office buildings there lingered pockets of jungle where men knew nothing of Yahweh, Allah, Jesus, or Shiva, or of iron, copper, gold, or bronze. They hunted with wooden spears and poison from reptiles, only now and then stupefied by the sight of big mechanical bulldozers mowing down the forest which was their world.

A flock of goats in the mountains of Judea still looked exactly like a flock of goats in the time of Cyrus the Persian. Shepherds tending sheep outside the city of Bethlehem looked exactly as they had when Jeremiah the Prophet raved.

Though East and West communicated and interacted continuously, each somehow held out against the other. Desert sheiks, rich from the oil discovered beneath their sands, still wore their headdress and robes as they drove about in automobiles. Vast numbers of the world's women still lived indoors almost entirely and only entered a public street if their faces were veiled.

In New York City, capital of the West and city of choice of the more clever and more powerful, the common person was utterly confident and utterly ignorant of 'science' at the same time.

What individual anywhere in the world knew the real meaning of binary code, semiconductor, triodes, electrolyte, or laser beam?

In the upper echelons a technological elite with the powers of a priesthood dealt in perfect faith with the invisible: ions, neutrinos, gamma rays, ultraviolet light, and black holes in space.

Icons shone bright for me in my awakening, bright as the eyes of Esther when she died.

'Servant of the Bones, listen,' she might as well have said. 'Servant of the Bones, come, see.'

All the material world was mine to behold, to know, without haste or alarm, as I slumbered, grieving for her, and angry, angry with her killers.

In invisibility and silence, I saw a man parked at Fifty-sixth and Fifth speaking on a tiny phone in his car, in the German language, to an employee of his in the city of Vienna.

One woman in a building in the city of Atlanta in the country of America talked for twenty-four hours before a camera about the weather all over the globe.

Esther Belkin, my lost one, was mourned by thousands who had never known her, her story broadcast to every country which could receive the Cable News Network, or, as it was mostly known, CNN. Members of the international

203

Temple of the Mind of God, to which she herself had not belonged, mourned for her.

Her stepfather, Gregory Belkin, a robust man of substantial height, the Temple's founder, wept before cameras and spoke of cults, terrorists, and plots. 'Why do they want to hurt us!' he said. His eyes were clear and brilliantly black, his hair close cut but thick as hers had been, and his skin was almost the perfect color of honey in sunlight.

The mother of the murdered Esther fled the public eye. White-clad nurses ushered Mrs. Belkin past screaming reporters. With the long unkempt hair of a girl, and thin beseeching hands, she looked little older than her daughter.

Law officers and elected officials condemned the violence of the times.

And the times were universally violent. In fact, violence came now like any other commodity, in all sizes and forms.

Robbery, rape, and battery were routine, if not rampant, beneath a canopy of civilization and peace. Small organized wars were in constant progress. People were fighting to the death in Somalia, in Afghanistan, in the Ukraine. Souls of the newly dead wreathed the earth like smoke.

The market for weapons was black, white, chaotic, endless. Struggling little countries vied with larger and more powerful nations to buy up legally or illegally the armaments and explosives of crumbling empires. Powerful nations sought to stop the proliferation of missiles, hand grenades, bullets, and canisters of poison gas, while they themselves continued to develop nuclear bombs which could destroy the earth.

Drugs were critical to people. Everyone talked of drugs. Drugs cured. Drugs killed. Drugs helped. Drugs hurt.

There were so many kinds of drugs and for so many purposes that no one being could grasp the significance of the sheer multiplicity itself.

In one New York hospital alone, the size of the inventory of drugs which saved lives daily through inoculation, injection, intravenous feed, or oral ingestion was almost beyond human count. Yet a computer system kept perfect track of it.

Worldwide, criminal overlords fought for the trade in illegal drugs – the wherewithal to develop, distribute, and market cocaine and heroin – chemicals with no other purpose than to make people feel an addictive euphoria or calm.

Cults. Cults were a matter of public obsession and fear. Cults were apparently unsanctioned religious organizations, that is, organizations to which people belonged, swearing allegiance generally to a leader of whose morals and purposes others were unsure. Cults could rise, seemingly from nothing, around the figure of one man – Gregory Belkin. Or cults could break off from large organized religions to form fanatical enclaves of their own.

Cults existed for peace and war.

Around the death of Esther Belkin swarmed the argument over cults.

Again and again, her face flashed on television screens.

She herself, a member of nothing, was related to everything – those who were anti-government, those who were anti-God, those who were anti-wealth.

Had her father's cult members actually killed Esther?

She herself had once been heard in private to remark that the Temple of the Mind of God had too much money, too much power, too many houses worldwide. Or had it been the enemies of Gregory Belkin and his Temple who sought through the death of Esther to hurt the father, to warn him and his powerful cohorts that his organization had become too big, and too dangerous, but to whom?

Cults could be liberal, radical, reactionary, old-fashioned.

Cults could do terrible things.

I drifted, I watched, I listened; I knew what people knew.

It was a world of empires, nations, countries, and gangs; and the smallest gang could dominate the television screens of the entire world with one well-planned explosion. The news would talk all day about the leader of fifty as easily as it might about the leader of millions.

Enemies were the beneficiaries of the same democratic and competitive scrutiny as victims.

The faces of the Evals – Billy Joel, Doby, and Hayden – rose to the fore, blazing as bright as Esther's on the television screens for brief seconds. Had these men who killed Esther

205

Belkin belonged to a secret movement? People spoke of backwoods 'survivalists' with barbed-wire fences and vicious dogs, who suspected all kinds of authority. Conspiracy. It might be anywhere in any form.

And then there were the Apocalyptic Christians, having more cause than ever before to say that Judgment Day was at hand.

Had the Eval brothers come from such organizations?

Gregory Belkin, the stepfather of Esther, spoke in a soft compelling voice of plots to hurt all God-fearing peoples. The innocence of Esther was significant and cried out to heaven. Terrorists, diamonds, fanatics – these words encircled the brief flicker of Esther's face and name.

The news in all forms – printed, broadcast, computerized on internets – was continuous, alarming, prophetic, fatalistic, detailed, ludicrous by intention and by accident in turns.

As I said, any ghost could have grasped these things.

The question with me was why was I thinking of *anything*? Why wake from my deep sleep, just short of death, always just short of death, and find myself walking amongst Billy Joel, Hayden, and Doby Eval – a sudden horrified witness to their crime?

Whatever the case, I had for the moment lost my taste for merely drifting, for merely existing, for merely hating.

I wanted to pay attention. I wanted to make full use of my mind unfettered by flesh and cast into eternity, a mind that had been gaining strength with each new awakening, taking back into the darkness with it not merely experience but emotion, and possibly a certain resolve.

Inevitably, it was a Master who would put all of this in order through his responses, his reactions, the vitality of his will.

But a very specific question tormented me. Yes, I was back and I wanted to be back. But had not I done things to ensure that I would never be brought back again?

If I wanted to, I think I could remember what I'd done. Forget the world and all its pomp and racket for a moment. I was Azriel. Azriel could remember what he'd done.

I had slain masters.

If I wanted to, I could remember more dead Magi than those I've already described here. I could smell again the camp of the Monguls, leather, elephants, scented oil – flicker of lights beneath the sagging silk, the chessboard overturned and tiny carved figures made of gold and silver rolling on a flowered carpet.

Cries of men. *Destroy it, it's a demon, drive it back into the bones!*

A series of windows in Baghdad looking out over a battle. *Back into the bones! Fiend from Hell.* A castle near Prague. A stone-cold room high in the Alps. And maybe even more – even after the vivid enchanting gaslight on the flowered wallpaper of the sorcerer's room in Paris.

This servant serves no more!

Yes, I'd proved to myself and them that I could slay any conjurer.

So where was the sly, covert consciousness which had brought me here to this presentation of power?

Oh, I could like to aver that I loathed being conscious again and forswore all life and everything that goes with it, but I couldn't really do that. I couldn't forget Esther's eyes, or the beautiful glass on Fifth Avenue, or the moment when the heat came through the soles of my shoes, and when the man, the kindly unknowing man had put his arm around me!

I was curious and free! In an orbit, I was bound to these bizarre events. But no Lord directed me.

Esther knew me but she hadn't called. Had it been someone on behalf of Esther, someone whom I had already tragically failed?

Two nights passed in real time before I realized I was once again awake, and moving through the air: the angel of might, the angel of evil, who knows?

This is what I saw:

Sixteen

This was a nearby city, in view of the other. The car moving through the rain was the car that had carried Esther to the place where the Evals surrounded her with their picks. Other cars traveled with it, filled with guards whose eyes roved dark and deserted buildings.

The procession was furtive yet full of authority.

Through the rain, I could actually see the shining towers of the street on which she had died. Grand as Alexandria, or Constantinople, this rock-hard capital of the Western world, New York – in its greedy nuclear splendor. Yet its soaring buildings reminded me of the weapons carried by the Evals. Hard and very sharp.

The man in the car was very proud of the car, proud of the guards who traveled with him, proud of his fine wool coat and the neat trim of his thick curly hair.

I drew in close to see him through the darkened glass: Gregory Belkin, her stepfather, founder of the Temple of the Mind of God, rich man. Rich beyond the dreams of kings in earlier times, because they couldn't fly on magic carpets.

The car? Mercedes-Benz, and the most unusual of its kind, made from a small sedan and elongated by three perfectly welded and padded parts so that it was twice the length of the engines all around it, shiny and black, deliberately glamorous, as if carved of obsidian and polished by hand.

It prowled for blocks before stopping, the driver quick to obey the rise of Belkin's hand.

Then this proud high priest or prophet or whatever he deemed himself stepped unaided out into the light of the street lamp as if he wanted it to shine on his youthful clean-shaven face, hair clipped short on the back of his neck like a Roman soldier, yet softly curly despite its length.

The full length of the dingy dirty block he walked, alone, past dismal boarded-up shops, past signs in Hebrew and in

208

English, to the place he meant to visit, his guards sweeping the night before him and behind him with their glances, the raindrops standing like jewels on the shoulders of his long coat.

All right. Was he the Master? If so, how could I not know it? I didn't like him. In my half sleep, I had seen him weep for Esther and talk of plots, and had not liked him.

Why was I so close I could touch his face? Handsome he was, no one would argue with this, and in the prime of life, square-shouldered, tall as a Norseman, though darker with jet-black eyes.

Are you the Master?

Mastermind of the Minders, that was what the flippant and cynical reporters called him, this billionaire Gregory Belkin. Now he reviewed in his head recent speeches he'd made before the bronze doors of his Manhattan Temple, 'My worse fear is that they weren't thieves at all and the necklace meant nothing to them. It's our church they want to hurt. They are evil.'

Necklace, I thought, I had seen no necklace.

The guards who watched Gregory from their nearby cars were his 'followers.' This was some church of peace and good. They wore guns, and they carried knives, and he himself the prophet carried a small gun, very shiny, like his car, deep in the left pocket of his coat.

He was like a King who is used to performing every gesture before a grand audience, but he didn't see me watching him. He had no sense of a ghost at his shoulder like a personal god.

Well, I was not this man's god. I was not this man's servant. But I was his observer, and I had to know why.

He stopped before a brick house. It was filled with glass windows, all of them covered. It had high-pitched roofs for snow. It was like thousands, possibly even millions, of other houses in this same arm of the city. The proportions of this time and place were truly beyond my easy measure.

I was fascinated. His perfect black leather shoes were speckled prettily with rain. Why was he bringing us here?

He went down a step and back the alleyway. A light shone

ahead of him. He had a key for a little gate. Then a key for a door between lighted windows in the deep bottom floor of the house.

We came in, he and I. I felt the warmth swoosh around me!

Ceiling overhead. The night locked out. An old man was seated at a wooden desk.

Smell of human beings, sweet and good. And so many other precious fragrances, too many to savor, or name.

All ghosts and gods and spirits feast on fragrance, as I have told you.

I had been starved, and nearly grew drunk on the smells of this place.

I *knew* I was here.

I was slowly taking form. But by whose direction? Who's decision? I loved it.

No old words issued from my lips; I was becoming solid. It was happening, as it had in New York when I chased her killers. I felt it. I felt myself enclosed in the good body, the body I liked, though what that meant I wasn't sure.

Now I know: I came visible and solid in my own body, or the body you see here now, the form I had when I was alive.

No one else here knew. Behind the bookcase I stood, watching.

Gregory Belkin had chosen for himself the very middle of the room, beneath a lightbulb with a frayed cord. And the old man at the desk, the old man could not possibly see me.

The old man's head was bowed. He wore the small black silk skull-cap of observant Jews. There was a green shaded lamp on his desk that was gentle and golden in its illumination.

His beard and hair were snow white and very pure and beautiful, and two long curled locks deliberately framed his face. The flesh of his scalp was pink beneath the thinnest part of his hair, but the beard was rich and flowing.

The books on the walls were in Hebrew and Arabic, Aramaic, Latin, Greek, German. I could smell the parchment and the leather. I drew in these fragrances and it

210

seemed for a moment memory would spring to life, or out of memory would come alive everything I'd tried to murder.

But this old man wasn't the Master either! I knew it immediately.

This old man had no sense that I had come, none at all, but was merely staring at the younger one who had just entered, the strong straight one who stood rather formally before the elder, and removed from his hands a pair of smooth gray gloves which he was careful to put in the right pocket of his coat. He patted the left pocket. The gun was in the left pocket. Little lethal gun. I had a desire to hear it go off. But he wasn't here to shoot it.

The room was so cluttered. Rows and rows of shelves divided me from the old man, but I could see over the tops of books. I smelled incense, and felt a flush of pleasure. I smelled iron, gold, ink. *Could the bones be in this place?*

The old man took off his glasses, which were of the simplest kind, rounded in silver wire, flexible, and fragile, and peered most directly at his visitor, without rising from his chair.

The old man's eyes were very pale, which struck me as it always does, as very pretty to look at – eyes that are more like water than stone. But they were small, and weak with age, and they didn't gleam so much as they accused from the heavy wrinkles of his face.

Stronger, you are getting stronger by the moment. You are almost completely visible.

I couldn't see the entire face of the younger man. I slipped even more to the far left side of him to conceal myself, and became whole and entire as I stood behind the bookcase, calculating my height at approximately his own.

The rain was all over his black coat, and the coat had a seam straight down the back, and next to his neck, pushing up at the black curls of his hair, was a white silk scarf as fine as the scarf she'd clutched in death, a scarf that was probably still in the emporium of her killing. I tried to remember it, the scarf for which she had reached in death not dreaming of the significance of that last gesture, if indeed there was any significance to it at all. The scarf she had wanted was black

211

but glittering, covered with beads. I think I told you this. But now I'm with them again, with them. Bear with me.

The old man spoke in Yiddish:

'You killed your daughter.'

I was astonished. So we come immediately to the point?

The love I felt for her tormented me, as if she herself had come up to me and dug her nails in my skin and said, Do not forget me, Azriel, only she would never, never have done such a thing. She had died in characteristic humility; when she had spoken my name it was with wonder.

That was too dreadful to see again, her dying.

Go, fly, spirit. Turn your back on them all – on her death and on the old man's accusation, on this fascinating room with its enticing colors and aromas. Let go, spirit. Let them struggle towards the Ladder of Heaven without your intervention. After all, do souls really need the Servant of the Bones to drag them into Sheol?

I wasn't going anywhere. I wanted to know what the old man meant.

The younger man merely laughed.

No disrespect, it was an uneasy, angry laugh of one who would not be forced to immediate response by these words. The dismissive wave of his hand was not surprise. He shook his head.

I wanted to move around him, look at him, but it was too late for that, I knew I had the full parts, that I stood, that my hands touched the books on the shelf in front of me, and I shifted very slowly to my left, so that the wall of books would hide me, lest the old man see me, though the old man showed no sign even now of realizing I was here with him.

The younger man sighed.

'Rebbe, why would I kill Rachel's daughter?' asked the younger man in Yiddish. 'Why would I kill the only child I had?' The language wasn't easy for him. 'Esther, my beautiful Esther,' he said, sounding heartfelt and strong. He didn't like to speak Yiddish. He wanted his English.

'But you did,' said the old man in return. It came from his dry lips with hatred. He spoke now in Hebrew: 'You are an idolator; you are a killer; you killed your child. You had her murdered. You walk with evil. You reek of it!'

I was slightly shaken. I could feel it physically, the jarring surprise at the old man's wrath.

The young man again played the game of patience, shuffling slightly, shaking his head as if humoring a half-naked prophet who won't stop raving on your doorstep.

'My teacher,' Gregory Belkin whispered in English, 'my model. My grandfather. And you blame me for her death?'

This put the old man in a fury.

He too spoke in English:

'What do you want of me, Gregory? You've never come to this house without a reason.' His fury was calm. This old man himself would do nothing about the death of this girl. He sat at his desk with his hands clasped on an open book. Tiny Hebrew letters.

I felt the loss of her again, as if I'd been kicked and I wanted to say out loud, 'Old man, I avenged her, I slew the three assassins with the leader's pick. I slew them all. They died on the pavements.'

I felt her as if I alone in this room held the candle in memory of her. Neither of these mourned her, accusations be damned.

Why are you allowing this to happen, Azriel? Grief for those you don't know is easy. Maybe it is even exciting. But to be alone? That is to be alive. And you are most certainly secret and alone here.

'You break my heart, Rebbe,' said Gregory in English. Obviously the current American language was much easier for him. His whole body sagged with his soft whisper of despair. His hands were deep in his pockets. His flesh was a little chilled from the cold outside, and the room itself was stifling. I thought he was lying, and telling the truth.

I fed upon the smell of them, never mind the wax, the parchment, the old reliable scents, I smelled the men – the old man's warm living skin that was so clear and fine, so free of disease that it had become silken in old age, pure like the bones of his living body inside it, which were no doubt so brittle now they could break at the slightest blow.

The young man was immaculate and anointed with fine

213

and subtle perfumes. The perfume rose from the pores of his skin, from the curls of his hair, from the clothing he wore, a subtle mingling of calculated scents. The fragrance of a modern monarch.

I drew closer to the younger one. I might have been now two feet from him, to his left, and slightly behind him. I saw his profile. Thick eyebrows, smooth and neatly groomed and well formed, fine features, molded in good proportion; we would have called him blessed. He had no scar or blemish. Something indefinable to me enriched him and enlarged his power. When he smiled, which he did now sadly and imploringly, his teeth were perfectly white.

His eyes were large, like her eyes had been, but not quite so beautiful. He lifted his hands, another form of plea, small, quiet. His fingers were fine, and the smoothness of his cheeks was fine; he had been nourished as she had, lovingly, as if the whole world all of his life had been his mother's breast. What did he lack? I couldn't find in him a fracture or sore, or break anywhere, only the indefinable enhancement.

Then I realized what it was. He had the prettiness of the young, but he was past fifty years! How dazzling it was. How wondrous the way age sharpened his physical virtues, and made the glare of his eyes so much the more strong.

'Speak to me, Gregory Belkin,' said the old man with contempt, 'and tell me why you've come, or leave my house now.'

I was again startled by the old man's wrath.

'All right, Rebbe,' the younger man answered, as if the tone and the manner were nothing new to him.

The old man waited.

'I have a check in my pocket, Rebbe,' said Gregory. 'I come to give it to you for the good of the whole Court.'

By this I knew he meant the Hebrews of the old man for whom the old man was the Rabbi, the zaddik, the leader.

Flashes of memory came at me, rather like jagged pieces of glass – glimpses of my long dead Master Samuel. But it didn't mean anything and I pushed it aside. At this point, keep in mind, I could not recall anything of my past. Nothing. But I knew what this man was – venerable, powerful in holy ways, perhaps a magician, but if he was a magician, why hadn't he sensed that I was there?

'You always have a check for us, Gregory,' said the old one. 'Your checks come to the bank without you. We take your money in honor of your dead mother, and your dead father, who was my beloved son. We take your money for what it can do for those whom they once loved, your mother and father. Go back to your Temple. Go back to your computers. Go back to your worldwide church. Go home, Gregory! Hold your wife's hand. Her daughter has been murdered. Mourn with Rachel Belkin. Is she not entitled to that much?'

The younger man gave a little nod, as if to say, ah, things aren't going to improve here, and then he tilted his head to the right and shrugged respectfully and spoke again:

'I need something from you, Rebbe,' he said. Direct as it was, it was smooth.

The old man lifted his hands and shrugged. He shifted in the light of the electric lamp, and sighed. His lips were full for the lips of an old man. A faint sheen of sweat appeared on the top of his head.

Behind him stood more shelves of books. The room was so crowded with books it might as well have been made of books. The chairs were big, with their frames hidden inside their leather, and all were surrounded by books. There were scrolls, and scrolls in sacks, and scrolls of leather.

One cannot after all burn or discard old scrolls of the Torah. These must be buried, and properly, or kept in some place like this.

Who knew what this old man had brought through the world with him? His English was not pure and sharp like that of Gregory, but carried with it the speaking habits of other tongues. Poland. I saw Poland and I saw snow.

Gregory slipped his left hand into his pocket. There was the check, the piece of paper, the banknote, the gift that he wanted to give so badly. I heard it crackle as his fingers touched it. It was folded right beside the gun.

The old man said nothing.

'Rebbe, when I was very little,' said Gregory, 'I heard you

215

tell a particular tale. Only once did I hear this story. But I remember it. I remember the words.'

The old man made no reply. The loose folds of his skin were shiny in the light, but when he lifted his white eyebrows he lifted the folds of his forehead too.

'Rebbe,' said Gregory, 'you spoke once to my aunt of a legend, a secret . . . a family treasure. I've come here to ask you about what I heard.'

The old man was surprised. No. It wasn't that. The old man was surprised only that the younger man's words had some interest for him. The old man gave the silence a moment, then spoke in Yiddish as before:

'A treasure? You and your brother – you were the treasures of your mother and father. What would bring you to Brooklyn to ask me about tales of treasure? Treasure you have beyond any man's dreams.'

'Yes, Rebbe,' said Gregory patiently.

'I hear your church swims in money, that your missions in foreign lands are lavish resorts for the rich who would visit and give to the poor. Indeed. I heard that your own fortune far outstrips that of your wife, or her daughter. I hear that no man can hold in his mind the exact amount of the money you possess and the money you control.'

'Yes, Rebbe,' said Gregory again, patiently in English. 'I'm as rich as you can imagine, and I know you don't choose to imagine it, nor to dwell on it, nor profit from it –'

'Well, then, come to the point,' said the old man in Yiddish. 'You waste my time. You waste the precious moments I have left to me, which I would rather spend in charity than in condemnation. What do you want?'

'You spoke of a family secret,' Gregory said. 'Rebbe, speak to me in English, please.'

The old man sneered.

'And what did I speak then, when you were a little boy?' the old man asked in Yiddish. 'Did I speak Yiddish or Polish, or was it English then too?'

'I don't remember,' said the young man. 'But I wish you'd speak English now.' He shrugged again, and then he said very quickly, 'Rebbe, I am grieving for Esther! It wasn't my

216

wealth that bought her the diamonds. I wasn't the cause of her wearing them carelessly. I wasn't to blame that the thieves caught her unawares.'

Diamonds? There was a lie in this. Esther had worn no diamonds. The Evals had taken from her no diamonds. But Gregory was as smooth-tongued at this as anything else.

How he played the part. How the old man studied him.

The old man moved back just a little, as if the strength of the words had pushed him, perhaps even annoyed him. He scrutinized the young man.

'You mistake my meaning, Gregory,' he said in English. 'I don't speak of your wealth or what she wore around her neck when they killed her. I mean you killed your daughter, Esther. You had her murdered.'

Silence.

In the dimness I saw my hands visible against the books; I saw the tiny creases in the skin of my knuckles, and in the place where a man would have a heart I felt pain.

The smooth-tongued one gave no sign of guilt or shame or even shock. Either infinite innocence or infinite evil suffused him and upheld him in quiet.

'Grandfather, that's madness. Why would I do such a thing? I am a man of God as you are, Grandfather!'

'Stop!' said the Rebbe. He lifted his hand.

'My followers would never hurt Esther, they –'

'Stop!' said the Rebbe again. 'Get on with it, what do you really want.'

Rattled and smiling uneasily, Gregory shook his head. He collected himself to begin again. His lip trembled, but I don't think the old man could see it as I could.

Gregory still held the check, an offering, poised, in his left hand.

'It's something I remember you saying once,' said Gregory, the English rapid and natural now. 'Nathan and I were in the room. I don't think Nathan heard it. He was with . . . someone else. I don't even remember who else was there, except my mother's sister Rivka, and it seemed there were old women. But it was here in Brooklyn, and we'd only just come. I could ask Nathan –'

217

'Leave your brother alone!' said the old man, and this time it was English, confident, low, as natural to his tongue as Yiddish. Anger can do that, strip a voice down to the best way that it knows to speak. 'Don't approach your brother Nathan. Leave your brother Nathan in peace! You just said yourself your brother didn't hear it.'

'Yes, I knew you would want it that way, Rebbe. I knew you wouldn't want me to contaminate Nathan.'

'Get on with this.'

'That's why I came to ask you. Explain it and I won't bother my beloved brother, but I must know.' He went on. 'That day, when I was a child, you spoke about a secret thing. A thing you called the Servant of the Bones.'

I was stricken. The words caught me utterly off guard. The shock only strengthened my form. I could not have been more stunned if he had turned and seen me. I called clothes to cover me, I called the clothes to cover me as he, the zaddik, was covered. And I felt myself immediately sheathed in black silk similar to his, warm and well fitted, and the air felt warm and the tiny lightbulb rocked on its frayed cord.

The Rebbe looked at the bulb for a long moment, then back at his grandson.

'Ah, be still, Azriel,' I commanded myself. 'And listen. The answers are coming now.'

'Do you remember?' asked the younger one. 'A family secret? A treasure called the Servant of the Bones?'

The old man remembered, but didn't speak.

'You said,' Gregory continued, 'that once a man had brought this thing to your father in Prague. The man was a Moslem, from the mountains. You said that this man had given this thing to your father in payment of a debt.'

Ah, this zaddik possessed the bones! But he wasn't the master, no, never would he be, either.

He looked hard and secretively at his grandson.

'You were talking to old Rivka,' Gregory pressed, 'and you told her the things the Moslem had said. You said that your father should not have accepted such a thing, but your father had been confused because the words on the wooden casket had been in Hebrew. You called it an abomination; you said it should be destroyed.'

I smiled. Did I feel relief or anger? An abomination. I am an abomination. And this abomination can destroy both of you and your room of books; it can tear your house to pieces to the rafters! *But who called me!*

I put my hand over my mouth in restraint. In the presence of a zaddik, I could not afford the most incidental sigh or sound. I couldn't afford to weep.

The zaddik was still holding his peace, letting the young man reveal himself more and more.

'Rivka asked you why you didn't destroy it,' said Gregory patiently, slowly, 'and you said that that was not an easy thing to do. You said it was like the old scrolls, this thing. It could not be destroyed irreverently. You spoke again of something written, a document. Do you remember this, Grandfather? Or do I dream?'

The old man's eyes were cold. 'You heard this at my knee?' he muttered. 'Why do you ask me of this now?'

Suddenly the old man raised his hand and made a fist and brought the fist down on the desk. Nothing moved, save the dust.

Gregory didn't blink.

'Why do you come here on the day of your daughter's funeral,' the old man raged, 'and ask me about this old tale! This tale, this secret or treasure, as you call it, that you heard when you were my *eloi*, my shining one, my chosen pupil, my pride! Why do you come speaking of this thing now!'

The old man was trembling dangerously.

Gregory calculated silently, then took a deep breath.

'Rebbe, the check will buy so many things,' said Gregory.

'Answer my question! Money we have. We are rich here. We were rich when we left Poland. We were rich when we left Israel. Answer my question. Why do you ask about this thing now?'

I could see no wealth in this room but I believed him.

I knew his kind. He lived only to study Torah and to keep the law, and to pray, and to advise those who came to him daily, those who believed he could see into souls and make miracles, those for whom he was the instrument of God. Wealth would make no change in the life of such a man whatsoever, except that he might study day and night as he chose.

I felt my pulse, very strong. I felt the air in me. My strength had been steadily increasing since the words had been spoken. The bones had to be here. Yes, he had them, and somehow he had called me up. He had laid hands on them, or read the words, or spoken the prayer . . . it had to be this old man, but how was such a thing accomplished and why had I not simply destroyed him out of hand?

Out of memory, like a comet came a face I knew and loved. Hundreds of years were bridged in a moment.

This was the face of Samuel, of whom I've told you. Samuel of Strasbourg. This was the Master who had sold me for his children as I had once sold myself perhaps for the children of God. In my memory I saw the casket.

Where was it now?

The memory was bitter, a fragment; I wouldn't have it. Accusations would distract me and nothing about this past, even with Samuel, could ever, ever be changed.

I stood in this warm room in Brooklyn, with another old scholar surrounded by dusty books, spells, charms, incantations, and I hated him. I despised him. He was far more virtuous, however, than Samuel had ever been, especially in the last moments when Samuel had told me to go my way to hell.

I hated this Rebbe almost as much as his grandson hated him.

And the grandson?

What was he to me, this smooth-tongued Gregory Belkin with his worldwide church? But if he had killed Esther –

I held fast. I let the temper and the pain melt in me; I asked of myself, be alive only, and be quiet.

This young one, groomed as well as a prince, waited in patience in the same manner for the temper of the zaddik to cool.

'Why ask me these things now?' the old man demanded.

I thought of the girl, the tender girl, her head turned on

220

the stretcher. How kind and awestruck had been her little whisper. *Servant of the Bones*.

The old man suddenly lost control of his anger. He gave Gregory no time to answer. He went on with his raving questions.

'What drives you, Gregory?' he asked in English. His tone was intimate suddenly, as if he really wanted to know. He rose from his chair and stood facing his grandson.

'You put a question to me,' he said. 'Let me put a question to you. What is it in the wide world that you would have? You are rich beyond imagining, so rich that you make our wealth a drop in the sea, yet you make a church to deceive thousands, you fashion laws which are no laws at all. You sell books and television programs that say nothing. You would be Mohammed or Christ! And then you kill your daughter. Yes, you did it. I see into you. I know you killed her. You sent those men. Her blood was on the very same weapon which killed them. Did you do away with them as well? Was it your followers who used those assassins and then dispatched them? What is your dream, Gregory, to bring down on all of us such evil and shame that the Messiah cannot stay away a moment longer! You would take away his choice!'

I smiled. It was a beautiful speech. Remembering nothing of Zurvan then, or anyone wise or eloquent, I nevertheless warmed to this speech, and to the conviction with which it had been made. I liked the old man just a little better.

Gregory adopted the softened attitude of sadness but remained silent. Let the old man rave.

'You think I don't know you did this?' said the Rebbe. He let himself slip back down into the chair. He had to. He was tired in his rage. 'I know. I know you and have known you as no one else from the day you were born. Nathan, your own twin, doesn't know you. Nathan prays for you, Gregory!'

'But you don't, do you, Grandfather? You said your prayers already for me, didn't you?'

'Yes, I said Kaddish when you left this house, and if I had only a sign from Heaven, I would bring an end to your life and your Temple of the Mind and your lies and your schemes with my own hands.'

'That's an easy claim to make, Grandfather,' said Gregory unperturbed. 'Anyone can do things when he has a sign from Heaven! I teach my followers to love in a world where there are no signs from Heaven!'

'You teach your followers to give you money. You teach your followers to sell your books. You raise your voice again to me and you'll leave my house without your answers. Your brother knows nothing of what you speak – this old childhood memory of yours. He wasn't there. My memory of that day is very clear. There is no one alive now who knows.'

Gregory raised his hand. Peace, forbearance.

I was enthralled and tormented. I waited for the next word.

'Grandfather, only tell me then what it means, "the Servant of the Bones." Am I such filth that to answer me is to desecrate yourself?'

The old man trembled. His shoulders narrowed and drew up under his black collarless coat. He shuddered and in the light his knuckles were pink and sore to look at. The light spilled down on his white beard and on the mustache which covered his upper lip, and on the translucent lids of his eyes as he shook his head and rocked back and forth as if he were praying.

Very smoothly came the voice of Gregory.

'Grandfather, my only child is dead, and I come to you with a simple question. Why would I kill my daughter, Esther? You yourself know there is no reason under God for me to have hurt Esther. What can I give you for the answer to my question? Do you remember this story, this thing, this Servant of the Bones? Did it have a name, was its name Azriel?'

The old man was stunned.

So was I.

'I never spoke that name,' said the old man.

'No, you didn't,' said Gregory, 'but someone else did.'

'Who has told you about this thing?' the old man demanded. 'Who could have done such a thing?'

Gregory was confused.

I leant my weight against the shelf of books, watching, my fingers catching the loose flaking leather of the bindings. Don't hurt them. Not the books.

The old man sounded hard and contemptuous.

'Has someone come to you with the legend?' asked the old man. 'Has someone told you a pretty tale of magic and power? Was this man Moslem? Was he a Gentile? Was he a Jew? Was he one of your New Age fanatic followers who has read your abracadabra about the Kabbalah?'

Gregory shook his head.

'Rebbe, you have it wrong,' he said with solemn sincerity. 'It was only your talk of this that I heard when I was a child. Then two days ago, someone else spoke the words before witnesses: Azriel, Servant of the Bones!'

I was afraid to guess.

'Who was this?' asked the old man.

'She said it, Rebbe,' Gregory told him. 'Esther said it as she was dying. The man in the ambulance heard it from her lips as she died. Esther said it, Rebbe. Esther said, "The Servant of the Bones." And the name "Azriel." Esther said it twice aloud, and two men heard her. Those men told me.'

I smiled. This was more of a mystery than I had ever imagined.

I watched them intently. My face teemed with heat. And I knew that I trembled as the old man trembled, as if my body were real.

The old man drew back. He was not willing to believe. His anger vanished. He peered into the younger man's face.

Then came the voice of Gregory, purposefully and cleverly tender.

'Who is he, Rebbe? Who is the Servant of the Bones? What is it, this thing, that Esther spoke of? That you spoke of? When I was a child playing on the floor at your feet? Esther said this name, "Azriel." Is that the name of the Servant of the Bones?'

My pulse throbbed so loud I could hear it with my own ears. I felt the fingers of my left hand bear down slightly on the tops of the books. I felt the shelf against my chest. I felt the cement floor under my shoes, and I didn't dare to look away from either of them.

My god, I thought, make the old man tell, make him tell so I will know, my god, if you are still there, make him tell Who and What is the Servant of the Bones? Make him tell me!

The old man was too stunned to reply.

'The police have this information,' said Gregory. 'They guard it jealously. They think she spoke of her killer.'

I almost cried aloud in denial.

The old man scowled, and his eyes moistened.

'Rebbe, don't you understand? They want to find who killed her – not that trash with the ice picks who stole her necklace, but those who put them up to it, those who knew the value of the jewels!'

Once again, the necklace. I saw no necklace then and I saw none in my memory now. There had been no necklace around her throat. They had taken nothing from her. What was this diversion of the necklace?

If only I knew these men better. I couldn't tell for sure when Gregory lied.

The voice of Gregory grew lower, colder, less conciliatory. He straightened his shoulders.

'Now let me speak plainly, Rebbe,' he said. 'I have always, at your behest kept our secret, my secret, our secret – that the founder of the Temple of the Mind was the grandson of the Rebbe of this Court of the Hasidim!' His voice rose now as if he couldn't quiet it. 'For your sake,' he said, 'I've kept this secret! For Nathan's sake. For the sake of the Court. For the sake of those who loved my mother and father and remembered them. I have kept this secret for you and for them!'

He paused, the tone of accusation hanging there sharply, the old man waiting, too wise to break the silence.

'Because you begged me,' said Gregory, 'I kept the secret. Because my brother begged me. And because I love my brother. And in my own way, Rebbe, I love you. I kept the secret so that you might not have the disgrace in your own eyes, and so that the cameras would not come poking in your windows, the reporters would not come crowding your stoop to demand of you how was it possible that out of your Torah and your Talmud and your Kabbalah came Gregory Belkin, the Messiah of the Temple of the Mind, whose voice is heard from the city of Lima to the towns of Nova Scotia, from Edinburgh to Zaire. How did your ritual, your prayer, your quaint black clothing, your black hats, your crazy dancing, your bowing and hollering – how did all of that loose upon the world the famous and immensely successful Gregory Belkin and the Temple of the Mind? For your sake, I kept quiet.'

Silence. The old man was sunk in silence, unforgiving, and filled with contempt.

I was as confused as ever. Nothing drew me to either man, not hate or love, nothing drew me to anything but the remembered eyes and voice of the dead girl.

Again, it was the younger man who spoke.

'Once in your entire life, you came to me of your own will,' Gregory said. 'You crossed the great bridge that divides my world from yours, as you call it. You came to me in my offices to beg me not to disclose my background! To keep it a secret, no matter how many reporters questioned me, no matter how they pried.'

The old man didn't answer.

'It would have benefited me to let the world know, Rebbe. How could it not have benefited me to say that I had come from such strong and observant roots! But long before you ever made your request of me, I buried my past with you. I covered it over with lies and fabrications so as to protect you! So that you would not be disgraced. You and my beloved Nathan, for whom I pray every night of my life. I did that, and I continue to do it . . . for you.'

He paused as if his anger had the better of him. I was mesmerized by both of them and the tale that unfolded.

'But as God is my witness, Rebbe,' Gregory said, 'and I do dare to speak of him in my Temple as you do in your yeshiva, let me tell you this. She said those words when she died! Now you know it was none of your black-clad saints clapping their hands and singing on Shabbes who killed Esther! It wasn't my doe-eyed brother who killed Esther. It was not a Hasid who killed Esther. When the Nazis shot my mother and my father, neither raised a hand to stop the arm or the gun, is that not so?'

The old man, perplexed and torn, actually nodded in agreement, as if they had moved far beyond their own mutual hatred now.

'But,' said Gregory, and he held up the check in his left hand, 'if you don't tell me the meaning of those words, Rebbe, and I do remember them, then I shall tell the police where I once heard them. That it was here in this house, among the Hasidim whom Gregory Belkin, the man of mystery, the Founder of the Temple of the Mind, was actually born!'

I was dumbfounded. I waited. I didn't dare to take my eyes off the old man.

Still he held out.

Gregory sighed. He shrugged. He walked a pace and turned and looked to Heaven and then dropped his hand. 'I will tell them, "Yes, sir, I've heard those words. Yes, once I heard them. At my grandfather's knee, and yes, he is living, and you must go to him to find out what they mean." I'll tell them – I'll send them to you and you can explain the meaning of those words to them.'

'Enough,' said the old man. 'You're a fool, you always were!' He sighed heavily, and then more in contemplation than consciously, he said, 'Esther said those words? Men heard her?'

'Her attendants thought she was looking at a man outside the window, a man with long black hair! That's a secret the police keep in their files, but the others saw him and they saw her look at him, and this man, Rebbe, he wept for her! He wept!'

It was I who trembled!

'Shut up. Stop. Don't . . .'

Gregory gave a soft laugh of nudging mockery. He stepped back, turning this way and that again, without ever lifting his eyes to see me, though his eyes might, in a better light, have passed over my shoes. He turned back to the Rebbe.

'I never thought to accuse you, any of you, of killing her!'

said Gregory. 'Such a thought never came to me, though where have I ever heard such words before except from your tongue! And I walk in your door and you accuse me of killing my stepdaughter! Why would I do such a thing? I come here out of respect for her dying words!'

The old man said very calmly, 'I believe you. The poor child spoke those words. The papers told of strange words. I believe you. But I also know you killed your daughter. You had it done.'

Gregory's arms tensed as do the arms of men who are about to strike others, but he couldn't and wouldn't strike the Rebbe. That would never happen with these two men, I knew. But Gregory was at the end of his tether, and the zaddik was certain of Gregory's guilt.

So was I. But what reason did I have for it? No more than the zaddik, perhaps.

I tried to peer into their souls, for surely they could boast of souls, the two of them, they were flesh and blood. I tried to look, as any human might look, as any ghost might plumb the depths of the soul of the living. I bent my head forward just a little as if the rhythm of their breathing would tell me, as if the beat of the heart would give away the secret. *Gregory, did you kill her?*

Did the old man ask the younger man the same thing? He leant forward in the light of his dusty bulb; his eyes were crinkled and bright.

He looked at Gregory again, and as he did so, quite by accident, and quite for certain, he saw *me*.

His eyes shifted very slowly and naturally from his grandson, to me.

He saw a man standing where I stood. He saw a young man with long curling dark hair and dark eyes. He saw a man of good height and good strength, very young, in fact, so young that some might have thought him still a boy. He saw *me*. He saw Azriel.

I smiled but only a little, like a man about to speak, not to mock. I let him see the white of my teeth. I confided to his secret gaze that I had no fear of him. Like him, I stood, with a full beard and in black silk, a kaftan or long coat. Like him and one of his own.

And though I didn't know why or how I knew, I did know that I was one of his own, more surely than I was kin to the Huckster Prophet before him.

A surge of strength passed through me, as if the old man had laid his hands on the bones and howled for me! So it often happens, when seen, I grow strong. I was almost as strong in those moments as I am now.

The old man gave no signal to Gregory of what he had seen. He gave no signal to me. He sat still. The drift of his eyes over the room seemed natural and to settle on nothing, in particular, and to have no emotion, except the dim veil of sorrow.

He stared at me again, in the veiled way that Gregory would never notice. He held fast to me in perfect quiet.

Louder came the rush of pulse inside me, tighter the perfect shell of my body closed its pores. I could feel that he saw me and he found me beautiful! Young and beautiful! I felt the silk I wore, the weight of my hair.

Ah, you see me, Rebbe, you hear me. I spoke without moving my tongue.

He didn't answer me. He stared at me as a man stares in thought. But he had heard. He was no fake preacher, but a true zaddik and he had heard my little prayer.

But the younger man, thoroughly deceived and with his back to me, talked again in English:

'Rebbe, did you tell anyone else the old story? Did Esther by chance ever come here seeking to know who you were, and maybe you –'

'Don't be such a fool, Gregory,' the old man said. He looked away from me for the moment. Then back at me as he went on. 'I did not know your stepdaughter,' he said. 'She never came here. Neither has your wife. You know this.' He sighed, staring at me as if he feared to take his eyes away.

'Is it a tale of the Hasidim or the Lubavitch?' asked Gregory. 'Something one of the Misnagdim might have told Esther –'

'No.'

We stared at one another. The old man, alive, and the young spirit, robust, growing ever more vivid, and strong.

'Rebbe, who else . . .?'

'No one,' said the old man, fixing me steadily as I fixed him. 'What you remember is true and your brother was far from hearing, and your aunt Rivka is dead. No one could have told Esther.'

Only now he looked away from me, and up at Gregory.

'It's a cursed thing you speak of,' he said. 'It's a demon, a thing that can be summoned by powerful magic and do evil things.'

And his eyes returned to me, though the young man remained intent on him.

'Then other Jews know these stories. Nathan knows . . .'

'No, no one. Look, don't take me for an idiot. Don't you think I know you asked far and wide among the other Jews? You called this court and that, and you called the professors of the universities. I know your ways. You're too clever. You have telephones in every room of your life. You came here as the last resort.'

The younger man nodded. 'You're right. I thought it would be common knowledge. I made my inquiries. So have the authorities. But it isn't common knowledge. And so I am here.'

Gregory bent his head to the side, and thrust the folded bank draft at the Rebbe.

This gave the old man one second to gesture to me, one second, merely to make the little gesture with his right index finger of Hide or Stay Quiet. It came with a swift negation with the eyes and the smallest move of his head. Yet it was no command, and no threat. It was something closer to a prayer.

Then I heard him. *Don't reveal yourself, spirit.*

Very well, old man, for the time being, as you request.

Gregory – his back to me still – opened the check. 'Explain the thing to me, Rebbe. Tell me what it is and if you still have it. What you told Rivka, you said it wasn't an easy thing to destroy.'

The old man looked up at Gregory again, trusting me apparently to keep my place.

'Maybe I'll tell you all you want to know,' said the old man. 'Maybe I will deliver it into your hands, what you speak of. But not for that sum. We have more than plenty. You have to give us what matters to us.'

Gregory was much excited. 'How much, Rebbe!' he said. 'You speak as if you still have this thing.'

'I do,' said the old man. 'I have it.'

I was astonished, but not surprised.

'I want it!' said Gregory fiercely, so fiercely that I feared he had overplayed his hand. 'Name your price!'

The old man considered. His eyes fixed me again and then drifted past me, and I could see the color brighten in his withered face, and I could see his hands move restlessly. Slowly he let his eyes fasten on me and me alone.

For one precious second, as we gazed at one another, all the past threatened to become visible. I saw centuries beyond Samuel. I think I saw a glimmer of Zurvan. I think I saw the procession itself. I glimpsed the figure of a golden god smiling at me, and I felt terror, terror to know and to be as men are, with memory and in pain.

If this did not stop in me, I would know such agony that I would howl, like a dog, howl as the driver had howled when he saw the fallen body of Esther, I would howl forever. The wind would come. The wind would take me with all its other lost and howling souls. When I'd struck down the evil Mameluk master in Cairo, the wind had come for me, and I had fought through it to oblivion.

Stay alive, Azriel. The past will wait. The pain can wait. The wind will wait. The wind can wait forever. Stay alive in this place. Know this.

I am here, old man.

Calmly, he regarded me, unmarked by his grandson. He spoke now without taking his eyes off me, though Gregory bent to listen to his words:

'Go there, behind me and in the back of these books,' he said in English, 'and open the cabinet you see there. Inside

230

you'll see a cloth. Lift it. And bring the thing that is beneath it. It is heavy, but you can carry it. You are strong enough.'

I gasped. I heard it myself, and I felt my heart crying. The bones were here! Right here.

Gregory hesitated for one moment, perhaps not accustomed to taking orders, or even doing the smallest things for himself. I don't know. But then he sped into action. He hurried behind the bookcase at the old man's back.

I heard the creak of wood, and I smelled the cedar and the incense again. I heard the snap of metal latches. I felt myself rise on the balls of my feet, and then sink down again to a firm stance.

The old man and I stared at one another without pause. I stepped free of the bookcase completely so that he might see me in my long coat that was like his, and he showed only the tiniest fear for an instant, then urged me, with a polite nod of his head, to please return to my hiding place.

Behind him, out of sight, Gregory fumbled and cursed.

'Move the books,' said the Rebbe. 'Move them out of the way, all of them,' said the old man as he looked at me, as if he held me in check with his eyes. 'Do you see it now?'

The smell of dust rose in my nostrils. I could see the dust rising beneath the light. I heard the books tumble. Oh, it was sweet to hear with ears and to see with eyes. Don't weep, Azriel, not in the presence of this man who despises you.

I lifted my fingers to my lips without willing it. I just did it, natural, as if I were ready to pray in the face of disaster. I felt the hair above my mouth, and the thick mass of my beard. I liked it. *Like yours, Rebbe, when you were young?*

The old man was rigid, indestructible, superior, and wary.

Gregory stepped out from behind the bookcase, and back into the light.

In his arms he held the casket!

I saw the gold still thick on the cedar. I saw it, and I saw it bound carelessly in chains of iron.

Iron! So they thought that could hold me? Azriel! Iron could hold such a thing as me? I wanted to laugh. But I looked at it, the casket in Gregory's arms, which he held like an infant, the casket still covered with gold.

A faint memory of its making came back to me, but I did not see anyone clearly in this memory. I only remembered the sunlight on marble and kind words. Love, a world of love, and love made me think again of Esther.

How proud and fascinated Gregory was. He cared nothing that his wool coat was fool of dust. That dust was in his hair. He stared down at this thing, this treasure, and he turned to lay it before the old man like an infant.

'No!' The old man raised both hands. 'Set it there on the floor and back away from it.'

Bitterly, I smiled. *Don't defile yourself with it.*

He paid no heed to me, but looked down at the casket as Gregory put it on the floor.

'Good God, do you think it will burst into flame?' asked Gregory. Carefully he positioned the casket directly under the light, directly before the old man's desk. 'This is ancient, this writing, this writing isn't Hebrew, this is Sumerian!' He drew back his hands and rubbed them together.

He was passionate and overcome.

'Rebbe, this is priceless.'

'I know what it is,' said the old man, his eyes moving freely from me to the casket. I did not change. I did not even smile.

Gregory stared rapt at this thing as though it were the Christ child in the Manger and he were one of those shepherds come to see the Son of God made flesh.

'What is it, Grandfather? What's written on it?' He touched the iron chains, slowly, as if ready to be commanded by the old man to stop. He touched the links, which were thick and ugly, and he touched a scroll that was tucked beneath the iron chains, where links crossed links.

This I hadn't seen till now, this scroll, until Gregory's fingers gently tested the edges of it. The gold of the casket itself blinded me and made the water come up in my eyes. I smelled the cedar and the spices and the smoke that saturated the wood beneath its plating. I smelled the flesh of other humans, and I smelled the perfume of offerings.

My head swam suddenly.

I smelled the bones.

Oh, my own god, who has called me? If only I could see

his cheerful face for a minute, my god, my own god. My own god who used to walk with me, the god that each man has unto himself, his own god, as I had seen mine, and if only he would come now!

This wasn't really memory, you understand, it was a sudden longing without explanation that left me cold and confused.

But I kept thinking of this person, 'my god.' Would he laugh? Would he say, 'So your god has failed you, Azriel, and even amongst the Chosen, you call to me again? Didn't I warn you? Didn't I caution you to escape while you could, Azriel?'

But he wasn't there, my god, whoever that had ever been, and he wasn't smiling. He wasn't at my side, like a friend who'd been walking with me in the cool of the evening along the banks of the river. And he didn't say those things. But he had been with me once, and I knew it. The past was like a deluge that wanted me to fall into it, and be drowned.

A wild hope grew in me, a hope that made my breath come quickly, and the scents of the room suffocated me in my passion.

Maybe nobody has called you, Azriel! Maybe you have come on your own, and you are your own master! And you may hate and disregard these two men to your heart's content!

It was so sweet, this strength, this smile, this seeming joke that I should at last have that power myself. I almost heard my own little laugh. I closed my right fingers over the curls of my beard and tugged ever so gently.

'This scroll is intact, Rebbe,' said Gregory eagerly. 'Look, I can slip it out of these chains. Can you read it?'

The old man looked up at me as if I'd spoken.

Do you find me beautiful, old man? I know what you see. I don't have to see it. It's Azriel, not made to measure by a Master, not shifted into this or that shape for a Master, but Azriel as God made me once, when Azriel was soul and spirit and body in one.

The old man glared. *I command you! Don't show yourself, spirit.*

Do you, indeed, old man, and I hate your cold heart! Some link binds us one to the other, but you are so full of hate and so am I, how are we ever to know if God had his hand in this, for her, for Esther!

Spellbound, he stared at me unable to answer.

Gregory crouched over his trophy, and touched the scroll gingerly and fearfully.

'Rebbe, this alone is worth a fortune,' he said. 'Name your price. Let me open the scroll.' He laid his hand suddenly right on the wood, and opened his fingers, in love with this thing.

'No!' said the old man. 'Not under my roof.'

I looked into his pale filmy eyes. *I hate you. Do you think I asked to be this thing that I am? Were you ever young? Was your hair ever this black and your lips this ruddy?*

He didn't answer, but he had heard.

'Sit down there,' he said to his grandson, pointing to the nearby leather chair. 'Sit there and write the checks I tell you to write. And then this thing – and all I know of it – is yours.'

I almost laughed out loud. So that was it! That was it! He knew I was here and he would sell me to this grandson whom he despised. That would be his awful price for every wrong done him and his God by the grandson. He would put me in the grandson's unsuspecting hands. I think I did laugh, but soundlessly, only so that he could see it, see a twinkling in my eye perhaps and a curl to my lip as I sneered at him, and shook my head in reverence for his cleverness, his coldness, his loveless heart.

Gregory backed up, found the chair, and sat down slowly, the old leather peeling and flaking. He was overcome with excitement.

'Name your price.'

My smile must have been bitter, knowing. But I was calm. My old god would have been proud. *Well done, my brave one, fight them! What have you to lose? You think your God is merciful? Listen to what they have in mind for you!* But who spoke those words down the long length of the years? Who spoke them? What was it near me and filled with love that tried to warn me? I stared at Gregory. I would not be distracted, drawn away into the mesh of hurt, I would get to the bottom of this mystery first. My own mystery could wait.

I let the nails of my right fingers dig just a little into the hardened flesh of my palm. Yes, here. You are here, Azriel, whether the old man despises you or not, whether the young man is a murderer and a fool, and whether you are being sold once more as if you had no soul of your own and never had and never would. You are here. Not in the bones which lie in the casket!

I pretended my god was there. We stood together. Hadn't I done that with other Masters, without ever telling them, just brought my god close up to be near me, but had he ever really come?

In a cloud of smoke, I saw my god turning, weeping for me. It was in a chamber, and the heat rose from a boiling cauldron! My god, help me! But this was an image without a frame. That was something unspeakable that must never be relived! I had to see things here now.

Gregory drew a long leather wallet from his pocket. He opened it on his knee, and with his right hand held a golden pen.

The old man spoke the sums in American dollars. Huge sums. He gave the parties to whom these checks were to be written. Hospitals, institutions of learning, a company which would then pass the money on to the yeshiva in which the young men of the Court studied Torah. Money would be sent to the Court in Israel. Money would be sent to the new community of the Hasidim who tried to make their own village in the hills not far from this city. The Rebbe spoke all the words with the briefest of explanations.

Without a single question, Gregory began to write, carving the letters into the bank drafts with his sharp, gold pen, then flipping one check up so that he might write another, and another, scrawling his name as mighty men are wont to do.

Gregory finally laid the checks on the desk before the Rebbe. The Rebbe stared at them carefully. He moved them wide apart in a long row, and he studied them and seemed ever so slightly surprised.

'You would give me this much,' the Rebbe asked, 'for something about which you know and understand nothing?'

'His name was the last word my daughter spoke.'

'No, you want this thing! You want its power.'

'Why should I believe in its power? Yes, yes, I want it, to

see it, to try to figure how she knew about it, and yes, yes, I give those sums.'

'Take the scroll out of the chains, and give it to me.'

Like a boy, Gregory obeyed, so eager. The scroll was not old, not old like the casket of the bones. Gregory put the scroll into the old man's hand.

Will you wash your hands afterwards?

The Rebbe didn't acknowledge me. He carefully unrolled the vellum, moving his hands to the left and to the right, so that he had the full writing before him, and then he began to speak, translating the words in English carefully for his grandson to hear:

'"Return this thing to the Hebrews for it is their magic and only they can put it deep into Hell where it belongs. The Servant of the Bones no longer heeds his Master. Old vows no longer bind him. Old charms no longer banish him. Once summoned, he destroys all that he sees. Only the Hebrews know the meaning of this thing. Only the Hebrews can harness its fury. Give it freely to them.'''

Again I smiled. I couldn't help it. I think I closed my eyes with relief, and then opened them, looking at the old man who looked only at the vellum.

But have I truly come on my own? I didn't dare believe it yet. No. There could be some secret to snare me, some trap in which Esther's death was merely the bait.

The old man sat with the scroll open, staring down at it. He said no more.

Gregory broke the silence.

'Then why haven't you destroyed it!' He was so excited he could scarcely stand there at attention. 'What else does it say! What is the language!'

The old man looked up at him and then at me, and then back to the scroll.

'Listen to what I read now,' said the old man, 'because I will translate it for you only once:

'"Woe unto him who destroys these bones, for if it can be done, which is not known even to the wisest, that one should loose into the world a spirit of incalculable power, masterless and ungovernable, doomed to remain in the air forever,

236

unable to mount the Ladder to Heaven, or unlock the gates of Perdition. And who knows what shall be the cruelty of this spirit against God's children? Are there not demons enough in this world?"'

Dramatically, he looked up at his grandson, who evinced only fascination.

Gregory did everything but rub his hands together in greed.

The old man spoke again, slowly.

'My father took it because he felt that he must take it. And now you come to me and you ask for it. Well, it is almost yours.'

The younger man seemed delirious suddenly, or possessed of a divine joy.

'Oh, Rebbe, this is too marvelous, too wondrous,' said Gregory. 'But how could she have known, my poor Esther?'

'That's for you to discover,' said the old man coldly. 'For I cannot possibly know. Never have I called it forth, this spirit, nor would my father. Nor would the Moslem who gave it over into my father's hands.'

'Give me the scroll. I'll take it now.'

'No.'

'Grandfather, I want it! Look, the checks are there!'

'And tomorrow the money will be in the bank, will it not? Tomorrow, when the sums are transferred, when the transaction is finished –'

'Grandfather, let me have it now!'

'Tomorrow, then you come to me, and you take it, and it's yours. And you will be the Master of the Servant of the Bones.'

'You stubborn, impossible old man. You know these checks are good. Give it to me!'

'Oh, you are so anxious!' said the elder.

He looked at me. I could have sworn he would have shared a smile with me had I invited him to do it, but I didn't.

Then he looked again at his grandson, who was in a paroxysm of frustration, staring at the golden casket at his feet, not daring to touch it, but wanting it so much he groaned.

'Why did you kill her?' the old man said.

'What?'

'Why did you have your daughter killed? I want to know. I should have made that my price!'

'Oh, you're a fool, all of you are fools, belligerent and superstitious, the idiots of your god!'

The old man was outraged.

'Your temples, Gregory, are the houses of the deceived and the damned,' he said. 'But let's have no more invectives. We know each other. Tomorrow night, when my bankers tell me that your money is in our hands, you come and you take this thing away. And keep the secret. Keep the vow. Tell no one that you are . . . that you were . . . my grandson.'

Gregory smiled, shrugged, opened his hands in a gesture of acceptance. He turned to go, never so much as glancing in the direction of where I stood.

He stopped before the door and looked back at his grandfather.

'Tell my brother Nathan for me that I thank him that he called me with his condolences.'

'He didn't do this!' cried the Rebbe.

'Oh, yes, he did. He called me and spoke to me, and tried to comfort me in my loss, and to comfort my wife.'

'He has no traffic with you and your kind!'

'And I don't tell you this, Rebbe, to bring your anger down on him, no, not for that reason, but just so that you know that my brother Nathan loved me enough to call me and to tell me he was sorry that the girl was dead.'

Gregory opened the door. The cold of the night waited uneasily.

'Stay away from your brother!' The old man rose, his fists on the desk.

'Save your words!' said Gregory. 'Save them for your flock. My church preaches love.'

'Your brother walks with God,' said the old man, but his voice was frail now. He was weary. He was spent.

He chanced a glance at me. I caught and held his eye.

'Don't try to cheat me, Rebbe,' said Gregory as the cold air moved into the room past him. 'If I don't find this thing here tomorrow night as promised, I'll stand on your doorstep with the cameras. I'll print the stories of my childhood among the Hasidim in my next book.'

'Mock me if it pleases you, Gregory,' said the old man, drawing himself up. 'But the bargain's done, and the Servant of the Bones will be here for you tomorrow. And you will take this thing from me. You who are evil. You who do evil. You who walk with the Devil. Your church walks with the Devil. The Minders are of the Devil. Welcome to this demon and its ilk. Get out of my house.'

'All right, my teacher,' said Gregory, 'my Abraham.' He opened the door wide and stepped through it, leaning back into the room so that the light clearly revealed his smiling face.

'My Patriarch, my Moses! You give my love to my brother. Shall I give your condolences to my grieving wife?' He stepped back, slamming the door after him.

There was faint vibration of glass and metal things quivering.

I stayed where I was.

We looked at one another, I and the old man, across the dusty little room, I stepped partway from behind the bookcase and the old man remained fixed behind his desk.

The old man trembled.

Go back into the bones, Spirit. I never called you. I don't speak to you, except to send you away from me.

'Why?' I pleaded. I spoke the old Hebrew knowing he would know it. 'Why do you so despise me, old one? What have I done? I don't speak now of the spirit that destroys the magicians, I speak of myself, me, Azriel! What did I do?'

He was astonished and shaken. I stood before his desk; I wore clothes like his clothes, and I looked down and I saw that my foot had almost touched the casket, and how small it looked, and the smell of boiling water rose in my nostrils.

'Marduk, my god,' I cried out in the old Chaldean. He knew the words, the zaddik! Let him glare at me in horror.

'Oh, my god, they will not help me!' I sang out the words

in Chaldean. 'I am here again and there is no righteous path!'

The old man stood rapt, and repelled. He was full of shock and loathing. He threw out his hands:

'Be gone, spirit, out of here, out of the air, and back into the bones whence you came!'

I felt a silken thrill through my limbs. I held firm.

'Rebbe, you said he killed her. Tell me if he did. I slew the men who stabbed her!'

'Be gone, spirit.' He threw up his hands over his face, and turned his head. His voice grew stronger. He stepped from behind his desk and walked about me in a circle, shouting the words again, louder, more clearly, his hands flashing in front of me. I felt myself weaken. I felt the tears on my face.

'Why did you say, Rebbe, that he had killed Esther? Tell me and I shall avenge her! I killed the hirelings! Oh, Lord God of Hosts, when Yahweh spoke to Saul and David, he said slay them all to the last man, woman, and child! And Saul and David obeyed him. Was it not right to slay those three filthy men who murdered an innocent girl?'

'Be gone, Spirit!' he cried. 'Be gone! Be gone. I will have no traffic with you. Go back into the bones!'

'I curse you, I hate you!' I said to him, but it had no sound.

I was dissolving. All that I had gathered to myself was dispersed, as if the wind had found its way beneath the door and caught hold of me.

'Be gone, Spirit, be gone from here, be gone from my house and from me!'

Blackness.

Yet I couldn't stop thinking.

I couldn't stop being.

I will see you again, old man.

Dreams came to me as if I were human and I slept, and my mind had opened its doors to living teachers. No, Azriel, no, perish, but don't dream.

Yet there came the face of Samuel; Strasbourg; another sanctuary of scrolls and books and it was in flames. I heard my voice. 'Take my hand, Master, take me with you into death.' Damn you, Samuel! Damn you, old man.

Damn you, all you Masters!

From the top of a hill I looked down on the small city of Strasbourg. Oh, it was nothing so clear then as it was when I described it to you.

But it was there, I saw it. I knew that all the Jews were suffering. I knew I was one of them. And yet I couldn't be one of them. And the bells pealed. The arrogant bells of murderers came from their churches. And the sky was the silent heavy sky of olden days – six hundred years ago – perhaps when the air didn't talk and so clearly I heard the bells.

'Azriel.' Chatter. Wind. The invisible were coming, they were coming to me in smoky mist, surrounding me, closing in, smelling the weakness, the fear, and the suffering. 'Azriel!' The rumblings of the jealous earthbound surrounded me. The greedy desperate earthbound dead.

Get away from me. Let me remember.

I wanted to know, I wanted to push past all of them as I had the people on the sidewalk when Esther had looked at me. I wanted to remember, I wanted to . . .

For one instant, I stood bright, staring at the Rebbe, but the Rebbe was huge, and his voice was louder than the wind.

Be gone, Spirit! I command you! The old man's face was blood red with his fury.

Be gone, Spirit!

His words struck me. They hurt me. They hurt me. They lashed me. Give me silence for now. If there can be no peace, there can be silence and there can be the darkness. It could be worse, Azriel.

It could be worse.

To be wounded is bad, but not so bad as to kill the innocent and to smile with hate.

241

Seventeen

There are several things I should have attempted. I should have tried to leave the room, intact, and follow Gregory. I had a visible body! I had clothed it perfectly. I should have hung on. I should have tried to wander freely in the streets of Brooklyn and discover more about the world, simply by asking more specific questions of it.

I should have discovered specifics about Gregory Belkin and the Temple of the Mind. People in the streets would have talked to me about these things. I looked like a man. I could have watched the television broadcasts in taverns. I could have spent a night of fruitful, focused learning instead of letting the old Rebbe drive me away from my own self, and into nothingness once more.

Whatever, when the Rebbe sought to destroy me, I should not have wasted time calling out to 'my god.'

That had been an unthinkable thing for the Servant of the Bones – to call upon my god – for my god had never been with me in my years of evil spectral service. I don't think the Servant of the Bones who cursed Samuel even remembered my god, because he did not remember being human, as I remembered now. My god had been mine when I was a man, a young man living in the city of Babylon where I had died.

Indeed, though I hate to admit it, if I bring to mind Samuel, I remember only how proud I was to be his genii, a ghost of remarkable powers such as simple dead souls almost never acquire. I was the mighty culmination of ancient magic and men who knew how to use it.

Of human life, I had recalled nothing. I could not even recall a Master before Samuel, though surely there had been such men. Back to Babylon there must have been a lineage of such magicians, all of whom I'd served and outlived.

It had to be so. It was so. The Servant of the Bones was passed hand to hand.

And at some point, as the Rebbe had so graciously explained for Gregory's benefit, the Servant of the Bones had rebelled against his solemn purpose. He had turned around in the very midst of his magic and lashed out at the one who had called him into being, and the Servant of the Bones had done this more than once.

But what had preceded all this? Had I not once been human?

What did my memories want of me? What did Esther want of me? Why was it seductive to have eyes and ears, to feel pain, and to hate again, and to want to kill? Yes, I very much wanted to kill.

I wanted to kill the Rebbe, but then again I could not. I held him to be a good man, a man perhaps without blemish, except for want of kindness, and I couldn't do it. There is only so much evil for which you can blame others. I couldn't kill him. I was glad I had not.

But you can imagine what a mystery I was to myself, caught between Heaven and Hell and not knowing why I had come.

But I was not of God, no, I was not of God and I had no god, and when the Rebbe banished me, when he used his considerable power to dissolve my form and addle my wits so that I could not oppose him, he had done so in the name of God and I had not dared to call upon that same God, the God of my father, the Lord God of Hosts, the God above and before all Gods.

No, in that moment of weakness, Azriel, man and ghost, had called upon his pagan god of old, from a human time, a god whom he had loved.

As the Rebbe cursed me, I deliberately called on Marduk in Chaldean. I wanted the Rebbe to hear the pagan tongue. Anger burnt me up as it has so often done. I knew my god wouldn't help me.

Some parting of the ways had occurred with me and my god.

Must I now recall everything? Must I know the story from the start?

Well, if I sought to put it together, to understand it, to know who I had been and how I'd been made the Servant of the Bones, there should be but one reason: so that I might die.

Really, really die.

Not just retreat into blackness again, to be called forth into another lurid drama, and surely not to be trapped, earthbound, with the lost souls who murmured and stammered and screeched as they clung to mortality. But to die. To be given at last what had somehow been denied me years ago by a trick I couldn't recall.

'Azriel, I warn you.' Who had spoken those words then, thousands of years ago? A phantom? Who was the man I saw dimly at the richly carved table who cried and cried? Who was the King? There had been a great king . . .

But my anger and my rage had weakened me so that I was shocked and dispersed by the Rebbe. My mind was blown apart as surely as my form. My capacity to reason was shattered, and I rose into the night formless, aimless, drifting once more among the electric voices, tumbling as it were above the magnet that holds us all – the spinning world.

But I never let go. I never really let go.

As I came to myself, as I gathered strength again, as I set my eyes upon a destination, I thought of all these various aspects of my situation – that I very well might be utterly Masterless, that I wouldn't fail Esther, that I was stronger than I'd ever been – and I was determined to fight harder this time to be free of either of these two men – the Rebbe or his grandson Gregory – I was determined that if I could not die, I would gain life apart from them.

Who knows what nourishes a spirit, in the flesh or out of it?

Men and women in this time, who would have laughed at our old customs, believed in absolutely preposterous explanations of things – take, for example, how a hailstone comes to form, from a speck of dust in the upper atmosphere, falling, then rising, gathering ice to itself, falling again, then rising again, and becoming larger and larger, till some perfect moment is reached at which the hailstone breaks the circuit and falls to earth and then, after all of that, all of that wondrous process, melts to nothing. Dust to dust.

Someday these people – these clever minds of today – will know all about spirits. They will know as they knew about genes and neutrinos and other things they cannot see. Doctors at the bedside will see the spirit rise, the tzelem, as I saw it rise from Esther. It will not take a sorcerer to drive a spirit heavenward. There will be men clever enough to exterminate or extinguish even something like me.

Note this, Jonathan.

Scientists of your time have isolated the gene for a fruit fly that is eyeless. And when they take his genes and inject them into other fruit flies – God have mercy on his tiny creatures – do you know that these fruit flies produce eyes all over their bodies? Eyes on their elbows? And on their wings?

Doesn't that make you love scientists? Don't you feel tenderness towards them and respect for them?

Believe you me, coming back to myself the following night, taking form again, diaphanous but optimistic and hatefully calm, I did not think to seek the help of scientists any more than sorcerers to effect my final death. No. I was done with all practitioners of the unseen; I was done with everything except justice for a girl I'd never known. And I would find a way to die, even if it meant I had to remember everything, every painful moment of what I'd suffered when death should have come to me, when death should have been granted, when the Ladder to Heaven might have fallen down, or at least the Gates of Hell swung wide.

Stay alive long enough to understand!

It was exciting! It was perhaps the only truly exciting thing that I could at that moment imagine or recall.

On the sidewalk, the next night, in Brooklyn, I took form whole and swift as if some modern man had flicked a light switch. Invisible to mortal eyes, but in the very shape that would soon enough become solid.

I wanted it this way. But still, to come forth on my own? I

couldn't quite trust it. But tonight I would make strides in my search for the truth.

Brooklyn again, the house of the Rebbe and his family, and Gregory's car sliding to the curb.

Invisible, I drifted close to Gregory, fairly wrapping myself around him, though never touching him really, escorting him back the alley-way, almost touching his fingers as he unlocked the gate.

When the door opened, I entered with him, beside him, buoyant and fearless, breathing in the smell of his skin, inspecting him as never before.

I think I was luxuriating for a moment in the invisibility, which in general I hate, and came close to see how very well groomed and strong this man was, and that he had the glow of a king. His black eyes were uncommonly bright in his face, unencumbered by fleshly wrinkles that suggest weariness or an attitude, and his mouth in particular was very beautiful, more beautiful than I had realized. He wore fine clothes as before, the simple garments of this era, a long coat of soft fleecy wool, fine linen beneath it, and around his neck, the same scarf.

I went to the far left corner of the room, a much better place than I had occupied the night before, this time quite far to the left of both men and the dingy lamps beside and above them, and the small circle of intimacy which they so unwillingly shared.

Indeed I could see the old man's profile as I saw Gregory's, the two facing each other, and the casket gleaming on the desk, the desk this time which had been stripped of all its sacred books and would no doubt be purified after by a thousand words and gestures and candles, but what was that to me?

I was making the air move. The old man would know it within seconds. I had to be still and resist the lure of my growing strength. Remain diaphanous, quick to move, rather than to be scattered, willing to pass through the wall intact, rather than frightened once more or hurt into disintegration as I had been the night before.

I was near the wall that was closest to the street outside,

against a wooden door that appeared unused, its brass handle covered with dust, and I could see my own shape, my folded arms, my shoes. I called the duplicates of Gregory's clothes to form themselves easily around me, in so far as I knew the details.

The Rebbe rested on his elbows, staring at the casket before him, and the black chains looked ugly against the plated gold.

I felt nothing in me that he was so near to the bones. I felt nothing that either man spoke of them, or moved about them, or stared at the casket which held them, and this I noted.

Behave now as if you are living, and as if it matters to go on living. Be careful as the living. Take your time.

My own advice to myself amused me a little. But then I settled in, deep into the corner, beyond where the light fell, beyond where it might even touch my half-visible shoe or inevitably gleaming eye.

Old man, just try it! I was ready for him. I was ready for anyone or anything.

Gregory stepped anxiously into the light. He looked directly at the casket. The old man behaved as though Gregory were not there. Gregory might have been the spirit. The old man stared at the gold plating; he stared at the iron chains.

Gregory reached out, and without asking permission he put his hands on the casket. Then I did feel a shimmer, much as I loathed it, and I was stronger, instantly stronger.

The old man stared right at Gregory's hands. Then he sat back, sighing heavily as if for effect or punctuation, and he reached for a sheaf of papers – rather cheap and light paper, nothing as good as parchment – and he thrust this group of papers at Gregory, holding them up above the casket.

Gregory took the papers.

'What's this?'

'Everything written on the casket,' said the old man in English. 'Don't you see the letters?' His voice was full of despair. 'The words are written in three tongues. Call the

247

first Sumerian, the second Aramaic, and the last Hebrew, though they are ancient tongues.'

'Ah! This was more than kind of you. I never expected such cooperation from you.'

I thought so too. What had moved the old man to be so helpful?

Gregory could barely hold the papers steady. He shuffled them, put them back in order, and started to speak.

'No!' said the old man. 'Not here. It's yours now and you take it. And you say the words when and where you will, but not under my roof, and from you I exact one last promise, in exchange for these documents which I have prepared for you. You know what they are, don't you? They let you call the spirit. They tell you how.'

Gregory made a soft laugh. 'Once again, your kindness overwhelms me,' he said. 'I know your disinclination to touch even trifles which are not clean.'

'This is no trifle,' said the old man.

'Ah, then, when I say these words the Servant of the Bones will rise?'

'If you don't believe it, why do you want it?' asked the old man.

The shock went through me. I was fully visible.

I cleaved to the wall, not daring even to try to see my own limbs. The cloth wound itself around me without a whisper. 'Make the shoes to shine even brighter, give me the gold for my wrist, and make my face as clean of hair, yet give me the hair of my youth,' I asked silently.

I felt my full weight, denser perhaps than it had even been the night before. I wanted to look down at myself but I dared not make myself known.

'You don't seriously think I believe in it,' Gregory replied politely. He folded the sheaf of papers and put them carefully into the breast of his coat.

The old man made no reply.

'I want to know about it, I want to know what she was talking about, I want it. I covet it. I covet it because it's precious and it's unique and she spoke of it with her dying words.'

'Yes, that does convey upon it an added value,' said the old man, his voice harder and clearer than I had ever heard it before.

I could feel my hair against my shoulders. I could feel the dampness from the concrete wall as it chilled my neck. I made the scarf at my neck thicker. I made it fit higher. The lightbulb stirred. Things creaked in the room, but neither man appeared to notice, so intent were they on the casket and on each other.

'The chains are rusted, aren't they?' Gregory said, raising his right finger. 'May I take them off?'

'Not here.'

'All right, then I presume we have concluded our bargain. But you want something else, don't you? A final promise. I know. I can see it in you. Speak. I want to take home my treasure and open it. Speak. What more do you want?'

'Promise me, you will not come back to this house. You'll never seek my company again. You'll never seek the company of your brother. You will never tell anyone of how you were born one of us. You will keep your world away as you have always done. If your brother calls you, you will not receive his call. If your brother visits you, you will not receive him. Promise all of this to me.'

'You ask that of me every time I see you,' said Gregory. He laughed. 'It's always the final thing you ask, and I always promise.'

He cocked his head and smiled affectionately at the old man, patronizingly, with maddening impudence.

'You won't see me again, Grandfather. Never, never again. When you die, I won't cross the bridge to come to your graveside. Is that what you want to hear? I won't come to Nathan to mourn with him. I won't risk exposing him, or any of you. Very well?'

The old man nodded.

'But I have one last demand of you,' said Gregory, 'if I am never to speak to or see Nathan again.'

The old man made a little questing gesture with both hands.

'Tell my brother I love him. I insist you tell him.'

'I'll tell him,' said the old man.

Then Gregory moved swiftly, gathering up the casket, letting the chains scrape on the desk as he stood upright with it in his arms.

I felt again the tremors, the strengthening, moving down my arms and my legs. I felt my fingers moving, I felt a tingling as if tiny needles were being touched to me all over. I didn't like it, that it came from his touch. But maybe it came from all of us here, our sense of purpose, our concentration.

'Goodbye, Grandfather,' said Gregory. 'Someday, you know, they will come to write about you – my biographers, those who tell the story of the Temple of the Mind.' He tightened his grip on the casket. The rusted chains left red dust on his lapels but he didn't care. 'They'll write your epitaph because you are my grandfather. And you'll deserve that recognition.'

'Get out of my house.'

'Of course, you needn't worry for the moment. No record exists of the boy you mourned thirty years ago. On my deathbed I'll tell them.'

The old man shook his head slowly, but resisted a reply.

'But tell me, aren't you the least bit curious about this casket, about what's in it, about what may happen when I read the incantations?'

'No.'

Gregory's smile faded. He studied the old man, and then he said:

'All right, Grandfather. Then we have nothing to talk about, do we? Nothing at all.'

The old man nodded.

The anger beat in Gregory's cheeks, wet and red. But he had no time for this. He looked at the thing in his arms and he turned and hurried out the door, kicking it open with his knee and letting it slam behind him.

The old man sat exactly as before. I think he looked at the dust on his desk. I think he stared at the flakes of rust from the iron which had been left on his polished wood. But I couldn't tell.

I felt nothing. I neither moved nor was strengthened, as

Gregory with his casket of bones moved away from me. No, he was not Master, never, never, by any means. But this old man? I had to know.

Gregory's steps died away in the alley.

I came forward, and walked to the old man's desk and stood in front of it.

The old man was aghast.

The moment for an outcry passed in rigid silence, his eyes contracting, and when he spoke it was a whisper.

'Go back to the bones, Spirit,' he said.

I drew on all my strength to hold out against him, I thought nothing of his hatred, and I thought of no moment in my long miserable existence when I had been either wronged or loved. I looked at him and I stood firm. I barely heard him.

'Why did you pass the bones to him?' I asked. 'What is your purpose! If you called me up to destroy him, tell me!'

He turned his face away, so as not to see me.

'Be gone, Spirit!' he declared in Hebrew.

I watched him stand up and move the chair back out of his way, and I saw his hands fly up, and I knew that he was speaking Hebrew, and then the Chaldean, yes, he knew that too, and he spoke it with perfect cadence, but I didn't hear the words. The words didn't touch me.

'Why did you say he killed Esther? Why, Rebbe, tell me!'

Silence. He had ceased to speak. He didn't even pray in his mind or his heart. He stood transfixed, his mouth closed tight beneath his white mustache, the locks of his hair shivering slightly, the light showing the yellowed hairs of his beard as well as the snow white.

His eyes were closed. He began to whisper his prayers in Hebrew, davening, or bowing, that is, very quickly over and over again.

His fear and fury were equal; his hatred outstripped them both.

'Do you want justice for her?' I shouted at him. But nothing would break his prayers and his closed eyes and his bowing.

Now I spoke, softly in Chaldean,

'Fly from me,' I said in a whisper, 'all you tiny parts of land and air and mountain and sea, and of the living and of the dead, which have come to give me this form, fly from me but not so far that I cannot summon you at will, and leave me my shape that this mortal man may see me and be afraid.'

The light above shivered again on its raw cord. I saw the air move the old man's beard. I saw it make him blink.

I looked down through my own translucent hands and saw the floor beyond them.

'Fly from me,' I whispered, 'and stay close to me to return at my summons, that God Himself would not know me from a man that He had made!'

I vanished.

I threw out my disappearing hands to frighten him. I wanted so to hurt him, just a little. I wanted so to defy him. On and on he prayed with eyes closed.

But there was no time for idle play with him. I didn't know if there was energy enough for what I meant to do.

Passing through the walls I went upwards, rising over the rooftops, passing through tingling wires, and into the cool air of the night.

'Gregory,' I said, as surely as if my old master Samuel had sent me to say it. 'Gregory!'

And there below in the stream of traffic on the bridge I saw the car, moving amongst its guardians, for there were many. I saw it, sleek and long, keeping perfect pace with the cars before it and behind it and beside it, as if they were birds together in a flock and flew straight, without having to play the wind.

'Down there, beside him and so that he cannot see.'

No Master could have said it with more determination, pointing his finger at the victim that I was to rob, or murder, or put to flight.

'Come now, Azriel, as I command you,' I said.

And gently I descended, into the soft warm interior of the car, a world of dark synthetic velvet and tinted glass that made the night outside die a little, as if a deep mist had covered all things.

Opposite him, I took my place, my back to the leather wall which divided us from the driver, folding my arms again as I watched him, crouched as it were, with the casket in his arms. He had broken off the useless rusted iron chains, and they lay dirty and fragmented on the carpeted floor.

I could have wept with happiness. I had been so afraid! I had been so sure I could not do it! All of my will had been so fixed on the effort, that I scarce had breath in me to realize it had been done.

We rode together, the ghost watching him, and he, the man clutching his treasure, balancing it carefully on his knees, and reaching in his coat for the papers, and then shoving them back in his excitement and steadying the casket again and rubbing his hands on it, as if the very gold excited him as it had the ancients. As gold had once excited me.

Gold.

A blast of heat came to me, but this was memory.

Hold firm. Begin. From land and sea, from the living and the dead, from all that God has made, come to me, what I require to make of me an apparition, thin as air, to make of me a barely visible yet strong being.

I looked down and saw the shape of my legs, I had hands again, I made clothes like Gregory's clothes. I could almost feel the padded seat of the car. Almost feel it, and I longed to touch it, longed for garments to wrap me round.

I saw buttons, the shining semblance of buttons, and fingernails. And I lifted my invisible hand to my face to make sure that it was clean shaven as his. But give me my hair, my long hair, like Samson's hair, thick hair. I caught my fingers in the ringlets. I wanted so to finish it but not yet –

I had to say when Azriel would come, didn't I? I had to say it. I was the Master.

Suddenly Gregory lowered the casket. He fell down on his knees on the very floor of the car and laid the casket before him, rocking with the motion of the car, steadying himself against the seat, his right hand so close to me he almost touched me, and then he ripped off the lid of the casket.

He pulled it up and off, and it flew off, rotted, dried, a shell of gold almost, and there – there on their bed of rotted cloth lay the bones.

I felt a shock as though blood had been infused into me. My heart had only to beat. *No, not yet.*

I looked down at the remnants of my body. I looked down at the bones that held my tzelem locked within them, coated with gold, chained together, and formed like a child asleep in the womb.

A dimness threatened me, a dissolution. What was the reason? Pain. We were in a great room. I knew this room. I felt the heat of the boiling cauldron. No. Don't let this come now. Don't let this weaken you.

Look at the man on his knees right in front of you, and the bones that he all but worships, which are your bones.

'Body be my own,' I whispered. 'Be solid and strong enough to make angels burn with envy. Mold me into the man I would be in my happiest hour, if I held the looking glass before my own face.'

He paused. He had heard the whisper. But in the dark he saw nothing but the casket. What were creaks and bumps and whispers to him? The car sped along. The city hissed and throbbed.

His eyes were locked to the bones.

'My Lord God,' said Gregory, and leaning back on his heels so that he wouldn't tumble, he reached out for the skull.

I felt it. I felt his hands on my head. But it was only a stroking of the thick black hair that was already there, hair I had called to me.

'Lord God!' he said again. 'Servant of the Bones? You have a new Master. It is Gregory Belkin and his entire flock. It is Gregory Belkin of the Temple of the Mind of God who calls you. Come to me, Spirit! Come to me!'

I said:

'Perhaps yes, perhaps no to all those words. I am already here.'

He looked up, saw me sitting composed and opposite to him and he let out a loud cry and tumbled over against the door of the car. He let go of the casket altogether.

Nothing changed in me except that I grew stronger and

brighter. I reached over towards him and down carefully and put the fragile lid over the curling skeleton of the bones. I covered them up with my hands, and I drew back and up and folded my arms, and I sighed.

He sat slumped still on the floor of the car, the seat behind him, the door beside him, his knees up, staring at me, merely staring, and then as filled with wonder as any human I could ever remember, fearless and mad with glee.

'Servant of the Bones!' he said, flashing his teeth to me.

'Yes, Gregory,' I answered with the tongue in my mouth, my voice speaking his English. 'I am here, as you see.'

I studied him carefully. I had outdone his garments, my coat was soft and flawless silk, and my buttons were jasper, and my hair was long on my shoulders. Heavy! And I was composed and he sat in disarray.

Slowly, very slowly he rose, grasping the handle of the door to aid himself, as he sat back down on the velvet seat and looked first at the casket on the floor and then at me.

I turned sharply for one instant. I had to. I was afraid. But I had to. I had to see if I could see myself in the dark tinted glass.

Beyond, the night moved in a splendid dreamy flight, the city of towers clustering near us, bright orange electric lights blazing as fiercely as torches.

But there was Azriel, looking at himself with sharp black eyes, smooth shaven, his hair a regular mantle on his head, and his thick eyebrows dipping as they always did when he smiled.

Without haste, I let my eyes return to him. I let him see my smile.

My heart beat and I could move my tongue easily on my lips. I sat back and felt the comfort of this cushioned seat, and I felt the engine of the car vibrating through me, vibrating through the soft, exquisite velvet beneath me.

I heard his breath rise and fall. I saw his chest heave. I looked into his eyes again.

He was rapt. His arms had not even tensed; his fingers lay open on his knees. He did not even bend his back as if to brace himself from a shock or a blow. His eyes were fully opened and he too was almost smiling.

'You're a brave man, Gregory,' I said. 'I have reduced other men to stuttering lunatics with such tricks as this.'

'Oh, I bet you have,' he answered.

'But don't call me the Servant of the Bones again. I don't like it. Call me Azriel. That's my name.'

'Why did she say it?' he asked at once. 'Why did she say it in the ambulance? She said "Azriel," just as you said it.'

'Because she saw me,' I said. 'I watched her die. She saw me and she spoke to say my name twice, and then that was all she said and she was dead.'

He tumbled gently back against the seat. He stared upwards now, past me, resisting the inevitable rocking of the car, and its sudden jerks as it slowed, perhaps blocked by the traffic. He stared and only slowly lowered his eyes to me in the most fearless and casual manner I have ever seen in a man.

Then, lifting his hand, he began to tremble. But it wasn't cowardice. It wasn't even shock. It was glee, the pure mad glee he'd felt when he looked at the skull.

He wanted to touch me. He rubbed his hands together, and he reached out and then he drew back.

'Go ahead,' I said. 'I don't care. Do it. I would like you to do it.'

I reached forward and grabbed his right hand before he could stop me and I lifted it as he stared amazed. His mouth opened. I lifted his hand and pushed it against my thick hair, and laid it on my cheek, and then against my chest.

'You feel a heartbeat?' I asked. 'There is none. Only a living pulse as if I were whole and entire a heart, made of a heart, when the very opposite is surely the truth. I feel your pulse, true enough, and it races. I feel your strength and you have much.'

He tried to free his hand, but only politely, and I wouldn't let him do it; I held his hand now so that I could see the palm of it in the flashing light coming through the windows.

The car went very slowly.

I saw the lines in his palm, and then I opened my right

hand which was free, and I saw the lines in my palm too. I had done well. No Master had ever done better. But I didn't know how to read these lines, only that they had come to me in glorious detail.

Then I made a decision to do something which I could not explain to myself. I kissed the palm of his hand. I kissed this tender flesh of his hand; I pressed my lips right against it and when I felt the shiver pass through him, I gloried in it, almost the way he was glorying in my presence.

I looked into his eyes and saw something of my own eyes in them, in their largeness, their darkness, even in the thick fringe of lashes of which I, once alive, had been so very proud.

I wanted to kiss his lips, to lock hold of them, and to kiss as enemies kiss before one tries to kill the other.

Indeed, if there had ever been a moment for the Servant of the Bones like this with any mortal, I didn't remember it. Not a wisp of such a memory remained; indeed, I felt nothing now except a fascination with him, and all that came to trouble it was her face, Esther's and her lips and her dying words.

'And what makes you think that I am not Master!' he whispered. A shining smile spread on his lips, almost rapturous.

I released his hand and he slipped it away, and brought his own two hands together as if to protect them against me, but this was done with graceful composure.

'I'm the Master and you know it,' he said it gently. But his voice was eager and loving. 'Azriel! You're mine.'

There wasn't even a sensible particle of fear in him. Indeed the wonder he knew now seemed the kernel of his person, the part of him which had always defied the Rebbe and had defied a legion of others, and would defy me. The wonder in him was . . . what? The monstrous arrogance of an Emperor?

'I am not the Master?' he asked me.

I looked at him calmly. I was thinking about him in wholly new ways, not ways of rage, but ways of wanting to know:

who and what was he? Had he killed her? What if he had not?

'I say not, Gregory,' I answered his question. 'You're not the Master. But then I don't know everything. Ghosts must be forgiven that they know so much and so little at the same time.'

'Rather like mortal men,' he said with a delicate touch of sadness. 'And were you ever one of them?'

A chill caught me off guard, rippling over new skin. Dimness. The cries of people echoing up glazed brick walls. I shook myself all over.

Certainly I had once been a mortal man! And so what.

I was here now in the car with him. The process of incarnation continued in me, with the thickening of the sinews and the deepening of the minerals within the new bones which were now in my fleshly body, and the hair that formed on the backs of my arms and on my fingers, and the soft remnant of beard on my cheek.

And this process had to be of my doing. He sang no songs to make it happen; he recited no chants. He didn't even know it was happening. If there was an alchemy coming from him, it was the alchemy of his expression, his wonder, his obvious love.

Again came the dimness. It came swift and titanic – a procession, a great street with high blue-glazed walls, and the scent of flowers everywhere, and people waving, and a dreadful sadness, so bitter, so total, that for one moment I felt myself begin to dissolve.

The car around me seemed insubstantial, which meant that I was leaving it.

In the memory I raised my arm and voices cried in praise.

My god wouldn't look at me. My god turned his back on me and on the procession, and he wept.

I shook my head. Gregory Belkin was watching all this, keenly sensing it.

'Something troubles you, Spirit,' he said gently. 'Or is it merely so hard to become flesh again?'

I took hold of the door handle. I looked at the glass and at my face.

I was the one who made myself stay.

The car shuddered and rumbled as it moved over the roughened street. He took no notice. But new light had come in from both sides, penetrating even the black glaze of the windows, and it showed how jubilant he was, and how easy, and how young he looked in his wonder and joy.

'Very well,' he said with charm, eyebrows lifted, 'so I am not the Master. Then tell me, beautiful one, and you are quite the handsome Spirit, why have you come to me?'

Once again, his teeth flashed white and there seemed a moment near magical when the various ornaments he wore – small and made of gold, at his wrists, on his tie – flickered as if struck by a note of music, and he looked very good, as good perhaps as he thought I looked.

Masters. . . . Who were masters to me? Old men?

I spoke before I thought.

'There was never a Master as brave as you, Gregory,' I said, 'not that I can remember, though so much lies beyond my reach. No, your bravery is different, and fresh. And you are not the Master. It seems, like it or not, that I have come to you on my own and for my reasons.'

This pleased him immensely.

I grew warmer and I felt the fibers of my clothes against me, I felt the snug certainty of being there. My foot flexed in my shoe.

'I like that you're not afraid of me,' I said. 'I like that you know what I am from the start as any Master might, but you're not the Master. I've been watching you. I've been learning things from you.'

'Have you?' he said. He did not so much as flinch. He was in near ecstasy. 'Tell me what you've seen.' At the moment it seemed there was only one thing he found more fascinating than me, and that was himself.

I smiled at him.

He wasn't a man unused to happiness. He knew well how to enjoy things, both minute and momentous. And though nothing like this had ever happened to him, his life had educated him to enjoy this too.

'Yes,' he said, smiling broadly. 'Yes!'

259

I hadn't spoken. We both knew it. Yet he had read my thoughts? What else is in there to read, I wonder?

The big car slid to a stop.

I was glad. I was frightened by his charm, frightened by the fact that I warmed to him, frightened that somehow in talking to him I gained strength. He didn't have to want it or wish it, only perhaps to witness it. But this I couldn't tolerate. I had been there when Esther died and he had not. He had not been there to see me, yet I had been strong enough to take the lives of her killers each in turn.

He stared out the windows, to the right and left. An immense crowd surrounded us, roaring, shouting, pushing up against the car so that it rocked suddenly on its wheels as a boat in water.

He was not concerned. He turned and looked at me. I felt that dimness come again, because this crowd reminded me of that old crowd, the crowd attending the procession, and the petals falling in the light, the incense rising, and people on the flat rooftops, standing at the very edge, with their arms outstretched.

Jonathan, you know now what I remembered, but I didn't remember then, you see. It was confusion. It was as if something were trying to force me to see my existence as a continuum. But I didn't trust it. I must have been very close to Zurvan's teachings a thousand times over the years and never knew it, never remembering Zurvan. Why else did I want to avenge this girl? Why else did I despise the Rebbe for his lack of mercy on me? Why else was this man's evil fascinating me so much that I hadn't already killed him?

He broke in with his gentle, beguiling voice.

'And so we're here, at my home, Azriel,' he said.

He pulled me back fast.

'We are at my very door.' He made a dreamy, weary gesture towards the people on either side of us. 'Don't let them frighten you. I must invite you, please, to come in.'

I saw rows of lighted windows high above.

The doors of the car had been unlocked with a loud distinct click. Now someone meant to open the door to my right and his left. In a split second, I saw a pathway made for him, beneath an awning. Ropes hung from bronze stanchions held back the multitude. There were television cameras bearing down upon us. I saw men in uniforms restraining those who screamed and cheered.

'But can they see you?' Gregory asked now, confidentially, as if we shared a secret.

It was a break in an almost perfect chain of gestures for him. Out of generosity I was tempted to let it go. But I didn't.

'See for yourself whether or not they can see me, Gregory,' I answered. I reached down and gathered up the casket, and holding it firmly under my left arm, I took a grip of the door handle and stepped over him and out of the car before him onto the sidewalk in the blazing electric light.

I stood on the sidewalk. A great building rose before me. I held the casket of the bones tight to my chest. I could barely see the top of this building.

Everywhere I looked were shouting faces. Everywhere I looked, I looked at those who looked at me. It was a babble of people calling for Gregory, and others calling for blood for Esther, and I couldn't untangle the prayers.

Cameras and microphones descended; a woman shouted questions furiously at me and far too rapidly for me to understand. The crowd almost broke the ropes, but more uniformed men came to restore order. The people were both the young and the old.

The television lights gave off a powerful heat that hurt the skin of my face. I raised my hand to shield my eyes.

A thunderous and united cry rose as Gregory appeared now, with the helping hand of his driver, brushing his coat that was covered with dust from the casket, and he took his place at my side.

His lips came close to my ear.

'Indeed, they do see you,' he said.

The dimness hovered, cries in other tongues deafened me, and I shook away again the mantle of sadness and looked right into the blaring lights and screaming faces that were here.

'Gregory, Gregory, Gregory,' the people chanted. 'One Temple, One God, One Mind.'

First it overlapped, prayer atop prayer, as if it were meant to do so, coming at us in waves, but then the crowd brought their voices together:

'Gregory, Gregory, Gregory. One Temple, One God, One Mind.'

He lifted his hand and waved, turning from left to right and all around, nodding and smiling and waving to those who stood behind him, and to those far off, and he kissed his hand, the very hand I'd kissed, and threw this kiss and a thousand other such kisses to the people who shrieked and called his name in delight.

'Blood, blood, blood for Esther!' someone screamed.

'Yes, blood for her! Who killed her!'

The prayer came roaring over it, but others had taken it up, 'Blood for Esther,' stamping their feet in time with their words.

'Blood, blood, blood for Esther.'

Those with cameras and microphones broke through the ropes, pressing against us.

'Gregory, who killed her?'

'Gregory who is this with you?'

'Gregory, who is your friend?'

'Sir, are you a member of the Temple?'

They were talking to me!

'Sir, tell us who you are!'

'Sir, what is in the box you're carrying?'

'Gregory, tell us what the church will do?'

He turned and faced the cameras.

A trained squadron of dark-dressed men rushed to surround us and separate us from those questioning us, and en masse they pushed us gently up the lighted path, past the throng.

But Gregory spoke loudly:

'Esther was the lamb! The lamb was slain by our enemies. Esther was the lamb!'

The crowd went into a frenzy of approbation and applause.

Beside him, I stared right at the cameras, at the lights

beaming down, at the flash of thousands of small hand-held cameras snapping out still pictures.

He drew in his breath to speak, in full command, as any ruler might, standing before his own throne. Loudly, he intoned his words:

'The murder of Esther was only their warning; they have let us know that the time is come when any righteous person will be destroyed!'

Again, the crowd screamed and cheered, vows were declared, chants were taken up.

'Don't give them an excuse!' Gregory declared. 'No excuse to enter our churches or our homes. They come clothed in many disguises!'

The crowd pressed in on us in a dangerous surge.

Gregory's arm closed around me, caressingly.

I looked up. The building pierced the sky.

'Azriel, come inside,' he said, again speaking close to my ear.

There came the loud sound of shattering glass. An alarm bell clanged. The crowd had pushed in one of the lower windows of the tower. Attendants rushed to the spot. Whistles sounded. I could see garbed police on horseback in the street.

We were drawn in through the doors across a floor of shimmering marble. Others held back the crowd. But still others surrounded us, making it near impossible for us to do anything but go where they forced us to go.

I was madly exhilarated, alive in the midst of this. Astonished and invigorated. Something told me that my former masters had been men of stealth, wise, keeping their power to themselves.

Here we stood in the capital of the world: Gregory sparkled with the surety of his power, and I walked beside him, drunk on being alive, drunk on all the eyes turned to us.

At last a pair of bronze doors rose up before us, carved with angels, and when they parted we were thrust together inside a mirrored chamber, and Gregory gestured for all the others to remain outside.

The doors swept closed. It was an elevator. It began to

rise. I saw myself in the mirrors, shocked by my long and thick hair and the seeming ferocity of my expression, and I saw him, cold and commanding as ever, watching me, and watching himself. I appeared years younger than him, and just as human – but we might have been brothers, both of us swarthy, with sun-darkened skin.

His features were finer, eyebrows thinner and combed; I saw the prominent bones of my forehead and my jaw. But still, it was as if we were of the same tribe.

As the elevator moved higher and higher, I realized we were now completely alone, staring at one another, in a floating cabin of mirrored light.

But no sooner had I absorbed this little shock, this one of many, and no sooner had I righted myself and anchored my weight against the slight swaying of the elevator, than the doors were opened again upon a large sanctuary that appeared both splendid and private: a demilune entranceway of inlaid marble, doorways opening to left and right, and just before us a broad corridor leading to a distant chamber whose windows were wide open to the twinkling night.

We were higher than the mightiest ziggurat, castle, or forest. We were in the realm of the airy spirits.

'My humble abode,' Gregory murmured. He had to rip his eyes from me. But he recovered.

From the doorways came the sounds of voices, and padded feet. A woman cried somewhere in agony. Doors were shut. No one appeared.

'It's the mother crying, isn't it?' I said. 'The mother of Esther.'

Gregory's face went blank then grew sad. No, it was something more painful than sadness, something he had never revealed in the presence of the Rebbe when they spoke of the dead daughter. He hesitated, seemed on the verge of saying something and then merely nodded. The sadness consumed him, his face, his body, even his hand, which hung limp at his side.

He nodded.

'We should go to her, should we not?' I said.

'And why would we do that?' he asked patiently.

'Because she's crying. She's sad. Listen to the voices. Someone is being unkind to her –'

'No, only trying to give her medicine that she needs –'

'I want to tell her that Esther didn't suffer, that I was there, and Esther's spirit went up so light it was like air itself in the Pathway of Heaven. I want to tell her.'

He pondered this. The voices died down somewhat. I couldn't hear the woman crying anymore.

'Heed my advice,' he said, reaching out for me and taking a firm grip of my arm. 'Come into my parlor first and talk to me. Your words won't mean anything to her anyway.'

I didn't like this. But I knew we must talk, he and I.

'Still, later at your leisure,' I said, 'I want to see her and comfort her. I want to –'

No words. No human cunning, suddenly, nothing but the crashing realization that I was on my own. Why in the name of Heaven had I been allowed to return with the full strength of a man? Or strength even greater.

Gregory studied me.

In a thinly lighted anteroom, I saw two women clothed in white. A man's voice rose husky and angry behind a door.

'The casket,' said Gregory, pointing to the golden box in my arms. 'Don't let her see such a thing. It would alarm her. Come with me first.'

'Yes, it's a strange thing, this,' I said, looking at the casket, at the gold flaking from it.

Dimness. Grief. The light changed just a fraction.

Go away from me, all doubt, and worry, and fear of failure, I said in a whisper in a tongue that he could not possibly understand.

There came the familiar reek of boiling liquid, of a golden mist rising. You know why. But I didn't. I turned and shut my eyes, and then looked again down the hallway, to the far window open to the night sky.

'Look at that,' I said. I had only a vague point in mind, something to do with the raiment of Heaven being as beautiful as the marble that surrounded us, the archways above us, the pilasters flanking every door. 'The stars beyond, look,' I said again, 'the stars.'

All was quiet in the house. He watched me, studying me, listening to my every breath.

'Yes, the stars,' he said dreamily, with seeming respect.

His quick dark eyes broadened and there came his smile again, loving and tender.

'We'll talk to her later, I promise you,' he said. He grasped my arm firmly and pointed. 'But come now to my study, come now and let's talk together. It's time, is it not?'

'I wish I knew,' I said in a half murmur. 'She's still crying, isn't she?'

'She'll cry till she dies,' he said. His shoulders were heavy with sorrow. His whole soul ached with it. I let him lead me down the hall. I wanted to know things from him. I wanted to know everything.

I didn't respond.

Eighteen

We made our way down this corridor, Gregory leading boldly, letting his feet ring on the marble, and I coming behind him, dazzled by the peach-colored silk panels affixed to the walls. The floor itself was this same lovely nourishing color.

We passed numerous doors, and one of them to our right lay open. It was her room. She was in there.

I came to a halt and peered in, rudely, but the sight which struck me amazed me.

It was a lavish bedchamber, done wildly in crimson with festoons of red silk coming from its ceilings down over the pillars of the bed. The floor was again marble and this time snow white.

But this in itself was not as remarkable as the sight of a woman – the woman who had been crying – sitting on a low couch, her gown airy and shimmering and as red as the trappings of the room. She had jet-black hair, like the hair of Esther, like my hair for that matter – and the same immense eyes of Esther with near glistening whites to them. But her hair was stranded through and through with silver; it seemed almost decorated by greater age. It spilled down behind her back. Nurses in white surrounded her. One moved quickly to shut the door.

But she looked up, saw me. Her face was drawn and sallow and wet with tears. But she was not old. She'd been very young when she'd given birth to Esther. At once she sat up.

The door was shut, the lock turned. I heard her call out: 'Gregory!'

He walked on, reaching back for my hand, his own warm and smooth and leading me alongside him.

Others whispered behind other doors. There were wires in the walls that carried whispers. I couldn't hear the woman crying.

We entered the main room, a grand demilune of splendid detail with a lofty half dome of a ceiling. A row of floor-length windows, each cut into twelve different panes of glass, ran across the street side of it, which was flat, and behind us doors of the same frame punctuated the half circle at equal intervals.

It was more than magnificent.

But the view of the night caught me with all its timeless sweetness. Across a deep dark divide I saw towers, patterned with lights set in rows of incredible regularity, but then I came to realize that all of these buildings had these straight rows of windows, that this age was very mathematically precise.

My head was swimming. Information was pouring in on me.

I saw that the room faced not a dark river, as I had supposed, but a broad dark park. I could smell the trees. I looked down and was amazed to see how truly far we were above the earth, from the tiny crowd still clogging the little thoroughfare and the mounted police-men moving awkwardly like trapped cavalry amid a battle. A swarm of ants.

I turned around.

The doors behind us, in the curved wall were closed now. I couldn't even tell which door had been our door. I was distracted and obsessed suddenly with the brief glimpse of the weeping mother.

But I cleared this for the present.

In the very center of the half circle wall stood a hearth, monstrous, made of the usual white marble and cold and grand as an altar. Lions were carved into this hearth, and a shelf stood above it and above that a huge mirror which caught the reflection of the windows.

Indeed reflections bounced about all around me. The twelve-paned doors of the rear wall were mirrored, rather than glassed! What an illusion it was. We were drifting in this palace, and comforted by the city as if it had taken us in its arms.

A great heap of wood stood ready in the hearth, as if it were cruel winter, which it was not.

All the doors, both real and mirrored, were double doors with gracefully twisted handles of plated gold, and fancy curving frames for their narrow and shining panes of mirror or glass.

I turned around and around, absorbing everything, drawing out of each item every inference that I could, and no doubt drawing as always upon sources of knowledge inexplicable to me. I was startled by each new object. Then I knew what it was. Statues from China, a Grecian urn very familiar to me and comforting, and lavish glass vases of flowers – these things stood on pedestals.

Strewn about us were couches and chairs of peach and gold velvet, tables with lustrous tops, more vases of magnificent lilies and great golden daisies, or so they seemed to me, and beneath all was a sprawling square carpet, reaching almost from the windows over the park to the edge of the circle in the rear.

The carpet was sewn in magnificent detail with the tree of life, full of the birds of Heaven, and the fruit of Heaven, and figures walking beneath the tree limbs, figures in Asian dress.

So it was always; the world changed; the world became more complex; the world increased in invention and sometimes in ugliness, yet the forms of my time were always embedded in the surfaces around me. Every object in the room was connected in some way to the oldest aesthetic principles ever known to me.

I imagined suddenly that the lost tribes of Israel lived in the carpet, those sold when Nebuchadnezzar came down upon the northern kingdom, but that had been before Jerusalem had been taken. Images of battle, of fire.

Azriel, master thyself.

'Tell me,' I said, disguising my delight in all this, my weakness and hunger for it. 'What is the Temple of the Mind that its High Priest lives in this splendor? These are private rooms. Are you the thief and the charlatan, as your grandfather said?'

He didn't answer me, but he was most delighted. He walked about me, watching me, waiting eagerly for me to speak again.

'There lies a newspaper from the streets opened where you left it,' I said. 'Ah, there is Esther's face. Esther smiles for the historians. For the public. And beside the paper, what is this pitcher? Bitter coffee. Your taste is on the cup. I smell it. This is all private, your place of recollection. Yours is a rich God, Mind or no Mind.' I took the time to smile. 'And you a rich priest.'

'I'm not a priest,' he said.

Two men appeared suddenly, gawky youths in white stiff shirts and dark trousers. They entered out of the wall of doors, and Gregory was flustered.

He made some quick gestures to them that they must go away. The mirrored doors closed again.

We were alone. I felt my breath and my eyes moving in my skull, and I felt such desire for all things material and sensuous that I could have wept. If I had been alone I would have wept.

I regarded him suspiciously. The night, both real and in reflection, pulsed with twinkling lights. Indeed lights were as plentiful and vital in this time as water had been perhaps in earlier times. Even in this room the lamps were powerful, sculpted pieces of bronze work with heavily adorned glass shades the color of parchment. Light, light, light.

His excitement was palpable to me. He could scarce hold his tongue. He wanted to inundate me with questions, drink all the knowledge he could from me. I stood obdurate, as if I were really human and had every right as any man to be quiet and myself.

Air moved in the room, full of the smell of trees and horses and of the fumes rising from the engines; the engines filled the night with discord. If he were to shut the window, it would go away, this noise, but then so would the fragrance of green grass.

Finally he could contain himself no longer.

'Who called you?' he said. He was not unpleasant. Indeed, he seemed now to slip into a childlike candor but with too much ease for it not to be a style. 'Who brought you out of the bones?' he asked. 'Tell me, you have to. I am the Master now.'

'Don't take such a foolish tack,' I answered. 'It will be nothing for me to kill you. It would be too simple.' I felt no weakening in myself as I resisted him.

What if the world was my Master now? What if each and every human were my master? I saw a blazing fire suddenly, a fire not of the world, but of the gods.

The bones which I still held all this time were heavy in my arms. Did they want me to see them? I looked down at the old battered casket. It had soiled my garments. I didn't care.

'May I set down the bones?' I asked. 'Here, on your table, beside your newspaper and your pitcher of bitter coffee and your dead daughter's face, so pretty to look at, with no veil?'

He nodded, lips parted, straining to keep quiet, to think, and yet too exultant really to do either in any organized way.

I laid down the casket. I felt a ripple of sensation pass through me, just from the proximity of the bones, and the thought suddenly that they were mine own, and I was dead and a ghost, and that I was walking the earth again.

My god, don't let me be taken before I understand this!

He approached. I didn't wait for him. I boldly took off the frail cover of the casket, just as he had before. I laid down the cover on the big table, crushing the newspaper a little, and I stared at the bones.

They were as golden and brilliant as they had been the day I died. But when had that been?

'The day I died!' I whispered. 'Am I to find out everything now? Is that part of the plan?'

I thought again of Esther's mother, the woman in red silk. I could sense her presence under this roof. She had most definitely seen me and I tried to imagine how I looked to her. I wanted her to come in here, or to find some way to go to her.

'What are you saying?' He questioned me eagerly. 'The day you died, when was it? Tell me. Who made you a ghost? What plan do you speak of?'

'I don't know those answers,' I said. 'I wouldn't bother with you if I did. The Rebbe told you more than I knew when he translated those inscriptions.'

'Not bother with me!' he said. 'Not bother with me! Don't

you see that if there is a plan, a plan even greater than that which I have designed, you are part of it?'

It gave me pleasure to see his mounting excitement. It was invigorating, beyond doubt. His fine eyebrows rose a little, and I saw that the charm of his eyes was not merely their depth, but their length. I was a person of rounded features; the lines of his face came to beautiful trajectories and points.

'When did you first come? How could Esther have seen you?'

'If I was sent to save her I failed. But why did you call her the lamb? Why did you use those words? Who are these enemies you speak of?'

'You'll learn soon enough. We're all surrounded by enemies. All we have to do to rouse them is show a little power, resist the interjecting plans which they have laid with all the solemnity of a god, plans which are only the routine, the ritual, the tradition, the law, the normal, the regular, the sane ... You know what I mean, you understand me.'

I did understand him.

'Well, I have gone against them and they would come against me, only I'm too powerful for them, and I have dreams that dwarf their petty evil!'

'My, but you speak with a silken tongue,' I said, 'and you give so much in your words. Why to me?'

'To you? Because you're a spirit, a god, an angel sent to me. You witnessed her death because she was a lamb. Don't you see? You came when she died, as if a god to receive a sacrifice!'

'I hated her death,' I said. 'I slew the three men who killed her.'

This astonished him. 'You did that?'

'Yes, Billy Joel, Hayden, and Doby Eval. I killed them. The papers know. The news talks of her blood on their weapons and their blood mingled with it now. I did that! Because I had failed to stop them from their evil plan. What sacrifice do you speak of? Why call her the lamb? Where was the altar and if you think I'm a god, you're a fool! I hate God and all gods. I hate them.'

272

He was enthralled. He drew close to me, and then stepped back, and then walked around, too excited to be still.

If he was guilty of killing his daughter, he gave no clue. He looked at me with pure delight in our exchange.

Something struck me suddenly. The skin of his face had been moved! A surgeon had tightened it over all his bones. I laughed at the ingenuity of it and the implications, that things in this age could be done so simply. And with a sudden sinking terror, I thought, What if I have been brought to this age for a reason that has to do with his horrors and the world's wonders, and this *is* the chance to stay whole and alive from now on?

I winced, and he started to question me again. I put my hands up for him to be quiet.

I backed away from my own thought. I turned and stared at the gleaming bones, and I bent down and laid my own fingers, my material fingers, upon my own bones.

At once I felt as if someone were touching me as I touched them. I felt someone's touch on my own legs. I felt my own hands on my own face as I touched the skull. I sank my thumbs into the empty sockets defiantly, where my eyes had been, my eyes ... something boiling, something too ghastly to think of – I uttered a small sound that made me ashamed.

The room quivered, brightened, then contracted as though it were receding. No, stay here. Stay in this room. Stay here with him! But I was imagining things, as humans say. My body had not weakened at all. I was standing tall.

I opened my eyes slowly and closed them and looked down at the golden bones. Iron fastened them to the rotted cloth beneath them, iron fastened them to the old wood of the casket, but it was the same casket, permeated with all the oils that would make it last unto the end of time, like the bones. An image of Zurvan flashed through me, and with it came a flood of words ... to love, to learn, to know, to love ...

Once again came the huge city walls of blue-glazed bricks, the golden lions and the cries of voices, and one of them pointing his finger and screaming at me in the old Hebrew – the prophet – and the chants rose and fell.

Something had happened! I had done something, something unspeakable to be made this ghost, this old ghost who had served Masters beyond recollection.

But if I dwelt on this, I might vanish. Or I might not.

I stood very still, but no more memories came. I withdrew my hands. I stood looking down at the bones.

Gregory brought me out of it.

He moved closer and he put his hands on me. He wanted so much to do this. How his pulse raced. It felt wondrously erotic, these fleshly hands touching my newly formed arms. If I was still gaining in strength, I didn't feel it anymore.

I felt the world. Safe inside it for now.

His fingers clenched the sleeves of this coat. He was staring at it, the precision of it, the dazzle of the buttons, the fine stitches. And all of this I'd drawn to me in haste with the old commands that rolled off my tongue like nothing. I could have made myself a woman suddenly to frighten him. But I didn't want to do that. I was too happy to be Azriel, and Azriel was too afraid.

Yet again . . . what was the limit of this masterless power? I contrived a joke, an evil joke. I smiled, and then whispering all the words I knew, fashioning the most mellifluous incantations I could, I changed myself into Esther.

The image of Esther. I felt her small body, and peered through her big eyes and smiled, and even felt the tightness of her garments on that last day, the flash of the painted animal coat in my eye.

Thank God, I didn't have to see this myself! I felt sorry for him.

'Stop it!' he roared. He fell back onto the floor, scrambling away from me, and then leaning back on his elbows.

I returned to my own shape. I had done this and he had no control of it! I had control of it. I felt proud and wicked suddenly.

'Why did you call her the lamb? Why did the Rebbe say you killed her?'

'Azriel,' he said. 'Listen carefully to what I say.' He climbed to his feet as effortlessly as a dancer. He walked

274

towards me. 'Whatever happens after, whatever happens, remember this. The world is ours. *The world*, Azriel.'

I was startled.

'The world, Gregory?' I asked. I tried to sound hard and clever. 'What do you mean, the world?'

'I mean all of it, I mean the world as Alexander meant the world when he went out to conquer it.' He appealed to me, patiently. 'What do you know, Spirit Friend? Do you know the names Bonaparte or Peter the Great or Alexander? Do you know the name Akhenaton? Constantine? What are the names you know?'

'All of those and more, Gregory,' I answered. 'Those were emperors, conquerors. Add to them Tamerlane and Scander-beg, and after him Hitler, Hitler, who slew our people by the millions.'

'Our people,' he said with a smile. 'Yes, we are of the same people, aren't we? I knew we were. I knew it.'

'What do you mean, you knew it? The Rebbe told you. He read the scroll. What are these conquerors to you? Who rules in this electric paradise called New York? You are a churchman, so says the Rebbe. You are a merchant. You have billions in every currency recognized on earth. You think Scanderbeg in his castle in the Balkans ever had the wealth you have here? You think Peter the Great ever brought back to Russia with him the luxuries you possess? They didn't have your power! They couldn't. Their world wasn't an electrical web of voices and lights.'

He laughed with delight, his eyes sparkling, and beautiful.

'Ah, that's just it,' he said. 'And now in this world so filled with wonders, no one has their power! No one has the force of Alexander when he brought the philosophy of the Greeks to Asia. No one dares to kill as Peter the Great killed, chopping off the heads of his bad soldiers until the blood covered his arms.'

'Your times are not the worst of times,' I said. 'You have leaders; you have talk; you have the rich being kind to the poor; you have men the world wide who fear evil and want goodness.'

'We have madness,' he said. 'Look again. Madness!'

'What does this mean to you? Is this the mission of your church to gain control of the whole world? Is that what drives you, as the old man asked? You want the power to chop off the heads of men? You want that?'

'I want to change everything,' he said. 'Look back over those conquerors. Look back over their accomplishments. Use the finest reach of your spirit mind.'

'I will. Go on.'

'Who really changed the world forever? Who changed it more than any single man?'

I didn't answer.

'Alexander,' he said. 'Alexander the Great did it! He dared to kill empires that blocked his path. He dared to force Asian to marry Greek. He dared to break the Gordian knot with a sword.'

I considered. I thought. I saw the Greek cities along the Asian coast, long after Alexander had died in Babylon; I saw the world as if I were standing back from it. I saw it in patches of light and dark.

'Alexander changed your world,' I said. 'The world of the West. I see what you see. Alexander is the cornerstone of the rise of the West. But the West isn't the world, Gregory.'

'Oh, yes, it is,' he answered. 'Because the West that Alexander built has changed Asia. No part of the globe has not been changed by the West that Alexander built. And no mind today stands ready to change the world as he would, and I . . . as I would.'

He drew in close to me, then suddenly with a darting motion, pushed me with both hands. I didn't move. It was like a child pushing a man. He was pleased and sobered. He took a step back.

I pushed him with one hand. I pushed him into a stumble and then a fall, from which he rose slowly, unshaken, refusing to be shaken.

He didn't become angry. He was knocked back a step, but he planted his feet squarely and he waited.

'Why are you testing me?' he asked. 'I didn't say I was a god or an angel. But you've been sent to me, don't you see? You've been sent on the eve of the transformation of the world, you are sent as a sign! As was King Cyrus of old, that the people would go home to Jerusalem!'

Cyrus, the Persian. My whole frame ached; my mind ached. I struggled to be still.

'Don't speak of that!' I whispered. My mind went blank with rage. You can well imagine. I was beside myself. 'Speak of Alexander if you will. But don't speak of Cyrus. You know nothing of those times!'

'Do you?'

'I want to know why I am here now,' I went on, holding firm. 'I don't accept your fervent prophecies and proclamations. Did you kill Esther? Did you send those men to kill her?'

Gregory seemed torn. He reflected. I could read nothing from him. 'I didn't want for her to die,' he said. 'I loved her. The greater good called for her death.'

Now this was a lie, a brittle, technical lie.

'What would you do if I told you, yes, I did kill Esther?' he said. 'For the world, I killed her, for the new world that will rise from the ashes of the dying world, the world that is killing itself with small men and small dreams and small empires?'

'I swore I'd avenge her death,' I said. 'And now I know you're guilty. I'll kill you. But not now. When I want to.'

He laughed. 'You kill me? You think you can?'

'Of course,' I said. 'Remember what the Rebbe told you. I have killed those who have called me.'

'But I didn't call you, don't you see, it was the plan, it was the world! It was the design! You were sent to me because I need you, and can use you, and you will do what I will that you do.'

It was the world. Those were the very words I'd said to myself in desperate hope. But was it to be Gregory's world?

'Surely you must help me,' he said. 'I don't need to be your Master. I need you! I need you to witness and understand. Oh, but this is too remarkable that you came alive to see Esther murdered, and to kill those three, you did say that to me, that you killed those three.'

'You loved Esther, didn't you?' I asked.

'Oh, yes, very much,' he said. 'But Esther had no vision.

277

Neither does Rachel. That's why you've come. That's why you were given to our people, to my grandfather's father, don't you see? You were meant to appear before me in all your glory. You are the witness. You are "He who will understand everything."'

I was puzzled by his words. Plan, scheme, design. 'But what is it I am to witness?' I asked. 'You have your church. And what does Esther have to do with it?'

He thought a long moment, and then he said with innocent candor:

'Of course, you were meant for me. No wonder you struck down others.' He laughed. 'Azriel, you're worthy of me, don't you see? This is what's so supremely beautiful, you're worthy of me, of my time, my brilliance, my effort. We are on a par. You are a prince of ghosts, I suspect. I know it.'

He reached to touch my hair.

'I'm not so sure.'

'Hmmm, a prince, I'm sure, and you've been sent to me. All those old men; they kept you, passed you down through the generations. It was for me.'

He seemed almost moved to tears by his own sentiment. His face was soft and radiant and confident.

'You have the pride and decisiveness of a king, Gregory.'

'Of course I do. What does the Master usually say to you, Spirit?' he asked. 'What do you remember?'

'Nothing,' I said adamantly. A lie of my own. 'I wouldn't be with you if I could,' I said. 'I stay with you now because I'm trying to remember and to know. I should kill you now. That would probably be like your precious Alexander when he cut the Gordian knot.'

'No, that won't happen,' he said calmly. 'That cannot possibly be meant. If God wanted for me to die, anyone could do it. You don't realize the scale of my dreams. Alexander would have understood.'

'I am not yours,' I said. 'I know that much. Yes, I want to know the scale of your dreams, yes. I don't want to kill you without understanding why you had Esther murdered. But I am not yours. Not meant for you. Not necessarily meant . . . for anything.'

278

Somewhere the mother was crying again. That I'm sure I could hear. I turned my head.

'Do as I say,' he said, touching me again, clamping his hand on my arm.

I pulled away. I hurt him a little.

My strength had gone past exhilaration. I was restless. I wanted to walk, to touch things. I wanted to touch these couches of velvet, and run my hand on the marble. I wanted simply to look at my hands. I was holding utterly fast. I wasn't sure that I could dissolve now if I wanted to.

It was a strange feeling, to be so strong, and not to know if the old tricks would work. But then I had only lately made myself Esther. I was tempted . . .

. . . But no, this was not the time.

I glare at the bones. I reached down and covered up the bones with the fragile lid. There lay the Sumerian letters for me to read.

'Why did you do that?' he demanded.

'I don't like the sight of the bones,' I said.

'Why?'

'Because they're mine.' I looked at him. 'Somebody killed me. Someone did it against my will. I don't like you either, necessarily. Why should I believe you that I am something worthy of you? What is your scheme? Where is your Alexandrian sword?'

I was sweating. My heart was pounding. (I didn't really have a heart but it felt like it was pounding.) I peeled off this coat, admiring my own handiwork as I did it. I could see how different it was from his clothing, though modeled completely upon it.

Perhaps he noticed the difference too.

'Who sewed these clothes for you, Azriel?' he ordered. 'Were they done by invisible angels on invisible looms?' He laughed as if this was the most preposterous idea.

'You'd better think of clever things to say. I may not kill you, but I very well may leave you.'

'You can't! You know you can't!'

I turned my back on him. Let me see what else I could do. I looked at the walls, the ceiling, the peach silk of the drapes, and the great tree of life blazing in the carpet. I drew near the window and the air moved my hair. The coolness came down on my skin and on my hair.

Slowly, I closed my eyes, though I could still take small steps, for I knew where everything was, and I clothed myself, envisioning a robe of red silk, with a sash of silk, and jeweled slippers. I took *her* shade of red, wrapped myself in it, and brought the gold to me for the sleeves and for the hem and for the slippers. I was now clothed in her violent red. Perhaps the mothers here mourned in red.

It was conceivable.

I heard him sigh. I heard his shock. I saw myself reflected in the mirrored panes of the ornate doors, a tall, black-haired youth in a long, red Chaldean robe. No beard, no, no hair on the face. I liked the smooth face. But this would not do, these garments, too antique; I needed freedom and power.

I turned around.

Again, I closed my eyes. I imagined a coat of his cut in this brilliant red but of the finest wool, tailored as his coat was tailored, with buttons of simple and perfect gold, almost pure gold. I imagined the trousers looser and smooth, as a Persian would want them to be, and the slippers I stripped of their embroidery.

Beneath the coat, I drew to myself, against my skin, a shirt like his, only of far whiter silk even than his, its buttons made of gold as well, and round my neck on my chest, beneath the wings of this coat, against the shirt, I brought two full strands of beads which I took from all the opaque stones of the world I loved – jasper and lapis lazuli, beryl, garnet, jade, and ivory. I put amber with this, on these two strings, until I felt the weight against my chest, and then I raised my hand and touched the beads, and when I let my shoulders fall easy, the coat almost closed over this secret bit of vanity, these ancient beads. My shoes I made identical to his shoes, only of the softest cloth, and lined with silk.

He was shocked by these simple magic acts. I had found them easier than ever.

'A silken man,' he said. He said it in Yiddish. '*Zadener yinder mantchik.*'

'Shall I cap it off?' I asked. 'By walking out of here?'

He drew himself up. His voice was shaky now. If it was not humility, it was some form of respect.

'There's time for you to show me every trick you know, but for now, you must listen to me.'

'More interested in your schemes than seeing me vanish?' I asked.

'Alexander would be more interested in his own schemes, wouldn't he? Everything is ready. Everything in place, and now you come, the right hand of God.'

'Don't be so hasty. What God!'

'Ah, so you despise your origins and all the evil you've done, do you?'

'I do.'

'Well, then, you should welcome the world that I place in your hands. Oh, I see more by the moment. You are here to teach us after the Last Days, I see it.'

'What Last Days! When the hell are mortal men going to shut up about the Last Days! Do you know how many centuries ago men yammered on about the Last Days?'

'Ah, but I know the very dates of the Last Days,' he said calmly. 'I've chosen them. I see no reason to delay in telling you the whole scheme. I see no reason not to make it all known. You recoil from me, deride me, but you'll learn. You are a learning spirit, aren't you?'

A learning spirit.

'Yes,' I said. I liked this concept.

I listened to the sound of steps in the passage. I thought I heard the mother's voice, low and urgent, and I didn't like it that she was still crying.

Coldly, I observed that his proximity to me did not matter. He could be one foot away or ten. I was just as strong. I was quite independent of him, which was perfect. As he watched, I covered my fingers with gold rings, and those fine stones I liked for rings, emeralds, diamonds, Eye of the Sea, or pearl, and ruby.

The mirrors were full of us. I would have bound my hair with a leather thong, and should have done it, but I didn't care just now, and again, I felt my face, to be sure it was smooth as was his face, because for all my love of a long beard, I liked this naked skin better.

He walked around me. He took his steps silently and made a circle as if he could close me in this way, with my power. But he knew nothing of magic, circles, pentagrams.

I asked my memory: Had ever I seen a Master more excited than he was, more proud, and more hot for glory? I saw crowds of faces. I heard songs. I saw ecstasy; but those had been masses and masses, and it had been a lie. And my god had been weeping. That was no answer.

The answer was this: I couldn't kill him, not yet. I couldn't. I wanted to know what he had to teach. But I had to be certain of the limits of his power. What if he were to command me now as the Rebbe had done?

I moved away from him.

'You fear me suddenly?' he asked. 'Why.'

'I don't fear you. I've never served a King, not as a spirit on any account. I've seen them. I saw Alexander when he was dying . . .'

'You saw this?'

'I was there in Babylon and I walked past him with his men, guised as one of them. He lifted his left hand again and again. His eyes were completely ready for death. I don't think he had any more great dreams in his head. Maybe that's why he died. But you are full of dreams. And you do burn bright like Alexander, that is true, and I fight you yet I . . . I think I *could* love you.'

I sat down and remained still on a hassock of velvet, and I thought.

I sat there, elbows on my knees. He took his stand in front of me, allowing plenty of room, perhaps ten paces, and then he folded his arms. Take charge.

'You already love me,' he said. 'Almost everyone who sees me loves me. Even my grandfather loves me.'

'You think so?' I said. 'You know he knew I was there when he sold you the bones, he saw me.'

This stunned him into utter silence. He shook his head, then went to speak, then was silent again.

'I was in the room and visible, and when he saw me with

his mean little blue eyes, that was when he agreed to tell you what you wanted to know of the Servant of the Bones and to sell me to you.'

The full hurt of it hit him. The full hurt. I thought he would weep. He turned and walked this way and that. 'He saw you . . .' he whispered. 'He knew the spirit could be brought forth from the bones and he gave the bones to me.'

'He knew the spirit was there in his room, and he sold you the bones in the hope that I would go with them. Yes, he did that to you. I know, it's pain, unendurable pain to realize that such a trick could be done. For a mortal man to hurt a mortal man, that's one thing. But for a zaddik to see a demon and know that demon can destroy you, and to pass on that demon to you –'

'All right, you've made your point!' he said bitterly. 'So he despises me, so he did as soon as I questioned him. By twelve I was hurling my questions at him, and by thirteen gone from his house, and dead and buried in his Court.' He shivered all over. 'He saw you and he passed the bones to me. He saw you!'

'That's right,' I said.

He grew calm with amazing speed. His face took on renewed confidence and he pondered, easily showing aside hate and hurt, as I knew that I had to do.

'Will you give me some simple facts?' he asked. His voice went lower. He was radiant with his pleasure. 'When did you first see me or anyone connected with me? Tell me.'

'I told you. I came alive with Billy Joel Eval, and Hayden and Doby Eval on their way to kill the rich girl. They stuck their picks in her before I knew it. I went after them. I killed them. She saw me as she died, she said my name. Her soul went right up into the light, as I told you. Next I saw you was in the room of the Rebbe, no, as you approached, as you came towards it out of your car, with your guards all around you. I followed you into the room. The next night I did the same. And here we are. The rest I've explained. I became visible to the old Rebbe. I became flesh as I am now, and he struck his bargain.'

283

'You exchanged words with him?' he asked, looking away as if this hurt was something he couldn't quite fight.

'He cursed me, he said he would have no traffic with demons. He wouldn't help me. He wouldn't have mercy on me or answer my questions. He wouldn't recognize me!'

I left out the part that the old man had made me disappear the first time, and that on the second occasion I had left on my own.

His face truly actually changed for the first time.

That is, his next expression seemed a great leap from where he'd been in his feelings and intentions. Something was stripped away from him. It was not the humor, it was not the jubilation, it was not the strength. It certainly wasn't the courage. But something was uncovered in him that was ruthless, and it made me think of my own fingers when they had tightened around the wooden handle of the pick and when I had shoved it into the soft swishy stomach of Billy Joel, right beneath his ribs.

He turned and walked a few steps away from me, and again I felt nothing. I watched; I felt my blood run through my veins. I felt the flesh of my face tighten as I myself smiled a tiny secret smile that aided my thoughts.

All of this is illusion, Jonathan, but the details meant it was very good illusion! As good as now, as I sit before you. Now, it takes strength, great strength, to do it, as you know. And though by the time I came to you, Jonathan, I was used to that strength; I was not so used to it then.

Yes, I'm independent of him, I thought with a great surge of courage, but what about the bones? How does it all figure? Could it be true, that I had been destined for him? In a moment Gregory would realize that the zaddik's seeing me and passing me on did not really contradict Gregory's own theory that I was intended for him.

'Right,' he said suddenly, answering my thought. 'He was merely the instrument. He had no idea. No idea at all that it was for me that he kept the bones. And Esther's words, that's what made the link. Esther gave me the link as she died; she sent me to him to get the bones, and to get you from him, you see. You are destined for me, and worthy of me.'

He paced and stroked the flesh beneath his lower lip with his finger. 'Esther's death was inevitable, necessary. I didn't realize it myself. She was the lamb. And she brought you to me. It is I who must make plain to you your full destiny.'

'You know, maybe you do have something,' I said, 'with this talk of my being worthy of you. I mean, perhaps you are worthy of *me*. You are so surprising. I wonder.'

I paused, then went on:

'Those masters, maybe they weren't worthy of me.'

'They couldn't have been,' he said with chilling smoothness. 'But I am. And now you're beginning to understand, and you're helping me to understand. I am the Master, but only in so far as I'm your destination, I'm your . . . your. . . .'

'Responsibility?' I said.

'Ah, yes, perhaps that's exactly the word.'

'That's why I don't kill you now, even though you sanctify the murder of that poor girl with some fancy babbling?'

'It's facts. She brought you to me, through my grandfather. She sent me to you, and you to me! She did it! That means the plan will work, the plan will be realized. She was a martyr, a sacrifice, and an oracle.'

'God guides in all this?' I asked derisively.

'I will guide things as I think God wants me to,' he answered. 'Who can do better?'

'You *would* seduce me to love you, wouldn't you? You are so used to love, love from people who open your doors and pour your drink and drive your car . . .'

'I have to have it,' he whispered. 'I have to have the love and recognition of millions. I love it. I love it when the camera shines on me. I love when I see my grand scheme ever expanding.'

'Well, maybe you won't get it from me for very long. Before I ever saw Esther die, I was damned tired of being a ghost! I'm tired of serving masters. I don't see any reason for me to do what it says on the casket!'

Anger again. Heat. But it was no more than might come from the body of a man.

I stared at the casket. I ran back my own words through my head. Had I said such a bold thing? Yes, I had, and it had

285

been true, and it had been no curse or supplication to anyone.

Silence. If he said anything I didn't hear him. I heard something, but it was a cry of pain, or worse. What's worse than pain? Panic? I heard a cry that was right between the ultimate agony one can feel and the madness which is about to obliterate all sense of it. I heard a fine scream, you might say, right there between the light and the dark, like a vein of ore on a horizon.

'You saw your own murder?' He was talking to me. 'Azriel, perhaps now you will come to see the reason for it.'

I could hear the fire beneath the cauldron. I could smell the potions thrown into the boiling gold!

I couldn't answer. I knew that I had, but to speak it, to think on it, was to realize and remember too much. I couldn't. I had tried before. I had memory upon memory of trying to remember and not being able to remember at all.

'Listen, you miserable creature,' I said to him in a fury. 'I've been here forever. I sleep. I dream. I wake. I don't remember. Maybe I was murdered. Maybe I was never born. But I am forever and I'm tired. I'm sick to death of this half death! I'm sick of all things that stop short of the full measure!'

I was flushed. My eyes were wet. The clothes felt rich and embracing, and it was good to fold my arms, to clutch at my shoulders with my crossed hands, and to look up suddenly and see the faintest shadow of the tangle of my own hair, to be alive, even flooded with this pain.

'Oh, Esther. Who were you, my darling?' I asked aloud. 'What did you want of me?'

He was enrapt and silent.

'You ask the wrong person,' he said, 'and you know you do. She doesn't want vengeance. What can I do to convince you, you were destined for me?'

'Tell me what you want of me. I am to witness something? What? Another murder?'

'Yes, let's proceed. You have to come with me into my secret office. You have to see the maps for yourself. All the plans.'

'And I'll forget about her death, forget about avenging her?'

'No, you'll see why she died. For great empires somebody must die.'

This sent a rivet of pain through my chest. I bent forward.

'What is it?' he asked. 'What good would it do to avenge the death of one girl? If you're an avenging angel, why don't you walk out there in the streets? There are deaths happening now. You can avenge them. Come out of the pages of a comic book! Kill bad guys. Go ahead. Do it till you're tired of it, the way you're tired of being a ghost. Go on.'

'Oh, you are one fearless man.'

'And you're one tenacious spirit,' he said.

We stood glaring at one another.

He spoke first:

'Yes, you are strong, but you're also stupid.'

'Say this to me again?'

'Stupid. You know and you don't know. And you know I'm right. You gather your knowledge from the air, the way you do the matter that creates your clothing, even your flesh perhaps, and the knowledge rains on you too fast. You are confused. Is that the better word? I can hear it in your questions and your answers. You long for the clarity you feel when you talk to me. But you're afraid that you need me. Gregory is necessary for you. You wouldn't kill me or do what I don't want.'

He drew in closer, eyes growing wide.

'Know this thing first before you learn any more,' he said. 'I have everything in the world a man could want. I am rich. I have money beyond counting. You were right. I have money the Pharaohs never had, nor the Emperors of Rome, or even the most powerful wizard who ever bombarded you with his Sumerian poetry! The Temple of the Mind of God I invented, whole and entire and worldwide. I have millions of followers. Do you know what the word means? Millions? What does this mean? It means this, Spirit. What I want is what I want! Not some fancy, or longing, or need! It's what I want, a man who has everything.'

He looked me up and down.

'Are you worthy of *me*?' he demanded. 'Are you? Are you part of what I want and what I'll have? Or should I destroy you? You don't think I can. Let me try. Others have gotten rid of you. I could get rid of you. What are you to me when I want the world, the whole world! You're nothing!'

'I will not serve you,' I said. 'I won't even stay here with you.'

He had been all too right. I was beginning to love him and there was something deeply horrible in him, something fiercely destructive which I'd never encountered in any human.

I turned my back on him. I didn't have to understand the loathing I felt or the rage. He was abhorrent to me and that was enough. I had no reason now, only pain, only anger.

I went to the casket, opened the lid, and looked down at the grinning skull of gold that had been me and still had me somehow, like a flask has its liquid. I took the casket up into my arms.

He came after me, but before he could stop me I carried the casket and its loose cover to the marble hearth. I shoved it noisily on the pyre of wood, and watched the sticks tumble as the heap shifted to receive it. The lid fell to one side.

He stood right beside me, studying me, and then looking down at it. We were looking to the side at each other, each of us, to the side of the hearth.

'You wouldn't dare to burn it,' he said.

'I would if I had a bit of flame,' I said. 'I would bring flame, only if I bring flame I may hurt that woman, and those others who don't deserve it –'

'Never mind, my bumbling one.'

My heart pounded. Candles. There were no burning candles in this room.

There came a snap. I saw the light in my eye. He held a tiny burning stick, a match.

'Here, take it,' he said. 'If you're so sure.'

I took the stick from him. I cradled the flame in my fingers. 'Oh, this is so pretty,' I said, 'and so warm. Oh, I feel it . . .'

'It's going to go out if you don't hurry. Light the fire. Light the crumpled paper there. The fire's built up. The boys do it. It's made to roar up the chimney. Go ahead. Burn the bones. Do it.'

'You know, Gregory,' I said, 'I can't stop myself from doing it.' I bent down and touched the dying flame to the edge of the paper, and at once the paper was laced with flame and rising and collapsing. Little burning bits flew up the chimney. The thin wood caught with a loud crackling sound and the blast of heat came at me. The flames curled up around the casket. They blackened the gold, oh, God! What a sight, the cloth inside caught fire. The lid began to curl.

I couldn't see my own bones for the flames!

'No!' He screamed. 'No.' He reached over, chest heaving, and dragged the casket and the lid out onto the floor, dragging some of the fire with them, but this was only paper fire, and he stamped it out angrily. His fingers were burnt.

He stood astride the casket and he licked at his fingers. The skeleton had spilt out, into a weak and gangling figure. The bones lay unburnt, smoking, glowing. The lid was charred.

He dropped to his knees, and drawing a white napkin from his pocket, he beat out all tiny bits of smoldering fire. He was muttering in his annoyance and rage. The lid was blackened but the Sumerian I could still read.

My bones lay amid ashes.

'Damn you,' he said.

I had never seen him really angry at all, and he was more angry now than most angry people I'd ever seen. He was raging inside, worse than the Rebbe had raged. He glared at me. He glanced down at the casket to make sure it wasn't burning. It wasn't. It was only very slightly scorched.

'The smell is bitumen,' I said.

'I know what it is,' he said. 'And I know where it comes from, and I know how it was used.' His voice trembled. 'So you've proved yourself. You don't care if the bones are burned.'

He climbed to his feet. His brushed off his pants. Ashes fell

289

to the floor. The floor was filthy with ashes. The fire in the fireplace burned on, consuming itself, purposeless, wasted.

'Let me throw them in the fire,' I said. I reached for the skull, and picked up the gangling dead thing.

'Enough, Azriel. You do me wrong! Don't be so quick! Don't do it!'

I stopped. That was all it took, and I too was afraid, or the moment had passed. Five minutes after the battle, can you still slice a man in half with a sword? The wind blows. You stand there. He is lying among the dead, but not dead, and he opens his eyes, and murmurs to you thinking you're his friend. Can you kill him?

'Oh, but if we do it then we will both know,' I said. 'And I would like to know. Yes, I'm afraid, but I want to know. You know what I suspect?'

'Yes. That this time it doesn't matter about the bones!'

I didn't respond.

'Not even,' he said, 'if they are crushed to powder with a mortar and pestle.'

I didn't reply.

'The bones have completed their journey, my friend,' he said. 'The bones have come down to me! This is my time, and your time. This is what is meant. If we burnt the bones, and you were still here, solid, and beautiful and strong – impertinent and sarcastic, yes, but still here as you are now, able to breathe and see and wind yourself with shrouds of velvet – would that deliver you into my hands? Would you acknowledge the destiny?'

We glared at one another. I didn't want to take the chance. I didn't even want to think of the whirlwind of the restless dead. The words came back to me, the words engraved on the casket. I shivered, in terror of being formless, impotent, wandering, knocking against spirits I knew were everywhere. I did nothing.

He went down on his knees, and he gathered up the casket and the lid, then rose, one knee at a time, walked over to the table, gently laid down the casket, put the burnt shriveled lid on top of it, carefully, and then he sat down on the floor, leaning against his table, legs sprawled, but looking remarkably formal still in his seamed and buttoned clothes.

He looked up. I saw his teeth flash, and bite. I think he bit down on his lip to his own blood.

He stood up and ran at me.

He came so fast, it was like a dancer leaping to catch another, and though he stumbled, he caught me with both his hands, around my neck, and I felt his thumbs press against me, and I hated it and ripped his arms away. He smacked my face hard this way and that and drove his knee into my abdomen. He knew how to fight. With all his polish and money, he knew the dancing way to fight, like the Orientals.

I backed away from these blows, barely hurt, only amazed at his grace, and how he reared back now and kicked me full in the face sending me many paces back.

Then came his worst blow, elbow rising, hand straight, the arm swinging around to knock me backwards.

I caught his arm, and twisted it so that he went down on his knees with a snarl of rage. I pushed him flat to the carpet and held him pinned with my foot.

'You're no match for me in that realm,' I said. I stepped back and offered him my hand.

He climbed to his feet. His eyes never moved from me. Not for one second had he really forgotten himself. I mean, even in these failed attempts he held a dignity and lust for the struggle and for winning it, too.

'All right,' he said. 'You've proven yourself. You aren't a man, you're better than a man, stronger. Your soul's as complex as my soul. You want to do right, you have some fixed and foolish notion of right.'

'Everybody has a fixed and foolish notion of right,' I answered softly. I was humbled. And I did at that moment feel doubt, doubt of anything except that I was enjoying this, and the enjoyment seemed a sin. It seemed a sin that I should breathe. But why, what had I done? I determined not to look anymore into memory. I pushed the images away, the same ones I've described to you, Samuel's face, the boiling cauldron, all of it. I just said, Be done with it, Azriel!

I stood in the room vowing from then on to solve this mystery there and then with no looking back.

'You're flattered that I said you had a soul, aren't you?' he asked. 'Or is it merely that you're relieved that I recognize such a thing? That I don't consider you a demon like my grandfather did. That's what he did, right? He banished you from his sight, as if you had no soul.'

I was speechless with wondering, and with longing. To have a soul, to be good, to mount the Stairs to Heaven. *The purpose of life is to love and better know the beauty and intricacy of all things.*

He sat down on the velvet hassock. He was out of breath. I had been slow to realize this. I wasn't out of breath at all.

I was hot all over again, with a thin sweat, but I was not soiled yet. And of course some of what I had been saying to him was bluff and lies.

I didn't want to go into darkness or nothingness. I couldn't even bear the thought of it. A soul, to think I might truly have a soul, a soul that could be saved . . .

But I wasn't serving him! This plan, I had to know what it was; the world, how did he mean to get it when armies fought each other all over it? Did he mean the spiritual world?

There were voices in the hall. I could pick out the mother's voice easily, but he ignored it, just as if this were nothing. He only looked at me, and marveled at me, and pondered what I had said.

He was radiant in his curiosity and in what he had allowed to happen here without fear.

'You see how it lures me,' I said. 'The marble, the carpet, the breeze through the windows. Being alive, the great lure.'

'Yes, and there's me to know and love, too, and I lure you.'

'Yes, you do.' I said. 'And something tells me that life has lured me in the past, lured me to serve evil men and men I can't recall. I am lured each time by life itself and flesh itself and when there comes a moment and the door opens to Heaven, and I cannot go through. I'm not allowed to go through. My Masters may go through. Their beautiful

292

daughters may go through. Esther may go through. But I don't go through.'

He drew in his breath. 'You've seen the Door to Heaven?' he asked calmly.

'As surely as you've seen a ghost appear to you,' I said.

'So have I,' he said. 'I've seen the Door to Heaven. And I've seen Heaven here on earth. Stay with me, stay with me, and I swear to you when the door opens, I'll take you with me. You'll be deserving of it.'

The voices came loudly from the hall. But I looked at him, trying to answer what he said. He seemed as resolute, as without conflict, as determined and courageous as he had been before our fight.

The voices were too loud to be ignored. The woman was angry. Others talked to her as if she were a fool. It was all far away. Beyond the windows lay the black night with the lights of New York so bright that the sky itself was reddened like the dawn coming when there was no dawn. The breeze sang.

I looked down at the box. I could have wept. He had me and the world had me. At least for now, for as long as I would allow it.

He drew close to me. And I turned, letting him come close, and between us there was a tenderness and a sudden quiet. I looked into his eyes, and I saw the round black circle within his eyes, and I wondered if he saw in my eyes only blackness.

'You want the body you have now,' he said. 'You want the body and the power. You were meant to have it. You were meant to be mine, but as of this moment and forever, I respect you. You're no servant to me. You are Azriel.'

He clasped my arm. He raised his hand and clasped the side of my face. I felt his kiss, hot and sweet on my skin. I turned and locked my mouth on his for one instant, and then let him go and his face blazed with love for me. Did I feel the same heat for him?

There was a loud noise from beyond the doors.

He made a gesture to me, as if to say, be patient, and then I suppose he would have gone to the door, but it opened, and the woman appeared there, the mother with the black-and-silver hair who before had been wrapped in red silk.

She was sick, but she had groomed and clothed herself in a proper stiff way, and she marched forward. Wet and pale, and trembling, she carried a bundle, a purse, a portmanteau that was too heavy for her.

'Help me!' she cried. She said this to me! And she looked directly at me. She came up to me, turning her back on him. 'You, you help me!'

She was dressed in gray wool, and the only silk on her was wrapped high around her neck, and her shoes were fancy with raised heels and beautiful straps across her arched feet, so thin, so full of blue veins beneath the skin. She gave off a deep and rich perfume, and the smell of chemicals unknown to me, and of decay and death, very advanced, death all through her, struggling to wrap its tendrils around her heart and brain and make them go to sleep forever.

'Help me now get out of here!' She grabbed my hand, wet and warm and as seductive as he was.

'Rachel,' said Gregory, biting his tongue. 'This is the medicine talking.' His voice grew hard. 'Go back to your bed.'

Female attendants in white had come into the room, also gawky boys, in stiff servile little coats, but this entire assemblage stood about idle and frightened of her, nurses and lackeys, and waiting upon his every gesture.

She wrapped her arm around me. She implored me.

'You help me, please, just to get out of here, help me to the elevator, to the street.' She tried to make her words careful and persuasive, and they sounded soft, drunken, and full of misery. 'Help me, and I'll pay you, you know that! I want to leave my own house! I am not a prisoner. I don't want to die here! Don't I have the right to die in a place of my own choosing?'

'Take her back,' said Gregory furiously to the others. 'Go on, get her out of here and don't hurt her.'

'Mrs. Belkin,' cried one of the women. The gawky youths closed in on her like a flock that had to move as one or be scattered.

'No!' she cried out. Her voice took on youthful strength.

As the four of them set upon her, all with anxious and tentative hands, she cried out to me:

'You have to help me. I don't care who you are. He is killing me. He's poisoning me. He's hastening my death by his clock! Stop him! Help me!'

The women's murmuring, lying voices rose to drown her out.

'She's sick,' said one woman in full and true distress. And other voices came like tiresome echoes of every word. 'She's so drugged, she doesn't know what she's doing. Doing. Doing.'

There came a babble as the boys and Gregory spoke, and then Rachel Belkin shouted over all, and the nurse tried to make her own voice even louder.

I rushed forward and pulled one of the women loose from her, and accidentally pushed this woman to the floor. The others were all paralyzed, except for Rachel herself who reached out to me, and grabbed my very head with her right hand, as if she would make me look at her.

She was sickly and raging with fever. She was no older than Gregory – fifty-five at most. A powerful and elegant woman, in spite of it all.

Gregory cursed at her. 'Damn it, Rachel. Azriel, back away.' He waved his arms at the others. 'Get Mrs. Belkin back to her bed.'

'No,' I said.

I pushed two of the others away from her effortlessly and they stumbled and drew back, clinging to one another. 'No,' I said. 'I'll help you.'

'Azriel,' she said. 'Azriel!' She recognized the name but couldn't place it.

'Goodbye, Gregory,' I said. 'We shall see if I have to come back to you and your bones,' I said. 'She wants to die under a different roof. That's her right. I agree with her. And for Esther, I must, you see. Farewell until I come back to you.'

Gregory was aghast.

The servants were helpless.

Rachel Belkin threw her arm around me and I held her firmly in the circle of my right arm.

She seemed about to collapse and one of her ankles turned on the shiny floor. She cried out in pain. I held her. Her hair was loosed and hanging all around her, brushed, lustrous, the silver as beautiful as the black. She was thin and delicate in her years, and had the stubborn beauty of a willow tree, or torn and shining leaves left on a beach by the waves, ruined yet gleaming.

We moved swiftly towards the door together.

'You can't do this,' said Gregory. He was purple with rage. I turned to see him sputtering and staring and making his hands into fists, all grace lost. 'Stop him,' he said to the others.

'Don't make me hurt you, Gregory,' I said. 'It would be too much of a pleasure.'

He ran at me. I swung around so that I could hold her and strike him with my left hand.

And I dealt him one fine blow with my left fist that knocked him on his back, so that his head struck the hearth.

For one breathless second I thought he was dead, but he wasn't only dazed, but so badly hurt that all of the little cowards present ran to attend him.

This was our moment, and the woman knew it and so did I, and we left the room together.

We hurried down to the corridor. I saw the distant bronze doors but this time they had no angels, only the tree of life once more with all its limbs, which was now rent down the middle as they opened.

I felt nothing but strength coursing through me. I could have carried her in one arm, but she walked fast and straight, as if she had to do it, clutching the leather purse or bundle to her.

We went into the elevator. The doors closed. She fell against me. And I took the bundle and held her. We were alone in this chamber as it traveled down and down, through the palace.

'He is killing me,' she said. She was up close to my face. Her eyes were swimmingly beautiful. Her flesh was smooth and youthful. 'He is poisoning me. I promise you, you'll be glad you did this for me. I promise you, you will be glad.'

I looked at her, seeing the eyes of her daughter, just so big, so extraordinary, even with the thinner paler skin now around them. How could she be so strong at forty years? Obviously she'd fought her age and her disease.

'Who are you, Azriel?' she asked. 'Who are you? I heard this name. I know it.' There was trust in the way she said my name. 'Tell me, who are you! Quick. Talk to me.'

I held her up. She would have fallen if not for me.

'When your daughter died,' I said, 'she spoke something, did they tell you?'

'Ah, Lord God. Azriel, the Servant of the Bones,' she said, bitterly, her eyes suddenly welling with tears. 'That's what she said.'

'I am he,' I said. 'I'm Azriel, the one she saw as she lay dying. I cried as you cry now. I saw her and wept for her, and couldn't help her. But I can help you.'

Nineteen

This stopped her grief, but I couldn't tell what she made of this revelation or of me. Sick as she was, she definitely contained the full flower of the seeds of beauty in Esther.

As the doors opened again, we saw an army brought out against her – heavily uniformed men, most of them old, all apparently concerned, and most rather noisy. It was an easy matter for me to push the diffident bunch aside sharply – indeed to scatter them far and wide. But this did make them hysterical with fear. She alarmed them further with her voice.

'Get me my car now,' she said. 'Do you hear? And get out of our way.' They didn't dare to reassemble. She fired orders. 'Henry, I want you out of here. George, go upstairs. My husband needs you. You, there, what are you doing –'

As they argued with one another, she marched ahead of me, towards the open doors. A man to our right picked up a gilded telephone from a marble-top table. She turned and shot him the Evil Eye and he dropped the phone. I laughed. I loved her strength. But she didn't notice these things.

Through the glass to the street, I saw the tall gray-haired one who had driven the car earlier, the tall thin one who had mourned for Esther. But he could not see us. The car was there.

The men came flying at us with solicitous words for a new assault – 'Come now, Mrs. Belkin, you're sick' – 'Rachel, this isn't going to help you.'

I pointed out a mourner.

'Look, he's there, the one who was with Esther,' I said. 'That one, who cried for her. He'll do what we say.'

'Ritchie!' she sang out, standing on her tiptoes, pushing the others away still. 'Ritchie, I want to leave now.'

It was indeed the same man with the deeply wrinkled face, and I hadn't been wrong in my judgment. He opened the door at once as we moved towards him.

Outside the building, the crowd pressed in close to the ropes with their candles and their singing; lights flashed on; giant one-eyed cameras appeared, like so many insects, closing in. They produced no confusion in Rachel any more than they had in Gregory.

Great clusters of these people bowed from the waist to her; others were giving cries of mourning.

'Come on, Rachel, come on,' the driver said, addressing her as if she were kindred. 'Let her pass,' he told the straggling troops, who couldn't make up their minds what to do. He shouted a command to an elderly man at the edge of the pavement.

'Open the door of the car now for Mrs. Belkin!'

On both sides the crowd became frenzied. It seemed they would break through the ropes. Loud greetings to Rachel were called out, but this was in profound respect.

She disappeared into the car ahead of me, and I followed her, coming down beside her, close to her on the seat of black velvet, the two of us suddenly locking our hands together, her left and my right. The door was slammed shut. I squeezed tight her hand.

It was indeed the same long Mercedes-Benz, the same in which Esther had ridden to the palace of death, and in which I had appeared to Gregory. No surprises here. The motor was running. The crowd could not stop such a vehicle even in its devotion. Candles flickered around the windows.

The elderly driver was already behind the wheel in front of us, the little wall that once divided this compartment from his having gone away.

'Take me to my plane, Ritchie,' she said. Her voice had deepened and taken on courage. 'I've already called! And don't listen to anyone else. The plane's waiting and I'm going.'

Plane. I knew this word of course.

'Yes, ma'am,' he said, with a hint of enjoyment, or mere exhilaration in his expression. Her word was obviously law.

The car edged forward, crushing back the singing crowd, and then lurched for the center of the street, and moved ahead, throwing us against each other.

299

The wall went up, shutting us off from the driver, giving us a private carriage in which to ride. The intimacy made me flush.

I felt her hand, and saw how loose the skin was, how white. Hands tell age. Her knuckles were swollen but her fingernails were beautifully painted with red paint, and perfectly tapered. I hadn't noticed this before, and it sent a pleasant chill through me. Her face was five times younger than her hands. Her face had been stretched like Gregory's face, tightened and made youthful, and it was a face that had profited by all these enhancements because her bones had such a symmetry, and her eyes, her eyes were for all time.

I cocked my ear, so to speak, for any call from Gregory, for any changes in my physical self as the result of what he might be saying or thundering or doing to the bones.

Nothing. I was completely independent of him as I had supposed. Nothing restraining me.

Indeed, I put my right arm around her and held her tight to me and felt love for her and a tremendous need to help her.

She gave in to all this with childlike abandon, her body far more frail than I'd expected. Or was it simply that mine was becoming ever more solid?

'I'm here,' I said, as if I'd been called to attention by my god, or by my master.

She had an ivory beauty in her illness. But it was bad, this illness. I could smell the sickness – not a repulsive smell but the smell of the body dying. Only her massive black-and-silver hair seemed immune; even the glistening whites of her eyes were dimming.

'He's poisoning me,' she said, as if she'd read my mind, and her eyes looked up searchingly. 'He controls what I eat, what I drink!' she said. 'I'm dying, of course. He has that on his side, but he wants me dead now. I don't want to be with him and his minions when I die, his Minders.'

'You won't be. I'll see to it. I'll stay with you for as long as you want.' I realized suddenly that this was the first time in this incarnation that I had touched a woman, and her softness was enticing me. Indeed, I could feel changes in my body like those a normal man might experience with a frail full-breasted creature pressed against him. I felt myself grow hard for her.

Could such a thing happen, I thought, not wondering about her virtue, but my limitations. All I got for my pains was a gang of confused memories, that I had indeed had women in this spirit form, and that my masters had railed against it because of its weakening effect. Again the memories were faceless and frameless.

I didn't loosen my grip on her, but my senses were flooded with the sight of her white thighs, her throat, and her breasts.

She was impatient with the drugs that still hobbled her.

'Why did my daughter say your name?' she asked. 'She saw you? You saw her die?'

'Her spirit went straight into the light,' I said. 'Don't grieve for her. And she did speak to me before she died, but I don't know why. Avenging her death, that's clearly only part of what I am here to do.'

This baffled her but another point concerned her as much. 'She wasn't wearing any diamond necklace, was she?'

'No,' I said. 'What is this talk of diamonds? There was no necklace. Those three men killed her painlessly, if it is possible. There was no robbery. She suffered such loss of blood that her mind drifted. I think she died without ever realizing that anyone had done her evil.'

She looked hard at me, as though she didn't entirely believe me, and she didn't welcome this intimacy I offered her.

'I killed the three men,' I said. 'Surely you read about it in the papers. I killed them with the ice pick they used to kill her. There were no diamonds. I saw her go into the store. I saw her before I knew just how quickly they would act.'

'Who are you? Why would you have been there? What were you doing with Gregory?'

'I'm a spirit,' I said. 'A very strong spirit with a will and some form of conscience. This is not human, this body,' I explained. 'It's a collection of elements, drawn together by power. Don't get frightened, whatever I say. I'm with you and not against you. I came out of a long sleep as the three murderers made their way towards Esther. I did not catch on quickly enough to how they meant to do the deed.'

She didn't react in fear and she didn't scoff. 'How did my daughter know you?' she asked.

'I don't know. There are numerous mysteries surrounding my presence here. I've come, seemingly on my own, but obviously with a purpose.'

'Then you don't belong to Gregory in any way?'

'Of course not, no. You saw me defy him. Why do you ask?'

'And this body here,' she said with a slight smile, 'you're telling me this body is not real?'

Indeed, she stared fixedly at me as if she could learn the truth with her eyes. I could feel the heat building between us.

Then she did a most intimate thing that astonished me. She came forward, surprising me, and she kissed me on the mouth. She kissed me as I had kissed Gregory only seconds before she had come into his room. Her lips were damp and hot and small.

I think my mouth was lax and gave back nothing, but then I cupped my hand behind her head, loving the large rustling nest of her hair, and I kissed her, pressing her mouth as hard and sweet as I could. I drew back.

I felt a deep pang of desire for her. The body seemed in perfect condition. Once again, a few echoes of admonition and advice came to me . . . 'lest you vanish in her arms,' or some other antique rot. But I was now through with trying to remember, as I've explained.

What was her pleasure?

As for her, she had the passion of a young woman, whether she was dying or not, or perhaps more truly the passion of a woman in full flower. Her lips were still firm and open, as if she were kissing me still or ready to do it. She was shrewd and not afraid of men or of passion. She was like a queen who has had many lovers. Exactly that way.

'Why did you do that?' I asked her. 'Why the kiss?' The kiss had strengthened me, enlivened parts of me for specific human function. I call that strength.

302

'You're human,' she said, dismissively, her voice deep and a little hard.

'You flatter me but I am a spirit. I want to avenge Esther, but there's something more involved.'

'How did you get to an upper floor with Gregory?' she asked. 'You know his power, his influence. The Lord's Right Hand, the Founder of the Temple of the Mind of God,' she said contemptuously. 'The Savior of the World, the anointed one. The liar, the cheat, the owner of the largest fleet of pleasure cruise ships in the Caribbean and the Mediterranean, the Messiah of merchandising and gourmet food. You're really telling me you're not one of his men?'

'Ships,' I said. 'Why would a church have ships?'

'They're pleasure boats but they also carry cargo. I don't understand what he's doing, and I'll die before I understand. But what were you doing with him?' She went on. 'His ships dock at every major port in the world. Don't you know all about it? It's not that I don't believe you, that you're not a Minder. I saw you defy him, yes, and you got me out of there.

'But everyone in that building is a Minder. Everyone in my life. Everybody's one of his church,' she went on, her words becoming rushed and full of distress. 'The nurses are from his church. The doormen, the messengers, the entire staff of the building. Those people chanting, did you see them, they're part of his church. His church covers the world. His planes drop leaflets over jungles and nameless islands.' She sighed, then continued:

'What I'm saying is, if you're not one of his, and haven't lured me off to some other place to be locked up, how did you ever get to the upper floor?'

The car was moving away from the crowded streets. I smelled the river.

She didn't believe me. But she was telling me many things. Many intriguing things. I could see something beyond her words that she didn't see.

She distracted me slightly from my thoughts. She found me an attractive male. I could feel this, and I could feel in her a despair that comes with the knowledge of approaching death. There was a careless passion in her, a dream it seemed, to possess me.

I was remarkably excited by it.

'Your accent?' she asked. 'What is it? You're not an Israeli?'

'Look, this is trivial,' I said. 'I'm speaking the best English I can. I told you, I'm a spirit. I want to avenge your daughter. Do you want me to do that? This necklace, why does he say there was a necklace? Why did you ask me about the necklace?'

'Probably one of his cruel jokes,' she said. 'The necklace started the big fight between him and Esther a long time before. Esther had a weakness for diamonds – that was certainly true. She was always shopping in the diamond district. She loved to go there more than to the fancy jewelers.

The day she was killed, she must have taken the necklace with her. The maid said she did. He latched on to that little detail. He almost sacrificed his big theories of the terrorists killing Esther with all his talk about the necklace. But then the three men, when they were found, they didn't have the diamonds. You really killed those three men?'

'They took nothing from her,' I said. 'I went right after them and killed them. Your papers tell you they were stabbed in rapid succession by one of their own weapons. Look, don't believe me if that's your wish, but keep explaining to me. About Esther and Gregory. Did he have her killed? Do you think he did?'

'I know he did,' she said. Her entire demeanor changed. Her face darkened. 'But I think he tripped up on the necklace. I have a suspicion that she took the necklace somewhere before she stopped at the store. And if she did that, then the necklace is in the hands of someone who knows that part of the story is a lie. But I can't get to that person.'

This greatly intrigued me. I wanted to question her.

But she was distracted again by physical desire. She examined me, my hair, and my skin. Her grief for Esther was heavy inside her but it warred with a simple human need for levity.

I loved her looking at me.

When I've reached this stage, when I'm this apparently alive, humans notice the same things about me that they would have when I was a true man and walking the earth in an ordinary life that God had given me. They notice the prominent bones of my forehead, that my eyebrows are black and tend to dip in a frown even as I smile but to rise as they move towards the ends of my eyes, that I have a baby's mouth, though it's large, with a square jaw. It's a touch of the baby face with strong bones, and eyes that laugh easily.

She was powerfully drawn to these attributes, and there came again that rush of memory, of ancient people talking and saying things of the utmost importance, and someone saying, 'If one has to do it, where could we find a man more beautiful! One who more resembles the god?'

The car moved faster and faster through empty streets. Other engines were quiet, and the pavements of New York were lined with thin, spindly little trees that fluttered with little leaves, almost like offerings before their lordly buildings. Stone and iron were the makings of this place. How fragile the leaves looked when the wind caught them – forlorn, tiny, and colorless.

We took on greater speed. We had come to a wide road, and I could smell more strongly the stench of the river. The sweet smell of water was barely detectable, but it made me powerfully thirsty. I'd passed over this river with Gregory but had not known thirst then. I knew it now. Thirst meant the body was really strong.

'Whoever you are,' she said, 'I'll tell you this. If we make it to that plane, and I think we're going to, you'll never want for anything again in your life.'

'Explain about the necklace,' I said gently.

'Gregory has a past, a big secret past, a past I knew nothing about and Esther stumbled on it when she bought the necklace. She bought the necklace from a Hasidic Jew who looked exactly like Gregory. And the man told her he was actually Gregory's twin.'

'Yes, Nathan, of course,' I said, 'among the diamond merchants, a Hasid, of course.'

'Nathan! You know this man?'

'Well, I don't know him, but I know the grandfather, the Rebbe, because Gregory went to him to find out what the words meant, the words Esther had said.'

'What Rebbe!'

'His grandfather, Gregory's grandfather. The Rebbe's name is Avram, but they have some title for him. Look, you said she stumbled on his past, that he had this big family in Brooklyn.'

'It's a big family?' she asked.

'Yes, very big, a whole Court of Hasidim, a clan, a tribe. You don't know anything of this at all?'

'Ah,' she sat back. 'Well, I knew it was a family. I understood that from their quarrels. But I didn't know much else about it. He and Esther quarreled. She had found out about this family. It wasn't just the brother Nathan who sold her the necklace. My God, there was this whole secret. Could he have killed her because she knew about his brother? His family?'

'One problem with it,' I said.

'Which is what?'

'Why would Gregory want to keep his past secret? When I was there with him and the Rebbe, his grandfather, it was the Rebbe who begged for secrecy. Now surely the Hasidim didn't kill Esther. That's too stupid to consider.'

She was overwhelmed.

The car had crossed the river and was plunging down into the hellish place of multistoried brick buildings, full of the cheap and mournful light.

She pondered, shook her head.

'Look, why were you with Gregory and this Rebbe?'

'Gregory went to him to find out the meaning of the words Esther spoke. The Rebbe knew. The Rebbe had the bones. Gregory has the bones now. I am called the Servant of the Bones. The Rebbe sold the bones to Gregory on the promise that he would never speak to his brother Nathan again, or come near the court, or expose them as connected to Gregory's childhood or his church.'

'Good God!' she said. She was scrutinizing me harshly.

306

'Look, the Rebbe never called me to come forth. The Rebbe wanted no part of me. But he had had custody of the bones all his life from his father, from years in Poland at the end of the last century. I gathered this from listening to them. I had been asleep in the bones!'

She was speechless. 'You obviously believe what you're saying,' she said. 'You believe it.'

'You talk,' I said, 'about Esther and Nathan –'

Esther came home and had this fight with Gregory, screaming at him that if he had kindred across the bridge he should acknowledge them, that the love of his brother was a real thing. I heard this. I didn't pay any attention. She came in and talked to me about it. I said if they were Hasidim they'd recited Kaddish for him long ago. I was so sick. I was drugged. Gregory was furious with her. But they had their fights, you know. But he . . . he has something to do with her dying, I know it! That necklace. She would never have worn the necklace in midday.'

'Why?'

'Very simple reason. Esther was brought up in the best schools, and made her debut as a girl. Diamonds are for after six o'clock. Esther would have never worn a diamond necklace on Fifth Avenue at high noon. It wouldn't have been proper. But why did he hurt her? Why? Could it have been over this family? No, I don't understand it. And he weaves in the diamonds, why? Why bring up the necklace in the middle of all this!'

'Keep telling me these things. I'm seeing the pattern. Ships, planes, a past that is a secret as much for Gregory as for the innocent Hasidim. I see something . . . but it's not clear.'

She stared at me.

'Talk,' I said. 'You talk. You trust in me. You know I'm your guardian, I'm for your good. I love you and I love your daughter because you're good and you're just and people have done cruelty to you. I don't like cruelty. It makes me edgy and wanting to hurt . . .'

This stunned her. But she believed it. Then she tried to speak and couldn't. Her mind was flooded, and she began to tremble. I touched her face with comforting hands. I hoped they were warm and sweet to her.

'Let me alone now,' she begged kindly. But she put her hand on my arm, patting me, comforting me, and she let her body lean on my shoulder. She made a fist of her right hand.

She curled up against me, and crossed her legs so that I could see her naked knee against mine, firm and fair beneath her hem. She gave a low moan and a terrible outcry of grief.

The car was slowing to a crawl.

We had come to a strange sprawling field full of evil fumes and planes, yes, planes. Planes now explained themselves to me in all their shuddering, keening glory, giant metal birds on tiny preposterous wheels, with wings laden with oil enough to burn the entire world in its fire. Planes flew. Planes crept. Planes lay about empty with gaping doors and ugly stairways leading into the night. Planes slept.

'Come on,' she said. She clenched my hand. 'Whatever you are, you and I are together in this. I believe you.'

'Well you should,' I whispered.

But I was dazed.

As we got out of the car, I knew only my thoughts, following her, hearing voices, paying no attention, looking up at the stars. The air was so full of smoke, it was like the smoke in war when everything is burning.

Amid deafening noise we approached the plane. She gave orders but I couldn't hear her words; the wind just snatched them up. The stairs spilled down in one firm piece like the Ladder to Heaven, only it was merely the metal ladder into this plane.

Suddenly, as we began to climb together, she closed her eyes and stopped. She groped, sightless, for my neck with her hands and held me tight, as if feeling for the arteries in my neck. She was sick and in pain.

'I have you,' I whispered.

Ritchie, the driver, waited behind me, eager to help.

She caught her breath.

She rushed up the steps.

I had to hurry to catch up with her.

We entered a low doorway together, into a sanctum of

intolerable sound. A young woman with brave, cold eyes said:

'Mrs Belkin, your husband wants you to come home.'

'No, we're going to my home now,' she said.

Two uniformed men stepped out of the front of the plane. I glimpsed a tiny chamber there, in the plane's nose, full of buttons and lights.

The cold pale-eyed woman led me towards the back of the plane, but I took my time, listening so that I could be there if needed.

'Do what I tell you,' Rachel said. I heard the rapid capitulation of the men. 'Get off the ground as soon as possible.'

The pale woman had left me standing beneath the roof and doubled back to stop Rachel. Ritchie, the loyal driver, hovered over Rachel.

'Leave the magazines and the papers there!' Rachel said. 'What do you think, she'll come back to life if I read about her? Get off the ground as fast as you can!'

There was a little chorus of weakening rebellion – men, women, even the elderly gray-haired Ritchie.

'You just come with me, that's all!' she said, and once again the silence fell around her as if she were the Queen.

She took my hand, and I was led by her into a small chamber padded in glistening leather. Everything here was smooth. The leather was tender, and the place glowed with refinements: thick glass goblets on a small table, hassocks for our feet, deep chairs that would hold us as dearly as couches.

The voices died away, or sank low and conspiratorial, behind curtains.

The little windows were the only ugliness, so thick and scratched and dirty that they revealed nothing of the night outside. The noise was the night. The stars weren't visible.

She told me to sit down.

I obeyed, sinking into an awkward couch of odoriferous dyed leather that caught me up as if it wanted to render me helpless and awkward, as a father might pick up his son by the ankle into the air.

We faced each other now in these scooped and oddly

comfortable couches. I became used to it, the seeming indignity. I grasped that for the severity of the materials, this was a form of opulence. We were lounging here, like potentates. Brilliantly colored magazines lay on the table before us, one neatly overlapping the other. Folded newspapers that had been arranged in a carefully designed circle. Stale air blew upon us as if it were some sort of deliberate blessing.

'You really have never seen a plane before, have you?' she asked.

'No,' I said. 'I don't need them. This is all so very luxurious,' I said. 'I couldn't sit up straight if I wanted to.'

The woman with the pale cold eyes had come, and she was reaching down beside me for tethers, a strap with a buckle. I was fascinated by her skin and her hands. All of these people were so very nearly perfect. How?

'Safety belt,' said Rachel. She snapped the buckle of her own, and now she did a thing which seduced me.

She kicked off her shoes, her beautiful ornate shoes with their high thin heels. She pushed at them, one foot at the other, till they fell loose, and on her narrow white feet I saw the imprint of the straps that had covered her feet, and I wanted to touch them. I wanted to kiss them.

Was this perhaps one of the most well-developed bodies I'd ever had?

The cold woman looked at me uncomfortably and shifted, and then only reluctantly went away.

Rachel ignored all this.

I couldn't take my eyes off her, vivid and somber in the dim light of this sanctuary, this plane, and I desired her. I wanted to touch the inner flesh of her thighs, and see whether the fleece-covered flower there was as well preserved as everything else.

This was disconcerting and shameful. Another realization came to me. Diseased things can be so beautiful. Perhaps a flame is a diseased thing, if you think about it, a flame dancing on its wick, eating up the wax beneath it, the way this disease was eating up her body from around her soul.

She made a dazzling heat in her fever and the keenness of her mind.

'And so we fly in this,' I said, 'we go up, and we travel faster than we can on the ground, like a javelin hurled through space, only we have the means of directing ourselves.'

'Yes,' she said. 'It's going to take us to the southern tip of this country in less than two hours,' she said. 'We'll be in my home, my little home which all these years has been mine alone, and there I'll die. And I know it.'

'You want to?'

'Yes,' she said. 'My head's clearing even now. I can feel pain. I can feel his poison clearing from my system. Yes, I want to know it. I want to be a witness to what happens to me.'

I wanted to say that I didn't think death was like that for most human beings, but I didn't want to say anything I wasn't sure of, and certainly nothing to bring her more pain.

She gestured to the woman, who must have been lingering somewhere behind me. The plane had begun to roll, presumably on its tiny wheels. It didn't roll easily.

'Something to drink,' Rachel said. 'What would you like?' And suddenly she smiled. She wanted to make a joke. 'What do ghosts like to drink?'

I said, 'Water. I'm so relieved that you asked me. I'm parched with thirst. This body is dense and delicately put together. I think it's growing true parts!'

She laughed out loud. 'I wonder what parts those could be!' she said.

This water had come. Lots of it. Glorious water.

The clear bottle was nestled in a huge bucket of ice, and the ice was beautiful. Ripping my eyes off the water itself, I stared at the ice. Of everything I had seen in this modern age, nothing, simply nothing, compared to the simple beauty of this ice, glittering and sparkling around this strangely dull container of water.

The young woman who had just set down this bucket of wondrous ice now drew the bottle of water out of it, so that the ice fell and crunched and made a gorgeous twinkling in the light. I could see that the bottle was made of something soft, not glass at all; it didn't have the shimmer or the strength of glass; it was plastic. You could squash the bottle flat when it was empty. It was the lightest container for this water, like a bladder filled with milk strapped to a donkey, the thinnest, finest bladder you could find.

The woman poured the water into two glass goblets. Ritchie appeared. He bent down and whispered something in Rachel's ear. It had to do with Gregory and his rage.

'We're on schedule,' he said. He pointed to the magazines, 'There's something –'

'Leave all that alone, I don't care, I've read it all, what does it matter? It comforts me that her picture is on every magazine cover. Why not?'

He tried to protest but she told him firmly to go. The plane was taking off. Someone called him. He had to buckle up.

I drank the water, greedily, the way you've seen me drink. She was amused. The plane was leaving the ground.

'Drink it all,' she said, 'there's plenty of it.'

I took her at her word and drained the entire plastic bottle. My body absorbed all of this and was still thirsty, its strongest indicator of growing strength.

So what was Gregory doing? Fuming over the bones? Didn't matter! Or did it?

It suddenly occurred to me that almost every delicate maneuver I had ever performed had been under the direction of a magician. Even taking a woman, I'd done with their grudging leave. I could rise, I could kill, then dissolve. Yes. That is not delicate, but the direct arousal of passion I felt for this woman – the strengthening that came to me from this water – this was new.

It struck me with total clarity that I had to find out just how strong I was on my own, and I hadn't taken any serious steps to do so. I felt as strong in the presence of this woman's carnal attraction to me as I had in Gregory's fascination.

As I put the bottle down, I realized I had let drops of water fall on the papers and magazines. I looked at them.

Then I saw what had so concerned the others about these

312

magazines. The pictures on them were of Esther at the worst moment. There were pictures of Esther almost dead!

Yes, there on the cover of one newsmagazine was the picture of Esther on her stretcher, and the crowds around her.

Someone said we were on course for Miami and cleared for an immediate landing when we got there.

'Miami.' The sound made me laugh. 'Miami.' It was like a joke word you say to little children to make them laugh. 'Miami.'

The plane was bouncing along. But the pale-eyed girl came with another bottle of water. It was cold. It didn't need the ice. I took it and drank it in easy patient swallows.

I sat back, filling with the water. Oh, this was the most divine moment, a moment almost on a par with kissing Rachel, to feel this water move down my throat and through the coils inside of me made by will and by magic. I breathed deep.

I opened my eyes, and saw that Rachel was watching me. The girl was gone. The glasses were gone. The only water that remained was the bottle I clutched in my hands.

A great pressure bore down on me, fondling me, pushing me against the leather, and teasing me almost with a sweet strength that was mysterious.

The plane was rising fast into the sky, very fast. The pressure increased and my head suddenly ached, but this I sent away from me. I looked at her. She sat still as if praying, as if this were a ceremonial moment, and she did not speak or move until the plane had found some comfortable height and ceased to rise.

I knew the moment by the way she relaxed, and by the sounds of the engines. I didn't much like this plane. Yet the experience was thrilling.

You're alive, Azriel, you are alive! I must have laughed. Or maybe I wept. I needed more water. No, I would have liked to have more water. I needed nothing.

But I had to know what Gregory was doing with my bones. Was he trying at this very moment to call me back?

He had to be doing something, though I felt no reverberations. I wanted to know. And I also wanted to know if, strong as this body was, I could at will dissolve it and recall it. I wanted badly to know.

I ran my tongue on my lips, which were cold from the water. I realized that my attraction to this woman, this delicate pale creature, had brought my anger and my confusion to the limit. I had to stop wondering about this and that and simply declare myself master. That's what I had to do. I wanted her. It was all connected in a human way – the carnal desire for her, and the desire to strive against Gregory and defy him, prove to myself he did not control me merely because the bones were now in his possession.

'You're frightened,' Rachel said. 'Don't be frightened of the plane. The plane is routine.' Then a mischievous smile came on her again, and she said, 'Of course it could explode at any minute, but, well, so far, it never has.' She gave an easy bitter laugh.

'Listen, you have an expression in English, kill two birds with one stone?' I said. 'I'm going to do it. I'm going to leave you now, and come back. That will prove to you that I'm a spirit and you'll stop worrying that you're consorting in desperation with a madman, and also I'll find out what Gregory is up to. Because he does have those bones, and he is a strange, strange man.'

'You're going to disappear from here? Inside this plane?'

'Yes. Now tell me our destination in Miami. What is Miami? I'll meet you at the door of your home in Miami.'

'Don't try this,' she said.

'I have to. We can't go on with your suspicions. I see now Esther is like a diamond herself in the middle of a huge necklace, and the necklace is intricate. Where are we going? Where do I find Miami?'

'Tip end of the East Coast of the United States. My home is in a tower at the very end of the town called Miami Beach. It's in a high-rise. I'm on the top floor. There is a pink beacon on the tower above my apartment. Further south are the islands called the Florida Keys and then the Caribbean.'

'That's enough; I'll see you there.'

I looked down at the spilled droplets of water, at the horrifying picture of Esther on the stretcher and then in absolute shock I saw that I was in the picture! I was there! I had been caught by the camera as I had raised my hands to my head and howled in grief for Esther. This was before the stretcher had been put inside the ambulance.

'Look,' I said. 'That's me.'

She picked up the magazine, stared at the picture and at me.

'Now I'm going to prove to you that I'm on your side, and I want to give that devil Gregory a good scare. You want something from your house? I'll bring it to you.'

She couldn't speak.

I realized that I had frightened her and silenced her. She was merely watching me. I pictured her body without clothing. The shape of her limbs was pleasing and firm. Her legs in particular had a muscularity to them in their slender form which was graceful. I wanted to touch the backs of her legs, her calves, and squeeze them.

This was quite a lot of strength for me, a lot, and I had to resolve the issue of my freedom now.

'You're changing,' she said in a suspicious voice, 'but you're certainly not disappearing.'

'Oh? What do you see?' I asked. I wanted to add with pride that I hadn't tried to disappear yet, but this was obvious.

'Your skin; the sweat's drying. Oh, it isn't much sweat. It's on your hands and your face and it's gone and you look, you look different. I could swear that there's more dark hair on your hands, you know, just the normal hair of a hirsute man.'

'That I am,' I said. I lifted my hand, looking at the black hairs on my fingers, and I reached down into my shirt and felt the thick curls on my chest. I pulled at them, pulled them again and again. That was my chest, the rough scratchiness of the hair when it was flat, the silkiness of it when I tugged on it, and played with it. 'I am alive,' I whispered. 'Listen to me,' I said.

'I'm listening. I couldn't be more attentive. What is it you

315

see – about Esther's death and this necklace? You were saying something –'

'Your daughter. She touched a scarf before she died. Do you want it? It was beautiful. She reached out for it right at the moment that the Evals surrounded her, the killers, I mean. She wanted it, and she died with it in her hand.'

'How do you know this!'

'I saw it!'

'I have that scarf,' she said. She went white with shock. 'The saleswoman brought it to me. She said that Esther had reached for it, that Esther said she wanted it! How could you know this?'

'I didn't know that part. I just saw Esther reach for the scarf. I was going to ask you if you wanted the scarf. I was going to bring it to you for the same reasons as this merchant woman.'

'I do want it!' she said. 'It's in my room, the room I was in when you first saw me. It . . . no. It's in Esther's room. It's lying on her bed. Yes, that's where I left it.'

'Okay, when I see you in Miami I will have it.'

The look on her face was a terrible thing to see.

In a whisper she said, 'She went there to get that scarf!' Her voice was so small. 'She told me she had seen it and couldn't forget it. She had told me she wanted that scarf.'

'In a gesture of love, I'll bring it to you.'

'Yes, I want to die holding it.'

'You don't think I'm going to disappear, do you?'

'No, not at all.'

'Keep yourself in check. I am. Whether I come back, that's the question.' I said something under my breath. 'But I'll try, try with all my might. This must be tested now.'

I leaned over and took with her the liberty she'd taken with me. I kissed her. Her passion passed through me completely. It burned in me.

Now in my heart I spoke the requisite words, *Depart from me, all particles of this earthly body, yet do not return to where you belong, but await my command that you come together instantly when I would have you.*

I vanished.

At once the body dispersed, sending out a fine mist to all the inner surfaces of the plane, leaving a shimmering spray upon the leather, the windows, the ceiling.

I floated above, free, fully shaped and strong, and I looked down at the empty seat, and I saw the top of Rachel's head, and I heard her scream.

I rose up, through the plane. It was no harder than passing through anything else. But I felt the passing, I felt the shivering energy and heat of the plane, and then the plane shot onwards at such terrific velocity that I fell towards the earth as if I had weight. Down, down, through the dark until I swung free, spreading my arms, and moving towards:

Gregory. *Find the Bones, Servant. Find your Bones. Look after the Bones.*

In the wind, as always I glimpsed other souls. I saw them struggling to see me and to make themselves visible. I knew they sensed my vigor, my direction, and for a moment they flashed and glittered and blinked, and then they were gone. I had passed through them and their world, their horrid layer of smoke that surrounded the earth like the filth hanging over burning dung, and I sped forward, like singing, towards the Bones. Towards Gregory.

'The Bones,' I said. 'The Bones,' I said into the wind.

The lights of the city of New York spread out in all directions, more magnificent and tremendous than the lights of Rome at its greatest, or of Calcutta now full of millions upon millions of lamps. I could hear Gregory's voice.

And then before me in the dark, there appeared the Bones, tiny, distant, certain, and golden.

Twenty

It was a large room, not in the apartments of Gregory and Rachel, but higher in the building. I realized for the first time that the building itself *was* the Temple of the Mind of God and it throbbed throughout its many floors with people.

The room itself glistened with steel and glass and tables made of manipulated stone, hard as anything mined from the earth; machines lined the walls, and cameras which moved as the inhabitants of the room moved.

There were plenty of inhabitants.

I entered invisible, easily passing through all barriers, as if I were made of tiny fish and the walls were nets. I wandered among the tables, eyeing the video screens in rows on the walls, the computers set into niches, and other devices which I couldn't understand.

Silently, broadcasts from all over the planet came in on these video screens. Some of them showed the news that all people can receive. Others were obviously monitoring particular and private places. The spy monitors were the most dull, greenish, murky.

The Bones lay in the very middle of the room on a sterile table. The casket, empty, lay to the side. The men surrounding Gregory were obviously physicians. They had the poise and attitude of learned men.

Gregory was in mid-conversation, describing the Bones as a relic, which must be analyzed in every conceivable way without bringing harm to it, X-rayed, carbon-dated, minute scrapings made for contents. Attempt at aspiration if anything inside were liquid.

Gregory was shaken, disheveled. He wore the same clothes as before but he was not the same man.

'You're not listening to me!' he said fiercely to these his loyal court physicians. 'Treat this as priceless,' he said. 'I want no mishaps. I want no leaks to the press. I want no leaks

318

within this building. Do this work yourself. Keep the jabber-mouth technicians away from it.'

The men took all this in stride. Not fawning like lackeys, they wrote notes on their clipboards, exchanged glances of agreement with one another, and nodded with dignity to the man who paid the bills.

I knew their kind. Very modern scientists who are just learned enough to be certain that nothing spiritual exists, that the world is completely material, self-created, or the result of some 'big bang,' and that ghosts, spells, God, and the Devil were useless concepts.

They weren't by nature kind. In fact, there was a peculiar hardness which they all shared, not a sinister quality so much as a moral deformity. It was in their demeanor, but I caught it merely from scanning them carefully. All these men had committed crimes of some kind, with medicine, and their status was entirely dependent upon the protection of Gregory Belkin.

In other words, this was a gang of fugitive doctors hand-picked to do special jobs for Gregory.

It struck me as marvelously good luck that he had committed the Bones to this pack of fools, rather than to magicians. But then where would he find a magician?

What a different scene this might have been if he had called upon the Hasidim – zaddiks who didn't hate or fear him – or on Buddhists or Zoroastrians. Even a Hindu doctor of Western mind might have been a danger.

I took an upright stance, still invisible, then drew close, until I was touching Gregory's shoulder. I smelled his perfumed skin, his fine silken face. His voice was crisp and angry, concealing all his anxiety as if it were a cloud that he could collect and swallow and let out only in a perfect narrow stream of fluid speech.

The Bones. I felt nothing as I saw them. Do some good mischief here, get the scarf and get back to Rachel. Obviously the moving of the Bones had no effect on me; neither did the prying eyes of these doctors.

Am I finished with you now? I spoke to the Bones, but the Bones gave no answer.

They were not in order. They were a haphazardly gathered skeleton, tumbled, their gold brilliant under the electric lights. Flecks of cloth clung to them, like bits of leaves or dirt. Ashes clung to them, but they seemed as solid as ever, as enduring. *For all time.*

Was my soul, my tzelem, locked within them?

Do I need you anymore? Can you hurt me, Master?

Gregory knew I was there! He turned from right to left, but he couldn't see me. The others – and there were six noted his agitation, questioned him.

One man touched the casket.

'Don't do it!' said Gregory. He was wonderfully afraid. I loved this too much!

There is always an element of pride in tormenting the solid and the living, but really, it was so easy, I had to restrain myself.

To test him and to test myself – that was my mission here, and I must not play games.

'We'll handle them with extreme care, Gregory,' said a young doctor amongst them. 'But we're going to have to take some substantial scrapings; we've been through that. In order to get carbon dating and DNA, we may have to take –'

'And you want full DNA, don't you,' asked another, eager for the eye and the favor of the leader. 'You want everything we can come up with about this skeleton – gender, age, cause of death, anything that might be locked inside there –'

'– You're going to be amazed what we can find out.'

'– the Mummy project in Manchester, you saw all that?'

Gregory gave them nods and stiff affirmations in silence because he knew I was there. I was invisible still, but now formed in all my parts and wearing my garments of choice, fluid enough to pass through him if I wanted to, which would have sickened him and hurt him and made him fall.

I touched Gregory's cheek. He felt it, and he was petrified. I pushed my fingers into his hair. He drew in his breath.

On and on came the science babble –

'Size of the skull, a male, and the pelvis, probably, you realize . . .'

'Be careful with them!' Gregory burst out suddenly. The

scientists were silenced. 'I mean, treat them like a relic, you hear me?'

'Yes, sir, we understand, sir.'

'Look, the scientists who do this work on Egyptian and –'

'Don't tell me how. Just tell me what! Keep it secret. We don't have many days left, gentlemen.'

What could this mean?

'I don't like stopping work for this, so do it at once.'

'Everything's going splendidly,' said an older doctor. 'Don't worry about time. A day or two won't matter.'

'I suppose you're right,' Gregory said, crestfallen. 'But something can still go wrong, very wrong.'

They nodded only because they feared to lose his favor. They debated now, speak, don't speak, nod, bow, do what?

I drew in my breath and resolved to be visible; the air moved; there was a faint noise. The room felt a vague commotion as the particles gathered with tremendous force, yet I was taking no more than the first stage, the airy form.

The doctors looked about in confusion; the first to see me pointed. I was transparent, but vividly colored, and perfectly detailed.

Then the others saw me.

Gregory spun around to his right and looked at me.

I gave him my soft evil smile. I think it was evil anyway. I floated. In airy form, I had no need to stand, or to anchor. I was a thousand degrees from the density that obeys gravity. I stood on the ground, but I didn't need to. This was a choice, like the position of a flower in a painting.

He glared at me, seeing the thin mirage of a long-haired man, clothed as I had been when I left him, but thinner than glass.

'This is a holograph, Gregory,' said one of the doctors.

'It's being projected from somewhere,' said another.

The men began to look around the room. 'Yeah, it's one of those cameras up there.'

'. . . it's some sort of trick.'

'Well, who the hell would dare pull a thing like this in your own . . .'

'Quiet!' Gregory said.

321

He raised his hand for absolute obedience and he got it. His face was locked with fear and despair.

'Remember,' I said aloud, 'I'm watching you.'

The cohorts heard me and commenced whispering and shuffling.

'Put your hand through it,' said the white-coated one closest to me. When Gregory failed to obey, the young man approached and moved to do it, and I merely looked at him and watched him and wondered what he felt, if it was a chill, or electric. His hand penetrated me, easily, causing no seam in the vision.

He drew back his hand.

'Somebody's gotten into security,' he said quickly, looking me directly in the eyes. They were all babbling again, that someone was controlling the image, that someone somehow had figured a way to do this, and that it was probably –

Gregory couldn't bring himself to answer.

I had accomplished my purpose.

He struggled desperately for some command, some powerful verbal weapon against me that wouldn't make him the fool in the eyes of the others. Then he spoke in a cold voice.

'When you give me your reports, tell me exactly how these bones could be destroyed,' he said.

'Gregory, this is a holograph, this thing. I want to call security . . .'

'No,' he declared. 'I know who is responsible for this little trick. I have it covered. It merely caught me off guard. There's no breach. Get to work.'

His self-confidence and quiet air of command really were kingly.

I laughed softly. I kissed his cheek. It was rough and he drew back. But he faced me. The men were astonished by the gesture.

The men merely came closer, surrounding me, absolutely certain in their incredible ignorance and bigotry that I was an apparition being made electrically by someone else. For a moment, I scanned their faces. I saw wickedness in their faces, but it was a brand of wickedness I didn't fully understand. It was too connected with power. These men loved their power. They loved their purpose, but what exactly was it that they did when they weren't analyzing relics?

I let them study me, looking from face to face. Then I struck upon the mastermind. The tall emaciated doctor, who in fact blackened his hair with dye, and who looked older than he was on account of his thinness. He was the brilliant one; his gaze was far more critical and suspicious than that of the others. And he monitored Gregory's responses with a cold calculation.

'Look, this is all very fancy,' said this one, 'this holograph, but we can get on this analysis tonight. You realize we can give you an image like this, this holograph, of the man who once had these bones?'

'Can you really do that?' I asked.

'Yes, of course –' He stopped, realizing he was talking to me. He began to make gestures all around me. So did the others. They were trying to interrupt the projection of the beam that they thought had created me.

'Simple forensic procedure,' said another, boldly ignoring the continuing strangeness of all this.

'And we'll get on this security thing immediately.'

Others continued to search the ceilings and the walls.

A man moved to a telephone.

'No!' Gregory said. He stared at the Bones.

'. . . permeated with something, some chemical obviously; well, we can have all of that analyzed, I mean, we'll be able to tell you –'

Gregory turned and looked at me. A clearer comprehension of him came to me.

This was a man who could only use everything that came to him; he was not passive in any meaning of that word. The frustration he felt now would fuel his rage and his invention; it would drive him to greater lengths; he was only holding firm now, biding his time. And what he learned now would enhance his cunning and his capacity to surprise.

I turned to the doctors. 'Let me know the outcome of your tests, will you?' I said, being a deliberately dreadful devil.

This caused quite a flurry.

I dissolved. I did it instantly.

The heat passed out of me, and the particles swarmed, too tiny no doubt for them to see. But the men felt the change in temperature; they felt the movement of the air. They were in confusion, looking around for another projected figure, perhaps, among them, for a switch in the direction of the light beam which they thought had made me appear.

I understood something further about them. They regarded their science as omnipotent. Science was the explanation not only for me but for anything and everything. In other words, they were materialists who beheld their science as magic.

The irony of this was very funny to me. Anything I did they would perceive to be science beyond their understanding. And I had been made by those who had been convinced that magic had the power of 'science,' if you just knew all the right words!

I went up and up, through the ceiling and the floor above it, rising through the shiny, bustling, crowded layers of the building, until I could not see the Bones any longer. The golden glimmer was gone.

I was in the fresh and cool night sky. Find Rachel, I thought. Your test is accomplished. You know now you are free.

He can't stop you. Go now where you will.

But in truth, the experiment would only be complete if I could make myself fully solid once more.

The scarf. I had forgotten about the scarf.

I drew down closer to the building. Only now did I really see its full height and grandeur. Covered all over even to its top floors with granite, it sloped majestically as it rose, rather like an ancient place of worship. There must have been fifty floors. Numbers don't come to me automatically. We had been on the twenty-fifth floor just now.

I descended, peering into the windows as I went, looking for the private living chambers. Offices, I saw hundreds of offices. I moved easily from right to left, amazed at the rooms filled with computers, and then I saw laboratories, highly elaborate laboratories in which serious people were diligently studying tiny things beneath microscopes and measuring potions into vials, which they carefully sealed.

What was this, part of Gregory's religious rackets? Drugs for his followers? Spiritual medicines, like the Soma of the Persian sun worshipers?

But there were so many laboratories! There were men and women in sterile white suits and masks, their hair carefully covered with white caps. There were giant refrigerators and warning signs against 'Contamination.' There were animals in cages – little gray monkeys with wide, frightened eyes. Doctors were feeding them.

In one area, humans moved sluggishly, encased in very bright colored plastic suits and with ominous windowed helmets worthy of modern warriors. Their hands were covered with giant clumsy gloves.

At their mercy, the monkeys chattered desperately and in vain in their little prisons. Some monkeys lay prostrate with illness or fright.

Most curious. Some Temple of the Mind, I thought.

As last I came down to perhaps the twelfth floor and there I saw the great demilune of a living room in which he and I had quarreled. I moved through the window easily, and through the corridors, moving the doors back slowly and lightly so that it would seem a breeze.

I saw Esther's bed. I saw her bed, and her picture beside it, a smiling girl with others in a silver frame, and I saw across her snow-white bedspread the black beaded scarf, folded neatly. I was overcome with delight. As I entered the room physically, I sensed the perfume of Esther. Here she had slept; here she had dreamed.

On her dressing table, there lay diamond rings and earrings with diamonds, and bracelets with diamonds, a scattering of finery, all delicate and pretty with silver or gold. On the walls were photographs – Gregory, Rachel, Esther – together year after year. One picture had been taken on a boat, another on a beach, another at some ceremony or party which required gowns for the women.

'Esther, tell me! Who did it? Why? Would he kill you

325

simply because you learned about his brother Nathan? Why would that matter to him, Esther?'

But nothing came back from the surfaces of this room. The soul had gone straight into the light and taken every particle of pain or joy it had ever known along with it. It had left nothing. Ah, to be murdered and to rise so cleanly!

I drifted towards the scarf. My hand grew denser and more visible as the weight of the fabric tumbled into it; it was beautifully woven, made of lace in its center, long, and trimmed all over with fine small black beads, exactly as I remembered. It was heavy, very heavy. It was almost a shawl. It was strange and unlike other things of this time. Perhaps she had thought it exotic.

The darkness moved around me. *Make yourself whole and flesh.* I did. Something brushed me and flashed before me, dimly and uncertainly. But it was only a lost soul, the soul of an unburied man perhaps, mistaking me in the mist for an angel then moving on. Nothing to do with the chamber.

I uttered a curse against the lost souls, and took my stand with the material world.

I wound the scarf tight in my hands, dazzled again that I was formed and answerable to no one. And then once more, keeping this scarf tight within my grip, I let the particles fly from me, and rolled my spirit round and round this scarf, this heavy scarf so that I might carry it with me.

I soared through the noise and smoke hovering over the city. For one moment I saw its lights below sprinkled exquisitely amid the clouds, the scarf like a great heavy stone in the very midst of my being, slowing me, giving me a rise and fall with the wind that felt oddly good.

Like the birds perhaps, I mused.

Rachel, Rachel, Rachel. I pictured her as I'd left her, not below me, screaming at my disappearance, but how she had been when she was seated across from me, with large hard eyes and all the silver shimmering in her hair, as if it had been threaded there deliberately by twenty slaves to make her magnificent in age.

Within seconds I felt close to her. I could almost see her. She moved through the night as swiftly as I did, and I circled her, rising high above her and then drawing near. I couldn't see her clearly enough. Her image was tangled with movement and light.

It was the plane.

I couldn't enter the plane. I wasn't sure enough to enter it. It was just going too fast. I didn't know if I had the strength. I didn't know if I could bring together the matter for a body in the compartment of such a swiftly moving machine. The whole technology of the plane seemed too full of contradictions, and precarious adjustments. I imagined some hideous catastrophe in which I'd be knocked back once more into oblivion, unable to revive.

If that happened, the scarf would fall to earth, like a bit of burnt black forest, moving back and forth on the wind until it entered the lower atmosphere and then pooled on the ground. Esther's scarf, divorced from all things that had to do with her, and those who loved her. Esther's scarf in some strange city – we were high above small cities.

I drifted without making a choice. I wasn't uncertain however. I would meet her, I resolved.

I waited and I followed; the plane led me like a tiny firefly in the night.

We were above the southern seas. The plane was circling and descending. I saw then the great sprawl of Miami as I came down under the clouds. Glorious in this warm air, this sea-filled, watery air, air as lovely as some ancient city where I had once been very happy as a spirit, learning from a wise man. I could almost . . .

But I had to concentrate. I saw the long stream of eerie colored lights that made the Ocean Drive of Miami Beach. I saw it as clearly as if she'd drawn me a map, and I saw the building with the pink beacon atop it, the very last one on the bony finger of the peninsula.

Slowly I descended, not close to the building, but a few blocks from it, drifting quickly into the large crowd that moved along the street, between the beach and the cafes. The warm air was grand and exhilarating. I almost cried for the sweetness of it, and the sight of the great sea, and the

327

beautiful billowing clouds of the sky. I thought if I had to die, I should like to die here too.

It was a remarkable mix of humans which surrounded me, wholly unlike the busy people of New York. These were pleasure seekers, all rather agreeable, and all eyes for one another, yet most tolerant of the great casual variety of styles intermingled here, and the obvious mix of the very young in ostentatious seductive attire, right along with the commonplace and the very old.

But my clothes were not right. I glanced about at the men. Men wore loose garments, short pants, sandals. No. There was a man in a beautiful white suit, like Gregory's suit, with a shirt and open collar.

I took that style. When my feet hit the pavement, I was dressed like that man and carrying the scarf in my hand and walking south on Ocean Drive towards Esther's building.

Heads turned, people smiled, people here looked at each other, people here wanted to see beauty. There was an atmosphere of festivity. Suddenly a girl grasped my arm. I was startled. I wheeled around and stopped and bowed.

'Yes, what is it?' I asked.

She was little more than a child with huge breasts, almost naked under her pink cotton tunic. Her hair was blond and fleecy and gathered back with a big pink bow.

'Your hair, your beautiful hair,' she said. She had a dreamy look.

'In this breeze, it's a nuisance,' I said, laughing.

'I thought that was it,' she said. 'When I saw you coming, you looked so happy, except your hair kept blowing in your face. Here, let me give you this.' She laughed with simple gaiety as she removed a long gold chain from around her neck.

'But I have nothing to give you for it,' I said.

'Your smile is what you gave me,' she said, and rushing behind me, she gathered my hair back at the nape of my neck and looped the chain around it. 'Ah, now, you look cooler and more comfortable,' she said, jumping in front of me. Her little tunic barely covered her underwear, and she danced on naked legs and sandals that had only one buckle to them.

'Thank you, thank you most kindly,' I said with a deep bow. 'Oh, I wish I had something, I don't know where to . . .' How could I bring to myself some valuable object without stealing it? I felt ashamed as I looked at the scarf.

'Oh, I would give you this . . .'

'I don't want anything from you!' she said, laying a little hand on mine and on the scarf. 'Smile again!' And when I did she cried out with laughter.

'I wish you blessings all your life,' I said. 'I wish I could kiss you.'

She stood on tiptoe, threw her arms around my neck, and planted on me a luscious kiss that woke every molecule of the body. I trembled, not able to gently remove her from me, but fast becoming her utter slave, and all this on the brightly lighted street in the brisk ocean breeze, with hundreds meandering on both sides.

Something distracted me. It was a call. It was Rachel's call to me, and Rachel was very close, and she was crying.

'I have to go now, pretty girl,' I said. 'You lovely girl.' And I kissed her again and hurried down the street, trying to remember to walk at a human pace. I could see Rachel's building up the slope.

I was there in less than five minutes. The kiss of the girl had been like a drink of wine for a mortal man. I was laughing to myself. I was so happy to be alive suddenly that I even felt a morsel of compassion for all those who had ever wronged me or anyone. But that passed fast enough. Hate was too much a part of my character.

These kind gentle people might melt it, however. These kind ones.

Approaching the garden terraces of the building, I looked up at its glorious height. Then I climbed quickly over the fence and sprinted on the drive, hardly realizing that I had bypassed a security gate as I headed for the front doors of Rachel's home.

A huge white limousine was parked there and Rachel was just getting out of it. Ritchie, the faithful driver, had her by the arm. He was agitated though silent. No reporters or anyone around. Only the building attendants in white uniforms, and the breeze rippling through the purple Egyptian lilies.

I turned and saw the sea again stretching forever under the white clouds. This was like heaven to me. Then in the other direction beyond the building I saw an inland bay. More gleaming, dreamy beautiful water, and beyond it towers of light.

I loved this world.

As I drew up to her, I babbled with joy.

'Look, Rachel, there's water all around us,' I said. 'And the sky is so visible, so high, look at the curling and rolling clouds. You can see their shapes and their whiteness as if it's day here.'

She was rigid. She stared.

I slipped the scarf into her hands, and wound her hands up with it.

'That's the scarf,' I said. 'It was on Esther's bed.'

She shook her head. She wanted to say things. She and the somber Ritchie both stared at me in plain shock.

'I've never fainted in my life,' she said. 'I think I might now.'

'No, no, it's only me. I've come back. I saw Gregory, I know what he's up to, this is the scarf. Don't faint. But if you want to faint, go ahead. I'll carry you.'

The wide glass doors swung open. Attendants preceded her with her leather bundle and some other suitcase I'd never seen before. Ritchie stared at me and shook his head. His wrinkled face showed anger.

Then she came close.

'Now you see,' I said, 'all I've told you is true.'

'Is it?' she whispered. She was dead white.

'Come on, let's get inside,' said Ritchie. He did pick her up, and he carried her in front of me to the elevator. Old as he was, he carried her inside easily in his arms.

'Let me in,' I said as the doors started to close. But Ritchie glared at me with a darkly furrowed brow, and jabbed the button and blocked my path.

330

'All right, have it your way,' I said.

I met them at the top. It was just a speedy rush up the steps, rather like racing when I was a boy.

Dumbfounded and enraged, and still carrying her, as she stared at me, Ritchie rushed to her doors and put the key in the lock. The attendants went in with her luggage.

'Put me down now, Ritchie,' she said. 'It's okay. Wait downstairs. Take the others with you.'

'Rachel!' he said. He was staunch, suffering. His gnarled old fingers were curled for a fight.

'Why are you so afraid of me?' I asked. 'You think I would hurt her?'

'I don't know what to think!' he said in a roughened, aged voice. 'I'm *not* thinking.'

She pulled me into the door. 'All of you, go,' she said.

I saw a blurred panorama of beautiful rooms, many open to the sea, and others open to a garden, just like the courtyard of our house when I was a boy, and the courtyard I could almost remember from that Greek city on the sea where I'd been most unhappy and then happy. I was dazed.

The loveliness of the place, its warmth, its windows framing Heaven is almost impossible to describe. It flooded me with love, and I think the memory of Zurvan touched me, not with words but with revelations. I was washed clean by love and felt a sense of ease. I understood that there could be a world in which only love was the significant virtue. A sense of well-being overcame me. But I did not try to remember anything.

Everywhere soft white curtains waved in the wind. The courtyard exploded with giant red African flowers, lovely purple vines, and the most lacy and soft trees, dancing in the captured breeze. The place was full of the scent of the flowers.

Rachel slammed the front door on those outside, including her driver angel, and she slid the lock and put up a little chain, and then she looked at me.

'You believe me now?' I asked.

She leaned towards me.

'Let me hold you.'

She tumbled softly against me. 'Take me to my bed,' she said. 'There, through the garden and over there, to the left, my bed.'

She put her arms around my neck and I did as she said. She was light, perfumed, tender.

It was the most marvelous room, open to the sea on all three sides, it was windows and windows; a rush of remembered warmth overcame me again. But where in the world had I ever seen such clouds, and tossed among them in the glowing light the stars, so friendly and small, and kindly.

I set her down on a huge bed of silk, covered with silk blankets and pillows; a soft golden color seemed to be in every fabric or tapestry or design in some way, and the room was filled with soft molded chairs, Turkish luxury.

I smelled the salt, and her perfumed sweetness, and I looked down on her, her wax-pure face. Tenderly as I could, I kissed her forehead.

'Don't be afraid, darling one,' I said. 'Everything I told you was true. You must believe me. You must tell me what you know about Esther and Nathan.'

She began to sob, and then turned, faint, and shivering, and nestled into the pillows. I sat there. I pulled up a silken cover over her, something full of the French flowers. But she didn't need it.

'No, the air itself,' she said. 'The air. Kiss me again. Hold me again. Be with me.'

'I have you in my arms. My lips touch your forehead, your cheek, your chin, your shoulder, your hand . . .' I said. Truth was, I could hardly resist her. I wanted to loosen her fancy clothes, release her in my power.

I softly locked my hand around her fragile wrist. She really was dying.

'Don't fear me, beloved,' I said, 'unless it eases the pain. Sometimes it does, to fear one thing instead of others.'

In answer, she turned and kissed me again, tugging my head down close to her, so that she could push her tongue into my mouth. It was a luscious kiss, full of passion and utter yielding. I kissed her longingly. I felt her hips lift against me. I felt my own body hard for her.

I had to have her, I had to make her happy. And the world would let me know my power in this as it had let me know in everything else. If I lost all power in her arms, so be it.

There was too much human heat here for anything but love-making now. The sky itself, the dreamy stars, the high white clouds – these things as well – decreed it.

Twenty-one

She pulled weakly at the buttons of her blouse. 'Undress me, please, help me,' she said. I quickly removed all her clothes as she wished. She guided me and assisted me. She sank deep in the pillows, pale, but with a body as firm to touch as a young woman's body.

I kissed the calves of her legs, her thighs. The garden rustled and sighed behind me. For the first time I heard a waterfall, its gentle trickle, and then I listened to the sound of water touching leaves, but my body was an engine of desire, and what drove me was her naked breasts, rather small, with the pink nipples of a girl, and the smell of death, rising sweet like a crushing lily. It was not that the death attracted me; it was that it made her all the more precious, something to be lost in a moment.

She lay back, heaving a deep sigh. The angles of her face were tight and delicate and precise in the dimness.

'Let me see you without your clothes,' she said. She reached for buttons, but I gestured there was no need. I stood up and back from her.

Not an electric light burned in the place. It was the dreamiest darkness.

I stretched out my arms and looked up at the sky. Though suddenly aware of a fatigue from all the night's tricks, I nevertheless told my clothes to assemble themselves nearby and await my command. I would be naked.

It worked even more swiftly and completely than last time. I looked down for the first time on my own chest, pubic hair, erect organ. I was too happy for humility, and to feel the sinews in my arms tighten was to be among living things, and surely some of those things must be good things.

She sat up on the bed, her breasts amazingly firm, and the pink nipples turned up. Her silver-and-black hair made a rumpled mass down her back and displayed a long neck.

'Splendid,' she whispered.

A rain of doubts descended on me.

But I had to do it. What was the point of warning her that I might dissolve in the process? I was going to do it.

I sat down beside her, embracing her. I felt the moist thin silkiness of her skin, not healthy in a woman too thin, yet delicious. Even the bones of her wrists were beautiful.

She tugged at my hair, and kissed me with her eyes closed, all over my face, and quite suddenly I realized with a shock that my beard and mustache were on my face.

She drew back, staring at it. I told this hair to go away. 'No,' she said. 'Bring it back! It makes your mouth sweeter and damper.' I felt the hair return as if it wanted to! I couldn't quite figure this out, why the hair had come of its own, but that was the whole story so far, my body came on its own, and in its own form. One lapse in my will, one drifting into pride in my physical self, and the hair had come.

Well, she loved it. I took a long breath, feeling the toll of all this changing and magic, but I was as hard as a statue for her. I wanted to pounce on her. Instead I let her bury her face in the hair of my chest, and kiss my nipples, and the pleasure went right to my loins.

I took her breasts in my hands, enchanted by their smallness, their delicacy. So pink, girlish pink.

'It's all drugs, my love,' she said, as though feeling my wonder. She kissed my beard, kissing it along the bone of my jaw. 'It's hormones and modern science; I have a woman's chemicals inside me, that's all. They can make me look young, but they can't save my life.'

I kissed her and held her, my hands free and rough over her thighs and stealing into the secret crevice, to feel there the firmness of a young woman's secret body. Chemicals, was it? Modern science?

'Those things preserve,' I said, 'but you make the beauty.'

'Sweet God,' she whispered, kissing me all over my face. I had my hands beneath her small backside, and cuddled it.

'Yes,' I said, 'God, capricious as He is; he lavished his blessings on you and on your daughter, Esther.'

'And you were the last thing,' she breathed into my ear,

her hands clawing gently at my back. 'You were the last thing she saw. How good that was for her.'

A savage strength rose in me, the realization that I had her completely at my mercy, this precious creature, and that no words from anyone could command me away from her. Only her words would hold sway with me now, and only because I would defer to her.

It was like fruit between her legs, like peaches or plums, it was just wet enough. I brought my fingers to my nostrils.

'I can't hold back, my love,' I said.

She parted her legs, and lifted her hips, and this was paradise suddenly, to be inside her, inside this hot throbbing fruit, and to have her mouth at the same time, to have both her mouths, to cover her, with hair and strength. I began the manly rhythm. Alive, alive, alive. I was blinded. Pleasure drenched all my senses.

'Yes, now, yes, do it,' she said. She lifted her hips against me. I rose up on my elbows so as not to hurt her with my weight, and looking down at her, I felt the seed explode inside her. My jerking motions surely hurt her. But then I saw the blush I wanted in her face, I felt the throbbing in her throat, and knew she was as happy as I was. The tight little core of fruit squeezed the last drop out of me, and I fell over on my back, whole and alive, staring at the ceiling of this room, or staring into airy dark.

Whatever had been my life, spirit or man, I could not recall a pleasure as delicious as this one, as totally humiliating in the way it took over, in the way that it made me feel the slave and the master simultaneously. I didn't ask myself what men felt.

Her head turned from side to side; she was blood red. 'Come to me again, please, now,' she said.

Overjoyed, I rolled back on top of her and entered her. I didn't need a rest. The fruity secret part was more luscious, tighter than before, throbbing more fully. Again I came and her face flooded with blood, and then finally she scratched my back hard with both her hands, she beat on me with fists, and when I lifted up to thrust, she came with me just far enough, and then lay back, to make it ecstasy.

'Harder,' she said. 'Harder. Make this a battlefield, make me a boy you've found, a girl, I don't care.'

It was too inviting. I slammed against her, harshly, over and over, feeling the seed spill again, the sight of her red face filling me with an all-too-human sense of power. Yes, to have her, to make her come, to make her come, yes, again, and again.

I filled her up. I was so tight inside her, I dragged her hips up off the bed with me, and then in her wetness she let me slide back and forth, and like a brute soldier, I came down, driving her into the silken pillows, and I saw through my half-closed eyes that she smiled.

'Surrender, that's what I want,' I said through my teeth. She could not stop the pleasure coming in her; it came and came as if her heart would break. She was red and tossing, and I wouldn't let her go, slamming again and again against her sweet fruitlike lips, and then she lifted both her arms to cover her face, as if she would hide from me.

This sublime gesture, this maidenly gesture, this sweet gesture stripped me of the very last control I ever possessed in this or any other body, and I shot forth my seed for the third time, groaning aloud.

Now I was spent. I was tired. And she grew pale in the light of the moon and the white billowing clouds, and we lay there together. My cock was dripping.

She turned over and in the tenderest way, like a little girl almost, she kissed my shoulder. She ran her fingers through the hair on my chest.

'My darling,' I said. I spoke to her in old languages, natural to me, Chaldean, Aramaic, I spoke words of love and testaments of fidelity and devotion, and cooed against her ear, and she rippled with delight against me, and tore at my hair again.

Pillows had tumbled to the side. The air swirled around her, full of the scents of the garden. It stirred beneath the low, white ceiling, and suddenly, as if the wind had changed its direction, there came the song of the sea, the full great sea, relentless, the deceptive song of water, water gurgling in the waterfall that seems to be talking to you when it is saying

337

nothing, has no syllables, and water pounding the beach as if to say I am coming, I am coming. But there was no I.

'If I could die now, I would do it,' she said. 'But there are things you have to know.'

I drifted, I dreamed. I felt my fatigue. I shook myself awake. Did I have my body still? I feared sleep. Yet I felt the need of it, the assembled body needed it, as it needed water. I sat up.

'Don't talk of dying,' I said. 'It's going to happen soon enough.' I turned and looked down at her.

She looked composed, intelligent, all mind with angular collected limbs, quite incapable of the passion we'd just shared. I blurted out:

'I have no power to cure, not a disease this far advanced.'

'Have I asked you?'

'You must want to know, you must wonder.'

'I'll tell you why I didn't ask,' she said, reaching up and playfully tugging at the hair on my chest. 'I knew if you had the power, you would have helped me the moment you had the chance.'

'You're right, you're absolutely right.'

She closed her eyes, and tightened her lids. It was pain.

'What can I do?' I said.

'Nothing. I want these drugs to wear off. I want to die on my own.'

'I'm ready to bring you anything I can,' I said. I was shaken to the bone by the sight of her suffering, but it seemed to melt, and her face was waxen again and perfect.

'You talked about Esther, you said that you wanted to know –'

'Yes, why do you think your husband killed her?'

'I don't know! That's just it. They quarreled but I don't know. I can't believe it was on account of the family. Esther and Gregory fought all the time. It was normal. I don't know.'

'Tell me everything you remember about Esther and Gregory and this diamond necklace. You said she discovered his brother Nathan when she bought the necklace.'

'She met Nathan in the diamond district. She could see his

resemblance to Gregory and when she mentioned it, he confessed he was Gregory's identical twin.'

'Ah, identical.'

'But what could it all mean? He told her he was Gregory's twin. He told her to give Gregory his love. She was amazed. She liked him. She met the other Hasidim who work in the store with him. She liked Nathan very much. She said it was like looking at the man Gregory could have been, all filled up with gentleness and kindness.

'The day she died, I'm sure she took the necklace back to Nathan. I think I remember her saying that she had to drop it off, because some small thing was wrong and Nathan would fix it, and she said, "Don't tell the Messiah that I'm going to visit his brother," and she laughed. I think she dropped it off before those killers got her. Gregory knew she was shopping that day at Henri Bendel. He knew that. But I don't think he knew about the necklace. It wasn't till yesterday that the whole issue of the necklace came up. I didn't even know the necklace was gone. Nobody did. Then Gregory brought it up, that the terrorists had seized her necklace and killed her. Sure enough, the necklace was gone, but I couldn't reach Nathan to find out if he had it. Besides, he would have called. I know Nathan only by voice, but I know him now, through one phone call.'

'Go back now to the earlier part. Esther quarreled with Gregory about his brother, and the brother was an identical twin.'

'She had wanted him to meet with his brother. He had been frantic that she tell no one about the Hasidim, no one. He told her it was a matter of life or death. He tried to frighten her. I know Gregory. I know him when he's weak and not thinking too clearly, when he's caught off guard, and is furious and desperate.'

'I've seen this too,' I said, 'a glimpse of it.'

'Well, that's how he was with her. "No, no, no, you didn't meet any brother, I have no brother!" Then he came storming into me and desperately appealed to me in Yiddish to explain to her how the Hasidim would not want to be connected with him. But he was furious about the whole

339

affair. She didn't speak Yiddish, Esther. She came into the room, and I remember he turned and he said, "You ever tell anyone about Nathan and I'll never forgive you!"

'She was so confused. I drew her aside, tried to explain how the Observant Jews would not like Jews like us, who didn't pray each day, or observe the laws of the Talmud. She listened but I could see she didn't grasp this. She said, "But Nathan said he loved Gregory. He said he would love to see his brother. He said that from time to time he tries to call Gregory but he can't get through."

'I thought Gregory would go out of his mind. "I don't want to hear any more of this," he said. "If you gave him my private number tell me now! These people hurt me. I left when I was a boy. They hurt me! I made my own church, my own tribe, my own way. I am my Messiah!"

'I tried to calm him down, I said, "Gregory, please, we're not in a television pulpit. Sit down. Rest."

'Then Esther demanded to know why Gregory had been so kind to Nathan in taking him to the hospital. She said Nathan had told her all about that, this time in the hospital – how Gregory had checked Nathan into the hospital under his own name, and had paid all his expenses, and kept Nathan in a private suite, and didn't want to worry the Rebbe or his wife about it, took care of all of it. She said, "Nathan said you were so generous."

'I swear to you, I thought he would go crazy.

'I started to see how complex this was. Gregory had something at stake other than mere publicity. In fact, it was perfectly obvious to me that the Hasid connection would be a help to Gregory with his church, a form of . . . occult status . . . do you know what I mean?'

'Yes, I do exactly. Exotic and pure roots had grown this great leader.'

'Yes. So I sat up and tried to ask a few questions, "Why had Nathan been in the hospital?" And Esther said that Gregory had suggested it, Gregory had told Nathan that they were both at risk for something inherited in their family, and knowing the Rebbe would never agree, he had spirited Nathan away and had all the tests done under Gregory's name. For Nathan it had been a dream, the beautiful hospital suite, kosher food, all the proprieties observed, and the people thinking he was Gregory. He found it amusing. Of course he didn't have the hereditary disease, whatever that was. God, what on earth –'

'Ah, I see,' I said.

'What does all this amount to?'

'Keep telling me everything about Nathan and Esther,' I said. 'What else do you know?'

'Oh, that first night, we fought for hours about it. Finally she agreed she wouldn't tell anyone, or try to bring the families together, but she would see Nathan from time to time and give him Gregory's good wishes. Gregory began to cry with relief. Gregory can cry on cue, and on camera. He went into how his people had cast him out. The Temple was everything to him, his meaning, his life.

'Whenever he went into that speech, Esther and I would just roll our eyes. We knew that he had compiled the teachings of the Temple of the Mind with a computer program. He had programmed in all the information he could about other cults, and which commandments had given the members the most comfort, and then he had chosen a list of the most acceptable and likable commandments. Other aspects of the Temple were created the same way, through secret surveys and computer compilation of the most appealing aspects of other religions. It was a joke to Esther and me. But that night he wept and wept. It was his whole life. God had guided him and his computer.

'I went to sleep. Two days Esther and Gregory didn't speak to each other. But that was nothing unusual. They could have fought over some little political question and scream. It was the way they acted together.'

'What else?'

'Two nights later, Gregory woke me at four o'clock. He was in one of his rages. He said, "Take the phone, talk to him, listen to him yourself." I didn't know what the hell he meant.

'The voice coming through the phone sounded exactly like Gregory! I mean exactly. I could scarcely believe it was another person, but it was, and he introduced himself as Nathan, Gregory's brother. He asked me kindly explain to Esther that the families couldn't get together. "This breaks my heart, that I must say this to my brother's wife," he said, "but our grandfather doesn't have long to live and the Court depends on him. He is the Rebbe. Tell Esther that it can't be, and give her my love, and in time I will see her when she comes to visit me."

'I told him I understood perfectly. "You have my love too, brother-in-law. I too lost my parents in the camps. I wish you only well."

'Then in Yiddish he said we were in his prayers and in his thoughts, and if we ever needed him, if Gregory was ever ill or afraid, we must call him.

'I told him how good it was to hear a Yiddish voice, and to talk with him. He laughed and said something like "Gregory thinks he has everything, and thank God he has a good wife, but you never know when a brother will need a brother. Gregory has never been sick a day in his life, never been inside a hospital, except to visit me of course and take care of me, but I will come if he ever calls."

'I remember thinking about this hospital stay, these tests. Had Gregory himself had such tests? What was this hereditary disease? I knew it was true that Gregory had never been in a hospital. Gregory had a private doctor, hardly what I would call a licensed practitioner of medicine, but he had never to my knowledge been in a hospital. I said to Nathan how kind he was, and I asked how I might reach him, and then Gregory grabbed the phone back.

'He carried it out of the room with him but I could hear him talking Yiddish in a simple natural way, and intimately, in a way Gregory never spoke to anyone. I was really for the first time hearing him speak to a brother. I had never heard that. I had always been told that all Gregory's people were dead. All of them.'

'How long ago was all this?' I asked.

'About a month ago. But I didn't even think of it before now, all this. I mean, I knew in my heart that he had been responsible for Esther's death, I knew when I heard him make his speech about terrorism and enemies that he'd been lying. He was too *prepared* for Esther's death! But honestly, frankly, do you think he *would* kill his own daughter because of all this?'

'Yes, I do, but I see a large design here,' I said. 'And the Rebbe. You never met or spoke to the Rebbe?'

'No,' she said. 'I wouldn't go over there to be rejected. I have great reverence for those people, my parents were Hasidim from Poland. But no, I know that kind of old man.'

'Well, let me tell you this. That old man also accused Gregory of killing Esther. And he wanted to know the same thing you wanted to know, why.'

'Do you realize what this means?' she said. 'If he would kill Esther to protect the family secret, then he might kill Nathan!'

'Has there been no call from Nathan concerning this necklace?' I asked. 'I know how the Hasidim live, but this is news, diamonds, you know, talk of valuable diamonds snatched by terrorists.'

'No, no call that I know of, but you see, I'm cut off, I was surrounded by the Minders. And Gregory himself didn't even come up with the necklace part till the day after the murder. In his first speech, all he did was talk about enemies. Then the next day he ... my god, maybe that's when Nathan called him, but then he wouldn't have told such a lie or ... Why in the hell did he bring up the necklace?'

I was quietly absorbing all these words.

'I think I can figure it out,' I said. 'One thing is true, I foiled his plan. His plan is big. His design is big. I foiled it by killing those tramps that murdered her. So that blurred his attempt at calling it all terrorism. Those men cannot be traced to terrorists, can they?'

'No, not at all. Half the world is crying with him, and others are laughing at him. The men were bums out of some town in south Texas, bums. Now Gregory claims his enemies will use any means to hurt him and these bums were part of it and the theft was to give them badly needed wealth to fight his church.'

'Let's leave the necklace for a moment. He still played up

the terrorist part, and for some strange reason included the necklace. Now listen, I have to ask you. Why are there laboratories in the Temple of the Mind? Why?'

'Laboratories?' she asked. 'I have no idea. I didn't even know there were. Of course there's Gregory own doctor, who pumps him up with Human Growth Hormone and special protein drinks and anything else he can to keep his youth and strength, and they do have some kind of hospital room so that if Gregory runs a temperature one degree above normal, his doctor can examine him in it, but there are no laboratories as such, not as far as I know.'

'No, no, I mean big laboratories where people are working with chemicals and computers. Huge laboratories with sterile storage and people even dressed in funny clothes to protect themselves. I saw this tonight. I saw this in the Temple of the Mind. I saw some people wearing orange clothes that covered their whole bodies. I didn't think of it at the time. I was just looking for Gregory . . .'

'Orange suits, you're talking about suits that protect people from viruses. Good Lord, is there disease at the heart of this? Gregory has some disease? What the hell did he do to Nathan in the hospital!'

'I think I know. He didn't hurt his brother. And there is no disease in Gregory, I can tell you that for sure, or in the Rebbe. I would have known the moment I saw them. I sense these things.'

She winced, the mere thought of her own sickness suddenly confusing her and muddling her mind.

'What does the Temple do that would require a team of doctors, a big team of brilliant men ever ready at Gregory's command? Research geniuses with microscopes and all kinds of equipment?'

'I don't know,' she said again. 'Of course one time they did contemplate a line of products, you know, trash like spiritually cleansing shampoo and "wash away evil vibrations soap" —'

I laughed, I couldn't help it. She smiled.

'But we talked him out of that. He struck some incredibly

344

lucrative deal with a New York designer for all the stock at his resorts and on his boats, and in his jungles . . .'

'There we are again, boats, planes, jungles, doctors, a necklace, a twin brother.'

'What are you saying?'

'Look, Rachel, an identical twin is not just a brother, he is a duplicate of the man, and here we have a twin unknown to the world, and not recognized every day of the week perhaps because he wears the beard and the locks of the Hasidim. There are things one can do with an identical twin.'

She stared at me. She was silent. Then a wince of pain came again.

'Look, I have to have water,' I said. 'I'll bring you some water.'

'That would be good. Cold water. My throat is sore, I can't . . .'

She sank back down.

I hurried through the beautiful garden, and entered what seemed a grand storage place for fine foods, and sure enough, there were plastic bottles of water galore in the refrigerator. I brought two of these bottles and a lovely crystal glass which I picked off a shelf.

I sat down by her and gave her water first. She had covered herself now. She drank. I drank.

I really was exhausted. This was not the time to be exhausted, not the time to risk sleeping and letting this body disappear. I drank more of the water, and I wondered what had come out of my body into her, had it been real seed, or just a semblance?

I remembered something about Samuel. Samuel laughing at the Catholic nuns who claimed to be made pregnant by spirits. I remembered that from Strasbourg and then another lovely memory came, it was all sensory, it had to do with Zurvan, and I remember him saying, "You can do it, yes, but it will take away your energy and you are never to seek a woman without my permission."'

I couldn't remember the speaker, only the love, and the garden, and the words, and how much it was like this. *It will take away your energy*. I had to stay awake.

'What if we're wrong?' she said. 'And he had nothing to do with Esther's death. He's a man who uses everything. He used her death but that doesn't mean –'

'The Rebbe said he killed her. I think he killed her. But there's more at stake. This temple of his, does it preach anything unique or of unique value?'

'Not really; as I explained, he invented the creed with a computer program. It's the nearest thing to a creedless creed you can imagine.'

She sighed. She told me there was a dressing gown in the closet. Would I bring it to her? She was feeling a little cold. She said there were robes, too, if I wanted them. I did, but not because I was cold. It was a Persian or Babylonian disinclination to be naked.

I found a thick blue robe that fell to the floor, with a tie for the waist, and wrapped myself in this, feeling a little trapped, but it was fine for now, and I needed all my power.

I brought the negligee to her. It was gold like so much in the room, and pure silk and full of beaded work rather like that of the dark scarf. She sat up and I helped her put it on, and I buttoned the pearl buttons for her, and then tied the sash. I buttoned the pearls at her wrists.

She stared at me.

'I have something else,' she said, 'that I want you to know.'

'Tell me,' I said, sitting beside her and taking her hand.

'Gregory called me tonight right before the plane landed in Miami. He told me *you* killed Esther. He said you were seen at the scene of the crime. I'd seen your picture in the magazine, but I knew it was a stupid lie. I was about to hang up on him. It's useless, you know, asking him to be reasonable, but then he really went off the deep end. He said you were a ghost, and you needed to take Esther's place in the world, that's how you got in.'

'That is trash!' I whispered. 'He is a smooth-tongued man.'

'That's what I thought. I just didn't believe it. But something seemed very certain to me then. You are here because of Esther's death. You are, and you're here to kill Gregory. I wish you would promise me, whatever happens, you'll kill him. I know it's a terrible thing I'm saying.'

'Not to me,' I said. 'I would like to kill him but not before this mystery is solved.'

'Can you possibly see to Nathan? See that he's safe?'

'I can do that,' I said, 'but I have grave suspicions on that. Never mind. Be assured, whatever happens, I will get to the bottom of it, and Gregory will pay with his life.'

'Laboratories,' she said. 'You know he's crazy, Gregory. He believes he is here to save the world. He goes to other countries, he asks for reception by dictators and establishes temples in countries that ... and then all this about terrorism. You know,' she said as she lay back down on the pillows. 'You can't go wrong killing him. This Temple is a racket. It's garbage, and it bleeds people, takes their savings, their fortunes ...'

She closed her eyes, and suddenly went still, so still that her eyes half-opened and I could see only the whites.

'Rachel!' I said. 'Rachel!' I shook her shoulder.

'I'm alive, Azriel,' she said softly without moving anything but her lips. Her dark brows moved just a little. She didn't open her eyes. 'I'm here,' she said. 'Will you cover me, Azriel? Even now I'm cold. It's warm, isn't it?'

'The breeze is wondrously warm,' I said.

'Open all the windows then. But cover me. What is it? What's the matter with you?'

All the windows *were* open, even the big window doors to my left that looked out on a terrace above the ocean. But I didn't disturb her by saying so.

I was suddenly startled. I noticed her arms for the first time. Really beheld them beneath the sheer silk.

'Your arms, I've covered them with bruises! Look what I've done to you.'

'That doesn't matter,' she said. 'That's nothing. It's only one of the drugs thinning the blood, makes me bruise without feeling it. I loved it, your being in my arms. Come here, will you stay with me? You know, I suspect I'm going to die right away. I left behind all the drugs that were keeping me going.'

I didn't answer her but I knew she was going to die. Her heartbeat was too slow. Her fingers had a bluish tinge to them.

I lay down beside her, and covered her with the tapestried draperies that lay all over the bed, what are called 'throws' and 'lap blankets,' though I had not realized it or thought of it.

She was nice and warm and she lay against me.

'I laughed so hard when he said you were a ghost and you killed Esther to get into the world. And yet I knew you weren't a human being. I knew it. You'd vanished from the plane. I knew it. And yet I thought Gregory was so hysterically funny telling me all this black magic, that Esther had to be sacrificed like a lamb so that you could come into the world and evil beings had done it. He said you'd kill me. He said if I didn't come back, he'd alert the police. I don't want him coming in here, disturbing me. I don't want him to.'

'I won't let him,' I said. 'Rest now. I want to think. I want to remember the laboratories and the men in the orange suits. I want to see the great scheme.'

It was a horrid thing to look at, her purplish bruises, and I felt shame that I hadn't been more delicate, hadn't even watched for such a thing, hadn't looked for anything but the age-old juiciness, and for all the rest, what did I care.

I held her arms. I kissed these places, and I could see where needles had made holes in her, and I could see where bandages had been ripped from her, and all the fleece was gone.

'Rachel, you are suffering, and I've made this worse for you,' I said. 'Let me get for you what you need. Send me. Tell me. I can get anything in the world for you, Rachel. That's my nature. Do you have doctors of great skill? Only tell me who they are. I'll be lost in the winds if I roam searching for doctors and magicians. Guide me. Send me. Send me now for whatever it is . . .'

'No.'

I studied her silent face; her smile had not changed. She seemed half-asleep; I realized she was singing, or humming with her lips closed. Her hands were too cold.

I sighed; this was the agony that comes with loving; this was just as fresh as if it had never happened to me before.

This was just as hurtful and cruel as if I were breathing and young.

'Don't worry,' she whispered. 'All the best doctors in the world have done their damnedest to cure Gregory Belkin's wife. Besides . . . I want to . . .'

'. . . be with Esther.'

'Yes, do you think I will be?'

'Yes, I do,' I said. 'I saw her go up in a pure light.' I wanted to add, 'One way or another, you'll be with her.' But I didn't add it. I didn't know whether she believed we were all tiny flames that went back into God, or that we had a Paradise where we could kiss and hold each other. As for me, I believed we had a Paradise, and I had a dim memory of flying high once, to the very heights, and of gentle spirits up there concealing something from me.

I lay back. I had been so sure I wanted to die. And now the flame of life that blazed still in her, melting her like a candle, seemed utterly precious to me.

I wanted to try to cure her. I looked at her and tried to see all the workings of her, each thing connected to the next thing, and all bound with veins like woven gold thread.

I did lay my hands on her, and I did pray. I let my hair rest on her face. I prayed in my heart to all the gods.

She stirred. 'What did you say, Azriel?' she said. She uttered some words. At first I didn't understand them. Then I realized it was Yiddish she was speaking. 'Were you speaking Hebrew?' she asked me.

'Just praying, my darling,' I said. 'Think nothing of it.' She took a deep breath and laid her hand on my chest, as if the very act of lifting her hand and setting it down exhausted her. I put my hand over hers. Too cold, her little hands. I made a heat for us both.

'You're really staying with me, aren't you?'

'Why does that surprise you?' I asked.

'I don't know. Because people try to get away from you when they know you're really dying. Those bad nights, when I was at my worst, the doctors didn't come, the nurses stayed away. Even Gregory wouldn't come. The crisis would pass, and then they would all come. And you, you are staying with

349

me. Doesn't the air smell good? And the light. Just the light of the night sky.'

'It's beautiful, a foreshadowing of Paradise.'

She laughed a little laugh. 'I'm ready to be nothing,' she said.

What could I say?

Somewhere a bell rang. It throbbed. I sat up. I didn't like it. I was staring into the garden, at the big red flowers, like trumpets, and realized for the first time that there were dim electric lights there on these flowers. Everything was perfect. There came the bell again.

'Don't answer it,' she said. She was damp all over.

'Look,' she said. 'Stop him, you stop the church. He's what we call a charismatic leader. He's evil. Laboratories. I don't like it. And these cults, these cults have killed people, have killed their own members.'

'I know,' I said. 'It was always that way. Always.'

'But Nathan, Nathan is so innocent,' she said. 'I can remember his voice, it was beautiful, and I thought of what Esther had said, that it was like seeing the man Gregory could have been. That's what the voice was like . . .'

'I'll find him and make sure he is safe,' I said. 'I'll find out what he knows, what he saw.'

'The old man, is he so terrible?'

'Holy and old,' I said. I shrugged.

She laughed a sweet delighted laugh. It was wondrous to hear it. I bent down and kissed her lips. They were dry. I gave her some more water, holding her head up so she could drink.

She lay back. She looked at me and only gradually did I realize that her expression meant nothing. It was only a mask for her pain. The pain was in her lungs and in her heart and in her bones. The pain was all through her. The soothing drugs she'd taken before she left New York were gone out of her body. Her heart was faint.

I cradled her hands in mine.

There came that noise again, the bell ringing, the alarm buzzing, and this time there was more than one. I heard the noise of a motor. It came from the elevator shaft.

350

'Ignore it,' she said. 'They can't get in.' She pushed at the covers with her hands.

'What is it?' I asked.

'Help me, help me get up. Get my heavier robe for me, the heavy silk. Please . . .'

I got the robe, the one to which she pointed, and she put it on. She stood trembling beneath the weight of the ornate robe.

There was huge noise outside the main door.

'Are you sure they can't get in?'

'You don't have to fear, do you?' she asked.

'No, not at all, but I don't want them . . .'

'I know . . . ruining my death,' she said.

'Yes.'

She was completely white.

'You're going to fall down.'

'I know,' she said. 'But I intend to fall where I want to fall. Help me out there, I want to look at the ocean.'

I picked her up and carried her out the doors to the balcony. This was due east. The doors faced not the bay but the true sea. I realized it was the same sea that washed the banks of Europe, the shores of ruined Greek cities, the sands of Alexandria.

A pounding noise came from behind us. I turned around. It was coming from within the elevator. There were people in the car of the elevator. But the doors were locked.

The breeze ripped across the broad terrace. Under my feet the tiles felt cool. She seemed to love it, putting her head against my shoulder, looking out over the dark sea. A great ship, hung with lights, glided by, just short of the horizon, and above, the clouds made their spectacle.

I cuddled her and held her, and started to pick her up.

'No, let me stand,' she said. She tugged herself gently free of me and put her hands on the high stone railing. She looked down. I saw a garden far down there, immaculate and full of trees and bright lights. Egyptian lilies galore, and large fanlike plants, all waving just a little in the breeze.

'It's empty down there, isn't it?' she asked.

'What?'

351

'The garden. It's so private. Only the flowers beneath us, and beyond, the sea.'

'Yes,' I said.

The elevator door was being forced open.

'Remember what I said,' she said. 'You can't go wrong killing him. I mean it. He'll try to seduce you, or destroy you, or use you in some way. You can bet he is already thinking in those terms, how best to use you.'

'I understand him perfectly,' I said. 'Don't worry. I will do what is right. Who knows? Maybe I will teach him right and wrong. Maybe I know what they are. Maybe I'll save his soul.' I laughed. 'That would be lovely.'

'Yes, it would,' she said. 'But you're craving life, craving it. Which means you can be lured by him with all his fiery life, the same way you were lured by mine.'

'Never, I told you. I'll put it right.'

'All of it, put it all to right.'

Several men had just broken through the front door, with a clumsy pounding noise. I heard the wood splinter.

She sighed. 'Maybe Esther did call you down. Maybe she did,' she said. 'My angel.'

I kissed her.

The men were blundering into the room behind us. I didn't have to look at them to know they were there. They stopped short; there was a rumble of urgent voices. Then Gregory's voice carried.

'Rachel, thank God you're all right.'

I turned and I saw him and he saw me, and he looked hard and determined, and cold. 'Let my wife go,' he said. Liar.

He was blazing with anger, and anger made him evil; anger took away his charm. I suppose it had done that to mine before. And I realized slowly as I stood there that I loved again, and didn't hate. I loved Esther and I loved Rachel. I didn't hate even him.

'Go to the door and stand between us,' Rachel said. 'Do that for me, please.' She kissed me on the cheek. 'Do that, my angel.'

I obeyed. I put my hand up on the steel frame. 'You can't pass,' I said.

Gregory roared. He let out a terrible roar, a roar from the soul, and the whole company of men rushed towards me. I turned around as they buffeted my shoulders, passing me. But I knew already what had made them cry out.

She had jumped.

I went to the railing, pushing them aside, and I looked down into the garden and I saw her tiny empty shell of a body. The light hovered around her.

'Oh, God, take her, please,' I prayed in my ancient tongue.

Then the light blazed and went straight up and for a moment it seemed that lightning lashed the southern sky, exploded behind the clouds, but it was only her passing. She'd gone up, and for one second perhaps I'd seen the Door of Heaven.

The garden held nothing but its bed of Egyptian flowers and her empty flesh, her face unhurt, intact, staring blindly upward.

Go up, Rachel, please, Esther, take her up the ladder. I deliberately envisioned the Ladder, the Stairway, replete with all the hanging remnants of memory.

Gregory cried in agony. Men took hold of me by the arms. Gregory screamed and cried and sobbed and there was no artifice to it. The man stared down at her and roared in pain and hit the railing with his fists.

'Rachel, Rachel, Rachel!'

I shook off the hands of the men. They fell backwards, stunned by the strength of it, and not knowing what to do, seemingly embarrassed by the figure of Gregory roaring in grief.

Suddenly there was havoc all around me. More men had come, poor Ritchie had come, and Gregory wailed and wailed and leaned over the railing. He was davening, bowing like a Hebrew and crying out in Yiddish.

I shoved off the men again, hurling some of them to the end of the terrace, I pushed and I pushed at them till they simply backed off.

I said to Gregory:

'You really loved her, didn't you?'

He turned and looked at me, and tried to speak but he was choked with grief. 'She was . . . my queen of Sheba,' he said. 'She was my queen . . .' And then he wailed again, and said the same prayers.

'I'm leaving you now,' I said, 'with all your armed men.'

A crowd was climbing up the slope of the garden below. Men with flashlights shone them on her dead face.

Then I went up and up.

Where would I go? What would I do?

It was time to walk on my own.

I looked back once at the tiny men down on the terrace, confounded now by my disappearance. Gregory had actually collapsed and sat down rocking, holding his head.

Then I went high, so high that the joyous spirits were there, and it seemed as I flew north that they stared at me with great interest.

I knew what I had to do first of all. Find Nathan.

Twenty-two

By the time I reached New York the need for sleep was weighing me down. I would have to give in to it before further explorations.

But I was fiercely worried about Nathan. Before taking on a body, I prowled invisibly all through the Temple of the Mind.

Just as I expected, there was much chemical research being done there, and there were numerous restricted areas, and there were people working in the night in the strange rubbery orange plastic suits I had seen, and these suits seemed to be filled with air. These suited beings peered through their helmets as they worked with chemicals which they obviously did not mean to breathe or touch. They were loading these into what seemed very lightweight plastic cartridges.

I studied everything else that was going on.

In an antiseptic laboratory, my bones lay on a hard table, being studied by the evil Mastermind doctor, the thin one with the bottleblack hair. He had no hint of my invisible presence as I circled him. I could not make out his notes. I felt nothing for the Bones, except the desire to destroy them so that I could never be driven back into them again. But I might die if that happened. It was much too soon for such a risk.

Other parts of the building were obviously communication centers. There were people watching monitors, speaking on phones and working with maps. There were great electrified maps of the world on the wall, filled with pinpoints of light.

There was a great air of urgency and commotion among these night workers.

All spoke in a completely guarded way, as if they thought they were being monitored by enemies, and their statements were maddeningly vague. 'We have to hurry.' 'This is going to be glorious.' 'This has to be loaded by four a.m.' 'Everything at Point 17 is perfectly in line.'

I could not make something sensible or sophisticated out of what they said. I managed to discover from one slip of the tongue that the project they all shared was called Last Days.

Last Days.

All I saw alarmed me and repelled me. I suspected the chemicals in the canisters were filoviruses, or some other lethal agent only recently discovered through technology, and the entire Temple stank of murder.

I passed many empty floors, many sleeping dormitories filled with young Minders, and a huge chapel where Minders prayed silently like contemplative monks, on their knees with their hands pressed to their foreheads. The image over the altar was a great Brain. The Mind of God, I presume. It was a mere outline in gold. It was strangely uninspiring. It looked anatomical and bizarre.

I passed rooms where men slept alone, in dimness. In one room was a man covered up and bandaged, with a nurse in attendance. In other chambers, there were other sick people, swathed in sheeting, hooked to gleaming tubes connected to tiny computers. Many solitary rooms contained sleeping members of the church. Some were so luxurious as to rival Gregory's rooms. They had floors of marble tile and gilded furniture; they had sumptuous bathrooms with great square tubs.

I had many unanswered questions about what I saw in the building, and could have spent much more time.

But now I had to go on to Brooklyn. I felt I could see what was happening. Surely, Nathan was in danger.

It was two a.m. Invisible I passed into the Rebbe's house and found him sound asleep in his bed, but he woke the minute I entered the room. He knew I was there. He was at once alarmed and climbed out of the bed. I simply went very far away from the house. There was no time to search for Nathan or to look for more sympathetic members of the family.

Besides, I was growing more tired by the minute. I couldn't dare retreat to the Bones; in fact, I had no intention

356

of ever retreating to them again, not the way that I felt now, and I feared my weakness in sleep, that I might be called back or dissolved by Gregory or even somehow by the Rebbe.

I went back into Manhattan, found a lake in the middle of Central Park not very far at all from the huge Temple of the Mind. Indeed, I could see all its lighted windows. I took form as a man, dressed myself in the finest garb I could conceive of – red velvet suit, fine linen shirt, all manner of exotic gold embellishments – and then I drank huge amounts of water from the lake. I knelt and drank it in handfuls. I was filled with water, and felt very powerful. I lay down on the grass under a tree to rest, in the open, telling my body to hold firm and to wake if there was any natural or supernatural assault on it. I told it it must answer no one's call but my own.

When I woke it was eight o'clock in the morning by the city's clocks, and I was whole, intact, with my clothes, and I was rested. Just as I supposed, I had appeared far too strange for prowling mortal men to attack, and far too puzzling to be disturbed by beggars. Whatever the case, I was strong and unharmed in my velvet suit and shining black shoes.

I had survived the hours of sleep in material form, outside the bones, and this was another triumph.

I danced for joy on the grass for a few minutes, then brushed off the clothes, dissolved with the requisite enchantments, and re-formed, velvet clad, bearded, and free of bits of grass and dirt in the living room of the Rebbe's house. I did not want the beard, but the beard and mustache came as they had before. And maybe they'd even been there when I woke. In fact, I'm sure they had. They had been there all along. They wanted to be there. Very well.

The house was modern, cramped, made of many smallish rooms.

It struck me as most remarkable how conventional this house was. It was filled with rather ordinary furniture, none of it ugly or beautiful. Comfortable and well lighted. Immediately people waiting in the parlor stared at me and began to whisper. A man approached, and in Yiddish I said I had to see Nathan immediately.

I realized I didn't know Nathan's real last name. Or even if they called him Nathan here. Obviously his last name wasn't Belkin. Belkin was a made-up name of Gregory. I said in Yiddish that it was a matter of life and death that I see Nathan.

The Rebbe flung open the doors of his study. He was in a fury. Two elderly women stood with him, and two young men, all of these people Hasidim, the women wigged to cover their natural hair, the young men with locks and silk suits. There was no one about who was not Hasidim.

The Rebbe's face was trembling with outrage. He began to try to exorcise me from the house, and I stood firm and put up my hand.

'I have to speak to Nathan,' I said in Yiddish. 'Nathan could be in danger. Gregory is a dangerous man. I have to speak to Nathan. I won't leave here until I find him. Perhaps his is a compassionate and fearless heart and he will hear me. Whatever the case, I will speak to him in love. Perhaps Nathan walks with God, and if I save him, so shall I.'

Everyone fell silent. Then the men bid the women to go, which they did, and they called several old men from the parlor, and they pointed for me to go into the Rebbe's study.

I was now among an assemblage of elders.

One of these men took a piece of white chalk and drew a circle on the carpet and told me to stand in it.

I said:

'No. I am here to love, to avert harm, I am here having loved two people who are now dead. I learned love from them. I will not be the Servant of the Bones. I will do no evil. I will not be driven any longer by anger, hatred, or bitterness. And I will not be confined by you and your magic to that circle. I am too strong for that circle. It means nothing to me. The love of Nathan is what calls me now.'

The Rebbe sank down at his desk, a rather large formal one compared to his desk in the basement, where I had first seen him. He seemed in despair.

'Rachel Belkin is dead,' I told him in Yiddish. 'She took her own life.'

358

'The news says you took her life!' said the Rebbe in Yiddish. The other men murmured, nodding.

A very very old man, balding and thin with a head like a skull covered in black silk, came forward and looked into my eyes. 'We don't watch television; we don't do it. But the news spread fast. That you killed her and you killed her daughter.'

'That is a lie,' I said. 'Esther Belkin met Nathan, Gregory's brother, in the diamond district. She bought a necklace from him. I believe Gregory Belkin had her murdered because she knew of his family and in particular of his twin brother. Nathan is in danger.'

They all stood motionless. I couldn't predict what was going to happen. I knew I made a strange sight in the dark red velvet with so much gold ornament on the cuffs and with my dark hair and long beard, but so did they make a strange sight, all of them bearded and wearing hats, either small- or large-brimmed, and in long black silk suits all their own style.

They gradually formed a circle around me.

They began to hurl questions at me. At first I didn't realize what this was. Then it became clear that it was a test. The first question was, Could I quote from this or that book of the Torah. They used letters and names I understood completely. I answered all their questions, throwing out the quotations first in Hebrew and then in Greek, and then sometimes, to really startle them, in older Aramaic.

'Name the prophets,' they said.

I did, including Enoch, who had been a prophet in my time in Babylon, whom they didn't know. They were shocked at this.

'Babylon?'

'I can't remember!' I said. 'I have to stop Gregory Belkin from hurting his brother, Nathan. I'm convinced he killed Esther because she met Nathan and knew of Nathan, and there are other suspicious things.'

Now they began to question me on the Talmud: What were the Mitzvot? I told them there were 613, and they were laws or rules in general concerned with attitude, what one does, good behavior, and what one says.

The questions went on and on. They had to do with ritual

and cleanliness, and what is forbidden, and with the heretic rabbis, and with the Kabbalah. I answered everything rapidly, lapsing into Aramaic over and over, then coming back to Yiddish. When I quoted from the Septuagint, I used the Greek.

I referred sometimes to the Babylonian Talmud and sometimes to the old Jerusalem Talmud. I answered all questions about sacred numbers, and the points of discussion became finer and finer. It seemed each man was trying to outdo the other with the delicacy of his question.

Finally I became impatient.

'Do you realize while we carry on like this, as if we were in the yeshiva, that Nathan may be in danger? What is Nathan's name among you? Help me save Nathan, in the name of God.'

'Nathan is gone,' said the Rebbe. 'He is far far away, where Gregory cannot find him. He is safe in the Lord's city.'

'How do you know he's safe?'

'The day after the death of Esther he left here for Israel. Gregory cannot find him there. Gregory could never track him down.'

'The day after . . . you mean then the day before you first saw me?'

'Yes, if you aren't a dybbuk, what are you?'

'I don't know. What I want to be is an angel and that is what I intend to be. And God will judge whether I have done His Will. What made Nathan go to Israel?'

The old men looked at the Rebbe, obviously confused. The Rebbe said that he wasn't sure why Nathan wanted to take the trip just then, but it seemed in his grief for Esther, Nathan was eager to go and said something about doing his yearly work early in Israel. His work had to do with copies of the Torah which he would bring back. Routine.

'Can you reach him?' I said.

'Why should we tell you more?' said the Rebbe. 'He's safe from Gregory.'

'I don't think so,' I said. 'Now that you are all here, I want you to answer. Did any of you call upon the Servant of the Bones? Did Nathan?'

They all shook their heads and looked at the Rebbe.

'Nathan would never do such an unholy thing.'

'Am I unholy?' I lifted my hands. 'Come,' I said, 'I invite you. Try to exorcise me, try in the name of the Lord God of Hosts. I'll stand here firm in my love for Nathan and for Esther and Rachel Belkin. I want to avert harm. I will stand firm. Go on, give me your abracadabra Kabbalah magic!'

This roused them all to whispering and murmuring, and the Rebbe, who was still furious, did begin a loud chant to exorcise me, and then all the men joined in and I watched them, feeling nothing, not letting any anger come to the fore, only feeling love for them, and thinking with love of my Master Samuel, and how I had hated him for something perhaps that was only human. I couldn't remember it. I remembered Babylon. I remembered the prophet Enoch, but each time sadness or hate or bitterness came to me I pushed it away and thought of love, love profane, love sacred, love of the good . . .

I still could not recall Zurvan distinctly, only the feeling, but I quoted him now out loud as best I could. Each time it seemed I used new words but it was the same quote: 'The purpose of life is to love and to increase our knowledge of the intricacies of creation. Kindness is the way of God.'

They kept up the exorcism, and I searched my mind, closing my eyes, and sought for the proper words, calling to the world to yield to me the proper words that would quiet them, just the way that it yielded to me the clothing I wore, or the skin that appeared human.

Then I saw the words. I saw the room. I didn't know where it was then. Now I realize that it was the scriptorium in my father's house. All I knew was that it was familiar and I began to sing the words, as I had sung them long ago, with the harp on my knee. As I had written them over and over.

I sang them now in the ancient tongue in which I learned them, loudly and with rhythm, rocking as I sang:

> *I will love thee, O Lord, my strength.*
> *The Lord is my rock, and my fortress and my*
> *deliverer; my God, my strength,*

in whom I will trust, my buckler
and the horn of my salvation and my high tower.

The sorrows of death compassed me,
and the floods of ungodly men made me afraid
The sorrows of hell compassed me about:
the snares of death prevented me
In my distress I called upon the Lord,
And cried unto my God; he heard my voice . . .

This silenced them. They stood staring in wonder, not afraid and not full of hate. Even the Rebbe's soul was stilled and had lost its hate.

I spoke in Aramaic: 'I forgive those who made of me a demon, whoever they were, and to whatever purpose. Learning to love from Esther and Rachel, I come in love and to love Nathan and to love God. To love is to know love, and that is to love God. Amen.'

The old man looked suspicious suddenly, but it was not of me. He looked at the telephone on his desk. Then he glanced at me.

The very old one said, in Hebrew, 'So he was a demon who would be an angel? Is such a thing possible?'

The Rebbe didn't answer.

Then suddenly the Rebbe picked up the phone and punched in a long series of numbers, too long for me to follow or remember, and then he began to talk in Yiddish.

He asked if Nathan was there. Had Nathan arrived safely? He assumed that someone would have called, had Nathan not arrived, but he wanted to speak to his grandson.

Then shock came over his face. The room was silent. All the men looked at him and seemed to know what he was thinking.

The Rebbe spoke into the phone in Yiddish:

'He didn't tell you that he was coming? You have not heard from him, one single word?'

The old men were distressed. So was I.

'He's not there,' I said. 'He's not there!'

The old man went over all the details with those at the

362

other end of the line. They knew nothing about Nathan coming to Israel. Last they heard, Nathan would come at his regular time later in the year. All was in readiness for Nathan's regular visit. They had received no calls from Nathan about an early visit.

The Rebbe put down the phone. 'Don't tell Sarah!' he said with his hand raised. All the others nodded. He then told the youngest of the men to go for Sarah. 'I'll speak with Sarah.'

Sarah came into the room, a modest and humble woman, very beautiful, her natural hair covered by an ugly brown wig. She had narrow almond-shaped eyes, and a lovely soft mouth. She emanated kindness and when she glanced at me shyly she made no judgment.

She looked at the Rebbe.

'Your husband has called you since he left?'

She said no.

'You went with him and Jacob and Joseph to the plane?'

She said no.

Silence.

She looked at me and then looked down.

'Please, forgive me,' I said, 'but did Nathan tell you he was going to Israel?'

She said yes, and that a car had come for him, from a rich friend in the city to take him, and he had said he would be back very soon.

'Did he tell you who this friend was?' I asked. 'Please tell me, Sarah, please.'

She seemed utterly reassured and something inside her was suddenly unlocked. I saw in her eyes the same gentleness that I had seen in the girl on the street in the southern city, and in Esther herself, and in Rachel. The pure gentleness of women, which is wholly different from the pure gentleness of men.

Maybe this is what happens when you love, really love, I thought. People love you in return! I felt so free of hatred and anger suddenly that I shivered, but I implored her with my eyes to speak.

She looked shaken and then she glanced at the Rebbe, and bowed her head and blushed. She was about to cry.

'He had with him her diamond necklace,' she said, 'the necklace of his brother's daughter, Esther Belkin. He was taking it to his brother.'

She began to cry.

'When he had heard of the necklace being stolen,' she said, 'when he heard this tale, he knew it wasn't true. He had the necklace. Esther Belkin had given it to him for mending.' She swallowed her tears and continued. 'Rebbe, he didn't want anyone to be angry. He called his brother to tell him. He said his brother was crying. The car came to take him to his brother so that he might restore the necklace to him which had been Esther's, and then his brother wanted Nathan to come with him to Israel that they stand together at the Wailing Wall. Nathan promised me that when he had comforted his brother, he would return. Perhaps, he said, he could bring his brother back home.'

'Ah, of course,' I said.

'Quiet,' said the Rebbe. 'Sarah, don't be sorry or sad. Don't worry. I'm not angry that he went with his brother. He went in love, with good intentions.'

'He did, Rebbe,' she said. 'He did.'

'Leave this to us.'

'I'm so sorry, Rebbe. But he loved his brother and was so stricken with grief for the girl. He said the girl would one day have come to us and would have wanted to be one of us. He was sure of it. He had seen it in her eyes.'

'I see, Sarah. Don't think any more about it. Go out now.'

She turned her head, still crying, glanced back at me once, and then left the room.

I felt so sorry for her, so very sorry! She knew something was wrong, but she had no idea what was wrong, how bad it was. She was loving by nature. Maybe Nathan was too. Very likely so, as Rachel and Esther had said he was.

'It's just as I thought,' I said.

The old man waited on me in silence.

'Gregory used the necklace to lure Nathan to him. Gregory published that stupid story of the stolen necklace so that Nathan would call him, and he could persuade Nathan to meet with him and stay with him. Nathan prepared you for his prolonged absence. Gregory put him up to this. I will do everything in my power to see that Nathan is returned unharmed. I can't stay with you now. Will you give me your blessing, all of you? I won't linger begging for it, but if you want to give it, I will receive it with love in the name of the Lord. My name is Azriel.'

They cried out, throwing up their hands and backing away. It was the fear of knowing the name of a spirit, though I hadn't expected such alarm at this point. I put my hands to my temples and thought again, 'Yield to me the words! Yield to me the words. I know my name is not evil.'

Then I declared. 'I was named Azriel by my father when I was circumcised in our own house of prayer at Babylon. We were the last tribes taken hostage out of Jerusalem by Nebuchadnezzar. The name was good enough for God and for the Tribe and for my father! Nabonidus was King and we practiced our faith in peace under his rule. We sang the Lord's Song in that strange land every day.'

A great flush of energy passed through me, but again the memory lacked substance, color. I knew only that what I said was true, and that if I could solve this blasted mystery, this horror, then perhaps in time I could recall other things, just as I had recalled this, and all my past would come to me. Not in hatred, but in love. I was now fascinated by love. No doubt of it.

They fell to murmuring, it is his Hebrew name, it is his human name, it is his own name blessed by God, and some arguing that to know my name only gave them power over me and others whispered that I was an angel.

Then with a nod from the Rebbe, they all gave me their blessings. I felt nothing, but at least I didn't dislike them anymore; I loved them and saw them for what they were and feared all the more for Nathan.

'But what is Gregory doing?' the Rebbe whispered, more to himself than to me.

'I don't know,' I admitted again. 'But Nathan is an identical twin, is he not? And your grandson Gregory would be the Messiah, would he not? He would change the whole world.'

The old man was perplexed and horrified.

I asked, 'If I need you, for Nathan's sake, for the sake of the love of all God's creatures, will you come?'

'Yes,' said the Rebbe.

I was about to walk out of the room. But I decided for obvious reasons that it was best to vanish. I did so slowly so as to amaze them, growing transparent, rising, extending my arms, then vanishing altogether. I don't think they saw the tiny bits of moisture all through the air. They probably only felt the coolness and then the heat when a spirit vanishes.

I left them staring solemnly at the place where I'd stood. I wanted desperately to comfort Sarah, whom I saw crying at the kitchen table, but there was no way, no time.

I went up higher and higher.

'Gregory!' I said, and I set my destination to that place where the Master of the Bones might be – his Temple. To search, as a spirit, for Nathan was impossible. I had never laid eyes on him, caught his scent, seen or touched him or his garments. He might have been sleeping in one of those rooms in the Temple which I roamed, invisibly, the night before. But I had not lingered on faces. There had been hundreds of faces.

Go to Gregory. The danger to Nathan was with his brother, and that was where I had to be now. I had one comforting thought. Whatever was in store for Nathan had probably not transpired yet.

On the other hand, the people in the Temple had been working full speed on the project called the Last Days.

Twenty-three

A huge mob surrounded the Temple of the Mind. I came down into it invisible, amid the cameras and the radio people and understood that Gregory Belkin was to appear to make a momentous statement at six p.m. or before and that he knew the identity of his enemies and the enemies of the Temple. He intended to name his terrorist enemies and try to prevent their new plan of destruction.

The crowd spilled out, blocking Fifth Avenue, and many of the Minders, virtually pushed away by the press, were in the park praying.

I went up and into the building and found Gregory seated in a huge room with five men, amid the big electric maps and numerous monitors, and he was hard at work going over the final directions. The room itself was soundproof, and before I made myself visible I saw that no camera monitored the room itself. All monitors revealed the outside, and the walls in the rooms didn't have ears either.

As I descended, Gregory spoke:

'Nothing will happen until two hours after I'm declared officially dead –' he said, and these words immediately galvanized me.

I appeared in my full Babylonian robes of blue velvet and gold, and my long hair and beard, and I snatched him up from the chair.

The men raced at me, and I threw them back. Through another door came a small group of heavily armed soldiers. Someone fired a gun. Gregory shouted no. No. This little cadre of ruthless guards surrounded me with powerful modern guns, the kind that fix you in a beam of light before they shoot you. All these men had the look of killers.

As for those who had been gathered at the table, they were the milder sort, though equally as serious, that included the Mastermind Doctor, and they reeked of resentment and suspicion and absolute desperation that I had interrupted them.

'No, be calm,' said Gregory. 'This is inevitable and this will not stop us. This is an angel sent from God to help us.'

'Is that so?' I said. 'What have you done with your brother? If you don't talk the truth to me, I'll tear you limb from limb and all these men will die with you. That's the only alternative you give me. What is this about your official death? Talk now, or I will destroy.'

Gregory sighed and then he told the other men to go. 'Everything will go as planned; only this angel needs to know the scope of his power,' he said. 'Go on, man your desks in the building and see that my brother is comfortable and not afraid. Everything will be glorious. We are in the time of miracles. This creature you see here is a miracle from God. Say nothing to anyone.'

The men at the table left with amazing speed, but the soldiers took a little more firm persuading from him that he knew what he was doing.

I flung him back down in his chair.

'You lying monster,' I said. 'How could you tell the world I killed your wife and your daughter? Tell me now where Nathan is, tell me now what you mean to do.'

I scanned the monitors all along the tops of the walls. They covered entryways, the lobby, elevators that were not in operation. I could see nothing but empty space in most. And guards passing.

The maps were dazzling and filled with pulsing neon colors, countries done in scarlet and yellow and rivers drawn in light like lightning. But there was no time to admire these things.

'Haven't you guessed it, clever spirit?' he said. He smiled up at me. 'How glad I am to see you. What took you so long? I need you, and time is running out.'

'I know you're going to do something with your brother,' I said, 'put him in your place to be killed, so that you can rise from the dead! That much is easy to figure and six is the hour you've marked for it. Six or before, what does that mean? I want your brother now, safe and in my arms to be taken back to his people.'

'No, you don't, Azriel,' he said with great reasonableness, his confidence flaring up in him like an unquenchable fire. 'Sit down and let me tell you what is to happen. You cannot imagine the beauty of it, and Nathan will suffer no pain. He is sedated and hardly knows what will happen to him.'

'I'm sure he is!' I said with great contempt, and a memory came back to me of people giving me something to drink, and saying, 'You will not suffer.' They were painting gold on my skin.

'If you kill me,' Gregory said, 'you will change nothing. The plan goes into operation after my death. If you want me to die before six o'clock then you will simply move up the time of the Last Days. Everything is set into motion. Only I can stop it. You'd be a fool to kill me.' He gestured for me to sit down.

'This room is soundproof, it has no security monitor,' he said. 'What we say here is private, utterly. And I want your attention and your sympathy.'

'The soldiers?'

'I pressed a button, here under the table. They won't come in again, but what I tell you must be secret, secret from all the world. You must be one of us when we leave this room. We have to leave it together.'

'You're dreaming.'

'No. You lack vision, Spirit, you always have. You've spent too many centuries a slave. Now, only in my time, have you known your full strength. Admit it. The doctors found living seed in my wife. You've lost your glaze-eyed confused look, Spirit. My wife taught you how to be a man?'

I said nothing. But I did have a strong sense of something – that I couldn't simply solve this by chopping him up like the Gordian knot.

'Right you are!' be said. 'Sit down, and listen to me.'

I took the first chair to his left.

He picked up a small multi-buttoned remote control device. I placed my hand on it.

'It controls the monitors, nothing more. Most are security.

369

Only two have film in them. Look directly up there, over the central map.'

At once two of the screens began to fill with still shots – frozen for about two seconds each – of people who were starving, or the dead, battlefields, bombed-out buildings, trash heaps. I recognized that these photos were a steady panorama from all over the world. I could see the Mayan temples in one picture of gathered villagers. In another I saw ruins I knew to be in Cambodia.

He watched these almost serenely, as if he'd forgotten my presence or took me utterly for granted.

'Assure me nothing will happen to Nathan,' I said, 'as we talk.'

'I assure you,' he said. 'Nothing will happen, until six o'clock and even then it depends on my signal. But I should let you know, angelic one, you have no bargaining power.'

'Oh?'

As he turned and smiled graciously at me, he was now preening and full of happiness.

'I've waited so long for this to come,' he said, 'and to think that you arrived in the midst of it. I do think God sent you as an answer to the sacrifice of Esther. I myself didn't see the symmetry of it or the genius until later. I offered up Esther, whom I loved, truly loved, and you came through the break from the Heavens.' He seemed perfectly sincere.

'I have not been in Heaven,' I said. 'Where is Nathan?'

'First,' he said, 'let us think intelligently. If you should lose your angelic temper and kill me, you'll only trigger the plan automatically. If you destroy this building you'll trigger the plan automatically. If you want any chance of understanding, acceptance, or modification, you need me. And hear me out.'

'All right,' I said. 'But you do plan to kill Nathan at six o'clock. You admit it. And you could do it before. That's why you put him in the hospital under your name, to create DNA evidence and dental evidence to identify Nathan as you, so that your death would be certified, didn't you?'

He didn't seem at all happy to hear this much figuring.

'That's a crude version of what I accomplished,' he said.

'But look, the world is at stake, Azriel, the world itself. Dear God, you must be my Divine Witness.'

'Don't get romantic, Gregory, tell me the plan. Somewhere else you have DNA documents that will be used to cleverly replace Nathan's set, and these documents will confirm you when you have risen. You have many people involved in erasing and moving data.'

'I'm beginning to love your intelligence,' he said. 'Now really use it. This is for the world itself! It's for that that we do what we do. And you cannot prevent what will happen, and you must keep it in your mind that when the Last Days come, and they will begin sometime before midnight this night, you will need me. You will need me desperately, just as everyone alive and meant to live will need me. Otherwise only disaster can follow upon disaster.'

'Okay, what is this Last Days? What's to happen? You're going to have him assassinated. Then what? Appear to rise from the dead?'

'In three days,' he said. 'Isn't that the way the other Messiah did it?' He was cooler.

Three days. Blurry horrid images filled with – lions, a loathsome swarm of bees, dancing. I shivered and fought it off. I saw the cross of Christ. I saw the risen Christ in paintings old and new. I heard Christian words in Greek and Latin.

'I'm eager to have you understand this,' he said. 'You know, it's occurred to me several times that you are the only one who will fully appreciate this.'

'And why's that?'

'Azriel, nobody else alive has my courage. No one. It takes courage to kill. You know it does. You know time and the world, and have probably witnessed war, starvation, injustice. But first, allow me to caution you. If you don't hear me out, if you decide that my death is appropriate and that you don't care what happens to the world, there's the question of the Bones.'

'Yes?'

'They are in a kiln in this building, and a word from me

371

will roast them and melt them into running liquid. Oh, and I should tell you the results of our tests on them, shouldn't I?'

'If you want to waste the time. I'd rather hear about the Last Days.'

'Don't you want to know what's inside your bones?'

'I know. My bones.'

He shook his head and smiled. 'No more,' he said. 'The human bone is almost entirely devoured by the metals in which it was encased. There is very little if anything left. Which means I think that as soon as the metal is headed it will easily incinerate and obliterate any trace of the human remaining.'

'That's what it means to you?' I smiled. 'How amusing. Your test results have an entirely different meaning for me. Did you find enough there to do your DNA magic?'

He shook his head. 'There's almost nothing left.'

'That's good news. But go on.'

He studied me most intensely. He reached out to take my hand, which I more or less allowed. All his charm was in play now, and his eyes had the depth of greatness, and the sincerity of greatness. Very alluring. Rachel had warned me of this.

But I loathed him. For Esther and Nathan alone, as if all the world didn't matter, or as if to mourn them was to mourn all injustice.

'Azriel, this is a dream of unparalleled greatness. It has harshness in it and death, but so did the conquests of Alexander. So did the conquests of Constantine. You know they did. You know the land of Egypt lived in peace for two thousand years because of harshness and the willingness to kill. You know or remember those long times of peace. The Peace of Alexander, and after him the Pax Romana.'

'Tell me the plan.'

He pointed to the big map on the wall, the map of the world that was filled with pinpoints of light. The pinpoints were red and blue mostly, though some were yellow. They were in stark contrast to the lights of the map, but I saw now much drawing and marking on the map. Much detail.

'Those are my headquarters throughout the world,' he

said. 'Those are my Temples, my so-called resorts, my so-called business offices. Airports. Islands.'

'God, why does ambition come to such a man?' I said. 'Think of the good you could do, you blithering moral idiot!'

He laughed sincerely and like a child. 'But that's just it, my tactless and impulsive one, I am a moral genius.' He pointed to the maps:

'They are ready within two hours of confirmation of my death to destroy two-thirds of the world's population completely. Now, before you object, let me explain that this will be done by a filovirus perfected here by us which is already in place in those various temples. Don't interrupt.'

He raised his hand and went on.

'It is a virus which kills within five minutes or less; it is airborne only as long as its host breathes, which is no more than five minutes; its first immediate action is to fog the brain and to fill the victim with a feeling of peace and ecstasy.'

He smiled gently, his eyes glazed suddenly, as though he were listening to grand and majestic music.

'No one will suffer, Azriel, at least not more than a few moments. Oh, it is such perfection compared to the hideous, bumbling stupidity of Hitler when he bludgeoned, shot, and tormented the Jews. What a crude, cruel monster he was. A digger of graves, a ragman, a fiend who tinkered with the gold in the mouths of his millions of victims.' He shrugged, 'Ah, maybe it simply wasn't the time. We didn't have the technology.'

He resumed:

'The virus will be dropped along with a lethal gas that tends to dissipate within four hours. These combined should kill everything living and human in the area. My planes and helicopters are ready worldwide to perform the annihilations. They will go over and over the territories involved until all people in them are exterminated.

'Foot battalions have been organized in some densely populated cities, like Baghdad and Cairo and Calcutta. They will insert the gas and the virus into large buildings through their air systems. Some of these people are themselves willing to die. Others will wear protective clothing.'

'Good God, how many cities, countries, people, are you talking about?'

'Most of the world, Azriel. I told you. Two-thirds of the world's population. Think of it as an inevitable plague, if you will, a plague which comes in angelic form, to clear the planet of the debris as other plagues have done in the past. Do you know what the Black Death did to Europe?'

'How could I not?' I thought of Samuel and the burning houses of Strasbourg.

'What you don't know is that Europe would be a desert now were it not for that plague. You don't know how many died in the flu epidemic early in our century. You don't know that AIDS was meant. You don't know that it takes courage to learn from nature and rise above it, rather than simply tamper with it, and make chaos out of it as you destroy it.'

'What countries of the world; you speak of Asia?'

'Oh, yes,' he said. 'Definitely. Asia, the Orient, all of those people will be wiped off the face of the earth. All of northern Russia. Only some of eastern Russia will be saved, and even on that score I haven't entirely made up my mind. There will be no more Japan.'

He didn't want to stop for breath, he went right on, excited now. I could swear that a light emanated from him.

'You haven't been here long enough to know the logic of it. First and foremost, everything in populated areas on the African continent will be wiped out. Think of it. Emptying Africa. Villages have been targeted, all areas where men and women live. The only animals who will survive are those which are far from populated areas. It's brilliant. You see, the filovirus won't affect most animals anyway, and the gas will dissipate soon enough for most animals to survive it. Oh, it's very complex. It has stages. But everything has been done to avoid panic or pain or knowledge among those who are dying. They will not suffer, no, they will not endure the absolute agony of our parents and others in the German camps. That was hideous, beastly.'

I didn't dare interrupt him. But, Jonathan, you can imagine my feelings at this moment. Panic rose in me, but something harder overcame it: a determination that this madness was not going to happen! Absolutely not going to happen! I kept a mask of a face:

'You truly have an immense vision, Gregory.'

'Every living person in India and Pakistan will be wiped out,' he continued with rapturous enthusiasm. 'In fact, almost every living person in Nepal, too, and up into the mountains. Of course Israel will be destroyed because Palestine has to be destroyed, and Iraq and Iran. In fact, all of that world will go – the Armenians, the Turks . . . the Greeks, the Balkans, where the war goes on, Saudi Arabia, Yemen . . .'

'The Third World, as you call it,' I said. 'The poor world. That's what you're talking about.'

'I'm talking about the world that is fatally diseased, always at war, courting famine, and dragging us all down with it. The great unsalvageable world – the world that Alexander couldn't save, or Rome, or Constantine, or the President of this country, or the United Nations, or all the weak fumbling liberal kindhearted peacemakers of today who do nothing but preside over massacres!'

He sighed.

'Yes,' he said, 'the disease ridden, the uncontrollable, and the unredeemable. It's absolutely essential. They will all die. By midnight tonight most will be dead. But the Temples are ready for a renewed gas attack on all areas again tomorrow. Our vans, our planes, our helicopters – all are disguised as medical vehicles. Our people are clothed as medical people. Anyone seeing them will think they are trying to help. People will come to them for help and shelter, and they will kill these people without torturing them or frightening them. It's going to work brilliantly. We have worked out our estimates. All of Cairo will be dead in two hours. Calcutta will take longer.'

He looked sad as he continued:

'The third day will be the worst, because we have to hunt down those who might have somehow survived and it will be difficult. People will know fear. But it will be brief. There may be bullets used then, even bombs, but we hope not. We envision a beautiful and silent world by the end of the third day.'

His hand fell warm and firm on mine, his eyes glowed.

'Imagine it, Azriel, all of the African continent still and quiet, the beautiful pyramids of Egypt standing in silence, the smog and filth of Cairo settled down like so much sand. Imagine Zaire with no more epidemics and secret filoviruses brewing to destroy the world. Imagine the starving put to sleep in silence. Imagine the great rain forests allowed once again to grow, the dense jungle blooming without intrusion, the wild animals of the interior allowed to multiply as God planned for them to do.

'Oh, Azriel, my dream is as great as Yahweh's dream when he told Noah to build the ark. I have even sheltered critical species. Very talented geniuses and scientists have already been lured here for a convention so that they might be saved as their people die. This, my country, is my ark. But the rest must die. There is absolutely no other beautiful or elegant or merciful way out of our present state.'

'Israel must die, you would do this to your own people?'

'Have to, no way around it. Besides . . . We must reclaim the Holy Places in peace and stillness. But don't you see, many Jews here will survive. Everyone in the United States and Canada will survive. No one in this country will be hurt at all.

'The attacks in this hemisphere will wipe out only the southern lands – all of Mexico, Central America, and the Caribbean. All those islands peaceful again and beautiful, where the poinsettia can bloom a deep red, and the palms can blow in the wind.

'But everything that is in our country and Canada will survive. The filovirus dies quickly. We've perfected our formula out of all three strains of Ebola and some we've found ourselves. The gas dissipates. I told you. It breaks down utterly. You don't know the lengths we've gone to to perfect our formula so that horses and cattle will be immune. You don't know how we have worked to make this merciful.'

He sighed, with a little shake of his head, then said:

'There will be spot exterminations of villages in the Amazon jungle – yes, that will happen – but in general the wildlife will rebound. It won't be hurt by these clever poisons. Azriel, do you realize the geniuses I have working for me, men who worked in government germ-warfare programs for years, men who know things you and I know nothing of?'

'And Europe?' I asked. 'You will kill Asia Minor? You will kill the Balkan countries. What will you do with Europe?'

'That is our biggest problem strategically. Because we must wipe out the Germans, we must do that on account of what they did with Hitler to the Jews. The Germans have to die. They have to. All of them. Absolutely.

'But we want to spare all other European countries. Except Spain. I just don't like Spain, and Spain has had too much Moslem influence. But the extermination in Germany will be very stealthy, involve more foot workers than anyplace else, and there may be some unavoidable casualties among the French and the English, especially those traveling in Germany at the time.'

He stood up and he walked to the map. 'It's all prepared. It's all in place. The final chemicals have been shipped. What remains here in the building can be used to attack anyone who enters the building. There are areas that can be sealed off where police and authorities can be gassed.

'You realize of course,' he said, 'that from most of these condemned areas, we will be the only broadcast that the United States receives. We will have the advantage in describing this gentle plague. We have written our poetry, which is worthy to be remembered, like the story of the battles of Darius carved in rock.'

He pointed to the various monitors whose cameras remained fixed on corridors or empty rooms or elevators. 'All killing traps. We are a fortress here.

'On the third day,' he said, 'as the United States weeps in confusion for the rest of the world, while secretly sighing in relief to be rid of it, I will rise from the Dead, and I will tell what I have seen of these deaths everywhere, and that this plague was inevitable and the will of God. All the members of my Temple are prepared to take positions of leadership.'

'Do they know it's a hoax!' I demanded. 'Your own idiot followers? Do they know it's Nathan, an identical twin, who will be killed?'

377

He smiled patiently at me, his back to the map, his arms folded.

'You tricked him into the hospital to acquire the DNA you need to verify your own death,' I said. 'How many know about the fraud? How many are there involved in exchanging the DNA records at the key moments in order to verify your resurrection?'

'Enough key people know. Of course the great mass of my followers don't know. They know who I am, and when I appear they will know it's Gregory. I take the responsibility for this on my own shoulders. I take the guilt of the murder of the world, and the burden of a new myth of my journey to hell and back. I am the new Messiah. I am the anointed one. And my secret things are mine, as Yahweh's secrets were His.'

He took the time to calm himself. His eyes were wet with emotion. 'You're beautiful, Azriel. I need you. You've been sent to be at my side. You've been sent.'

'Get on with this plan. Who knows what?' I demanded.

'Only a few in this location know that the death and the resurrection are a trick. Isn't that how it probably happened the first time?'

'The first time,' I whispered. 'And what was the first time? Was it Calvary? Is that what you think?'

'Even the people distributing the gas throughout India do not really know what it will do. Only those in charge know. There are levels of knowledge. Mine is a world of zealots willing to die for me, don't you see, die for me and for a new world. Now listen to what I say. Listen!

'Imagine the relief when people realize what has taken place. I mean it. Think of the relief in the minds of all intelligent Americans and Europeans, all Westerners, or whatever you want to call us.'

He sat down again and leaned towards me. 'Azriel, people will be overjoyed when the Great Death has passed. They will be overjoyed! Only the West with all its resources will remain, that's all. All the poverty, the disease, the tribal war, gone. Gone from the earth. A new beginning.

'We, the Temple of the Mind, will take control. We

outnumber those in Washington who might at first resist us. We will have no problem in other places. We know what has happened. We have the knowledge. We will go on the airwaves describing that the will of God has been done, and that the earth is now at peace, and free of millions who covered it like termites and parasites.'

'And you think the President of this country is going to take your hand for this?'

'Well, we'll probably have to kill him. But at least we'll give him a chance. At the moment he is an extremely brilliant man and rather beautiful. But our Temple people in Washington are ready. There are three thousand of them within blocks of the White House, and the nearby Pentagon. I presume you know these are our important buildings. We can gas everyone in those buildings. If necessary the entire population of Washington can be gassed. I've agonized over this. I believe that we should not do this to our own people.'

'How merciful.'

'Just wise. We want the government to realize it has been spared by the prophet Gregory at the will of the Lord to help rebuild a new and bountiful world order. At least, we want to give the President and our congressmen time to visualize these empty continents where the lilies of the field can bloom again in all their glory.'

He implored me with his eyes. He was truly moved. When he trembled it wasn't fear, but a great anticipation.

'Don't you see, my friend?' he asked. 'This is what everybody wants. When a man turns on television at night and sees the war in the Balkans, it fills him with despair. Well, there won't be any more war. Bosnians and Serbs alike will be dead.

'Imagine never having to worry again about the naked millions, the hunger, the floods, the disasters in India. All gone. All of those beautiful cities and temples lying virgin and ready to be reawakened. No one wants to hear any more about petty genocide in Iraq, or street riots in Tel Aviv, or massacres in Cambodia. We're all sick of watching the Third World struggle, while we remain impotent, castrated by our superiority and refined values.

379

'Everyone wants this!

'It is what Alexander would do! It is what Constantine would do! No one has the means, the guts, the wisdom, or the courage to do it but me! I alone will do this. I alone will do it! I will strike as the Pharaoh struck when he rode down on those who invaded the Valley of the Nile.'

I said nothing. A clock was ticking in my brain, a clock. Six or before. What time was it now?

'You've got to consider it,' he continued. 'You've got to carefully consider it. Imagine the jungles of Indochina and those beautiful ruins, with all the warlike people gone! Imagine the majesty of a city like Berlin. Imagine its resources. In fact Germany will be filled with resources. And those the Germans hurt in the World War will be so happy that Germany is gone!

'All these people have brought this on themselves! I was born to do this, you're proof of it.'

'How can you be so sure of that?' I asked. 'Doesn't my presence make you pause even an instant!'

'No. Not when I picture the world after the Last Days. The Paradise. Imagine the quiet sweet earth, growing with grass again, and only those of the West preserved to reinvent, and to save, to rebuild nations without ever letting the chaos of the past redevelop. America will colonize these peaceful and beautiful worlds. Under my leadership. If the government helps, that will be good. We need the help. If not, we take over the government.'

'And the people in this country, you think they will let you do this?'

'Trust me, they will be very happy once it has sunk in, once they know all that is gone, once they know we are living in a world filled again with natural resources, and abundant land, and beautiful monuments, and fertile and magnificent places to be colonized. Even our Afro-Americans will be delighted that they don't have to worry any more about Africa. American members of all our minority populations will be saved. No people or race exists that does not have a colony in America. This country is the Ark! Cooperate! They'll worship us. They'll worship the risen Messiah, and

380

then his Hasid roots can be known, and it will all be written down; it will become the great turning point in history.'

I let him go on: he was truly in his own grip now, nothing could have shut him up, this was his aria.

'Azriel, if you only knew how much we have tried to help these poor nations. If you only knew the conditions in Baghdad and Israel. If you only knew the impossible state of things.

'The first half of this century, we saw fascist madmen like Hitler and Mussolini, and Franco and Stalin. We saw their crude methods fail and pitch Europe into agony.

'Now there are no more such men in the West. There isn't a single leader in the West capable of the clarity of Franco.

'One must go to ragged poor places like Baghdad to find little dictators, like Saddam Hussein, or to the Balkans to find those who would fight to the death. Even Russia itself has no great Stalin, no Lenin, no Peter the Great.'

'And you saw these men as great?' I asked. 'You see them as great?'

'No, they were evil. They did harm, and by the way, they annihilated millions. Don't think for a minute Stalin didn't kill as many people as Hitler. They killed and they killed and they killed. But it was crude, sadistic, ugly, primitive. I don't count them as great.

'Now the West is led by people who are caught in the trap of their own conscience and benevolence. They know they should bomb Iraq and Iran off the map, but nobody has the guts to do it! Everybody knows Africa is a breeding place for plagues that can kill the world. No one has the guts to annihilate the population.'

'And here, what of the poor and the ragged here?'

'We are the Ark, I told you. In the New World, our small population of unredeemables will be given a new chance. Or executed. It won't be a problem. It's nothing. It's a gnat in the face, our problems here.

'That the beauty of it. America, New York itself, contains people of all races. They can begin the new world order with us. If some do rebel, out of sentiment for their lost lands, we kill them. But we have gone against no race, no tribe, and will in this safe haven protect the remnants of all peoples.

'And remember our campaign through television is extensive. It's all worked out. As the horrible deaths are reported, we will control the news from those areas completely. The President and his Army will be helpless. There will be no overseas connections or allies. Only the Temple of the Mind of God.'

'And during these Last Days,' I said, 'people here will be in a panic that they too are going to be exterminated. All America will be in panic and fear of this plague.'

'Exactly, then they will discover that they are blessed. And I have come back from the Dead and have brought with me a vision of a New World. They will learn that God's will decreed these things, that God chose the Temple as His instrument, but I have been among the Dead! Believe me, when this thing is over, the Temple of the Mind of God will be the only worldwide institution left in existence, and resistance to us will be simple to block. We have it all planned, we have our leaders, we have our stations, we have everything in order.

'Nathan has to die in my place at six o'clock, and if I die before that, if anything happens to me, if I give a signal, the world extermination process will begin automatically. And I have a thousand ways of giving that signal.'

'Like, name one, for instance?'

'I beg your pardon?'

'What if I simply kill you now and save Nathan and reveal the plot.'

'You can't. Don't you realize there are soldiers at all the doors? And the Bones, remember, I've told them, if you begin to fight us, they are to cremate the Bones. That will end your existence.'

'What if it doesn't?'

'What can you do? You can't stop all these people worldwide, you can't even betray this building into the hands of the enemy. We have it under control perfectly. Don't you see? You can only be in one place at one time, spirit or not, and your abilities are limited. When Rachel committed suicide right behind your back you didn't even know it.'

'And you think I'm just going to let you do this,' I said. 'You think I won't try to stop you. You think I will be a party to this horror? You count yourself among the wrong leaders. Cyrus rose to power by tolerance of the religions in his Persian empire. Alexander brought Hellenism to Asia, he married Asian to Greek. The Pax Romana was a time of tolerance. Don't you see, you filth, you take your place with the destroyers!'

I couldn't hold my temper. He looked hurt, deeply hurt but more than that, disappointed and sad, a man committed.

'You take your place with Attila the Hun,' I said. 'You take your place with Tamerlane, who built walls out of the live bodies of the conquered. You do indeed take your place with the Black Death and with Ebola and with AIDS. You are destruction!'

He shook his hands. He put them up to his face.

'Azriel, try to comprehend the beauty of this. The scope. It is what the world needs, and the only thing that can save the world. Nations have always been annihilated to make way for other nations. The Indians of America were wiped out so that this great nation could rise. Must I remind you what Yahweh told Joshua and Saul and David? To annihilate their enemies to the last man, woman, and child.

'Don't you see, Azriel, this takes brilliance and courage. Unbelievable courage. And I have it. I have it and the means and I can see it through. I can endure the condemnations, the outcries. I have the vision!'

He stood up again, and went to the map as if musing.

'You know, once it's begun, perhaps then you'll see.'

'It isn't going to begin!' I declared. I stood up.

There was a little star at the very center of the map. I saw it too late. White, the Star of David or the Star of Magicians. It had had much significance down through the years. He stared at it lovingly.

Too late, I realized that he had pressed it! It was a button. He had triggered something!

'What have you done?' I demanded.

'Merely sent Nathan to his death. He's groomed and ready. He'll be assassinated in front of the building within five minutes. That starts the worldwide countdown of two hours. You have that time to learn from me, and pray you do, and become my helper.'

I stood up, dumbfounded.

'My God!' I declared in prayer and utter horror.

'Well, what are you going to do? Stay here? Kill me? Try to save Nathan? Nathan is going down in the elevator now. Look at that monitor. You see it?'

I did. High up in a far corner I saw a blurry picture of Nathan, the true identical clone of Gregory now, his beard and locks shorn, held up by those who stood next to him. He wore Gregory's clothes. I could even see the slight bulge of Gregory's personal gun in the coat pocket. To my horror I realized that the front elevator doors were opening. To my horror I realized that the figures were moving towards the front doors of the Temple, towards the crowd.

'You can't do anything, Azriel. You came back to life to be my messenger. If you kill me now you kill the one man who might be persuaded to stop this a little later on. I won't of course, but you'll make it a fait accompli, as we say, if you kill me. You need me. You know you do. You need me badly.'

In desperation, I gave a cry for the iron to come to me that I needed. I held two nails in my hands. I kicked him back against the map, then threw him against the wall, lest the map be full of triggers and buttons.

I drove the nails through his hands. He winced but he didn't cry out.

'You fool!' he said. He shut his eyes as if savoring the pain. Then became enraged.

'Well, you wanted to be the Messiah, didn't you?' I said.

He cursed and snarled, writhing, hands nailed to the wall.

On the monitor I saw the figure of 'Gregory,' Nathan in disguise, stepping out into the crowd.

I dissolved and moved myself to that spot with all my power, invisible.

But even as I did, I heard the rifle shots. I heard the hail of bullets that descended upon the innocent Nathan. I heard the screams rising from the street.

Twenty-four

Nathan lay in a pool of blood, eyes blinking at the bright summer sky, as the crowd panicked around him. The assassins had been snared by the mob. Sirens screamed. The Minders wailed.

I stared down at the body of Nathan. I saw the confusion in his bright dark eyes. Memory swam over me, threatening to pull me from the moment.

Then I realized that everything around me had changed. The building had faded. The crowd was gone.

Up before me into the beautiful sky rose the gleaming and unmistakable Stairway to Heaven.

With my own eyes, I tell you, I saw a light that others have told you over and over is indescribable. I saw a light so full of warmth and love and understanding that it filled me in my invisibility, reached me at my core. And I saw Nathan slowly walking up the Ladder.

At the top Rachel and Esther appeared. There were others I didn't know, and suddenly I realized in this blinding and beautiful brightness that they were telling Nathan he had to go back, he couldn't die, he had to return.

Nathan turned around obedient and began to cry; he cried and cried with his hands to his eyes. His image now was Hasid; he had the beard and locks they'd shaved from him. He had his black hat. But he was a spirit returning to the ravaged body that lay on the ground, in which the heart had just ceased to beat.

Suddenly Rachel called to me. I found myself running up the Staircase. Nothing stopped me. I was on it, I tell you, Jonathan, I was on the golden stairs and there above they stood, I saw them all, not only Rachel and Esther, but my father, my own father, and Zurvan, my first teacher, and Samuel and others. I saw them; in a flickering my whole memory was restored to me.

386

My life passed through youth and innocence into the horror of my murder in which I knew each personage and his or her role, and then all Zurvan's teachings returned to me. Everything I had ever done I saw, good and evil.

I was almost to the top, and Nathan was staring at me in astonishment. Rachel stepped forward.

'Azriel,' she said, 'you go back, into Nathan's body. Azriel, he's not strong enough to fight Gregory, but you are. You can keep the body alive! Azriel, I beg you.'

Nathan turned to me; he was so like Gregory and yet so pure and clean and full of love, utter love. He looked searchingly at all those gathered at the top of the stairs, only a few feet away, where the garden began and the light rose with limitless brilliance.

'You mean I could stay with you?' he asked the others. He looked at Rachel and Esther, and other Hasidim I did not know, Elders, and my elders too!

I wanted to throw myself into my father's arms. 'Can't we both come now?' I cried. 'Please, Father!'

Suddenly Zurvan spoke, 'Azriel, you have to go back in that body and make it get off the ground. Even if it means you never get out of it. You must do it.'

'Azriel, please,' said my beautiful Esther, 'please, you know how evil Gregory is. Only an angel of God can stop him.'

My father was crying as he had thousands of years ago. 'My son, I love you, but they need you so badly. They need you, Azriel! Only if that slain body rises now can the plot be undone!'

I saw the rationale of it in an instant. I saw what they meant. To foil the assassination now and seize the cameras, that was the only way to warn the world.

I turned, nodding, 'Go with God, Nathan!' I cried, and I heard their lovely voices behind me thanking me and praying for me.

Then suddenly from both sides I saw the malcontent spirits tearing at me, faces twisted in hate, my former Masters by the dozen whom I'd forgotten, men for whom I had done evil.

'Why do this?'

'Why should you?'

'Let the madman destroy the world.'

'What do you care!' demanded the magician from Paris.

'They're using you again. They're using you!' declared my Mameluk master, whom I'd slain on sight.

'You'll lose your spirit strength, don't you see?'

'You'll be mortal in that body, trapped; you'll die in it of the wounds it sustained.'

'Why suffer mortality like that when you are a free spirit!'

And behind these faces and voices were legions of swarming angry, envious, and hateful spirits.

I glanced back up the Stairway. I saw them all gathered, and Nathan had his arms around the others, and they around him. Rachel raised her hand and sent to me a kiss. And in a childlike manner Esther waved. They were fading into utter brilliance. My father had become pure illumination.

I looked at the light and I let it fill me. I treasured just one fraction of a second of understanding, at peace with all things, at peace with all that had been done to me, and that I had done, and all that had ever happened; the world had meaning then. It had a full and magnificent meaning. And the millions of the poor, the hungry, the angry, the warriors – they were not parasites as Gregory had said; they were souls!

'No,' I said to the angry spirits. 'I have to do it.'

'Go into his body, resurrect it,' said Zurvan, 'even if it means you lose everything.'

'Azriel, my love goes with you!' cried Nathan. He had begun to glow like the others.

Blackness. I felt myself sucked down as if by the most powerful mechanical force, and suddenly I was filled with pain, pain in my lungs, pain in my heart, pain in every limb, and I was blinking at the sky as men put me on a stretcher, just as they had done with Esther.

I lurched, rolled over, even though they were astonished, and saw no more stairway and no more light, only the Temple itself, and the mob screaming.

I sat up on the stretcher and then I climbed off it. The

medical men backed away in pure astonishment. I knew why. The wounds were fatal. More than one was fatal.

I saw the cameras and I beckoned to the reporters. I reached out for their hands.

'Your government, your agencies. Surround this building and search it at once. An impostor has taken my place. An impostor has tried to kill me. This building is loaded with fatal viruses; and there are Temples of the Mind throughout the world ready to discharge them. Stop them. You must reach the thirty-ninth floor. You must reach the room with the map, and the impostor nailed to the wall. Hurry now! I give you permission to enter the Temple of the Mind. Take guns with you.'

I turned around. Everywhere I looked, people had whipped out those little phones that open up and they were screaming into them. The police rushed at the building. Sirens screamed.

'It is an impostor,' I said, 'it is a twin, and he plans destruction you cannot imagine.'

I could see the television cameras coming down on me. 'The Temple of the Mind in every country must be stopped. Every building contains poison gas, and deadly viruses. You must stop the Temple of the Mind wherever it is, and beware their lies, beware their lies. Look what they have done to me, and I am living to tell you this.'

I felt myself growing weak. The blood was pumping right out of my heart. I realized I was undone. I reached out and grabbed for a microphone. I heard my own voice, tinged with Nathan's tone, rise in volume.

'Minders, your leader has been shot and tricked. Minders, you have been infiltrated. Go inside, destroy the people who have deceived you!'

I was about to collapse. I grabbed hold of a young woman, a reporter who stood beside me with her cameraman catching every breath I took or lost.

'The Armed Services, the people who deal in deadly disease. Worldwide. Alert them. There is enough in any one Temple building to destroy a city, even this one!'

In a blur I saw them all distracted, turning away from me.

389

A riot of screams broke out. I turned, almost falling, supported in fact by the doctors around me. There in front of the glass doors, held back by confused and frightened followers, stood Gregory, bleeding from the wounds in his hands, screaming:

'I'm Gregory Belkin!' he cried. 'That man is an impostor! Look, I bleed like Christ from my hands! Stop the Devil. Stop the Liar.'

I faltered. I was almost going down. I looked around me, and then I remembered there was the gun in the left pocket of my coat. He had outfitted the drugged Nathan to perfection, as he himself would have been outfitted, even to his personal gun. It was his little gun, the one he carried the first night I ever saw him, the one he always carried.

I took the gun out, and people screamed and fell back. I staggered towards Gregory and before the bodyguards could think what to do, before anyone could, I began to shoot Gregory. I shot him over and over again. Astonished, he stared as the first bullet struck his chest, then with the second he went up in the air as if calling for help; the third hit his head. I shot another one, before anyone could stop me. He fell dead on the pavement.

There was noise all around me. Someone had taken the gun, very carefully, from me. I heard the endless babble of voices into the phones. I saw armed men running towards the doors of the Temple and the dead body. I saw men putting down their guns and throwing up their hands. I heard shots. I turned and found myself falling into the arms of a young doctor, horrified and staring at me with awe.

I tried to search his soul. 'Act fast,' I said. 'Act fast! The Temple will annihilate the peoples of whole countries. It is poised and ready! That man I killed is a madman. It was all his evil plan. Hurry.'

Then I felt myself sinking, not down into the numb indistinct darkness of spirit sleep, but into mortal agony, into a pain that made it impossible for me to talk. I tasted mortal blood in my mouth.

'Call the Rebbe Avram,' I said. 'Call for Nathan's wife.' I begged for the words to come, the names of the community and Court in Brooklyn. Someone said a name for the Rebbe Avram and that was correct, and I said, 'Yes, call him to bear witness that I killed the impostor.'

I was on the stretcher again blinking at the sky. Is it enough? Will it stop? I closed my eyes. I felt the ambulance rolling, and I felt oxygen pouring into my lungs. I saw above me an innocent face.

I pushed aside the plastic mask. 'Connect me now to the people who can stop the Temple.'

A phone was thrust at me. I didn't know the person to whom I poured out my last appeal:

'It's the Ebola virus,' I said, 'a mixture of old and new strains, developed to kill in five minutes. It's in canisters. Hurry. The gas and the virus are in Temples in cities in Asia, the Middle East, Africa. On the ships. The planes are ready to go out. The helicopters. Tell all the good Minders they must cooperate with you. Ninety-nine percent of the cult is innocent! Bell them to turn on their local leaders! Everywhere. You've got to surround and reach them all before it begins. These people mean to kill.'

I lost consciousness. I went on speaking, struggling, feeling pain, but I was really unconscious. The human body had broken down, and I was on the brink of death. I was so glad. But had I done enough?

I woke in the emergency room. Again people surrounded me. The Rebbe stood over me. I saw his white beard, the tears in his eyes, I saw Sarah, Nathan's wife. I spoke in Yiddish. 'Tell them I speak the truth,' I said, 'that I am your grandson Gregory, and declare the dead body that of an impostor. You have to. He has arranged for this body, of Nathan, to be verified as his own. Say only that I am your good grandson if you will. It's dark. It's tangled. And I think I'm dying.'

Then Sarah's face flickered before me: 'Nathan?' she whispered.

I turned close and beckoned for her to come down near my lips.

'Nathan walks with God, and Nathan is no more,' I said. 'I

saw him go into the arms of those he loved. Don't fear. Don't fear at all. I'll keep this body alive as long as I can. Help me.'

She sobbed and sobbed and her hands stroked my forehead.

I heard a voice, 'We're losing him! Everyone out! Out!'

The world went dim. All things were known to me yet dim, and I felt only the peace I'd known in the light, the memory as fresh as a fragrance. The dimness thickened and then loosened. I knew I was being moved.

I knew we were going up in an elevator. And then all went very dim, and a shadowy figure appeared near me. I wasn't certain whether it was good or bad, and then I recognized its voice and the Greek it spoke.

'The purpose is to love and to understand, to value . . .' it whispered.

All was blackness. I think I was thinking, Will the Stairway come now? Will it? Can it do that for me after all I've done? Then nothing.

I awoke in a room in what they call Intensive Care. I was hooked to machines. Nurses surrounded me. Great men were waiting to speak to me, heads of armies and heads of state.

I realized that my pain was dulled, and my tongue thick. I was mortal, utterly helplessly mortal! And I had to stay in this body. It was the only body they would continue to listen to.

The Rebbe appeared. I saw the black clothes and white hair and beard before I recognized the face. Then I felt the nearness of his lips. This time he spoke in the ancient Aramaic for me alone:

'They've been stopped. DNA on file in the hospital confirms that you are Gregory. I have declared the dead man a demon who took the place of my grandson. This is, in its own way, the perfect truth. The Temples all over are being seized. The scientists and masterminds are surrendering. Arrests are being made. In all lands the evil work is at a halt.' He gave a great sigh. 'You have accomplished it.'

I tried to squeeze his hand, but I couldn't feel my own hands, and only gradually did I realize they were taped to the sides of the bed. I sighed and closed my eyes.

'I want to die here, if I may,' I said to the Rebbe. I spoke

Aramaic again. 'I want to die in this, your grandson's flesh. If God will have me. Will you bury me?'

He nodded. And then I slept – troubled, thin, mortal sleep, living sleep.

It was very late in the night when I awoke. All the nurses were beyond the glass. Only the monitors and the machines sustained and befriended me. In a nearby chair, the Rebbe slept.

With absolute shock I realized I was in my own body. I was Azriel. With all my will, I transformed myself back into Nathan. But the flesh of Nathan was dead. This was only an illusion. I could surround the flesh and make it move, but possession as such had ended.

I turned my head, I began to cry. 'Where is the Stairway, My Lord? I haven't suffered enough, have I?'

Then I was Azriel again, as easy as taking a breath, and the needles and other medical connections were not connected to me. I stood up, strong, solid, healed in my own sound body, and in my favorite Babylonian robes of blue with gold. My beard, mustache, all there. I was Azriel.

I looked at the sleeping Rebbe. I saw the figure of Sarah, asleep, her hand on a pillow, on the cold floor.

I walked out of the room. Two nurses noticed and came to me gently and told me I couldn't be here without permission, the man in the room behind me was very sick.

I looked back. There lay his body. He was dead, as he had been since the bullets had struck him. Suddenly they heard the alarms go off. They heard the signals.

The Rebbe woke. Sarah climbed to her feet. They stared at the dead body of Nathan.

'He died at peace,' I said, and I kissed the nurse on the forehead. 'You did everything you could.'

I walked out of the hospital.

Twenty-five

I walked through the city of New York. When I came to the Temple, I found it surrounded by police and military men of many different kinds. Clearly the building had been taken and evacuated of all the evil ones.

Nobody noticed me much – just a crazy man in velvet robes, I suppose. There were Minders everywhere weeping and crying.

I went into the park where the Minders lay weeping on the grass and under the trees and singing hymns and declaring they didn't believe it was all a lie. They couldn't. The message of the Temple had been love, be kind, be good.

I stood still for a moment, and then using all my power I changed my shape into Gregory.

I found this surprisingly difficult to do, and difficult to sustain.

I walked towards them and as they stood up, I told them to be quiet.

In Gregory's voice I told them that I was a messenger sent to tell them their leader had been deranged, but the age-old message of love still had its full truth.

There was soon a huge crowd around me. I talked on and on answering simple questions about their platitudes, love, sharing, the planet's health, all of this, confirming that this was good. Then finally I spoke Zurvan's words.

'To love and to learn and to be kind,' I said.

I was exhausted.

I vanished.

I drifted invisible up past the windows of the Temple of the Mind. 'The Bones,' I whispered. 'Take me to the Bones.'

I found myself in a room with a kiln. But it was empty and unmonitored now, for the whole system seemed to have been arrested. I opened the door of the kiln and I saw the Bones unharmed. Just the old skeleton.

I pulled the skeleton out, letting it flip and flop about on its new wires as I did so, and then I called for the strength I needed to make my hands like steel and I crushed the skull to pieces, rubbing the pieces harder and harder together till it was powder dropping from my hands, gold powder.

All this I did invisibly, and to each and every bone, grinding it between my hands until there was only dust left, a glittering tiny scattering of golden dust, I saw it swirl up into the ventilating system. I opened the window to the street, and it flew out, this dust, on a great gust of fresh air.

I stood watching until I could see no more dust, only tiny points here and there of gold, and I called down a wind to cleanse the room, to carry it all away into the world, and soon there was not one tiny pinpoint of gold remaining.

I stood thinking, studying.

Then I discovered that I was visible, whole, dressed.

I walked out of the room. But there were so many police now. There were lots of people from the Centers for Disease Control here, and members of the army. No use to parade through these panicstricken men.

Besides, I had work to do. I felt no taste for it. But I had to do it. Too much poison was stashed in too many vulnerable places. Too many madmen had a head start upon the officials and soldiers who were coming after them.

I threw off the body – again the effort surprised me – and went up and out of the building and high over the world, and then descended to the Temple of the Mind in Tel Aviv.

Soldiers had it surrounded. I entered invisibly and slew every last follower of Gregory who resisted. I slew the doctors who guarded the toxic weapons. I moved fast with swift and certain blows. I made no noise. Death lay in my wake. It was wearisome and sad, but done well and completely.

At once I moved on to Jerusalem and there found that Gregory's followers had all surrendered. The city was safe.

Not so in Tehran. Once again, I slew the resisters, and here I must confess to an evil indulgence. I took lavish and splashy physical form to kill, so that some of the more superstitious Persian Minders – converts of Gregory's from desert religions – would be especially affrighted. Vanity, ah, vanity. I disgusted myself with this fancy show. Blood had lost the shine of rubies. Fear in the eyes of my victims wasn't so pretty.

So I suppose my games were instructive to me, and therefore had benefit. Whatever, I slew everyone in the Tehran Temple who did not bow down and beg for mercy, who did not throw down a weapon and crawl towards surrender.

There were other temples which required my intervention.

But I am not going to give you this litany of slaughter.

Let me say only that I assessed each Temple, whether or not it had been 'neutralized,' as modern military men would say, and I gave my assistance where I thought it was imperative. I grew more and more tired.

I knew the modern world must complete this work. I knew that it must appear as if the world itself had conquered Gregory Belkin and the Temple of the Mind. I left the certain victories to the human beings.

I learnt from this rampage. I learnt that I did not love at all to kill anymore. Nothing of the Mal'ak remained in me.

My fascination was with love, my obsession was with love.

And the truth is, that the very last of these murderous tasks – the killing of a few very dangerous Minders in Berlin and in Spain – I did with weariness and no small demand on my own endurance and fortitude.

Temple battles would continue.

I was finished.

A great relaxation overcame me. It was easy to return to my own fleshly form. It was the natural result of preoccupation or distraction – to become physical, the creature you see and hear, to feel and smell, and to walk in the world. Invisibility became a feat. I found this compelling.

For a week I wandered the Earth.

I wandered and wandered.

I went into the lonely sands of Iraq. I went to the ruins of the Greek cities. I went to the museums which held the finest of the art of my times and gazed on these things in quiet.

It took energy to move from place to place in spirit form,

but in either state I was quite strong. Indeed to take on any other form than my own became harder.

And as you know – as you saw yourself earlier – when I called back the body of Nathan to me, there was no wedding of my cells with his cells. His flesh was putrid and from the grave, and I sent it back, humbled, and ashamed that I had troubled it.

I studied all the time I wandered. I went into the bookstores and the libraries. I read through many nights, without sleep. I watched the television endlessly as the Temples were contained and destroyed in various countries. I heard of the mass suicides. I saw it all blended finally with the other news all over the world. It was headlines at the beginning of the week. By the end it was still first page of *The New York Times* but much further down.

And the magazines burst forth with their great flower-colored covers, and then a new issue came out and it was another story.

The world went on. I knew your books. I read them in the night. I went to your home in New York City.

I came here after you, to find you. You remember. You had a deep fever.

All the rest you know. I can still change my shape. I can still travel invisibly. But it gets harder and harder to change into anyone else. You see?

You understand? I'm not human. I am the full spirit that I dreamed I would be – in those dark terrible moments when rebellion and hate seemed my only source of vitality.

I don't know what will happen now. You have the tale. I could tell you more, about those bad masters, about little things I saw, but all will be revealed in God's good time.

That's the end of my adventure. That's the end. And I am not dead. I am strong, I am seemingly without flaw. I am perhaps immortal. Why do you think? What more does God want of me?

Will Rachel and Esther and Nathan forget me? Is that the nature of the bliss that lies beyond the light, that you forget and only come when you are called?

I've called. I called and called and called. But they don't

answer. I know they are safe. I know someday I may see that light. Beyond that, the purpose of life is to learn to love and that is all I intend to do now.

Is it the blood of Gregory himself that keeps me the wanderer? I don't know. I only know I am whole and that this time I served myself as best I could.

I killed, yes, but it was not for a cause, but to stop one. It was not for a master, but to stop one. It was not for an idea, but for many ideas. It was not for a solution, but for the slow unfolding mystery around us. It was not for death, death which I wanted above all, the rest, the grandeur of the ultimate election to die. No, what I did was not for that. I did it for life – so that others may struggle for it. I turned my back on the light and then I shot to death the man with the great plan.

Never forget that, Jonathan, when you write the story. I shot Gregory Belkin. I took his life.

Has God made a special place for me? Has he made it easy for me? Did he give me vision and signs? Was my god Marduk a guardian spirit? Or was he and were all the spirits I saw merely dreams of the lonely human heart that endlessly refurbishes heaven?

Perhaps the story is chaos. It is another chapter in the endless saga of the blunted yet stunning accomplishments of vicious human wills, the stunted yet dazzling ambitions of little souls. Mine, Gregory's . . .

Perhaps we are all little souls. But remember, I told you I've seen these things. And as I turned my back on the Light of Heaven, I committed yet another murder. Death was mixed up in my story from its earliest days.

And I don't know any more about death finally than any mortal man living knows. Perhaps less than you do.

Part IV

LAMENT

Cry not, my baby.
Cry.
I know a frog ate a white moth.
The frog did not cry.
That's why he's a frog.
The moth did not cry.
Now moth is not.
My baby, cry not. Cry. There is much to do.
I will cry too.
I will cry for you.

Stan Rice, *Some Lamb* 1975

Twenty-six

It was morning again, cold and clear and still. He said he had
to sleep again, but not before fixing me my breakfast. I ate
the hot hominy again, prepared by him, and then we lay
down together and slept.

When he awoke he smiled at me, and he said:

'Jonathan, I'm not leaving you here. You're too sick and
you must go home.'

'I know, Azriel,' I said. 'I wish I could concern myself with
such things, but all I can think about is the story. It's all
there, isn't it, on the tapes?'

'Yes, in duplicate,' he said with a laugh. 'You'll write it for
me when you're ready, and, Jonathan, if you don't you will
pass it on to someone, won't you? Now, I think we should get
ready and I should drive you home.'

Within the hour we were packed and in the jeep. He had
shut down the fire and all the candles in the cabin. I was
running a temperature still, but he'd bundled me up well in
the back so I could sleep, and I had the tapes tight in my
arms.

He drove fast, fast as a madman, I suppose, but I don't
imagine he put anyone in danger.

Every now and then I'd look up, roll over, and see him in
the driver's seat, see his long thick hair, and he'd turn and
give me a smile.

'Sleep, Jonathan.'

When we pulled into the driveway of my house, my wife
ran out to greet us. She helped me from the back of the jeep
and my two children came, the young ones who are still at
home, and they helped me upstairs to the bedroom.

I was afraid he would go now, forever. But he came with
us, walking through the house as if it were the most normal
thing in the world.

He kissed my wife's forehead, he kissed each of my children.

'Your husband couldn't stay up there. Terrible storm. He got a fever.'

'But how did you find him?' my wife asked.

'I saw the light coming from his chimney. He and I have had pleasant talks together.'

'Where are you going?' I asked him. I was sitting up against a heap of pillows.

'I don't know,' he said. He came up to the side of the bed. I was covered with two quilts, and the little house, set to my wife's temperature, seemed intolerably warm, but I was greatly relieved to be home.

'Don't go, Azriel,' I said.

'Jonathan, I have to. I have to wander. I want to travel and learn. I want to see things. Now that I remember everything, I am in a position to really study, to really comprehend. Without memory there can be no insight. Without love, there can be no appreciation.

'Don't worry for me. I'm going back to the sands of Iraq to the ruins of Babylon. I have the strangest feeling, that Marduk is there, lost, with no worshipers and no shrine and no temple, and that I can find him. I don't know. It's probably a foolish dream. But everyone I ever loved – except you – is dead.'

'What about the Hasidim?'

'I may go to them in time, I don't know. I'll see whether it does good or makes fear. I only want to do good now.'

'I owe you my life, and nothing in my life will ever be the same. I'll write your story,' I told him. 'You know what you are now.'

'A son of God?' he asked. He laughed. 'I don't know. I know this. That Zurvan was right, in the end there is one Creator, somewhere beyond the light I saw the truth of this, and only love and goodness matter.

'I don't ever want to be swallowed by anger or hate again, and I won't be, no matter how long or hard my journey. If I can just live by that one word it will be enough. Remember?

Altashheth. Do Not Destroy. That alone would be enough. Altashheth.

He leaned down and kissed me.

'When you write my story, don't be afraid to call me the Servant of the Bones, for that is what I still am, only not the servant of the bones of one doomed boy in Babylon, or some evil magician in a candlelighted room, or a scheming high priest, or a king dreaming of glory.

'I am the Servant of the Bones that lie in the great field that Ezekiel described, the bones of all our human brothers and sisters.'

He spoke the words of Ezekiel in Hebrew, words which the wide world knows as the following from the King James edition:

> *The hand of the Lord was*
> *upon me, and carried me out*
> *in the spirit of the Lord, and set*
> *me down in the midst of the valley*
> *which was full of bones,*
>
> *. . . and behold,*
> there were *very many in the open*
> *valley; and, lo,* they were *very dry.*

'Who knows?' he continued. 'Maybe some day the breath *will* come into them? Or perhaps the old prophet meant only that one day all mysteries would be explained, that all bones shall be revered, that all who have lived will know a reason for what we suffer in this world.'

He looked down at me and smiled.

'Perhaps someday,' he said, 'the bones of man will yield the DNA of God.'

I could find no answer. I too smiled, however. And I simply let him go on.

'But I must confess, as I leave you, I am dreaming of a time when the division between life and death will be no more and ours will be the eternity we imagine. Goodbye, Jonathan, my gentle friend. I love you.'

* * *

That was a year ago.

It was the last time I actually spoke with him.

Three times I've seen him since, and two of those times were on the television news.

The first time I saw him was among the medical workers in a cholera epidemic in South America. He was in simple white medical garments, and he was helping to feed the sick children. His hair, his eyes – it was unmistakable.

The next time I saw him, it was in news footage of Jerusalem. Yitzhak Rabin, the Prime Minister of Israel, had been assassinated the day before.

Azriel was a face in the crowd that saw the CNN camera and turned and moved towards it.

He seemed to peer directly through the lense at me.

The newscaster spoke of a city and a country weeping for its murdered leader. The world wept for the man who had wanted peace with the Arabs, and was now dead.

Azriel stared at the camera, and the camera lingered. Azriel was silent – thoughtful – looking right at me. He was dressed in plain black clothes.

The camera and the news moved on.

The third time was merely a glimpse. But I knew that it was Azriel. It was in New York. I was in a cab speeding downtown, navigating wildly through the early afternoon traffic, and off to the side I saw Azriel walking on the street.

He was handsomely dressed, with his hair untamed, and looked magnificent, striding along, carefree and full of wonder. He turned suddenly as if he had felt me see him; he looked around puzzled. But the cab shot on. Trucks blocked my view. We traveled blocks, weaving in and out of other cars. I couldn't have told where it was even, the place where I saw him.

Maybe it wasn't Azriel, I wasn't sure, or so I told myself.

And then, of course, I knew that he could reach me if he wanted me. I did not go back to look for him.

* * *

404

It's taken twelve months to prepare this book for publication, and then to publish it effectively under the cloak of anonymity so that my own colleagues won't laugh me out of the university, and those who need to hear this tale won't be hampered by knowing my identity.

There you have it. The Tale of the Servant of the Bones. And the story of what really happened with the cult of the Temple of the Mind. Or you have one story of one soul and its agonies and its refusal to give up, and its ultimate victory.

Azriel, if you read this, if you are pleased, let me know. A call; a small written note; your presence. Anything. My life has never been as it was.

But I am confident that wherever you are, you are both happy and good. And that is what matters to you most, I am sure of it.

Altashheth.

11:50 p.m.
July 11, 1995

THE FEAST OF
ALL SAINTS

*This book is dedicated with love to
Stan Rice, Carolyn Doty, and my parents,
Howard and Katherine O'Brien*

Batter my heart, three-person'd God; for, you
As yet but knocke, breathe, shine, and seeke to mend;
That I may rise, and stand, o'erthrow mee', and bend
Your force, to breake, blowe, burn and make me new.
John Dunne

VOLUME
ONE

PART ONE

I

ONE MORNING in New Orleans, in that part of the Rue Ste. Anne before it crosses Condé and becomes the lower boundary of the Place d'Armes, a young boy who had been running full tilt down the middle of the street stopped suddenly, his chest heaving, and began to deliberately and obviously follow a tall woman.

This was the street in which he lived, though he was blocks from home, and the woman lived in it also. So a number of people on the way to market—or lounging in the doors of their shops to garner a little breeze—knew the pair of them and thought as they glanced at the boy, that is Marcel Ste. Marie, Cecile's son, and what is he doing now?

These were the riverfront streets of the 1840s, packed with immigrants, where the worlds met over the back fence, and gallery to gallery; yet despite the throng, and the wilderness of masts above the levee markets, the French Quarter was then as forever a small town. And the woman was famous in it.

But all were used to her occasional meandering, a senselessly disheveled figure with beauty and money enough to make her a public offense. It was Marcel they worried about when they saw them together (the woman didn't know they were together). And dozens of others stared at him, too, not knowing him, just for the sake of staring because he was a striking figure.

That he was part African, a quadroon most likely, anyone could figure, and the white and the black blood in him had combined in an unusual way that was extremely handsome and clearly undesirable. For though his skin was lighter than honey, indeed lighter than that of many white people who were forever studying him, he had large vivid blue eyes which made it dusky. And his blond hair, tightly kinked and hugging his round head like a cap, was distinctly African. He had ridgeless eyebrows which were high and gave his expression an appealing openness, a delicate nose with small flared nostrils, and a full mouth like a child's even to the pale rose color. Later it might be sensual, but now, in his fourteenth year, it was a Cupid's bow without a single hard line to it, and the down on his upper lip was smoky as was the bit of curling hair that made up his sideburns.

In short, his was an appearance of contrasts, but everyone knew darker men could pass for white while Marcel would never, and those bound to believe him deprived of a coveted asset were disturbed at times to find themselves so drawn to looking at him, unable to anatomize him in a glance. And women thought him positively exquisite.

The yellow skin on the backs of his hands appeared silky and translucent, and he tended to grasp things that interested him, suddenly, with long fingers that appeared reverent. And sometimes if he turned to look up at you abruptly from a glass display case under a lamp, the light would make his close-cropped hair a halo around his head, and he stared with the serious radiance of those roundfaced Byzantine saints who are rapt with the Beatific Vision.

In fact, this expression was fast becoming habitual with him. He had it now as he hurried across the Rue Condé after the woman, his hands unconsciously formed into fists, his mouth slack. He saw only what was ahead of him, or his own thoughts, you couldn't always tell which, but he never seemed to see himself in the eyes of others, to sense the power of the impression he made.

And it was indeed a powerful impression. For though such dreaminess might have been past all patience in a poor man, or some drifting nuisance for whom things had endlessly to be repeated, it was perfectly fine in Marcel because he was by no means poor, as everyone knew, and was invariably well dressed.

For years he'd been the gentleman in miniature in the streets, on errands or carrying his missal to Mass, his frock coats too perfectly fitted as if he weren't sure to outgrow them in half a year, linen immaculate, waistcoats so smooth over his narrow chest that they hadn't the slightest bulge or wrinkle. On Sundays, he wore a small jeweled stickpin in his silk tie, and had lately been carrying a gold pocket watch which he sometimes stopped dead in the streets to study, teeth pressed to his lower lip, his blond eyebrows knit in a sharp look of distress that strained the taut skin of his forehead. His boots were always new.

In short, slaves of the same color knew at once he was free, and white men thought him at a glance a "fine boy," but when all that is put aside, which is only the beginning, his preoccupation seemed the absence of pride, he was no snob, but possessed a genuine and precocious gentility.

You couldn't imagine him climbing a tree, or playing stick ball, or wetting his hands except to wash them. The books he carried eternally were ancient and tattered, leather covers bound with ribbon or string; but even this was elegant. And he had about him often the subtle scent of a cologne seldom lavished on boys.

Of course Marcel was the son of a white planter, Philippe Ferronaire, Creole gentleman to his fingertips, and in debt on the next crop to the hilt, his white children crowding the family box at the opera every season. And though no one would have thought of calling the man "Marcel's father," that is what he was, and the sight of his carriage listing in the narrow Rue Ste. Anne before the Ste. Marie cottage was somewhat regular.

So people thinking Marcel splendid and rich forgave him his slight peculiarity, and merely smiled when he ran smack into them on the banquette, or leaning forward, snapped their fingers, hissing gently "Hey Marcel!" And he would wake to the solid and familiar to go on being unfailingly polite.

He paid his mother's bills promptly, tipped generously for the slightest service, and on his own brought her flowers from the florist which everyone thought powerfully romantic; and often in the past, though seldom lately, had escorted about his sister, Marie, with an affection and obvious pride in her uncommon in a brother so young. Marie at thirteen was an ivory beauty, ripening beneath a child's lace and pearl buttons.

But people if they knew Marcel at all, had begun to worry

(12)

about him. He seemed in the last six months bound to ruin himself, for with his fourteenth birthday in the last fall, he had been transformed from the innocent to the mysterious without apparent explanation.

It was a gradual thing, however, and fourteen is a difficult age.

Besides it wasn't ordinary mischief. It had a curious flair.

He was seen all around the French Quarter at odd hours, roaming for the sake of roaming, and several times recently he had appeared in the rear pew of the Cathedral, staring at every detail of the statues and paintings as if he were a baffled immigrant off the ship and not a boy who'd been baptized there and made his Communion in the same place only a year before.

He bought tobacco he wasn't supposed to smoke, read a folded newspaper while walking, watched with fascination the butchers under the eaves of the French Market hacking bloody sides of beef into parcels, and wandered astonished along the levee the day that the H.M.S. *Catherine* docked, her load of starving Irish the scandal of the summer. Wraiths too weak to walk, they were carted to the Charity Hospital and some of them right to the Bayou Cemetery, where Marcel stood watching the burials, and all this when he must have seen it so many times in the past with yellow fever coming on every summer and the stench from the cemeteries so thick in the steaming streets that it became the breath of life. Death was everywhere in New Orleans, what of it? Why go stare at it?

In a cabaret, he was served absinthe before the owner recognized him and sent him home. So he took to worse places, waterfront bistros where in the smoke-filled shadows he would pull out a morocco-bound book in which to write, and sometimes with the same book, wander into the Place d'Armes, fall on a bit of grass under a tree as if he were a derelict and there commence the same scribbling or what might have a been the drawing of pictures as he squinted at the birds, the trees, the sky. This was ridiculous.

And yet he didn't seem to know it.

And worse was the sight of his sister, Marie, on tiptoe at the doors of the dram shops, shuffled in such a crowd, her hair down to her waist, her childish dresses hardly concealing the fullness of her figure, beckoning for him to come out.

Mother and daughter came alone to Sunday Mass where there had always been three.

But who knew much about Cecile Ste. Marie, Marcel's mother, except that she was a stunning lady, laced so tight beneath her taffeta that her heart seemed forever fighting for breath beneath the frill at her throat. Her black hair parted in the middle and pulled back over the tips of her ears, she would stand proudly with arms folded at the back door, fighting with butcher and fishmonger before pointing their merchandise to the kitchen. Hers was a French face, petite, sharp of feature, with no trace of the African, except of course for her beautifully textured and very dark skin. She seldom went out, occasionally clipped roses in her garden and confided to no one.

The Ste. Marie cottage gleamed with respectability beyond its short fence and dense banana trees, a sprawl of magnolia limbs over its pitched roof. And one could only speculate, was she worried about her son, Marcel? And what did she say to the white man, Monsieur Philippe, Marcel's father, when he came, if she said anything at all? But neighbors said there was occasional shouting behind the lace curtains and even the slamming of doors.

And what would she think now if she saw her son following this woman, the infamous Juliet Mercier? Should he come too close Juliet might just strike him with her market basket, or scratch his face. She was mad.

And any speculation on her made Marcel at once the paragon. He was, after all, just a boy, and a good one at that. He'd straighten up. He was high in the small private academy of Monsieur De Latte, which cost a fortune, and would undoubtedly come to his senses.

But Juliet was shameful, she had "no excuse," people shunned her, he ought to shun her, certainly shouldn't be following her, she had become the object of absolute scorn. How dare she retreat in her listing mansion on the corner of Ste. Anne and Dauphine and nail boards over the windows that fronted the street, vanishing so totally from life that neighbors thought her dead and beat down the gate? And then to come racing toward them with an ax, her hair streaming like an Ophelia, a gaggle of hens in a swirl of feathers screeching at her wake? So let her be shut up with chickens and flies. Let the cats roam the top of her sagging courtyard walls. One and all banged their shutters shut on her as if she hadn't already bolted her own.

She was not old by any means, had the slender figure of a girl at forty, hair of gleaming black with skin so light she might have passed to the untutored eye, and rings on her fingers when she chose. It was outrageous, this waste of prime and property...but worst of all, worst of all...it was the matter of her son, Christophe.

He was the one whose name was on everyone's lips these days, a star in this constellation where he had not been for a decade. Because gone to Paris years before, he was now a famous man. For three years his essays and stories had appeared in the Paris press, along with colorful accounts of his Eastern travels, reviews of the theater, art, music. And his novel, *Nuits de Charlotte*, had taken the city by storm. He was a dandy in dress, veritably lived in the cafés of the Rue Saint Jacques, surrounded eternally by exotic and scribbling friends. Children abroad sent home his articles, his stories in the *Revue des Deux Mondes*, copies of his novel and the reviews which sang his praises as a "master of the language," or a "new and unbridled imagination, Shakespearean in power, Byronic in tone." And even those who understood not a particle of the ravings of his bizarre characters nodded with respect at the mention of him and among many he was no longer Christophe Mercier, but merely Christophe, as if he had become familiar and a friend to all those who admired him.

Even the white planters' sons carried his novel in their pockets when they got off the boat and told stories of having seen him emerge from a cabriolet before the Porte-Saint-Martin Theatre, a white actress on his sleeve. And slaves overhearing these stories at table brought them to town.

But among the colored community there was more than a special pride. Many could remember the boy he had been when the dreary house in the Rue Dauphine had blazed with lights, and handsome men were forever at the gate to take the hand of his mother. And most concurred he might have buried his past had he chosen, there was light skin enough and money, and the warm embrace of fame. But he did not. Over and over in this or that notice or bit of article, there appeared the fact that he was a native of this city, that he was a man of color, and that he had a mother residing here still.

Of course, he was in Paris. When you die...you go to Paris.

He drank champagne with Victor Hugo, dined with Louis Philippe in the Hall of Mirrors, and danced at the Tuileries. White women were seen occasionally to draw back the curtains from his high windows on the Ile St. Louis and look over the quay toward Notre Dame. He sent home trunks brought in cabs from the customhouse to vanish through his mother's gate. And she, the wretch, unkempt, distracted, wandered to market with her black cat, in the rich and ragged costume of a beggar at the opera.

Marcel was familiar with these tales. He had been at his front gate the day she swung the ax in the dirt corner where their streets met. And knew the letters for "Christophe" that his friends put through the gate were beaten white of ink on the garden path by the falling rain.

What he really didn't know was how things had been before. Though one evening at home, Monsieur Philippe in his blue robe, lounging at table the way Marcel would never have thought to do in his own house even if no one were there, said idly through his aura of cigar smoke, "Perhaps that boy, Christophe, was destined for great things."

"How so?" asked Cecile politely. It was that hour when she sat across from him, her face softened and serene in the light of the candles, enthralled as Philippe unwound his lustrous chatter, and Marcel pretended to read at the open *secrétaire*.

What had the boy, Christophe, been like?

The picture dazzled.

Of how the little one was forever falling asleep in his mother's box at the opera when his legs weren't long enough yet to reach the floor, or at midnight suppers was left to doze on a settee against the folded coat of a gentleman caller, or a visiting ship's captain who had brought with him a parrot in a cage. Men of all hues and shades took their turns at the late night soirees while restaurants of any reputation sooner or later sent steaming trays up the wooden stairs.

And it was the waiters often enough who, having gathered the stained linen and the silver dollars, put the child to bed, removing his shoes.

They said he drew on the walls, collected the feathers of birds, and played in his mother's dresses, acting Henry IV on the dining-room table.

What a figure! Marcel had let his book close. He shut his eyes, thought of those times when this heroic presence had reigned at the very corner of the block. What friends they might have been! And what was there now in his world but well-behaved children! If only he could have spoken directly to Monsieur Philippe, the questions he might have asked.

But the subject made Cecile nervous, it was clear, Marcel could tell. She didn't remember those times, no, she shook her head, as if the world ended at her front gate.

But the story took its turn. Monsieur Philippe loved the sound of his own voice.

And when Christophe was thirteen, a final guest arrived who stayed, though forever shrouded in mystery, a black veteran of the Haitian wars.

"You remember him, that old man." Monsieur Philippe bit off the tip of his cigar and spat it in the grate. Marcel knew those subtle sounds by heart. Like the chink of the neck of the bottle hitting the rim of the glass, and that soft breath of satisfaction after each drink. "Of course we were suspicious of him, who needs these rebel slaves from Haiti...Haiti! It was Saint-Domingue when my great-uncle owned the biggest plantation on the Plaine du Nord. Ah, but the point is, the man was abroad so long, money in Paris, New York, Charleston...banks here, uptown. Hardly the one to set fire to every sugar plantation on the coast and lead a band of ragged blacks to cut our throats."

In the mirror, Marcel saw his mother shudder; she rubbed the backs of her arms, her head to one side, eyes on the lace tablecloth. Ragged army of blacks to cut our throats, the words struck some sudden excitement in Marcel, what was Monsieur Philippe talking about? But it was Christophe that interested him, not that mysterious history of Haiti of which Marcel got bits and pieces at odd moments, never enough to make a picture of anything except rebel slaves and blood.

And he was old besides, this black Haitian, and crippled. And soon sick of seeing Christophe feast on chocolates and white wine, accustomed to sleep in his mother's bed when he chose, and permitted to lie on the sloped roof at night, three stories above the street to study the stars, he sent the boy abroad.

Christophe was fourteen when he left, and people argued about the rest. It was uncertain, some saying he boarded in England for a while, others that no, he went to Paris, having *in loco parentis* the white family of a hotelkeeper who kept him in a veritable closet under the stairs, without even a candle let alone heat on winter nights. He was beaten there some insisted, others that, spoiled as always, he had had his own way, lashing out at these poor bourgeoisie any time they tried to restrain him.

But one thing was sure, that at sixteen he had run away

to Egypt, wandered through Greece and returned to Paris in the company of a wealthy Englishman, white of course, to become an artist. He'd written of these exotic lands, Monsieur Philippe had an article somewhere sent home by his young brother-in-law, Vincent, where was it (what Marcel wouldn't have given to lay hands on it). But back to those times when he was wandering, and slaves over the back fence said the old Haitian, now bedridden, had disowned him. What claim had he over that beautiful Juliet, who could imagine? She with that pale golden skin and delicate face...but Philippe merely touched on that lightly, she had died on the vine. Cecile nodded.

And they said she drank sherry and fell to merely watching the rain.

And that she was mean to the old Haitian in the last year of his life, yes, Cecile had heard that too, when paralyzed he had to lie there to be fed softboiled egg with a spoon. The blinds were shut forever. Children of five and six thought the house haunted and loved to run past it squealing. Ah, look at it now, a jungle behind those cracked brick walls, and a peeling hulk on the busy corner.

But at just this time, across the sea, Christophe's star rose.

Marcel could remember the rest.

And long after Monsieur Philippe had let the tale drop, he traced the thread in his own memory—how people had gathered to watch the old man's casket come out because of the son's fame. And only when it was all over, and a ghastly, worn Juliet walked back from the cemetery in the scorching sun, did people begin to whisper the truth. It was on the tombstone. The old Haitian had been her father!

So didn't he have some rights over the boy, his own grandson?

But what would she do now, take lovers? Get new servants for those sold off or dead, patch the walls, bring the drapers and painters up the steps? No one doubted she could do it. She was so-o-o-o lovely still, Marcel at twelve was mad to get a glimpse of her. He didn't really understand about Christophe then. He was "in love" with something or someone else. It did not come to him as having meaning yet that a famous man had lived there, walked there, breathed there.

And she did nothing. Her windows crusted with dirt, her garden wall became a menace. The vines that pushed it out miraculously held it up. She did not answer notes or knocks, and soon the hatred commenced. It was unfair! Christophe's

Nuits de Charlotte stood open in the windows of the book-sellers. Stupid, silly... but most of all unfair.

How wonderful it would have been, after all, to "receive" her and hear about the young man firsthand, be her friend. But she became a witch in time, her lone-ness not only absurd but unfathomable. How, after all, could she endure it? The last of her slaves was put to rest in the Old St. Louis. The house was empty save for the cats.

Pity went fast, however, for she was too vicious if you spoke to her on the street, turning away at once, her head bowed, her cat in the basket on her arm. And with her son's fame, increased the hatred.

But the boys Marcel's age were now on fire for Christophe. They worshiped him, and sternly forbidden to go near his mother they nevertheless lingered at her gate, hoping to put but one question, and always in vain. If she came out at all, they scattered. She looked too dreadful with her diamond rings in the noonday sun, an inch of petticoat beneath her hem. The mailman brought her letters from France, they got that out of him, but did she even pick them up from the gravel path? Straining to see through a chink in the wood, they had the worst fears.

But she was Christophe's mother after all. They couldn't despise her out of loyalty, and they had other things on their minds. Like writing stories in his "style," making scrapbooks of clippings sent home by older brothers, uncles, cousins. And lounging about in each others' parlors on afternoons when adults were out, they dreamed aloud with pilfered brandy of the day they would make the fabled pilgrimage to Paris, might knock on his black lacquered door on the Ile St. Louis and reverently, politely, gently, unimposingly, hand him their sheaf of manuscript pages.

Occasionally there was an uncle or a brother home who had, in fact, drunk with him in some crowded café, and then the rumors went wild.

He smoked hashish, talked in riddles, could be seen quar-reling in the streets, and staying drunk for twenty-four hours at a stretch, he talked to himself, and sometimes fell into a stupor at a café table. And there would appear that English-man, "white of course," who would pick him up, slap his face gently with a few drops of water, and slinging Christophe's arm over his shoulder, carry him home.

But he was kind to his countrymen always. He never read stories shoved at him across tables, but gave gentle general advice, and when a tactful introduction here or there could be effected, did that with grace. He showed no shame of race, clasped dark hands, asked about New Orleans, and certainly seemed to listen. But he was quick to be bored, to grow silent and then be gone. You clanged his bell in vain after that. He knew when he had done all he could and you had nothing to offer.

Ah, admire him if you will, but imitate him never, said the parents to the enamored children. Marcel worshiped him, and those who watched his recent wanderings wondered if it were some mad emulating of the famous man that sent Marcel off the track.

For Christophe set the other boys on the straight and narrow when they thought of him. They wanted the tools to be like him, and in the scattered private schools around the town, here under a white teacher, there under a colored, they strove tensely, the lessons expensive, the classes select. They must be educated when they stepped off the boat, they had to be men.

And that Marcel would make the journey to Paris, that he would have his chance—all that was certain. A promise made by Monsieur Philippe at his birth was the guarantee. And sooner or later, at least once a year, that promise was reiterated. Cecile saw to that. She had no concern for her daughter Marie, she said, Marie would "do well." Lips pressed tight, she dismissed that subject abruptly. But in the warmest and best moments would broach the matter of her son. Marcel, lying awake on smothering summer nights when the mosquito netting, gleaming gold in the faint spluttering nightlight, became the only walls dividing them, would hear Monsieur Philippe murmur on the pillow, "I'll send the boy in style..." It was a vintage promise, a part of life. So why not work toward it?

But Marcel daydreamed in class, provoked the teacher with obscure questions, and the sight of his empty chair a dozen times in the last month filled everyone with a vague dread. He was too well liked for the other boys to enjoy it. And his best friend, Richard Lermontant, seemed rather miserable. But what made this fall from grace all the more confusing, especially to Richard, was that Marcel himself seemed not the least confused by it. He was hardly helpless in the face of youthful passion. He did not, for instance, court his sister's pretty friends and then, giggling, yank their hair. Nor did he pound his fist on tree trunks declaring, "I don't know what got into me!" And never once, in a welter of confusion, did he call on God to explain how he could make the races different colors, or demand an explanation for why the world was cruel.

Rather he seemed privy to some terrible secret that set him apart, and bound to calmly pursue his course.

Which this morning seemed hell-bent for disaster.

It was a warm summer day, and he had only caught his breath as he drew closer and closer to the volatile Juliet when she stopped at the fruit stands beneath the arcade. And putting his left hand up against the slender iron post in front of him, he pressed his lips against his hand and gazed at her with wide blue eyes. He did not realize it, but he seemed to want to hide behind the colonette, as if such a narrow thing could hide him, and he had covered all of his face except his eyes.

There was pain in his eyes, but the kind that reveals itself in a flicker, the puckering of the eyelid underneath, a flinching at one's own thoughts. Looking at Juliet, he knew full well what he was expected to see, and understood full well what he, in fact, perceived. Not squalor and wickedness but some radiant and splendid spectacle of neglect that laid his heart waste. But this had been today a matter of glimpses....

Running breathless to her gate from school, he'd pounded on it for the first time in his life, only to be told by a shouting neighbor that she'd gone to market. But he'd caught the first sight of her only a block away. And she was tall and he could trace her easily.

Now, when the flock of bonneted women broke between them, and she stepped out again into the cobblestone street, he saw her clearly for the first time.

He started, all of a piece, like a man jumping to the clang of a bell, and moved as if he might go up to her. Then he lapsed back, lips pressed again to the back of his hand, as she made her way under the clear sun to the iron fence of the square. He seemed lost to her in every detail and silently shuddered.

She was slow if not languid as she walked, her market basket riding gently on her arm, and as he had seen her a thousand times, fantastical, her frayed shawl a blaze of peacocks and silver against her red silk dress, flounces torn and dragging the stones, her fine brunette hair falling in hopeless tangles from the grip of a pearl comb. Diamonds sparkled on

(21)

the fingers of her right hand with which she gathered her skirts at the curb, and as she turned toward the long row of sketches for sale on the pickets, Marcel could see her profile for an instant and the flash of the gold loop in her ear.

Suddenly, a great lumbering hack rattled by, obliterating her, and maddened, he darted across the street behind it, coming to a slapping halt so that she turned around.

Someone called his name. He didn't hear it, but then he did, and couldn't remember it. She was looking at him, and he had lapsed again into the utter passivity of a staring child.

Only a yard stood between them. It seemed in years he had never been so close to her, her amber face as smooth as a girl's, deepset black eyes fringed with lashes, the high smooth expanse of her forehead broken by a widow's peak from which her hair grew back in lustrous waves. She was mildly curious as she looked at him. Then, her thin rouged lips drew back into the curve of her cheek and the supple flesh around her eyes was etched with fine lines as she smiled.

A tiny heart pounded in Marcel's temple. Someone brushed his shoulder, yet he didn't move. Someone said his name.

But suddenly as if something had distracted her Juliet bowed her head, tilting it strangely to one side and groped with her fingers in her hair. She was searching for the comb as though it had begun to hurt her. And as she jerked it out and looked at it, all of her black hair fell down over her shoulders in a cascade.

A soft excited sound escaped Marcel's lips. Someone had a hold on his arm, but he merely flinched, stiffened, and let his eyes grow wide again, ignoring the young man at his side.

All he could feel was the pounding of his own heart and he had the distinct impression that the rush of horses and wheels in the street had become deafening. There was shouting somewhere, and from the riverfront before him came those echoing booms from the unloading ships. But he saw none of this. He was seeing only Juliet, though not right now. Rather it was another time, long long ago, before he was the villain he had become of late, the outcast. But it was a time so palpable that whenever it came back to him, it engulfed him and was memory no longer, but pure sensation. His tongue pressed against his teeth and he felt flushed and stunned. He might even be sick. And just for a moment he didn't know for certain where he was, which might lead to terror. But groping for a hold, he found the memory which was a spell.

Running home years ago, he'd stubbed his boot on a fallen lump of coal in the street and been thrown right into her arms. In fact he'd pushed her backwards as he gripped the taffeta of her soft waist and then seeing it was she, Juliet, let go in such panic he would have fallen if she hadn't clasped his shoulder. Looking up into her eyes like beads of jet, he saw the buttons all undone from her throat, and the mound of her naked breast pushed against the placket of shimmering cloth. There was a darkness there beneath the undercurve where he could see the soft meeting of chest and bosom. And an alien surge had made him shudder. He had felt her thumb against his cheek like sealskin, and then the open palm of her hand rubbing gently back and forth, back and forth against his tight curly hair. Her eyes seemed blind then. Her fine small waist was flesh beneath the cloth only, an astonishing nakedness. And the scent of spice and flowers lingered afterwards on his hands. He almost died.

He was almost dying now. And then and now, he watched baffled, weak, as she moved away from him like a tall ship, upstream.

"But this has nothing to do with it!" he whispered, the shame burning in his cheeks, unable to keep his lips from moving (he was a great one for talking right out loud to himself, and was forever relieved when others, coming upon him unawares assumed he had been singing). "It's Christophe," he went on. "I have to talk to her about Christophe!"

But the mere vision of her swaying skirts was stunning him again and he murmured in French out loud with a melodramatic air, "I *am* a criminal," and felt some mild relief at being the abject object of his own condemnation. Too many nights had he indulged himself thinking of that chance childhood collision—the naked breast, uncorseted waist, wild perfume—so that now he had to draw himself up like a gentleman who, having glimpsed an unclad lady at her bath, shuts the door and quickly walks away.

This was the Place d'Armes, someone was trying to break his arm.

He stared astonished at the breast buttons of Richard Lermontant, his best friend.

"No, go on, Richard," he said quickly, as if they'd been arguing all the while, "go on back to school," and craning his neck to see Juliet disappear in the throng at the market, tried to wrench himself free.

"You are telling *me* to go back to school?" demanded Richard, holding him fast. His voice was low and deep, all but a whisper on the word of emphasis. "Marcel, look at me!" It was always Richard's habit to lower his voice precisely at that point where others raise theirs, and it was invariably effective, perhaps because he was so tall. He towered over Marcel, though he was only sixteen. In fact, he towered over everyone in the street. "Monsieur De Latte's furious!" he confided, drawing close. "You've got to come back with me now."

"No!" Marcel said shortly, and lurched forward freeing himself and stifling the urge to rub the upper part of his arm. Seldom in his life had he been touched except in anger, and he had a healthy distrust of being held, loathing it in fact, though it was impossible for him to loathe Richard. They were more than friends, and he simply couldn't bear to be angry with Richard or to have Richard angry with him. "Be a good friend to me," he turned pleading, "and go. I don't care what you tell Monsieur De Latte. Tell him anything." And he started off fast for the corner.

Richard overtook him quickly.

"But why are you doing this? What's the point of it?" he pleaded, his shoulders slightly bent so he could be near Marcel's ear. "You ran out in the middle of class, do you realize what you've done?"

"Yes, I realize it. I did it, I did it," Marcel said, blundering into the traffic of the riverfront street, so that he was at once forced back on the curb. "But let me go please." He could just make out the top of Juliet's head at the fish market. *"Give up on me, please!"*

Richard let him go, and clasping his hands behind his back he gained at once what seemed a characteristic composure so that nothing of the sixteen-year-old boy was left in him. In fact he had an ageless look most of the time so that strangers might think him twenty, perhaps older. He had never asked for his height, in fact, had prayed against it, but a manly spirit had some time ago invaded his long limbs; and as he stood very still with one foot forward, and his shoulders only a little bent, his lean face with its prominent cheekbones and slanting black eyes made him appear at once majestic and exotic. He was darker than Marcel, all of an olive complexion, his hair wavy and black. But this suggested the Turk, the Spaniard perhaps, or even the Italian, and almost nothing of the French and the Senegalese from whom he was descended.

Gesturing with a languid hand, fingers sloping gracefully from the wrist, he whispered. "You have to come back, Marcel, you have to!" But Marcel was looking toward the market again where a great flock of birds rose suddenly from the tiled roof, looping and descending on the masts above the dock. His eyes narrowed. Juliet had emerged from the crowd feeding fish on her fingers to her cat.

Startled, Richard said. "You aren't following her!"

An involuntary look of distaste passed over his face, which he quickly banished, but not before Marcel had seen it. "But why?"

"What do you mean, why? You know why," Marcel said. "I have to ask her if it's true...I have to know now."

"This is all my fault," Richard murmured.

"Go back." Marcel started off again. And again Richard clutched his arm.

"She won't know, Marcel...and if she does what makes you think she'll tell you! She's not in her right mind!" he whispered, and glancing at her, dropped his eyes politely as if she were a cripple.

Her hair was in streams now like that of an immigrant, and she wandered through the crowd letting her feet find her path so that people all but stumbled over her as she crooned to the cat. Richard's thin, large-boned frame stiffened as he shifted his weight. The boy in him wanted to cry.

"You won't turn to stone, looking at her!" Marcel whispered. And astonished, Richard saw a vicious spark in Marcel's eyes, and heard a driving impatience in his voice.

"This is craziness," Richard muttered, and almost turned to go. Then he said, "If you don't come back with me now...you'll be sent home from school for good."

"For good?" Marcel reeled half off the curb. "Well then, good!" And he started across the street to her.

Richard was speechless. He stared beyond the row of crawling carts that worked against the crowds from the market, and as Marcel approached Christophe's mother, Richard went after him.

"Well, then give me back the clipping!" he said, his voice thick. "You know perfectly well it's Antoine's, I want it."

At once Marcel rummaged in his pockets and drew out a crumpled bit of newspaper with neatly trimmed edges. He tried desperately to smooth it in the palm of his hand. "I didn't mean to steal it," he said. "I was excited...I meant to put it back on your desk..."

Richard's face was dark with anger. He glanced from second to second at the figure of Juliet, and then at the ground.

"I would have brought it to you before supper," Marcel insisted. "You have to believe that."

"It's not even mine, it's Antoine's, and you stuffed it in your pocket and ran out."

"If you don't believe me," Marcel insisted, "you wound me in my heart."

"I know perfectly well where your heart is," Richard murmured, with a glance at the *mea culpa* fist Marcel touched to his breast. "And you're in for a lot more than pangs there, I'll tell you. You're going to be expelled!"

Marcel didn't even seem to understand.

"And suppose it's true," Richard went on, "suppose Christophe is coming back here...What kind of a recommendation is it—to be bounced out of Monsieur De Latte's school on your ear?"

Richard folded the clipping, but not without reading it quickly again. It seemed a flimsy piece of evidence to push Marcel to ruin. But, how splendid it had seemed that morning, when Antoine, Richard's cousin, cutting open the letter from Paris, had given it to Richard at the table. Christophe coming back at last. They had always dreamed of it, hoped for it, told themselves the day would come when he would learn of his mother's madness and if nothing else had done the trick, his love for her would bring him home. But there was so much more to it than that. One was left no room for fantasy, for speculation. It was spelled out plainly that Christophe Mercier planned no simple visit, but a real return. He was coming home to "found a school for the members of his race."

By evening all the community of the *gens de couleur* would be aflame with it, this news which had sent Richard flying toward Monsieur De Latte's classroom to share it with Marcel. And now this turn had been taken, this bolting by Marcel through the open doorway with Monsieur De Latte shouting for order and cracking his stick on the lectern.

It seemed sour now, painful. A cloud hung over Richard that made the very streets dreary, like soot on the bricks.

But he looked up suddenly and was mortified. Juliet not a yard away was staring at them both. He felt his cheek flame. And Marcel was moving suddenly toward her! Richard turned, darting through the stagnant stream of mules and wagons until he was rushing fast along the Place d'Armes, headed back to school the way he'd come.

But it pounded in his head with every step: this is my fault, this is all my fault. I should have kept it till the right time. This is my fault.

II

THE RIVERFRONT streets were a quagmire that Richard detested, and the fact that he had to pass through them to return to an infuriated schoolmaster weighed on him like the noonday sun. Already distraught, he stopped in the middle of one of these squalid alleys, hung with laundry and echoing with the harsh German and Irish voices, and considered for the first time in his life going into a public house and getting totally drunk.

That he could get away with it, he had no doubt. He had long ago outgrown his father, and his grandfather, a wizened man who had been taller in his youth. But on the wall of the parlor at home was a portrait of his great-grandfather Jean Baptiste, a mulatto slave freed in the days before the Spanish took the colony of Louisiana from the French in 1769, and on his free papers, tucked in a mahogany *secrétaire* with other treasured records, Jean Baptiste was described as "a mulatto, servant to Lermontant, known also as 'the titan' on account of his uncommon height being full seven feet."

His portrait showed broad African features, more drawn than painted, the stilted landscape behind him darkening and cracking with age so that soon the few distinct traces of river and cloud would disappear and only Jean Baptiste's brown face would remain, with the same gently slanting eyes that marked Richard's face and a flaking white ruff at his throat.

It was a precious thing to everyone, his industry having founded the family, his legend dominating its long climb. But Richard never looked at him of late without dreading that one morning, he would stand before the beveled mirror of his armoire at last unable to see his own face reflected there because he had gained the final inches to match Jean Baptiste's height. Jean Baptiste's mother, the African woman,

(27)

Zanzi, had been a towering figure also. And after all, though Richard had not inherited Jean Baptiste's broad nose or African mouth, he alone had his great-grandfather's slanting eyes.

And being one of those big velvet-voiced creatures who can quiet a screaming infant with a bare touch to the belly and a rumbling song, or reassemble silently the scattered works of a pocket watch and hand it back to you ticking, a faint smile on his lips, Richard dreaded becoming the local giant.

But he could use his height well enough to get into the most dismal of waterfront places where the free Negroes drank along with everyone else. And a wild anger drove him to it now, a passionate fear for Marcel, a dread of Monsieur De Latte, and *something...something else,* a tangle of thoughts and pain which he could not fully examine.

He turned around in the street and went toward the levee. Monsieur De Latte was surely well into the day's lessons. Certainly he wasn't waiting for Richard. And if there was anyone who was never suspected of anything, it was Richard. Everyone knew his father the formidable Monsieur Rudolphe Lermontant, had long ago measured the route from his home to the school with his pocket watch and that he allowed his son no more than five minutes variance coming and going for rainy weather. But the thought of this trust was hardly a comfort. Richard was a boy at heart, and never questioned authority, though he was often looking down on its embodiment, and deceit for its own sake had no savor.

The mere thought of his father, looming suddenly amid these vague considerations made his head ache. Richard knew well what Rudolphe would say when Marcel's latest disgrace was discovered. And the whole dreadful mess was too much suddenly, as he turned along the market (though much below where he had left Marcel), and spied a nice dark filthy place in which to commit mortal sin.

He had a pint in no time and seated himself at a wooden table that threatened to collapse, the chair dark with grease, and poured himself a glass. Irishmen were raging at the bar, and the black laborers kept apart. But he had trouble understanding what the Irish raged against, and no trouble whatsoever shutting them out. He tried to understand what had happened to Marcel, and more than that, this confusing tangle of thought which was causing him pain.

It had begun with occasional absences, Marcel's daydreaming in class. And then Richard could hear in the too carefully constructed explanations that Marcel was merely implying his mother had kept him home, and soon Monsieur De Latte realized this as well. Marcel refused to tell a lie. Very soon he refused to do almost anything, his vague and fragmented murmurings only calculated to bring down the teacher's wrath.

And then there was the death of old Jean Jacques, the carpenter, when Marcel stole wine from his mother's cabinet and got drunk so they found him sick in the morning at the cistern. Marcel's mother was in tears; Richard held his hand while he retched. And then slumping against the steps, Marcel merely murmured, "I am a criminal, give up on me," which thereafter became a slogan. That all this had to do with Jean Jacques seemed clear, but even this was a mystery. A fine cabinetmaker he had been, an old mulatto from Saint-Domingue who'd kept a shop ever since they could remember, but hardly a man to incur the devotion of an educated boy like Marcel.

Even Anna Bella Monroe, the dearest of Marcel's childhood friends, could not account for the changes in him. He had always come to her in the past, but she shook her head now, with a desperate click of the tongue, to hear of his vagrant wanderings. And these things did not stop with the passing of grief, but went on.

But Marcel at home could easily read the works he neglected in school, translate verses which confounded others, and whenever he and Richard exchanged their poems, Richard knew without pain that Marcel's were incomparably the best. They had a sharp vitality within the honored forms that made Richard's flat and stilted by comparison. It seemed at times that Marcel, once so perfect and now so wildly bound to destroy himself, was cursed with the ability to succeed at whatever he chose.

Richard leaned his head against the wall of this dingy place feeling delightfully anonymous in his misery, eyes lowered against the smoke that hovered in the motionless air, and felt the whiskey burn his chest.

His way had always been one way, and that was aiming for excellence through constant striving. He knew nothing else. It had been bred into him not only by Rudolphe, but by his grandpère, Jean Baptiste's only son, whose example was the prevailing spirit of the home now, the warm flame that illuminated the ancient portrait on the parlor wall.

Richard had seen Grandpère's guns crossed beneath that picture all his life, proud symbol of the War of 1812 when Grandpère had fought with the Light Colored Battalion under Andy Jackson to save New Orleans from the British. And men of color had proved themselves loyal citizens of the new American state. He'd been decorated, and had come home to buy with Jean Baptiste's savings a failing undertaker's shop from a white man, shutting down the old tavern in the Tchoupitoulas Road in which Jean Baptiste had made his fortune. And nursing the old man in his dotage, Grandpère had made a name in this business from which he had only retired in recent years when arthritis so crippled his hands that he no longer cared to keep the books himself, or tend to the dead. Yet even now he read the papers daily, in French and English, and spent the afternoons, hands warmed even in summer over the coal stove, writing painstaking letters to the Congress on the subject of the colored veterans, their pensions, their land grants, their rights. He remembered birthdays, visited widows and chatted from time to time with other old men in the parlor.

And on long winter evenings, when the family lingered at table, the children given brandy in crystal glasses, he would leave the lovely warmth at the stroke of nine always, wrapping his cravat around his neck, and begin his long walk to say his rosary. Beads clutched in his right pocket, he wound slowly through familiar streets, never failing to nod at this neighbor at her window, or that man passing, collar up against the wind, though his lips moved only with his prayers. He ran the family investments, told the little ones history before they were old enough to go to school. And up before everyone at dawn, it was he who lit the fires and woke the slaves.

His only son, Rudolphe, Richard's father, a booming man who slammed doors if the soup was cold, had greatly expanded the business, buying a tombstone yard and fostering his young colored sculptors. He had long ago delegated the actual tending of the dead to his nephews Antoine and Pierre. And spent his time in the parlors with the mourners, seeing they had the best black to wear and nothing to worry them of future or finance till the dead were laid to rest. A bear with his family, he was gentle with the bereaved, thought them worthy of the only real patience he could muster. And over the door of the prosperous establishment in the Rue

Royale hung the name of the white man who had freed the long dead Jean Baptiste: Lermontant.

Richard raised his eyebrows listlessly over his whiskey glass, his vision pleasantly blurred, and noticed with a slight twist to his generous mouth that the glass was dirty. It had the fingerprints of others, and, if he was wont to speculate, the stench of others' spit. Beyond the open door, the blue sky exploded over the market, and squinting, he bowed his head. He wondered for the first time in his life if Hell were not a filthy place, unpurified by fire, and quickly drank the whiskey down.

The sweet aroma of damnation was enough. And then came the tension as before, the fear for Marcel which was compelling him to do this to himself. And that *something,* that *something else,* that morbid tangle of neglected thought, a needle suddenly in his brain. He wasn't meant for this kind of felonious activity. That the Irishmen at the bar were all staggering drunk before noon amused him vaguely.

He thought of how his father would shake him by the collar if he knew he had gone to this place. And that vaguely amused him too. His last spurt of height had apparently conferred on him an immunity from being beaten senseless. He was too big and too heavy to shove around. He smiled to himself and drank another glass.

But he knew that he could not endure this long. He did not have Marcel's capacity for it. Even if the entire Lermontant heritage had been swept away in one blast, Richard would always be the same. He was formed and obedient and possessed of a constant and incurable anxiety that made it impossible for him to remain in a room that was not straight, or to begin a job without finishing it, or to put down a book that he did not fully understand.

But one thing saved him every day of his life, as he sprang from bed before the light, and only lay down when his clothes had been smoothed on their hooks in his armoire, and his lessons laid out flawless on the dining-room table. He knew somewhere in his heart of hearts that nothing could ever really be perfect, and that this tension which was his daily companion was never actually meant to end. Does that sound simple?

He thought sometimes his father did not know it, or that his mother, Suzette, bustling back and forth from kitchen to supper table, her sleeves pinned back, her brow moist, really thought the day would come when she might rest. But Richard understood in some wordless way it was the manner in which life was to be constantly lived, and so often he seemed possessed of a maddening calm when others were furious, and he performed his duties in a manner that was resigned and sometimes mechanical. He didn't know yet this would become harder as time passed.

His head split. Yet the whiskey gave none of the sweet pleasure of sherry or port.

But only the vague awareness that some figure, that of a white man, detached from the bar, was watching him caused him to push the glass away.

Christophe really coming back here! Christophe really opening a school! Richard's dreams had never reached that height. In fact, they had always been rather modest dreams in which a pilgrimage to Paris had not even played a part.

Fixed on the backdrop of his imagination, rigidly and perfectly drawn, was a picture of Grandpère by the fire, pushing the Paris review of Christophe's *Nuits de Charlotte* away from him. Antoine had taken it silently.

"Passe blanc!" the old man spat into the grate.

"No, Grandpère!" Richard urged softly. "He has never...it's always mentioned he's a man of color..." But then he saw Antoine shake his head.

"Ten years..." the old man whispered. And from somewhere in the shadows, Richard's father, pacing, laughed. Coming to hover over Richard's chair, Rudolphe whispered dryly, "What do you think Paris is, some paradise where you grow angel's wings? Where your skin turns to milk?" Richard was stunned and silent. Everyone spoke of going to Paris. Why, his brothers had gone...

It was then that the words, "Ten years..." came to him and he looked at Grandpère's face. No one ever spoke about them anymore, those brothers. Richard could not even remember when this silence had commenced.

"Passe blanc," the grandfather whispered in disgust.

Richard stared mutely at the grate. It was something he had always known, something terribly wrong that hung in the air. Something that hovered very near his mother when she dusted their pictures by the stair. Richard had never seen these brothers, never seen a letter from them, never really thought...

"They live in Bordeaux, now, I think," Antoine said later when they had gone upstairs. "A while back, a man came into the shop. He said they were there, wanted news of us. They're married to white women, of course..."

He lay in bed that night thinking of them for the first time, André and Michel. Married to white women. And when at last he pinched the candle out, he knew he would never go to Paris, that he would never leave this house as they had done, breaking Grandpère's heart, and though he never thought of his father as possessing a heart at all, there was something there equally strong which bound them together. But Grandpère he adored. This year Richard had learned the books at the shop from him with ease and had gone occasionally to attend the mourners, always amazed when they seemed glad to see him, and pulling him down near them on chairs beside the coffin, patted frantically his hand.

Compulsively he swallowed more whiskey. He had an irresistible urge to smile again, though his thoughts had hit the point of pain, and he saw it clearly. All right, Paris no. But the great man's coming back. And anxious mothers will crowd his sitting room eager to place their little ones in the warmth of his light. He shut his eyes and then narrowing them stared at the glaring sky. But would he, Richard, ever go to that school? Would his parents ever allow it? With Antoine's constant stream of florid anecdotes: hashish, white women, Christophe in battered velvet veritably living from café to café, sometimes never finding a bed for days at a time? The others might forgive, talk to the great man about Victor Hugo, ply him with questions about his famed travels, but the Lermontants? It was not what they wanted for Richard, or what they would tolerate. That was the whole truth of it. He'd known it even running to class this morning with the news.

And what he felt now, and had felt when he left Marcel wandering at the Place d'Armes was simply this: jealousy. This was the repulsive tangle of pain and confusion he'd been bound to unravel: jealousy.

He forced his gaze on the sky and felt his eyes water. He couldn't see the dark arcade of the market at all in his blindness, only knew there were bales there, men at work, that wobbling carts creaked under their heavy loads, and on the air came the strong, sour smell of boiling cabbage.

Jealousy of Marcel! A fine thing, Richard! Drink another glass.

But it was true. It was jealousy of that flair with which Marcel could hiss, *"Je suis un criminel!"* and set off, glaze-eyed after mad Juliet. Richard envied him, bitterly envied him whatever wild adventure he was courting now at midday. And worse yet, he envied the strength that would lead Marcel to break Juliet's silence. Marcel would succeed. Richard hated himself. Marcel had to succeed. Marcel always did, always—somehow—got what he wanted.

Richard shoved the bottle away suddenly and was rising to go. But at that moment, the white man who had been watching him from the bar became real again, a visible thing lurching forward and slumping down in the chair beside him. An Irishman with reddened blistered face and blasted hair. For the first time since Richard had entered the bar he felt wary.

He'd been using this luxurious danger. He didn't think it could touch him. And now this man had a hand on his arm. The fact that Richard couldn't see him clearly made it worse.

The man, drunk, drunker than Richard, displayed a few coins in his other hand. Richard hesitated, fearing any move might provoke a fight.

"Not enough even for a stinkin' glass," the man breathed. "And in such a town as this, where a man can't make enough for a bed at night even if he works all day for it." He glanced over his shoulder as though an enemy lurked at the bar.

Richard pushed the glass toward him and tried to edge away. "Please..." he said, gesturing to the bottle.

"Oh, you're a gentleman, sir, to be sure..." said the Irishman. He poured a drink, but clung to Richard at the same time, patting him now, then clutching him. He wasn't old but he looked old, his eyes shot with veins, his reddish hair greasy and thinning. He wore the rough, shapeless clothes of a workman and his nails were black with dirt. He was mumbling something now about the work in the streets, the laying of stones and mortar.

"Damn niggers!" he cried in a burst of coherence. "Damn free niggers getting five dollars a day as waiters in the hotels when a man's working in the heat of day in the streets...!"

Richard's face flamed. A profound instinct told him not to play into this man's hand, that he would be the loser for it. But he was cold with rage, his arm trembling under the man's fingers, that this man would say such things expecting him, a Negro, to listen. He slid back against the wall. But then the man said innocently:

"How do you stand it, man, living with them niggers as free as you please?"

Richard's mouth went slack. Something began to dawn on him, but he could not yet believe it.

"And then the quadroon wenches, whatever they call themselves, up there in them ballrooms in silks and satins, not letting a man in lest he's a fancy gentlemen, as if I'd want to dance with the filthy nigger wenches ...'cause that's what they are, nigger wenches. But how do you people stand it, not to have them whipped and sold off, or better yet sent back ..."

"Excuse me, Monsieur," Richard was on his feet at once, steadying the bottle. "Help yourself to the whiskey, please." He rushed out the door and into the breeze from the river, blind for an instant, but unable to repress a smile, and then a sudden burst of laughter. Hurrying up the Rue de la Levee he forgot for a moment all his trouble. Never before had he had such an experience. The bastard thought he was white.

III

FROM A NEGRO BARBER in the Rue Bourbon, Richard got a basin of water with a towel for his face, a splash of cologne and a cold drink. And when the man wasn't looking he put the cologne in the drink and washed out his mouth. He was already thoroughly contrite, and sick.

Monsieur De Latte did not condescend to even take notice of him as he slipped to the back of the class. But rather went on with the lesson in a foul temper, and somehow, somehow the afternoon passed.

"You are going to take this bill to Marcel's mother for me, immediately," he said to Richard as the others filed out. And scribbling it quickly he then removed his spectacles and rubbed the sore red imprint on his pale flesh. "I don't have to tolerate this!" he muttered to no one. "I don't have to put up with it for a minute! Tell her she is to make other arrangements for her son!"

Richard was already on the hot sidewalk walking doggedly for home before any rebellion could take form in him, any voice could protest in vain now, "I will not, I will not be the one to tell her."

But Marcel could do this himself. He had to be home by the time Richard got there, Richard was convinced. And he vowed to slip behind the cottage quickly before Cecile Ste.

Marie might see him, and go up to Marcel's room over the kitchen in the *garçonnière*. It had been six months since Marcel had moved out of the cottage proper to these private quarters in the rear—a fabulous luxury in Richard's eyes— yet never had Richard skirted the proper entrance to the house to seek him there. But the thought of giving this bill to Cecile, of explaining the expulsion...all that was intolerable.

However, as soon as he reached the garden gate in the Rue Ste. Anne, he was foiled. Cecile stood at her door, head cocked to one side, her black eyes wild with distress, as he approached by the gravel path.

She was startling in her lemon muslin, two tiny pearls pressed into the tender flesh of her earlobes, and the heat of the day had not touched her. He had never known a woman more delicate, more fragile, and he felt in her presence now a familiar awe that often rendered him awkward and speechless. With some shame he knew it was all bound up with her being the kept woman of a white man, the dark "wife" of a wealthy planter, but that could not fully explain it. A faint cologne emanated from her like breath as she brought her handkerchief to her lips and whispered faintly in French, "Where is Marcel?"

He fumbled for the bill, and had it half extended when he saw her turn, tears starting in her eyes, and heard the door crack back against the wall. This was going to be unbearable.

She moved awkwardly into the small parlor, and let out a gasp when she reached the china closet and heard the vast contents chatter. She put out a hand to steady it on its tiny legs and then looked, imploring, into Richard's eyes.

"What is this?" she said. "What are you giving me?" She sank down on the settee in a perfect circle of crumpling muslin, her prim breasts heaving as though she were going to faint. "What has he done now?" She looked up. "Just tell me, Richard, what has he done?"

Richard stared stupidly at the small curling hand in her lap, the tight bands of gold. It was perfectly useless to glance about for Marcel, to beg time to look for him, "Madame," he whispered. "Madame..." He cursed Monsieur De Latte! He cursed himself that he had undertaken this duty. But it was too late for all that. She snatched the bill from him suddenly and seeing the sum written out, slammed it down on the side table.

"I pay this always, what does this mean!" she demanded.

All the crystal in the room tinkled, and the dimming sun flashed in the shivering glassed portraits on the wall.

"He's been...well, he's been asked...I mean I am to tell you..." Richard stammered. But something intervened. There was the glimmer of salvation. For in the shadows beyond the arch that divided this small parlor from the dining room, Marcel's sister, Marie, had silently appeared. She held an open book against her breast as though she'd been reading. And her hair was loose, as though she'd just taken it down. Richard stared helplessly at her, but Cecile, rising, took his wrist. "What is it, Richard, what are you telling me!" she demanded angrily. 'For the love of heaven, what has he done!'"

"He's been expelled, Madame," Richard whispered. "Monsieur De Latte has asked that he make arrangements at some other..."

She shrieked. So sudden and so loud that he jumped backwards, all but upsetting a small table. Clumsily he reached for a teetering lamp, and turning, caught his foot on the leg of a chair. She was crying in choking sobs. His heart was in his mouth.

But Marie had come forward and stood beside her mother. Face burning, Richard stared blindly through the open door.

"Get out!" Cecile shouted suddenly, her voice hoarse and cold. "Get out!"

He glanced at her, at her bowed head, her clenched fist which pounded soundlessly against the carved roses of the settee, her foot stomping dully against the floor. "Get out!" she roared again, the voice coarse with anger. And he felt his temper rise. Marie was drawing back, and suddenly turned her face away. Not for the best of friends am I going to endure this a moment longer, Richard thought. Get out, indeed! With a muttered, *"Bonjour, Madame,"* he marched down the front step and down the path.

It was only very late that night as he lay in bed that a thought came to him. It was long after the lengthy agonizing dinner when the family had railed against Marcel, and Rudolphe had dragged in the cook, who trembled to admit that Richard's mother, Suzette, might have "ruined the shrimp" with her own "special touches" and Antoine had glowered across the table at Richard, saying with his eyes, this all has to do with Christophe, doesn't it, this getting expelled, you romantic imbeciles, all of you. And Richard, sick, had begged to go upstairs just when his mother, throwing up her hands

(37)

to scream, "It's the way I have made it for ten years!" over-turned her wine.

Nothing much out of the ordinary, really. And they hadn't guessed Richard's waterfront debauchery—and he had not expected to feel so little guilt for it—and Grandpère said finally that Marcel was a good boy, better perhaps than one might expect, what he needed was a father.

And then as Richard lay awake, the windows up despite the familiar noises of the street, this thought had come to him. It was something about the way Marie had backed away from her mother, the way that Marie had bowed her head at the moment when Cecile's words had stung him so, when Cecile had said, "Get out!" It was something to do with the very tone of Cecile's voice, a ferocious intimacy.

She wasn't talking to me at all, he realized, she was talking to Marie.

He was certain. And opening his eyes wide, he looked at the pale ceiling. The light of a lantern below threw the shadow of a lace curtain shivering across the plaster. And the shadow slid down the wall and away as the lantern passed at the pace of a weary horse. The sting of the words went away. But this was yet another mystery. Because why would Cecile speak that way to her own daughter? And uncomfortable suddenly, Richard wished that he had not heard it. He felt all the more the intruder, and the sting came back. But it was worse.

What had Marie felt, and with him there? No, he must be wrong, he thought suddenly, but he was not wrong. And there was some powerful resonance to those stinging words, "Get out," that he felt now with all he had ever known of Cecile and her daughter. He was most definitely uncomfortable, he wished he had not ever had such thoughts.

He loved the Ste. Marie family, all of them, not just Marcel who was his closest friend, his only real brother, but the lovely Cecile, such a lady, and the beautiful quiet young girl that Marie had become. She'd been the story-book child of his life in years past, the vision of sashes and ribbons and shining slippers that one seldom sees except on painted pages bordered with roses, the companion of verses and songs. And now she was as tall as her mother, swan-necked and round-armed, with eyes like the marble angels at the church doors that hold the holy water out to you in deep shells.

It took his breath away suddenly, thinking of her. Marie. The sheer simplicity of the name seemed perfect. He'd written poems to her and torn them up at once as though the room were full of spies.

He couldn't bear it suddenly, the thought that she'd been scourged by a cross word. But they were a close family, he knew them too well to think...? But then.... His thoughts were making circles. He shut his eyes, but could not sleep. He was coming back and back to the same place. So that he turned over, shifting the pillow to feel something fresh and cool beneath his face, and he let himself slip into some fragment of fantasy. He was sitting with Marie on the back steps of the *garçonnière* as they had done years before one day when he had buttoned the little strap of her slipper. Only now they were not children, and they were speaking together intimately so that he reached out and.... No. He saw the angels again at the church doors. Marcel was in trouble, she was in trouble, Cecile had been crying, crying when he left. He sighed, and carrying now only one of the thousands of burdens to which he had grown daily accustomed, he sank slowly through his care, into a thin, restless sleep.

IV

IT WAS a long time after Richard left him at the market before Marcel actually accosted Juliet. Marcel had memorized the newspaper clipping, and there was no doubt in his feverish mind that he had the momentum needed to carry him across the barrier that separated her from all the world. But he waited for his moment, letting her see him from time to time, as she had, again, just before Richard bolted, and watching expressionless, as her gaze drifted and she went on her way. With the infinite misery and patience of a lover, he followed her, thinking let it take a day, or a year.

He had nothing but disgust for the profligate he had so recently become, but at the same time he understood what was happening to him, and was curiously without regret. His childhood had become a wasteland; or rather he had finally become aware of just how barren and desolate it had always been, and following Juliet, he felt as if he moved toward life itself, the drudgery of his day-to-day disobedience left behind.

She bought clucking hens and ripe tomatoes, oysters in the shell and writhing shrimps, her cat darting in and out of the market stalls, arching its back against her dragging skirts. And for all this, she took money from the tight silk over her breasts under which Marcel could see the tiny raisins of her nipples so that he grew dizzy from the heat and lounged against the hogsheads like a roustabout, never taking his eyes from her straight back or from the men who leered at her, or stopped in their hacking or sweeping to watch her pass.

Of course the market men stared at him also, carters stared at him, black men with bushel baskets on their shoulders stared at him, this stiff-starched little gentleman getting hay all over his fine coat, with such wide and wild blue eyes fixed to the figure in front of him.

But Marcel did not see this. He saw only that Juliet had at last filled her basket, heaped it with yams and carrots and bunches of greens, tethering two hens to the handle by their feet so that they squawked and fluttered as she swung the whole enterprise up high onto the top of her head, and then dropping her hands idly at her sides, managed to walk swiftly through the bustling crowd, the basket perfectly balanced, her back straight, her steps rhythmic as those of a common African *vendeuse*.

"Mon Dieu," Marcel whispered. "She can do that!" Better than those slaves who came to market day after day from the outlying farms.

Of course it was positively shocking.

He was delighted by it! And mesmerized by her grace, he went after her out of the shocks and smells of the market, the gap closing between them, so that he was all but hovering in her wake with an air of protective menace. Let some sneering shopkeeper utter one word as he stopped to lean on his broom in an open door. Marcel would kill him.

But soon he was sick to see that they had all but reached the Rue Dauphine, and her gate lay only a few paces ahead of them. He drew up behind her so that he could almost touch the fringe of her shawl.

She stopped. Her arm went up, graceful, the wrist bent, and steadying the load on the top of her head, she turned as if on an axis.

"You're following me!" she said. He was stunned.

Shoppers pushed past them, but she didn't move. She was looking down at him, seemed in fact to tower over him, though they were almost the same height. She adjusted the teetering basket and he saw that her face was not cross at all, merely inquisitive.

(40)

"Come now, why?" she asked, and as she studied him her lips drew back in a cunning smile. He felt his heart slowing gradually to its regular pace. Her voice was lilting, rich with some suppressed laughter. "You are going to tell me?" she asked with a gentle lift to her eyebrows. There was something in her speech which made him think of his aunts, even his mother, something that he connected with the wilds of Saint-Domingue where all of these women had been born.

And suddenly he felt the thrust he had awaited all the long day.

"Madame Mercier," he said. "It's a matter of what I've read in the Paris papers! Today! I have to speak to you about it, please, please forgive me for approaching you this way, but I have to..."

She was regarding him with mild astonishment, but seemed at once bored, as though she could not understand what he was saying. She gestured to something at his feet.

It was the black cat. It had been following them all the while, sometimes ahead, sometimes behind, and now it rubbed its back on Marcel's boot. He gathered it at once and lifted it to her outstretched hand. Clasping it to her bosom, she turned away and stepped off the curb.

"But it's about Christophe!" Marcel said desperately.

"Christophe," she whispered. She turned her head majestically to look at him over her shoulder. Something vicious showed itself in her eyes, and the change of expression was altogether so violent that he was frightened.

But with an indefinable sense of what must work, he went on, "The papers...they say he is coming home."

That was it.

"No!" she gasped, turning full round again. "They say this, Paris papers?" Behind her a cart had come to a halt, and a red-faced white man was shouting at her.

"But tell me, *cher*—" she started. The horse shied, and whinnied. "Where is this Paris paper, what does it say?" She looked Marcel up and down, on the verge of frenzy, as if she might see the paper bulging from his pockets and attack him in an instant to lay hands on it. He felt a ruthless regret suddenly for ever having surrendered the clipping to Richard.

"I saw it this morning, Madame, with my own eyes. I don't have it with me, but I read it so many times I memorized it, I can tell it to you word for word."

"Tell me, tell me!" she burst out. And at that moment the driver of the cart began to bellow. He raised his whip over

(41)

Juliet's head, shearing the leafy stems from the load in her basket. Marcel clenched his fist and started forward in a rage; but Juliet, faster by far, jerked around and lifted the black cat in her right hand, heaved it over the horse's head into the man's face.

A cry went up from the loose crowd on the banquette and someone in the door of a shop laughed. The carter was furious. The cat scratched wildly, only to get a hold, and he could not get it loose until there was blood streaming down his cheek and the horse had lurched backward forcing the wheel of the cart up over the edge of the banquette. He was cursing Juliet in a strange guttural tongue.

And then in fast French came the warning from a black man on the pavement, "You beware, Monsieur, she put the evil eye on you, you beware, Monsieur..." only he'd broken into laughter.

But Juliet had reached out for Marcel's hand and was dragging him across the street. "Come, *cher,* come..." she said. The carter was scrambling down to the pavement. Her grip was moist and amazingly strong. She pulled Marcel forward and to her garden gate. Someone on the far banquette had taken hold of the carter, was trying to reason with him. And they were inside the yard suddenly with the gate shut and Marcel found himself in a narrow passage where the ivy spilling from the wall had long ago found the side of the house and made the walkway a soft fluttering leafy bed.

Juliet stepped daintily through it ahead of him, and the black cat appeared behind her, its tail high in the air.

For a moment Marcel hesitated. Looking up he saw the stained walls, the weathered blinds, and beyond nothing but the blue sky. The tall banana fronds obliterated those high buildings which he knew to be across the street still, and he seemed alone for the moment in this alien place. There was a small window in the gate, partially covered with slime. He had strained to see through it many times before, as had others, and he found himself peering through it now. There was only a dim glimmer of shapes beyond.

"Come, *cher,*" she called to him. He turned, confused, and hurried toward her. She went into the backyard.

As he reached the end of the passage, the sun for an instant blinded him. Shutting his eyes, he saw the blazing outline of a ruined cistern clinging to the far fence, and the sloping roof of an ancient shed. He reached out to steady himself against the plastered brick, and realized he had been running

(42)

almost all day, but it was only an annoyance, this momentary weakness, this threat of a pain behind the eyes. He was within her walls! And with a reverent throbbing of the heart, he looked up into her sun-drenched yard.

It was a cistern he saw again, rising high beside the three stories of the house, its gray boards splintered against the sky, and hung with the writhing tentacles of the Queen's Wreath, a bright pink flowering vine. Rust stained the rotting wood in long streaks from iron bands that had fallen away, and the soft dark of the broad base showed that it was still partially filled with water.

He did not like the look of it, to think of it, and had the awful sensation that it was falling slowly down on him, and on the woman who stood in the high weeds before him, tending an iron pot that simmered over a heap of coals. She bent gingerly to taste from a large wood spoon as if that hulk did not menace them both. But she was troubled, brooding, and looked quickly, fiercely toward Marcel.

"Come, monkey," she said. "You read the Paris papers, then you can read to me!" And quickly getting him by the wrist again, pulled him into the dark house.

It was ruin everywhere.

The rain had long beaten through the rotted shutters, and they walked softly along stained and buckling floors through desolate rooms where wallpaper, once flowers and ribbons, hung in yellowed strips from the damp ceilings and laid bare holes in the crumbling walls. Paint peeled from the frames of mirrors, cushions had fallen from the seats of chairs. A gossamer thing which had once been a curtain fell like dust from a window frame as if they had violently stirred the air.

But someone lived here still, that was the horror of it. A pair of new shoes stood before a gaping marble grate, and here lay a plate and a glass glittering with ants.

A packing case sat stranded on a faded carpet, and from its contents, still wrapped in yellow paper, protruded one large green glass vase. All the rest was left and under dust.

"Upstairs," she whispered, and pointed to the banister beyond the parlor door.

It was unsteady when he grasped it. Tall windows let in only bursts of leafy light. Pausing, he shuddered at the rustle and the scent of rats. And from beyond the dusty slats there came the day-to-day chorus of the street—a man cursing at his mule, a child's sudden sharp cry, and under all the rumble of wooden wheels. Gazing upward at a dim light on paneled doors that lay ajar, he felt himself would up in the warp and woof of dream.

She led him to a dining room. Mosquitoes swarmed over a china pitcher which she stirred with an easy gesture of her hand as she passed, and reached to let in a stream of burning yellow sun on a chest that sat there, beneath the window, dusted and somewhat new. The table here still had its polish and a soiled napkin lay crumpled on a chair. The gilt-framed portrait of a black man in military dress hung on the wall.

"The Old Haitian," Marcel whispered, remembering Monsieur Philippe's long tale. But the sun pouring in had rendered the surface of it opaque and Marcel could make out nothing of him at all.

"Here, *cher,* here . . ." Juliet said quickly, as though he might forget why he had come. And dropping to her knees, she raised the lid of the chest.

It was letters, hundreds of letters. The correspondence of years!

And Marcel had no doubt from whom all these letters had come. He was breathless as he knelt down. He lifted one, then another, shifted a mass of them here and there to reveal the varied scribbled words, Istanbul, Rome, Cairo, London, and Paris. Paris, Paris, Paris. And dozens, scores of them, had never even been unsealed!

"No, no," she whispered. "Here, these new ones . . . see." She picked them up and put them into his hand. One had been torn open and from its bulk and creases he could see it had once contained something larger than a letter. A mere note was inside.

But the other was more recent, he could tell. The date was at the top of the page as he unfolded it, it was this year, this spring.

"Read it to me, *cher,*" she said. "Read it . . . hurry, now."

She sank down sitting back on her heels and gazed at him, her hands clasped in her skirt, with the open expression of a child. She did not see the dizziness that swept over him, the vague disconcerting fear. It was awful the sight of these letters, sealed and piled here. Yet some pounding excitement dissipated the sadness that threatened at the edges of things, and he was staring now at the creased parchment page. It was Christophe's letter all right, there was the scrawled signature at the bottom.

What would all of those on the outside have given for this

moment, Richard, Fantin, Emile, so many of his friends. But there was no "outside." There was only this place, and this awful waste, and something akin to tragedy. He looked at Juliet who lost in her thoughts or fears did not see him. It had its wild magnetism. His voice did not sound like his own as he began:

"Maman..."

"Go on!" she said; he hesitated. It was too personal. He felt it a crime.

"Read it to me, *cher!*" she clasped his wrist. Of course, he realized, she could not read any more than his own mother could read. She had no idea, no idea at all...

You've won. It's as simple as that. Sometimes when I am distraught I imagine you are dead. But then some traveler I meet in the street tells me different, that he's only been away from New Orleans a matter of months, and you're alive, he's seen you with his own eyes. Still no answer from you, no response. Charbonnet goes to call on you from the bank, and you do not answer the door. For six months you do not answer the door.

Well, I won't say that I'm giving up everything for you, that you haunt my waking thoughts and make my dreams nightmares. Nor will I say I love you. I sail at the end of the month.

Chris

He showed it to her. But she had turned away, and let out a long sigh. She whispered softly that it was true then.

"Shall I read any more of them?" he asked.

"Why?" she murmured. She was not happy, not excited. He watched her rise slowly, steadying herself for an instant on the sill of the window. "He's coming home then," she said. She passed silently out of the room.

He looked after her, watching the low flounce of her dress move on the dusty floor, and he did not know what to do. Something held him where he was, near this chest with its hundreds of unopened letters, and looking down at it again, his fingers involuntarily closing, he was aware of a bright light at the end of the passage, and what seemed the flash of her shadow against the gray wall.

He could well imagine what these letters contained. He could see packets, some torn, some sealed, the thick folded

(45)

pages of journals protruding from their wrapping, it was a treasure, and yet he could not touch these things. He had no leave. He got to his feet, wiped the dust from his pants, and reaching for the open blinds gently pulled them shut. It seemed the darkness gathered around him like a cloud.

He stood still for a moment. He was excited, perhaps more excited than he had ever been. Outside lay the everyday life that so frustrated him, driving him, pushing him toward all manner of petty mischief and petty defeat. Yet here he felt alive, marvelously alive, and he was afraid of being sent away. He turned quickly, brushing again at the dust on his pants, and went in search of Juliet.

A soft sunlight flooded the end of the passage, aflicker with the shapes of leaves, and shading his eyes with his hand he found himself on the threshold of a vast room, and heard Juliet say to him, "*Cher*...come in."

She was sitting at a wicker table, her back to the open windows where the wild arcs of the Queen's Wreath shivered with their tiny pink blossoms in the breeze. The air was cool here, and not stale, and had the tang of freshly cut oranges. Gradually he made out the shadowed features of Juliet's brooding face. She was holding something small in her hands, a mirror perhaps, and was whispering to it though he could not make out the words. There was a bowl of fruit in front of her. But he was quickly distracted by the scattered contents of the room.

A stack of feather mattresses made up her bed, and it was littered with the lovely fabrics she often wore—tarleton, silk, and flowered silk, flimsy things for which he did not know the name. The windows above it were shaded by the thick-leaved branches of the trees and bathed all in a green-tinted light. While along the walls sat trunks sprung and bursting, and here and there packing crates, papered boxes, clusters of bonnets with wide tangled ribbons, and bunches of crinkled shoes. Before a cluttered marble-top dresser there stood a magnificent Chinese screen. It was alive with slant-eyed maidens sketched in gold against painted clouds.

Marcel drew in his breath. Every instinct in him responded to this place and to the silent beautiful woman who sat there, her rippling dark hair like a veil over her arms, intent upon the small object in her hands. Her deepset lids were languid with heat or with sadness.

But one splendid detail touched him more deeply perhaps than all the rest. Throughout this place there stood vases of

(46)

flowers: roses, lilies, fragile bunches of lavender, and wild clumps of jasmine withering there among the sturdier blooms with the thick arching fronds of ferns. She must have gathered these herself, and only she could have placed them so carefully amid this chaos. The table before her was shining clean as was the dresser mirror between the windows behind her head.

A breeze stirred the dark leaves beyond the windows. It lifted the spun gold of the mosquito netting that hung above the mattresses from a peg, sighing with the netting, and dropping it softly back against the wall. It seemed an insignificant thing, yet made the hair on the back of his neck rise.

Juliet leaned wearily to one side on her hand. And raising her eyes to Marcel slowly with a sweep of dark lashes, she smiled. "Look, *cher*," she whispered, and held the small framed object out to him so that it exploded all at once with the light.

He sank down in the chair beside her own. It was not a mirror at all.

In fact, it was a portrait so finely drawn and so lifelike in its little ornate frame that it gave him an almost unpleasant start. All painting broke his heart over his own crude sketches, but this was quite beyond belief.

"But what..." he murmured.

"Christophe, *cher*..." she said. "My Christophe...he's a man now, look at him. The boy is all gone..." She herself looked mournfully away.

Marcel had realized this, of course. He had seen that face in numerous engravings, the frontispiece in his novel, on the published text of two essays, and once in a journal, and he had copied it himself in ink a dozen times. Pictures of Christophe covered the wall above Marcel's desk. He had even cheated for the making of these pictures, using paper to trace or crude devices rigged from lamps to throw the printed image on fresh paper for him to copy it there with his pen.

But here was such a lively picture and so perfect that the technique staggered the imagination. Marcel could all but feel the smoothness of the small square face, and the rougher texture of the dark coat. He rose, almost upsetting the chair behind him, and held the picture at the window in the light.

The man was breathing there, and only the eyes seemed lifeless, like gems in the marvelous plasticity of the face. "But this can't be a painting!" Marcel sighed. And with his nail he tapped it lightly to discover that it was made of glass.

(47)

However, the most baffling aspect of it was the color; it was done entirely in muted tones of black and white. And suddenly with a loud gasp, he realized what he was holding in his hands. "Monsieur Daguerre!" he whispered. This was not a painting at all. It was the living Christophe in the frame, captured in Paris by Monsieur Daguerre's magic box! All the newspapers had been on fire with the news of this invention, and yet he had not believed it until now! And as he realized he was looking upon a genuine photographic likeness, even to the slight scuff on Christophe's boot, he felt the blood drain from his face. The implications of the picture dazed him, never had the world known such a miracle, by which men and women could be captured exactly as they were and the pictures, clear as the reflection in a mirror, kept for all time. And the papers had spoken of Daguerreotypes of buildings, whole crowds of human beings, the streets of Paris, moments in time fixed forever from the clouds in the sky to the expression on a man's face.

"Perhaps he lies in his letter," came the voice, weary and rather deep behind him.

Marcel was startled. "Oh, no, Madame, he's coming home, I read this in the papers," he said. He sat down beside her and placed the portrait against the bowl. It took an act of will for him to detach himself from it and look into her eyes. "They said he was coming back here to found a school, Madame...for us." He touched his breast lightly when he said this. "You can imagine what this means to us, Madame...the way that we admire him, the way that everyone admires him. Why, we follow him through every bit and piece of news that we can find."

Again he glanced at the little Daguerreotype, Christophe in Paris as he lived and breathed. Christophe among the men who invented such magic, and on his way home.

She was looking at him with that same dreamy expression that he had seen before in the street. It wasn't clear that she was listening to him at all. "He's a hero to us, Madame," he went on anxiously, eyes lighting again and again on the small image. "We have his novel, copies of his stories, articles he's written for the journals...I read everything I can lay hands on. I read his *Nuits de Charlotte,* it was magnificent, like Shakespeare in the novel form, Madame, I could see it happening before my eyes, and when Charlotte died, I died too."

She's going to ask me to go, he thought, and I don't want

to go, not now, not yet. There was something severe in the tiny face in the picture, the eyes fixing him fiercely.

"Of course, I copy his essays,..." he said quickly, "I have a notebook full of them, and sometimes I write essays—well I try—on my own. If he begins a school here...well, there is no telling how many pupils he'll have."

He could tutor the best white families, Marcel thought sullenly, perhaps he doesn't realize that....But he said the school was for us, for the *gens de couleur*... Marcel put that thought out of his mind. "There's no telling how many pupils will want to enroll. I imagine your parlor will be crowded with applicants."

"What parlor?" she asked in a flat, leaden voice.

He was shocked. He had offended her.

"There's nothing here anymore," she sighed, her voice so low that without realizing it he bent toward her. Her eyes were moving around the room slowly. "There's only ruin here."

"But all that can be changed, perhaps..." He was afraid. She would lose her temper in a minute, tell him he was impertinent and that he should get out. He stared dismally, helplessly, at the surface of the table before him, and then at that little portrait of the man sitting so regally in the chair. Even the boots were so expertly rendered, and the boards of some polished floor a thousand miles across the sea. He shut his eyes.

When he opened them again he saw that she was taking a ripe peach from the bowl. "Are you hungry, *cher?*" she whispered. It seemed little more than a soft explosion of breath.

"No, thank you, Madame," he murmured.

She stared at him as her teeth cut through the skin of the peach and he saw the ripe bright fruit against her lips.

"You were telling me things, *cher*..." she said in that same low voice. She ate the peach in great bites, the peeling and fruit, with no other movement than the movement of her delicate jaw, her lips, her tongue...He felt some vague stirring in himself and shifted his weight in the chair.

"About my essays, Madame," he said without really hearing himself speak. "I was thinking perhaps that I could bring my work so that when the students begin to come..." He stopped. She was studying him, and she was frightening him. He did not want to admit this but it was true.

(**49**)

"And when the students come..." she breathed softly, "...he would take you as one of them."

He found he was amazed that she had followed his line of thinking at all. "Yes, that's it exactly, Madame. I want so much to be one of his pupils," he said.

She began to lick her fingers. The peach was gone. Only the rough kernel lay on the table, picked clean. And he was astonished, even embarrassed, as he had never seen a lady do this before, and he had never seen anyone, not even a child, do it quite like this. She licked the first finger, drawing it straight across her tongue, and then the second. Then holding her hand like a fan, her tongue found the nook between finger and thumb and sucked there. Gradually as he watched, she licked the whole hand as though it were only natural, and dainty, and then she rested her chin on her clasped fingers, elbows on the table. Her eyes had never left him once.

"You want to go to the school," she sighed. The gold hoops in her ears moved ever so slightly against the dark waves that hung down her back.

"Oh, yes, Madame, more than anything. I want to try!"

"Hmmmm..." she took a long breath. "And this is why he comes home, then," she said in an expressionless voice that made her steady gaze even more unnerving..."not what he says in his letter at all."

"Oh, no, no, that can't be true," he said at once. "I'm sure what he says in the letter is true, Madame. He's coming home because...because of you."

This was dreadful, he had been saying all the wrong things to her and didn't know it. He saw her again as he had seen her when he entered the room, holding the portrait, and talking to it in a whisper.

The only sound now was the sound of the breeze. Trees swelling, rustling against the glass, then dying back. Her dark eyes were fixed on him as they had been all along, and her narrow face had that youthful smoothness that was always hers. Not a line of care marked her forehead. Only some subtle softness around her eyes and around her throat betrayed her age.

Then low, with the barest movement of her lips, her voice came again, "You are hot, *cher?*" she asked. "You are tired?" A snakelike arm extended across the table between them, and her long fingers played with the buttons on his vest. He had never seen a woman in his life as beautiful as she was; even the tiny lines around her eyes were exquisite, the flesh

(50)

a little paler there, very soft perhaps to touch. He looked down suddenly with the first hint of shyness and found himself gazing at her breasts. The tips of the nipples showed through the silk, he could even see the dark circle of flesh around the nipples, and as her hand found the back of his neck, as her fingers actually touched his skin, he felt a tremor pass over him that contracted to a sudden forbidden excitement swelling uncomfortably, unmistakably between his legs.

She was feeling his hair. He saw nothing before him for an instant, except the gathered silk of her sleeve where her arm pressed against the bulge of her breast. But he made up his mind to look into her eyes, to be the gentleman if he could not be the child she apparently thought that he was. However, she was rising now, and though she had let him go, she was beckoning for him to get up also. And he could still feel the touch of her fingers as if she'd never moved.

A cloud passed over the sun. And then came another. The room was dim, and she was standing by the bed, drinking from a silver pitcher. She turned to him, holding it in both hands as she extended it. He walked toward her, his feet deafening on the bare boards and taking it from her, he drank. His thirst was far worse than he had realized, and in a moment the pitcher was empty. And when he looked up again, he was dumbfounded.

A rapid explosion of rips that he had heard were the hooks of her dress. And she had stepped out of it, and held it loose, gathered against her naked shoulders. He could see the thin margin of her naked leg, the curve of her hip; the fixed expression of her dark eyes might have struck terror.

But never in his life would he be able to describe the physical sensation that overcame him, the immediate grinding passion that obliterated every other sense, any scintilla of judgment. He knew he should run from the room, and he had no intention of doing so.

And as she drew near to him, as her arm went around his waist, he became some single-minded thing that wanted nothing but to rip away that red silk dress. With a gentle tug she opened the buttons of his shirt.

He did not remember getting undressed. Except that he had never done it so fast, with so little regard. She had let the dress drop and slipped between the sheets. Sinking down beside her, he felt the breeze from the darkling windows cool on his arms and on his face. It stirred the tendrils of her hair.

She kissed him on the mouth, and he felt at once clumsy

(51)

and stiff in his passion, the blood pounding in his head as
her hard tiny nipples pressed against his chest. It seemed
then for one moment when he did not know how to proceed,
that all the voices of his childhood were murmuring anxiously
to him, commanding him to rise and go, to grab his clothes
and flee. "This is without honor!" said the chorus. But over
its slowing and predictable rumble, there came another voice
echoing through the long halls of time that needed no vernacular to declare with a stentorian authority: Man, are you
mad? Go to it!

He had in his hand the gorgeous satin weight of her breast,
the very contour that had driven him to distraction in his
dreams, and pressing his lips there, he stopped breathless
and afraid. Even the friction of the sheets against him might
be too much. He could not hold back. But with a shift beneath
him and the swift subtle movement of her hand, she guided
him to the moist hair between her legs and into the place
where he belonged. He clenched his teeth, moaning as he
went in. Never had he ever seen this place! And he did not
see it now, only felt himself slide into the perfect pulsing
opening, the embrace toward which he had been moving all
of his life, and in a mounting rapture, all the fantasies of his
childhood burnt dim, and forever went out.

Then he heard her cry.

She was blood-red and suffering, her breasts and face
flushed, a low hoarse sound coming out of her as if she struggled for breath. She was dying in his arms! Yet when he
struggled to free her, her hands held him fast, and the sudden
sharp movements of her hips sent him straight to heaven.

It seemed to go on forever.

And then to be more over than anything he had ever
known.

On his back in the gloom, the breeze moving over him like
water, he kissed her hair as her forehead pressed against his
cheek. She was pleased; she lay still. And together they
drifted off.

It was a deep sleep at first that left no dreams to mark
the length; and then he was conscious of loving her, of her
arms around him, and that she held his back against her
breast, her legs tucked beneath his, so that they slept tight
together spoon-fashion and again he drifted off. He had never
slept with another person that he could remember, not even
when he was very small, and was ill, and this seemed luscious
to him and natural and very sweet. But thin dreams came

to him that were hardly dreams at all, in which he roamed the house, found gaping holes in the stairs, had the disconcerting vision of rats. And some time before the room grew dark, he knew the cistern was near, gaping by the leaf-shrouded windows. He opened his eyes once and saw her profile against the distant vines, and in sleep found her even more beautiful than she had been before. A dusky cologne emanated from her skin. He found himself savoring the scent it left on his fingertips.

Hours must have passed, he didn't know. Only that at some point, when he was dreaming of the letters in the chest, and of trivial intruding things, he had turned over, very hot, and seen the flowers in a vase on the round table. Only they were enormous; the magnificent blooms one gets from florists, and vaguely he had thought my eyes are not actually open, I am dreaming this, these perfect roses and their mist of delicate fern. But all the room was there in the shadows, as sometimes happens between sleep and dream. And there were the flowers, white, all but luminous, and beside the table, there stood a man.

A man.

A man! Marcel sat bolt upright in the dark, the sheet sliding down to his lap, and stared straight ahead, his fists clenched in an instinctual protective fury.

It was a man most definitely, medium of height, and apparently dressed in a smartly cut frock coat with a starched white shirt collar and something loose over his shoulders like a wool cravat. But his face was so dark that nothing could be seen save the barest glint of light in his eyes. And beside him, on the floor, stood a bulky valise.

Juliet stirred, turning over and touching Marcel's naked back. And rigid with alarm, he realized, beyond a shadow of a doubt, who this man was. All the air went out of him suddenly as Juliet cried out.

He did not need for her to say the name as she snatched the sheet from his naked legs, threw it around her, and ran to the center of the room. "Chris!" she burst out, and "Chris!" over and over.

Marcel watched petrified as they embraced. It seemed Christophe turned her around and around in his arms, his laughter coming soft and rich and low under her gasps and cries. She was kissing him all over the face and neck; she was beating gently on his shoulders with her fists.

Suddenly her cries slowed, became deeper, and an awful

sorrow broke loose in her voice. Christophe sat slowly in the wicker chair at the table and folded her against him so that she buried her head in his neck.

"Maman," he said to her softly, stroking her as she sobbed against him, saying over and over, as if with a broken heart, "Chris, Chris..."

Marcel pulled on his pants and his shirt at once. There was no time for his vest, watch, comb. Jamming his unfastened cuffs into his jacket sleeves, he turned around, shirt open at the throat and saw the man's large dark eyes fixed on him in the gloom. Juliet cried still, and Christophe's hand patted her gently. He looked down at her, much to Marcel's relief, and lifted her chin so he could look into her eyes. The light fell on his profile, gleamed for an instant on his forehead as he said to her, "Maman..." as if that word alone conveyed all the eloquence that he might need.

She was feeling his face, kissing his cheekbones, then his eyelids.

Shaking and on the verge of tears himself, Marcel pulled on his boots, and shoving his socks down into his jacket pockets turned toward the door.

"But who is this?" Christophe asked. Marcel froze.

"Oh, yes..." Juliet wiped at the tears on her cheek with the back of her hand. "Oh, yes, come here, *cher*, it's Christophe..." and when she said her son's name again her voice broke. She appeared to shudder, to kiss him again and then hold him tightly. Marcel was utterly miserable. But then she said, "Come here, *cher*, come come come!" and held her hand out toward him.

Marcel's legs were trembling so violently that he could only make himself approach the table by a severe act of will. And when he felt Juliet's hand slip into his and clasp it, he looked deliberately into Christophe's eyes.

It was the face he'd only just seen in the little picture, of course. A somewhat square face, the tightly curled hair making a neat frame for it with a straight line across the forehead and carefully trimmed sideburns. It was a common enough face where Mediterranean and African blood combine, the features small, the skin a light brown and supple, the jaw square, the whole effect being one of evenness, the kind of face which in later years is often rendered powerfully distinguished by its frame of graying hair, and the grizzled line of a mustache.

But the expression of that face was hardly the lifeless

rendering of the portrait. It had rather a fire to it that seemed all but menacing in the twilight, something of mockery or absolute rage.

Marcel withered.

"This is a smart boy," Juliet said. She was crying still, and in another burst of excitement she kissed Christophe again. He was holding her firmly in his right arm, as if she weighed nothing on his lap, and with his left hand now he smoothed back her hair.

"I can well imagine," he said under his breath as he glanced up at Marcel, but his mother did not appear to hear.

"He read your letter to me, told me you were coming home, of Paris papers saying this, that you were coming home," and again she began to shake with sobs.

But Christophe was gazing levelly at Marcel, and he raised his eyebrows dramatically, pretending to study him with interest.

"These boys, they worship you, they put letters under the gate," she said excitedly, "But this one, Cecile's son, he came to me like a gentleman! No peeping at the windows..."

Cecile's son. It was like feeling the noose slip around his neck. How in the hell could she have known he was Cecile's son! She seemed not to know the time of day, the day of the month, the month of the year! And yet she knew he was Cecile's son! Her words went on, but Marcel did not hear them. For one vain moment, it occurred to him there might be something to say, some magnificent explanation. But it died before it was born.

"And this school, he talks of this school..." she was saying. "And wants to meet you so, of course..."

A short ironic laugh came from Christophe's lips, and with an icy smile, he extended his hand. "Indeed? And so we meet."

Marcel took his hand mechanically. It felt powerful and somewhat cold. Perfect enough, Marcel was thinking and convulsively he drew back too soon while Christophe let his hand drop rather slowly again to his mother's waist.

"You know what I think of this school?" she was saying, wiping at her eyes with the edge of the sheet. She had loosened it slightly over her breasts. Marcel looked away. "I think this is the reason you have come back here, this school. Not your mother, I am not the reason..."

"Ah, Maman!" he said, shaking his head. He kissed her. It was the first spontaneous thing that he had said, and he looked at her now as if he were seeing her for the first time.

And then taking her in his arms he held her as if he were doing this for the first time.

Marcel murmured quickly that he should take his leave. And had started for the door when she said, "I'll talk to him about the school, *cher*. Christophe listen to me, he wants to go to your school."

"He seems a bit precocious for school," came the rich-voiced sarcastic reply beside the upturned innocent gaze of the mother.

"Ah!" she waved away words she didn't understand. "Go, *cher,* come tomorrow."

"Oh, yes, do come again," said the man with a purely malignant smile.

Marcel could feel the tears just behind his eyes. But again, as he turned, she reached out for him, and tugging him gently close to her, she put her cheek against his chest.

He broke away slowly and with a gentlemanly murmur, went swiftly through the dark house, clattering down the hollow stairway and blundering out into the shadowy street. The sky was red with the sunset over the river, and he was crying now, so that as he reached the banana grove inside his gate, he stopped and choked back his tears, resolutely refusing to let them flow any longer, to let anyone see them, to let anyone know where he had been and what he had done.

V

IT WAS DARK. The breeze was damp from the river and carried with it the scent of rain. All the day's heat was lessened now, and the long loose lace curtains rose and fell against the back window of Marcel's room, and the sounds of the evening meal below were just past. The lamp on the desk flickered dimly. Then there came Lisette's familiar steps up from the kitchen, and he heard her quick tread along the porch.

"Better eat something, Michie," she coaxed lightly in the Creole French. "Come on now, Michie, open this door."

He lay still staring at the shadowy ceiling. She had moved to the window. So let her try to see him through the blinds, he didn't care.

"All right, then Michie! Starve to death!" she shouted at him and was gone.

"Mon Dieu!" he sighed, his teeth biting into his lip. He

(56)

was going to cry again if he didn't get a hold on himself. His mother had flown at him as he ran up the stairs to his room. She had beat against his door while he stood inside, his hand trembling on the bolt. "How could you do it, how could you do it!" she had shrieked until he covered his ears. It had taken him a moment to realize that she couldn't have known what he had *really* done, any of it. It was the school that mattered to her. He'd been expelled, so be it. And now Lisette shouting at him as if he were a child. She'd burn his bacon in the morning and serve his coffee cold. He was becoming completely furious about it when he realized with a dry laugh that he was very shortly scheduled to die.

And then that familiar oppression descended upon him, that dull misery that had been with him all evening, more bleak perhaps than almost any depression that he had ever known. He'd ruined himself utterly with Christophe, and Christophe, if he did not kill him, would surely beat him within an inch of his life. He had thought it over from every vantage point and was sure of this beating if nothing else. And there would be dreadful humiliation afterwards and all the questions which he would never answer. And soon the world would know what he already knew, that he was shut out from Christophe's new school forever, shut out, in fact, from Christophe's world.

He rose suddenly as he had done a dozen times that evening, and holding the backs of his arms he paced the room.

The pungent atmosphere of Juliet's bed enveloped him, and he felt again her nakedness, that musky perfume, and warm hands that pulled him close so that he shuddered violently at the obscenity of it, was almost sickened, and the entire soft debacle was a rape. She was mad, everyone knew she was mad, he knew she was mad, had he ever heard so much as a smattering of the gossip about her without that word, *mad?* And oh, how miserable she had been, how forlorn as she had sat at that table gazing at Christophe's portrait. No, he'd taken full advantage of her distress, abused her in her loneliness and her distraction, and Christophe had caught him, was going to kill him, and he deserved to die.

He saw himself quite clearly standing in a field before Christophe, it was bleak and windy, and he was saying, "Monsieur, I deserve it. I shall not lift a finger to prevent it. I deserve to die." Perhaps he should go there to the house and say these words, perhaps he should go there now. He would ring the bell, if there was still a bell, and wait on the banquette, his hands clasped behind his back, until Christophe came down.

But no, this would smack of some cheap dissimulation, some plea for mercy of which he was not capable, and must not be capable. No, the man would choose the moment. He had to wait.

He shut his eyes. He was leaning against the frame of the back window, letting the breeze cool him, still hugging his arms. That was the simplest part, perhaps, that first violent encounter. It was the aftermath that was to be his real punishment, his hell. He tried to imagine for a moment the Christophe he had known before this afternoon, that distant and heroic novelist whose ink portraits still covered the walls of his room, he tried to savor the old excitement at the mere saying of the name. But that voiceless, remote, and endlessly glamorous Parisian writer was flesh and blood now, the cold-eyed ironical man who had glared at him through the shadows of Juliet's bedroom with unveiled contempt. And Marcel had cut himself off from both of those enigmatic figures, and what he felt was not so much fear for himself as a misery that was akin to grief.

Lights twinkled beyond, through the thick forest of oak and cypress that rose behind the *garçonnière*, a swamplike growth that divided all the cottages of the Rue Ste. Anne from those of the Rue Dumaine. It was a lovely thing this wild untended place of knotted figs and knife-blade banana, of wild roses and the ivy that hung from the branches of the oaks in heavy drifts that often lifted all of a piece with the breeze. Crickets sang here at twilight, and obliterating the rattle and chatter of supper tables, and the cry of children, they lent a graceful privacy to this close and crowded block. It was sweet now to see no more of distant windows than a sudden tiny burst of yellow light among the shifting leaves, somewhat like the blinking of a star. Marcel had always loved these rooms, and as a little child came here to watch the sundown or rush from room to room over vistas of dusty floor. Last summer, Monsieur Philippe had begun to call it, quite suddenly, the *garçonnière*. And in a matter of weeks, he was saying with a weary shrug, "Why the cottage is so small, he ought to be out there now and leave this place to you and Marie." Cecile was shocked. "Why, *ma chère*, on the plantation, he would have been moved before now. It's *de rigueur*."

"*De rigueur!*" Marcel had said to Richard with the same

(58)

weary gesture. Richard had laughed. Of course the man did not want to go on making love to Cecile within the hearing of an adolescent son, what did that matter? Marcel was ecstatic, and Monsieur Philippe, whatever his motives, had some sense himself that the move for Marcel was a splendid thing. A narrow convent bed was made especially for the small room, a desk sent up, and he came one evening from the plantation with a series of old framed paintings, dim beneath their crazed varnish, saying they might look quite good on those walls. *"Eh bien,"* he sighed when he saw Marcel's sketches everywhere. He drew on his cigar and letting the ash fall, he smiled. "Do as you like, *mon fils,* after all, the place is yours." A Turkey carpet arrived a day later, worn, but quite beautiful still and very soft.

Eh bien ... it had been a refuge since the beginning, but now? Marcel would have lost his mind had he not had that door with its latch behind him. It was sanctuary.

"Je suis un criminel," he tested the lovely epithet on the empty air. Tears came again. Turning, he bent gently to the lamp on his desk and lowered the small flame. Then taking the chair in both hands he brought it near to the back window, and sat so he might look out, his feet propped on the sill.

It was not guilt he felt for what he'd done so much as sorrow. He had lost Christophe, and he had known this kind of loss only once before in his life, and he had been as lonely in it then as he was now. This was the loss of Jean Jacques, the cabinetmaker, when Marcel was thirteen years old.

PART TWO

I

THE YEAR had been begun well enough, it seemed. Nothing unlucky in the thirteen candles. Nevertheless his mother, teasing him, had winked her eye, and said, "A bad age."

And then came an afternoon, remarkably like many others, on which Marcel had been walking with his Tante Josette to church. She had just come in from the country, her carriage full of baskets of fruit from the orchards of her plantation, *Sans Souci.* He loved the name of her plantation, and was saying it over and over to himself as they drifted slowly through the winter street toward the Cathedral. She went always as soon as she arrived to the altar of the Virgin Mary and said a rosary there in thanks for the safe journey from Saint-Domingue years ago before Marcel had been born. Her sisters, Tante Colette and Tante Louisa, were in a paroxysm for days before these visits, and with Cecile's help veritably renovated their dress shop in the Rue Bourbon and the long flat in which they lived, above. These women had reared Cecile, having brought her with them in that flight from Saint-Domingue for which Tante Josette gave thanks.

What had there been in his life before that afternoon, when he and Tante Josette had set out for church? Only routine and wondrous events such as the beginning of school, suppers with the family of his new classmate, Richard Lermontant, the change of the seasons, the Mardi Gras, and those long afternoons he had spent with his friend Anna Bella

Monroe reading English novels, talking of pirates, and walking out sometimes hand in hand like brother and sister along the broad ditches of the outlying streets where minnows swam and frogs croaked amid the high weeds. And boredom, utter and complete boredom, that made the blue sky a monstrous and eternal roof and the miracle of white butterflies in wild vacant lots hypnotic and somehow grating.

Tante Josette was an eccentric woman, preferring grace in old age to nonsense in manner of dress, wore her gray hair back in a chignon, and was in dark blue always regardless of the weather, though this was sometimes trimmed with a little lace, but more often with jet. And she was talking, low and steady, to him as they walked, reading the signs over shops and the funeral notices tacked to the lamp posts, and picking out places where the brick banquettes were "a disgrace," and lifting her skirts carefully above her long thin leather boots, then she stopped short and with a quick bow nodded to the cabinetmaker, Jean Jacques, at his door, and said low, under her breath, "That man taught himself everything that he knows."

Marcel heard these words, as if they had flashed clear suddenly from so much that was of no concern to him and turning back he looked at the man, Jean Jacques.

"Even to read and to write," she said. And no more about it.

Of course he had seen Jean Jacques a hundred times: an old mulatto from Saint-Domingue with skin far darker than Cecile's and gray hair perfectly like wool around his ancient skull, he had often frightened the children, walking as he did with hands behind his back, a rusty wide-pocketed coat hanging well below his knees, the heavy folds of his brown skin lending him a brooding expression, so you feared he would stamp his foot at you if you came near: he never did. His thick lips moved silently as he turned the pages of his missal at Mass, and from a worn cloth purse he drew coins for each collection, and sometimes soiled dollar bills.

And there had always been his shop with its shingle in the Rue Bourbon. He made all manner of furniture to order, including pieces that he covered with damask and velvet as well as those crafted entirely from wood.

But it was later that afternoon when the winter dusk was dreary, and Marcel had broken away to wander by himself in the streets, that he saw—really saw—Jean Jacques.

His doors lay open to the bustling street, and the potbellied stove showed a heap of red coals behind him, while in the warm light of his smoking lamps, his sleeves rolled above the elbow, he bent on one knee in the fragrant shavings, his arm moving the silver chisel so smoothly and regularly along the leg of the delicate chair before him that it seemed he didn't carve the piece at all, rather merely discovered under the wood the marvelous curve that had been hidden there all the time. Chairs for sale stood in a row by the door; and others hung in the shadows along the walls, while bolts of cloth gleamed on high shelves, and on a small desk as fine as anything that might carry a price, its French polish shining dully in the light, lay an open ledger in which Marcel could see the long lines of slanting purple script. Here and there were thick catalogues and engravings taken from them of fine furniture which must have been his models, and on a sturdy simple bench lay all his tools which he would lift with reverence now and again in the manner of the priest gone to the side altar for the washing of his hands.

"That man taught himself all that he knows..." came the low and enigmatic voice, all the more rich with meaning for its monotone, "even to read and to write." And the words were mingled with this vibrant and aromatic place that shone in the thin winter rain with the magic of a stage; and passersby became blind men.

It was not long after that Jean Jacques, having seen Marcel so often stranded for a half hour or more in the open doorway, asked him to come inside.

He made strong coffee on the iron stove, and poured it with the hot milk in one stream into the china cups, giving one to the boy and taking the other, though he stood always with a knotted fist on his hip as he drank and went back to work when the cup was yet half full. Marcel, stiff in a straightback chair, asked politely the name of this tool, that style of chest, what kind of wood was this? He waited patiently for the slow replies, the pauses so long sometimes he'd thought the man had forgotten, only to hear the answer finally: this chisel is tempered for wood, you see, and this one for stone. Jean Jacques placed a square of marble into the neat frame of a table top, having made the four sides smooth to touch.

Rudolphe Lermontant, Richard's father, came in one afternoon carrying a batch of slats bound with cord. "Look at this," he said angrily, as the old man cut the bundle loose and lifted the lacquered pieces. "A fine little table, and they let it fall

from the cart on the way from Charleston, sometimes I..."
he smacked his fist into the palm of his hand. "And then they
say it was already ruined, all the glue come undone, I don't
believe it. That's my daughter for you." He threw a furious
glance at Marcel who stood decorously and self-consciously
on the edge of the room. "You know Giselle, aaaahhh!"

The old man had it done by the end of the week when
Marcel came after school, a jewel of inlaid rosewood and
glinting mahogany, the tiny drawer sliding back and forth,
back and forth beneath the table top as if it were on magic
wheels. Even the key turned again in the polished brass of
the lock where it had once been rusted tight. "Ah, so many
of them no longer have the key," said Jean Jacques with slow
wonder as if this were the remarkable aspect of it all, this
good luck. Rudolphe, stunned, said. "Monsieur, name your
price. My grandmother bought this table when this place was
a walled colonial town."

Jean Jacques' heavy shoulders shook with silent laughter.
"Don't say such a thing to a shopkeeper, Monsieur," he said.
But then serious, he wrote some figures on a slip of yellow
paper. Rudolphe pait it at once from his pocket.

Later, that Sunday afternoon, Marcel, entering the Lermontant house for dinner, saw that small table nestled between the heavily draped French windows. A brass lamp
stood in the center of it casting a loving light on the curved
drawer, its shining key, the tapered legs. "And this was
made," he whispered, approaching it. He touched the surface
which felt like wax. "Made!"

"Marcel!" Rudolphe snapped his fingers behind him. All
the room was filled with things that were made, made by
someone with chisels, saws, the pot of glue and the bottles
of oil, and the soft cloths and the tiny pegs, and hands that
felt the object all over as if it were living, breathing, growing
into its perfect shape.

"Sometimes, my boy," Rudolphe whispered to him as he
reached for his shoulders, "you have the perfect vacant stare
of the village idiot!"

It was easy between them, Marcel and Jean Jacques.
There was never any explanation for Marcel's being there.
Time and again he slipped in while the man worked, or talked
with his customers, or seated at his desk, filled that ledger
not with long columns of figures but neat sentences, para-
graphs, which he wrote with quite rapid dips of his pen. Never

(63)

was much said. There was no need. But Marcel burned with the one question he could not ask, how did you do it, how did you learn all of this yourself?

From a picture in a book, Jean Jacques made a rounded and gilded fern stand for the rich Celestina Roget who was so delighted she clapped her hands like a child, and visiting the parlor of an old white woman in the Rue Dumaine he came back to make three more chairs for her to match the one and only that had survived the crossing from France. With knotted fingers sometimes he threaded his own needle and bound the edges of the flowered damask before he stretched it to fit the rounded seat of a settee. But how did it all begin, was Tante Josette right? She had said it with such authority, and gone home again to *Sans Souci,* her plantation in the Cane River country, before Marcel could catch her alone.

No matter if he had teachers really. What had enabled him to learn? What had removed this man from the commonplace and given him the gift of spinning straw into gold?

Learning for Marcel was agony at times. It was only after a long tutelage with his friend Anna Bella and hard work in Monsieur De Latte's class that the magnificent world of books had opened to him, and even now he struggled, against all his native inclinations, to make something coherent, if not beautiful from the Latin verses he did not really understand. Oh, how he envied Anna Bella that she could read English by the hour, as easily as French, and curling up in a chair by her bed, laugh aloud to herself over the pages of *Robinson Crusoe,* or fall into the spell of a penny romance.

But there was no way this boy in starched Irish linen and velvet waistcoat could ask the working man such questions. And how tastelessly it would have betrayed an admiration that was fast growing into love. He longed to take the broom from the man's hands at the end of the day's work, or help him wipe the oil again and again from the chair leg as it slowly darkened. But Marcel had never touched a broom in his life; his hands lay still at his sides, there was no dark stain in the fine lines of his fingers, nor beneath his carefully trimmed nails.

No one understood what he was doing there. Richard would leave him at the corner on the way home from class with a shrug. The streets were filled with the shops of such free colored craftsmen, good men all of course, but they worked with their hands, what was the fascination? Especially for Marcel who possessed for Richard always, the panache of a planter's son, born for drawing rooms and crystal glasses, as if he had been nurtured in the big house itself, and not in the demimonde.

Cecile, observing Marcel once at the back of the shop, turned beneath her parasol with a stiff back. Marcel was humiliated until he was sure that Jean Jacques had not seen.

"Well, they told me you made yourself at home in that shop," she said that night at dinner. "Would you please be so kind as to tell me why?"

Marcel played with the food on his plate.

"I don't want you hanging about a shop," she said, as she gestured to Lisette for more soup. "Marcel, are you listening to me? I don't want you with that old man."

"But why?" He looked up as if from a dream.

"That's what I asked you, Monsieur. To tell me why?"

He paid her no mind whatsoever. It never occurred to him to do so. Sundays were unspeakably dreary to him because Jean Jacques' shop was closed, and every other day now he was there at one time or another, and sometimes, swelling with pride, was left to watch for a moment or two while Jean Jacques in the backyard fed the fire with the day's debris.

At last one afternoon as he sat on a stool by the stove, staring at that open ledger, Jean Jacques, who had been writing in it since he had come in, turned to say, "It's my diary," as if he had heard the wordless question aloud.

Marcel was amazed. Writers kept diaries, and so did the planters, and so did Jean Jacques. He would get a diary himself at once, why hadn't he thought of it before now?

Jean Jacques laughed lightly, soundlessly at the expression on Marcel's face.

"Why, you stare at this book as if it were alive!" said the old man. He shook his head and closed the ledger carefully, running his hand along the cover. "Well, it's precious enough to me. Forty-nine years ago when I left Cap François, I didn't have anything with me but the clothes on my back and a diary just like this one in my hands. See there?" He pointed beyond the front room of the shop to the small rear bedroom. Marcel saw a shelf above the neatly made bed and on it was a row of such ledgers. "That's the very same book there, which I began in Cap François, and next to it are those I've filled for forty-nine years."

"But what do you write in it, Monsieur?" Marcel asked.

"Everything," Jean Jacques smiled. "How the day begins

and how it ends. What I do that day and what happens to others. All those events that took place in Saint-Domingue, those I saw with my own eyes, and those that were told to me by others." All this he said slowly, thoughtfully, his eyes off to one side as though he were seeing the things of which he spoke. "I imagine you've heard plenty about those times," he went on glancing at Marcel. He rose from the chair, and pressing his hands to the small of his back, he stretched.

He looked like a young man when he did this. But then his shoulders came forward as they'd been before, his vest sagged open as he stooped, and he was the old man again, his steps slow as he approached the bench and looked at the tools before him.

He had said more in these few moments than the sum of all that had ever passed between them, and Marcel had liked his manner of speech. His French was not formal but almost perfect. In short, he spoke like a gentleman. "Your aunts must have told you enough," he said. "I mean Madame Colette and Madame Louisa. I remember them when they came, and your Maman when she came, she was just a baby...like that." He made the gesture with his hand to indicate she had been so high.

Of course they spoke of Saint-Domingue, Tante Colette and Tante Louisa, but Cecile had been too young to remember anything and never said a word. They spoke of rich plantations on the Plaine du Nord and their house in Port-au-Prince where they had entertained the French officers in their regal uniforms, drinking champagne with the generals, and gossiping about the wild orgies of Napoleon's sister, Pauline, who had dined and danced through the entire war. All the names of Saint-Domingue thrilled Marcel along with these images of balls until dawn, and ships with billowing sails striking out across the blue Caribbean for the port of New Orleans. And then there had been the buccaneers. "Tell me about the buccaneers," he had said once when nestled among their immense skirts in the cottage parlor. They had laughed wildly, but Anna Bella had read him an English story about buccaneers.

"Oh, yes, Monsieur," Marcel said, speaking lightly and quickly of French officers, champagne, and how the black slaves had risen and burnt it all and finally the French officers had left with the army, and his aunts had left, too. He meant to sound knowledgeable, but even as he spoke he sensed that all he knew was flimsy, simple phrases often

repeated and never explained. He was ashamed suddenly of
how foolish he had sounded.

Jean Jacques' face had changed. He stood very still over
the workbench looking at Marcel. "French officers," he said
under his breath. "French officers, and parties till dawn." He
shook his head. "These are some historians your good aunts,
but please understand I mean no disrespect." He turned back
to the chair he had been fixing, and going down on one knee
as if in genuflection, he pressed the damask where he had
been tacking it down. The box of brass tacks lay beside him,
and in his hand he held a small hammer.

"They had a great plantation on the Plaine du Nord,"
Marcel went on. "Tante Josette lived there, but the others,
Tante Louisa and Tante Colette, they lived in the city of Port-
au-Prince. Of course, they lost everything. Everything was
lost."

"*Eh bien,* everything was lost," Jean Jacques sighed. "I
could tell you a lot about French officers, I could tell you a
slightly different story, of the French officers who killed my
master at Grand Rivière, and broke his commander on the
wheel."

This was said simply and for a moment Marcel was not
certain that he had heard. Then it was as if every sound from
the street had died. He strained forward, and then a shock
went through him and he felt himself shudder. He had heard
it all right, Jean Jacques had said the words, "my master."
Jean Jacques had been a slave! Never in all his life had
Marcel heard anyone refer to a time when he or she had been
a slave. Of course there were mulatto slaves and quadroon
slaves and slaves as light as Marcel, as well as there were
black slaves, but these were not *gens de couleur, Creole gens
de couleur* who had been free for generations, free always,
free so far back that no one could remember—or hadn't
they???

"Do those good ladies ever talk about that, the battle at
Grand Rivière?" Jean Jacques asked gently. There was no
judgment in his voice, merely in the choice of his words. He
lifted a tack from the box, fitted it between two fingers of his
left hand which held the cloth in its place. "Do they ever
speak of the mulatto, Ogé, and how he led the men of color
in battle at Grand Rivière and how the French captured him
and broke him on the wheel?"

It seemed the shame Marcel was feeling was palpable and
hot. It burned his cheeks. The palms of his hands were damp

with it. What does it matter that Jean Jacques was a slave, what does it matter, he was struggling with it, hearing quite distinctly his mother's tone at table, so *sans façon*, "I don't want you with that old man." He loathed himself at this moment. He would die before he let Jean Jacques know what he was feeling. He cast back though the confusion of his mind for the words Jean Jacques had only just spoken and said quickly, nervously.

"No, Monsieur, they never spoke of Ogé." He was afraid of the tremor in his voice.

"No, I don't suppose they would," Jean Jacques said. "But it seems they might have. That a young man should know something of those times, of those men of color that died."

Only now was the meaning of the words penetrating to Marcel.

"What does it mean, Monsieur, broken on the wheel?" Men of color fighting a battle with white men, he could not envision this. He knew nothing of it.

Jean Jacques stopped. He held the hammer poised above the brass crown of the tack, and in a low voice said,

"'... while alive to have his arms, legs, thighs, and spine broken; and afterward to be placed on a wheel, his face toward Heaven and there to stay as long as it would please God to preserve his life.'" He paused. Without looking up, he went on. "I was in Cap François then, but I didn't go to the Place d'Armes. There were too many white people in the Place d'Armes to see it happen. Planters drove in from the countryside to see it happen. I went later, after they'd hanged the other men of color they'd captured with him. But they didn't capture my master. My master died on the battlefield, and no one got to hang him, nor break him on a wheel."

Marcel was stunned. His eyes were riveted to Jean Jacques.

"But how did this happen?" Marcel whispered. "Colored men fighting white men?"

Jean Jacques glanced at him, and slowly a smile broke over his wrinkled features. "Some historians those good aunts of yours, *mon fils*," he said gently as before. "It was colored men fighting white men who commenced the revolution in Saint-Domingue *before* the slaves rose. You see, it really began in France. It began with *Liberté, Egalité, Fraternité*, those magic words. And this man, Ogé, quite an educated man, had been in Paris and wined and dined by those men who were the friends of the blacks in the colonies and believed in their protection and their rights." Jean Jacques suddenly put the tack and the little hammer down. He closed the top of the box of tacks, and then rising slowly as if his knees ached, he turned the chair toward him and rested back on it, his hands on his thighs. He sighed heavily with a movement of his shoulders.

"Well, it must have made a lot of sense in Paris, that Ogé should come home to Saint-Domingue and demand the rights of his people, the *gens de couleur.* Mind you, nobody had said too much yet about freedom for the slaves. But I don't have to tell you, *mon fils,* young as you are, that there was no way the white planters of Saint-Domingue were going to give the *gens de couleur* the same rights as they had themselves. So Ogé gathered a fighting force at Grand Rivière, and my master was there. Oh, I'd begged him not to go. I'd begged him not to be so foolish! And he wasn't my master then anymore, I was free, and he respected me, he really did." He looked at Marcel, his eyes moved slowly over Marcel's face. "But he went on, and with that small force met the French and the French defeated them like that.

"But by the time it was all over, by the time your good aunts had left with your mamma and come here ... why, thirteen years had passed, and white had fought colored, and colored had fought black, and black had fought white. And black and colored had finally joined together to drive out the French ... those French officers your aunts have told you about ... and that famous Madame Pauline, Napoleon's sister ... they drove them out.

"I wonder if there was an acre of farmland left ... of coffee or sugar or anything a man can grow ... I wonder if there was an acre of it on that island that hadn't been burned ten times over before it was finished. I don't know. It was in the very beginning that I left, set sail from Cap François during the first days of the black revolt."

He sat still. His eyes left Marcel and he stared forward as if seeing those times.

Marcel was speechless. And when Jean Jacques looked at him again, his dark eyes appeared to search Marcel's face for some glimmer of response, some little indication that he had understood. But Marcel had never heard a word of this before, he had believed his people to have been one with the whites, to have been driven out along with the whites, and he had that overwhelming sense which had come over him of late of all that he did not know or comprehend.

(69)

Jean Jacques glanced at the open door. "Do you feel that breeze?" he asked. "Winter's over, and none too soon." He rose and stretched as he had done before. "That's the Angelus, *mon fils,*" he said.

Marcel had heard it, the dull clanking of the Cathedral bell. "But Monsieur," he began, "it went on for thirteen years, this war, this revolution?"

"You've got to get on home, *mon fils,*" Jean Jacques said. "You're usually gone by this time."

Marcel did not move.

All the while he had imagined it so simply. One night the slaves had risen, and burned it all. "White, colored, it didn't make any difference," Tante Colette so often said with a weary wave of her fan. "They burned everything that we had."

He was excited. And yet he was frightened at the same time. It seemed he hovered on the edge of an awful, dismal feeling as he sat there, conjured by this vision of men of color in arms, and black men fighting with them. He barely heard Jean Jacques' voice:

"Go on, *mon fils,* your mother will be one angry woman if you don't go on."

"But will you tell me tomorrow?" Marcel asked. He got to his feet but stood there looking intently at Jean Jacques.

Jean Jacques was thinking. And that dismal feeling in Marcel deepened, something akin to the dusk in the street and the fading light around them within the shop. He watched Jean Jacques' dark face and regretted that he had asked with such feeling. Marcel had made it seem too important by asking, and as so often happened when you wanted something desperately, then you couldn't have it.

"I don't know, *mon fils,*" Jean Jacques said. "Maybe that's enough history for a while. Maybe I've said too much as it is." He was looking at Marcel. He appeared to wait and then Marcel said,

"But Monsieur..."

"No, *mon fils,* one day you can read all of that in books on your own. It seems you ought to know something about it. Those were your people." He shook his head. "But you read it in books on your own."

"But Monsieur, I have no such books, I've never even seen them," Marcel said. "I could go into the bookstores and ask them..."

"Oh no, no, *mon fils.* Don't do that, you mustn't do that,

don't you ever go into bookstores and ask," Jean Jacques said. His face had settled into that brooding frown of his that Marcel had known so often in years before. "Some day I'll give you those to read." He gestured to the diaries on the shelf. "When I die, I'll leave those books to you." He looked at Marcel. "Would you read them if I did that, would they mean something to you?"

When Marcel did not answer, he asked again,

"Mon fils?"

"I don't want you to die," Marcel said.

Jean Jacques smiled. But he was already turning to get the shutters, and said again under his breath that it was time for Marcel to go home.

II

MARCEL HAD BEGUN to change. Cecile saw it, and sighed, *"Eh bien,* he's thirteen." He took unexplained walks, and went out of his own accord to the flat of his aunts over the dress shop. And at table on Sundays (they were always at the cottage for supper if Monsieur Philippe was not there) he asked them simple questions about Saint-Domingue, seemed bored by their accounts of all the practical wealth left behind, reminiscences of those lovely courtyards crowded with flowers where you could pick the ripe yellow bananas right from the trees.

"But the revolution, what was it like?" he asked quite suddenly one afternoon.

"I'm sure I have no idea, *mon petit,* since it was mostly in the north and we were all so thankful Josette escaped!" Tante Louisa said haughtily.

And Cecile nervously turned the talk to the subject of Marie's birthday. That white eyelet lace was too expensive, she said suddenly, she was thinking of something a little more practical, and Marie was growing so fast besides.

Richard, a frequent guest, felt the tension in Cecile at such gatherings. The tall aunts fascinated him with their ripples of laughter, rustling and tinkling with pearls and gold, even the white streaks in their straight dark hair seemed decorative. While Cecile, cutting the cake for dessert, brought down the knife a little too hard making a strangely attractive "chink" against the plate. But never, never did any of them

(71)

speak of anything that was more than the practical, more than the materially real. "Oh, we had such chandeliers in that house, and champagne each night, and that young French officer, what was his name, Louisa, you remember he brought up the little orchestra. Why, we had music every night, all night. Richard, here have some more cake. Cecile, give that boy another piece of cake, Richard, if you get an inch taller you won't fit through the door."

And before he could even answer these quick flashing statements, their eyes were elsewhere, their hands eternally busy. Cecile in particular fussed with the flowers in the center of the table, or examined the immaculate linen napkin in her hands as if for some tiny and all-important flaw. And if the boys, alone after dinner, lapsed into some low-voiced talk of what they had read at school, she was at once uncomfortable, quick to clear the table, as if listening to some abrasive foreign tongue.

Richard had not thought of it before. And it was Marcel's taut face that made him think of it then, how empty at times all that chatter seemed, and how quickly it left the mind. Richard was only vaguely aware of his own ability to think about abstract things and to talk of them, but the whole tone of the Lermontants' suppers was different. You could count on it, trivial or not, conversation with the Lermontants revolved around the invisible. And Marcel, who had once sipped his soup quietly waiting to be excused so that he and Richard might slip off alone, now stared fixedly at Rudolphe who waved a folded newspaper over the steaming plates, crying, "Read what they say, read it!" while Grandpère Lermontant tried to quiet him with a quick, "It won't pass, Rudolphe, I tell you the legislature will never pass it."

"It's the country parishes, every time it's the country parishes: strip the *gens de couleur* of their right to own property!" Rudolphe all but rose straight into the air with rage. "To think that they..."

"It won't pass," said the old man.

"But why, what does it mean?" Marcel asked.

"That the country whites are afraid of the free negro," Grandpère explained patiently. "It's been the same since 1803, since we became Americans," he went on with a slight twist to his smile, never missing a bite, reaching now and then for his glass: "They bring one bill after another before the legislature in Baton Rouge to try to take away our rights, limit our rights, what have you. It's all because some colored barber in their town has a finer horse than they have, or a prettier daughter."

Madame Suzette, Richard's mother, shook her head, deplored ignorance under her breath, and motioned to the cook for more rice. Marcel read the column in the paper when he could get his hands on it. And Richard mused silently that he had never even heard the word "color" at Cecile's table. He felt a momentary discomfort to think that he would not mention it in her presence.

"It's not the old families," Rudolphe was saying. "I can tell you that. It's men come here to make money off slaves, that's the long and short of it. It's not a system they inherited! They've no respect for a way of life, for traditions that go with it. And every free man of color's a threat to them. Well, I'll tell you one thing, that this family was the *Famille Lermontant* when half that cracker rabble were packed in the convict ships landing off the coast of Georgia."

Marcel's head jerked round toward Rudolphe, and he let the folded newspaper all but slip from his hand.

Rudolphe lifted his glass ever so slightly toward the framed portrait of his Arrière-Grandpère Jean Baptiste, beyond the double doors. "We had our tavern in the Tchoupitoulas Road, and money in the banks when they were splitting kindling for a living and clearing the fields."

"Let's go upstairs," Richard bent to whisper in Marcel's ear. But Marcel stared off, his face as still as if it were made of wax.

It was days later when wandering into the parlor of the cottage as young men do, absorbed in his thoughts and annoyed by the very sight and sounds of the house, he glanced at the pictures of Tante Josette and Tante Louisa above the buffet and said,

"But they are not our real aunts, are they?"

Cecile, positively afraid of him of late, dropped the embroidery she held in her hand.

"They brought me up from a child that high!" she burst out, "gave me my trousseau, how dare you speak of them in that manner!" It was a rare moment. She had never spoken of being indebted to anyone. And once in a while she would remark when having her measurements taken how she hated, herself, to sew. She had done it for twenty-one years in their shop, Marcel knew.

Tante Louisa, two days later, as she passed him a glass

of sherry, said, "Of course I'm your aunt, who's to say I'm not? Who's been putting such ideas in your head?"

Her black hair was curled fastidiously at the temples, her pale brown face old but still lovely with the faintest blush of rouge. She had sent her last lover off three years ago. An old white widower from Charleston who loved to play with one side of his waxed mustache, had fighting cocks, race horses, and taught Marcel to play faro.

"But there is no blood connection," Marcel said to her. They were in her rear sitting room, its high windows open to the court so that there rose over the distant noises of the street the constant trickling of the fountain.

"There's a connection," she said to him calmly. And rising, she stood behind his chair and slowly massaged his shoulders, his neck, "You're my little boy," she said in his ear. "That's the connection."

But Tante Colette, always the more practical and the more outspoken said without looking up from her book of accounts, "Now don't you worry your maman with all that, Marcel. All the questions you've been asking about Saint-Domingue, what do you know about Saint-Domingue? Your maman was just a child when she left, but children remember." Then she removed her gold-rimmed eyeglass and let it fall on its long blue ribbon, looking at him gravely. "Why we hardly had the time to take the clothes on our backs... and the pewter and the silver we left behind... Oh, it makes me ill to this day!"

His lips were moving with her words, he had heard them so many times, but she did not see, and there was nothing of mockery in his eyes.

"But how did you happen, then, to bring my mother?" he asked.

They were stunned.

"Marcel," Colette began, "do you honestly think we would have left that baby there!"

"Her parents, then, they were your friends?"

They were studying him as if they had not ever really taken stock of him before, and then Louisa bending over the evening paper seemed at once absorbed as though he had never come in.

"Why, *cher*, your mother's father had the biggest plantation north of Port-au-Prince," Colette said simply. "He was everybody's friend, 'course that man didn't have the sense he was born with..."

"Marcel, you haven't touched that glass," said Louisa, her

(74)

eyes on the paper, "you're always asking for a glass of wine like a proper gentleman—"

Marcel sipped it hastily, spilling a drop or two as he set the glass down. "He was white, this man, her father?"

"*Cher,* don't you even know that?" Colette asked. "Of course he was white. And a fine white man at that, though a bit dumb."

"Oh, my head is aching," Louisa said. "Go shut those blinds, *cher.*"

"But what do you mean a bit dumb?"

"Oh, to stay there at all after that," Colette said, "after the French army leaving, with the blacks taking over, every white man who had any sense left. But no, that black devil, General Dessalines, that black devil, he told the white planters to stay, said he needed them to go back to their lands, rebuild the plantations, and they believed him, they believed that black devil. Well, *cher,* he hated them, and he hated us too, hated everyone that wasn't black as he was. He'd been a black man's slave, that's what he'd been, before he became the powerful General Dessalines!"

"I just don't want to talk about these things, my head aches!" Louisa dropped the paper, putting her fingers to her temples. She turned stiffly in her chair to her sister.

"Well, he just wants to know!" Colette said. "*Cher,* don't you say a word of this to your mother, do you hear me? Why, they massacred every white French man, woman and child in the city of Port-au-Prince! Why, there was this colored officer running through the streets just to kill the children, can you imagine, just to kill those babies! I saw that with my own eyes! And there was that baby, your maman, out there in the street. 'Course she wasn't white, you could see that, but all around..."

"Oh, stop this now!" Louisa burst out.

"No, no, please." Marcel turned quickly and placed his hand on hers and pressed her hand against the table. "Go on, Tante Colette, where was my mother?"

"Out there in the street, with people dying right there all around her. Marcel, I swear to you, I've told you many a foolish tale in my life, but I swear to you, the water running in the gutter down the middle of that street was the color of blood."

Louisa's face was very still. She had removed her hand from Marcel's hand, and she sat looking at her hands which were now clasped in her lap. "Cecile's my little girl," she said softly. "My little girl."

"...and that white man, your maman's father, they had hung him on a hook right over the door! Right opposite our house this was, Marcel, and there he was, that hook run up through his chin, and blood streaming down the front of his clothes. 'Course he was dead, been dead for hours, I hope to God he was dead before they hung him up there, but there was that baby, your maman, just clinging to that door post and that colored officer up at the top of the street, sticking his bayonet into the bodies of those other babies. They were everywhere, they had dragged those people out of the houses, women, children, they didn't care . . . just so they were French and just so they were white."

"I feel sick in here," Louisa said softly. She put her hand to her lips. "Those blinds, shut those blinds, Marcel."

"Never mind about those damned blinds!" Colette said. "Well, there was that baby like I told you," she went on. "And Josette, she was the one, Marcel, yes, she was the one..."

"Will you stop this for the love of heaven!" Louisa said.

"I will not. I say if he's old enough to ask the question then he's old enough to know. Might just stop him from driving his maman out of her mind, all those questions about Saint-Domingue. Look at me, Marcel, don't you tell your mother, your mother won't ever talk about those times."

"What did Tante Josette do?" Marcel asked.

Louisa walked crisply across the polished floor and pulled the blinds shut with a clat. She went to the second window and to the third, as the room was darkening around them.

"Well, she looked out there into that street," Colette said, "and she saw that baby down there, poor little baby in her bare feet, that man never took any care of that baby at all, just fed her right off his own plate in the tavern, that's all he ever did, never combed that pretty hair, never washed her face. That baby didn't even have shoes, I bet that baby had never even worn shoes. Will you stop it, Louisa, I can't see a thing in here, will you open those blinds!"

"But what happened?" Marcel asked.

"Well, Josette was never scared of the devil in hell. We were terrified, Marcel, 'Oh, don't go out there,' we said to her, 'they won't hurt that baby, they're killing white babies...' But she took the bolt down off that door and marched right down those steps. 'I'm going to get that baby,' she said, and walked right out there into that street, right up to that dead man hanging on that hook, and she grabbed that baby in her arms. Why, she had to bend down right under that dead man, knocked his body around on that hook to get that baby in her arms. And oh, to hear that child scream! It made no difference that that man was dead, she did not want to leave that man! Oh, to hear that child scream...."

"Don't say another word!" Louisa said.

Colette turned. Louisa merely stood with her back to the blinds, her hands clasped in front of her, her face dark.

Marcel was staring ahead of him. He was looking at the droplets from the sherry, and very slowly he moved his fingers toward them, and then his hand closed around the glass.

"We never let that baby out of our sight after that," Colette said quietly. "Your Tante Louisa and me... And when Josette went upriver again to *Sans Souci,* she wanted to take your maman but that baby got under this table right here in this room, and clung to the leg of this table, she didn't want to go. She wanted to stay here with us. Strange, it was as if she turned on Josette, she wanted to stay here with us. 'Well, that baby's been through enough,' Josette said. 'If she wants to stay here in New Orleans with you, then she can stay.'"

They were quiet.

Marcel was looking at the glass of sherry, and then very slowly he lifted it to his lips. He drank it all down, and put the glass back very carefully, and putting his elbow on the table he rested his forehead in his hand.

"Go home, Marcel," Louisa said. Her voice was thick and low.

"Leave him alone," Colette said.

"You go on home," Louisa said. "And don't you ever say a word to your maman, you hear me?"

It was late afternoon when he came home. A bundle of white lace lay on the dining table. And the long slanting rays of the sun found all the glass in the cottage.

It seemed at such times when it was hot and cloudless that the brilliance of light combined with the moving air to make the clutter of mahogany and shining what-nots shabby in the swirls of dust. Sun shone in a pool on the waxed floor, and rendered the gilt framed picture of *Sans Souci* a glaring mirror.

Marcel, sitting very still with his hands on his knees, merely looked at his own slender fingers, the few veins drawn on the backs of his hands. There was no sound except the buzzing of flies.

Then the tread of boots on the path and the sharp sound of his mother opening the latch.

He saw her silhouetted against the sun, a black hourglass of a woman, tiny wrists, fine fingers that delicately closed the parasol and set it by the door. She moved closer to him, brows knit, her eyes gleaming in her dark face, one hand neatly gathering the pleats of her green taffeta skirt. She wore a cameo at her throat on a band of black velvet, and the white lace beneath it lay in scallops over her breast. "Marcel?"

His impassive face gave no sign that he had heard. She seemed to him a timeless being as she stood poised there, someone who had not been born at all but had come into life full-blown when fashion reached some perfect peak that suited her, so that moving toward him she was like the bric-a-brac and petit-point that everywhere surrounded her, something solid, exquisite and unsubtractable from the whole.

A great gulf lay beyond her. As if the door of the Ste. Marie cottage swung open onto chaos, and rushing there on some pretext of normal errand, Marcel might find himself clinging to the knob above a chasm. History stirred in the awesome dark, the stench of burning fields, drums, the black faces of slaves.

He shuddered as he rose to his feet. It seemed the very walls were disintegrating, the baubles of the crystal candlesticks were on fire. Going out the front gate, he heard her for the first time calling his name.

III

RAIN FLOODED the streets. By midday it had overflowed the low brick banquettes, poured into the shops, lapped at the steps of the cottages, and made of the narrow mud thoroughfares flat lakes spreading beneath the pelting drops from one side to the other. The fenced garden of the Ste. Marie cottage was a swamp.

But with the afternoon it had stopped; the sun poured down on the receding waters, and Jean Jacques, after sweeping out the shop and bringing down again the chairs he had

(78)

hung on hooks around the walls, went back to work. In the past he had sent his fine pieces out to be gilded, but this year, whether out of boredom or simple fascination, he did not know, he was going to do it himself. He dipped his brush into the pot of glue he had softened on his stove and painted invisible wet curlicues along the oval frame of a mirror. And now, raising the gold leaf ever so carefully on the tip of a dry brush, he blew it in a fine spray so that those curlicues seemed to Marcel to come to life perfect and golden along the mirror's polished border.

He would rest from time to time, light a cigar for a few puffs and continue to talk.

"...I don't know that anyone would have taught me if I hadn't shown the will to learn. It was more than will, to tell the truth, it was a passion, a passion..." The word was uncommon to him, he said it with emphasis. "I wouldn't leave that old carpenter alone. Of course he didn't want to bother with me. My mother had been nothing but a field hand, and me one of the barefoot bunch that played at the back door."

Marcel studied his profile against the fiery light outside. A sheet of water still lay at the corner of the Rue Bourbon and the Rue Ste. Anne, and a hack turning fast in the softened ruts below sent a flashing spray toward the shop. Children squealed with laughter.

"But I wouldn't leave his tools alone. 'Don't you touch my tools,' he would say, but I wouldn't pay him any mind. I'd stay right there, planted by his side asking him over and over, 'what are you going to do with that, what are those pegs for...' 'Course he didn't make furniture like this furniture. He fixed things, fixed the porch railings and the wooden blinds, and he'd make simple chairs, rocking chairs and tables and benches for the kitchen and sometimes for the other slaves."

"But how did you learn, then, to make fine furniture?" Marcel asked.

Jean Jacques was thinking. "I learned simple things first, then I went on to those things I really wanted to make. You see, I have the belief, *mon fils,* that if a man can learn any one thing well, then he can learn most anything else that he puts his mind to."

He glanced at Marcel. Marcel sat on the high stool by the stove as always. The fire for the melting of the glue had long gone out and a clean breeze blew through the front doors and out those open to the yard in back. He seemed hardly wilted by the day's heat or the day's damp. On such days as this he had learned to move slowly, to walk slowly, and his clothing retained its crispness, though the high polish of his new boots had not survived the mud of the streets. Jean Jacques smiled at him almost wistfully and the change of expression took Marcel by surprise. But then Jean Jacques went on.

"There were field hands on my master's land, men who came over from Africa who made things in the evening after all the work was done, objects..." his hand opened, palm up and fingers somewhat rounded as if he were trying to grasp the thing of which he spoke... "pieces of art," he said as if he had found the proper word. "They made these things with a simple knife, out of the hardest mahogany. Heads is what they were, African-looking heads with lips that were bigger than any Negro's really, and eyes that were no more than slits, and the hair would be made into braids on the tops of these long heads, braids that were coiled round and round and came down sometimes to loop around the ears. To look at it, what would you think, that it was a savage thing, a...a...an *African* thing," he said. "Yet I tell you the workmanship on that head was as fine as any I've ever seen. I mean the way that those braids of hair were carved, the way that the ear on one side of that face was perfectly balanced with the other... why, I can remember the smoothness of those faces when they were polished, and the way that they would appear in the firelight in the corners of those small cabins. Well, I tell you, if a man can make that object so perfect, that piece of art... because art is what it was... then he could make anything with his hands that he wanted to make. He could make this little *secrétaire* here, or that *fauteuil*. If he wanted to do it! If he wanted to."

"But how did you learn to read, Monsieur? And write?" Marcel had done it at last—he had found the moment for that question.

"The way a hundred men have learned," Jean Jacques laughed. "I got a book.... It was an old Bible that the master gave to me, in fact, its cover had come off, and I wanted to have it, and he said well, you can have that if you want it. And I took that Bible and sat down by the front steps. I was older then, and I helped around the house. There were lots of times when no one needed me, why there were whole days when all I did was to go from one room to another to find the master's pipe for him, or run upstairs to get his tobacco. So I found this place in the honeysuckle by the gallery, and every time I had a chance to ask the master to tell me the meaning of one word, I would do it. Of course I had to ask him the same words more than once, but by the end of month I could read three lines of that Bible by myself, and I knew those words wherever else in that book that they would ever appear. By the end of the year I could read four pages. Don't look so surprised, *mon fils,* many men have learned that way. And then there came this special afternoon. It was nothing special to anyone but me, but my master was on his long couch on the gallery and looking up from under his hat, he said, 'Jean Jacques, you're always reading that Bible, why don't you read it to me?' I came up on the porch beside him and read him those four pages, clearly, and the few lines I'd learned besides. 'Jean Jacques,' he said, 'when you can read any page in that Bible to me, any page from beginning to the end...I'll set you free.'" Jean Jacques laughed softly, "Well, there was no stopping me then."

Marcel could not conceal the exquisite pleasure this moment in the story had given him.

"'What do you want to be, Jean Jacques?' he asked me when the time came...."

"When you could read any page!"

"Mon fils," Jean Jacques leaned forward nodding and winking his eyes. "I read him St. John's Apocalypse!"

Marcel laughed in spite of himself, hunching his shoulders and thrusting his clasped hands down between his legs.

"Well, 'I want to be a carpenter,' is what I said to him. 'Our Lord Jesus Christ was a carpenter, and that's good enough for me.' But you know, I think when I look back on it I just wanted to spite that old man, that mean old slave carpenter who would never show me how to use those tools. I wanted to show him I could be as good as he was. And later on, my master sent me into Cap François to really learn the trade. I became a builder of stairways, I learned to build the finest stairways in the houses of the richest in the town. And the furniture, I came to make it in the time that I could call my own." He paused; he appeared to be studying Marcel. Marcel was picturing with a special pleasure all the lovely stairways he had seen. There was in particular that long stairway in the Lermontant house that curved so gracefully at the small landing to double back above itself to the second floor. "But the best furniture making, that was done here in New Orleans after I came," Jean Jacques said. "I made it from the furniture I saw in peoples' houses when I went to make their staircases or to repair them, and I made it from the pictures I saw in books. I made a stairway once for your Tante Josette," he paused again, watching Marcel's face. "She came down here one summer from the Cane River and said, 'Jean Jacques I want you to come up and make me a good staircase, a fine staircase at *Sans Souci.*'"

Marcel thought of the times she had invited them all to visit her, of Cecile's excuses and his own passion for his day-to-day city life. He had thought the country would be so dull. But he would go there, he would see this staircase, walk upon it and feel its newel posts, he would study how it was made.

"We came on the same ship here," Jean Jacques said. "Your Tante Josette and me, did you know that? And I remember thirteen years later when she went back to Saint-Domingue determined to find her sisters, and she brought them here and brought your maman here too."

A shadow passed over Marcel's face.

"What is it?" asked the old man.

Marcel shrugged quickly, "But tell me, Monsieur, with writing, how did you learn to write?"

"You ask the strangest questions," Jean Jacques said. Marcel was looking at the open diary. He himself had tried a diary and had written such empty foolish things as "Rose, breakfasted at seven, walked to school."

"How do you think I learned?" Jean Jacques laughed. "By copying the words I read on pages other people had written and in the pages of books."

A silence passed between them as often it did. It seemed Jean Jacques had the tissue of thin gold leaf poised on the tip of his dry brush again. A bit of the leaf clung to his fingertips. He looked at the oval mirror before him.

"You have heavy thoughts, *mon fils.*"

"Will you tell me...explain to me...about the battles in Saint-Domingue?"

Jean Jacques paused. Then he shook his head. His hand, however, did not move. The gold leaf on the tip of the bristles did not move.

"Can't do that anymore, *mon fils,* maybe I should have never done it before..." His expression was brooding, unpleasant.

"But why?" Marcel asked.

"It's not my decision, *mon fils,*" he said. "I can't decide when you're to learn those things. But remember, when I die, I leave all my books to you."

"Don't talk about death, Monsieur ..." Marcel couldn't contain himself.

"And why not?" Jean Jacques asked simply. "I've lived too long as it is. Seen too much. I guess I remember too much of those old times." He went on with his work.

"But it's better now, isn't it?" Marcel asked. "I mean those wars, those battles, they're past. It's peaceful now, and we can talk about it, can't we?"

"Peaceful now? You misunderstand me, *mon fils*. The memories don't hurt my soul." He had carefully replaced the little leaf of gold as though he despaired now with this conversation of getting anything done. And setting down the brush, he took a rag from the bench beside him and carefully wiped his hands. "In some way, those times were better than these. There were battles all right, there was bloodshed, and I don't want to think of the number of men who died on all sides. But in a way those times were better than these." He narrowed his eyes as if peering into his history, "because for all the roughness and cruelty of that land, men's ideas weren't so fixed. They tortured their slaves, they murdered them on that island in ways no planter would ever try to use here; and when those slaves rose they gave that cruelty back in kind. But men's ideas were not so fixed. There was hope that the *gens de couleur*, that the whites ... that even a hardworking slave getting his freedom might ..." he stopped. He shook his head. "I've lived too long," he said. "Just too damned long."

IV

MARCEL WAS SOBBING on the steps of the *garçonnière*. Cecile at her wits' end had sent Marie to the Lermontants.

"They looked everywhere for you!" She was wringing her hands, "If you'd been in school, they might have found you! What is the matter with you that you carry on like this?" But as she reached for him, he jerked away and smashed his fist against the cistern.

It was Rudolphe Lermontant himself in his black broadcloth coat who stepped into the courtyard. His face was somewhat hard and fixed until he saw Marcel.

"But he can't be dead, not just like that, no one can die just like that! He was there last night, I was talking to him, he was right there, everything was the same last night..."

"Listen to me, Marcel," Rudolphe began in a low voice. "Jean Jacques died in his sleep. He was probably dead long before midnight, if I'm any judge of such things, most likely he never even took his supper. And this is midsummer, you know perfectly well that I couldn't keep him in this heat. But for you, Marcel, for you I would have kept him as long as I could. I sent to school for you, you were not there, I sent to the house for you, you were not there. Now come with me. Pull yourself together and come with me now. I'll take you to the cemetery and show you the stone and you can pay your respects..."

Marcel drew back from Rudolphe's hand. A momentary indignation passed over Rudolphe's heavy features and then he let out a little explosion of breath between his lips and pressed them tightly together.

"The shop's empty, empty," Marcel gasped. "He can't just disappear as if he was never there! I don't want to see his grave, I won't look at it, he can't be shut up in it like that."

"At three o'clock this afternoon that shop wasn't empty," Rudolphe said. "It was jammed with mourners. He was much loved."

Marcel struggled to stifle the sob in his throat. "And his books, Monsieur," he pleaded. "They're gone, and that old charwoman, she just told me to get out." He clenched his teeth over a cry.

He did not see Rudolphe's sudden inquiring glance to Cecile, or the haughty lift of his mother's chin and the imperious jerk of her head. Lisette at the kitchen door was looking from one to the other of them.

Cecile clasped her hands at her waist, her eyebrows raised as she stared at Rudolphe, her hands making a lock.

"What books?" Rudolphe murmured, his eyes fixed on Cecile.

"His diaries, Monsieur, he promised them to me, he left them to me, he told me he wanted me to have them. I went to the *presbytère,* the priest knew nothing about them! They were gone..."

"Get up, Marcel," Cecile said quickly.

Rudolphe's eyes were still fixed on her. And under his breath he said, "The wishes of the dead are sacred, Madame."

"I don't take orders from shopkeepers!" she said. "Books, what do I know of books!"

Lisette had turned to the alleyway which led to the yard in back.

Marcel looked up. He saw them, their eyes holding one another, and then Rudolphe's face contorted with rage.

"Shopkeeper or no, it was his will," Rudolphe whispered.

"I am not referring to the cabinetmaker, Monsieur, I am referring to you!"

"Maman, what are you saying?" Marcel's tone was impatient, desperate as if to say What now?

Rudolphe was furious. He remained a moment longer, his hands curling at his sides, then forming into fists. He strode toward the alleyway and then turned.

"What is it?" Marcel rose, his hand on the banister, wiping the tears from his face. "What are you saying?" His mother was angry, he could see it in the tremor of her lip, the narrowing of her eyes. "Maman!"

"You had best go, Monsieur, and leave me to care for my son," she said coldly.

Rudolphe's voice was equally cold and controlled. "You destroyed those books!" he glared at her.

"Leave this house," she answered.

Late that night, drunk to incoherence, Marcel lay across the bed. All the long evening he had been with his friend, Anna Bella Monroe, in her little parlor behind the boardinghouse at the corner. And it was she who had taken the wine away finally and locked it up. "You haven't lost him," she had said, and when he protested through his tears that he did not believe "those things," she had shaken her head patiently.

She seemed a lady to him then through the glaze of his pain, not merely his Anna Bella, but then she had always been so, perhaps, deeper and better than childhood allowed, and at fifteen a lovely equanimity shone in her eyes that often drained the tumult out of him. "I mean you'll always have what passed between you, no one can take that," she said, "what you remember *in here!*" Her small curled hand tapped her breast, her face a perfect sweetheart amid the soft fullness of her black hair. It seemed he had kissed her then, just to let her know how much he loved her. She had always understood about Jean Jacques, even when Richard did not understand, when no one could understand, and as he felt the baby roundness of her chin, the plumpness of her cheeks, all the exquisite pain of loss dissolved for him. But a warning

(85)

hand had pressed him gently away. And from a dim bedroom beyond, her ancient guardian, Madame Elsie, pounded the floor with her cane. He could not have gotten to his own gate without Anna Bella's supporting arm.

Now he was only vaguely aware that she was, in fact, gone from him, not holding him, that he was in his room, and that Lisette had silently opened his door. She had a bundle folded in her soiled apron and approaching him she held it out. He squinted at her, feeling a vague fear of that reverent posture, the way that she held the folded apron as if it had some power. It put him in mind of fetishes, those foul-smelling objects she sewed into his pillows when he was sick, her magic powders.

"The dead are the dead," he whispered. "Get me a bottle of whiskey, Lisette, get it. I'll give you a dollar."

"You've had enough whiskey, now sit up and look here."

And flipping back the apron she showed him the charred remains of a ledger, its corners blacked and burned off, the leather of the cover blistered. "I dug through those ashes with my own hands for this, Michie, I burned my hands for this, sit up."

He snatched it from her, cracking it open to see Jean Jacques' script.

"Richard Lermontant brought it for you, Michie, never you mind what *she* says!" she spoke now of his mother. "There was a note on every one of them with your name, I can read that much, Michie. That old man left them for you and I saw *her* light that fire with her own hands. I got this one for you, Michie, digging in those ashes myself, all the rest is gone."

What was there? Fragments.

All through the hot summer he pored over it, finding not a single sentence complete for all that had been burnt away around it. Observations of the weather, bits of a transaction, some purchases of imported woods further on, the note of a public hanging. And here and there the dates that fixed the year at 1829 with all the rest gone forever.

This the only document left of a life, this the only relic of fine slanting script replete with curlicues, and some fine relationship between the exquisite purple ink and the cleanliness that had been the page, as though the man who had taught himself all he knew had liked to lift the pen, to form the words as well as he had done everything.

October came. Marcel was fourteen.

MARCEL READ night and day, dreamed at school, listened with bright attention to the chatter of fishmongers, and wandering at random found the world alien with wonders.

Before a clock shop at noon, he strained to see and hear all the clocks strike at once behind the plate glass windows. And reading the newspapers in French and English, ate his breakfast with one hand, speaking to no one. In bitter October rains, he trudged through the high grass in the cemetery and gazed with head turned from the corner of his eye down the aisle at the stone of Jean Jacques' high crypt, one of a hundred fixed into the crumbling whitewashed walls.

Only for Marie's First Communion did he affect a human face and kiss her afterwards on both cheeks, refusing for a moment to let her go, then drinking sherry with the party, sharing cakes, and smiling stiffly at his aunts and their pleasantries, words he instantly and effortlessly forgot.

Writing his name, Marcel Ste. Marie, in his diary, he found his hand stopped. Where had Cecile got the surname, anyway? From her prayers? *Bare feet, dirty face, tangled hair.* After supper he watched her at the head of the table as she pinned up her taffeta sleeves. The slaves set a basin of warm water before her as always, and carefully she washed each painted china plate herself, only entrusting them to Marie's waiting hands. Drying her long fingers afterwards, she fanned them on her palms to inspect the perfect ovals of her nails.

How many times in the long summer nights of his childhood when the damp heat made his sheets limp and the air close, had he heard her suddenly moan in her sleep, and through the open doorway saw her rise from the pillow like a doll thrown forward, her hands in her hair. She would pad silently across the boards, her chemise luminous in the dim flicker of the night-lamp, and taking the pitcher in both hands drink it down. *"And oh, to hear that child scream! It made no difference to that baby that that man was dead, oh, to hear that child scream ..."* And even setting the pitcher by, seemed still heavy with her dreams, turning, and turning again as if she could not find her bed.

People still called Marcel an angel, dutiful son, sometimes even yet a perfect child, were they out of their minds? He glared as if they uttered abominations. In this new blaze of clarity that threatened to consume the most mundane objects, he turned his relentless gaze upon himself and realized that he had always known the truth about his world, breathed it like the very air.

Who had told him a pedigree lay behind the endless washing of hands, suffering of starched collars, the lowering of voices in this tiny parlor, leaving the last of the soup when you are hungry, never daring to tip the edge of the plate? The world was glass like angels on the mantel, bound to shatter at the thrust of a crude word. *"Why did you burn those books, how could you burn those books!"*

"Don't you raise your voice to me, Monsieur! May I remind you that I am your mother!"

She shivered in his arms. He felt the stays of her corset, the prickling layers of lace. Her hands clung to his thick hair, her lips quivering against his neck. *"You did a bad thing, Maman."* She cried bitterly, *"I didn't know, I didn't know."*

And I am a part of this, he hissed to himself in the oval of a mirror, affecting the stiffness of an ancestral portrait until the image fired before his eyes with a separate life and turned him away, his fingers digging into the back of his neck, his breath halting.

But how could he have imbibed this desperate need to build a respectable world as if it were Cecile's passion for chocolates, her wild aversion to the color red? So he breathed this. It was the very air. But some flaw in him must have made him the all-too-perfect player of parts, *what was it?* He saw himself poised on that stool in the back of Jean Jacques' shop, hands immaculate, gloss and gleam like the polished tables, Queen Anne chairs on tiptoe, armoire doors inlaid with mirrors. Some flaw in him, *what was it?* He dipped his own pen to write, to make his own diary.

That he had loathed childhood from the beginning? That he had absolutely hated being a "little boy?" And bruised and confounded by those stifling limits, put himself by will upon another path? Games bored him eternally. The dullwitted repetitions of his teacher, Monsieur De Latte, made him grit his teeth. But with a monster's mind he had perceived the workings, what was wanted, and settled on a subtle subterfuge that had no use for innocence. He would be perfect out of rage, bow of his own accord to kiss the ladies' hands, scorn chatter in the back pews, and look upon humiliations from aloft, seeking eternally for reason. *That's such a good boy, that is the best boy, why that's Madame Cecile's little man, that boy.*

(88)

My little man, your little man, her little man.

He belonged to the adults, he was their darling, with un-
canny calm, and a perfect liar.

But he hadn't known it then. It had seemed so natural.
As natural as it had been to seek those long afternoons with
Anna Bella, away with the din of the boys of the street,
listening to her read from the English novels, his foot against
her coal stove, his eyes on the woven plaster wreaths of her
ceiling. She was a woman at twelve. They had played at lady
and gentleman, and with a grown woman's impeccable grace
she had understood his new passion for the cabinetmaker
and had not begrudged him the new world away from her in
the cabinetmaker's shop. She made him English tea, when
he came to call, from a china pot.

And then there was Richard who was, in fact, the gentleman and had treated Marcel like a man from the moment
they met, coming forward out of the cold-eyed pale-skinned
gathering in the new classroom at Monsieur De Latte's to
show Marcel to an empty seat, welcome him to the new school,
remark that they might walk home afterward the same way.
And Marcel, frightened to the marrow of his bones in that
new world, would never all his life forget this kindness, the
clasp of this hand which said, "We are young men, we are
brothers." Theirs was a bond that would last a lifetime.

And so the strife between them was all the more painful
now. *"Je suis un criminel!"* Marcel would stop suddenly with
a shudder as they walked in the street, gripping the backs
of his arms as though he were cold, and Richard astonished
would murmur steadily of the time of day. And with some
frantic movement like that of a bird, Marcel might bolt
through the crowded streets, crossing the Rue Canal, finding
the depot of the Carrollton Railroad and riding for hours up
the shell road through a world he had never seen, tall oaks,
the white columns of the homes of the Americans. Nothing
had been real in childhood. And things were so real now that
he could have spoken aloud to the very trees.

On the street one day, he met Anna Bella in a splendid
dress of plum taffeta, hair swept up beneath a lady's broad
brimmed bonnet. She carried a parasol that threw lace shadows on the bricks behind her. And startled to see her the
grown woman with her fine small velvet gloves, he was
speechless as she reached to take his hand. Madame Elsie,
her guardian, always a mean woman, urged her forward.

"Now wait, please, Madame Elsie," Anna Bella had said in her soft always slurred American voice, "Marcel, why don't you walk a ways with us?" But he had seen the look in the old woman's eyes, her gnarled hand pressing Anna Bella on.

Had she seen that kiss in the parlor, had she overheard those drunken tears for Jean Jacques? He had stood stock-still among the jostling passersby, to watch that small-waisted figure make its way into a crowded shop.

And calling for Anna Bella soon for evening church, he was told simply she could no longer go. He stood silent before the old woman as she adjusted the quilt over her lap, until finally, brushing her gray hair back from her temple, she said under her breath with a shrug, *"Mais non,* you are no longer children, hmmmm?"

Something was over.

But why? With some silent, almost obdurate instinct he would not question it, he would not dare to bring it to the surface of his mind, and leaving his gate each day turned sharply not to see the shuttered boarding house, not to risk a glimpse of Anna Bella at her door.

But walking back from Benediction one night alone he found himself by no accident standing before the high facade of the Salle d'Orléans, swept up at once by the music, violins raw and lovely in the cold air, so that he did what he had never done before which was to linger in this spot, turning his head slowly but boldly toward the commotion in the open doors. Carriages crowded the cobblestoned streets, and black capes glistened as they shook off the rain. Young white men, sometimes arm in arm, talked rapidly as they pushed through the candlelit vestibule, and beyond Marcel saw the bare shoulders of a dark woman on the broad stairs.

The music swung violently with a waltz, and through the high French windows above he could make out the shadows of swaying couples on the walls, women he knew to be colored, men that he knew to be white.

Overhead the stars went out behind the winter clouds and a voice beat beneath the gentle pounding of the rain, speaking to him of what he'd always known, that he would never be admitted to this place. White men only were admitted to this place, and all places like it. Though of course even now he could glimpse the colored musicians against the windows and just catch the rise and fall of the bows of their violins. But there had always been such balls, they were a tradition as old as New Orleans, why think of it? He felt the sudden shame of someone who invites misery, it was senseless. Yet it was at such an affair as this perhaps that Cecile had met Monsieur Philippe, and perhaps it was beneath this very roof that Tante Colette had approved Philippe's promises, promises that built the Ste. Marie cottage, promises that would send Marcel to Paris when he was of age. Paris, it struck him with a new searing intensity, and in a mercurial vision he saw all doors opened to him, dim places of fashion where dark men might dance with beautiful women while music this sweet cut the winter air. "What is this to me?" he all but whispered aloud. "Why, in Paris, soon enough..." But he'd been distracted from some other path, some other thought which came back to torment him now, like the press of a child's face against a windowpane.

It was Anna Bella he had been thinking of, Anna Bella who should have been with him tonight but could not be. They would have walked hand and hand through this sprinkling rain, his arm from time to time about her waist, talking softly, listening to one another. He might have shared his anguished soul and come to understand it better. And it was Anna Bella whom he saw now, above, in some vague vision of that whirling ballroom, Anna Bella with the glint of a woman's jewels, those rounded arms bare.

His pulse quickened. He turned to go. But all along he had been wondering, why not admit it, was she now destined for this—white men kissing that dimpled hand, white men whispering in that tiny ear? His mind said stop this. Shut the door. Why, after all, should you care? "Paris," he whispered as if it were a charm, "Paris, *la cité de la lumière...*" But he had lost her, lost her! In all the fine confusion of this dreadful year, she'd been snatched away, long before the pain of leaving her for the world abroad had ever come to test him. It was as if he'd turned his back, and she'd grown up. But if it was to be so, why had he not known it, why must every commonplace truth become a shock? Did this not happen around him day after day? Where had he gotten those blue eyes that stared at him morning and night in the mirror, white men, dark women! It was the alchemy of his history. But Anna Bella, he'd taken her for granted, years of childhood binding them tight, that arm about his shoulder as he wept for Jean Jacques, that blinding sweetness when at last he'd dared to kiss her. Stop this, shut the door. Yet it seemed suddenly that it was something in himself that had thrust her out of reach, as surely as Madame Elsie's malignant sneer, some mounting force within him that brought their lips together. *Mais, non, you are no longer children, hmmmm?* No. He was astonished to feel the blood flow from the palms of his hands, and lifting them suddenly in the slanting silver rain he saw that his own nails had broken the flesh. No longer children, no. But what if... what if he were not going, if foreign portals didn't await him over *wine-dark seas?* The rain pelted his palms; the blood vanished only to reappear.

And above the music surged, while the wind came in cold gusts. It was lovely music, was it not? He pressed his lips to make a thin, fine whistle, and moving on was vaguely conscious of another melody in the air, the high-pitched falsetto of a black voice near him, singing faintly, softly as he slowed his pace. And through the dark he saw the glittering eyes of the black coachman leaning against the side of the carriage. Marcel knew the tune, he knew the words, and the Creole patois in which they were sung, and he knew it was meant for him:

> *Milatraisse courri dans bal,*
> *Cocodrie po'té fanal,*
> > *Trouloulou!*
> *C'est pas zaffaire à tou,*
> *C'est pas zaffaire à tou,*
> > *Trouloulou!*

> *Yellow girl goes to the ball,*
> *Black man lights her to the hall,*
> > *Yellow man!*
> *Now, that's no affair for you,*
> *Say, that's no affair for you,*
> > *Yellow man!*

Jean Jacques had been dead three months before Marcel caught Tante Colette at the door of the dress shop at dawn.

"But her mother..."

"What is it now, Marcel? I'm busy as it is, can't you see that?" She was going through the mail. "Look at this, I paid this."

"My mother's mother, who was she?" he said in a low voice, his eye on the shop behind her. He could see the dark swish of Tante Louisa's skirts through the glass. And hear a rumbling of heavy heels.

"What's the matter with you, *cher?*" she reached for his

forehead. "You have a fever, *cher,* now don't do that." He shut his eyes, his lips tense, his head going to one side in a near imperceptible negation.

"I don't have a fever," he said softly. "Tell me, surely you must have seen her mother sometime or other...you saw so much of her father."

"Her father, *cher,* was the richest planter north of Port-au-Prince," she said, feeling his cheek. He pulled back.

Tante Louisa had called his name.

"Please, Tante Colette," he said earnestly, and in an uncommon gesture he clasped her wrist.

"Oh *cher,* what mother?" She sighed...

"Surely she had a mother!"

"I don't know, *cher,*" she shook her head, but her eyes held him steady. "It's cold out here, you come inside."

"No." He reached beyond her and pulled the door to.

"Marcel!" she said.

"Tante Louisa won't tell me," he said glancing beyond her at the glass windows, "You know she won't. And if you won't tell me I'll ask maman myself."

"Don't you do that, Marcel," she said. "I tell you since that old cabinetmaker died, you've been a handful." But as he turned to go, she caught his sleeve.

"She was one of those slave women, *cher,* I don't know who she was, a slave on that plantation. 'Course they weren't slaves by that time, oh, no, they were all free, she didn't care anything for that baby the way I remember it, God only knows where she was when we took that baby, probably run off with that black army of General Dessalines for all I know, she was nothing for you to think about, *cher,* that woman had nothing to do with you...Marcel!"

He was a pace away looking at her. His lips had formed words, but she didn't hear them, and she bit her lip as she watched him walk swiftly off, the crowd closing around him, his pale blond head glinting suddenly in a faint shaft of the winter sun.

Slave women, one of those slave women. The words refused to be made flesh:

Behind the *garçonnière,* he watched the slave women he had known all of his life gather the billowing sheets from the line, Lisette, running with arms out, letting the wooden clothespins pop in the air, while Zazu, her mother, blacker, thinner, handsome, swung the wicker basket on her agile hip.

(93)

Droplets everywhere turned the beaten earth black and a dusty scent rose on the cold air. Wandering under the bent banana fronds, listening to the tap-tap-tap and a storm in the cistern, he saw them lighting the kitchen lamps, putting the flat irons on the glowing coals. Lisette, hands on her narrow waist, came to the door to scowl at him with a lowering head. "Someone put a spell on you, Michie," she said voice deep-throated, scornful. "So you *want* pneumonia!"

It was Lisette, the copperskinned one who sometimes sulked, begged for gold earrings, and tied her yellow *tignon* in glamorous knots around her reddish hair while Zazu doted, loving to dress Cecile, to brush her long straight black tresses and wind them into soft curls. It was Lisette who whispered of voodoo, terrified Cecile with the mention of spells, and from time to time in a rage banged the kettle and vanished for a whole night, only to reappear at some odd hour the next day, her apron stiff with ruffles, hands busy with a dust rag as if nothing had happened. These women had rocked Marcel's cradle. Monsieur Philippe had brought them from *Bontemps,* his plantation, before Marcel was born.

Ah, *Bontemps,* that was the life, the picnics on the bayou and the dances, ah the dances, it was a whispered recrimination which Marcel had long ago ceased to hear. Occasionally, he said sardonically to Lisette, "And I suppose you don't enjoy your Saturday nights on the town." But when Felix the coachman came bringing Monsieur Philippe from the country, then it was party time in the back kitchen with *Bontemps* gossip, white linen on the deal table and chicken roasting in the pot. Felix in nifty black with brass buttons, said, "*Bonjour,* Michie!" with a slight sarcastic bow to Marcel and took his place at once on the stool by the door not waiting for a child to tell him he might sit down.

But on those days when Cecile with wringing hands whispered of waste and sass, or found some frightening bundle of mysterious feathers sewn into the hem of a sheet, Philippe would saunter out to them, shaking his head, rout Felix, and settling in his place draw the women near. "What's happening to my girls?" he would begin, but soon sent them, with his low whispers, into peals of confidential laughter. "Now make your daughter mind," he would turn eventually to the serious vein, his arm encircling Zazu's waist.

"I don't know what to do with that girl, Michie," she would say in her soft deep voice, a tone mellow like the expression on her stoical black face. But then he would insist,

"Be good to my Cecile."

He gave them dollar bills, declared the gumbo was better than in the country, and warned them over his shoulder at the cottage door, "Stay away from those voodooiennes!" But then he winked his eye.

Slaves.

From the corner of a narrow eye, Marcel watched the black prisoners in chains who bent their backs to shovel filth from the open ditches, winced at the snarl of the overseer, affecting a casual air, burned with shame for staring at a common spectacle he had been taught to ignore since childhood.

Was it possible he had thought suffering vulgar before this? And bondage merely degrading?

His eyes watered too easily in the cold wind, and wrapping his cravat high, he bent forward as he made his way to the City Exchange, hands numbed in his pockets.

He had a letter with him should anyone question his presence, he'd never hung about the place before, and wandered baffled through the open doors into the smoky din, gazing up at the high dome, and then from one auction block to another. Pushing his way through the rumbling crowd until he stood before the block itself, he did not know that he had clenched his teeth, and then stared astonished at the smoothness of the wood before him. For a moment he couldn't fathom it, that smoothness, that perfect gleam. He thought of all the hours that Jean Jacques' hand would rub a surface, folding and refolding the small square of cloth soaked soft with oil. Until with a sickening jolt he realized this wonder. That it was the work of bare feet. A vague nausea threatened him. He needed the outside air. But slowly he lifted his eyes to the row of bright dressed men and women beyond, blue calico, tailcoats, and dark eyes that watched him from impassive faces. A child clinging to his mother's skirts let out a wail. Marcel had frightened him with the mere intensity of his stare. He turned to go, the blood rushing in his chilled face and hands, but like a gun came the auctioneer's bark. It was ten o'clock. The day's business was beginning.

A tall freckled mulatto had stepped up before the tightening assemblage, rolling his pants above the knees and stripping the shirt from his back as he walked up and down, up and down, to show that he had no marks from the whip. "Now what am I offered for this lively boy," came the guttural English. "What am I offered for this fine healthy boy, master hates to part with him, reared from a baby, right here in the city of New Orleans, but *needs money!*" And then in rapid rhythmic bursts of French: "The master's misfortune is your good fortune, a household slave but strong as an ox, baptized right here at the St. Louis Cathedral, never missed Sunday Mass in his life, this is a fine boy, this is a good boy..."

And the boy, turning round and round on the polished block, as though completing a dance, bowed to the crowd, a smile like a spasm in his taut flesh. He bowed low and whipped the shirt up, deftly closing the first two buttons with one hand. Then his eyes moved furtively over the shifting faces, down over the rows that surrounded him, and fixed suddenly on the face more nearly like his own, looking up at him, blue eyes into blue eyes.

Marcel, motionless, lips slack, was unable to move toward the winter street.

Slaves.

He had never seen the country fields, knew nothing of the coffles trudging overland with children wailing, and had never breathed the stench of the slave ships long relegated to the distant and thriving smugglers' coves.

Passing the slave yards, he saw what he was meant to see: bright turbans, top hats, rows of men and women in idle conversation eyeing him casually as if he were on display, not they. But what went on inside the walls? Where mother was ripped from daughter, or listless old men, their grizzled sideburns stuck with bootblack, hunched to hide from the probing buyer a racking cough; or gentlemen, gesturing with walking sticks, insisted perfunctorily they must see this bright mulatto girl stripped if you please, the price was exorbitant, what if there were some hidden disease? Would you please step inside? Of these and other things, he could only guess.

What he did know was New Orleans, and all around him the city's poor—black, white, immigrant, Creole—cooks driving bargains for fowl at market, the chimney sweepers roaming door to door, carters and cabmen, dark faces blank with sleep in the shadows of the *presbytère* arches, hands limply anchoring the lap basket of spices for sale. In dim sheds nearby, black men forged the iron railings to grace the balconies that lined the Rue Bourbon or the Rue Royale, and amid showers of sparks beat with rhythmic hammers on horseshoes in the stables after dark.

And all through the back streets near his home there had always been those hundreds upon hundreds of independent slaves who hired out their services, renting a modest room with wages, only sending a sum now and then to a master they seldom saw. Waiters, masons, laundrywomen, barbers, you gave their grog shops a wide berth in the evenings, if you had to pass them at all, hardly noticing the eternal rattle of dice, the aroma of cigar smoke, high-pitched laughter. And in those same streets, here and there the softened silhouettes of scant-clad black women against lamplit doorways, beckoning languidly, then letting the curled fingers lazily drop.

It was prosperous slave men who often came, spruced and shining, to hurry with Lisette on Sundays to the Pontchartrain railroad for the ride in the starred Negro cars to the lake. And on holidays, in hired carriages, they came clattering to the gate, bright in new broadcloth waistcoats while she in her fine red dress would run to meet them, sidestepping the rain puddles in the narrow alley as if in a dance, her picnic basket rocking on her arm.

Slaves.

The papers complained of them, the world was filled with them, New Orleans sold more of them than any city in the Southland, and they had been here for two hundred years before Marcel was born.

Roaming aimlessly at a rapid pace, his eyes searched the faces that passed him, as if for some sudden illumination, some undeniable truth. "I am a part of this, I am a part..." he whispered aloud, and sat at last among the books and clutter of his darkened room, cold, but unwilling to light the fire, staring at nothing, as if the power to do the simplest things had left him.

He was afraid.

All his life he had known that he was not white, but snug in the tender advantages of his special world he had never for a moment dreamed that he was black. A great gulf separated him from the throngs on either side, but oh, how dimly he had miscalculated, misunderstood. And pushing his fingers to the roots of his hair, he gripped it, pulled it, until he could no longer stand the pain.

As winter wore on, he knew what it was to be fourteen. Richard's sister Giselle had come home with her husband from Charleston for the opera, and the family invited Marcel to go with them for the first time.

And weak with anticipation, he had been led through the brightly lit lobby of the Théâtre d'Orléans, directed to the loges *pour gens de couleur* and hurried to take the seat given him in the very front of the Lermontant box. The spectacle of his people ringing the horseshoe tier stunned him as he raised his eyes, silk flashing in the flicker of candles, white linen all but luminous in the azure gloom. Faces both light and dark glowed above the beat of feather fans, and there hung about him, as it were, a wreath of low, sonorous chatter sweet to breathe like the perfume in the air.

Richard in his white gloves was a gentleman of the world with his elbow on the arm of the chair, legs easily crossed, and Giselle wore a cluster of tiny pearls on a chain around her neck like the buds of a flower set among gold leaves. Bending forward, she raised a pair of ivory opera glasses before her eyes, the thick glossy corkscrews of her curls shivering against her pale olive throat; and the scent of camellias suddenly surrounded her like an aureole.

Marcel let out his breath slowly, resting at last against the back of the chair. Across the gulf he caught the animated face of Tante Colette and the subtle persistent wave of her gloved hand. He smiled. It had been months since he had seen her, though she had asked for him again and again. He had not seen her since that day he'd spoken to her at the door of the shop. But some sweet exhilaration warmed her distant features. She was happy to see him here. All but imperceptibly he gestured with the fingers that clung to the rail.

But at that vibrant moment when the lights went slowly dim, he found himself passing the inevitable glance across the parquet, and the white tier below, and realized with a start that he was staring down into his father's upturned gaze.

His heart stopped. All around Philippe were his white family, women with petal cheeks, young men with Philippe's long French nose and the same golden thatch of hair. Marcel could remember nothing of them afterward, only his father's eyes. He felt himself a yellow flame against the mellow backdrop of the Lermontants. And shut his eyes as the lights at last went out. Only the sudden glow of the distant tiny stage soothed the pounding of his heart.

There was a world come alive above the footlamps, of painted windows, doors, bright candles, a brilliant and ornate room. A woman with outstretched arms unwound a plaintive lilting song that caught him at once with its power. He felt the chills rise. But it was when the orchestra swelled beneath her bright soprano that the tears suddenly blurred Marcel's vision. Music rose violently and beautifully in the dreamy gloom. Diamonds winked like stars. It was too solid, too perfect ever to have been, this music. Its rich and startling rhythms were like pure gold, something mined from the earth, and burnt to send its vapor heavenward. He had only known it in flashes in the past, like glints of sun in winter windows, felt the mere promise of its spell at High Mass, or in those thin and distant ballroom violins. It was a discovery, this music, something inevitable, that might in fact devour him; he must know it forever, breathe it always, never let it get away.

Dragging his feet on the way home, he sang softly all the melodies he could remember, dreaming of Paris when he would stand with other gentlemen, on the parquet, so near to those magnificent instruments he could feel their vibrant music like the beating of a heart. He would stroll the boulevards afterward, or chat amiably of this or that brilliant new talent in glittering crowded cafés.

For days this music stayed with him, he sang it, whistled it, hummed it, until gradually one by one the phrases had slipped away.

He remembered now with a bitter bite of his lip how little he had paid attention the evening that Philippe had offered to buy Marie a small spinet, she was studying music with the Carmelites, he might enjoy a little music himself. "Monsieur, you are too generous, no, indeed, you go too far," Cecile had said so quickly, "These children, sometimes I think they have only to close their eyes and wish for things, not even to speak." The sisters had said that at school Marie showed promise, played well.

But one afternoon finding the parlor empty at the Lermontants', he approached the piano stealthily, and tried the keys. Dissonance echoed through the room, and strain as he might he could make nothing of melody, only discovering, after long effort, a few simple but priceless chords.

It was almost summer when Philippe came again, and taking Marcel aside with a gravity that frightened him, told him only he should go to a notary in the Rue Royale every month from now on to get the money for the bills. It was foolish for Cecile to have such sums in the cottage, and Marcel was old enough to take this worry from her shoulders.

They never gave him anything to sign.

And there was something all but felonious about the envelope of cash that he slipped into his breast pocket, coming

as it did from strangers. Stepping back out into the sun,
Marcel was pricked again by a revelation of what he felt he
had always known: not a scrap of paper kept the golden barge
of day-to-day life afloat. He walked on water.

V

SO IT WAS this frame of mind that brought Marcel to misery
in Monsieur De Latte's class where the four walls of the
classroom suffocated and the constant recitation of the
younger boys scratched at him like insects on the blinds.
With the crack of a ruler the old white man taught by rote,
gave back without a spark of comprehension those basics
dealt out to him some half century before, and disliking ex-
tremes, resenting questions, assigned again and again to his
older pupils the same verses, theorems, platitudes and lies.

Marcel saved his money from week to week for the sec-
ondhand booksellers, and finding old texts of Latin, philosophy, metaphysics, brought these home and set to serious
work on his own.

Trimming his lamp, and cutting himself a set of new pens,
he turned to his Greek early on these warmer evenings, only
to realize when the clock chimed ten that he had daydreamed
for an hour after struggling with a few thick meaningless
words, or had even drifted into sleep, obsessed in thin dreams
with some simple phrase that Jean Jacques had spoken or
that disturbing image of the African head, its slits for eyes,
gleaming by the firelight in some slave cabin in the land that
was drenched with blood.

And turning to Thomas Aquinas, he would soon nod over
the pages. *The Divine Comedy* confused him, the jests of
Shakespeare's clowns were unfathomable, and the couplets
of Longinus stiff and without life.

But day after day he struggled in this manner. And week
after week. While the afternoons found him drawing pictures
idly in the Place d'Armes, the quick scratching of his charcoal
pencil somehow soothing to the driving misery inside of him,
or wandering along the levee bewitched as it were by the
vision of black children and white children in the lapping
brown water, dancing with thin legs atop a dipping, turning
log.

But at last he came upon an inescapable truth about the

shape and limits of his own mind, and he was seized with an awful despair. He could learn the rudiments of anything if he chose, but he could not progress. He needed teaching, guidance, the blazing flash of another intellect to stir the chilled waters of his own thoughts. *He was incapable of learning on his own.*

And if ever there was a time when he longed for Anna Bella, when he needed her, it was now. But this, in his private cataclysmic world was fast becoming an old pain. He was burying it deep within the recesses of his soul. While she, with her head bowed and a cautious hand on her lovely summer bonnet, never passed his gate without the old woman, Madame Elsie, clinging to her arm. He pretended he had not seen, and pretending, soon did not see her at all.

Late on still nights, when the cottages of the Rue Ste. Anne lay dark under the cloudy sky, he would emerge on the gallery outside his room and gaze beyond the rooftops at the distant rosy glow that hovered over the gaslit streets, listening for the subtle faraway sounds so often lost at midevening, the rumble of carriages, the fleeting melody of violins. It was Paris that he saw beyond the dark whispering trees, Paris of the *Quartier Latin,* the Sorbonne, the endless corridors of the Louvre. It was the Paris of Christophe Mercier. The years that lay between him and his dreams seemed endless and dreary, and his heart ached as he clung to the wooden railings feeling the comfortless river breeze. Oh, the wasted hours, the wasted days. He did not know what his life was supposed to be! And thinking of the white planters' sons who at this moment sent the billiard balls rolling in the casinos of the Rue Bourbon or rushed up the stairs of the ballroom in the Rue Orleans, he wondered what vast stores of knowledge lined the walls of their palatial homes from which their tutors must have plucked books like flowers, rolling the Latin phrases on their tongues, explaining at breakfast this marvelous philosophical point, that stunning historical conclusion.

Oh, if he had only known the truth! Of all Philippe's children he was the only one who had even the pretense of an education, but comparisons were not the point.

He burned to be a part of the Great World, where empires fell, and poetry rang from the great stages; to argue in cafés the way to paint the human form, and stand breathless in the presence of the monuments of the masters. But it was not the surface that fascinated him. He had seen to the heart of things; a door had cracked on an endless vista, a door that now threatened to swing shut on him forever.

He could not, would not presume, to ask Philippe if he might make the voyage early. These things had been agreed to the year before he was born. A gentleman's tour when he was eighteen, the Sorbonne if he should so desire, an income naturally, letters and introduction might even be arranged ... Tante Colette had seen to that, she would say with Cecile's approving nod. But God, if it could only be now!

VI

SO A YEAR had passed since Jean Jacques' death, a year since life had been unalterably changed for Marcel.

And now in one day, all the bleak and terrifying confusion of that year had come to its mystifying climax. Marcel had been expelled once and for all from Monsieur De Latte's class, he had ravaged the exquisite and helpless Juliet Mercier, and he had lost her famous son, Christophe, forever. He had lost Christophe just as as he had lost Jean Jacques. And as he stood in the shadowy bedroom of the *garçonnière*, peering down through the blinds at the courtyard below, it was grief that Marcel felt, and it was harrowing.

The clock in the cottage chimed eleven times, and the lamps went out. A small hand pushed the shutters back from Cecile's window and the breeze stirred the lace curtains of her darkened room.

Marcel waited for the faint flicker of her night lamp, and then silently he opened his door.

A splendid and terrible vision was taking hold of him, and for the moment his agony was finding a direction in a perverse and beautiful plan. In all this time, he had never approached Jean Jacques' narrow raised crypt in the St. Louis, never ventured down that weed-choked walkway to actually touch the engraved letters he knew to be there.

And in all this time he had never crept out at night from this room. Well, he was to do both now. He would slip out down the steps through the alleyway and along the deserted Rue Ste. Anne across the Rue Rampart all the way to the St. Louis Cemetery, and there scale the short thick wall, find Jean Jacques' tomb and pour out his soul. Alone in the dark he would tell Jean Jacques what had happened to him today, how he had lost Christophe, and how he had loved Christophe as he had loved Jean Jacques, and that he had lost them both. His pain was already soothed by the boldness of this vision, the obvious tortures ahead of him, the dark near-moonless night, and his own natural fears.

And who knows what he would do afterwards, ruined as he was with his mother and his friends, and slated for an hour of reckoning with the famous man? Perhaps he would find one of his favorite filthy little cabarets. So delicious on his truant afternoons, what would they be at night, those haunts full of Irish cutthroats and runaway slaves? He had two dollars in his pocket. He would get drunk. He would smoke cigars.

Quickly, he padded down the wooden steps, bracing himself for the inevitable creaking, and moved gracefully, his shoulders bent forward, into the courtyard. A twig crackled beneath his boot and he froze, eyes fixed on his mother's windows. But all was still. However, just as he darted toward the mouth of the alley, the great ancient fig that hung above the side fence stirred, its leaves rustling all at once so that he spun around.

For an instant it seemed a shape loomed from the dark, some concealed figure that moved among the immense limbs only a pace from where he stood. But by the dim quarter moon, Marcel could see merely a thousand menacing configurations, and drawing up, he clenched his teeth. If you are so damned frightened in your own backyard, how in the name of God will you ever scale that cemetery wall! And turning, he ran.

He was sprinting when he hit the street and seeing ahead a broken and broadly spaced path of dimly lit windows, followed the old brick banquette that he knew so well by day that it would not fail him now in the dark.

Only when he had crossed the Rue Rampart, did he slow his pace. His throat was burning, but for the first time since he had left Juliet, he was not utterly miserable. And the fear subsided. Then he saw ahead the faint chalk white of the cemetery walls.

He stopped. A score of subtle sounds replaced the dull tromping of his own feet. The sidewalks were gunwales now, rotting here and there from the constant rain, and creaked even as he stood still, but he heard steps somewhere, and beyond, far off, the clanking of a bell. He turned around. But there was nothing in the dark behind him except the faintest gleam of the slanting roofs, the dim outline of a massive oak. All right, coward! He spun round again and ran full speed, feet splashing through the open gutter until he could lay his hands right on the rough whitewashed wall.

He was panting and for the moment could only rest there. A cloud was over the moon and must surely move as all clouds do on the wind from the river, but he couldn't wait for this, he had to go on, to remember how he had done such things as this when he was ten years old, or better yet, forget. Just do it, don't try to think how. He backed up, utterly terrified suddenly of the dark and the graves and the night and the dead and of everything that had ever terrified him, and running at the wall, leapt up to catch an inside edge, his arms across the top of the soft moldering bricks. He shut his eyes, breathed heavily, and hung tight. Then with all his strength he brought himself up on his arms, swinging his legs up behind him so that he was lying out straight. And letting out an awful moan for what he was about to do, he crawled over the broad width of the vaults lining the wall and let himself drop into the cemetery below.

"Mon Dieu, Mon Dieu!" he shivered, his hands trembling over his eyes, the sweat pouring down the sides of his face. His chest heaved, and his legs felt weak and light as if they might give way. But then a splendid exhilaration came over him. He was inside, he had done it, he was alone in this place, alone with Jean Jacques, and with himself. And turning slowly he opened his eyes. The shapes around him appeared gradually. But all of a sudden he heard sounds in the dark, a chorus of rustling, scuffling noises at once above him and beside him that caused his heart to rise in his throat. The dim white crypts gleamed dully before his eyes, and then he drew back, his breath a gasp. Some amorphous shape loomed above him, something rose and moved against the distant sky.

No conscious will need tell him to turn, no intelligence that he must escape. He pivoted, his boots sinking into the marsh of high weeds, and he ran. But with a thick crashing, the thing behind him hit the sloshing path; and with a cry, Marcel felt hands clutch his arm. "O God!" he whispered, his teeth biting down into his lower lip to draw blood.

"What in *hell*," said the voice low behind him, all but a whisper, "what in *hell* are you doing?"

Marcel went weak, his breath a series of gasps. It was a wonderful sound, that sound, of some human adult voice at wits' ends with him as usual, nothing else! And the voice, didn't he know the voice? "Oooo God!" he whispered again as the tremor passed through his arms and his legs. His arms ached under the tight hands that held him, and slowly, lifting his boot out of the mire he turned round.

"Why did you run from me? And why in *hell* did you jump over this wall?" It was Christophe, of course.

"Run from you??" Marcel's voice was a pant, a whisper. "Run?"

"You saw me in the tree!" The voice was exasperated. Marcel could see nothing of the face, except a tiny spark of light in the eyes.

"O *Mon Dieu*..." Marcel sighed. The pain in his chest was excruciating and every breath seemed to aggravate it, not alleviate it. "But you were in the tree?"

"I was waiting for your mother to retire. I wanted to talk to you! There was a light in your room," he said.

"In the tree?" Marcel repeated weakly.

"Well, where else? Did you expect me to sit on the wet ground? I was sitting in the tree. You mean you didn't see me? You looked right at me!"

"No," Marcel shook his head.

"Then why the hell did you run?"

Marcel put his hand up as if to ask for mercy. He groped in his pocket for his handkerchief and wiped the sweat from his face.

"My mother told me you were quite the burning cauldron of youthful passion but this is beyond belief. What are you planning to do here, for God sakes?" Christophe had let go of him, and was looking about. He looked up at the wall of crypts, and then around at the faint whiteness of the high peristyled tombs clustered about them like so many small houses. He reached out suddenly to the dull gleam of a stone door. Marcel, breathing heavily, watched the hand moving down the stone, touching the shadowy indentations of the carved script. He looked into Christophe's eyes, but he could see nothing there, he could see only the outlines of the partially turned face, and oddly enough the sparkle of his eyelashes against the remote backdrop of gray clouds.

"Ah, Monsieur," he sighed, his voice weakened still and very low, "I have nothing but the utmost respect for your mother, she is a great lady, I have only profound respect for her, for your house, this is the bitterest of misunderstandings, you mustn't consider me a base intruder in your house, I swear on my honor, I have known your mother all of my life, grown up in her shadow and have always considered her a great lady, I would throw myself at your feet if that would cause you to believe me..."

"Oh, do!" Christophe said flatly. "Throw yourself at my feet." He laughed shortly. And lifting his boot he brought it down with an ugly splash.

Marcel said quickly, "You have no compassion, Monsieur," before he could stop himself. It was precisely the sort of thing he would have said to Richard if Richard had been making fun of him. "I am at your mercy, but I am not a buffoon."

Christophe dissolved into soft laughter, but then he said in a cold inflectionless voice, "Don't be so damned quick to come to the point. Now, is there an easier way of getting out of this city of the dead? A gate somewhere without a guard at it? I've ripped my pants as it is."

"There's a guard, to be sure, and he might summon the police," Marcel said.

"Well, if it's all the same to you, *mon ami,* I am going to try to bribe him, and get out of here now. Would you care to come with me and continue this conversation, or do you prefer to go on with whatever madness prompted you to come here in the first place?" He waited.

"I'll go with you," Marcel said timidly.

"Ah, what a refreshing display of common sense," Christophe answered. The gatekeeper's lantern had already appeared at the end of the path.

It was midnight when they drew near the waterfront and the roaring cabarets stood open along the banquette, the crowds dense around the long bars, air thick with smoke. Pianos tinkled in the din, and the shades of the flickering oil lamps were black with soot. White men and black men stood jostling on the stoops, gesturing, shouting, or gathered on the damp bricks in the leaking light of the doorways, squatted on their haunches over games of dice or coins flipped in the air. An impromptu cockfight was in progress a pace from the markets, and suddenly the knot of men there let out a roar.

"I want a drink," Christophe said at once. He had made the same remark on leaving the cemetery and had not spoken again until now. Marcel's eyes were wide. He had seen these streets often enough by day when they were just as heavily thronged, but the night gave them a savage aspect which he instantly and absolutely loved.

He was powerfully excited by Christophe as well as by everything around him, and in the dingy light he saw Christophe's face clearly for the first time. It appeared as hard as it had seemed in the shadows of Juliet's room, but it was by no means a cruel or insensitive face, in fact, the neat even features had a somewhat agreeable aspect, there was nothing out of proportion, yet the eyes blazed as if they must make up in intensity for their rather common color and size. They were curious, however, though suspicious, wide though a little flinty, and something about the straight mouth with its faint bit of horizontal mustache suggested anger, though why Marcel could not have said.

He wasn't so afraid of Christophe now; rather he was utterly absorbed. And studied everything about him. There was something defiant about his walk, the ramrod straightness of his back and the manner in which the compact chest was thrust forward. It reminded Marcel more of the Spaniards he had seen than any Frenchman. It was almost arrogant. Yet Christophe seemed little conscious of the finely cut brown coat and lavish silk stock he wore, or the great streaks of whitewash and dirt on his dove-gray pants. His eyes lingered on no one and nothing with any particular judgment or challenge, and he had a somewhat selfless interest in all about him which attracted Marcel to him rather easily. He was darker than Juliet, could never have passed, rumor was wrong.

"There," Marcel said suddenly, "Madame Lelaud's." He realized that he was burning with thirst. He could all but taste the beer already.

Christophe hesitated. The double doors were wide over the banquette, and the place was packed. They could hear the crack of the billiard balls over the low strumming of a banjo, and the vibrations of the piano within.

"This is not a place for white men?" Christophe asked in a low voice. An undefinable emotion flickered in his eye.

"There are men of color in there, too," Marcel said and offered to lead the way.

Madame Lelaud herself was at the bar, a brilliant red *tignon* around her dark hair so that with the wide gold loops in her ears she looked somewhat the gypsy. Her black hair in tight waves fell to thin wisps over her shoulders and she had soft caramel skin finely wrinkled. "Aah, *mon petit,*" she waved to Marcel. The air about them was rife with foreign voices, Irish brogues, the guttural Dutch, the softer rapid

Italian, and everywhere the Creole patois. Negroes in black broadcloth and top hats drank at the bar, foot upon the rail, and beyond in the open billiard parlor congregated about the luscious soft green felt were a handful of splendidly dressed dark men, their striped coats and vests of silk gleaming beneath the low-hung lamps. Dark faces everywhere mingled with the white, and might have been Greek, Hindu, Spanish.

Madame Lelaud had come around the end of the bar and moved toward them with a gentle sway of her red skirts, her white apron streaked and soiled though she placed a hand on her hip as if smartly dressed and reached for Marcel's hair. *"Mon petit,"* she said again. "You want a quiet table, hmmmmm?"

Christophe was smiling at him coldly, one eyebrow slightly raised. "Just how old *are* you?" he asked.

A long row of small tables lined the rear wall where a door lay open to the yard allowing a weak but welcome breeze. Men played cards here and there around them, and at the front doors a great shouting commenced all at once, a stomping on the bare cypress boards, as a brilliantly colored rooster, flapping and squawking helplessly, was thrust for an instant over the heads of the crowd. Near the door of the billiard room an old black man played the spinet while a tall and very tired quadroon woman rested her weight against it, a glass of amber-colored whiskey clutched in her heavily jeweled hand. Her clothes were tawdry, her eyes half-closed. These people appeared and disappeared as the assemblage parted and came together in front of them, and a steady stream of men trooped to the rear stairs, their boots clomping heavily as they went up.

"Well?" Christophe said, settling back against the wall, his arm on the table. He surveyed the place and seemed to like it. Marcel had been on tenterhooks. He wondered if Christophe had already ventured into the Rue Chartres or the Rue Royale and seen the dozens of places of fashion where no one of color would have been served. "How old are you?" His face was somewhat gentler now.

"Fourteen, Monsieur," Marcel murmured.

"Say that again," Christophe leaned forward.

"Fourteen!" Marcel confessed. Now Christophe would know what a degenerate he was, and wonder naturally enough what would such a boy be doing at sixteen, and eighteen, and twenty.

"I'm to go to Paris, Monsieur," he blurted suddenly looking

up into the cold yellow-brown eyes. "For my education when I'm of age. I'll be sent to the Sorbonne."

"Splendid," Christophe said with a rise of the eyebrows. He had drunk half of his beer in one swallow and already gestured for another round.

Marcel realized with a sudden lightness in the head that he had not eaten all day. He drained his glass.

"And in the meantime, you want to go to my school?"

Courage, Marcel thought. "Yes, Monsieur, I want that more than anything in this world. I can't tell you what this means to me, to attend your school, I only learned of it this morning from a little article in the Paris papers, of course everyone will know about it by tomorrow, the news will be everywhere, you can pick and choose your pupils..." he stopped.

A shadow had fallen over Christophe's face.

"They really do know of me here, then?" he asked.

"Monsieur, you're as famous here as you are in Paris. Well, not that famous perhaps, but *very famous*." Marcel was amazed. And that this did not seem to please Christophe amazed him further.

Christophe let out a long sigh. He let his eyes move over the throng at the bar as he drew a very narrow brown cigar out of his inside pocket and biting off the end of it spat it easily on the floor. He struck a match on the sole of his boot.

Madame Lelaud set two foaming mugs before them as Christophe was doing this and with a corner of her apron took a symbolic wipe at the wet table. "What's the matter with you, *mon petite?*" she drawled, her hand going out for Marcel's hair. He moved slightly to one side but gave her a strained smile. "What, no pictures?" she asked. "Where are all your pictures?" Marcel was mortified, especially when Christophe asked,

"What pictures are you talking about?" And when he did it, there was a slight sparkle in his eye, just the trace of a smile for Madame Lelaud. She turned, appearing to notice Christophe for the first time.

"This one is an artist," she said drawing nearer so that her skirts brushed Christophe's knee. "Sits here every afternoon and draws everything in the bar, little people who look like ducks, but you, I haven't seen you before, what's your name?"

"Every afternoon?" Christophe said, eyeing Marcel with mock suspicion.

"You don't want to tell me your name?"

"Melmoth," he said to her, "they call me the wanderer. Every afternoon," he turned again to Marcel, "then you're not in school now at all?"

Marcel shook his head. Madame Lelaud had been distracted, drawn away, letting her skirts dust quickly over Christophe's leg. He looked after her but only for an instant.

"Monsieur," Marcel went on rapidly, "If you know how we admire you, we've read your essays, your novel..."

"Oh, you have my condolences, I can't say I've shared your suffering," Christophe laughed. "It's much easier to write those things than to read them. But what sort of pictures do you draw?"

"They're dreadful," Marcel said at once. "The people look like little ducks..." he was ashamed of his pictures and showed them to no one except for those few more perfect sketches he had placed on his bedroom wall, and in those he'd cheated, with tracing paper and all manner of tricks. What he drew in the bar was so childish it humiliated him, and he had only allowed Madame Lelaud to see it because Madame Lelaud's was a secret world of his, where no one knew to look for him, and he was dreadfully confused now, wondering why in the hell he'd brought Christophe here. But it was the best drinking place for men of color of which he knew.

"Monsieur when the news makes the rounds, I mean about the school, you'll have more students than you can ever accept," Marcel said. "It was our dream you would someday come home. But a school, we never so much as thought of that..."

Christophe made a short ironic sound. He put the beer to his lips for a deep swallow. His long narrow cigar had a sweet aroma.

"I feel stupid trying to put all this into words," Marcel said.

"You do well enough," Christophe said. "But why aren't you in some sort of school now? Are things so bad here that there are no schools for you at all?"

"Oh, no, Monsieur, there's a number," and quickly Marcel told him of those he knew, all private academies like that of Monsieur De Latte, some taught by white men, some by men of color, some very much sought after and expensive, others not so. It was the fashion to seek Monsieur De Latte among those that Marcel knew, all his friends attended Monsieur De Latte's, Monsieur De Latte was...well, an old man.

"Monsieur, you'll be turning people away," Marcel said finally. "If you would only give me a chance."

"But why?" Christophe asked, and his eyes were hard again though the voice was sincere. "Why in particular my school? Because I'm famous? Because I wrote a novel, and got my name in the fashionable journals? What do you think will happen in my classroom, alchemy? That you'll be swept up into some eternal after-theater crowd where the glasses are clicking and the wit is rippling and the actors and actresses never take off their paint?" He bent forward, "What do you want to learn from me there? Your name is Marcel, isn't it? What do you want to learn, Marcel?"

Marcel's face was suddenly a knot. He did not see the smile on Christophe's lips.

"Hmmm!" Marcel began finally, "You have accomplished things of which most men dream, Monsieur. Your words have been printed, they've been read by thousands. I would think that would make for a different...a different point of view." He looked up. "My teacher, Monsieur De Latte, the man who was my teacher...he handles books as if they were dead! Yes, dead." He looked into Christophe's eyes, saying this last word with a slight grimace. He could see perfectly what he wanted to say, and felt miserable that he couldn't express it. Finally he decided to be true to the image that was in his mind. "My teacher believes in those books only because they occupy space, I mean he can hold them in his hand. And they are solid enough that when thrown against the wall they make a...a clonk!" He shrugged. "I want to know what's inside of them, the way...what they actually mean. We forget all the time, I think, that things are made, that this table was made by someone for instance, with hammer and nails, and that what's in books was made by someone, someone flesh and blood like ourselves wrote those lines, they were alive, they might have gone this way or that with a different word." He stopped, bitterly disappointed in himself, and thought, This man is going to think me a fool. "I think, Monsieur, people forget this, and all that's in books, it's something dead to them, something to be acquired. I want to understand it, I want to...to find some key."

Christophe's lips were on the verge of a smile.

"You're very clever for your age, Marcel, you understand

something about the material and the spiritual which others often never come to understand, no matter how long they live or where they go."

"That's it, the spiritual and the material," Marcel said, more intent on the idea than the compliment which Christophe had just paid him. "I have this feeling of late that all things are alive. I believed at one time that furniture was just furniture, objects that we used, and thought nothing more about it, as a matter of fact I loathed furniture and people who spoke about it with all manner of allusions to the price..."

Christophe's eyes were wide.

"...until I watched a man make it and I learned that the curve of the leg of the chair can be a spiritual thing."

Marcel had never spoken these words to himself before, they had just taken shape from all the chaos and pain in his mind. And they gave a beautiful order to his thoughts suddenly so that he sat back lost for a moment in the vision of Jean Jacques at work in his shop, balancing the gold leaf on the tips of the brush. "But there is some point where the spiritual act creates a material object and that object gets away from it and is merely material again for those around it. It does not continue to be spiritual...chairs, tables, books, what's inside books. But if ever there was something that is obviously supposed to remain spiritual it's the contents of books. Chairs could fool the best of us, I suppose. We take them for granted. But the contents of the books...it's by its very nature spiritual, poetry, philosophy, etc...." He lifted his full glass of beer and suddenly drank it completely down.

"Wait," Christophe said, "you're going to get drunk."

"Oh, no, no, I can hold much more than this," he said. He felt reckless and wonderful. He gestured for Madame Lelaud.

"Some disciplinarian this Monsieur De Latte must be, do you report back to him after your afternoons here on how much you can hold? Maybe he sends you here to draw pictures?"

"Oooh!" Marcel put his hands to his head. "There's something more I have to tell you. A lie right now would be a spiritual disaster. I have never spoken to anyone of all these things, my head is bursting. I was expelled from school, I was thrown out. So I have a bad record, a bad reputation, Monsieur De Latte will say terrible things about me if you ask him, or worse yet write a letter calling me names. These things came about because I couldn't endure being there any longer, listening to those endless recitations…I *know* the multiplication tables, I *know* the names of the states and their capitals, I *know* the basic theorems of Euclid, I *know* the Seven Acts of Mercy, the Seven Deadly Sins, the Twelve Gifts of the Holy Ghost, the Six Precepts of the Church, 'early to bed, early to rise, makes a man healthy, wealthy and wise,' 'We the people of the United States in order to form a more perfect government,' 'All Gaul is divided into three parts,'…'I came, I saw, I conquered.'"

"So he kicked you out, did he?" Christophe laughed. "The man's a fool, obviuusly, how could I possibly believe a word that he might say?"

Madame Lelaud had brought their mugs. "Next time, *cher,* you draw my picture," she said as she moved away.

"Of course," Marcel said. "Madame Duck, and Monsieur Duck, and all the little Ducks!" He reached for the beer. "I'm in disgrace, Monsieur. But if you give me a new start…"

"Start by not drinking that down in one gulp," Christophe said gently, extending his hand above the glass. Marcel nodded.

"This is the greatest night of my life," he whispered.

"And you read my novel," Christophe mused, "and you admire me…"

"Monsieur, I lived *Nuits de Charlotte!* I was Antonio with Charlotte in my arms! When Randolph killed Charlotte, it was the death of innocence, I wanted to destroy him with my bare hands!…"

"Calm yourself," Christophe smiled. "I was the one who killed Charlotte, and I should have killed Randolph and Antonio too."

"Are you mocking me, Monsieur?"

"No," Christophe shook his head. There was something sad in his laugh, but something whimsical. "And when were you expelled, may I ask?"

"I'll never miss a day of class, Monsieur, I will be a changed person," he said. He lifted the glass carefully so as not to spill the slipping foam and barely tasted it. Then he took a deeper drink. "A changed person," he murmured again.

Christophe was studying him. His arms were folded on the table and he looked directly at Marcel. "I don't care about that, Marcel," he said. "If you care so little for what happens in my classroom that you absent yourself, that's your affair. I won't be teaching little boys, I won't be training or disciplining anyone. I'll teach the older boys, the ones who can appreciate

(113)

it. And if what you say is true about there being so many students, it sounds as if I'll have it the way I want it. They aren't all as spirited as you are, though, are they?" he smiled.

"You mock me, Monsieur, for certain."

"You are drunk, and you have to go home."

"Oh, no, I don't want to go home. My mother is sound asleep, besides, nothing wakes her in the night..." he stopped. The first lie. She was always waking in the night. "But my door is locked, she'll think that I'm inside." Had he remembered to lock it, he wasn't sure. *"Je suis un criminel,"* he murmured.

"There's something I want to take up with you first, and then I'll walk you to the end of the block and you're to go home. But this first, the matter of what happened in my house this afternoon."

Marcel drew in his breath. His expression changed like that of a soldier being called to attention, and through the dreamy exhilaration induced by the beer, he felt quite clear-headed suddenly and miserable.

"Monsieur, I have only the most profound respect..." he began. He was vaguely conscious of putting his hand over his heart. He saw her again, beautiful, asleep against her pillows and he shut his eyes. He had the overwhelming physical sense of that soft flesh right where her arm pressed against her breast. The room moved.

"Yes, I remember that," Christophe said. "But are you a gentleman?" the voice was harsh. Marcel looked up again to see Christophe's face somewhat hard as it had been before. "Well?"

"Ma foi, I mean to be always!" Marcel said. "I'll never darken your door again, I swear it."

"That's not my meaning. Shall I make it clear?"

"Yes?"

"If I ever hear one word spoken by you, or by anyone...about what passed beneath my roof this afternoon, I will know that you are no gentleman. And I'll break your neck."

"On my honor, Monsieur, I swear."

"Good. Because I mean what I say. And if you mean what you say then we can both look forward to the school. Now come on, your mother's likely to send for the police if she finds you're gone. Get up, get up! You're going home."

Marcel nodded submissively. "You don't despise me," he whispered, as he all but fell off the stoop into the cooler air of the street. He found himself gazing up at the women on the overhanging porches, dark shapes against the dimly lit windows beyond. A thinning but still spirited crowd moved on the banquettes under a silent and faintly fragrant rain. Marcel extended the open palm of his hand to feel the droplets.

"Now do I need to walk with you?" Christophe asked. He drew on his delicate cigar. It was clear he did not wish to leave.

"Oh, no," Marcel said, cocking his head, "I'm quite myself. When shall I come?"

"It will be a while, I have to fix the house, you know what state my house is in, it's about to collapse, but in a few days I can give you some studying to do on your own. Tell your mother, if you wish, that I've accepted you, that is, if it will help with your disgrace. I'll be advertising the school. Now go on, it's raining on top of everything else, I want to see you off."

Marcel moved swiftly away. There was a small tavern at the end of the next block, a tarnished light in the darkness. He moved toward that light, and then turned to see if Christophe was still there. Christophe stood on the brick banquette before the cabaret and with his arms folded appeared to be looking at the sky, or perhaps at the windows of the bordellos across the way. He dropped the butt of the cigar and ground it into the brick with his boot. And without looking after Marcel, he went back into Madame Lelaud's. Marcel meantime pushed his way into the tavern, jostled on all sides by the massive shoulders of the workingmen and getting his elbows onto the bar and his boot onto the slippery rail, managed to down three mugs of beer in rapid succession. Now certain he could feel no pain he plowed through the dark muddy streets toward home.

Cecile sat in his room, clutching a blue satin wrapper about her, and cried bitterly as he fell headlong onto the bed. "I'm too tired, Maman," he said, as his eyes closed. For a little while he knew she was still there, walking back and forth. He could hear her choked and angry sobs. But then he was gone.

PART THREE

I

AT TWELVE NOON a mild breeze from the river carried the ringing of the Angelus over the rooftops so that Marie on the settee in the parlor of the cottage put down her needle and thread, and shutting her eyes, began the prayers to herself without the movement of her lips. Her long straight black hair was parted simply in the middle, unbraided, undone; and casually, without thinking of it, she ran her hand beneath its silky weight and shook it loose over her shoulders. It descended like a veil on either side of her face.

She did not feel well, and invested the prayers with her full concentration, her mind for the moment cleared of all that tortured her, her face devoid of expression. She had slept miserably the night before, a prey to thin dreams of Marcel's troubles, and she had heard her mother crying in the night. At dawn she had been awakened to be sent on a peculiar errand to Monsieur Jacquemine, her father's notary, in the Rue Royale, an errand which violently confused her, and coming home had had the misfortune to meet Richard Lermontant in the street and cry in his presence, and even now, some hours later, she was still on the verge of tears.

In addition, the Rue Ste. Anne was in an uncommon commotion. Juliet Mercier's son, Christophe, the famous Paris writer, had returned the night before, and this morning he and his mother had been quarreling so fiercely that glass was broken, screams erupted from the townhouse, and finally

(116)

the famous man himself, his shirt open at the throat and tie streaming, had run into the street shouting with a clenched fist at his mother over the garden wall, while she with wild witch's hair banged shut the blinds of a high window with such force that they broke, clattering down to the flags below.

A crowd had gathered, neighbors hovered at their gates, and Mercier at last stomped off, but only after demanding of one and all where a man might order a decent meal with something to drink without being thrown out of the establishment for being a nigger. Trunks lay helter-skelter on the corner for thieves to steal, and five different women had come to the cottage to relate to Cecile these amazing details.

Marie showed no interest in this matter, but merely continued to make small embroidery stitches in a scarf as though she liked this kind of work when in fact she loathed it. Far from distracting her from her fears for Marcel, this confusion in the street seemed rather some absurd amplification of what was in her mind. She stopped occasionally, taking deep silent breaths, and stretched her long fingers out against the muslin of her skirt.

Cecile, muttering disdain for such disturbances, and pacing as she had since morning, at last took up her parasol and on the pretext of an errand went out, obviously to see some of the spectacle for herself.

Of course Marie knew who Christophe Mercier was.

She had seen his *Nuits de Charlotte* on her brother's desk, and one evening Marcel had come bounding down the steps of the *garçonnière* with a freshly done ink sketch of the man which he turned over and held up to the shade of her lamp, demanding to know if she could detect in it the slightest disproportion. Impressed with his skill, she confessed she saw none, and gave him quickly from her armoire an empty oval frame with glass intact that he accepted at once as if it were a jewel. Dazed for the moment by her brother's passion she had thought little of the subject of the portrait at all.

Until on long slow nights this summer, she had overheard that name again and again as Richard and Marcel, lingering after supper, spoke of his wild Parisian life, often forgetting that she was near. Richard's voice was a deep rumble at such times, and lounging with legs outstretched, his large heavy fingers gesturing against the lamp, he cast a man's shadow, and now and then filled the small rooms of the cottage with a man's laughter. Of all the young boys she knew, brothers and cousins of friends, or the few companions Marcel brought home, Richard alone had stirred in Marie some new and painful fascination.

She had always been fond of him, and had always known that Marcel loved him. And loving Marcel as she did, she could not help but see Richard bathed in a flattering light. But there was more to it than that, he had become a presence to her, something baffling in its intensity, and on dreary afternoons when she was dull and tense from the silence of the cottage and her mother's unspoken irritations, she found herself more and more often wondering if Richard would not come by. She listened for his voice at the door, for the sound of his foot on the path.

Quite recently, after the death of a mother of a friend, she had seen him presiding with his father at the wake when he had not known that she was there, a man among the mourners, attending to all manner of details with an adult's ease and something gentle and reverent that struck in her a resonating chord. Later on the steps of that house, his father had taken her hands, called her Mademoiselle, and expressed his affection for Marcel. She with downcast eyes had felt a sudden anguish, a desperation as if something utterly precious, something more than she had ever wanted in her life before, might be torn from her for reasons she could not know. In the night she would awake with a start to her empty room, the tiny porcelain light flickering on the tester, and find that she had been thinking of Richard, not dreaming of him, merely thinking of him, in her sleep.

So hanging on his words on balmy evenings, when the candles burned low, and the smell of strong coffee rose deliciously from the steaming pot, she had learned something of Monsieur Christophe Mercier without ever meaning to learn it—that he was a famous novelist and a writer of pamphlets about the arts, that the boys idolized him and lived for the day that he might come home.

Well, he was home and quarreling in the street. And it was no wonder. His mother, Juliet, was as terrifying as a voodooienne, and it seemed to Marie, something evil lurked in the long and ruined house at the corner. The silhouette of that reclusive woman moving from one dim window to another was repellent, like the slime that oozed from the crevices of her walls.

Could it be that the famous Christophe, having been gone so long, had failed upon coming home to realize what everyone knew full well, that the woman was mad? It was tragic if he did not know.

But it was remote. Marie thought of Marcel who by noon had still not come down from the *garçonnière,* and when the closeness of the parlor became too much for her, or the sewing had put her teeth intolerably on edge, she put it aside and wandered to the back of the cottage to look up at the shuttered window of her brother's room.

It was all the same.

Sun glared in puddles from a morning rain that had cooled nothing, and the fronds of the banana trees hung listlessly against the plastered walls. Behind drawn blinds, Lisette and Zazu dozed while the pots simmered in the open hearth, and above Marcel's room on the great thatch of blue Morning Glory that dipped its tendrils to his door, a swarm of insects gave off the only sound, a murmur that seemed the murmur of the heat itself.

Still as a statue, her hands loosely clasped before her skirt, Marie looked at these things, wanting to wake Marcel but never dreaming of actually doing it, afraid as she was of the scene that might inevitably follow, when he learned how things stood.

Early that morning, Cecile had dictated a note to Marie for the notary, Monsieur Jacquemine, demanding that he attempt to reach Monsieur Philippe at once on urgent business. Cecile's face was drawn, and though primly dressed, her hair was yet undone and disheveled and there was a slight puffiness beneath her eyes. She had paced, summoning up her words with effort, and at last concluded, "It is a matter concerning Marcel Ste. Marie who has been expelled from school and behaves badly." Marie was appalled. For an instant she had stopped, bent over the *secrétaire* so that her mother could not see this, and when she went on the writing was uneven, a word misspelled. Of course she had known Marcel was expelled, she had learned it the night before, but what shocked her and to some extent even for the moment revolted her was that her mother would report this to Monsieur Philippe.

"Take that to his office, go!" Cecile had said, and her back to Marie, she moved into the dark bedroom where the blinds had been drawn against the heat. Marie had turned slowly and looked at her mother, at the hunched shoulders, at the flared and flounced muslin skirts.

It was then that Cecile had spun round and flashing a similar virulence to that she had shown the evening before in Richard's presence, hissed at her daughter, "Go, do you hear me, go!" Her teeth were clenched and she had made of her hands two small trembling fists.

A peculiar sensation passed through Marie then. She felt chills. They moved over her arms, up her back, and up the back of her neck. And looking up, she met her mother's eyes for the first time since Richard had blundered out of the cottage the night before. There was a subtle alteration in Cecile's expression, no more than a flicker, and hastily she turned her back again.

Marie watched her calmly, watched her lift the soft mass of her skirts and blend with the shadows, leaving behind her in the air only the sound of her hasty halting breath, the sudden gurgle of water being poured from a pitcher into a glass. It seemed then Cecile made some sound, something that was almost a cry. But Marie merely folded the note and left.

Walking steadily toward the Rue Royale, her parasol too far back on her shoulder to shelter her from the clear sun, the heat of the bricks rising through the thin leather of her slippers, she felt herself blinded by an uncommon emotion, uncommon in kind and uncommon in intensity: this was anger, an anger bordering on rage.

Marie did not think in words as Marcel did. She did not talk to the mirror, nor write out "thoughts" on paper, and even in the Cathedral where she often went alone on Saturday afternoons to kneel for an hour in a pew nearest the altar of the Virgin Mary, there was no outpouring of her soul that was articulate, she did not pray in words.

And those rote prayers she uttered at such times—as she did each morning and each night and with the ringing of the Angelus, or when the beads of her rosary passed through her hands—those rote prayers had precisely that effect they were intended to have when invented centuries and centuries before: they ceased to be language and merely became sound, a rhythmic repetitious sound that lulled the mind and slowly allowed it to empty itself. So that divorced from what others call thought it was free to know itself in terms of the infinite, in terms of that which language has only begun to approximate if not destroy. Marie saw images at such times like blazing icons. Eyes fixed inwardly on the sufferings of Christ, she pierced all the mundane visions of the dusty Jerusalem streets through which He dragged His Cross and felt with a violent chill what was beyond the words of the missal in her hands: the pure nature of suffering for others, the meaning of the Incarnation: *and the Word was made Flesh.* The concept of goodness was real to her, as was the concept of the good life.

She understood this, just as throughout her life she knew her own feelings, was not given to self-doubt, spoke with quiet confidence, and seemed to possess no need to confide. In crowded rooms she could often through her own veil of silence perceive keenly the feelings of others—this one's hurt, and that one's anxiety—and the meaning of rapid verbal exchanges here and there, their injustice, their superficiality, their basic lie.

But when she was confused, when some emotion swept her violently for which she was utterly unprepared, Marie became lost in it, groping for a language that might help her discuss it in her own mind, and finding none, was shaken as if some force inside of her might rend her limb from limb.

It had been this way for her that morning, as she pushed steadily with the note through the muddy streets, toward the office of Monsieur Jacquemine, stopping mechanically at curbs for carts she did not see, oblivious to the shouts from a gallery doorway, her eyebrows raised, her lids lowered, in what seemed between the long shadows of her shimmering hair the very countenance of calm.

Envisioning over and over her mother's face, hearing again and again that hiss of her words, she felt once more that extraordinary chill that had come over her at the *secrétaire,* the very chill she felt at keen moments in her prayers, a tiny rising of the delicate down on her flesh, a shock that seemed to paralyze, though somehow the body moved, step by step with unerring instinct, on its way.

She could not abide what she felt; yet she could not stop it. All she could do was continue her violent pace, and that movement alone soothed her, seemed constructive, though the nature of the errand filled her with loathing and with fear.

There had never been closeness between them, Marie and Cecile. They had never talked to each other, did not seek each other's company, and moving swiftly through what had to be done in life—sewing, dressing, straightening, the preparations of a fine feast day table—they fitted hand in glove in the cottage, knew nothing of argument, and held for each other not the slightest surprise.

Childhood had seemed timeless in this regard. It was the way it was. But of late, a shadow was between them, growing in depth, a shadow thick and cumulative like a cloud. It was perhaps that Marie had begun to think about their life, and roaming sometimes after school through rooms of other families, mothers and daughters at cluttered dressing tables with pins and cologne, had begun to see beyond the seemingly inevitable fortress of family to other worlds.

It was little things. Gabriella Roget with her fingers clasped tight to her mother's eyes, steering her with waltzing flounces to the mirror, saying, "Not yet, not yet, very well now, look!" Peals of laughter at a birthday table, brothers and sisters quarreling for the last bit of cake with pinches and mischievous looks; or young Fantin on Gabriella's bed, teasing, "I know what Maman wants to do, Maman wants to get ahold of that hair," so that "Maman" turning from the dresser said, "Oh, do let me brush it, Marie, just let me take it down once, your mother won't know, oh, just look at that thick straight hair."

Things that ran to nonsense, kisses, defied memory or made up afternoons unmarked, so that a vague feeling collected in Marie, something that felt subversive, must stop, but did not.

At home with a rigid face Cecile watched the ticking clock over the covered dishes and when at last Marcel's step hit the door, motioned again for the reheated soup to be served. He was animated, cross, picked at things; yet all the worse was his absence, when silence lapsed back like dreary waves on a winter beach. He must have his bath water hot, not so much milk in his coffee, you know how he dislikes it, call him again, did you forget to darn his shirt? So that at odd moments, when mother and daughter wandered alone from room to room with no sound but the soft closing of the armoire doors or the rattle of a rosary drawn from a small chest, a sense of dread overcame Marie. It was awful this dread, it was like fear of the dark when she was a child, that amorphous something that lurked in shadow beyond the dull glow of the Virgin's face above a vigil flame, or guardian angels in a brass oval on the wall paper, clustered with giant feather wings about the tiny figure of a golden-haired white child.

This dread. It called in question all that was warm, seemingly solid, and sometimes when it was at its worst, she felt a weakness in her toward all the world, as if she could not reach out for cold water right in front of her on a burning day.

"Come home with me," Gabriella squeezed her arm too tight, and yet she felt powerless to do the simple thing of walking through the cottage door to ask her mother, "I should like, I should like to go..."

At times when Cecile thrust at her some ribbons or lace left by her aunts, Colette or Louisa, murmuring indifferently she should try this out, Marie would look at these bits and pieces numbly, from the center of that weakness, and finally only by an austere act of will, manage to touch them long enough to put them away.

In recent weeks there had been argument among the women, begun amid all the sherry and cakes of Marie's First Communion while she sat alone at the foot of her bed, paging slowly through the prayer book given her by Marcel, running her fingers over its cover of laminated pearl. They talked of the opera, of Marie's clothes, and like the nuns at school insisted it was time, surely, for corsets, and a change in dress.

"She's thirteen, that's sheer nonsense," Cecile said coldly. "I'm weary of this subject, all this attention to an impressionable girl."

"But look at her, look at her," came the shrill voices beyond the closed door.

And Tante Colette that afternoon had flung a corset across the poster bed, laying out with ceremony a dress of pale blue flounces trimmed with the most delicate white ribbon, the center of each little bow a masterfully folded rose. She waved a warning finger as she left with heavy steps that made the mirrors shiver. Marie alone in the shadows, felt the backs of her arms, her hair shrouding her bare shoulders. And turning slowly to see if in fact her aunt was gone, encountered instead her own dark shape in the tilted glass, the swell of breasts against the white eyelet of her chemise.

Dress her properly, Cecile, Mon Dieu!

Properly.

The word hung in the air. Cecile, slamming the fluff and whalebone into the broad armoire drawer, paused for a moment with a bent back adjusting the cameo on its velvet ribbon at her throat. Marie, in the corner of her eye, was not there.

On the streets she loomed monstrous, turned her head

(123)

from the darkened reflective windows of shops, could feel her stockinged ankles as though they were naked beneath her short girlish hem, and at night the pressure of her bosom, loose and large in her flannel gown against the mattress filled her with a vague disgust. She could see a dusky down on her arms, a bit of fleece on the backs of her fingers, and lay awake picking out of the dense gloom the distant roses on the tester of her bed, wondering vaguely what if Marcel had not finally gone to the *garçonnière,* had not left her the luxury of this small middle room, how could they have gone on, mother and daughter, sharing that other larger bed? It was as if they had never slept together, flannel against flannel, huddled in winter for warmth. Some splendid simplicity was gone, a surface broken. She did not sense as yet that it would never be mended.

But all this might have lain dormant within her. Mothers after all make mistakes. Gabriella laced to nineteen inches and in *décolleté* at dusk for the first soiree shook her head at the bad judgment of mothers, and with a furtive glance took the white camellias out of her hair, "Just too many!" And Sister Marie Therese taking girls aside at school had so often whispered, "And your mother said you might wear this, indeed I don't think..."

But was it a matter of that? Kneeling at the small bedside altar her hands clasped against the marble top, feeling the barest warmth from the votive candle, Marie in the flickering dark forgot her prayers at times, sensing instead some terrible illumination that fell back, back through the corridors of memory where there was hardly memory at all, as she was overcome with a profound listlessness liken to that of the infant in its crib, who, fed only at the whim of others, soon ceases its own cries because those cries have never brought it anything at all.

Oh, this must pass!

But it did not.

One evening late she climbed the stairs to Marcel's room and sat still in the corner watching him at his desk, listening to the scraping of his pen. He put it down at last bending toward her, "What is it, Marie?" And when she could not answer, with both hands he stroked her hair and kissed her eyelids quickly as he clasped her hands.

She loved him. It was nothing to defer to him, wait supper for him, take the buttons off his worn shirts, saving them carefully in a wicker box. She went to church when he wished, tied his four-in-hands, waited on warm evenings until he had had his bath, gave him in winter the chair by the fire. He was the only person in truth whom she did love now, she was sure of it; and she would find herself thinking, more often than she was aware, of afternoon naps long years before when climbing onto his bed she had curled up by his side, his knees tucked beneath her own, and felt the gentle pressure of his arm around her waist. He had smelt of pressed linen, rose-water, and something warm that was all his own. Rain fell outside the open windows with the soft rumble of thunder, and jasmine, pounded softly on the sills, filled the room with yet another sultry perfume. He had held her tightly in his sleep, and often kissed her hair. She liked the smooth golden flesh of his face, the lips ashen and rose, and all this so taut and satin in repose that she could not imagine it fired with waking laughter. Then stirring, he might rise and stare before him with such utterly blue eyes.

No, jealousy of him, it was impossible, it was not this constant favoritism she begrudged her mother, it had always seemed so natural that he should be first, and now if anything this only brought her to the brink of a new sharp pain:

After all, what was the matter with him now, why did he roam the streets at all hours, why had he finally been expelled from school?

She felt she knew the answer only too well. It had come with the abrupt end of childhood. One day childhood was gone and that was all. And in the new world of harsh adult distinctions, everyone she did not know believed Marie to be white, while no one who laid eyes on Marcel believed for a moment that he was.

It sent a shock through her to think of it; it was impossible that he did not know. Though she herself could never pinpoint that exact moment when she had found it out. And it was hurting him now, she was certain, causing him to shun her, to say always at the cottage door when she came in that he was going out. He passed her in the streets without a glimmer of recognition, and she had even glimpsed him on a Sunday afternoon, wandering in the Place Congo. Drums beat, incessant, urged on it seemed by the constant tink of the tambourines, the rattle of bones, and somewhere in the midst of that thick and common crowd, of Yanquis, tourists, slaves, vendors, the blacks danced just as they must have done in African villages, something wild and terrible that she herself

(125)

had never seen. And there he was on the periphery, her brother, his hands clasped behind his back, his brow furrowed, he had seemed at once a child and an old man. He turned one way, then the next, eyes wild or in the midst of some blinding concentration, she could not tell. It seemed the crowd opened to envelop him and toward that pulsing terrifying center he had moved. She could hardly stand it. All she knew of love, its pleasure and its sublime pain, were wound up with Marcel alone.

That anyone could see him as any less desirable than her was inconceivable to her, the attraction was so strong, so rooted in detail when she studied him, hung on his words, relaxed easily into his casual embrace. He was beautiful to her, and must be to all the world, precious in fact, his hands when he spoke enchanted her, so that to some extent prejudices of color had become for her at this early age something highly suspect, something all too caught up with ideas.

But she knew well how her world worked, heard more of it from sharp tongues of pale friends than ever did the world's victims. Indeed it seemed sometimes that angels protected the victims, as they did children and fools. Or so it seemed with Anna Bella, who with her broad African features and American drawl seemed for all the world unaware of how Marie's schoolmates snubbed her, and ever-pleasant with smiles, took not the slightest offense when others for sheer meanness, some idiot righteousness, had intended for her to do so. Girls on the way home from school turned their heads as Anna Bella waved from her courtyard gate.

And Marie, a quiet person who said little ever to anyone, despised herself at such times for this natural inclination. It was cowardice not to say, "Why, that's Anna Bella Monroe, she's our friend." Anna Bella, who brought preserves in flowered porcelain crocks and tureens of this special soup, that special brew to cure a fever, leaning on the doorjamb, ever so gracefully, one shoulder higher than the other, her neck so very long, said in a lilting voice, "Well, you just get better now Ma'ame Cecile, and if there's the slightest thing...I don't go to school anymore, you just send for me..."

But no such gathering of angel wings sheltered Marcel who, on the sly, slipped away with Monsieur Philippe's newspaper and left it open under the lamp to an article on the special feeding for African slaves, Marcel, who took command when Lisette ran away insisting that no one say a word to her, after all, she's come back, hasn't she? But then he had a way with Lisette as he had a way with everyone, and when she would not work it was Marcel who brought her round, and later gently hinted to Cecile, "Monsieur Philippe will be so tired from the long trip when he comes, he won't want to hear complaints, isn't it better he not know?" The man of the house, her brother!

He could have anything, do anything, even now when he acted the madman and frightened everyone, he still had that power...

No, it wasn't jealousy of him for a moment that could explain this awesome dark thing that lay between herself and Cecile, this throbbing violence of emotion that seemed to threaten the very coordination of Marie's limbs.

She was nearing the notary's office without thinking of where she was going, and through the tears that stood in her eyes the Rue Royale had become some avenue of the grotesque where men and women worried each other with ludicrous errands.

She could not stop seeing her mother, could not stop hearing her voice at that moment when she had turned, her head lowered, the veins in her neck standing out, and her lips taut with hissing. "Take that to his office, go!" And the vision of Cecile had been the very same the evening before, all semblance of the lady lost in one blazing instant in Richard's presence when she had said those unmistakable words, "Get out!" Not one syllable had passed between them all the long night afterwards, not once had Cecile so much as given Marie a glance. She had learned of Marcel's expulsion from Cecile's cries outside his door. And withering after into a corner of the bedroom, had listened for an hour to her mother pacing the floor.

Her mother disliked her, *disliked* her! The word formed instantaneously from the chaos of her conscious with stunning cold. Disliked her, it was manifest at last in those flashing eyes, the lips drawn back from the teeth, the quick turning of the head with that overpowering aversion, dissolving utterly all myths of family love, and all that which had been mere pretense crumbled at once like something splendid, painted on ancient paper, come apart at the touch. But ah, to reveal this in the presence of another, with blind impatience to display it, this which should have been the deepest of family secrets! It was unforgivable! Marie, shaken, throbbing, in fact, from the sting of it, felt for her mother suddenly the most profound contempt. And this contempt, like all else between them, was as cold as a barren hearth.

(127)

She stopped in the street, astonished to discover that she was at the notary's door.

She did not for an instant know why or what she was doing, and then the necessities of the moment flooded back to her, and she felt, if anything, more helpless and confused than before. This note, this foolish, if not disastrous, note! Her fingers, moist from the heat, had disfigured it but not enough. She was mildly amazed to feel her hand shaking as she grasped for the latch.

It was here that her rage should have focused all along, she felt it in a flash, and there came a vague relief as this passion was deflected from her own behalf. After all, what was being done here to Marcel with this note? What a rash and utterly foolish action this was. Who was Monsieur Philippe really, this gentle man she called *mon Père* when he bent to kiss her cheek? He was a white man, a protector, a benefactor upon whose whim Marcel's fortune utterly depended, and for the moment the child in her who had loved this man gave way to the woman who felt that the other woman was committing a stupid and absurdly destructive act. She felt superior to Cecile in that moment, worldly and peculiarly strong.

But what could she do about it? How could she stop it? Go back now, not to the cottage, but to Anna Bella's right by, where she might borrow pen and paper and write another letter, something milder, that would give her brother time? Cecile who could neither read nor write might never actually know. But this was inconceivable really. She had never done such a thing, and she was powerless to do it now.

And seeing her father in these moments as some remote and powerful personage from another world, she loathed the sheer reality of these thoughts, her own calculations, and their sordid resonance and resented all at once the whole circumstance that had made her think of lies and tricks, such words as indiscretion and the very practical phrase, common sense. It was repulsive, as repulsive as that moment when Richard had hurried from the cottage door, an unwilling witness to hostile words.

She bowed her head. She did not know it but she appeared ill as if the steaming street with its ripening smells had made her weak, and the clerk having seen her through the shadowy glass came to open the door.

"Mademoiselle?" he whispered. He extended his arm. She

didn't see him. She took the chair he offered and sank down in cooler air, breathing the clean fragrance of leather and ink, and watching dumbly as he neatly closed the silk folds of her parasol.

When he brought her water, she did not drink it, but merely looked at the glass in her hand. He thought she was white, naturally, and there was another aspect to his gentle attentions which made her drop her eyes.

"Monsieur Jacquemine, I have to see him, please," she explained at once.

There was nothing to be done.

"Ah, Mademoiselle, forgive me. I don't believe I have had the pleasure," the notary came blustering from an inner office, and imprisoning her hand needlessly touched the palm of it with rough fingers that set her teeth on end. She rose.

"Marie Ste. Marie, Monsieur, I believe you know my brother."

His thick mossy brows lifted, and his reddened cheeks plumped with his smile. "Aah, I would not have guessed." he whispered.

She was furious. She could feel the smarting of her own face. That he should think this a compliment. And thrusting the note quickly into his hand, she turned to go.

"But wait, *ma petite*," he insisted. She had moved to the door. "Expelled from school?" he held the note at arm's length, feeling for his spectacles, no doubt, in a breast pocket. "But what school is this, ah, this is serious...what school does your brother attend?"

"Monsieur, if you can reach Monsieur Ferronaire." She had never said her father's surname before. Even this hurt her, shocked her. She reached for the latch.

He came close to her, a hand pressing the door shut. His sleeve brushed her arm, and turning slowly toward him she looked up into his eyes. She could see him shying backward, see the effect of her chilly expression and felt not the slightest regret.

"Ah, Mademoiselle, I'm sure I don't know if Monsieur is in the city, if he is not in the city, it might be some time..." he smiled confidentially, "these matters..." he murmured.

"Merci, Monsieur," she whispered and found herself in the crowded street.

He was insisting upon something, calling her. She did not hear. Glancing back suddenly, she saw that smile again, confidential, seemingly tender, and his gaze passed furtively over her yellow muslin dress.

Tears formed in her eyes as she moved quickly away, but they did not come.

The crowd was blurred, indistinct. Someone brushed her shoulder and mumbling apologies gave her a wide berth so that she felt unsteady and reached out for the bricks of the wall. But she did not like to touch such things. Her fingers dropped, closing instead on the folds of her dress. She had forgotten about her hair, and saw it suddenly in flat tresses against her bosom and whispered to the raucous rumbling about her, *"Mon Dieu, mon Dieu."*

Through the open doors of the St. Louis Hotel came a press of white women, clambering into open carriages, one behind the other at the curb, so that she was obliged to stand with others for a moment as they passed, and turned her head she became aware of a strange noise.

It was as if an orchestra were playing already at this early hour, and all but the thick vibrations of the bass were drowned by the murmur of the lobby crowds. Above this came the faint high-pitched nasal cries of the auctioneers at war with one another under the high rotunda. Lifting her hand to her cheek, she was astonished to see on her fingertips the bright wetness of tears.

The crowd moved. And she was forced to move with it. She had never fainted in her life, but felt for the first time a rising darkness and a weakness in her limbs. Her mouth was curiously moist, and loose. She was afraid. But then a hand reached for her, steadied her, and meant to guide her closer to the wall. This was dreadful. She was going to pull away, most certainly had to pull away when with stinging eyes she saw that this was Richard Lermontant.

Had it been anyone else, anyone at all, it would not have mattered. Strangers did not frighten her, not in the Rue Royale. She could have gotten away and gone home. But when she saw him leaning forward, saw the passionate concern in his large brown eyes, and felt again the mild press of his fingers on her arm, she commenced to shake. Humiliated, she turned her back on him and on the crowd, stared mutely at the red bricks before her, and gave way to silent sobs.

"But Marie, what is it?" he whispered. He held a clean linen handkerchief out to her.

She did not know it but she had pulled her hair close around her, as if it might cover her up, and then she thought distinctly in bright flashes, I am not here, I cannot be here, not with Richard in this street, crying. I must somehow get away.

"Tell me Marie, what is it, what can I do?" he whispered.

She shook her head. Turning, she was peculiarly affected by this closeness to him. She stared at the sudden whiteness of his starched front, the glossy buttons of his black broadcloth coat. With some immense effort she raised her eyes to his, wanted to let him know that she was all right. But she experienced a weightless feeling, and a throbbing in her ears. It was as if she were hearing the rush of a waterfall, the great gush of rain through flooded passages, a sweet and stunning cessation of all matters in time. His face above the dark silk of his tie was not young, it was immaculate with youth certainly, but it was older in its tenderness, its obvious solicitude and something that must surely be wise.

But there was an intrusion, a man's hand. Stepping back impulsively she saw Monsieur Rudolphe, Richard's father, beside him, dressed in that same proper wintry black. Even against the extraordinary height of his son, the man seemed massive, his great chest and belly smooth beneath his curved waistcoat, his large somewhat long face with its slightly protuberant eyes looming over her. The clear Caucasian voice was immediately commanding.

"Ahh Marie, come across to the shop, out of this heat, at once," he took her arm.

She drew back in spite of herself. "No, Monsieur, thank you," she murmured. She swallowed quickly, and took Richard's handkerchief. "I'm expected home right now." She wiped the tears quickly from her eyes. "It's only the heat, yes, I was walking too fast..."

Monsieur Rudolphe accepted this more easily than she had expected, and Richard merely nodding stepped aside from her, gesturing at once that she must keep the handkerchief.

"You should have a sunshade, Mademoiselle," Monsieur Rudolphe said. And she realized with a sudden sense of defeat that she had left her parasol with the notary. Well, Marcel would have to get it, she was not going back. "Walk slowly and keep under the galleries."

Richard's face when she last glimpsed it was the picture of distress. She felt faint, sick, as she walked on, and actually dreaded some stupid accident. She took in her breaths deeply, and by the time she had reached the corner she was all right.

But in a moment she was thinking of nothing but Richard, and her mind, exhausted, gave in gradually to a melancholy that was almost sadness. They were wealthy, the Lermontants, with their shop, their stables, their stone yards. Their new Spanish style house in the Rue St. Louis had large lacquered double doors and at night through floating lace curtains one could glimpse a spectacle of gaslight. And he their only son could pick and choose.

There would be talk of dowries at their supper table, of how many weddings between this and that name, entered in the ledgers of the St. Louis Cathedral for this many generations back. At thirteen she would soon be old enough to be courted, and at sixteen Richard was not old enough to give it a thought.

How tired her mind was! Giselle, his sister, had gone off to marry into a fine colored family in Charleston taking with her a dowry of rosewood furniture and ten household slaves. And Madame Suzette Lermontant had come from those wealthy colored planters of Saint-Domingue who had all but dominated the province of Jeremie.

At any other time, how this would have made her heart beat, how miserable it might have made her feel. But now it merely made her head droop. Turning the corner into the Rue Ste. Anne, she moved on steadily to the Rue Dauphine, where she saw a light-skinned colored man dragging with angry grunts a heavy trunk toward the Mercier gate. He stopped when he saw her, as though struck by something about her. This must be the man, she thought, as she hurried past, eyes down, this famous Christophe. She could feel his eyes on her back as she moved down the narrow street and crossed to her own gate. One quick glance told her he was still watching her, had stopped dead still to watch her and she turned her eyes away from him angrily with a haughty lift to her head.

II

RICHARD STOOD WATCHING Marie as she moved away along the crowded banquette, into the shade of one overhanging balcony after another. She had square shoulders, nothing of artifice in her walk, only a natural grace and dignity of which she herself seemed utterly unaware. Her hair flowed to her waist, and the thick ruffles of her shorter girlish skirts showed a bit of narrow white-stockinged ankle above the bright heel of her slipper that caused him quickly to drop his eyes.

Then folding his handkerchief carefully, he put it in his pocket and followed his father across the Rue Royale and into the undertaker's shop.

"I would have insisted that girl sit down, but who knows, this place might have unsettled her," Rudolphe murmured, glancing at his watch, "and if I don't get some of my work done, I'm going to be unsettled. Why don't they post it, tell me that?" he said angrily to Richard. "Do you hear?"

He was listening to the bells. The mortuary chapel had been tolling steadily since morning, and the Cathedral was tolling, and no doubt other churches all over town. "Yet they don't post it!" Rudolphe said with a sneer.

He meant by this the notices at the Board of Health that the yearly scourge, yellow fever, had reached the proportions of an epidemic, the news that would send the last of the gentry scurrying for the country where they should have been before now. Deaths were worst among the immigrants, but the Lermontants would be busy round the clock. They had only just come from the cemetery, and Richard was already changing his boots so that they could be blacked again. This would happen perhaps three times this day, maybe more.

As Antoine, his cousin, gathered these, and Rudolphe's as well, Richard went at once to the high stool before his slanting desk and began to go through the bills that had accumulated in the past few days. He would have to put the books in order before Monday when he returned to school.

"She's prettier than I remembered, really she is," Rudolphe murmured, and Richard stopped, held the brass letter opener poised for an instant, and then went on. It seemed Antoine, gone into the back office to black the boots, uttered a short laugh.

"Well, I don't suppose you haven't noticed!" Rudolphe said to Richard. "You heard what I said, didn't you? Or have you gone deaf?"

"No, *mon Père*," Richard whispered.

Again came that derisive laugh. Richard glanced at the open door.

"Never mind him, I'm talking to you," Rudolphe said, but at that moment there was a tap at the glass and a tall Negro, in the same gentlemanly black as the Lermontants, entered, the bell jingling.

"That little girl's gone, Michie, went at nine o'clock, and that Madame Dolly is out of her mind," he said.

This was Placide, valet, butler, and assistant in a thousand capacities, bought for Rudolphe when Rudolphe was born. He was an old man, his very dark face heavily creased, and he removed his hat at once and held it in his thin hand. "And they say there's nothing in that flat, Michie, not even chairs to sit on, seems Madame Dolly's been selling everything piece by piece for a long time."

"*Mon Dieu!*" Rudolphe shook his head. "And that little child?"

"Nine o'clock this morning, Michie, with three doctors there, at this time of the year, with three doctors there," he held up three fingers.

"Get in here, Placide, and black these boots," came a low disgruntled voice from the back room. Antoine emerged, wiping the bootblack from his fingers. "You wait until my hands are filthy before you finally show up."

"I only have one body, Michie," said the tall Negro, "I can't be two places at the same time," and he moved slowly toward the rear door, his walk uneven as though it hurt him to bend his knees.

"This is Dolly Rose's daughter?" Richard asked.

"Lockjaw." Rudolphe shook his head. "I'll go there first."

Richard sat slightly hunched on the stool, his eyes on the desk. He looked up, eyes moving languidly over the shop. A dull light fell over the smooth mahogany of the long counters, the stacks of folded crepe, the black cloaks on hooks, and bundles of bombazine along the shelves. "Lockjaw," he whispered.

"All right," said Rudolphe, "enough, the child's in heaven to be sure, which is more than we could say with any certainty of anyone else. Now I want to finish what I was saying to you, listen to me. I've seen you looking at that girl! I've seen you gawking at her on the street the way you did just now, and gawking at her in church when your mind should be on the Mass."

Richard's brows knit. He lifted the letter opener again and slid it quickly into the envelope in his hand.

"Put that down and turn around," Rudolphe said furiously. "You're too big for your age, that's your trouble, people take you for a man, and you're nothing but a child. Now, listen to me, you know perfectly well what I mean."

Richard drew himself up, taking a long silent breath, and slowly raised his eyes to his father's. He summoned all his self-control to make his face a mask of calm. Even the slightest resistance, he knew, would make this worse.

"*Mon Père,* I never meant..." he began.

"Don't talk to me as if I were a fool!" Rudolphe said.

Antoine had emerged again from the rear door, and now wore his black coat. He was smoothing his straight dark hair with one hand.

Richard pressed his lips together and again fixed his eyes on his father. The muscles of his face were taut. "Yes, *mon Père?*" he whispered. Anyone but Rudolphe might have caught the timbre of sarcasm in the polite tone.

"Oh, so you're angry now, well, good, because then you'll pay some attention. All the rest of the time you dream! A girl like that—!"

Richard started. Before he could stop himself, he said, "*Mon Père,* she's Marcel's sister."

"I'm not insulting her, don't be an imbecile," Rudolphe said. Both of them heard Antoine's derisive murmur, and Rudolphe turning sharply to his nephew said coolly, "If you are ready, go on to the LeClairs', they're waiting for you. The Mass is at eleven, go on!"

With a faint smile, a superior and knowing smile, Antoine walked slowly out of the shop. When the door had shut Rudolphe turned to his son who sat slightly hunched over the desk, all but crushing the envelope in his large fingers. Richard had been staring at the words written there but they made no sense, they might as well have been a foreign language.

"I mean no insult," Rudolphe said with annoyance. "If I didn't approve of Marcel you wouldn't be his friend. I like Marcel, I always have. I feel sorry for him, if you want the truth, though that would curdle his mother's blood, wouldn't it, a 'shopkeeper' feeling sorry for Marcel!" He made a short laugh. He turned, and reaching into the corner behind his rolltop desk, he produced a small bottle of rose water and pouring it into his handkerchief blotted his lips and his face. "But my point is simply this," he went on. "I'm tired of being the one to state the obvious to people, tired of being the one to bring them face to face with facts that ought to be already known..."

"She is above reproach, *mon Père*," Richard whispered. "I have never so much as spoken to her except in the presence of others, her mother...Marcel..."

"Above reproach, of course she's above reproach, virtuous, ladylike and beautiful! Beautiful beyond compare!" Rudolphe glowered at him. "Isn't she? Well, isn't she...*beautiful?*"

"Yes, yes!" Richard whispered. The blood pounded in his temples. He looked at his father helplessly, desperately. And again dropping his voice to that velvet tone that was just above a whisper, the invariable characteristic of him when he was furious, he said, "If I looked at her in some way, it was nothing, I assure you..."

For a moment their eyes met directly and in silence. There was a change so subtle but unusual in Rudolphe's expression that Richard was bewildered. *"Mon fils,"* Rudolphe said, his voice low, softer, "don't you understand? I know perfectly well what you're thinking about that girl, I'm no fool. And don't you understand that girls like that, girls like Marie Ste. Marie, yes, yes, Marie...girls like that *always* follow in the footsteps of their mothers?"

Richard's eyes moved slowly down. The entire posture of resistance to his father which was more than habit, rather something inveterate, was softly broken.

"But no," he shook his head. "No, *mon Père,* not Marie. No."

"Oh, son," Rudolphe sighed. He had never taken this tone with Richard before. "Don't break your heart."

III

IT WAS ONE O'CLOCK before Marcel came down, and rushing into the cottage, he stared amazed at the brass clock on the sideboard, whispering, *"Mon Dieu,* I slept like the dead. And the truth is, I've been reborn. I've been reborn!" He snapped his fingers and turned to Marie. "And you look lovely this afternoon." He approached her with brisk steps. "It's been too long since I told you that you were lovely, that I derive the sweetest *constant* pleasure from your loveliness. Am I too old for us to kiss, no, we'll never be too old to kiss, will we, you and I?" and reaching down so that he lifted her by her shoulders, he kissed her on one cheek and then the other and let her drop. He laughed. "What's the matter with you?" he asked, suddenly becoming serious. "You're crying?"

"No," she shook her head, turning away. But again she looked up at him as if he were mad.

"Oh, my head is splitting," he said in another quick shift, "and I'm starving, where's Lisette, I'm starving."

"Where's Lisette, I'm starving," came Lisette's echo in disgust from the back room. "As if I didn't hear you get out of bed, it's a wonder you don't go right through the floor." Her face was puffy from napping. But she had a tray in hand and was setting his silver and napkin at the head of the table. The steam from the soup rose in her face. "You better want your dinner, too, don't tell me you want breakfast."

"Of course I don't want breakfast, dinner's fine, and I'm sorry that I wouldn't answer you last night, Lisette, sometimes I don't think I appreciate you as I should—"

She laughed loudly. "Eat that before it gets cold."

"I was in despair last night," Marcel went on, approaching the chair. He glanced at the soup. "In utter despair. But I'm no longer in despair, and I'm sorry."

"In despair," she repeated, her hand on her hip. "You were *in despair,*" she said again. "And now you're not *in despair,* Michie?"

"No, absolutely not. As a matter of fact, I feel wonderful! Except for my head, my head's splitting, you know that white wine that's in the water barrel, the bottle I put there, get it, please, my head's coming off. But what is this, one place? Am I dining alone, where's Maman? Marie, are you ill?"

Lisette's eyebrows went up in mock astonishment, and Marie from the settee regarded him with round eyes, her mouth open.

"You look dreadful," he said to Marie, "what is it?"

"Well now, Michie," said Lisette swaggering again toward the table, her eyes darting quickly to the front door and back to Marcel. "There's two ways of explaining it, this dining alone. First off, your sister and your mother have been just a little too upset to want any dinner???? Hmmmm? What with you doing so well these days in school???? And staying out all night? But then I hustled to fix your soup the best I could as soon as I heard your foot hit the floor because I knew, no matter how grave the crime, there is always got to be that final meal for the condemned man. Now eat up, Michie, before that platform drops from under your feet."

Marcel burst out laughing. "Lisette, this is no meal for a

condemned man!" he said. And seating himself quickly he drew his napkin from the silver ring. "Now please get that wine, this is a celebration, and my head's throbbing."

Lisette was staring at the door. A shadow loomed on the path.

"Wine, Michie?" she murmured, and backed slowly toward the bedroom.

"Wine, wine!" he said. "Hurry!"

"WINE!"

Marie put her face in her hands.

Marcel rose at once, his eyes fixed on Cecile as she entered the room, but nothing changed in the brightness of his expression. His lips narrowed with a smile.

"You are asking for wine!" Cecile screamed again. The door banged shut behind her.

"I was asking for you, too, Maman," he said softly. "I have some news for you, but what's the matter?"

"WHAT'S THE MATTER!" She ripped off her lace gloves, the seams splitting, and flung them impotently in the direction of the far wall.

"Oh, I know I've worried you," he said in a small voice. "I know I've been dreadful." He stopped, biting his lip so that he looked like a small boy. "But Maman, it's going to be different now, you must believe me, all that's past, and I have some good news for you, wonderful news!" He began to pace the flowered carpet suddenly as if he were lost in thought, his hands rubbing together, his face the picture of acute concentration. But then turning to her again, he smiled. "I won't worry you again, I promise you. Please, come have dinner now..."

Cecile was petrified. Marie was speechless.

He waited, his expression open, looking from one to the other of them.

"Have dinner!" Cecile gasped, her hands rising to cover her ears. "Have dinner!" she screamed. And suddenly stomping her feet in rapid staccato she let out one low shriek after another until finally she clenched her teeth and burst into tears. Lisette at the dining-room door, turned and ran.

For a moment Marcel did nothing. He bit his lip again, turning it slightly inward, and then he folded his arms. He walked solemnly to his place at the table and turned to face Cecile. "Tell me, Maman," he said with the voice of reason, "what must I do, what explanation can I give you, what assurances, how can I prove to you that I love you and I'll never distress you again?"

"AAAAAHHHH!" she screamed. "You are expelled from school, expelled from school, and you say this to me! You stay out till dawn and come home drunk and you say this to me!"

He appeared to meditate on this, as if it were all new and unexpected, and then with a resolution that Marie had not seen in him in months, he approached his mother and took her firmly by the arms, saying in a commanding voice, "Of course you're angry with me, and of course you're worried. Come sit down, please!"

For a moment it seemed she might. But then she drew back, her hands in tight fists as she let out her breath in a long moan, "Ooohh, you have gone too far, Monsieur, you have done just too well this time!" she cried. "Don't you play the little gentleman with me! You will not take one meal in this house, you will not sit at that table! You will go to your room, at once, that's what you will do. And you will stay there! Until Monsieur Philippe arrives here, whether that is a week from now, or a month! I don't care what it is, this heart will not soften!" She choked. "I have sent for him, Monsieur, I've sent for Monsieur Philippe and he's coming, he's coming to deal with you at last. This very morning I wrote to him, and told him everything!"

She stood poised as if she might continue. She was on tiptoe, her fists pressed into the flowing folds of muslin that flared from her waist, the tears luminous on her cheeks. The room was utterly silent. And Marcel with his hands on the back of the chair was staring at her. His face had lost its vigor. It was dark suddenly, the eyes widened gradually and the mouth was perfectly still.

"You did that?" he asked simply.

She let out a small cry, then stopped, gazing at him. She raised her finger to her lips.

"You wrote to Monsieur Philippe?"

A whimper escaped her. Her lower lip trembled violently. "Yes!" she blurted at last, "Yes I did that," she nodded, lifting her chin, "I wrote to him, and told him everything!"

He remained as before, his hands clasped on the back of the chair, regarding her. His face had changed to the coldest consternation, and in his expression were all those small, near imperceptible changes that meant mounting anger. Marie had never seen such an expression on his face, it was as frightening as his former gaiety.

"Yes," Cecile repeated, her body shaking violently with a choked sob, "I did it. I sent your sister this morning to the office of the notary."

Marcel looked at Marie. She sat still, her hands folded in her lap, the tears coursing down her cheeks. She looked away from him and the moment lengthened and the silence was broken only by a sudden soft cry from Cecile.

At last Marcel spoke in a cold voice.

"You should not have done that, Maman."

Cecile shuddered, gasped, her hand pressed against her mouth. "I'm at my wits' end with you," she wailed. It sounded suddenly like a plea.

"You shouldn't have done it!" he said wearily, angrily.

"Roaming the streets at all hours..." she sobbed, "drinking in taverns, expelled from school."

He shook his head as though disappointed, disapproving and immovable. She rushed forward leaning over the table between them, "What was I to do then, tell me!" she begged.

"Punish me, yes, anything that you wanted," he said with vague indifference, the voice slightly bitter. "You should never have written to Monsieur Philippe."

"He's your father..." she began.

"Aaahh, Maman!" he said in disgust, turning his head. "Really!" His lips were twisted. His eyes moved over the ceiling as if he were praying for patience.

There was a great relief in Marie, a pleasurable emotion she had not expected to feel when he said this. She watched Cecile waver, saw the fear in Cecile's eyes. Sinking down into the chair, Cecile laid her face against her arms on the table and cried softly, almost brokenheartedly, while Marcel taking his place as before, his hands in his lap, stared forward, his eyebrows slightly raised as if in deep thought.

"I didn't know what to do," Cecile pleaded, "I didn't know...I can't always know what to do, can I? It's too much, too much..." and on and on, the cries too muffled to be articulate. Finally she raised her head and said helplessly, "He'll come...he'll talk to you...he'll advise you!"

Marcel's face was cold. He studied her as if he did not know her. And then he uttered a dry laugh.

"O mon Dieu," she covered her mouth, crying again, trembling again. "What...what do you think he'll do, then?"

"I'm sure I don't know," Marcel said. "You know him far better than I do, Maman, to be sure."

She put her head down as before, her shoulders rising and

falling with her sobs. It had a desperate sound, as if she had only just begun to understand what she had done.

"Ah, but don't go on," he said suddenly, and reaching out, found her hand beneath her dark hair and clasped it. "When he comes, I shall have to explain to him why I was expelled, and that it is actually quite all right."

"What?" she lifted her head. "Yes, you can explain?" she asked pathetically. "You can explain, yes. Perhaps it was all a misunderstanding, you were such a good student..."

"Yes, yes," he said gently, patting her fingers.

She reached for his napkin and put it quickly to her nose. "I didn't know what to do!" she shook her head. "You can explain! Tell him it was all some sort of mistake, that you'll behave now."

He smiled, the same bright smile that Marie had seen when he first entered the cottage.

"I was so frightened..." Cecile cried.

"I know, I understand," he said. "But don't you worry about it anymore, Maman, you let me worry about it, all right?"

She sighed, immensely relieved, her fingers clutching at his wrist, shaking his hand, pulling it near to her. "You'll be the gentleman with him, Marcel, you'll explain."

"That's right," he said. "And you see, it's all happened for the best. There's to be a new school, a far better school than Monsieur De Latte's. Christophe Mercier's come home, it's his school, and I've already been accepted into it."

She brightened at once, but was obviously confused at the same time. "But how, what?"

"I was with him last night, Maman, you know who he is, he's famous. Monsieur Philippe knows who he is, all about him."

"Aah, yes," she sighed, remembering. "And he's accepted you, he knows about the other?"

"Of course, I told him," Marcel said calmly. "Now if you don't mind Maman, I'm starving?"

"Oh, but of course," she burst out, "Lisette! Where is that girl, anyway, didn't she hear you tell her to bring the wine? Marie, go at once and tell her to bring Marcel's wine, tell her to set this table!"

But Marie for the moment was too astonished to move. It was not merely that his old manner had returned, that blithe ability to hold everyone in the palm of his hand. There was a new conviction, a new calm. Even as he lapsed into some private world now, his eyes remote and blind, he still patted his mother's hand gently, and as Marie finally rose, he looked up to her.

"Well, you're having dinner with us, are you not?"

It was after the meal, when the table was cleared and Marie was standing alone in her room looking mutely at the little altar, that she again saw the shadow of worry in his face.

"What did the note say? Now don't cry Marie, you never cry. Just tell me what it said."

"I had to take it," she said. "I didn't know what to do."

"Of course you had to," he said. He kissed her again. "But was it so bad as all that?"

He listened patiently as she explained, nodded, and then said: "I'll take care of it, but you must promise me one thing."

"Anything," she answered.

"That you won't worry, and you won't think again about having to take it, and that you'll leave it all to me."

He was all right again, he was himself again, as he had been a year before, when the old cabinetmaker was still alive, and when they had still been children. Of course she could not conceivably guess that in one day he had slept with a beautiful woman, leapt the wall of a cemetery in the dead of night, and toasted in a wild waterfront cabaret with a famous Parisian writer. She only knew as he walked away from her and across the yard to his room that he resembled more than ever a man.

She turned and opened the drawer at the bottom of her armoire. There lay the corset Tante Colette had brought and the small-waisted dress of blue ruffles with its tiny white satin bows. She drew these out with careful hands as though they might break and spread them on the bed.

There was no hallway in the cottage, there is never a hallway in such houses in New Orleans, one room opening onto another, so that Lisette, going by with the last cleanup from the dinner table had to pass through the room.

"Wait, I need you," Marie said and gestured to the corset. "To lace..."

She slipped behind the flowered screen beside her bed. This was a party dress, really, but it would take her as far as the dress shop. And it was late afternoon now, besides, who was to know why she wore it?

Sometime before they had finished, Cecile came to the door.

"Now you forget everything you ever knew about breathing," Lisette had said as she jerked the strings. But Marie, fascinated by the snug contour enclosing her, found the pressure had its allure.

As the dress dropped down like froth over her arms and settled in layers about her waist, she saw a woman in the mirror, and let out a gasp. Her body softened, grew smaller, and she was privy to a subtle but titillating strength.

Cecile, staring coldly from the edge of the parlor, spoke not one word as she watched her daughter, with Lisette behind her, leave the house.

IV

IT WAS ALMOST DARK when Richard finally left the undertaker's shop that evening to attend to the wake of Dolly Rose's little girl. All day he had been busy with the mourners or the burying of the dead, had gulped meals in the back room, changed his linen five times in deference to the July heat, and was tired to the marrow of his bones. A late afternoon rain had inundated the cemeteries so that one burial for the parish had to be made in a veritable pool of muddy water; and the bodies of the yellow fever victims were beginning to pile up at the gates, giving off a stench sufficient to sicken the oldest citizen who had seen it summer after summer. Of course there had been worse years, years when the entire city seemed a charnel house. This summer was nothing extraordinary at all.

But in spite of all this, Richard had thought of Marcel all day, and tormented by the spectacle of Marie's tears in the street, he feared the worst for him. Now he knew it might be very late before he had any chance to pass the cottage, and he had little hope of finding a lighted window even in the *garçonnière*.

Also the matter of this wake had him on edge. He was not used yet to going alone, but Antoine and his father were both busy with other families. And this was the wake of a little girl.

Four years ago in the spring his little sister had died, and he could remember all of that illness vividly, including some details which he had never confided to anyone and which time had not dimmed in the slightest.

The Lermontant house was a new one, built entirely according to the wishes of his parents, and in the back courtyard was laid out a long somewhat formal garden in rectangular patches and flagstone walks. There were vegetables to the far end near the kitchen and the cistern, but everything else was flowers, and when the camellias and hibiscus were in bloom, the children loved to play there, darting through the tunnels of abundant foliage, hiding in the narrow space between the cistern and the back walls, or making secret caves amid a border of chinaberry trees whose lower branches were worn bare and shiny from the children's hands and knees.

Richard often took his book out into the shade of the overhanging gallery so that he could watch them, his mother showering him with grateful kisses, and he rather liked the sound of their play. He was patient, could hold a squirming nephew or niece easily in one arm for a moment while he finished his sentence, then tend to the scratched knee or say it was nothing, and go right on reading without losing the sense.

But he could remember with a vividness that seemed a curse the first afternoon his little sister, Françoise, had come to him and told him that she was too tired to play. She was not yet four years old then, a quick-witted little girl who liked to roughhouse with the boys, though she had about her always a certain near prim femininity that came naturally from her long loose black curls, thick eyelashes, and also the starched lace that her mother labored over even for backyard play.

On this afternoon she had come trailing alone from the back of the yard, her hands dangling at her sides, and leaning close to his chest had said with that rather adult phrase that she was "just too tired." It was not something a child said; it was something the parents told the child when they saw it was cranky and overwrought, and Richard would remember all his life the shadow falling over his heart when he heard her say these words. He had lifted her face and seen the flesh was dark and seemingly tender beneath her eyes, and there was something listless and vague in the eyes themselves.

It was not an isolated moment. She had complained a little now and then for days, fallen asleep on the parlor couch, and whereas in the past she was always up with Grandpère at the first light, they had had to wake her each morning. She complained that her arms ached, and as he led her now from the courtyard she did not even want him to touch her shoulder because it hurt.

Richard had said nothing much about it at the time, but in a matter of days she was clearly wasting, and a raging fever took her before the end of the following week. He could remember the last nights of her illness perfectly, her crying, his mother's steps up and down, up and down the stairs. "Go to bed," she had said to him every time he asked to come in, until he realized finally that he might help the most by being out of the way. Opening his eyes at four o'clock that morning, he had been startled by the silence of the house. And gone at once to his sister's door. He knew the moment he saw her so still on the pillow, and the figure of his mother sitting at the window, that she was dead.

It was never any relief to him, the platitudes, that she would cry no more, suffer no more aching in her arms and legs, was with God.

A wretched weakness came over him at the thought of her, and for him the story would always begin at that moment in the garden, a nightmare burgeoning from that point which no one had the power to stop. Every time he stepped into the yard, he saw her there, coming up the long central path among the ripe and swelling flowers, her dark curls flowing down the front of her pale blue dress, her head to one side as though her neck were a weakening stem. He felt some impulse over and over to take her again in his arms, as if he might then perform some desperate action that would change all of time since that day; and every year on her birthday, he thought, ah, she would have been this old. No one had to remind him to go to Mass on that occasion, or to think of her; he knew when it was coming long before. He had some locks of her hair in his prayer book, could remember her pet phrases, and still distinctly hear her ringing laugh. When people complimented the sharpness of his recollections, which they often did, he thought of her, that he would have liked to forget, but then again not for the world. Until then death had been what happened to other people, but in those days it had come home. It was ever after always personal, and the grief of the parents at the funerals of children struck his very soul.

He wondered sometimes how his father endured it, how he could not when taking the measure of these small bodies think of his own little girl. But much as Richard sometimes resented Rudolphe, resented him particularly today for all his wisdom in the matter of Marie Ste. Marie, he respected him in his profession as everyone did. He knew his father had never attempted to escape an obligation in his life, and would not have shifted the responsibility of this wake to his son had he the choice. There were old families who needed Rudolphe tonight, people who would have been wounded if he did not come himself.

"You'll do well, you always do," he had said to Richard earlier. "Every time I step into the street, it seems someone takes my arm and praises you. You have a special gift in this regard so use it, and pity your cousin Antoine who hasn't the slightest smattering."

Richard didn't really believe all this. It was business perhaps, building him up to do his job. He did not believe it because to him real grief was the most awful feeling he had ever known, and his own miserable mumblings at funerals seemed an insult. He did not understand that he radiated a depth of genuine concern that people sensed, in his manner as well as in his words.

So walking up the Rue Dumaine in the twilight, he felt an awful apprehension, redolent with memories of his own sister, and knew from much past experience that he was all the more susceptible to it at this time of day, this quiet dreary sensual time between the sun and the moon when the Saturday night excitement of the Quarter had not yet begun though the business was all but concluded and the lamps were lit beneath a sky the color of blood.

It was deepening to purple over the river, descending in layers of violent gold and red clouds behind the masts of the ships; and cicadas sang in the dense foliage of walled courtyards, while from open windows came occasional billowing curtains, and the sounds of supper, tinkling, the scrape of a knife.

Without realizing it, he turned his eyes to everyday things, a horse and cart passing, a woman on an upstairs gallery who stopped beating the dust from a small Turkey rug long enough for him to pass.

But when he reached the block where Dolly Rose lived, the mother of the dead child, he came upon a strange pocket even at this quiet time, a stretch of some ten or twelve doors where the only sound was the song of the insects and the remote melancholy ringing of a church bell. The sky darkened; the stars seemed low, and yet the distant corner lamp remained dismal against the azure gloom, unable to shed its full light until the real night. He quickened his pace, as if someone, something were following him.

And it was with relief at last that he reached the archway of Dolly Rose's courtyard drive.

A man stood there, a lean square-shouldered man of color, dressed in a coat that seemed quite fresh for the balmy summer and very smartly cut. He wore a slight mustache, no more than a line of dark hair, and his eyes, flashing on Richard quite suddenly from the shadows of the archway gave him a mild shock. They looked at one another, and it seemed the man was uncomfortable, on the verge of saying something, yet did not know how to begin. The man was also obviously struck by Richard's height.

"Can I be of service, Monsieur?" Richard asked.

"Can you tell me, is there a wake here tonight?" the man asked. His pronunciation was slightly sharp but what marked the voice more distinctly was its flat, inflectionless tone. For some reason this made his words rather expressive.

"Yes, Monsieur." Richard answered. This the man might have learned very simply from the black-bordered notices that fluttered on the lamp posts nearby, on the trunks of the trees. These had been posted all about the Quarter in the late afternoon. "It's upstairs."

"But is this wake open to all the friends of the family?" the man asked.

Ah, that was the problem. "Monsieur, it's open to everyone who knows Madame Rose or her family, it is not merely for close friends. I'm sure if you know them at all you would be most welcome, there will be many many people there."

The man nodded. He seemed relieved, yet uncomfortable, and a little annoyed with himself for that discomfort. And there was something distinctly familiar about his face. Richard was certain he had seen him before. As for the clothes, he was quite sure they were from Paris. Paris maintained such a vast lead in fashion, it seemed you could always tell these gentlemen who had just come home.

"Permit me, Monsieur, I'm Richard Lermontant, the undertaker," Richard said quietly. "If you will follow me?" he gestured to the door.

The man bowed his head, did not say his name and behaved as if this were of no consequence, following Richard into the short hallway and up the carpeted stairs. Entering

(147)

the parlor, he moved quickly away behind a crowd of men and women along the wall and Richard at once turned his eyes to the small bed surrounded by white chrysanthemums on which the child was laid.

Because funerals had been his life for years, Richard never associated these particular flowers with funerals. That is, they had for him no morbid resonance, and were always just what they were meant to be when brought into such a room; something lush, beautiful, and alive—springtime—an offering amid the sorrow that brought to mind the cycle of life and death at the very time when death weighed so heavily on the soul. He was glad to see them now. And quickly greeting Antoine who took his leave, Richard moved silently, invisibly along the borders of the room, around the clusters of whispering women in black dresses and gentlemen with hat in hand, until he stood over the large fragile bouquets and looked down through the perfume, and through the smoke of the wax candles, at the dead child.

She was a little older than his sister had been, and perhaps every bit as pretty. In fact, her beauty shocked him. He had seen her often enough on the high seat of Dolly Rose's carriage, her bonnet ribbons whipped in the wind, but she was all clothes then, bundled up except for a dimpled cheek. And he saw for the first time here her rounded bare arms and pale throat. Of course she appeared to be asleep. They all did, no matter what the manner of death, no matter how acute the suffering. This child had died of lockjaw, and yet she lay serene in this lifelike posture. It never failed to give him a moment's pause. And he was surprised as he brushed a loose strand of hair from her forehead to realize that she was already stiff. But there was no odor, in spite of the heat, except that of the rose leaves and orange leaves beneath the sheets, and the heavy flowers.

And pleased with this and a dozen other minor details (Antoine did this sort of thing perfectly), he was relieved of everything for the moment but his contemplation of her face. She was baby-round still and very white, could have been a white child for all a stranger knew, and her brows seemed a bit too dark against her forehead so that her expression in death was too serious. It was as if she were having an absorbing dream. There was a sound then that he could not have identified, but he realized that it was a series of narrow white petals breaking loose from a flower and falling down to the pillow beside her head. He moved to pick these up, but an unusual thought struck him. They were soft as the child had been in life, but was no longer. He felt the impulse to leave them there. But no one else would have understood. Then he saw nestled with the thick chrysanthemums a prim spray of white rosebuds. He took one of these and quickly breaking its long stem, tucked it in with the pearl rosary beads intertwined in her folded hands. He touched it lightly and drew back.

Dolly Rose was not there. Her godmother Celestina Roget, haggard and pale, rose now to go, whispering to Richard that she had been up three nights and three days with the sick baby and must see to her own house. "You watch her!" she said, and gestured as she left to a rear bedroom beyond the arch of the hallway. Muted voices came from that room. And when at last the door was flung open Dolly Rose did not come out. Rather a white man appeared who came down the long passage, went up to the coffin, looked down, and then retired to a far corner of the room.

He was a striking man, young, perhaps twenty-five, his black hair gleaming with pomade and curling just above his collar. A thick mustache and a fullness to his sideburns gave him a distinction that was rare in one so young, but having a hawklike expression he carried it well. His eyes now found some indefinable spot in front of him and he remained fixed on it, even when Dolly Rose finally entered the room. She glared at him from the doorway and was ushered, even pulled, by two other women to a nearby couch where she buried her face in her hands.

Richard could see at once that she was drunk. She was at that point of grief and drunkenness, in fact, where there might be trouble. And I have Antoine to thank for warning me, he thought bitterly, and Madame Celestina for leaving me to handle this on my own. Dolly looked up from time to time at the white man as if she were going to shout something at him, but she did not. And the other ladies, none of whom seemed quite to have her glamour, even in these moments, were clearly afraid as they held her by the arms.

Dolly Rose had, in fact, been a remarkable beauty, that kind of quadroon who had given the Salle d'Orléans its fame, but hardly the legendary faithful mistress who weeps upon hearing of the marriage of her white lover or throws herself beneath the wheels of a passing cabriolet. Rather she had gone through white admirers as through pairs of gloves, spending lavishly with each new connection, and never

thinking to save for the future, often gave to her slaves taffeta
and merino dresses that had scarce been worn. She had provoked duels, neglected creditors, adored only her mother and
her daughter, both of whom were now dead, and had in the
last few years been on bad times, though everyone said she
might make a perfectly fine connection at any moment that
she chose.

Once she had been friends with Richard's sister, Giselle,
and even come to dinner often at the Lermontant house, and
Richard could remember them as grown-up girls of fifteen
exchanging secrets behind the curtains of a bed. The little
boys used to sing to her, chanting as they surrounded her
skirts, DOLLY Dolly, DOLLY Dolly, DOLLY DOLLY
ROOOOSE! Richard could still remember that engaging
rhythm and how she had laughed. And from all the talk he
had heard of her waning beauty, he was quite impressed to
see she was very lovely still.

Hers was an unusual face, not so much for its pale *café
au lait* skin, nor its diminutive nose and mouth. But rather
for its shape, not being lean like the faces of so many Creole
girls, but rather square with high rounded temples beneath
her dark waves, and eyebrows very flat across the almond
shape of her eyes, rising slightly at the outside before they
curved down. It was this straightness of the eyebrow, and the
manner in which it set off the eye beneath it that had always
intrigued him. Pretty was the word he thought of when he
looked at Dolly, because there was a gaiety and loveliness
in her looks that sometimes beautiful women lack.

But her friendship with Giselle had ended badly. One summer Dolly had left the convent school and commenced to
appear at the "quadroon balls." Rudolphe forbade Giselle to
see her. And Dolly was not invited when Giselle was married
at Nuptial Mass. Old Madame Rose, Dolly's mother, was rude
to the family, and Dolly took her first white lover in due
time. But everyone had liked Dolly. And Richard would have
known, even if he hadn't been told, that half the furnishings
of the room had been supplied for the funeral by his father.
There were the Lermontant mirrors brought around merely
to be draped, and the clocks set out merely to be stopped,
extra chairs from the Lermontant storerooms, and even the
settee beneath the front windows, as well as tables, the decanters of sherry and the glasses. It had all been brought up
late that afternoon in a covered cart by Placide, the old valet,
and passed quietly through the carriageway to the back so

that no one was the wiser. And though it was of no consequence to him personally, Richard was rather certain that the bill for all this would not be paid.

Now, taking a deep breath, he approached Dolly tentatively only to discover that she did not know him, in fact, did not appear to know anyone, and the women who surrounded her appeared anxious and somewhat put out. Meanwhile, people entering turned their heads to the white man as though his face were a light. And he sat rigid, eyes on the floor.

In short, it was not a good situation. But as Richard slipped into the far corner behind the white man where the shadows might conceal him, the man of color in the Parisian coat approached.

"Vincent," he said to the white man and he extended his hand.

Slowly the white man lifted his head. There was about him an air of wariness which was suddenly dispelled.

"Christophe!" he whispered, and at once they clasped hands.

A mild shock passed through Richard. It was Christophe Mercier! At once he recognized the smooth square face, and he understood completely the manner which bordered on the arrogant as the man stood before the white man's chair. But their clasp was warm, lingering. "You came on my account?" the white man asked.

"And for Dolly," Christophe nodded.

"Ah, then you know her."

"For many years. If there is anything I can do, you must tell me." Christophe's voice was low, inflectionless as before. "But here, this is the undertaker," he gestured for Richard to step forward, "his name is Lermontant."

The man gazed up into Richard's face and only then did Richard sense his torment, shrouded as it was by the shadow of his dark hair and black brows, the deepset eyes peering like lights.

"Lermontant, Monsieur," Richard whispered with a slight bow.

The man nodded, and from his waistcoat he drew out a small card. The name was Vincent Dazincourt and Richard knew it at once. It was an old Louisiana family, and the name of the first lover that Dolly had taken years before. He was the father of the child. "Anything," the man said, "any expense, the best hearse, the best horses..."

"It's arranged, Monsieur," Richard assured him. But at this moment, Dolly Rose came across the room.

A cluster of reluctant women attempted to stop her, but gasped indignantly as she pushed them off. And sitting down beside the white man, she hissed in a low voice.

"So you'll pay for everything, will you? Now...now that she's dead?"

Backs turned to them politely.

"And where were you when she was alive, when she called for you, 'Papa, Papa,'" she hissed. "Get out!"

The room had fallen silent. Richard bent to touch her shoulder, summoning his greatest reserve. "Madame Dolly," he said gently. "Why don't you come now and rest, this is the best time."

"Let me alone, Richard!" she shrugged him off, her eyes fixed on Dazincourt. "Get out," she said again, "out of my house, do you hear?"

He glared at her from under his black brows, only his mouth seeming soft and a little boyish as he twisted it into a bitter grin.

"I'm not leaving here until Lisa's buried," he said in a low contemptuous voice.

It seemed she would strike him then, but one of the women attempted to take her arm. Her hand flew out smacking the woman's face. And at once she was abandoned as soft shuffling skirts drew away from her all around.

"Dolly, please," Richard addressed her as he had a thousand times when he was a little boy. He went to take her by the waist, but she jerked from him violently, the wine sour on her breath, the flesh that slipped from his hand feverish. He was afraid of her, and what right had he to hold her, this was after all, her house as she had said. He watched helplessly as she reached for Dazincourt who had turned away as if she weren't there.

But it was Christophe who slipped between them, whispering low to her upturned cheek, "Dolly, you don't want to do this." It was a tone of simple command.

She wavered, and put her hand uncertainly to her brow. "Christophe!" she whispered, "wild little Christophe!"

"Come on, Dolly," he said, and as angry, scornful faces looked on he lifted her gently to Richard's arms. Her eyes were vague, dazed, but with a wan smile she gave herself over to Richard, gesturing to a doorway down the hall.

It was a disaster of a room, clothes heaped amid crumpled

sheets, which at once made Richard mad. Old liquor reeked in glasses everywhere and thrown helter-skelter over the screen were a corset, chemises, scarves. The house was rudderless, the woman friendless, and as he guided her gingerly to the high bed, he was ashamed for her, ashamed that she would be alone in this room with him and with Christophe at the door.

"I want brandy there!" she declared and would not lie down. He turned to see a bottle beside the sputtering lamp. Without glancing at Christophe for approval, he filled the glass and gave it to her as if it were milk for a child. Her hair fell over her broad high forehead and her fingers made him think of claws.

"Rest now, Dolly," Richard said, and he covered her shoulders as she settled back.

"Maman," she groaned suddenly into the stained pillow. And then, shuddering, opened her eyes wide. "Christophe!" she said. "I want to talk to Christophe."

"You can talk to me anytime, Dolly," Christophe said. "I'm not going anywhere for a long while."

"You bastard," she said, straining to make him out in the gloom. Richard shuddered. Her face was pale, her eyes glittering. "You threw me in the river!" she said.

"Ah," Christophe answered softly. "You threw me down the stairs first."

Her laughter was light, girlish. "Why the hell did you come back here, anyway?" she asked. "They had you dancing with the Queen."

"I came back to throw you in the river again, Dolly," he said.

She closed her eyes, shivering, but the smile on her lips remained. "Only white men can throw me in the river now, Christophe," she answered. "You've been away too long. Get out of my bedroom." She turned her head to one side.

"Don't get rough, Dolly," Christophe said, backing silently toward the door. "It's only white men now who can throw me down the stairs."

She laughed again, her eyelids fluttering.

"How many white women did you have over there, Christophe?" she asked, smiling up at him again. "Come now, how many did you have? They told me you danced with the Queen."

"Not so many, Dolly," he said. "Just the Queen."

Her head rolled on the pillow as she laughed again. Richard all this while was mortified. He was emptying the contents of various glasses into the pitcher, shoving shoes and slippers beneath the skirts of the bed. But it was beyond him, this chaos, and she was moaning and snuggling down into the pillows, her face altered in one of those complete shifts which drunkenness makes possible, "Maman, Maman," coming like a moan from her parted lips. The tone was so helpless, so piteous that it made him breathless to hear it and to see her moist and quivering face.

But she began to breathe deeply, silently. And the face became smooth. He opened the high blinds to let in a little air and made his way to the door.

Only two of the women were there to meet him, older women, old as Dolly's mother had been before she died. Their inquiries were cold, perfunctory and hearing that she was sleeping now, they hurriedly took their leave.

Christophe meantime had rested his weight easily on the frame of the door opposite, and a warmth shone in his eyes as he glanced at Richard and gave him a weary smile. Richard was ashamed now for having been so shaken, ashamed for having depended so on this man who for all his fame was a stranger to Richard still.

"And Madame Rose, her mother?" Christophe asked.

"She died last year, Monsieur, a stroke." It had never been his habit to gossip about the bereaved, but his cheeks were still burning from the rawness of Dolly's language, and he found himself struggling now to make some guarded explanation for the woman who was so alone in the next room. "She was devoted to her mother, Monsieur. And devoted to the little girl. Now they are both gone and...?" he let the words hang there as he made a subtle heavy shrug.

Christophe's eyes held him intently for a moment. Then he removed a thin cigar from his inside pocket and glanced toward the distant door which stood open to the yard.

"A stroke, was it?" said the monotone voice. "I thought that woman was made of iron." And his eyes moved eloquently over the walls as if probing some childhood memory and there was faint mystery in his smile. "You should have seen her face the day I threw Dolly in the river," he said. "But then you should have seen my face the day Dolly threw me down the stairs."

Richard laughed softly before he could stop himself, and it took him a moment to regain his composure under the man's playful eye. He felt strangely at ease with Christophe, the man's manner was compelling, even spouting this blasphemy outside Dolly's door.

"I want to thank you, Monsieur," Richard said, "for helping me as you did."

"De rien," Christophe shrugged.

"If it weren't so soon after Madame Rose's death, perhaps Dolly could manage better, but they were so close, closer I think than mother and daughter usually are."

There came that mystery again to Christophe's expression. "She was a witch!" he said.

Richard was stunned.

"And I'll tell you something else," Christophe said simply. "Dolly hated her." He turned, cigar and match in hand, and walked quietly toward the back door.

As Richard returned to the parlor, more and more callers were coming up the stairs. A short line formed behind the little prie-dieu before the child, and it seemed order had returned to the universe, the rosary soon commenced, and a decorous wake proceeded as smoothly as before. Christophe, coming in from the gallery, brought a chair up beside the white man, so they were soon tête-à-tête and as the hours passed, a faint picture emerged from the murmuring pair: they had known one another in Paris, had acquaintances in common, and had returned home together on the same boat. But this was subdued, slow conversation, and Vincent Dazincourt, obviously comforted by Christophe's presence, soon lapsed into his own heavy thoughts.

And burning to tell Marcel of Christophe, and burning to know more of Christophe himself, Richard would have forgotten the white man altogether after this night had it not been for another occurrence which left its imprint on Richard's mind.

At a very late hour, when the crowd had thinned somewhat and the rosary had already been said, another white man came up the stairs from the back courtyard, walking with a heavy tread down the high-ceilinged hall, his dark cape flaring to touch the walls on either side. This was Marcel's father, Philippe Ferronaire.

Richard had seen this man many times in the Rue Ste. Anne, and he recognized him at once. His yellow hair was unmistakable as was his large somewhat affable face with its pale blue eyes. Philippe Ferronaire appeared to know him also, and gave him a nod as he hesitated at the door. Richard could not know it, but Philippe had marked him often in the past, not only for his height but for the exotic slant of his eyes, the fine bones of his face and an overall beauty that struck Philippe as regal, reminding him of those African "princes" among his slaves who kept the women in thrall. Now he surveyed the small company, and turned to Vincent Dazincourt.

He drew up a chair beside the listless figure, and Dazincourt turned with a start. His face evinced a faint and evanescent pleasure at being so surprised.

Christophe, however, distracted him by choosing this moment to go. With a nod, he was headed for the stairs. Dazincourt rose for the first time during all these long hours and followed him. "Thank you for coming," he whispered as he took Christophe's hand. And after a moment's hesitation he said gravely, "I wish you well." For an instant Christophe merely stared at him. The words were ceremonious and final. And Richard felt himself stiffen as he looked away. But Christophe merely murmured his thanks and was gone.

"Ah yes ... the novelist, 'sweet Charlotte' ..." Philippe Ferronaire whispered afterwards when the two white men were again alone. They spoke in hushed voices until Philippe rose, his heavy cape unfolding thickly around him, and moving to the hallway, beckoned for Richard to follow him as he proceeded to the rear gallery over the yard.

Richard's limbs were stiff and his back ached. He wanted to stretch when he stepped out under the black sky but he did not, only breathing deeply as he looked up at the faint stars.

Philippe Ferronaire lit a cigar and moving from the light of the hallway, leaned his elbows on the iron rail. A gas lamp flickered at the bottom of the curving stair, and beneath it in the rippling waters of a fountain Richard could see the sudden flash of goldfish beneath the pads of the lilies. The lilies were as white as the moon. The small stone figure of a child, dark with moss, poured water over all from the mouth of a pitcher and that low trickling seemed somehow by its sound to cool the air. Yet there were weeds everywhere, sticks of weatherworn furniture, and the buckling broken flags that signaled ruin all around.

Richard glanced at Philippe who was also looking down. The man fascinated him because he was Marcel's father, yet he had been thinking since Philippe arrived that it was rotten luck, pure and simple, for Marcel that the man was in town at this time.

"Listen to me," said Philippe in a low drawling voice. "There's a boardinghouse in the Rue Ste. Anne...for gentlemen, a respectable place...oh, you know the place, right near the Rue Burgundy...that's that young girl there, very pretty girl."

"Oh, Anna Bella," Richard said emerging from his thoughts. The man had avoided saying this is just near the Ste. Marie cottage, or that the girl was Marcel's friend. "It's Madame Elsie's, Monsieur, at the corner."

"Ah, that's the one, you know it then."

"In passing, Monsieur."

"But you could get him a room there tonight, in spite of the hour?" He referred to Dazincourt obviously. He drew his pocket watch out, and facing the door again, checked the time. "He has to sleep, he can't stay here till morning. And he won't go back to the hotel, doesn't want to be with his friends."

"I can try, Monsieur, and of course there are other respectable boarding houses."

The man sighed heavily and leaning on the banister appeared to be looking at the dark sky. Lights glimmered behind slatted blinds across the courtyard; there was, as always, noise from the nearby cabarets that were sprinkled throughout the Quarter among shops and quite lavish townhouses. He moved his jaw a little as though chewing his thoughts. There was something heavy about him beyond his build, though in fact he was rather firm. It was more in his slow casual manner and the deep voice that drawled as he spoke. It seemed his most natural gesture would be the shrug, a gesture that would consume him easily, even to the loose twist of the mouth and a droop to the heavy eyelids and a rise to the mossy brows. Richard did not find him compelling in any way, could see nothing certainly of the Ste. Marie children in him, but he was not insensible to the fact that the man had the aura of immense wealth. There was something powerful about him, too. Perhaps it was merely that he was a planter, that he wore high riding boots even now, and this heavy black serge cape that no doubt protected him even in this sweltering heat from the cold winds on the River Road. He smelt of leather and tobacco, and seemed made for the saddle and some seemingly romantic ride through the fields of cane. There was gold on his fingers, and a bright

(157)

green silk cravat, which he had apparently taken off in deference to the funeral, bulged from his jacket pocket. "Anna
Bella, is it?" he whispered now. "What does she do there?"

"She's an orphan, Monsieur, but well provided for. Madame Elsie is her guardian. I do not think that she works in
the house."

"Hmmmm..." he drew on his cigar, and the fragrance was
sweet but strong, hovering about them in a cloud.

"Pretty thing..." he muttered. "Well, you take him there
when you leave, you can do that now, can't you?"

It wasn't until near midnight that Richard's cousin, Pierre,
at last came to relieve Richard, and he set out for Madame
Elsie's with Monsieur Dazincourt. The man said nothing as
they walked, seemed to be brooding and deadly tired, and
though he was shorter than Richard—as was almost everybody—he was by no means of small stature. He had a near
military stiffness to his back.

As they passed the Ste. Marie cottage it was completely
dark, as Richard had expected, but he realized now that Philippe Ferronaire was not stopping there, and it was for this
reason no doubt that he had not taken Dazincourt to the
boardinghouse himself. He had not wished to be seen passing,
naturally. At least Marcel might have some time.

V

IT HAD BEEN A LONG while since Richard had seen Anna Bella,
except at Sunday Mass, and he was rather surprised when
it was she who answered the front door. He was glad. He
wanted a chance to talk with her alone.

In the normal course of his life, Anna Bella was a person
Richard would never have known and never have noticed. But
Richard did not fully realize this. It was Marcel who had made
them close, they were his best friends, and Richard had grown
fond of her in the last few years, trusted her certainly, and was
eager in his concern for Marcel to speak with her now.

Anna Bella was to him, however, an American Negro having been born and brought up in the north of Louisiana in
a small country town. Her father, the only free colored barber
there and a very prosperous one, had been shot down one day
in the street by a man who owed him money; and her mother

having died some time before, Anna Bella fell into the hands of a kindly white man whom she always called Old Captain who brought her down to New Orleans to board with an elderly quadroon, Madame Elsie Clavière.

In times gone by, Madame Elsie had been more than a landlady to Old Captain, but that was all past. He had white whiskers and a bald head, could speak eloquently of the days when Indians still attacked the walls of Nouvelle Orléans, and Madame Elsie, crippled in the damp mornings with arthritis, walked with a cane. But she had been a wise woman when young, saved her money, and turned her townhouse into a fine boarding establishment for white gentlemen, from which she herself retired to a parlor and several bedrooms beyond the courtyard in back.

It was there that Anna Bella grew up, played with the neighborhood children, and had lessons in French and in the making of Alençon lace. She made her First Communion with the Carmelites, studied for a while with a Bostonian Protestant who couldn't pay his rent, and drew from her father's estate at a downtown bank all that she required.

She was ladylike in dress and manner, wearing her raven hair in a thick chignon, and though she spoke French now fluently, English was still her native tongue, and to Richard she was most definitely as foreign as the Americans who settled the *faubourg* uptown.

Of course, technically, he was as American as she was, but though born in the United States, Richard was a Creole *homme de couleur,* spoke French almost exclusively, and had lived all his life in the "old city" bounded on the one side by the Boulevard Esplanade and on the other by the Rue Canal.

But there were more profound reasons why Anna Bella would never have gotten more than a glance from him had it not been for Marcel.

For though she had skin the color of wax candles, a perpetual bloom in her cheeks that was a rose, and large liquid brown eyes heavily fringed with a sweep of soft lashes, she had an African nose, broad and somewhat flat, and a full African mouth. In addition there was about her stance, her long neck and the easy sway of her hips, something that reminded him all too much of the black *vendeuses* who carried their wares to market in baskets atop their heads. All things African frightened him and put him off.

But this was not really known to him. If anyone had accused him of looking down on Anna Bella he would have been mortified, steadfastly denying it, and perhaps have gone so far as to insist that no such superficial judgment on the basis of appearance could cause him to dismiss a feeling, thinking human being, or even run the risk of hurting feelings as tender as hers. Was he not a man of color, he might have asked, did he not understand prejudice all too well, feeling its sting day after day?

But the truth is he did not understand it. He did not understand that its nature is that it is insidious, a vast collection of vague feelings that can wind their way into notions that are seemingly practical in nature, all too human, and have sometimes the deceptive aura of being common sense.

And in his heart of hearts, without ever voicing it to himself, Richard was repelled by Anna Bella's Africanness because of what it represented to him, the degraded state of slavery that was all round, and he would never have considered for an instant infusing by marriage into his own line those strong indications of Negro blood which had proved so obvious and profound a disadvantage for three generations and had now all but passed from the Lermontants.

These feelings, unknown, unexamined, led all too easily to a sense on his part that they were different, could have little in common, must move in different worlds. But the sum of it was that he did not consider Anna Bella his equal and the measure of it was the courtly manner in which he invariably treated her, the near fussy politeness that governed his actions in her regard.

Of course had he fallen in love with her, he might well have thrown all this to the winds. But he couldn't have fallen in love with her. And in fact pitied her slightly.

But again, of all these things, he was unaware. And when Marcel once remarked in one of those dreamy and disturbing conversations that Anna Bella came nearest in his estimation to being "the perfect person," Richard had been baffled in the extreme.

"What do you mean, 'perfect person'?" Richard had asked. Thereby opening the door to one of Marcel's longest, most abstract and rambling speeches which seemed to culminate in this: she was honest in a selfless way, and would tell Marcel the truth when he needed it, even if it made him mad.

"Well, it's sometimes very hard to tell you the truth, I'll admit that," Richard had murmured with a smile. But the rest he didn't understand. Anna Bella was a sweet girl, he'd

(160)

break the neck of anybody that hurt her; she'd make some hardworking man a good wife.

But he'd been a little surprised to hear Monsieur Philippe call her a pretty girl. And even now, watching her climb the steps ahead of Monsieur Dazincourt, throwing the light of her oil lamp before her, he found in the elastic movement of her hips, and the long low slope of her shoulders, something animalian and disconcerting. It was as if despite her carefully clustered curls and the pressed folds of her blue cotton skirt flaring so neatly from her whalebone waist, she was the black woman in the fields, the black woman swaying to the Sunday African Drums in the Place Congo. Very pretty? Well, actually...yes. He was not aware that Dazincourt who was plodding upward and down the long hallway after her had on the same matter decidedly more robust thoughts.

"Richard," she hissed at him from the top of the stairs when she was alone. He turned in the dim light from the fan window and saw her coming down in a hurry, like a little girl, her boots making not the slightest sound, the lamp held miraculously still at arm's length.

"You'll spill that!" he said, taking it and setting it down.

"Oh, I'm so glad to see you. I wanted to talk to you Sunday but I just couldn't get the chance. Come in here Richard, Madame Elsie's gone to bed; she's all crippled with this damp weather, she can barely walk."

She drew him into the parlor which was for the boarders and told him to sit down. He disliked being here. He had never visited her in these rooms.

"You've got to take a message for me to Marcel," she said.

"Then you haven't seen him...I mean today." There had always been the chance. In times past, when hurt, Marcel always went to Anna Bella. But that was before he had started to deliberately lose his mind.

"Oh, I haven't seen him in months!" she said, her head inclining to one side, her hands clasped in her lap.

He murmured awkwardly that it was one of Marcel's moods. It was a shame to treat her shabbily when before Marcel had visited her almost every afternoon.

"It's got nothing to do with moods," she shook her head. "It's Madame Elsie, she drove him off."

"But why?" he whispered.

Oh, I don't know," she said disgustedly. "She says we're too old now just to be friends, me and Marcel. Imagine that, me and Marcel, you know how it is with me and Marcel. Oh,

(161)

I don't pay her any mind, not really, not when it comes to something like this. But I can't get to see him long enough to tell him that. I can't just go down there to his house anymore, she doesn't need to tell me that, we're not children."

He nodded at once. He was embarrassed. He was not at all sure that Madame Elsie might not appear at the slightest moment and here they sat in this shadowy parlor with the light behind Anna Bella's rounded shoulder, and he was wildly distracted by her breasts. It seemed that she sat with them deliberately thrust forward and her head back so that a sloping line ran from the tip of her chin to the tip of what was almost brushing his arm. He did not like it, did not approve of it. And if anyone had pointed out to him that his own sister Giselle carried herself in much the same manner he would have been amazed. All he saw when he looked at Giselle was Giselle.

"Of course I'll take a message to him for you," he said at once, feeling guilty for these thoughts. She seemed trusting, simple, and her eyes were like those of a doe.

"Just tell him that I have to see him, Richard..." she began.

The door handle turned in the hallway. Several white men entered with the heavy tread of boots. Richard was on his feet at once and Anna Bella, taking the lamp showed the men up the stairs, leaving Richard in darkness. As soon as she returned, he headed for the door.

"I'll tell him as soon as I see him, but that might not be for a little while."

"Oh, but you'll tell him for sure?" she asked. And again she dropped her head to one side. A long loose lock made a perfect curl against her pale neck. "Seems like I can't go to market or to church anymore without Madame Elsie has to go with me, I can't even get out the door. And then when he comes, she's right there with him in the parlor and wants to know why he's there. You never saw such nonsense..." she dropped her voice. "And then she leaves me here late to let the gentlemen in!"

He did not answer her. He was staring at her, and then stammering, "I'll tell him," as he glanced at the floor. Above he heard the creak of the floorboards, the click of a lock. The house seemed vast, dark, and treacherous to him then as he slowly raised his eyes, and he felt an anger rising in him slowly and somewhat coldly so that he could not quite understand her words.

(162)

"...that he should come at supper time, Richard," she was saying, "Madame Elsie's always busy then, sitting in the pantry, watching everything, she wouldn't even know. Marcel and I could talk in the back..."

"Surely there are the maids about," he murmured now, his voice thick. "You're not here at night all alone."

"Zurlina's sleeping in the back," Anna Bella waved that away. "Don't you worry about that. But tell Marcel, Richard, tell him I have to talk to him now."

He did not relax until he heard the door close behind him and he was alone in the empty street.

Turning he saw through the fanlight her lamp moving upward and then the glass went dark. He stood motionless for a moment, anger gripping him, thinking of nothing but the words that she had said. So Marcel wasn't to call on her anymore, was he, so they were too old for that, were they, so Marcel mustn't come around. And yet she was alone in that house, "to let the gentlemen in." No, Marcel wasn't good enough, what young man of color *would* be good enough, even for that simple country girl, the daughter of a freed slave? No, but she had to stay up late to let the "gentlemen" in. "There's a young girl there, a pretty girl," Philippe Ferronaire had said, pretty girl, pretty girl, pretty girl.

Richard turned on his heel toward the Rue Burgundy, his head down, his hands hanging heavily at his sides. He would speak to Marcel at once. But by the time he had reached the corner it was his father's image that was speaking to him, Rudolphe in the close heat of the shop this morning speaking so cynically, so earnestly of Marie Ste. Marie and the world. That sudden warm admonition that had shocked Richard to the core, "Son, don't break your heart."

Well, perhaps Rudolphe did know the world, the world of Dolly Rose and old Madame Rose, and Madame Elsie with her thumping cane. But he did not know Marie. He did not know Marie! The world was one thing, but all people are not of it. Some are better than it, apart from it, more splendid, untouchable and pure.

And as he finally mounted the steps of his home, he was dogged by a rasping fragment of all the long day's exhaustions and frustrations: Dolly, glazed-eyed as she lay against her pillow, saying so crudely to Christophe, "Only white men," only white men, only white men. Well, Christophe, welcome home.

PART FOUR

I

A WEEK PASSED before Marcel saw Christophe again. All the
while he had been afraid to knock at the gate, afraid that
Christophe would not want to see him and that he would be
sent away. At times it occurred to him that Christophe had
been drunk the night of their clandestine meeting in the St.
Louis Cemetery and might have forgotten the later confer-
ence at Madame Lelaud's. Marcel believed this because he
himself had been so drunk, yet he did remember every marvelous detail even to the morning sun falling on his eyelids
when he had at last thrown himself across his bed.

Each day after that he had risen, dressed excitedly and
walked at the slowest pace humanly possible past the Mercier
townhouse, only to see the usual shuttered windows and the
vines threatening to close the old gate. Then he would go on
to Madame Lelaud's, taking the route along the waterfront
so he might pass in and out of the bustle of the market, and
once inside the smoky cabaret, he would begin with coffee,
later swallowing some gumbo for lunch, and spend the afternoon sipping beer, his sketchbook spread upon the greasy
table, his pencil working constantly, his eyes returning again
and again to the page.

Who knew but that Christophe might come through the
door? He'd suffer the chastisement for being there, but it
would be worth it just to see Christophe again.

And after all, he told himself, these gala days were coming to an end, it was good-bye to the delicious foam on the beer and the click of the ivories, he was a serious student now, and would soon be so busy with lessons that he would have no time to degenerate at all. It had to be so. Because he had to be at the head of his class by the time Monsieur Philippe came to town. That was the cloud that hung over him, the coming of his father.

But meanwhile, it seemed he heard news of Christophe everywhere that he turned and all of it was good.

Christophe, for example, had already called upon the Lermontants, seeking Rudolphe's advice on how he might advertise the new academy. And Rudolphe, after some hours closeted with the new teacher in the parlor, had emerged to announce that he was much impressed. Indeed, he thought Richard should prepare himself for the change from Monsieur De Latte's.

Richard was flabbergasted, and Marcel who came that evening for supper was too excited to risk an impetuous word.

Only Antoine, Richard's cousin, spoke forcefully against the idea, hinting again and again that the boys really knew nothing of this Paris Bohemian. "You can admire a writer who is quite far from you, but schoolboys imitate their teachers, which is quite a different thing."

"I don't care how the man lived in Paris," Rudolphe had boomed impatiently at last. "That was Paris, the *Quartier Latin*, where he was the dilettante and probably too popular for his own good. So he drank, so he kept company with actresses." Rudolphe shrugged. "He's home now, in New Orleans, and obviously prepared to be a serious man."

Antoine had not yielded, however. The family had never seen him in such opposition to Rudolphe, and even Marcel had to admit later that there was about him some sincerity in all this, which was rare. Antoine was jealous of Richard, at least so Marcel thought. But here Antoine seemed genuinely concerned. And finally giving his uncle a frankly incredulous look had said,

"But you're not really considering it!..."

"Hold your tongue!" Rudolphe had pointed to his nephew. And then lapsing into a more practical tone of voice went on. "The man reads and writes ancient Greek fluently, he can recite from Aeschylus... from memory! His Latin is perfect, he knows all the poets, and Cicero, Caesar as well. And he's fluent in English, besides. Richard has to learn English. I can't understand him when he speaks English and I'm his father! The man deserves his chance, and if he's half as good as he sounds, we're fortunate to have him."

But it was when Antoine pressed, his vague but angry statements obviously circling some point that he feared to make, that Rudolphe lost his temper. "I deplore gossip!" he said, leaning with wide eyes toward Antoine. "I tell you I will not listen to one more word about this teacher, do you hear me?"

It was finished. And both boys knew of course that as soon as Rudolphe let it be known that Richard would attend the new school, many of the other old families would follow his example.

But Christophe with a shrewdness they might not have expected of him had also called upon Dolly Rose's godmother, the rich and independent Celestina Roget. Might she consider enrolling Fantin who had not been in school for years? Of course if Celestina were to do this, her quadroon friends might follow her example just as the old families followed Rudolphe.

And Celestina was indeed considering such a move. After all, Fantin was a young man of property, and though that property was well managed, shouldn't he perhaps know a little more of the basic skills, he didn't read so well, Fantin, he couldn't read English newspapers at all.

But what had influenced her in this decision—Fantin having proven "too nervous" for any extended educational effort so far—was her personal feeling for Christophe. She had known him as a boy. And Dolly, her godchild, had known him as a boy. And on that recent Sunday, at the funeral of Dolly's little Lisa, it was Christophe who had saved the day.

Of course Richard had witnessed the events at the funeral just as he had witnessed Christophe's meeting with Dolly at the wake the night before. But he could not tell anything of this to Marcel. He did not even tell Marcel that he had seen Christophe at all. The Lermontants never spoke of the private affairs of their clients, what happened in their homes was sacred, whether it be violent grief or quiet heroism, no mention was ever made. And Richard had been so strongly inculcated with this professional stance since childhood that he did not dare to say even utterly harmless things for fear this would lead him toward that bizarre bedroom conversation when Dolly had teased Christophe from her pillow and Christophe had teased her in return.

But Celestina had told the story of the funeral many times over. Everyone knew it by the week's end.

It seems the white father of little Lisa had been there on Sunday over Dolly's vociferous objections, and Christophe had come as well. And when the time came to nail shut the little coffin, Dolly began to scream. She tried to force her hand between the wood and the nails, and was pulled away. "Go on with it," said the white man, and the Lermontants, believing it was best for everyone, including Dolly, began to drive in the nails, Monsieur Rudolphe comforting Dolly all the while. "No, no, don't do it yet, stop it," Dolly kept screaming, however, until finally they hoisted the little box onto the shoulders of the pallbearers and Dolly went wild. Then Christophe appeared, "You want it opened, Dolly?" he had asked. And Dolly, covering her mouth with her hand, nodded her head. "Monsieur," Christophe turned to Rudolphe. "Dolly won't see that child again in this life. Open the coffin. Let her say her farewell. She'll be brief, I promise you, and then you can go on."

And all this had sounded perfectly reasonable to those who'd thought Dolly hysterical a moment before. The coffin was opened, Dolly kissed her daughter and touched her daughter's hair, and then bending low appeared to whisper a little chant to her daughter, telling her good-bye under all the little pet names the child had ever had, it was a poem coming from Dolly, they said, then it was over, and falling back on Christophe's chest, she let them take the coffin away.

But Celestina was not above adding, good friend to Dolly though she was, that Christophe had remained alone in that flat with Dolly when all the other women had finally gone home.

"Imagine that!" Tante Colette had laughed later with Cecile. Cecile was disapproving of the turn this conversation had taken and glanced pointedly at Marcel. No one had to explain to Marcel that Dolly Rose had never been seen "in the company" of a man who wasn't white.

"I'm quite sure he was there to comfort her," said Tante Louisa. "The man's to teach school after all, he has to think of his reputation."

"His reputation?" Tante Colette had laughed. "What about hers?"

It would have been difficult to define Dolly's reputation

at any time before that, but by the following Friday it was damned near impossible, if Dolly had any reputation left at all. For on that evening, only five days after little Lisa's death, she had dressed to the teeth and strolled boldly through the streets to the Salle d'Orleans where she danced the night away at the "quadroon ball."

Eh bien.

Meanwhile, workmen had begun to swarm over Christophe's house, stripping paint from the streaked walls, hammering on the broken roof, filling the lazy afternoon with the clatter and boom of debris heaved from the heights onto the flags below. One could hear the scrape of shovels within the yard. And Juliet had been seen rushing to and from the market with her basket, properly dressed, her hair no longer a nest for the birds. Very soon fresh paint brightened the scraped shutters, clean glass sparkled in the sun, and from the back kitchen chimney rose the regular evening belch of smoke.

And on Saturday morning, just when Marcel's excitement had reached a painful peak, Christophe himself appeared at the cottage door, bowing courteously to Cecile, the faint scent of pomade emanating from his brown curly hair, to ask if he might see Marcel that day, might Marcel consent to take him about the city for a while, be his guide?

Marcel was in heaven.

Christophe was amiable as they walked but very quiet, and when deep in his thoughts, his face would acquire that hardness that Marcel had noted when they first met. But now and again he would ask some question, or nodding to Marcel's tentative commentary, would smile. They roamed the market, stopping for a small cup of very black, very strong coffee which they drank on their feet, and went on, wandering finally into Exchange Alley, the domain of the fencing academies, and glimpsed that famous quadroon Maitre d'Armes, Basile Crockere, just stepping out of his fencing salon in the midst of his white students. A handsome man he was and a collector of cameos which he wore all about his person. And though no white man would fight a real duel with him, it was rumored he had buried quite a few opponents on foreign soil.

It was noon when they reached the Rue Canal, and early afternoon when they took the Carrollton Railroad uptown, past the massive Grecian mansions of the Faubourg Ste.

Marie, where all was still beneath the spreading oaks, as if the white families had fled, one and all, to the country to escape the summer's inevitable scourge of yellow fever. Early evening found them passing slowly through the glittering coffee shops, confectioners and cabarets of the Rue Chartres, where occasionally Christophe would glance through the plate glass at the flicker of gaslight, at the white faces, at the spirited movement within. Marcel's heart contracted. He hastened to point out the sky, gone a rare and exquisite purple over the river, all but luminous behind the darkening trees, as if its extraordinary glow had nothing whatsoever to do with the dying sun. A serene smile softened Christophe's features, and reaching out he did that inevitable thing which Marcel so hated from others, he touched Marcel's tight yellow hair, "*Ti* Marcel," he murmured. Marcel was indignant and deeply moved at the same time. Yet Christophe seemed to savor the evening, its fragrances, the coolness of the air, and as they stood beneath an old magnolia leaning out over the arch of a Spanish house, his eyes narrowed to pick out the distant white blooms. Marcel murmured that they had always frustrated him, because they were so high. Children sold them sometimes in wagons, but the waxy white petals were invariably bruised then, perhaps from being thrown from the heights. Christophe seemed heavy, almost sad. And then with the shameless agility of a street urchin, he climbed the wrought-iron carriage gate, and mounting the stone arch, broke loose an immense flower at its brittle stem. "Give that to your mother," he said softly as he landed on his feet beside Marcel.

"Merci, Monsieur," Marcel smiled, taking it in both hands.

"And grant me one very special request," Christophe said, putting his hand on Marcel's shoulder as they walked home. "Don't ever call me Monsieur again, call me Christophe."

What had Christophe thought to hear of Dolly's return to the "quadroon balls," what had Christophe thought of all those gilded billiard parlors, white men and women sipping chocolate through the windows of the fashionable Vincent's, what was Christophe discovering all about him now that he was home?

Marcel shuddered.

Alone again in Madame Lelaud's on a Monday afternoon, his sketchbook before him, he let the pencil move sluggishly as he felt himself numbed by a vague and familiar pain. He

(169)

had long ago erected between himself and the white world a wall that he was not eager to penetrate, but the thought of Christophe penetrated it for him, thrust him acutely against the doors that were closed to him, the lines of caste and race that he felt powerless to change. He thought of Rudolphe, shutting up the undertakers shop on days when death did not detain him, who might stop into the Hotel St. Louis long enough to gather the newspapers of the day, nod to white acquaintances, or even speak with them a moment under the rotunda, then walk quietly to his immense house in the Rue St. Louis where his valet, Placide, had ready for him his small glass of amontillado, the day's mail. Would he give a thought to the bars where he could not drink, the restaurants where he could not dine? Rudolphe did not set foot in the shabby waterfront cabarets that served the common black man, and perhaps Marcel would not either as the years passed. Nor ride in the starred public cars for Negroes even if he must walk the length of the town.

But what does all this mean to a man who has strolled with other white-gloved gentlemen on the parquet of the Paris opera, to a man who has danced at the Tuileries?

Only that spring, another such world traveler had returned to New Orleans, and Marcel could well remember the outcome of that visit, as would others. This had been Charles Roget, Celestina's eldest son.

All the Roget family was excited, of course, though Charles had warned by letter that his stay would be brief. And on the great day when he at last arrived with presents for everyone, a party was given that spilled over onto the front banquettes while the courtyard of the Roget house roared with gentle voices, the tinkle of glasses, and the shrill sound of violins. Marcel had glimpsed Charles hugging his brother, Fantin, bestowing kiss after kiss on his little sister, Gabriella, and chatting now and again with two white men who stood near the back gate smoking cigars. The young boys studied him, approving his elegant dress and the pomade that he wore in his hair. There seemed no touch of the Louisianian in his speech, he was a Parisian, had strolled the boulevards.

But as the party wore on with talk of supper and Celestina pressed Marie and Marcel to stay, Charles at last took the family aside to confess that he was returning to France that very night on the same ship that had brought him in before dawn. He had spent the morning in law offices untangling his recent inheritance and he was going "home."

Celestina fainted. Gabriella broke into uncontrolled sobs, while Fantin, playing the man at once, implored his brother to change his mind. This was cruel, really! But Charles, his arms folded as he stood against the curving banister of the iron steps, swore he had seen enough of New Orleans on his journey from the docks, he was a man, he would not spend one night on southern soil. It was then that he confessed that he had a white fiancée abroad, whom he could not even bring to visit his mother as his wife. To appear in public with her in this savage place, why he would risk insult, assault more than likely, possibly even arrest. *Mais non! Adieu.*

Months after, Gabriella, drifting into Marie's bedroom, flung herself with flounces and tears on the bed and cried that Charles had written insisting they all move to Marseilles. "I don't know anything about Marseilles, I don't want to go to Marseilles!" She beat the pillow and yanked her hair. Even Cecile who generally greeted her with a subtle disdain had spoken some comforting words though later she muttered to Marcel, "Such nonsense over that spoilt yellow brat, so let him live where he wants."

Marcel had winced. And couldn't help but note silently that Charles, that "spoilt yellow brat" was somewhat less yellow than himself. But that was not the point. His mother's sentiments offended him. They were gross and out of place. One did not use such language especially not when speaking of those one knew. And meanwhile Gabriella lost herself in a round of soirees after her fourteenth birthday and Celestina having mourned a little while for Charles' father (she had always liked him "the best") began to keep company with an old white gentleman from Natchez. They had turned Charles' pictures to the wall.

But Marcel could not forget the biting determination on that young man's face when he had announced his departure, the ringing sarcasm in that laugh when he had been pressed to remain. And thinking of all this now in the dingy light of Madame Lelaud's, a sparkle of sun occasionally blinding him when the rear door opened and shut, his pencil working, his lips occasionally moved with a fragment of his thoughts, he envisioned Christophe as he had left him that first night in front of this bar, standing in the thin rain. The posture had struck him then, Christophe's stance, eyes fixed upward as if on the pale stars. And he had a strong sense suddenly of the quiet, soft-voiced man who had followed him everywhere for a day without complaint, and then leapt so suddenly atop that carriageway to bring down the fragrant magnolia flower in his hand.

And suddenly Marcel slammed shut the sketchbook, and all but upsetting the chair, left the bar. So what if Christophe had told him to wait, he could not wait, he must find Christophe now.

The gate was open, the long narrow bed of ivy cleared to reveal a path of jagged but even purple flags. And a door lay ajar, far at the back, to the dimly lit hall.

No answer came when Marcel called. A black slave, naked to the waist, fed random broken boards to a smoldering fire in the yard. He eyed Marcel indifferently, and through the dirty gray smoke, his body drenched with sweat, his large black head all but bald, he presented some image to Marcel of souls suffering in Hell. Marcel took a cautious step into the gloomy house and moved toward the front room. "Monsieur Christophe?" he called. "Madame Juliet?" It echoed in the uncarpeted emptiness as did a distant hammer somewhere, and a wrenching sound of something pulled apart.

A broad path had been cleared in the thick dust of the parquet and sensing that a dozen workmen had followed that path he followed it, turning now to the open doors of the great front room.

He could not resist a smile. What had been a shadowy ruin was so completely transformed. Rows of desks stood perfectly along the polished boards, each with its small glittering glass inkwell, and in the dusty shafts of sun that fell from the slatted blinds he saw along the freshly painted walls a gallery of framed engravings, maps, and dim paintings where shepherds piped amid placid lakes under rosy gilt-edged clouds. A lectern stood before the marble fireplace. And beyond, fitted around those high windows that faced the street, were rows of books, and a marble bust of some Caesar staring forward with smooth blind eyes.

But in the midst of this, at parade rest, hands clasped behind his back, there stood a tall white man in a dove gray coat. His golden yellow hair was brilliant in the rays of the sun that appeared to truly bathe his slender face, his green eyes. Never had Marcel understood this concept of the sun, that it might "bathe" an object or a person, until this instant. It seemed the man was luxuriating in it and set off by it as actors are when "playing their lights." He was looking upward, this man, perhaps at his own thoughts, eyelashes sparse and golden, his lips forming some private word, when he turned, quite aware of Marcel standing there, and said, "Monsieur Christophe?"

"I am looking for him, Monsieur," Marcel said.

"Ah, then we are looking for the same person," said the man, this coming in an English far unlike the hard American twang heard so often, and Marcel knew at once that it was British, and educated, and it was slightly sardonic in tone.

The man turned and walked the length of the classroom, his steps precise as though he enjoyed the sound of his boots.

"Ah, well, then," Marcel began carefully in English, "perhaps I should ask one of the workmen, sir."

"I've consulted them already but they are not workmen, they are slaves," the man said, and shifting effortlessly into French continued, "and it seems the master is not at home. Are you acquainted with 'Monsieur' Christophe?" There was clear mockery in the way that he said Monsieur. There had been mockery in it before when he had said Monsieur Christophe. There was, in fact, a deep ironical tone to all his words, and Marcel felt uneasy. He could not place it, but he had heard this very tone before, and recently. "Perhaps in the meantime," said the man, "you can explain to me the meaning of these quaint little desks."

Who this man was Marcel could not imagine, and yet something nagged at his memory. But suppose he were some bigoted person, newly arrived and suspicious of this school? There were places in the Southland where free Negroes were not allowed education any more than slaves. And though this was somewhat unreal to Marcel, he was wary.

"Perhaps I should look for Madame Juliet, Monsieur," Marcel turned to go.

"You waste your time. She's gone to market, charming woman that she is, and so very hospitable," came the answer.

And it was at this moment that Marcel realized, in utter confusion, that this ironical tone reminded him of Christophe.

The Englishman came forward, moving in and out of the slanting light.

He was considering Marcel, perhaps carefully, and Marcel, sensing some danger, felt his eyes mist over and everything become indistinct. Then he saw the man stroking the newly finished wood of one of the desks. He did not sneer at all this, but it seemed he did. A delicate map of blue veins showed

(173)

at his temples and on the backs of his hands. They were very mature hands. The man was older, much older than he seemed, but lithe and youthful, and extremely handsome. Marcel did not like him.

"What is this place, a school? I know it's 'Monsieur' Christophe's house but is it also a school?" came that perfect French again but without a characteristic Gallic thrust.

"If you'll excuse me, Monsieur, I'll come back another time," Marcel said, and went out.

But as soon as he stepped into the street, he saw Christophe. Head bowed, he was walking doggedly up the Rue Dauphine, sidestepping the rain puddles, his arms filled with parcels. He almost tripped at the curb.

"Ah, Marcel!" he said. "Give me a hand with this." His face brightened.

Marcel quickly shifted two of the bulky bundles into his left arm. "Monsieur, there's a man waiting for you..."

"Did you see the classroom?" Christophe asked. "I was looking for you today, and a very lovely young woman—your sister, I believe—told me you were out walking. Seems you spend your days walking, or so she let me know. Where were you, Madame Lelaud's?"

"Who, me, Monsieur, in a place like that!" Marcel laughed. "The classroom is splendid, Monsieur, but it's enormous."

"Well, you were right in your predictions, I've been turning people away, that is, when I haven't been tearing my hair out by the roots. The place is falling apart...no, no, let's go in by the gate." He gestured for Marcel to pass first, following him back the alley. "There's not a window that doesn't stick, a door that isn't warped, and a board that isn't infested with termites, there are rats..."

"But that's nothing out of the ordinary here, Monsieur," Marcel said, "they can fix it. But excuse me, there's a man waiting..."

"So let him wait," Christophe gestured as they entered the hallway opposite the door of the back room. "Open that, please, will you? I want to get these books unpacked. I've been talking to people all week. I set the tuition at ten dollars a month and it discouraged no one. Where is my mother," and dropping his voice to a whisper, "she's in a terrible mood."

Marcel felt a spasm. "But why?" Out of the corner of his eye, he had seen the Englishman at the far end of the hall before they entered the room.

"Open those windows, will you?" Christophe dropped the

bundles on a large table already stacked with books. "She's in a terrible mood because she doesn't want to let me out of her sight. She would like to put me in a bell jar. There are twenty students now at least." He took a deep breath, looking about himself. "Well, we'll see what happens on the first day of class. Someone will drop, no doubt, and there will be room for others, if I haven't lost the waiting list, hmmm." He stuffed his hands into his pockets. His eyes were afire.

The blinds were new and opened easily to emit the same gentle sun that had illuminated that front room, pouring as it did into a deep alleyway dividing the townhouse from the one next to it, a place still alive with much of the lush greenery that had been cleared from the other side. And the room in this new light appeared cluttered with all manner of fascinating objects, busts of Voltaire, Napoleon, Grecian goddesses, and a distinguished head Marcel had never known. Books were heaped all over, there were the trunks and crates Marcel had glimpsed before, and framed pictures in leaning stacks against the walls.

"For years," Christophe said, just catching his breath. "I sent home packages from all over the world. And I never really knew why. Why would my mother want a small marble bust of Marcus Aurelius, for instance? What would she do with Shakespeare's works? I'm lucky she didn't put them by the chamberpot. It was as if I knew I was coming back, and as if I knew it was all meant for something, all those boxes traveling the Atlantic, it was all destined for this moment, this place. I have the distinct impression that life can be worthwhile." He smiled at Marcel, and then let out a low excited laugh. "Imagine," he said. "Life being worthwhile. You know, Marcel, there is a line in St. Augustine, the only line I remember from St. Augustine, as a matter of fact; it is 'God triumphs on the ruins of our plans.' Ever read that? Well, I can't explain it now ..."

"Monsieur," Marcel whispered. The gray-suited Englishman had come into the door.

Christophe reached forward and clasped Marcel's neck. "Christophe," he said, "you were going to call me Christophe, remember? Not Monsieur, but Christophe, hmmmmm? Now I want you to tell me frankly how these books compare with those you've used in the past, there's a penknife somewhere in all this mess, I'm going to send abroad for more books, but remember, from here on out, it's Christophe."

"Christophe," echoed the Englishman behind him. Christophe turned.

The Englishman stood as before, hands clasped behind his back, but the ironical lift of his eyebrows was gone, and the green eyes were softened with a radiance that emanated from his entire expression as he surveyed the man before him who was undergoing a dramatic change.

It was a change so complete and remarkable in Christophe that Marcel felt it, as if some current had zipped through the air between the two men.

Color danced in the Englishman's face. "Well," he stepped into the room glancing disdainfully at a heap of books that fell to one side at the brush of his boot. "This is an awfully long way to go for the morning papers and a litre of white wine."

The muscles of Christophe's face tensed, and the eyes became moist, and as he remained motionless staring at the Englishman, the veins slowly corded in his temples and his neck.

"That was it, wasn't it?" the Englishman asked, his speech crisp as his eyes scanned the clutter of the room. "You were going out for the newspapers, and a litre of white wine?"

"How did you get here?" Christophe whispered. The voice was low and thick and had a slight resonance Marcel had never heard. "What are you doing here?"

The Englishman was stung. "I might ask you that question, Chris," he said, and the color in his pale cheeks darkened, emphasizing the bright cornsilk of his eyebrows and his hair. He flashed his warm and wounded expression around the room, and reaching out for a small ivory statuette on the cluttered table picked it up, turning it easily in one hand. "Istanbul?" he asked, and set it down. His pale fingers touched the forehead of a marble bust. "This we bought in Florence, didn't we?"

"*You* bought it in Florence! Why did you come here!" Christophe turned, however, before the man could answer; and he closed his hand over his eyes as if he were squeezing his temples tight between thumb and fingers, letting out a moan at the same time. Then looking at the ceiling he said loudly between clenched teeth, "Oooo God." With his back to the Englishman and to Marcel, he appeared to be pounding his fist into the palm of the other hand.

The emotion in the room was palpable, and the Englishman's lips were suddenly trembling as with a sudden violent impatience, he snatched one thing after another from the table and tossed it about, a statue, a handful of chessmen that he let drop like pebbles, a rolled tapestry he flung out as if it were wet and then threw to the floor. He overturned a stack of books and ran his hand lightly over the gilt titles, his voice spiteful, biting, as he read, *"Histoire de Rome, simples et composés de la langue anglaise, leçons d'analyse grammaticale,* what is this, Christophe, some missionary outpost among the natives, where is your cassock, your crucifix? And when does the local populace string you up for educating slaves?"

"I'm not here to educate slaves, Michael." Christophe's voice was dull. He stood still with his back to the man, his shoulders slightly slumped, while Marcel watched, afire himself with rage. He felt the Englishman's eyes on him now, on the disordered bookshelves behind his head. The pale, sharp-featured face showed some indignation, some thin and righteous disgust, and everything around the man appeared shabby suddenly, to have nothing of his own vibrant and gilded person. It infuriated Marcel, the sight of Christophe's bent shoulders infuriated him, and above all it infuriated him that the room once so fabulous in its jumble of treasures was now dusty and smelled of mold.

With a thumb hooked in his pants pocket and a hand curled on his chin, Christophe was thinking. He drew himself up and said calmly,

"Go back to Paris, Michael. It's a bad thing, your coming here. I should have written you, and I would have written in time. Now you must forgive me for that, and you must leave here. You can't accomplish anything here. You had best get right on the boat for France now, this isn't the place for you, any other place in the world, perhaps, but not here..."

"It's the place for you, Christophe?" the man asked. He strode about the room glaring at the shelves, at the sawdust that overlay the windowsills, and kicked a heap of curled maps with his foot. "It's a marvelous measure of character the debris a man collects about him. We went through Greece with a knapsack if I remember, and in Cairo we had a small leather valise."

Marcel had to rip his eyes off this man with an effort. It was as if the hatred he felt for him and the fear he felt of him kept him riveted. "I'll come back, Monsieur," he said striding toward the door.

"No!" Christophe pivoted. "I need you today! That is, I want you...I would prefer if you stay..." he was all but stammering, his eyes watery and gleaming. "There's a knife somewhere," he snapped his fingers... "those parcels, Marcel, the school's to start on Monday, I'm not even close to prepared, the knife's...the knife," he snapped his fingers again, the voice barely under control.

"And who's to come to this school, then, you're teaching white students?" came the indignant voice. "Tell me what you are doing here, Chris!"

Marcel quickly drew out his keychain and the small silver knife attached to it, and cut through the twine of a loose bundle of books. He removed them from the crumpled paper, his hands awkward and fumbling under the Englishman's hard gaze. He had to defy the man. He had to look at him. And as he ripped the twine of the next bundle, he looked up.

But the Englishman wasn't looking at him at all. He was staring almost stupidly forward, the color still dark in his face. And he was suffering.

And Christophe, as if he couldn't risk a moment's hesitation, was snatching the books from the table and stuffing them into the shelves. His hands smoothed the rows, brought the spines out deftly to sit even with the edge. All his gestures said this man isn't here, he's not even here. But his face was stricken, and there was something hunted and miserable in his eyes. When a book slipped from his grasp, he snatched it angrily from the floor.

"Stop that!" the man said. He slapped the book out of Christophe's hand. And then lowering his head as he bore down on Christophe, his voice went soft. "You did this to spite me, Chris? But why!"

"It has nothing to do with you, Michael!" Christopher was all but groaning. "Don't you see! It's what I want to do! It has nothing to do with you! I told you I was going home, I told you I was leaving Paris, I tried to talk with you before I left, you wouldn't listen to me, I was in a glass box shouting at the top of my lungs, for God's sakes, Michael, get out of here, go back to Paris, and let me alone!"

At that moment Juliet appeared at the door, and for an instant Marcel did not know who she was. A corseted lady stood there, immaculate in new muslin and all that lovely hair was drawn up in a wreath of braids on the back of her head. But there was no time for savoring this. She was looking intently at the Englishman.

And the Englishman was brutally stunned.

He had stepped back and moved by himself, in his thoughts, about the room. He took slow shuffling steps. Christophe was beside himself. He was struggling for control, and running a hand back through his hair now he turned toward the man, quite oblivious to Juliet or to Marcel.

"Look, I...I wasn't prepared for this," he said gently, "Michael, I didn't expect you to come. I thought you'd write, yes, but...you've got to give me a little time to talk to you calmly, not now, later...when we can sit down...I've done nothing to spite you. I left without telling you, that was bad."

"You've tried over and over to spite me, Christophe," the man said calmly. "But when you ruin yourself to spite me, when you give up your life in Paris, when you leave your future there...you have found the perfect way." And then looking up with an entreaty to reason, he said, "You can't stay in this place." He shrugged. "It's out of the question, you can't remain here."

"No," Juliet said suddenly. She lowered her heavy market basket to the floor and moved quickly toward her son. "Who is this man?" she said.

"Not now, Maman, not now," Christophe shook her off.

"Do you know what they are doing in the rotunda of my hotel?" the Englishman asked softly.

"I know, I know," Christophe nodded wearily, shutting his eyes.

The Englishman sighed. He shook his head. "They're auctioning slaves, Christophe. Do you know when we last saw that? It was in the hellholes of Egypt where all that remains of civilization lies in ruin, and this is America, Christophe, America!"

"Christophe," Juliet whispered, "who is this man!"

"That has nothing to do with it," Christophe said. "It's got nothing to do with my being here or not being here, because it was the same before I was born and it will be the same after I'm dead...that's not..."

"That you would come here, to live in this place," said the Englishman softly, "to spite me—that has everything to do with it, Chris. I'm going back to the hotel now, a hotel where it is illegal for you to be lodged. And I am going to take my dinner in a room where it is illegal for you to share my table. And I am going to wait for you to come to me. Up the backstairs, no doubt, the human chattels who staff the place will show you the way. And then you can explain to me what this exile is all about. Now, do I have your word you will come!" His green eyes gleamed with a sense of power.

And Christophe nodded, running that hand through his hair again. "Yes... later... tonight."

The Englishman started towards the door. But then he stopped. He drew something out of his coat, a packet of papers. "Oh, yes, your publishers want to talk to you, about adapting *Nuits de Charlotte* for the stage..."

Christophe grimaced with disgust.

"...Frederich LerMarque wants to play Randolphe. Frederich LerMarque! And he's willing to help you to adapt it, there's a guarantee naturally, do you know what this means?"

"Nothing," Christophe shook his head, "I cannot do it."

The Englishman's face showed a momentary flicker of rage. He glanced at Marcel coldly and Marcel at once looked away. Juliet was studying the man as if he were not a human creature at all.

"This is an author's dream, Christophe," the Englishman said with renewed patience. "LerMarque could pack the Porte-Saint-Martin, he could pack the Théâtre Français. Thousands would see your work, thousands who've never read a book in their lives..."

Christophe did not move. Then he turned to face the Englishman, and with an effort he made his face very calm and said gently, "No."

"The flat in Paris is as you left it," the Englishman said, "the rooms are as you left them... your desk, your pens, it's all still there. And I have infinite patience, Christophe, though at times I lose my temper. I am here to wait this out." Leaving the packet on the table, he left.

A heavy silence lay over them.

Marcel was miserable. He found himself studying the small silver knife on his chain and realized he had deliberately cut the tip of his finger with it, and it was bleeding. He felt listless staring at it as though all the enthusiasm had been drained from him, drained from the room. Christophe's eyes were leaden as he slumped into the chair.

"Egypt?" Juliet whispered. "You were with that man in Egypt?" Her brows knit like those of a child. Gently she placed her hands on Christophe's neck and commenced to massage the muscles. "Christophe, you were in Egypt with that man?" She reached suddenly for the packet of papers.

But Christophe jerked around and caught her wrist with careless violence.

"No, Maman, stop it, don't be crazy for once!" He got the packet back and threw it down.

She stared at him. "Answer me, Christophe," she said. Her voice was low and guttural, "Who is that man?"

"No, Maman, not now."

"Who?"

"Maman, it doesn't matter who is he. I'm not going back to Paris, I'm not going back!," he looked up at her, removing her hand from his neck. "Now, get me something to eat, get Marcel something...leave it alone."

She was not satisfied. Her eyes followed Christophe as he turned to Marcel, and began to murmur now, almost incoherently about the work at hand. Marcel was thinking dully of all the old stories he'd heard of the "tall Englishman" who lived with Christophe in Paris, the "the white Englishman" who carried him home from those glamorous *rive gauche* cafés. The should just clear this table, Christophe was saying, get this place in order, he had to have some twenty sets of texts by Monday morning and was sure to have to go back to the store at least twice. Juliet, her head cocked to one side, watched him and then, her lips moving silently with some angry speech, she lifted her skirts prettily and went out of the room.

Christophe was staring forward.

"Let me put these together by subject," Marcel said, turning to the volumes on the shelf. "Then we can examine them, Monsieur, I mean...Christophe."

Christophe looked up. He smiled. "Yes, Christophe, right," he said. "Yes...alphabetical order for now, it doesn't matter..." Some of the old vitality was struggling to return. There were trunks upstairs to be brought down, he said, and maps to be unrolled, pictures yet to be hung, it was so fortunate that Marcel was willing to help him, that Marcel had come by.

And it seemed by dusk that they had almost restored it, the excitement that Christophe had exuded when they had first entered this room. They drank coffee as the sun set, the windows open and that great twining Queen's Wreath, much cut back, but still luxurious, framed the windows, and the fresh boards of a new cistern rose abruptly to the far left as if to the very sky.

Inside the room was clean. Books filled all the shelves,

and in the hall, out of sight, lay the empty trunks. In a newly upholstered wing chair, Christophe sat beside the grate, looking about with a pleasant and relaxed air. He beamed at Marcel. And Marcel, having never done such work...the lugging of crates downstairs, the back-straining unpacking and sorting...was exhilarated and exhausted at the same time. They had had a fun time with the trunks, coming across random discoveries that sometimes made them laugh: a woman's slipper, scarves, a fan Christophe had bought in Spain, playing cards, mantillas, and ladies' buttons fixed to a card which in their tiny intricate carvings told a story of love won and love lost. Juliet had been delighted with these unexpected finds, having thought she had cleaned these trunks long ago of all their real treasures, and indifferent to the ancient names of Horace, Pliny, Homer that they dug from the depths, had held the mantilla to the window, smiling, to see the sun through black lace.

Marcel, at the window with his coffee, savored the aroma, let the steam sting his eyes for no good reason, except perhaps that he was ashamed of watching Juliet in the open kitchen across the yard as she stirred the pot in the dim light of the fire; and pretending not to watch her, his eyes moved now and then to the fluttering hens that scampered across the purple flags. It was cool now. Getting darker, and the evening star shone in the deepening blue of the sky.

"What are you thinking, Marcel?" Christophe asked.

"Ah...that I like this time of day." Marcel laughed. He'd been thinking that if he must live in torment this near to Juliet, he must watch his step. Now there was a whaleboned waist to clasp, as enticing as the flesh he knew to be inside of it. She drew down a black iron pan from the ghastly flickers at the kitchen ceiling, her back to him, her silhouette quite flat and utterly fetching.

"But what are you thinking, Christophe?" he asked.

"That you are my friend," Christophe said. "And that your shirt is torn, and your coat is soiled and your mother will be angry with you."

Marcel laughed, "My mother doesn't tend to those things, Monsieur," he said forgetting the old admonition. "She won't know. And if she did, she'd be relieved to hear I wasn't brawling in the streets, she's been at her wits' ends with me lately, though all of that is changed now."

"You've grown up," Christophe teased. There was a gleam in his eye. He tapped the ash from his cheroot into the grate.

His shirt was open at the throat, and he sat with legs comfortably apart, one foot on the fender.

"I have, Monsieur."

"You must like calling me Monsieur more than you like me," Christophe said.

"I'm sorry. I forgot."

He could hear that pan sizzling on the fire, smell the peppers, the onions, all mingled with the delicious aroma of the frying bacon. He filled his cup again and brought the pot to Christophe.

Christophe sat back, sipping his coffee, the room so dusky now that Marcel could not clearly make out his face. But he saw the gleam of his pocket watch as Christophe flicked it open.

"I have to go out for a while," he said.

"And I should be getting home," Marcel said.

"I want you to come back for supper, do you think your mother will let you do that?" Christophe rose. He stretched, groaning with the obvious fatigue of his muscles. He reminded Marcel of Jean Jacques. In fact the atmosphere of Jean Jacques' shop had been very much with Marcel this afternoon, coming and going, distant, sometimes violently clear. He had thought of all those times that he had sat on that stool watching Jean Jacques as if he were a mannequin on a shelf. He had worked today, actually worked, the way that Jean Jacques worked, and he had loved it.

"I'll ask her, Monsieur," he said excitedly.

"Good. In an hour then?" Christophe said. "Do try to come back."

Juliet was moving across the flags toward the back door. She came in as Christophe was adjusting his tie. And throwing up his hands, he turned it over to her, standing patiently as she quickly made it right.

"But where are you going?" she demanded.

"An errand, that's all," he said vaguely.

"Ah, but do this for me, now," she said holding him. Something gleamed in the palm of her hand. To Marcel at the window it looked like a jewel. And Christophe, guiding her toward Marcel and the light, quickly tilted her head to one side and drove the small hook which held the jewel through the soft lobe of her ear. Marcel winced. It caught him unexpectedly and he felt such a surge of brutal excitement that he backed off flustered, put the coffee cup down, and murmured his farewell.

(183)

"But where are you going?" she was demanding of Christophe as he moved away. "Tell me, where!"

An hour later to the minute, Marcel found her alone as he entered, candles on the mantel, the round table set with silver, and she with folded arms and bowed head crouched by the empty grate in all this warm air as if she were cold. The new clock on the wall had stopped, and drawing out his watch, Marcel opened the glass case and adjusted the hands. He gave the pendulum a gentle touch. Blood thudded in his ears. He knew he was alone with her, and kept thinking to himself that soon this pain would pass. He would grow accustomed to her. When Christophe had said, "you are my friend," he had known a rare and perfect happiness which he would not jeopardize for all the passion in the world.

He turned slowly, forming some conventional thing to say to her, when she shot him a glance with those strange feline eyes and said, "He's with that man."

"Do you think so, Madame?" he meant to treat it lightly.

"I know so," she said. "He thinks I don't know anything. He thinks I have no mind."

She was looking directly at him and when she said those last words, he had the strangest sensation. He himself had thought she had no mind.

It was a disturbing thought, for what did she have in her head if she didn't have a mind? What was it that was so terrifying about her? Her eyes appeared nearly malevolent in the candlelight. He would have liked a good oil lamp in this room right now, perhaps even two.

"Why don't you come here to me," she said, "and kiss me?"

"Because, Madame, if I do that...I won't be a gentleman with you for very long," he said.

"Why don't you let me be the judge of that?" she said contemptuously. It was not her usual voice, it was a voice with some quickness and social awareness that he hadn't heard from her before.

He was aware of his face being knotted, that he wasn't hiding his distress. He wanted her to know how much he wanted her. If he had to refuse her, he wouldn't have it any other way.

"Don't you want me?" she asked softly.

"Yes," he sighed. He shut his eyes. "Christophe is very likely to come in..."

"Well, then let's do it, if it will make him come in," she said.

She dropped back in the chair, defeated, eyes staring off.

"You're very clever, *cher*," she said in another vein, but he was so uncomfortably excited he hardly understood her words. "You know that man who was here?"

"I never saw him before this afternoon."

"But was he...was he an Englishman?" she looked up.

When he said yes, her face became cold, as hard as Christophe's face could be. "Aaahh," she said. She rose without the aid of her hands, and clutching the backs of her arms she moved slowly yet feverishly about the room. "And he comes to this house, he comes to this house." She turned to Marcel. "How old do you think he was, *cher?*"

"I don't know, Madame. Thirty-five, perhaps older."

"They think I have no mind," she whispered, her eyes narrowing. "They think I have no mind!" Her voice was trembling. "That he should dare to come into this house," she whispered, "That he should dare to come here. What am I, mad?"

"I don't understand," he shook his head.

"No, you don't understand. Well, let me tell you then. Years ago, ten years ago I sent my son to Paris..." her voice was breaking. She stopped and put her hands to her head. She appeared to be pressing hard against the sides of her head. "Oh, Christophe..." she moaned suddenly. "Not the same man."

"But what is it?" he asked.

The house was silent around them. She stood in the shadows, far from the candles, still pressing her hands to the sides of her head. It was as if she were trying to blot out some pain, her eyes closing, her teeth bared, for an instant white between her lips. "Christophe," she whispered again. It had the desperation of some terrible need. Then she dropped her hands at her sides. "He disappeared from the hotel where he was, I don't know, some family there, they were his guardians, I couldn't read his letters and then there were no letters. He would have been fourteen then, maybe older. He was young as you are, *cher*," she said. "And he disappeared."

The old tale was fresh in Marcel's mind..."And then he ran away, they said, he went wandering, all through Turkey, Egypt, Greece..."

"What happened, Madame?" he came forward.

"One day I was coming home..."she said..."I was coming

(185)

home and there were letters here again. It was years after. Those men at the bank, they read them to me, he was alive, he was all right. He was alive," she sighed. "It was years after," she said. "But he was alive!"

"Sit down," he said gently. And obediently, she settled in the chair. He was looking down at the nape of her neck, the soft curls there, and the thin chain that held the diamond that was over her breast. Her breasts heaved and she leaned, as if fading, to one side. "It couldn't be that same man, he would not dare to come here!" she said. She shook her head. "Not in my house, not that same man..."

A vague dreary feeling had descended upon Marcel. It was dark as this room was dark, and all the warmth here, the sheen of the leather books in the candlelight, silver gleaming on the table, was all gone. "What do you mean, Madame?" he asked her. He was seeing the Englishman, that violent intensity with which he had confronted Christophe and Christophe so weakened by it as he had begged the man to go. "What is it, Madame, about this man?"

"They said it was an Englishman," she whispered. "They said it was a strange Englishman who had been lodging there in that hotel with the family that kept him, at that hotel."

It was as if a winter wind had chilled the room. Marcel his brows knit was staring at the empty hearth. It was as if his hand were on a door and something that he did not know lay beyond that door, something he had no experience of, no knowledge of, though he had always known such things were there. He shuddered. "That's impossible," he whispered. She was crying, and when she heard him speak she stopped.

"What did you say?" she whispered.

Antoine Lermontant might as well have been beside him in this dark place saying with a cunning smile, *"I told you there were things you did not know about this man."*

"No," he whispered. "I don't believe it."

"What do you mean?" she asked. He looked down at her. He had forgotten that she was there. He wanted to speak to her and yet his lips couldn't form words. *But you're not really considering it, sending Richard to that school!*

"It was an Englishman," she whispered, mistaking his meaning. "They said it was. And *that* was a year after we received the word. My son was gone!" She was looking up to him, appealing to him. "It could be that man? That man? Come here, under this roof, into my house?" Her voice grew in strength with her outrage. "After he stole my son from me? After he disappeared?"

"No," he shook his head, forcing his lips into a smile. "It must not be the same man."

"I want you to do something for me," she said, turned now so that she gripped the back of the chair. She was looking up into his eyes. "I want you to find that man. Go to the hotels. I don't know where he is. Are you listening to me?"

He was looking through the open window at the rustling shapes now colorless and welded in the dark. *And what are you thinking, Monsieur? That you are my friend.* He saw that Englishman, that pain in his face, and between them that searing intensity, that struggle. "I don't believe it," he whispered.

"The flat in Paris is as you left it...the rooms are as you left them...your desk, your pens, it's all still there."

"I want you to find that man, find where he is, do you hear me, that he should dare to come to my house!" she breathed. "That man! Marcel, listen to me!"

It was the first time she had ever called him by name. He didn't even know that she knew his name. He was staring off, barely conscious of her hand touching his hand.

"You must do it. You must find him and tell me where he is," she said. "I will go to him."

A door slammed somewhere, a powerful distant echo. There was the strong stride of boots down the empty hall. Marcel's heart quickened.

He looked down at her. Her eyes were wide and dark in her pale face, distorted by this dim light so that for an instant she appeared to have the face of a skull. "No," he shook his head. "I don't believe it," he whispered to the air as if he were in a trance.

"I will tell him I *know,* I know what he is!" she whispered.

Christophe clicked his heels at the door.

Marcel lowered his eyes. Juliet had not turned away from him, her eyes were still searching his face. And the blood roaring in his ears, he finally made himself face the man in the door.

Christophe stepped out of the shadows into the light. "Maman?" he looked at Juliet. His eyes held a question as he turned to Marcel. He was bright, animated, as if he had been hurrying and eager to return to them. "What is it?" he whispered. And then angrily, he said, "Maman, get my supper now please!"

She had a stunned and bowed attitude as she left.

Christophe glared at Marcel.

"Are you playing your little games with my mother right under my nose?" he demanded.

It was a sudden blow.

"What?" Marcel whispered.

"What were you doing in here!" Christophe was furious. And striding to the door he slammed it, his back to it, as if he would not let Marcel escape.

"O mon Dieu!" A violent shudder passed over Marcel. He shook his head. "Monsieur, I swear!" he threw up his hands. Christophe's face was the picture of fury. And then bowing his head, Marcel burst into tears. He loathed himself for this, and hopelessly humiliated he turned his back, his choked sobs deafening in the silence, and by an iron act of will at last became quiet.

"I'm sorry, Marcel," Christophe said simply. He felt Christophe's hand on his shoulder. "I keep forgetting how young you are, you're too young really to even..." he sighed. Gently he turned Marcel around. "Be my friend in this," he said, and guiding Marcel to the chair insisted he sit down. He leaned forward to Marcel across the table. Marcel was sick. He fixed his eyes carefully on some point between them and let the nausea in himself subside.

"I've tried to play this with dignity, to act the gentleman," Christophe was saying. "But the fact is simply this, every slave on this block knew you were here that afternoon with my mother, don't deceive yourself for an instant that they didn't see you come, and go. And if that sassy girl of yours, Lisette, felt even the slightest affection for your mother, then your mother would know, too. And if you keep playing this little drama with my mother, my little academy will fold overnight like a bad play in competition with a spicier one at the theater upstairs."

Marcel shook his head. He wanted to say he would never let such a thing happen, but still he was sick, and fatigued and confused. It was easier just to listen to this firm and gentle voice coming from the man opposite.

"It seems everyone is against this little enterprise of mine, my friend from Paris, my mother, this house which is falling down around me, but not you. You mustn't be against it, not you!" He studied Marcel, his brows knit. "That first night when I came home, I was so discouraged, you cannot imagine. But you know how my mother was. You saw this house. I almost panicked, Marcel. I almost bundled her up and took her with me right to the docks.

"But then I looked around me, really looked around. I went roaming through these rooms where I'd grown up, I went up on the rooftop and lay there for a long time alone with the stars. I had the strangest feelings welling up in me. I wanted to touch the oak branches, the magnolias, I wanted to wander through the streets, caressing the old bricks and the gas lamps, and hammering with my fist on the heavy wooden shutters, slip my fingers through the slatted blinds. I'm home, home, home, I kept thinking to myself, but it was beyond thought, it was sensation, and I wanted to see *my people*, men and women of color, Creoles like ourselves. I wanted to go out and see them in the houses I remembered, hear their curious and languid accents, and their laughter, see the light flicker in their eyes.

"I tried to envision my school as I'd seen it in Paris, tried to see it as I'd planned it...and I went downstairs then and went to see you.

"And I discovered this: you wanted me to found the school, you told me there were other boys who wanted it, my people here might already know what I planned to do and welcome it with open arms. And I realized that others saw my little school as I saw it, I felt anchored suddenly after years and years of wandering, I felt I'd come home!

"Oh, I know this is hard for you. You're dreaming of the day when you'll go to Europe as a young gentleman, and I'll do my utmost to prepare you for it as your teacher in my own way. But someday I'll explain to you what overcame me in Paris, that feeling of utter rootlessness, that confusion when I thought of all the places I'd lived, the little cottages, the crumbling villas on the Mediterranean, all those damp and sometimes beautiful rooms! I wanted to come home!

"Now I'm telling you all this because I want you to know what it means to me! What you mean to me! What all the boys here who will come to this school mean to me! You've made my saving dream something real.

"But if you let my mother lure you up those steps, I won't be able to survive that little scandal, the prim and respectable *gens de couleur* will pull their children away from this house like that! Be patient, Marcel. The world is really filled with beautiful women, and something tells me you'll never have to want for them, never at all. Be gentle with my mother, be the gentleman with her, but don't let her seduce you! Not again!"

Marcel shook his head. "Never, Christophe," he whispered. "Never again." But he was barely conscious of the words he uttered because the immensity of his feeling could not be expressed in words. He loved Christophe, loved him as surely as he had ever loved Jean Jacques and it seemed to him that nothing must separate him from this man. He felt quickened and alive in Christophe's presence, and Christophe's words were utterly unlike the speech of those around him, they were like water in the desert, light piercing the inescapable darkness of a dungeon cell. That only a moment ago, Marcel had been the prey of some bleak and terrifying suspicion about Christophe seemed unreal to him, the Englishman's bizarre possessiveness meant nothing, and neither did Antoine's vague gossip, nor even the violent power of perceptions which were Marcel's own. It was all swept away before it could come to flower in the light of an intensifying spiritual desire: Marcel must know Christophe, learn from him, love him, all the rest be damned.

"Then you won't go back to Paris, you'll stay?"

Christophe was surprised. "Did you think I'd go back?"

"To adapt *Nuits de Charlotte* with Frederich LerMarque for the Paris stage? Yes, I thought you'd go back . . . when you thought it over."

"Never," Christophe said with a faint smile. "Revive those characters, lock myself up again in a Paris flat with those characters, live day in and day out with those dreary half-realized souls. Ah!" he shuddered. "Let someone else adapt it, I am through with that book, I couldn't do it, I'd lose my mind."

The doorknob turned. Juliet came in silently, a large heavy iron pot in her hands. She lowered it to the table and began to stir the steaming food.

"Now, let's toast to the school," Christophe said. All about him had a wholesome ring now, his eyes were youthful and chinked with laughter. "Sit down, Maman!" he burst out suddenly, and rising he caught Juliet by the waist, kissing her on both cheeks while she made to hit him with her spoon.

"Where were you that you kept us waiting?" she demanded. It had a nice everyday ring to it.

"An errand," he shrugged. He pushed her down into her chair. Then taking Marcel's plate he served it now with the rice and chicken bubbling in the pot. It had a voluptuous and spicy aroma, familiar enough with its blending of garlic, herbs, red pepper.

She filled their glasses for them, and commenced to butter their bread. It was only then that Marcel realized she had set no place for herself. She brought the candles from the mantel, and settling in the shadows seemed content to watch them dine.

And just as she leaned her face to one side, the soft skin of her cheek wrinkling against the knuckles of her right hand, there came a hard knock at the side door, across the hallway from them, and they heard it creak on its hinges.

Christophe stiffened.

But it was only a black slave who came into the dim light. Tall, very young, his clothes were miserably ill fitted, his shoes worn.

"Michie Christophe," he drawled in a voice so soft it was like a lump of chalk crumbling as one tries to write with it on a brick wall.

"Yes?"

"Here, Michie Christophe," he produced a brass key ring complete with a heavy set of household keys. "Madame Dolly says you left this just now, Michie Christophe, she said that you will pay me to bring this to you here. Just five cents, please, Michie Christophe, so I can buy a little something to eat."

Juliet let out a shriek.

Marcel turned his face away, attempting to keep it straight. But he felt weak with laughter and suddenly very light-headed, elated as he glanced slyly at Christophe.

Christophe, embarrassed, stuffed the key ring back into his pants pocket, and paying the slave turned, flustered, to his plate. Attempting to appear casual he picked up his spoon.

"An errand, was it?" Juliet murmured, leaning forward, "and with that vain stupid woman, no less, that china doll!"

Marcel was gazing at Christophe with undisguised admiration.

Juliet hissed, "I ought to cook you in the pot."

"And why, may I ask?" Christophe said. "When I left this city ten years ago, I may have been a little boy, Maman, but in the event that you haven't noticed, I have come back a man."

MADAME ELSIE CLAVIÈRE walked with a cane all the time now, dragging her left foot slowly as the consequence of a recent stroke. She was bent, her hair a fluffy white from the temples, and beneath a black veil, she struggled along Père Antoine's Alley, her right hand tightly clasped to Anna Bella's arm.

She had been born in the days of the French colony, remembered the old Indian attacks, and those times under the Spanish when Governor Miro, driven to it by the white ladies, had passed the famous "*tignon* law" restricting the quadroons to a simple scarf for a headdress as if that might stifle their charms. She laughed even now at that old tale. But New Orleans had grown around her into a vast city, brilliant perhaps as the Paris and London of travelers' talk. There were eighteen thousand *gens de couleur* in it today, only a part of its ever-shifting and motley population, and despising the Americans, she lamented those olden times, when Spanish officers had brought her Madeira and jeweled bracelets, and her daughters had been fair and spectacular, their meager offspring disappearing north into the white race. She was lonely in her old age. She often said this with a sneer. And with a firm grip on life and on Anna Bella's arm, she averred now that she was weary of this world, she wanted to be taken home.

"I don't see why you don't go visit Madame Colette," Anna Bella was saying in her slow but easy French. "Madame Colette is always asking for you, and Madame Louisa too."

As they struggled along the Rue St. Louis toward the Rue Royale, Anna Bella continued her campaign.

"Why, every time I see them at Mass, they ask about you, Madame Louisa says she means to come see you and with this and that, and the opera season, well they'll be busy all summer long."

"All right, then," Madame Elsie said finally. "I want to get off my feet."

The dress shop was thronged as usual, and Colette at the rear was making notes in an immense ledger, when seeing Madame Elsie and Anna Bella, she rose at once and brought them in. Of course she was glad to see Madame Elsie, and oh, what lovely white lace on Anna Bella's pretty dress, my, but she did make the most beautiful lace, please come on now into the back room.

"Now you just sit down here, Madame Elsie," Anna Bella eased the old woman into the chair. "Why, maybe you ought to be looking at a few of those bonnets while you're here. And I'll just go down the street now to get that sachet."

"Won't you have some coffee, Madame Elsie?" Colette asked. But Madame Elsie was glaring at Anna Bella from behind her veil.

"What sachet?"

"Don't you remember now, I told you. I wanted some sachet for the armoire, and some camphor, too. Don't you remember, and you said to get some blessed candles, why I've made a list." Anna Bella drew back toward the door, bowing to Colette. "You just rest yourself, Madame Elsie, you know, Madame Colette, she just has to get off her feet."

"You leave her to me, *chère,* you go on." Colette was clearing a heap of lace, and ribbons from the small table by Madame Elsie's chair.

"You come right back," said Madame Elsie.

"Yes, Madame Elsie, I sure will," Anna Bella answered, and quickly she rushed through the bustle and press of the little store.

Behind her she could hear Colette's voice, "My, but that girl's turned out to be a little lady."

"Eh, and whose doing was that!" rumbled Madame Elsie, "I tell you she doesn't know how to behave. However... well the face is not pretty, but you know, well, the figure is, something else..."

Anna Bella shut the door behind her and started back toward the Rue Ste. Anne. "The face is not pretty," she said to herself in a whisper, "but you know, well, the figure is something else!" She glanced to heaven for justice and shook her head. Passing the open doors of a restaurant with its black doorman, she heard him say as he pretended to tip his hat,

"Well, ain't that a pretty nigger gal, I say, ain't that a fancy nigger gal."

She dropped her eyes, her head tilted to one side, and walked fast as if she hadn't heard.

"I say that's one fine nigger gal," he said louder, mocking her, "bet that's a Creole lady for sure!"

It seemed the faster she walked, the slower she moved, his voice still in her ears, and when she saw her reflection in the

(193)

darkened windows of the undertaker's shop she lifted her head a little haughtily, lips quivering between sudden tears and a smile, as she held the deep folds of her light blue dress.

The Ste. Marie cottage looked deserted in the glaring sun, the long blinds loosely latched over the front door; and she didn't stop because she would have lost heart if she had, but went right up the path and tapped by the window, head down, eyes averted as if when she was discovered there someone would deal her a hard blow.

But there was no sound from within. She rocked for an instant on the balls of her feet, and then shaking her head, eyes still down, withdrew from the stone stoop and went back the alley along the windows toward the rear courtyard, "God help me," she whispered, "I've got to do it, I've got to..." but as she turned into the bright square of sun that fell on the flags, she stopped with a short cry.

Two figures moved quickly, awkwardly in the thick grove of banana trees behind the cistern, both of them startled by her as she had been startled by them. Richard Lermontant emerged, flustered, rubbing his hand nervously and senselessly against the side of his leg.

"*Bonjour,* Anna Bella," he murmured in that low languid voice of his. And then, utterly at a loss, he made a quick bow to the figure in the grove behind him and hurried out of the yard.

"O, my lord," Anna Bella whispered. There was a young woman in the grove, her broad skirts flickering amid the slender bright green trunks, a broken veil of ivy obscuring her face as she lifted it now and stepped out, her arms bare in her fluttering short sleeves except for a very thin white woven shawl.

Anna Bella, glancing desperately in the direction of Marcel's windows, turned to go. She was certain Richard was well ahead of her, they would not collide again. But the woman said, "Anna Bella?"

And turning Anna Bella was astonished to see that this was Marie Ste. Marie. She put her hand to her lips, unable to suppress a gentle laugh. "Why, it's you!" she said, glancing shyly at the lovely ruffled afternoon dress, the pale arms.

Marie was pressing the palm of her hand to her cheek. She looked steadily at Anna Bella, her eyes as they had always been, black, almond in shape, and cold.

"I'm sorry to be here like this," Anna Bella said. "I'm just so sorry. I knocked at the door and when there wasn't any answer, why, I thought I'd leave a note up there on the door for Marcel." This was a lie.

Marie moved toward her. With her hair combed back severely from her perfect face she looked so much older, older perhaps than any of the girls they both knew.

"I don't want to disturb Madame Cecile," Anna Bella said, knowing full well that Madame Cecile was not there.

"Come inside," Marie said.

It was more a command than an invitation, but Anna Bella could sense that the tone was not intentional. She followed her through the darkened bedrooms with their gleaming white coverlets, a faint clean smell of wax rising from the little altar of the Virgin, and into the front rooms. Anna Bella had always loved this little house, its sweet scents, its spotlessness, the exquisite touches of luxury everywhere, and she felt with pain how long it had been since she had seen it, how long since she had sat in this chair. This last year had been the longest of her life, and she was bitter all at once that she had not caught Marcel alone here as she hoped, it had taken her weeks to get Madame Elsie to the dress shop, her plan was ruined, she ought to go. And she was annoyed at the same time by the sight of those two together, that handsome and polished Richard Lermontant and this beautiful cold-eyed girl. It struck her to the heart, actually. But she had cried so often in the last few weeks that she would not allow herself to feel it. She started to rise. "I should go home."

"No," Marie said. "Please. I'm glad that you've come." She was standing by the window blinds as if to catch a little fresh air, that hand still pressed to her cheek. And what she said was true.

Richard had just kissed Marie, and she had never felt a physical sensation akin to what she'd experienced when he was holding her lightly, gently, as if he might break her, in his arms. His hands had spread out firmly against her back, pressing her to his chest so that the buttons of his frock coat had touched her breasts. And when that had happened a shock had passed through her, so keenly pleasurable that she had let her head fall back, her lips part, and felt that shock's consummation in one shuddering instant as his lips pressed against hers. His arms had closed around her. He had lifted her off her feet. And she had been obliterated in that instant, everything she'd ever been taught had been obliterated, all that she was before was simply gone away. She might have fallen if he had not held her, because the shock had weakened her legs. They had no strength at all and seemed in fact to be closed tightly together, in the blessed secrecy of her skirts, of their own accord. She remembered breaking loose from him, however, and leaning against the trunks of the trees, shuddering, her lips tingling and then numb. His hands were on her waist. He had kissed her shoulders, her neck.

Anna Bella had come at that instant, and if Anna Bella had not, Marie might have given herself over to this pleasure without reserve, something that would have been unthinkable for her only moments before. She was in the act of turning to him again when Anna Bella stepped into the yard. And she was still weak from this now, her lips were still numb. There was yet a humming in her ears, and Anna Bella's voice and Anna Bella's person were remote from her, outside of her. And so unaccustomed was she in her life to gaining anything for herself, to desiring anything for herself, that she could not quite accept the extraordinary elation that she felt.

She could not accept that this had happened to her.

That Richard having seen her at Mass that Sunday in her new grown-up dresses had asked if he might call on her, and indeed had come to the door only minutes ago, and that she knowing she must not sit with him alone in the cottage, and not wanting to let him go, had led him with low awkward words, senseless small talk, into the back courtyard. And that there, she herself had moved toward the cover of those soft, nodding, banana leaves, the ivy spilling down from the roof of the *garçonnière*, and that in some sudden and perfect moment their eyes had met and she had let him, led him, by subtle gestures she might never duplicate, to take her in his arms. "I love you...I love you," he had whispered. And then this kiss, this shrill and palpitating ecstasy that had almost been pain. It struck her as monstrous but absolutely true that she might go to hell for what she'd done, just as a man who had murdered another man, or a woman who had murdered her own child. These were mortal sins, all. But that was an *idea*. And there was something so immense, so overwhelming and sweet about those moments that she could not feel guilt for him, but rather saw calmly a vision of her soul having become as a stagnant swamp filled with foul and breeding things, and there he was at the same moment, breathing "I love you, I love," his own body filled with some marvelous vibrant power that made his fingers warm and shocking against her bare skin, her clothes. Her words moved in a silent prayer. Don't let this be wrong. She closed her eyes.

And when she opened them, she saw Anna Bella in that little curly-legged chair by the fire where she herself never sat. Anna Bella's elbow was on the arm, and her fingers pressed into the soft flesh of her cheek, her pretty eyes so large and so mournful, so sad.

"I don't know where he is, Anna Bella," she said. And Anna Bella started, looking up at her. Marie had lost all track of time, how long had they been there together in their own thoughts? "He's gone all day every day," she said, knowing this was what Anna Bella wanted. "He may be at the corner helping Monsieur Christophe, he's been going there often, to prepare for the school."

"Hmmmm..."Anna Bella felt sick. She had come this far, why not go there? It was impossible. Marie had already discovered her, she couldn't enter that house with that strange mad woman, and that famous man. It was bad enough as it was, and yet thinking about it, she almost burst into tears. "I've got to talk to him!" she whispered in English. She didn't know if Marie had heard. She clasped her hands together in her lap and let her head fall to one side.

"I'll tell him that you came," Marie said.

"No, no, don't do that!" she looked up. "I don't want him...I think..."

Discreetly, Marie nodded.

She was aware then of Marie's eyes on her and again she looked up into Marie's cold face. All the girls had thought her so vain, so proud of her incomparable beauty, her white skin, her satin hair. Anna Bella had always defended her, she's such a sweet girl! And yet at this moment she felt the most violent and disturbing resentment of her. What would she ever know of these troubles, she or Richard Lermontant, she thought, and without realizing it, she shook her head. She would have to get up, leave without seeing Marcel, go find Madame Elsie and go home.

"What is it, Anna Bella?" Marie asked. Her voice was smooth, like a breeze blowing over the waters of a lake.

"I have troubles, Marie, troubles within myself." She looked up. "Marcel's my friend, he's always been my best friend, I'm not talking about courting and foolishness like that now, I'm talking about us always being the best of friends."

"I know," she said. And it seemed for a moment that maybe she did.

"Why we were always together, I never had a girl friend that was close to me like Marcel, and now Marcel won't come back. Madame Elsie said something to him, something mean, I don't know what it was, I don't listen to Madame Elsie, I mean...well, I listen to her but not all the time! And I just can't figure out all these things alone, I can't think. I used to believe that I could think in my head when I was alone. It's not that way anymore, I have to talk with him to figure things out. If Madame Elsie knew I'd come over here to his house on my own..."

"No one will tell her," Marie said at once.

Anna Bella regarded her for a silent moment. It penetrated to her slowly that Marie was on her side.

"Tell me, Marie, what would you think if I went up there to Monsieur Mercier's right now and just asked for Marcel? There's workmen all over that place, and I don't know those people, that woman and her son, but what would you think if I just went right to the gate..."

"No," Marie advised gently. "Don't do that, Anna Bella." She sat in the chair opposite. "Let me explain to him that you want to see him. He need not know you were here."

"O, my lord," Anna Bella clicked her tongue. "I just have to see him."

"But what is it?" Marie asked her.

"Oh, I can't...I don't want to trouble you with my affairs, I...it's just I'm all alone these days and Madame Elsie's getting on, and I have to think things out!" If she didn't stop, it might all come out of her now which she knew would be a dreadful error. How could she speak of all those white gentlemen boarders and their appraising eyes to this girl, this girl who had everything at her fingertips, in the palm of her hand?

"Would you tell Marcel something for me?" she asked, rising now and smoothing her skirts. She went to the door. "Would you promise me you'll never tell a living soul what I'm going to say, except Marcel? That you'll tell him just what I say?"

"Of course I will," Marie whispered. But her smooth procelain face showed little of the warm inflection in her voice, and once the words had died on the air there was nothing.

"You tell Marcel for me that Madame Elsie's forcing me to those white gentlemen, that Madame Elsie's made up her mind for me, and that's not what I want. Tell him I've got to talk to him, I need him, he's my friend." She searched Marie's face for the slightest glimmer of feeling. Marie dropped her eyes. It seemed she sighed but Anna Bella wasn't sure. And overcome with shame Anna Bella turned around, eyes stinging, and unlatching the narrow blinds hurried out across the yard.

The gate must have closed. There was the sound of it, and of a carriage rattling unevenly through the rutted street. Marie was looking at the pattern of the sun on the floorboards, and when she looked up the sky showed blue over the far roof of the cottage across the way, a blinding blue among the shifting shapes of green leaves.

She sucked in her breath. Her hands were moist, the thin muslin of her tight bodice clung to her and the heavy weight of the chignon on the back of her head pulled at her. She turned on her heel, walking fast across the little parlor, jerking pins from her hair all the while with both hands. And when she reached her bed, she lay down heavily, her hair descending all around her, and she began to cry.

A long time after, she was conscious that she was not alone. She heard her mother's step in the front room. She wondered if her mother had heard her tears, and she wished that this question had not entered her mind. A strange peace came over her, devoid of the slightest shame. She felt a wordless and consuming desire for Richard and she said those words, "I love, I love you," just loud enough so that she alone could hear them, and closing her eyes, she felt his lips again and his hands against the small of her back lifting her into the air. If life were such that you could want something and *you could work to get it*—then, she wanted Richard more than anything in the world.

It was terrifying to want and terrifying to think that that "want" could be fulfilled. So terrifying perhaps that what struck her suddenly with the immediacy of an apparition was Anna Bella's face at the door. Anna Bella's poignant and desperate confession just as she had turned to go. She felt so sorry for Anna Bella! Yet she was bruised by the reality of those words just as she had been bruised weeks before by the raw reality of those moments in the shop of the notary, Monsieur Jacquemine. They brought the world home to Marie— Anna Bella and Jacquemine each in their own way—the

(199)

world Marie had witnessed all her life with a defeat that was too profound for her years.

Now something was crystallizing in her as she lay on this bed. Her eyes shut and she yielded to a dim and ethereal vision of her wedding, the altar before her resplendent with flowers, and Richard's face above hers, the play of candles beautifully obscured as if by the soft whiteness of a veil. There had been such a moment at her First Communion only the year before when she had risen from the marble rail, the Host on her tongue and all the world about her was softened with the scent of roses, and pure. That Christ was with her, inside of her, had been the only thought in her mind as she walked down the aisle. The magic of the splendid painted church had merely resonated with her prayers. And all the guilt she had felt moments before for those seconds in Richard's arms was gone now as the conviction of his goodness took hold of her, the conviction that nothing so ineffably sweet could have been evil at all. That he might love her, really love her...that she might have that moment at the altar—it astonished her, and drew from her now a conviction that had always been latent there. Yes, conviction. She felt it growing stronger and stronger; she felt the powers of her will.

Never, never would she be forced into the arms of a man she could not marry, never would she stand with Anna Bella on that awful brink. And never, never would any child of hers know the shame she'd known when she walked into that notary's office with a note for a white father who could never give her his legal name.

Maybe she had always known it, known every morning of her life as she hurried through the streets to Mass, known it when rising for Communion, she saw those "respectable" quadroons about her remaining impassively in their pews as the young girls took the Sacrament which they themselves had been unable to receive for years. All those prosperous and genteel women waiting the days, the weeks, the months, for those white "protectors" to come unexpectedly and desperately welcomed through their doors.

No, perhaps she'd always known it, and her heart was breaking for Anna Bella, breaking for the misery in Anna Bella's face. But those words spoken to her today, "I love you, I love you," had given her the courage to make it a solemn vow. All right, then, she had learned to say "no" with strength. But how to say "yes, I want him, I want *him!*" She found herself rising suddenly from the pillow and staring, flustered ahead of her into the shuttered gloom.

For the first few moments after he left the Ste. Marie courtyard, Richard was not aware of the direction he took, or that he had stopped at the corner of the Rue Ste. Anne and the Rue Dauphine, one foot on the curb, the other in the gutter, staring about him like a man who had never seen these streets before. He started violently when a white man with blond hair brushed his arm. And was in the midst of a stammered apology when he realized that the man was already across the street and disappearing into Christophe Mercier's gate. This appeared to mean something, this white man, but he could not figure what. A man of color, meantime, had passed Richard and tipped his hat. That meant something, too, but he could not figure what.

At last, unable to think anything coherent at all, he realized he was walking straight for the Cathedral, and that only the incessant movement of his legs could bring his body into check.

And his body was almost under his conscious command again when he reached the doors of the church. He almost laughed out loud as he dipped his fingers into the holy water and made his way across the vestibule, nodding again to someone whom surely he must have known. Dolly Rose was in a rear pew, and this seemed to mean something, too, but he could not figure what.

It was only when he had finally found a nice dark niche for himself in the far side of the Cathedral that he realized Dolly Rose had been frightfully pale. Her usual caramel color had been sallow. And she had been bent over the pew in front of her, her knuckles almost white, while holding firm to her waist with her other arm. This meant something, but what?

All he could think—truly think—was this. Marie had let him kiss her. She had drawn him into that grove. Her face had been inexplicably innocent and desperate at the same time and she had let him do it, even putting her arms about him as if she had actually wanted it, as if she, beautiful and distant Marie whom he had loved all his life from afar, could actually love him. He almost laughed—almost gasped aloud. He fell down on his knees, clasping his hands before him as if he were praying so that he might hide his face.

But this was only part of the shock that gripped him. The other was too complex for him to understand. In fact, he had no private vocabulary for straightening it out at all. Suffice it to say, he had had women, women he could not even think about under this church roof, and women he could never think about when thinking of Marie. But they had been just about the best women a man of color could buy. And somehow, somewhere, it had been made known to him that that forbidden pleasure—arranged for with rather lavish sums—was just about the keenest passion a man might expect. Yes, that was the way it was supposed to be. Because when one took the woman of one's dreams to bed, the mother of one's children, that irreproachable and convent-bred woman with whom one was to share one's life and one's home, she would endure it with all the forbearance of a brittle china doll. Well, someone—and he could not for the life of him think who had told him such things—was very simply a damned fool.

He had known fire in Marie's arms, physical fire which came from her, and which ignited in him a miraculous and carnal blaze which he had been all but unable to control. And that, now inseparable from his chilling and beautiful vision of her, left him shuddering as he tried to comprehend it. But it was too much. Too splendid. Too rare.

Love, that was the only explanation, it was what love could do. And the world was as the poets described it, not cynical, not disappointed men. It was love. And it brought, very slowly, the tears to his eyes.

"Could she love...?" he wanted to whisper aloud. He let his head, unconsciously tilt to one side. "Could she love me?" And then with his eyes fixed on the distant tabernacle of the main altar, he was saying a prayer. Dear God, I want to try! And if my heart is broken in that effort, I don't care!

There was one last baffling aspect to it, wonderful perhaps as all the rest. He was astonished, he was shaken by what had passed between them, but in some very real way he was not surprised. Her eyes had spoken to him more eloquently perhaps than the arms that had closed around him. And the eyes had said, "Don't you know? Haven't you always known that you were the one?"

He was puzzling this out, a weary hand massaging his temples now, lightly, when he started to see beside him an animate and dark form.

It was Dolly Rose. She had let her long mourning veil down over her face, and through it he saw her features indistinctly, the shuttering movement of her lips, the dark of her eyes. She settled in the pew beside him, her bombazine skirts rustling against him, and trying to speak, stopped as if she could not, her hand closing on his wrist.

"Dolly, what is it!" he whispered. The scent of verbena came from her. Her hand was ice cold.

"Help me home, Richard, I cannot..." she whispered, stopping again, her lips pressed together. "Help me. Let me lean on your arm."

He rose at once, ushering her out into the sun.

She didn't speak. She had to stop twice. Once to catch her breath, and another time, she put her arm about her waist as if she were in pain. It was only three blocks to her house and finally he had tucked her against him, his right hand under her right elbow as he lifted her weight from her feet.

It did not surprise him to find no servant for the door. Or to see the house dark behind closed blinds and in some disarray. A lot of new furniture stood about the parlor and flies swarmed over a ruined dinner beyond the double doors.

He settled her in a chair by the window, telling her he would get water for her at once.

"You're kind, Richard, you're always kind," she whispered, and lifted up her veil to take a deep breath.

He was just turning to go when he stopped with a start.

In the shadows he had not seen that a man lay sleeping on the couch. And the man was rising now on his elbow, squinting at the distant blinds. Seams of light lay across his face. It was Christophe.

"Dolly?" he asked, shielding his eyes from the thin glaring light.

"It's gone," Dolly said. "It's gone."

"She's ill, Monsieur," Richard whispered. He didn't understand Dolly's words.

"Did you see the doctor?" Christophe scrambled to his feet. He smoothed his jacket haphazardly.

"It's no use," she whispered. "It started last night."

Richard was looking everywhere for a pitcher and a glass.

"You shouldn't have gone out," Christophe said almost angrily. He was beside her and she let her forehead rest against him.

"It doesn't matter," she was saying as Richard went down the passage. "It's always the same. One month, two... and then it's over. I don't know why I let myself hope. I don't know why I thought that it would be any different this time."

There was a pitcher by the bed in her room. Richard filled

the glass and brought it to her, and she took it, trembling, and put it to her lips.

"Should I call Madame Celestina?" he asked.

"No," she shook her head. And Christophe, so that Dolly could not see, made a more emphatic negation to Richard with a jerk of his head.

"Come, lie down," Christophe said, helping her to her feet.

Richard waited silently at the door of the parlor until Christophe had returned.

"You're a marvel with women in distress, has anyone ever told you that?" Christophe asked.

"Monsieur, she is in bad pain."

"I know that," Christophe said. "I'll go for Celestina if it gets worse. She is not close with Celestina now."

Richard said nothing. He too had heard the story of Dolly's infamous return to the "quadroon balls" the week after little Lisa died.

"But she is very ill, Monsieur," he said. He could feel nothing but compassion for the fragile woman who had clung to him all the way from the Cathedral. He could tell his mother about this. His mother would come. Celestina wouldn't stop his mother. Nothing would if Dolly was really ill. Richard's mother spent half her life visiting the sick, caring for the aged, her small Benevolent Society of women of color was her life outside the family, the only life she had. "Monsieur," he asked now. "Do you know what is wrong?"

This caught Christophe slightly off guard. He studied Richard's face. And Richard realized that Christophe did know what was wrong and that Christophe was a little surprised that Richard did not.

"It will pass," he said.

That evening, when the supper was finished, Richard sat with his mother on the rear gallery over the garden and told her the story of his meeting with Dolly Rose. When he came to the mention of Christophe in the house, he told this as delicately as he could. He repeated Dolly's conversation. His mother's face had stiffened at this mention of a man alone with a woman in her flat, but now her face became remarkably sad.

"She is ill, Maman," he said to try to explain why he had burdened her with this indelicate tale. "And there was only Christophe."

His mother sighed. She rose and put her hands on the

railing as she looked down into the yard. *"Mon fils,"* she said, "Dolly can have no more children. She cannot carry them. I've heard this from Celestina before. Now it's happened again."

For a moment Richard felt no compassion when he heard this. It confused him. It was dreadful to think that she had lost a little baby just so soon after little Lisa's death, but it was dreadful to think that she had gone to the "quadroon balls," too. It was dreadful to think of all the scandalous things that were said of her and the endless procession of men in her life. "Is it such a tragedy, Maman?" he asked gently.

"She was a good mother, Richard," Madame Suzette said. "She would have been a good mother till the day she died. You see, for a woman like Dolly that is everything. Men mean little. They come and go. Nothing of honor or dignity endures there. But the child, that is *la famille,* that is all."

She took her place in the rocker beside him, straightening her skirts. "I'll call on her, of course, but there is nothing anyone can do."

Richard knew so little of bearing children and losing children that he naturally accepted this without a word. But he was strangely unsatisfied. He felt uncomfortable that he had told his mother this tale, uncomfortable that he had spoken so plainly of Christophe sleeping in Dolly's parlor, quite at home there when they had come in.

"You'll forgive me, Maman?" he whispered slowly, "for burdening you with all of this...this matter of Christophe..." his voice had deepened, trailing off.

"I know why you mentioned it, Richard," she said. She tilted her embroidery ring slightly toward the light from the window behind her.

Richard felt his cheeks burn. He tried to make out her face, but the light behind her illuminated only the loose fine hairs of her coif.

"You mentioned it because you wanted me to tell your father. You wanted your father to know that your teacher is courting Dolly Rose, and all of Antoine's vicious gossip about him is therefore a lie."

Richard was speechless. He should have known this could not be kept from his mother, no matter how rank and shocking it was. And if she was right, that he had told her this tale tonight to counter Antoine's gossip, he was amazed. He had not known it himself. But she knew it. She knew it all.

(205)

She had witnessed Antoine's horrified expression at the supper table, observed those whispered sessions with Rudolphe behind closed doors, and Antoine's shock when this Paris Englishman whom he accused of the vilest, most appalling, and most mysterious proclivities had appeared in New Orleans at Christophe's door. But that Richard and his mother should speak of these things was out of the question. Richard and his father couldn't speak of them. And Rudolphe had only vaguely alluded to them to try to warn his son that Antoine was "losing his mind." "It's the dirt people talk in the *Quartier Latin* in Paris," Rudolphe had waved it away, indignant. "Don't you listen to it, and don't you think of it. And above all, don't you repeat it for it could ruin young Christophe."

Richard, thunderstruck, had been all too willing to obey. He sat stunned now, unable to look his mother in the eye.

"Don't worry, *mon fils,*" Madame Suzette went on in a hushed voice. "Your teacher is apparently quite enamored with Dolly Rose. That Dolly has reciprocated his affections is the reason that her godmother, Celestina, is so put out. Celestina!" she sighed. "Celestina was not so shocked as you might think that Dolly returned so soon to the 'quadroon balls,' those women are so very practical!" She paused as though considering, and her voice was intimate, unusually candid as she went on. It was the voice reserved for other women when sewing together they confessed the vulgar facts of this world to one another with a weary shake of the head. "But a man of color courting the lovely Dolly, how is Celestina to abide that? Why the good Celestina and the good Dolly have never put anything into their coffee but the purest white milk."

Richard winced. His eyes were fixed on the shifting trees, and the sudden flicker of a star beyond which was as suddenly lost.

"It won't come to anything," Madame Suzette sighed. "Dolly is already being seen in the evenings by a white gentleman, and I trust your clever schoolteacher knows what to expect. They are all the same, those dear ladies, they and their mothers before them, and their grandmothers before they were born." She reached out to touch the back of her son's hand. Richard's fingers clasped hers, but otherwise he didn't move. "Celestina," she whispered, "and Dolly...and old Madame Elsie," and dropping her voice for emphasis, "and the proud Madame Cecile Ste. Marie."

Long after her hand had withdrawn from his he remained perfectly still. He was staring out over the darkened yard. Love her as he did, he could not tell her what he was thinking, he could not confide. She reminded him softly that his Vacquerie cousins were coming to dinner soon, lovely girls. Theirs was a family as old as her own, as respectable, older than the *Famille Lermontant*. He didn't speak. He was not there. He was standing in the grove behind Marie's house. He was holding Marie in his arms.

III

IT WAS OVER FINALLY, the first day of class. Marcel was the last to rise, and a knot of students still lingered with Christophe at the lectern, waiting their turn for a few words as Marcel went out of the room. He stood in the hallway on the new Aubusson carpet gazing through the door of that long back study where two of the oldest boys, colored planters' sons both, sat at the round table leafing through the papers and periodicals that Christophe had put there. This was the table where Christophe, Juliet, and Marcel had dined together every evening for a week. No one but Marcel knew that Christophe, his funds dangerously low, had stripped to the waist and gotten down on his knees to bring the polish up in the hardwood floor. Or that Marcel had cleaned and dusted the marble busts that gleamed in the shadowy shelves, or that the two of them together had put all those long rows of novels, classics, poetry in order. Now this room would be open for all of their benefit until supper each day, the class ending at four o'clock, and a copy of *Nuits de Charlotte* lay on the table, there were back issues of the Paris journals, stacks of the New York and the London *Times*.

Marcel was tingling. And with something more painful than a twinge of jealousy he finally let go of Christophe at the lectern, surrounded by his eager students, and went out into the sunlit street. A group of the youngest, those twelve- and thirteen-year-old boys, were just heading home down the Rue Dauphine their loud laughter and animated talk in wild contrast to their demeanor only moments before. Richard was waiting for Marcel and when their eyes met they knew at once that they were in perfect triumphant agreement about

(207)

the events of the day. They walked in silence toward the Ste. Marie gate.

For four hours they had sat still among the class of twenty, gripped by Christophe's opening address. Not a hand had stirred unnecessarily, there was no whispering in the back row, no flutter of pages, no idle and irritating sharpening of quills. No one shuffled his feet, or gazed out the window. In fact the air was so different from that of the schools they had known that they were at a loss to explain how they and all those around them might have been transformed into adults overnight.

The fact was that in one day they had been graduated from the uneven discipline of an elementary schoolroom to the serious atmosphere of the university class. And it was Christophe's tone and bearing which had brought about this transformation. They had known from the very first words spoken by him that he expected them to behave as young men.

"You will be responsible for all that I say in this room," he had explained, his eyes moving with complete command from one eager face to another, "you will each keep a notebook for each subject of study, writing in it as you wish to record for yourselves the lectures of each day. At any time I may ask to see these notebooks, and when I do I expect to find evidence there that you have profited by the time spent here.

"The texts for general history and the physical sciences are on your desk, as well as your Latin Grammar and your Greek. And as you can see on the blackboard behind me, there is the schedule of your assignments for the summer which you will copy at the end of this day's class."

Never had they been instructed so directly and never had they been spoken to as if they themselves might take some responsibility for what they were going to learn.

But it was only the beginning. They were soon told that during the hours spent here they would be regarded as serious scholars no matter where they were to go afterward, or what they were to do. Whether they went on to the university, or to work in some profession or trade did not matter. They were to devote themselves with equal fervor to all the subjects taught here so that when they eventually left this small academy they would be educated men.

Marcel, his eyes lowered shyly, had been swelling with pride. Christophe spoke with an easy perfection, his sentences as crisp and articulate as if all had been prepared in advance, and yet it flowed as if spontaneous, the voice so natural and eager in its inflections that it kept them riveted to his neat and commanding person as he paced slowly back and forth at the front of the room.

Again and again he paused at the perfect moment, his eyes engaging their eyes, and went on to elaborate in the same thoughtful manner on this or that point that might not be so clear.

His speech was slower than usual, an excitement for the task at hand emanated from him, along with the same muted power that Marcel had felt all along.

And only Marcel knew of the torment Christophe had endured that week, the endless frustrations, the long visits of the Englishman, Michael Larson-Roberts who would come upon them in the midst of their work in the sweltering heat and disparage the school without even speaking a single word. Marcel despised this man.

Yet there was something utterly compelling about him. That was the trouble. He would stride into the dusty townhouse, its long corridors echoing with the sound of hammers, his dove-gray clothing immaculate as though he had been miraculously conveyed above the muddy quagmire of the streets to this spot, and stepping with exaggerated care through dirt and broken boards, he would take up some lonesome position in the corner of the empty classroom, a Paris paper spread out before his bowed head, and there read in deafening silence as all around him paled, became confused, as if the angle of the world at large were the angle of his narrow green eyes. Christophe was monstrous. He caused Christophe's power to go dim.

And in one long afternoon at Madame Lelaud's Marcel had been curled over his sketchbook, drawing all manner of ugly things, as the two men argued furiously in English, Michael Larson-Roberts hitting Christophe with one ripe sally after another, such as "You're vain, that's what you are, vain and frightened of the critics, frightened of your talents, frightened to go on risking that talent in the world. This isn't the world, this place, this is self-immolation, don't preach that rot to me about a school for your race, you don't believe in your race, you don't believe in anything but art, and even in that you don't believe enough or you wouldn't have turned your back on it..."

"You say that to me because you believe in nothing!"

Christophe came back at him through clenched teeth, "you think you've stripped me of the faith in simple things, the faith that sustains every human being, because *you* have no such faith and never have had. Don't talk to me about art, what do you really know about art, have you ever written anything, painted anything, understood anything! If you had, you'd know that everything I wrote was trash. It was written for effect, that's why it was written, there was no passion to it, no soul. I tell you what I do here has a soul to it! Somewhere during one of those long binges I woke up to see the difference between us. I understand art and you don't and I can't abide bad art whereas you have never known what that was, yes, you, for all your sophistication, your education, your taste! You don't know!"

Often the rifts of English were too fast for Marcel to comprehened or lapsed into phrases so informal and violent he didn't catch them at all. But never had he seen a man attempt to exert such force over another, while that other resisted so bitterly though falling again and again into stammers and at last a sullen silence which seemed the only really successful resistance he could accomplish. Was it perhaps that they argued like a father and son???

No, more truly priest and sinner. For there was something violently religious about the Englishman, something desperately dogmatic about his pronouncements. Christophe was being lost as a soul is lost, Christophe was damning himself, and this cesspool of a city around him with its sullen slaves and wary *gens de couleur* was hell.

"It's a dangerous thing to really love someone," Christophe had said finally after a half hour's silence at the dirty little table, his back to the wall, staring at Michael Larson-Roberts, "it's a dangerous thing to be young and malleable and let that someone give you a consummate vision of the world."

"I never meant to give you a consummate vision of the world," the Englishman said, barely moving his lips. Marcel had never seen him so spent. "I meant to give you an education, that was all."

"...because all your life after that, the vision haunts you," Christophe went on. "You'll hear that deprecating and defining voice in your ears saying, 'this isn't what I taught you to value, this isn't what I taught you to respect'..."

"And what are you going to teach those precious little coffee-colored bourgeoisie of yours in that classroom?" the Englishman had asked with a sudden flush of anger.

"To think for themselves!" Christophe said. "I'm twenty-three years old and I'd never once thought for myself until I got on that boat for New Orleans!"

The Englishman's bright eyes held his steadily as he brought up a clutch of bills from his pocket and dropping them on the table, he said, "You do this to wound me, Chris. And you've succeeded, but you could have been a great writer, you could have done anything you wanted with your talent. Wounding me is a pathetic accomplishment in comparison!" And rising he left.

Christophe was furious and impotent in his fury as he watched the Englishman disappear through the crowd at the door.

But after a long while of sipping his beer slowly and moving his lips now and then as though communing with himself he said to Marcel wearily in French, "Forgive me for all this arguing in a language you don't understand."

"But Christophe," Marcel said in English, "You are a great writer, isn't that true?"

"Marcel, I just know this, that if I hadn't gotten out of Paris and the *Quartier Latin* when I did, I would have died. If I am destined to be a great writer, all I need is pen and paper and the solitude occasionally of my own room. Now come on, let's get out of here."

His stride had been swift then. His hand was firm and casual on Marcel's shoulder as he led Marcel, quite to his surprise, down the Rue Dumaine to meet Madame Dolly Rose.

They drank coffee with her in the shade of her patio. She was shamelessly dressed in a yellow sprigged muslin though it was only three weeks since the death of her little daughter, and an equally shameless piano music carried out of the windows of her flat. But she was pale, had dark shadows under her eyes, and her hands shook. She laughed sometimes with a forced gaiety and teased Marcel about his blond hair. She called him "Blue Eyes" while Christophe smiled serenely, and she spiked their coffee with brandy which she drank herself, desperately and lustily as a man, without effect.

A lovely woman, delicate of feature and voice, she could speak the patois one minute and her usual Parisian French the next, laughing in sudden frantic but alluring spurts as she reminded him of the characters of the streets in their childhood, the old chimney sweeper who had threatened them with his broom when he had caught Dolly and Christophe marching behind him, mimicking his gestures and his sing-song voice. "Well, Blue Eyes!" she had said once when she caught Marcel watching her. She had kissed him on the cheek. "Women," he thought with an uncomfortable shift in his chair. But he beamed at her. And did not like to see her lapse suddenly into silence. Christophe was content here. He clasped his hands behind his neck, and when the music within had stopped, looked up with interest to see that strange tattered black slave coming down the steps, that painfully thin boy who had brought his key chain from Dolly's house weeks before. Dolly called him Bubbles, gave him small coins now for his dinner and sent him off. "Well, I finally bought him outright," she said. "But he just runs away." He had been cheap, and tuned pianos perfectly, but never brought the money back to her; it had been a failure, buying him, she ought to sell him to the fields.

"You don't mean that," Christophe scoffed. "Sell him to the fields."

"But he was not the one playing the piano, was he?" Marcel asked.

"He can play anything," Dolly said. "That is, when he's here."

"Buy him a decent coat, some shoes..." Christophe said.

"And then I'd never see him!" Dolly snapped. "You buy him a decent coat!" She was suddenly crestfallen and distant. But Christophe had leaned across the table and given her a slow gentle kiss as Marcel took a bit of a walk about the yard.

And after that Christophe had hired the slave, Bubbles, to help him with his work at the house, and given him an old serviceable suit of clothes. That got him into decent houses again with his tuning wrenches, and the day before the school had opened he had tuned the spinet in the Lermontant parlor and played an eerie song for Marcel and Richard, his fingers like spiders on the keys as he rocked back and forth on the stool, his eyes closed, humming along with the obscure melodies through clenched teeth. And he had not run away.

But these bits and pieces of Christophe's life which Marcel witnessed before the school began were but the tip of the iceberg. Much had gone on behind closed doors. Rumors had rippled through Marcel's small world that Christophe took to spending late nights with the Englishman after that quarrel at Madame Lelaud's, that he was wined and dined in the Englishman's suite at the St. Charles Hotel with the slaves dismissed before he took his place at a table set for two in the privacy of the Englishman's room. And Dolly Rose had had Christophe often as a guest in the afternoon, even walking out with him around the Place d'Armes, while everyone knew that she was receiving a white military officer in the hours after dark.

And just when all had expected that man to take up informal residence with Dolly (he was refurbishing the flat), she had broken off this connection violently, and gone dancing again at the "quadroon balls." All this frightened Marcel, he would have preferred for Christophe not to be seen so much there. Dolly caused trouble for men, men were dead on account of Dolly—of course up until now, they had all been white—yet it fascinated Marcel that Christophe was obviously quite pleasing to the demanding Dolly, and Dolly was pleasing enough to Christophe.

Meantime Juliet had been in a rage. Only Christophe's threat to "throw everything up" if she did not show some courtesy to Michael Larson-Roberts had succeeded in calming her. If she remembered her little boudoir encounter with Marcel she did not show it; her son was now the man in her life. And the very night before the school opened, there had been another fight in the townhouse, complete once more with the breaking of glass. Lisette had told Marcel at dawn, when he was dressed and ready hours before, that Juliet had disappeared around midnight and had still not come home.

"Oh, you don't know that, that's foolishness," he had answered sharply. "You were sound asleep at midnight yourself."

"I might have been but there's lots of others who were awake!" she said knowingly. "I tell you if that fancy schoolteacher doesn't get that woman in hand..."

"I won't listen to this!" Marcel had stormed, playing the master, "Take that tray out of here and go!" It was foolish to argue with her. She knew everything, it was true, and lying down for a while, as neatly dressed and still as a corpse on his bed, he thought to himself, maybe some day she'll know something that I want to know. Lisette was warm to him even if downright disrespectful, but her face could be as sullen and unreadable as that of any other slave when she chose.

But as soon as he had entered the new classroom, first to

arrive, one glance at Christophe's drawn face had told him this must be true. The teacher was spiffily dressed for the first day, sporting a new silk tie, and a rich beige vest beneath his chocolate brown coat. But he looked debonair and half-dead.

"Have you seen my mother?" he had asked in a whisper. And then before the others had begun to arrive, he vanished to the rooms upstairs.

The Englishman had passed the front windows at seven-forty-five A.M., a bent figure, hands clasped behind his back as usual, clearly recognizable even through the half-open shutters, but he had not stopped.

Then when the room was filled and waiting, Christophe had made his swift entrance right on the hour, face radiant, and there began this exciting day for all of them which went without a mishap or a dull moment until the stroke of twelve. One half hour before they were to be dismissed, early on this first day, he had begun their Greek instruction with a short and moving recitation of a verse in translation and then in the original tongue. Marcel had never heard classical Greek recited; he could not read a syllable of it. But listening to this beautiful and impassioned speech, he had felt the heart of the poem as one feels it with music. Above the blackboard between the two front windows there hung an engraving of a Greek theater carved into the deep side of a hill. The audience sat in flowing robes; a lone figure stood in the center of the field below. Listening he had been transported to that place, and he was full to the brim at last when the noon Angelus had rung. He had bowed his head. A sudden burst of applause rang from the back of the room. It was those older boys, the colored planters' sons, who had thought to do it. Christophe smiled gratefully, demurring, and let them go.

Only one aspect of all this had disappointed Marcel. And that was his jealousy of all these students who were encountering his teacher for the first time. There had been no sign to him that he was special, that he was Christophe's friend. Of course he hadn't expected it. He knew that he was to be treated as anyone else. Yet it hurt him and he was angry with himself for it and did not want this to show on his face. He thought he might hang about, offering perhaps to look for Juliet. But what if he were brushed off, Christophe after all was so very busy. He wasn't really worried about Juliet besides. He felt an anger with her that grew out of this week's long intimacy of working together in the schoolrooms, dining together at the little round table, easy with one another in their pride and their exhaustion, as she called him *"cher"* always, and sometimes rubbed the top of his head. It was too mean to have run off on this all-important night. He was certain she was all right.

"Well I hope Antoine hears of today's proceedings," Marcel said to Richard with spirit. "I hope he hears that Christophe is the most brilliant teacher since Socrates, and the school is going to be a success."

Richard shrugged. They had just reached the Ste. Marie gate. "The hell with Antoine," he whispered.

"Come on, let's go to my room."

Richard was reluctant. He had refused Marcel's invitations several times this week, and at first Marcel had not noticed this, but it was very clear that again Richard did not wish to accept.

"What's the matter with you?" Marcel pressed. He was so elated, he wanted to share this with Richard. And not to worry about the Englishman or Juliet. They could talk about the class, mull it over, make it endure.

But Richard struck an unusual pose. He lowered the bundle of books in his arm, straightened up to his full height of six feet and six inches and with his right hand behind his back made Marcel a civil bow. "I must speak with you, Marcel," he said, "on an important matter, now, in your room."

"Well, perfect!" Marcel said. "I just invited you, didn't I?"

Richard hesitated. Then he nodded. "Yes, you did. However it would have been better..." he stopped. He was embarrassed. "It would have been better had I come to call. Nevertheless, may I speak to you? It's a pressing matter. May I speak to you now?"

Marcel was beginning to laugh. Then his face became somber. "Just so long as it isn't about Anna Bella," he murmured. "About my going to see her."

"No," Richard shook his head. "Because I assume and justly so that you went to see her. You're a gentleman. You wouldn't ignore her request."

A momentary anger flashed in Marcel's eye. He opened the gate and led the way back the alley to the *garçonnière*.

Pulling off his newer, stiffer boots at once, he settled on the bed as he selected an older pair, and gestured for Richard to take the chair at the desk. He was quite surprised to see that Richard merely stood in the door. Richard had set his

(215)

books down, but his hands were clasped behind his back and he was staring at Marcel.

"Richard," Marcel said calmly "I will go to see her in my own good time."

A faint shadow of pain passed over Richard's face.

"Make it soon, Marcel," he said.

"Is this all you think about? Anna Bella? I know Anna Bella better than you do." Marcel could feel his face reddening. He thrust the discarded boots aside and strode heavily to the back of the room, sitting on the windowsill against the close trees, his back to the frame, his knee crooked, one foot on the sill before him. "No one has to tell me when to see Anna Bella," he said coldly.

Richard remained motionless, his demeanor utterly formal. "Have you seen her?" he asked, his voice so low that the question was almost inaudible.

Marcel turned his head. He looked down into the bracken, into the drifts of ivy hanging from the oaks. "Let's talk about school, Richard, it's going to be rough," he said.

When Richard didn't answer, he went on.

"Those boys, Dumanoir and the other one from the country, do you realize they've both studied in France for a year. Dumanoir was at the Lycée Louis le-Grand..."

"They told everyone that four times," Richard murmured. "Let us settle this...about Anna Bella. Because it's not the subject of this call. I must talk to you about something else."

"Good lord, what next!" Marcel sighed.

"All right, let me be rude," Richard said. "If you don't go to see her, she will think that I didn't give you her message."

"She's given the same message to Marie. Believe me, she knows her messages have been relayed."

"I don't understand this!" Richard insisted. He was becoming heated and his voice was lower, softer than before. He stepped into the room. "When the rest of us were running from girls and making faces at them, you were fast friends with her, Marcel! You spent half the day at her house all summer long. Now that you're old enough to..."

"Old enough to what!" Marcel turned on him suddenly. The edge on his voice startled Richard.

Richard looked down. "She wants to talk to you..." he murmured.

Marcel's face was darkly flushed. He removed his foot from the frame of the window and stood. Richard studied him uneasily.

"Madame Elsie won't let me near Anna Bella. I can't see Anna Bella!" Marcel said. "And if I could...what would I say?"

"But there is a situation there, Marcel..."

"I know that, my fine gentlemanly friend," Marcel answered. "I know all about it. I know more about it than you know about it. But what can I *do* about it!" He was astonished to realize that he was trembling, that a sweat had broken out all over him, and that he was glaring at Richard as if he meant to strike him. Richard was not the one to strike.

Richard was mystified. There was something here that he could not comprehend.

"But Marcel," he said uncertainly, "if you could just be a brother to her..."

"A brother! A brother..." Marcel was staring at him in disbelief. "If I were her brother, do you think she'd be in that situation? Up late at night...how did you put it...to let the gentlemen in?"

At this, a peculiar light came into Richard's eye. He was silent. Marcel seated himself on the windowsill again. He was looking out at the trees. "Madame Elsie can't force Anna Bella," he said in a low voice. "Anna Bella has a mind of her own."

"But who will help her to stand up to Madame Elsie, who will be on her side?" Richard asked. "That old woman is mean. She needs a brother, Marcel, you...you are like a brother to her!"

"Damn!" Marcel burst out. "Will you stop using that word!"

Richard was astonished. His brows knit. He was probing Marcel's agitated and darkened face. It seemed a latent emotion had overcome Marcel, something inimical to the round childlike face, the clear innocent blue eyes. Richard's lips moved as if something were just dawning on him, and then he stopped.

"We aren't brother and sister," Marcel whispered, the voice thick and slow. "We never were. If we had been, it would be simple, and I would do as you say. But we are not brother and sister! Anna Bella's a woman and I'm not yet...not yet a man." He stopped, as if so volatile that he could not continue, and then the voice even lower than before resumed. "She'll be spoken for while I'm still sitting in the schoolroom, she'll be spoken for before I set foot on that boat for France, she'll be spoken for and gone and we are not

(217)

brother and sister, and there is nothing, nothing that I can do!" He turned his head and once again looked out into the trees.

Richard stared at him helplessly. Every muscle in Richard's being reflected his distress, his heavy frame sagging though he stood erect, and a subtle light in his dark eyes flickered as if detached from the older, sadder face around it.

"I didn't understand," he whispered. "I...didn't understand." He reached for his books.

For a long moment Marcel was silent.

"Now what was it you wanted to speak to me about?" Marcel asked. "This other matter that was on your mind?"

"Not now," Richard said.

"Why not now?" Marcel asked. The tone was bitter but he didn't mean it to be so. He was conscious of Richard standing in the doorway and suddenly, he resented Richard very much. There were times when Richard's life struck him as profoundly simple and this could irritate him almost beyond words. "What is it?" he asked again, and for vanity, or reasons he did not know, he attempted to regain his control.

"I'll come tomorrow, after school," Richard said.

But Marcel's face was calm. He wiped his forehead almost casually with his folded handkerchief, and then he made some semblance of a polite smile.

Richard hesitated. He set the books down again and clasping his hands behind him in that deferential manner he said, "It's about Marie."

Marcel's expression was utterly innocent. Uncomprehending. "Marie?"

"I want to call on her," said the deep voice, barely louder than an ordinary breath. "Your mother...I'm afraid..." He stopped. "I'm afraid," he went on, swallowing, "that she will think it unimportant, that we are too young...but if I could just call on her, with your blessing, when you were there! I mean, however you would want it...however you..." the large shoulders shrugged. And the face was mortified.

Marcel's eyes were wide. He had assumed that blank and obsessed expression that so often frightened people.

"Marie?" he whispered.

"Good lord, Marcel!" Richard stammered. "Good lord!"

"I'm sorry. It's my turn not to understand," Marcel was almost laughing. But Richard's face was so ominous that he didn't dare. Richard looked menacing. As if he might grab

(218)

Marcel and shake him as he'd done so often in the past. "Of course you can see her, if she wants!" he smiled. A calming sensation was surprising him. Marie and Richard . . . But then he drew himself up. He left the window and stood firmly in the middle of the floor.

"She'll be fourteen soon. You should really wait until then," he said seriously. "There'll be a party for her naturally and of course you'll come. After that . . . anytime. Before that, well, if you wish, I'll see."

"But your mother . . ."

"Don't worry about my mother," Marcel smiled. "Just leave that to me."

Richard, miserably uncomfortable and relieved at the same time, now moved to go. He made a quick bow much like the bow he'd given Marcel at the gate and turned to the porch.

"Well," Marcel said.

Richard looked back.

"You see what a good brother I can be?"

For a long time after Richard had gone, Marcel sat at the window looking out on those moving drifts of ivy and the winding, knotted branches of the old figs. Then wiping his face again with his handkerchief, he buttoned his jacket and went out.

In the dappled shade of the overhanging magnolias two white men sat at the painted wrought-iron tables of Madame Elsie's courtyard, their tall glasses of bourbon a pale amber in the afternoon light. A row of airy crepe myrtle trees separated this small court from the path to the back outbuilding where Anna Bella lived. And its long porches were screened by these same light green branches though Marcel could see that the windows were open, the lace curtains drawn back. But when he noticed the white gentlemen with their drinks, and heard their low voices, he paused, quite invisible beyond the edge of the flagstones, and stood still looking up at that distant porch. He was barely conscious of their drawling French, the playful compulsive tapping of a key against the rim of a glass.

Then he went up the gravel path to the stair.

Out of the corner of his eye, he saw a dark figure in the kitchen door far across the yard, but he took no notice of it as he mounted the steps. The figure rushed forward with lifted skirts. But he was already on the porch before he heard her hiss for his attention, the snapping of her fingers, the whispered and urgent: "Marcel!"

He was staring through the low windows of Madame Elsie's sitting room as he moved toward the door. And he saw Anna Bella on the settee, her lap covered with a long thick ribbon of white lace. It had been months since he had laid eyes on her. He no longer went to Mass at all with his mother and sister and their paths did not cross. But at this moment when he saw her, the love he felt for her was so exquisite that it left him weak. And he felt the ugly sting of shame. How could she know what he was feeling? How could she know why he had never come? How could she know when Richard didn't know and Marie didn't know and he himself could only dimly understand? He did not plan what he would say now. He didn't rehearse his words. He knew only that he must be with her, he must sit beside her in this room, close to her, and somehow make her understand. *Mais, non, we are not children.* And no longer children, what have we become? Oh, there were so many other moments, so many other times when they had opened their souls to one another, when in those long and mysterious tête-à-têtes they had come on truths together that neither, perhaps, would have ever known alone. So surely now they could take this step together. If any two people on earth could lay bare the adult travesties that had befallen them, entangling their lives, separating them, he and Anna Bella could. Just take her hand.

He moved forward, his fist already tight to knock, when suddenly inside the window just beside the door, a dark head distinguished itself from the familiar shapes of the room. A young white man, his black whiskers sleek and shining, his thick hair parted in the middle and curling fastidiously above his collar gazed up with severe hawk eyes. Marcel drew back and, his legs weakening under him, quickly left the porch.

He was still trembling when he reached his own room. He sat at his desk, the notebook for the day's class where he had left it, the Greek text, the case for his new pens. He moved to take a pen, to dip it in the ink. But then his arm tightened around his waist and putting his head down, he shut his eyes and dissolved into private tears.

IT WAS THE WITCHING HOUR, or so it seemed. Lights out, and only the far-off sounds: a woman laughing hysterically, the crack of a gun. It seemed for a while there had been the faint thudding of drums, those persistent voodoo drums, from a meeting lost within the maze of the neighborhood fences and walls. Marcel awoke. Lisette was standing over him, he was hot, covered with sweat, he stretched uneasily in his clothes.

He had fallen asleep, his books spread at the foot of the bed. He had been poring over his Greek, as he had done every night for three weeks since the school opened, striving to maintain his precarious lead at the top of the class, and now with some measure of relief he realized this was Friday night again, he could rest though the work was unfinished, he wouldn't be on the rack again until Monday morn.

"All right," he said grumpily to Lisette, ready for her lecture. He struggled up, stiffened, and wanted to fall back again asleep.

"That teacher wants you," she said.

"What?" He had his face in the pillow again, a warm rumpled pillow. The heat was unbearable in the little room. "What?" he rose up.

"He sent that no 'count Bubbles down here, said for you to come on up to his place if you were awake, and if your Maman said it was all right. Well, your Maman's asleep. It's nine o'clock. You going or not?"

"Yes," he said, "of course I'm going. Get me a fresh shirt." He was truly asleep. But he hadn't really spoken alone to Christophe since school started. He'd been dreaming of men on horseback for no reason at all. "You scared me," he murmured.

"How did I scare you?" she stood in front of the open armoire. His clothes were peeling off, soiled by the summer heat and his own skin. At the end of the class today that tall polished Augustin Dumanoir, the colored planter's son, had said with a sigh that the August heat was unbearable, perhaps the school should have opened in the fall. But then it was all worth it, really, heat or no heat. Marcel knew why Christophe had not waited. Christophe had had to prove to himself that the school could be done, and to prove it to the Englishman, who was still lodged at the St. Charles, as well. The Englishman was no longer coming to the townhouse. But

Christophe, at the dinner hour, was seen more than once to meet him a block from the house and walk with him fast uptown.

"I thought Monsieur Philippe had come, that's how you scared me," Marcel sighed. He must still be asleep. His own words surprised him. He had thought Monsieur Philippe was far from his thoughts, but now something of the atmosphere of his dream returned to him, a man riding in country fields, but it was all mixed up with that Augustin Dumanoir, who lingered after class each day to chat with Christophe as though they were both men. That boy had brought his hounds with him to New Orleans, and Marcel had seen him early last Saturday riding out with a clatter over the cobblestoned street, his hunting gun in its holster, his lean bronze face squinting in the sun. The horse was magnificent. The hounds had been streaking alongside it, darting in and out of the sparse crowds. But it was Monsieur Philippe's presence that lingered from the dream, and the old fear, had Monsieur Philippe been angered by Cecile's note? He had received the note for sure, the notary let Marcel know that, though how it was accomplished Marcel did not ask. The notary had been prying, where did Marcel study now, what was his teacher's name, and how old was his sister, my, she was lovely. "But I'm in the new school," Marcel thought, straining to open his eyes. He drank the hot coffee Lisette had just given him. "I'm at the top of my class, and Monsieur Philippe knows of Christophe." He shut his eyes tight and opened them again. The coffee, sweet with sugar and cream, went down deliciously.

His work these three weeks had taxed him to the fullest: his old habits had given him a bad time. He dreamed too much, thought too much, slept too much, had to struggle desperately to complete his assignments, his head ached. Yet in some quiet way he was happier than he had ever been. The day-to-day life in the classroom had surpassed his most romantic dreams. Christophe was infinite in his patience with the basics, but it was when he spoke of vast systems of ideas that he came into his own. History wasn't date and name to him; rather he spoke of cultural cataclysm, revolutions that divided the world in art, architecture, all expressions of the human mind. Marcel was dazed. He should have liked to wander through the streets again, thinking luxuriously for hours of a mere sentence which Christophe had spoken, a mere phrase. His only pain was the same pain he had experienced that first day: Christophe was his teacher

(222)

now, formal and demanding as with everyone, adding no particular warmth of inflection to his voice when he called on Marcel by name. There was no time to say even a word to him in the afternoons, and calling at the townhouse on Sundays, he had twice found Christophe gone, and Juliet, wild-eyed and worn, much resembling her former self, had worried him with her indifferent invitation to come in. And it was the Englishman himself who, meeting Marcel one late afternoon when the school let out, explained to him sarcastically that indeed, he was no longer even "permitted" to visit Christophe in his mother's house.

There was but one treasured consolation: Marcel led the class. Each morning when their corrected assignments were returned to them, and the grades announced, Marcel's was the highest. His translations were perfect, his geometry completely correct. He wished he could tell Christophe with a swelling heart how much the teacher's skill meant to him, his infinite patience with the most obtuse questions, his repeated inquiry, "Now is there anyone who does not understand, tell me if you do not understand." Monsieur De Latte had punished questions, berating the boy who asked them as lazy or dim-witted. The pretense of understanding when he did not understand was something that Marcel had to unlearn.

"What time is it?" he asked Lisette. The fresh shirt was cool but stiff.

"Nine o'clock, I told you," she said. "And Michie Philippe's not in town." He looked up at her as he buttoned his vest, saw her face sullen in the lamplight, the pecan skin with its rash of freckles glinting red like her copper hair.

"How do you know he's not in town?" he asked wearily. She pretended to know everything, where everyone was, what went on. Christophe's words came back to him, *every slave on this block knew you were here that afternoon with my mother.*

"Drink another cup." She handed him the coffee, and put his new boots beside the bed. "I haven't had time to get to those others, they're crusty. What with your sister's birthday coming I don't have time to breathe."

He nodded. His new boots. They hurt like hell. "But why is the birthday party being held at Tante Colette's?" he asked wearily. He too didn't have time to breathe. Marie's birthday was the fifteenth of August, the Feast of the Assumption of the Blessed Virgin, it was the birthday and name day that always brought the most elaborate celebrations, with a special cake, a reception, even presents for the slaves. And this year it was quite special because Marie was to be fourteen; she would become a young woman as if she weren't that already, as if Lisette didn't spend all day these days ironing her clothes, as if Richard hadn't come twice already to call. Lisette, who had loathed the simplest personal tasks for Cecile, went everywhere with Marie, was becoming, on her own, Marie's maid.

"You don't even know what goes on under your nose," Lisette said. "Your mother says the cottage is too small." There was contempt when she had said those words, "your mother." "Don't stay there too long," she whispered. It was a strange shift, but she still spoke to him protectively as if he were a child.

"Don't be foolish," he said. "I'll do as I damn well please." This affair of the cottage being too small, it didn't make sense.

"And if your mother wakes up, that's what I'm to tell her, he's off doing what he damn well pleases?"

"If you want to be mean about it," he said. He pulled on his boots, combed his hair. "Is Maman angry with Marie?" He asked it over his shoulder, as if it were not important at all.

Lisette made a short sound, not quite a laugh. "Don't be long," she said again in that same whisper.

"Now, what the hell is really on your mind?" he stopped as he put the comb in his pocket. It seemed the breeze had shifted, or some intervening sound had died away, so that faintly again he heard those voodoo drums. "You want to sneak away, don't you?" he whispered. "You want to go to that meeting, wherever it is..."

The drums were louder, or was it just that they had gotten a hold on his mind? They had a maddening monotonous rhythm.

"Don't you ever wonder what goes on there?" she asked. Her tone was insinuating.

He shot her an indignant glance. "Why should I care about that barbarous superstition?" he demanded. He could feel his eyes become hard. But she didn't budge.

There was something insolent and cunning in her face, something proud. "You'd be surprised, Michie, what fine company is dancing with those savages," she said with a slow smile, "even such fine gentlemen as yourself!"

(224)

He looked at her. At the smile on her face, the manner in which she stood against the door with her arms folded.

"You hate us, don't you, Lisette?" he whispered. "You hate all of us, even Marie...And if we were white we could beat you twice a day, and you'd lick our boots."

The smile died on her face. He was trembling. She stared at him almost blankly. And he felt a chill pass over him. Never had things gone so far between them before, never had he spoken these sentiments even to himself. But he was amazed to see the change in her. Her brows came together, it was as if he had struck her.

"I like you well enough, Michie," she said softly. "Haven't I always done right by you?" She was shaken, positively shaken. "You don't know my pain, Michie!" She looked away.

"I'm sorry, Lisette," he said. Flustered, his hands formed fists. He'd hurt her all right when he never dreamed he had the power to do so. She was playing with her earring, her head to one side, she would not look at him.

"I'm sorry," he said again. "And you've taken fine care of Marie these last few weeks..." he murmured.

A sullen smile showed gradually on her heavy features. "Well now," she whispered, "Doesn't that just make your mother boil!"

The slave, Bubbles, admitted him through the side door, and with the eyes of a cat led him through complete darkness to the stairs. "You go there, Michie," he whispered, and appeared to drop off silently as if in a void.

In all the time he had worked with Christophe, Marcel had not returned to the second floor. A bare bit of moonlight showed him the paneled door to Juliet's room was closed, and turning, his hand on the newel post, he saw the swell of a lamp far down the hall. Christophe beckoned him, and when he reached the door, he realized he was entering Christophe's room.

The teacher sat at his desk against the far wall, the lamp on a shelf slightly above his head. And above that lamp, covering the wall as high as a man might reach, were pages fluttering from tacks, all covered with a purple script. This writing had the obvious form of verse, with words crossed out here and there, lines scribbled in the broad margins. And beneath them, the desk itself was hopelessly cluttered with opened books, heaps of paper, feather pens, a chaos utterly different from the shining neatness of the classroom on the floor below, and a chaos that seemed to emanate out from the desk enveloping this entire room. The bed itself was unmade, papers were weighted down in random piles over the humps of the thrown-back spread, and an ashtray had spilled there distributing burnt matches and cigar butts. But it was comfortable, marvelously comfortable, all of it, the mantel crowded with figurines, the walls hung with maps and engravings helter-skelter, and before the grate was a rumpled pillow, and an empty glass, as though disdaining the bed, Christophe sometimes slept on the cooler floor.

He himself was dressed, dressed as formally as if he might be conducting class, and he sat with his back to the desk, one arm leaning on it, his hands clasped. He looked as poised and composed as he had in that small black and white Daguerreotype that Juliet had shown to Marcel the first afternoon in her room. Christophe had since presented the same picture to the class, explaining what it was, and how, through light and chemicals, the image had been made. Everyone had been amazed, and this lecture was but one of several that week on the new inventions and developments in Paris, a part of their education that kept the boys enthralled.

But something was wrong with Christophe. He sat too still, was too perfectly dressed, stood out too clearly amid the room's disorder, face in shadow against the lamp.

"I've missed you at supper," Christophe said.

"I've missed you, too, Monsieur," Marcel said. "I didn't want to disturb you, and I've been studying till midnight every night."

"It's hard for you, too hard," Christophe said. "And one of these days I want to have a talk with you about all that staring out of the window you do in class, but not now. You're my star, besides."

Marcel flushed.

"Right now, scolding you for daydreaming is the farthest thing from my mind. I wish I knew what was on my mind, then I wouldn't be rambling about things that don't matter to either of us. Sit down."

Marcel took the armchair near the grate. He couldn't keep his eyes from those fluttering poems. And when Christophe said nothing, he asked gently, "But what is it, Christophe?"

Christophe sighed. "Well, how has it been, Marcel? Have I been a good teacher, is the school worth a damn?"

Marcel was astonished. A good teacher. Everyone was talking of Christophe. Rudolphe stopped at the cottage gate to sing his praises and even the high-strung and spoilt Fantin was actually attempting to learn to read. Augustin Dumanoir and his cronies had sent back to the plantations for their trunks.

Marcel cocked his head to one side. "Are you playing with me, Christophe?" he asked.

Christophe uttered a dry laugh. "No," he shook his head. "Maybe the teacher needs a little assurance from the pupil, maybe he needs to see a little admiration in those blue eyes." The voice was softer than usual, a little vibrant with emotion as it had been in argument with the Englishman often before.

"You have that admiration!" Marcel said. "You know you have it."

Christophe was thoughtful. "I'm to see my friend, Michael, tonight," he said. "And if I refuse again to go back with him, I think he may leave tomorrow morning, with the tide." His eyes moved across the walls and looked down. "Which means...I may never see him again."

"Aaah," Marcel whispered. He understood the raw and vibrant voice, the still, composed form that was holding emotion in check.

"You know it's easy for me to forget that you're so young," Christophe went on. "You have some God-given confidence which is an inner flame. I don't have that confidence, though I have been told I possess a certain flair."

The compliment did not warm Marcel. He was afraid. His voice was uneven when he spoke.

"You want to go back to Paris, don't you?" he asked.

"O God, no!" Christophe shook his head. "That has nothing to do with it. Never, no!"

"But are you certain? You haven't had regrets?" Marcel's eyes probed fearfully for the slightest doubt.

Christophe made a weary smile. "You can't understand now. If you'd spent your youth traveling the world, and years in Paris, drunk night after night as you stumbled from one café to another, smoking hashish with people you couldn't remember, making love to people you'd never even met, if you'd written enough garbage that you yourself couldn't even recall committing to paper, ah, well, then, you might begin to comprehend. You might find yourself right back here on the corner of the Rue Dauphine and the Rue Ste. Anne with an idiotic smile on your lips, whispering the word, 'home.'"

But then he broke the contained pose for an instant and ran his hands over his hair. "Maybe I wasted Paris," he murmured. "It became a foul taste in the mouth and an endless throbbing in the head."

Marcel studied him, studied the way that he lifted a pencil from his desk and meant to break it firmly with both hands.

"Then it is just parting from the Englishman, then, just saying good-bye?"

"*Just* parting from the Englishman?" Christophe looked up. "*Just* parting from the Englishman?" His lips lengthened in a grimace.

Shyly, Marcel looked away. "If you want to be here with us," he said, "and we want you here—need you—then why is it so hard for the Englishman to understand?"

Christophe's brows came together in a tense frown. "Because he needs me," he sighed. "He needs me to need him again. And there's a monstrous injustice in all this, a monstrous injustice which no one comprehends here except me."

"I know he's not good for you," Marcel blurted suddenly, "and when he does leave this place, you'll be better off!"

He pressed his lips together tightly. He had gone too far. But he could hardly bear to see Christophe as he was now, and only the Englishman could reduce the resolute and quick-witted teacher to a diffident and miserable young boy.

"I'm sorry," Marcel muttered.

"You despise him, don't you?" Christophe asked. "The same as Maman. You glare at him as if he were some menace and she curses him, threatens him with voodoo magic, calls him names..."

"Christophe, that's because she's afraid of him, she's afraid he'll persuade you to leave here, just as I'm afraid. Besides, she believes him to be... well, a man, who took you away from your home in Paris years ago!"

Now he had done it! But he had the distinct impression he was fighting some sort of battle here, Christophe was asking him to fight it, and he didn't fully understand the terms.

"My home in Paris!" Christophe bent forward. "My home in Paris, did she use those words! Good God, such sublime simplicity of mind! You know, sometimes I think I understand my mother's madness perfectly. It is the perfect self-ishness, she will not understand what she does not wish to understand!"

"Christophe, she'll hear you," Marcel cautioned.

"So, let her hear me! Let me bring down the rafters on her head. My home in Paris, for the love of heaven! That hotel

and those people, I'd been there two years in that place without a letter from New Orleans, the bank clerk who left me
there was gone! I stole to get the paper to write her! Now,
Marcel, there are shops in this very street where a woman
can dictate a letter and have that letter sent abroad."

"But what did happen?" Marcel asked.

Christophe ran his hand back through his hair again, fingers raking the tight close-cropped brown waves. "I sometimes wonder myself," he said. "But I'm not being honest, the
whole truth is, I know too well." He drew himself up, clearing
his throat slightly. "It was her father's idea. And it must
have sounded terribly official when he spoke to his lawyers;
but you see, by the time I'd crossed the ocean and passed
through a succession of strangers, there was little left of the
original design. A family took me for the money offered, and
kept me out of school to work in the hotel. I didn't have shoes
by the time Michael came to lodge there, I'd run off twice and
come back rather than starve. I can't talk about those times
even now," he shifted uneasily. "But I can tell you this, I was
younger than you are when I arrived there, and two years
seemed the length and breadth of the world."

"I didn't know…" Marcel whispered.

"I don't expect you to know," he said. "But she doesn't
know either, that's the tragedy of it. But if only she'd had a
little strength, if only she had stood up to that man. She was
always the prey of the lovers of her life, but I always knew
with her that I came first. That no matter what happened,
she was my mother and I belonged to her and she belonged
to me. I'd look at them with their fancy carriages and their
presents, they'd pay the rent, they'd order me around. But
I knew I'd outlast them, all her lovers, and if they ever dared
lay hands on me, well that would be the end. They could slap
her around all right, I listened to enough of that through
these walls. But she belonged to me and I belonged to her,
until he came, her father, that glowering ghost from the past.
A brigand was what he'd been, one of these wild Haitians
who've lived for generations in the hills, runaway slaves in
one century and rebels in the next. That man was made of
iron, with all that blood on his hands, and all that gold in
the banks.

"Oh, how the laywers impressed him, I can remember the
offices here myself. Lots of leather and green velvet, a little
good sherry, I was to be educated abroad. *In loco parentis*, I
was to have a good French family. And then that bleak little

hotel, those grim-faced peasants with their leather straps, and the cot under the stairs."

Christophe made a short bitter sound.

"The first night Michael came, he let me warm my hands and feet at the grate when I brought up his supper. Then claiming he wasn't hungry, he watched me devour every morsel on that tray." He shook his head, musing, his eyes quite remote from Marcel. "Strange, I've never written a word about that. Mr. Charles Dickens would probably have written about it, but then he isn't scribbling nonsense between puffs of a hashish pipe."

Marcel said nothing. It was all as gossip had told it, he could almost hear Monsieur Philippe's drawling voice at table recounting the old tale. Only the Englishman had never been part of it. And until this moment, perhaps, Marcel had still doubted Juliet's fears. Now he was riveted to Christophe, and at the same time afraid. "He felt sorry for you, then..." he whispered.

"Sorry for me? He became my life. He bought me clothes, a warm blanket, gave me something to eat, took me everywhere he went. Then the day came that I dreaded, the day he told me he was going away." He sighed. He grasped the pencil again in one hand as if he wanted to break it against his fingers with the pressure of his thumb. Marcel could all but feel the pressure he exerted upon it. But Christophe continued, "I thought I was going to die. I told him I'd run away as soon as he was gone, I couldn't stay there any longer, I didn't care what happened to me, I was going away. Well, I don't think I'll ever forget that moment. He was sitting by the window in his room. I remember this as if it were happening now.

"'I've come to a decision, Christophe,' he said. 'It's a decision the world would not understand. But I've come to it, the struggle is over. Pack your belongings now quietly, and be ready to leave with me tonight.'"

The hand that held the pencil suddenly broke it in half. Christophe watched it drop to the desk. "I wonder what would have become of me if he'd left me there." His eyes moved slowly to Marcel. "Three years passed before I walked into the offices of a solicitor in London and had him write to Maman. I had wanted to punish her, I had wanted her to believe I was dead."

Marcel bowed his head. Something stirred in his soul, a vague excitement as he thought of those "three years" and the names so often mentioned by the two men, Istanbul, Athens, Tangier.

Then Christophe asked in a small voice, "Do you know my worst fear?"

Marcel looked up.

"That *she* was dead. That I'd lost her. That maybe she'd disappeared. I couldn't stop thinking about her. And oddly enough, as time passed, she became more and more real. I could remember all manner of things about her that I did not even know I had known. I would awake in different cities feeling the atmosphere of this house around me. I would dream of her. She was with me, at last, night and day. I was trembling the day I went to the solicitors for their answer. They had contacted a law office here, in the Rue Camp uptown. The old bastard, her father, was bedridden, paralyzed from a stroke and she had cried uncontrollably when they let her understand I was alive. All she ever said to any of them was 'Tell him to come home.'

"Well," Christophe shrugged with the same bitterness he had evinced before. "We had already booked passage to Istanbul and I had no intention of crossing the sea for her, after what she'd done to me, not while that bloody Haitian was still alive. I instructed the solicitors to let me know as soon as he'd departed this earth, but by that time, well, I was in Paris, I was famous for writing nonsense about an improbable heroine named Charlotte and her preposterous lover, Randolphe. Michael had educated me, outfitted me, instructed me in the fine points of manners, polite conversation, vintage wines. It was he who dealt with the publishers, managed the rent, and carried me home on his arm from the cafés.

"I couldn't teach you or anyone else a damned thing if it weren't for Michael. I wouldn't be a teacher, a writer, I wouldn't have the money in my pockets for a dram of absinthe!"

He turned his head sharply to the side.

Below and far to the back of the house, a clock chimed, so faint that a sigh would have obliterated it. Marcel listened, but did not note the time. As a matter of fact it seemed to go on forever.

He took no note of anything around him, not even of Christophe who rested his forehead against his open hand, the heel of his boot hooked in the rung of his chair. The story had left him miserable and vaguely excited and he did not know why. He loathed the Englishman, positively loathed him, but he

(231)

had a profound and numbing sense of two people together, wandering over land and sea, together, the one sheltering the other, caring for the other and *just how that might be!* It was so alluring suddenly that without realizing it he gave a slight shake of the head. And he felt pain for the Englishman that this was ended, utterly ended, and he felt terrible pain for Christophe.

There was one great flaw in the story, however, a hideous flaw. Why hadn't the Englishman written to the mother in New Orleans, why hadn't he tried to help the boy get home?

Christophe drew himself up. His voice was thick, heavy. "It's time for me to go."

For a moment, Marcel didn't answer. He was feeling a dull palpitation. Then he said softly, "But surely you'll see him again."

Christophe shook his head. "I think not."

He stared at Christophe who sat stiff again, like the model for the Daguerreotype in the chair.

"But why must it be so final, Chris, I don't understand!"

"Because it's finished!" Christophe whispered, his eyes widening on the shadows before him. "Because I owe him my life! And that is simply too much to bear!"

He rose. He stretched his arms out, clenched his fists, and then let them drop at his side.

Marcel stared at his straight back, the square shoulders, the head that faced the wall of poems. The night seemed empty around them except for some soft, distant rustling sound. Marcel blinked as if the story had been a sudden blaze that had blinded him, and he must regain his sight.

"Do you want to walk with me...part of the way?" Christophe murmured over his shoulder. "We could find one of those little riverfront bistros you so love and have a cool beer."

"Yes," Marcel rose slowly. "Maybe I could wait for you...outside the hotel."

"No," Christophe shook his head. "I'll see him off," he said, and reached out for the package of cheroots on the desk.

But there was a soft tread in the hallway. And the tall, willowy figure of the slave Bubbles appeared in the door.

"Michie, a man's here," said the slave, "come from the St. Charles Hotel."

"Damn," Christophe muttered. "Anger on top of everything else."

Marcel followed him through the dark hallway at a slow pace.

He didn't welcome the sight of the angry Englishman cursing Christophe for not coming sooner. However, it was a black man at the foot of the stairs, with a lantern in his hand. Christophe turned to Marcel, and at first Marcel thought the light had distorted the expression on his face.

"Michie, you best move him out of there right now," said the black man. "They say he's far gone with it, and when it gets these Englishmen, Michie, they drop like flies."

"No!" Christophe staring wide-eyed. He shook his head, and said again, "No. He's been in Cairo with the cholera, with the plague. This is nothing, surely..."

"Michie, he's got it, and they want him out of the hotel."

"Got what?" Marcel whispered.

But he already knew.

V

THE ENGLISHMAN was delirious. He did not know that he was being taken into the carriage, nor out of it, up the stairs into Christophe's room. A tousled and sleepy Juliet came into the hallway, a flowered shawl over her long silk gown. Pushing her hair back angrily she padded toward them, passing Marcel in the open doorway and looked down at the Englishman in Christophe's bed. His head lay limp against the pillow, his hair wet and dark against his high forehead, eyes at half-mast. The breath came from him in slow, measured gasps.

Bubbles, having gone for water, brought the pitcher to Christophe who wet his handkerchief and laid it on the Englishman's head. "Michael, can you understand me?" he said in English. He had asked this over and over on the way to the house. "Oh, where is the doctor, for the love of God!" He turned to them with clenched teeth.

"He's coming, Michie," said Bubbles in that soft, eternally calm voice. "The fever is all over tonight, Michie, he will come when he can."

Christophe tore at the Englishman's shirt, loosening the buttons at his throat, then wrapped the robe more tightly around him.

"It isn't a doctor he needs, Christophe," Marcel said. "It's a good nurse. Our people are the best for that, the doctor will tell you this when he gets here, to get him a nurse."

Christophe turned to Juliet. She was leaning against the door frame staring down at the Englishman from the corner of her eye.

"You know what to do for him, Maman, you know yellow fever, you've seen it here and in Saint-Domingue."

She turned her gaze slowly to Christophe, eyes widening as if with disbelief. "You ask that of me!" she whispered. "Me, and that man!"

"Maman!" he grabbed her suddenly by the arms, as if he meant to hurt her. She merely let her head drop to one side.

"Christophe, listen to me," Marcel interjected. "I can find a nurse. My aunts will know, the Lermontants will know..."

"No!" Christophe shuddered. "Don't go near those people." For a second, Marcel did not understand. It was superstition, the mention of the Lermontants, of course. But behind them, the Englishman let out a moan. His thin body looked so slight under the covers, and his cheeks flushed with the fever made him appear all the more wasted and white.

"Michael, the doctor is coming, a nurse will be here soon," Christophe said to him in a barely controlled voice. "This is some tropical fever, Michael, you've seen this before, you'll shake it off."

The Englishman grimaced, and his lips formed the whisper, "Yellow jack."

A soft indefinable sound came from Juliet. She left the room.

Christophe was after her in an instant, catching her in the hall. "Maman, help me!" he pleaded.

"Get your hands off me," she groaned, but her eyes were on fire. "You dare to bring that man here, here to me?" her voice broke. "In my house."

"No, no, don't look away from me, please, Maman, I've told you over and over what happened in Paris, Maman, I'm begging you..."

She jerked away from him, pulling her shawl up over her shoulders, hair falling down in her face. "There isn't anything I can do!" She shook her head. "It's yellow fever, your friend knows it, they all know it!" she threw up her hand. "He is going to die!"

Christophe gasped. He let her go. He backed away from her. And turning, her head down, she padded softly away from him into the darkness of her room.

One half hour later the doctor, weary, overworked, and plagued with a wracking cough himself, confirmed Marcel's advice. A nurse would work no miracles, but it was the best anyone could do.

"But I saw him at noon today," Christophe whispered. "He complained of a headache from walking in the sun, that was all, a headache." Bubbles and Marcel stared at him. It was clear he could not accept the situation. The Englishman had begun to have violent chills.

A terrified Tante Louisa opened the door for Marcel at midnight, greatly relieved it was only that Englishman friend of Christophe's who was ill. Of course she knew nurses, but all of them had their hands full, ah, this heat, this rain. Nevertheless, Marcel took the names from her and began going door to door.

It was near dawn when tired and discouraged he rang Rudolphe Lermontant's bell. Rudolphe in his nightshirt wiped the shaving soap from his face as he stood in the door, a stub of candle in one hand, a peculiar expression passing over his features, his eyes almost dreamy as he looked at the deserted street. "I told that man," he said wearily and without pride, "to get out of the city, to go out to the lake for a while until the end of summer. Every day he walked past the shop with his head uncovered in the heat of the afternoon. He uttered some poetry to me, some mad English foolishness about the Hounds of Hell! All the nurses are employed by now, even the old women who ought to be retired." Marcel, studying his wide musing eyes, was suddenly struck by a faint shudder. Rudolphe knew the Englishman was a dead man, he knew that he would be bathing that body, dressing it perhaps before this day had passed.

"You must know some names, just anyone..." Marcel murmured. "Christophe's caring for that man by himself."

Rudolphe shook his head. "There is one young lady I can think of, but your chances of getting Madame Elsie to let her go up there are as good as mine," he said.

"Ah, Anna Bella."

"You remember '37, Madame Elsie's was almost a hospital, and every time I came to pick up a body, that poor little girl was there. She knows as much about nursing fever victims as anyone around. But Madame Elsie, well, now that's another affair."

"She'll do it for me," Marcel said, and turning he ran, forgetting to offer Rudolphe his thanks.

The sun was just rising over the river and the sky resembled perfectly a sunset as Marcel entered Madame Elsie's yard. A mist hung over the flagstoned garden, and beyond through the gray branches of the crepe myrtles a light already burned in Madame Elsie's windows, and against the backdrop of that light Marcel could see the outline of a figure on the porch, a lone woman in a chair. The creak of the rocker sounded clearly in the stillness. He stopped at the edge of the path. A pain throbbed inside him like a heart. But then a faint voice reached him, a voice singing low, a voice that did not know it could be heard. It was not Madame Elsie in the rocker, it was Anna Bella.

She rose as he pounded up the steps. She wore an airy dress, replete with her usual lace, a thin crocheted shawl over her shoulders, her heavy hair undone. And as she turned to him, he saw that she had been crying.

"Why Marcel!" she whispered.

"Anna Bella," he said as he took both her hands. "You've got to forgive me, but I need you now, Anna Bella," and without guile or craft or stammered apologies he told her at once all about the Englishman in Christophe's house.

"Just you wait right here, Marcel, while I get my bag," she said.

He was so relieved that he squeezed her hands before he let her go, and then, forgetting everything, he clasped her tight, kissing her quickly, innocently, on both cheeks.

"But what about Madame Elsie?" he whispered.

"To hell with Madame Elsie," she whispered back.

As they hurried up the block, she asked a few rapid questions about when the Englishman had been stricken and how.

"The man's been all over the world, he wasn't the least afraid of yellow fever, he's been in the tropics before," Marcel explained.

But when they reached the gate, Anna Bella hesitated, looking up at the shuttered windows, the dark outline of the chimneys against the pale but brightening sky.

"I'm here with you," he said.

She turned to him, her eyes large and soulful and just for an instant there was her silent reproach. Then she went in.

She had the sickroom in order at once, told Christophe to shutter the windows but to let in the air. The sheets had to be changed, they were damp, and there ought to be more blankets and drinking water, and water for compresses for the man's head. "Quinine won't do this man any good," she

(236)

said when Christophe suggested it, "leeches neither, you just got to keep him really warm." She sent Bubbles on to the pharmacy to get a glass feeder for the drinking water, and told Christophe he was no longer acclimated after all this time, he ought to get out of the room.

"I'm not leaving here!" he said with mild astonishment. "The fever never affects us, besides."

"'Course it does...sometimes. But I knew you'd say that. If you're going to stay here go to sleep, you'll have to spell me for a while later on."

Just before noon, Marcel was awakened abruptly. He had been slumped up against the wall in the corner of the room. Now Bubbles told him that Lisette was downstairs with Madame Elsie's girl, Zurlina. They wanted Anna Bella to come home. The Englishman was shuddering violently and did not know where he was. He murmured names that no one knew.

The day looked unreal to Marcel when he went outside. His head ached violently, and the sun seemed to cut brutally through an uncommonly clear sky. Zurlina was haranguing him, demanding that Anna Bella come out, and without realizing it he was leading her back toward his own gate. His mother stood in the shade of the banana grove. "What is all this?" she asked. And when he told her, stammering, speaking in fragments, he saw a resolution forming in her face. "That old crow," she said, as she gazed with narrow eyes toward Madame Elsie's door.

"She's coming down here herself to get that girl, if you don't bring her out," said Zurlina.

"The hell she is," hissed Cecile and barely lifting her majestic skirts she marched toward the boardinghouse at the end of the block.

When Marcel returned, cradling a pot of hot coffee between two towels, the Englishman was vomiting black blood. And Christophe was trembling so violently that at first Marcel thought he was ill. The Englishman's face was gleaming, his eyes rolled up into his head. Chest heaving beneath the blankets, his hands twisted the covers, the knuckles white.

It was late afternoon when Marcel stumbled out again, too tired to protest when Christophe told him to take some supper before he came back, that they would send for him if there was a change. He had the best of intentions of returning with soup and bread for all of them, but once at home he fell across his bed. Lisette had promised to wake him in an hour. He went into a deep sleep.

*　　*　　*

It was dark when he awoke, the cicadas were singing in the trees. He jumped up, almost cried out. The evening star hung in the sky and the night seemed strangely empty around him. He was certain the Englishman was dead. An awful anguish overcame him, that falling to sleep, he had let the man die.

Rushing up the dark stairs and along the empty hall, he found Anna Bella sitting quietly in the bedroom, her rosary beads in her hand. Dim candles flickered on a small makeshift altar, with a prayer book propped open to a picture of the Virgin, the whole set on a linen napkin on Christophe's desk. The corpse lay neatly against a snow-white pillow. Marcel let out a low moan.

"Marcel," she whispered drowsily, rolling her head to one side as if it were heavy on her neck.

He walked softly toward her as if somehow the dead man would be upset by the sound of his steps. Her hand burned against his, and feeling the weight of her forehead against him, he clasped her shoulders and held her, trying not to give way to tears.

"Where is Christophe?" he whispered.

"I don't know," she answered. "It was terrible, Marcel, it was the worst!"

She rose, leading him to the doorway, but just outside she stopped. She was looking back at the man on the bed, and obviously did not wish to leave the body all alone.

"Oh, Marcel, it was the worst ever that I've seen," she said, her voice very low. "I tell you when that man died, I thought Michie Christophe was going to lose his mind. He just stood there staring at that man as if he couldn't believe his eyes. And then she came in, that crazy woman." Anna Bella shook her head. Her voice dropped to a whisper. "She just walked in here real slowly as if she didn't have anything in particular on her mind. And there was Michie Christophe just holding onto his own head and staring down at that man. And then, shrugging her shoulders, just like this, she says to him, 'I told you, didn't I, that he was going to die.' I tell you, Marcel, she might as well have been saying the weather was hot, or come to dinner or shut that door. And I thought that man would kill her, Marcel, he started screaming at her, he called her names I never heard a man call a woman, and his own mother, Marcel, why, he called her words I wouldn't say to you right here. He ran at her, trying to get a hold of her and

(238)

she went down on the floor, sliding right down the wall, to get away of him, Marcel, it's a wonder they didn't knock that poor dead man right off the bed. Well, I got my arms around his waist, I held onto him with both hands, I said, 'I'm not going to let you go, Michie Christophe,' and he just slammed me back against the door. I tell you my head's still spinning from that."

Marcel murmured a negation, his head shaking.

"Oh, the language that that man was using to that woman. Well, she got up fast enough on her hands and knees and then she ran out. I don't know where she went. And Michie Christophe just stood there staring again at the bed. It was like he didn't even know I was there. 'Michael,' he said to that Englishman, not moaning for him, Marcel, talking to him. 'Michael,' he kept saying, and then he jerked him up by the shoulders, shaking him like he could wake him up. 'This is a mistake,' he said, 'Michael, we've got to get out of here, this is a mistake!' Then he was turning to me and saying it, like he could convince me that it was all a mistake. 'That man's not coming back, Michie Christophe,' I said. 'Let him go. That man's dead.' And oh, when I said that to him, Marcel, why he broke down just like a child. He was crying, crying, like a little boy. He kept looking at me, I swear he looked just like a little boy. I put my arms around him and held onto him, he was just rocking back and forth. One minute I'd been scared to death of him, and then I was just holding him like a child. I don't know how long that went on. It was a long time before he got quiet. He just wandered out here by the stairs. He had his hands on his head again. I told that worthless Bubbles to get on over to Michie Rudolphe's and get you on the way. And when I turned around Michie Christophe was gone."

"Gone?" Marcel made a soft, weary moan. "But where?"

"I looked all through this house, they were both of them gone. I came back here to wash and lay out the body. Michie Rudolphe's gone up to the hotel to see if he can find some papers in the man's room. And that Bubbles, I don't know where he is!"

"Forgive me," he shook his head. "Forgive me. For asking this of you, for leaving you here alone..."

"No!" she said emphatically. "I'm the last one to worry about, Marcel. You put that out of your mind." Her eyes were clear, honest. And it was so like her, and so unlike anyone else that he knew, that as he looked down at her he felt a peculiar catch in his throat. He wanted to kiss her, just gently, innocently, and he resented all the voices now which told him he must not. But hesitating only for a moment, he found that his hands were on her arms, her small plump arms, and his lips had brushed the rounded firm deliciousness of her small cheek. Everything about her was roundness, ripeness, and he was overcome suddenly with all the bold and bewildering physical awareness of her that he had so long denied. Only now did he realize how he had held himself back, how his eyes had resisted her, how his imagination had refused to weave this voluptuous flesh into the fantasies in which Juliet had become his queen. He had clenched his teeth now, his hands still holding her, and he was wrestling with some violent ugly anger against the whole world: against Madame Elsie, against Richard, but above all against himself, the young boy who couldn't have her, and wouldn't have her for all his dreams of Paris instead. A shameless sound escaped his lips, he could feel her cheek against his chin, feel the roughness of his own neglected beard against that ripe fruit. But even now he might have won this battle had she not drawn up on tiptoe and kissed his lips.

Her mouth was soft, guileless, utterly innocent as it opened, sucking gently, daintily at his breath. And in the sudden mounting of his passion, the battle was lost. He had lifted her, and turned her, drawing her close against the wall as if he meant to conceal her while he kissed her over and over, his hands fumbling through the pleated muslin of her skirts for the contour of her hips. The house lay deserted around him, dark rooms gaping onto the hall. He might enfold her, carry her, but then his thoughts became one with the movement of his limbs. And so purely, sweetly, she gave herself over to him, that precious virginal innocence terrifying him, maddening him, heightening his desire. "No!" he whispered suddenly, and drew back from her, roughly pushing her away.

"Damn you, Anna Bella!" he stammered. He felt for the post at the top of the stairs. "Damn you!" he clutched the railing, his back to her, holding tight to it with both hands. "I can't, I can't...I can't let it happen!" he whispered. A throbbing in his head blinded him and became a dizzying pain. "Why in hell do you think I've stayed away from you, why in hell..." He turned on her suddenly to see her staring at him with immense glimmering brown eyes.

She didn't move. Her lips quivered. The tears poured down

her cheeks. And then, her white teeth cutting into that tender vulnerable lip, she came forward, and lifting her right hand cracked him hard across the face.

He winced, shut his eyes. It seemed, as he heard her moving away from him, he positively savored the pain. And when he looked up she was gone.

Approaching the door of Christophe's room, he saw her sitting before the candles, her rosary in her left hand. With her right, she waved languidly, steadily at the flies that buzzed over the dead man's face.

She was sad and distant as if he were not even there to see it, her cheeks glistening with tears. He stared at the dead man, stared at the candles, and then blindly he took up his position to wait for Rudolphe at the foot of the stairs.

VI

MADAME SUZETTE LERMONTANT HATED her husband Rudolphe with all her heart. She hated him and resented him as she did no other human being in the world. And she loved him at the same time. With a love laced with admiration, submission, and appalling need. She could not endure a word of criticism against him, though for twenty-five years not a day had passed during which she did not wish at once time or another to beat him to death with her bare hands. Or better yet, stab herself in the breast to spite him, or blow her own head off in his presence with Grandpère's 1812 gun.

Since the very first day of their marriage she had endured his ranting, his criticism, his scathing judgments and violent rejections of all she believed, all she held sacred, and she was no more used to it now than when it had all begun. Year after year he attacked her manner of speech, her manner of dress, threw her favorite volumes of poetry across the room in disgust, called her an idiot and a fool in front of family at table, and glared in SILENCE at her nervous, chattering friends.

Somewhere during the long years of quarreling and tears, she had come to realize an all-important point: none of this was personal with Rudolphe. *He would have treated any wife the same way.* But far from easing her anger and pain, this revelation made her bitter, deepened her outrage. Because she realized that in all her ruthless self-examinations resulting from his condemnation, and all of her intense striving to make herself understood, she had been utterly wasting her time. Rudolphe ground her to powder for the benefit of some audience in his imagination for which her part might have been played by anyone, it was merely a supporting role. And sometimes screaming at her with his fist clenched as he strode back and forth across the room, he seemed some savage giant who might consume the earth, the water, the very air she breathed.

Had she been a more submissive woman she might have learned to accept Rudolphe's flamboyant fury the way one accepts the weather. In fact she might have undermined it with indifference and affection astutely combined. And had she been completely strong on the other hand she might have beaten him somewhere, or drawn back, content to live along-side him within a fortress of herself, sneering from aloft. But she was the perfect mixture of the two dispositions, a woman of strong personality and marked temperament, who never-theless did not wish, and had never expected, to stand on her own two feet. She wanted Rudolphe's love and approval, and she wanted him to tell her what to do.

And among all the men she'd ever known, there was no one figure whom she respected, trusted, as she did Rudolphe. He had given her uncommon security, and was admired by everyone around him not only for his business sense, which was splendid, but for his professional decorum, his family loyalties, his stunning capacity to lead and calm others, his remarkable wits. He was a man of substance. And handsome to boot.

They had shared joys and sorrows together, suffered the loss of a daughter, the complete defection of two sons, and theirs remained a passionate marriage when they had the time for it, complete with a great deal of commonplace af-fection, kisses, snuggling together under the covers, shared enjoyment of the good Creole cooking, exotic flowers for the garden, imported wines.

But constant were the ripping arguments. Suzette had only to declare a preference for it to be trampled, and she was berated day in and day out for being spineless in those matters where she had become clever enough to declare no preference at all. In all these years, she had never caught on herself to what others had sometimes hinted: Rudolphe was a little afraid of her, and of his love for her; he thought that all women were something slightly subversive that had at all times to be controlled.

Yet in one particular aspect of their life together she had recently decided that she would not be the loser even if he were to burst a blood vessel from temper on the spot. She was prepared to deceive him if necessary to gain her ends. But first she would try the truth. And this was in the matter of Marie Ste. Marie and their son, Richard, whom Suzette absolutely adored.

A week ago an invitation had come from the Ste. Marie family inviting the Lermontants to attend a reception for Marie's birthday and name day, August fifteenth. Rudolphe had said at once that he could not attend, he would be busy as always in August, and the war was on. By that evening he was raving that Suzette would not attend this reception either and at last that even Richard must not be allowed to go alone. But Suzette did not decline the invitation. And fighting with Rudolphe night and day behind closed doors, she told Richard softly but firmly not to give it another thought.

So on Monday at half past one, only a half hour before the reception was to begin, she was frightened to discover that Rudolphe had come unexpectedly through the front door. She was dressed and waiting for Richard who was still upstairs, and she had not expected her husband to drop in at home.

"All right," he said wearily as he removed his black frock coat. "I don't want coffee, get me a little cool wine." He dropped into a chair in the second parlor.

She brought him the wine, along with his lighter coat which he always wore in the house. But he merely threw this aside.

"That was holy hell," he whispered. "The Girod cemetery is worse than the St. Louis, what with the Yanqui Protestants dropping like flies."

"Hmmmmm," she said. She knew that he had just buried the Englishman, Michael Larson-Roberts, who had been Christophe Mercier's white friend.

"Mon Dieu," Rudolphe shook his head. "Get me the decanter for heaven sake's, what does this hold, a thimbleful?"

"It will make you tired," she warned.

"Madame, I am not an idiot." He sat back and reaching for the palmetto fan at his side, waved it limply before his face. "Every one of the students came," he said, lowering his voice as he always did when he discussed his profession and

(243)

those details concerning it which were never discussed outside the house. "I don't believe any of those boys welcome this unexpected little vacation," he said. "He's managed to make quite an impression on them in three short weeks."

"And Christophe himself?" she asked.

Rudolphe shook his head.

"You mean he didn't come?" She knew that Christophe had disappeared and that Marcel had been searching for him everywhere. But with the notices in the papers, and the announcements posted around the Quarter, they had all hoped that Christophe would return.

"The man blames himself, it's obvious." Rudolphe shrugged. "The Englishman followed him here from Paris."

"And Ma'ame Juliet?" she asked.

"She's gone out with Marcel to search the docks. She goes on board the steamboats and the foreign ships. She's convinced he's booked passage out of here and is never coming back. He hasn't been home at all, nothing in his room has been touched."

"Ah, no, he wouldn't leave the school, not after all this work, I don't believe it," Suzette said sadly. "After all, the Englishman... why, they were only friends."

Rudolphe's face was thoughtful. She watched him curiously. But he made no comment. Then he said,

"Well! The boys believe he's in mourning. I suppose that's perfectly true."

He turned, hearing Richard's heavy rapid rush down the stairs. Richard did not hurry in this fashion when he knew that his father was at home, and caught in the act, he stopped. Obviously he was dressed for the birthday reception, and obviously Suzette was dressed for it too. Richard glanced at his mother desperately. The clock in the hallway chimed lightly for the quarter hour. It was time for them to leave.

"Monsieur," Suzette began, drawing herself up to be firm.

"I know, Madame," Rudolphe sighed. "Well! Get me my coat. Don't just stand there, get me my coat. I can't very well go to a birthday reception in my shirtsleeves."

Suzette kissed him twice before he could brush her away.

It was crowded already when they arrived. Celestina Roget was there with her pretty daughter, Gabriella, and her frail but cheerful son, Fantin. Old lady friends of the aunts were already nestled comfortably into the more ample chairs. Young Augustin Dumanoir was there with his father, and his very lovely younger sister, Marie Therese, just in from the country, who was a dark-haired girl with pecan skin and bluish green eyes. Monsieur Dumanoir had only just come in from his plantation to meet the new teacher, Christophe, and with a letter of introduction had called upon the Lermontants the night before. *"Quel dommage,"* he was sighing now. The death of this poor Englishman, no wonder the teacher "would see no one."

Anna Bella Monroe was in the corner and she rose at once to be kissed by Suzette on both cheeks. She was fresh, lovely, and yes, blushing, thank you, she had made the lovely green muslin with its pearl buttons herself.

Nanette and Marie Louise LeMond were there, and Magloire Rousseau, the tailor's son who had just proposed marriage to Marie Louise and been accepted, the banns having been announced in church that week. Nanette smiled when she saw Richard and gave him a rather graceful curtsy which he did not appear to note.

But Marie Ste. Marie, the celebrity of the day, outshone all around her as she sat demurely beside her Tante Colette, the massive flounces of her new dress threaded with pink ribbon, her dark full black hair drawn back softly to its chignon so that it covered the tips of her ears. A startling girl, this Marie Ste. Marie, one could not help but wonder when such beauty would reach its peak, and there was a flicker of pain in the eyes which she turned to Suzette. *"Bonjour, ma petite,"* Suzette kissed her, "you are very lovely, very lovely indeed."

A touch of color flared in the girl's white cheeks, her voice was barely audible as she murmured her thanks, and then she flushed outright as the shadow of Richard loomed over his mother's shoulder. Suzette saw her son bend to kiss Marie's hand.

She is not vain, Suzette was musing, no, she is not vain at all. It's almost as if she cannot guess that she's beautiful. And frankly the girl's beauty was too much. In drawing rooms around the world, she might have been presented as an Italian countess. A Spanish heiress, any dark nationality but that which she truly was.

"Ah well, Michie Rudi," Colette was pulling Rudolphe toward the crystal punch bowl, "did they bury that poor Englishman?" It was a stage whisper. "And where on earth is this famous Christophe! And does the man have any people, had he left anything, who will..."

"His lawyers will attend to all that," Rudolphe grumbled. He detested this sort of questioning. He never divulged this sort of information about the deceased and yet he was eternally asked. It was polite to ask, to show concern. "Where's Marcel!" he demanded now. "And his mother?" He glanced with irritation at the beautiful belle of the ball who was not looking at him. She was looking at his son.

"My niece is ill," said Colette. "She rarely goes out, some women are like that, I don't know why. As for Marcel, talk some sense to him, he's been out all night looking for Christophe!" She gestured to the open French doors. Marcel stood on the gallery, his back to the assemblage, the taller Fantin Roget towering over him as he talked rapidly, rocking now and then on his heels.

"Hmmm," Rudolphe grunted. "Let me talk to Marcel."

Suzette, settling beside Louisa and an ancient quadroon woman who was completely deaf, played idly with a small bit of cake. It was not *the* cake. *The* cake stood resplendent in the center of the nearby table, a majestic script spelling out on the white icing the words *Sainte-Marie*. This referred of course to the Virgin Mary whose feast day it was, and it struck Suzette as slightly disconcerting that it was the birthday girl's last name as well. Her eyes moved over the assemblage returning furtively to the lean figure of the young Augustin Dumanoir who had just come between Richard and Marie, and bending over somewhat unctuously, it seemed to Suzette, meant to crowd her son away. Richard gave easily. He dropped back finding a seat beside Anna Bella and fell into conversation with her at once. Suzette studied Dumanoir. So this is the competition, she was thinking, that sprawling new house in the Parish of St. Landry and fields of sugarcane. Fantin had come in to take his place behind Marie's chair, and from afar, young Justin Rousseau watched with obvious interest. Old families, good families, and this girl herself did not need family, her beauty speaking for itself.

"Well!" Louisa laughed suddenly.

"What is it!" Suzette experienced an uncomfortable start. Nanette LeMond was such a lovely girl, and from such fine parents, why couldn't Richard—

"Why, you're staring at that cake as if it were poison, that's what. Eat, eat, eat!" Louisa said.

"And you keep your figure following that advice yourself!" Suzette cut into the cake with her spoon. Augustin Dumanoir was not going to let Marie's attention go. He was darker than Richard, but not very much darker. His long thin nose flared at the nostrils elegantly, his lips were small. Yet his father with heavier, flatter features was the more distinguished, smiling almost haughtily as he nodded to Celestina Roget as if he were perfectly proud of his broad African mouth. Both men had tight rippling hair, shining with pomade, and she caught, through the tinkle and hum, the father's sonorous tones, "Oh, yes, indeed, everything for the table grown right on my own land."

Suzette felt weary suddenly. She wanted to get rid of this cake. Her calculations struck her as inhuman and ugly, she wanted her son to be happy, and imagining him wounded, she felt at once an unbearable pain. She had made it a fixed rule with herself never to envision her older boys, and yet the memory of them descended upon her as surely as if they had come into the room. Boys! They had married white women in Bordeaux, they might as well have gone to China, or been lost at sea. Listing ever so slightly with her thoughts, she was suddenly startled to realize that Richard had been watching her and their eyes had met. A little smile played on his lips. He seemed not to have the slightest fear. If half the world thought her son as handsome as she thought him...her thoughts stopped. "Beauty, beauty everywhere," she whispered, "and not a drop to drink."

"Why, what on earth are you saying?" Louisa asked her.

"I don't know," she said. And staring at the door in amazement, she said. "Why, there's Dolly Rose."

"No one had expected her. That she could cast aside her mourning often enough for the "quadroon balls" everyone knew, but to come here? Yet there she stood, two white camellias in her jet-black hair, her creamy bosom swelling above a taut border of lavender watered silk.

"Good lord!" Louisa whispered.

And had not Dolly moved swiftly to fill the silence that followed, it would have been a scene. But she kissed her godmother, Celestina, immediately, embraced Gabriella, and murmured a festive greeting to the two aunts. Only for an instant did a desperate light disfigure her composure and then she saw Suzette. She put her arms out.

"Why, come here, Dolly," Suzette said. "How good you look, *ma chère*." Her voice dropped as Dolly bent to kiss her. "How good it is to see you well."

Louisa stared in horror. She rose quickly, leaving the chair for Dolly who settled beside Suzette at once. It seemed young Augustin, who knew nothing of all this, commenced his chatter with Marie again, Colette had begun to laugh, the party rippled on.

"Do you think me a monster!" Dolly's eyes blazed. Again she kissed Suzette on the cheek. "I should stay home, should I not, I should wither on the vine. That would bring her back, wouldn't it, she would breathe, she would have life again."

"Dolly," Suzette whispered taking her hand, "believe me, if anyone knows the loss of a child I know it. Time is the healer. This is God's will."

"God's will, do you believe that, Madame Suzette?" Dolly would not lower her voice. Drops of moisture glistened on her high forehead, the pupils of her eyes danced. "Or is that just our way of saying it is out of our hands?" There was wine on her breath, a ruddy color to her lips. "I don't believe in anything except myself. Yet everything is out of my hands."

"Dolly, Dolly..." Suzette patted her arm.

"Is Giselle happy?" Dolly asked now, her eyes moving across the ceiling. They settled fiercely on Suzette. "Oh, you don't know how I cried that year...when we were no longer friends."

"I cried, too, Dolly," Suzette whispered, drawing near to her, hoping that that shrill clarion voice could be stilled. "You are not well..."

"Oh, I am very well!" she said. "I am free!"

Out of the corner of her eye, Suzette could see that Celestina was glowering at Dolly from across the room.

"No more children," Dolly mused, "no more children, who would have ever guessed? And now it doesn't matter all that rot Maman used to talk. If there can't be children..."

"Dolly, there are other things to live for!"

"Yes, love," Dolly smiled. "Live for love. I suppose you've heard of my white officer, Captain Hamilton from Charleston," she laughed, and throwing back her head said it again in English mocking the southern American drawl. "Oh, yes, he's going to take care of everything, 'my dear, you leave it all to me!'"

She stopped, frozen, as if distracted by some awesome thought. Suzette gazed patiently at her tortured face, the dancing eyes, the high forehead with its moist wisps of raven hair.

"Maman would have loved him," Dolly whispered, her eyes moving blindly over the assemblage. It was as if she'd forgotten that Suzette was even there. "But I do not love him!" she whispered. "I do not love him!" she pleaded. "I do not love him at all."

"You need rest," Suzette said softly.

But Marcel had appeared. He had come up before Dolly and stood staring down at her, his small face clouded with a scowl.

"Have you seen him?" he whispered frantically. "Christophe!" he said, when she did not appear to understand.

"Of course I've seen him," she said, her voice suddenly guttural and alien. Her mouth was hard. "He's been at my house all the time."

Marcel was speechless. It was as if he had heard wrong.

"I left him there to entertain Captain Hamilton," she said now, with an immediate innocent smile. "I do hope they get on together. The Captain is due in this afternoon."

Marie had gone back the passage to the rear gallery, and not pausing to see whether or not she was followed descended the curving iron stair. Her steps were rapid. She moved under the porch in the shadows where she could not be seen, but was not at all surprised to see a pair of boots descending and then Richard's large hand on the rail.

"Did you receive my note?" he whispered. He stood a pace away from her near the rear door of the dress shop which was shut. And it took a moment for him to realize that her face was flushed, that her eyes were red. "Why, what is it, Marie!"

Marie shook her head. She wiped her eyes with her handkerchief, turning ever so slightly away. "It's all right," she breathed softly. He could hardly hear her. "It's just...it's only...Dolly Rose."

"She shouldn't have come!" Richard said.

"No, no. I don't condemn her!" Marie whispered. She was suddenly quite frustrated and then, swallowing, said in the same soft voice, "It's only all the wretched things that people say. I feel...I feel so sorry for her!"

Richard dropped his eyes. He did not feel sorry for Dolly at all now. Or if he did, he did not expect that Marie could feel sorry for her. Dolly's presence here was unforgivable. That anything of Dolly should touch Marie—it was more than he could bear.

But he was immensely relieved now to see that Marie had

turned to him and her face brightened with just a touch of a smile.

"You needn't have written that note," she said. "I wanted so to tell you, but...but..."

"Marcel was there..."

"And Maman was there..." she said.

"And then Marcel was there..." he smiled.

They both laughed.

"Why is no one *here?*" she whispered with just a touch of the mischievous.

He experienced such a lovely pleasure then that he didn't realize it was the first time he had ever heard Marie laugh. Hers was a wintry beauty, he would have known, had he ever thought to anatomize it; but she was radiant at this moment and she was looking directly into his eyes.

But then her face became morbidly serious. It had a frightening coldness about it, and he felt the same spasm of fear he'd experienced only moments before when he had seen her red-rimmed eyes.

"You needn't have written it," she said gravely.

"If I ever lose your trust, Marie..." he said to her.

"But you haven't lost it. You couldn't lose it," she said, and she said this with such seriousness that it astonished him.

"Richard," she went on, "I am torn in half."

"But why?" he asked at once.

"Because I do not know how to behave with you!" she said. "I don't know how to behave with anyone! I never have. That room upstairs, I find it an agony to be there. And every Thursday now we are to receive friends, my aunts and myself, every Thursday there are to be little fêtes. Tante Louisa says she's getting old, she wants to see young people, it would be fun for her to make dresses for me, to receive my friends. I don't want this!" she looked at him miserably. The voice was her voice which he had known all his life, low, vibrant, and pure. But never had he heard such heat in it; never had he seen such heat in her face. "The truth is, it's your company I want and yours alone, and yet I'm a fool for telling you so. I should be cold to you and coy with you, I should give you smiles begrudgingly, look away when our eyes meet, hide my real feelings behind a feathered fan. I detest it! I don't know how to do it. And I cannot smile at Augustin, at Fantin, at those I despise. Why should I receive them? I don't understand."

Richard could never have found a name for the emotion he felt as he heard this. When she stopped speaking, he was looking at her as someone might perceive an apparition, as if its loveliness and perfection were quite apart from him and this time and this place, as if he had been granted some extraordinary revelation and to speak would tarnish it, dissipate it, cause it to leave him as before.

"You are pure of heart, Marie," he whispered. He couldn't know that his face appeared unspeakably sad, that it had the melancholy and the wonder of much older men whose faith has been bruised at times, if not almost lost. "You are pure of heart."

"Then why am I in such pain?" she answered softly.

"Because the world doesn't understand people who are pure of heart, it's made for people who cannot trust each other, and are not trustworthy themselves."

"Did you mean what you said to me...the last time we were alone?"

"Yes."

"Then say it now."

"I love you," he whispered.

"Then why can't you kiss me again?" she whispered. "Why is it wrong?" And as she said this she turned toward him assuming that same near-indefinable attitude that had brought him close to her that day in the grove. He reached out for her; as soon as his hand touched her flesh through the cloth of her dress, a fire passed through his fingers so that that humming sound commenced in her ears. She felt his lips on her forehead but this produced no profound sensation. It was his hands, his body drawing closer against her. It was his cheek now pressed to her forehead, and the strength with which he held her, inclining her backward as he kissed her lips.

It built slowly, and somehow more strongly than it had the first time, so when they at last kissed, she felt an even more powerful sensation of weightlessness and exquisite drifting, along with a shuddering pleasure all through her form. "Marie, Marie," he was whispering to her, and then came that moment when he seemed to pass out of his gentlemanly guise, to lose control. He might have crushed her, he was so strong, and all at once, that shuddering pleasure consumed her. She could not affect the pulsing of her body and was limp in his arms. She felt the most extraordinary excitement and was powerless to stop its radiating from the

(251)

center of her all through her limbs. It seemed she would die, shocked, delirious, and then violently it climaxed and subsided leaving her stunned. She had been moaning aloud. He was frenzied, kissing her limp neck, returning again and again to her lips, his fingers all but bruising her waist and her arms. And then with a loud catch in his throat, he stopped. He held her close, she couldn't see his face, and his breaths came heavy, anxious, so that he trembled as he slowly let her go. "I love you, Richard," she heard herself say from some dreamy place that had nothing to do with this secret spot at all. Collapsed against him, she felt him stroke her hair, felt his heaving grow less anxious and at last they were both of them perfectly still.

When she looked up at him, there came an exquisite shock. He was against the brick wall and looking down at her, his eyes slightly glazed, his lips drawn back in a serene smile. For a moment, it did not seem to be Richard at all. He stroked her hair, and then pressed her against his chest. The expression on his face had been utterly loving as if love itself were very near to pain. She could not know that he had not experienced the full climax of passion that she had just experienced, and that he only dimly understood that she was capable of it, only dimly understood just how he had been swept up again by her fire. Only her subsiding passion had enabled him to still himself, to command his own excitement to die down. "I love you," he whispered over and over now, soft to her ear. And then, growing agitated, he drew slowly, gently away.

There was a clatter above them on the porch. Tante Colette was calling Marie's name. At once Marie tried to smooth her mussed hair.

But before she could answer, Marcel clattered down with Rudolphe behind him and the two of them, deep in some agitated conversation, swept right past through the courtyard arch and out toward the street.

With an air of resignation Marie put her hand on the railing. But as she mounted the third step she looked across to Richard in the shade near the wall. He was leaning on the wall, and his face was rent with pain. It so shocked her, that she stopped.

"Marie!" Tante Colette was angry above.

But Marie did not move. Richard came forward as if he gave no thought at all to being seen. He slipped his hands around the iron railings as if they were bars. Then he faltered. And with the same look of pain and appalling fear, he reached out for her taking her by the waist.

"But what is it?" she whispered.

"I don't know," he answered. "I don't know."

Rudolphe was grim. He pounded along the sun-drenched street in silence, occasionally coughing from the dust that swirled in the air, his chest heaving with his pace, as Marcel struggled to keep up with his long legs.

"Damn that woman," he whispered finally. "I don't have to tell you what a mess this is, do I?" Marcel knew that Rudolphe was speaking to him man to man. Rudolphe would have never taken that tone with his own son. "That harlot," he went on. "White men quarreling over her year in and year out, and now she plays this lovely act with Christophe and this Captain Hamilton, I hope that woman burns in hell."

"She said he was drunk, Monsieur," Marcel said, out of breath. "She said he'd been drunk for days."

"I heard what she said," Rudolphe stammered. He darted across a crowded street forcing a carter to slow before him, pulling Marcel by the arm. "I heard every word. She's left him in that flat for that white man to find."

The few short blocks to the Rue Dumaine took forever. But at last they were rushing back Dolly's open carriageway and up the rear stairs. The door to the flat lay open, lending it a neglected look, but it was far from neglected inside. Evidence of young Captain Hamilton's affections were everywhere, new tables, mirrors, the smell of fresh enamel, and bright new wallpaper on the walls. Rudolphe tapped at one door after another, cautiously examining each room to find it empty until he paused at Dolly's bedroom door. He knocked once. And then turned the knob.

It was a sumptuous room, with a wilderness of perfumes on the immense dresser and the gleam of new velvet over the blinds. Bottles crowded the bedside table, their dark liquid catching the bits of afternoon light that filtered through the shutters, and beyond them in the high poster with its red silk trappings lay Christophe, asleep, his face in the pillow, his slender brown body naked and uncovered on the white sheet.

"Get up," Rudolphe said to him at once, and commenced to shake his shoulder violently and then to tug on his arm. "Christophe!" he said, "Christophe, wake up."

(253)

"Go to hell," Christophe answered, and slipped heavily and shapelessly from Rudolphe's hands.

"Listen to me, Christophe, and listen now. Captain Hamilton's coming here, do you know who that is..."

"...he's in Charleston," came the slurred voice from the pillow.

"...not according to your sweet friend. He's expected here today. Now. Get up!" And jerking Christophe's arm, he brought him to a sitting position where he fell forward and stared now not at Rudolphe but at Marcel. His brown eyes widened and then appeared very calm. He was looking at Marcel just as if he had seen him for the first time, as if there were no urgency, as if he were merely watching him in some timeless and safe place. Then very slowly he smiled. When Rudolphe slapped him now he was not prepared for it and awoke as if from a dream.

"Don't do that to me!" Christophe whispered. He looked about, his eyes reddened, squinting as if he did not know where he was. The flesh of his lips were so badly cracked that it was bleeding. It hurt Marcel to see it. It hurt him to see Rudolphe slap Christophe's face.

"Listen to me, you fool," Rudolphe was furious now. "You've got to get out of here. That Captain Hamilton is keeping Dolly! Do you understand. He is keeping Dolly!"

"And he wouldn't like to find a nigger in her bed," Christophe sneered. He was about to lie down again.

"If he finds one," Rudolphe said, leaning over him now with a grim, sardonic smile, "that nigger is just very likely going to be dead."

"Come on, Chris," Marcel said suddenly. He thrust Christophe's limp arm through the sleeve of his shirt. "Get up, Chris," he said. "If you don't that man will find us all here, don't do this to us, Chris, come on."

The mere thought of some ugly confrontation with a white man sickened Marcel. It was not the violence he feared, that was theoretical to him, it was the humiliation that his mind found quite real. Christophe rose, shakily, letting Marcel button his shirt. He commenced to dress himself now, shoving them belligerently away.

They gathered his watch, his tie, and his keys and put them into his pockets; and starting unsteadily for the door, their arms around him, they stopped at the shrill crying of a bell.

"Damn," Rudolphe murmured. Christophe attempted to

straighten himself but his legs would not support him and he crashed heavily into the wall. Again there came the shrill sound of the bell.

Then with some preternatural effort, Rudolphe lifted him out of the bedroom and toward the rear door of the flat. They could hear the grinding of a key in the lock, a distinct metallic sound that echoed through the empty passage from the front of the house. But they had reached the back gallery then, and within seconds were halfway down the stairs.

Marcel was trembling when they reached the carriageway, but he was not trembling with fear, he was trembling with some other awful and degrading emotion that he'd never known in his life. He had never really run from anything before, and in all his follies had never been accused of cowardice in the face of any challenge, discipline, or trial. Leaning against the wall, waiting as Rudolphe said to wait, with Christophe slumped against his shoulder, he felt a curious loathing, not for Dolly, not for Christophe, and not for this Captain Hamilton, but strangely, for himself.

"Let's go now," Rudolphe said. And together, arms locked around Christophe, they went out to the right, away from the house, walking fast until Rudolphe could signal a hack.

VII

THAT EVENING was the longest of Marcel's life. He did not dare take Christophe into his own room where the Englishman had died, but Rudolphe insisted that he do this, and laid Christophe right down on the same bed. Of course it had been thoroughly cleaned, and the room was immaculately straight. It resembled more a room in the Lermontant house than Christophe's cluttered study now, but Christophe did not seem to notice any of this, or to care. When he tried to get hold of his bottle of whiskey, Rudolphe stopped him and sent Marcel for a keg of beer.

When he returned, Christophe was propped against the headboard of his narrow bed beside the desk and he was staring glaze-eyed and still at Rudolphe who strode back and forth, back and forth, across the room. "Give him the beer," Rudolphe said. Juliet, terrified of her son, hovered with a tear-streaked face just outside the door. She had all the look of madness and neglect of the years before Christophe came home.

"Now you listen to me," Rudolphe boomed, "and you," he said, pointing to Marcel, "I want you to hear this too. Now," he turned to Christophe, "you know it's not going to do you any good getting drunk like this. Sooner or later you've got to sober up and face it, your English friend is dead."

Marcel drew in his breath. But Christophe remained motionless, his eyes like pieces of glass.

"Now your mother needs you," Rudolphe went on. "She's out of her mind. So if you blunder out that front door again, if you wander back to Madame Dolly Rose and her hotheaded young 'protector' and get yourself killed, well, then, you've killed your mother too. Not to mention this boy here who thinks you hang the moon, and two dozen other boys like him whom you've abandoned for this little escapade as if there weren't a school downstairs and as if you weren't the schoolmaster whom they all adore! Now, just keep this up! Just see how many people you can drag down with you, we'll keep count."

"Please, Monsieur," Marcel said. He couldn't bear this, and the gradual alteration of Christophe's expression, as Rudolphe went on.

"Did you bury Michael?" Christophe whispered. He raised his eyebrows ever so slightly, but otherwise he did not move.

"Of course we buried him, but with no help from you. And I'll tell you something else, Monsieur, you get yourself in another fix with Dolly Rose and you're on your own." He stopped. His temper was getting the best of him, and again he strode back and forth across the room. Rudolphe was a massive man, not as tall as Richard, but strong of build and larger than anyone else there. He was ominous in this temper; his voice, though deep, had absolutely no African timbre to it, but a clear almost sharp Caucasian tone. Now he drew himself up, as if he found it difficult to say what he must.

"I have never been in such a position," he declared, "as I was in . . . with you . . . this afternoon! I have never never . . . cowered before any white man in my life! And never have I had to! And never, never will I endure that again!" He turned, unable to go on. Marcel could not look at him. He could not look at Christophe. Much as his heart was rent and much as he was afraid, he knew these sentiments were his own. But he was a boy, Rudolphe was a man. Rudolphe was a man of substance and one of the strongest men that Marcel knew.

Christophe's lips, whitened and cracked, barely parted and softly, very soflty, he chanted. "DOLLY Dolly, DOLLY Dolly, DOLLY DOLLY ROOOOSE." His voice trailed off. Rudolphe staring through the open door, his back to Christophe, had not moved. Then he sighed.

"Come lock the doors after me, Marcel, and don't let anyone in."

Christophe was sick. For hours he lay in fitful sleep awakening only to give up the bile in his stomach and to drink the heavy draughts of beer. But he did not ask for whiskey, he did not move to try to find it, and Marcel, sitting patiently beside the grate, watched the windows darken around them as night came on. The twilight terrified him, it seemed an immense resonance with the darkness in his soul. He put his face in his hands.

From time to time Juliet appeared at the door, and he would gesture to her that all was well. But all was far from well, and he was afraid. He lit the lamp by the bed finally, and drew himself a glass of the beer. It was still cool, and tasted good to him, and he felt he was going to cry. He had just settled in the chair again beyond the circle of the lamp's light when he realized that Christophe was sitting up, against the carved headboard of the bed, and that he was staring at him with those same unnatural glazed eyes.

Marcel began to talk. He could never have remembered how he began. He simply tried to tell Christophe how much he needed him, how much all the boys needed him, and how Juliet was again going out of her mind. She had roamed the city night and day while he was gone. She'd boarded the ships convinced that he had booked passage to leave her forever, she had worn out the leather of her shoes, and her feet bled. "She loves you, she loves..." Marcel said, his voice breaking and he realized that he wanted to say "I love you" but felt he could not.

"My life here is over if you don't come back, I mean come back to us, to the boys. I tell you I'll run away. I won't wait for my chance to go to Paris, I'll run away. Remember what you planned when you were in Paris when you were a boy, that's what I'll do now." He ran on through long descriptions of how he could become a cabin boy or a common seaman just to escape "this place," how he would be abused on the ships that took him, beaten probably, maybe he would starve. No doubt he would fall from the mast, and there would be rats in the hold, and they would all get scurvy, but he didn't care. Sometime during all of this, he drew another glass of beer for Christophe, but Christophe sitting propped against his pillow did not move. His beard was thick and rough, darkening his face, and the eyes glittered in the gloomy light of the lamp.

It seemed the Cathedral bell clanged the hour over and over again, and still Christophe sat there, and after long pauses, Marcel would resume again, running through the old refrains to a slightly different tune.

Finally in a very soft voice, Christophe asked;

"Where did they bury him?"

And Marcel explained. It was the Protestant Cemetery uptown because from all his papers they had discerned he was Episcopalian and he had left some money for Christophe, too, in a packet marked "Property of Christophe Mercier, return to him in the event of my death." It was a clever ruse, the lawyer had remarked, as the man had a good income but no capital which he might will on his own. Marcel could read no response to this in Christophe's face. And only when the eyes closed again, did Marcel allow himself to drift into sleep.

When he woke the first impression he received was that of the sun flowing in through the open windows. "He's escaped!" he thought, and jumped to his feet. But then he saw Christophe, freshly dressed, smooth-shaven, sitting with his legs crossed on the length of the bed. A pot of fresh coffee steamed on the desk beside him. And he drank from a heavy mug, a cheroot in his other hand which he lifted now and then to his lips. He appeared perfectly calm.

"Go on home now, *mon ami*," he said.

"No!" Marcel protested. Christophe's eyes were bloodshot, the lip was still bleeding slightly where it had cracked.

"I'm all right," his voice was, as before, very soft. "And by the way, *mon ami*, you'd be quite the sensation on the Paris stage, you could move the most jaded audience to tears with those speeches of yours, all that about the roaches crawling over you in the hold of the ship."

He turned then to fix a cup of the coffee for Marcel. But his hands were shaking so badly that he couldn't quite manage to pour the warm milk, and Marcel took it over at once. Christophe's eyes had an unusual fire in them. He seemed elated as he watched Marcel, and then he reached out and clasped Marcel's arm tight. Marcel was looking down at him, and Christophe still holding him, bowed his head. And then Marcel yielded to an overwhelming impulse and put his arm around Christophe's shoulder in a quick but firm embrace.

When he drew back, Christophe began to speak. He was exhilarated and his words came too rapidly, with too much feeling as Marcel settled into his chair.

"A long time ago in Greece," Christophe said, "I saw a funeral for a peasant in the hills. This was near Sounion, the very tip of Greece. It was where we'd come to see the temple of Neptune where the poet Byron had carved his name. We were living almost in the shadow of the temple in a peasant hut. And I saw this funeral. With the women dressed all in black and crying wildly, wildly, as they tore their hair.

"It had a ritual sound, that crying. But something of blind anguish in it too. They wanted their cries to reach heaven, they wailed in outrage, they gave full vent to their grief. Well..." he stopped as though considering, and carefully lifted his coffee to his lips. A bit of it spilt but he did not seem to notice this. His hand shook even more violently as he set it down.

"Well, I had to mourn that way for Michael," he said. "I had to cry out, I had to let out the pain. Well, it's done. I don't even know what day this is. I don't know how long I was with Dolly, but it's over now, it's done."

Marcel was relieved but wary. He didn't understand that this exhilaration in Christophe came from so many days of drunkenness that Christophe was in an unnatural state in which all things leapt out at him, beautiful or tragic, and seemed somehow sublime. But he could see some fear in Christophe's eyes, and he sensed that Christophe's pain had only just begun.

"How will I ever repay you, *mon ami?*" Christophe asked. "Pray the world never gives me the chance."

"Just come back to us," Marcel said. "Just be all right again. That's more than enough."

He felt the embarrassing urge to cry again. But Christophe was on his feet now and taking the empty coffee cup from him said, "You've got to get on home. Your mother... you must go on."

"But Christophe, you won't go out, will you? I mean you'll stay here... for a few days until this man... this Captain Hamilton..."

Christophe nodded with a touch of resentful resignation.

"Don't worry about that," he said, his voice a little raw. "The illustrious Captain Hamilton has taught me a couple of lessons. One, that I don't invest enough in whiskey...his is incomparably better. And secondly, that I don't really wish to die."

Marcel rose. He looked Christophe straight in the eyes. "It was not your fault that Englishman died," he said.

"I know that," Christophe surprised him. "Believe me, that's quite far from my mind. I have a heavier burden to bear: and it is simply that, regardless of who or what is to blame, Michael is really dead."

Marcel shuddered. Christophe clasped his arm and led him to the stairs. And Marcel was already deep into some thought of what he was going to say to Cecile, when opening the front door, he found himself face to face with a tall white man in the street.

His body underwent a powerful shock. For an instant he was aware of only two sensations: fear that this was Captain Hamilton and the very unpleasant feeling that he had, somewhere, sometime or other, seen this white man before. But this white man was in no rage. He was standing quite still and composed as though he had been about to ring the bell. He had black hair and was remarkably fair-skinned with deepset and disturbing black eyes. Marcel felt positively weakened, almost unable to speak.

"It's all right," Christophe's voice came from the stairway along with the dull thud of his steps on the carpet. "Come in, Vincent," he said.

The white man stepped into the hall.

Marcel didn't trust this situation. Christophe was unsteady, his bloodshot eyes were all but maniacal in the harsh sunlight, and that he was volatile and could be rash seemed more than likely. He invited the man to step into the back parlor behind the school.

The white man said nothing for the moment, and when he did speak, his tone was decorous, his words dramatic for their pace.

"I cannot stay, Christophe," he said.

Christophe's face evinced no surprise at this and no change of the veiled expression.

"I wish to speak with you about a Captain Hamilton, are you familiar with the Captain Hamilton to whom I refer?"

He waited, but Christophe did not answer. Christophe's face had become fixed and somewhat cold. He folded his arms across his chest and adopted an attitude of chilled patience, offering nothing to what the man was obviously struggling to convey.

The man appeared to take a deep breath. He was finely dressed in a green frock coat and cream-colored trousers and he carried a silver walking stick which he touched lightly now to the parquet floor. If he was conscious of Marcel behind him, he was equally conscious that Christophe had not told Marcel to go.

"Captain Hamilton is not a man with good sense," he remarked now in the same measured manner. "But then Dolly Rose is a woman quite given to causing a man to lose his good sense."

These last words were strongly emphasized, however, there was not the slightest change in Christophe's face.

"Captain Hamilton has been informed," the man went on, "by a number of his more pleasure-loving companions that Dolly Rose has played him for the fool. Your name was mentioned in this affair, and Captain Hamilton and I have discussed it at length."

There was a pause.

"I have explained to Captain Hamilton," the slow steady voice continued, "that you and I are acquainted, that certainly his quarrel must be entirely with Dolly Rose. I have explained to Captain Hamilton that he will come to understand this more clearly when he has been longer in these parts. I have explained that a man..." he hesitated, "a man of color cannot defend himself upon the field of honor, that, in fact, a man of color cannot defend himself against a white man at all. I have explained that in some circles it is judged an act of cowardice to quarrel with a man who cannot defend himself. That is, if allowances can be made at all."

Christophe's eyebrows rose. "And he believed that, Vincent?"

"He accepted it," answered the white man. "As I said, he hasn't been long in these parts." But then, dropping his voice, he added gravely, "However, you have."

And turning, he said under his breath and without conviction, "Don't make the same mistake again."

Christophe's eyes narrowed, his mouth tensed. He glared at the back of the man's head and then suddenly he spoke,

"Do you want a receipt from me, Vincent?"

The white man, reaching for the doorknob, stopped. Marcel saw the shock in his face, saw the sudden rise in his color as he looked back. He glared at Christophe.

"What did you say?" he whispered.

"I asked if you wanted a receipt. After all, you're paying me off, are you not?"

The man was stunned. His face flushed, and he stared at Christophe in disbelief.

"For all those suppers in Paris," Christophe's voice came low, inflectionless, "all those long walks by the river, those conversations at sea? What did you think I would do, Vincent, come to call on you at your plantation, set myself down at your table, ask your sisters to dance? What was it you said to me that night at Dolly's, ah, yes, 'I wish you well.' You should have known better, Vincent. I was born here the same as you were. You don't have to pay me off!"

The man was trembling. His eyes were moist and large with anger. "You take advantage of me, Christophe!" he declared, the voice vibrant with a suppressed rage. "If you were born here the same as I, you know then you take advantage of me! Because you have insulted me!" His lip quivered. "You have insulted me under your roof. And you know that I can't demand satisfaction for it, and that if I could, I would!" He spit these last words. And turning, wrenched the door back, letting it crack into the plaster of the wall.

Christophe's face was contorted, and he too was trembling as he squinted into the sunlight. "You go to hell!" he said between clenched teeth. "You and your fucking Captain Hamilton, you go to hell!"

The man froze. He turned, more outraged than angry, wildly frustrated and amazed. But something happened in his face. The struggle there gave way to some desperate consternation. "Why in the name of God did you come back here!" he said. His eyes widened as if he must somehow understand. "Why did you ever come back!"

"Because this is *my home,* you bastard!" Christophe's eyes were blinded by tears. "This is *my home,* the same as it is yours!"

The man was speechless and somehow defeated. He stared for a moment more. They stood staring at one another, Christophe's face working violently with his inner torment. And then the white man turned abruptly and withdrew, his crisp steps quickly dying away.

By the end of the week, Dolly Rose had broken with Captain Hamilton, pitching out of the windows of her flat in the

(262)

Rue Dumaine a good deal of the furniture he'd bought for her before the shopkeepers could come to take it away. Celestina Roget had spoken harsh words to Dolly at Marie's birthday fête and would no longer receive Dolly in her home. No one would receive Dolly.

But two quadroon girls, newly from the country, were invited to share her flat and soon men were entertained there in the evenings, and Dolly commenced to refurnish the house on her own.

PART FIVE

I

THE AUTUMN CAME ON, chilly as always at first, with falling leaves. But then one morning ice appeared on the surfaces of the open ditches while the tender fronds of the banana trees were scarred brown with frost.

It was the kind of winter that no one really talks about who visits New Orleans, as if the steaming heat of summer obliterates all memory and all anticipation of it from the mind. But it was bleak and damp as always and only a little more cold. Yellow fever had gone with the first brisk winds, never having reached the point of epidemic, and the city had about it now the air of new cleanliness, and those who had moved sluggishly through the shimmering August streets darted about with frozen hands in fists in their pockets and women rushing into the warmth of crowded shops were radiant with rosy cheeks.

Even the Yanquis suffered, saying this cold penetrated, it was worse than New England, and huddling about their small coal grates, looked with despair at the tendrils of damp working their way beneath the flowered paper on the walls. The breath of horses steamed in the streets, and the rain seemed to freeze in the air.

Yet everywhere still were the full green-leafed oaks, often trailing with ivy, while in the corners of courtyards roses clung shuddering to the vine. And there were the lush sheltered ferns. Honeysuckle still struggled in the dense grove beneath Marcel's window. And the sky was often brilliantly blue with clean white clouds blowing fast from the river, letting through the weak sun to warm the spirit if not the frosty air.

Marcel loved these days, and buying himself a gentleman's great-coat, walked for hours after school along the shining wet banquettes excited by the spectacle of gaslight and plate glass windows, the smell of chimneys and the bustle of commerce in the early dark. At home coal burned in all the small grates, and approaching with his books under his arm, he saw in the windows the inviting glimmer of blue flames. He drank too much cocoa, slept soundly after hours of study, and only now and then with a start would think of that inevitable meeting with Monsieur Philippe.

It seemed it hung over him as it did over Cecile, and then again it did not. Monsieur Philippe had always come at times of his own choosing and six months might pass before he was seen again. But the harvest was over at *Bontemps,* thousands of hogheads of sugar had already come down the river to crowd the levee, and soon all the grinding and refining would be done. Cecile's drumming fingers reminded everyone that it might be anytime now, and all the cottage around her seemed to wait, mirrors reflecting empty mirrors, silence taut as the string of a violin.

Christophe's class, meanwhile, had swelled to twenty-five students against his better judgment, and the reading room in back was always full. He had not returned to teaching for two weeks after the Englishman was buried, but when he again appeared at the head of the classroom it was with a new fervor, and just a little impatience which his students appeared to understand. He shook Marcel once, violently, for daydreaming and Marcel could not meet his glance for two days.

He was still suffering, however, everyone knew it. And made no remark on it when they chanced to see him sometimes after hours weaving alone through the streets, drunk.

Meanwhile he had called on the ferocious Madame Elsie and soothed her burnt pride with a thousand thanks for Anna Bella's kindness in nursing his English friend. And having heard of Anna Bella's passion for reading offered her the newest novel of the famed Mr. Charles Dickens, begging her gently to accept. Madame Elsie pondered the propriety of this but clearly confused by his exquisite manners and remarkable confidence, murmured finally, *"Eh bien,* she may read it." The whole affair was the fault of that miserable Marcel Ste. Marie, she was to tell her maid, Zurlina, afterward, never was that boy to be allowed in this house. How was she to know "a gentleman" was lodged with the schoolteacher at the end of the block? And as for Christophe, well at least these men of color who had been to Paris conducted themselves as if they were men.

At the same time Rudolphe Lermontant brought old newspapers for Christophe's reading room, stopping now and then to read there himself with the older boys, and Augustin Dumanoir's father visited whenever he was in town, perusing the Paris journals as he smoked his pipe. Christophe had two published poems in a recently received issue, full of obscure imagery and veiled references to demons which he absolutely refused to explain. No one understood a word of it, but it was greatly admired. Other men began to drop in, fathers of the students, friends. So that it was soon a regular sight to see them moving quietly back the hallway past the classroom doors, or later ranged about the round table or in the leather wing chairs beside the little fire.

There were dinners in the upstairs dining room, now quite magnificently restored, even to the portrait of the Old Haitian, Christophe's grandfather, who scowled from his refurbished frame. Augustin Dumanoir's father and the other country planters were frequent guests, while Marcel, always included, listened to their endless drawling conversation with a combination of fascination and gloom. They would have had Christophe lodged on their paradisal arpents, privately educating their sons. He might visit anytime that he liked, stay for a month or a year. "I cannot see myself away from New Orleans," he would answer politely. And beneath the Old Haitian's furious gaze, they would speak of the problems of the weather, the sale and the care of slaves. Christophe showed no taste for this subject, and sometimes gave Marcel a bitterly amused glance.

Juliet served on such occasions, with Bubbles to assist her, but never sat at the table herself. And Bubbles had become a regular part of the household for which Christophe paid him a dollar a week, and bought all the slave's clothes.

Marcel was fifteen on the fourth of October, and Christophe, invited to the birthday celebration, was received in the cottage for the first time. Aglow with wine he composed a poem on the spot for Tante Louisa, and astonished everyone by addressing a great many of his comments to Marie, who was, as always, rather stonily quiet.

A lavish amount of money had been deposited with Monsieur Jacquemine, the notary, so that Marcel, for this occasion, might buy himself a horse. Marcel had never ridden a horse. Marcel actually crossed the street to avoid them when he could. They were monsters to Marcel. He was terrified they might step on his foot or even bite him. He laughed at the whole idea, aloud.

But what if he were to take that same money, he mused, and purchase with it not some chomping treacherous beast but the magic box!

For the "magic box" invented by Monsieur Daguerre in Paris, the "magic box" which had taken the little black and white miniature of Christophe was all the rage. The French government had paid Monsieur Daguerre for his secrets and was now making them known to all the world. Christophe had ordered copies of Daguerre's magnificently illustrated treatise and set them out for his students to read, while Jules Lion, a mulatto from France had been producing Daguerreotypes right here in New Orleans for some time. And *The New York Times* and the *New Orleans Daily Picayune* both indicated one could order the new Daguerre camera along with all the necessary equipment and chemicals for the making of pictures on one's own. Ah, an end to the world of crude sketches and men that looked like ducks, and pencil portraits so disappointing that Marcel burnt them in the secrecy of his own room.

How it tempted, dazzled, and there was the money in the notary's hands. But what of the other costs, plates, frames, bottles of chemicals whose stench would inevitably waft from the *garçonnière* to the cottage, and the stove that had to be kept going all night, what if the *garçonnière* should burn down? No, this was hardly the time for Marcel to ask such allowances, and when would there be time for him to go mad with the new camera when his studies kept him up late into the night? Reluctantly, he let the matter drop, let the excitement subside in his veins.

"But don't you think it's a good sign?" he said afterward to Cecile. "I mean, Monsieur Philippe can't be too angry, then, after all."

She was not so sure.

The clock ticked on the mantel. The rain beat on the panes.

On the Feast of All Saints when the Creoles crowded the

cemeteries, bustling among the high peristyled tombs with their bouquets of flowers, tête-à-tête to speak of this departed uncle, that poor dear dead *cousine,* Cecile went alone to St. Louis, late, to tend with Zazu the graves of two infants who had died long years ago before Marcel was born.

Finding the cottage dark and cold in her absence, he lit the fire, and set a warm lamp in the window, sitting back to listen to the rain. Then came her tread on the path, and entering the parlor alone she covered her face with her hands.

Marcel by the shadows of the grate laid the poker by and took her in his arms.

He was the man again in her life as he had been before— never the lover, of course—but the man.

It was obvious to all that he had regained some old sense of proportion, the clouds were gone from his face, and added to that easy courtesy which had so beguiled them when he was a child was a new maturity, a quiet strength. He was not the wanderer and the truant any longer, and presiding at the head of the table each night he kept the conversation quick, sometimes delighting his aunts with teasing witticisms, giving them interesting bits of the daily news. Of course they themselves never read the papers, they did not consider it very nice for a lady to read the papers, so he had for them all that distinct aura of a man who knew the world.

It was surprising to Marcel, then, that when they began to talk of the opera season, of Marie's presentation there, they did not expect him to go.

He had not forgotten that dazzling experience of the season before, and when they began to laugh at him, he felt a sudden sharp pain.

"You're just a baby," said Tante Louisa playfully, "what do you know about the opera? Why, young men go to sleep in the opera, women have to pinch their husbands to keep them awake."

"But no, I want to go..." he insisted.

"This is foolishness, really," Cecile interjected. They had finished supper and she gestured for Lisette to take the plates. "Marcel loves music, what does Marie know about music?"

Tante Colette laughed lightly, "Cecile, she's to be seen, *chère,*" she explained. *"Mon Dieu,* you know perfectly well she's to be seen!"

"She's too young for all that," Cecile said flatly. "Marcel

if you wish to go, I am sure that it can be arranged. Monsieur Rudolphe can arrange it..."

"Cecile," Louisa said gently, "we were talking about Marie. She'll have to have a dress made and..."

"Oh, talk, talk, talk about Marie. You're turning her head with all your ribbons and taffetas and pearls. I never heard such foolishness in my life." And then, bending forward, her eyes narrow, she demanded of Marie:

"Do you *want* to attend this opera! Is this what you want, all this nonsense? Well?"

Marie's face tensed. Then the color rose in her cheeks as she looked at her mother. Marcel could see that she was unable to speak, yet she did not look away as she did so often. And as she at last moved her lips to form some words, Louisa spoke.

"Don't leave it up to her, Cecile, why it's all arranged." And then lowering her voice to project an utter seriousness, she confided, "Cecile, the best families wouldn't consider not presenting their girls. You should have seen Giselle Lermontant the year she was fourteen, and Gabriella Roget last year."

"You don't have to talk to me as if I were a fool," Cecile said coldly. "We do not do everything that other people do. It's time and money wasted, if you ask me."

"Well, it seems to me that time and money are two commodities which you have," Louisa answered.

Colette who had been watching all this as closely as Marcel was watching it, leaned over to Marie and asked her to look in the bedroom for a dress that had to be mended. "Go on," she whispered, "I want to talk to your mother."

"You make too much fuss over that girl," Cecile was saying as Marie quietly left, "you turn her head."

"Maman," Marcel said gently. "I doubt that anyone could turn Marie's head."

"You keep an eye on your friends, Monsieur," Cecile said sharply. "Imagine that Augustin Dumanoir coming here, asking if he might call! And Suzette Lermontant asking if Richard might walk with Marie to church..."

"They are all asking, and I told them at the birthday party that after the opera..." Louisa said.

"You had no right to tell them!" Cecile said. Her voice had become shrill. A silence fell over the little group. At some point this had passed from the usual suppertime argument to something unpleasant. Colette's face was darkly angry as she studied Cecile. Louisa, however, in a patient manner, went on.

"I had to tell them something, *chère,* because you were not there!" she said. "She is the belle of this season, *chère,* don't you realize that? And Richard and all those boys..."

"Of all the foolishness, that boy doesn't come to this house to see her, he comes to see Marcel, he's Marcel's closest friend, why they've been friends for years, he doesn't pay any mind to her, he's seen her since she was that high."

"Maman," Marcel said, "perhaps Marie is old enough, perhaps she would like..."

"Marie, Marie, Marie!" Cecile wrung her hands. "I should think you'd be sick of hearing it, Monsieur, so much talk of your sister as if she were a queen! I detest all this talk at supper."

"Seems to me you detest it anytime," Colette said in a low voice. "Seems to me you never want to talk about that girl, whether it's her birthday or the opera, or First Communion ... seems to me..."

Cecile's face was changing. "You think you can arrange these matters without my consent, do you?" she said, her voice savage, and low.

"Somebody has to arrange them," said Colette.

"You think you can coif and drape that girl as if she were a princess, parading her back and forth for your own vanity, that's what it is, your own vanity, you think you can treat her like royalty, with her brother in the shadow! Well, I tell you I won't have it, I won't listen to this anymore, I won't see her preened and strutting like a peacock, her brother goes with her to that opera, he has a seat in the front row of that box, or by God your little marionette doesn't go."

Both the aunts were silent.

Colette was the first to rise, gathering her shawl up quickly, and putting on her gloves. Louisa murmured some brief words about the time, and the likelihood of rain, they ought to be going.

"Maman, I didn't mean for there to be a quarrel," Marcel whispered. "I can go to the opera with Richard, perhaps...I'll see."

"You can go with us, baby," Louisa said, "Of course, you can, why we've arranged for an entire box, you can sit with us." She slipped her cape over her shoulders adjusting the hood. Colette had paused at the door. She was looking back at Cecile with that same dark expression that had marked

(270)

her face throughout the conversation when she had been quiet.

"You're jealous of your daughter," she said suddenly. All heads turned to her. Marcel was stunned.

"You're jealous of her," Colette said again, "you've been jealous of her since the day she was born."

Cecile rose, upsetting the coffee cups. "You dare say this to me, in my own house!"

"You're unnatural," Colette said, and turning went out the door.

Cecile, in a paroxysm of rage turned her back as Louisa followed, and Marcel took his mother gently in his arms.

"Maman," he said, "sit down, this is just an argument, sit down."

She was trembling, and struggling to get out her handkerchief pressed it to her nose. As she settled again in the chair, she reached for his lapels and pulled him down opposite her.

"I'm going to make things right with Monsieur Philippe," she said in a low, choking voice, "I'll explain to him I was distraught when I wrote the note, that I missed him. He'll understand. There's so much that passes between that man and myself, you don't know," she forced a strange glittering smile, her hand stroking his lapel. "No one knows, only the woman knows who is alone with the man. It will be all right." Her voice became rapid, a little feverish, and with both hands now she held the lapels of his coat. "You know, once Monsieur Philippe told me that he'd write letters for you, letters to gentlemen in Paris that he knew, why letters of introduction so you could be received. You know when I saw you in the crib, when they first brought you to me, I made a vow, I told Monsieur Philippe that vow, he promised me, I swear to you, no one is going to break that promise..."

"Maman," he took her hands and clasping them tightly laid them on the table. "You mustn't worry," he said. "I'm not in Marie's shadow."

She let out a sharp sigh, and running her hand up through the tight hair over her temple seemed to be scratching at a deep pain.

"Maman, I never even think of her, I'm ashamed to say it," he went on. "Why, I neglect her. We all neglect her. Why, I've never even thought of boys wanting to call on Marie, until Richard...Why, it's only Tante Louisa and Tante Colette who make a fuss over her, and even then it's not so much, not really. Why, when I think of Ma'ame Celestina with that lovely idiot, Gabriella," he uttered a low laugh. "And Dolly Rose, the way her mother used to parade her, never the same dress twice..."

Cecile drew him close, her hand clasped to the back of his neck. She smoothed his cheek, his hair. "It's vanity, all of it," she said. "They've never had children, either of them, and now they want to pretend she's their daughter, that gives them pleasure to show her off in that box..." She kissed him.

"Well, why not, Maman, is it such a bad thing? I feel sorry for Marie, sometimes. I have the strangest feeling that none of this makes Marie happy, I have an awful feeling at times, that Marie has never been happy at all."

This had stopped her. She was looking into his eyes as if straining to find something there, and then with a little shake of her head, she drew back. But then she took his hands in hers and held them together. That strange glittering smile came back to her, her mouth twisting down at the ends and when she spoke, her voice was low and acidic and very unlike her.

"Don't you understand that your sister is beautiful!" she whispered. Her lips went back into a grimace, and her face appeared malignant, losing all semblance to that of the woman he knew. "Your sister turns every head when she passes, can't you see that?" she hissed. "Your sister is the kind of woman who drives men mad." She was frightening him. There was venom in her eyes and in her voice. "Your sister has always . . . and everywhere . . . and at all times . . . passed for white!"

He was conscious of lowering his eyes, and of a peculiar blurring of his vision, her words reverberating in his ears, as if he had been daydreaming and had only heard her when the words at last penetrated his dreams. Yet he had not been daydreaming at all. "Well," he murmured softly. He was looking at his hand. Her nails were cutting into his hand but she didn't know it, and he was feeling a slight sharp pain. "That's the way it turned out, Maman," he said. He meant to shrug his shoulders. "It just turned out that way."

"Feel sorry for her, do you?" she whispered, lips drawn back from her teeth, her eyes monstrously large. "Your sister will have anything in this world that she wants."

Lisette stood in the kitchen, one hand on the flat iron which she had just lifted from the fire. She ran it along the

(272)

rumpled width of a white sheet. The warm air engulfed him as he pushed the door wide. "Don't let the cold in!" Lisette scowled at him, "now fix that back, Michie, the way it was."

"Is Marie here?" he asked.

Lisette studied him for a moment so that he almost became impatient, and then he saw Marie, in the small cell off the kitchen where Zazu and Lisette slept. Marie was sitting on Lisette's narrow bed. Candles spluttered beyond her, throwing ghastly light over the wall where Lisette pinned her holy pictures, and a small cheaply painted statue of the Virgin stood on a stand of two worn books.

Marie wore a winter dress of blue wool, the neck high and adorned only by a small cameo. There were no rings or bracelets on her long white hands. She had taken down her hair and it flowed over her shoulders, becoming part of the shadows around her, so that the face with its slight blush to the cheeks appeared almost luminous like that of a marble virgin in the church. Or rather the downcast face of the Mater Dolorosa beneath her dim veil, among lilies, weeping for the dead Christ. She turned slowly, shyly, and looked up to see her brother standing in the door. Her lips never touched by paint were the color of a deep pink rose. And as he stood there, not speaking, his brows knit, his blue eyes wide as if with wonder, she became frightened of him, and said, "What is it?" so that he shook his head.

"I won't go if you don't go!" she whispered. "I won't go."

"I'm going," he said, sitting down beside her. "We'll go together, with Tante Louisa and Tante Colette." He spoke slowly, seriously. "I'll tell you about the singers, the story of it all, so that you'll enjoy it, it's going to be something special that night, you're going to enjoy it, you're going to have a splendid time."

II

IT WAS NOT VERY LONG until the opening of the opera, and the aunts soon soothed Cecile's ruffled feelings by a series of ritual gestures, so that the cottage buzzed with talk of dresses, the perfect fabric and the perfect color, the choice of jewels. And Marie, raw and wary since the recent quarrel, found herself again and again turning to discover her brother's attentive blue eyes.

(273)

It surprised her mildly that he came often to kiss her, to sit by her in the evenings by the fire. And more than once in the weeks that followed he coaxed her up the stairs to the *garçonnière* to do her sewing in that smaller, warmer room. It was more than his old protectiveness, something quite unknown or not fully understood by her had brought them closer, and during one of these long evenings, when she sat with the rise and the fall of her needle, and he with the turning of the pages of his book, she almost, almost confided to him her love for Richard Lermontant. But it was the unspoken bond that she treasured. Words had never satisfied her, and something deeper, finer, satisfied her now. And that Marcel would be with her on that frightening opera night when she was to be displayed like a doll in a shop window gave her a new peace of mind.

But as the very day of the opera drew near, events had conspired to separate them, the opera was far from Marcel's thoughts, and all of this had to do with the slave, Bubbles, whom Christophe Mercier had hired outright in September from the disreputable Dolly Rose.

It was not clear in Marcel's mind whether Christophe had really wanted Bubbles, or any slave, in his service, as even his chance remarks on the subject smacked of abolition or disgust. But Dolly had given Bubbles such a beating one Sunday that he had come to Christophe with weals on his face and blood showing through his ragged shirt. She had locked up his tuning wrenches on the argument that he held back his earnings. And in a rage, Christophe had written her a caustic letter with some dollars enclosed for the slave's hire. No one, of course, had ever seen Christophe and Dolly exchange a civil word since the affair after the Englishman's death, and Bubbles just came to be Christophe's devoted servant after that, and devoted to Christophe he was, beyond doubt. If anyone ever heard the slave moan for anything, it was for the tuning wrenches which Dolly kept locked in her flat.

And soon such a transformation was worked in Bubbles that people who had taken no notice of the slave before came to stare at him in the streets. He had always been a striking figure, wiry and so black that his skin had glints of blue, and his small somewhat yellowish eyes under brooding ridges gave him a wise somber look unbroken by the slightest expression in his thin wide mouth. He resembled, in truth, a monkey.

But this requires some explaining.

As there was nothing comical or grotesque about him at all. He looked as monkeys really look when they are not clowning for organ grinders or doing tricks in ink cartoons.

They have wise faces, seem unusually meditative when they examine things carefully with their long-fingered black hands, and often frown under heavy brows as if in profound thought.

Bubbles had this manner, and as is the case in human beings often, this did in fact signify a depth of mind whereas in monkeys obviously, it may not.

But he was exactly that kind of young black man whose extraordinary grace and beauty was so alien to the Caucasian mode that brutal slave traders would have called him "a black ape" and uncorrupted children, not having been told yet what to think, would see him as exquisitely feline and dignified. He had skin like fine old kid gloves, a tight cap of woolly hair on his perfectly round head, and he glided like a dancer through streets and rooms with hands so limp that they appeared too heavy for his narrow wrists.

But under Christophe's wing, he had acquired a further distinction, that of Parisian coats and waistcoats, and linen shirts and new boots. And no one knew except Marcel that most of these came from the Englishman's old trunk. Those personal effects of Michael Larson-Roberts had never been claimed by his family in England. And so Bubbles, small of frame as the Englishman had been, and also tall, was seen following Juliet to market in black broadcloth and Irish linen the élan of a valet *par excellence.*

Everyone admired Christophe for this, just as they abhorred Dolly for her cruelty and for not giving up the tuning wrenches. That is, everyone admired Christophe until the Monday before the opera when Bubbles appeared seated in the back row of Christophe's classroom with notebook and pencil in his spider hands.

Then no one admired Christophe at all!

Fantin Roget was the first to drop, not even finishing the day's class, but leaving abruptly at noon. And when his mother's letter came the next day to give some vague excuse for her son's change of plans, three other letters of withdrawal accompanied it in the same mail. By Wednesday, all of the poorer students were gone, and Augustin Dumanoir, seeing

Bubbles again seated and ready with pencil in hand asked to talk privately with Christophe in the hall. "This is all nonsense," Christophe's voice was barely audible in the classroom. "What harm can he do anyone sitting in the back of the room?"

"It's going to be all right," Marcel had at once whispered to Richard. "People will get used to it, it will be all right!" But the alien expression on Richard's face gave him a shock. Dumanoir left the class at midday, and that night, Rudolphe learning of all this from other parents lit into Richard in a rage, insisting that he remain at home.

At last on Friday the day before the opera, Christophe was stunned to discover himself at eight o'clock standing before an empty room. Marcel, after a night of exhausting argument with his mother and his aunts sat grimly beside the fire in the reading room not even bothering to go to his desk. Bubbles was at the round table, face narrow and heavily carved with sorrow like that of a medieval saint. He was the first to rise, to walk silently into the classroom and take his place in the last row.

Marcel could see Christophe clearly from where he sat. He saw Christophe looking at his watch; then at the clock on the wall. And then at the small stack of hand-delivered letters on his desk. Christophe's face then became as mobile and agitated as that of a fiercely humiliated child. He slumped into his armchair and stared at the empty desks as if he could not quite believe his eyes. Finally Marcel rose and came through the double doors walking softly down the center aisle.

"Damn!" Christophe whispered. "Damned insufferable bourgeoisie!" He ran his hands back through his hair.

Marcel leaned his shoulders against the wall and with folded arms waited.

"I'll take new students!" Christophe said.

"They won't come," Marcel answered.

"And when the others see this room is filled again, they'll come back."

"They will never come back."

Christophe glared at him.

"That is," Marcel said, "unless you put Bubbles out of the class."

"But this is madness! What harm is he doing!" Christophe demanded, but before giving Marcel a chance to answer he glanced at the dark brooding figure of the young slave in the remote corner of the room and told him gently to go upstairs.

"I am his master," Christophe said as soon as the steps had died on the stairs. "If possession is nine-tenths of the law I am his master, and if I decide he may be educated that is enough to satisfy the law."

"It will satisfy the law, Christophe, but it will never satisfy the parents of the other boys."

"And why are you still here, Marcel!"

"Ah, Christophe!" Marcel said in disgust.

But the hurt in Christophe's eyes was more than he could bear.

It seemed a half hour passed that they remained there, Christophe muttering from time to time under his breath and then pacing the room.

Finally Marcel said quietly, "Christophe, do you remember the day that you showed us the rug?" This was a little Kerman rug, a treasure, which Christophe had brought down from his room. All the class had been dazzled by the medallion and the flowers, their intricacy and violent colors, and Christophe had astonished them by telling them this thing had been made for the dirt floor of a tent. "You told us the key to understanding this world was to realize it was made of a thousand varying cultures, many so alien to the others, that no one code of brotherhood or standard of art would ever be accepted by all men," Marcel said. "You remember? Well, this is our culture, Christophe, and if you ignore it, or try to go blindly against it, you'll accomplish nothing but the ruination of the school."

"Marcel, there is not one of us," Christophe burst out, "not one of us who is not descended from a slave! To my knowledge no coterie of African aristocrats ever settled willingly on these shores!"

"Chris, don't make me the spokesman for people I don't admire! If you don't send Bubbles out of the class, then there will be no class."

At that point, Christophe shot Marcel such a venomous look that Marcel backed off and rested his forehead against the frame of the front door.

"Go to Monsieur Rudolphe," Marcel said. "Tell him you'll take Bubbles out. If he sends Richard back, then others will follow. Go to Celestina. If she sends Fantin back, then the other quadroons will follow, too."

Five minutes later, walking at great speed, Christophe and Marcel had reached the Lermontant shop.

Rudolphe, who had just finished showing a series of veils and bombazine yardage to an elderly white woman, took his time as he let her out the door. The winter sun was bright through the front windows and seemed irreverent as it fell on so much folded crepe and items of mourning on display.

"What can I do for you, Christophe?" Rudolphe asked stiffly as if nothing had happened. He gestured for the teacher to take a chair and ignored Marcel as if he were not there.

"You know damned good and well why I'm here, Rudolphe, my classroom is empty! My students have withdrawn!"

"You should have known better, Christophe." Rudolphe dropped his pose at once.

"You're a leader in this community," Christophe said coldly, "if you hadn't withdrawn Richard, the exodus would not have occurred."

"Oh, no, Christophe, there are some barriers no one will cross regardless of what I should do, I assure you. But I don't want to mislead you. There are barriers I have no intention of crossing myself. You brought a slave into your class, you sat him down with my son and my son's friends..."

"Because he wanted to learn! He wanted to make something of himself..."

"Christophe, that might draw a tear in a Paris drawing room but not here."

"You mean to tell me you don't believe the boy should learn? Suppose a white man named Lermontant had taken that attitude towards a certain famous slave of his by the name of Jean Baptiste!"

"Don't twist my meaning," Rudolphe said. "I've taught my black apprentices to read and write myself at this very desk, I've trained them in accounting, business management, so that when they finally got their freedom they could make a living on their own. I've given two of my slaves their freedom in my time and each has paid me back by his own labors with the knowledge he took from this shop. Teach that boy in private and everyone will respect you for it. Give him a fine education if you like, but do not sit him down in a classroom with our boys. Don't you understand what's at stake here, don't you understand these times?"

"I understand that you're a bigot and a hypocrite!" Christophe said.

"Monsieur, you try my patience more than any man I've

ever met!" Rudolphe rose suddenly and stalked to the door. Marcel was frightened. He was on a verge of going after him, thinking that Rudolphe was storming out of his own shop in his confusion, when Rudolphe merely gestured through the glass.

"Do you see those men in the street, the men patching the banquette, there!"

"Of course I can see them, I'm not blind."

"Then you can see they're Irish immigrants, and you can see that everywhere you go, there are Irish immigrants, patching the bricks, digging the canals, waiting the tables in the big restaurants, and in the hotels. Irish or Yanqui or some other Anglo-Saxon, and do you remember who used to wait the tables and drive the hacks here when you left? Our people used to do that, *gens de couleur,* the honest laboring *gens de couleur* from whom these people in a never-ending tide have taken the jobs! They'd take my job, too, if they could. Had they the capital and the wits, they'd set up an undertaking store right beside this one and take my white customers away from me and my colored ones too. And do you know what we look like to those Yanquis, Christophe, do you know what they say about us to the foremen on the construction gangs and the bell captains in the big hotels, 'why, they're niggers, free or not, and we're white, they're no better than slaves, give those jobs to us.' We're an offense to them, Christophe, and they'd take any opportunity they could get to push us right back into the morass of poverty and misery from which a lot of us came."

"Rudolphe, what has that to do with a handful of wealthy young men who've been born with silver spoons in their mouths, we're talking about an *élite de couleur!* The *cordon bleu.*"

"No," Rudolphe shook his head. "We're talking about a caste, Christophe, that has won its precarious place in this corrupt quagmire by asserting over and over that it is composed of men who are better than and different from the slaves! We get respect in one way, Christophe, and that is by insisting ourselves on what we are. Men of property, men of breeding, men of education, and men of family. But if we drink with slaves, marry slaves, sit down in our parlors with slaves or in our dining rooms or in our classrooms, then men will treat us as if we were no better! And all that we've gained since the days when New Orleans was a fort on the river, all that, will be lost."

"It's wrong what you're saying, it's logical, practical, and wrong," Christophe averred. "That boy's part of us."

"No," Rudolphe shook his head. "He's a slave."

Christophe sighed.

"You've defeated me, Rudolphe," he said. "I expected pomposity, talk of inherent superiority, of white blood. But you're no such fool. You're a Machiavelli in a shopkeeper's guise; you do what works best."

Rudolphe raised his eyebrows thoughtfully.

Christophe rose and jerked open the door without a word.

"I have a paternal feeling for you, Christophe." Rudolphe put a hand on his shoulder. "Send that boy out of the class, teach him on your own time, and I'll let it be known you made a simple error in judgment. I'll call on the LeMonds and the LeComptes, myself."

As soon as Christophe reached the classroom, he wrote out a simple notice stating that school would be resumed with a special Saturday session the following day, and posted it on the outside door. Then he wrote a brief letter which he folded and gave to Marcel. "You do too many favors for me, but here's another," he said. "Take this to your good friend, Rudolphe Lermontant."

"All right," Marcel said. "But will you be here when I get back?"

Christophe shook his head. "I've got to call on Celestina," he said with a bitter smile. "And old Brisson, the grocer, and a few other good parents, And after that I want to spend a little time with Bubbles and explain this to him."

"He understands," Marcel said.

"No," Christophe shook his head. "He can't imagine anyone taking so much notice of him, or caring so much whether he's alive or dead, or sitting in a room or not sitting in it. And after that, I want to be alone. I'm not good company for anyone." He looked up at Marcel. "Don't worry," he said. "I've made up my mind to compromise myself and I won't waver. I've done it before. Now, go on."

Marcel had not seen such an expression on Christophe's face since the Englishman had died, and three times that evening he had knocked on the townhouse doors without result.

But the morning before the opening night of the opera, the classroom, without Bubbles, was filled as before. The first lectures were cold, brilliant, and without a flicker of passion, and only toward the afternoon did some of Christophe's usual spirit return. As the day wore on, Marcel became more and more anxious that Christophe would climax with some bitter denouncement, but at four o'clock they were dismissed without any extraordinary words. The students clustered for an hour afterward, talking warmly and affectionately of all manner of unessential things as if they wanted to assure their teacher of their devotion (now that he had given in) and Marcel could see that Christophe got through it with obvious strain.

As soon as the school was empty Christophe stalked into the back reading room, making no acknowledgment of Marcel by the fire, and got his bottle of whiskey out of the press. He set it down on the round table, shoving the papers and journals aside angrily and filled a glass.

"Don't do this, Chris," Marcel said after Christophe had drunk two glasses as if they were water.

"I'm in the privacy of my own home right now, I can preach sedition and abolition to the rafters here if I like, and I can also get drunk!"

"Tonight's the opera, Christophe. You told me once you were counting on the opera to keep you sane..."

"Only a Creole could think of the opera at a time like this," Christophe said, draining another glass. He sat back obviously calmed for the moment by some six to eight ounces of pure whiskey. "Well, I shall be at the opera!" he said. "My soul may be in hell but I shall be at the opera."

"Drunk?" Marcel asked. "Christophe, people will be watching you, they'll be looking for some gesture from you because of all this, and they'll be looking for the opportunity to make some gesture themselves..."

"Go home," Christophe said drearily. "I told you I'd be there," and without theatricality, he removed a crumpled note from his pocket, rolled it into a ball in one hand and shot it to Marcel. It read in large childish print:

> MICHIE, I AM ONLY TROUBLE TO YOU I HAVE GONE
> BACK TO M. ROSE.
>> AFFECTIONATELY, B.

Marcel studied it. Yesterday morning in this very room, he had spelt out the word, "affectionately" for Bubbles never dreaming for what. "He'll come back," he said. "He's run away before and he'll run away again. Besides, Dolly Rose has never been able to keep a male slave. Tougher blacks than Bubbles would rather clean the ditches than stay with her."

But Christophe merely sat there, drinking the whiskey and suddenly both of them were roused by a loud knock on the door. It was followed immediately by the impatient tapping of something metallic on the glass. And then the door opened with a click and through the long vista of the deserted classroom Marcel saw the figure of Dolly Rose.

She wore a dress of lilac taffeta and a loose black cape over her shoulders, head bare, and her cheeks ruddy from the cold. Christophe, too, saw her, but he did not move, slouched back in his chair behind the table, watching her through the double doors.

"Chrissssstophe!" she sang out softly, moving lightly through the wilderness of desks. She did not appear to know that she was being watched, and seemed to enjoy being alone in the vast room. With a series of little pirouettes, she moved behind the lectern and suddenly with a gesture so genuine of feeling that it was startling, brought her clasped hands up to her bowed head. As she raised her eyes, her voice rang out dramatically as if before an immense audience.

"Randolphe, Randolphe, kill me then, for if I cannot go with Antonio, I do not wish to live!" she cried. "Kill your beloved Charlotte! For death alone shall possess her if Antonio cannot possess her." And then grabbing herself about the throat she proceeded to struggle as if being strangled by her own hands. But a deep false masculine voice boomed from her at the same time, "Yes, die, Charlotte, die! Not because you want to go with Antonio! But because you are the heroine of a bad novel!" And strangling, she fell over "dead" on the lectern.

Marcel could hardly restrain his laughter.

"All right, Dolly!" Christophe said, and even on his lips there was the slight twist of a smile.

She slowly lifted her head, staring at him from the corner of her eye. Then she marched back the center aisle, eyes appraising the walls with their engravings and maps, and the great world globe in its corner, and entered the reading room as Marcel, resentfully, rose to his feet.

"Bonjour Blue Eyes," she said winking at him. Her face was radiant, the old shadows gone, the lips faintly rouged enticingly. But then she became serious and said to Christophe who had not risen, "Peace?"

"Go to hell," he said.

"You want your little bootblack, don't you?" she said. The tender flesh beneath her eyes quivered. She was lovely enough to make Marcel forget what she'd done. All the gossip about her "waning beauty" was spite. Warily, he looked down.

"Yes," Christophe sighed.

"Then take me to the opera tonight," she said.

Christophe studied her, his own eyes flinty, suspicious.

"I am accompanying my mother, but thank you, Madame, you flatter me," he said.

"Your mother. How tender!" she said with a mock dramatic tilt of her head. "Why, I thought you might have planned to take Bubbles!" she laughed. "You're so fond of him, after all."

Christophe's face darkened with anger. The swelling of a vein showed against his temple. "Get out of my house, Dolly." he said.

She approached the table and just as he reached for it, snatched the glass of whiskey and took a drink.

"Hmmmm...you must be one very rich schoolteacher," she said, running her tongue over her glistening lip. Again Marcel looked away, only to look quickly back at her. "Or did your English friend leave that?" she asked.

Her eyes glistened without a scintilla of deeper feeling. And she was so fresh, her *café au lait* skin so clear and creamy that she seemed the embodiment of seduction, something inherently dangerous and irresponsible which could never be held to account. Marcel disliked these thoughts and tried to think on *who she was*. There were soirees at her house nightly now, with white men trooping up the steps. "Take me to the opera," she said gravely.

Christophe frowned. "Madame, you're mad."

"I do as I like these days," she said quite seriously. Then uncertain, she drifted about the room, her fingers playing with the back of the wing chair. She flashed a sudden brilliant smile at Marcel. But then she was to the point again. "No one owns me anymore, Christophe, no one tells me with whom I can be seen. I am mistress of my own house. *I do as I please.*"

"Not with me," Christophe shook his head.

"Not even for Bubbles?" she asked.

Marcel turned his face toward the windows. She was a Circe. If Christophe were to appear with her, it would be the finish. The white men on the parquet might not give a damn

(283)

about it anymore, but all the colored community would see this. Dolly Rose's house might as well have had a shingle over its door.

"What do you want, Dolly," Christophe sighed. "What do you really want!"

At these words her façade appeared to crack. Marcel saw the sudden involuntary pout of her lip, the flicker in her eyes. She pulled back the chair across from Christophe, and seated at the table drew a sheet of paper out of her muff. She handed it to him. One glance over Christophe's shoulder told Marcel it was the title to the slave.

"Sold to Christophe Mercier for the sum of one dollar," she said. "One slave Bubbles, Senegalese. Hmmmm? Go on, take it."

Warily, Christophe studied the paper. Then he folded it, and slowly he removed a silver dollar from his pocket and reaching across the table put it in her open hand.

A wicked smile brightened her face.

"Christophe is a slave owner!" she sang suddenly. And jumping up, "Christophe is a slave owner!"

"I intend to set him free!" Christophe growled.

"You can't set him free, he's fourteen years old and unskilled, and been in the Parish prison seven times, they'd never grant your petition even if you had the money to post bond for him, no, my *cher* Christophe, you're his master!" She let out a husky laugh and backed out the door.

"Lord, God," Christophe sighed.

"Christophe is a slave owner, Christophe is a slave owner," she sang as she twirled through the classroom. But she stopped suddenly, only halfway to the front door.

"Don't take me to the opera, then, if you don't want to," she said coldly. And then in a small voice, marked by mock sincerity, "All your little secrets are safe with me."

"Get out of my house," Christophe flashed. His hand clutching the paper almost crumpled it. "And I want those tuning wrenches," he said contemptuously, "I want them now."

"They're under my bed," she said. Her voice was dry as if burnt by feeling. "You know what you have to do to get them? Can you figure that out? Have you read about it in books!"

"Get out of here!" He rose, all but upsetting the table.

She took a step backward, almost afraid. She was shaking

(284)

her head. She was on the verge of tears, and Christophe didn't move as if he didn't trust himself to move.

"I wish Captain Hamilton had killed you!" her voice rang out over the classroom.

"So do I!" Christophe said. "So do I!"

But she had already turned, and banging the front door behind her, she was gone.

Christophe slumped in the chair. He tilted the bottle to the glass.

"Christophe..." Marcel came forward. He put his hand around the neck of the bottle... "don't do this. Don't let her...she's nothing but a..."

"Don't you dare purport to tell me what she is!" Christophe hissed. He jerked the bottle from Marcel and rose, glowering into Marcel's eyes. "Don't you say one word about her. You and your miserable bourgeois friends, don't give me any more of your bourgeois estimations of anything, slavery, manners, morals, women! She's worth more than the lot of you, indolent planters' brats and shopkeepers all!" He stopped, his mouth open.

Marcel was so stricken that the tears came at once. He backed away from the table, his fists clenched, and trembling turned and went through the door.

"Marcel, don't go!" Christophe said. "Don't go. Please, don't go."

Marcel turned to see him standing beside the table, his face as defenseless as that of a child. His voice was simple, without pride. "I'm sorry," he said. "I don't know why I said that to you, to you above all. I didn't mean it, Marcel."

Marcel wiped his mouth with the back of his hand. He couldn't have refused Christophe anything at this moment. Yet he was bruised. "But why did you defend her, Christophe!" he asked.

"You don't know the whole story," Christophe said softly. He paused, his level brown eyes merely holding Marcel, and Marcel felt the most unexpected sense of foreboding. It was as if Christophe were trying to make him understand something here, beyond the words, and Marcel was filled with fear.

But Christophe had looked away, and when he spoke again it was as if he were speaking to himself. "I wounded Dolly," he said. "She expected something of me, something I just couldn't give." He stopped, and then in a low voice added, "I *disappointed* her."

"So you didn't love her!" Marcel blurted out. "And if you had, she would have wounded *you!*"

"You think so?" Christophe's eyes fixed on him.

"She's a damned soul!" Marcel insisted.

"So am I," Christophe answered.

"I don't believe that!" Marcel said, his voice breaking. "I don't believe that anymore than I believe we're all . . . we're all indolent planters' brats, whatever you called us! I don't believe anything you say today. You should stop talking altogether!"

There was a flicker, a flinching in Christophe's eyes. He took a slow drink of the whiskey. "You're my star pupil, Marcel," he said. "You're the one face out there in the crowded classroom that means the world."

"Then don't disappoint *me,* Chris!" Marcel said. "Not for Dolly Rose!"

Christophe winced. He sat still for a moment, and then with a soft sound more subtle than a sigh, he took the bottle of whiskey and locked it in the press. He rested his back against the press and looked calmly at Marcel.

"I'll see you tonight," he said. His voice was low, devoid of irony. "And tomorrow and tomorrow . . . and tomorrow, I'll be here."

III

IT WAS ONLY A FEW HOURS later that Marcel entered the cottage parlor, dressed for the opera, his serge cape over his shoulders, his white gloves clasped in one hand. He had no spirit for it, and could not remember his passion for the music he had heard the year before. The image of Dolly Rose twirling her skirts in the empty classroom had commenced to obsess him for reasons that weren't clear to him. And he was thinking only of his duty now to Marie. His aunts were fluttering about, assisting Lisette with all the boudoir preparations while Cecile sat collected by the fire.

But as he was sipping his brandy, and had just lit a cheroot by the coals, he raised his eyes to see, quite unexpectedly, a woman he did not know emerging from the bedroom door. And it was with a flush of embarrassment that he realized this was his sister Marie. Forgetting himself entirely he rose in one fluid unconscious gesture from the chair.

Her black hair was brought up and back from her forehead to descend in deep waves on either side of her temples before being swept to the wreath of braids behind her head. Lisette had threaded these braids exquisitely with pearls, and pearls dangled as well from the pendants in the delicate lobes of her ears. The deep ruffle of her emerald green dress plunged to reveal for the first time the full swell of her breasts. And the skin was flawless there, set off by the iridescence of the watered silk, and it was as smooth and as fair as her naked arms. Marcel drew in his breath. She was a vision standing before him, in an excess of ornament that only a goddess might have supported, and as she lifted her eyes to him he saw that these were her real jewels. He was proud beyond words. And he felt such a rush of tender love for her that he realized he was brimming with tears. He forgot Dolly, forgot Christophe, forgot all the world. She reached out for him. He drew close to her as Lisette brought her velvet cape.

"Mademoiselle," he said, "let me kiss your hand."

But it was not until they had settled in the box at the opera house and he saw the heads turn throughout the crowded tier that he began to feel a pounding excitement for her, an exultation when he looked at her, which he could not conceal. He could all but feel the eyes upon her, they seemed to give her cheeks a glow. And as she gazed for the first time on the spectacle around her, the commotion everywhere of painted fans and flashing jewels, and heads bowed beneath tiaras, she seemed to feel some genuine pleasure of her own. That old doleful aura had been dissipated. She was not that funereal angel that had always made him sad. In fact she was looking boldly across the dim gulf that divided the arms of the balcony to the Lermontant box.

At once the visits commenced. She had been the last to arrive, perhaps by some marvelous timing on the part of the aunts, and Marcel could see Celestina and Gabriella making small motions of greeting, and the Rousseau family, wife and daughters of the rich tailor, and the LeMonds with their cigar factories, and the colored planters who had come in from Iberville and St. Landry and Cane River were all settled comfortably in their chairs.

But behind him, Augustin Dumanoir had just entered to pay his respects with his father, that impressive, chocolate-colored man, his gaunt face and powerful African features rendered all the more dramatic by his silver hair. The young Augustin was the color of bronze. He wore a small ruby ring on the little finger of his right hand. And no sooner had they withdrawn than Marcel had risen to greet the LeMond brothers, and then came young men from the Cane River with a note of introduction from Tante Josette. And here was Fantin Roget, clever enough to flatter Colette and Louisa enormously before turning ecstatic and simple eyes on Marie. His face as he bent to greet her was as fair, as white as her own.

But something had distracted Marcel. It was faintly disturbing, but he had to get back to it, and as soon as he could he looked out again across the house. It was a familiar figure in a far box, and there were other figures with it, one of them pathetically small, bent. It was Anna Bella, he realized, with Madame Elsie behind her stooped over her cane. And it was the slim, square-shouldered figure of Christophe that stood above her as she looked up. The endearing tilt of the head was unmistakable; she was laughing now without bothering to lift her fan, and even at this great remove, Marcel was overcome with a sense of her, of that sweetness, that slow, mellow voice that Christophe must be hearing now. Lightly, her white-gloved hand touched the sparkle of a pendant on her breast. And her breast was the color of ivory and flowed beautifully into the low bodice of apricot silk.

But the light was sputtering, going out. He could not tell if the distant face saw him as it turned, if the eyes were meeting his as Christophe withdrew. He saw the pale slope of rounded shoulders, that long graceful neck, the full bouffant of heavy black hair. And dropping his eyes, he peered at the distant glimmer of the musicians' lights, and sighing, let the anticipation all around lull the fever in his veins. But there was pain in this. He did not feel enchantment. He could not lose himself, even as the music came at last, with a lovely surge, it was as if he could not care.

At each intermission, the admirers came. Marie was the sensation of the evening, and Marcel spent every minute clasping hands. Even Christophe came before the last act, reciting another little poem for Louisa which thrilled her so that she coquetted as Marcel hadn't seen her do in years. The poem was straight from Lord Byron, and Christophe had a mocking smile. But Louisa had never heard of Lord Byron, and doubtless forgot the words as soon as they were recited. "Go visit with Juliet!" she struck Marcel's shoulders with her fan. "Go on now," she bent to whisper. "Your teacher's mother hasn't been here in ten years. And she so loved the opera, go on. I made her new dress."

(288)

Richard had just lifted the green curtain and silently entered the box.

Marie shifted without the slightest coyness, *"Eh bien,"* she said under her breath. "I thought you had forgotten me, Richard." And Marcel could see the blood rush to Richard's face. He was radiant, teasing her in return. "Ah Marie Ste. Marie, but we've met before, haven't we?" He bent to kiss her hand without even lifting it. "Surely...or was it in my dreams?"

Marcel was on the verge of laughing. Sooner or later he had to start teasing Richard mercilessly about all this. Christophe, beside him as they moved down the carpeted corridor, said, "They are in love!"

"Then you see it, too!" Marcel said. But as Christophe lifted the curtain of his box, Marcel paused. It seemed no happiness tonight could be more than evanescent, he didn't understand himself and this sudden apprehension, this sudden compulsion. "And why not?" he whispered defiantly, "Why not?"

"What is it, Blue Eyes?" Christophe whispered.

But how with that old witch right at Anna Bella's side? And if we are not children, then what in hell are we, if I cannot call upon her between acts as it's always done, if I cannot visit with her in her box? But he did not allow these thoughts to become confused. He turned, telling Christophe softly, urgently, he would be back.

Neither Anna Bella nor Madame Elsie saw him as he entered. And, as he drew close behind Anna Bella's chair, the bell was sounded for the last act. Her head was slightly bowed, and those curling wisps that always escaped her coif lay on the fair nape of her neck. The old woman was stirring with the dry rustle of taffeta and some clicking noise from her throat.

"Aaah!" she let out that scornful sound as if for a vocal chord she had only her long hooked nose. And gently, just beneath him, Anna Bella looked up. Her breasts, so full, were actually plumped against the apricot silk and between them lay a deep well of shadow with the sparkle of the diamond, cold, against the flesh. But it was her bright face that obliterated this, the light gathered in the irises of her enormous eyes.

"Marcel," she whispered, and the lights all around went dim. The old woman was speaking rapidly, viciously, she brought her cane down with a thump.

"Stop it, Madame Elsie!" came the insistent plea, the face

the perfect shape of a sweetheart now rent with distress. She reached out for Madame Elsie's cane. The stage lights had risen far below leaving them in a dusky cloud. Then without thinking Marcel lifted his fingers to his lips, placed a kiss on them and touched her baby-soft cheek. He heard her desperate whisper, "Marcel!" as he left the box.

The passage was dark. He was all but stumbling toward Christophe quite far ahead of him, and then into the loges, Christophe directing him to sit beside his mother as he took the other chair.

The music was all around him, the wild and tragic theme of the closing act. He bowed his head. He saw nothing, and felt an immense suffocating lump in his throat. It was noise, deafening noise, this music. Painfully obliterating all else except the sensation that he was standing in the unlit hallway of the Mercier house and that Anna Bella was glaring at him from the wall, tears on her cheeks, and then came that right hand up toward his face. And what had this to do with the figure of Dolly Rose in lilac taffeta twirling through that classroom today as if she were a young girl? And what had this to do with the woman beside him, Juliet in black velvet, her gown so much a part of the dark that she was nothing but radiant flesh and otherwise naked, conceivably, an animalian posture nevertheless visible against that ornate little chair. He blinked at the distant stage, saw its colors running as if on a rain-drenched window pane. He could remember nothing of the sensation of Anna Bella's hand against his face then and all of the sensation of having held her in his arms. All he had to do now to see Anna Bella was ever so slightly turn his head.

All he had to do to see beauty all around him was ever so slightly turn his head, Gabriella and Celestina, Nanette LeMond with her russet curls, and Dolly, Dolly whom he'd glimpsed before with those country quadroons done up in their Paris gowns, and Marie whose silhouette he could still see against the glow of the stage. Beauty was all around, beauty which seemed the very nature of his people in its infinite variety, splendid mixtures, that unabashed blend of the genteel and exotic that had made his women famous for two centuries and brought the aristocratic white blood again and again into their veins.

He sucked in his breath. This was unbearable to him, and he stared at the opera glasses in his hand. Juliet's fingers had placed them there, and withdrawing stroked him lightly

(290)

as they disappeared. The music sang of foreboding, tragedy, death. A Charlotte was being overcome by a Randolphe, while an Antonio wept in the wings.

And then one image imprinted itself clearly upon his eye. It was that of a white man, against the wall of a box below where women in front of him could not see him, looking up directly, unmistakably, at the colored tier. It seemed he lifted his glasses now to probe one certain spot. That box to the far left and down the length of the balcony where a girl with snow-white shoulders sat looking serenely at the stage. And Marcel, turning his glance to her, picked his sister out of the gloom. Dream on, Marcel thought suddenly, acidly, look while you can. She's no immigrant off the boat from Saint-Domingue, no vain and vicious Dolly Rose. A gasp went up from the audience. Another Charlotte had met her inevitable violence, what had he said that night to Christophe when Christophe had only just come home? It was the death of innocence. He shook his head.

"But what is it?" Christophe whispered to him. The opera was over. All around men rose to their feet. "Bravo, Bravo." There was stomping on the hollow wooden floors.

There was a party afterwards at the aunts' flat to which all were invited, the Lermontants with Giselle and her children, the Rogets, the Dumanoirs. Fiddlers had been hired and a spinet rented, Lendamain the caterer had rolled back the carpets for dancing, brought gallons of champagne.

Marcel realized at once that it was so crowded he could easily slip away, and Christophe did not surprise him by coming on alone.

"But where is that Juliet, I made her gown," Tante Colette said to him, and he after a few polite excuses whispered to Marcel. "I can't trust her at these affairs, you know how she is. She saw Dolly on the street a week ago and tried to catch her by the hair."

Small wonder, Marcel thought. It seemed he should be loving all this, how exciting it would have been the year before when he'd gone home with all that music playing triumphantly in his brain. And now he could remember nothing of the opera, it had become a din.

"So she cannot be trusted at these affairs," he thought irritably, and when Christophe spoke to him again he was almost rude.

At last, bad company for himself as well as anyone else,

he went to take his leave of his aunts. The music had commenced, and Christophe had asked Marie to dance. They had just begun to move, gracefully, swiftly about the polished floor as Marcel headed for the stairs. Richard in the shadows, his arms folded, watched Marie, her skirts swaying with the waltz, his face serene with absorption, his lips just touched with a smile.

For an hour Marcel roamed.

He walked around the iron fence of the Place d'Armes, then through streets no wider than alleys, oblivious to the mud that spattered his boots, winding his way along the riverfront, imagining now and again and unsuccessfully that he was walking along the Rue St.-Jacques in Paris to cross the Seine and make his way to the Tuileries. But he was in the city of New Orleans, and outside the fashionable billiard parlors in the Rue Royale, he watched the white men milling about the tables, heard the crash of the balls. He melted into the shadows as they swept past him, top hats glistening in the rain.

It was sweet to know he might return at any moment to the crowded party and yet it was not sweet at all. He gazed up at the lighted windows of the Hotel St. Louis, watched the carriages stopping, heard the music of the salons.

The Mercier house was dark when he turned the corner into the Rue Dauphine. Then drawing near the end of the wall in back, he saw a light in Juliet's window above. Curtains were drawn, a phantom smoke rose in gusts from the brick chimney against the gray sky. Catching his hand in the thick vines that still covered the bricks, he gazed upward, musing, wanting, but not really daring to sound the bell. So she could not be trusted at these affairs, so she had tried to catch that sorceress, Dolly, by the hair! It made him smile.

All of her life was Christophe's now, she cooked for him, ironed his shirts with her own hands, worked like a servant in the back kitchen and seemed content with a white apron tied across her skirts, her hair gathered under a red *tignon*. And yet she could emerge that magnificent lady in black velvet who had smiled at him tonight as he entered the box. She had hummed once with the opera, and he had been touched by it, soothed by it, in spite of the complexity of his thoughts. "Ah, think of it if you like," he whispered aloud in the dark street, "no one can stop you from dreaming, dreaming about them all." But closing his eyes, a torturous sensation intruded. It was Anna Bella he was holding, Anna

Bella he was kissing, and then he remembered with a surge of anger that guileless virginal sweetness, those trusting little arms. In this very street, he could have pressed his head against the vines until their thorns cut him, he could have cried.

But even as he turned to go, the light went out above. He took one last look. A dull glow swelled in the window above the stairs. It appeared next in the window at the landing. And then he heard the heavy muffled sound of the front door. She was coming out at this hour, alone?

But a man appeared under the gas lamp. He stopped, his opera cape folding in against him as he lit a cigar and then putting it to his lips lifted his head. Marcel's eyes strained to make him out, the dark skin, the shock of white hair beneath the brim of the top hat, combed back to curl above the high collar of his cape. It was Augustin Dumanoir's father, that man! Marcel wanted to kill him, tear him apart with his bare hands. But he stood rooted to the spot, watching the flare of that black cape as the man crossed the street, passing under another gas lamp and disappearing into the darkness as he moved toward the river along the Rue Ste. Anne.

A flame burst in Marcel. There was nothing of reason about it. He was moving before he could stop himself toward the garden gate. And knowing that old latch would easily give, he forced it with his shoulders and strode back the path to the side door. He felt his teeth clenched so tight his jaw ached and all the long night's frustrations were mounting to some volatile and unknown pitch. So she was mad, was she? So she couldn't be trusted in all that fine company above the dress shop, so she had tried to pull Dolly's precious hair. And every slave on the block knew he had had her, did they? And so it would bring down the roof. But it was fine for that proud planter who whipped his slaves and rode to hounds. He hit the knob of the door upward with his knee, thrust his weight against the panels, and felt it give.

She was at the threshold of her room when he appeared, holding the lamp in her hand. Her long peignoir was open down the front and he could see a slice of her long naked leg.

"Cher," she whispered with amazement. Then lowering the lamp so that it threw an unsteady light on her face, she smiled. This was madness, he had no right to be here, he was insane. And she was heartbreakingly beautiful, hair loose and light on her shoulders, the peignoir slipping over the

(293)

dark shadows of her nipples under the silk. Christophe would make a grand entrance at the perfect moment and murder him, and what was his excuse, that he'd seen that rich colored planter, her lover, going down the stairs? But even as his brain teemed, the peignoir swung loose and he saw she was completely naked, saw the dark tuft of hair between her legs. She had backed easily into the room, which like all the chambers of the house had been restored. And entering it now for the first time since the first debacle he was maddened even in this near-blinding passion by the lady's bower which it had become. A majestic frame held the soft mattresses, there was the tester with its wreath of roses, and in the mirror beyond her, above her marble dresser, he could see her reflection, hair rippling to the curve of her hips which moved beneath the thin flowered fabric, birds and birds of paradise glittering with the light.

"So at last," she whispered.

He glared angrily at the table with its wine in the silver bucket, and the glasses still in place.

"So it takes another man to make you mad enough?" she laughed softly. "Hmmmmm? Another man to make you come to me? I should have known."

He could feel his chest heaving, his own breath giving away what might have still been hidden beneath his clothes.

"And what if I told you, I didn't let him touch me, hmmmm?" she whispered, eyes quivering with laughter. She gestured toward the bed. The coverlet was untouched, pillows in place. Her clothes lay in a heap over the painted screen. "And what if I told you that I would let you touch me," she was smiling, "what would you think, then? Would you be angry, then?" She backed toward the bed, the peignoir completely open, the soft roundness of her belly gleaming above that tuft of dark hair. The lamp flickered behind the thickly carved post, and as she reached to turn down the coverlet, the peignoir slid from her shoulders hanging loosely on her arms.

He had lost all power to reason. He was merely moving toward her, and had taken the lamp out of her hand. He blew out the flame. He shut his eyes. And as he looked again, she materialized in the darkness, her own hands, lifting, offering her high firm breasts.

Having her again, having her again, he was breathing against her neck, realizing it was going to happen, nothing could stop it, no matter what the price. It was no bitter fantasy in his narrow bed, it was happening. He was dropping his clothes behind him and climbing in beside her under the coverlet, sinking into a voluptuous softness of feather pillows and mattress as she shifted away from him, as if teasing him, to one side. He would not let this end too soon. He would savor it as if it had to last him a year, as if it had to last him all his young life. Christophe was a stranger, everyone else was a stranger. *"Je t'adore, je t'adore,"* he whispered, holding her face upturned on the pillow as he felt her breasts with rapid, frantic gestures and bent to kiss her lips. He heard her low, maddening laughter, and suddenly she very lightly slapped his cheek. She pushed at his shoulder, she ran her hand roughly over his hair, she arched her back, and leaning upward let her teeth close on his ear. "I could kill you," he whispered, "I've wanted you every second, I'd commit murder for you, I'd murder that man."

"Don't do it," she said drawing him down, letting him kiss her neck and her shoulders, "Just come to me, come to me." And then slapping him again, pushing him, she released the roughness in him so that he caught her wrists in one hand and held them over her head. She was laughing, undulating, her legs between his legs, that moist tuft of hair against his thigh. He slid his hand down fearfully and felt that place, shutting his eyes, for the sheer sweet warm wetness of it, as his breath caught in his throat. He couldn't endure this, he couldn't, couldn't make it last. And thrusting home again powerfully, he heard her let out an awful inhuman moan and felt her shuddering as he had gone to Paradise again.

When he opened his eyes, she was on her elbow over him, against the gray light from the window so that he couldn't see her face. She ran a finger over his cheek. She kissed him, pushing his lips apart with her tongue. He was too tired to move. Again he told her that he adored her, but she didn't want him to speak. She wanted to begin again. He wanted to say that he couldn't do it, it was all over, what was she doing? But he felt the passion mounting, slower, sweeter, and every bit as bestial as he rose up pushing her softly back. He could sense the difference, how it was happening, more piquant and protracted and ecstasy just the same. "Juliet, Juliet," he breathed into her neck, "say that you love me, say that you are my slave."

"Lovely one," she whispered, "pretty, pretty Marcel. Make me your slave if you want me to be your slave," she pushed against him, dug her knee into his leg. "Make me your slave!"

she gritted her teeth, and harder, wilder than before, he took her again.

She lay sleeping finally, hair out over the pillow. He could see nothing of the woman in her at all. She was as old as his own mother, and yet in the dim glow from the window she was as a young girl. Her flesh, so sweet and yielding, had its own drowsy, musky perfume. He stood by the window, and looked out at the rain. It thrilled him to be in this warm room with her, quieted by love, and almost sleepy, while all about him the rain fell, rushing in the gutters overhead, running with a gurgle into the cistern, teeming on the flags below. He stepped into his boots, shirt still unbuttoned, his coat loose, and poked at the coals in the grate. They were dead. A door slammed below.

Then another door closed, and there was the sliding of a latch. "Maman!" came the alarmed whisper on the stairs.

Marcel froze, still clutching the poker as Juliet, rising on her elbows, cried out,

"Go 'way, Chris, your mother is not alone." She fell back as if asleep. And then Christophe, standing in the doorway, saw through the murky light the figure by the grate.

"You bastard!" he whispered, and pitched forward straight at Marcel.

"Christophe!" Juliet shouted. But he had Marcel by the shoulders and had thrown him back against the wall. His fist shot out, but Marcel ducked this and attempting to get around him, was caught suddenly in his strong hands. But Juliet was up, peignoir flying loose around her, and she had hold of her son's neck. "Let him go, let him go!" she was screaming, and then commenced to slap him over and over with both hands.

"You think you own me!" she growled and then grabbing him by the hair, swung him around. Her teeth gritted, her voice raging, she was speaking a patois which Marcel could not fully understand.

"Stop it, stop it," Marcel pleaded with her as she slapped Christophe again. And Christophe, dizzy, stumbling, moved away from her finally, his head in his hands.

It seemed it was over then, and all were breathless, staring at one another in the dark. But then Christophe let his hands down slowly and as they both waited, uncertain, he sprang at Juliet. He caught her off guard with the back of his hand, flinging her against the bed. She let out a second cry as

(296)

Marcel rushed to stop him, but Christophe had struck her again. She fell down on her knees.

"Don't, Chris, my God," Marcel said throwing his arm about Christophe's chest, "it's me you want to hit, not her!"

And Christophe obliged him with one fine blow that sent him back to the floor.

Marcel had never lost consciousness before. He had no idea how it felt. He only knew that he was sitting against the wall and it seemed a long long time had passed, that surely he must be in another time and place. But he was right there, nothing had changed, except that Juliet was holding onto the lamp threatening to throw it at Christophe if he came a step closer and that Christophe, trembling, had slumped into a chair.

"All right," he said. Marcel was just climbing to his feet. He had hold of the marble mantelpiece and his legs were refusing to support his weight. "Sleep with him then if you want to, sleep with them all," Christophe said in a low voice.

"I don't want them all," Juliet whispered from beside the bed.

"Why don't you invite them up right after class? Why don't you just invite them up in the middle of the afternoon?" He was rubbing his forehead with his hands.

"It was my doing," Marcel whispered. "All my doing." He tried to stand erect. "There's no one to blame but me, Christophe," he said. He realized for the first time that Juliet was crying.

"You hit me like that, your own mother," she moaned softly, her breath catching with sobs.

"Mother, mother," he said in a low voice.

"They wanted me to kill you before you were born, you know that, they wanted me to kill you when you were in my body and I said no."

"Well, that's what they would want in a whorehouse, isn't it?" he turned toward her, rising, upsetting the chair.

"Christophe, if you try to hit her again..." Marcel said simply, "I'll kill you, I promise you. I've got this poker in my hand." He didn't have it, however. He didn't even know where it was. He had dropped it when Christophe ran at him. But he stood resolute, as if he himself were some marvelous weapon.

"It's not *me* you care about! You don't care about *me*," Juliet whispered, still crying. "Why don't you tell him the truth, instead of calling me names, you and your English

(297)

friend," she said contemptuously. "Do you think *I* don't know it, do you think I have no mind?"

"If you dare..." Christophe whispered, shaking his head. He had his fists clenched. "If you say one more word..."

"Christophe, please..." Marcel said.

"Tell him the reason you're so angry, the real reason..." she taunted.

"I swear I'll kill you..." Christophe said, "if you say another word."

For a long, tense moment they stared at each other in silence, mother and son, and then he turned and went out of the room. Marcel followed him until they had reached the head of the steps. Then Marcel watched him disappear in the darkness of the hallway, and heard the latch of his bedroom door slide into place. Marcel wanted to die.

He went down the steps, aware that Juliet was behind him, and felt her brushing against him as she reached to unlock the front door. "Go back up," he whispered, "and lock your door while he's calm."

"He isn't going to hurt me," she said quietly. "So he bruised my face, so what?" she sighed. "He's jealous."

"He loves you, he's your son," Marcel said. "He's only thinking what any son would think." He bowed his head. He couldn't put it into words, that the world thought she had no right with a boy his age, which meant that he as a boy had no right with her, that he could ruin everything that Christophe had built up, that that gray-haired Dumanoir had the right somehow but he did not have the right.

He had no right with Anna Bella, no right with Juliet, no right with anyone!

"The hell he is," she said with a deep voice. "You don't know him," she whispered.

"I know he loves you," Marcel whispered.

"Oh, yes, he loves me," she whispered. "He'll be all right tomorrow, I promise you. Come around."

Rain was flooding the Rue Dauphine when he stepped out. He stopped in the deep niche of the door to straighten his clothes, fix his tie and his shirt, and properly right the cape on his shoulders. His mother might be up waiting on this special night, "playing the candle" and he only hoped there were no bruises on his face. But then, touching his chin, he felt the wetness of blood there. Well, marvelous! And then as if they had been waiting for some cue, all the aches and pains of his body chose to manifest themselves. The back of his head hurt, and so did his shoulder. And dizzy, he all but fell as he stepped into the rain. All he wanted in the world was to die, or fall into bed.

It felt almost good to step into the downpour. The rain pounded his head and slowly he turned his face up to the dark sky. It drenched him, pouring into his collar, splashing into his outstretched hands. An icy coldness crept over him, and half closing his eyes, he let the street become a blur.

He was walking through that blur toward his own gate when he saw the glimmer of lights through the trees. The parlor was ablaze and so were his mother's rooms. "Lord," he whispered, "if I can just get through this, just manage to answer her questions and get to bed."

"*Mon Dieu*, Marcel!" she let out a cry when she saw him. He shook off his cape before turning to her, and when he did turn to her, he felt all the blood drain from his face.

"Where the hell have you been, *mons fils?*" came Monsieur Philippe's drawling voice.

IV

HE SAT AT THE TABLE, his foot on the seat of a dining-room chair, his black cape loose over his shoulders as if he were chilly, and he was drinking wine from a stem glass. Through the haze of cigar smoke, his blue eyes appeared uncommonly brilliant and though he had acquired a touch of gray at the sideburns, his hair was as golden as ever, thick, a bit long, and moist on his forehead. He was drunk.

Marcel felt his teeth clench on all the abominable oaths he knew. What in the name of God was the man doing here? It was the opening night of the opera season, why the hell wasn't he dancing at the St. Louis Hotel? Surely the family had come to town, they always came to town, didn't they? But as Cecile bore down on him, Marcel went limp under a veritable swaddling of towels, and being shaken to near senselessness, he stood mutely wiping his face.

"Your pretty sister's been home for hours," said Monsieur Philippe pleasantly enough. He stretched, the chair creaked, and he clasped his hands behind his head. The room was redolent with the tobacco and something else which might have been cedar chips thrown on the fire. There were presents on the table, as always, sweets, jams, and a small shining lap *secrétaire*.

"Come here, and let me have a look at you," Monsieur Philippe said, motioning limply with his right hand. "Come here."

His face was mere geniality, nothing of threat whatsoever in the drowsy blue eyes. But Marcel could feel that Cecile was afraid. She had transformed herself quite agreeably since early evening. She was in *décolleté* with rhinestones, with just a hint of rouge on her lips. She brushed at his coat nervously. *"Mon Dieu,"* she said again, "you'll catch pneumonia from this."

"Well, get the boy some brandy," said Monsieur Philippe quite gaily. "Either you've grown or I'm getting wizened with old age. Now I know why adults say that to children, you've grown. But you have grown!"

"Bonsoir, Monsieur," Marcel gave him a short bow.

The man laughed. "Brandy, brandy, where's Lisette?" he demanded. "I am of the opinion that all young men are infinitely improved by a little brandy, here, *mon fils,* sit down." And laughing at his own magnanimity, he lifted his own drink.

Marcel eyed him warily. Where was the anger he'd been expecting? If Cecile had handled this, why was she afraid?

"Now tell me, where have you been!" Monsieur Philippe demanded. It was almost a mockery of a parent's solicitude.

"Walking, Monsieur," Marcel murmured.

Leaning over the nearby candle, Monsieur Philippe lit another cigar. He sat back, drawing in the smoke. His cheeks were ruddy, and he had about him the smell of leather and horses which always mingled distinctly with his pomade, his cologne.

"Walking on a night like this, hmmmm," he breathed, the air suddenly smelling like wine. Lisette had filled Marcel's glass. And without waiting to be told, Marcel took a stiff drink. The brandy burned his throat, and stung his eyes.

"Another, another," Monsieur Philippe motioned to Lisette. "Your mother tells me you went to the opera tonight, don't tell me you enjoyed it," he laughed, but with head wagging slightly, added, "But then you would!" His mouth turned down at the ends as he appeared to roll his wine on his tongue. "I expect one of these days I'll be getting a little bill for a pair of those delicate spectacles," he said pinching his fingers, "octagonal with gold rims. That would suit you," he nodded, laughter cracking in his throat. "Such a boy, such a boy. What do people know of the world, I wonder, but then again what was that song?" He cocked his head as though listening to music, and suddenly began to sing. Marcel did not know the song, except it was an aria, and Monsieur Philippe seemed to handle it right on key. If anyone else in the world had been singing it, at any other time, Marcel would have liked it a great deal.

But he was numb as he listened. There was water in his boots and his shirt clung to his chest. He drank the brandy and motioned this time himself for Lisette to give him some more. On and on Monsieur Philippe was singing, his eyes moving over the ceiling, mossy blond brows gleaming in the firelight, his voice becoming high and thin with the words which were Italian, most likely, Marcel could not be sure. But the melody descended so that he became louder, clearer, and more poignant until at last he brought his fist down in time with the rhythm and shook all the china in the room.

Cecile laughed and clapped her hands.

"Come here," Monsieur Philippe said, opening his arms. He hugged her tight and then set her down in the chair beside him, opposite Marcel.

"I have a book for you, my little scholar, where's that book?" Lisette handed it to him from the buffet, and he thrust it at Marcel. It was a handsome volume, old, with gold letters fading in the leather cover. And opening it Marcel discovered it was a history of ancient Rome, complete with the most splendid engravings, each covered with its own thin tissue which he touched reverently.

"Thank you, Monsieur," he whispered.

"And I'll tell you a little secret," Monsieur Philippe said, "you'll be the first person to read it, though it's fifty years old. I always think of you when I see books," he winked his eye. He said the word, books, with a special emphasis, continuing, "I saw some book the other day, what was it, ah, some splendid nonsense, *The Anatomy of Melancholy*, yes, that's exactly what it was. Found it with some others in an old trunk, should have brought it to you. But, well, next time!"

"You're very generous," Marcel said.

"You know he's studying now with Christophe Mercier, the novelist from Paris, you remember?" Cecile whispered. She poured some wine into Monsieur Philippe's glass.

"Oh, yes, yes, that fellow came back on the same boat with

my brother-in-law, did very well for himself in Paris," he said, raising his eyebrows. "How's that mother of his, still playing the mad Ophelia with all that...all that hair?" he made a wandering gesture about the head, and then laughed as though this were a capital joke.

"She's better," Cecile said with a slight air of condescension. "He's a good teacher for the boys, Monsieur, a very good teacher, everyone sings his praises."

Monsieur Philippe nodded and shrugged. He sat back, crossing his boots on the seat of the chair in front of him.

"And he tells you all about Paris, hmmmm? The Sorbonne!" he said exaggerating his voice. "The university, hmmmm? Well, tell me this, if this is such a dreadful place for them, why do they always come home?"

Marcel smiled and shook his head, muttering something respectful.

"And you, I suppose you're anxious as ever to get on that boat, hmmm, to leave your poor mother all alone?"

"Oh, it's my fault, Monsieur, I've talked so much about it," said Cecile. "All the boys dream of it, but perhaps if I didn't make such a fuss."

Again came that magnanimous smile. He was eyeing Marcel up and down and Marcel could feel his wet shirt cold against his back and the sting of the cut on his chin. But in this smoky light, well, he tried to keep calm.

"Even soaking wet you're all right," Monsieur Philippe nodded approvingly. "You're all right. Now go on to bed, take that book with you, and oh, and here..." He reached into his pocket withdrawing a wad of bills in a clip. "If you're so crazy about this opera, here, then, this ought to get you a good seat." Marcel was a little stunned at the amount.

"You're generous, Monsieur," he said again.

"You are pleased," his mother said anxiously, "about this new school?"

"But, of course, why not?" said Monsieur Philippe. "Though I don't see what was the matter with the old one. This young Mercier, he's sensible, not giving them airs."

"Oh, never," she said. "Why, Lermontant, the undertaker, he's sending his son," she said, watching his face.

Monsieur Philippe was looking at Marcel with the most dreamy smile. Suddenly he laughed. "A scholar of all things," he said. "You know, Marcel, once when I was fourteen I actually read a book all the way through." Laughter erupted again. "Can't even remember what it was. That was the first and only time I ever fell off a horse, and I'd broken my foot. One of these days you have to tell me what you think of this English fellow, Dickens, I have an old aunt from Baltimore, more American you know, she brought this fellow Dickens down with her in her portmanteau, and she started to read him and she cried!"

Marcel couldn't help laughing for the first time. He had to make himself stop, and even then he couldn't keep his face straight and had to look away.

"I know that Lermontant," said the father, his mind wandering, "he does his job well, all right." He nodded, glancing at Cecile. "And that son of his, a fine looking young boy..."

"Forgive me just a moment, Monsieur," Cecile said following Marcel out of the room.

Marcel was trying hard not to laugh. He felt lightheaded, miserable, and was elated at the same time. As soon as he had reached the back door, he covered his mouth and began to shake with laughter.

"What's the matter with you!" Cecile hissed, drawing up to him. "Stop it, stop it."

"But he doesn't remember!" Marcel said, trying to keep his voice down. He doubled over with laughter. "He doesn't even remember the note!"

It was a full minute before he realized his mother was standing very still except that she was wringing her hands.

"Well, he must not," he whispered. "Either that or he never got it."

"He did get it, you told me that man...that notary said that he did," she said.

"Maman, it's too perfect!" he bent to kiss her.

"It is not perfect!" she burst out, then turned afraid that Monsieur Philippe might have heard.

"O my God, why not?" Marcel sighed wearily. A reprieve after all this time. He kissed Cecile. "Maybe he'll think of it in the morning."

"No," she shook her head. "He's forgotten it, if it ever made any difference to him at all."

"Ah, now don't worry," he said.

"Cecee?" Monsieur Philippe called from the dining room. Putting his cape over his head, Marcel ran for the *garçonnière*.

Only a few hours later, when Lisette stood over him shaking him, he awoke quite cross.

(303)

"What's the matter with you?" he demanded. "Haven't you enough to do in the cottage? I only just fell asleep."

"Well, get up and on your feet," she whispered. "And look down there right now."

"At what?" he demanded, pulling on his robe. "Light the fire, for God's sakes, this is a tomb."

"Look down there!" she said, pushing him.

And wrapping the robe quickly around him, he followed her angrily to the open door.

The rain had stopped, the morning was gray and cold. He stuffed his hands in his pockets as he went to the rail.

Anna Bella was staring up at him from the wet flags below.

V

HIS VERY FIRST IMPRESSION was that her face was not her own. She was over near the cistern, an utterly unlikely figure standing still beneath the wet banana leaves, her dark blue merino dress and cape blending, it seemed, with the mist that enveloped the yard. And the expression with which she looked up at him was simply not that of the Anna Bella he knew.

Only once before had Marcel seen the expression of a human being alter in that way. It had been on the morning that Richard's sister, Françoise, had died. He had met Richard at Mass, and the change in Richard was so complete that it was terrifying. It seemed a supernatural being walked in Richard's shape and clothing, and Marcel had never forgotten it. The memory swept over him now, palpably, as he looked down at this young woman whose black-gloved hands were clasped on the knob of her umbrella, and he felt this besides: enormous love for her, protective love. He had to know the reason for this at once.

"Tell her I'm coming, go on ... I'll be right down," he said to Lisette as he hurried back into the room.

"Down! Where am I going to put her if you go down!" Lisette demanded. "Get your clothes on so she can come up here! What's she doing here, anyway, at this hour? Michie Philippe's asleep down there! What's your mother going to think if she sees her out there!"

"All right, all right," he stammered as he dressed hurriedly and Lisette bent to make the fire.

Anna Bella slipped off her cape as soon as she entered, not waiting for anyone to help her, and laid it neatly over the back of the chair. She sat down, in front of the desk, though he offered her the more comfortable armchair by the grate, and when he asked her to have coffee she merely shook her head.

Lisette, returning with a full pot and hot milk, urged it on her anyway, and set the cup by her side.

"Would you leave me alone with him, please?" Anna Bella asked. Lisette studied her for a moment, obviously surprised, and then went away.

The room was warming. Anna Bella, removing her gloves carefully as though they were a peeling, stretched her small dimpled hand toward the hearth.

"What is it, what's happened?" Marcel said.

Her face had relaxed only slightly.

"I thought you were my friend, Marcel," she said. Her voice was calm, devoid of drama. "I thought we would be friends all of our lives."

He felt an odd catch in his throat, had the sensation that if he tried to speak nothing would come out. "We are friends," the voice was weak. "We will always be friends," he said.

"That's foolishness and you know it!" she said.

"Anna Bella, have you forgotten what happened last night when I stepped into the box?"

"Don't you give me that foolishness, Marcel!" She glared at him, her teeth biting into her lip. "This has got nothing to do with Madame Elsie, you aren't scared of Madame Elsie, there're a hundred times you could have come to see me, when she's at supper, when she's asleep..."

"Asleep, asleep!" he could feel his face growing hot, his voice still maddeningly unsteady. "And have what happened that night in Christophe's house happen again..."

She meant to answer, but it seemed her voice broke. She turned away from him struggling violently, her chin quivering, her hand shielding her eyes.

"Anna Bella, I can't see you anymore," he said desperately. "It's past between us, don't you understand? It's just the way it happened, Anna Bella!" he said. If she began to cry, he was afraid that he would cry too. "What do you want of me, Anna Bella!" he demanded. "What can I do!"

"Talk to me, Marcel!" she burst out, the tears clinging to

her lashes. "You can care about me, what happens to me, I'm your friend!"

"I do care," he said. "But what can I do? You don't know what you're asking of me... You're a young woman now, you shouldn't even be here with me alone in this room! You're to be chaperoned, guarded..."

"No!" she shook her head. Her lashes were matted with the tears that were coursing down her cheeks. "Don't you tell me all that, I don't believe it, I won't believe that what we had, you and me, what we had between us is just gone like that! Marcel, look at me. We cared about each other, it was like we were kin. And now you're trying to tell... tell me..." she stammered, her hands out, her eyes glancing helplessly at her own breasts, her skirts... "You're trying to tell me that because we're grown-up, all that's gone? I don't believe that! If that's what growing up is, I don't ever want to grow up, I just want to be a child all my life!" Again her hand went to shield her eyes. Her head rested in her hand, and she shook with her choked sobs. Her voice came again, weak, pleading, "Don't you remember how it was between you and me?" She looked up at him, her head bent, limp on her neck. "You were with me the night Jean Jacques died, don't you remember? We were always together..." the voice just died away.

He was looking at her through a film of tears. It was terrible to watch her cry, to hear it, to see it, the way that she gave herself to it so completely, so defenselessly. He had seen it before, but never had it been so important, and never had it been over something that they could not share. She exaggerated nothing in what she'd said. If anything, she had not touched the heart of it, that they had understood each other, known each other as very few people in this world ever did. There was no way he could tell her how he had missed all of it, how he had missed not only her but the person he had been when he was with her.

"Don't you tell me that growing up can destroy that!" she whispered now through her tears. "It's just not true, it's just not fair." She was dabbing at the flow from her eyes. "What happened that night in Michie Christophe's house... that was my fault..." she whimpered. "I did it!"

"Don't say that!" he burst out. "Don't ever say that!" He put his hands out, wanting to take her by the arms, but then he let his hands drop.

"But how can that count for so much?" she pleaded, her

head inclining to the right as she looked up at him. "So much that it can just destroy everything else?"

"It's not that," he whispered. "You didn't do it, don't you understand? It would have happened sooner or later, sometime, anytime that we were alone. I did it! I could do it again. I can't be alone with you without wanting to do it! I want to kiss you, take you in my arms now!" he said.

She was amazed. She was staring at him, the fingers of her right hand just touching her lips. "But why..." she started.

"Anna Bella, don't you see? It can't *be* between us!" he said. The tears were flowing for him now, too, he couldn't stop them, but as he swallowed thickly, he began to speak to her in a man's voice. "All this has happened too soon, it's happened at the wrong time. I haven't come into my own! I can't court you, I can't even tell you how I feel. And yet I am a man, a man with nothing, nothing but his dreams. You know what those dreams are, you've always known. Anna Bella, that is all I have."

She did not understand, he could see that. She did not really see the point of this, but sensed only that he cared for her, he could see the warmth, the passion in her eyes.

"I'd wait for you," she whispered, her voice heartbreaking, "if only, if only you would..."

"You don't know what you're saying!" he stepped back, his hands forming into fists. "Wait for me how long, ten years? Twenty? Anna Bella, it may be three years before I even leave for France, and God only knows when and if I'll come back!" He shook his head. "What would you wait *for!*"

A calm settled over her when he spoke these words. She was crying, but quietly, her face unspeakably sad. It was the old truth, she couldn't claim surprise. But no real relief had come to her, she was merely defeated, and turning in the chair it was as if she were turning her crying inward, her hands limp in her lap.

He was desperate watching her, and the solitary figure that she made amid her blue skirts, her shoulders heaving softly and those silent sobs. And then a wild thought came to him, that nothing mattered as long as they were alone in this room. To hell with everyone and everything outside of it, even the passage of time. He moved toward her, knowing that he would not hurt her, never hurt her, he wouldn't leave her "ruined merchandise" for the fine white men of Madame Elsie's or the husband she might ultimately love. But he

(307)

would have her, somehow have her, at least just to kiss her, to abandon himself just for this little while to her arms. Improper, reckless, he did not care. Last night, perhaps it would have been impossible when maddened and aching he had broken Juliet's door. But this was the quiet of the morning, she was here in the room with him, the gray mist nudging on the windows beyond. He would hold her close to his chest. They were entitled to this, were they not? Why in hell had he ever let anyone take it away?

But she did not see him move. She didn't see him coming silently across the floor. And just as he reached for her, she said, alone in her thoughts and in a heavy voice,

"There is this man."

He stopped. The fingers that had almost touched her settled instead on the back of the chair.

"...he's already spoken to Madame Elsie," came the small, weakened voice, "and with Old Captain dying upstate, well Old Captain's not coming down here anymore. It's just Madame Elsie now, so it's all arranged. That is, if I say yes to him," and then plaintively she looked up to Marcel.

She saw nothing but the blue eyes staring at her, saw the smooth tan face with its pale shadowing of gold, the mouth still, as if in wonder.

"...that is, if I say yes to him today. He's from your father's people, Vincent Dazincourt's his name."

Vincent, Vincent, it was like something grating, a scratching that persisted like some animal scraping at the door. Vincent, Vincent, the hawk-eyed white man who had risen that day in Madame Elsie's parlor just as Marcel had touched the knob, oh, yes, he had to be, because he was the same "Vincent" with those black eyes who had come to Christophe's with the silver walking stick: *Don't make the same mistake again.*

"...a fine gentleman like your father," she was saying, her eyes down, her forehead furrowed, her hand rubbing anxiously at her hair, "from his wife's people . . . Dazincourt . . . his wife's brother, actually . . . from *Bontemps.*"

"*Bontemps?*" he whispered.

"...well-to-do..." she was saying, "and young. Well, he has the front rooms up yonder, the upstairs suite. He and Madame Elsie they talked about it for hours already, and he wants my answer today." Her eyes narrowed for a second as her teeth touched her lip. "It's the old-fashioned way, she saw to that, I'd have my own house, and with Old Captain dying

(308)

upstate, and Madame Elsie as old as she is..." Teardrops
hung in her lashes as she lifted her eyes. The eyes were
imploring and slowly she rose from the chair. "I have to tell
him today..." she whispered, and then faltering, she burst
out, "I don't care anything about him!" She sobbed. "I don't
care anything about that man!"

"Then say no to him!" Marcel gasped furiously. "Tell him
to leave you alone! My God, Anna Bella stand up to him, I
can't do this for you!" he declared.

"But why!" she was crying. "Why stand up to him? For
what! Why!"

He turned his back on her, the fists he'd made striking
one another painfully until finally he turned on the wall. He
smashed his fist into the plaster. And smashed it again.

"Marcel," she cried behind him. "Marcel."

"No!" he said, turning. "No!" He was staring at her with
wide eyes. "Anna Bella when I am eighteen years old I am
leaving this place! I am going to France or so help me I will
die. And nothing, nothing is going to stop that, not you, not
the devil in hell, not God. I will not tie that millstone around
my neck, I will not do it!" he cried.

He could no longer see her, he was utterly blinded by his
own tears. But he knew she was moving away from him, that
she had turned like someone brutally wounded and she was
reaching for the door. His tongue thickened and failed him
when he tried to say her name, but he had hold of her, just
in time, and with his arm slammed the door shut again.

And now he had buried his face in her neck and it was he
who was crying uncontrollably while she caressed him, her
timid hands stroking ever so slowly, her firm breasts crushed
against him as he was wracked with his own sobs. And it
was she who comforted him, let him lean upon her, she whose
lips touched his cheek as her fingers touched the back of his
neck.

"Listen to me..." he was whispering now as he caught his
breath. "If he's a gentleman, if you are sure..." he was stammering... "If it is what you want to do, if it is what's best...
but you musn't do it foolishly, you musn't do it in haste." A
slow sigh came out of him, shuddering, it was just what Richard had wanted, what Marie had told him to do, *be a brother
to her,* preside over it, help in it, give his consent. "Are you
listening to me?" he asked her. Resentfully and roughly he
wiped away his own tears. "You don't have to do it unless
it's arranged as you want it, do you understand!"

(309)

She was just crying, and she laid her head to one side against his shoulder so that he could feel the silken resilience of her bouffant hair.

"If only I were older, wiser..." he said. "Then I could...I could..."

"I know," she whispered, "I know..."

"But you musn't let that man force you, don't you understand me, Anna Bella, swear to me, if he tries to force you, I'll go to Monsieur Philippe, I'll go to my mother, I swear to you..."

She let out a soft sound against him. Calming, slow. And then he felt her drawing back. He was dazed, and curiously tired. She had taken his face in both her hands and then she kissed him on the forehead.

"You know how it would have been," he whispered, not looking at her but looking off to some distant and fabled boulevard where he saw carriages rolling over the Pont St.-Michel, where he saw the rose window of Notre Dame. "It would have been just a little house somewhere right in these streets..." He was alighting from one of those carriages, in his dream he wore a top hat, a sweeping cape. And in his dream he went into the foyer of Notre Dame. The bells sounded above, the people moved like ghosts beneath the immense arches, "and we would have had children, so many children, and I would have...I would have been so bitter! Bitter that I had never gone, never seen..." In top hat and cape he turned again to the open church doors. Sun streamed on the square before him, streamed on the winding walled river Seine, streamed on the high roofs. The entire city of Paris gleamed in that sunlight as he stepped into the open air. "I just couldn't give that up, Anna Bella, I just couldn't. But if that man hurts you, I swear to God...!"

And again she was holding him, almost rocking him in her arms.

When he drew up, he felt sickened and still.

"I'll never see you again, will I?" Anna Bella asked. "I mean, not really, not like this."

He shook his head.

"You know I told him once that I would think on it, think on it, living with him, but only if after I could still see 'my friend.' He asked me who that friend was. I told him it was you. I told him all about you, 'course, I never said who your father was. I wouldn't say anything like that, him being well...he's your father's brother-in-law, I would never make that mistake. But I told him how it was with you and me, at least, at least the way that it used to be."

Again Marcel shook his head. "He may say it's all right now because he's wooing you. If I were wooing you, I'd kneel at your feet. But he won't say that a month from now, he won't want to come in from the country to find me in his house."

He saw her brows knit, saw the tears welling again.

"Besides," he whispered, "you can't ask that of me."

"No, I guess not," she answered softly, almost dreamily. "Good-bye, Marcel," she whispered.

And as he stood, seemingly unable to move, she withdrew, silently closing the door. It seemed a full minute passed that he stood there, and then suddenly, he cried out, "Anna Bella, wait!"

He came after her, but stopped in his tracks.

She had already reached the foot of the steps, and Monsieur Philippe stood at the back door of the cottage, his blue satin robe tied carelessly in front, as he leaned on the frame, cigar in hand. He was staring at her as she cut across the courtyard in front of him, her hands working fast to pull on her gloves. Never once did she look at him, her small head bowed. A little rain was falling, so light it couldn't be heard. But she stopped boldly to open her umbrella and as the droplets began to speckle the black silk, she went on.

Monsieur Philippe raised his eyes to the gallery above. He regarded Marcel coldly before turning back into the cottage and shutting the door.

VI

MONSIEUR PHILIPPE had a late breakfast. He scattered the newspapers over the table, and downing three and four glasses of beer, sat smoking until the afternoon. Marie, home from Mass, put on her opera gown again at his request so that he might have another look at it, and showering her with kisses, he presented her with the little portable *secrétaire*. It was a gem of a thing with lacquer and gilt, come down several generations, he explained to her, she must treat it with love. She might set it on a table to write a letter, or even use it on her lap when sitting in bed. It had a crystal inkwell, a packet of parchment paper for notes, and several new feather pens. He was delighted with the changes in her, asked if she needed more money for the hairdresser. The aunts, he said, were to spare nothing for her new dresses, and should just send the bill to old Jacquemine.

Cecile, aloof and weary, sat nestled into the settee observing all this, saying not a word. And when they were alone in the parlor, the three of them, Marcel, Philippe, and herself, she quietly mentioned that Marcel had had some difficulties with the old teacher which is why she had put him in the new school.

"Ah... I knew there was something," Philippe snapped his fingers. He turned the large page of the newspaper, carefully flattening it. "And it's all straightened out? You're behaving yourself?" he glanced at Marcel.

"Studying very hard, Monsieur," Marcel said dully. He dreaded the moment when he might have to explain about Anna Bella. He hadn't the faintest idea what he was going to say.

"Hmm..." his father said. He made some notes in a leather-bound book, murmuring aloud. "Repair the gutters, hmmmm, dresses for Marie, and you, I suppose you're growing an inch a day, you didn't buy that horse, hmmmm? What's the matter with you? Well, *ma chérie, ma petite,* I have to go."

Cecile sighed as she put her arms around him. Marcel made to vanish but Philippe called over his shoulder, *"Mon fils,* wait for me in the yard." He had already sent Felix to fetch his carriage from the stables.

"Monsieur," Cecile asked gently. "When do you think that he should go? When he's eighteen? Is that when they want them to enter the universities?"

"Eighteen is plenty of time," he said. "And here," he drew out that wad of bills again in the gold clip. "Let him go to the theater if he likes, that Booth will be coming through with Shakespeare, let him learn English, too. Is that man teaching him English, we all have to give way to it, learn it sooner or later, does this Christophe teach him anything practical at all?"

Well, it's coming now, Marcel was thinking when they finally met on the front path. The rain had stopped. The banana trees were glistening and clean. And the air with the brightening afternoon sun was not so cold.

"That little girl," Monsieur Philippe said, looking warily up and down the narrow street. He stepped back into the gate. "What was she doing in your room this morning, would you tell me, please?"

His blue eyes, shot with red from the night's drinking, were strikingly cold. He had seldom taken such a tone with Marcel and Marcel felt a curious humiliation.

"Monsieur, she and I are like brother and sister, we played together when we were children, why, she lives just up the street..."

"I know where she lives," said Monsieur Philippe, his voice flat, and somehow filled with meaning. "You're spoilt," he said, his lips moving in a loose smile. It was a smile of the mouth only. "That's your trouble, spoilt from the day you were born. Have you ever wanted for anything?" he asked with a haughty lift of his head.

"No, Monsieur," Marcel muttered.

"You're just a boy, you don't know anything about this world, do you?" And doubling his large white hand into a fist, he tapped Marcel's shoulder playfully. Marcel felt a peculiar chill. "That little girl's too old for you now, she's a young woman!" he said. "Now I don't want to hear of her being back there again."

The carriage had appeared at the corner, turning from the Rue Burgundy into the Rue Ste. Anne. It stopped before the boardinghouse four doors away.

"No, Monsieur, never again," Marcel murmured mechanically.

A slender young man with jet black hair came down the boardinghouse steps, bounding easily to the granite carriage block over the water that still ran in the street.

So they're going back to *Bontemps* together, or to their family in the St. Louis Hotel. And they've conferred in this little matter of Anna Bella, Monsieur Philippe had known of it when he saw her in the yard. An unpleasant shock went through Marcel. He did not immediately understand why he was so astonished when the carriage lumbered to the gate, or why his lips drew back in an irresistibly bitter smile. Felix had jumped down to open the door. Marcel looked away.

"You remember what I said to you," Monsieur Philippe said with a warning finger. "You study your lessons, and be good to your mother. And don't forget Lisette's birthday this week, that girl will be twenty-three if you can believe it, buy her something nice." He fetched that money clip for the third time. Marcel stuffed the bills into his pocket murmuring that he would take care of it, of course.

(313)

"And you watch out for your sister!" Monsieur Philippe said lastly. "You see she doesn't go out without Lisette or Zazu, or you go with her yourself." Sister, sister, the word emerged with clarity in the swirl of Marcel's thoughts. His wife's brother, that was who this Dazincourt was, the brother of Philippe's white wife. And he brings the man here to the gate of his mistress's house. Marcel regarded him as if Monsieur Philippe were not still murmuring some vague admonition, as if he were not squeezing Marcel's arm a little too hard as he mounted the carriage step.

It disgusted him suddenly, these two fine gentlemen, this brother, who must surely sit at his sister's table to eat her food, to drink her wine, and here he comes to town with her unfaithful husband and takes a mistress only a few doors from his brother-in-law's mistress. The door of the carriage had shut. The whip cracked, and the great wheels ground into the deep ruts as it moved slowly forward and gaining speed with the trotting hooves passed from his sight.

Oh, what did he care about these white people, their entanglements, their lies? Didn't he know that they had shaped his very world with their domestic treachery, built the cottage in which he lived, hung the very pictures on the walls? Yet he stood still at the gate, gazing toward Madame Elsie's boardinghouse, Anna Bella's words running like a thread through his mind. "He's a gentleman just like your father, a fine gentleman just like your father." Gentleman, indeed. Would he kiss his sister when he saw her next, having just passed the gate where he had seen her husband's bastard child? Mistress, bastard, he abhorred these words, what had they to do with him? *I love you, Anna Bella.*

Go inside, put on your Sunday best, the table will be prepared for dinner, white lace, silver, Tante Louisa will be along shortly with pastries for dessert. Look at that gilt-framed picture of *Sans Souci* in the country, white columns, he ought to write Tante Josette a letter, they would all be talking about the opera, he had one hundred dollars in his pocket for the theater, so he'd ruined his new suit, there were half a dozen frock coats in his armoire and shirts with collars stiff as a board. *I love you, Anna Bella.* "He's a fine gentleman just like your father," that's the point! *Don't do it.*

He saw those hawk eyes peering through the shadows of Christophe's hallway, that white skin, the hand clutching the silver walking stick... *"that a man of color cannot defend himself upon the field of honor...that a man of color cannot defend himself against a white man at all." I love you, Anna Bella, don't!*

Down the Rue Ste. Anne came a cluster of *gens de couleur* wandering home from twelve o'clock Mass, pink and blue dresses lifted carefully over the mud, black frock coats, umbrellas picking at the wet brick banquette like walking sticks. *"Bonjour, Marcel, and how is your Maman?" Don't, Anna Bella, don't.* He stood nodding, arms folded, as if in a dream. *Bonjour, Madame, Bonjour, Monsieur. I won't ever see you again, will I? Not like this.* Sunday dinner, white linen, red wine.

He turned suddenly, leaving the cottage yard behind him and walked steadily toward the Rue Dauphine.

He wasn't thinking anymore. It did not matter if Christophe cursed him, or what he would have to sweat on his knees. He found the latch of the gate broken just as he had left it the night before. The side door was open still where he had broken the lock, too. But he turned just before he entered. He looked down the narrow alley with its ivy spilling over the brick wall. Above hung those slatted blinds bolted over the windows as they had always been, and as he had seen them the first time he had ever passed into this yard. And the tall banana trees, wet and flapping in the chill breeze, still hid all of the world outside except for the gray sky. The slime had been washed from the tiny window in the gate, and he could see only a blur of color there of the street beyond. Only he was not frightened this time as he had been on that first afternoon. He felt nothing of that instinctual wariness. Rather, turning to the door, he could not wait to push it back and enter the long hall.

It seemed they both saw him as soon as he appeared in the reading room door. Christophe at the round table ate his breakfast, the folded newspaper in his hand. And Juliet, her shawl drawn over her shoulders, huddled in the great wing chair by the fire. Coffee steamed on the fender. The air was warm here. Frost covered the panes.

"Cher!" she said. "Come in."

Christophe lifted his cup, eyes fixed on Marcel.

"Cher!" she said again with that same vague amazement. "Sit down." She came round to him as he settled at the table, she lifted his face, inspecting the cut on his chin. "Not so bad," she whispered, "why, it's hardly there at all."

"Did you read the reviews of the opera?" Christophe asked in a low voice.

She had set a cup before Marcel and was filling it with coffee and cream. "Here, *cher*," she said.

"What did I tell you, the baritone stole the show." Christophe said. "Get him something to eat." She lifted a piece of cake from the plate with a knife.

"You ought to read it," Christophe sighed, laying the paper aside. He sat musing. His brown eyes appeared tired. He pushed his cup forward and his mother filled it. Then she moved slowly back to the fire. Her hair was loose over her shoulders, the light glinting on her face, and she wore that same peacock shawl threaded with silver that she had worn on the day Marcel first met her in the street.

"Go on," Christophe said softly, "have a little coffee, you look as if you're still asleep."

Marcel parted his lips. He wanted to say something. But suddenly there were no words. He started to speak, but it was as if his voice had left him, words had left him, he could only sit there, staring forward, his lips working silently, and then, his brows knit, he was still.

Christophe rose, stretching, and said that he would go out.

"But it's raining again," Juliet said.

"Hmmm, it's always raining," Christophe answered, buttoning his coat. He looked down at Marcel.

"You stay here with my mother," he said in a low voice. "Keep her company for a while. I don't know when I'll be back. And I haven't fixed those locks yet. I don't like to leave her alone."

Their eyes met as Christophe took his wool scarf from the back of the chair. He put his hand on Marcel's shoulder, "Just keep her company for a little while."

Marcel looked at Juliet as Christophe left the room. He could hear Christophe's step in the hallway, and then the closing of the front door.

"Come on upstairs with me, *cher*," she breathed as she came toward him. "We'll build a little fire in my room and make it warm."

VOLUME
TWO

PART ONE

I

MONSIEUR PHILIPPE FERRONAIRE had reached his full five feet eleven inches by eighteen years, a majestic height in those times for which he was very much admired, along with his golden hair and blue eyes, these traits being not at all common among the white Creole aristocracy, rife with French ancestors, who were his people and his friends along the prospering river coast.

His was the world of the Creole sugar plantation, come into its own at the turn of the century, with its rambling raised cottage of white columnettes and broad verandas over which the roses twined and the river breezes blew. Seated on these deep porches on summer evenings, one could watch the boats beyond the levee on the high water of the river, moving as if they floated against the sky. Being the youngest of four brothers he was the baby there, and evinced from childhood that mixture of sparkle and easy charm which endears itself at once to adults, so that he grew up on the laps of doting aunts who pushed cake on him at table and sent for a portrait painter from New Orleans to fix him forever in a gilt frame on the wall.

He rode his pony on rampages through the oaks, flushed the ducks from the marshes with the crack of his gun, and dancing at his brothers' weddings, drew squeals from his little nieces with the golden coins he plucked magically from their curls.

(318)

Months passed in the languid rural summers of his twenties when disdaining to make the Grand Tour, he seldom rose before noon in the lonely luxury of the *garçonnière*, lingered at table with his white wine and tobacco, and at last rode off to race friends along the spine of the levee or call upon the local belles. He was good to his mother in her old age, liking to stroll with her through the orange trees, and evenings found him spruced to go to town.

Of course there was the Mardi Gras, plays at the Theatre St. Philippe, billiards at which he proved to be excellent to a degree, and finally his perennial luck at cards. He had missed the war of 1814, obliged as he was to take the women out of the battlefields, but he fought a duel when he was twenty-one and seeing his opponent die instantly in the damp morning mist beneath the Metairie Oaks was overcome with horror for this senseless act. It had not seemed real to him before. After that he still played with the rapier, loving to advance with perfect form and rapid steps across the polished floor, but this he confined to Saturdays in fashionable upstairs city salons.

At twilight, pleasantly exhausted so that the muscles of his long legs tingled, he would wander back to the flat of his city cousins, singing aloud the saccharine airs of the Italian opera, and grooming for an hour or two, sup late, and then appear at the "quadroon balls."

He loved the *sang-melées* with whom he danced, certain that any one of them would have been his mistress, but being young yet, and free, and loath finally to tie himself in any alliance, he settled for listening with a smile to the gossip of his glamorously fettered friends. He liked his life, might visit for months on the plantations upriver, loving the luxury of long days on the steamboats, and at home was the pampered darling of his brothers' wives.

After all, he had time to be courtly, made amusing stories, and sometimes in the dim light of some waning party found himself falling in love with a cousin who was about to be married so that he sighed sadly to the night air.

But what were his prospects, actually, asked the mothers of the girls with whom he danced the cotillions, though he had made such a handsome figure in the saddle riding to the front door. Of course he was graceful on the dance floor, played with the little ones, and always on hand to please the fathers, could while away the night with brandy, dominoes, cards. But Ferronaire was a struggling plantation, grown up with the industry, suffering with its experiments, and desperate at times still for capital, then swimming in the profits of a flush season which must sustain it through more mercurial times.

It was his brothers who had built the noisy mill with its belching chimneys and it was they who brooded over the bubbling vats. They led the blacks at dawn through the icy fields to slash the ripening cane before the coming of the frost. He did not care for these things, Philippe, grew bored around the plantation office, and only once in a while, lounging rather arrogantly in his saddle, with gleaming spurs, did he ride out with a friend or two through the fields.

Of course he had his share of these arpents, but what was that, and each of his brothers now with a wife, and children running through the garden and those airy immense rooms?

But Philippe's name was as old as Louisiana, a commodity that was priceless to the ancient families, and he spent his life in the parlors, on the veranda, sipping *eau de sucre* as he bided his time. And kissed the ladies' hands.

Then one evening in New Orleans, meeting his older and very distant cousin Magloire Dazincourt among the quadroons of the ballroom, he perceived in an instant the poverty of this bachelor existence. It had wearied him in the extreme. For here was his cousin at sixty, master of twenty thousand arpents, and though a widower, had the consolation of one small son and four marriageable girls. *La famille* was all, really.

And by summer, Philippe had married Aglae, the eldest and Magloire's favorite, journeying upriver to the endless cane fields of his father-in-law's plantation, *Bontemps*. Its wealth astonished him. Five hundred attended the wedding, dining on plate.

But before that happy event united two remote branches of the family, Magloire had become fast friends with his future son-in-law and entrusted to him (it was a simple matter for a bachelor who lived so much in town) a certain series of duties with regard to a beautiful little mulatto woman whom he kept in a flat in the Rue Rampart. He was building a house for her in the Rue Ste. Anne.

Kitchen and *garçonnière* having survived an old Spanish dwelling recently destroyed by fire, he had got the land cheap and was building a cottage in front, a comfortable but modest establishment to have four principal rooms. But all was to be done as *Ti* Cecile wanted it, his dark beauty, it was her future home. Could Philippe supervise these proceedings, that is, ride in at the first of each week to show these men the master was near at hand? He would appreciate it all the more, however, if on those days Philippe could bring himself to look in on the poor little woman herself, as she was all alone in the flat, and having lost two babies in the past, was again expecting a child.

Philippe smiled. And his respect for his father-in-law mounted. After all, the man was past sixty and worn out, and now in the midstream of such a romance. He had long suspected his own father had known such pleasures when he was young, and his brothers as well. But these were early escapades, and were supposedly stopped at the inevitable marriage, youth being the time for these luxurious alliances of the demi-monde. But whatever the man wanted, he was a widower after all. So one day in 1824, Philippe rode up the Rue Rampart and lifted the brass knocker of this woman's door.

That afternoon in the parlor left him with a lasting and somewhat seductive impression. Of course he had known the lovely quadroons, women so white no real trace of the African remained, and others darker but as charming with their heavily lashed eyes and mellow caramel skin reminding him of the pictures he had seen of Hindu women in books. There was about them an aura of the exotic and wild; and whirling with them over the polished floorboards, his hand lightly caressing this small waist or that rounded arm, he had dreamed of some savage pleasure he had never known. Pity they were so closely guarded, one had to "set them up" to have them, it was the custom, *plaçage*. Promises, rituals, and long-term means. Yet others, pale and stunning in their lofty refinement, struck him as white to the soul; they were all too much like the good women who surrounded him at home, he reasoned. Who would want such a mistress? One could see them shuddering on the pillow as they reached to make the Sign of the Cross.

But here in this long somewhat sumptuous flat maintained by his future father-in-law and cousin, Philippe encountered a piquant combination unexamined before. It was to enter his dreams. For though this woman was fragile and diminutive as a porcelain doll, and done up in the primmest fashion, she was dark, very dark, with skin the color of stained walnut such as one sees in the full-blooded Africans in the fields. It intrigued him, the fineness of her features, her small mouth with its lower lip trembling slightly as she approached him with all the shyness of a child. She was a petite white woman carved in dark stone. And he found himself drawn by this darkness, this glinting brown skin, and

(321)

stifled the near-maddening desire to feel the backs of her hands for their texture, that silkiness perhaps that he had loved in all the black nurses of his youth.

Her eyes were wild with fear like those of some small animal captured in the wood; yet she was older, past twenty to be certain, and did not possess that irritating and dangerous flirtatiousness of ignorant young girls.

She spoke good French, would not sit in his presence until he insisted on it, and smiled now and again with an alluring spontaneity as he endeavored to put her at ease. Her tiny fingers played sometimes with a brooch at her throat; he had never seen such small hands. It would be a pleasure looking after her, and touched by what seemed her near reverence for him, he took his leave reluctantly for the long ride home. Winding his way in the slanting sun, he smiled, thinking his future father-in-law even more the man than he had known him to be before. Cecile, it was a lovely name, Cecile.

But Magloire was ailing by the time of the nuptials and knew it; and eager to acquaint his son-in-law with every detail of his vast plantation, he rode too long, stayed up too late, and at last went to bed with the first winter chill. His little boy Vincent he entrusted to Philippe and Aglae to rear as if he were their own son, and before New Year's, he was carried to the parish cemetery after a well-attended Requiem Mass. Philippe sitting alone that evening on the broad veranda saw in all directions nothing but land which belonged now to him.

He worked hard in these first few months. It was not only the newness of it, the power of ordering so many people about, but he was afraid. Nothing had prepared him for the immensities of responsibility all around. His brothers came when they could, he set his mind on nothing but management and riding the fields all day, ended with ledgers at midnight, almost blind.

And it was time to cut the cane lest the frost come early and destroy it, the vast team of slaves galvanized and ready for the heaviest labor, cords of wood gathered from the mud beaches of the river and the back swampland to stock the roaring furnaces of the grinding house, the wind already sweeping the galleries with icy draughts.

His back ached, it seemed he lived in the saddle, his feet tingling when they at last touched the ground.

But he was resentful of all that fell on his shoulders. It seemed to him time and again that someone else ought to be doing all this, why should he? But under close examination, this made no sense finally. He was wealthy, master of twenty thousand arpents, the scepter was in his hand. But when was there time to enjoy the pleasures of this palatial home he had acquired, dwarfing as it did the old Creole style house in which he'd been born? Here were Grecian columns so wide he couldn't span them with his arms, the grace of spiral stairways, and all about, the sun striking prisms in the baubles of crystal chandeliers. He would have liked to take his ease as in the old days, becoming familiar at leisure with these fine things.

But his brothers drove him worse than he might ever have driven himself, the overseer was at his shoulder constantly, and he was visibly irritated at last with those around him and under him, becoming something of a gruff bully with his slaves. It was fear that lay behind this, naturally. He would rather be loved by them all. But doling out whippings which he himself would not watch, becoming imperious with his cook and his footman, he nevertheless at times lapsed into familiarity with everyone still hoping to be served and liked at the same time.

Yet by the end of the harvest he had learned the plantation. Her yield was enviable, fantastic. Consulting old diaries on the minutest problems, and the changing of the weather in past years, he buried the cane for the coming season, built up the levees, repaired the irrigation canals. A great ball was given just before Advent, with carriages crowding the broad drive beneath the oaks. And Aglae was expecting a child.

Aglae.

Had he been a man of reflection he might have wondered afterward, could he not have seen her character in those first meetings, could he not have been wiser, could he not have opened his eyes?

What marvelous luck it had seemed that she was so pretty, this wealthy cousin, and that she ran her father's house with a firm hand. He liked the dishes she ordered in those early days especially for his pleasure, and at night sinking down into the massive mattresses of her immense and ornate bed, he found her pliant like a child.

But she was more than level-headed and submissive, this dark-eyed girl who sat across from him at table, listening impassively to his rambling conversations, or boasts of overwork to his brothers, without so much as a nod of her head. There was something flinty and cold about her small mouth, her drawn cheeks, something calculating and mocking about those steady eyes. Twice she caught him in obvious exaggerations with a few frigid well-chosen words.

(323)

He would have liked her to laugh at his witticisms, think him splendid in his new riding coats, and cater to his exhaustion when at last he collapsed each night at her side. It was wise to be firm with her, he decided finally, find details where her domestic management was lacking as he had often seen his brothers do at home with their wives. He must make it clear to this remote girl he was not so easily pleased as she supposed.

But all this brought from her was an icy incredulity, and a near-venomous smile. Her mother had died when she was twelve. When she walked up the aisle in bridal white, she had been mistress of *Bontemps* for five years. And realizing the stupidity of much of what he'd said, Philippe was pink with frustration to the roots of his hair. He sat sullenly at the breakfast table in his vast bedroom wishing he were home again in his mother's house.

Aglae's voice was monotone and low as she retaliated soon enough, reporting that the slaves complained of his contradictions, she would not allow her kitchen staff to be beaten, the overseer, old Langlois, were he not placated at once, might leave when he was in fact indispensable, having been at *Bontemps* since before she was born.

This was spoilt behavior, unforgivably arrogant, Philippe declared. Was he not aching in every muscle? He would not tolerate such talk from his wife a moment longer. She merely laughed as she walked out the door.

But she left him in painful confusion. He was injured and awkward in her presence and despised her for it from then on. She seemed forever in the background when he greeted family and friends, measuring him in her silence so that she became cruel in his mind, a vindictive and ungrateful girl. Had he not taken on this monstrous feudal paradise for her sake, and now he lived in dread that she should catch him in some small humiliation or find some evidence of his untutored judgment to throw in his face.

Dinners were agony for him, her sisters buzzing softly of unimportant things, he loathed the sound of her spoon hitting the dish. And he drank late until the recurrent need, flamed in these long hours, to subdue her would lead him time and again to the bedroom door. There was no warmth between the sheets.

As the year passed it grew plain that she did not respect him. Those little witticisms of his, which had so warmed others, sounded ridiculous when uttered in her presence. His charm seemed to wither, and even at Christmas, with the house crowded, he could not escape some stumbling, inept vision of

(324)

himself reflected in her hard eye. While she all the time grew in power, devoted mother to little Vincent and then after uncomplaining labor exemplary with her own child. People admired her at all turns for her poise and domestic capabilities, the slaves adored her, and she became the darling even of Philippe's mother and his aunts. And all the while he kept this secret to himself that she was mean and even vicious to him, trying from time to time to find some way to correct her in the presence of the others, only to bungle this so that apologies were required as he felt the censure of silence all around. If only they knew! A wife should bolster her husband, wipe his brow. She, on the other hand, showed him eternally a deceitful outward respect. And once, alone in his study, he put his fist right through the plaster wall.

Oh, the loneliness of it.

But in his heart of hearts he feared sometimes he knew why her contempt for him had bitten so deep. There was something in himself that he accepted readily enough but did not admire. He didn't really *want* to run *Bontemps*. He had no passion to emulate the dead Magloire, or his own brothers. And ashamed, he also wondered why he had let himself give up that life which had been so dear. He lived in fear of others perceiving this lack of ambition, or of making mistakes through carelessness that he might not be able to correct. And little Vincent, it would be years before he could lend a hand.

But by the end of summer, he was in a state of perpetual fury toward his wife, and wondered at the extraordinary independence with which she could go on from day to day pretending he was not even there. He was sorry for himself and wanted to spite her. And the limp passivity that was offered him at night, that which had so appealed to him in the beginning, seemed now a worse insult than all else he had had to bear. Well, she would give him children, a son already, and another on the way. But this merely added to her glory. He took to sleeping on the study couch.

But when his mother died, he sent at once for a young black maid who had been his favorite at home, and by whom some years before he had fathered a child. Of course he would not soil himself with such sordidness in the future, who would think of it, he'd been a boy (and terrified, his brothers having threatened to send him away to school), but he needed some touch of warmth beneath his roof, and that dear sweet black girl had cried when he left. No one need know more about it, he wanted her there to arrange his clothes as she had done in years past.

However, Aglae upon seeing the woman's copper-skinned little girl had given him such a withering smile that he convinced himself she was of low mind. He would not dream of humiliating himself with some household maid, but he did not shrink from giving everyone the impression through special favors to this woman that he had.

It was near winter again before he went to New Orleans, the second harvest over, the money in the bank. Two of the girls were married off, he was sick of the country. And riding through the narrow muddy streets of the "old city," found himself at the gate of Magloire's little mistress, that sweet Cecile who had lost both her protector and her expected child.

It had been too long since he had looked in on her, he told himself, this was a matter of concern. After all Magloire had been devoted to her, lawyers could not always be trusted to follow through in such matters. But he forgot all this when she opened the door.

"Michie Philippe!" she had cried out, and catching herself in the act of rushing toward him, stopped, her face in her hands.

"Now, now, *ma chère*," he pressed her small head to his cashmere vest. Old Magloire could turn in his grave.

It did not always please him to think of the old man afterwards. There had been a bond between them, a trust. Aglae was his favorite daughter though little Vincent of course was the favorite child.

But Philippe had come to live for these days in New Orleans when entering that small cottage he felt himself grow so that reaching out, it seemed, he might touch the four walls. There were his slippers, his tobacco, the few liqueurs he preferred to brandy; and this soft scented woman who hung on his every word. He thought sometimes he had fallen in love with her eyes. So wide and mournful they seemed to him, never leaving him for an instant, and firing so magnificently when she smiled.

Even the birth of Marcel with all its inconveniences gave him some pleasure. Because he so loved the sight of the petite mother, and enjoyed the sound of the singing as he lay patiently across the bed.

And he was not out of sorts either when those shrewd aunts, Louisa and Colette, cornered him, making him promise to provide a European education for the boy. They were practical women, they had not been consulted in this little arrangement, but indeed they had had many a conversation with Monsieur Magloire, such a fine old gentleman, didn't he agree? "You know, Monsieur, what can the boy do here in Louisiana?" said that clever Colette, cocking her head to one side. "For a girl it's different. But for the boy? An education in Paris, Monsieur, a few years abroad, four I should think, and perhaps the boy might be settled there someday, who knows?"

All right, all right, he would deposit money in the bank for him, he shrugged, opening his coat with both hands. Did they wish to take it out of his pockets? Must he pledge his faith in blood? "Stop it, stop it," whispered his pretty little ladylove Cecile. She came to his rescue, and warmly he beamed down at her from his lofty height. "Forgive them, Monsieur," she said.

"You will provide for the boy, Monsieur, four years in Paris when he is eighteen?"

"Mais oui, but of course!"

II

THERE IS A SAYING in the Catholic Church; "Give me a child until he's six years old and I'll give you a Catholic forever." Vincent Dazincourt was Magloire's son till he was six years old and he remained Magloire's son till the day he died.

No one had to turn him against the kindly blond-haired brother-in-law who told him the best bedtime stories he had ever heard; he was simply cut from a different cloth. He adored his sister Aglae with all the warmth and trust he might have shown his own mother, and she became for him as he matured at *Bontemps* the model of the woman he would one day take for his wife.

At fifteen he was riding the fields every day with the overseer, reading avidly the agricultural journals, and having spent years with Magloire's diaries knew the failure and success of every refining experiment, every innovation in the planting, harvesting, grinding of the cane. Nights often found him accompanying Aglae to a slave's sickbed, and as he rode the vast plantation from its river beaches to its back forest, he knew the names and the histories of every black man and woman whom he passed.

He'd been bookish as a young boy, read the contents of

Magloire's dusty library, went to school for a year in Baltimore and then on to Europe for fifteen months when he was twenty. In short, he traveled, was exposed to new ideas.

But he did not come home to consider the institution of slavery an evil, and being born to it, reasoned that he was a "Christian" planter in the act of civilizing the heathen, so that he carried out his "duty" with conscience and a firm hand. The waste and suffering of Europe's industrial cities had appalled him, and in the midst of his own orderly world he remained convinced that "the peculiar institution" had been misunderstood. But cruelty disgusted him as did all excess, so that he supervised the whip himself whenever possible and observing with a silent thoughtful face all cause and effect in the running of *Bontemps* believed in moderation, consistency, and reasonable demand. This made him to his slaves a more admirable master; at least they knew with young Michie Vince how things stood.

It was possible, in fact, to pass a year in his service without punishment, indeed a lifetime, and anyone might knock anytime at his office door. He saw the black babies baptized, rewarded wit and skill with promotion, but never, never did he set a slave free.

Philippe meanwhile regarded Vincent's ambition with humor, was pleased with his quiet outward respect, and liking to encourage him in worthwhile ways shifted the burdens to his shoulders without argument whenever he showed the slightest interest in assuming them, the slightest good will.

But Vincent went to town as a young man, of course, and not dreaming of any complex alliances, fell hopelessly in love with the volatile Dolly Rose. Never had he known such a woman, dazzling in her high-pitched melancholy, and passionate beyond his wildest dreams. She danced with him at midnight around the spacious rooms of her elegant flat, singing between clenched teeth to the music of hired fiddlers, to fall exhausted finally against his chest. Morning was the time she liked for love, with the sun falling on her shameless nakedness. He buried his face in her perfumed hair.

But after the birth of their daughter she had been unfaithful to him, made him something of the laughing stock, was hostile and arrogant when questioned, only to throw herself into his arms declaring a love that consumed her to the bone. It brought him unbearable pain. He was not destined to understand her desperation and her cruelty. It was doubtful to him that she would ever understand it herself.

Once on a Sunday morning, she had risen naked and slipped into his frock coat, walking straightbacked and jaunty about the room, her smooth naked legs like stems beneath the flaring serge, her hair tousled above the broad shoulders. And seating herself at last on a chair near him, she had drunk champagne from a china cup and said, "Nothing matters really except the ties of blood. All the rest is vanity, all the rest is lies." He was to remember it afterward as his ship plowed the gray Atlantic, those pale stem legs crossed like a man's, the bulge of her breast against the heavy black wool of that coat, and the Sunday sun spilling from the half-opened window onto her loose hair. He had kissed his little daughter before he left, squeezed her arms through puffed sleeves and cried. And then wandering the drawing rooms of Paris and Rome, sought to forget the one while cherishing the other, and coming home found his daughter had just died. It was a judgment on both of them from God.

The night he followed the tall undertaker, Richard Lermontant, to Madame Elsie's boardinghouse, he had been softly coaxed in the direction of Anna Bella by Philippe who had seen her often in the Rue Ste. Anne. But Vincent could hardly think of this because he was bitter and contrite and more miserable than he had ever been. He was done with wild affairs, he had murmured to his brother-in-law whom he had been somewhat glad to see at last among those distant colored faces at his daughter's wake, nevertheless he felt the need more keenly than ever for loving hands.

Those days were agony for him, the days of coming home to little Lisa's funeral. He would remember them always with a vague sense of horror and dread. He had wanted desperately to be with Aglae in some fantastical world where he might somehow speak to her of what he had "done." Yet he shuddered at the thought of going home to *Bontemps*. After all these months in Europe, he would have to endure the most passionate welcome, nieces about his neck, sisters caressing him, when he could think of nothing but that little girl, his Lisa, dead. On the morning after the funeral he awoke in Madame Elsie's boardinghouse to the sound of the child's laughter as if she had been in the room. He could hear it so perfectly that for a moment he wanted nothing but to surrender to sleep, to hold her again in his dreams. He would have given her the world. She had her mother's beauty, and the perfect heart of a pearl. He rose to wander numb about the boardinghouse corridors, the parlors, the open rooms.

Flowers shivered on the empty dining tables, the smell of warm biscuits came from the pantry, and across that sea of round white linen tablecloths, he saw her, Anna Bella, that girl. She sat in a shaft of sunlight working with a needle a small band of lace, and looked up suddenly to him when he came into the double doors. She said something simple to fill the silence. She rose to get for him whatever he might want. It was so hot, she was saying, her voice liquid and sweet and flowing easily into some mellow rhythm of conversation that soothed him as though she had been touching him, stroking his fevered temples, telling his aching heart it was all right. He remembered afterward that he had made her sit down, that he had asked her some feeble, foolish question and that at last assured of the warmth of her voice, he had lapsed into himself again, near in his strangled silence to someone who would talk to him, someone who was warm to him, someone who would give him the tenderest, the most genuine smile.

He was there the following night and for all the rest of the week. Philippe had not exaggerated the special appeal of this American colored girl, he had to admit, as he lay with his coffee, thinking in his bed, this girl with a baby's cheeks, who spoke French so slowly but so nicely, devoid of vanity, as batting her long thick lashes she seemed the natural model for this gesture so often cultivated by women Vincent had never liked. She was not cunning and exquisite as Dolly had been, she did not go to the veins like champagne. But an ineffable sweetness seemed to suffuse her speech and her subtlest gestures, so that he was almost painfully drawn to her in his grief, and felt a near-delicious calm when he merely glimpsed her moving about the rooms.

However, something else stirred deep inside him as he dozed, thinking of her, against his white pillows, something of which he had never before been aware.

He had grown up among black nurses, cooks, coachmen, soft African-voiced beings who surrounded him with gentleness and attentive care. He had felt warmed by their laughter and their hands. And though he would never truly have given in to the desire to force himself upon one of his slave women, he had known that desire in someplace a little less obscure to him than his dreams: that image of the yielding black girl as she sinks into the shadows of the cabin, firelight glinting on her long neck and soulful eyes, begging, "Please, Michie, please don't..." It exploded in his brain as Anna Bella came forward, hips swaying under those scalloped skirts. Yes...this was precisely the brand of nymph that, flushed sighing from the wood, lurked beneath Anna Bella's lace.

Only when he had to, did he return to *Bontemps*. Excuses couldn't cover it any longer. Aglae knew he had arrived, he had picked up his messages at the St. Louis Hotel. So he boarded the crowded steamboat at five o'clock in the evening, intoxicated by the breadth of the mighty river, glad for the first time to be home. He had presents for everyone, sat down to the table laden with his favorite dishes, and clasped in both hands his little nieces and nephews who buried their kisses in his neck. How sweet it had been to mount the front steps, between those majestic columns, to hear the click of his heels on these marble floors. The wealth of Europe could not dim the perfection of all that lay about him, and the priceless devotion of his own kin. He told foolish stories, absurd details of trunks lost, packets behind time, little hotels where he had had to make signs for a razor and basin, and laughing, kissed Aglae again and again.

She was older, remarkably older, and never given to *en-bonpoint* as one might expect at this age, seemed almost painfully drawn. He felt such a rush of relief at the sound of her steps ahead of him in the corridor, the vision of her throwing back the doors to his room. The familiar tone of her voice brought him several times to the verge of tears.

But that night, slipping out of the netting that draped his bed, he wandered out onto the broad upstairs gallery facing the river and thought of his little girl. Over a year ago, he had taken her into his room at the Hotel St. Louis the night before he was to sail. He had fed her himself with a spoon from the supper table, and much to her nurse's disapproval brought her to sleep in his own bed. So Dolly would be furious with him for keeping her overnight. He did not care. He nestled her against his chest in the dark, and when the heavy rap came on his door before dawn, he opened his eyes to see her smile. She had been waiting for him to awaken, she laughed with a shrill and perfect delight.

Now on the cool breeze-swept gallery, gazing out at the distant river which he could no longer subtract from the darkness, the image of Anna Bella wound its way into his grief. He saw those lovely rounded cheeks, the delicate waist, those deft little fingers reaching for the needle and pulling it through the cloth. *Mon Dieu*, he didn't understand life. Patterns did not soothe him because he suspected them. He rubbed his eyes. He would go back to Madame Elsie's before the week was ended, he would think of some excuse. It was as if that colored girl's sweetness mingled with the heavy atmosphere of death that lay over him, like the flowers beside the coffin; only he could not make that distinction, he merely saw those chrysanthemums again, and Anna Bella, in that shaft of sunlight, sewing, alone in that empty room.

Then Aglae came onto the gallery. He felt strangely shaken to see her coming along the rail. She wore a high-necked dressing gown that ruffled out from her ankles in the breeze. She stood quietly for a while as though she knew that he would rather be alone. And then turning, she looked into his eyes.

Only a little light seeped from the bedroom, enough to see all, but not clearly; however, she was in that light as she turned. "Any death is hard, Vincent," she said. "And one of the worst is the death of an innocent child."

He turned away from her, catching his breath.

"Mon frère," she said, "learn by your mistakes." And then kissing him, she left him alone.

He was never to know by what intricate grapevine this news had reached her, or what precisely she had heard. It was unthinkable that Philippe could have told her, no use even considering that. And Vincent and Aglae never spoke of it again. But sometimes in the weeks that followed, when she asked whether he took proper care of himself in New Orleans, might not be coming home too tired for his health and his rigorous schedule, he felt she was pleading with him. And he heard again that admonition, "learn by your mistakes."

Without coyness, he gave her assurances at once. He needed the lights of the city now and then, he wasn't ready after months abroad to settle into the country routine. And forfeiting an occasional plan to visit Anna Bella, he read stories to his nieces and nephews by the home fires instead. He would sit up late in the library, leave his brother-in-law alone to the pleasures of the bottle, and riding out early down along the gray mud beach of the river he looked at the cold sky like a man saying his prayers.

Bontemps had never been so beautiful, so rich. The death of Langlois, the old overseer who had succumbed in his absence, was a sadness. But there was the new man and the new harvest and when had the cane looked so high, so hardy, so green? He would break in this new overseer to his ways, he was home again, went out at night with his lantern to see the foal delivered of his favorite mare, and roaming through the rose garden in the early mist, drank thick soup for breakfast while Cook in her snow-white bandanna pouring the milk for him, said, "Michie, don't you ever leave us again."

Months later, Philippe from the carriage window pointed out the Ste. Marie cottage in the Rue Ste. Anne. The carriage had creaked to a stop. Vincent's soul shriveled as he turned his head. At first he did not believe that he had understood, that here his brother-in-law kept a colored family! And would tell him this casually as they passed the gate!

But the morning after, stopping for Philippe again, he had seen the fruits of this alliance plain enough. There stood the blond-haired boy with the honey-colored skin staring at him with those shameless blue eyes. Kinky hair like that of a fieldhand, only it was the color of his father's. Vincent's cheeks burned.

He adored Aglae! Philippe knew this. But even if they had despised each other, brother and sister, this should never have been revealed to him, this little slope-roofed cottage under the magnolia tree and that oddly handsome blue-eyed quadroon in Sunday best at the gate.

It was more than Vincent could bear. He had ridden back to *Bontemps* in unyielding silence. And in the plantation library at night, he brooded on the promises he had made that very day. Anna Bella Monroe was his now. But by God, that alliance would end with honor and dignity at the very moment he contracted for a proper marriage, and striking the poker on the grate, he made that vow to a wife he had not yet laid eyes upon, a woman he did not yet even know. Anna Bella's house would not be in that street, he would tell Madame Elsie this was his one requirement, he must not have to pass through the Rue Ste. Anne.

III

WHEN ANNA BELLA told Marcel that she didn't care anything for "that man," she had not been telling a lie. She had not let herself care for Vincent Dazincourt because she was convinced that the life he offered her was wrong.

This was not a heartfelt religious conviction, though Anna Bella was devoted to the Virgin and made special novenas to her on her own. She could have lived without the sacraments and was preparing to live without them now. On the

Sunday morning that she saw Marcel, she did not receive Communion but she felt some personal and unshakable confidence that God still heard her prayers. She would go to Mass all her life no matter what she did, and light candles before the saints for all the causes that she knew.

But the Catholic Church was not the church to which she'd been born, and it seemed ornate and alien at times of real trouble, it was a luxury like the lace she'd learned to make, the French language she had acquired. And when she received the offer from Vincent Dazincourt, she had a strong instinct that *plaçage*, that age-old alliance of a white man and a dark woman, was an evil and unwholesome life.

She had seen it all around her, this alliance, with its promises, its luxuries, its ties. And she had known the haughty dashing ladies of the demi-monde, Dolly Rose and her indomitable mother; and such proud and enduring women as Cecile Ste. Marie. But she had seen the insecurity also, and the ultimate unhappiness that such knots spawn. She had never thought of this for herself.

For Anna Bella, there shone across the vista of childhood the warm light of an earlier time when her father and mother had been with her, and there had been simple hearty meals at the deal table, and soft family conversation by a dying kitchen fire. She could remember snatches of things that still conveyed extraordinary pleasure . . . white starched curtains, rag dolls in gingham dresses with shining button eyes. Her mother could swing her up on the hip with one arm, and throw the clothes over the line with the other hand. She didn't remember her mother's death clearly, it seems they sent her out to play. And coming back into the house, she had seen the mattress stripped of its sheet and had known that her mother was gone forever. She could not remember a funeral or a grave.

But all the rough edges had been worn from these remembrances, and so was the sense of time. She had been innocent in a perfect world, and had those parents lived, Emma and Martin Monroe, Anna Bella was convinced she would not be drawn out of innocence now.

But she had been at the barbershop window when the bullet hit her father, and she had seen him, the blood splattering from his skull, as he fell in the street. He had stepped out with his white barber's jacket on, saying to the customer in the chair, "Just you wait." Just you wait. She never forgot those words. It seemed to her, though it must have been wrong, that Old Captain brought her down to New Orleans that very night, stopping at a roadside tavern where she'd been sick and feverish and cried. She had one dress in which she slept, and she'd forgotten her precious doll. She could never remember anyone telling her Old Captain was her father's father, but she knew it, and that he had an old white family in those parts so that he couldn't take her in.

Madame Elsie gave her new clothes, a silver-backed mirror, and put her out alone on the gallery in the dark when she cried. And that mean Zurlina, Madame Elsie's maid, said, "Eat that cake!" as if it were something bad when it tasted sweet. Zurlina tied her sash too tight, yanked with the brush at her hair. "Look at those lips, those thick lips," she would say under her breath, "and that nose of yours, like to cover your face." She herself was a thin-faced mulatto slave. She dragged Anna Bella along the porch saying, "Now don't you get that pinafore dirty, don't you touch anything, be still."

But in bed at night, Anna Bella turned the pages of old books, and hummed the Latin hymns she had heard in church. Madame Elsie gave her a doll dressed as a princess. She held it as she slept deeply in her feather bed. The world was scented soap, starched dresses. Madame Elsie appeared in the dark over her pillow holding a candle. "Come, read to me, child, read to me," she said, her cane scraping on the boards. She sat slumped on the side of her great bed, lace-trimmed flannel gown sagging over her gaunt bosom, too tired it seemed to move the covers over her lap. "See that girl?" she held an oval porcelain of a white woman, "That's my daughter, my girl," she would sigh, her nostrils quivering, and toss the gray braid that hung down her back. "Come on, child." She put Anna Bella on the pillow. They went to sleep.

The gentlemen boarders picked her up, put coins in her hand, remembered in town to buy her a little sweet. And Old Captain coming up the stairs with a thump said, "How is my little one?" Zurlina whispered, brushing her long black hair, "Look at that nigger mouth!"

She was busy all the time, learning French from the neighborhood children, even that mean little stuck-up Marcel Ste. Marie. Always dressed for Sunday Mass, he passed with a solemn face, engaged in the burial of a dead bird he'd found in the yard. She studied for a while with Mr. Parkington, that drunk man from Boston who couldn't otherwise pay his bills. 'Course he was never drunk in the mornings, and she liked to make lace, loved it when the Mesdames Louisa and Colette came to call, showing her the patterns engraved on paper, in their bulging valises they had the needles and the thread.

She read poems to Madame Elsie, learned to walk back and forth across the boudoir with a book on her head for perfect posture, and the Boston tutor had a stroke in his bed.

One afternoon, having finished the lace for a Sunday collar, she wandered out the garden gate. There was that mean little Marcel sitting on the step, his arms wrapped around his knees. His blue eyes blazed under the scowl of golden brows as he watched the game of ball in the street. Someone had cheated, it had gone unnoticed, he murmured when she asked him, he would not "debase" himself with all this again. She understood though she'd never heard the word. She knew the meanness of children perfectly, nobody had to tell her. "Oh, don't play with Anna Bella, oh, don't let's play with Anna Bella. Anna Bellllla! where's your mamma and daddy! Well, she may belong to Madame Elsie, but she's not Madame Elsie's little girl!"

"Come inside," she said to Marcel. "Come on inside and talk to me."

His blue eyes shifted. He looked so mean. Not half as mean as that white sister of his, but awfully mean. Yet getting up from the steps he brushed his pants and said that he would come in. She served him tea like an English lady, she sat amazed with her hands in her lap when he talked of buried treasure, of pirates up and down the Spanish Main. "I know these things," he said with raised eyebrows, "I have heard of these pirates, they used to come storming through this very city, that's why there are gun holes in the walls."

"Fancy that," she said laughing, "it's like I was just reading in this book. See this book?" she took it off the shelf. "I think sometimes I was brought here by pirates. And someday those pirates are going to come back."

They would laugh about it afterward, he didn't know anything about the buccaneers! He lay stupefied as she turned the pages of *Robinson Crusoe*. She made voices for the characters. Sometimes she cried. "Like that, and like that, and like that," he shouted as he showed her how to wield the rapier. Madame Elsie said "Hmp!" in the door. But he had been mortally wounded in the heart (outnumbered) and fell dead.

There were years after that when she expected him daily, putting down her lace if he weren't there by half past four to ask with mild astonishment, "Now, where's Marcel?" He brought her engravings which they colored, showed her how to do very special things with drawings, to make the folds of drapery real, to draw profiles, to draw ducks. He read the papers in French to her, they sneaked away together to view an execution in the Place d'Armes. And were both confined to their separate houses afterward, but he sent her a note by his sister Marie.

When it was that he had ceased to be that sexless golden childhood friend she could not have precisely said. Like so many girls in this steaming tropical climate, she could have borne children at the age of twelve. She loved him. He poked a trash fire in the street, the flames glinting on his rounded forehead and spoke of the end of the world. They stood in the dark yard together in summer looking at the stars. "Do you think it will be like that," she asked hugging herself anxiously, "at the end of the world?"

"I think it will end in our lifetime!" he said triumphantly. "You and I shall not know death at all."

On the day of his First Communion, he sat quite still among all the fuss and celebration and said to her later, "I had the living Lord in my soul." She bowed her head, and said, "I know, I know."

Something to laugh at? All of that? The boy who came last year and walked restlessly around the parlor. The boy who read her the newspapers and listened so attentively when she confessed those childhood memories, how the colored barber of that small town, her father, had carried her on his shoulders down the main street to his shop. "Each one of those rich men, they had a shaving mug with their own name. My Daddy wore a fresh white apron. It was the cleanest shop." She lay with her head back against the wall. "You know sometimes I want to go back to that town, just walk down that dirt street."

"I'll take you there, Anna Bella," he said.

"I just want to see my Daddy's shop again. I just would like to walk out there, you know, where they buried him, you know..." she sighed, hugging her arms.

She loved him. He loved her. They even said so to each other, but there was something virginal in the way that he had spoken the words, something that sensed its own nobility in transcending whatever older people might mean by such utterances. Older people cheapened them with kisses and embraces. In short, she thought once in the night air under the stars, her hands on the gallery railing, "He really loves me for myself, Marcel. And that's just not enough!"

But he was a child yet, despite the waistcoats and his

pocket watch and the long dreams he unfolded of Paris, the Sorbonne, flats above the waters of the Seine. Time was all around them she told herself, until the day that Jean Jacques, the cabinetmaker, died in his sleep.

It was a young man who came to her that night to pour out his sorrow, it was a young man's terror that she witnessed, a young man's first understanding of death. And as the hours ticked to midnight, it was a young man, bleary and raw with pain, who had told her in a soft and musing voice,

"You know, Anna Bella, if I hadn't been born rich, I could have learned the cabinetmaker's trade from him...learned to make things as well as he made them...and I might have been happy with that all my life."

But his future was to be that of a man of means, how could she tell him that it made her heart ache to think of his leaving her, to know that someday he would go away? And then had come that moment when their lips touched, when drowsy, his sorrow softened by wine, his eyes had burnt with a low fire as if he were seeing her for the first time. He loved her, loved her in the new and disturbing way that she had loved him for so long. And Madame Elsie saw it all through the crack of the door.

In the months that followed, Madame Elsie insulted him, rebuffed him, but Anna Bella was sure that it would be rectified. It never was.

She would see him in the streets, his face painfully knotted, a bundle of leatherbound books under his arm. Or in the Place d'Armes once where he stood with legs apart, drawing in the dry dust with a long stick. He turned a tense face toward her during Mass, seemed on the verge of speaking even there, of slipping out of the pew and moving toward her, but he never did. His legs grew long, his face lost its early roundness, and he cut a sharp figure, almost dramatic, so that people marked him when he passed.

But week followed week without his calling, and soon the long months had made a year. And realizing desperately that she had lost him, somehow long before the appointed time, she gave way again and again to tears. She would have run away with him then, done anything with him, but the pure fact of it was that these were wild imaginings. Why after all should he leave the snug world in which he had such a lustrous future, and when had they last been alone together, even exchanged words? No, she had lost him, not just the young man who had kissed her in the parlor, but the boy who had been her closest, truest friend. She was at a loss to un-

derstand it, but understood at the same time that her own
life was changing in a manner she could not prevent.

Madame Elsie whispered to her of the "quadroon balls"
and the old ways, scoffing at any talk of a colored husband,
that was disgusting to her, "for the common," she said as she
sent Anna Bella out at night to let "the gentlemen" in. "My
rents are thirty dollars a month," she said with lowered lids
and an ugly baring of her yellowed teeth. "My gentlemen are
the best!" And letters came from Old Captain's parish priest
that said he would not get up from his broken hip, and might
not see his little Anna Bella again.

Sometimes she thought of the sons of the old families of the
gens de couleur, families she had known for a little while when
she was still studying with the Carmelites in school. But theirs
seemed a remote and exclusive world, and she was the daughter
of freed slaves. She was not invited to those homes, not even as
a little girl to play. Yet she was frightened of the hardworking
free Negroes around her, men like her father who'd bought their
freedom and learned a trade. These were the men who came to
repair the plaster, spread the new wallpaper in the parlor, or in
the little shops that lined the Rue Royale, fitted her new boots
for her, or took her order for a new four poster for the best upstairs rooms. Good men with money in their pockets, they
tipped their hats to her after Mass and called her Mamselle. So
why did they frighten her? Because she dressed so well, spoke
so well, carried herself like a lady, had the hairdresser in each
Saturday afternoon, and had grown accustomed to directing a
household of slaves?

One night late when she was alone in the parlor of the
big house—fearing at any moment the bell at the door and
the long walk down the polished corridors with some strange
white man who might whisper an irritating familiarity which
she would be bound to ignore—tears came to her eyes. What
was it that she herself wanted, she asked. What would she
have, were there the choice? But the answer eluded her.
Pushed and pulled she had no clear vision; she could think
only of the traps that awaited her. And helplessly, she felt
the need of time.

That Marcel could have left her so completely made her
angry, suddenly, and a little bitter. Perhaps it was a lesson;
perhaps life was full of such lessons. People left you one at
a time and forever all along the way, mother, father, Old
Captain, and your only real friend.

Then came that moment in the Mercier hallway, outside

(339)

the room where the Englishman lay dead. There was no doubt then that Marcel loved her, and it was his love for her as much as anything else which had kept him away. Even as he cursed her, she'd known it and known that he would never come back. It was inconceivable to her afterward that she had slapped him, and that night alone in her room, she had known the deepest anguish of her life. No matter that Madame Elsie had shaken her when she returned home, called her "cheap," declared that Monsieur Vincent Dazincourt had been asking for her, and had gone back to the country disappointed, Anna Bella was a little fool!

And there were the flowers from Monsieur Vincent on the table, and a bottle of French perfume. Monsieur Vincent had family, fortune, fine manners, had courted and abandoned the beautiful Dolly Rose. "He wanted to see you!" Madame Elsie snarled as she slammed the door.

The days after had been agony. But Anna Bella had to see Marcel. Foolishly she had gone to the little birthday fête for Marie Ste. Marie only to witness the bitter controversy between Dolly Rose and her godmother, Celestina, to learn what treachery she had worked on the distraught Michie Christophe. On the verge of tears, she had returned only to come face to face with Monsieur Vincent in the front hall. She could not talk to him now, she could not talk to anyone, and rudely, almost rudely, she turned her head.

But in a low voice, all propriety at the expense of feeling he was complimenting her, telling her that he had only just learned of her nursing the unfortunate Englishman who had died at the schoolteacher's house. She was admirable, generous, he was saying, to have taken this into her own hands. Indeed, he had known the Englishman in Paris, and had seen him once or twice here at home before his death. Indeed, he had heard much praise of Christophe, the schoolteacher who was now quite in Anna Bella's debt.

But at those words, she turned to face him quite unable any longer to restrain herself or her tears. "Michie, he's in bad trouble, the schoolteacher!" she had cried. "He's out of his mind since that Englishman died because he thinks it's his fault. Michie, it's Dolly Rose he's gotten mixed up with, with that mean Dolly Rose! And she's got a gentleman, a Captain Hamilton, coming back from Charleston to find it out this very afternoon."

There was no caution at this moment. That no decent well-bred girl of either color should speak so to a man, Anna Bella knew, but it did not enter her mind. Cheapen herself in his eyes? She didn't care. Monsieur Vincent knew Dolly, had quarreled with her, enough people had told Anna Bella this, and she was imploring now as she said, "She's nothing but trouble for a colored man, Michie! She's the meanest woman I ever knew."

But never would she forget the seriousness of his expression as he took her outstretched hands, the immediate comprehension in his eyes. "Don't you upset yourself a moment longer," his voice had been hushed as he went to the door. "I shall see to this, rest assured."

It was the next afternoon before she saw him again. She had just come up the stairs to find him watching her from the door of his room. "You must not worry anymore about your schoolteacher," he had said to her softly, gravely. "He has only his grief to trouble him now."

"Oh, Michie," she had smiled, breathless, and utterly trusting. And silently he had stood before her, his hands at his sides. Behind him the snow-white bed with its great drifts of netting seemed a cloud in the late afternoon sun. He cut a black figure against it, except for his pale face, his pale hands. But something flickered in his black eyes as he watched her so that she stopped, at a loss. Slowly he turned and shut the door.

That night he asked Madame Elsie if he might speak to her, and she was quite surprised to see them both enter her little upstairs parlor, to see Madame Elsie nod and withdraw.

Vague speech followed, so proper, so veiled that finally, very frustrated, he stopped. "A flat was what I had in mind," he murmured, looking out the window. He turned his back to her. His meaning was just dawning on her. She stared at him with wide eyes. Then he said a strange thing. "I would like very much to have one of those flats along the Rue Royale, with the high windows, to have a fern in the window on a marble-topped stand. I've always admired those windows with the lace curtains drawn back, and the ferns on the marble-top stands. Do you like such things?" He turned toward her, his face open, seemingly innocent. He looked like a boy.

"It would be lovely, Monsieur," she said.

"But Madame Elsie insists that I purchase a small house. Of course I have no objection, the house would be in your name. She knows of a likely cottage... If you were to have a look..." He stopped.

She was crying. She had put her fingers to her temples.

He was shaken. "I have to go home now, back to the country," he murmured. "It will be November, after the harvest, before I return. You can give me your answer then. And if that answer is no, I won't trouble you after that. You won't see me again."

"Yes," she whispered through her tears, nodding her head. "Let me think, Monsieur." She couldn't flatter him, even say good-bye. She was thinking of Marcel, and a little key had turned in her heart.

But on the day she left Marcel's yard, smarting to feel the eyes of Monsieur Philippe on her as she passed the cottage door, she came home to strike a bargain with her whole soul.

Vincent was breakfasting with friends in the vast dining room, and only rose to come to her in the boardinghouse parlor when they were completly alone. It was that hour when the slaves would change the linen tablecloths, sweep out the corridor and begin the preparations for Sunday dinner, the week's most sumptuous meal. He shut the double doors. November rain flooded the alleyway along the house, and the steam rose on the panes around them till there seemed no place but this one empty room. He soon gave up as he stood behind her, murmuring respectful assurances. He had discerned from her bowed head that the answer was no.

"Will you be gentle with me, Monsieur?" she whispered, turning suddenly.

"Ma belle Anna Bella," he breathed as he drew close to her. She felt in his vibrant fingers the first glimmer of the passion that had motivated him all along. *"Ma belle* Anna Bella," he sighed, touching her cheek. "Just give me the chance."

IV

MARIE LOVED HIM. Marie *loved* him. Marie loved *him!* Not Fantin Roget who had brought her flowers this very afternoon, nor Augustin Dumanoir who again, and in vain, invited her to the country, nor even Christophe, yes, Christophe, who stopped in at the little soirees with amazing frequency, always with some small gift for the aunts though he gazed at Marie as one might at a work of art, and bent with a peculiar poise to kiss her hand. No, Marie loved him, Richard Lermontant, and it was not impulsive, it was not passing, it was not subject to change! He was dreaming as he moved through the crowded Rue Royale, vaguely annoyed by the traffic, vaguely annoyed by the insistent Marcel who repeatedly tugged at his arm.

"But aren't you even curious about it, actual pictures of people and things as they appear? Why, this is the most marvelous invention to come out of Paris, and only from Paris could such a miracle have come, I tell you, Richard, this is something which will change the course of history, the world . . ."

"But Marcel, I haven't time . . ." Richard murmured. "I should be at the shop now. And frankly, sitting still for five minutes with my head in a clamp, well . . ."

"You had time to see Marie, didn't you?" Marcel pointed to the door. A small and dingy dormer was fixed next to it with an ornate sign:

PICARD, MASTER OF THE DAGUERREOTYPE
MINIATURES IN FOUR SIZES
Upstairs

Richard was stopped, staring at the small collection of pictures on display, all of them monstrous actually, the people staring from their silvery background as if dead. "No, I simply see no reason . . ." he turned, resolute, his shoulders rising in a shrug.

Marcel pressed his lips together angrily, there was something of desperation in it as he searched Richard's face. "We never do anything much together anymore, do we?" he asked. "We never even see each other, you don't come to school but two days a week."

"That's not true," Richard said, the voice now softened with its intensity, "we see each other all the time." But this lacked conviction, Marcel's words had the real truth to them, and why they were growing apart just now Richard didn't know. "Listen, come home with me for supper, come on, you haven't been home with me in weeks."

"I will if you come upstairs now with me," Marcel answered. "Richard . . ." he bent his head to one side, elongating the name. "Richaaard, suppose I told you that I brought Marie here last week, and that she had a beautiful picture made, of course she's not going to be the one to suggest an exchange . . ." he raised his eyebrows with a slight shake of the head, a smile. "Come on!" he started up the hollow wooden stairway at a run, and Richard sighing, went after him. A picture of Marie, she hadn't even mentioned it, but surely, no, absolutely not, she would never have given it to anyone else.

"But what maddens me," Marcel was saying over his shoulder as he turned on the landing, "is that you don't care about this, and it's utterly remarkable, Richard, that you have no curiosity, that you don't even want to see the camera and how it works for yourself." Richard didn't bother to answer, and it seemed they had had this very same conversation two years ago, only then it had been furniture, stairways, aren't you even curious about how these things are made, how wood is joined together, lacquered to bring out the beauty of the grain? No!—he had shrugged his shoulders then and NO!—he was shrugging them now. Suddenly, on the second staircase, he drew up, catching his breath.

"Mon Dieu!"

"Oh, those are just the chemicals, come on," Marcel said impatiently, and he rushed up and into the waiting room, a foul blast of warm air hitting Richard as he followed. He drew out his handkerchief quickly and placed it over his nose. It was an ugly room, the carpet looking somewhat ridiculous on the poorly painted floor, the few fine chairs obvious remnants from some more harmoniously decorated past. And here again on the walls were the Daguerreotypes, dead people, except for one very remarkable picture of a church, beautifully detailed, that did startle him and draw him to it, just as Marcel was reaching to take it right off the wall.

"Marcel," Richard whispered. "Don't do that!"

But the Daguerreotypist had already poked his head through the velvet curtain, a white-haired Frenchman with very pink skin and octagonal spectacles, "Ah, it's you," he said to Marcel. "I should have known."

"Half plate for my friend, Monsieur, please, if you want to start preparing it," Marcel answered, but he was staring at the picture so that his lips slurred the last few words.

It was the St. Louis Cathedral taken obviously from the center of the Place d'Armes, and looking over Marcel's shoulder, Richard could not help but be impressed. It was extraordinary the clarity of it, the details down to the cobblestoned street, the blades of grass in the square and the leaves, the individual leaves on the trees. "Did you do this, Monsieur?" Marcel called after the man.

"No!" came the deep disgusted reply from behind the curtain. "It was Duval, and he took twenty plates to do it, at least!"

"I'll buy it!" Marcel followed him, and Richard tightening the handkerchief entered the studio cautiously, the stench of the chemicals positively sickening him so that he felt weak. The light from the undraped windows was garish, and showed a bare floor at the far end of which was a small stage as if set for a play, with a chair, table, wallpapered board propped behind it, and just enough drapery to suggest a window where there was none.

"... And what should we charge for it!" Picard, the Daguerreotypist, was grumbling as he wiped frost from the panes, "With all the chemicals he wasted, it's priceless!" Heat from the roaring stove brought out the moisture on the top of his balding head.

"And Monsieur Duval, is he here, will he sell it?" Marcel asked. He was carrying the picture about with him as he made a nervous circle on the floor. "Sit there, Richard," he said off-handedly pointing to the carved chair. And then a voice came from beneath a small tent of black muslin saying,

"Yes, I am here, Marcel, I won't sell it."

"You know, it's one in a thousand that captures this quality," Marcel said to Richard revealing the picture again as Richard moved to sit down. If it wasn't the chemicals, it was heat, he was going to be ill. "I mean most of them are merely pictures, but this is more than a picture ..." Marcel went on.

"And twenty plates to do it," said Picard again. But Marcel, as if jerked by a string, had put the picture down on a work table against the wall and advanced suddenly on the small muslin enclosure from which the voice had only just come.

"Monsieur," he spoke to the black cloth, "let me in?" A laugh echoed from inside, "Come in."

"Your friend is mad for the Daguerreotype," the old man said. He reached over Richard's shoulder to make some small adjustment of the velvet drape. The chair was short for Richard, naturally, and he had to stretch his legs to the limit of the stage. "I tell you he brings us a new customer every few days."

"Monsieur, you don't think you could open a window, do you, just a little, perhaps?"

"I'm sorry, my boy, the dampness, it's impossible. But you'll get used to it, just take a deep breath, and put your head back against the brace, you won't be here very long."

"Five minutes?" Richard grimaced, removing the handkerchief. He felt his stomach was rising to his throat.

"That was last year, my boy, forty seconds at the most," Picard said. "A small price to pay for a work of art."

"Ah, so you believe it's art, then," Marcel's voice rang out from the tent of black muslin. And there came a low laugh from this invisible person, Duval.

"I said to you *sometimes* it's an art!" Picard pointed a didactic finger at the tent. "I said to you sometimes, when a man has nothing better to do than destroy any plate which doesn't meet with his personal approval or stand for two hours in the Place d'Armes making a spectacle of himself to get a picture of the St. Louis Cathedral in the proper light. But not when a man has to keep clothes on his back and food on the table, it's not an art then." He stalked toward the camera, and for the first time Richard observed it, a wooden box on an ornate pedestal with three legs.

"Art, art," murmured Picard, "with people complaining every day about the fact that it renders them precisely as they look. 'Go to a painter, then' I say, 'if you've got the money!'" The camera was large and in the front of it was a rimmed aperture with the glint of glass. The man adjusted this now, cranking the stand to get the camera higher and then, staring with a bit of visible irritation at the tall boy in the chair, picked up the entire apparatus to move it back.

What if it were halfway decent, what if he could give it to her, Richard was thinking, what if it didn't look like a corpse? He felt the most profound humiliation on that point, he would never, never entrust it to her if it had the slightest hint of his profession, he clamped the handkerchief over his mouth again and convulsively held his breath.

Beneath the muslin of the little enclosure, Duval, a lean white Creole in a threadbare coat, was whispering confidentially to Marcel, "But don't tell the proportions, I feel strongly this influences everything, and I do not want it known . . ."

"Of course not," Marcel whispered, his eyes intent on the plate which had just been lifted from the first of the coating boxes to be placed into the next. "I would not tell anyone," he said. Light leaked upon them from the seams of the tent, it sparkled in the loose weave of the fabric.

"And I'll tell you another little secret," Duval whispered, his eyes as wide, as intense as Marcel's, "just a bit of grease when I buff the plate, suet, nothing more than suet from the butcher's, it has a decided effect."

"Have you ever thought of opening your own . . ."

"Shhhhhh!" the white man grimaced at Marcel, bent suddenly with the effort not to laugh as his eyes rolled quickly to indicate Monsieur Picard beyond the cloth. "In time," he made the words silently with his lips. "In time."

Marcel was gazing at him with an acute case of admiration, the way he often gazed at Christophe.

"Let me take the picture," he said suddenly. "Just this once."

"No!" came Picard's loud voice from outside. "Young man, you go too far."

"But Monsieur," Duval emerged, throwing back the flap. He slipped the plate quickly into the camera as Marcel stepped out. "Why don't you let him take it?" Duval's face was young, appealing with something of the charm that softens others, and good breeding which provided a certain lubrication to his words. "It's the preparation, really, and what happens after, that matters, and well, he brings us so many new customers..."

Picard threw up his hands.

Triumphant, Marcel stepped up to the camera and suddenly squinted at Richard in such a manner that Richard was frankly exasperated, Marcel looked as if he were mad. Richard could not possibly know that Marcel was deliberately forcing his eyes out of focus so that he could see the scene before him entirely in terms of light and dark shapes. And Richard was further confounded when Marcel bounded toward him, ripping the heavy velvet drape away. This rendered the outline of Richard's black coat perfectly distinct against the wallpaper, and his face of deep olive complexion, partially framed by raven hair, was now equally clear. "No, don't sit so rigidly," Marcel said now, the voice gentle, slower than usual, "let everything about you soften, even go limp, your eyes, your lids. And think, think of something that is more beautiful to you than anything else," the grave voice went on, the face utterly intense, "do you have it? Good, then don't see me at all, see that beautiful thing that calms you and lulls you while I count. One, two, three..."

All the way home to the Lermontant house, Marcel continued to stop to look at the results. He would pull up short as Richard pressed his lips together in exasperation, and pulling open the pressed paper cover stare at the small plate. "Dreadful, dreadful," he would mutter with perfect sincerity at this image which had positively amazed Richard, flattered him, in fact, and had him burning to give it, in spite of his inveterate modesty, to Marie. He would put her picture by his bed, no, under his pillow where no one would see it, no, in the drawer of his chest.

"She'll think it's quite fine," Richard shrugged. His feet were getting numb from the December cold. He was hungry besides. And to be late for supper in the Lermontant house was a mortal sin.

"I overexposed it," Marcel sighed. "I should have asked Duval before I started counting, I should have stopped when he said."

Richard laughed lightly. He could not understand the intensity with which Marcel invested the slightest task or experience, and sometimes he felt a vague relief to live devoid of those peaks and valleys himself.

"When you see the picture of Marie which Duval took, then you'll understand." Marcel shut the cover for the seventh time and handed it wearily to Richard. "If you want to know the frank truth it would take Marie these days to get you to notice anything."

"Oh, don't be so foolish," Richard said softly. "If *you* want to know the frank truth, you are simply too young to understand."

Marcel gave him such an acidic smile then he was startled by it, even a little wounded. "Richard," he said, "what you know about women could be placed in a thimble, and I've just taken you to witness one of the finest inventions in the history of the world and you paid not the slightest . . ."

"You exaggerate," Richard said, as they turned into the Rue St. Louis. The house was just ahead. "You have always exaggerated, and you think anything which comes from Paris has to be wonderful, Paris, Paris, Paris!"

"Marie, Marie, Marie," Marcel muttered. But then he clasped Richard's hand and said sharply, "Look."

Both boys came to a halt. There was a small crowd ahead on the banquette before the Lermontant house, there were shouts. And then, clearly, Richard could see two men scuffling, others attempting to stop them and one of them was Rudolphe, to be sure. Richard bolted, easily outrunning Marcel with long strides, so that he reached the scene first.

There was a white man lying on the banquette, his yellowish face twisted with a snarl, his top hat floating in the gutter, as Le Blanc, a white neighbor held Rudolphe around the waist. "Stop him, Richard, stop him," Le Blanc was shouting, "Get him into the house."

"You filthy nigger," the white man was shouting as he struggled to his feet. "You damned nigger, call the police!"

Doors were opening everywhere, people rushing out on the galleries, as Richard quickly lifted his father back into the front hall. Marcel could see Grandpère standing there, and behind him Giselle's husband, Raimond, looking positively stupefied, as Richard and his white neighbor, Le Blanc, forced Rudolphe into the front room. Marcel slammed the door.

Giselle was hysterical. She was sitting by the fire, her bonnet half off, tears streaming down her swollen face, while at the table, her smallest son, Charles, had begun to howl.

"He wouldn't leave me alone, he followed me, he wouldn't leave me alone," Giselle choked. "I just tried to make him stop following me, to leave alone, I told him I was going home. I know enough English to know what he was saying to me, to know what he thought I was!" She shuddered, screaming, her eyes closed, and stomped both her feet.

Rudolphe's chest heaved, blood streamed from a cut on his temple, and furiously he pushed Richard and Le Blanc away. "Damned Yanqui trash!" he roared. "Damned Yanqui trash!" But then he turned on Giselle. "And you, you flighty stupid little baggage, no, you can't wait for your mother to go out with you, you can't wait for your husband to go out with you, you've got a brother six-and-a-half feet tall but you can't wait for him to go out with you, you have to go tearing around the streets, shaking those flounces..."

"Rudolphe!" Madame Suzette was aghast. "For the love of God!"

But Rudolphe suddenly grabbed Giselle by the shoulder and was shaking her, "Don't you tell me you didn't do anything to give that man ideas!" Giselle put her hands over her ears and screamed.

Marcel was mortified, and Raimond stared helplessly. But all at once and quite without warning, Richard reached for his father and tore him away from Giselle. Richard was furious as he took his father by the lapels. Everyone went quiet at the sight of it.

"Don't you do that to her!" came the low voice which might as well have been a bell in the silent room. He was trembling with rage. "Don't you do that to her! She's not to blame for that common trash, don't you know that! Leave her alone!"

For a long moment Rudolphe merely stared dully at his son. And then Giselle, letting out one miserable wail, ran from the room. Rudolphe jerked his coat loose with a resentful gesture and turning his head slowly, almost stupidly, he settled down at the head of the dining table in his chair. The white neighbor excused himself at once to Madame Suzette, assuring her that he would be "right next door." And Raimond gathering little Charles' hand led him after Giselle, up the stairs.

Richard had gone to the front windows. His huge shoulders were hunched as he stood with his back to the room. And Marcel was thoroughly miserable, loving the family but not being part of it, and quite unable to help.

"What sort of a man was he?" Grandpère's voice broke the silence. He moved slowly and somewhat painfully back to his usual chair at the table, his shoulders bent beneath the coat he always wore in winter, his neck protected by a wool scarf.

Rudolphe made only a weary gesture of disgust.

"A ruffian or what?"

"Ah, top hat, frock coat," Marcel murmured. "Well dressed at least."

But at those words Madame Suzette glanced sharply at her husband and then at his father. And Grandpère pressed his glasses, thoughtfully, to the bridge of his nose. It was precisely what he had wanted to know. And within twenty minutes the police had rung the bell.

By nine o'clock, they had obtained Rudolphe's release. Marcel had gone with Richard to find Remarque, the family lawyer, a white man of considerable influence, and bail had been set and paid. The Yanqui was in fact from Virginia, and well-to-do, it seemed, since he was staying at the St. Louis Hotel. Rudolphe was charged with verbally insulting a white man, a crime in itself, and physical assault with intent to murder, and trial was set for the following week. But he said nothing to the boys as he walked home from jail, he gave no hint as to whether or not he had been imprisoned with slaves, runaways, or the lower sort of criminals, and he said nothing of his handling by the police. He entered the parlor long enough to tell Madame Suzette that he wished to be alone now, to rest, and he advised Marcel to go on home.

Nevertheless, Madame Suzette followed him upstairs. And when she came down she found the house dark, and Richard sitting alone by the fire.

"How is Giselle now?" he asked her.

"Asleep, finally." She stood for a moment at the small table by the windows, opening the cover of the Daguerreotype which Marcel had salvaged from the front banquette, and when she saw there the image of her son, very lifelike and extremely pleasing to her, she made a wan and evanescent smile. Then she closed the picture and came silently over to settle in the chair opposite Richard, her feet on the edge of the hearth. "The man ... actually laid his hands on her," she said with determined simplicity and calm. "He tore the lace of her sleeve. *Mon Dieu*, I feel so very very tired!" She pressed her forehead with the fingers of her left hand. Richard thrust the poker beneath the soft layer of gray coals and a latent flame brightened so that his mother could see the expression on his brooding face.

"And *mon Père?*" he asked.

(350)

Her eyebrows knit, her forehead creasing with the long heavy lines that always indicated intense distress. She shook her head.

After a moment, she said,

"I want to tell you something about your father. Your father didn't really mean what he said to Giselle."

"Maman, I'm so worried about him now that I can't possibly be angry with him for what he said. I'm angry with myself that I laid hands on him, raised my voice to him . . ."

"No, *mon fils,*" she said almost crossly. "You did the right thing. Your father should never have taken out his anger on Giselle. But you see, your father felt helpless. If that had been a man of color you know very well what he would have done . . ."

"I know that, Maman," Richard said.

"But he was helpless. He knew the minute he struck the man that he'd be arrested. And don't you see, that helplessness was more than he could bear. If he could blame Giselle, if he could somehow say that it was all her doing, then the burden of defending her passed from him. And he couldn't defend her. He couldn't call the man out as any white man would have done."

Richard was thinking. In his own wordless way he knew that this was true. But he relived the moment; he saw his father shaking his sister, he heard those words, vulgar, insolent, spoken in the presence of the entire family, in front of that floundering and stupid Raimond, in front of Marcel, in front of old Le Blanc. He tried to erase this from his mind. Wasn't it enough to picture his father's somber face when he had emerged from the jail, wasn't it enough to realize what this hearing in court could mean? But he was angry with his father, and it seemed that Rudolphe always had some splendid excuse for his outbursts, that in his rages and his injustices he was always somehow on the right hand of God. It confused Richard hopelessly.

"I have to tell him somehow that I'm sorry," he said softly. "I have to let him know . . ."

"No, *mon fils,* you do not!" Madame Suzette said. "Leave it. And your father will respect you for leaving it."

"You really believe that, Maman?"

"Richard, there's something you must come to understand. I had hoped that by this time you would have already perceived it and that the perception of it would have given you some inner peace. But I see now you are not going to understand without my help. Your father in many respects is simply not the man that you are."

Richard was amazed. Scanning his mother skeptically though respectfully, he inclined his head to one side.

"Maman," he almost laughed, "what I have perceived a thousand times is that I am not the man my father is, and never will be! I lack his vigor, his force. And tonight, when only for an instant I evinced that force, it left me shaken and in doubt. Do you think *mon Père* would ever doubt himself for such an action? Do you think he doubts himself for what he said to Giselle?"

"Yes, I do think that he doubts himself for it. I think he doubted himself at once. But he'll never say so to you and he will never say so to Giselle. And that, *mon fils,* is not always the mark of strength."

Richard's brow was furrowed. He was watching the fire.

"You have your own brand of strength, Richard," she went on, "and has it never occurred to you that it is finer, and more honorable than that of your father? Has that never crossed your mind? You do not realize the gulf that separates you from your father. *Mon fils,* to build a house such as this by the sweat of one's brow is a great accomplishment, but to be born in a house such as this and to all the advantages that surround it, that is another world. Your father is a gentleman and a man of honor because he has worked to become a gentleman and a man of honor. But you were born to it, Richard, it's bred into you without a flaw. You are of a different ilk."

Madame Suzette could see that she had stirred deep waters, and she was not surprised to see that Richard was displeased.

"It's a strange thing we do to our children. We work tirelessly to make them better than we are. And if I ever thought that you would come to look down on your father, I wouldn't dream of speaking to you as I do now. But you're too much the gentleman even for that. You're too wise already, that would be too base for your soul. But something else is happening, something I've watched with frustration for years. Your father's force, as you call it, intimidates you. You do not value yourself for the wiser, surer person that you already are.

"Believe me when I tell you that your father is not angry with you for standing up to him as you did tonight. And you must remember, Richard, you must remember in the future, that when you stood up to your father, your father backed down without a word. Again, if I had less faith in you I would

(352)

never speak to you in this way. But my faith in you, I know, will never be betrayed."

She waited for a long moment, but it was clear to her that Richard could think of no answer. It would take time for her words to penetrate which was of course as she had hoped. It occurred to her that in all these years, she had never once felt that her counsel was lost on her son.

"I have one more bit of advice for you," she said, rising, and placing her hand on Richard's shoulder when he started to get up. "Don't talk to your father of the court hearing unless he wants to talk of it. And for the time being, don't say much to him with regard to Marie Ste. Marie. But remember, you are his only son, and his cherished son. And though he berates you night and day, though sometimes I see nothing but blind anger in your eyes when you are looking at him, remember, he lives for you, Richard. You and Giselle...you give your father's life its real meaning. And I know you'll never abuse the power of that position. But for God's sake, use it when you must. Now I must go to your father. And you should go to bed."

"Maman," he stopped her at the door. "What if they...if the judge rules against him?"

"That won't happen!" she said. But her voice lacked conviction, and her shoulders were bent as she went silently up the stairs.

She was right.

On the morning of the hearing the courtroom was packed. All of Rudolphe's white neighbors had turned out, together with a dozen white customers, and a large body of the rich and respectable *gens de couleur*. A score of character witnesses could be called, and to spare Giselle an appearance in court, a sworn statement from her was in Monsieur Le Blanc's hands.

And the American from Virginia, a prosperous but uneducated man by the name of Bridgeman, appeared with an expensive lawyer of a fine old law firm much patronized by the white Creole gentry, a man who knew the courts of the First Municipality and spoke fluent French. But before he could state the case clearly, the white man, Bridgeman, spoke for himself.

He had been attacked by a "negra," he declared, in a public street. And before witnesses and in the plain light of day that "negra" had tried to kill him and that "negra" was still walking around free. In his own state, they would have strung that "negra" from the nearest tree branch and lit a fire be-

(**353**)

neath him to send him on his way. What was this place, New Orleans, what with the abolitionists in the north and "negras" attacking white men on the street?

The faces of the *gens de couleur* were impassive, Rudolphe's expression as if it had been carved in stone. Bridgeman's lawyer finally succeeded in getting him to be quiet, and in rapid French he commenced to state the real elements of the case.

A man of color had here verbally insulted a white man which was of itself against the law. In addition there had been a violent physical assault in the presence of witnesses from which Bridgeman was fortunate to escape with his life. His client meantime had merely attempted polite conversation with the daughter of the defendant thereby opening himself to this shameful abuse. In simple, untheatrical language, the lawyer reminded the judge that the city's vast free Negro population was increasing daily in numbers and constituted a perpetual nuisance, if not a threat to the white race.

Monsieur Remarque, Rudolphe's lawyer, was equally restrained in his presentation, his nasal French droning through the court. He had a sworn statement from Giselle Lermontant that this man Bridgeman had followed her from the front of the St. Louis Hotel insulting her, annoying her, frightening her until she reached her very door. He refused to believe the house in the Rue St. Louis was her home, and at the appearance of her father heaped him with abuse. By the man's own admission he had never seen "nigger women got up like southern belles" and wanted to know "what manner of house is this?" Witnesses would be produced both white and colored to state that Bridgeman had refused to leave the Lermontant doorstep, that he had laid hands on Rudolphe Lermontant's daughter, and all those who could attest to the substance and character of the entire Lermontant family were too numerous to appear in this court. Jacques Le Blanc, a white neighbor, was to be the first of these witnesses, as he had seen the whole affair.

But the proceedings had only been underway for some three-quarters of an hour, commencing with Rudolphe's own calm and rehearsed statement, and witnesses following one another and lawyer countered lawyer, when the judge at last raised a weary hand. All the while he had been listening as if half asleep, his soft wrinkled cheek resting on his knuckles, fingers occasionally stroking his white beard. And now he awoke from this sublime stupor and held forth in droning English marked by such a heavy French accent that all strained to hear.

(354)

That free men of color were bound under the law to show respect for white persons, indeed, never to deem themselves equal to white persons, of course, this was plain enough. But the law extended protection to free men of color also, respecting their property and their families, their persons, their lives. It was never the intent of the State of Louisiana that such persons, though inferior, should become the victims of wanton violence at a white man's whim. Rudolphe Lermontant had been protecting his household and his daughter. Case dismissed. He banged his gavel, gathered his papers, and shuffled through the rear door.

A soft roar rose from the assembled crowd and it seemed all were on their feet at once. Bridgeman stood flabbergasted, his face engorged with blood, though his lawyer obviously was not, and urged him to keep his mouth shut.

But the man forged through the thickening crowd in the aisle, turning theatrically to the white onlookers and declared in a booming voice, "A negra standing up to me in a court of law. A negra laying hands on me in a public street!"

Marcel was almost to the door when this commenced, but both he and Christophe turned to look back. The man, his eyes red and brimming with tears, stood staring at all around him in disbelief. "And what am I, then," he demanded, the fleshy mouth quivering with self-pity, "if a negra can stand up to me in a court of law?"

Marcel was struck silent watching him. The face so full of outrage, the voice sincere beyond doubt. "A negra, a negra!" Bridgeman nodded as he insisted again. The man was actually hurt.

But then Marcel saw that Rudolphe, too, was staring at the man with the same awful fascination that Marcel himself felt. Rudolphe's face was blank, solemn, and then without a word he walked out of the court. Marcel forced himself to look away from the white man, and only in passing now did he see Christophe's face.

And Christophe's face was unlike the face of anyone else at hand. Because Christophe was about to laugh. Only some weariness prevented him from doing so, something akin to boredom, and suppressing a smile, he merely shook his head. It was so frankly disdainful that for a moment Marcel clung to it, and attempted to work his own mouth into a smile that he could not feel.

It seemed everyone was happy then as they spilled into the Rue Chartres. Madame Suzette came quickly from the back pew in the Cathedral where she had been waiting, and people pressed to shake Rudolphe's hand.

"I want to stay with Richard for a while," Marcel said, and Christophe, shrugging as if he found the role of disciplinarian unpleasant, said, "Of course."

But Rudolphe did not appear to share the common relief, and as soon as he could, he took his leave for the shop, telling Richard to accompany his mother home. Marcel watched him walk off alone down the Rue Chartres, and the vision of the man, though there was nothing remarkable about it, filled Marcel with gloom.

A celebration was called for. As soon as they reached the house, Richard got a bottle of good wine from the back and brought it up to his room. Marcel had already built the fire and the two of them toasted the victory right off, settling back in their chairs. The Lermontant house had about it an almost antiseptic cleanliness which Marcel had always found appealing, softened as it was by the sheen of fine furniture and waxed floors. But this room he loved above all others because its high lace-curtained windows looked over the Rue St. Louis; and Richard's immense desk, packed as it was with bills and other business of the undertaker's shop, was the picture of order even to the small brass cylinder which held a cluster of quill pens. The coverlet of the bed was green satin and in winter, drifts of velvet hung in deep folds from the canopy above.

But Marcel was quite surprised to note, as he surveyed all this with the usual pleasure, that the sharp clear Daguerreotype of Marie had been added to the room's few ornaments. She peered at him from the center of the small ornate case which stood open on the marble top table beside the bed.

So the exchange had been made in spite of everything, Marcel thought, and as always he admired Duval's work, the man's sense, not only of how long to expose the plate itself, but of every element of the picture, every detail of the background which provided a shadow, a line. Of course what Marcel had never bothered to tell Richard about that little session at the picture studio was that Duval and Picard had thought Marie was white, and there had been an inevitable shock when it became clear that she was Marcel's sister, a shock which both men had taken pains to disguise. And though Marcel smiled faintly now at the perfection of the portrait, that memory lent its particular darkness to the gray cloud that was fast settling over him, a cloud which was settling over Richard as well.

"To victory!" he said again, attempting to dispel that cloud, and Richard did not answer, nor did he lift his glass.

"*Mon Dieu,* we ought to be celebrating!" Marcel tried again in a moment. And to this Richard merely nodded as he stared off.

But it was coming clear to Marcel, as he sat there, what was wrong. They had never been brought close to the law before, any of them, not Marcel, not anyone that he knew, certainly not the mighty Lermontants. And it had reminded him that they were people of color living in a white man's world. Their own world was magnificently constructed for forgetting that, the Lermontant house itself a veritable citadel, but all of them were fortified in a thousand ways. And today, those fortifications had been besieged. And it was not only Bridgeman who had penetrated the battlements, it was the judge with that weary and heartless recitation of their "inferior status," as much as it was the white man in his heartfelt declarations, who had brought the realities of the situation crashing home.

Marcel was scowling now into the dregs of his wine. And had no spirit to reach for the bottle on his own. Any white Creole father might have killed Bridgeman for his insult to Giselle, not even waiting perhaps for a formal appointment at the dueling oaks. But there was to be no satisfaction for the Lermontants. And what would it have been for a poor man of color, for any one of the thousands of hardworking free Negroes who were hauled into the recorder's office daily for squabbles on streetcorners or arguments in bars? A crime to verbally insult a white man, Marcel grimaced in disgust. And found himself again envisioning that bored and distant expression on Christophe's face in the court.

Well, it was all well and good for Christophe to find it amusing. Christophe seemed forever "above it" because Christophe was here by choice. Marcel reached for the bottle without thinking, without realizing he had let out a sharp little sound of anger, despair.

Richard hastened to pour the wine for him like a good host.

"It's at times like this that I think of one thing," Marcel murmured. "And that is setting foot on that boat for France." Why pretend anymore this was a celebration? Why pretend the "victory" had been enough?

Richard only nodded at this, as if he were quite unconscious of Marcel's probing stare.

"And you know," Marcel murmured, the voice devoid of feeling, "you don't talk much about that anymore, our going

(357)

to Paris. In fact, it's been months since you spoke of it at all. In a way, that's what we were getting to the afternoon all of this started when Uncle Rudolphe got into the fight."

"Paris, Paris, Paris," Richard said softly to indicate that he remembered. "Marcel, it's far from my thoughts."

"Is that why you haven't been coming to class regularly? Is that why you're spending more and more time in the shop?" Marcel's tone was mildly accusatory.

Richard's eyes shifted dreamily to him and attempted to fix on him, as if to fix on the subject at hand. "I'm not going, Marcel," he said. "I'm not going with you to the Sorbonne, and I'm not going with you on the Grand Tour, and we've both known that for a long time..."

"But Richard, you're not even needed in the shop!"

"No," Richard took a swallow of wine. "But I am needed here. In this house. I don't know," he shrugged, looking away again. "Perhaps I've known this all along and it was just fun to plan with you, and dream with you, it made school so much easier, and so I did it, knowing I would never go."

Marcel's face appeared almost angry. But a languor lay over both boys, a sense of defeat. "I couldn't live here," Marcel whispered, "not one more day if I didn't know I was going to France. If I didn't know that at least there would be those years when I could live and breathe as a free man."

Richard's expression was serene and detached. He put his elbow on the arm of the chair and stared at the subtle movement of the curtains against the glass. Cold air seeped in at the windowsills, and he could feel it despite the fire. He was startled suddenly to see Marcel's expression underscored with something bitter, something bordering on rage.

Marcel rose silently and moved across the room, lifting the Daguerreotype of Marie from beside the table.

"And I thought you felt the same way I did. Until you became enamored of my sister." He glared at the fine white image in the frame, and then he put it down abruptly as if distracted, exacerbated in this vein. "Richard, you know this is the time of temptation, this is the time when young men forget all about the vows they made in childhood, not just the vows they made to each other, but the vows they made to themselves. The world has a way of closing in on us now, inundating us with the practical, and the enticing, and sometimes even the small."

Richard listened to this patiently. He was struck by the conviction of Marcel's tone as well as by the uncommon maturity of the words. Marcel who so often eluded and discouraged Richard with a scintillating passion, seemed to have struck something undeniable and just a little too complex. But there was quiet resignation in Richard's tone when he answered.

"I know what you're saying," he said. "But believe me, Marie has little to do with this, Marcel. I always knew I wouldn't be going with you to Paris, I knew it as soon as I was old enough to understand what my brothers had done."

"Richard, I'm not saying go for the rest of your life! I'm not saying you should leave your family as your brothers did. I'm only saying that while we're young still we can do things that in later years will be impossible..." He stopped, and again there was that distraction in his expression as if he had touched on an inner pain, a secret stress. "Now I'll be saying good-bye to you, too..."

"I've taken on more and more responsibility in the shop because I want it," Richard said calmly. "I'm not the scholar you are, Marcel, and not the dreamer besides. I never was, and even if my mother and father insisted that I go abroad for a while, I'm not sure that I would accept. It isn't merely that I'm their only son now or that I wouldn't recognize those brothers of mine—wherever they are—were I to meet them in the street. It's that I have a feeling for my father's profession, it's become my profession, too. My life's settled, Marcel. It's like a puzzle, and all the pieces are fitted into place. Except one. Marriage, that's the remaining piece. And if Marie, if she will actually consent, if I can bring her home as my bride...well, that will be my Paris. Don't you see?"

"So it's come to that, has it?" Marcel said.

"I love her," Richard whispered. "Didn't you know that? Could you forgive me were I to tell you that she loves me?"

"Forgive you!" Marcel's smile was bitter. But then it became light. He settled easily into the chair and watched Richard fill his glass for him, feeling now there was something a little felonious about drinking at midday. "You and Marie." He was absorbing it, of course he'd seen it, yet to hear it stated in such a great perspective, it gave him a feeling of solemnity and somehow a feeling of peace. If he could leave his sister, his beautiful and strangely sad little sister married to Richard...why, the future was becoming too inevitable, too articulated, as childhood melted away all around him and dreams became a matter of certain steps.

"Then you approve?" Richard whispered.

"Of course I approve. But you're sincere, aren't you, really sincere when you say that your life is here?"

"I'll be content with that life," Richard said. "I'm content now."

"Well," Marcel rose slowly leaving the glass untouched. There was still time to go to school. "I don't know whether you are simply more courageous than I am, Richard, or whether you've just had better luck. One way or the other I envy you."

"Envy me, you?"

"You have a place in this world, Richard, a place where you truly belong."

V

IT WAS THE WEEK before Christmas. Anna Bella sat at the marble top dresser in the only ball gown she had ever owned. The little parlor of the cottage glistened. Zurlina had just given the furniture a last dusting, and had beaten the art square before stretching it out on the waxed floor before the hearth. Decanters of bourbon and sherry stood on the sideboard with glasses in a shining row.

All of the furniture Anna Bella had chosen was light in feel, she preferred petit-point to damask, and had hung lace curtains with only a strip of velvet around each window at the edge. A Queen Anne table stood on tiptoe in the small dining room, already set with gold-edged china, and ornate sterling service and brand new napkins in their heavy rings.

Only the bed was out of scale to these small rooms, rearing its high mahogany back almost to the ceiling. The tester writhed with Cupids frolicking in scalloped garlands. It was a bride's canopy, the sort made specially for the wedding night.

Now and then, when Zurlina opened the back door, a waft of supper came with the cold wind. Gumbo was simmering in the low slope-roofed kitchen, there was chicken roasted in the iron pot, two dozen oysters scrubbed and waiting to be opened, warm bread in baskets on the back of the stove. Zurlina would sleep in the room beside the kitchen for these next weeks until Vincent Dazincourt provided Anna Bella with slaves of her own. She was not happy with this at all, though Anna Bella had bought her an expensive brass bed.

However, since Dazincourt had chosen Anna Bella, Zurlina had shown her a new begrudging respect.

"How long do you think he'll stay?" Anna Bella asked, looking at herself in the mirror between a pair of candles. The hairdresser had very skillfully layered the waves along the side of her face. Madame Colette had come late in the afternoon to make the very last adjustments on this tight and perfectly fitted blue silk gown.

"He can stay as long as he wants to!" Zurlina said. "He can stay till Mardi Gras next year if he has a mind!" she laughed coldly, bending down to open the bottom drawer of the armoire. Anna Bella, through the mirror, saw her lift out the white nightgown to which she had so carefully sewn the intricate lace. There was a catch in her throat at the sight of it being laid across the bed.

"Now don't you ring that bell unless he wants some supper," Zurlina said. "You serve him the coffee yourself, and don't you sit till he tells you to sit, and remember just how he likes that coffee, and how he wants his bourbon, so you don't ever have to ask him again. Now he just might not want any supper, he's up at the boardinghouse now."

"Oh, I hope not," Anna Bella bit her lip. She couldn't endure the thought of it, the long meal as if nothing were to happen afterwards. She had been living in the cottage for a week and she was sick with waiting.

However, her days had not been unpleasant. Old friends of Madame Elsie's had come to visit her with gifts, and to her utter amazement Marie Ste. Marie had come, too. She had brought Anna Bella a very beautiful little lap *secrétaire*, inlaid with gold, apologizing for a broken edge saying it had been passed through many loving hands. Anna Bella had been delighted. The very next day she had used it to write a note to Marie in thanks. And Gabriella Roget had stopped in one afternoon with her mother to present Anna Bella with a silver dish for sweets.

In fact, it seemed all the world was abuzz with news of this alliance, people had complimented Madame Elsie on her shrewdness, and Dazincourt's affections had cast Anna Bella in a new and somewhat flattering light. Women who hardly noticed her before nodded after Mass.

Zurlina poured a little perfume into the palm of her hand and massaged this gently into Anna Bella's shoulders. Anna Bella seeing that thin haughty face in the mirror looked away.

"Don't be anxious," said the old woman. Still Anna Bella didn't look at her. She didn't want to hear any unkind words.

Zurlina took a tiny bit of cream on her fingers now and tilting Anna Bella's head touched it to her eyelashes to make them seem darker, longer. Anna Bella held still patiently. "You are prettier than I thought," said Zurlina, with a lift of her chin, "yes, very pretty indeed."

Anna Bella's large black eyes studied her, searching her face for some meanness.

"Everybody's been very good to me," she whispered.

The old woman snorted as if this were foolishness. She pulled a long pin out from her *tignon* and made some little adjustment with Anna Bella's hair. "Be smart for once," she said in Anna Bella's ear. "Get that gloomy look off your face. Learn to smile! They're jealous of you, all of them, you got what they want." Zurlina picked up Anna Bella's hand and slipped another gold ring, set with a pearl, on her finger. "Stop thinking about that Marcel Ste. Marie."

"Oh, stop it," Anna Bella went to pull away, she had known some meanness was coming.

"I heard you ask Michie Vincent if he could come and visit you, you're a fool!" Zurlina said. Their eyes met through the mirror.

"What passes between Michie Vincent and me is my business," Anna Bella said attempting to look hard, her lip quivering. "And if you don't like what you hear, then don't bend down by the keyhole."

"I don't have to bend down by any keyholes to know what that boy is up to," Zurlina smiled. The candles below did not flatter her face, her eyes were too much in shadow, the expression was eerie. Anna Bella drew herself up, rubbing the backs of her arms.

"Seems to me you ought to build up that fire," she whispered, eyeing Zurlina.

"It's that Juliet," said Zurlina in a dry whisper. "Night after night." She gave a low hollow laugh. "He plays the good schoolboy by day and that man plays the good teacher. And then when Madame Cecile's asleep, he slips down those stairs ..."

"Stop it, I don't believe anything you say."

"... and up to that bedroom, night after night. Sometimes in the morning he goes, just before sunup, he has his own key to the gate." Her wrinkled face was crimped with laughter. "They dine together, those three, alone in that house, just one big happy family," she sneered, "and she has that boy to warm her bed, night after night."

"That's a lie," Anna Bella whispered. "Michie Christophe wouldn't let that happen. Michie Christophe's one of the nicest men I ever knew."

"Michie Christophe!" Zurlina snorted. "Michie Christophe! He can't get that crazy woman in line. So he gives her the boy." She shrugged.

Anna Bella shook her head.

"Did you think that boy wanted you?" Zurlina hissed.

Anna Bella's eyes narrowed. She peered up at Zurlina through the mirror, saw the evil play of the candles on her cheeks. "You stop it!" Anna Bella said. "Don't you say one more word to me about Marcel Ste. Marie!" she said.

But nothing changed in the woman's smile.

Anna Bella rose abruptly, pushing the chair against her and went into the parlor alone. She lit the candles on the mantel, those on the sideboard, and took her place by the fire.

"You don't know what you have, you!" Zurlina hovered in the doorway. "Don't you be the fool and throw it away."

Anna Bella turning her back said nothing. It had been over a month since she had seen Michie Vincent, she wished she could remember anything special about him except that he was handsome and that she had resolved to give herself to him with a pure heart.

He was late in coming. It had been raining for hours, Zurlina was gone. The cold air swept through the rooms as he opened the door, and she saw his shadow leap suddenly forward from the fire. He held a bouquet of roses in his hand, the only dash of color about him except the soft ashen pink of his lips. She had forgotten the man's presence, his strong steady gaze, his black eyes. An elusive perfume seemed to rise as he removed his black serge cape and threw it carelessly over a chair. She went to take it, her hand out, when he stopped her.

"Do you want some supper, Monsieur?" she whispered. "Why, there's gumbo and oysters and, why, there's anything you ..."

"I've never seen you in silk," he whispered. And touching her shoulders lightly he moved her as though she was a statue planted in the center of the room. He had not touched her since that last day in the parlor of the boardinghouse, he had come and gone, visiting only with Madame Elsie in the back upstairs. His white cheeks looked utterly smooth above the sleek black of

(363)

his whiskers and the eyes, deepset, gleamed from the neat lines of his eyelids as if these had been drawn with a pen. It seemed the sense of belonging to him passed over her for the first time, and at that same moment she smiled.

She took a step back and began to cry.

"I'm afraid, Monsieur!" she whispered, all dignity and coquetry utterly lost. He would be so disappointed. She looked up at him through the glaze of her tears.

But he was smiling still. "Of me, Anna Bella?" he whispered. "Of me? Why, you're frightening me, now, Anna Bella, come here."

But this was mere nonsense he said to make her laugh. He was all confidence and gentleness. He guided her directly past the carefully set little table into the bedroom and toward the bed. She could feel his eyes moving lovingly over her, hungrily, she could feel an urgency in his hands. He stood behind her, his hands on her naked shoulders, and then on her naked arms. He kissed the back of her neck and waited and then breathing deeply he kissed it again. "O Lord," he whispered. A startling chill moved over her flesh, and without meaning to, she became nearly drowsy, head falling to one side.

"You'll be gentle, Monsieur . . ." she whispered. He turned her around. She could see the flames in his cheeks, hear that rapid, urgent breath. And suddenly she understood as he held her how much he wanted her, how much he wanted all of this.

"Sweet, sweet, that's what you are, the word is sweet," he breathed, kissing her. And then his hands moved rapidly over her hair. He pulled the pins out, he caught the curls as they unraveled. "Please, take it off . . . no, here," he sat on the side of the bed, "let me watch you, I won't hurt you. No, don't touch the candle. I want to see you. You don't know how pretty you are."

He ripped at the strings of her corset, and sliding her chemise off onto the floor, clasped her tightly, almost painfully at the waist. He ran his fingers over the soft marks left in the flesh by the whalebone, and lifted her quickly into the bed. She closed her eyes as he undressed, and did not open them until she felt his kisses again on her naked breasts. He was stroking her all over as if he could not see enough, feel enough, savor enough. And she was suffused with a drowsiness that seemed to come from the way that he said, over and over, *"Ma belle* Anna Bella, *ma pauvre petite* Anna Bella."* It was almost an hour before, unable to contain himself any longer, he seemed to become rigid from his shoulders

to the tips of his toes, mounting gently, gracefully, careful
not to crush her with his weight, as he gathered her under
him in his arm. But she was yearning for it, the pain was
nothing, she could hardly feel it at all. Her head was thrown
back in some delicious paralysis in which he had become the
mover of her limbs. She let out a little laugh when it was
finished. His pleasure had been acute, and he was lying back
on the pillow beside her, his face smooth in contentment, his
hand gathering hers by his side. "Was I gentle?" he smiled.

"Yes, Monsieur, very gentle," she said.

She was drifting into sleep when she realized he was dressing by the firelight. He put on the robe that Zurlina had laid
out for him, and ran a comb through his long hair.

It seemed a gift of the gods that he was so uncommonly
handsome, "Go to sleep, *ma bébé,*" he said leaning over her.

"Are you happy with me, Monsieur?" she asked. Zurlina
would have been so furious if she had heard.

"Splendidly happy," he said. "Can't you tell?"

She was asleep again when he came back into the room.
She thought she should get up, attend him at once in whatever he wanted, and struggling she broke the surface of her
dream. She'd been riding south with Old Captain, stopping
at one plantation after another where she'd slept in spacious
bedrooms in his arms. A black woman in a white kerchief
had been saying, "Let me rub that child's feet, look at that
child's feet, those feet are cold!"

"I'm coming," she said sitting up so the counterpane nearly
slipped away. She had to catch it at her breasts. He sat beside
her. He was holding something in the dark, too large to be
a book, she couldn't see what it was.

"Where did you get this?" he answered. She put out her
hand.

"Oh, Marie, brought it to me, she's my friend..." she
stopped. "You put it on a table to write letters, or on your
lap in bed."

It occurred to her then, without much reality, that he
might not know that she could read and write, and she wondered if he could disapprove. What would he think when he
saw her books that were still in the trunk, or her little diary
with its gold clasp?

"Marie?" he asked.

"Marie Ste. Marie," she said. She wondered if he would
know the name. It frightened her suddenly. She knew his
relation to Michie Philippe, she knew all about it. Madame

Elsie had investigated him completely. She wished now she hadn't brought the name into it at all.

"Aaah..." he answered after a while, and kissing her told her to go back to sleep.

She watched him standing in the firelight with it for a while before he went out the door. He had put it on her dresser after rubbing some small spot beneath the lock that no longer had a key.

Later in the morning while he still slept clutching the rumpled pillows, she picked it up and tilting it toward the gray window saw the letters there that spelt *Aglae* all but rubbed away. It meant nothing to her this name, only perhaps that some lady had owned this long ago, it had a fine patina that might have been enhanced by this person named Aglae. Yet she wondered at it, and the way he had held it, as she put it aside.

When he went out finally, promising to be back for supper, she had wrapped her cape around her, ignoring Zurlina's outraged protests, and walked the long windy streets to Madame Elsie's where she wandered alone in the rain in the backyard. A nest of ferns still grew in the shelter of the cistern. She dug up the best of these herself. It was in the window in a porcelain pot, its spears spreading in the steamy warmth of the cottage, when Monsieur Vincent came home.

VI

IT WAS A MONTH after Madame Elsie died that Anna Bella learned she was pregnant. This was early spring, and the winter having retreated slowly still gave them chill damp days. Not a fortnight had passed without a visit from Monsieur Vincent. He would come swinging through the gate with quick hard steps, carrying flowers, and sugar liqueurs in his arms. He had bought Zurlina after Madame Elsie's passing, gotten Anna Bella's modest settlement from her out of the tangle of the courts, and matters had settled into a routine. He ate heartily, rose early, studied late by the fire. Sometimes in bed naked from the waist he read the papers he had come to New Orleans expressly to buy or went through treatises on economics, and the cultivation of sugar in other lands.

He had papers from the land office which he examined, always locking them up afterward, and went off to lawyers in the St. Louis Hotel, bringing back candy for Anna Bella

or some fine article from a shop window he imagined that
she might like. Sometimes she laughed at these gifts, they
were so strange, so luxurious in their uselessness, little statues, a foreign coin in a minute rosewood stand, ancient bits
of lace for her to copy that were themselves so fragile they
required a frame.

As the weather warmed and the garden blossomed she felt
as if she'd always known him, and she couldn't even remember him as that earlier remote and frightening young man.
He seemed very young to her at times, a boy of twenty-two;
yet at others, he was a specter at her door with his gleaming
black hair, those magnetic eyes, his dark cape wrapped
around him as if he were the figment of doom.

But in their day-to-day domesticity, he had taken on a
perfection in her eyes. She loved the sight of him at leisure,
his linen shirt undone at the throat so she could see the thin
curls of hair on his chest. He had this same soft growth on
his wrists where she liked to play with it and move her fingers
through it as if it were a wild land of tall grass and they were
little creatures on the run. But it was his face that was the
perfect part, she often thought, loving the high cheekbones
and the graven eyelids, and eyes like beads of jet.

The mere sight of him, unexpected at the gate, could make
her weak. A shock passed through her body often in her
dreams, and opening her eyes in the empty bed she felt a
craving all over when he was not there.

He would kiss her all the time as if he could not get enough
of it, not in passion but some lovely pleasurable tenderness
such as one lavishes on little girls. And she, loving to touch
him in any way, would come round him in his busiest moments to work the tired muscles of his neck and shoulders,
even once in a while to run her hairbrush gently through his
thick hair. She liked to roll his curls on her finger until with
a tightening of his lips, he looked at the ceiling and reached
out for her hand. But even then he smiled, kissing her fingers,
it was impossible to think of him in a temper, the mere idea
of it could fill her with dread.

But on the night that she was to tell him of the coming
baby, she was uneasy. She had realized some time ago that
he was skilled at interrupting the act of love just at the
crucial point to prevent conception, and he had not consulted
her in this, nor had she wanted to question him. But now
that she knew for certain she was pregnant she was filled
with a dull misery, fearing his unhappiness, and her own

unhappiness, and that he would not be pleased, nor would he love this child.

The night was warm when he came, and he asked at once for a bath. Zurlina had long ago set up his broad boatlike iron tub in the small unused back bedroom of the cottage, and he peeled off his clothes as the water on the stove began to boil. Anna Bella got his soap and the towels and filled the tub. She lit the candle on the washstand, and turned her back demurely as he came from behind the screen and slipped into the steaming water. He let out a moan of pleasure. She picked up the soap and leaning over daintily rubbed it into the washcloth that she brought along his back.

"Do you love me?" he asked playfully.

"You know I love you, Michie Vince, why do you tease?" she said. She rubbed the soap well into his neck, lifting his dark curls and holding them up until she rinsed him. She touched them lovingly with the towel.

"And what do you do when I'm gone?"

"Think about you," she said.

"And when you're not thinking about me?" Vincent laid his head back on the curled edge of the bathtub, sliding deeper into the water, and looked up into her eyes.

She came round the tub, dropping down on her knees with the grace of a curtsy, and began to gently soap his chest.

"So, tell me why you're not glad to see me," he said in a low voice.

"Why, Michie Vince, what do you mean?" she asked. But it was no use trying to hide it. He took the washcloth out of her hand. "Leave that, I'm clean enough," he said. "Talk to me, Anna Bella, what's wrong?"

She rose slowly, her hand instinctively moving around her waist. "I do so want a little baby, Michie Vince, I guess, I guess I would never want anything that made you unhappy with me..."

"Is that it, then?" he asked softly. She didn't dare to look at his face. She moved slowly to the coal stove and opened the door just a crack to let out some heat. He had stepped out of the tub behind her and drying quickly, slipped into his robe. She heard him padding across the bedroom, and took a deep breath. A strange thought passed over her, clear and wordless, that gave her exquisite pain. She had not planned to love this man really. She had not ever expected it. She loved Marcel too much. And she knew too little of Michie Vince to expect anything, besides. But she had been utterly won over in the past months by his genuine gentility and his brooding charm. She loved him. It was that simple. She loved him and respected him, respected all that was decent in him, honorable, a code of behavior that seemed to extend to all human beings who had not lost his trust. She had sensed before now that this man would treat her decently long after he had ceased to want her, as he treated everyone decently, and that respect had so warmed her affection for him that somewhere, mysteriously it had turned to love.

That he was ecstatically happy with her she understood, but did he love her? She was not so sure.

When she went into the dining room, she found him sitting in his armchair by the empty parlor grate.

"Come here," he said wearily. And as she obeyed he put his arm around her waist. "It isn't fair of me, is it? To ask you to wait?"

"Michie Vince," she said. "It's already done."

"Aah," he sat back. She could see his relief. He hesitated for a moment and then rising wound her in his arms. He kissed her fervently, and sweetly at the same time.

"You know, I'm a fool," he said. "I can already see it, I can see the glow in your cheeks."

She shook her head, this was all flattery.

"No," he said. "It's true. You've got to have everything, do you hear me, everything that will make you comfortable. Do you understand?"

They dined early. She had not told Zurlina this news, and he seemed to sense at once that she didn't want to talk about it when Zurlina was near.

"And how long will it be, then?" he asked. "Before you must...well, stay in?"

"Oh, a few months," she said. "I'm not worried about all that."

"I am," he answered.

"But why?"

"Because I know that when I'm not here, you're very alone."

She laughed suddenly with delight. "Well, when that little baby comes, it won't be that way anymore, then I'll have part of you here with me all the time." She stopped, not sure what she had read in his face. Perhaps she'd said too much.

"What about that girl?" he asked, leaning forward on his elbows, "the girl who gave you that little *secrétaire?*"

"She only came that once," Anna Bella shrugged. "We

were never really good friends, it was Marcel who was my friend, Marcel, her brother, you remember me telling you all about Marcel."

"And does he come...when I'm not here?" He had given his permission for this quite explicitly and there was nothing of suspicion now in his tone.

"No, he doesn't come," she said. She didn't want to talk of this, even to think about it, she wanted to think of the baby, or think of nothing at all. Just be in this room, with the light of the candles and Michie Vince sitting comfortably across from her, and she was very surprised when he said,

"Would it help if I were to speak to him, to tell him that he might visit you if he likes?"

"Would you do that!" she whispered, amazed.

"I'm going to be gone for long periods this summer, there'll be too much work at *Bontemps*. There'll be months when I can't come to see you at all. You told me once he was a brother to you, that you were the closest of friends..."

She studied his innocent, trusting face. His quick black eyes moved expressively as he spoke. He had met this boy once, Marcel, he was saying, it would be a small matter putting him at ease.

She experienced a jarring sensation then because she was suddenly flooded with memories that seemed to come from another world. And as these memories inundated her, she had the odd experience of thinking about two incidents at the same time. On the one hand, she was exquisitely aware of Marcel's presence as if he were in this room, not the Marcel who had kissed her, but the raw and deeply trusting friend who had parted from her that last time they'd been together alone in the *garçonnière*. And on the other hand, she had an immediate and unexamined recollection of Lisette laughing in the back kitchen as she reported to Zurlina that Marcel was indeed spending his nights with Juliet Mèrcier. A sadness came over her. She was still looking at Michie Vince, and her love for him was so strong and so undoubted that she felt a bitter-sweet longing for Marcel as one might for a loved one who was actually dead. But was it possible that some ugly carnality had only arisen for a short time to mar that friendship which had been finer, more vigorous than any she'd ever known? Was it possible to somehow regain that innocence, that trust? Here she was with child, and there he was with a mistress, and in her mind she went back, way back to some evening in the parlor behind the boardinghouse when the two of them as children had been alone. The subject of the conversation had long escaped her leaving behind only the impression of closeness, of pure and certain love.

"Would you do that, Michie Vince?" she asked. "Would you really do it? I think if you were to tell him it was all right, he might come."

"You know, *ma chère*," he said with a peculiar look of wonder, "for you I'd do almost anything, anything that is within my power to do."

He wanted to make love. He had given the series of indefinable little signals, rising without a word, wandering into the darkened bedroom without the candle. She heard the faint soft sounds of the quilts being folded back. As soon as she was in his arms, he alarmed her with his passion, stunned her with rapid kisses, his hands exploring her body with a new boldness that neither of them had known. She did not realize that her condition had excited him and relieved him. He didn't have to be careful anymore, the blood was teeming in his brain.

Later she found him again in the parlor, alone. He turned to embrace her at once with such a frightening urgency that she brought up the candle and looked into his face.

"What is it, Michie Vince?" she asked. "Is it the baby?"

"No, no," he shook his head shutting his eyes. She believed him. Often she had seen this struggle in his face. And now, as always, he said it was "nothing, nothing."

"Just hold me," he whispered. It seemed that passion did nothing to quiet this. But strangely enough she felt closer to him in these moments, when he needed her, clung to her. And all that was between them passed through their bodies to one another, it had been the same many times when they'd parted at the gate and a forlorn being she did not know had peered at her from his black eyes.

It was that strange being, gentle, relentless in his silent and consuming need, who lived with her for the next few days.

And when it came time for him to leave again, she watched him go in the grip of his dark feeling, and felt a gnawing pain. She knew him better than she had ever known anyone, and yet something divided them, hopelessly, something she knew instinctively had little to do with any fault in herself.

But what she failed to understand about Vincent was this. All her life it had been easy for her to tell her troubles to others, to lay her head on Old Captain's chest, or let the tears flow from her eyes on the first night of love, whispering,

"Monsieur, I'm afraid." She knew at once what troubled her, or broke her heart, just as she knew what was dishonest and wore on her nerves.

But for a man of Vincent's makeup such confidences were a luxury he would never enjoy. And even if he had somehow managed to overcome his profound disinclination, there were reasons why he could not confess to her the particular troubles on his mind. She knew the Ste. Marie family, his brother-in-law, Philippe. It was unthinkable that he could burden her with the turmoil at *Bontemps.*

For in the months after his return from Europe he had found that the new overseer, far less scrupulous or experienced than the deceased Langlois, had been given a free hand. Money was missing from the coffers obviously, or wasted in inefficiencies, Vincent could not at first tell. And during his months abroad a pregnant slave woman had been beaten to death. A hole had been dug in the ground over which her body had been stretched for the whipping so as to protect the child. But she'd aborted during the night and been found in the morning dead. Older slaves took this to Michie Vince just as soon as they could find the chance with him alone. Nonc Pierre and Nonc Gaston, the elders in the cabins, laying it all out for him in low reverent whispers, didn't have to tell him that he was the only court of appeals. She'd been a lost soul, that poor slave woman, no man could claim or would claim to have been the father of that child, else the slaves might have been in a worse state than they were.

But these considerations barely entered Vincent's mind. She was a human being and Vincent had been horrified by this brutality and his subsequent discovery that without benefit of ceremony her body and that of the infant had been hauled away in a filthy cart. This struck to the heart of the very thing that terrified him about the entire system of slavery, the utter callousness and inhumanity which it bred in the worst of those in command. And clearly this overseer, having spent his early years on the vast industrial sugar plantations of the state, had learned to work his chattels as if they were mules. He had to be taught what was expected here! These were Creole Negroes, and they were the "people" of *Bontemps.*

Yet none of this had been mentioned by Philippe to Vincent, not even in passing, and Vincent's antipathy for Philippe, which had grown so strong in its early years of dormancy had been fanned to a flame.

And of course there was the vexing matter of Aglae who

was beside herself with her maids. Someone (someone!) had senselessly stolen her little antique lap *secrétaire*, a treasure left her by Grandmère Antoinette. It seemed hardly worth pawning, yet it had broken her heart. That Vincent could say nothing about this infuriated him, he had seen it in the parlor of the house he had bought for Anna Bella, he had no doubt who had given it to Marie Ste. Marie.

And had he not grown up under his brother-in-law's gentle authority, always the recipient of extraordinary kindness, he might have been less thoroughly confused, He respected Philippe, but had the long months in Europe given him a sharper perspective, a man's perspective? Had he been blind? Now all this was too momentous for a mention; were he to drag it out between himself and his brother-in-law, he could not have gone on living under the same roof. And of course he had no intention of leaving *Bontemps*. It was his father's house. And he was not to dream of leaving Aglae who wept softly over the stolen heirloom, "It's always little things, your father's gold watch, books that he treasured, and now that little *secrétaire*. Why don't they steal my jewels for the love of heaven? And who is behind it?" In her desperation she ran off the names of the black girls she'd reared from childhood. Vincent glowered at the fire.

But there was the master of the house, night after night, presiding at the supper table, lavishing on Vincent a splendid allowance both for his private needs and that new "petit household" sensing not the slightest hostility from wife and brother-in-law, or if he did, giving no sign. He was now taking two fifths of red wine with his dinner, and brandy afterwards without fail.

No, Vincent could not have told Anna Bella any of it, he could not have told anyone. Duty bound him to silence even as he calculated, becoming aware in himself of some vague but persistent ambition of which he was not entirely proud. He had long known he would not divide his inheritance from the rest of the plantation, so early marriage was quite far from his mind. *Bontemps* was a grand enterprise which must continue as Magloire had designed it, to provide income for his sisters, their children, a life for them all. *Bontemps* would always be *Bontemps*, and for now Vincent was just a part of it, content to instruct his young nieces and nephews, to groom young Leon, Philippe's eldest, for the inevitable trip abroad. Yet he would continue to learn all that he could about the cultivation and management of this sprawling land. He would watch this new overseer, and break him if possible, he knew more of the workings of *Bontemps* than anyone now that old Langlois had died. And Philippe with a careless shrug tipped the neck of the bottle to the glass, murmuring *"eh bien."*

But yet another burden, bittersweet and baffling weighed on his soul. Much as he had been drawn to Anna Bella in the beginning, he was amazed to discover that he loved her now far more than he should. He had never really thought to find virtue in this alliance, nobility, or anything particularly fine. It was the satiation of passion that he wanted, and some companionship in its least sordid form. And finding Anna Bella so sweet and pure, he had made the mistake of thinking her a simpleton of sorts. Actually, he'd thought Anna Bella was a fool.

He believed all Negroes were fools.

Not that God had made them inferior so much as they had somehow developed into a childlike race foolish enough to submit to the yoke of slavery. Born to the regimen of the immense plantation, he had judged them by their chains. He knew nothing of the horrors of the Middle Passage from Africa, the utter dehumanizing brutality of the coffles and the auction blocks, and he did not even fully appreciate the extent of the tyrannical efficiency developed by his own father on his own land. And he had never guessed that those slaves closest to him, having long ago come to terms with their condition—that is, choosing to accept it rather than run the miseries of a fugitive's existence—knew that he believed them to be fools, and shrewdly chose not to disillusion him in the slightest. After all, he was benevolent when not challenged: they could do a lot worse.

Of course the *gens de couleur* posed a special problem and always had. Well bred and educated, they often invited optimism. Vincent, in fact, had only just installed on his plantation a refining process invented by a brilliant young man of color, Norbert Rillieux. But how could one account for their living here generation after generation in a country and a region that did not want them, that would never permit them equality, and sought ultimately to crush their heads? How could anyone as clever as Christophe come back to this place declaring sentimentally that it was his home? And still smarting from that humiliating encounter with him of the summer before, Vincent could not think of him without anger, embarrassment, and scorn.

But the women of color, they were more pathetic really as

(374)

women are always more pathetic, not the movers or the changers but merely the victims. Better that they be sweet, accepting, and unobtrusively pragmatic as women always are.

But quick-witted? Profound? Possessed of any real substance of mind or character? He had never expected it.

And Anna Bella had disillusioned him at once.

He had perceived in no time that her sweet passivity was not indicative of a lack of intellect or a lack of character at all. And far from being some sow's ear fashioned into a Creole belle, she was a lady to the tips of her fingers, having imbibed the principles of gentility for the very best and most profound of reasons: that gentility makes life graceful and good. That gentility depends in its truest sense upon respect for others, love of others, it is the daily practice of charity refracted into manners with the most profound moral principle at its core.

She was admirable, this simple and pretty girl who did not comprehend the scope of her own passionate appeal; and day in and day out she impressed him more and more with her candor, clear intelligence, and the very gracefulness of mind and manner that he might have wanted in his wife.

Yes, that was the worst of it, it was all that he might have wanted in a wife. In fact she was all that he could *ever* have wanted in a wife, and his happiness, despite himself and the gloomy exterior he often offered to her, knew no bounds.

When she had told him in the parlor that she was with child, he had one tormenting thought. Had she been white and all else been equal, he would have flaunted the old tradition and brought her, orphan that she was, to *Bontemps*. But she was not white. And this was unthinkable. So that the very extent of his love for her, its peculiar profound composition, seeming as it did far more appropriate to the state of matrimony, weighed on his soul. *What had he done?* He could barely endure being away from her, he needed her, how would he ever give her up?

Eh bien, what had it been, half a year? He could pray that it would pass. But he knew theirs was a perfect match, it would not.

So pounding out the front gate to find Marcel Ste. Marie on this morning in May, he had only one desire, to obtain for her something that she wanted, some companionship to which he felt she was entitled. He shuddered at all thoughts of a lover's possessiveness and a colored mistress's subservience. He wanted this woman whom he loved to receive her friends with dignity, to have some measure of the full life he possessed. If someone had told him then that he had another idea in mind, he would have denied it. He did not understand the full character of his own fears.

It was only when he reached the Rue Ste. Anne, that he became aware that he had no immediate or practical plan. Certainly he would not enter the gate of that little cottage. He moved on. But a shock visited him as he headed towards the Hotel St. Louis. He and Philippe had long honored an understanding that they would not leave *Bontemps* at the same time. Yet there was his brother-in-law walking slowly toward the corner of the Rue Ste. Anne and the Rue Dauphine with Felix, the coachman, who carried bottles of wine, and gaily wrapped parcels in his arms.

"*Bonsoir,* Monsieur," Vincent gave Philippe a slight, courteous bow.

"*Eh bien, mon fils,*" said Philippe wearily. "I couldn't wait on you forever, besides I lost at cards to your cousin, and he's told his wife, and she's told your sister, and these days I never have any peace at all." But then he drew him close, affectionately, "You'll hurry back, won't you? I knew you would be back today or tomorrow, hmmmm?"

"I was on my way back now," Vincent said with his usual formality. He would have liked to point out that his brother-in-law had been absent only last week for several days, and the week before, and the week before. Indeed, it seemed Philippe had spent the better part of spring in New Orleans, it seemed they were never together at *Bontemps* at all.

"No, truly, listen to me," Philippe said confidentially as if they were the best of friends. "It's Zazu, the black woman I gave them years ago," he gestured vaguely toward the distant cottage with its banana trees pressing on the white picket fence. "She's failing, badly. I don't want to be gone too long until we see if the hot weather will bring some improvement, she was born on my father's land."

Vincent nodded when Philippe uttered a short laugh. He pointed with a quick unobtrusive gesture toward a bright blond-haired quadroon boy who was coming down the opposite side of the street. "Can you believe that is *Ti* Marcel? He's grown an inch a month for the past year."

Vincent's face flamed with a sudden and jarring humiliation. He saw that the boy, having averted his brilliant blue eyes, was walking on as if he had not seen the two men. A loathing came over Vincent, not for the immaculate young quadroon who passed them as if he did not know them, but for all of this, his brother-in-law smiling covertly at his bastard son, Felix with that cache of presents, Felix who would be driving Aglae to Mass next Sunday, and the proximity of that little cottage, and his own position here, dallying with all of this around him in this street. A revulsion gripped him so that he was hardly conscious of his perfunctory farewells, and walking fast for the hotel he did not look back.

It was only when the steamboat was at last churning upriver that, standing on the deck he resolved not to keep his promise to Anna Bella, that he realized he could not bring himself to speak with Philippe's bastard, Marcel. He did not want the Ste. Marie family to touch his Anna Bella, and he would have liked to believe that she was not of their world. But she *was* of their world! He had only to think of that little *secrétaire*, Aglae's *secrétaire*, which sat so proudly on Anna Bella's bedside table to realize that of course it was Anna Bella's world, too. And as dusk obscured the banks of the river, and the waters beneath him turned the color of the darkening sky, he realized more keenly the source of his pain. *He* did not wish to be connected with that world.

With Dolly Rose he had had no sense of it, knew nothing really of those who surrounded her, and his pale and lovely daughter had been for him a creature fixed in some complex and ornate frame, painfully separated from him, but untouched by anyone else. And even so, her death had been a reprieve.

But this was over, Anna Bella was pregnant, he had surrounded her with a house which was his home. And in so many months she would bear a child who might very well be a boy-child, a child who would become a young man. And that young man would be half-caste, just as the blond-haired son of Philippe's was a half-caste, and that young man would be Vincent's son!

His youthful adventure with Dolly had never struck him with this curious intensity, he had never seen its implications, he had never understood. The thought of the boy-child made him positively shudder, and he wrapped his cape about him vainly, turning his back to the river wind. Pray it were a girl. But what did this really matter! He had made the same tragic mistake again. He had forged a chain for himself linking him inextricably to that dark society which was all too real to him now, and which for all the distinction and appealing rhythm of those words, *gens de couleur libre*, was the Negro world.

By the time the plank dropped at *Bontemps*, he had resolved to give Anna Bella only a simple explanation. He did
not wish to speak to her friend, Marcel Ste. Marie. Sensitive
and clever as she had always been, she would not question
him, and might quite likely even understand. Surely she
knew of the connection. And it was the only promise to her
he'd ever broken. She would forget in time.

And as soon as he set foot on his own land he put it out
of his mind.

Old Nonc Pierre was waiting with two young black boys
to take his bags, and the old slave led the way with a lantern,
saying the usual, that he was glad to welcome the young
master home.

"Things are well, then?" Vincent murmured, more out of
courtesy than anything else. A sense of security slowly
thawed his depression as they moved toward the warm lights
of the big house.

"So, so, Michie," said the old slave. He did not turn to look
Vincent in the eye.

"What's wrong, then?" Vincent asked almost irritably. He
was dead tired. But nothing more could be gotten out of Nonc
Pierre. And Vincent entered the house wearily, knowing
there would be some unpleasant surprises for him in the
morning when he stepped into the office and tracked that
overseer down. Nothing out of the ordinary, he thought
grimly, and Philippe gone for the week, no doubt.

Aglae was waiting for him in the big parlor, a wood fire
blazing strongly beneath the high mantel. He could see she
had been studying the plantation ledgers, which were always
kept under lock and key. The sight of these bulky books
annoyed him. He would have liked to change clothes before
sitting opposite her, but she gestured for him to come in.

There was a wasted look to her as she poured his brandy,
the firelight harsh against her sharp features. The brief ruffle
at her neck, her only ornament, did not soften her but rather
served to emphasize the heavy lines of her narrow face, the
inevitable evening shadows under her eyes. And her countenance didn't brighten with affection as it so often did when
he came home. Instead, she merely produced a letter from a
packet of letters, all neatly opened, no doubt by the small
ivory handled knife in her hand.

"Read it," she said.

(378)

He hesitated. Clearly, it was addressed to Philippe. But she said again, "Read it," and he did.

"Mon Dieu!" he whispered. He folded the letter and gave it back to her. There was nothing of overt alarm in her slim, pale face. Her eyes held him steadily.

"Did you have any idea he had mortgaged *so much?*" she asked.

"That's incredible!" he whispered.

"No, not incredible," she answered simply, "not if after years of negligence, one has consolidated a series of older outstanding notes."

PART TWO

I

IT WAS THE WORST of days for Rudolphe, there was never any
denying it, and certainly never any accepting it, and in fact,
Grandpère's quiet acceptance of it, and Richard's complete
dismissal of it only served to torment Rudolphe so that now
at five o'clock in the evening on this balmy June day he did
not wish to seek the refuge of his own home. Yet everywhere
that he walked he saw the lines before the polls. Lines of
men who owned property such as he owned, men who paid
taxes such as he paid, men who shared with him a concern
for the political and economic issues of the day, men who had
much in common with him in all respects save one: he was
colored; they were white. They could vote; he could not.

"Monsieur, take your mind off of it," Suzette would say
with that maddening aristocratic calm at supper tonight. And
Grandpère would discuss the elections, newspaper in hand,
as if nothing were amiss, as if no monstrous injustice separated the prosperous *gens de couleur* from their fellowmen.

Of course the battle was over for Grandpère. It had been
fought bitterly in the early years of the Territory of Louisiana
when the *gens de couleur* had struggled to be fully enfranchised citizens under the new flag. In the year 1814, it seemed
General Andrew Jackson had all but promised full citizen-
ship to the members of the colored battalions who had gone
with him to vanquish the British below the city on the battlefield of Chalmette. And this when certain white Creoles

were grumbling behind closed doors, afraid that Jackson was fighting "a Russian war," and would burn New Orleans as the Czar had burned Moscow rather than surrender it to a foreign power.

Well, the war had been won with the lives of colored soldiers fighting valiantly side by side with white, and the hopes of the *gens de couleur* for the franchise had been utterly lost.

In the years that followed it was clear that the Anglo-Saxon American despised and distrusted the "free Negro," and the colored battalions had been deceived and used. The new government had never really planned to strengthen and maintain these proud fighting units, which had existed for years under the Spanish and the French, because it feared the very sight of armed Negroes, and the State of Louisiana, denying them the vote, had put more and more restrictions on her people of color than they had ever known.

Yes, the war was won and the battle lost, and Grandpère would never pit himself against the white Anglo again.

There would be an air of grim superiority about him tonight if Rudolphe were to mention the election. And Richard, deep in his studies, would not even acknowledge the subject at all. No, hot and tired and angry as he was on this Tuesday evening, Rudolphe did not wish to go home.

And if there was any man whom he did wish to see, it was Christophe, though why he was not entirely sure. Certainly Christophe didn't share his anxiety over the state of the *gens de couleur* and never had. Shortly after his return from France Christophe had told Rudolphe simply that such matters did not concern him; he had made peace with all of this, and had he not made peace he would never have come back. The incident of Bubbles in the classroom did not weaken Christophe's commitment to his students, he had accepted its outcome with an amazing equanimity, never broaching the subject again.

But there was something beyond resignation in Christophe's manner. It was not the same as Grandpère's bitter silence or Richard's genteel disdain. Christophe was not wounded by the inequities around him. Though eminently successful in day-to-day life he appeared, nevertheless, to exist on a different plane. Yet he had always respected Rudolphe for his concern, respected Rudolphe even for his honest opposition to bringing a slave into the schoolroom, and at other times uttered sympathy for Rudolphe's frustrations in the face of what he was powerless to change.

And Rudolphe felt that if he could talk with Christophe tonight, the man would listen, offer understanding and ultimate solace to Rudolphe's soul.

But unfortunately other matters came first. It was Dolly Rose whom Rudolphe had to see now on a matter that could not be postponed nor delegated to anyone else. It concerned the grave of Dolly's daughter, Lisa, for which a magnificent statue had been ordered without Dolly's knowledge by the wealthy and somewhat condescending Vincent Dazincourt. For months, Narcisse Cruzat, Rudolphe's finest sculptor, had been at work on this monument, now it was ready, and Dolly of course must be told.

Of course Dolly herself did not go to the cemetery. On the Feast of All Saints last November she had come into the shop to make arrangements for the flowers, her hands trembling, her face shimmering from drink. Rudolphe who was still thoroughly angry with her for the affair of Christophe and Captain Hamilton would have shunned her had duty allowed for it, but she was frail then in her grief. "You take care of this for me, Michie Rudolphe," she had said without guile, the voice soft, stripped of its flamboyant cynicism and contempt. She had a charm in those moments, the charm of the young Dolly who had come so often to the Lermontant house in days past to visit with Giselle. Dolly simply being Dolly, not the wild *belle dame sans merci* bound to be the tragic heroine of a glamorous and sordid life.

Well, grief did that to people. And Rudolphe himself had tended little Lisa's grave.

But he had no illusions now, some seven months later, of how he might find the grieving mother, if indeed, he could speak with her at all. The house in the Rue Dumaine was infamous, carriages stopping all evening before the doors, as champagne by the case went up the back stairs, and the white gentlemen callers paid lavishly for their refreshments, sums adequate for entertainment and companionship should they so desire. Neighbors were outraged, but Dolly's clientele was the richest, and this was the "old city," what could be done?

But Rudolphe who had never used a servants' entrance in his life was contemplating using one this evening with relief.

Five-fifteen. The clock over his desk struck just as he opened the shop door. Antoine was deep in conversation with a white woman from Boston who had only just lost her brother and wanted two score pair of black silk gloves made for all the mourners which they might then keep. It could be done, anything could be done, that is, if the seamstresses worked night and day. Rudolphe surveyed the merchandise quickly, swept dust from the counters, set the clock in accordance with his infallible watch, and left for the stoneyard a block away.

It had been too long since he had spoken with Narcisse, his young colored sculptor, and besides he was longing to see the completed monument for little Lisa's grave himself.

Narcisse was the best of them.

Twenty-five and the son of a freed slave woman and a white father, he had already sprinkled the cemeteries of the First Municipality with astonishing funereal art, fresh, delicate, and exquisitely crafted, so that people were coming to the Lermontant yards to place their orders from all over the city and even the parishes beyond.

And Rudolphe, brimming with admiration for young Narcisse, felt a profound interest in him, his talent, the scope of his life. It was time to bring the young man to his house for supper, to present him socially as his gifts had merited and not stand upon ceremony and custom with the old families, as aloof and exclusive as they were. Rudolphe's social world, of course, was composed of such people, the LeMonds, Vacqueries, Rousseaus, and lately, the Dumanoirs. Naturally enough, the prosperous and respectable quadroon women were included, those whose white connections brought their children breeding, education, wealth. But rarely if ever was this *cordon bleu* atmosphere challenged by the inclusion of humbler men, and in the case of this brilliantly talented young sculptor, an exception must be made. His was a natural gentility, something inevitable in such a sublime sensibility, resonating fully with the God-given ability in his hands.

And when Rudolphe, entering the work yard behind the shed, laid eyes upon the new monument, his breath was literally taken away. It was just getting dusk. Lanterns burned beneath the nearby roof, and the sky above was perfectly lavender behind the darkening trees. But the light of the sun was not yet gone, and in fact, at this moment seemed to pulse from all the color that it could yet find. The red bougainvillea that clung to the weather-beaten fence, the wild lilies in clumps behind the small cistern, the grass beneath Rudolphe's feet. And in this radiant twilight moment, softened by the balm of the summer air, Rudolphe saw the marble angel, gleaming and white, its head bent as its arm descended to embrace the small figure of a child. Sorrow marked the

(383)

angel's face, seemingly inexplicable sorrow. And the child, her gown descending in classical folds, turned inward beneath the angel's wing, her eyes closed.

Only little sounds came from afar. It seemed Rudolphe was alone in this place with the angel and the little girl, and the pair before him on the high wooden pedestal was alive. He took a step forward, strangely conscious of the crunch of the grass beneath his boot, and gently, gently, he extended his hand. It hurt him to look at the expression of the angel, he felt anguish at the slope of the child's neck. And standing there, quite lost in this unexpected experience, he did not hear Narcisse come from the shed.

Slowly Rudolphe shifted his gaze. The young mulatto in work sleeves, a small hammer jutting from his vest pocket seemed altogether unreal. And Rudolphe had the disconcerting sensation that he had lost complete track of time. *"Eh bien,* Narcisse," he whispered. But his eyes returned to the angel, the lowered lids of the stricken face, the mouth half open in its cry. *"Eh bien,* Narcisse," he whispered again.

Narcisse was smiling at him. His dark brown skin was covered with a fine film of dust, and the large African mouth yielded easily to a serene expression of pleasure in what he perceived in his employer's eyes. Rudolphe worked every day of his life with monuments, with graves, with sorrow, and yet he stood all but speechless at the angel's feet.

And then, as if wrenching himself loose, Rudolphe turned and made a small slow circle about the yard. He was thinking, rubbing his chin.

Narcisse meanwhile had taken a receipt from his pocket, his roughened fingers opening it easily for Rudolphe to see. "He paid for it in full today, Monsieur," he said in very proper French, eschewing the Creole "Michie." "He was pleased."

"Indeed he should have been," Rudolphe was nodding, surveying the pair from afar. The sun had left the flowers. The trees were shapeless in the dark. But the statue, some five feet in height and perfectly polished, had become itself a source of light.

He was barely conscious of Narcisse speaking to him, of Narcisse telling him there was some matter he must take up with him now. The French was decorous, slow, the boy uneasy, a little sad. At last Rudolphe pressed his fingers to the bridge of his nose, made a small shrug, and said almost irritably, "But what...?"

"...that we have at last raised the money, Monsieur, my

mother, my uncles, our Craftsman's Society, it's been done.
I could be leaving any day, Monsieur, that is, when it is best
for you, Monsieur, that I take my leave, when you will
permit..."

Now the boy appeared quite clear to Rudolphe as he stood
before the sculpture, the dust clinging to his dark lashes and
the tight halo of his black hair. His words were soft and
winding and unobtrusive and Rudolphe without even hearing
them suddenly realized what they meant. The boy was going
to Europe, he was going to Italy to study art.

That he would be disappointed now to see his employer
bow his head, that he would be disappointed to see his employer turn his back, all this Rudolphe knew. But just for a
moment Rudolphe could say nothing, and it seemed all the
bitterness that had been building in him all the long day
came up like the taste of poison in his mouth. "Going," Rudolphe whispered. "Going. Like all the rest."

"Pardonnez, Monsieur?" the boy whispered behind him.

Rudolphe shook his head. Turning he saw the sculpture
had become slightly indistinct, shadows obscured the beautiful face.

"Monsieur, I have worked for years for this..."

"Yes, yes, yes!" Rudolphe said wearily, and without thinking to explain, he walked heavily past the boy, past the angel,
into the shed. He found a chair there without worrying about
dust or dirt and sat down, his arm on the deal table against
the wall. The boy was taking his time as he came from the
yard, sensing Rudolphe's displeasure, and it was the boy who
now bowed his head.

"What can I do here, Monsieur?" came the voice as the
figure, quite completely dark, stood against the open door.
"In Rome, I can study with the masters, Monsieur, I can have
the future..." The words without sound or meaning rumbled
on.

It seemed a long time before Rudolphe finally spoke.

"I know, Narcisse, I know." His hand moved into his coat
pocket. He felt his leather wallet there and drew it out. He
let it rest on his knee. "It's just that all the young talented
ones leave us, Narcisse. Or so it seems." He sighed.

"Monsieur," came the soft reasonable voice. "What is there
here for me? My work is admired, but I will never be admired!"

It was all the same old story. Why put it into words again?
You can go whenever you want, Rudolphe was explaining,

Jacques would take over the remaining orders, and if there is anything special, well, then tomorrow we will go over the books together, we'll talk. Drowsily, heavily, Rudolphe rose to his feet. He opened his wallet, and he heard the boy's frank gasp as he received the bills.

"But Monsieur..."

"No, no, no...you deserve it," Rudolphe was already on his way.

And it was night before he reached the Rue Dumaine.

He had given his mind over to practical thoughts. How tomorrow evening when meeting with his Benevolent Society he would introduce a resolution to raise a fund for the young sculptor to help him in Rome. Of course LeMond would be willing, and Vacquerie delighted, but Rousseau would probably balk. Didn't the boy already have his Craftsmen's Society? "You know very well they'd be grateful for our assistance!" Rudolphe would insist with pride. So on his thoughts went. But try as he might, he could not put the bitterness of the loss of Narcisse out of his mind, and as he approached Dolly's house with its blazing lights, he was eager for any distraction.

And Dolly was one of the more powerful distractions of which he knew.

The truth was that Rudolphe had always been fond of Dolly, and terribly fond of her when she was a young girl. He was a faithful man, deeply in love with Suzette, but fidelity had not always been easy for him. And being powerfully built and handsome in the Caucasian mode, with light brown skin, he had ample opportunity to stray. Only a few lapses had blemished his respect for himself, lapses without affection or warmth. And confessing these to Suzette after, he had endured her scornful condemnations almost gratefully, resolving never to travel sordid paths again.

But he had lusted, truly lusted, after a few very beautiful women in his heart, women whom he had never even thought to touch. One of these was Juliet Mercier in her youth who had all but bewitched him without the slightest knowledge of it, and another was Dolly Rose.

However, this was not the Dolly who had become Dazincourt's mistress, nor the spiteful crazed woman who had come drunk and wild-eyed to Marie Ste. Marie's birthday fête. It was the young Dolly, the honest Dolly, one of the purest, gentlest and truly innocent women Rudolphe had ever known. During those years when she had frequented his home with Giselle, Rudolphe was often in a private hell watching her, listening to her spirited laughter, feeling the bold and naive touch of her cheek when she rose on tiptoe to greet him with a simple kiss. And loving as she did to entertain the respectable young men of color who came to visit with her and with Giselle, Dolly would be the one, for certain, he had thought, to go against her mother's ways. Times were changing, after all, and these were not the days of *Les Sirènes* as Madame Rose and the old beauties from Saint-Domingue had been called. There was a sordid air in recent years about the Salle d'Orléans on those nights when women of color went there to meet their white "protectors" and surely this lovely Dolly, so fresh, and so strong in a perfectly feminine fashion, would not choose the old path.

But Dolly had chosen it. In her sixteenth year she had been presented at the "quadroon balls." Giselle had thrown herself across the bed sobbing when Rudolphe forbade the friends to meet. And on the day that Giselle was married at the St. Louis Cathedral, she had not seen Dolly watching the wedding from the back of the church. But Rudolphe had seen her, and would never forget that pretty figure, Dolly done up as if she were to be a bridesmaid, quite alone, watching all with tears in her eyes.

Of course she was rich then. Young Vincent Dazincourt kept her in silks and satins, she had a beautiful baby girl. A private orchestra was hired to play just for the pair whenever Dazincourt came to town.

Rudolphe seldom saw her after that. Dolly was a wild and bitter woman by the time she lost her mother. But he had never forgotten the vision of that pristine and blossoming girl.

And it was that girl, actually, who had flamed to rage the anger he felt for the woman she had become.

Walking back her carriageway now, he did not wish to see her, did not wish to battle with her over her daughter's gravestone, nor to hear her crude invectives on the matter of Vincent Dazincourt. Nevertheless he felt a certain grim curiosity about her. Despising her as he did for her behavior with Christophe, he had never guessed that her life would take this course. He had envisioned a series of broken romances for her, the quasi-respectable arrangements of *plaçage* fractured again and again by her whims. Advancing age would

(387)

have put an end to it, an end that might have been shabby indeed.

But Dolly's "house" and the word did indeed now merit that connotation, was one of the most prosperous in the Quarter, all the rage for its newness and for the luminary that Dolly had been. It was clever, all of it, yet dreadful. Dolly had thrown away everything. Yet Dolly had triumphed at the same time.

He was not at all surprised now to happen upon a courtyard strung with pretty lanterns, and candles on the iron tables about which a few white men were already gathered in the company of dark women whispering in the gloom. And it did not surprise him either that a pretty young mulatto girl came at once to ask his business and went to inform the mistress that he was here.

Led along the upstairs gallery of the servants' quarters he hesitated outside the appointed room. No one below took notice of him anymore than if he were a Negro servant, and he was too tired to be irritated, and felt merely the vaguest excitement at the prospect of seeing what Dolly really was.

It was her maid who threw open the heavy green shutters and said come in.

The bright lamps of the room blinded him for an instant and he was startled by what he then saw.

For in this smaller servant's boudoir was crowded all of Dolly's bedroom trappings from the big house across the yard. Here was the immense four poster from which Rudolphe had pulled the drunken Christophe the summer before. And here that immense dresser with its beveled mirrors, those painted screens. But at a rolltop desk against the wall at the foot of the bed sat Dolly quite collected in a blue dimity dressing gown. Her thick black hair hung loose in deep waves down her back, and as she turned to greet him, her face was bright, almost radiant, and youthful, without the trace of pain.

"Come in, Rudolphe," she said to him without mockery. She laid down her pen. Her ledgers were open there and he saw in one quick glimpse columns of figures. And a great deal of money, very likely a reckless amount of money, stacked in an open metal box. "Sit down, Rudolphe," she was saying. "What brings you here?" It was just as if they were old friends.

The sash of the dimity dressing gown was quite modestly wrapped and a froth of beige silk flounces rested high on her breast to the neck. He reflected in a moment of peculiar

(388)

intensity that sin was doing her good. In fact she looked better than she had in years. She looked almost like...quickly, he shook his head.

"It's a matter of the gravestone, Madame, for your daughter. It's a matter of a monument ordered for it by Monsieur Dazincourt."

There was a flicker in the clear black eyes, a flicker that made him stiffen, ready for all those excesses he had witnessed in the past. But she appeared to be thinking and said, "I didn't know of this."

"Well, it's quite beautiful, Madame, and more than fitting. He ordered it some months ago. I had thought it was your order until it was recently finished and the matter came to my attention yesterday afternoon. I've seen the sculpture in question and truly it is fitting. I think perhaps you should see it yourself."

In a few words then he attempted to describe it to her, but this could not touch it, and the atmosphere of the shed and the yard came back to him along with Narcisse's revelation that he would soon go abroad. He found that beautiful as the statue had been it was unpleasant to think about it, unpleasant to be overpowered again by that sense of anguish and the deepening dusk. He had stopped speaking and was scowling at the carpet before him, at her small morocco slipper and the dimity against the naked instep of her foot. "Madame, of course, we'll do as you wish," he said, looking up. "But before you make up your mind, see it first."

"I know Narcisse's work," she said. "Everyone knows it. Put the statue in place." Her manner was completely reasonable. She sat with her back to the desk, one elbow on the open ledger, her small pale hands clasped.

"Very well, Madame," he rose at once and reached for his hat.

"Rudolphe," she said suddenly. "Don't go so soon."

He was about to make some trivial excuse when he saw by her manner that this was not merely politeness on her part. Her eyes had an imploring expression while the face remained firm.

"How is Madame Suzette?" she asked. "How is Giselle?"

"Very well, Madame, all of them, very well."

"And Richard?" she asked. "You know Richard did me a great kindness once, bringing me home when I was ill."

Rudolphe nodded. He knew nothing about this, naturally enough, his gentleman of a son hadn't bothered to tell him, but *eh bien,* people were forever telling him how Richard had done this or that kindness, well, perfectly fine.

"Very well, Madame," he said in the same dull and discouraging tone.

"Is this true that he is courting the Ste. Marie girl?" she asked. He felt himself tense at this question, and he realized he was glowering at her, at the seeming openness of her expression.

"He's far too young for that," he murmured carelessly, and again he moved to go.

"And Christophe?" she asked.

He glanced at her over his shoulder. Only now was the calm breaking. Her eyebrows had knit in an intense frown. She was waiting for his answer, her chin lifted, her body inclined slightly forward in the chair. "You do see him, do you not? Richard goes to his school?"

"He's done very well, Madame," he said, unsure of his voice. He was not good at pretending events had never happened, not good at "carrying on" as if there weren't old wounds. "And you, Madame?" he said suddenly angry. "And how does it go with you?"

There was that flicker again, marring the steady gaze. And she looked down, her hand rising to find some imperfection in the paper of the ledger, her dark lashes casting the most delicate shadow on her cheeks. "I do not go out much anymore, Monsieur, I do not see anyone," she said her voice deepening. "I merely wondered if he...if his life is going well."

"Exemplary," Rudolphe murmured, the blood warm in his cheeks. "He turns students away, and gives private lessons in the evening. But of course it's hard. A schoolteacher is never a rich man."

She was pondering this. Or something else. And when she looked up again, her voice was soft and slightly sad. "Would you give him a message for me, Monsieur?" she asked.

He would certainly rather not. But how say so, he wondered. So he said nothing, and knew that it was perfectly plain.

But she rose from the desk and moving around the bed went down on her knees beneath the ruffles and drew out a large leather case.

"Here, allow me..." he mumbled resentfully, and took it from her as he also took her hand. It was moist and warm in his own and almost perfectly the same color.

"I want you to take this to him for me," she said. It was heavy, very heavy. He set it down by the door.

Why a slave couldn't have done that, he couldn't imagine, because now she certainly had slaves enough. And the image of himself lugging this case through the streets distressed him. "But what is it?" he asked.

"Tuning wrenches. They belong to Bubbles, and he can't do his work without them," she murmured. She stood beside the desk, her head to one side, looking down.

"Ahhh," he nodded. He had heard that story often enough. Stopping Bubbles in the street to ask if he might tune the new spinet, he had been told the slave's lament. Dolly Rose wouldn't give the wrenches back. And seeing now that all this was quite impulsive with her, that in this brightly lighted room at seven o'clock on a summer evening because he had dropped in, she had decided to do right by Bubbles, he murmured indeed he would take them to Christophe on his way home.

"You know, Rudolphe," she said, looking up at him suddenly with a little smile. "I never meant really to cause Christophe so much harm. I never meant really to cause him so much trouble, nor to bring trouble to you."

"It's past, Madame," he said almost sharply. And he reached to pick up the case.

But she came across the carpet then and taking his arm in one hand, pushed gently at his right hand with the other until he let the case go. "Rudolphe," she said. "Tell that to Christophe for me."

For a brief moment he merely looked into her eyes. And then without thinking, he whispered to her, heartfelt,

"Dolly, why! Why this house, why all of this! Wasn't there some other way?"

At first, she merely shook her head, the smile lengthening, brightening on her face. And then leaning against him, her hand on his shoulder, she said, "You know sometimes I think that if Christophe had been, well . . . if Christophe had been the marrying kind, maybe it would have all been different, maybe it would have been different indeed. But that's foolish isn't it, Rudolphe? To imagine that now?"

"Too easy, I think, Dolly," he said softly. He could not imagine her content with any man, let alone a man of color, it was absurd. In fact, the image of some sordid and miserable marriage between her and Christophe sickened him. But it was difficult to think of this clearly when he looked at her now. Her high forehead was as smooth and free of care as that of a child.

"Do you really believe in life after death?" she asked him. He was startled by the question, but answered immediately, "Yes."

"That the dead are somewhere...else?"

"Of course."

"That Lisa is somewhere...and that I'll see her again?" Her eyes were moist as she looked up.

"Definitely," he replied.

"And that my mother is somewhere...and she knows what I do?"

Ah, so that was it. He studied her, trying vainly to think of something comforting to say. He had no such trouble when dealing with the mourners at funerals and wakes. And he wondered that this ability, so often polished, should fail him now. Perhaps it was her expression. Her eyes were wide, musing, and there was nothing of the sentimental about her.

"Imagine," she said softly, staring forward, "what Maman would have thought had I married Christophe! Her precious Dolly with a man of..."

He turned away. His face was suddenly throbbing. It was an insult that she should speak thus to him and he wouldn't endure it. He had the case of wrenches in his right hand at once and nothing would keep him here now.

But she drew close to him right at the door, one arm sliding urgently about his waist. She was looking down, her head all but brushing his chest.

"I have to go, Madame," he said. A fast, light music came from the big house, and an indifferent murmur from the yard below.

"It doesn't much matter, does it?" she sighed. "Marrying him or not, does it? After all, Maman's turning in her grave."

"Life is for the living, *ma chère*," he said suddenly, not conscious that he had closed his hand on her small shoulder and was pressing it tightly. "What the dead think of us in God's time and wisdom is just fiction inour minds. Life is for the living, for us now. Close up this house for your own sake. That power is yours anytime."

He stepped onto the porch. Her arms dropped to her sides.

She smiled as she looked up at him, her hair so full it made a dark shadow behind her to her waist.

"Rudolphe, none of that concerns me," she said simply. "I've made my choice and I rather like it. And maybe, just maybe, it's the only real choice I've ever made."

"Dolly, Dolly," he shook his head.

But she was not sad, nor spiteful. There had been a conviction in those appalling words. She folded her arms and leaned against the frame of the door, obscuring for the moment the light behind her. "You know it is such a sublime feeling to do as one pleases for once, to own one's own person, one's own soul."

"How can you say this?" he protested.

"I don't go into that house over there, Rudolphe, I haven't been in it for months," she smiled. "I can do what I want, Rudolphe, what I like. And I'll tell you something. If I weren't so devoted to Madame Suzette, I'd beg you to stay for a while... here... with me. No one would take the slightest notice of that now, no one would care. Just you and me here alone. But then perhaps I underestimate Madame Suzette. She was always an understanding woman. Maybe she'd forgive, that is, if she ever found out..."

For an instant, he merely stared at her, his eyes wide. And then softly, he said, "*Adieu,* Madame," and was gone.

It was very late that night before he finally went home. Bubbles had been overjoyed to receive the wrenches. He had salvaged a ruined piano from a recent fire in the neighborhood and was in the process of restoring it in Christophe's kitchen shed. Now with the wrenches and other tools in his case, he would complete this task and his gratitude knew no bounds. He cut such an elegant figure these days, quite accustomed now to the fine clothes Christophe continued to give him, that he would soon be earning money for himself and for Christophe of which Christophe was sorely in need. The Mercier house after so many years of blatant neglect was a constant liability as well as a priceless asset; its ongoing repairs took every penny that Christophe made.

Christophe himself had not disappointed Rudolphe, and after accepting Dolly's expressions of good will with a gentlemanly nod, he had poured the wine and offered a sympathetic ear. He concurred with Rudolphe on political matters as he always did, but he himself seemed unmoved by the current state of affairs except for one point: it was so hard now to set a slave free. And Christophe wanted to set Bubbles free. Bubbles would have to be thirty years of age and self-sufficient unless a petition was filed and an exception granted, and this was becoming harder to accomplish all the time. Louisiana was afraid of her free Negro population and did not wish to see it increased. Meantime free blacks and people of color poured into New Orleans from all over the South seeking the anonymity and tolerance that the city had to offer. The legislature sought again and again to control this, to limit it, to prevent it. Their contempt for their colored population was abundantly clear.

But in all this Christophe was alert but calm, sympathetic but removed. And Rudolphe as he had hoped, felt better for having seen him and spoken to him, for having unburdened his soul. It had occurred to him just before leaving that Christophe's attitudes represented an alternative of which Rudolphe in the past had not been so keenly aware. Christophe knew exactly what was happening to his people, and he cared very much about it, but he was not personally diminished by it in any way. He saw his task as the education of his students and he felt he might strive to do that to perfection regardless of the injustices of this time and place.

And this time and place seemed far more bearable to Rudolphe as he finally went home. If a man could perceive that deeply, neither excusing nor ignoring it, and still have peace of mind, well, that was a worthwhile thing. Wisdom was the only word for it that Rudolphe knew.

And wisdom was on his mind to some extent when coming up the stairs that night, he passed his son's room.

The door was open to catch the cooling draughts of the house and a weary Richard was squinting by the light of the lamp over his books. He wore a dressing gown, open at the throat to show a bit of the dark hair on his chest, and as usual appeared to Rudolphe, when seen in a sudden unexpected glance, as a much older and somewhat impressive man.

Rudolphe paused. He attempted to put the imposing figure into perspective, this was his son, his youngest, a boy of seventeen.

"Mon Père," Richard murmured politely, rising from the desk. Rudolphe, disliking to look up to Richard, motioned for him to sit down. He came into the bedroom as Richard obeyed and made a small stiff survey of it with a furrowed brow.

This was always his manner in Richard's presence as it was his manner with his nephews, his employees, his slaves. Its effect was simply to produce a state of tension in others; this man of authority might find something here short of perfection and everyone knew that he would settle for nothing but perfection, he was all but impossible to please.

Richard felt that tension. His eyes moved furtively about the room after his father, and he saw with a sharp twinge that he had left his soiled boots on the hearth. Had he summoned Placide.... But his father was not taking note of the boots, nor the somewhat frivolous novel on the bedside table, but instead had fixed his attention on the Daguerreotype of Marie.

The anxiety in Richard made a knot inside him. He had verses to translate before retiring, and now this.

But it was with an unusual countenance that Rudolphe turned to him finally as he clasped his hands behind his back. *"Les Sirènes,"* Rudolphe murmured almost absently, and Richard inclining forward, asked,

"Mon Père?"

But suddenly the slight alteration in his father's face confused Richard. And he had a vague and painful memory of having seen such an alteration once before.

"You don't follow my advice, do you, *mon fils?"* The voice was gentle, quite unlike the blustering father of whom Richard lived in glum fear. Out of habit, as old as himself, Richard struggled to find the right diplomatic tone, the perfect placating phrase. But his father approached him, which was seldom his custom, and placed his hand on Richard's arm. Richard stared up at him in utter bewilderment.

"What is love to you, Richard?" Rudolphe sighed. The voice was sad. "Romance, women as pretty as spring flowers, the peal of bells?"

Rudolphe stopped. His eyes were wide, and he was not really conscious now of what he had just said. He was seeing the vestibule of the St. Louis Cathedral on the day of Giselle's wedding, and it seemed all those sounds and scents mingled for him, along with some vagrant image of Narcisse's perfect statue that put him in mind of love and love lost as much as his evening visit with Dolly Rose. He did not see that Richard was awestruck by this lapse of the decorum that forever divided them, and he was awakened, as it were, when Richard began to speak.

"Mon Père, it's more than love, it's something more splendid and more important than love ever was. I don't have the gift to explain it," came the slow, hesitant, and then carefully chosen words. "I never had your gift for explaining things and never will. But believe me, what you fear for me simply

will not come to pass." The tall figure was rising, unwinding from the chair, and looking down at Rudolphe now as if this were inevitable and Rudolphe glanced away disquieted and strangely raw. "It's not only love we feel for each other, we know each other!" The voice was a whisper. "And there is...there is trust!"

"Now, now there is trust!" Rudolphe whispered, shaking his head. He was losing control. He had not even wanted this conversation, he had so much on his mind from this fatiguing, and endless day. He glanced up at the wide black eyes that were gazing down on him; he wanted to say more. He wanted to reach across the years and years of sharp reprimands and brusque orders to say simply now, I love you, you are my son, my only son, you don't know how much I love you, and if this girl wounds you I cannot bear it, if she wounds you, she wounds me.

But Richard had begun to speak.

"Mon Père," he said, the voice soft but urgent. "It is so difficult for you to believe that she can love *me!* Is is so impossible for you to believe that she can respect *me!* I am not the son you wanted, I've always disappointed you, and I always will. But please believe me when I tell you that Marie sees in me the man you'll never see."

"Richard, no..." Rudolphe moaned. "No, no!" he shook his head. But the hand that he held out closed suddenly and dropped helplessly at his side. And before he could gather himself for this moment, before he could express the love that was so abundant and so accessible to him, Richard had begun to speak again.

"Mon Père, I want to tell you something which I myself don't understand. You see Marie with all the advantages, she's beautiful, she's courted by everyone, she can do whatever she wants. But I tell you there is some grave sadness in Marie, something dark and dreadful, and I sense it when I'm with her, I feel it as if it were a force lurking about her, seeking to do her harm. I don't know why I feel it, but I do feel it, and I feel that when we are together I stand between her and that force. And she knows it, knows it without words as I know it, and there is trust in her for me that she feels for no one else. It's not only that I love her or that I want her, it's that in some way she's already mine. Now is that spring flowers, *mon Père,* is that the peal of bells?"

When Rudolphe turned to look at him, Richard was staring off, unsatisfied as if his words had failed. He did not realize that his father was scrutinizing him from a vantage point entirely new to them both. He did not sense his father's amazement, he did not see the remarkable concentration in Rudolphe's face.

But some profound instinct in Rudolphe recognized the truth of Richard's words. Because Rudolphe, too, had sensed this inexplicable sadness in Marie Ste. Marie. He had even sensed that air of menace that seemed forever to encircle her like an aureole. But Rudolphe had mistaken the darkness at the core of knowing the girl for something that emanated from her, from within. He had not thought her the victim of it. Rather he mixed it completely with his fears for his son, his distrust of the girl's enticing beauty, his scorn for *Les Sirènes* in all their varied forms.

"No, Richard," he said softly. "It's not spring flowers nor the peal of bells."

"Mon Père!" Richard glanced at him directly. It was not clear that he'd even heard. "Give me your consent!" he said. "Let me ask for her now!"

Rudolphe's face was passive, uncommonly calm. He regarded Richard for a long moment without anger or impatience, but when he spoke it was with conviction.

"You are too young."

He could see that Richard had expected this. His son lapsed into his characteristic posture of acceptance, eyes down.

"There's only one sure test of love that I know," Rudolphe said. "That's the test of time. If this girl's affection for you is equal to your affection for her, then it will stand that test, and be all the stronger for it when you've reached the proper age."

"Then you will consent. You will give your blessing ... in time."

Rudolphe's gaze was steady, thoughtful.

"You can be certain of one thing," he said. "Whatever I decide it will be for you. For your happiness, for your good."

He reached up. His hand closed on the back of Richard's neck and he held him for a moment, eyes calm as before. Richard was astonished. Then the hand tightened affectionately, and leaving the room, Rudolphe said softly over his shoulder, "I have never, never been disappointed in you, my only son!"

IT WAS IMPOSSIBLE, she couldn't have run off at a time like this! Not even Lisette, bad as she'd been all year and getting worse all the time. Marcel dressed hurriedly. It was July and unbearable, he had spent a sleepless night on moist sheets, mosquitoes droning about the netting, and now as he drew on his limp white shirt, he realized it was already too small for him, and he threw it aside with annoyance. He would have to be visiting the seamstress again. Monsieur Philippe stood on the gallery of the *garçonnière*, his back to Marcel's door.

"If you don't find her in an hour, just come on back here," Monsieur Philippe said disgustedly. They had been arguing all morning, Lisette and Monsieur Philippe, a mystifying but familiar sound. Marcel had heard her low, rapid voice, muffled so that he could only catch an occasional word; and Monsieur Philippe's replies, a steady rumble from the kitchen before he finally left it, slamming the door.

He had been drinking beer since breakfast, and drank it now from an earthen mug, his vague blue eyes weary. But he held it well, considering that he had spent the night with Zazu who was so sick now that she thought she was at Ferronaire, Monsieur Phillipe's old home downriver, where she'd been born.

She had been failing at Christmastime, and then when a stroke crippled her left side, Monsieur Philippe had moved her up from the damp brick room beside the kitchen into the *garçonnière*. All through the spring and early summer Marcel had heard her wracking coughs through the walls. The warming weather had not improved her, and unable to move for the paralysis and the congestion in her lungs, she had soon wasted from the tall handsome black woman she had been to a wizened crone. It was the worst of deaths, Marcel thought, gradual, but not gradual enough. Madame Suzette Lermontant had sent maids to help; and after Madame Elsie died Anna Bella sent Zurlina whenever she could. Lisette was patient one minute and then wildly afraid the next.

"Do you have any notion where she's gone?" Monsieur Philippe gestured vaguely, contemptuous of the whole affair.

"I know a few places," Marcel murmured. But this was foolishness. Lisette knew dark alleys and dark secrets of which he had no more knowledge than a white man, in fact, in the past few years, he had steadfastly guarded that ignorance, shaking his head to see Lisette's puffy face on Sunday morning, and to mark the new earrings, silk *tignons*. She had money in her pockets whenever she wanted it, and stole nothing from them, he was sure. "I'll do my best, Monsieur," he said now. Then he stopped. The door of the sickroom was ajar and he could see that Marie had just lit the candles. The articles for Extreme Unction were set out. So it had come to that. Marie emerged and gently touched her father's arm.

"Shall I go now?" she asked. Marcel knew that it was for the priest.

"You find her!" Monsieur Philippe said to Marcel. "You tell her to get back here!" he muttered.

"I'll do my best, Monsieur," Marcel started off. Never in his life had he seen Monsieur Philippe even mildly angry, and he was surprised at the vehemence with which the man behind him swore, "Worthless, worthless girl!"

But it was more than an outburst of temper, it was fast becoming the truth. And there had been no real beginning to it, Marcel reasoned as he hurried toward the Place Congo, no real provocation for Lisette's behavior which he could fix in his mind. She had always been the grumbler, sullen, and sharp of tongue when she chose. But with Zazu's illness and all the burdens of the cottage descending upon her alone, she had become outright rebellious in the last fall. On her twenty-third birthday she had taken the silver dollars Marcel gave her and thrown them on the floor. He would have liked to be angry with her, now and then, but he was afraid. He loved Lisette, she'd been there when he was born, was part and parcel of his life. And in some private unconfessed way he had always felt painfully sorry for her, sorry for the keen mind behind that brooding, contemptuous face, for the shrewd and secretive person locked within the sulking slave.

But she was out of hand now. What did she want? Complaining of the simplest orders, she lavished all her attentions on Marie of late as if to say: I do this of my own will. Of course she obeyed Marcel, he had always had a way with her, but more and more, she flaunted, aggravated, provoked Cecile. And at last over some trivial matter of hairpins, mistress and maid had quarreled and Cecile in a unique display of temper had slapped Lisette's face.

"You pray your mother gets up from that sickbed," Cecile's words had flashed through the small rooms of the cottage,

(399)

"or so help me God, I'll see you on the block. I'll sell you downriver, do you hear me, I'll sell you myself into the fields!"

Even Lisette had been appalled. And a frantic Marcel ushered his sobbing mother from the room.

Of course it had been nonsense, vulgar, monstrous, but nonsense all the same. Talk of the block to Lisette who had grown up in this house, her mother born on Ferronaire land. Nevertheless it had lacerated the fabric of domestic tranquillity and there had been the unwholesome ring of long-repressed rage in Cecile's voice.

She had wept after that by the grate, Marcel stroking her hair. And that image came to him, an image which, in fact, had never really left him of the little girl rescued in Saint-Domingue from the blood-drenched street. "Maman," he said gently. He wished that he could somehow stroke her heart.

But he had been helpless. And helpless, too, later that night before a silent Lisette bent over Marie's dress on the ironing board who would not so much as look him in the eye.

This would pass, he told himself, but it did not. As the months moved into spring, Cecile sent out her garments to the laundress, and had the hairdresser twice a week. Marie laced her mother's corsets, gave the orders at the kitchen door. While Lisette went about the careful care of the two children as she had always done ever since they had been in the crib.

It wearied Marcel as it must have wearied Monsieur Philippe, who effected a chilly order by his presence, Lisette ministering in grim silence to a flint-hard Cecile. But sometimes the image of Lisette bent over Marie before the mirror, her yellow face slack with adoring preoccupation, etched itself on Marcel's heart. It seemed Lisette dreamed with Marie as little girls dream with pretty dolls. And Marie who had found these months of soirees since the opera rather agonizing had never needed Lisette more. Yet it was Marie who sought over and over to reconcile them both, attending to any small matter that she might herself, ashamed it seemed sometimes of Lisette's loving care.

"In time, in time," Monsieur Philippe whispered to Cecile softly, "I promise you another girl." But he was sad now over Zazu's worsening illness, he had always had a special affection for Zazu and wanted only that she should die in peace. In fact, Monsieur Philippe showed such devotion to her in these months that Marcel had not resented his presence in the house. And he was there so often now as spring moved into summer and summer to its peak, that his presence ceased to be the exception and became the rule.

No one had expected him that Sunday morning only a week after the opera last November when he had come back, riding his favorite black mare, having brought the horse down with him on the boat from *Bontemps*. He had parcels for everyone as though he hadn't been there only the Saturday before, and hardly a month went by, it seemed, when he hadn't come for days, even weeks. There were those slippers on the hearth, layers of pipe smoke floating at the dinner table, and empty kegs of beer in the yard.

He had even appeared the day after New Year's when everyone knew this was the greatest feast on the plantation, saying "As soon as I could get away, *mon petit chou*," while he pressed Cecile to his chest. And she in a perfect ecstasy had spent a winter of ordering special dishes, rushing out to shops to find him rare blends of tobacco, selecting for him new and fancily carved ivory pipes. Lisette was sent at dawn to market for the best oysters, and new dresses had been ordered for Cecile from her aunts. Monsieur couldn't have enough wax candles, tallow was intolerable, bought an argand lamp for the parlor, and a new Aubusson carpet for the boudoir. And in bed till afternoon on Sundays had Marcel read him the papers while he sipped his brandy, or his sherry, or his bourbon, or his beer.

"I've got a new pup at *Bontemps*, thinks he wants to play the master," he had remarked once with a confidential sneer to Marcel, "so let him get a taste of it. He's at odds with the overseer, nothing's done right, has to mend the levee his own way, let him get a taste of it. What are those cakes I like, you know, with the chocolate and the cream, get those for after dinner, here, take this, go yourself, Lisette's got her hands full with Zazu, here, buy yourself something while you're out."

So it's that black-haired white man with eyes like the devil, Marcel was thinking, "the young pup." And a vision disconcerting in its clarity visited him of Anna Bella in that man's arms. He could not think about it, Anna Bella puttering about her own small house, how soon would she be ... would she be with ... child? He wouldn't think about it. His mother was so happy these days, all was going too well.

Cecile in black lace cut low over her full bosom presided at their private midnight suppers, and seemed to Marcel in these months a perfect rose, the petals at their fullest with no hint of inevitable fall. Some unnatural froth or forced gaiety might have ruined this, but she was too clever for that, his mother, her instincts were too sound. She leaned against Monsieur Philippe when he had to go, and wept when he returned, unexpectedly and so soon! And "at home" with her, cherishing her, Monsieur Philippe dropped his ashes on the carpet and snored till noon.

Now and then, drunk and forgetting himself, he would ramble about that white family that Cecile had never seen. Marcel, bolting his dinner with a book at table could hear the deep voice in the afternoon quiet of the other room. His son, Leon, had just left for the continent with his great-uncle, it seems that opera gowns are made of money, why does every young woman these days have to have her own tilbury, and those trips to Baltimore were costing him a fortune, what with accommodations for five slaves. Cecile marked all this quietly, never uttering a question or a word.

And he was all the time urging money on her, would she like a new pearl necklace, then she should have it, he liked her so in pearls, but then she wore diamonds so well. Only a beautiful woman could wear diamonds, he whispered the words, Venus in Diorite, in her ear. On his return from *Bontemps* one week, he bought her a new ring. Marcel must go to the theater whenever he wished, and take that Lermontant boy with him if he liked, or his schoolteacher, yes, take the schoolteacher, how could anyone make a decent living as a teacher, here, they're playing Shakespeare aren't they, and Marie should have new gowns. He picked the cloth himself once or twice, of course Tante Louisa should charge him the full amount, why not, send Monsieur Jacquemine the bill. There was a slight defiant lift to his chin as he peeled off the dollar bills.

And meantime he teased Marcel about his books, admitted airily that he could not read a word of English, and seemed vaguely amused by the recitations of Latin poems. Marcel had won every prize in Latin and Greek that Christophe offered and would not have minded the nickname, "my little scholar," if he had not gotten it already from the boys in school. But even the older boys had said it with some measure of respect for him, while Monsieur Philippe's manner hinted that all these academic matters were foolishness really, they hadn't the pungent reality of horses' hooves beside the stalks of ripening cane. He swirled his bourbon in the firelight, slapping the cards down on the dining table. "Marcel. Come here, you play faro? Well it's time to learn." Even in ballooning sleeves, shirt open at the throat and tight black pants tapering to those soft blue slippers, there was an arrogant glamour to the man always, never dulled by the liquor that clouded his eyes. Marcel could see him sauntering among the fencing masters of Exchange Alley, a silver rapier clanking at his side. His spurs had rung on the flags when he came in one afternoon, and children up and down the Rue Ste. Anne hung on the gates to see his sleek black horse.

One's own world could shrink in the face of all that, Marcel mused. It was bitter to feel apologetic for the yearnings of one's soul. It seemed a miracle had been worked for Marcel in Christophe's class and Marcel, seeking the Mercier house whenever he could, slipped into his own skin there where he could be proud.

Because all the struggle of those early months, the books open past midnight, the hand cramped from the pen, all that struggle had indeed borne its fruit. History, that dark chaos of sublime secrets was at last yielding to Marcel a magnificent order; and the heavy classics that had once frightened and defeated him came clear under Christophe's light. But grander, more important, and so important in fact that Marcel shuddered to think of it, was simply this: Marcel had learned how to learn. He had begun to really use the powers of his own mind. He could feel the sheer exhilaration of his progress in all the subjects he had undertaken and his day-to-day world of lectures, books, and even the old street-roaming, was one of momentous and meaningful shocks.

So did it matter when that robust smiling planter, reins in one hand, trotted his mare through these narrow streets as if they were his own fields?

Of course Monsieur Philippe approved when Marcel spoke of his determination to sit for the examinations of the Ecole Normale in Paris. A year ago, Marcel could not have hoped to pass. But it was more than possible now. Christophe had told him so. "You'll be prepared by the time you go."

"Then I could teach at a French *lycée,* perhaps go into the university itself some day," Marcel explained as Monsieur Philippe blew the foam from the mug. "I would have my profession!" the word had a gilded ring. Of course the salary for such positions was nothing, most likely, he murmured. Monsieur Philippe said, "No matter," under his breath. "Very

(403)

good, very good indeed. But does that teacher ever teach you anything practical?" Philippe shrugged. "Sums, acccounting, whatever," he snapped his fingers to summon some intangible from the air.

He was pleased then to hear that Christophe had them read the English papers twice a week aloud in class, discuss the reportage, the political and financial events. And that Christophe had taken them all to see the Daguerreotypist, Jules Lion, who lectured on this magnificent new process, did Monsieur know of this man, a man of color, who had introduced the Daguerre method here from France?

"Ah, he is mad for all this, Monsieur," Cecile laughed, almost as if slightly ill at ease to see Marcel go on so.

"But here, Monsieur," Marcel was undaunted. "I insisted we all have a portrait made, together, to commemorate the school." And Marcel produced the large shining full plate of these twenty individuals staring stiffly at the camera, a dark spectrum from the near-black Gaston, son of the shoemaker, to the snow-white Fantin Roget. Monsieur Philippe laughed.

"Magic, magic," he said to Marcel with the characteristic twinkle in his eye. "One no longer has to sit for the painter, I always loathed it, so boring," and then squinting he found Marcel among the assemblage with a playful laugh. "Ah, those Dumanoirs," he said recognizing the son of the planter, "I tell you they do better than I!"

Cecile laughed as though this were capital wit. And in spite of Marcel's increasing height, he discovered his father could still reach to pat him on the head.

Marcel smiled. *Ti* Marcel indeed. On the balmy nights of summer when he heard their lovemaking across the little courtyard, the heavy breaths, the creak of the giant bed, he lay calm in the shadows of his upstairs room waiting for them to fall asleep. He was too much the gentleman to have said it even to himself, but the truth was, he had a mistress as beautiful as Monsieur Philippe's.

No one knew it. If Lisette knew it, and if other slaves knew it, as Christophe had once indicated they might, they had never said a word. Not to anyone that mattered, that is, not to anyone who might care.

And all winter long he had gone to Juliet, slipping out of his room when it was quiet to admit himself to the Mercier house with his own key. Over and over he had climbed anxiously into the smoky warmth of that second floor to find her

(404)

barefoot by the glowing grate, an angel in white flannel with
high neck and long sleeves contrived to drive him mad. He
would lose himself in caressing her, feeling those small angular limbs through the soft cloth as if he'd never seen them
naked before.

And sometimes miserable and restless he had come to her
just before dawn, already dressed for the day's demands,
wandering in the dark trickling garden under her window,
singing her name. "Come up," she would whisper to him, a
ghost above, and he would find her carelessly dressed in one
of Christophe's cast-off shirts, its flared hem stroking her
pubic down. She made coffee for him on the hissing stove,
laughed when he reached for her legs. They would breakfast
on fruits and bits of cheese in bed, and coming up after school,
he would find her sleeping still in the perfumed room.

And Christophe all the while came and went, finding
Marcel at home with no more comment than if they were one
family, and Marcel had always been there. They studied together, argued philosophy over supper, went through old
trunks and old books, played chess and would end on the
floor of Christophe's room before the fire with their wine.

Juliet was always near, bringing supper to them, mending
some cuff or collar for Christophe as they talked, or sewing
a button to Marcel's coat. She brought cake to them when
they were glassy-eyed and frenzied in their arguments and
had forgotten that they must eat. And fluffing the pillows of
Christophe's bed, lay there at times to listen to them, her
eyes on the ceiling, her hands beneath her hair. She would
crook her legs under her flared skirts exactly as if she were
a boy. And at table she was ever the servant with Bubbles'
silent assistance, anticipating their slightest need.

Collecting Christophe's bruised books she scolded him for
slopping the pages when he drank, saying, "Look at what
you've done to this," as she set it near the stove to dry. She
urged heavy coats on him when he went out, or sent Bubbles
rushing after with his wool cravat. And had the slave not
cleaned his master's boots she would have done that with her
own hands.

All this Christophe took, meantime, as if it came to him
on the open air. He was the magician who merely wishes for
a full glass to find it in his hand. And Marcel had long come
to realize and accept that Christophe was her first love when
he was there. "Anyone coming into this house right now
would think they were the lovers," he mused, "her eyes never

leave him for an instant." And he felt both jealous and content.

From time to time, he remembered that letter Christophe had written to her from Paris to tell her he was coming back. He wished now that he could see it again, just by chance perhaps lying open on a table or a desk. For in all Christophe's long diatribes about his return home, he had never mentioned his mother with all the warmth, the feeling that had been written there. And here he was slumped in study by the fire letting her massage the muscles of his neck, stir the sugar into his coffee, even touch the cheroot with the match.

Yes, it was enough to make a lover jealous, but after all, when they were alone together in that bedroom, Juliet belonged to Marcel.

She was his completely between the sheets, showing him all manner of secrets with her lips and her hands. He thought some of it perverse at first and lay awake afterward uneasy and afraid. But gradually he became accustomed to her wild variations and saw them as the piquant delicacies known only to mature lovers, even as was her passion. He had not known before that women could so relish the act of love, in fact, Richard had told him quite simply once that they did not. And there she was, this woman who had had her pick of men, her head thrown back, her lids fluttering, dying over and over in his arms. He glanced in the mirror proudly, put a slender cigar to his lips, drank his wine with lusty despairing swallows, and laughed.

The waning season had found them a regular trio at the opera, Juliet in red silk and laced to make her waist a mere handful which he could not gather for himself save in the dark.

He had never dreamed that life could be this way.

It astonished him the contentment he knew when he was in that now familiar house, its nooks and crannies comfortable as his own. And time after time he would leave her fragrant bed and wandering down the hall, find Christophe writing by the dingy light of his smoking lamp. They would talk. The clock would tick, the wind made a mournful sound in the chimneys, Christophe scratched at the verses in front of him, then might crumple the paper into a ball and toss it into the fire. Once on the frostiest night, Christophe had all but dragged Marcel up on the sloping roof to look at the stars. He was afraid of falling, but the wilderness of glistening roofs spread out before him magically; and he would have liked to run from one to another, peering down through alleys at yellow windows, listening for mingled voices rising unevenly up the airwells, to find the river from this height and watch the steamboats, a spectacle of vague and dazzling lights in winter mists. Christophe knew the constellations, discovering each easily, and told him how much he would love the absolute clarity of the heavens when he first saw them over the open sea.

"But let's not talk of that now," Marcel had whispered, "of going, parting." And realizing later that never had he said such a thing to anyone, he pondered the wordless feeling he had for Christophe which was love as surely as his passion for Juliet, and in some ways just as volatile, sweet, with the ebb and flow of each new encounter be it argument, laughter, hours alone together reading in a silent room. They had seen pain together after all, even death, the excesses of temper and drink, and had fallen into some simple and utterly explicit language as do the more trusting members of a family who cannot conceive of life without each other and think nothing of it as time goes on.

And yet daily there was the relentless and demanding teacher at the podium who with a sharp accusing finger would catch Marcel as he lapsed into his habitual dreams. And once begging off an assignment late at night, Marcel was lacerated by such a venomous glance that he went at once to beg Christophe's forgiveness and home to do the appointed work.

Yet there were times when a darkness came over Marcel, and waking up in Juliet's bed, he saw the world through her shuttered windows, slits of green leaf and sun seemingly beyond him, and feeling stifled suddenly he sought the open air.

It was spring, the damp winter was dying in warmer though brisk winds. He found himself wandering back of town, out beyond the Place Congo to the Bayou Cemetery and sometimes back again through the Rue St. Louis past the cottage he knew to be Anna Bella's home. His steps would quicken then, his eyes averted, and he would embroil himself in other thoughts, wondering after, why he had chosen that path. Everyone said she was happy. Some said now she was expecting a child. He would roam the markets and wharves as he used to do before, thinking vaguely, ah, well she will be indoors after this and I won't see her, but there came some recurrent sensation of being with her in some sunny place, of white china, and some wholesome rippling talk. And dropping in at the Lermontants for dinner—he was always welcome and he knew it—he would immerse himself in their interminable and interesting conversations, occasionally looking around the orderly table—Richard's mother beckoning with whispers to Placide, Rudolphe in the midst of some adamant point on the economy, and Richard musing with his glass—and thinking of Juliet, he would wonder: what would they do if they knew? What would they think? Rudolphe came so often to the back reading room of Christophe's house, Giselle's oldest boy, Frederick, had been allowed to sit in on class when in town. What would they think? It almost brought a smile to his lips, but then again it did not. Who could understand this madness, a woman past forty, a boy of fifteen? And then he felt disloyal to his love, and later would take Juliet flowers which he dropped one by one along the length of her bed.

Once wakening by himself near the very stroke of midnight he had been possessed by a disembodied thought: Anna Bella was no longer innocent; Anna Bella was a woman; Anna Bella was carrying a child.

But his mistress in the half-light stretched her long brown limbs and shifted like a feline against his chest. She didn't question the urgency with which he awakened her, nor the exhaustion with which he finally fell to sleep.

"If only I could speak of it to one living soul," he thought once dismally seeing Juliet in the street. Alphonse LeMond the tailor had come with her to the door of his shop, entrusting a parcel to Bubbles' hands. It was sweet to watch her unnoticed, her sprightly figure in shimmering taffeta and the lean graceful black servant at her side. "If only I could speak of it to a living soul.

"But I can't. If I could I would speak of it to Chris, but I can't, and I never will."

Because in all those months Christophe had never acknowledged the affair with a single word. There were three subjects one did not speak of in this house which had become Marcel's home: the first was the Englishman, the second was Juliet's father, the black Haitian, the third was this day-to-day affair.

And remembering that awful fight between mother and son when Juliet had taunted Christophe, "Tell him the real reason you don't want us together!" Marcel would not dare

(408)

to break this silence on any of the three scores. That she had been taunting Christophe with a son's natural jealousy of his mother, Marcel had no doubt.

But sometime in the early summer, Marcel could not precisely recall, he had wandered up the stairs in the small hours and found Christophe in her bed. Dressed, of course, and rumpled, with the wine bottle beside him on the floor. He'd fallen asleep there obviously, and she, seeing no earthly reason to move him, lay curled against him under his arm. A shocking impropriety anywhere else, but why not under this roof? It seemed similar to so much that happened here, a matter the world would misunderstand. Juliet had risen, gestured for silence, and covering her son's shoulders, led Marcel down the hall. In Christophe's bed they'd made love and this being new and different it excited Marcel wildly. He couldn't hold her tight enough, wanted to make her cry out. It happened again. And again.

And even once he had awakened to find the three of them nestled in the same bed, Christophe in shirtsleeves beside his mother who between them had slipped into the modesty of her gown. It was Christophe who rose before anyone and, as if shocked to find himself there, left at once.

But what pleasure had Christophe in his life right now other than this simple affection? What would his rigid discipline allow? Aside from the occasional excess of the bottle, his was a monk's life, and his room with its books, narrow bed, and crowded desk had become a cell. Rarely if ever did the evenings find him gone, he was writing, studying, shuffling his students' pages on the dining table or roaming about the house as if it had become a cloister, his lips moving silently with his thoughts. And then some physical task would obsess him, he must change every picture on the wall of the classroom, or wrestle trunks about the damp and leaking attic rooms. Bubbles must not be allowed to scrub the grates without help, it was too much for him; and Christophe, much to Bubbles' misery, took the rake from him time after time to pull the weeds from the flags. A shocking thing this, a gentleman with callouses on his hands. And Bubbles said so whenever he could.

But Christophe was in the grip of a magnificent asceticism, Marcel sensed this, extreme perhaps as the excesses he had described abroad. In fact, he was forever shuffling through volumes of Augustine and Marcus Aurelius with his spy glass for some lost quotation that would give him no peace.

And once in a while Marcel, surprising him with a light step, would find him with a manuscript on his desk. A large sheaf of papers one time, a smaller at another, but always unmistakably a work over which Christophe was murmuring with a poised pen. But Christophe locking it away at once commenced some forceful discussion, cutting Marcel coldly though politely should he ask the slightest question on what he had just seen.

If there was loneliness Marcel did not see it; if there was an empty place Christophe kept that knowledge within.

But as the months stretched to the half year, the nature of Marcel's secret life weighed upon him more and more heavily until it was, in fact, a persistent pain. If only he could talk to Chris, just put it into words! And it seemed the need was greatest, not when he was with them both in the Mercier house, but when he had to be at home.

Death permeated the atmosphere of the cottage as July came on, and Marcel could not and would not attempt to escape it as Zazu grew worse. But a glass divided him from those he loved. He saw his sister suffering sometimes beyond that glass, and Richard struggling with a boy's restraints and a man's work. And Lisette, in the shadows of the sickroom, head averted, staring in horror at her mother's wracked and heaving frame. Cecile visiting the sickroom left it hurriedly, wringing her hands with short breaths under the night sky.

And Marcel, hearing those vibrating coughs through the walls, stared at the familiar objects of his own room. But why did it weigh on him, his secret love, he would ask himself pacing later, picking up his pen only to set it down and find the windowsill in back with its moist breeze. He loved her; she loved him, and what harm could this possibly bring? He ached to be with them both now where it would not matter, and wondered at the fear that gripped him when he thought of it here alone.

Something was coming back to him, fainter than memory as he considered this, some picture conjured by Christophe of a man sitting in a Paris room. "It's a decision the world would not understand," the man had said. "I've come to it, the struggle is over . . . a decision the world would not understand." And it was that word, decision, which loomed large, obscuring the picture as it grew more and more familiar, the

Englishman Michael Larson-Roberts in that phantom hotel in Paris the night he'd vowed to take Christophe away.

"If I could only make that decision," Marcel had murmured over and over, and finally, reckless and willing to jeopardize all the splendor of his clandestine world, he left the *garçonnière* the night before Lisette ran away, and found Christophe alone in the yard behind the Mercier house.

A lantern burned in the shed beyond the trees and there Bubbles sat playing the old piano which he had now restrung, and an eerie music, soft, tinkling, filled the yard. Christophe himself lay on a cot under the sky, his hands behind his head, one knee crooked, the arc of a lighted cheroot descending to his lips as Marcel approached.

"And how is she?" Christophe asked, the voice tender. Then, his eyes accustomed to the partial light, he could see that Marcel had not heard.

"Zazu," Christophe whispered.

Marcel said, "The same." Then finding a wooden stool by the shed he brought it near, sitting so that he might rest his back against the bark of a slender leafy tree. The night was alive with the sound of insects, but the mosquitoes for reasons unbeknownst to man, if known to God, were not their worst.

"We never speak of it," Marcel said softly. "Your mother and me."

Christophe said nothing. The lantern in the shed made a moon in his eye. Marcel heard the soft explosion of the smoke from his lips and breathed the sweet aroma of tobacco. He wanted to reach into his own pocket for a smoke, but somehow or other he could not move.

"Is silence consent?" he asked now, looking up at the dark windows of Juliet's room.

Again Christophe did not answer. Marcel rose to pace the flags.

"It isn't that I believe it's wrong," Marcel declared. "It isn't that I have the slightest qualm about it! It isn't that it does me harm. You would say if you thought it did me harm... or Juliet harm... or you harm, you would say..."

Again silence.

Then Christophe asked in a low monotone, "So what is it, then?"

"That it seems somehow impossible, impossible that it should be so easy and so forbidden, so good and yet supposedly wrong. That I flourish doing what others would think patently evil, and it goes on under their noses and they don't suspect. That's what it is. It goes against the order of things!"

Christophe took another long draw on the cheroot and then sent it arching slowly across the yard. In the shed Bubbles' music became lower and melancholy. As always it sounded disturbingly familiar as if made of fragments from a recent opera or theatrical that were altered and interwoven in undefinable ways.

"Is it that way, really? There is no real order to things!" Marcel asked. "There's nothing, is there? You knew that when you conceded on the matter of bringing Bubbles into the classroom, didn't you? You knew there was no undying principle, nothing for which you would go to the barricades like the mobs in the Paris streets..."

"You are very clever, my star pupil," Christophe said softly. "But you may not thrust this responsibility into my hands. I refuse to accept it and you may interpret my silence as you please..."

"Christophe, help me!"

"Marcel," Christophe laughed, "that is like the ocean asking for help." He turned over on the cot, raising himself on his elbows and stared into the dark clump of leaf and tree that obscured the shape of the rising cistern. There was the rustling of paper, a hand in the pocket, and then the bright explosion of a match: his profile visible for an instant in casual concentration and then gone.

"I'm afraid," Marcel said.

"Why?"

"Because if it's really true that there's no order, then anything can happen to us. Anything at all. There's no real natural law, no right and wrong that's immutable, and the world is suddenly a savage place where any number of things can go wrong."

He walked slowly back and forth pondering this, and then continued quickly, "Juliet told me a story once of something she witnessed in Saint-Domingue. It wasn't actually a story, it was one of those strange little details she lets slip sometimes in an airy way as if it's been floating for years in her mind. It was an account of an execution, of three black men burned alive before a crowd. She told me..."

"I've heard," Christophe stopped him.

"But the point is I couldn't get it out of my mind for days after she'd told me, the vision she conjured, it was unspeakable to me that men could die like that, that people would

(412)

watch...and if there is no real right and wrong, if there is no natural law that is immutable, then things like that can happen all over this world...dreadful things, worse things if there are worse things, and somehow it would never ever be made all right. There wouldn't be any justice, and suffering ultimately would have no meaning, no meaning at all."

"And suppose it's the opposite," Christophe said. "That there is a natural law, a real right and wrong?"

"Then I should not be sleeping with her because she is a woman of forty and I'm a boy of fifteen, and she's your mother and you are my teacher and pupils come to this house every day, and those who might discover it would abhor her and abhor me. And yet it seems sweet and harmless, and I...I don't want to give it up! I won't give it up, not unless you force me to give it up or she sends me away."

"But don't you see?" Christophe said calmly. "It doesn't really come to that day-to-day." He sat up on the cot and faced Marcel. The light from the shed threw the shifting shadows of the leaves across his face distorting his expression, rendering it impossible to read. "When you find out that there is no ultimate good and evil in which you can place your faith, the world does not fall apart at the seams. It simply means that every decision is more difficult, more critical, because you are creating the good and evil yourself and they are very real."

"Decision..." Marcel murmured, "the Englishman's word."

Christophe did not answer.

"In Paris, the night he took you with him," Marcel said tentatively, "'it's a decision the world will not understand.'"

It seemed to him Christophe nodded but he couldn't be sure. He was very sorry he'd mentioned the Englishman. Bubbles' music had died in the interval and Christophe appeared almost unnaturally still.

"Did you say?" Marcel murmured, "a moment before, did you say that the good and evil were very real?"

"I said it," Christophe whispered.

"It's never going to be easy, is it?"

"No," Christophe answered.

"Not even when it's only love."

"...and when you really come to understand that," Christophe said, "then whether it's love or not love, you are really alone."

* * *

Alone. The night had been restless, Zazu's hoarse breaths, Monsieur Philippe's tread on the porch, and the steaming heat that rendered the slowest gesture heavy and exhausting, until finally the morning had come with its wilting sun and Marcel had commenced his search for Lisette.

III

By MIDMORNING he had been all through the market and past a dozen or more of the little grog shops in which he'd caught her before. He had stopped at the neighborhood kitchens, conferred with Bubbles, but Lisette had not been seen. And finally, after putting it off to the very last, he walked steadily and anxiously toward Anna Bella's gate. However, the sight of the neat little cottage with its whitewashed walls and green shutters, the crepe myrtles sheltering its front path, stopped him in his tracks. He could not imagine himself slipping past those windows to find Zurlina in the back kitchen, and yet he could not bring himself even to knock on the door. It seemed the pendulum in his mind swung back and forth: he must ask, Zazu was receiving the Last Sacraments, and yet would Anna Bella want him here on this errand, unable even to remain for a moment's talk? And then again the pendulum swung: he wanted to see her, to see her! And beneath that fragile conviction lay some sense of her now as settled in her new life and of himself so content in his own. Whether he would have gone up or not he was never to know for, within minutes, Zurlina had opend the front blinds, and come down the path.

She wore her snow-white *tignon* like a turban and her face against that stark linen was very much the pale wax of some gnarled tree trunk, lined, yellow, and seemingly hard.

"Et Zazu?" she rubbed her hands on her white apron.

"Where is Lisette, is she here?" he asked, and without realizing it, he ripped his eyes from the front shutters behind her, and turned to go. Anna Bella might be there, Anna Bella might see him at the gate.

A mean laugh escaped Zurlina's thin lips, the skin above them wrinkled in vertical lines. Marcel despised this woman, she had been haughty to him always, some proud and blistering extension of her old mistress, and

(414)

he turned his back on her now.

"Lola Dedé," she said in a low scornful voice. "Go to Lola Dedé if you want Lisette."

Marcel nodded but he did not look back. "Lola Dedé!" he muttered contemptuously. He had heard the name. So that was the voodooienne to whom Lisette returned again and again for powders and charms; he had often passed her dilapidated gray house sagging upon its long lot near the Rue Rampart and it disgusted him as did all of the voodoo about him, the whispers among the servants, those random nighttime drums. But he knew he must go there. "Tell your mistress," he turned now to the departing Zurlina, "tell her I give her my best."

The thin lips drew back in an ugly grimace and the low nasal voice, caricature of the dead Madame Elsie, snorted a vague assent.

Marcel took his time about it but at last he came to the shell yard outside Lola Dedé's door and approaching with a bowed head, he knocked hard on the weathered wood.

Only an eye showed itself in the crack, and a rank smell, soiled bodies, soiled clothes, seeped out into the fresher air. "She's not here," said the voice.

"You tell her for me her mother's dying," he said placing a hand against the door.

"She's not here!" the voice averred again, and it seemed a rumbling commenced within, soft laughter. Marcel told himself this was fancy.

"You tell her to come home!" he said, as the door slammed shut in his face. He looked up in despair at the gray rainwashed shutters, the sagging roof, and then with a sudden sense of relief turned fast for home.

As soon as he reached the *garçonnière* he knew it was the end.

Marie and Cecile stood quietly on the porch and Monsieur Philippe was at the bedside alone.

"Go in now, if you want to take your leave of her," Cecile whispered anxiously. She had twisted her handkerchief into a piece of ragged string. There was panic in her eyes, and her skin was moist.

"And Lisette, did she come back?" Marcel asked.

"No," Marie shook her head. "Go in, Marcel," she said gently.

He hesitated at the door. He had gotten off easy with Jean Jacques, he realized that now, and he had gotten off easy with the Englishman, but he wasn't to get off now. For a moment he was absolutely incapable of moving into the room. Then Monsieur Philippe, looking up, motioned for him.

Zazu lay with her mouth open, the white of her lower teeth showing against her dark lip, her breath coming in labored gasps. And when his father pressed him against the bed, she opened her eyes. She knew him at once, she had come round, and feebly she took his hand.

It seemed his voice left him, and only when Monsieur Philippe said that he ought to go on out now, did he kneel down and say to her softly how much he'd loved her, how well she'd cared for him all these years. The sudden thought came to him that this would alarm her, but again she smiled. Her heavy black lids closed, but not all the way. And he whispered quickly, "Monsieur!"

Philippe bent over her. Then she opened her eyes again. "Look out for my girl, Michie, look out for my Lisette." she said, her voice so faint it was barely clear.

"I will, my poor dear," he said to her. It seemed her eyes rolled up in her head. Marcel was shaken.

"Look out for her, Michie," she whispered again as if she would not give in. The voice was dry and seemed to scratch inside her throat. "Michie!" her eyes widened. "Michie, she's your girl, too!"

"Yes, yes, my poor dear," Monsieur Philippe said.

She was dead.

For a long moment Marcel stood staring down at her. He had never seen the life go out of any living being, and as he watched her face relax in death, he felt the tears come.

With a solicitude that amazed him, Monsieur Philippe drew Zazu's rosary from the covers, and slipped it over her fingers. "*Adieu, ma chère,*" he whispered heavily. Then he folded her hands atop the counterpane and he brought the lids of her eyes down gently, letting her head sink to one side.

And when he stepped out on the gallery with Marcel behind him, he struck a match hard to light his cigar. "Damn that girl!" he said.

Cecile turned, shuddering, and walked swiftly down the length of the porch to the stairs. Marie had gone into Zazu's room at once.

Then Marcel touched his father's arm. Lisette stood at the entrance of the alleyway, her yellow *tignon* bright against the green brush. She was glowering at them, and even from where he stood Marcel could see she was unsteady.

"Is my Maman dead?" she asked in a low voice.

Monsieur Philippe moved so fast Marcel was nearly knocked off balance by him. But Lisette turned and ran. She was gone before Monsieur Philippe ever reached the bottom of the steps. He stamped out the butt of his cigar and beckoning angrily for Marcel, he stalked into the cottage.

"I have to get back to the country," he said. He was picking up his cape and putting his flat black wallet into the pocket of his coat. Cecile sat in the corner of the parlor, her head bowed.

"Your mother can't take care of this, go get your friends, the Lermontants," Monsieur Philippe said with his eyes on her. Indeed, she looked miserable, and extremely weak.

"I imagine they've taken care of a few devoted servants in their time."

"Yes, Monsieur."

"So get them to do it right." He slipped several twenty-dollar bills into Marcel's hand. "And when you see that girl, you tell her to do what you say. You be the master here now, you get her in line!" He pointed a warning finger at Marcel. "I'd do it myself if I didn't have to get back to the country and discover what little surprise my young brother-in-law has cooked up for me now. He's had time enough to flood the entire plantation in my absence and turn the crop to rice!" He gathered his keys, and removing his watch checked it by the clock over the mantel.

"But Monsieur, what's the matter with her!" Marcel whispered. He was not in the habit of asking his father questions, but this was too much. And there had been those muted arguments for months.

"She wants her freedom, that's what's the matter, wants it on a silver platter now!" Monsieur Philippe declared. "Got some fancy notion I should tell poor Zazu on her deathbed that I was setting her daughter free."

"Freedom!" Marcel gasped. That she should want it was hardly a surprise to him, but was this the way to get it? Lisette who had been nothing but trouble all her life, Lisette who was rebellious to the marrow of her bones? And now to do this? He shook his head. It was more than folly. It was insane.

"Run off with that woman on her deathbed," Monsieur Philippe was muttering. "I took that girl out of the kitchen yard at *Bontemps,* gave her money, brought her to live in town!" His face was working with his anger. "Well, she's not

(417)

playing games with me! And what would she do if she were free, I've seen the nigger trash she runs with and the white trash too!" He hesitated, his lips working angrily, his eyes casting a protective and pointed glance at Cecile. "Don't you take any sass from her," he said to Marcel under his breath. "I've never whipped a house slave in my life, but by God, I'll whip her if she doesn't get back here before you put Zazu in the ground. Go to those Lermontants," he said over his shoulder. He approached Cecile, his hand out for her shoulder. "And you tell her if she ever wants a petition from me for her freedom, she's to do as you say!"

It wasn't until the morning of the funeral that Lisette finally appeared. The Lermontants had buried many a loyal and faithful servant for their white and colored clients alike, and they did well as always, a procession of neighboring servants and friends following the coffin to the grave.

Cecile was trembling violently as the coffin left the house and quickly shut up the windows and the doors as if to keep some unnamed menace away. Marcel disliked leaving her, knowing Marie could be of no comfort to her, and after the brief ceremonies at the St. Louis Cemetery, he hurried home.

A note had come from Anna Bella. His mother behind a veil of netting, her head against her pillow appeared asleep. For a moment all he saw of the note was an ornate and curling script replete with beautiful capitals, and then slowly the sentiments, perfectly and briefly expressed, made their impression on him with a peculiar pain. Anna Bella had commenced her confinement. She had been unable to come. He held the note for a moment, quite unwilling to let any thought form in his mind. Rather, he saw himself in the Rue St. Louis approaching Anna Bella's gate. But Lisette. Lisette. He slipped the note into his pocket and went out to cross the courtyard to his room.

She did not disappoint him. She came wandering in, her eyes red, her dress filthy and carrying a tattered broken bouquet in her hands. But as soon as he saw her, her head to one side like a bruised flower, and saw the way that she picked the petals from the chrysanthemums that she carried, letting them fall on the shells of the alleyway, all the anger went out of him.

"They covered her up already, Michie," she said.

Marcel followed her into the kitchen and into her room.

"You'd better sleep it off, Lisette," he said.

(418)

"Go to hell," she answered.

He watched her. She was throwing these flowers all around the floor. Now she was tramping on them with her feet. Now she tore the *tignon* off her head, and her copper hair poofed out in thick tight ripples and she scratched at it, shaking her head.

He sighed and sat down in the corner in Zazu's old rocker.

"You remember after Jean Jacques died?" he started. "You got that diary for me out of the fire."

She stood in the center of the room scratching at her head.

"I remember it, if you don't," he said.

"Well, bless you now, Maitre, you're one kind man."

"Lisette, look, I know it's grief that's eating at you, and I know what grief is. But Michie Philippe's really put out at you, Lisette, you've got to get yourself in hand!"

"Oh, come on now, Michie. You scared of Michie Philippe?" she demanded.

He sighed. "If it's your freedom you want, this is no way to get it." He rose to go.

"Get it, get it?" she came after him. "And what should I do to get it?" she hissed at him. Reluctantly, he turned his head.

"Act like you'd know what to do with it, that's what! Running off like that with your mother dying. Michie Philippe's at his wits' ends with you, don't you know that?"

But instantly he regretted this. He could see the fury in her eyes.

"He promised me my freedom!" she said, her fists striking at her own breast. "He promised me when I was a little girl, he'd set me free when I was grown! Well, I passed my twenty-third birthday, Michie, I've been grown for years, and he broke that promise to me!"

"You can't get it this way!" he pleaded with her. "You're being a fool!"

"No, you're the fool! You're the fool to believe anything that man ever said. Sending you to Paris, putting you up like a gentleman, don't you believe it, Michie," she shook her head. "My Maman served that man for fifty years of her life, she licked his boots, he promised her she'd see me free before she died and he broke that promise to her! If he wouldn't set me free before she shut her eyes on this world, he's never going to set me free. 'Oh, you just be patient, Lisette, you just be a good girl, you just take care of your Maman, what you want with freedom anyways, Lisette where you going go?'"

She spat on the brick floor, her face twisted with contempt.

"He's been good to you," Marcel said in a low voice. He started for the kitchen door.

"Has he, Michie?" She came after him and reaching out swung the door shut behind her, facing him, so that for an instant he was blinded and saw only a sparkle of light in the rough cracks.

"Now stop this, Lisette," he said. He felt the first real urge to slap her. He moved to push the door. She clutched at the latch. He could hardly make out the features of her face, and the kitchen seemed at once damp and suffocating. He took a deep breath. "Get out of the way, Lisette." The sweat broke out on his forehead. "If Maman hears all this, she's sure to tell him."

It seemed the faint light gathered slowly in her eyes as he became accustomed to it; her face was a grimace. He could smell the wine on her breath.

"If he can break his promise to me, Michie, he can break it to you," she said. "You think you're so special, don't you, Michie, you think 'cause his blood's running in your veins, he wouldn't do you dirt. Well, let me tell you that with all those books of yours and schooling of yours, and that fancy teacher of yours, and that fancy lady you keep up there right under everybody's nose, you're not so smart! 'Cause that same blood's running in my veins, Michie, and you never so much as guessed. We got that in common, my fine little gentleman, I'm his child just as sure as you are! He slept with my Maman same as he slept with yours. And that's how come he hustled us off *Bontemps* years ago, 'cause his wife caught right on to what you never guessed in fifteen years!"

There was no sound then except that of her breathing. He was staring into the darkness, seeing nothing.

"I don't believe that," he whispered.

She was perfectly still.

"I don't believe that!" he whispered. "He wouldn't have brought you here!"

"The hell he wouldn't," she growled. "Madame Aglae said to him 'you trouble your house bringing that copper-colored baby into it, I won't have my children growing up with that copper-colored baby, you trouble your house, you inherit the wind...'"

"No," Marcel shook his head. "He wouldn't..." *I never*

(420)

*whipped a house slave in my life, but by God I'll whip her,
you be the master with her!* "Not here!"

"Yes, here, Michie, here! And your Maman, your pretty
black Maman, when she saw me, she said, she said, 'you ever
tell anybody you're his whelp so help me I'll kill you!' digging
those fingernails into my arm. I tell you, Michie, men are
blind as bats but women can see in the dark! So what do you
have to say to your sister now!"

Marcel let out a long raw moan.

He was not conscious of the turns he took. He only knew
that he was walking and that he would continue to walk
until some of the tumult in him died away. And the awareness that it was early evening meant little to him, any more
than the awareness that he was wandering in the Rue St.
Louis not far from the Lermontant house. Only he was not
going to the Lermontant house. He felt if he had to sit down
to supper with them tonight he would lose his mind. He was
going somewhere else, but perhaps not, he could make another decision, there was no law against passing the gate.
And what if he stopped when he got there, overcome with the
perfume of the jasmine, wanting just to enjoy it for a little
while? Two neat crepe myrtles stood on either side of the
gate, their hard waxy limbs as clean as bones beneath the
lacy foliage, crepe myrtles just like those in Madame Elsie's
yard. Maybe Anna Bella had picked the cottage for those
crepe myrtles with their fragile red blooms. A rich wave of
the jasmine passed over him, and drifting out into the street,
he made a small circle under the night sky. It seemed the
world pulsed with the cicadas' scratching song, and beyond
the crepe myrtles was the glow of Anna Bella's windows, and
he had no doubt that she was there. If ever there had been
a time in his life when he wanted to fall into her arms, it
was now. He did not know whether this was shame or simply
horror. And when he thought of Lisette sleeping in that back
kitchen room, her dress stained with dirt, her body moist and
shuddering from the drink she'd had for three days, it was
for him a perfect of image of misery, if not hell.

When he saw a dark shape in Anna Bella's window, he
did not look away. And hearing the heavy shutters of the
front door creak, he watched for a movement on the path.
The moon spilling through the trees made shifting shadows
on the figure, on the pale face and the white shawl.

Now he saw her clearly at the gate.

(421)

"Marcel," she beckoned. "Marcel, come inside."

"Is he there?" he asked.

"No," she said. "You come on inside!"

It seemed an hour that he talked, he did not know.

Anna Bella, her thickening waist covered with a light quilt, sat in the rocker to one side of the open doorway, tendrils of her soft hair moving in the breeze. She had put out the one candle. And Zurlina to make her disapproval known, puttered in another room. They paid no attention to her. The door was shut. She could not have heard. There had been no real greeting, he had not so much as touched her hand, none of that polite kissing on either cheek, and she did not seem to expect it, she had merely led him to his chair. He felt exhilarated as he talked, certain of her understanding, and when he saw by the light of the moon the tenderness of her large brown eyes he was not surprised.

"Never tell anyone," he said thickly. "I can't stand for anyone to know this! I just can't bear the thought of it. You must swear to me, you'll never tell a soul."

"You know I won't, Marcel," she said. "But where is she now? How are you going to stop her from being crazy, and from doing herself some harm?"

"I don't know. I don't know what to do with her! Why she hasn't run away for good before this, I don't know."

"This is her town, Marcel, where would she go? Away from New Orleans and her own people? No. She wants to be free right here, Marcel, not living hand-to-mouth, but set up nicely somewhere right here. That's not to say she couldn't ruin herself, ruin any chance she's got. But you don't think Michie Philippe would send the police after her if she did run away..."

"Anna Bella," he laughed. "What do I know? Had you asked me yesterday could he put his own daughter, black or colored, to licking her brother's and sister's boots, I would have said never. Ties of blood mean something to the man, he wouldn't stoop so low. But that's just what he's done. She's my sister! And my mother knows this, has always known." He stopped. This was one salient aspect of the entire revelation that caused him private and particular grief. "Marie doesn't guess," he said in a calmer voice. "Anna Bella, I tell you I can't go on under the same roof with Lisette now that I know this, and with Marie it would be the same way. Do you know she brushes Marie's hair every night, she takes her dresses from the laundress, swears they're not done well enough and heats up the iron again after the supper's cleared away at night? I see her down there in the open kitchen ironing those dresses while Marie sleeps. What am I going to do with her? What am I going to do with myself?"

He could not see the reservation in Anna Bella's face as he said these last words. He could not know that Anna Bella had overheard too much of Lisette's sharp tongue to believe Lisette had ever loved Marie. Lisette played with those pretty dresses as poor children play with dolls.

"There's only one thing you can do as I see it, and I think you know what that is," she said. "You've got to get Michie Philippe to keep his promise to her. She's got to get her freedom for your sake now as well as her own."

He was quiet. In all the day's interminable wanderings this single fact had never come clear in his mind.

"That girl's ruining herself in ways you don't even know," Anna Bella murmured, "what with that Lola Dedé the voodooienne..."

"I know that," Marcel said with a nod. "But how can I do this? No one demands anything of Monsieur Philippe! If you knew how things stood with me and..."

"I'm not talking about demands, Marcel, I'm talking about getting him to do it, they aren't the same thing. You've got to put it to him in the right way, don't you see, you've got to convince him it'd be best for all of you if Lisette wasn't around. Now don't tell me that man would put his own daughter on the block. Don't you see, you've got to put it like an advantage to the peace of the house if Lisette goes. You've got to work up to it, you've got to begin by asking him gently if he means to do it sometime, you've got to play it smart."

"I can't do that! I swear if he were in town now, I don't know that I could look him in the eye. I couldn't stay in the house with him."

"Stop that," she said. "Don't you ever say that. Don't you ever stop looking him in the eye or staying in the same house, and don't you ever let him know that you know! You just have to set your mind on one thing, the best way of getting that girl free without making the man mad. You've got to keep pride out of it, not just for her sake, but for your own."

She stopped, alarmed at her own heat. "Don't you let it come between you, Marcel, you and your father. You know what that could mean."

He was musing. He was thinking of Zazu, tall, slender and ebony black as she'd been when he was a little boy, thinking of that mute subservience, the decorous manner in which Zazu had always waited upon Cecile, and Cecile's quiet dismissal, while Zazu had once been...But he would become angry if he thought of it again, and blinded by that anger he would not be able to extricate Lisette from this, nor himself. Anna Bella was right the way Anna Bella was 'most always right.

"And what will she do if she gets free?" he murmured thoughtfully. "There was a time when the better slaves used to call on her, the blacksmith Gaston, you remember, and those blacks that worked at the hotels....But lately, what's happened to her with that Lola Dedé and those women in that house..."

"All that in time," Anna Bella said. "When that girl's free and on her own. She's a smart girl, smart as you and me, the way I see it, and with a little money in her pocket she can hire out as a cook, as a lady's maid. I'd hire her in a minute myself if you want to know it, and she'd have decent wages and..."

"You're right." I must think practically, I must be wily, I must accomplish this, he thought, with disgust.

They sat for a long while in silence. He lifted the glass of white wine she'd given him and tasted it for the first time. "You're right," he said again softly with resignation. "I will manage to get her free."

A mellow breeze moved through the open door, and the dull glow of the lights beyond the gate made a soft halo of the edges of her hair. She moved her palmetto fan drowsily.

"I want to know..." Marcel said finally. "How is it with you?"

He felt an anxious tremor as he asked this question, as if venturing into waters where he might be afraid. It had been easy to talk of Lisette, to let Lisette bring them together, but now—

"Well, you can see that for yourself, can't you?" she smiled. But she wasn't so big yet with the baby, and draped with the white shawl as she was, no one could have told. What was changed about her—he couldn't really put it into words. The voice was a woman's voice? But hadn't it been always? And there was that easy confidence about the way she moved, the way she spoke. And they were as close it seemed suddenly as they had ever been.

"No, you know what I mean, Anna Bella," he strained to make out her expression in the dark.

(424)

"He's more than a fine man, Marcel," she said, her voice low with feeling. "I am not fortunate, I am blessed!"

He did not answer. And she could not guess that he had been surprised to discover that this was not the response from her that he had wanted to hear. What did he want, he thought in disgust, for her to be miserable? "I'm glad," he said softly, but the words stuck in his throat. "Of course, it's what I've heard all along. I don't know what I would have done if I'd heard different." And why couldn't he mean that, after all this, the longest, most eventful year of his life? He wondered if those perceptive eyes could, in fact, see the lie in the dark.

"What sort of a man is he?" he asked dryly.

"I can't describe him, not in a few words, I don't know where to begin. He's a man that lives for his work, Marcel, that plantation, it's his life. I never knew there was so much to study in the cultivating of sugar cane, I never saw so many books and letters as he reads on that one subject, of how to grow it, cut it, refine it, ship it out. I wonder sometimes if all hardworking men don't have something in common, really, whether they're gentlemen or laborers or craftsmen like old Jean Jacques. I mean, that is, men who love what they do. It's an excitement, it's something almost magical in their lives. You remember, watching Jean Jacques in the shop with his chisels, his tools."

He nodded. Time would never diminish that.

"I remember my Daddy," she went on, "when he used to be working on his books, figuring how he could pay off the barber shop and that little farm we had outside of town. My Daddy had two pieces of property when he died and he was a young man. He loved his work, you know what I'm saying? I suppose it's like that with you when you're studying for school, and when you're in Michie Christophe's class. Everybody says you're the star pupil these days and that Augustin Dumanoir from St. Landry Parish is fit to be tied. Is that true? That he's always trying to do better than you and he never can?"

"It's Richard he'd like to best at the moment," Marcel smiled. "It's Richard who's gaining on the prize he really wants."

"I heard that too."

"But what were you saying about this man and your father?" he asked.

"Only that he puts me in mind of my father, when I'm watching him work. 'Course I wouldn't say that to Michie

(425)

Vince," she laughed with just a touch of slyness. "What I mean is, he's a hardworking planter, he's got his hopes and dreams wrapped up in *Bontemps, Bontemps* means everything to him, and he's earning what that land puts out, he's putting in his share. Every time he comes to town, seems he has to visit with his lawyers, he spreads maps out all over that table, he writes in his journal, he makes his plans. Right now, the whole plantation's working to lay enough wood by for the sugar mills in the fall. They have to get it early out of the back swamps, because it has to have time to dry. He's in the saddle these days, more than he's out. I never knew there was so much to it, I guess, I never thought much about those big plantations, it's an industry, he says, he says it will take as much as a man may give."

She regarded him quietly. "Come on now, you don't want to hear all this, you probably heard enough about *Bontemps* over the years to put you to sleep."

"Maps?" he asked. "Lawyers?"

"I don't understand any of it, he never goes into the complicated questions with me. I'll tell you one thing. He likes to hear me read in English just the way you did, which is nice, and I've been just reading myself blind. I have a pair of eyeglasses now, Zurlina says they're ugly, but he likes them, and I like them. Michie Vince says they look pretty, eyeglasses on women, he can't get used to the sight. Can you figure that?"

She lifted them out of her bodice on a little silver chain, a tiny pair of eyeglasses, round as coins with a light and flexible frame. She fitted them to her nose, and they flashed instantly like mirrors.

He smiled.

"Of course I only wear them when I'm reading," she said. "I've been reading Mr. Edgar Allan Poe to him, and some of those stories like to scare me to death."

"Were they maps of the plantation?" he asked thoughtfully.

"I think so, they must have been, big maps showing the whole outlay, the sugarhouse, the fields, I'm sure they were maps of *Bontemps,* why?"

"I don't know. I never saw a map of *Bontemps,*" he said. "Strange..."

"Strange?"

"You and I...and *Bontemps,*" he murmured.

Anna Bella sighed. She put the tiny pair of eyeglasses

(426)

into her bodice. "And you're dreaming of the day you can get on that boat for France."

"More than ever," he said. "More than ever."

It was late when he rose to go. Anna Bella had lit the candle and been startled by the clock. The house had grown quiet around them as had the neighborhood, and she figured that for spite, Zurlina had gone off to bed.

"Anna Bella," Marcel was not looking at her. He was looking out beyond the door. "I would like to come back..."

"Strange your saying that," she said. But she didn't say anything else. He bowed his head and was about to leave when she touched his arm. "Michie Vince comes on Fridays, late generally, but if he's not here by Fridays, then usually he doesn't come at all."

"It will be in the afternoons."

He was watching her, the candle behind her making a wreath of faint light about her head. Her eyes were downcast. There was so much he wanted to say to her but above all, this: that the frustrating passion he'd felt for her a year ago was now within his rein. Had it not been for his Juliet and her Michie Vince they could not have sat together, talked together, in this room. But whatever they had captured tonight it was fragile; he realized this, and he did not want to blemish it now.

"Do you want me to come back?" he asked.

"I want it to be as it was before," she said, eyes averted, her head to one side. She had her hand to her temple as though hearkening to her own thoughts. "When we were children," she looked up. "The way it was with us here tonight."

"I know that," he turned slightly angry. "you needn't have said it."

"But I thought if I didn't say it, if I didn't let you know, then you wouldn't come back," she said.

He was softened at once. "I'll come back," he said. He wondered if he might kiss her then, just gently, as he might kiss Marie. But realizing the light was behind them and they stood in the open cottage door, he found himself placing a kiss on the tips of his fingers exactly as he had done that night at the opera and touching those fingers to her shoulder as he went out.

But a strong feeling mounted in him as he walked away, his pace becoming quicker as he neared the Rue Ste. Anne. If he could rouse Christophe at all, he had urgent news for him. He would study round the clock from now on, take any private instruction Christophe could give. And as soon as Christophe told him he might pass the examinations for the Ecole Normale he would press to leave for Paris at once. And slowly, as he grew closer to the Mercier house, the sweetness of this long evening with Anna Bella, its desperate solace, became laced with something bitter that seemed part and parcel of all the tasks that lay ahead of him, the burdens he could not thrust off. Some somber reasonable voice said, "What of Marie? Will you leave before she's married, before Rudolphe even lets Richard ask?" And what of Cecile, then, would she be completely alone?

But this had always been just a matter of time, and never had he felt such an urgency to have that time concluded. What would it matter to Monsieur Philippe if he went a year early and wouldn't Marie say yes now to Richard, if Rudolphe would only allow the proposal to be made? A sweet peace came over him when he thought of Marie. She was the single person in this world who seemed untouched by the sordidness around him, unsullied by complexities that made his head ache. And it was not until he was started up the stairs of the Mercier house toward the light in Christophe's room that he thought vaguely of all that talk of lawyers, and maps. So Dazincourt, "the young pup," was giving Monsieur Philippe a hard time, was he? And might there even be some feud in the making, over inheritances and lines? The disgust Marcel felt for his father was too profound to admit of the slightest sympathy. And he could not care about it all once he was across the sea. Yes, get Lisette's freedom for her, and then go, he thought. Then go!

Anna Bella latched the front blinds and moved slowly toward the bedroom door. She prayed Zurlina had gone to bed—though Zurlina should not have gone—she did not wish to hear her predictable hostile words. She set the candle down on her dresser and as the flame steadied and the light spread out beyond her, she all but let out a scream. There was a man sitting on the bed, his legs crossed, the red glint of a cigar in his hand.

"Michie Vince!" she gasped.

She lifted the candle and saw his still, relatively calm face. He was in shirtsleeves, his coat laid neatly over the foot of the bed, "Michie Vince, if I had known..."

"I know that, *chère,*" he said. "It's quite all right."

(428)

"Why, I thought when you didn't come by supper. Why, I didn't have any idea..."

"Anna Bella, it's all right."

She sank down in the chair beside the dresser, and in spite of his words began to cry softly, inconsolably, covering her face. He slipped off the bed and lifted her by the arms.

"Anna Bella, come now," he said. "I could have sent Zurlina in, I chose not to. Now don't show me tears," he held her tightly. "I've come too far."

This seemed only to aggravate her misery. He led her to the bed, kissing her, smoothing her hair. She slipped her arm up around his neck. "I love you, Michie Vince," she said. "I love you, I love you, I love you!"

"Then why the tears?" he whispered. "Hmmmm, *ma belle* Anna Bella?"

They came in a torrent and she was powerless to stop it, only clinging to him and making that same affirmation of love again.

It was dawn when Marcel at last reached home. He had fallen asleep, not in Juliet's room, but in Christophe's on the rug before the hearth. Late talk, some wine, and then the tossing and turning to discover that they had both of them dropped off in their clothes. The air of the room was smothering. He slipped out without waking Christophe and went down the street sleepily toward his own bed.

But the city was awake already, the *vendeuses* on the way to market from the outlying farms, and the lamps lit in his mother's room. Well, if there was no time before class for sleep he might at least splash some water on his face, bathe his arms and chest. Study round the clock, indeed, this was a great beginning, and was Lisette still dead to the world in her room, he had to rouse her, reason with her, and a cold dread came over him as he thought to himself, what if she's gone?

Hurrying up the *garçonnière* steps, he couldn't wait to peel off his limp and rumpled clothes.

But just as he was removing his boots, he heard a rude rap at his door.

"Who is it?" he asked crossly. He was unbuttoning his shirt.

"Lisette, who do you think it is!" came the answer, and the door swung back.

She wore a bright fresh calico with a spotless apron,

(429)

starched and ruffled, as she stomped into the room. His coffee was steaming on the tray, and there was a special breakfast, the sort she whipped up for him when he'd been good to her, slabs of bacon, eggs perfectly done, the grits melting with butter, and warm bread. He was flabbergasted as he watched her set the tray on the desk. She picked up his soiled boots.

"Do you look for every mud puddle between here and that teacher's house!" she demanded.

He couldn't answer. He was staring at her as stupidly as he had ever stared at anyone in his life.

"Well!" she demanded, reaching for his soiled shirt. "You going to eat that or let it turn to stone?"

"You didn't...you didn't have to..." he whispered.

She was shaking her head in disgust as she held out the boots. Then their eyes met.

Her face was as sullen and unreadable as it had always been, the eyes brown and overcast with weariness, but sharp in the smooth copper-colored face. A snow-white *tignon* mashed her springy hair, and she was studying him as if it were any day of the week, any week of the year.

He swallowed, glancing away from her and suddenly back to her, and struggling to form words, he said nothing but the driest whisper of her name.

"Now, do you want these cleaned now, Michie," came the low matter-of-fact voice, hand on the hip. "With every china plate in this house stuck with food and the laundry stacked to the ceiling, or couldn't you manage with your old boots?"

But she didn't wait for his answer. She had seen the rumpled coat on the bed and was furious. "Look at that!" she swept it up as she went out the door. "What did you do, roll around in the street in that!" She was on her way downstairs.

IV

IT WAS THE SAME dream again, vague and bordering on nightmare, and that excitement mounting until Marie awoke, pushing her hands against the mattress, her body rigid, the excitement culminating in a series of delicious and reverberating shocks. She was jarred by the sound of her own moan. And stung with shame, she turned over on her back and gazed numbly through the gauze of the mosquito *baires* at the familiar furnishings of this narrow bedroom in her aunts' flat. So the dream had followed her here as well, and even through the immense and heavy cypress door, her aunts might have heard her soft sounds.

She sat up, leaned forward, and pressed her hand to her cheek. The excitement was only now subsiding and she felt a shudder as her heavy tresses fell over her shoulders and brushed the nipples of her breasts.

The dream had been happening for a year now, with its inevitable and shattering pleasure, and she knew without anyone telling her it was wrong. But what brought this peculiar and terrifying cross to her, that she could not understand. Behind a door in her mind lay the simple fact, quite unexamined, that never in all the years of her childhood had she heard from her mother's bed any sound other than Monsieur Philippe's laboring breath. And a sordid suspicion had begun to form behind that same door, form somewhat like a cartwheel spiderweb, that women who felt this debilitating and exquisite pleasure were wretched women, women such as Dolly Rose and the girls who had come to live in Dolly Rose's house. So abhorrent was this, and yet so obsessive, that in recent weeks it had terrified Marie even to see one of those women walking about, and that Dolly Rose herself was seldom seen in public anymore was quite a relief.

But Marie would begin to cry if she thought of this and as always her tears would be aggravated by a dull rage. And these tears would alleviate nothing, rather, they would produce a new chaos with which she would then have to contend.

She sat back against her pillow, the pleasure having drained away, the air of this narrow and darkly furnished room very still. And the dream in all its simplicity came back to her: she wandering in a strange house, Richard wandering in that same house, the two of them advancing across a vista of empty floors. That was all of it, really. Nothing brutal, nothing raw, and yet all was charged with that vanquishing pleasure that faded slowly afterwards as if of its own accord.

It was unpredictable. It might not visit her for a month and then it might come several nights in a row. She could interrupt the pleasure, however, were she to wake in time and sit up at once, slipping out of bed to stand on the floor. But often she didn't do this. This morning she didn't do it, and she felt a dreary anger against herself. No one had to tell her that, no matter whatever else was true of women, decent or indecent, this pleasure for an unmarried girl was a sin. And that it was merely a more brilliant and unham-

(431)

pered expression of the same pleasure she felt whenever she
touched Richard, whenever she was near him, well that much
was certain, too.

And Richard, had he begun to suspect? She ached for Richard now, positively ached for him, and she knew that had he
been present at the moment she awakened, she would not
have denied him anything for any reason in the world: not
for guile, not for cunning, not for reputation, not for God.
And she had the oppressive, near despairing fear that Richard in some wordless way had come to understand that she
felt these blinding passions and that because of them, he and
she must not be alone. She was not the proper lady protecting
her virtue and had not been for some time. Richard was
protecting it, meeting her only at the little soirees which her
aunts still gave for her, accompanying her without fail to
Sunday Mass. He would not risk a moment of privacy with
her, and she, often to distraction by the hum and chatter of
senseless conversation in a room about them, could think of
nothing else. But so be it, it was best.

Because the boy Richard whom she thought she loved a
year ago was merely a gentle precursor of the man, Richard,
whom she loved now. At one time, she had still been able to
count their meetings, the little stolen tête-à-têtes at the soirees, the leisurely walks, Lisette following, from church. She
had been able to summon to mind a dozen brilliant and subtle
images of him which had marked the stages of her deepening
love and savor them as one might Daguerreotypes and engravings memorizing every salient detail. But she had long
lost count, for too much had passed between them, too many
times together, hushed voices telling of their day-to-day
world, hers so neat and lackluster, his own so full of relentless
demands. Life and death beyond themselves had brought
them together, too, in other parlors where people wept and
Richard, never shy or effusive with her, managed the mourning, the burying of the dead with a man's hand. It was after
Zazu's death at the beginning of summer, however, that he
had made his most indelible impression upon her, coming
into the death room to take her quite by surprise. She'd been
frightened then. She didn't know how to prepare the body for
burial, and was praying that Zurlina would come to help her,
that Marcel had not gone wandering away to leave this burden to her alone.

And then Richard had come through the door. "You go out
now, Marie," he had said firmly as she floundered, "You leave

this to me." All night and the next day he had been there, directing the neighborhood cooks and maids up those steps, bending a patient ear to hear their soft eulogies, gathering the flowers they brought to be placed in water along the walls of that little room. There was no hint of intimacy even when he glanced at her, and yet no boy's awkwardness prevented him from telling her now and then she must sleep, take a glass of water, get in out of the heat. That wasn't Richard the boy of those first few dazzling encounters. No, it was the man for whom her admiration was as thorough as her love. She could not live without him.

And she would not live without him.

Be it an hour they might have together this week in her aunts' parlor, or five minutes snatched from their random errands to meet at the gates of the Place d'Armes. Richard had become her life just as this tormenting passion for him had become her life, and she would suffer it in silence, bury it, as she moved relentlessly toward a future which was Richard in which this pain would be dissolved. It was unthinkable that once they were united this pleasure could be wrong. And now a pure sense of his presence revisited her, nothing dreamlike, but the real Richard who would press her quite suddenly against him in the shadows near her front gate, his own body echoing that passion, yearning for it even as he stepped back and away. No, if he sensed it, it could not divide them; it was not shame that prompted his care, but rather the goodness that had always been in him, he would wait as she would wait.

She had gotten up from bed. Without even realizing it, she had risen, had taken the washcloth from the stand, submerged it in the tepid water of the basin and brought it up to bathe her face. No refreshment there. August was too damp, too warm. And she had to go out into the street now before the midday heat became too wearying, she had to make her way home.

For a week she had been living in this room. Of course Tante Josette never came down from the country anymore, never needed it, and her aunts were only too glad to have her stay. More and more often her mother suggested it, never in words to Marie, only obliquely to Monsieur Philippe, the cottage is so warm, Monsieur, why, Marie might stay with her aunts. And off she would go for a night there, two days there, now this time a week. And Monsieur Philippe

(433)

having been at the cottage for over a month showed no signs of going back to *Bontemps*.

Of course she was grateful for the privacy. This narrow shadowy bedroom with only rare shafts of sun piercing the alleyway beside it, its darkly stained furniture, Tante Josette's desk, Tante Josette's books. It was remote from the little thoroughfare that was her boudoir at home. Yet there were times when she resented it as if it were exile. Her mother did not want her at home! What obdurate pride, she wondered, kept Cecile from sending her here with her aunts for good? It was not Monsieur Philippe who was forever asking for her, nor Marcel who would sense a rift at once. It was some ironclad, yet elusive *persona* of respectability that hovered at her mother's shoulder, keeping that dull contempt for her daughter in check.

Again she put the washcloth into the water. Wringing it out tight she pressed it to her eyes. She needed clothes from the cottage, if Monsieur Philippe had been out at all, he would have some little gift for her and be sending for her, and she missed, positively missed Lisette. Since Zazu's death it seemed Lisette had been the perfect servant, sometimes even a little tender not only with her but with Marcel. And he as always took special pains to keep her content. It was Marcel naturally who had defended her earlier this summer from Monsieur Philippe's rage. He might have whipped her, he said, for leaving her mother's deathbed. Marie had been aghast. But Marcel had been as clever with him, it seemed, as ever Cecile had been, calming him with soft words, Lisette was being so good now, why she had a special dinner prepared for him and had worked all day to make it, would he, Monsieur, I beg you, give her just one more chance? And it was Marcel now that pleaded against Monsieur's latest and most ambitious domestic plan.

Yes, the household needed another servant, but he could not see bringing a strange slave woman in under this small roof, no, Lisette should train a nice healthy little girl. About twelve would be a good age, he stated one evening at supper, and Cecile could mold her as she chose. It seemed only Marie and Marcel saw the shadow pass over Lisette's face. "In a few years," Monsieur Philippe had been saying, "you'd have the finest lady's maid you could want, with all that Lisette could teach her, and in the meantime, well, Lisette would have another pair of hands. God knows it would be cheaper," but then he shuddered with distaste at his own word.

(434)

"But Monsieur, isn't it too much for her now?" Marcel had pressed him ever so gently. "Doesn't Lisette need a woman in the kitchen with her right away? To train a little girl, it would take so long." Softly, subtly, on other nights the subject would arise again while day after day there was no venture to the slave marts, no summons for the notary, Jacquemine. Monsieur Philippe drank bourbon at noon for breakfast, dropping his raw oysters deftly right into the glass. And Lisette, broom in hand, glared at him from beneath lowered lids in a flash of weary yellow eyes.

If I was there I could help her, Marie was thinking. She had always folded the linen, put the china away. No, even in the sedate comfort of Tante Josette's bedroom, she stood quietly at the washstand thinking of the cottage which for all the miserable hours she had spent there was still her home.

She was breathless as she rushed up the stairs. Anyone who ran through the streets at high noon in the month of August was a fool, and certainly, any young woman who had just celebrated her fifteenth birthday should not be running through the streets at all. But she had run all the way from the cottage to the dress shop, and she did not care. She stopped in the hallway of the flat to catch her breath, and to take Madame Suzette's letter out of her valise, and then sighing made her way to the parlor door. Tante Colette had been dozing by the window, the blinds loosely latched to keep out the sun while admitting the breeze. And Tante Louisa with the Parisian *Sylphes des Salons* hovered over the table, a monocle held to her eye. "Ah, Marie, *chère,*" she murmured as if the words must be said softly so as not to dissipate the cooler air that hovered motionless in the shadowy room. "Have you been home?"

"Tante," Marie kissed her breathlessly. She was seated quickly across from her as Tante Colette roused herself and peered, one hand shading her from a small burst of sunlight between shutters, at the distant mantel clock. "Don't read in that light, Lulu," she said. And to Marie, "Did you get all your things?"

"Yes, but you see, you see..." Marie started. Still she had not caught her breath, and there was so much to explain.

"And what is the matter with you?" Colette rose, rustling, as she came forward. She put her hand on Marie's head. *"Mon Dieu."*

"Tante, it's a letter," Marie said. "From Madame Suzette."

"Well, who is the letter for, *chère*." Colette took it, holding it quite far away so that she might read it, then clucking, she turned it toward the light.

"What did your Maman say, it's all right with her if you stay?" Louisa asked dreamily. She was turning the pages again.

"Yes, yes," Marie shook her head. Stuff and nonsense. It was always all right, but still they would always ask, "Did you ask your Maman, now are you sure that your Maman...?"

"Tante, Madame Suzette's asked us to coffee, all of us... this afternoon!" Marie said.

"This afternoon?" Louisa put down the monocle. She squinted at the clock. *"This* afternoon?"

"The invitation came last week," Marie shook her head again. "But there was no answer, the invitation must have been lost."

"Lost?" Louisa said. "Why it's twelve-thirty, *ma chère,* coffee this afternoon?"

Colette had taken the letter to the front window and held it to the thin bars of light. "Hmmmm, hmmmmp," she was saying. "And she just said to me after Mass Sunday, 'well I suppose I'll see you all on Tuesday afternoon,' and do you know I couldn't for the life of me figure what she meant, 'see you all Tuesday afternoon.'" She folded the letter. "What do you mean the invitation was lost!"

"But Tante, there's still time," Marie said. "It's not till three o'clock and..." Marie stopped. She was so hot now she was dizzy. She sat back abruptly causing the small Queen Anne chair to creak. She put her hands to her face. The weight of the chignon on the back of her head was painful and it seemed even her clothes were heavy, pulling her down with them. "Tante, I must write to her this minute, tell her that we'll be there, Jeannetta could take the letter now."

"Now just be patient, *chère,* just be patient," Louisa took the letter from Colette's hand.

"Lost indeed," Colette said. "Your Maman received that invitation, didn't she?"

Marie stared from one to the other of them. She started to speak and then stopped. Bending forward from the waist, she looked away from them down the long passage from the parlor door. The shutters were open at the end of the passage and the light forced her to close her eyes.

"It doesn't matter, does it?" she whispered, turning back to them. She was in pain.

"So what did she say!" Colette demanded.

Marie shook her head. Her shrug was subtle, not a consummate gesture. "She doesn't recall receiving it," she said, her voice faltering, weakening. She didn't want to speak of this, or even think of it. It wasn't important to her. "Ah..." she took a deep breath, "Monsieur Philippe received the letter this morning...Maman says...she cannot go."

"Hmmmmp, well that's understandable enough with Monsieur Philippe there," Colette conceded, "but not to answer that invitation, I bet she threw that invitation away."

"Doesn't matter, we'll just have to write to her and explain that we can't go now." Louisa said.

Marie was on her feet again. Red blotches appeared in her white cheeks. "Can't go? But we must go. She's expecting us, you said that Sunday...Sunday..." she looked at Colette. Her voice was unsteady, hoarse from her running, but her eyes were imploring and rather strong. "Tante, don't you see?" she said. "She's invited us, all of us, formally to coffee..."

"Why, *ma chère,* of course I see," Louisa interrupted. "And so does your Tante Colette, but it's twelve-thirty-five by the clock and we can't..."

Marie put her hands to her temples as if she were hearing a discordant sound.

"Now you listen to me, Marie," Colette said quite simply. "This is just a little bit of a mess, here with your mother unable to go, and the invitation not properly answered, things like this have to be attended to in the proper time..." she stopped. "Well," she said suddenly, and looked from her sister to her niece.

"The point is," Louisa said, opening the journal again and lifting her monocle, "this is a certain sort of invitation, I mean, considering the visits you've had from young Richard..."

"But that's just it," Marie said softly. "That's exactly it."

"And it's just not proper that we rush into something like this, not with people who are so, well, formal, like the Lermontants..."

"Now you have to understand," Colette interrupted gravely, "when you let a boy visit you like that so often, walk with you to Mass every single Sunday and you don't pay even the slightest mind to anyone else..."

"But I understand!" Marie was gasping. "I knew that sooner or later she might ask us, I was ... I was hoping ..." She pressed her knuckles to her lips.

Both the aunts remained silent for a moment. They were looking at her, and a slight frown marred Colette's rather smooth forehead. She had her head just a little to one side. It was an air of skepticism and then drawing herself up she began again, "Now you just can't do something like this without thinking it over ..."

"You're not saying you won't go!"

It was two o'clock before it ended. Marie sat numbly in her chair. For a long time she had said nothing, the early arguments had been easy to counter, that she must not be hasty, that there were so many fine boys, and Augustin Dumanoir was a planter's son, and she was so young, yes, again and again, she was so young. But some time or other in the room matters had changed. It was a tone of voice perhaps, something impatient in Colette's tone. Marie did not even know then but she had commenced to shake all over as she heard that voice altering, the words becoming slower, weighted with the necessity for truth. Marie had run her hands into her hair, palms pressed to her forehead. She did not believe it! But it was always Colette who would finally come to the point.

"... parties are good for a young girl, they give a young girl poise, why, there's nothing wrong with your receiving all the boys, as long as all the boys are invited, as long as ..." And so on it went, until deeper and closer it came to the heart of the matter as the clock ticked, as the tiny golden hand moved from one to two.

Silence in the room except for the ticking. Colette was scratching at a note at the desk.

Louisa was trying to soften it, make it all seem rather matter-of-fact, "You see, even if you were to marry a colored boy, I mean if you were to make up your mind that that was what you wanted for yourself, and Michie Philippe was willing and your Maman was willing and ... well, you see Augustin Dumanoir is a planter's son, *chère*, a planter's son, with land that goes on farther back from the river than the eye can see, and I'm not saying that Richard Lermontant won't make some nice girl a fine husband, why if you want to know the perfect truth, *chère*, I have always liked Richard Lermontant just about the best."

Colette put down the pen. She rose from the desk.

"Now I have taken care of this," she said gravely. "You mustn't worry about things. I have known these old families all my life, I've known them on the Cane River and I've known them here. Madame Suzette will understand. Now do you want to take this down to Jeannetta or shall I take it on down myself?"

"I'll take it," Louisa said rising. Marie had not moved. She was staring at the note. And she did not know it, but the drawn and grave expression of her face sobered and frightened her aunts. Louisa made a patient gesture of "let her be" and Colette made a little shake of the head.

"*Chère*, someday when you're older, and that will come awfully soon," Colette said, "you will thank me for this. I don't expect you to believe that, but I know it's a fact."

"Give me the note," Louisa said quickly.

But Marie reached out her hand.

"I'll take it," she said softly. And she rose from the chair.

"Well, then, now that's better," Tante Colette embraced her, kissed her on both cheeks.

"We're not saying you can't still see that boy...long as you see him with all the others..." Louisa had commenced again as Marie went out the door.

She was in the back of the shop for a full five minutes before Jeannetta down on her knees to pin up a hem for a white lady rose quickly to her beckoning finger.

"Is my new green muslin ready?" Marie whispered.

"Oh, yes, Mamzelle," the girl answered. The other seamstresses looked after her a bit resentfully, as she took Marie into the small dressing room opposite, "See, perfect, Mamzelle!"

Marie's eyes moved coldly over the ruffles. "Then help me dress quickly." she said. She had already crumpled the note into a ball.

She had never been in the house. She had passed it a hundred times, it seemed, and never crossed that threshold and at times she had lain awake at night knowing her brother was there.

Her world was made up of flats and cottages, finely furnished always, but nothing of the grandeur of this immense façade rising three stories above the Rue St. Louis, a broad fan light above its paneled door. She did not stop to look at it now, to look up at the high attic windows, or the lace curtains that fluttered a bit carelessly from an upper room. Because if she did stop, she would be afraid.

And since she had left the shop, all fear had been obliterated in her by an anger so perfect in its clarity that it had impelled her on without pause for the slightest question of her course. Now she lifted her hand to pull the bell. Far off it rang, and clearer yet was the sound of a clock, an immense clock, ringing the hour of three. Her eyes fixed on the granite step before her. She refused to think a moment ahead. And when Placide, the old valet, opened the door for her, she did not know what words she murmured to him except that they were polite. A great stairway rose before her, winding its way up beyond a landing where a high window looked upon a lace of leaf and sky. And her eyes turned slowly, steadily, to follow the old man's back as he led her into a large room. Madame Suzette was there, she knew it before she lifted her eyes. Very slowly, timelessly it seemed, the room impressed itself on her. The low table before the marble fireplace set with cake, the china cups, and the lone woman rising to her feet, the pale creamy brown skin of her folded hands against her blue dress. And there was that face, serene, not beautiful perhaps, but pleasing with its large dark eyes, the long and generous Caucasian mouth, the gray streaks in the deep chestnut hair. There was anger in the eyes, just a touch of outrage, as they shifted uneasily to the figure of Marie in the door. The lips didn't move. The expression shifted subtly from one of anger to patience and then a deliberate and wary smile.

"So you've come, after all," the voice was courtesy.

"Madame, my aunts and my mother regret..." Marie started. "Madame, my aunts and my mother regret that they cannot come. I have...I have come alone."

The eyes were wide with wonder, the figure contained as if it would not make some hasty move. And then all at once it seemed, soundlessly and gracefully, the figure came toward her, the hands out slowly to take her by the shoulders, "Why, *ma chère,*" she said softly, hesitating, "I'm so glad, then, that you could come."

It was never awkward which seemed a wonder afterwards. Madame Suzette had commenced at once to talk. Not once had she mentioned the aunts or Cecile, there were no questions, in fact, and it seemed rather that she could carry the afternoon's conversation with only the sparest of monosyl-

(440)

labic answers on her own. She had talked softly of the weather at first as people do, moving gently into all the proper little subjects, did Marie sew, and wasn't it a lovely dress? Had she left school altogether after her First Communion, well, perhaps that was just as well.

It seemed at some perfect interval they had risen, and begun to move about the house. It was easier then, easy to ask about the crystal on the sideboard, the dining table which had come from France. And the garden was so beautiful that Marie at once smiled. They had wandered up the stairs finally, talking softly of Jean Jacques who had made the small table in the upper hall.

"And this, *ma chère,* is my son's room." Madame Suzette threw open the double doors. Marie had felt such a strange pleasure to see it, to think suddenly, incoherently, yes, Richard's place. For one instant, she had been startled by the sight of the small Daguerreotype of herself by the bed. "You see," Madame Suzette had laughed lightly lifting it, "you are very much admired."

Her own bedroom was to the back of the house, and lovely perhaps, Marie was not sure. For no sooner had they entered it than Madame Suzette had taken her into a small adjacent room. This had been the nursery once, but it was the room where she worked now. Her voice had become grave then, simpler. She had begun to explain about the Benevolent Society and the work that they did. Some two dozen women they were from the old families and some new, she made a little shrug, but united for one purpose, one and all. And that was to see no colored child went hungry, no colored child went without shoes. Even the poorest young girls were to have pretty dresses for their First Communion and if there was a single elderly woman of this parish alone somewhere neglected in a room they must know about it at once. She didn't say these things with pride. She said them with absorption. She had been sewing on the Communion dresses already for next year. Her hands lifted the sheer netting which would be made into veils. Marie was looking at her now more intently, certainly more directly than before. Because Madame Suzette was no longer meeting her gaze and forcing it away from her without realizing it, and Marie could see her as if she were close and quite far at the same time. They had the responsibility now for some seventeen orphans, she was saying softly with the faintest touch of concern, and she wasn't sure they were all so well cared for, two in particular were very little to be working so hard in the homes where they were kept. "It's so important that they learn a means of livelihood," she was explaining, and then suddenly lost in her thoughts, she let a silence fall in the room.

Marie saw her perfectly against the shelves of folded white cloth, baskets, balls of yarn, her tall and rounded form dully reflected in the immaculate floor. Sunlight poured through the thinly veiled windows, and she said almost to herself, "There is never an end to it really, it will take all that you can give."

Somewhere in the house a small clock chimed. And then came the grandfather clock below. Madame Suzette was staring at Marie, her eyes vague and wondering and utterly kind. Marie knew that Madame Suzette had moved toward her but it was so silent and swift, she realized only that Madame Suzette's lips had brushed her cheek. And suddenly Marie was trembling, lifting her hand to her eyes. No, this was unthinkable, this just couldn't happen to her now, not after all the day's struggles could she weaken at this moment and lose control.

But she was shaking violently, she couldn't even be silent, she could not, would not lift her eyes. She knew Madame Suzette was guiding her out of that small workroom and across the bedroom floor. Through her tears she saw the flowers of the carpet and their curling leaves that seemed to flow outward as if the room could not end.

"I am so sorry, so sorry..." she was whispering, "I am so sorry..." over and over again. It seemed warm words were spoken to her, sincere words that stroked her, but they stroked only the outside of her, and left the inside dark and tangled and miserable as the tears continued to flow.

And then a voice came, so low, she thought perhaps it was an illusion. A voice very deep and soft that said with the touch of a great warm hand on her wrist, "Marie!"

"It's Richard, *ma chère...*" his mother said softly.

And stupidly, blindly, ignoring the proper and generous woman at her side, she reached out, clutched him and buried her face in his neck. She could feel the soft rumble of his voice against her, the world be damned.

"Marie, Marie," he said almost as if speaking to a little child.

It had been half past four when she left, and the three of them, Richard, his mother, and she, had sat talking quietly

(442)

as if nothing had happened, as if she had not, without explanation, commenced to cry. There had been fresh coffee, cake, and Richard arguing intimately with his mother that, indeed, if he were to take three spoons of sugar now he might as well throw his supper away. She had had time to collect herself, Madame Suzette holding her hand warmly, the sweet stream of conversation moving on.

At one point she had feared she must explain, how in that moment in the workroom when Madame Suzette was speaking of the orphans, she had felt a longing so immense and so desperate that her soul and her body had become one. But she couldn't explain this because she did not understand it herself. The Benevolent Societies were nothing new to her, she had heard of them for years, her aunts gave fabric for their sewing, her mother now and then gave old clothes, but perhaps her view of such things had been ironical, distant and trivializing, she was unsure. But one conviction struggled for articulation inside of her even should it never come out: never in her life had she felt such respect, such trust for another woman as she had felt then for Madame Suzette; never had she known a woman could have substance, simplicity, and vigor which all her life she had associated entirely with men. And this it seemed amid the usual feminine trappings which for her had spelt vanity in the past, unendurable hours with the needle, making lace to grace the backs of chairs.

But they had expected nothing of her then, Richard and his mother, only that she sit quietly if indeed she wanted that, and raw as she was she would have known it had Madame Suzette's soft and dignified concern for her been not so perfectly pure. She was glad she had come! She was almost happy sitting with them in that large front room.

At last she had risen to go. Madame Suzette's embrace was tense, lingering as was her gaze when she looked into Marie's eyes. She would send her maid, Yvette, to see Marie home.

Richard had come out on the steps with her, however, refusing to let go of her hand. "I'll walk with you!" he said almost righteously.

"No!" she'd shaken her head at once. For one moment Richard's eyes met her eyes and nothing more was said. "I love you" was spelt there with the understanding that she could not let herself be alone with him and he could not let himself be alone with her. Even in the crowded streets they

(443)

would have found some place to kiss, to touch. Turning her head, she was gone.

All the afternoon was beautiful to her. The sun was mellow even in the high windows of the townhouses where it turned to solid gold. And then the rain commenced, lightly suffusing all with a cooler, sweeter air. Flowers bent their necks along the garden walls, tiny blossoms broke and fell, shuddering in her path. She was walking fast as always, but uplifted and no longer angry, no longer afraid. It was as if all the gloom that she had ever known was remote from her. It belonged with her aunts and with her mother in some other world.

The Lermontant house with its soft scents and polished surfaces seemed to descend upon her, surrounding her like a fragrance wafted on the breeze. She could feel Madame Suzette's arm about her shoulder, feel that hand which held hers to the very end. She could see Richard's eyes.

And not remembering the little maid, Yvette, who followed her faithfully to her gate in the Rue Ste. Anne, she went in without looking back and shut the parlor door. She would not see her aunts today. She would not answer their questions, and Monsieur Philippe would be here, a great and pleasant force between her and her mother. She need not speak to anyone, actually, she would settle at her dresser, she would pull the pins from her hair. And maybe, just maybe, the time had come for her to talk to Marcel. Maybe, just maybe, she would mount the steps of the *garçonnière* later and knock at the door of his room. He would not betray her, he would never betray her, and maybe it was time, now, to tell him what she already knew, that she would marry Richard Lermontant.

But the house was quiet, and Marcel, home early from the Merciers it seemed, sat at the dining table glaring at the floor.

She removed her white shawl. "What is it?" she whispered as she came forward. But he was scowling past her as if she weren't there.

"Lisette's in jail," he said. "Monsieur Philippe's gone to get her out."

For one moment the words did not register—"in jail."

"But why?" she gasped. "How?"

"Drunk, fighting somewhere in a cabaret," he murmured. Still he did not look at her.

(444)

"But she's been so good since Zazu died. Why, she hasn't been in any trouble at all."

Marcel was ruminating. His eyes danced back and forth and then slowly he began to speak again as if he himself could not quite comprehend his own words. "It seems they quarreled, she and Maman, over something stupid, small. And Maman tore off Lisette's gold earring... ripped it down... gashing open the flesh."

V

IT WAS A HELL OF A MESS, wasn't it? Philippe drained the glass, drowsy but just beginning to feel himself again as he always did by noon, the early hours full of tremor, headache. He'd have a little gumbo in a while, perhaps, that is, if Lisette would stop crying and deign to fix it for him. He bit the tip off his cigar. "I said when you were grown!" he stabbed the air with his finger, "and you know the law as well as I do, that means when you're thirty years old."

She threw up her hands and as she turned for the match he saw that scar on the side of her face where the lobe of the ear had been cut away. "Pull this down," he said to her now more gently, attempting not to grimace at the sight of it, but he could not prevent himself from sucking in his breath. He reached for the red silk *tignon* and brought it over the hideous little gnarl. Her eyes were watery, her face puffy. "Hmmmm," he shook his head. But it was her own fault, wasn't it, drunk, dirty in the Parish prison. For days after the ear had festered until finally Marcel had all but dragged her to the physician. She was burning with fever and so afraid. "Hmmmp," he shook his head. "Now, that's not so bad," he mumbled to himself as she put the match before him, as he drew in the smoke. "I mean I've seen lots of likely girls with one earring, the *tignon* tied quite prettily over the other ear." Lisette didn't answer. She was pouring the bourbon in the glass. He didn't know he had said this to her a hundred times in the past month never recollecting having said it even once. The fact was he felt sorry for her, and the scar on the side of her face made him sick. He had always felt sorry for her, sorry for her since she was born. She had inherited nothing of Zazu's remarkable African beauty, and certainly no decent Caucasian looks from his blood. It was the worst of luck that

(445)

copper skin, those yellow freckles, and now that dreadful little scar.

"Come on now, come on," he crooned as he rested back on the pillows, his large soft hand beckoning for her. "You sit here by me." She settled almost shyly on the side of the bed, swiping roughly with her apron at her watering eyes. A hell of a mess, to put it mildly, he thought, it wearied him attempting to keep all the disparate elements clear in his mind.

"Michie," she was saying with a sniffle. "I'll be an old woman when I'm thirty, Michie, I'm a young woman now."

She didn't begin to understand it. Three-fourths of the Parish police jury had to rule on it, and then only for meritorious service could she be emancipated unless he was to post some bond, some outrageous bond of a thousand dollars and she would have to leave the state. Lisette, meritorious service, *Mon Dieu.*

"I can earn my own way," she was almost whining, "I can cook and clean, I can dress a lady's hair, I can earn my own way..." It was an awful sound.

"Earn your own way, now don't start that!" he said roughly, teeth on edge. He drank a swallow of the bourbon, it was smooth and perfectly delicious. He was just beginning to really want some good breakfast, some nice soup. He lowered his voice as he bent forward, he wouldn't have Marie or Cecile hear a word of this. "You and that Lola woman, that voodooienne, don't speak to me about earning your own way. Is that what you'll be up to if you're set free!"

"Michie," she shook her head frantically, the voice still that low whine. "I don't go there anymore, I swear it. Michie, I've been good, I've been taking care of everything, Michie, I don't even go out, I swear it."

Again he drained the glass. He couldn't bear it, that whining. He was waving at her coarsely with his left hand. It was worse than some field hand begging not to be whipped, it disgusted him, he'd rather hear her banging pots and pans. And what did all this mean about meritorious service, Marcel had explained it but it wasn't clear. Meritorious service if she was under thirty and born in the state, then she wouldn't have to be deported, no bond. Meritorious service, Lisette? Fined and imprisoned for brawling in a public street?

"...I've tried to be good, good as gold," she was saying, "and Michie, it's four months now since my Maman died."

"Now don't start that again," he said. He couldn't even keep one thought straight and now she was changing her attack. "Your mother was born the same year I was born," he said with that didactic finger, "I didn't know she'd die before you were thirty, I didn't know she'd die when you were still a girl." Maybe all this foolishness about meritorious service was a formality, Jacquemine could take care of it, write it on the petition, and he would sign it.

"But I'm not a girl, Michie," her teeth cut into that thick lower lip. *Mon Dieu*, it wasn't her fault she'd been born so ugly, he looked away from her shaking his head. "Fill this glass." And suppose he would have to post some bond, where was Marcel, Marcel had all this straight, what was the bond, one thousand dollars, *Mon Dieu!* And what would it cost him, a new serving girl?

"Don't, *chère*, don't!" he said now as she sat there crying, tears squeezed from the large protuberant eyes. "Lisette, *ma chère...*" He hugged her shoulder, shook her lightly.

"Please, Michie," the voice was low and shuddering, "Michie, please let me go!"

Suddenly she rose. He had the full glass again to his lips and was for a moment confused to see her standing on the other side of the room.

But Cecile had just entered, with Marcel behind her, and had come to straighten the light coverlet on the bed.

"Ah, *petit chou*," he reached up to stroke her face.

"Monsieur, there's a message for you," she said.

"And you, brat, what are you doing home from school?"

Marcel glanced uneasily at his mother. "Monsieur Jacquemine sent a boy to school, Monsieur, asking that I please find you, that there is urgent business, and he requests..."

"Find me? Find me?" Philippe gave in to a wild laugh. "Lisette, soup!" he said now, the finger pointing straight at the tester. She moved silently, almost gratefully out of the room. "Why, I've been here for two months, what does he mean, find me!"

"Apparently, it's very important," Marcel shrugged lightly. Cecile was wiping Philippe's face. He slipped his arm about her waist. "He asks that you come to his office as soon as you can."

"Ah, that's impossible, not today," Philippe took another swallow of bourbon. Jacquemine, urgent business. Jacquemine could answer all these questions about the Parish police jury, and just might likely know the cost of a new maid. He couldn't have some black sloven about this place, no, it would make his *petit chou*, Cecile, miserable and frankly he could

(447)

not endure soiled bodies and fumbling service himself. No, it would have to be a fancy girl, a thousand dollars at least, *Mon Dieu!*

"But Monsieur," Cecile was saying gently. "If it's urgent business, Monsieur, perhaps if you were to have some dinner and then a little nap..."

"Oh, urgent business, urgent business, what could be urgent business!"

Cecile's eyes narrowed for an instant, considering. He did not see her turn quickly to look at Marcel. He threw the coverlet back and gestured for his blue robe. Marcel held it open for him, and Cecile tied the sash.

"I only meant, Monsieur, if it were urgent business perhaps it concerns the country, Monsieur..."

Lisette had just come in with the tray.

"You want to see me go back to the country, *mon petit chou?*"

"Ah, Monsieur, never!" she whispered slipping her hands under his arms, her head inclined to his chest.

"They don't need me in the country, *ma chère,*" he said moving with her into the dining room. "I assure you, *Bontemps* has never been in more capable hands!" He made a great dramatic gesture as he pulled back the chair. The aroma of the hot gumbo, shrimp, spices, the green pepper, filled the room. "No, they don't need me and they won't see me until the harvest, urgent business, they can go to hell."

Cecile pulled the napkin from the ring and placed it in his lap.

"And you," Philippe said now, regarding Marcel who stood patiently at the door. "We talk tonight, you and me, all that about the Parish jury, do you think you'd show a particle of common sense when it comes to purchasing a decent slave?"

Marcel's face drained. He glanced at Lisette whose steady brown eyes were fixed on Philippe.

"Well...I...yes," Marcel swallowed. "I could..."

Philippe was studying him, then he laughed as he picked up his spoon. "Oh, never mind, my little scholar," he said, "I'll put this in Jacquemine's hands. If I have to see him, I will put it in his hands. Urgent business. He can straighten all this out... *Mon Dieu,* I guess it's time."

Marcel followed Lisette from the room. Cecile was talking softly. He should dress, rest a little before walking uptown.

"Well," Marcel said taking her arm. "He's going to do it! Now, when he goes to see Jacquemine."

(448)

"I'll believe it when I see it, when I have those papers in my hand," Lisette turned away from him. "What's all that urgent business about anyway?" she asked as she started across the yard.

Marcel murmured softly, "I don't know."

At half past two he helped his father with his boots. He was talking in a low voice, telling him that Lisette had been a good girl all summer, and she knew it wasn't going to be easy for her when she was free, but she'd work hard, she wouldn't come to him for anything and Monsieur Philippe nodded, his eyes glassy, as he ran the comb through his hair. "My coat," he gestured. Cecile had just brushed it. It was days since he had even gone out of the house. "Just a little white wine," he said now as he inspected the faint glimmer of a gold beard. Cecile had shaved him that morning and done it well.

"Monsieur," she said so sweetly, "no more wine now, hmmmm? The sun's so hot."

"Walk with me a ways," he gestured for Marcel. "Business in this heat. All business ought to be suspended until October, anybody with any sense is at the lake." But he laughed and clasped Cecile again as he rose to go. "That is, anybody, but me."

He took his time in the Rue Royale, leaving Marcel long before he reached the Hotel St. Louis where he went to the long elaborate bar at once. The air was cool under the lofty ceiling, and though the day's auctions were over, he nevertheless found himself considering the block. Jacquemine could handle all that well, of course, and he himself disliked buying slaves, in fact he hated it, especially if some family were to be separated and there would be a piteous squalling child and a mother frantic, ah, it was too much. But what if Jacquemine made a mistake? Some haughty girl that would take on airs about serving a colored mistress, *Mon Dieu*, that was all he would need, and *Ti* Marcel, *Ti* Marcel haggling with a slave trader? The way he went on about Lisette he was more likely to buy some downtrodden creature out of pity than a good mulatto maid. Mulatto maid, now that was a luxury, she didn't have to be a mulatto, but then what would Cecile think, he had never stinted on anything with Cecile, Cecile had from him the best! But the price, it could damn well be a thousand dollars in these times, couldn't it, and with that quick shift, a series of figures invaded his

brain, bills for Marcel's fall coats, he'd have to come up with
something when he freed Lisette, bond or no bond, she'd need
a start somewhere, a few months rent before she'd find a
position, and his son, Leon, had just written home for some
enormous sum, he was buying Europe apparently, piece by
piece. Cold beer, he had told the bartender and now it was
gone. He gestured for another glass.

And those gowns for Marie again, and what exactly was
that witch Colette up to, coming and whispering to him that
Marie was getting herself into deep waters with a colored
boy? What colored boy? While Marcel had come to see him
one evening, played a hand of faro, and talked vaguely of a
"good marriage" with one of "the old colored families." The
matter of dowries, that was it, dowries, he had been calculating roughly these expenses, dowries, these old colored families, they were as fussy and proud as any white family, of
course he'd have to see to that, his Marie would not be married without a dowry, but what in the world did Colette mean
with all that foolishness about "some colored boy?" Didn't Colette and Marcel speak to each other, what was this about? He
would certainly rather see his *belle* Marie married to some
good upstanding colored planter or tradesman than... than
hmmm, take that Lermontant boy, for instance, that beautiful
giant of a boy. Dowry, those Lermontants with their mansion
in the Rue St. Louis, they'd want his eyeteeth.

It gave him a pleasant though minor sensation to envision
Marie in a bride's white, and it crossed his mind swiftly as
he downed the second beer—deliciously cold, he ordered a
third—that she ought to be the child he sent abroad, really,
it would make more sense. But in all probability it wouldn't
save him a dime. In fact, the cost of Marcel's up and coming
venture would be staggering, a *pension* in the Quartier Latin,
his allowance, the proposed travel, and all those years at the
Ecole Normale. Of course he approved of the Ecole Normale,
whatever the Ecole Normale was! He laughed suddenly at
the riotous thought of his son, Leon's face, should he ever
discover the identity of this *petit* scholar who could read four
languages and was his father's... ah, well! Leon had all the
education a planter could use. He drank the third beer down.
But it was important Marcel come home four years from now
with some means of supporting himself, at least in part, or
there would be no end to all this in sight. Of course, he could
set him up, some rental property, but he had mortgaged that
property to pay for something, well, maybe Marcel could

manage those properties for a reasonable commission, the question was, how to manage the formidable sum of four thousand dollars at the moment, or should it actually be five?

He had just opened the door of the notary's and moved into the cool shade of the office when he was aware that something was not right. He turned, unsteady on his feet, a drinker's sweat breaking out uncomfortably all over his face, and peered into the sparse crowds of the street. It was Felix, his coachman, he was sure of it, he'd seen him and Felix had looked away! Felix should have been at *Bontemps,* and Felix had looked away. Perhaps that damned Vincent had sent him on some errand, but Felix had pretended not to recognize his master, this was absurd.

"Won't you step inside, Monsieur?" came the grating voice of Jacquemine from the door of his inner office.

"I'll have a drink, that's what I'll do," Philippe murmured. His eyes widened as he saw through the open door. A cluster of dark-clad figures surrounded the mahogany desk, there was his sister-in-law Francine, her husband Gustave, and a tall gentleman with very familiar white whiskers clutching a leatherbound folder. Aglae was sitting in front of this man, Aglae! And beside her, rising slowly and ceremoniously with a remarkable intensity of expression on his silent features, was Vincent.

"What is this?" Philippe's eyes narrowed.

"Please sit down, Monsieur," the notary mopped his forehead. "Please, please, Monsieur, please..."

It was almost dusk when Philippe emerged from the office. He glared at Felix and before the coachman could turn away, Philippe had snapped his fingers and beckoned for him with such a dour expression that the man didn't dare ignore the command. "Go to my woman's house in the Rue Ste. Anne and get my valise," Philippe said in a low voice, oblivious to the family filing out of the office behind him. "And bring it to my room in the hotel. I want you there in one half hour." He strode across the Rue Royale and toward the St. Louis, and within a matter of minutes had been shown to the cool solitude of his regular suite, stuffing a few coins in the bellhop's hand.

"Your usual, Monsieur?" the drowsy black face waited.

Philippe stood glaring into space. "Yes," he said after a moment's hesitation. He was cold sober now, his head throbbing, and he knew that if he did not have a taste of beer he was going to be ill. He fell heavily into the large *fauteuil* by the grate and folded his arms. His mind struggled for some calculated analysis among a morass of emotions not the least of which was fear. He had almost signed those papers. During the first few moments, confused, weary as he was, he had almost signed! And drunk, yes, drunk. And they had known he was drunk when they put the pen in his hand. There had been that moment of total sentimental weakness when he had been almost willing to do what they wanted him to do. A serpent's tooth, that Vincent! Even in the privacy of this room, Philippe's face flushed to the roots of his yellow hair. And Aglae, that reptile in the gentle guise of a woman. He had almost dipped that pen! It was no use attempting to rest, he could not sit still there, he could not stand still. He ended pacing the floor, and when Felix entered he took him roughly by the lapel.

"You go to my wife's suite, you hear me," he all but snarled. "You tell her that I will dine with her in the main salon. I request the presence of her brother along with her. And then we shall go back to *Bontemps*."

Felix nodded quickly. His coachman's dignity did not give way easily to fear. "Yes, Michie," he said calmly enough and stood waiting to be released.

"And as soon as you've delivered that message, you go back to the Rue Ste. Anne. You tell my woman that I won't be back for a while, perhaps not until after the harvest. And you find that damned Lisette and you tell her to behave. If my boy is there..." he stopped. He let Felix go. "Never mind, don't say anything to my boy. Just do as I told you, now go on."

The dining room was crowded when he came down. Aglae and Vincent sat together waiting for him, and Aglae's eyes met his boldly as he pulled back his chair.

He smiled almost sweetly as he removed his napkin from the ring, and then with the same composed and pleasant expression he turned to his brother-in-law.

"A serpent's tooth, Monsieur, is what you are. So you would have my land, would you, and everything that I own."

He noted the immediate pain in Vincent's face. The flush to the smooth white cheeks. The young's man's eyes, however, were as cool as his sister's eyes.

"Philippe," he whispered. "You may never believe this, but I did what I thought was best."

(452)

Again Philippe smiled at his wife. His head was very clear, and the small amount of cold beer he had consumed had steadied him in his sobriety and soothed his grinding stomach. "And you, Madame, how disappointed you must be that your little plan has failed."

"Monsieur," she said at once as she straightened her napkin and reached slowly for her glass. "I do not care to know the reasons for your extravagances, the neglect of your responsibilities, or why you have all but lost my father's plantation including that portion of it which belongs now and has always belonged to his only son. And you are very right in assuming that I do not wish to push this to a suit. But if you do not set your affairs in order, if you do not clear every debt against the house and land which my brother and my children stand to inherit, I assure you that though it may kill me to do so, I will proceed against you in a court of law. You have not won any battle today, Monsieur, *you are on trial.*"

The tender flesh surrounding Philippe's pale blue eyes quivered, and there was something both skeptical and imploring in his expression. He looked away from her, in his own good time, to Vincent who sat mortified, his eyes on his plate.

"I loathe you, the pair of you," Philippe whispered. His voice broke. Yet his lips remained fixed in that same polite saccharine smile.

"Be that as it may, Monsieur, set your affairs in order," Aglae said. "Or I will do it for you. Once and for all."

VI

"COME IN." Richard had answered the door himself. He followed Marcel into the parlor and gestured almost ceremoniously for him to sit down.

Marcel felt in his pocket for a cheroot, noting quickly that Grandpère was not about, neither was Madame Suzette. "May I smoke?"

"Of course," Richard was pacing the floor.

Marcel was irritated, not good company. The last few days had been all but unendurable to him, and there was more to come. Monsieur Philippe had left near the first of September without a farewell so that Cecile had been on edge for weeks, and absolutely nothing had been done about Lisette. On the contrary, the notary Jacquemine denied any knowledge of Monsieur Philippe's intent to emancipate her when Marcel approached him, and he claimed he could not reach Monsieur Philippe in the country which Marcel knew was untrue.

Meanwhile at school all hummed with the excitement of Augustin Dumanoir's departure for France, and a party was to be given for him tonight in the Mercier flat. In fact, school had been canceled today in honor of Augustin's voyage, the entire Dumanoir family had come in from the country, and it was they who would provide the catering and the musicians for this evening's fête. Even Juliet shared the enthusiasm though she could not recall from moment to moment who the Dumanoirs were. She had bought herself a new dress.

Of course Marcel upbraided himself daily for his jealousy, and he was ashamed when Christophe had taken him into the dining room one night, spread out a map of Paris on the table and tried to draw him into talk of the streets, the famous places, the boulevards. "This isn't like you to envy someone's good fortune," Christophe had said finally giving Marcel's shoulder a squeeze. "You've worked too hard all summer, you need a little rest. And maybe I haven't told you how well you've done. The fact is, you'll be ready for your examinations by spring." A little sadness had come over Christophe then, and over Marcel as well. Of course Marcel knew the time was drawing near. Of course he knew it was foolish to envy Augustin. But how explain that the very pain of having to say farewell made him anxious for it to commence?

Perhaps in these weeks if he could have spent a little time with Anna Bella it might have been better for him, but her child had been born at the end of August, and the community let him know through hushed whispers that it had been difficult for her, though the baby was a healthy boy. "Who would have thought?" Louisa had said to Colette. "A girl like that, it should have been as easy as a field hand."

Mon Dieu, Marcel had looked to heaven, counting the days until his sixteenth birthday in October, thinking yes, leave, with the early spring. That is, if Marie...if Marie and Richard...?

"Are you going to tell me?" he said suddenly, looking up at the giant figure that was moving relentlessly back and forth across the parlor, "What is it?" Marcel struck the match on the sole of his shoe, lit the cheroot, and let out the smoke.

"Don't you know?" Richard asked. He had knocked on Marcel's bedroom door at dawn, making Marcel promise to come up to the house as soon as he could. "We must talk about it," he had said.

"But what?" Marcel asked now. "Is it Marie?"

"Then you know nothing about it?" Richard stopped. He was in the middle of the room, hands clasped behind his back as usual, the face remarkably lined for that of a boy of eighteen, the expression commanding an uncompromising respect.

"She hasn't spoken to me," Marcel said. "Why, she's been with my aunts..."

"She hasn't spoken to you because she doesn't know what's happened," Richard said. "Because I cannot get near her to tell her. And the time has come for me to speak to you directly and for *mon Père* to speak to you directly. He'll be here within the hour."

"But tell me..."

"Your aunts have refused to receive me any longer in their flat. They say that I am no longer permitted to call on Marie there or in her own home. You know I have never been able to see her in her own home. Well, don't you see what this means, Marcel, I want to marry your sister! And they know that."

Marcel could feel the blood rushing to his face. A surge of protective feeling for his sister was warming him, angering him.

"This is foolishness and I'll stop it," he said. "They can't make this decision for Marie."

"But they have made it," Richard said turning, his hands clasped before him now as if to tighten the grip of one hand on the other helped him to think. He walked slowly in a small circle about the center of the room. "They said unimportant things at first, she was too young, I was too young, the little soirees were intended for all the young people, perhaps we'd misunderstood..."

"I'll take care of it!" Marcel said furiously. He moved to go. "You leave this entirely to me."

"But you don't understand," Richard said. "They've had words with my father, it's gone too far."

Marcel stopped. He was attempting to consider all the elements coolly as he settled back into his chair. He knew that Cecile was somehow incapable of even recognizing the prospect of this marriage: Marie to a man of color, it ran against some impregnable wall in Cecile's mind. But his aunts, all along he had counted on his aunts! They had been so good to Marie, and he had relied upon them to supply for her all the mysterious feminine machinery that a wedding would require.

"They simply don't understand that Marie is old enough to know her own mind," Marcel said flatly. "And they don't know that I have already spoken of this to Monsieur Philippe."

At that Richard's head made a sharp decisive turn toward Marcel. "You have done that?"

"Without the mention of names," Marcel shrugged. "After all, you haven't formally proposed."

"That's what I mean to do this morning," Richard said, "As soon as *mon Père* comes home, we mean to present the proposal to you."

"You have my blessing, you know that!" Marcel said. But he was so angry with his aunts that it was difficult to contain himself.

"But what did you say to your father?" Richard's voice had sunk to that baritone whisper so that Marcel could barely hear the words. "Did you make it clear to him that you were speaking of a marriage, you were speaking of a man of color," the voice all but died on the word. "Did he think you were speaking... of something else?"

"No!" Marcel said. But even as he made the negation he was recalling that dim conversation, the drunken blue-eyed man across from him who was winning from him at cards. The whiskey, and those large white fingers that could still snap, snap, snap, so sharply, in spite of their softness, for Lisette to fill the glass.

"He's coming back before the harvest, he's bound to," Marcel said gravely, drawing himself up to his full height, "and when he does I shall make it absolutely clear to him, Marie's wishes, your intentions, your family, your name. There won't be any difficulty, Richard, let me promise you that. I promised it to Marie a long time ago."

Richard was looking down at him almost dreamily, his dark eyebrows coming together in the smallest frown.

"But you see, Marcel, your aunts have insulted us, and they themselves have gone to Monsieur Philippe's notary, and they have threatened us with Monsieur Philippe's anger when he comes to town. It is Monsieur Philippe, they say, who will put a stop to this once and for all."

Marcel turned.

His eyes moved toward the lace curtains and, his shoulders

lifting, he let out a heavy breath. Had Jacquemine taken a message from them, when he had steadfastly insisted that he could take no message regarding Lisette? But that wasn't important, was it? It was the content of the message that mattered. It was the attitude that had been engendered in Monsieur Philippe, the degree of distortion, the quality of the lie. What did Monsieur Philippe know of this community, its better families, the future that lay within Marie's reach? To Monsieur Philippe, the *gens de couleur* were women, beautiful women, with occasional sons shipped off as soon as possible for other worlds abroad. A whirling confusion was rising in Marcel, something fed and fanned by frustration, a confusion he'd known keenly only once before. It had to do with Anna Bella and the sharp vision of two white men riding in a barouche through the narrow dirt street that was the Rue Ste. Anne.

"No!" Marcel whispered. "No!" This will not happen to my sister, this will not happen! He turned to see Richard's face unchanged, the same softly tragic expression drawn there as if by a knife. "I will talk to Monsieur Philippe," Marcel averred. "Monsieur Philippe will listen to me!" He put his hand to his temple as if to collect his thoughts he must somehow touch them, massage them, and when he spoke, his voice was private, barely audible. "He's been good to my mother, but he can't, he can't wish that for Marie!" And he stared into Richard's eyes as if imploring Richard to concur with him, assure him.

Richard's mobile features evinced a ripple of fear.

The front door had opened. There were those heavy and urgent steps that always signaled Rudolphe, and then the slamming of the door, the tinkling of china somewhere beyond the dining room arch, glasses on a glass shelf.

Rudolphe's face was haggard, all but unrecognizable so that it gave Marcel a start. "Well, let's go on then, now," he said at once as if in the midst of a conversation that, in fact, had not begun.

"But where?" Richard whispered.

"Not you, I'm not talking to you, you stay in this house," he said roughly. "I'm talking to Marcel. Your father's notary just sent his clerk to my shop for me. He wants to see me, and he wants to see Christophe, and he wants to see you!"

Marcel didn't move.

It wasn't fear, and yet some instinct in him, wild, unreasoning, held him to the spot. In years after he would remember this, remember it with a certain awe.

He did not say farewell to Richard. He stepped forward slowly to follow Rudolphe out into the sun, to follow Rudolphe silently, rapidly through the hot dusty streets to the school.

Christophe, of course, had no idea why this summons and wanted to know.

"I have no answer!" Rudolphe cleared his throat, walking too fast for the others with little regard for the heat. "Perhaps he wants to inquire as to my son's character!" He was furious. "My son's character!" His hand beat his chest in a convulsive gesture. "And he inquires of you!"

Christophe, patient as usual, said nothing.

But when they reached the notary's office, Jacquemine greeting them with an unctuous smile said, "Ah, Marcel. You wait over there, *mon fils,* across the street under the awning in the shade. I must talk to these two, the undertaker," he nodded affectedly, "the schoolteacher," he nodded affectedly, "and you wait, *mon fils,* please, until I call."

"No!" Marcel said.

The man was startled. His mossy gray eyebrows rose.

"Go on, do as he says," Rudolphe whispered and he reached out to reassure Marcel with a gentle pressure on his arm.

He could see nothing over the green curtains that covered the lower half of the glass. The heat was relentless even in the shade. And when his watch told him he had waited for half an hour, he stepped into the street. But no one had emerged from the little office, no other client had gone in. He ran his hand through his tight closely cropped hair and turning took up his vigil again by the wall.

Suddenly the door opened and Rudolphe emerged only long enough to gesture for him to come in. But then there was that hesitation, as unpredictable and irrational, as it had been in the parlor of the Lermontant house before. He stood still, staring at the office. He could not have explained it to anyone, and it seemed his mind was empty of thought as he finally crossed the street.

"Sit down." Jacquemine wore the same unctuous and artificial smile. Rudolphe sat opposite the man, in front of his desk, Christophe stood against the wall.

"Monsieur Philippe," the notary began, though Marcel remained standing, "is pleased to take up the matter of the marriage of Marie Ste. Marie to Lermontant's son. He will

(458)

discuss this in due time when he can do so in person, that is, with the Longemarre sisters...your aunts, I believe...and your mother, of course."

Marcel looked at Rudolphe. Rudolphe's eyes were fixed on the notary. They were glazed with fury, and Christophe's face was grimly set. There was no relief, no happiness. What on earth had been said?

"Get to the point, Monsieur," Christophe said suddenly. The notary was startled, insulted.

"I had asked you..." Jacquemine said... "to take this matter into your own hands!"

"No!" Rudolphe shook his head adamantly. "This is your job, Monsieur. I think you should explain it to Marcel now as quickly and as simply as you can."

VII

"...and it is Monsieur Ferronaire's wish that you do not discuss this with your mother, that you do not burden her, he has been thoroughly explicit on this point, that he wishes to make it plain that he will only support you in this enterprise if you assure her that you have chosen to learn the undertaker's trade." He tipped the brown bottle upward, and the last of it flowed like water into his mouth. The light exploded as the door to the yard opened and it gleamed on the cypress boards. A loud peal of laughter shook the rafters, and suddenly in one instant of silence came the distant peal of the Sunday morning bells. *"Now, listen to me, Marcel, this isn't the end of the world, and you've got to face it, that silver spoon you were born with...it's been taken away, Marcel listen to me, in two years, two years, I know this isn't what you wanted, but we've got to talk business now, in two years you can be earning a decent wage on your own..."* On your own, on your own, on your own. The ivory balls crashed across the table. Here, he held up the bill, she slipped the bottle of whiskey into his hand. Well, open it, a fresh glass. The sight of the grease on the glass disgusted him. A splendid looking Negro was talking to Marcel, a Jamaican with a shining black skin and a high-bridged nose. He wore a waistcoat of bright striped silk, and a glistening camellia in the lapel of his long flaring coat, don't play billiards, thank you, the whiskey exactly like water not the slightest sting. *"Has been extremely generous*

in this matter, but wishes to make it clear that you must earnestly work for two years at the undertaker's trade, the terms of the apprenticeship..." That soft bleary-eyed son-of-a-bitch, those damned kegs in the yard, those slippers, coward, coward. Here, buy yourself tickets for the opera, take that schoolteacher if you like, schoolteachers don't make much, get your mother some flowers, new suit, new gown, new candles, linen napkin, goose down, *"Now listen to me, Marcel, I know what you're thinking, this isn't the end of the world, you've got to face it, you are like a son to me, I'll teach you everything I know, you know when you are ready you'll earn the best wages I can pay you under the circumstances,"* Shades of Antoine, on the edges of things, that bitter smiling poor relation, never, never!

Madame Lelaud stirred the gumbo in front of him, "Eat," her lips formed the words, "Your friend Christophe was looking for you." *You told him I was not here. I'm not here!*

"Marcel, do you remember that first night, when I came home from Paris, and we talked in Madame Lelaud's... I told you, you knew more of the difference between the physical and the spiritual than most men know in a lifetime. I know, I know, the wound's too raw now, the disappointment is too appalling, but you must listen to me..."

"You've been drunk for two days, you are a bad boy, my boy, drink that soup now, hmmmmmmm? Your friends will be coming again, looking for you." I'm not here!

A girl lay on the steps at the top near the rafters, peering at him again through the rude splintery banisters, the sun skittering along the perfect shape of her bare calf. She made the words, "come up" with her lips. He lifted the bottle to his mouth, aware with a shudder he had been with her already, it was perfect this enticing brutality of women for hire, you need not care anything for them, they did not expect it, his own cruelty had surprised him, but it had not surprised her. The door opened, the light exploded, she vanished. This had been going on forever, he saw the flame appear at the tip of his cheroot before he had succeeded in lighting the match.... *"must understand that it is Monsieur Ferronaire's wish that you apply yourself without reservation to this apprenticeship with the view to being entirely self-sufficient within two years."* I always knew it, he was lying, lying all the time, those dead blue eyes, that wad of bills, the silver money clip, and now this, the coward, while he's in the country, *"...to make it plain that he will not support you in this endeavor unless you assure your mother that you wish to learn the undertaker's trade."* That back room, those chemicals, Antoine with his sleeves rolled above the elbows, arm around the dead man, tipping him forward, other hand squeezing the fluid from the rag. *"...the disappointment is simply too raw now, you cannot think, and you mustn't think, you must give yourself time, do you remember the words from St. Augustine, I gave them to you, 'God triumphs on the ruin of our plans,'"* our plans, our plans... "Drunk for two days, *mon fils*, your friends will be... drink it." *Coward, bloody, rotten coward, send the boy in style, the Ecole Normale, of course, why not, excellent, of course, send the boy in style.* "You are going to be sick, *mon fils*, eat, eat."

"You're a beautiful woman, did you know that?"

"You are drunk, my blue-eyed *bébé*, and I am always beautiful on Sunday mornings. But your friends, they are going to be looking for you, and the schoolteacher, you promised him..."

"...drink it off, then, drown it for a while, then come to your senses, this is not the end of the world, 'God triumphs, triumphs...'" DO YOU BELIEVE THAT? *"Listen to me, Marcel, I know what this means to you, all right, that silver spoon, it's gone, you've got to work now, and you know it's as if you were my flesh and blood, your sister and Richard, but there is nothing dishonorable, there has never been anything dishonorable in trade."* I knew it, always knew it, I would never get out of here! Illusions, don't you understand, all the accoutrements of family but no family, all the accoutrements of a gentleman but not a gentleman, all the accoutrements of wealth but no wealth... *"too raw right now, don't expect resignation, God triumphs..."* *"as if you were one of the family already."* *"...entirely self-sufficient in two years."*

"That's right you go home now, *mon bébé*, your Maman will be pleased, hmmm, kiss me." "Not without a flask for this pocket and this pocket." Laughter. "Of course, *bébé*, put that money away before someone sees you, all those bills." "Why, Madame, I'm a rich man!" *"Marcel, I should like very much to correspond with you from Paris, I'll be staying in the Rue l'Estrapade, the Pension Menard, you must write to me, let me write it down for you, 'Augustin Dumanoir, Pension...'"* *"Too raw right now, this disappointment but when you come out of this, go on get drunk, when you come out of this, you will understand that nothing, really, is changed."* ARE YOU MAD TO SAY THAT TO ME, NOTHING HAS CHANGED!

That bleary-eyed lying son-of-a-bitch, *eh bien, send the boy in style.*

Madame Lelaud put the flasks into his pockets, patting his chest, "You go on home now, *mon bébé,* before your friends come..."

"Do you love me?"

"I adore you, *mon bébé...*" She turned his shoulders, facing him toward the street, away from that girl near the rafters, that handsome Negro with the pool cue, bowing again as the balls crashed behind him, never, thank you, I do not gamble, "Be careful with that clip of money, *mon bébé,* get off the waterfront." "You are beautiful!"

He was standing in the street. A man lay dead, look, that man's dead, but she was just smiling in the doorway, her hands on her hips, those gold loops shivering, "You never mind him, *mon bébé...*" "But he's dead, look he's dead." "They'll come for him, *mon bébé...*" She ran her hand along the stubble of his chin, he'd seen it already in the mirror behind the bar, that golden fuzz. "My blue-eyed *bébé.* Get off the waterfront." He put one foot in front of the other, the flasks clanking heavily in his pockets, the street vanishing beneath his feet, faster, heels clicking loudly on the flagstones, crowds flooding out of the Cathedral, in and around the Place d'Armes, absolutely do not wish to encounter Rudolphe or Madame Suzette. It was amazing the speed with which he had crossed the square, the sky flashing in the Rue Chartres, waves of laughter from the Sunday morning confectioners. That bleary-eyed coward, letting that simpering Jacquemine do it, calling Rudolphe and Christophe to do it, all those years, those little dinners, the bills peeling off that bundle, *"If he can break his promise to me, Michie, he can break it to you, Michie, you think you're so special, don't you, Michie, you think 'cause his blood's running in your veins."* YOU ARE MY FATHER, YOU LIED TO ME!

He turned into the shadowy alcove of the shut-up pharmacy and tipped the bottle upward, his throat burning for this perfect stream. Don't take the steamboat, that will make you think, walk, walk, walk. You can't get there on the steamboat, simply walk, as if nothing can stop you, nothing can stop you, walk. *"If he can lie to me, Michie, he can lie to you... set me free, promised, your sister, Michie, yes, your sister, me!"*

Liar. Same streets, same houses, same faces, I will not, I

(462)

will not...it's unthinkable, this hellhole, I refuse...I will never!

And here it was already the Rue Canal with the bells from Christ Church and a sea of lumbering carriages, streamers from those broad-brimmed bonnets fluttering in the wind. I will not live out my life in New Orleans, I will not die in New Orleans, this will not happen. *"That you yourself have chosen the undertaker's trade, two years, two years entirely self-sufficient, there has never been anything dishonorable in trade."*

Now everybody was speaking English, it's quite impossible to walk there, but what if you just put one foot in front of the other, no, don't take the car uptown, just walk, walk. Walk as if nothing can stop you.

"Now, you listen to me, Marcel, he brought you up in the planter's tradition, you've never gotten those hands of yours wet except to wash them, well that's over now, and you'd best face it, there is nothing dishonorable..." I will not do it, I refuse to do it, tell him I refuse the apprenticeship. *"You're not thinking."* *"Leave him alone, Rudolphe, it's too raw, it's too deep a wound."* I REFUSE!

You knew it was not going to happen, didn't you? You knew in those months before Christophe ever came home, you were never getting out of here, it was just something to believe to keep you going, to make youth tolerable, to make life possible, Rue l'Estrapade, the Pension Menard, Ecole Normale, Quartier Latin, Théâtre Athenée, Musée de Louvre. Don't cut back to the river now, this is the Irish Channel, and they'll kill you, that cesspool, those filthy immigrants, no, stay in the Nyades Road, walk, walk, as if nothing can stop you.

He stopped in the shade of an oak, tipped the bottle again, one full flask left in the right pocket, one full flask left in the left, the Carrollton car chugging by on the shimmering track, steam against the blazing sky, the clang of church bells. I am walking to the Parish of St. Jacques.

To understand this properly, one has to have lived with him, seen him day after day in those soft slippers, that blue robe, pipe smoke layered over the dining room, that wad of bills. *"Ti Marcel, my little scholar..."* *"He took my Maman to bed, Michie, same as he took yours!"* One has to have seen him marching up that garden path, the cape flaring to the rustling leaves, that horse chomping in the Rue Ste. Anne, those presents, those parcels, peeling off those bills, send the boy in style, style, style, style!

(463)

What is it, noon? Take out that splendid pocket watch with the small curling inscription from Hamlet and read it, don't even bother to smooth your vest, it fits too perfectly, noon, and this is the old city of Lafayette already, you are making good time.

Somewhere before he reached the city of Carrollton at the bend of the river, he threw the first bottle away, seeing it shatter on a rock, this was country now, the swamp encroaching, those little kitchen gardens, a cow with an immense eye and delicate lashes peering at him from the high grass behind a broken fence. Over and over the cars passed on the tracks, and now he was passing those frothy verandas and ladies with pink parasols, this is the country now, you are moving through the Parish of Jefferson toward the Parish of St. Jacques.

It seemed the steady motion of his feet obliterated thoughts, all those voices had become music, and what was cutting and ugly had melted slowly into a rasp and then a hum, one foot placed in front of the other, the soles of the boots getting thinner, he knew perfectly well that were he to stop, there would be pain, the shells were actually cutting through these boots, this expensive leather, and a white dust adhered to the edges of these trousers. *"... some measure of responsibility with regard to your means, Monsieur Ferronaire has been quite generous, means suited to an apprentice in the undertaking trade, perhaps Lermontant can be some guide, you understand, of course, to date Monsieur Ferronaire has been, well, shall we say, very generous, but as of now, some measure of practicality with regard to your means, apprenticeship, proper attire of course, but these bills outstanding, some measure of reduced means..."*

And with each carriage rolling, crunching in the white shells, the dust rose, a wagon with people staring, an old black man gesturing, no, thank you, I prefer to walk. I wonder if this is an impossibility, all the way to St. Jacques, I suspect it might be considered so, but not for me. He uncapped the second bottle, drinking without having to stop, he should have thought of this before, and why not mount the levee, go ahead, feel that chill wind coming off the river, cutting this drench of sun. He started up through the grass, a swarm of insects rising, and with a careless hand slapped at his face, at the sudden sting on the back of his hand. Another drink, and there it lay, the Mississippi, that immense sluggish gray current, and riding downstream with all the speed of the

(464)

current, a lofty, beautiful steamboat, twin stacks belching into the clouds. The breeze was cold, positively cold, imagine that. But it was perfect now, the way that everything was outside of him, the stones cutting through his boots, the thin layer of sweat beneath his shirt, that itching stubble on his face, this chilling wind. I have always been terrified of those trees falling like that right into the river, the current eating at the land, carrying off something that immense and so solid, a tree that inland could lift the brick banquette right over its roots, but it does not frighten me now.

A white man stopped him.

He saw the horse coming a long way off along the river road below and ahead and then the horse took a path to the top of the levee, and Marcel stopped, waiting, as the horse bore down on him, again it was so distant, those pounding hooves, and looking at the man, it was as though he had heard the request without the words.

He'd never shown those papers to anyone, did he have them, he always carried them. His hand slid mechanically into his breast pocket while his eyes stared out over the river, at a great mass of logs and dead vine borne downstream like a perfect raft. The man's voice was surly, something not to be borne, and in an instant, he knew it without even looking up, the man couldn't read. "Born in New Orleans, Monsieur, of free parents, Baptismal certificate, St. Louis Cathedral, no, Monsieur, business, Monsieur, in the Parish of St. Jacques."

"You're walking to the Parish of St. Jacques!" The horse lurched and danced, the papers shoved down into his face. It was like snatching for the brass ring to get a hold of them, *runaway niggers with free papers*. He cleared his throat, eyes raised cautiously, decorously, yes, that is a better word, decorously, this man cannot possibly hurt me, he has nothing to do with me. "On the Ferronaire plantation, Monsieur, business." Those papers of yours better not be fake. *But you can't read them, can you, you swaggering fool*. No, Monsieur, in the Rue Ste. Anne, all my life, at the corner of the Rue Dauphine. *Merci*, Monsieur, *Bonjour!*

I told you he couldn't hurt you, he has nothing to do with you, and without looking back, go ahead, lift the bottle to your lips, he's gone anyway. This breeze is positively cold. A bell clanged somewhere, and round the bend it came, another of those magnificent steamboats, with faint music floating over the water, carried past his ears on that chill wind.

It seemed they were waving from the decks, to him? He looked down across the river road, the white columns of a distant house peeping through the trees, an open carriage passing soundlessly below and out of this wind, a woman waving, her skirts made of some soft green. Don't look at the house, don't look at the carriage, look at the river and keep moving, your feet are on fire.

It was what time now, three o'clock? You see, it means absolutely nothing. He drank the rest of the second bottle and threw it out so it disappeared into the gray water. And men riding along the mud beach below gave him a friendly wave. He stopped, stunned at this gesture, and slowly, limply, he lifted his arm. His boots were white with dust, and the leather was breaking open. Don't think about it, walk.

But when a cart stopped on the road beneath him, and an old Negro gestured again, not the same one as before, impossible, and the black woman beside gazed up at him, mute, waiting, he walked slowly down the embankment, those heavy careless drunken steps, quite impossible for him to fall over anything at this point, very likely he might have taken wing. "St. Jacques."

"Get in then, young man" came that heavy American voice, those yellowed eyes studying him, appraising him, "this ain't no fine carriage, but I reckon it's a damn sight better than walking clear to St. Jacques, where you headed in St. Jacques, young man, you just sit in the back." There was time for a murmured answer over his shoulder, before it began to rattle, and rock, the wheels lurching violently over the rough road which disappeared behind him, mile after mile after mile. He became skilled at lifting the bottle, tensing his lips so the glass could not possibly hurt his teeth, wondering if this old black man wanted a drink, perhaps not with his wife there, in her best Sunday black, her basket covered up there with a white cloth.

Iron fences, wrought iron gates, white columns flashing beyond the trees, the road winding so there was never a vista, the sun teeming on his head, his feet swaying above the dust that rose around him as the wagon jogged on. Hour after hour, don't look at anything around you, don't lose courage, a lone *vendeuse* on the road, her basket teetering, that lovely motion to the spine, long-necked, arms dangling, somber, unreadable black face as she passed and receded and became a speck on the white shells and was gone round the bend.

(466)

In all the years he had heard the word *Bontemps* he had never pictured the house in his mind.

How explain this to anyone, how even the most casual questions about it offended, much better to pretend it was no concern of his. A very rich plantation, yes, Augustin Dumanoir had said once, and he had not wanted to discuss it, he lived in the Rue Ste. Anne, what had that to do with him?

And even when Tante Josette remarked on having seen it from the deck of the steamboat coming downriver from *Sans Souci,* he had turned his head. "When a man's that comfortable in the Rue Ste. Anne," Louisa laughed, "you can be sure he's not so comfortable at *Bontemps.*"

So now as he jumped off the cart, all that rattling and dust finally at an end, and saw his hand shove the dollar bill toward that bowed and grateful old black man, his wife's eye a slit in her puffy face, he turned for the first time, even in imagination, toward those immense iron gates.

Don't stop because it's so beautiful, don't stop because those oaks are dripping moss along that perfect avenue, and you can see those magnificent white columns, this is a temple, a citadel, don't stop, he jerked the bottle out, his back to it, the cart creaking and clattering out of sight, and drank again, deeper, deeper, feeling the whiskey go down into his bowels.

Whether it was the largest house he had passed in this endless pilgrimage he could not have said, he was too blind, and moved even now in a trance. It was merely the largest house he had ever seen. And something flickered down that long vista, there was a swish and flash of color between two rounded rising columns, things stirred, people stirred on those verandas hooked to those Grecian columns, the sun a splinter in some elaborate glass. Don't stop, don't even move toward that immense and open central gate, that path inviting you to the tiny tabernacle door. He moved slowly, steadily, feet blistered and in pain that did not touch him, toward the side alleyway, rutted by hooves and carts, and once passing through that side gate, drew closer and closer to the house.

There was music from somewhere, the sharp rise and fall of a Sunday fiddler? And fragrances rising, mingling with the river breeze. A soft triangle of color shifted on the upper veranda, then flashed from one column to another and a faint tiny figure showed itself at the rail.

Don't think, don't plan it, don't think, don't lose your nerve. Did you think he was the only one who inhabited this palace, that he would be all alone somewhere inside with his pipe and his slippers and those decanters of bourbon, sherry, kegs of beer? Living like some rooting pig in deteriorating rooms? Leon, Elizabeth, Aglae, names came back to him, nothing to do with me, I have but one purpose that guides me, one foot before the other, the path carrying him quite far afield of the house itself, roses rising between this path and the house itself, and some soft cluster of figures up there, perhaps with batting fans, and small talk, and drinks tinkling with expensive liqueurs. Smoke rose from chimneys beyond it, a thick squat building emerged through the branches of the oaks, the rising banks of roses, and beyond that a man was coming toward him just as he drew nearer and nearer to the side of that house only those Corinthian capitols in all their detailed splendor visible now above these trellises, he could see it was the mill that brick building, and some squat old-fashioned bungalow was there, with its slender columnettes and beyond that some little town of roofs and chimneys, the man drew closer and closer, a black face, a familiar dark coat, Sunday best. The man was running, the man was afraid.

"Don't, get away from me!"

"Michie, what are you doing, Michie, you gone crazy!"

"Let me go, Felix."

Others were watching, a white man in a shapeless hat, his face invisible beneath the brim, as he turned his horse, its chestnut flanks gleaming in the slanting afternoon sun, and then took off into that little town of cabins, shacks.

"Michie, are you crazy?" came that same voice and Felix's frantic face. His powerful hand closed on Marcel's shoulder, and he moved him bodily and easily toward those shacks. Through the trees dancers flickered and there came that shrill sound of a country violin, voices carrying over the high fluttering leaves.

"Let go of me," Marcel said again between his teeth his fingers trying to pick loose that hand. A shock went through him, near to nausea, time is of the essence, don't try to stop me, I must see him, I must hear it from him, all those promises. He stood rigid, his feet being dragged through the high grass away from those distant snatches of color and laughter and above the house rising monstrous against the sky, cornices, Acanthus leaves, and gables peering down from that lofty roof, windows blind in the sun.

"Let me go!" he turned on Felix, his throat painfully dry,

but the coachman had slipped an arm under his and had him firmly around the chest. In a moment he was shifted roughly into the close darkness of a large cabin and saw a woman in a red dress rise uncertainly at the hearth.

"Get out, get out!" Felix said to her, as Marcel tried to swing himself loose, his eyes again turned toward the sky. The woman shied past them, and a horse was bearing down the little avenue between the rows of sloped roofs, porches, gaping doors. Marcel could feel his feet sliding backward against his will as he struck at the coachman, and now he dug his heels into the boards. He knew that horse, it was Monsieur Philippe's black mare.

And for one instant their eyes met. Monsieur Philippe, hatless, shirt open at the front, clutching the rein. His hair was blown back from his gray-blue eyes, and they were narrow and without a glimmer of recognition, the jaw set as he dug in his knees and rode on.

"Damn you," Felix threw him back against the hearth where he caught himself and stood up absolutely sick to the pit of his stomach. The room went round and round, and suddenly he was sitting on the stone his back to the fire.

"Now he's seen you, you damned crazy boy!" Black face glistening in the light of the fire. "What did you come here for, you gone out of your head!" He whipped the bucket of water off the hob.

"Don't you throw that at me!" Marcel rose, moving mindlessly toward the open door. Felix caught him just as the sky vanished, and the door shut with a crash, Monsieur Philippe with his back to it, his blond hair blazing in the uneven light.

"I got him, Michie, I'll get him out of here," Felix said desperately. "I'll take him, Michie, he don't know what he's doing, Michie, he's crazy, drunk."

"Liar!" Marcel stared up into those pale eyes. "LIAR!" the word leapt out of him, a convulsive gasp.

Monsieur Philippe was flushed and shuddering, the lips moving in a silent rage. He lifted the riding crop, the long tender leather strap doubled over to the handle and brought it down across Marcel's face. It cut deep, deep through the waves of drunkenness. Marcel was sprawled on the floor, his hands behind him, and still he looked up. "LIAR," he cried again, and again it came down across his face.

"Michie, don't, please, Michie!" the slave was begging him, his arm out taking the third blow of the crop. A warm wet blood was trickling down into Marcel's eyes, he felt himself losing consciousness, and lurched forward trying to get up on his feet. "Michie, please, please," the slave had both his arms out against which the crop struck again.

"Bastard, rotten! Spoilt rotten!" Monsieur Philippe growled, and gave the slave one decisive shove. He brought the crop down against the side of Marcel's face and Marcel felt the shock of the weight of the handle more than the flesh opening. He could not see. "You dare, you dare!" Philippe roared, his teeth clenched. "You dare!" The crop hit Marcel across the shoulder, across the neck, and the back of the neck, each blow so distant and vibrating, the sting and the pain outside the mind. Again he was losing consciousness. He saw blood on the boards. "You dare, you dare, you dare, spoilt rotten, you dare!"

That slave was bawling; he had himself again in front of the master taking those blows, "Please, Michie, I'll get him out of here, put him in the wagon, get him back to town." *Why for me!* And seeing that boot coming up toward his face, Marcel threw up his hands.

He heard his jaw pop, felt the wrenching pain in the back of his neck, and then that last shattering blow to the temple. He rose up and fell foward, and it was finished.

PART THREE

I

THIS WAS MARIE'S ROOM. It seemed everyone was in the parlor, Rudolphe, Christophe, Tante Louisa, and Cecile. Marie wrung out a rag in the basin by the bed and touched it to his cheek. The throbbing in his head was so intense when he turned to look at her that he almost moaned. But he felt a consummate relief that he was here, and no longer in that wagon bumping down the road. It must be midnight. He had the sudden fear that if he turned his head too far to the right he would see that Felix was in the room.

"Is Felix here?" he asked.

"Out back with Lisette," Marie said. She was frightened. He reflected he had seen a thousand shades of sadness in her, but he could not recall seeing this fear. So Felix had told them everything, and it was bad enough to bring them all together, bad enough for them to have summoned Rudolphe who was speaking now beyond the open door.

"Well, I suggest you write to her at once, then, and in the meantime I will take him home with me," he said.

"There's no need to write to her," Louisa answered haughtily, "she's my sister and he's welcome there anytime, we just need to put him on the boat."

Cecile was crying.

"I don't want him going upriver unless she knows he's coming," Rudolphe insisted.

"But the point is," Christophe said patiently, "he should

(471)

not remain here, not even tonight. If Ferronaire should come here, he should not find Marcel."

Cecile murmured something choked and inaudible through her low sobs. Rudolphe was saying again he would take Marcel home now.

Marcel struggled to sit up, but Marie said to him quickly, "Lie still."

"No, I'm not going," he murmured, and then Christophe stepped into the room. The taller broader figure of Rudolphe appeared behind him, and his voice with its insistence upon reason said,

"Marcel, I'm taking you home with me. You're to stay there for a few days, get up. You can walk, come on."

"I'm not going," Marcel said. He was sick to his stomach and felt that if he climbed to his feet he might fall.

"Do you know what you've done today, do you realize?..."

"So I won't cause you or anyone else any more trouble," Marcel murmured. "I'm not going to your house, I do not accept your invitation, that's all."

"All right," Christophe intervened, "then come on home with me," his voice was quite calm and devoid of anger or urgency. "You're not going to say no to me, are you?" He did not appear to see the expression on Rudolphe's face, but went on explaining in a low voice to Marcel that he must stay there for a few days until it could be arranged for him to go to the country. If he sees that expression, Marcel was thinking, if he sees the manner in which Rudolphe is studying him, I'll never forgive Rudolphe as long as I live. It was that old suspicion, which still infected Antoine whenever the teacher's name was spoken, and clearly, in this dejected state, Marcel admitted to himself what that suspicion was. But it paralyzed him, this look in Rudolphe's eye, and when Christophe turned and the men now stared at one another, Marcel almost let out a small warning sound.

"You have room for him there?" Rudolphe asked dully. But before Christophe could answer, he said decisively, "I think Marcel should come with me."

Marie had risen and gone out.

A dark expression passed over Christophe.

"My God, man," he whispered. "If you still don't trust me with the tender youth of this community, why don't you shut down my school!"

Rudolphe was stunned. He glanced pointedly at Marcel as if to say how can you speak this way before the boy. His mouth pressed shut. "I admire you, Monsieur," he said coldly. "This was simply my advice."

"Oncle Rudolphe," Marcel said, climbing slowly to his feet and steadying himself by the bedside table. "I want to go with Christophe. Oncle Rudolphe, you must allow me *not* to be a burden to you just now."

"Marcel, Marcel," Rudolphe sighed, shaking his head. "You are never half the burden to anyone that you are to yourself. Will you stay quietly at Christophe's until we can reach your Tante Josette at *Sans Souci,* do I have your promise, will you behave for just a little while as if you were in your right mind?"

Marcel's wretched confusion was aggravated by these sharp and loving words, and one perfect and distinct moment was yielded to him, that of Monsieur Philippe with that riding crop, and the boot, and those words, *you dare, you dare, you dare.* What in the name of God have I done? Christophe slid a firm arm around his shoulder and urged him forward; he moved without saying a word.

Cecile was in the door, and her face was streaming with tears. Marcel shut his eyes. If she says something angry, I will deserve it and I cannot bear it, he thought. But her hands stroked tenderly at the sides of his face, ignoring the rough beard there and she kissed him quickly and pressed him close.

"Stay at Christophe's, she whispered. "Promise me..."

Marie had come in with a valise, and he realized it contained his clothes. He wanted to say something to Marie, to Cecile, to all of them, but he could think of no words.

Rudolphe was giving orders as he left, the coachman Felix was not to be told where Marcel was, he was to tell his master, if asked, that Marcel was "no longer at home." It had a dreadful finality to it, and Marcel thought vaguely, yes, that's it. I have not brought the roof crashing in on them, no matter how outraged he is, he will never desert them, it's merely that I can never live under his roof again.

Juliet dragged her long boat-shaped tub across the carpet and stoked the fire. She peeled off his clothes and told him to get into the water when it was hot enough and she soaped him all over, rubbing the suds well into his hair. He could see the soot on his hands and how it had become sticky when Marie had tried to clean it off. He lay back against the rim of the tub and shut his eyes.

"Do you know what I've done?" he asked wearily. The cuts on his feet burned in this hot water and he could not decide whether this was pleasure or pain.

"Hmmmm, we are a fine pair, *mon cher,*" she said, "both mad it seems."

When she had dried him off and wrapped him in a thick white robe, she sat him against her many ruffled pillows, and brought the straight razor and the basin, and put a towel around his neck.

"Lie back." she whispered, and deft as a barber began to lather his face. He put his hand up to feel the cuts. It seemed the swelling had died down some, and it felt again like the contours of his own face. "Close your eyes," Juliet said. "Go to sleep." And as if he had just discovered this was permissible, he fell into it, only vaguely aware that she had finally finished and had put the covers up over him, and blown out the lamp.

Remorse. It was one of those words he'd heard but never actually made his own. Guilt he understood, but remorse? He felt it now, however, he was certain, and with it the most agitated dread. With the days of drinking sending tremors through his limbs, and all the house quiet, the streets beyond quiet, and Juliet sleeping deeply in the barest glint of the moon, he lay awake trying to reconstruct the why and the wherefore of what he had done.

It had seemed he had had to go to *Bontemps,* but why? No one knew the etiquette of this strangely stratified Creole world better than Marcel knew it, so why? What had he hoped to do to his white father, what had he expected that outraged and anxious white man to do to him? He shuddered, inflicting those blows again in his mind, his sickened and exhausted body unable to sleep anymore, the image of Philippe's convulsed face confronting him again and again. He wanted to hate Philippe, but he could not. He could not see himself as he had been before he entered the gates of *Bontemps,* he could see himself only as Philippe had seen him. And his actions were senseless, utter folly, and had brought misery on himself, his mother, his sister, on them all.

Finally, unable to bear his thoughts a moment longer he rose, pulling on his pants and a soft full-sleeved linen shirt that was Christophe's and in his bare feet he padded silently to the door.

A meager relief touched him as soon as he saw the light

at the end of the hall. There was the smell of the kerosene of Christophe's lamp, there was the barely audible but steady scratch of Christophe's pen. And savoring this relief Marcel let his eyes drift over the ceiling and the walls. The passage was barren and damp as always, but it was warmly familiar as was everything about him, even the moonlit face of the Old Haitian peering from the open dining room door. And only now did it come clear to Marcel that the day's violence was over, and that somehow the sanctuary of this house had been yielded to him again. He was in his refuge. And just possibly, as it had happened in the past, the world outside would become blurred, unimportant, even a little unreal. He moved impulsively toward Christophe and felt his relief deepen as he saw the figure bent over the desk, shadow leaping on the wall as he dipped his pen.

A soft grace emanated from the figure. It wasn't merely Christophe. Rather it was Christophe carrying on in spite of the day's insanity, Christophe undeterred from the usual and very significant tasks. It suggested balance, well-being. And Marcel, standing silently in the doorway, felt an overpowering desire to fall into Christophe's arms.

There had never been real touching between them. Not even the jostling which boys might occasionally enjoy. And in fact, Marcel had never embraced another man in his life. But he wished now that he could overcome the reticence that seemed inveterate to both of them, and that he could just hold Chris for a moment or rather be held by him in some natural way as brother might embrace brother, as a father might hold a son. Those old suspicions were remote to him, they were trivial and mildly irritating, and seemed something that was part of a confused and dimming world beyond these walls. But he sensed this reticence in him had never been part of those concealed fears; it had nothing to do with gossip or the specter of the Englishman; it was merely his nature, and more or less the nature of all the men he knew. But the desire for this embrace, the need for it was so acute now that he would have left Christophe's door if Christophe hadn't laid down the pen and turned around.

He turned the small brass key on the lamp so that he might see Marcel in the shadows, and he gestured for him to come in. "Drink a little of this," he said turning to the wine on his desk. "But slowly, it will help."

It was that same calm he had evinced in the cottage, miraculously at odds with Rudolphe's disgust and Cecile's tears. Marcel took the glass from him and drank deeply.

"Slowly," Christophe insisted. He gestured for the chair.

"Rather stand," Marcel whispered. He moved to the mantel, setting the glass before him, and stood over the empty hearth. It was quite possible that the pressure of the boards against the blisters of his feet felt good.

Christophe was watching him. "Rudolphe's already written to your Tante Josette," he said. "Have you ever been upriver to this plantation, *Sans Souci?*"

At the mention of the place a bitter tremor passed over Marcel. It seemed quite impossible that he was going there.

"I don't know those people," he said in a low voice. "Or rather I know them and that's all. They aren't my family, they snatched my mother off the street in Port-au-Prince when the war was on, when Dessalines was massacring the French. That's the connection. She was four years old. They brought her up." He winced. He had never told this to anyone, not even to Marie who did not know it, and without realizing it he shut his eyes.

"They're your family then," Christophe said. The tone was unobtrusive, gentle. "It's been that way all these years, hasn't it?" The voice was perfect compassion, devoid of self-consciousness. It was intimate and easy and nothing more.

"They are not my family," Marcel whispered, but he stopped, unable to continue because that desire had welled in him again to reach out for Chris, and he wanted to say you are closer to me, more a part of me than they are, but he could not. He glanced at the figure who sat at the desk. It was that old posture, habitual with Christophe, so still and contained that it seemed he was posing for the Parisian Daguerreotype all over again.

"What are you really thinking?" Christophe asked.

Marcel shook his head. He rested his arm against the mantel. The room was thick with shadows and the gray night, misty perhaps, showed luminous against the black shutters over the street. But Christophe's face in the small dim circle of the lamp was gently illuminated and the yellow-brown eyes were probing and patient and calm.

"Thinking," Marcel sighed. "That I behaved like a fool," he said. "I hated him for what he did, and for letting me know it like that through the notary, Jacquemine. He never meant to send me to Paris. He lied. And now I've done something unpardonable, and he has the right to despise me for it, the right to disown me. I've earned my disinheritance as if I deserved it all along."

The world outside was coming back, in spite of the house, in spite of this room.

"But you didn't deserve it," Christophe said. "And I think you are punishing yourself much too much for what you did today, you need to rest in this place, *Sans Souci,* you need to think. But not about the exchange between you and this white man. It's finished. You frightened him, outraged him; he feared some humiliation before his white family which from all I've heard simply did not come about. They didn't see you, and more than likely if they had, they would not have guessed who you were. So don't go on with this, Marcel, turn your eyes ahead."

"Ahead, Chris!" Marcel demanded. "Ahead to what!"

The smooth flesh of Christophe's forehead contracted into a sharp frown. But he was as still as before. "I didn't educate you for the Ecole Normale in Paris," he said. "I educated you for yourself. And you will kill me—you will kill me!—if this has proved a waste. It I haven't given you something with which to fortify your soul now, well then truly, I've failed."

"You've never failed!" Marcel whispered. He looked away. It was excruciating to him that their talk had taken this turn. Unwillingly he thought of that night in Madame Lelaud's when Christophe first came home, he thought of all he had expected of his new teacher and of how the flesh-and-blood Christophe had put to shame the poverty of his dreams. He let his eyes return to the disarray of poems, books that made up Christophe's ·wall and then again to Christophe's face. It wasn't a severe look he found there, not even with a touch of the reprimand which had just barely sharpened Christophe's voice. "Why is it you're not angry with me?" Marcel demanded. "Why is it you're not disgusted with me for what I've done? Why do you go on believing in me when everyone else has probably given up?"

But Marcel didn't wait for an answer. If they could not embrace, he could still find some voice for his heart. "It could have been so different," he said. "You could have been the same teacher, and the school, it could have molded me in the same way. But why have you given me so much more than that, why have you demanded of me over and over just what I really wanted to demand of myself? You trusted me when you came home, trusted me when I'd disappointed and frightened everyone; and you trusted me later with Juliet, trusted

(477)

me to love her and not bring harm to any one of us, and you're trusting me now, aren't you, not to fail us both?"

"Is that so remarkable!" Christophe's face had changed. The calm had melted to agitation, and the voice was deepened as it always was at moments of emotion. "Why shouldn't I trust you!" he insisted. "Why shouldn't I believe in you as I always have? Marcel, is it that you fail to see what's really happened here? What is cutting you even now? I'll tell you then if you don't see it. It's that this man, Philippe Ferronaire, has dismissed you, that he doesn't give a damn about you, your accomplishments, your dreams. And you stumbled out to that plantation to make him see you, to force him to recognize you for the young man that you are! But Marcel, he'll never do that, and you must let him be a fool in his own world without destroying yours!"

He stopped. He had never once broken the still posture, never once even raised his voice. But his face was contorted and his eyes were moist. "He's a bastard for what he's done!" he whispered. "And you never deserved it, and it is no measure of what you are!"

Marcel was shaken. He knew that Christophe was watching him, waiting for some sign that he had been heard. And that desire in Marcel to embrace Christophe was almost more than he could surmount.

"It's not going to cripple you!" Christophe said. "It's not going to ruin you. Do you understand?"

Marcel nodded.

Their eyes met.

And the clearest perception occurred in Marcel then. So clear that it was never subject to doubt. He knew suddenly that Christophe wanted to rise, to come to him just as surely as Marcel wanted it, he knew that Christophe wanted desperately to underscore this moment with some vibrant and man-to-man warmth. He wanted to slip his arm around Marcel's shoulder, he wanted to say with a forthright gesture, yes, I trust you, and there is love, too. It was all there in Christophe's eyes. It passed between them unspoken. And just as surely as Marcel sensed this, he knew Christophe would never embrace him at such a moment. Christophe would never, never take the risk. Because all of the old suspicions about Christophe were true. And that rigid poise which over and over again simulated the Daguerreotype was simply the violent and obdurate check on physical desire.

Marcel didn't move. And yet the physical presence of

Christophe overwhelmed him. He felt drawn to Christophe as he had always been, to Christophe's quiet and compelling strength. And he knew that it had never been his fear which stood between them; rather it was Christophe's fear, and this seemed quite suddenly absurd. But what amazed Marcel was not this final realization, not the quiet admission that he had always known the truth, but rather that he had struggled against it for so long. What had he felt? That the world would become chaos should he admit what he could never deny? What world, and what chaos, he mused. Who had mattered more to him than Chris, what had mattered more? And any fear he had once known was obliterated, gone with the remnants of his dreams and his patronage which had never been there at all.

But even as Marcel stood still at the mantel, Christophe underwent a slow but cataclysmic change. His eyes narrowed for an instant, and he rose, moving impulsively away from the desk and toward the window where, resting his shoulder on the frame, he gazed through the narrow slats into the street.

These thoughts were too much for Marcel. It was all beyond him, and mingled with his love it was more than he could comprehend. He never once took his eyes from Chris, and now as only a yard lay between them, he moved silently forward. There seemed no reason on earth not to do that, not to defy the entire world.

Christophe's restraint yielded slowly. He put his arm around Marcel. But it was rough, warm, as any man's embrace might have been.

"Now, are you going to stand on your own?" Christophe whispered. His hand was almost hurting Marcel's shoulder with its urgent clasp. "Answer me, I want to hear you say it."

Marcel nodded.

"I won't fail you," Marcel said. "But you must tell me. Have I ever failed you in some other way?"

There was a flicker in Christophe's eyes. His arm didn't release Marcel; rather it tightened. "Never," he whispered, the eyes inquisitive, solicitous. "How could you think that you have?"

Marcel, wondering, gave a slight shake of the head. "Has there never been anything else you wanted of me, something perhaps for which you wouldn't ask?" He thought he saw just

(479)

the glimmer of pain in the shadowy face. "Take it," Marcel whispered. "It's already yours. It's been yours all along."

Christophe was incredulous, then slowly amazed. And then there was the light of recognition. He raised his right hand, gently, tentatively. And it seemed he made some soft sound. Then suddenly he drew himself up, and shoved Marcel backward and away.

The gesture was brutal. Marcel was stunned. "Christophe," he gasped. He had to reach for the mantel to prevent himself from falling. And he heard himself again say Christophe's name. But Christophe was gone. And by the time Marcel reached the head of the stairs, the door to the street had slammed shut.

It was six o'clock. It seemed there were sounds from below of the early morning churchgoers, those steady daily attendants at Mass. And carters headed for the waterfront markets and slaves, starched and pressed and on their way to the restaurants and the big hotels. That old man would be passing, most likely, who opened his shoe shop down the block long before anyone else. He would be outside on the stool reading last night's papers before the others unlocked their doors.

And Marcel who had been lying in Christophe's bed was dimly aware that he had fallen to sleep, and that on awakening he was not alone. He sat up slowly, pleased that the pain in his head did not blind him, and lifting the napkin from the glass beside him drank the water down. Then he drank the pitcher, too.

And looking forward, and slightly to the right, he saw Christophe's feet before the leather chair by the hearth. He stared vacantly at those boots, and felt a dull despair.

I've ruined it, he thought, ruined it all. He is going to tell me to go to the Lermontants, and that's unbearable and I'll have no choice. But more than that, greater than that, how can we go on being teacher and student, friends? Only silence made that possible, only pretending that I did not know what I knew.

He jerked the covers back and set his feet on the floor.

"I want you to know this," he said in a low voice, his eyes down. "I've always thought...perhaps wrongly...that you and the Englishman were more than friends. I thought ...I thought that you were lovers. And when I approached

(480)

you last night, it was from the heart." He rose and moved to the door.

"Wait," Christophe said.

"I'll never mention it again. I'll never say a word."

"Will you let me explain?" Christophe said softly. "Will you allow me that?"

Marcel sat listlessly on the bed. It was dawn all right, he could see the colors of the rug, the tiny flowers on the wall, and even as he sat there the light brightened around him almost magically. "Explain?" he asked. "Why in the hell should you explain anything to me? I am the one who presumed, not you."

"You were right," Christophe said. "Michael and I were lovers. But I never thought, never once, that I'd given you cause to believe I wanted that from you."

"You didn't give me cause!" Marcel looked up at Chris for the first time. "It was I who wanted it. *Mon Dieu*, isn't that plain?" He turned away almost angrily.

"No, you don't want it, that's just the trouble," Christophe said. "But I've always wanted you. From the first night I saw you, I wanted you. And it's been nothing, nothing but a bloody struggle ever since. I've lived in terror that the slightest gesture might betray it, that I'd lose our friendship, which was all I'd ever have. And then, out of despair, Marcel, out of despair, you approached me. Not out of love, not out of desire, but out of despair."

"That's not true," Marcel said bitterly. "I love you. And I'd do anything for you and if you don't know that, it's because you don't want to know it."

"Spare me the sacrifice!" Christophe's voice was sharp.

"But I don't know how to be your lover!" Marcel came back. "Sacrifice has nothing to do with it! You have to show me, you're my teacher, you have to show me what you want!"

"You damnable little son-of-bitch," Christophe bent forward. "Don't you understand! It's not me you want, it's that man who's eluded you all your life, the father that Ferronaire refused to be. That's what you want, that's what you were searching for the night I met you. Don't shake your head and look away from me. By God, I've kept my hands off you long enough and I'll turn your head around on your neck if you don't listen."

"And so we all want fathers and mothers," Marcel said with disgust, "tumbling in the dark and lost. My mother wants some dead father she left dangling from a hook in

Saint-Domingue so she lays her head on my father's chest. It's a father Marie wants when she looks up to Richard, so it's a father I want when I look to you."

Christophe stared at the barren fireplace, his boot thrust against the fender, his fist under his chin. And Marcel looked at the smooth brown skin of his face, his hands, the glittering and narrow eyes that were averted, shutting Marcel out and slightly maddening him. He had that same mounting feeling of the night before; if I touch you this ache in me, this misery, will be gone, and we'll be together in some new dimension of love; you'll be there with me if I'm afraid. He drew in his breath. But this had no immediate physical figment for him, which made it all the more alluring and strange.

"They may want a father, a mother, whatever you say," Christophe said. "But the need is not the same. It's the intensity that breaks the heart, the feeling of being lost in a world of fragmented dreams and aspirations without guidance, without some strong hand that can lead you to a maturity where you will feel self-reliant at last. I don't think you can really love anyone, Marcel, until you have that self-reliance, until the need is diminished. And I tell you right now that need in you is desperate. You laid your heart bare to that old cabinetmaker, Jean Jacques, and it was pure and unmingled with desire just as it was the first night I came home. You said to me from your soul, 'be my teacher, be my father, help me to become someone who is valuable, someone who is good...'"

Marcel let out a small desperate sound and motioned for Christophe to stop.

"But you see," Christophe continued, "now you are confusing that need with something else. You're confusing it with a physical love with which it doesn't belong. And that combination, Marcel, that need and that love, it would be the most appalling, the most dangerous mistake."

"It was a mistake between you and the Englishman?" Marcel demanded.

"Oh, was it ever!" Christophe whispered. "But I don't know what would have happened to me if I hadn't gone off with Michael. I wasn't as strong as you are, Marcel. All we had in common as boys was that terrible need.

"And Michael filled that need. He was father, lover, teacher, all blown into one magnificent figure that overpowered me and held me just like this in its hand. Oh, the world was born the day I left Paris with Michael, everything had meaning when Michael explained it, it was beautiful if Michael said it was beautiful, and as long as Michael was with me, anything, absolutely anything at all, could have been endured.

"But don't you see, his hold became so tight I was strangling! That's why I left Paris, surely you know that now. I was engulfed by him, I couldn't breathe. So I crossed the sea to break the hold. I went back to the only other person who had a grip on me and thought, well, at least that's a step towards freedom, and Maman for all the grubby power she's got over my soul has never wielded it with any conviction or any purpose whatsoever.

"But you know what happened. He came after me before I could break his hold, and he died here because of me. And he took half of me with him to the grave. I'll never be free of him, and the life I live now is an imitation of the life I dreamed of, nothing more.

"Now you must listen to me. You feel the same need that I felt. In your own way you are equally lost. You love your father, no, don't say you don't. I know you do, you've always been more or less in love with him and the whole idea of him, that powerful planter strewing your path with gold. But what you loathed was that he did not love you at all. And when that need in you went unsatisfied, you turned to others, to old Jean Jacques and then to me. I knew in every word you ever told me about that old cabinetmaker what it was you wanted. People always tell us what they want. I understood when you finally confessed to me that you'd jumped the cemetery wall that night to visit his grave. I understood it much better than you did. Just as I know now I cannot do to you what Michael did to me.

"I am facing the same moment that Michael faced in Paris. And this decision will not be Michael's decision. It will be my own.

"But what I'm going to tell you now is the hardest lesson of all. This need of which I've spoken all along, this need must never really be fulfilled. To be a man you are going to have to forget it, you are going to have to learn to live with the knowledge that the child in you has come to maturity without ever knowing that protective love.

"Someday, someday you may have a lover, someone you love above anyone else in the world and that could be a man. It doesn't much matter, not so much as people suppose. And there's always been something exquisitely discerning in you, something quite apart from the prejudices of the world. I do believe you when you say you came to me last night with your heart. But whether it be a man or a woman, you can only love that person fully when you no longer have that need."

He paused, the pupils of his eyes dancing, his fist curled under his chin. "Men and men, women and women," he said staring at the fireplace. "I've known the best brothels this world has to offer, and the best brothel boys from Istanbul to Tangier. I suppose I could make you overcome any antipathy with a skill the like of which you can't conceive. But mix a child's need and a man's desire, I will not do it. I've made my decision and the answer is now and forever simply no."

Marcel rose and walked slowly, back and forth across the room. The sun was just coming through the slats. And he stood for a while at the blind letting the sun warm his face and hands. A long interval passed, and finally he spoke.

"I love you, Chris," he said.

"I know you do," Christophe said. "And you know my answer..."

"But Chris," he looked down at Christophe in the chair, "it can't be as lonely as that. An imitation of the life you wanted, I can't accept it. When I think of you in the classroom, when I think of the passion and the power you've always shown us..."

"We're talking about my battle now, and frankly I'd rather not!" Christophe averred. But then his face softened, eyes still on the hearth. "Maybe I haven't worked hard enough," he murmured. "I don't know." And then he looked up at Marcel with an open, defenseless expression as if they were men of the same age. "I've got to stop loving you so much. I've got to stop constructing a little world of dreams around your comings and goings, and imagining every time you darken my mother's door you're coming to me."

Marcel's face was drawn into a scowl. "Christophe," he said. "You know you're just hanging onto the Englishman, don't you? You just don't want to let him go!"

Anger rent Christophe's face. His eyes became defiant at once. "And I asked you if you were going to stand on your own! Do you ever lie down!" he demanded. "Do you ever stop swinging? Well, don't take advantage of what I feel for you!" and in a rage he rose to go.

"And what about what I feel for you, Chris!" Marcel asked.

(484)

"I don't mean the blundering gesture I made last night. I mean what I really feel! Doesn't that give me some right to speak now? You've got to let the Englishman go. Of course you live in dreams of me because you know you'll never let those dreams come true. And that way you can be faithful to Michael forever, can't you? Well, how are you going to stop all of that if you don't love someone else?"

Christophe had slumped against the frame of the door. His eyes were weary, reddened from lack of sleep, and he stared forward listlessly. "Come here to me," he said softly with a gesture of his left hand.

Marcel stared for a moment, confused. And then quickly he moved forward closing the distance between them and felt Christophe's arm enfold him just as it had done the night before. He felt it strong, simple against his back with a reassuring pressure that suddenly softened him all over and made him feel a curious relief.

"Now I am going to demand something of you," Christophe said in a low voice, "With a lover's prerogative and a teacher's authority, and that is this. That you never, never mention any of this to me again"

II

Anna Bella had been crying on and off for days. Zurlina said it was nothing but the usual after the birth of a child. Yet Zurlina had told her in glowing detail of Marcel's long walk to *Bontemps* and that his father, Michie Philippe, had given him the flogging he deserved. Anna Bella did not have to ask each day whether or not Michie Philippe had come to town after Marcel, Zurlina let her know the goings on at the Ste. Marie cottage as always, replete with gossip of how that miserable Lisette was ruining herself again, sneaking off evenings to the house of Lola Dedé, the voodooienne, who was nothing but a harlot selling colored girls to white men in her house for good money, just as she sold voodoo candles, and powders and charms. And of course the Ste. Marie family didn't know any of this, didn't have the slightest idea.

Meanwhile Anna Bella was tired, dreadfully tired. She had not seen Michie Vince since the week after their son was born, and Anna Bella knew that he was disappointed that this baby had not been a little girl. He had stayed several days, however, and once in a while had held the little baby in his arms. It had been foolish of her to want to name it Vincent, she realized, though he had been tender with her in explaining that he might someday have another son who would be called by this name, perhaps she should give the child her father's name, Martin. This was done. He had filled the bedroom with flowers, and worked all day long in the parlor with his agricultural journals as usual, the aroma of fresh coffee wafting again and again through the small rooms. And though polite to her as always, there was a stiffness about him, and that old sense of foreboding came over her often when she looked into his pensive withdrawn face.

Then only hours after he had finally left, Zurlina came to tell her, it was Michie Vince's wish that she put the child out to nurse. The tears had come at once. "I don't believe that!" Anna Bella had said. "I won't believe it." She held little Martin tightly, her face averted, whispering, "You go away."

"Listen, girl," she had said. "You put that baby out to nurse now. When that man comes here, he wants to find that baby out to nurse."

"He won't even be back until after the harvest," Anna Bella said, her lip trembling, "and I want to hear that from him when he comes back, why didn't he say it to me?"

And so each day after that Zurlina warned her to find a wet nurse for the child. And each day Anna Bella rocked by the fire, attempting to affect her entire body with the love she felt for the baby so as to calm her body and not injure her milk.

Then there were the visitors, so many, day after day, Madame Elsie's old friends, Gabriella Roget and her mother, Madame Suzette with the ladies from her Benevolent Society, and even Marie Ste. Marie with her aunts. And over and over, from the little crowd about the bassinet came those shrill and sprightly observations, "Why that child's got his father's nose and mouth, and *good* hair! Course Anna Bella's got good hair, just look at that pretty child!" And what if it had gone another way, Anna Bella thought. It seemed it was all that concerned them, that mixture of the white and black, could this child perhaps pass?

But alone at night after Zurlina was asleep, she lifted the baby from the bassinet beside her bed and laid it sleeping still against her breast. "All right, then, Martin, since the world's the way it is," she thought, "you are certainly blessed. You won't know the pain I've known," and a glistening tear fell once on his tiny cheek as she brooded lovingly over him, "but when you grow up, son, what will you think when you look at me?" It seemed to her at such moments that it would have been better, actually better, if Anna Bella Monroe had never been born.

Her son's large dark eyes opened to reflect a mere particle of light from the little crackle of a fire on the hearth, and unseeing, uncomprehending, he lolled in the warmth of her arms. "I don't believe Michie Vince said such a thing," she whispered aloud to no one, "I won't give him up to a nurse, I won't do it," and at the faintest cry she put the nipple in his little mouth.

"You ought to be happy," Zurlina would say as she yanked Anna Bella's hair with the brush in the morning, "with all you've got! Don't you know you've got to please that man! Didn't you see the look on that man's face when he saw you nursing that baby! Why, girl, you've got to pay attention to that man."

Don't you be a fool, came the old refrain, that man's crazy for you but he won't be for long, you just better put that baby out, out, out, till Anna Bella angrily snatched the brush from Zurlina's hand.

"Why did you want to come here after Madame Elsie died?" she said bitterly. "Why didn't you stay on at the boardinghouse, those old women would have paid well for you, they told me so themselves, no, you had to tell Michie Vince you wanted to stay here."

"And you be damned glad I did," Zurlina said, looking down her long narrow nose, her thin lips pressed together. "Now give me that brush back, look at your hair. And I've got to go to market besides."

"You run this house, that's why you wanted Michie Vince to buy you," Anna Bella said. "Well, go on to market and leave me alone."

"Don't you be a fool." Be a fool, be a fool, be a fool.

And then two weeks after Michie Vince had left there came this word that Marcel had gotten wildly drunk and wandered right through the gates of *Bontemps*.

She sucked in her breath shuddering, and finally after two days had written him a letter. But his reply had been protective of her. "Don't worry, Anna Bella, I am going to the country for a few months, I have done myself no great injury, and not harmed anyone else besides." He had recounted simply for her the story of his altered prospects. He would not be apprenticed to Monsieur Rudolphe in the undertaking trade. He did not know now what he would do. She put down the letter and stared at the grate. And when she had read it several times, committed it to memory, in fact, she burnt it quickly though why she could not say.

And now alone in her little parlor, the child rocked to sleep in his draped cradle beside her, she watched the night shroud the open windows, the late September air at last touched with a real chill, and she felt her tears coming again. She had almost fallen asleep, her fire dead, her shawl tight over her shoulders and the trees black against the curtains, when she heard that familiar step on the walk. "Michie Vince," she whispered aloud and turned, rising, just for a moment groggy and confused with sleep.

He had slammed the door behind him, and without removing his cape he came across the parlor toward her until she could just make out the sharp features of his face.

"Have you heard!" his voice came in a terse whisper. "Have you heard what your friend Marcel has done?" It was rage that was emanating from the familiar figure as if an alien force had inhabited the body that was looming over her, the dark heavy cape distorting it into a great menacing shape.

"Michie Vince," she whispered softly in amazement.

"Don't you ever, ever, ever in your life let that child come on my property!" he said throwing a long white finger out toward the bassinet, his voice rising to a roar in the silence.

She gasped.

"You teach him, teach him from the day he is old enough to understand anything, you see that he understands, that he is never, never to do such a thing!"

From the lace over the cradle the child moaned and let out a wail.

"You teach him from the beginning never to come near me or my family, do you understand! That child is never to come near *Bontemps*, he is never to mention the name *Bontemps* to anyone, you are never to mention that name to him yourself!"

The baby had begun to scream.

She stood staring at Michie Vince, her hands clasped against her face, and suddenly she went past him, hands digging down into the covers to scoop up the little boy. She wound the blankets around him, awkwardly turning, and walked fast to the back of the cottage, stopping short helplessly before the back door. Her head bent forward and her forehead smacked the frame of the door. An instinctive motion of her arms soothed little Martin, and as she stood there, her eyes shut, her head against the door frame, the baby became quiet.

It must have been an hour that she sat alone in the dark bedroom in a small chair, only the upper part of her body moving back and forth, back and forth, cradling the child. She heard nothing from the living room not even the faintest sound. Once she imagined that she had fallen to sleep and that Michie Vince had actually gone. Then finally came the creak of those boots on the boards and out of the corner of her eye, without turning, she saw his dark shape in the door.

"Anna Bella," he started, the voice soft now, a little breathless, his own. "Anna Bella, I...I..." he stopped, with a sigh. After a long pause he came toward her slowly and his hand reached out for her shoulder finding it and clasping it tenderly as she sat there staring forward, still rocking the baby in her arms. She rose. She walked to the back door and looked out into the night. The cicadas still sang in the trees, those long rasping drifts of song that rose to one terrible pitch after another and then died away. She had not even heard them until this moment, and now suddenly they scraped at her nerves.

She could hear and feel Michie Vince drawing close to her, and now she felt the weight of his forehead against her head. It seemed he was turning his head from side to side against her, his hands on her arms.

"Michie Vince," she said her voice dry of tears now, "I realize this is your house even though you put it in my name. But if you were to ask me what I wanted most of all right now, Michie Vince, it would be that you go out of here and leave me alone. That's what I would really want, that you would just go out of here and leave me alone. Somebody told me that a gentleman never stays where he's not wanted, and I've always known you were a gentleman." She stared straight into the darkness, distinguishing nothing of tree or sky or stars; and she could feel his hands relax on her arms, and suddenly he was not touching her at all.

Some inveterate courage in her caused her to turn, and quite used to the dark now she could see his face. He was staring at her, his chin lifted, his eyes hard.

"I would be just very grateful," she said, "if you would be so kind as to just go out of here and leave me and my baby alone."

He raised his eyebrows slightly, his eyes down toward the floor. And turning without another word, he left.

It was near midnight when she heard him come in again.

He had left his cape, and when she had found it in the parlor, she had suspected he might return. She was sitting by the cradle in the bedroom and did not move. She could hear every step he took. She knew that he had taken the cape from the chair, she heard the scrape of the buttons, she knew by a dozen little soft sounds he had put the cape on. It seemed he moved toward the bedroom and then he stopped. Almost, almost she wanted to rise and to go to him and to speak some word, she did not know what. But she didn't move. And suddenly, those steps turned and walked swiftly out of the little parlor and down the walk, and were gone.

In the morning, when Zurlina came in she was surprised to find Anna Bella dressed and seated at her small lap *secrétaire* in the parlor. She held out a folded paper.

"What's this?" Zurlina stared at it.

"It's the paper that says you belong to me," Anna Bella answered. "Take it and get out of here, I don't care where you go, I never want to see you around here again. You've got money, you've always got money, Michie Vince is always giving you money, so take it and go. Go to work for those old women up at the boardinghouse or anywhere else you want, I don't care."

Zurlina narrowed her eyes, the corners of her long lean mouth twisted down. "You can't live here alone," she said. "Why, you can't even go out yet, you're..."

"The hell I can't. Now you get gone from here." Anna Bella said.

"I'll talk to Michie Vince first before I do," Zurlina answered.

"I wouldn't do that if I were you," Anna Bella said. "'Cause you see, this paper says you belong to me, but if I tell Michie Vince the pins you've been sticking in me and the meanness you've done to me behind his back, he just might ask me to sign this paper over to him, and who knows, you might just wind up chopping cane in those fields. If I was you, I'd get out of here, I'd take this paper with me, and go."

"You nigger bitch!" Zurlina rasped.

"You're free, I'm setting you free," Anna Bella said with a cold smile. "So get out."

(490)

THE DOCKS WERE BUSTLING as five o'clock approached, the gangplanks thronged, and the light of the shorter September day dimming to a red sunset over the scores of smokestacks that rose along the levee for as far as the eye could see. Marcel stood idly among the rushing passengers, his eyes on the high decks of the steamboat, *Arcadia Belle,* as Marie beside him squeezed his arm gently and said,

"Marcel, you're going to write to me, aren't you, every day."

"Of course I will," Marcel said. "But no matter what I've done, Monsieur Philippe and Rudolphe have agreed to the marriage, and Jacquemine has already conveyed Rudolphe's eagerness to set the date. It's all clear. Monsieur Philippe won't visit his anger on you."

"I know that," she sighed. "I only wish that you were here...and that there was no reason for you to go."

"There's Christophe," he said. "Kiss me, and go on." He touched her lips lightly and held her hand for an instant as if he didn't want to let it go.

Rudolphe was not far behind Christophe with Placide coming after with Marcel's trunk on a cart.

"Bonsoir, Michie," said the slave with a deep bow, "looks like you got enough clothes here to retire to the country for the rest of your days and it feels like it too."

"Get it on board," Rudolphe said with disgust. "Now, here's your ticket," he turned to Marcel, "and you've got a first-class stateroom though I dare say you paid a little more for it on account of the color of your skin. Have you got some coins, and some dollar bills?"

"Yes, Monsieur." He patted his breast pocket instinctively. He had taken some two hundred dollars from the strongbox in his desk, money saved from all those munificent handouts, and after seeing to it that Cecile had ample household money, had put the rest in large bills. It crossed his mind now as it had earlier that this was the last bit of fortune he might ever see. "But please, go on and take Marie before she begins to cry, and I begin to cry, too. Monsieur, will you look after her while I'm gone, I am leaving at a bad time."

"You don't have to tell me that. Your beloved mother called me a shopkeeper again today, and she says it with such a delightful ring!"

Marcel bit his lip and made a faint smile.

"All right," Rudolphe said, "now remember what I told you. If there are many *gens de couleur* on board, there will probably be a special seating for your meals. If there are only a few, they may set a table aside for you at the same dinner hour for everyone else. Just watch, and wait for the signals, and be generous with your money, but not a fool. You're a gentleman and expect to be treated like a gentleman, understand?"

Marcel nodded. He gave Rudolphe his hand.

"When you come back," Rudolphe said, "then we'll have a talk. Some decisions can be made then, after you have cooled somewhat, gotten a better view of things...well, there's time."

Marcel merely smiled again, the silent semblance of consent. He had already told Rudolphe quite firmly that he would not become his apprentice in the undertaking trade, and he had conveyed this as well to Jacquemine. And all of Rudolphe's kind actions, seen in the light of Marcel's altered prospects, cut Marcel and humiliated him as they would not have done in the past. The penniless in-law who just might become a stone around Rudolphe's neck? Marcel would starve first. He shook Rudolphe's hand warmly, but no more words would come.

At last, there had been a few more polite farewells, and Christophe and Marcel stood alone near the foot of the gangplank, out of the way of the trooping passengers and the procession of baggage and trunks. The lower deck of the steamboat was jammed with produce, bales of cotton, hogsheads, horses on short tether, and slaves. A coffle had been led on board, in fact, of miserable shackled human beings, a child or two wailing, and it had been as degraded a sight as Marcel's life had ever yielded to him, living in the heart of New Orleans as he had always been.

The state of his nerves was raw, and the vision of the slaves had put him in a particular gloom. He was not at all excited to be making this journey to *Sans Souci,* in fact, *Sans Souci* itself seemed a myth, while his last few days with Christophe had been sublime. It seemed a great burden had been lifted from Chris, and their talks had been more intimate, spirited, and exhilarating than before. Marcel didn't want to leave. And this afternoon, only hours before they left for the docks, Christophe had given him a very special gift.

At first it appeared to be an issue of a French journal, and

Marcel, touched by Christophe's brief but affectionate inscription had moved to tuck it into his valise.

"No, look at it," Christophe had said.

And Marcel opened it again, quite surprised to discover that it had been published in New Orleans. But in a moment, he was leafing through it with unrestrained excitement. He knew the names of some of these contributors, some of them he had even met, and suddenly, excitedly he looked up:

"Why, this is published by our people!" he said. "These are men of color!"

Christophe nodded with a smile. "It's the first number of a quarterly, and our people did it here," he said, "not in Paris, but in New Orleans."

Marcel was proud beyond words. *"L'Album littéraire, journal des jeunes gens, amateurs de la littérature,"* he read the title aloud and for a long time he sat reading the poems— they were in flawless Parisian French—and then reverently, carefully, he had wrapped the small magazine in brown paper and placed it with his belongings. An hour passed as he sat thinking of this little book, and not without some pain. He knew that one of the contributors had recently gone to Paris, and word had it that he was moving in literary circles there with some success. His father was a dry cleaning merchant whom Marcel had nodded to often enough in the street.

But this did not obsess Marcel, he did not dwell on the young man who had crossed the sea, rather he was thinking of the others here at home. And several times, he took out the little periodical, again leafed through it, and smoothing its cover with his hand, replaced it. He would read every word of it when he reached *Sans Souci,* Christophe would send him the next number, and perhaps, oh, yes, certainly, he would write to these men.

And now as the whistle sounded and people commenced to run toward the long gangplank, it did not surprise Marcel that he could find no words to tell Christophe farewell.

Their eyes met and Christophe gave him a firm clasp of the arm.

Marcel forced a thin smile, but he could feel the inevitable lump in his throat, and when Christophe, his eyes moist, made an emphatic gesture of release and turned away, Marcel started for the deck.

But when he reached the rail, he felt panic suddenly. He searched the crowd for Christophe, and picking out the small figure with arm raised, he waved broadly as the whistle gave another violent blast.

It was only when Christophe was out of sight that Marcel looked about himself, at the great swell of gray water pouring past the hull beneath him, and at the crowded stairs to the upper deck. In all his life, not five steps from the Mississippi River, he had never actually been on this water, and he had never heard the sudden violent blast of the whistle so close. It sent an immediate thrill through him. And even as he moved toward the stairs, he felt the immense floating palace shudder and as the hands on shore threw the ropes toward the heavy Negroes against the rails, he realized the boat was moving out.

Once on the upper deck he was amazed to see some yards already between the boat and the docks, the heavy boats at anchor rocking with the churning of the river around them, and the passengers shouting from the land becoming smaller as they received the last farewell from those on board.

Even after the others had dispersed, he clung to the rail, watching the city recede as the boat made for the very center of the immense river, and he was surprised to discover that he could see the towers of the Cathedral, the high fringe of trees among the mansard roofs, and that they were moving rapidly and steadily past the Rue Canal upstream. The boat seemed so apart from the current, its giant wheel turning hypnotically, the smokestacks gushing, and only that tremor throughout that he could feel with his feet.

It was dark before he'd left the deck. The boat had long passed the city of Lafayette and the town of Carrollton, leaving the urban landscape for the open country, and all that could be seen of the plantations beyond the ragged trees and the low hump of the levee were occasional twinkling lights. The stars were wondrously clear over the low land, and the wind was cold. Those who promenaded on the decks wore heavy coats or shawls and light laughter came from the open salons. Marcel had not gone to supper, reluctant to eat, for the first time in his life, at a table separated from white men, but he did not much care. He was excited now, and it was penetrating to him at last that he had left New Orleans, and was really on his way to *Sans Souci*.

Turning to find his stateroom, he was pleased to run upon a courteous porter who directed him graciously, and as he slipped his key into the lock, a tall white man coming down the passageway acknowledged his nod with a murmured greeting of his own. The little room was splendid with its garlanded wallpaper and sumptuous furnishings, and through the open window he could see the heavens again with those miraculous and low-hanging stars. *Sans Souci,* he sighed, and was struck by the actual meaning of those words. It had been a name and picture on the wall so long he had forgotten: *without care.* It made him smile. And though he had the strangest feeling that the acute happiness of his last few years would not come back to him for a long while, something new and perhaps far more exciting was taking its place. He had always wanted it to end, that limbo of childhood, and now it had all but come to its close. And it astonished him to realize slowly that the next time he saw the home he was leaving now he would be on his own.

What would he do? What would he make of himself? Strange that in the midst of a morass of difficulty that question kindled a flame in him, a flame that actually warmed his heart.

IV

THE RAIN CASCADED DOWN the panes, and again there came that hard insistent knock. "Michie," Felix said, rousing himself from a drowsy posture beside the mantel, his lean corded black hands loosely clasped over his bent knee. He had been looking out the windows at a landscape rendered shapeless and splendidly colored by the rain.

"I hear it," Philippe muttered. "Open that bottle." He turned up one more card. Red queen, red queen on a black king, he had been certain there was a black king. "Not that bottle, the Kentucky whiskey," he said. The knock came again.

Felix filled the glass. "It's the *Maîtresse,* Michie," he whispered. He regarded Philippe almost sleepily, and the distress that lined his gaunt black face was remote, as if not attached to this room and this time.

"Hmmmmm," Philippe gathered the cards again into a thick pack. He shuffled them easily, fancily. "Miss Betsy loves that," he laughed, glancing to Felix as he arched the divided pack, the cards falling into place. Miss Betsy was Philippe's daughter who was not there. "She loves that," Philippe laughed again. He always called her Miss Betsy because she spoke English so well, had so many American friends, the mere thought of Miss Betsy brought him a soft delicious smile. Miss Betsy had been ten years old the week before, the perfect little lady, with his blond hair, his blue eyes. "That's what I like," he said as he dealt the long line of solitaire across the shining surface of the table, stopping once for a large swallow from his glass. "That's what I like, two aces on the first go-round" and quickly he removed these from the line and placed them above. His eyes moved back and forth over these fine surfaces, the gilded cards, the polished table, the shimmer of the amber whiskey in the glass. Then he stopped, eyes vacant. There was the grind of the key in the lock. His heavy face, the cheeks bruised with a wilderness of broken blood vessels, became set. Aglae stepped into the room, her eyes scanning it at once, and she gestured for Felix to go out.

"Don't you move," Philippe said, his eyes fixed malevolently on his valet. Felix dropped back into the corner beyond the chimney where the fire illuminated nothing but the gleam of his patient eye. The mistress never countermanded the master's orders, disliked to challenge the master in the presence of the slaves.

"Well?" Philippe said. "So I have no privacy even here in the *garçonnière,* and where's your shadow, why didn't you bring your brother here to break down the door?" He reached for the queen of spades. "Ever have your fortune told with the cards, Madame?" he said with a smile so sweet and natural no stranger could have perceived its bitterness as he looked up to her. "I've had my fortune told a thousand times, and it's always the gambler's card that turns up. I am a man willing to take risks. Give me the unknown rather than the known."

"Monsieur," she said in a deliberate monotone, "you are gambling with the entire crop."

Philippe's eyes widened. The expression became thoughtful. Vincent had moved into the room, as reticent as Felix on the edge. Heaving a sigh, Philippe turned up another card. "Madame, there is enough wood to run the mill for three years," he said with that loose, gentle smile, "every fence is repaired, the..."

"That may be so, Monsieur, but you have been locked in this room for three days."

He studied the board, moved a black king into the empty

(496)

space left by the ace which he had placed above. Then he gazed at the palm of his hand, and holding it out to her by the light of the fire said, "Blisters, Madame, I was in the saddle for a week. Blisters take time to heal."

"Monsieur, if we do not harvest now, we are running a dreadful risk. If you would leave this room only long enough to..."

"It's too early," he said firmly. He had turned up the two of clubs, placed it on the ace.

"Monsieur, the temperature has dropped drastically," came the same monotone, Aglae's figure as straight as if it were cut from cardboard against the fire. "You have not been out of this room for three..."

"When have I ever waited too long?" he said. "Madame, I have run this plantation for eighteen years, I have never, never waited too long."

"I am losing patience, Monsieur."

"You are losing patience!" His eyes grew wider, a flush disfiguring his face so that his golden eyebrows became prominent against the pink flesh and gave a sharp intensity to his anger. "You are losing patience! And what about your husband, Madame, eighteen years of this icy courtesy, this venomous decorum. Tell me, Madame, what is the inside of your mind? What barren, wintry place," he spat the words, "that the fortress which surrounds it is so impregnable, so cold?"

"Aglae, come out," Vincent whispered.

"Ah, yes, and it's our blessed boy, is it, the joy of his father's old age." Philippe dealt another card. Good luck, a red seven. He laid it neatly in place, his hand deftly straightening the crooked rows before him. His eyes were glazed now with tears. He stared at Vincent who looked away from him. "All right, what do you want, cut the cane then, cut the cane! Go on, tell Rousseau to cut the cane!" he said with a powerful shrug. "And if the weather holds for another month, then what will you say, Madame, 'he cut the cane too soon, he is not the master here any longer,' and if there's a frost tomorrow, you'll say I waited too late." He laughed, a soft genuine laugh. "Do as you like. Ride the fields if you like. I'm tired, Madame, your unpaid overseer is tired...This room, Madame, this room is my New Orleans, now if you please..." he stopped. He let the little pack slip from his hand and brought his hands up to support his bowed head. "What do you want of me, Madame?" he whispered.

"That you stop this, Monsieur," Aglae said. "Your children have not seen you for three days. Miss Betsy is crying, Monsieur..."

"Miss Betsy loves me!"

"And Henri is old enough to know now..."

"Henri loves me!"

"You must eat, Monsieur...you must have a decent meal..."

He laughed, his head still bowed, the fleece on the backs of his fingers golden in the firelight. "I must have love, Madame," he whispered. "Why don't you tell your children what you think of their father, Madame, what you have always thought of him?" Vincent moved silently, slipping out onto the gallery against a backdrop of cold rain, the door closing behind him. "Why share that secret only with your brother?" Philippe asked. "No, Madame, it's time you made them privy to the hell of ice and snow in which they were all conceived..."

"You are a fool, Monsieur," Aglae said. "We begin the harvest tomorrow."

As soon as Aglae opened her eyes, she knew that Philippe was in the room, and Philippe had not been in this room in five years. But a fire burned on the hearth, and its warmth had awakened her, used as she was to order that fire only when she herself was up and dressed. Beside her, Miss Betsy slept, having awakened in the night afraid, and been taken into her mother's bed. Now Aglae rose carefully, smoothing the comforter over her daughter's shoulders, and stood beside the bed letting her lank flannel gown fall down around her ankles as she slipped on her robe. The long heavy braid of her salt and pepper hair had caused the familiar morning ache at the back of her head. She moved to the mirrored doors of her armoire, and saw through the mirrors the figure of Philippe sitting near the licking flames. He wore riding boots, his frock coat with the fur collar, and beneath a worn weary red-eyed face gleamed the brilliant azure of his silk tie. "Why are you here, Monsieur?" she asked. "I am going to dress now, Monsieur."

"Are you?" he said. His head wagged slightly as he looked at her through the same mirror. These were fancy clothes. The gold chains of his watch crisscrossed the buttons of his embroidered vest, and there mingled with the sour fermented breath the clean smell of his cologne.

(498)

"You propose to ride the fields when you have been awake all night?" she asked, opening the door. "I suggest you leave this day's work to Vincent, and Rousseau."

"I'm not riding the fields, Madame," he said with obvious amusement. "I'm going into New Orleans for an extended stay."

When he said this, her frail form slumped slightly in the empty hanging gown. She let her head rest for a moment against an outstretched arm, hand clutching a black broadcloth dress on its hook. "Monsieur, we begin cutting today!" she said through her teeth.

"Do we, Madame? Well, your unpaid overseer won't be here to manage it for you this year, he's taking a leave of absence. Do you see this?" and he drew out of his coat a folded sheaf of papers. "All signed, Madame, just as you wanted them, your beloved *Bontemps* is no longer in my hands. And as soon as you exercise your new power of attorney by writing several drafts on your bank for me, these papers are yours. One thousand each, I think, and six drafts, that should be quite fine. Date them a month apart. I've always known you to be a woman of your word."

"And what then, Monsieur!" she turned angrily. The little girl in the bed stirred, a sharp limb heaving the white comforter.

He shrugged, his blue eyes fired with a wild animation, red-rimmed as they were, and heavy and listless as his great frame appeared in the small curved-legged chair. "We'll see, hmmmm? Six drafts, Madame, one thousand each, and we'll see. I'm a gambling man."

"You're making a dreadful mistake," she said, her voice for the first time infected with a slight resonance.

He had risen and drawn near the bed, his arm sliding down under his little girl. "Miss Betsy," he whispered.

"Hmmmm, Papa..." the child whispered.

"Kiss me, *ma petite, ma chérie*..." he breathed, lifting the sleepy child. Aglae moved barefoot and silent into the dressing room and clutched her forehead in her right hand as if she meant to break by sheer force the bones of her own skull.

It was half an hour before she was dressed and had the drafts signed for him. The immense study of the lower floor was cold, without a fire, and a concealing fog rolled up the length of the French windows between their saffron draperies. Her hand was stiff as she signed her name. And Philippe, a glass of whiskey in hand, walked to and fro on the immense Turkey carpet, humming some sweet air from the opera that Aglae knew but did not know. She watched him dully, and when he made some turn so that he might see her, she held out the bank drafts, her eyes cast down.

"What will I tell the children?" she asked.

"I don't know, Madame," he set down his glass, the papers folded and placed in his pocket. "But whatever you tell them, think on it carefully, as they are most likely to believe it, every word." He went out the door.

Aglae sat still. Then she rose so quickly, she upset the random items of her desk, but took no notice, walking rapidly into the main hall. Her steps quickened until she was almost running as she passed out of the front door. Philippe had just mounted, and he gestured for Felix to ride on. The rolling fog from the river shrouded the entire avenue of the oaks so that almost nothing could be seen of it but the dim arching outline of the nearest trees.

"Monsieur," she cried, her voice barely carrying on the moving air. But he turned his horse, urging it backwards and to one side and then came toward her. "Don't do this, Monsieur," she cried. "Don't go!" She stood stiff, her hands clasping her skirts, looking up at him. "Don't do this!" she said firmly. "You were doing well, Monsieur, you had the reins again." The words came in tight blasts, the body tense as if something of immense value might escape. "You don't want to do this, Monsieur!"

But he only smiled as he urged the horse on again, the black mare shying to the side, and he looked above her, beyond her, as though surveying the immense façade of the white two-storied house. The smile was vague and unfamiliar and seemed to have nothing to do with this moment or with her. He dug his knees into the horse's flank, and the sharp hooves sent a spray against her dress from the wet grass. Her hand shot to her throat as though she were suffocated, and a cry died in a gasp on her lips. She saw the horse and its rider penetrate the limitless mist. They became colorless and without the faintest sound over the wind, and then vanished altogether right before her eyes.

It was getting dusk when Philippe reached the Rue Ste. Anne and he saw at once that the front rooms of the cottage were dark. His hand was all but frozen on the reins, and a frost clung to his hair and to the ruffled fur of his collar. He guided the mare back the shell-paved alley, Felix following him, and the dark wet banana fronds slapped at him lightly as wearily he put up his arm. Felix dismounted at once to fill the bucket at the cistern, and the kitchen door creaked open showing Lisette's face. Philippe gave her a nod and a wink as he jumped down, and said, "Ah, there's my girl."

A light swelled behind the lace curtains of Cecile's bedroom, and in an instant, Philippe had Cecile in his arms. She was soft, hair down, in her silk dressing gown, and so hot that her fingers all but burnt his freezing face.

"Precious, precious," he breathed to her, lifting her off her feet, the warmth of the little room seeping about him like a delicious fluid. "Don't cry now, my precious, there, there, don't cry," he breathed as he carried her toward the unmade bed and felt her shuddering as he covered her small mouth with his own. All of her rounded limbs yielded to him as her head slipped into the hollow of his neck. "Take off these wet clothes, precious," he whispered, and watched through a haze, it seemed, as those tiny dark fingers worked a miracle with the buttons, the coal fire glowing, blinding his watery eyes.

It was after midnight before he awoke against the pillow. She had a plate of oysters for him, hot bread with lots of butter, and a cup of thick soup which he drank, chewing the bits of meat with a slight moan. He stretched, his knuckles scraping the mahogany behind him, and snuggled back into the pillow, his eyes closing. "And Marcel?" he whispered drowsily, his head turned away from her, on the verge of sleep.

"Gone to the country, Monsieur, for a long visit," Cecile said. "Do you want your nightshirt, Monsieur?"

"No, *chère,* just your arms," he sighed. "A long visit, in the country, a nice long, long visit, that's good."

After a week, he sent the miserable and anxious Felix back to *Bontemps* for his trunk. Marcel had already been in the Cane River country for two months, and it would be three months more before he was to come home.

V

NONE OF THE NIECES and nephews, the cousins, aunts, and uncles had left *Sans Souci* though it was four days after New Year's. And the eleven rooms of the rambling mansion were fragrant with blazing fires, and the smell of roasting meat still wafted from the slave cabins on the cold air. The day was mild, however, for this time of year.

Marcel rose early despite a long night of toasting and dancing, and after a brief bit of small talk in the parlors, went off for a walk along the Cane River, alone. He was worried about the family in New Orleans, and he found it soothing to wander the banks of this broad swiftly moving stream, at times approaching the very edge of the water, at others roaming some thick bracken for a silent visit to an oak or a tall stiff magnolia which had become a milestone on his private landscape for mornings such as this.

He loved this river; far smaller that the Mississippi it was manageable for his heart. One could row across it, fish in it, wade in it, with none of that awe or reverence which the Mississippi inspired. The sky was streaked with clouds, and a pale blue, the sun slanting warm through the crisp air.

It was midmorning when he came back, and he was tempted to send for his horse and ride out beyond the borders of the plantation through an uncleared and eternally mysterious land just to the south. But he was still tentative with the horse. He had learned to ride in spite of his fear, and he rode well. But a tension always preceded the decision to mount. He thought better of it as he came up the broad front steps, and pushing open the double doors on the immediate warmth of the parlor, saw a letter from Christophe lying on Tante Josette's desk.

Christophe had written faithfully since Marcel had left, letters coming as often as three times a week by the steamboats that plied the river, and the letters were always candid, leaving nothing to doubt. Chris said things Rudolphe would have never committed to paper. Richard's notes contained no information, whatsoever, and Marie did not write at all. And often Christophe wrote, "Burn this when you are finished," and as Marcel tore open the soft blue paper and found the usual three pages crowded with a remarkably clear though ornate script, he saw these words again: "Burn this when you are finished." He had not burned a single letter and he would not burn this one.

It is as bad as rumor would have it. I can confirm this now because I met Monsieur P. last week and was invited up for cards in the *garçonnière*. Let me add that your mother gave me the evil eye when she saw me, but I accepted this invitation out of concern for you as you will understand. The man is drinking suicidally. He has sent for much furniture from the country and carved out a regular parlor for gambling next to your old room, taking over that as well for his wardrobe and that valet, Felix, who appears the most miserable of men. Monsieur P. has company continually there, and there were two white men when I arrived, both of them spiffily dressed with no breeding, river gamblers I suspect, though your father despite the amounts of liquor he pours down his throat, is sharp.

I lost fifty dollars before I had sense enough to become a spectator, and Monsieur P. lost two hundred, but it could have been much much more.

And this between Christmas and New Year's. He did not go to the country at all. Your mother is terrified, or so I'm told, now that she sees the man is seriously ill.

Lisette finally came back, and there is no doubt now she was earning something for her favors wherever she was lodged. I've pleaded again with her to be patient, not to quarrel or run off, to wait until you can come home.

Marie is gone completely to your aunts now. And meantime there can be no talk of the wedding while Monsieur P. is so ill. Rudolphe is furious, and Richard at school is a loss. Take this advice. Write to your mother and urge this marriage, now.

Don't be so much ashamed with me of enjoying the country life. There is nobility in every pleasure you describe to me, the riding, the hunting, the good company by the fire. Learn all that you can from this, and stop deriding your own weakness for loving it. You weren't sent there to suffer, and even if you were, you are free to do with any experience what you like. That you have "given yourself over to it" is a credit to you.

Au revoir, petit frère. Stop asking about Maman. Hers is a treacherous nature because it is so simple. And I have always relied upon you to be clever in this regard. But never mind, she misses you in her own way. She hit me with an iron pan the other day for teasing her. An iron pan.

Chris

Marcel put the letter into his pocket, and felt, as he always did after Christophe's letters, that he couldn't bear to stay away a moment longer, he had to find some way to go home. That he could be of no help to his mother or to Marie stung him. However, he was loving the life of the Cane River country, and when he had written Christophe that he had given himself up to it completely he had been telling the truth. But there was so much more that he wanted to tell Christophe, so much he was aching to tell, and soon after his arrival, he had realized he could not commit the real content of his feelings to paper. He simply lacked any gift with the pen. Another failing in a series of personal failings, which in some way was the real drama of his life: that discovering music in earnest that first year at the opera, he himself could do nothing with it; and loving art always as he trudged here and there with his sketchbooks, he himself could do nothing with it; and now it was the same with literary expression, his passion for literature not lending him the slightest gift for writing of his own. And his mind teemed. Not only with thoughts of those he loved at home, but with a thousand realizations that had come to him in the country, and he wanted so much to talk with Christophe, to feel the easy exchange of ideas between them, that this desire approached physical pain.

It was a Creole plantation, *Sans Souci,* not one of those massive Grecian temples, cold and indifferent, and come so late to Louisiana with the Americans. Rather it was the old style of house, simple, harmonious, and built for the climate and the terrain. And Marcel had come upon it quite unawares in the hour just before dawn as his packet wound its way through the Rivière aux Cannes, not knowing that this distant lovely house, a vision emerging from the mist beyond a thinning line of forest, was in fact his aunt's home.

He had left the great palatial steamboat on the Mississippi the night before, transferring to this smaller boat which then chugged inland on its serpentine route at an abominable pace, time and again stopping at a darkened pier beyond which the swamp, not so dense perhaps or so forbidding as it was one hundred miles south, nevertheless threw up its mysterious wall against the impenetrable and starless sky. And unable to sleep, he had come out on deck in the dark to find the morning warm and alive with whispering creatures and the slapping of the smaller paddle wheel somewhat soothing to the anxiety which had increased as he drew closer and closer to this unknown world. And then the sleepy porter had come out with the trunk behind him and as a slave appeared on the pier beyond, his lantern high in the clearing mist, had said, *"B'jour, Michie, c'est Sans Souci."*

High on a foundation of whitewashed pillars it stood, its broad verandas enclosing the main floor on three sides and supporting its deeply pitched roof with slender graceful columnettes. Narrow gabled attic windows looked out over the river, and a broad stairway ran down from the front gallery with its double doors to the avenue of young oaks below.

Marcel's heart was pounding as he mounted the steps. It had been years since he had seen his Tante Josette, and there came a sweet moment then when she took him in her arms. She was the eldest of the three sisters, and seemed vastly older than either Louisa or Colette, her hair pure white now, waving tightly back from her high forehead to a pair of pearl-studded combs. Tall, stiffly slender, she could look Marcel straight in the eyes in spite of his height, and when she kissed him there was a simple sincerity of affection to it which put him at once at ease. Memories came back to him, myriad impressions of her which had lain dormant in his childhood soul. The special perfume she always wore, a mixture of verbena and violets, and the particular feel of her firm hand.

She took him directly into the big parlor, its French doors open to the mild September air. There was strong coffee for him at once, and he sat back on a long couch and surveyed this high-ceilinged room with its immense old-fashioned fireplace (no mean coal grates here) and its many oil portraits hung over mantel, sideboard, between the windows, everywhere indeed that he might look. They were all dark faces, some bronze, amber, others the perfect cream of *café au lait,* and he recognized Tante Louisa and Tante Colette among them, and men and women he did not know. He had never seen such a vast collection of painted *gens de couleur,* and he was to remember the curious effect of it afterwards because it forecast the particular world to which he had just been admitted, the nature of which he could not have really guessed. In the coming months he was to study these pictures often, noting a style that ranged from a Parisian perfection to a cruder, ill-proportioned work, very expressive, however, which reminded him painfully of his own sketches. Tante Josette meantime settled at her high *secrétaire* against the wall, turning to face him in a Queen Anne chair. Her eyes had an intensity he remembered at once. They were youthful or timeless as was her voice which hadn't the slightest timbre of old age. But the face was lined, the cheeks slightly sunken, and the dark blue broadcloth dress with its somewhat narrow sleeves and proper white lace collar completed the figure of advancing age. None of that frivolity that marked her sisters, the abundance of rings and frills. Only the two pearl-studded combs.

"You're in good health," she said. "And you've got your father's height which is always an advantage and your mother's delicate bones. And I see an animation and intelligence in your face which seems the best of them both. So tell me why you did such a foolish thing as to go to your father's plantation, why you let that man humiliate you, why you let him put his boot in your face."

All this was said so calmly that it took Marcel's breath away.

But Tante Josette went on in the same even voice.

"Don't you know who you are, and who your people are, Marcel?" she gave a short sigh. "When you let a white man humiliate you, we are all humiliated. When you give that man the opportunity to degrade you, we are all degraded. He knocked you down on the floor of a slave cabin, and so he knocked us all down. Do you understand?"

Not even Rudolphe could have said it better, if Christophe had ever given him the chance. Marcel felt his cheeks grow hot but he didn't take his eyes off his aunt.

"Well," he said, "at least we come right to the point."

She uttered a small dry laugh. He himself did not realize he had said these words somewhat casually and confidently in a voice that was no longer the child's voice she remembered, and she respected him for it.

"I was angry and bitter, Tante," he continued. "I lived all my life with the idea I would go to Paris when I was of age, that I had a future. All that was changed, and I was angry, and bitter, and foolish."

"I know that," she said. "But had you no pride in yourself in the here and now, where you are? Paris may be the City of Light, Marcel, however, it is not the world. This is the world. Where was your pride?"

"I should have had it," he said. But he could divine from her expression that she knew he did not entirely mean what he said. This, the world? How could he live in this world? He wondered if his mouth showed the bitterness, the positive anguish he felt at being on her charity here, on her hands. After all, she was not really his aunt, these were not really his people, he found himself looking off and shaking his head. "I have no fortune now, Tante, and no future, but I have money enough that I won't be a burden to you while I'm here. I regret that..."

"Nonsense, you insult me. You are my nephew and this is my house."

"Tante, I know about my mother. Years ago I got it out of Tante Colette. I know you picked her up off a street in Port-au-Prince in the time of Dessalines. It's quite an accident my being here..."

"It's an accident any of us being here or anywhere," she said at once, with the same calm but quick manner. "It's all an accident and we don't care to realize that because it confuses us, overwhelms us, we couldn't live our lives day to day if we did not tell ourselves lies about cause and effect."

This he hadn't expected. He turned slowly to her again and saw her meditative face in profile, the white hair rippling back through those combs to the chignon on the nape of her neck. An uncomfortable realization confronted him which was at once exciting. Why had he thought this woman so peculiar in years past, so eccentric? Because she was intelligent?

"Tante, I wouldn't insult you for the world," he said. "I'm painfully aware, however, that I'm a burden to you whether you say so or not. I occupy space and I require food and drink. I'm on your hands. Please understand my anger in this helplessness and allow me my apologies. You've always treated me as if I were your own flesh and blood, my unhappiness now is no recrimination."

"Hush, Marcel," she said, but again she had been secretly impressed. "You're being a bit of a fool. I love you and your sister just as I love your mother, don't you understand the true nature of love?"

Of course he understood it. It was unselfish and unquestioning in the final analysis and it was loyal. He was humiliated by this love.

"You misunderstand it all," she said. She had made her narrow fingers into the steeple of a church which she touched

(507)

lightly to her lips, her eyes on the wall above her. "I know what my sisters told you, of how I snatched your mother from the shadow of that dead Frenchman in Port-au-Prince. But that's the mere bones of the matter, not the real flesh and blood. Love can be quite selfish, Marcel, love can serve itself."

She shifted in her chair so that she might see him. Her slight eyebrows were black still against her brown skin and arched lightly over the deepset black eyes. Her thin Caucasian mouth was only a line now in old age. But her expression leapt from the eyes. "I had no right to take your mother from that street. She was a dark child for all her French features, those soldiers of Dessalines would not have harmed her. Oh, starved and lost for a while she might have been, you cannot imagine the sheer clumsiness and confusion of war. But she was not orphaned. Yet I took her, took her as if she were the spoils of a battle in which I myself was not even engaged."

He looked away. This seemed absurd. But Tante Josette went on.

"I took her on the spur of the moment, Marcel, and plunged her into my world of my own will because I wanted to do it. She became my property at that moment, and *my responsibility* thereafter. More keenly perhaps than any child which God has sent to me since."

There was no doubt she meant these rather extraordinary sentiments. She was not speaking this way merely to put him at ease. And seen in this light, the sordid battle, the moaning frightened child, and the brave woman going down the stairs to rescue her from the torn street—these images changed in Marcel's mind slowly but richly; however, nothing distinct emerged. He attempted, just for a moment, to see it her way.

"Some would not have bothered, Tante," he said. "Some would have trampled her underfoot in the escape."

"I wanted her," she said, arching those fine eyebrows. *"Wanted her."* She studied him. "It was that desire for her, and certainly an impulsive desire, that lay at the root of the magnanimous act. I was widowed then, and barren. I wonder if she had not been such a beautiful child whether I would have noticed her at all."

Marcel's eyebrows knit tightly in a frown.

"Later, there was war between my sisters and myself when I came here to the country. They wanted to keep her, I wanted to take her with me. She decided it herself, loving Colette as she did and crying not to be taken with me here. Did you ever think what the lives of my sisters might be today if it weren't for your mother? If it weren't for your mother, and your sister, and you?"

He had never perceived it in that light. Of course Tante Louisa and Tante Colette had their lady friends. But they had lost all the babies they had ever carried, their lovers were long gone now, and it was the little Ste. Marie family that rooted them deeply and firmly into the community with its generations, it was the Ste. Marie family that was their world.

Of course Tante Josette had married again. Gaston Villier who had built *San Souci,* and one son born late in his mother's life had survived the scourges of childhood to run this plantation after his father's death with two sons of his own. But Louisa and Colette? Marcel, Marie, and Cecile were their life.

But how could he not be grateful for this, nevertheless? How could he wish himself back on that blood-torn island, if, in fact, he would ever have been born at all? Tante Josette was watching his expression, she was studying all of him as if she had only just had the vantage point from which to see the young man who he was. "You are part of me, Marcel," she said, "just as I am part of you. And you belong here now."

He wished he could believe it. He wished above all he could convince her that he believed it, so that he might stop causing her trouble, and find some corner here out of the way where he would not be underfoot for however long this exile must last.

"Thank you, Tante."

"You did not acquire this wit from your mother or your father, I suspect," she said, musing, her fingers made into the church steeple against her mouth. "You must have got it from God. Shall I make my point more keenly? Turn those blue eyes to me again, and let me see if you would really care to know the truth?"

"Don't I know it already?" he said. "Isn't the rest a matter of comprehension which must come with time?"

She gave a short negative shake of the head. "This will make it clear."

Just a flicker of fear showed in his eyes, but there was no shrinking.

"We didn't leave the island the day that we found your mother," Josette said. "The massacre of the French continued,

(509)

so did all the random and dreadful acts that are inevitable in war. But there were Americans left unmolested in Port-au-Prince, and it was with them that we planned to escape.

"Meantime our house was shuttered like a fortress. We bathed your mother, rocked her, combed her long hair. Whatever food we had we gave to her. But she was stunned. She whimpered like an animal. When she did say a few words they were African, quite distinctly African, though what tongue it was I couldn't have told you then nor could I tell you now.

"But it was on the morning before we were to leave that we heard a frightful banging below. I heard it all the way to the back of the house where I was sleeping with your mother. Your aunts, Colette and Louisa, were huddled together in the front room. Of course I demanded to know what was it, and why hadn't one of them even peeked from the shutters to the street. 'You leave it alone,' they said to me, both of them, 'just some mad woman down there, some savage right from Africa, don't even look.' Well, my sisters could never fool me for long. I knew there was more to this, and I was bound and determined to tell what."

"It was a savage all right, a tall woman, very black, handsome I suppose, I couldn't tell you, but dressed in nothing but a swath of red cloth and African to the marrow of her bones. She was pounding on the door with both fists and when she heard the shutter creak above she shouted in Gombo French, 'You give me back my child!'"

Tante Josette paused. Marcel was staring at her, enrapt.

"Others had seen us take your mother, others were standing about, watching, as this woman pounded on the door. But that house had survived years of siege, and we huddled inside of it not making the slightest sound. I crept to the back and gathered little Cecile in my arms again, covering her ears.

"An hour passed, perhaps more. Yet the woman would not give up. She threw stones, brickbats. And at last she attempted to wrench the door from its hinges with a wedge. My nerves were on the breaking point, and unable to bear it a moment longer, I threw open the shutters and looked down at her in the street.

"But understand Marcel before you judge: the smell of fire eternally in the air, the stench of rotting flesh. That woman in her bare feet, her breast naked, that Frenchman's body bloated, festering on the hook. And the little ebony child,

(510)

your mother, the flawless and beautiful little face with eyes closed against my bosom, hair in ringlets, skin like silk.

"I screamed at that woman, 'Your child's not here. Go away from here, your child's dead! They took her body away last night, they put her on the common pyre.'"

Tante Josette stopped. She was staring forward, and Marcel, speechless, watched her remote but agitated face.

She sighed. "I will never forget the sound of that woman's howl. I will never forget that face with the hands pressed on both sides of it, that round hole of a mouth."

"'Cecee, Cecee, Cecee!' she bellowed before she went down on her knees. And two days later when I said that name, 'Cecee' to your mother in the hold of the ship that was taking us to New Orleans, she smiled for the first time."

Marcel had brought his hand up to shield his eyes and he said nothing, nor did he move.

"Don't you understand?" she asked softly. "Your mother is more mine than any child I ever bore, and you belong to me, too. It was evil what I did, willful, wrong. You do not know the hours I have spent begging forgiveness for it, begging God to give me some sign that I was right. But God has been easy with me, easy with us all. And in telling the truth to you now, I should rather lose your love, Marcel, than have you come to believe that you are not my own."

Once alone in the spacious room of the *garçonnière* behind the house, Marcel cried like a child against his knotted fists while beyond the open windows the vast plantation with its spreading fields of cotton came awake.

It was a week before he could write of this to Christophe and how stiff and stilted the words seemed. Tante Josette's feeling eluded him, the voice so enriched with grief and remorse had not been his to convey.

Christophe's reply was prompt, however, and brief.

Pity your mother, she was old enough to remember all of it. And your Tante Josette, who if she could have put her conscience to rest would not have told you the tale.

But it was neither Cecile nor Josette who concerned him during those first few nights when darkness came so totally to the country, it was the black woman beating on the door in Port-au-Prince. The family portrait was now complete: the white Frenchman dangling eternally on his hook, and the

(511)

African with her bare breast howling as she dropped to her knees. How wish Josette had not done it? How reach back across four decades to touch that black hand? And finally sitting bolt upright in the dark one night he had wandered down to the main house just before dawn to find Tante Josette reading by the light of a lamp. She reached out for him when he came in. It was so easy to cry against her, to encircle her small waist and press his forehead to her withering breast. "You are my own," she said again softly. And this time, he answered, "Yes."

It seemed those early weeks at *Sans Souci* passed in confusion. He had been burnt by these early revelations, and the recent past in New Orleans was never far from his mind. And all he wanted finally was to speak with Tante Josette while instead he went through the elaborate motions of a visiting nephew in the midst of a large family as if he were an actor playing the part.

But in the next few months Marcel was to spend long mornings in Tante Josette's company during which she revealed to him her entire world. She had gone to Paris when she was very young with a white lover who had her educated by tutors in their Paris flat. She remembered another age of three-cornered hats and knee breeches and the turmoil of Paris under the Directory still vibrating with the horrors of the guillotine.

And unlike her sisters, and the pretty women who surrounded her all her life, she was an obsessive reader of papers and books. Her corner of the parlor at *Sans Souci* revealed a library behind locked cabinet doors, and it was from these carefully concealed shelves that she commenced Marcel's education on the history of his people and the island of Haiti or Saint-Domingue.

And baroque and filled with blood these books were. They were, some of them, violently opposed to the revolution, and painted the rising slaves as monsters, cruel beyond civilized reason, while others made heroes of these same men, detailing the life and speeches of Toussaint L'Ouverture, the little black general who had commanded the first great organized uprising, and his successors, Dessalines, who had given the island the name of Haiti, and its first emperor, the magnetic and enigmatic Henri Christophe.

Night after night, Marcel (forbidden to show these books in the house) fell asleep with these histories open beside him on the pillow and the chronicle of horrors bled into his dreams. And it was during this time that he first read of the brigands, those runaway slaves who had lived for so many generations in the mountains of the old French colony of Saint-Domingue that the Crown had finally recognized their independence, a status which in the days of the black revolution they had been loath to lose. They fought for the king at one point, the rebels at another, and sometimes it seemed only for themselves.

Juliet's father, the "Old Haitian," had been of this breed. And only now did Marcel come to understand, as Tante Josette answered his eager questions, all that had long puzzled him in Juliet herself. Had she been reared in those mountains, with a brigand band? Was it not natural then for her to wring the chickens' necks so easily, to pull the yams from the backyard, to carry her market basket with such perfect grace on her head? What kind of life had she lived there, what violence had seared her mind leaving her, as Christophe had often said, a mere shell? One thing was certain in Tante Josette's mind, that Juliet had believed her father murdered by one of the ever-changing factions in power when she had found her way to the Louisiana shore. And the name Mercier was that of the first white man who had put her up as his mistress in the house in the Rue Dauphine.

"A cunning woman, that," Tante Josette said, "She'd let them drag her by her hair across the floor if they liked, but she hid the money they gave her, and never let them lay hands on her son. I rather think the old man gave her a mortal fright when he appeared in New Orleans, and God only knows from whom he got the wealth he brought with him, and where he had been. The portrait painter, Belvedere, came up this way just after he had done the old man's portrait in that house in 1829, and what tales he told. Sometimes I think a traveling artist shouldn't talk anymore than a doctor should or anyone who comes to render a service in the privacy of a home."

"But tell me!" Marcel said with a characteristic impatience which, more than once, had made his aunt laugh.

"The old man drove off Juliet's lovers, he paid her debts, bought the house, and all of this in gold. But he beat that poor exuberant Christophe, and the pretty mother would burst into tears when he was shaking the boy and beat on the old man with her fists. There was a power to that man, think of all he survived. And a power to her, too, I should think. She was scrubbing floors when she first came, and God knows what else until she took a good look in the mirror and then around herself at what was to be had. Tell me, Marcel, does that power persist in your teacher, today?"

Marcel's short bitter laugh gave her the answer. How could one compare these generations? It dazzled the mind. "Christophe's a European," he said more to himself than to her. "Somewhere in the oldest capitals of the world, he contracted a fatal case of ennui."

"What does it all come to?" she sighed. And then after considering it for more than a moment she surprised Marcel. "And Juliet, my dear nephew?" she shot him a subtle smile. "Ah, but you're a gentleman and a gentleman shouldn't be tempted to tell tales."

Marcel made his face a mask.

"I don't know what you mean, Tante."

"Well, my dear nephew," she drawled slowly, "if I had seen those brilliant blue eyes of yours in my prime, I might have bent the rules and folded back the coverlet myself."

Marcel merely smiled and with a light graceful shrug shook his head.

But as Marcel read on, it was not the personal history of those around him that kept him enthralled. It was the unfolding tale of the revolution itself. Jean Jacques had been right when he had told Marcel it was the *gens de couleur* that lent the powder keg of the colony its spark. It amazed Marcel to discover the height to which his people had risen, the wealth, the number of plantations, how in such impressive numbers they were educated and burning finally for their full rights. Then came the French Revolution, *Liberté, Egalité, Fraternité*. How grand it must have seemed. Who could have guessed in 1791 that the island would reek with blood and fire for decades afterwards, its fantastical wealth consumed and scattered, its luxurious capitals burnt over and over to the ground?

Why did the whites come back and back? Why did any of them ever remain? It was the wealth that must have seduced them throughout the struggle, the old tales of fortunes made overnight, the *petite bourgeoisie* from Paris become millionaires with a single harvest of coffee, tobacco, cane. Napoleon's finest men had pitted all their strength and reserves to subdue the island and lost it forever in 1804, the richest colony of the French Crown.

And who could deny the measure of greatness that the

rebel slaves had produced? Toussaint himself a loyal servant to the age of forty-one; had the man ever dreamed of such a destiny? That he would take the reins of the rebel forces and bring them from savage pitched battle to a disciplined and often invincible army of soldiers willing with a fanatic's courage to fight to the death? The French had gotten him finally, lured him with lies. And Marcel felt anguish to read of Toussaint's death in some cold damp dungeon on French soil.

But what of the others, Dessalines, whom Marcel's aunts had once called "the black devil," the man who massacred the trusting whites who stayed to rebuild the Republic of Haiti? Who could deny that man's courage, quite larger than life, and the hold he had once maintained on his fighting men?

And the emperor, Henri Christophe. Born a servant, and destined to build at the northern tip of the island a mighty fortress where he was to reign in a fairy-tale kingdom ever ready for a French invasion which never came again?

But it was Marcel's own people who continued to touch him with a particular emotion. He understood their dilemma and how so often they were exploited and distrusted by both sides. They fought for the French for so long, and then against them, and for and against the blacks. It seemed no concept of brotherhood, born of necessity, had ever truly united the black men and the men of color until they realized that it was only their combined effort which could forever drive the European from Haitian soil. And even then the island was split in half, because as black Henri Christophe reigned in the north, so the man of color, Pétion, had ruled the south.

It seemed at times Marcel would never grasp the whole. He drew maps, made little charts of battles and events and read over and over the gruesome travelers' accounts. But what came clear to him again and again was that in Haiti his people had had a power and a history like nothing he had ever known in his native Louisiana in his own time. They had borne arms for their rights, and even today on that island in the Caribbean they lived along with the blacks in the Republic of Haiti as fully enfranchised men.

But how to separate a noble history from this world of horrors he did not precisely know. Haiti was drenched with all manner of human blood. Marcel shuddered to read of the slaves tortured, burnt, brutalized under the French; and the passion to which those slaves had been driven once they had rebelled.

But what had it finally to do with him? An earlier century with its near incomprehensible barbarity, a world of *gens de couleur* that dwarfed and sterilized his own?

One night late in October when he wandered into the front parlor to put a pair of volumes back into Tante Josette's shelf, he found her writing still in the plantation ledger by the light of a candle, her left hand rubbing at her reddened eyes.

"Read this to me, Marcel," she said sitting up very straight and pressing the heels of her palms against the side or her head. "Take the candle over there."

As soon as he was seated on the couch, he saw that it was a list of names made that day, and it was the numerical figure in the farthest column opposite each name that Tante Josette wished to hear. He had read perhaps half of it before he realized these were the names of her slaves, and the figures were the weight of the cotton which each man or woman had picked that day. A curious revulsion came over him. In his mind, he had been fighting pitched battles in the Haitian hills, but he realized that those battles too had filled him with revulsion and he felt an oppression that seemed almost endless as life itself.

"Is it good, Tante?" he asked.

She nodded, and the sigh that came out of her narrow heaving chest and her attitude as she sat back in the chair with her palms pressed to her forehead struck him as rather masculine and interesting.

"We lost so much in the depression of '37," she said. "It has to be a good crop. And it is a good crop. We'll be picking until January at least."

"Could it happen here, Tante? Could it happen as it did in Saint-Domingue?"

She sat still for a moment as if experiencing a concentration and allowing the new subject its just due.

"Never," she said. "Though how to convince the white population of these southern states, I do not know. We live in the shadow of those times every day. Give me the ledger, *mon cher,* you ought to go to bed."

"But how do we live in the shadow?" he rose and put the ledger in front of her.

"Marcel, each year it becomes harder for us, each year there are laws passed that seek to restrict us, each year as the abolition forces in the North increase in scope and volume, we are pushed and threatened on all sides. I suppose one would have had to see Saint-Domingue to know that these United States are a world apart, but there are hundreds of small planters and farmers through these backwoods who never saw it and never knew it, and they live in terror of just that sort of uprising. No, if you want my opinion, it will never happen here. Something different has happened here." She rose, shutting the ledger, and put the candle again in his hands. "Take this with you, if you like, I've been able to see in the dark all my life."

"But what's happened, how is it different?" he asked. Of course he had read of atrocities committed in the name of routine discipline on Saint-Domingue plantations of which Louisiana planters would not dream. But he wanted to hear from her. All this knowledge lay about him, all around him, he was blinded by it, and drained and somewhat lost.

She moved into the main hall and toward the delicate curved stairway that led to her attic room.

"Saint-Domingue was settled by unscrupulous men who worked the land only long enough to leave it in the hands of their overseers and live in luxury abroad," she said. "And it was paradise that land. You can't imagine it, the fruit there to be picked from the trees, the air forever mild, that clean wind from the sea. Fortunes were made too fast; men worked their slaves to death planning with pen and paper the profits of such a system when they could always buy more. This is a different country, it's gone a different way. People live on the land that they own, slaves have been bred for generation upon generation, domesticated and not by blatant atrocity, but by some system far more subtle and efficient, something akin to the cotton gin and the refining mill in its precision and its relentlessness. No, it could not happen here, because we've beaten them, cowed them, and ground them utterly *and completely into the dust.*"

Marcel blew out the candle as he stepped onto the porch. The night was black over the rural country, and alive with an endless sweep of tiny brilliant stars. Beyond the row of crepe myrtles behind the kitchen, he saw a flicker of light in the village of slave cabins he knew to be there. The barest snatch of laughter drifted to him on the night air, and it seemed he heard some faint mournful singing but he could not be sure. He had been at *Sans Souci* a month by this time, and never had he gone near that long row of bungalows, though sometimes from the window of his room in the morning he had looked out on the hundred distant tiny figures making their way through the low fields. The names he'd read from the plantation ledger came back to him, Sanitte, Lestan, Auguste, Mariette, Anton...and he let out a moan to himself in the shadows of the porch looking still at the distant light which suddenly dimmed beyond the branches of the trees and appeared to die out. What was it like there, was there a dreary submission, a sullen misery, such as he had so often seen in Lisette's face as she stood above the kitchen fire in summer, or was there some measure of peace in the hopelessness? He found himself frantic suddenly, wiping his lips with the back of his hand, unable to continue with these thoughts.

Of course he knew the household servants, saw them daily, pretty Toinette who brought his breakfast tray with its small bouquet of roses, and little Narci who groomed his mare. And Celeste who stood at old Gregoire's arm nightly to hand out the steaming plates as he served the supper just behind Tante Josette's chair. But they were the scrubbed and comely aristocracy of this little slave nation. What of Sanitte, Lestan, Auguste, Mariette, Anton...backs all but broken by those pounds of cotton, eyes inevitably squinting over a field which had become the wretched measure of the world?

It's an accident any of us being here or anywhere...it's all an accident and we don't care to realize that because it confuses us, overwhelms us, we couldn't live our lives day to day if we did not tell ourselves lies about cause and effect. An accident then, his consciousness emerging here among this rich and proper colored elite of New Orleans, an accident, an accident, his mind played with the cadence of the words, like a drum. And what if...what if his consciousness had emerged out there? He could not move toward those cabins, not tonight in this enfolding darkness, nor on any night. He could not run the risk of discovering there a system so thorough that it might have crushed him had it ever gotten him in its maw. And this was a small plantation, a human plantation, a vital community in comparison to those vast industrial enterprises that lined the banks of the Mississippi where anonymous slaves were driven like mules. He shoved his hands deep into his pockets, hunched as if the air were cool, and turning his back to the village that had vanished with its single light into the dark he made his way around the broad gallery until he settled in a chair at the front of the house. There he could

(518)

sit back, hands clasped behind his neck, and peer again at the limitless stars.

Only a trace of light gleamed on the distant rippling waters of the river. The trees were monsters against the sky. His mind went swift and free of all distractions to his home, and shot through the small community of the French Quarter like a ghost on tiptoe, surveying all those respectable friends of his, the Lermontants, the Rogets, the Dumanoirs. Christophe in love with his books and his students, Marie dreaming of marriage beneath a flowered tester, and weightless and immediately he returned to this silent rambling house and the generations of this family of the Rivière aux Cannes who had let a layer of dust accumulate on those secret Saint-Domingue histories, perhaps never dreaming that they were there. How could these be a part of armies clashing on the Plaine du Nord, or wild-eyed horsemen, torch in the wind, thundering through a burning town? My people, my people, my people, he heard the words pass his lips in the dark, tears flowing silently down his face. I wish, I wish, I wish I knew, I wish I knew what I am.

He had fallen asleep in the chair. The sky was gray over the river when he opened his eyes, and behind him the front doors opened, the porch reverberating with heavy steps. His cousins, Gaston and Pierre, were in their riding boots, their great shining guns over their shoulders. "Come on, Marcel," commenced the usual refrain with the warm clasp of a hand, "we've got a mare back there, Marcel, so old and so sleepy you could ride her with your hands behind your back, Narci, get that mare!" Little Narci had just brought their horses around, sleek chestnut geldings, and as they pranced and stomped on the shell path they looked like the most dangerous animals Marcel had yet seen. But some old restraint that had sustained him up until now in this new world was suddenly lost. He gave in.

And by Christmastime he had given himself up entirely, without vanity and with wariness, to the life of a country planter of these parts.

It was hunting twice a week, the exciting crack of the gun, and a peculiar flutter inside him when he saw the duck fall from the sky. Its heart still beat when he took it from the dog's awesome jaw, and broke the life out of it with his own hand. And fishing now and then with high-booted treks into the swamps to draw up the crawfish on long lines. And a delicious relaxation would come over him in the evenings, the long table aglow with candles where seldom less than fourteen sat down to supper, the conversation easy and languorous like the motion of the overhead punka, that great rectangular wooden fan suspended from the ceiling which moved back and forth, back and forth to the jerks of a drowsy slave child at the distant end of its long rope.

Here in these enormous rooms Marcel saw for the first time the proper setting for the immense furniture that had crowded the Ste. Marie cottage all of his life, it was for this space that the great four posters had been built, here the giant sideboard appeared graceful and adequate, and the towering armoires and cabinets in perfect scale. One could grow too accustomed to it, the breeze through the French doors, the last heat of the Indian summer rising toward the high ceiling, and the mingled voices of those pretty cousins, Clementine, Louise, Marguerite, who had taken to driving over more and more often from their father's plantation since Marcel had arrived.

Marguerite's voice was pretty. She played the spinet well as he turned the pages for her, mesmerized by the speed of her tiny fingers, and when she occasionally looked up into his eyes, he felt a peculiar weakness all over, something diffuse and romantic and very unlike the passion he missed so painfully with Juliet. Her eyes were black, slanted, her hair a collection of perfect finger curls around the ears, the skin *teint sauvage,* or reddish like that of an Indian, and her full mouth just touched with the color of rose. Once they went to the *pigeonnier* together, and as they gathered the furry baby birds, he was quite horrified to discover they were taking them to the kitchen for the evening meal. She laughed at him, and kissed his cheek.

It was not all leisure, this life. Everyone worked, in fact, the women constantly with the needle and cutting patterns on the dining table in the afternoon. Tante Josette supervised all the operations of the enterprise, there were the pickings through late December, repairs to a dozen outbuildings, the slaughter of the pigs when winter had at last set in. Gaston and Pierre often fell asleep in their parlor chairs, their rough hands folded on their chests, while Emile burnt the oil late over the books. Marcel wrote letters for anyone and everyone amid the sprawling family that seemed at times to encompass every plantation in the surrounding parts, and one afternoon, coming in with Gaston from the hunt at Marguerite's home upriver, found himself very much pressured to take up the education of the little ones of the family in earnest. A tutor was living with Tante Elizabeth but he had his hands full. There were Marguerite's little brothers, and Tante Josette's great-grandchildren, a brood of twelve whose names Marcel still confused. So the mornings soon turned to some elementary lessons, until impatient and anxious, Marcel went out to nap in his room.

A painter came in early December as so many had come before, offering to do a pair of portraits for a very small sum and room and board. He was a man of color from New Orleans whom Marcel had never had occasion to meet, and soon the rich smell of his linseed oil filled the lower rooms of the *garçonnière* and Marcel watched in fascination as the man dipped his brush into the palette of brilliant colors and brought the face of Cousine Elisa to life right before his eyes. He made her mouth too small, less African, and thereby sacrificed something of the sharp beauty of her face.

But it was the traveling Daguerreotypist who fascinated Marcel even more. He missed the picture salons of New Orleans as much as he missed anything at home, thought constantly of the illustrious Jules Lion, or old Picard and his brilliant assistant, Duval, wondering if the latter had ever managed the capital for a studio of his own. He longed for those expensive sittings, the chatter, the magic, and wondered would he ever be able to afford them again. But here in the country a man came through with his own cart on which the words were painted, Daguerreotypist Salon, and took pictures of all the family which were to be put up on the walls. Another brought his equipment into Marguerite's home finding a well-lighted room and fixing a blanket for the backdrop to produce an excellent portrait of the three sisters, Marguerite, Louise, and Clementine. But much of this work was woefully inferior to the artistry in New Orleans, and the one great advantage was that when lodged in the house, as they often were, these men talked freely of their adventures, of the pictures they had taken among the Indians out West, or of natural wonders, even the great Niagara Falls. Marcel sent a tolerable "specimen" to Christophe, an oval of himself in riding boots with his gun, describing a wagon salon in detail with notes on his analysis of the man's technique.

Meanwhile Marcel was meeting more and more of the

colored planters. His hunting excursion took him into new houses and new families as various men joined the party, and one morning he was surprised to discover that they were riding north to hunt with two white planters of the *Cote Joyeuse*. All was amicable and familiar. And later the entire party took supper at the house of a man of color, the white men and colored men at the table together, after which several hands of cards were played. No false formality intruded, there were old jokes familiar to all and tales of other hunts, talk of the crop this year, the lack of rain in the last summer and fall, and how they were all paying for it now. And Marcel studied all this, not quick to trust, and certain that in spite of this camaraderie strict lines here were still drawn.

But it was only one Sunday when Marcel and Tante Josette drove north into Isle Brevelle that Marcel was to grasp the actual size of the colored community all around. They had come to visit the Metoyer family whose plantations were quite famous in these parts. All through this country were colored Metoyers, in fact, and the Catholic church of St. Augustine on the Yucca plantation had been built by that family. And here it was that Tante Josette took Marcel with her to Mass. Only colored faces made up the congregation with the black slaves out under the spreading eaves adding their beautiful African timbre to the singing, and the only white face was that of the priest.

A curious peace came over Marcel in this church. His thoughts were not of God, in fact, he was barely conscious of the ceremony, kneeling, rising, murmuring only to please his aunt. But he realized that for months now he had lived almost exclusively among people of color so that the sight of the white Daguerreotypist or the hunters of the *Cote Joyeuse* had actually presented him with a gentle shock. Even in New Orleans where his people were everywhere in the narrow streets, some eighteen thousand in number, he had never felt this pleasant anonymity, this lovely concord. But what would his pretty *cousines* think, he wondered, as he watched them return one by one from the Communion rail, their heads bowed, their hands folded, but what would they think if they knew he hadn't a penny to his name? Name. Do I even have a name?

But after Mass as he walked with Tante Josette along the banks of the Cane River, and she told him the history of this family, his thoughts were much changed on this question of name. All of these Metoyers who filled this country known as Isle Brevelle, sprawling over many houses and prosperous plantations, were descended from one freed slave, Marie Therese CoinCoin who had built a small fortune on land granted her in the days of the Spanish and bought the freedom of her children one by one. Even Grandpère Augustin, her eldest, who had built the church of St. Augustine, had not been born free. And had been the grandson of the African-born slaves who had been the parents of Marie Therese, calling her CoinCoin which was, in fact, an African name. *These people had not inherited their world, they had created it!* Just as Richard Lermontant's ancestors had created theirs. They had made a life for themselves as gracious and prosperous as that of the white colonists who'd once held them in chains.

But that mellow and beautiful day might have passed into Marcel's varied collection of tender impressions of the Cane River along with many others had it not been for another small detail which made its imprint on his mind.

In the late afternoon, he had gone out alone on the back gallery of the big house at Yucca and looked over the land. There were the usual plantation buildings, sights, sounds. But as his eyes swept the familiar landscape, he saw a structure directly behind the main house—that is, right in front of him—that was quite different from the other outbuildings he had seen. Because, though it had an immense sloping roof like many a slave cabin or bungalow, no columns supported this roof and it rose very high, much higher than any he had observed, above the doors below. A short walk about the place revealed it to be even more amazing, for beneath this great roof another complete story to the little house was hidden, its windows peeping out into the shade. Rude beams projecting from the walls held the roof in place. Marcel did not know what to make of it, and riding home that night with Tante Josette was disappointed to hear that she did not know the purpose of the structure or why or how it had been made.

It lingered in his mind. It was reminiscent of buildings he had seen in some old book, engravings that he could not quite resurrect from memory, and sometime during the night he realized he had seen this same form in pictures of the wilds of Africa in the accounts of British travelers that Anna Bella so loved to read. Africa. The house had seemed like something built for such a climate—how that immense mushroon roof would have cooled the rooms within!—and there had been no evidence of metal in the construction anywhere, except perhaps the hinges on the blue painted doors. What slave had built that structure, what slave had remembered such a house in Africa which might even have been his home? This perplexed Marcel, for one transcendent feature of this house had added to its singular impression: it was very beautiful. It seemed finer than those other cabins whose roofs were supported by posts from the ground.

And as he thought of it, Jean Jacques' words of years ago came back to him, Jean Jacques' long description of the fine quality of that African sculpture made in the cabins of his old home in Saint-Domingue. Suddenly Marcel was burning to return to Yucca, to ask anyone and everyone about that curious little house. And he felt, as he fell asleep, more acutely than ever the loss of Jean Jacques. He wanted to show this house to Jean Jacques, to take him under that soaring roof, he wanted to talk to Jean Jacques about how this house had been built. Oh, how Rudolphe and Richard had teased him that summer when Marcel had been so obsessed with the craft of a simple chair, a table, the way that a staircase climbed the wall. But the miracle had never dimmed, not with Jean Jacques' death, or with the development of Marcel's mind. And it seemed to him the greatest of cruelties now that he hadn't even the talent to sketch the African house from memory, and dared not return to Yucca to draw a picture of it for fear that others might see. And then his mind roamed freely in half sleep with a delightful possibility, that of capturing one of the country Daguerreotypists to make a picture of the house for him when the light was just right. What a treasure that would be among his collection of plates that glinted on the bedroom wall at home.

Home. An ugly reality awakened him. Monsieur Philippe had returned to the cottage, and Marcel, when in the name of God would he see his room again? And why in the name of God hadn't he bought the magic box, the Daguerre camera, during that millennium when he had been a rich young man, his father filling his pockets with ten-dollar bills? He could have had it, that wonderful instrument to fix all that he could never draw, precisely as the eye saw it, as the eye chose to place it in the frame. But that was gone, wasn't it, the young gentleman who was forever hanging over Duval's shoulder with ten dollars for a whole plate whenever he chose. Sheer exhaustion called him back to the African house, and the gentle drifting into sleep commenced again. He found himself in Christophe's classroom, in the midst of one of those familiar lectures in which Christophe was striving to make the point anew: the world is filled with varying standards of beauty and civilization so that the edicts of one small time and place must never be accepted as supreme. Ah, he must ask about the African house, he must discover...

But there was much to be done the next day.

He was determined that his little charges would be able to read their French well for their grandmother before he was called back to New Orleans, and he had promised to help Marguerite copy out some poetry from a borrowed book. He liked Marguerite but was a little afraid of her, of that luscious and familial affection which she so easily displayed. So he forgot about the African house, and did not think of it until years after, knowing no more then of its origins than he did now.

Christmas had been heaven at *Sans Souci*. Days before, the slaves had made the effigy of a cow, marked with all the cuts of beef, and when this was mounted on a pole, shot at the animal to win the cuts as presents for their Christmas table, all this in a ceremony known as the *papagai*. The plantation rang with music within the great house and without, and all the family round came together for dancing, and on the solemn night itself they made the long carriage ride to the church of St. Augustine for Midnight Mass.

Marguerite had made a long knitted scarf for Marcel, and sometime in the hours after midnight on New Year's Day, when he was sick of the sweet punch and had gone to the pantry himself to see if there wasn't just one more bottle of vintage claret, Marguerite had pressed close to him, offering her tender child mouth for him to kiss. She was soft as a baby, and he felt shame afterwards, and resolved not to be alone with her again before he left.

So one week after New Year's, when he was still carrying Christophe's letter of two days before, and reading it over and over, and feeling impotent that he could not be with Cecile and Marie in New Orleans, he was quite surprised to find his aunt one morning at her desk with a grave expression, saying to him, "Sit down, Marcel, I want to talk to you about your cousin, Marguerite."

She had a letter in her hands. At first he thought perhaps it was something more from Christophe. But after folding it neatly, she laid it aside and told him to close the parlor doors.

"Tante, I meant no disrespect for her," Marcel said. After

all, this was just an innocent kiss. But what if her aunts had seen them, this penniless ne'er-do-well from New Orleans with their precious and pretty little girl.

His aunt's face was particularly tired this morning, and she flexed her fingers stiffly before turning in her chair so that she could see him.

"I have some news for you from home, but with your permission, let me put that aside," she said. "And I promise to be brief. You've made an excellent impression here, Marcel, you are much liked and much admired, and I think you know you could make a tolerable living as a schoolteacher in these parts."

He couldn't conceal the expression on his face. This wasn't the life he wanted, he had taught the children because their parents had wanted it, and it was all he had to offer.

"But there are other avenues open to you, and I should like to get directly to the point. Marguerite's father owns two plantations upriver, some 150 acres of cultivated land. The man is willing to settle one-fourth of that land on you, and to build a house upon it for you, should you enter into marriage with Marguerite."

"Marriage? With Marguerite!" Marcel was stunned. "But does he know my circumstances, that I could bring nothing to this marriage?"

"Marcel, you bring a gentleman's education and breeding, and a gentleman's honor. That would be quite enough."

She waited, then went on.

"Marcel, don't you see, ours is a small community, and we have intermarried over and over, and perhaps too much. My son married his second cousin, my grandsons were second and third cousins to their wives, and so it will probably go with their children as well..." But when she said this last about the grandchildren, a distress distracted her so that she made a little gesture of opening her eyes wide as if to clear them. "But let me make it simple. There are not many eligible men here for Marguerite to marry, and all of us would look with favor on this match. You need not give your answer now, Marcel. There's no doubt in my mind that you could manage a plantation, that you could learn the cultivation of cotton, the management of the slaves. You'd be under more of a watchful eye than you'd want, besides." She sighed as though reciting all this more from duty than anything else. "You'd have your own home. You would be the master on your own land."

She displayed no enthusiasm whatsoever and Marcel was perplexed. Surely she wasn't trying to convince him.

"Do you approve?" he asked.

Again she appeared distressed, distracted.

"Is it what you want, Marcel?" she asked.

"Tante, I can't stay here. I don't need to think it over. Oh, it's tempting, it's beautiful." He was feeling that peace again that he'd felt so strongly in the church of St. Augustine, that sense of community where one would never encounter a white face without the community's strength to bolster him, the community's warmth.

"I have to go home," Marcel said. "I have to go back to New Orleans to whatever future I can make there. I don't know what I will do or how I will do it, but it's the city to which I belong, with all its strife and its challenges."

And all it vicious injustice, too.

"When I came here, I brought with me a little book," he went on. "I believe I showed it to you, it was the first issue of a literary journal, published by men of color entirely. Christophe's sent me several numbers of it since."

"Marcel," she sighed. "Poetry doesn't mean anything in this world, it never has meant anything and it never will. If men of color in New Orleans write poetry it's because they can do precious little else! Don't give me that wounded look, that proud expression. It's true and you know it. What future has a man of color in New Orleans."

"I don't know," he said quietly. "And this little quarterly, it may have no significance as you've said, but I respect it. I respect it! And all my life I've been searching for something to respect. All my life I've been trying to understand what really matters, and I tell you, this book, *L'Album littéraire,* matters. And there are other things that matter... Christophe's school, the business that Rudolphe Lermontant has built... I don't want to enumerate these things. I don't want to be placed in a position of having to defend them. This country's beautiful, Tante, and I should like nothing better than to let it enfold me and protect me so that I could pretend all the world was people of color, but I can't do it. I can't cut myself off from what I perceive to be the real world. So I have to go home."

She appeared thoughtful and then she said,

"I have been alive too long."

"Don't say that, Tante!" he said. He did not remember it now, but these were the words Jean Jacques had used the night before he died.

"Why not?" she said. She began to murmur as if he weren't there... "Picture the Plaine du Nord where I was born, that splendid island, and La Belle France when I first went there, and this rude country when Monsieur Villier first brought me to this stretch of swamp and told me he'd make it our home. I don't believe in anything.

"I tell you after what I have seen in my life of Saint-Domingue and this place, I don't know what a man of color can do anywhere in the world. I don't know. We are a doomed people, Marcel. Whether you stay here or go to New Orleans it makes no difference finally. Oh, I don't tell my grandchildren these things. I tell them the world is a good place, that in their time they will enjoy a greater measure of equality with the whites than we do now. But this is a lie. There's no equality. And there never will be. Our only hope is to hold onto our land here, to buy and to cultivate more land so that we can keep our community as a world apart. Because the white Anglo-Saxon heart is so hardened against us that there's no hope for our descendants as the Anglo-Saxon takes over, as he supplants the French and the Spanish families around us who understood us and respected us. No, there is only one hope and that is for our descendants to pass when they can into the white race. And with each one who passes, we are diminished, our world and our class dies. That's what we are, Marcel, a dying people, if we are a people at all, flowers of the French and the Spanish and the African, and the Americans have put their boot in our face."

"Tante, stop this! What about the here and now?"

"Here and now, here and now? Each year it grows worse, the prejudice, the laws that restrict us. We live in a fool's paradise here, shut off from the world on our plantations, but the world is right there, outside. You don't know the reverses we suffered, all of us, in the depression of '37, and you do not know the constant struggle with the land itself. You don't know the mortages that underlie some of the prosperity you see. This 'here and now' is fragile, indeed, for us and when it crumbles, what awaits us but American Southland which is encroaching on all of us more day after day."

"Oh, I know how you feel, Marcel, you're a European in your heart and mind. That's what you've been all your young

(528)

life, a European. But you must understand that the only integrity that you can claim for that image of yourself is in the sanctuary of your own mind. I tell you, the worst hatred is racial hatred, the worst wars are racial wars, I see no end to it at hand."

"I am a man," Marcel said quietly, his voice thickened, the picture of her at the desk slightly blurred. "A *man!*"

It seemed his tone pulled her back. Into some awareness of the room about her. She was looking at him. She was perplexed. "Well," she said with raised eyebrows. "In all these years, with all my pronouncements I have never made anyone cry." She laughed dryly. "Perhaps it's a reason to go on living after all."

He did not answer.

He was aware that ever since he could remember, one illusion after another had been shattered. The world was never what it seemed. And yet again, here on the Cane River, he had been drawn into another illusion, of peace and solidarity and something inviolate, only to learn from this wise woman that this too was but an illusion sustained day in and day out by a collective act of faith. Perhaps he had gone about it in the wrong way over and over again. Nothing was anything until someone defined it. Nothing was inevitable. Nothing was inviolate. Everything existed, perhaps, by the act of faith, and we were always in the midst of creating our world, complete with the trappings of tradition that was nothing more than an invention like all the rest.

And for the first time it occurred to him that the world of the white Southerner with all its doors shut in the colored man's face might also be fragile, also dependent on the same enormous act of collective faith. It didn't seem so. It seemed the one aspect of this world not subject to change. He smiled.

"I admire your decision," Tante Josette said, her eyes on the windows beyond him. "I was old when I came here, I found a refuge in this country, a place where I could lay my head down. But you're too young for that, I admire you that you choose to go home." She flexed her hands again, slowly, as if the pain in the joints was bad, and then she lifted the letter she had put aside earlier, and opened it.

"But you cannot go now," she said, "I don't know how long your mother wishes you to remain here, or why, but she is adamant that you must not come home until she sends for you, though what I am about to tell you will certainly prove a trial."

He snapped out of his reverie. "What now?"

"Monsieur Philippe died two nights ago in your mother's house."

VOLUME
THREE

PART ONE

I

THIS HAD TAKEN AGLAE by surprise, this apparent physical inability to set foot into the room. She had short patience for such temperamental nonsense in others and feared some excess of emotion for which she was completely unprepared. But it had happened this way. She had gone down the stairs, and approaching the parlor doors she had been unable to go in. Miss Betsy was crying. She had her arm curled under her face and leaning on a table cried, while her Tante Antoinette stroked her hair. And the room was filled with black-dressed men and women, Philippe's brothers among them, who had turned to face Aglae at once as she stood there in the main hall. And beyond, along the far wall, stood the coffin with silver handles amid a veritable garden of fragrant flowers. She could see nothing of Philippe's face.

And then it happened. She could not move. She could not, simply could not, enter the room. And she had turned much like a marionette, she imagined, and made her way up the stairs. People had spoken to her, her sisters, little Rowena from the kitchen who was proving to be such an attentive maid. But she had been unable to answer. Unable, imagine that. She had felt a tension in the muscles of her face. She could not open her mouth. So sitting in her room now, her elbows on her leather-top desk, fingers meshed, she stared

(532)

straight forward, and was barely conscious that Vincent had come in behind her. It would be a fine thing if Vincent should speak to her and she would not be able to answer. With a gesture of impatience, she emphatically turned her head.

"Aglae," he said softly. He stood at the back of her chair.

A series of items passed through her mind, items of information to which she returned again and again. And without emotion, without emotion! This physical inability to speak was insane. That he had died in the bed of his colored mistress. That she had run out screaming into the street. That the body was so malnourished the face had darkened and collapsed. That it was the noteworthy skill of that colored undertaker, Lermontant, who had many rich white clients, which had restored the face so that the coffin might be open after all. That this mistress lived in the Rue St. Anne, and had two quadroon children! That she had been Philippe's mistress for some eighteen years! That Felix, their coachman had resided there and here with the master for some eighteen years!

She shut her eyes and said quite plainly,

"Philippe Ferronaire! To die like that! Philippe Ferronaire!"

"Aglae, if you are to blame yourself for this I will not allow it," Vincent said. "If you had not moved to take the reins of this plantation when you did, we might very well have lost it! Do you understand?"

Again she made that characteristic gesture of impatience with a slight scornful sound.

It seemed the motion was eternal. She could hear the clock ticking. And one carriage after another stopping below. Wind tugged at the French windows, and a frost obscured the sky beyond. Aglae had always liked the sound of a clock ticking.

"Did he die in this woman's arms?"

They had not discussed it, she had not discussed it with any man, it was from women that she got the story, her sister, Agnes Marie, and her maids.

She heard his proper sigh. He didn't want to speak of it, more properly, he did not want for her to speak of it.

"Did he die in this woman's arms!"

"In his sleep," Vincent said.

"And she awoke then to find him?"

"Yes."

She sat back.

"Did you see her?"

He had gone to get the body. The Lermontants had had the body, surely they didn't lay him out in that woman's house!

"Briefly, I saw her." He sighed. "Aglae, I went to the house so that you might never have to think of the house, so that you might never have to mention it. I went to the house to make certain that everything was as I had heard it. Do you understand? So that none of it would reach your ears? So that there would be no unfinished..."

"I should like to know your impression of her, Vincent, you may leave off the rest."

"Aglae, don't..."

"Vincent, when I am in my dotage you may expect my obedience. Until then, you will please answer the questions I put to you...what was your impression of this woman?"

"She was...ill. Philippe had...uncashed bank drafts, some clothes...she gave these to me. There was a sum of money which I told her she must keep. She did not answer me, so I left it there." Of course he had looked into the matter further, ascertained that she had family to provide for her, she would not be destitute. And he would clear Philippe's debts.

"The woman, her appearance, her age."

He drew himself up, emitting a small sigh again more or less without wishing it to be eloquent, and moved across the room. She was an attractive woman, more than likely, how at such a time could he tell? Petite, curvaceous, a marvelously delicate face rendered all the more remarkable by the texture of her very dark skin. A white woman with a black skin. How was he to put this into words, and for what?

"Don't torment yourself, Aglae, you owe these people nothing, you do not owe them the slightest thought."

"If you persist in playing the master of this house with me, Vincent, I shall go to the notary in New Orleans and find..."

He shook his head. "A good-looking woman, very well-bred," he shrugged. How else to put it, that she had been anxious, trembling, like any white lady at such a time in that pristine little parlor among whatnots and petit-point as delicate as herself. She had hardly managed a word. She had wrung her hands, her gold and pearl rings flashing, suffocating in her tight laces, and the daughter standing there, that beautiful young woman who looked completely white. It was the daughter who had confirmed the story for him,

(534)

and so properly had she rescued it from the sordid and the ghastly. "Monsieur had gone to bed early, Monsieur did not feel well. When it was time for Monsieur's breakfast, we went to awaken him, Monsieur would not wake up. Monsieur did not suffer... at all." The girl had her rosary beads in her hand, and the woman, crying, tore her handkerchief in shreds.

"Aglae, it was not a squalid place. It was *un plaçage* ...Aglae, this is not a reflection upon anyone but Philippe himself."

Again she made that impatient shake of her head. She was staring out the windows at the flutter of a branch against the frost.

"It was I who urged you to get the power of attorney," he said. "It was I who examined the books. Even then he had every chance...I don't believe he could have helped himself, even if he had wanted to. Aglae, the bottle had gotten him, all of his weaknesses had gotten him. His behavior was no longer acceptable anywhere else."

"Aaah," she said.

He drew close to her and put his hands lightly on her narrow shoulders. "Do you want to come down now?"

"Not just yet, but you must go down," she said. "You must look out for Henri. And Miss Betsy."

"They are in good hands," he said. "It's you I want to look out for."

She looked at him as if she did not know him, and then she looked down. She reached for his right hand and removed it from her shoulder so that he removed the hand on the left. "Go down, Vincent," she said.

He hesitated at the door. "There is something more I want to tell you. If you feel at all to blame for what we did last year, perhaps this will work some alchemy on your thoughts."

However, she wasn't listening. She was looking at the window. And murmured, "Last year?" as if she had hardly heard.

"When I visited that house, I saw in it a number of items which belong to you. The candles on the mantel were in the silver holders that were given to Grandmère by the Marquis. There were books which had been the property of our father. And on her neck the woman wore a small jet brooch, quite appropriate for mourning, which has been in the Dazincourt family for two hundred years. You remember that you could not find that brooch when Oncle Alcee died? There were other items, china, painted plates. He stole your treasures, Aglae,

(535)

small, priceless heirlooms, he was the one all along who was taking those things...the little lap *secrétaire*, the carved wooden rosary, it was on a table beside the woman even as I talked to her, the wooden rosary that had been Grandmère's, you remember that? Think on that if you are inclined to the slightest self-recrimination, think on the pettiness of it, the deceit..."

"You may go, Vincent!"

He went out closing the door.

She shut her eyes. Blame herself for what happened last year, the thought had never entered her mind. Blame herself for getting the power of attorney, the thought had never entered her mind. She had considered that action from every standpoint before she had taken it, and she was not a person given to regret. But something else loomed on the edges of her bleak considerations, something else hovered very near her that was alien to her and caused her to stare wide-eyed at nothing now as she looked up again, caused the muscles of her face to tense again as if she could not find the proper expression for herself, could not move, could not speak.

It was something immense, and so terrible that it could not, simply could not, be true. And her mind took her mercilessly back, as if she were a child with her heels dug in refusing to be dragged, and yet she was being dragged by some righteous stiff-backed woman who was also herself, back to the time when Philippe had first come into this house, when she had first seen him strolling along the gallery with her father, the figures reappearing in one window after another, those two men, the silver-haired man so cheered by the company of the younger, the hand on the shoulder, and that handsome blue-eyed smiling face. How the blue eyes had gleamed as Philippe bent to kiss her hand. The eyes said we have some secret you and I, as he called her *"Ma chère."* But oh, how at the same time those eyes had implored. That was it, they implored, always they implored, *love me, love me,* find me the man of your dreams, *love me*...and behind those quick witticisms and all that passed for charm among the others, there had always been that weakness, that dependence, those eyes saying *love me, love me,* oh, it gave her the wildest shudder of revulsion even now.

She writhed in her chair. Her hands were again on the sides of her head, and that tautness of her muscles went away. Her mouth was quivering with some terrible sadness. She could so keenly remember her sisters' laughter, their

(536)

heads coming together, "Why, he's so handsome, Aglae, he's so handsome," and Christine destined to marry Cousin Louis who was so old then and white as a bone. There had been tears in Christine's eyes when she said, "He is splendid, Aglae." Christine had been dancing with him until she was so dizzy she could hardly stand. But oh, how he had angered Aglae, maddened her with that need, those eyes flashing to her again and again from the end of the supper table, from across the crowded room, and how sheepish was that whisper when he drew near to her, and that smile and that look, "We share a secret, you and I." She had loathed him! No, No. She shook her head. "No!" she said aloud to the empty room. "It could not have been different, I am not to blame, I am not to blame, I am not to blame..."

II

AS SOON AS THEY ENTERED the cottage, Cecile looked at the clock. She stared so intently at it, her face drained and weary, that Tante Louisa took her by the arm and told her to sit down. They had all been in the Cathedral at the moment when in St. Jacques Parish, some fifty miles away, Philippe had been taken from the Requiem Mass in the St. Jacques chapel to his family grave. Friends had come to the Cathedral, Madame Suzette had been there with Giselle. Celestina had come with Gabriella and Fantin. And in the great empty church where there had been no service on this day, others moved about oblivious to this small gathering in the back pews. At last it was three o'clock. No doubt the stone had been set in place, and most likely no one even remained in the cemetery in St. Jacques Parish. So Louisa had said, "Let's go home."

And now having come into the cottage, Cecile stared at the clock and had to be told to sit down.

"I don't see why you stay in this house," Colette said, her voice light so that it sounded strange and sing-song among so much black bombazine. Marie took a pot of coffee from Lisette and poured it into four small gilt-edged cups.

"Put some brandy in that, *ma petite,*" Louisa said. And Colette, thinking that Cecile had been offered enough brandy and enough sherry and enough straight whiskey, shot her a disapproving and vain glance.

"I don't see why we just don't go right up to our place now," said Colette folding her shawl and laying it over the back of her chair. The cottage was cold, since Lisette had only just made the fire.

"You should go," Cecile said quite suddenly. Both the aunts were startled. Cecile's eyes were glassy, but calm. "You should both go now and leave Marie and me here alone."

For a moment they all studied her as if they had not properly heard.

"I want to be alone here with Marie," she said.

Marie's face was remote and cold. She set the coffee down for her mother and glanced from Louisa to Colette. There was as always now a defiance in Marie's expression. Louisa had several times told her that her haughty look was not feminine, and she ought to be more demure, but this did no good. And now Colette appeared exasperated.

"You've got plenty of time to be alone with Marie, you come up to the flat with us. Where's Lisette, seems like someone is always asking where's Lisette, get her to pack your things, you don't want to stay here right now..."

"This is my home and this is where I want to stay," Cecile said sharply, baring her teeth involuntarily as she clenched them. She drank the coffee down in one gulp.

Marie seated herself at the end of the table and stirred her coffee with a small silver spoon.

"All right, then," Louisa said. "But you send Lisette up there for us if you get to feeling bad. Has anyone taken the time to write to Marcel yet to tell him to come home?"

"No!" Cecile's teeth clenched again. "I'll take care of that when I want him home."

"Well, what difference does it make now, for God's sake?" Colette asked. "Those *Bontemps* people have been here and gone, they won't be coming back here, I don't see why he can't..."

"Will you leave that to me?" Cecile said.

"This lady's tired," Louisa said. "Come on, let's leave her alone." And she was halfway out the door before Colette could protest.

Marie had her back to her mother, more or less. She could see her mother out of the corner of her eye. She was not particularly afraid now, it seemed a time to forgive, if that were possible, or at least to pretend to forgive, but she was quite uncertain as to why her mother would want her here, why such a situation as this could thaw the hatred between them when her mother had others to lean on, when her mother had not spoken a civil word to Marie in a year. She herself was sickened by her father's death, sickened by the manner of it and the months of drinking that had preceded it, and was shamed and humiliated that he had died under this roof, not for herself, but for him.

She felt she had known he was going to die long before it had happened, and the sight of the man in those last weeks had horrified her, torn her heart. It had brought her to tears to see him stumbling, unable even to keep the cigar to his lip, her mother's terrified eyes gazing on. She drank a sip of the coffee into which she had put no brandy and wondered how long she must wait now for the marriage, if Cecile could conceivably throw another obstacle in her path, some decorous period of mourning, for instance, and just how long that might be. Rudolphe didn't care about a dowry, and in veiled gentlemanly terms had let her know. And now, having become quite adept at putting her mind someplace else when she was alone with her mother, Marie looked at the lace curtains, or at the papered walls, or at the whatnot shelf or the statues on the mantel and thought, I am with Richard, in Richard's house.

Her eyes moved numbly over the surface of the table when she heard her mother rise, saw the black dress in the corner of her eye drawing closer and closer and suddenly felt her mother's hand on her shoulder and heard her intake of breath. She looked up, and to her amazement her mother's face was completely sad. She was staring at the ceiling above Marie and she looked dreadfully softened and sad.

Marie hesitated and when the hand didn't go away, she lifted her left hand and slid it around her mother's waist. She felt stiff and cold doing this, and unnatural, and she wished that this extremely unusual moment could elicit more from her, but it could not.

"Wouldn't it be better to go up to the flat?" she asked.

"I have precisely seventy-five dollars and seventy-five cents," Cecile said in a simple voice, her eyes still on the ceiling, and her hand tightening on her daughter's shoulder. She looked down now into Marie's eyes so boldly that Marie flushed. "Now how long do you think we can live on that?"

"Marcel should come home, right home," Marie said.

"And what can Marcel do?" her mother asked without a trace of the usual acrimony, the voice strangely unaffected by anything but sincerity.

Marie was painfully conscious of the hand on her shoulder, painfully conscious of the closeness of her mother's body. In fact, her mother's breasts, very high and firm beneath the bombazine, aroused in her a vague disgust. She looked at the table, and opened her eyes wider as the hand actually clasped her arm and she felt her body tilted toward her mother and felt her mother trembling all over beneath the bombazine and the scent of roses.

"These are decisions we must all discuss together, we need Marcel," Marie said.

Suddenly her mother sat down and reaching out so that Marie was frightened, she suddenly pulled the pins from Marie's hair. She did this gently, deftly, her brows knit as she did it, so that her dark face, so devoid of wrinkles that it was almost a girl's face, became suddenly brooding with care. Marie was astonished. She felt the hair unraveling from her chignon, and that great sweet relief as it fell down on her shoulders. She could not resist lifting her fingers to massage the scalp suddenly while her mother sat looking at Marie's hair, her own hands clasping the pins. The fact that the mere touch of her mother's hands to her hair had given her the usual tingling pleasure she always experienced when her hair was touched confused her. She wanted nothing from her mother, least of all pleasure, intimacy, affection. Her mother hadn't touched her hair since she was a little girl.

"It's beautiful," her mother said, and took a handful of the dark tresses. This was quite amazing really.

"Like your own," Marie said coldly.

"Yes, but that is where the resemblance stops." Cecile looked her right in the eyes. Again, no venom. "You are as beautiful as everyone says you are. I've been jealous of you from the moment you were born."

"Maman, don't say these things," Marie drew back. She hadn't used that word, Maman, in years. Years! It was "you" and "she" or "Maman" in the third person when speaking of Cecile to others, but most often then "my mother" which she had often allowed herself to say with the faintest sneer. People were often puzzled by her expression when she spoke of her mother and she liked it, seeing the vague discomfort in Gabriella's eyes. But everyone must know, surely, we hate each other. Now Marie was flushed, and staring at the floor.

"But it's true," Cecile said. "I've hated you for being beautiful while other mothers would have been proud."

"Then don't talk of it, it's best if it's not talked about..."
Marie murmured.

"Why? Aren't you tired of the tension, tired of the hatred
between us? Don't you want it to end? We only have each
other now, you and me."

"We have Marcel." Marie glanced at her but couldn't continue to look into her eyes. She's mad, she thought. The grief
has driven her temporarily out of her mind. "I'm tired, I want
to lie down."

"Get me the sherry," her mother said.

Relieved to get away, she got it at once. She set a glass
down and filled it and was just a little alarmed to see her
mother drink that right away and refill the glass.

"That's warm," her mother said. It was a phrase Monsieur
Philippe had often used, when coming in on cold nights he
had taken a heavy drink of his whiskey. "That's warm."

Marie moved to the fireplace and taking the poker stoked
the coals. Her mother was drinking a third glass. "Did you
like him?" she asked as if she knew that Marie was thinking
of Monsieur Philippe. "I know that you loved him, but tell
me...did you like him?"

"Very much," Marie said.

Cecile sat back and let out a low moan. Her eyes moved
over the ceiling and her hands moved feverishly along the
stem of the glass. "If he hadn't died right there in that bed,
I don't think I'd believe he was dead. I think I'd spend the
rest of my life waiting for him to come in that door."

"Let's go up to the flat," Marie said.

"Hmmmmm, no. No, I want to be alone here now with
you," Cecile shook her head. "You don't know how shy I was
in the beginning, you have no idea. You only know the woman
who had grown accustomed to him, who loved him so. You
have no idea how it was in the beginning. I used to hide from
them, they wanted to take me to the balls, and I used to lock
my door and hide. I would have gotten under the bed to get
away from them, and I was twenty-four years old. I was
terrified! And all day long in the shop I spent my days on
my knees under those white women's hems. Pins in my
mouth, pins..." she looked at the tips of her fingers and
rubbed her thumb along the tips. "I used to be pricked all
over by those pins. Even now when I thread a needle, I can
hardly bear it." She shut her eyes and shook her head.

Marie was staring at her. She had never, never heard her

(541)

mother speak of any of this. Only once in a great while she had said in the past how she hated to sew.

"And then they brought that old man home to the flat, that old man..." Cecile mused.

"But what old man?" Marie asked. She was still holding the poker. A faint ray of sun came in through the close trees outside the window and struck the rings on her mother's hand. The sherry in the glass sparkled. Her mother's small mouth was wet and gleaming.

"Magloire Dazincourt," her mother said with mock dignity, "Magloire Dazincourt. Old enough to be my father, with yellow teeth. He built this house, not your father, and those are his babies in the cemetery, not your father's. You never knew that, did you? 'What are you going to do?' Colette kept saying to me, 'throw your corset on top the armoire and be an old maid? You're twenty-four years old, what are you going to do?'" She turned with wide eyes toward Marie and then with a strange sweet but bitter smile, she said, "They didn't want me on their hands forever, I don't blame them."

"Oh, but I don't believe that," Marie whispered. "They would have taken care of you forever, they will take care of you..." she stopped.

"Now?" Cecile whispered. "Is that what you were going to say?" And again braced for the malignant edge, Marie did not sense it and was confused.

Cecile drank more of the sherry, and bent her profile scowling in the ray of sun. Dust swirled about her in the light, dust which in church in similar rays of light had often put Marie in mind of the Annunciation, the word of God coming to the Virgin in a ray of light. Those tiny particles seemed to be a spirit in the light.

"I wasn't fortunate enough to have a child that lived during Monsieur Magloire's time, and he died the very day this house was complete. But the house is mine, and the furniture is mine, everything here is mine, he was a generous man. He had in fact a young friend who looked after me, a man so handsome people turned to look at him when he passed. That was your father, Monsieur Philippe." She glanced at her daughter, and Marie, quite fascinated by this tale, was staring at her.

"And so the old maid, you see, at the age of twenty-five, had snared the handsome planter who could have his pick." Cecile smiled. "I did well."

Marie nodded.

"And I tell you," her mother sighed suddenly, her head thrown back so that her breasts seemed higher, fuller, and the sun gilded the edge of her throat, as the voice became low, husky, "in those days you have them in the palm of your hand. You can have anything, anything," she said. "Later? They become practical, they have other things to think about, but in the beginning..." she let out a low intimate laugh... "You've got them! And it's diamonds if you want them." Her right hand fingered the rings on her left. "Diamonds," she said, "and champagne."

Marie's eyes were wide with disbelief. Her mother was baring a soul to her that she had never even glimpsed. She found it abhorrent, and yet she was fascinated. She could not look away from Cecile.

"We are women, you and I," her mother was saying as if she spoke to the ray of sunlight. "We are women," she said again, running her tongue over her gleaming lip. She drank the sherry and looked at her glass. "I was lucky," she said, narrowing her eyes. "That's what they all said, 'she was in the right place at the right time.' They said the same vicious things about me that they said about that foolish Anna Bella," her eyes turned again on Marie with perfect candor. "I know they did because I know them, all of them," she made an angry gesture to the world.

"But you?" she went on softly. "You? No matter whatever happens to you, they won't call it luck, they couldn't. You can have anything you want, and they know that, all of them, Louisa, Colette, Celestina, any of them, all of them, what could they say? You've stripped the spite out of them with your beauty, if you walked into that ballroom, they would fall on their knees. Oh, they'd hate you, they'll hate you as I hated you, but where would they find the words to say anything except she's beautiful, look at that white skin, that hair, those eyes... she can have anything that she wants! It's there for the taking, she can just reach out for it. Philippe Ferronaire's daughter. I tell you every man in that ballroom would go down on his knees."

"No," Marie whispered.

"Come here," her mother said. She pushed the glass of sherry forward toward Marie. "Come here."

"No," Marie shook her head.

"It's true," her mother smiled. "But you don't believe it, do you? You've never known. Colette said once 'if you'd ever tell her she was beautiful, she'd believe it, you're her mother, she doesn't see it in your eyes,' and me all the time thinking with an aching heart, she'll despise me when she becomes a woman, when she sees this black skin!"

"Oh, no, never for that, never!" Marie whispered.

Cecile laughed. Her eyes were luminous. She sipped the sherry. "Sit by me then, have a glass with me, then," she said. "I need you, I need you now."

Marie stood stock-still. She tilted her head to one side, and then slowly she moved to the chair. Her mother moved the glass toward her and she picked it up thinking suddenly that her mother's lips had touched it and it was repellent to her and then she looked into Cecile's eyes.

"It's true," her mother said. "It's true. You were so, so pretty," her mother's eyes narrowed with pain. "You were so fair! Did you know when you were a little girl, and I'd be walking with you, those white women would stop me to compliment you, to lift you and kiss you, and those women thought that I was the servant sent out with you, did you know that? They thought I was your nurse!" She leaned forward, eyes narrow, "They thought I was your colored nurse."

Marie shook her head. She ran her hand up to her hair and it fell down like a veil. "O my Lord in heaven," she murmured.

"You know sometimes I wonder," Cecile threw back her head. Her hand moved nervously, almost unconsciously to her throat and pulled at the velvet ribbon there, the mourning brooch, until the ribbon came loose. Her hand slid down toward her breast pushing the fabric free from the jet buttons... "I wonder," she sighed, "how it would have been if he had been the fair one, and you had had that kinky hair, and I could have done nothing with it, Lisette would have ironed it on the board."

"Maman," Marie whispered. "He is a handsome man!"

"Hmmmm..." she disregarded this. "I wonder if I would have loved you then, and ironed that kinky hair, and tried to make it like cornsilk, and put powder on that yellow skin. I wonder if I would have held you to me, protected you, been afraid for you the way I've always been for him. Oh, I don't think a day passes that I don't fear for him," she shut her eyes, her teeth cutting her lower lip. She had made her arms into a cradle for an invisible child and now she rocked it back and forth making the faintest moan. "People look at you when you're together, I've seen men look at you, look at him. O God," she whispered squeezing her eyes shut again. "I've seen them staring at him thinking he was...and you were..." She grimaced with distaste and a shudder shook her frame.

"Yes," Marie whispered. Her eyes were brimming with tears.

"You know that same fear," Cecile whispered.

"Always..." With him, with Richard, with Rudolphe...

"If he could have just gone to Paris, if he could have just gotten away! And you, you who could have the moon and you're throwing it all away now, throwing it all away..."

"I love Richard Lermontant!"

Her mother turned away, grimacing again as if Marie had given her a blow. "You can't do it!" she whispered. "You can't do it to yourself, and you can't do it to him!" Her eyes widened, staring right into Marie's eyes. She took the glass from Marie's hand. "Don't you understand that, don't you see? The Lermontants are nothing, they'll make Marcel a clerk in that store, they'll pay him a pittance and he'll be threadbare and bitter all of his days. But you can change that! You can do anything, don't you understand? I tell you in that first year, when it's fresh, and they are crazy for you, you've got them in the palm of your hand! You walk into that ballroom and they will go down on their knees! They'll be all too glad to get rid of your brother, they'll send him to the ends of the earth if you ask them, Paris, what's that to them, they have wealth of which you've never even dreamed. Ooooooooh," she rocked back in her chair putting the glass to her lips. "You can do it, you can state it plain in the beginning." She brought her left hand down flat on the table. "They send him to Paris or they don't have you, and they will want you, *ma chère*, more than you can imagine, how they will want you, that white skin on a nigger wench, they will want you as you have never dreamed..."

Marie's hand had risen slowly to her mouth, and she spread her fingers over her mouth tight, pressing them into her own cheek, her eyes growing wider and wider as she glared at her mother.

"You've got to do it, and will your aunts love it," her mother said, the grimace wide, the taut lower lip trembling, "oh, they will turn you out for a *real* wedding day, they'll drag out the gold thread for you, the pearls, oh, how they will love it, oh, they will be in their glory, they'll be running to Celestina's, they'll be going through the old names, they'll be inspecting all those eager offers, picking over those old pedigrees..."

Marie upset the chair. She was backing away even before she had risen, and the chair fell backwards, teetering and then to one side. She stood in the corner of the room, her hand holding the frame of the bedroom door.

Her mother rose slowly.

"Get away from me," Marie whispered. "Get away from me!" She backed into the bedroom, the hem of her dress coming perilously close to the fire. "Get away!" she glared at the woman who stood in the door.

"Marie, Marie..." Cecile reached out toward her, her teeth drawing blood from her lip. "Marie, you can give him that," she said, the voice strained to a hissing sound, "you can give him Paris where he can be a man."

"Stop it," Marie snatched her shawl from the foot of the bed. She backed across the rear bedroom to the door. "How could you think I would do this!" she spit the words as Cecile advanced. "How could you believe I would live the way I've seen you live! How could you think I would take on that misery, the misery I've seen you suffer ever since I could remember, year after year? Never knowing when he was coming, if he was coming, if there'd be money again this month for the bills, if you could keep this roof over your head, and then to have him die like that, not leaving a scrap of a will, not even a scrap of paper in secret for you with Jacquemine. Seventy-five dollars and they called you lucky, did they? And you loved him? And you love him still? You're mad, mad if you think I would live like that, mad if you think I would turn my back on Richard for that. Oh, you would sell me on the auction block for my brother, wouldn't you? But you don't know me, you've never known me, or you wouldn't have shown your soul to me, your whore's soul!"

And as Cecile moaned, Marie had pulled open the door and she ran down the alleyway toward the street.

Without knocking she burst into the Mercier hallway, and through the open doors of the classroom saw Christophe. Quickly he came out to her, moving her to one side out of the prying eyes of the class.

"Michie Christophe," she said breathlessly, "please, write to my brother, write him now, tell him to come home, I need him..." she said. "I know my brother, I know my brother..." she stammered, vaguely aware that he could not possibly understand. She clasped his hand. "Tell my brother I am with my aunts, and that I need him now!"

III

IT WAS EARLY EVENING and Richard was tired. His mother had insisted he accompany her this afternoon to the house of her Vacquerie cousins, descendants of her mother's brother, on the grounds that since he had become a young man he had hardly called on these cousins at all. As a child, he had played there often, loving these mild-mannered people, a house of women except for Cousin Gregoire who ran the family business, a grocery store, but it had been three years now since he had seen them anywhere except on the church steps.

They were a refined family, without the bluster of the Lermontants, their modest flat furnished about a handful of treasures rescued from the Saint-Domingue revolution, and they spoke of the old plantation regime as if that world were alive today. In fact, little anecdotes of daily life had come down through the family with pet names for people who had been dead for fifty years. And one had the feeling in their sedate shadowy rooms of living in an old world that could somehow not make its peace with the thriving New Orleans of today.

There were no surprises for Richard. The shaded yard with its twin oaks in back was as Richard remembered it, and the little playhouse built for his daughters by Cousin Gregoire, though sagging from the relentless Louisiana weather, was still there. All was ruin within, however, broken toys, neglected dolls and dust, for Isabella, the youngest, was sixteen.

And it was while they sat in the parlor together, Isabella showing him with enthusiasm the new Daguerreotypes that had been made of all the family, that Richard perceived the reason for this visit, and grew silent thinking with a shocking immediacy what it would be like to be married to this sweet girl. She would have been a good wife for anyone; generosity emanated from her small drowsy brown eyes, and she had a combination of features which he had always found beguiling, a full African mouth with a long thin Caucasian nose. All of them would make good wives, he speculated dully, this Cousin Isabella, Raimond's cousins in Charleston, and even those green-eyed beauties, Renée Lermontant's daugh-

(547)

ters, descendants of Jean Baptiste's one illegitimate son, who had little to do with the Lermontants who had become *la famille*, but lived in luxury, Renée Lermontant owning a thriving tavern on the edge of the Faubourg Marigny.

And in the last few months, it seemed, his mother had seen to it that he called on every one of these cousins with the exception of the Charleston people who came to visit often enough. It was Madame Suzette's intent to distract Richard, to reassure him, to buffet him against the truculent and spiteful whims of Cecile Ste. Marie, and Richard knew it. But nothing could buffet him against the possible loss of Marie now. He had been desperate since Monsieur Philippe's death, and his mother ought to know this, Richard thought, her timing, for once, had not been so good.

When they rose to go, Isabella walked with them to the side gate.

"You must come to call on us." Madame Suzette kissed her on both cheeks. "Next Sunday, after Mass, I insist."

But the girl's soft yielding manner had a touch of melancholy to it as she made her curtsy. "And I am the cause of this," Richard thought darkly. He could add nothing to his mother's polite invitations except his polite farewells.

They walked along in silence, Richard taking his mother's arm in his as he guided her past the inevitable puddles and stones of the dirt street.

"I thought it was good for you to get out," she said finally.

"Maman," he said. "I must see Marie. I want to go to Madame Louisa's now."

"Son, don't do it," she said. "Wait until Marcel comes home. Marcel is head of that family now, whether he is prepared for it or not. Your father will speak to Marcel."

"No, Maman," he shook his head, his voice dropping to a whisper. "I must see her now."

This was unlike Richard, this obstinacy. He led Madame Suzette across the Rue Rampart, helping her gracefully over the deep waterfilled ditches, and lifted her slightly by the waist to the curb. A few steps ahead in the Rue St. Louis she saw the gas lamps beside the door of her home, burning already at five o'clock as the sky was leaden and dark.

"My son, there is no reason under God for us to endure insult," she said. "We are the Lermontants." And this last statement, spoken with simple pride, was as unlike Madame Suzette as obstinacy was unlike her son.

He stared ahead through the twilight, rendered so color-less by the winter sky.

"Maman, I cannot wait," he said and giving her his arm as she went up the front steps, he stayed on the banquette.

"What has this done to you?" she whispered. "What is it doing to you now?"

"I must go, Maman..." He stood firm.

"Don't let your father know," she opened the door. And he smiled faintly, realizing that this meant she would not tell.

A cold rain had begun by the time he reached the dress shop in the Rue Royale and pulled the bell. He pulled it again after a wait of approximately three minutes, stepping under the carriageway arch where he could not be seen from the shuttered windows above.

A third time he rang, and then a fourth, and the rain was coming now with a dull force.

An unpleasant sensation paralyzed him. He moved very slowly into the center of the banquette and looked up at the flat over the shop. Rain poured down the yellowed plaster of the façade, and ran along the dark green slats of the shutters before it shot out in little jets over the street. It fell on his forehead and pelted his eyelids as he squinted against it. And suddenly lifting his hands, he cupped them about his mouth and taking a slow breath raised his voice out of the deep organ of his chest. "Marie! Marie!"

Nothing stirred above.

"Marie!" he called again, only to hear a scraping sound behind the shutters of the house next door. "Marie!" he cried again.

He backed slowly into the street, almost bumping into a passing cart. A little cluster of passersby had stopped to stare at him from beneath an awning, and a woman passed in front of the dress shop scrutinizing him suspiciously from beneath a dark bonnet brim. "Marie!" he shouted once more. And not waiting for an answer, he suddenly reached down, picked up a glistening lump of coal from the slush, and heaved it overhand so it struck the high shutters and fell to the banquette below. A murmur rose from those around him, a wagon groaned behind him forcing him toward the curb. He saw another rock, grabbed it, and threw it as well.

"Lermontant!" a voice intruded suddenly.

He was jerked from some acute state of concentration to find himself looking down at the notary, Jacquemine. A pace behind him on the curb stood a dark-faced woman, her head slightly averted, gazing at Richard from above her wool cravat with one enormous expressionless eye. He felt a chill pass over him as he stared at her, in fact, he hardly heard the notary's voice. "Indeed, you are making a spectacle of yourself, Lermontant, what's the matter with you?" It was Cecile Ste. Marie, that dark-faced woman, that bundle of wool and bonnet brim that turned now with a lift of the head. Again the eye fixed him, wide, wild, like the eye of a bird.

"Get out of the street, for the love of heaven," said Jacquemine. But Cecile Ste. Marie had turned her face away and walked on and the notary ran to catch up with her, as the clop of a horse sent a spray of wet mud over Richard's coat.

Richard stood there motionless. A sickening spasm caught his stomach, as the two figures receded, the notary glancing nervously back as he panted to keep up with the marching woman.

And above, those windows shuttered as before like blind eyes.

Marie was crying. She sat in the darkened parlor with her elbows on the table. Tante Colette stood at the windows, looking through the glass and the dark slits of the shutters at the street below. "I want you to go out of here," she said over her shoulder to Louisa. Louisa said, "But why?"

"Because it's time I had a talk with this girl," Colette said. "It's time I had a talk with her alone."

Louisa didn't want to go. She stood watching her sister. But then Colette ushered her into the hallway and closed the door.

Two oil lamps burned on the mantel above Marie, and Colette turned the little brass key in these, one by one, to raise the flame. Then she looked at the girl who sat at the round table, her hair down, her face covered with her hands.

"It's time we cut out all this sweet talk," Colette said, "and get down to the facts."

"That *was* Richard, wasn't it?" Marie said through her tears. "I know it was."

"Stop asking me that question," Colette said. "For days now, it's been 'poor *bébé*,' and 'poor *bébé* just lost her papa,' and 'poor *bébé* has had such a shock,' and 'let poor *bébé* rest'..."

"It *was* Richard!" Marie said.

(550)

"Well, I think it's time we got down to the facts."

"Which are what!" Marie said bitterly, her eyes glimmering with her tears. She was shivering with her sobs. "That my mother wants me to take a white man for a protector? And that's what you want, too! That's what you always wanted, wasn't it?" She meant to look away, but something caught in the corner of her eye. It was a stiff expression on Colette's face, something quite alien to the soft chattering affection that perpetually filled this flat.

"It is what you want, too, isn't it?" Marie said. "All the time you would have approved of it. It was all hypocrisy your taking me to Mass, all hypocrisy your receiving Richard..."

"I've heard just about enough," said Colette. "I've heard just about enough tears and enough complaining and enough foolishness to make me sick."

Marie stared at her, stunned.

"'Course I took you to Mass, I go to Mass every Sunday of my life, don't I, every feast day, every day during Lent! But what's that got to do with the fact that your brother hasn't a cent to his name, that your mother can't put food in her mouth, that you've got nothing, none of you, but that cottage and the clothes on your backs! Now when your papa was alive," she said, drawing near to the table, "that was a different time. Your papa was rich, and your maman was rich, and if you wanted to throw away your life on some colored boy that was your whim! But I'm sick to death now of hearing this spoiled selfish talk! What do you mean to do, march up that aisle in a white dress with everyone in the church thinking you're a damned fool—and don't think they won't—and leave your mother and your brother to sell off the furniture for a living, end up selling that house? And what would your fancy people the Lermontants do, give Marcel some pittance for working for them with his sleeves rolled up, and enough to keep Cecile in a rented room? Or are they just supposed to be the poor relations? Living off the charity of the Benevolent Society with Marcel giving lessons to the children and escorting the old aunts to Mass? Are you crazy, girl! And you think your mother would ever live in that Lermontant house? Even if they would take her in and give her some attic room with the rats and spiders, your mother would rather die!"

She drew near to Marie, who sat mute staring up at her, and put her hands on the table as she leaned forward.

"Now you listen to me. For sixteen years, you've had the

best of everything, now I mean the best! Any dress you wanted, any jewelry I had in my box, you had it, pearls, diamonds, silks from Paris, the hats right off the boat, the slippers, the pomade, the perfume, the best! And you got that because your mother got it for you, and I got it for you, and Louisa got it for you! And now it's time for you to give something back! I haven't begun to fight for you, oh, no, I haven't begun. I haven't begun to give you up to some colored undertaker and his penny-pinching bourgeois people, oh, no, not for this world. You are going to those balls with me, you are meeting those white gentlemen who couldn't take their eyes off you in the Théâtre d'Orléans, who can't take their eyes off you when they see you coming down from that Communion rail at Mass! You are going there with me and you are going to make the best alliance this family can get! And you are going to get your brother on that boat for Paris, you are going to get him to a place where he can marry a woman who will respect him and look up to him as if he were a man! Now, why do you think, why do you think your maman made your papa swear he would send that boy to France? Education, Sorbonne, all that foolishness? There's no life for your brother here! And you are going to get him out of here, and you are going to get a comfortable income for your mother so that she can keep her house! And you can get all that, Marie, you can get it like that!" She snapped her fingers, holding out her hand. And as Marie stared at the fingers, Colette snapped them again with an unconscious tightening of her teeth. "Like that!" she said. And again, "Like that!"

She turned away. She folded her arms and commenced to pace the floor, her gray head slightly bowed, her lips pursed. Marie was not looking at her. She was staring at the surface of the table, her arms limp in her lap.

"Now, I tell you what you're going to do." Colette said. "You're going to rest a while. And we are going to wait until a little interval passes, a decent interval, and then you and I are going to call on Celestina Roget. I don't have to tell you who's courting Gabriella, you know all about it, Alcee LeMaitre, one of the richest white men on the coast. Well, we are going to talk to Celestina, we're going to talk about the balls, whether that's the best way to go. And then you are going to be the toast of this town."

Marie stood up. She looked slowly about the room. Her

shawl lay on the chair by the door. She walked to the door and drew the shawl up around her shoulders.

"You just go on to your room," Colette said. "And you leave the details to me."

"I'm going home," Marie said in a small voice. "I'm going to see if my brother's come back."

"Your brother's not coming home, not till your mother tells him to, and your mother does not want you at the house."

Marie drew the shawl up over her head. She turned to her aunt, her eyes level and wide.

Colette glanced anxiously at the lamp. When she looked back, Marie was still staring at her, and she looked away again with a slight shudder.

"You'll be back," she said, "soon as you get a taste of what your mother's got to say." She pursed her lips. "After all, where else have you got to go!"

IV

IT WAS LONG AFTER DARK when Marie rose to leave the Cathedral. The sacristan was putting out the lights. Thunder rumbled beyond the heavy doors, and dully, Marie thought of the black streets. But it was fear of her mother and her aunts that had kept her here till this alarming hour, and lingering in the vestibule of the church she stared numbly at the distant tabernacle, bewildered that the serenity which had always visited her under this roof had not visited her when she needed it most. A thousand desperate considerations had inundated her mind in the past hours, all of them floundering ultimately upon the same rock: Marcel was on his way home, she must wait for him, she must not make matters worse. But prayer had not fortified her, the figures and forms of her faith were beyond her reach. It was almost as if the hypocrisy of those around her had drained all of its meaning, or had her own anger cut her off from God, her own bitterness burnt her prayers dry? A chaos threatened her, gaping wider and wider with the mounting intensity of her anger, becoming fathomless with her rage.

And as she ran through the pitch blackness of Pirate's Alley toward the Rue Royale, she was dogged by one terrifying thought. What if he were not coming, what if they could keep Marcel away? And she must prevail against them night after night, day after day?

Lightning flashed as she turned into the Rue Ste. Anne, and as she ran toward the corner of the Rue Dauphine, there was a light crackle of it again, illuminating the street as if it were midday so that she could see the bleak deserted façade of the Mercier house. If there had only been a light there, she thought suddenly, she would have pounded on Michie Christophe's door, maybe even gone inside to stay for just a moment by his hearth. But the house lay dark beneath the pelting rain. Her shawl was soaked, her chest ached. And bracing herself against the swirling wind she went on toward the dull lights of the cottage ahead.

The rain came faster. Or was it just that it shot off the low roof and caught her in shimmering blasts? She stopped in the walkway beside her mother's window and saw her shadow on the blinds. Her mother was walking back and forth. Marie slumped exhausted against the wet wall and covered her face with her hands. Her shawl fell loose, the cold rain fell on her hair, and making a lattice of her fingers she saw in a sudden silent flicker of lightning the distant unlatched kitchen door.

"Lisette?" she whispered as she stepped inside. All was blackness save for a pulse of red light from the dying coals. But she could hear little sounds, near imperceptible sounds, breath in the dark, cloth folding against cloth. "Lisette?" she whispered again. "Let me come in?"

"Nobody's stopping you," came Lisette's low voice in the darkness. She sat against the wall, her legs stretched out across the width of her cot. Marie padded softly across the floor and settled in the wooden rocker by the stove. She saw a flash of gold in the shadows and knew it was whiskey in the glass. She saw Lisette's head now in a thin gleaming line of light from the kitchen coals. And that gleaming line followed the bulge of Lisette's breasts as a soft ugly sigh came from her lips. Marie, her elbow on the arm of the rocker, began to cry.

Lisette having been in this dark room for three hours could see Marie perfectly, her hair cascading down over her arm, the rustling shadow of her taffeta dress. The rain on the taffeta had given off a funny fragrance which mingled now with the heat from the coals in the kitchen and the coals in the stove. Lisette lifted the glass again and barely tasted the whiskey and then put it down. This was Michie Philippe's whiskey, delicious and strong. An elixir compared to the corn whiskey to which Lisette was accustomed or the drams of rum or wine which she could buy for herself. She had four bottles of this whiskey under the bed, stolen from his gambling rooms upstairs, and she saw no end to the warm and numbing feeling that had come over her sometime early this evening with her fifth glass.

Lisette was thinking, however, thinking. This calm and warmth had given the course of her deliberations a certain freedom and, strangely, a certain relief. At dark, her mistress had come home, with the notary to inform her that Michie Philippe had not left her free. "You belong to me, now." Cecile had hissed at her, the soul of the woman coiled like a snake in those fancy clothes, "Monsieur Dazincourt is sending your papers from *Bontemps* to me! And if you think Marcel can help you, you're wrong!" She had smiled as she leaned forward from the kitchen door: "Why don't you run off," she had said, "go on, run off the way you've done it before, go to that Lola Dedé, live hand to mouth in back alleys, go on. You think I won't find you, I'll post a notice on every wall, on every tree! You'll never work for a decent family in this city, not so long as I have breath. Go on. Run off, let me tell Marcel when he comes home, you've run off again."

Wild-eyed, panting, oh, if only the rest of them could have seen that ladylike face then. "Go into the country," the curling smile. "Go on, let them catch you and put you on those slave gangs, let them sell you when no one comes for you. But you won't do any of that! Even if I get that notary to execute copies of those papers, even if we don't wait for them to come from *Bontemps!* You're going to be a good girl, you're going to stay right here. Because when I take you to that yard, you want me to say you're a good girl, you're a good lady's maid, or else they'll sell you right into the fields!"

Smart she was, wasn't she? Smarter ten times over than Michie Philippe, oh, ten times over than that driveling sentimental lying man! My papa, the rich planter, going to take good care of me, going to set me free.

She let the whiskey slide down her throat.

And this one, look at her, poor Missie Marie, rocking, crying in that chair. She could see Marie's white hand gleaming like a light; and now the white skin of her forehead as she lowered her hand to the dark taffeta of her lap. What's it like to wear a dress like that, to feel that taffeta next to your skin? Marie's hair almost closed on the whiteness of her forehead, the dark taffeta almost enveloped the tiny white hand. There was the almond of the face flashing again as she lifted her head. "What am I to do, Lisette, what am I to do," to do, to do, to do.

In a way, it was good that it was over! It was good that all hope was gone. It seemed she'd been born with a fever and it had raged in her, raged in her, year in and year out ever since she had known. "He's your papa, honey, that's right, but don't you ever tell anybody, honey, he's going set you free when you're grown up, you're going to be free!" And how she had played it all out in those little dreams. She would work for some nice lady, she would take her wages every Friday afternoon to the bank, they would know her name there after a while, and when she made her little deposits the clerk would say something nice to her, like, "My, Lisette, aren't you a thrifty girl." "Oh, I have my own rooms, Monsieur," she'd explain. Maybe some day even, "I have my own little house." "Don't you take any liberties with this girl," she would say to the slaves who tipped their top hats, those arrogant swaggering men at the corner grog shop, "I'm free!"

Well, it was over, wasn't it? It was done.

"What am I to do, Lisette," Marie was crying. "What am I to do?" Other words, small dusty sorrowful little words about Richard Lermontant and that shrew Louisa and that shrew Colette and that shrew "Maman" and that knight in shining armor, "my brother," Marcel. What's it like to have a dress like that, hair like that, that skin! And she whines in that chair, helpless, never able to do the slightest thing for herself, weak, whining, "Lisette, what am I to do!" O God, to have that for an instant, to look like that, walk like that, speak that perfect lady's French. Back alleys, Lola Dedé's, cheap men and filth in bed, and back alleys. But not! Not the auction block!

No, there had never really been any question of that, had there? No, that wasn't it at all. And good Michie Christophe, begging her to be brave, promising her he would reach Michie Dazincourt himself, tell him the truth. You needn't bother, Michie, good as you are, you needn't put yourself out. Again her arm like a machine went out for the glass of whiskey and the whiskey came into her mouth. Some sudden impatience made her drink the glass down; and setting it back on the chest, she lifted the bottle with that same arm and filled the glass again. It had not been necessary for her to move any part of her body other than that left arm for two hours and a half. *Go on, run off, live from hand to mouth in back alleys, go to that Lola Dedé, why don't you?* Yes, that is exactly what is going to happen, and it will be just as terrible, just as dreadful as she said it would be.

"They want me to go to the balls, Lisette, they want me to give up Richard, to take a white man..." Oh, you poor baby! Such a dreadful fate!

"Lisette, what am I to do?"

Steal those dresses, why not, you're going, aren't you, she'll hunt you down no matter what you do. Steal those dresses, the green taffeta, the muslin, that rose silk... hmmmm... steal the pantaloons, the chemises, you've washed them, ironed them, washed them, ironed them, you know every bit of thread, every seam. And the money, what's she got in that *secrétaire*, one hundred dollars? Take it! *You'll never work for a decent family in this city, not so long as I have breath!*

"If only Marcel could come home, Lisette..." Marcel, Marcel, Marcel.

"What the hell damn can he do, Missie, he's just a child!"

And now Marie was sobbing, those white hands up to that white face. Steal it, steal it, those corsets, sachet, taffeta, silk, perfume. "He's got to help me, Lisette, he's always been on my side."

I'll make him set you free, Lisette, have faith in me, I'll get him to do it, but this takes time!

Ooooo God. But had she ever really done anything like that in her whole life, steal the dresses, steal the money, run. What did Lola Dedé say once, about a poison, you put that in your *maîtresse's* food and you just sit back, *chère,* and watch it work. Dreams, that's what it was, dreams of making that bitch suffer the way she made me suffer, making her afraid the way that she made me afraid. Only I'm not going, not going on that block!

But she'd never had the courage, never had the strength. Poison, charms, it was dreams over and over again so that it made her sick. Could you even steal those dresses, could she even break the lock on that *secrétaire? Lisette, why do you run off like this, why do you drink like this, you just hurt yourself!* Dreams of taking that black shrew by the neck, of breaking that neck, breaking it. *Honey, you have to be nice to the* Maîtresse, *that's the way it is now, and you just have to be patient, Michie Philippe's your papa, Michie Philippe's going to set you free!*

"I don't know what to do if Marcel doesn't get here, Lisette, I can't go back to them, I can't go into the house..."

Oh, poor helpless little white Missie Marie with all that beautiful long hair. Poor, poor, little Missie Marie who had never been anything but unhappy all her life! "Let me just sit here with you, Lisette, Lisette, he has to come home!"

"What you need is a charm, Missie." Again the arm raised the glass. "Some powerful magic to make them leave you alone till your brother comes home, to make those white men look away from you." That little waist, that red mouth, Lisette let out a husky mean laugh.

"No, no, don't talk of all that, Lisette, let me stay here with you in the kitchen, I can't go into the house."

"Get a charm," Lisette murmured. You know how it will probably turn out, you won't steal anything from them, nothing, no poison in the food, and no little free nigger going into the bank with her own money and her own little house and some nice spiffed-up free nigger coming to call on you on Sundays, "Well, good afternoon, Miss Lisette, you mind if I just sit with you for a while on your step??????"

Stop it, stop dreaming. Those papers might just be here tomorrow and you are not, not going on that block!

A strange thought came to her. She was holding the glass in her hand.

It was a sensation at first, something she felt in the muscles of her face and in the roots of her hair. A strange relaxation very like the relaxation of getting drunk. She could feel the air on her face, and her mouth partially open as, concealed by the darkness, she was peering into it, at a possibility that had never occurred to her before. Was it like all the rest, would there come that little catch when she knew it was all make-believe? No. This was so easy, so simple, and so big, bigger than anything she'd ever imagined, she was struck dumb. Her mind tried to back off and say, no, you'd never do that, not you, Lisette. It wanted her head to fall to the side with the "no" on her lips as she looked away. But what if you did it! What if you *do* it! And who can stop you, you can do it, you can do it now!

And suddenly it expanded in her vision; it blossomed from its first conception into something ripe and immense and evil, and splendid in its evil, splendid in all that it would do to all of them, that black shrew Cecile, that shrew Louisa, that shrew Colette, that knight in shining armor, that brother, who is not here! She let out her breath and drew it in deeply, it was magnificent, the like of which she had never never done.

"...don't believe in charms, please don't talk of charms, Lisette, just let me sit here with you..." Marie was crying, poor, poor little rich, white, beautiful Marie!

"Poor Missie," Lisette's eyes grew wide looking at the white ghost of the girl across from her. She ran her tongue along her lips. "But there are such charms. Just a little thing that can make them not want you anymore, they won't even look at you when you pass in the street, makes no difference what your aunts say, they can talk themselves sick to those fine gentlemen..." her voice trailed off. And she slid her legs off the cot. She felt her feet find the slippers, and rose in the darkness, moving toward Marie, there was that splendid evil before her, the chance of a lifetime, there was no doubt any longer. As she lifted Marie by the arm, *it was done*.

V

MARIE STOPPED AT THE MOUTH of the passage, as for one second the silent glimmer of lightning showed the small peeling cottage in the slanting rain. She blinked in the darkness. Music pounded from within and behind the colored cloth that masked the windows, she could see figures dancing to the rhythm of the drums. "What is this place?" she whispered.

"Come on, out of the rain." Lisette put her arm around Marie's shoulders and forced her forward into the alley. "We aren't going in there!" she said with contempt. "We're going to see Lola Dedé in the back."

"But I don't believe it, how can it make men look away from me?" Marie stopped again.

"You leave that to Lola Dedé," Lisette said, "you leave everything to Lola Dedé and me!"

Someone in the little cottage was shouting and figures leaped against the red cloth on the windows, as Lisette pulled her back through the crunching shells, under the wet branches of the fig trees toward the huge hulk of the house in back. Long galleries ran the length of the yard, two stories high with glowing windows against the falling rain, and a yellow door lay open from a townhouse whose façade opened on another street. A figure was standing in the door and it was to that figure now that Lisette and Marie ran.

"Let this girl sit down, Ma'ame Lola," Lisette said. They had come into a cluttered room. A brass bed stood against a row of lace curtains. A long altar there was crowded with statues of the saints. "Voodoo saints," Marie whispered. She pushed back against Lisette toward the door.

"You just rest yourself," Lisette said. "You don't have to stay here if you don't like it, you just let me talk to Ma'ame Lola."

A man was laughing somewhere, and there were steps on those galleries in back, and the music thudding from the little cottage beyond. Marie had been offered a chair. Scarves hung over it, a fringed shawl, but a black woman snatched these away. And sitting, her hands smoothing the rain-spotted flounces of her skirts, she looked up to see some shadowy figure beyond a thin veil of beads at the door. It seemed a man with a top hat was talking to another man there, but then this brown-skinned woman in a brilliant red silk dress drew a tapestried curtain over that door. "Lisette, I want to go!" Marie said.

"Now, *bébé*, why you want to go and leave us on a night like this when you only just came in?" said this brown-skinned woman, her long dark tendrils of hair winding down her back beneath her flowered *tignon*. Her voice was like a song.

"This is my mistress, Ma'ame Lola, Marie Ste. Marie," Lisette said.

"Oh, I know who this girl is," sang the brown-skinned woman. "Now Lisette, gal, get your mistress some tea. You talk to me, pretty girl!" The brown-skinned woman dropped onto a piano stool in front of Marie and clasped Marie's hands in her own. "Child of grace," she said, and reached out to touch Marie's cheek. Marie drew back, and looked at the hands that were holding hers, the small serpent ring that wound about the woman's finger so that she pulled away. This was a mistake, all of it, a dreadful mistake!

"Now what this girl needs is a charm, Ma'ame Lola, you know what her Maman and her aunts want her to do, they want those white men to fix her up, they want those white men quarreling over her at the Salle d'Orléans, at the balls."

"Lisette, I want to go," Marie said in a timid whisper. She tried to pull her hands loose, but the woman, Lola, held them fast. She was a pretty woman, she had perfect teeth. Again she lifted a hand to brush Marie's cheek. She brushed Marie's hair back from her face. "Don't you like those fancy gentlemen, precious *bébé?*" she asked. But something had distracted Marie. It was a statue of the Virgin on that altar, complete with blue veil and white gown, and the hands outstretched lovingly and around it was wound the dead skin of a snake. Marie gasped, and Lola Dedé was taken by surprise when Marie jerked loose and stood up.

"Now why you want to go and make a fool of me in front of my friends," Lisette whispered. She had her arm around Marie's waist. "It isn't going to do any good for you to go home now. Your aunts are probably there by this time, and then it will be the three of them on you, you best stay with me. Now sit down, you just sit down and wait now while I talk to Ma'ame Lola, you hear me? Sit down!"

Madame Lola had shut the door to the yard. "Cold wind," she sang out, "cold wind, you and this girl like to caught your death."

And Marie turning saw the two women's heads together as Lisette whispered in the woman's ear. "Get that girl some hot brandy with her tea," sang Ma'ame Lola's voice and a black woman who had snatched the scarves from the chair set them down now and returned, the ivory white of her eye growing huge in her head. Madame Lola took the cup from the black girl as soon as it was poured and taking a brown bottle from the marble dresser by the bed tilted it into the tea. A piano began above. Marie looked at the ceiling, at the faded paper with its wreath of painted roses about the chain that held the candles in the brass chandelier.

"Don't you be rude now!" Lisette scowled with the cup in her hands. "You drink this now, you be polite to my friends!" Marie could smell the brandy wafting up with the steam and meant to turn her head when Lisette raised it to her lips.

"You let me cool that for that girl," said Madame Lola, "you let me put a little sweetness in it." and taking the cup she poured a dark syrup into it and gave it back. It smelt strange but good. Marie let her eyes close just for an instant feeling the steam on her face. Her hands and feet were cold and she was wet all over from the rain which had soaked through the shoulders of her dress and run down her bodice and her back. She sighed, exasperated, weary, and took the smallest drink of the tea. "I want to go," she whispered to Lisette. Lisette glowered at her. "You drink that first!" came the intimate whisper. "What you want to do, shame me in front of my friends! Drink it, I told you, then we can go!"

"Drink it, pretty child," said Ma'ame Lola, "drink it down."

And then with a smile, she lounged back against the high
brass footboard of the bed and drank her own tea from a
broken cup.

It was good, the taste, laced with peppermint perhaps,
Marie was not sure. She stared at the murky substance in
the bottle and saw the little spout of the teapot in front of
her and the pouring liquid stirring the sediment again as the
cup grew heavy in her hands. Her ears began to ring with
the pain that had been in her head all the long afternoon.
Lisette was talking in a low rapid voice about a charm, a
charm to take away her charms. "And those charms," Madame Lola said, "such charms as those charms, you can't kill
those charms without a powerful charm." The cup had almost
slipped from Marie's hands! The black woman gave it to her
again, and Madame Lola sang out, "Yes, drink that, *chérie,*
precious *chérie,*" and this time the tea burnt her mouth but
strangely enough this burning was outside of her and she
almost liked the sensation of this in her chest. She rested
back against the chair and stared forward at the flowers on
the wall. The flowers danced on the wall, thousands and
thousands of tiny roses marched upward at long angles toward the ceiling and there it seemed a yellow smoke gathered, a smoke that she had not seen before. It wound itself
about the candles in wreaths and was alive but dissipating
rapidly into the shimmering air. And just below the candles
as it vanished in an ever-thinning haze were the two women,
Lisette and Madame Lola, with their heads together again,
each tilted toward the other, Lisette's breasts almost touching this woman's breasts and their skirts descending in long
flowing lines. Little paisley tails of gold wound in and out
on the red silk of Madame Lola's skirts, had Marie even seen
these before? She wanted to remark that she had not even
seen them, seen only the redness, but she had the most curious sensation of not being able to open her lips. And the
two women had become perfectly flat.

They were perfectly flat. They could have been cut from
cardboard and placed there together, or no, rather cut from
the same piece as nothing showed of the room behind them
where they were joined, Madame Lola's dark hair filling the
gap between the flesh of their cheeks. And they had been
standing there for the longest time perfectly, perfectly still.
And Marie had been sitting here watching them. She had
been sitting forever here, her back against the chair, her
head thrown to one side, her hair trailing down on her

(562)

breasts. Slowly, ever so slowly she shifted her gaze down and saw the teacup lying on the floor. Tea ran out over the cypress boards, tea ran in rivulets into the cracks between the boards and tea had stained her taffeta dress, tea had burned her hands. Lisette's voice was a rumble, urgent, argumentative, then soft, and right before Marie's eyes the cardboard cutout of the two women was broken and Ma'ame Lola bending now to the open drawer of her chest drew out dollar bills. One of these bills fell to the floor. That tapestry was drawn back, and the black woman had gone out. But then again it seemed the tapestry had not been drawn back because it was perfectly in place, and Madame Lola was facing her, leaning against the brass bars of her bed again, smiling at her, and Lisette was gone.

Lisette, Marie thought, Lisette, and she brought her tongue up between her teeth. She could feel the first syllable forming and then it came out of her in a long, never-ending hiss.

"You best drink some more tea, gal," Madame Lola's face was right in front of hers suddenly. And the most magical thing had happened. The tea was all back in the cup again, and the cup was in her hands. Marie wanted to say, I cannot do it, I cannot even move my lips, but the tea was in her mouth and Madame Lola's hand did the most intimate and slightly repulsive thing of touching her on the throat.

When she looked down, afraid of vomiting the tea, she had drunk it and Madame Lola's hand was on her breast. This was quite out of the question, unbuttoning her dress for her, she did not wish to stay here, she did not wish to be lifted out of the chair like this, and suddenly she opened her mouth wide to scream but her mouth didn't open. It was as if the scream rolled up and filled her mouth, pressing against the teeth, she saw her naked breasts when she looked down and the opened buttons of her white chemise. Her dress was on a chair across the room.

Sometime during the long night Marie was awake and knew exactly what had happened.

There were five white men, gentlemen all of them with their stinking breath and their stinking pomade, this big one with the black whiskers digging his knee against the inside of her thigh, his thumbs pressed down into the flesh under her raised arms so that she arched her body, that scream rising again to suffocate her, a stream of vomit rolling up with it that leapt out in silence to make peaks on the walls. They didn't bother to take off their clothes.

The young one with the blond hair wept in his wine until the tall one threw the wine in his face, and he sat there, long arms hung between his sprawling knees, the tears and the wine dripping from his swollen face, little whines coming out of him. The man beside her on his elbow said, "Now you're not going to try to hit me now, no, you don't want to do that," and untied her hands. Darkness. Only to awaken to that room again. And again. And again.

Until in darkness, she heard the morning sounds.

Sun shone on the mud-streaked floor, and the rain teeming on the shell yard became a glare as it hit the puddles in the sun. Not one particle of this had been imagined, it was all true. And the blond-haired man, drunk, blubbering, listed still in the chair with his wine-soaked cravat, his opera cape with its white satin lining hanging down so far it was caught under the leg of the chair. He tilted his head to one side, crying, murmuring, crying. Everyone else was gone. Except that singsong voice that sang to him, "You go home now, Michie DeLande, you just go on home now, Michie, you got to get some sleep now, Michie, party's over now, Michie," while he sat there, head to one side, whining and murmuring, and sobbing with a sudden shift of his shoulders, the snot and the spit on his lips and his face.

Marie watched that woman moving about the room. She watched her emptying the whiskey from the glasses into a brown bottle, she saw her pitch the butts of the cigars out the open door. She saw her nudge the drunken man again and to her surprise the drunken man did not get out of the chair. His gray red-rimmed eyes were still fixed on Marie, and his mouth shuddered, thick and the color of salmon, with his whimpering cries. "You go home now, Michie, you best get out of here, your brother's going to come looking for you, Michie, party's over." So that was it, he was not a man, he was a boy.

Ever so slowly Marie moved her left hand. She lay with her head twisted so that her neck ached, but she did not move her head, her eyes following the woman, she merely lifted, slowly, her left hand. She could feel the strap of her chemise and moved it up ever so slowly to her shoulder. She could feel the other strap and moved it ever so slowly up over her shoulder and let her hand drop then as the woman turned,

'Michie, now you got to get out of here, Elsa get that boy to take this man out of here, Elsa?" Ever so slowly, Marie's hand tugged at the white muslin until the button loop closed over the button, it would have been infinitely easier with her right hand, but her right hand was twisted upside down under the bar, and she could not move it without turning over, so she just kept on working with her left hand. One button. Two buttons, three buttons, four. She could see her naked knee against the wall, and the thigh black with bruises and the smears of blood. With her left hand, she slid the muslin down. There was blood over it, it was impossible to get out of here like this. She stared at the blond-haired man.

But Madame Lola had seen her eyes. "You just lie back, girl," she was saying in that singsong voice, and had snapped her fingers. Another woman had come into the room. There was the sound of a rag being squeezed through water, and beside Marie there was a bottle of green glass with a long narrow neck. If she reached out quick with her left hand ... But now this woman had touched her right wrist and was turning her hand painfully under the brass bar and had it free. It was absolutely essential to act before they got rid of that man.

Her head nearly pitched to the floor when she turned over but she had that bottle and it took two slams at the corner of the marble to break it. She was sitting up with it, and staring at the voodooienne for the first time.

"Now why you want to go and do that now, _chérie_," said Madame Lola. "Now why you don't want to lie still now?" She came forward motioning to that other woman who was wringing the rag in the water, "You put that down, _chérie_, you got to have a nice bath now, you got to rest."

"Don't you hurt her!" The drunken man blurted out. But he could not stand. He had put his hand on the back of the chair and nearly fallen just as the woman with the rag had reached out and Marie scraped the broken bottle down the length of her arm. Both women stood still. "Don't you hurt her!" he was roaring, trying to get up on his feet, his opera cape dragging on the muddy floor.

"You get out of here, Michie!" Madame Lola growled at him over her shoulder. "You're in bad trouble, Michie, now you want to make it worse, you just stay, this ain't no nigger girl, this is a white girl ..." Perfectly stupid, the man didn't hear a word she was saying. But that other woman had run

(565)

out of the room. It was absolutely essential to get up before that woman brought someone else back.

And Marie sprang off the bed and rushing past Madame Lola with the bottle clenched in her right hand, got behind the white man, her left fingers digging right through his coat.

"You leave her alone!" he said at once, and reached back behind himself to hold onto her. She pulled him toward the door, his big stumbling feet crushing down on her toes; no time to think about that, she felt herself back suddenly into the cold downpour of the rain.

She grabbed the cloak off his neck nearly pulling him over and he helped to put it on her shoulders now, the hem of her chemise and the hem of the cape disappearing into the great sheet of water that was spreading out endlessly in the alleyway and in the yard.

"Now, you come back here, girl." Madame Lola put a hand up against the rain, eyes squinting, "Where you think you're going, girl? You belong with us, girl, your Maman don't want you now, you belong with us, now you come back in here, girl, you got to have a nice bath and lie down."

Marie was stepping backwards through the water, the shells cutting into her feet, the big cumbersome drunken man soft and stumbling as he backed away with her, his hand fluttering behind him trying to catch hold of her as reaching under his coat, she dug her fingernails into his side right through the linen of his shirt.

"Animals, animals!" he bawled at the advancing woman. They had reached the street.

The water spread in all directions obliterating the banquettes, streaming from the gutters along the galleries, flooding down the dirty plaster of the houses, shooting off the ends of the sloping roofs. Figures stood behind the half-opened doors, men clustered under the eaves of the little grocery, and someone had come out splashing in the rain, and at the edge of the wall the woman stopped.

Marie could see the dark folds of the cape coming together as slowly she let down the bottle, and let go of the drunken man. She held the cape together from the inside and squinting at the buildings around her, the rain blinding her, felt that scream rising again in her throat like a convulsion until again it curled against the roof of her mouth as she had to reach out again, get hold of that man's shoulder or fall down. He was babbling foolishness that he would protect her while

(566)

her eyes moved back and forth from one side of the street to the other and at last she knew where she was, this was the Rue St. Peter at Rampart, she knew where she was, and how to get home.

She saw him fall as she ran, splashing through the water toward the alleyway that would lead her to the bracken at the middle of the block. He was trying to get to his feet, but seeing that great mass of snarled vines and trees ahead of her, she ran.

And it was from that bracken behind the Ste. Marie cottage, that she finally emerged to limp across the courtyard toward the back door.

She saw the bed first. She did not see her mother but then she knew her mother was there, and that her mother was screaming and Tante Louisa was telling her to wait, to be still. "I know it's her, it's her, it's her..." her mother was saying, but her mother did not know she was in the house, did not know that she was holding on to the post of the bed and falling forward toward the white spread.

Then again she heard her mother scream. When she turned it seemed they were at a great remove from her, her mother screaming and Tante Louisa with her arm around her mother's waist. Tante Louisa was lifting her mother right off the floor. And then her mother got free and tore at the bloody chemise with both her hands. Marie felt her mouth open, she felt it open and the scream inside filled it silently so that she couldn't breathe.

"RUINED, RUINED!" Cecile roared, "RUINED, RUINED," it seemed the roar was filling the room and Marie reached to cover up her ears. "RUINED, RUINED," her mother bellowed, and rising again and again in Tante Louisa's arms brought her feet down with a clonk against the floor. Marie was gasping, choking, at her effort to scream, her eyes growing wider and wider, her mother's face convulsed and swollen as suddenly her hand flew out and caught Marie on the side of the face. Marie clutched at the neck of the broken bottle only to realize that she had lost the broken bottle, her hand was empty, her mother's hand struck her again and her forehead hit the heavy post of the bed. She had dropped the bottle in the street. "RUINED, RUINED." came that bellow again and again until it was one great insensate roar through her mother's clenched teeth in time with the

(567)

blows that struck Marie until Marie reeled again and grabbed for the far post of the bed with both hands.

"Stop it, Cecile, stop it, stop it!" Tante Louisa was grabbing at her mother, but her mother lunged forward, and when she lunged forward, Marie was ready this time. That scream was throbbing DON'T YOU TOUCH ME, DON'T YOU HIT ME, DON'T YOU SAY THAT TO ME RUINED RUINED DON'T YOU COME NEAR ME all the while not a syllable of sound was passing her lips, as she swung her hand right against her mother's face and felt her mother's teeth cut the flesh. She saw her mother's head jerked around and up as if it were going to be broken right off her body, DON'T YOU HIT ME, DON'T YOU HIT ME, DON'T YOU SAY THAT TO ME RUINED RUINED. And her fingers got her mother's hair, dug right down to the scalp and rushing forward she banged that head into the wall. Again and again she banged it, her mother's eyes were rolling, and with her right hand she slapped that swollen cheek, that shoulder, DON'T YOU HIT ME, DON'T YOU HIT ME, DAMN YOU, DAMN YOU, DAMN YOU, DAMN YOU. And when her fingers were rigid, the strength of her mother's hair tangled around her fingers was not enough and tore loose as her mother slid free down the wall to the floor. She let Tante Louisa have the back of her hand and Tante Louise broke the kerosene lamp with her elbow as she toppled over and crouched down behind the dresser, whimpering, on her knees.

She wanted to kick her mother. But she did not have on her shoes. Shoes. Put on shoes. Everyone was perfectly still. And someone was beating at the front door. All the blinds of the house rattled, someone was beating with both fists. Marie turned around. She had to put on her shoes, and backing toward the bed, felt beneath the dust ruffle for those old slippers. She got down on her knees and pulled them out. She ripped her dress off the hook and tore the sleeve as she pulled it over her arm. This was foolish, smoothing it down like this, but she could not stop her hands from smoothing it over the bloody chemise and had to grab one hand with the other and make them deal with the buttons, that scream coming out only as an awful muted syllable, an animal sound that wasn't even a sound, as she tried to breathe.

She was clutching her shoulders with her hands, arms crossed over her bosom, the buttons half undone, the silk transparent and clinging to her arms with the heavy cold rain when she stumbled, her foot cut and bleeding, into Dolly Rose's yard.

Everyone was on the galleries, women all over the gallery of the back of the house and the gallery of the quarters, women in peignoirs and dressing gowns, and black women and no Dolly. And then she saw Dolly gripping the iron railing with both hands. Dolly shoved the women and ran along the gallery and Marie reached up as she put her foot on the stairs, her legs vibrating and weak under her as she attempted to mount the steps. She reached out, that single muted syllable, that grunting sound coming from behind her closed lips. "Hm, hm, hm, hm," as she reached up for Dolly Rose who was crying, "O my God, my God, my God!" She could explain this if she could only get her mouth open, RUINED, RUINED, she reached out for Dolly Rose, Dolly Rose had to understand, but she could not get her mouth open, and as she reached out for Dolly Rose, her hands went up instead to her own mouth, trying to get it open, Dolly Rose had to take her, RUINED, RUINED, it was not possible that those women who had done this, RUINED, RUINED, Dolly Rose had to take her in with her women, RUINED, RUINED, she felt Dolly lifting her by the elbows, saying, "O my God, O my God, go get Christophe, O my God," tears streaming down Dolly's face as she lifted her and someone else lifted her, carrying her under the painted roof of the gallery on running feet, under the papered ceiling of this room.

She rose up on the bed. Dolly Rose tried to push her back down, that same sound, "Hm, hm, hm, hm," until suddenly, suddenly, rising up again, she felt her lips parting, she felt her teeth opening, she felt the scream escaping, the giant curling scream coming out of her throat and out of her mouth. It poured out of her, deafening her, blinding her, rising in one great loop after another until she fell back, the scream throbbing and soaring to fill the room, to fill the yard, to fill the world.

PART TWO

I

MARCEL HADN'T EXPECTED anyone really, how would they know when he would come in? But there was Bubbles, moving swiftly toward him through the crowd. "I have a cab for you, Michie," he said, and quickly heaved the heavy trunk up on his back. "You come with me to Michie Christophe."

"I should go home first..." he said.

"No, Michie, you come with me to Michie Christophe." The slave was insistent, his usual feline grace strained by a certain urgency. Marcel could hear him giving the driver Christophe's number in the Rue Dauphine.

And as soon as they reached the townhouse, Marcel saw Christophe at the top of the stairs.

"I couldn't get here any sooner," Marcel said, hurrying upward. "The day your letter arrived there was one also from my mother saying I must not come home. I had a devil of a time convincing my aunt that you wouldn't have written without a reason..."

Christophe was walking away from him toward his room. He gestured for Marcel to enter.

"But what is the reason?" Marcel was studying the impassive face.

Christophe took his key ring out of his pocket, and without answering he locked the door to the hall. Then he put the key ring back into his pocket and before Marcel could question this, he said,

"I want you to promise me that when I'm finished you will not try to do anything without my knowledge or permission. You understand? Your friend Richard is locked in his grandfather's bedroom in the attic of the Lermontant house and for two days he has been trying to get out. Rudolphe and Antoine haven't left the house, and they have left off trying to reason with him and they merely watch the door. I don't want to go through that with you. I want you to do exactly as I say. Is that clear?"

Marcel moved slowly to the desk. He sat in Christophe's chair. He started to speak, but then said nothing. He tried to read Christophe's expresson and could not, and he realized he was experiencing the very unpleasant sensation of fear.

"Two days ago," Christophe began, "in the house of that voodooienne, Lola Dedé, your sister was assaulted by five white men. They paid for the privilege, and your sister was drugged and forced. She's alive. And she's sustained no serious injury and she's with Dolly Rose.

"How and why she got into the hands of Lola Dedé is a mystery but all points to the fact that Lisette took her there. She was seen leaving home with Lisette that night and Lisette has disappeared.

"Now, yesterday, Vincent Dazincourt had that house raided by the police and shut down. And yesterday, Dazincourt also shot and killed young Alcee LeMaitre who was apparently the leader of the five men. He called him out right at his plantation, and settled the affair on the bayou some five miles away. At three o'clock this afternoon, he shot and killed Charles Dupre who was also among the five, calling him out in the bar at the St. Louis Hotel and threatening to kill him on the spot if he didn't defend himself. Two of the other men, D'Arcy Fontaine and Randolphe Prevost have both disappeared. The families are letting it out they were called away on business; the rumor is they are already at sea, bound for France. And the fifth and last of the group, a boy of nineteen named Henri DeLande will meet Dazincourt at six o'clock tomorrow morning before the Metairie Oaks. The DeLande family is trying everything in its power to stop the duel, but the husbands of Dazincourt's sisters will not intervene. All of these men have claimed of course that they did not know who your sister was, that they didn't know she was Philippe Feronnaire's daughter, or that they were seduced. The former is true, the latter's a damnable lie. Your sister is black and blue with bruises, her wrist broken, her

(571)

lip split. DeLande claims he had no part in it, and that he helped your sister escape. This may or may not be true, no one knows.

"But the morning after it happened, with or without the noble Monsieur DeLande, your sister wandered back to the cottage alone. Your mother and your aunt had already heard the tale, everyone had heard it, it was flying over the back fences even before your sister got away. So they knew what had happened when your sister came into the house. A battle of sorts ensued and a crowd gathered outside. But when I got there your sister was gone. Your mother was badly hurt, and your aunts told me that your sister tried to kill her, but when the truth was got out a little further, it was your mother who attacked your sister, beating her until your sister fought back. She stopped long enough then to get a dress and shoes and went to Dolly Rose. Dolly won't let me see her, she won't let anyone see her, your sister has tried repeatedly to destroy herself, but Dolly is keeping a good watch on her, she's caring for her. Your sister is safe."

He watched Marcel's face, and Marcel staring up at him registered no expression at all.

"Now, there's nothing you can do against the men who did this," Christophe went on, "two are dead and a third is going to die, or kill Dazincourt, at dawn. The others are out of the country for sure. You have got to leave this in Dazincourt's hands. But I want your word you will attempt nothing on your own. You know as well as I do that there's nothing you can do."

Marcel did not answer immediately. He had risen and was standing with his back to the desk, his face utterly blank. His eyes were fixed on the space before him, and when he spoke his voice was reasonable and low.

"Did my sister know what was happening to her?" he asked. "You said she was drugged, did she know?"

"Yes," Christophe said. "She has described it to Dolly Rose."

Again Marcel appeared to reflect. And the changes in him were so gradual, so slight that at first Christophe didn't perceive them—the closing of the fists, the mouth shuddering, and then though the mouth was closed, Christophe heard the low roar. It grew louder and louder, Marcel turning his back to Christophe. And Christophe took hold of him by the arms.

Felix came in quietly, having pushed the door to without a sound. Vincent sat at the desk writing, the thin curtains drawn over the Rue Royale. His pistols lay before him in their satin-lined case. He had cleaned them, loaded them, checked them, and put them there where he could see them, as dipping his pen, he commenced again to write. A single sheet of paper lay on the desk. The words, "Dear Aglae," were inscribed carefully with purple ink.

"Not now," Vincent said softly as he looked up into Felix's eyes. The slave's face was worn, furrowed, his shoulders stooped.

"It's the boy to see you, Michie Vince," the slave persisted, the loose mouth letting the words go slowly, "Michie's boy."

Vincent did not move. For four hours he had been sitting at this desk, the pen in his hand. His lips barely parted as he whispered, "Michie's boy?"

But the slave had opened the door. And "Michie's boy" had passed silently into the vivid colors of this room. He wore a greatcoat speckled with rain, the mud had been hastily wiped from his boots. He came forward with measured steps to the desk.

Twice before, Vincent had seen him. Glimpses when his mind was set on other men. But in the wintry light from the windows, the boy was revealed to him entirely, an extraordinary *sang-mêlé* beauty of honey skin, ashen hair, blue eyes. Eyes bluer than Philippe's had ever been, and altogether penetrating, sharp. The young man was tall, fine of feature, with a face that evinced breeding, grace. Vincent's mind produced for him an image simultaneously of the boy's sister, that striking and coldly beautiful girl who had spoken so politely, so bloodlessly of Philippe's death. The mere thought of her conjured the horror of Lola Dedé's house, the sneering humor in Alcee LeMaitre's face before he raised the pistol to shoot. A slumbering rage awakened in Vincent, whispering to him, I am here, I have been here all the time, I shall be with you in the morning, I shall steady your hand. And his thoughts, proceeding slowly, ever so slowly in the great clarity produced by imminent danger moved on: this brother and sister were wildly unlike each other, and yet very much the same, they had the demeanor of that dark ladylike woman who was their mother, that haughtiness that reminded him of men and women he had known in Paris, aristocrats for generations who bereft of all wealth and title by recurrent revolution nevertheless commanded subservience all around.

He was struck suddenly by the casual progression of his thoughts, the vision of the boy being allowed to stand there, the odd sharpness of every detail of this hotel room. There was no urgency, there was no ticking clock. One single fact reigned supreme. At six o'clock in the morning, he would meet Henri DeLande at the Metairie Oaks and Henri De Lande was the most dangerous of opponents, young volatile, and afraid.

"You go to defend Monsieur Philippe's honor tomorrow," the young man said suddenly, softly. "And I wish to inform you that should it go against you, I will kill Henri DeLande."

Vincent didn't answer. He had brought his knuckles up to his lip, thinking, thinking. The boy's voice was Caucasian like that of his sister, the boy's eyes like two stones. And Vincent could say, But Henri DeLande will never meet you in the field, you know that, and then the proud quadroon would say, Then I shall shoot him down, and Vincent could say, They'll kill you, regardless of your cause, and the quadroon would say, This doesn't matter, I will do what I must do. And something in Vincent which was more man than white man thought, Well, I respect you for it and I know that if it goes against me as you say, you are doomed.

"It will not go against me," he said. It was quite out of the question. "And until such time as it's finished, you must leave it in my hands."

Something contemptuous, despairing, flickered in the quadroon's face. His voice was low. "If it goes against you," he repeated, "I will avenge my sister's honor on my own."

Vincent rose. It was rather unconscious, his rising. He realized that he was standing at the desk. He was leaning forward looking into this young man's eyes. His lips were pressed together, but they were straining to form some crucial statement which would not come to his mind. "I go to avenge your sister's honor," he whispered. "Not merely your father's honor, your father is dead."

And there was that contempt again, deepened, that despair. The young quadroon was leaving the room. The door opened soundlessly, shut. And Vincent was again sitting in the chair.

And if she did not need me, if she did not need me, Marcel was walking fast through the corridor, if she did not need me, the tears welling in his eyes, if she did not need me, I would kill that man now! Damn you, damn you all to hell, all of you, he didn't see the immense stairs before him, the great drifts of men and women moving under the rotunda, as his feet carried him down, faster and faster toward the front doors. That roar was rising in his throat, that roar escaping through his teeth. And she won't even talk to me, won't even see me, how can I tell her that I am here now, that I'll care for her, she must let me see her, and Dolly says they can't let her alone, that with a knife, with a scissors, with the splinter of a mirror...Marie, Marie! I'll take care of you, I am here! He stopped in the very center of the immense lobby, the crowd blinding and confusing him, he did not know where he was. He could not see the doors. Dolly said maybe in a week, maybe in a month, she had screamed when Dolly said Marcel was there! Marie, Marie, he whispered, he was moving belligerently forward, he could smell the rain in the street, he felt the draft from the open doors. "Promise me you will not try to do anything," Christophe had said. "What in the name of God," he had answered, "can I do!" Marie, please! She had screamed when Dolly said his name.

He stopped suddenly. It was raining all around him, the street ran with mud, he was on the curb. And there was the undertaker's shop across the street from him, the rain streaming down the windows, streaming over the carefully inscribed letters: LERMONTANT. She tried to cut her wrists, she tried to cut her throat, she broke a glass, a mirror, she screamed when she heard his name. "I won't let her come to the slightest harm."

"Are you going to bury my sister!" Marcel leered at those windows, eyes glazed, the street a lumbering procession of carts through which the letters flashed, LERMONTANT. "You were going to marry her, are you going to bury her!" He had moved forward without willing it, "Promise me you will not do anything." "What in the name of God can I do!"

"Are you going to bury her!" he shouted at the windows rising up before him, the black curtains in their gold rods. And suddenly he pitched forward, elbow, shoulder slamming into the glass, the glass shivered, then he heard the loud crack, the crash as it split and fell shattering around him, the giant heavy pieces coming down on him, slicing through the leather of his boots. "Are you going to bury her, bury her!" the roar came through his clenched teeth. The crowd was pressing on him, the wind whipping the black serge curtains, the door pulled back, its bell jangling, Placide rush-

ing at him, "No, Michie, no Michie, Michie, don't." He had
Marcel by the arms, Marcel reaching for the jagged pieces
still stuck in the frame, while above at the window of his
room on the St. Louis, Vincent Dazincourt stood behind the
glass staring numbly down at Marcel in the street.

It was Felix who managed to get Marcel home. He had
rushed down from the hotel and taken him quickly by means
of an iron grip out of the thickening crowd. Placide had his
hands full with the broken window and, to be sure, the police
were on their way. But as they entered the stone-cold parlor
of the little Ste. Marie cottage, Felix tightened his hold on
Marcel. The place was deserted, had been deserted for days.
A damp musty smell pervaded all as if doors or windows had
been open to the rain, and as Felix's eyes picked the indefinite
shape of the furnishings out of the gloom, he saw the little
shelves were barren of their bric-a-brac, the candles gone
from the mantel. However, the scuttle still held coal. "Now,
stop that, Michie!" he said to the young man whose slight
frame stiffened in his grip. "I got to find something now to
bind those hands."
However, quite suddenly, he felt the boy's struggling
cease, and he saw the cause of it, that there was a woman
sitting at the dining-room table in the icy gloom and she had
risen, a silhouette against the dim rain on the panes.
"What's the matter with those hands?" came the voice. It
was that one, Michie Vince's Anna Bella, well, thank God.
"Cut clear to the bone, that's all," Felix said. "Breaking
down the undertaker's window, and the glass like to cut clean
through his boots, too."
"You had better get out of here," Marcel said thickly, sitting down heavily in a chair by the grate. "Go on, get out of
here, before your white planter finds out you're here."
Anna Bella regarded him calmly. "Felix, you know there's
pillowcases back there somewhere, just tear one of those pillowcases up, don't matter whether it's a good one or not," she
said. "Let me see your hands, Marcel." She dropped down on
one knee in front of him.
"Anna Bella, go."
"Seems like you haven't heard then," she said. "No, I guess
you haven't since I asked Michie Christophe not to tell you,
and since I made Richard promise he wouldn't tell you, and
I never wrote to you and told you myself." The cuts weren't
deep, but they were bleeding wildly. "Felix!" she cried out.

She couldn't know that the slave was standing aghast in the wreck of the back bedroom, surveying the broken lamp, the kerosene that had sunk into the carpet and eaten the wax from the floor. The windowpane was broken out, the mirror cracked and dark smears of blood streaked the carpet's gray flowers that writhed beneath the bed's fancy skirts. He pulled the pillow from beneath the coverlet and brought the case to her. Women knew how to tear cloth better, they found some weak spot, nipped it with their teeth. And then...as he bent to shovel the coal in the grate he heard the sharp rip.

"I got to go now, Missie," he said a moment later when he had the fire started, and he could see Marcel was sitting quietly as she bandaged his hand.

"Ah!" she let out a little groan as she climbed to her feet. The fire was quickening with the few sticks he had placed under the coals.

"Where you going, Felix," she asked, "back up to the St. Louis Hotel?"

He nodded. That's where he is, Missie, was what he knew he was saying.

"You tell your master one thing for me," she said. "You tell him Anna Bella will be praying for him tomorrow, that she's been praying for him all along."

"I'll tell him afterward, Missie," he said. "So as not to worry him one way or the other."

She smiled.

She saw him out and shut the door.

For a long time she merely watched Marcel who was sitting there with the palms of his hands wrapped in white. Then she came around again in front of him and dropped down slowly, sitting under her voluminous skirts on her heels.

"You want to hold on to me?" she whispered. "Just for a little while?"

He shook his head. But he was losing control again. "I want to kill them," he was barely able to articulate. "I want to kill them all."

There was nothing to do but wait. Perhaps there was food in the back kitchen, but it was bolted from the inside. And some bits of fruit which she had found, lovely hothouse peaches almost too ripe, he simply let lie there where she had cut them and arranged them on a plate. The bread was old, the wine as good as ever, and he drank a little of that from time to time as he watched the fire, and the clock above it, its painted face showing the hour of six, then seven, and eight. Her breasts were heavy with milk, so now and then, secretly she pressed her arms against them, as if she were merely clasping her hands and stiffening, he would never guess. While meantime, back at her little house in the Rue St. Louis, Idabel, that sweet young slave girl she'd bought from the mart in the Rue Canal, was taking good care of little Martin with cow's milk and a sugar tit.

It had been five months since she had seen Michi Vince, five months since he had walked out her door, and five months since his lawyers had come round to tell her she must put her affairs in their hands, that there would be regular deposits for her at the bank. But she had led an independent life from then on, managing her own money, thank you, Monsieur. And drawing on the small pension left to her by Old Captain and the remnants of her father's property, she seldom touched the money Michie Vince left for her on account. Once it occurred to her to take it out, and redeposit it in her son's name. But she had never brought herself to do that, and the fact was, as the months passed and the love for Michie Vince and the longing for Michie Vince were alchemized totally into pain, she didn't think of little Martin as Michie Vince's child anymore.

And it seemed at times when she woke in the night thinking of him wanting him, that she clung to the misery of missing him because it shut another worse suffering out. If he was gone forever, if he was never coming back, then she would want Marcel again, Marcel, whose dreams had been shattered, Marcel, who was bitter and penniless and wouldn't be Michie Rudolphe's poor relation, and who would suffer again when he learned that his walk to *Bontemps* had forced Michie Vince out of her life. But he hadn't done it, really. She had done it, the night she had not gone to Michie Vince when he stepped into that room. When he stood silently in her parlor waiting for the slightest word. Often, so often, she had thought of those moments, and one image only would illuminate for her the reason for her silence: it was that of the little baby in her arms.

Now all such personal considerations had left her. They had been obliterated in her for days. She thought of nothing so simple and so self-serving as she sat still in the little dining room, her hands clasped, watching the tall man by

the fire, this man whose height had so astonished her when
Felix had brought him in, this man whom Marcel had become. And who was the boy, Marcel, very much still. She
was thinking listlessly and morbidly, rather, of Marie Ste.
Marie shivering and sobbing they said with Dolly Rose behind closed doors. And lamps everywhere in Dolly's room
burning all night long because Marie couldn't endure the
dark, Marie who just kept crying and wouldn't eat the slightest morsel of food. She had driven her hand right down into
the water pitcher, feeling all around, before she would even
trust the clear water which she then held to the light. Marie
who at the sound of her brother's name had put her hands
over her ears and begun to scream.

And Richard, she was thinking of Richard, too, locked in
that attic bedroom with its barred windows on the roof, trying
again and again to break that cypress door. "Did you hear,"
Marie Anais that pretty quadroon had said, "they tried to go
in last night, he knocked his father to the floor. Took all
three of the Lermontant men to hold him, even the old
grandpère, but they got him locked up again."

And Michie Vince, what about Michie Vince, who just
might get killed at dawn? Yesterday she had been crying
over all of it, bawling, her rosary beads in her hands. And
at some indeterminate hour—she had never thought to look
at the clock—she had felt a dread so palpable, so sudden, and
so abysmal that she had cried out. She had risen, frozen for
a moment, staring into the air. And then rushing to little
Martin's crib, grabbed him up in her arms. But he was all
right, little Martin, sleepy, glad to be against her breast. Yet
the sense of danger was all about her, hovering like a presence unseen. And three hours had passed before they came
to tell her, her neighbor, Madame Lucy, and then pretty
Marie Anais from the cottage across the street: Michie Vince
had just fought a duel with Alcee LeMaitre, the son of a
wealthy planter of the same parish as himself, and it was
LeMaitre who had fired the first shot, singeing the hair right
from Michie Vince's temple; then Michie Vince had taken
his turn. Only then had that sense of danger dissipated, and
only then had Anna Bella known that as glad as she was for
Michie Vince, she was trembling with relief that this dread
that had so gripped her had not signaled a threat to Marcel.

Now what was there to say to him? What was there to do?
He might sit all night as he was sitting now, could she per-

suade him perhaps to come with her to her own house in the Rue St. Louis, or was it best just to stay here at his side?

She rose now wearily but quickly, and commenced to straighten the rear rooms. She swept up broken glass with the torn pillowcase, and brought a lighted lamp back with her to the parlor where she found him unchanged.

But just when her heart was sinking and she was not sure he wanted her there, he put his hand out and slipped it into hers. She looked at the bandage which was white still, clean. And resolved to sit there for as long as he needed her, even if it were the whole night.

There was a knock at the door. It opened before she could even rise, and Christophe came, without a word, into the room. Marcel's eyes never moved from the fire.

"Did you talk to her?" he asked quietly.

"She won't see me. It's too soon," Christophe said. "It's just too soon."

Marcel merely sighed.

"And you, *ma chère,* how are you?" Christophe said gently. And reaching out took Anna Bella by the shoulders. He kissed her on both cheeks. "I'm very glad to see you here."

"Michie Christophe, this boy's got to eat something, I figure, though you'd never get him to allow that, if you just help me get that kitchen open, I'm sure there's yams or something inside."

Christophe nodded.

Neither of them took note of Marcel's slight alteration of expression. The bolt on the outside of the kitchen was simple, you could lift it with one hand.

"That shouldn't be any problem," Christophe said, and having started to peel off his leather gloves, he put them back on.

"No, it's locked from the inside, we've got to pry it, get a fence post..." Anna Bella explained. She had already started for the back door.

"Locked from the inside?" Marcel murmured. "Locked from the inside?"

"You just sit there, rest yourself, don't start those hands to bleeding..." Anna Bella said.

"But you can't lock it from the inside unless you're in it," Marcel said. And the three of them were struck suddenly and silently by the same thought.

Marcel rose. His eyes narrowed, his jaw set.

(580)

"Now, don't...don't do anything wild or crazy!" Anna Bella whispered. "If she's in there, she's drunk."

"She's in there!" he said and started for the back door.

They had caught up with him before he reached the kitchen and it was true, the heavy rough-hewn wooden door was shut tight. Rain was coming down in silver needles all around them, blown directionless by the wind. Christophe drew a knife from his pocket and popped open a long blade. He was able to pry the wood loose just enough to get a good grip on it with his hand.

"Now, be still, just wait..." Anna Bella took hold of Marcel. "You give her a chance to tell, you just don't know..." she whispered. But the door yawned back on utter darkness, and pulling loose from her and brushing aside Christophe, Marcel rushed inside.

"Lisette!" he said. "Lisette!" And then they both heard him gasp. He staggered backwards with his hand over his mouth.

Christophe could see nothing in the dark and then coming forward, step after step, he too felt the sudden heavy shape which had hit Marcel softly in the face. His hand groped before him. And he felt the coarse wool stocking of Lisette's leg. She was hanging from the rafters, her feet already curling up.

II

DOLLY ROSE RAISED the back of her hand to her eyes as she entered the room. Lamps blazed on the dresser, reflected brilliantly in the polished mirror; they blazed on the tables, atop the armoire, beside the bed. "You can go," she said to her maid, Sanitte, as she looked down at Marie crouched in the far corner against the wall. Marie wore a soft silk dressing gown which Dolly had given her, threaded with lavender ribbon at the neck. She would not look at her own clothes. Dolly's maids had found dresses in the cottage, where there was no one to stop them, but Marie had screamed when she saw them, screamed as she had at the mention of her brother's name. Marcel had cried like a baby on the gallery, begging Dolly, let me see her, let me in.

"I can't, *cher*," Dolly had gently turned him away.

And as she stood looking down at this beautiful girl who

had crept into the far corner of the room, bringing her feet up under the beige silk of the gown, Dolly's eyes were softened with tears.

"Come, Marie," she said as she padded softly forward. She held a tray of food in her hand, the white meat of the chicken, slices of tomato, fruit. She set this down beside the bed, and dropping to a crouch, took Marie's hands.

Marie stared dully at the wall, at the skirts of the bed. Her eyes would not meet Dolly's and with one hand she drew her long flat black hair down over her face as if to hide herself from Dolly's gaze.

She was thinking that she had never known anyone in her life like Dolly, that all the world misunderstood Dolly, did not know Dolly's goodness, that Dolly was all the perfumed kisses of women at weddings and christenings and funerals, Dolly was verbena and lace and soft hands, the tickle of Gabriella's lashes when she whispered a secret, the touch of Celestina's hands on her hair. All things affectionate, yielding, ineffably sweet, that was Dolly, this woman whom everyone branded outcast, Dolly to whom she had wandered thinking well if I am ruined then I will go to Dolly, I will go the *cordon bleu* of ruined women. I will go to the illustrious DOLLY Dolly DOLLY Dolly DOLLY DOLLY ROOOOOSE!

But there was more to Dolly, something infinitely more vigorous about this affection which had never been a component of the affection Marie had known. Something self-appointed and self-sustained, unfettered by the estimation of others, yet without defiance, and Marie believed it, believed it, believed it when Dolly said, "You may stay here forever, safe in this room."

And the truth was Marie was terrified of the very reason that she had come here. That men could touch her again, that she should endure this as one of Dolly's girls was beyond comprehension, and yet this was why she had come. This was where she belonged. And Dolly didn't know how much she belonged here, no one knew, but Marie knew and stared dully past Dolly at the skirts of the bed.

But Dolly would not be refused.

"Come up here with me," she said. She lifted Marie's hand, tugging her gently to her feet. And leading Marie to the bed, she positioned her against the pillows, bringing the coverlet up over her lap. Then sitting next to her, Dolly showed her the plate.

Marie's eyes moved sluggishly over the white meat of the

(582)

chicken, she was reasoning that insects couldn't be hidden there, but the sight of the tomato with those writhing seeds forced her eyes away. Since she had come she had eaten nothing, drunk nothing but clear water, opaque liquids terrifying her because she was overcome with the horror that insects lurked beneath the surface, big brown roaches with floppy wings that would rise to crawl into her mouth as soon as her lips touched the glass. Or one of these might appear wobbling, flapping on the spoon. She could not bear the sight of milk or soup, nor meats drowned in gravy, and sitting now against the cream-colored pillows of Dolly's bed, the room ablaze with light, she was suddenly jarred by the sensation, no, the memory, that a man was trying to force her mouth open as he straddled her, his knee crushing her arm. She shuddered, sitting forward, turning away from Dolly Rose.

"Marie, tell me," Dolly insisted, "don't shut me out."

Could men do that? Had they done that? Her mouth was sealed shut as she covered it with her hand, her shoulders hunched, her mouth sealed shut again as it happened every time that sensation or memory came back to her. Her nostrils were filled with a personal stench, she was in that dim smoky light, a man's voice talking casually, almost tenderly to her, her teeth clenched, she began to shake.

"Marie, Marie," Dolly said softly. She felt Dolly's hand on her arm. "There is nothing so dreadful that you cannot tell me, that you cannot put this burden in my hands."

Oh, but that's where Dolly was so wrong! There was something she could never tell anyone, not even Dolly, something worse than that man straddling her, that pain as his knee bore down on her arm, much worse, something that rendered it all perfectly just, perfectly just and disenfranchised all rage, she was about to scream again.

But she had sunk down into the pillows. She curled up, her forehead pressed against Dolly's wool dressing gown, her eyes shut.

"I belong in this house," she whispered. "I belong in this house."

A heavy listless sigh escaped Dolly. The hand that brushed Marie's hair from her forehead was warm, light.

Don't feel sorry for me, don't feel pity for me, Marie thought dully, her eyes half-mast as she stared forward, the green of Dolly's gown a pulsing blur. But I can't go across the yard, can't let those men, I...I...And without realizing

(583)

it, she had rolled on her face and away from Dolly, burrowing her head into the pillow, forehead moving back and forth as if she meant to bore through the bed.

"Marie, stop this!" Dolly grabbed her suddenly, lifting her. Marie gasped.

"Listen to me," Dolly turned her roughly, shaking her back and forth, her head bobbing on her neck. "You must talk to me, you must let it out!"

Marie's head fell to the side. She whispered, "I want to die."

"No," Dolly's eyes were glassy, her lips trembling. "You don't want to, *ma chère*, you don't want to die. They haven't killed you, they haven't touched you, not you!" And that hand, always so gentle, touched the well between Marie's breasts. "Now, listen to me, the day you came here, you talked to me, you told me what they'd done..."

Marie drew herself up, a shriek rising behind her clenched teeth.

"...you've got to let it out like that now, again. It's a wound that must be lanced, the poison must be let to drain away..."

"I didn't know then, I didn't know," Marie whispered, the words barely escaping her lips, her eyes rolling listlessly to the side.

"What, Marie!" Dolly pleaded. "What didn't you know?" Her hand enfolded the back of Marie's head and brought her close. "Don't you see, *ma chère*, they can't make you into something by what they did, they can't make you into what they say." Her voice was low, the words carefully emphasized. "They take the pen in hand, they write the play for us, they tell us to take the parts, *placée*, white protector, virgin girl. But we can turn our backs on it, we can take the pen from their hand. We are free really, free to live as we want to live." Her lips pressed against Marie's hair. "We are alive, look at us, listen to the beat of our hearts, Marie..." she lifted Marie's chin in her hand. The girl was shuddering, the eyes struggling as if to peer through the heavy lids, and suddenly seeing Dolly, Marie drew up gasping, "No, no," backing away as if she might fall from the bed.

"Stop it, Marie." Dolly lifted her hand as if to slap her, but then her lips pressed together, the tears glimmering in Dolly's eyes. She took Marie by the shoulders and again she shook her hard.

"No, no!" Marie's mouth fell open, the cry coming louder

and louder, "They knew, they knew, they knew when they saw me, stop it, Dolly, they knew, that's why they did it to me!" she was screaming, the voice rising, dying, rising again. "Don't you see, I deserved it!" she roared, "I deserved what happened to me!"

Dolly stared at her uncomprehending, holding her still. The girl was sobbing in her tight grasp, the head thrown back, the body heaving as she repeated those words again and again. "Why, *chère,* why, how could you say such a thing! Talk to me. Marie, tell me!" And desperate, she clutched Marie to her so that Marie's head fell against her own.

The lips were moving there, the words so low, rapid, feverish that Dolly couldn't hear. "I can't stand it any longer, I can't stand it any longer," came the rough panting breaths, and then Marie, exhausted, hysterical, turned her lips to Dolly's ear.

Dolly was staring forward, listening. At first her brows puckered and then gradually her eyes opened wide. "O God, *chère,"* she whispered. "Oh, *bébé,"* she whispered, the tears slowly welling from her eyes. "Poor innocent baby," she cried.

"But Dolly," Marie lifted her head, looked at Dolly, the whisper thin, shuddering, "don't you see, I felt those things every time Richard...I felt them even in my dreams, and they knew when they saw me, they *knew!* They knew they could do that to me!"

She didn't see Dolly shake her head, she didn't see the tears slipping down Dolly's cheeks. She only felt the hands that stroked her hair back from her forehead, the warm body next to her and she knew that at last, at last she had confessed it, she had told someone why she deserved no pity, no love, why it had happened, and limp she lay finally in Dolly's arms. Dolly rocked her back and forth, she felt the rise and fall of Dolly's breath. And then as if from some vast distance came Dolly's voice, simple devoid of guile or solicitude, saying only, "Now I understand, *ma chère,* now we have a place to begin."

III

SIX O'CLOCK AND MARCEL was gone. The windows graying, the sound of a rooster over the back fence. An hour ago, he had risen from the bed, silently, slipping into his clothes. "Don't go out there," Anna Bella had whispered. *"Must* go!" he had said. For a long moment they had embraced, her arm encircling his slender chest, her head against his warm neck. And when their lips met, all the night's desperate intimacy overwhelmed her again. But he had taken his leave, kissing the tips of her fingers as gently, he let them go. It seemed only minutes ago the sound of his horse at a gallop had left the yard.

But here it was six o'clock, a cart lumbering through the Rue St. Louis, bumping over the deepening ruts, and the clock on the mantel tinking the hour when Michie Vince just might, just might die. Martin stirred beneath the airy lace of his broad wicker bassinet, so that Anna Bella moved it subtly, the wheels not even making the slightest creak.

She rose, pulling her silk peignoir over her flannel gown and taking her rosary with her, tiptoed to the chair.

How long did it take to do these things, fire one shot, two shots? For somebody deliberately to die. And what would Marcel do, what would he do if Vincent were the one to fall? Anna Bella moaned, eyes shut, bent almost double in the chair.

Far off, a heavy bell echoed the tiny clock, and from all the kitchen gardens round came the same monotonous clarion of the rooster, faint, repetitive, dull. Little Martin cried beneath his lace, and the wicker basket began to rock. With the rosary still in hand, Anna Bella gathered him up before he could begin to howl. Moving the silk back from her breast, she felt his firm little sucking mouth close on it, hard and big though it was with all the night's milk that he had not drunk while she was gone. It was soothing that soft sucking, soothing to the ache in the breast, and a sympathetic trickle now flowed from the other side which she had to press firmly with her hand.

When the clock tinked the half hour, the baby was dozing, and Anna Bella had reached the fifth of the Sorrowful Mysteries of the rosary, "The Crucifixion," her hand moving silently over the beads as the words of the Hail Mary went through her mind. How long would it be before there came that knock to tell her, would it be her neighbors, Madame Lucy or pretty Marie Anais, or would it be Marcel! The windows were a cold blue by the time the clock struck seven and the rain came in splinters of glass in the gleam beyond the clouds.

Knock, knock, for the love of God, somebody knock! But what she had never expected was the sound of the key in the door. She shut her eyes, teeth biting into her lip at the sound of those boots. It was unmistakable. "Michie Vince!" she whispered. "Michie Vince!" she cried out. Closing the peignoir under a slumbering Martin she carried the baby with her into the front room.

Vincent was a shadowy figure at the mantel, his hair sleek and shining from the rain. She saw the glimmer of light in his eye first and then his face fully illuminated by the flowing window as he came toward her, his deepset black eyes fixing on the configuration of the infant in the blanket in her arms. The child's ivory face shone against the snow-white of the wrappings, eyelashes beautifully long, the features in their sixth month exquisitely formed.

Anna Bella's lip would not stop quivering, and she saw the tears veritably dropping on the child's head. She let out a little moan as Vincent kissed her forehead and quite suddenly he crushed her against him, the child against his chest. He was cold all over, cold hands, cold cheek, the clothes smelling of winter and wind, and rain.

For a long time she just let him be.

But even after she had gotten off his wet boots and put the coffee to heat and made the fire, still he hadn't spoken. He could see that she was crying; he could tell from her warm hands that took his head and pressed it against her the depth of her pain and relief.

Even when Martin awakened again, he did not speak. He followed her into the bedroom and watched her put the baby to her breast. Finally, it was she who broke the silence.

"Is that Henri DeLande, is he...?"

Vincent nodded. He was looking at the child. He did not tell her that Henri DeLande had been shot stupidly, miserably in the stomach, and that it had taken him twenty minutes to die. They didn't attempt to move him, and he couldn't have endured the pain. Nineteen years old and blinded by the rain, the boy's own shot had gone wild.

It seemed he wanted to take the baby from her. She herself was looking down at the puckered rounded little lids, the long lashes, moist-matted, and the tiny mouth. She was trying to see what Vincent saw, a skin as fair as her own, the hair softly curled, the dimpled hand opening and closing as if in thought. Now, as if perceiving that a stranger was near, Martin jerked loose from the breast and stared at Vincent. And when he saw no smile on Vincent's face, when

Vincent stared at him with the same seriousness with which the baby stared at him, little Martin began to scream.

"Hush, now, don't you do that." Anna Bella pushed him back to the breast. "He doesn't mean anything by that," she said. "He just doesn't know who you are!"

But Vincent's face was stricken. And he stood up turning away from her and his shoulders commenced to heave with an awful silent crying that seemed to shake him completely and to shake the room. Anna Bella watched, helpless. It was as if some great strong dam had been broken and Vincent's entire body was shattered by the release while vainly he struggled against it, unable and unwilling to give it voice.

Finally Anna Bella put the baby down, finding the sugar tit hastily among the covers, and turned her attention to the man.

But turning his back to her as he sank down on the side of the bed, he would not face her until he was still.

"Anna Bella," he said, "Anna Bella, I came here to tell you I was sorry, sorry that it ended the way it did. To tell you myself that I would always provide for you, and for the baby, but that you would never see me again. It was wretched having my lawyers tell you these things. It was wretched of me to put it, as I did, in legal hands." It seemed he was going to lose his restraint again, but he took his linen handkerchief and wiped impatiently at his lips. That simple gesture sustained him.

"All of this...these Ste. Marie children, the boy coming to *Bontemps* as he did, and now the girl...it should never have happened!" he insisted. "I mean these children, they should never have been! My brother-in-law was an evil man, selfish and lacking in fiber because he did not care for anyone but himself. It was carelessness and carnality that produced that family, and left it, penniless, to fend for itself. Anna Bella, you and I...that baby...it should never have happened either. It's wrong! I tell you it should never have happened no matter how great the loneliness, and how great finally...the love!" He stopped. She had her arm about his shoulder, had been holding him all this time, but at his slightest gesture she would have let him go. Her face was mellow and thoughtful, but why, he could never guess. She was thinking of her own reservations, of the day she had gone to the *garçonnière* and made Marcel take the decision in his hands. Only the slight turning of his head, the pressure of his hand against the small of her back brought her back to this moment. "I understand, Michie Vince," she said.

He appeared softly handsome to her as he sat there, the morning sun at last warming the windows beyond him, his face slightly gaunt from sleep, eyes touched with sadness like those of a much older man. And a strange thought came to her as she watched him, that he had killed three men in two days, and the last not more than two hours ago. And yet it was not this that tormented him. He did not even think of it now. She looked at the slender white hand, nails trimmed so neatly, that lay upon his knee and thought of this hand holding the pistol, pulling the trigger back. "I understand, Michie Vince," she murmured, feeling some dull sorrow for her own awakened desire. She was straining to understand the allure of his power, the infinite power and freedom that infused that elegant hand, that white brow. "I understand."

"But you see, if I had come back to you to tell you myself, I was afraid I wouldn't be able to walk out that door. Anna Bella, I've needed you so much. I have loved you so much. God, why did I ever do this to you, why did I do it to myself?"

"Don't make me cry again, Michie Vince," she whispered. He drew her close, his left hand pressing her, urging her as if he wanted her to pass out of herself and into his very flesh. His right hand felt the roundness of her cheek as if he could not get over it, the texture, as the skin, firm and silken, resisted the press of his thumb.

"I don't know if I can leave you, Anna Bella," he spoke into her ear. "But by God, I cannot bring another child into this, I cannot!"

She sighed. She was looking past him at the sun on the window, the windy shifts of the golden rain. She was thinking of all those times before when he had fallen silent, brooding and haunted, and had held her tight like this in a wordless anxiety when it was time for them to part, and she knew that if she continued to think of that, more that than all he was saying to her now, she could not keep herself from yearning toward him with her whole soul.

But it was past, it was over! Over before the death knell had been dealt it in this very bed last night.

"Michie Vince," she said looking into his eyes. "You don't want me and you don't want this!"

"Lord God, if only they weren't one and the same!"

"But they are, and you don't want it, and you don't want

(589)

that little baby there in that crib. You can't even look at it or touch it, you can't claim it as your own."

He could not deny this, he could only draw up into himself now, turning away from her, his clasped hands thrust between his knees.

"What are you asking of me," she said softly, "that I try to change your mind? That I make this bed soft for you again, so there will be nothing but misery for you now and in some part of your life till the end of your days?"

She could see his eyes warming with a curious light that she had often seen in them in the past.

"You've never done anything but right by me, have you, Anna Bella?"

"Michie," she sighed. "I want to do right by us all."

"But you never thought for a moment that I would let that child want . . . that I would let you want?" he asked.

She made a quick negation with her head. It had been a rhetorical question. He was making the only gesture with regard to little Martin that he could.

His voice was measured, calm now as he commenced to speak, there was an air of relief about him as though his struggle were past. He took Anna Bella's hand and looked at it.

"I want him to be educated. And I want him to leave this place when he's old enough, perhaps when he's twelve, thirteen, before he's a man. I want him to live somewhere on this earth where the races can achieve some amalgamation, or at least some peace . . . The legal precautions I have taken for you and him cannot be overturned by a probate court, and they are known to others in my family who will protect them, if or when I die, on your behalf."

Her large slow brown eyes lingered on his face, and he did not perceive that as they left it, they moved over him remotely, dispassionately, as if seeing the entire man that he was.

"No, Michie Vince," she said quietly.

Startled, his expression sharpened, his brows knit.

"Michie Vince," she said, "I know you're one of the finest men I've met, and I may live my whole life through without knowing your kind again. But I'm not rearing my baby boy to go to France because you want him to, I'm not filling his childhood with dreams of some rosy world where he can be a man. I'm teaching him to be a man right here, Michie Vince, where his mamma grew up and where he was born.

I'm teaching him how to live among his people right here in the world they've made for themselves. And someday, someday if that boy wants to seek his fortune in another country, well, I'll be the first to give him a helping hand. But nobody's taking him away from me before that time, and nobody's teaching him to despise what he is."

He was quietly stunned. He looked down at her, the level brown eyes, the large silken mouth that was quite still.

"But don't you worry, Michie Vince," she said. "He'll know his father was a fine white gentleman who provided for him always, but he won't know your name."

It stung him those words. He was incredulous. He studied her as if he could not believe that she had meant to hurt him and then he perceived that, indeed, she had not. And a peculiar thought struck him for which he was not prepared. He didn't turn his head to the sleeping child in the bassinet but he thought of him, saw him, and it penetrated to him for the very first time that this was, indeed, his own child! And it penetrated for one simple reason. She had just told him, reasonably enough, that she would do with that child what she, and she alone, thought best.

He rose slowly, letting her hand go with deliberate gentleness and found himself stranded in the center of the room. All around was the dull roar of the sunny rain, and she was sitting quite collected there before him, her pretty silk peignoir tied modestly at the throat, her ivory-white hands clasped over her knee.

"That's what you want," he said softly.

And as she spoke now she reminded him of another raw and painful moment which had occurred for him not so very long ago. In fact the feel of that moment, its undefined confusion descended upon him as she said, "Michie, I don't expect you to understand this, but this place, right here and now, is that baby's home."

He did not leave abruptly. He was aware that that would have been entirely wrong. It would have left an edge on things that he himself could not have borne. She followed him into the parlor, she smoothed his cape for him as he slung it over his shoulders, she put his boots before him and waited, her arms folded, and then accompanied him to the door.

He had thought this would be a painful moment. Wrenching, terrible, the inevitable price of seeing her again. And he wondered if she had thought so, too. But he could not reach the great swell of love he felt for her, or rather it could not reach him. But then looking to her bravely, expecting nothing more than that dispassionate face, he saw instead those tears welling again in her eyes. He saw her bite her lip, and he saw her head incline helplessly to the side.

"I love you, Michie Vince," she whispered.

And he felt that tidal wave rising in him, and he knew it was really, really the end. "*Ma belle* Anna Bella," he whispered, holding her, and then kissing her once more and forever he moved blindly and doggedly out the door.

A sleepy little Idabel came in from the kitchen, her flat and lanky twelve-year-old body done up prettily in a maid's blue serge with white apron. She was sable in color, her tightly kinked hair drawn back to a little bun with two pins. She set the coffee down on the table, looking at her mistress's bowed head, face hidden by her arms.

"Shush that baby, will you, honey, hold him for a little while?" Anna Bella said in English.

"Why you crying, Missie?" the child asked.

"Never mind, honey, but if you were to hush that baby, I'd feel a lot better, would you do that now?"

Idabel picked him up easily, "What are *you* crying about?" she said with a scowl, bouncing him as she made a small circle in the room. "Missie, that colored man was here," she said. "I mean that colored gentleman, you know the one."

Anna Bella lifted her head, eyes squinting at the wet and glaring light from the windows. "What are you talking about, Idabel?"

"That colored gentleman, Missie, with the blue eyes. He come riding in while Michie Vince was here, he was soaked to the bone. He come to the back door and he ask, was that white man here? I told him I didn't know anything about any white man, and he says, 'Well, you tiptoe to the door and see.' Then he just went away, Missie, got on his horse, soaked through and rode off."

The little girl stopped, the baby shushed and playing with the buttons of her dress.

"Now, don't cry Missie, don't cry!" she said with a fearful rise in her voice. But then she just stood there, her lips pressed together, watching her mistress's shoulders shake as Anna Bella buried her sobs in her arms.

III

IT WAS ALMOST DARK. And the steamboats blazed along the levee, passengers scurrying toward these lights in a thin gray rain. Marcel stood on the high deck outside the stateroom, the rain cutting his face, his eyelids, cutting his hand on the rail. He was about to turn toward the open door when Tante Louisa emerged, turning her back to the icy wind off the water so that she might catch her cape around her with both hands. She drew near to him, head inclining toward him, and to avoid this moment, he attempted to break away. But she caught his hand.

"You're not going to leave your Maman like this. Not after all the things you said to her, Marcel, when will you see her again?"

His face was tense. It had been an awful battle, and in some dreadful way it had been the worst of his life. He could remember little of what really passed between them now, only that Tante Louisa and Tante Colette had tried to prevent him from seeing her and that he had threatened to break down the door of her room. She had run from him, hidden her face from him, denied his accusations, refused to answer his questions, and at last she'd begun to scream. "I did it for you, I did it for you," she had roared over and over, and at last, forced to the far corner of the room and cowering, she had weakened so that he had taken her arms and looked into her eyes. He would never forget that moment, never forget the moment of turning from her and seeing the two of them, his aunts, with that same terrified expression. And he had known then that all his words were wasted words, all his anger lost. They simply could not understand what had happened, they simply could not understand what they had done. They were staring at him as if he was a madman, and with the same maddening practicality with which Colette had first told him "the whole story," she had commenced again to talk to him plainly, idiotically, then. He ought to leave his mother alone now if he had any decency in him, and he ought never, never to mention his sister's name to her again. All the outrage had drained out of him at that moment. He had turned to the shivering little woman who seeing him towering over her raised her arms to shelter her head. He had thought clearly, calmly, this is my mother, this is the woman who bore me. And silently he had walked out of the room.

That he would eat nothing, drink nothing, say nothing in their flat after that, that he would not touch them, or allow himself to be touched did not come to him as a decision at all. He had gone through the motions of taking Louisa and his mother to the steamboat dock in silence, and now he wondered as he stood there on the deck that Louisa meant to provoke his tenuous control.

The whistle sounded above, mercifully, and he removed his hand from hers without a word. His mother was standing in the stateroom door. He watched her dully as she came toward him and put her hands on his lapels. He did not draw back though he wanted to draw back, and his eyes felt to him as if they were made of lead.

"Remember," she said, "the cottage is yours now. But don't sell the cottage unless you have to. And if you have to, go ahead." She was not looking at him as she repeated this refrain. "And what you gain from it, you keep," her head moved emphatically. "I will be quite all right where I am."

He nodded. You will be quite all right, he thought coldly, and I will never see Tante Josette again. I will never set eyes upon her, or *Sans Souci* as long as you are there. And you will die there, the money you possess—the pittance left in Monsieur Philippe's pockets—will be a fortune for you in the country and provide for all those little expenses, gifts for birthdays or weddings, store-bought fabric, pins for your hair, all you will ever need among that infinite procession of aunts and cousins and nieces and nephews until the end of your days. And of course you will grow old with your whatnots, your jewelry, all that fine jewelry, and all those lovely clothes. You'll grow old with these things rapidly, hands forever busy with the sewing you have always so detested, making an endless round of First Communion lace, collars, scarves, doilies for the backs of chairs. And all around you, every time you turn your head, you will be confronted with men of color married to women of color, which you have always abhorred to the marrow of your bones. But no one will ask your views of these matters, no one will even care. You will simply be old Tante Cecile, proud old Tante Cecile, bent over her needle, with her graying hair.

She was old even now as she stood beneath the cabin door, the rain drenching the rim of her bonnet with its persistent thin torrent, and putting her hands to her ears to shield herself from the deafening whistle, she had a slowness about her, a vagueness that he had never before seen. "You will come to *Sans Souci?*" she whispered, blinking at the wet boards of the deck before her, her head listing slightly as if she felt some nagging pain.

"Marcel!" Louisa's voice pleaded. "Marcel! Tell your mother you'll come to see her, tell her farewell."

"And what shall I tell my sister for both of you?" he gasped suddenly, his eyes wide. "Tell me. What am I to say to my sister for both of you?"

His mother lifted her head. The dark eyes were suddenly brilliant in the deep brown face, and the lips drew back slowly from her white teeth. "You tell her for me," came the guttural voice, "I wish to hell she was dead!"

"God help you," he whispered. "God help you both."

Tante Louisa's shrill voice sang out over the deck, over the crowded stairway, over the mounting passengers and the rushing wind. But within seconds he could no longer hear her, he was rushing across the lower deck and down the gangplank to the shore.

Quickly, he had crossed the Rue Canal and one blast after another sounded from the great steamboats so that it was not possible to distinguish one from another, and he was in his own streets on the way home.

Home. It was Christophe's house he entered, and it was Juliet who took his coat and his cravat. She offered her soft cheek to him, innocently, and left him quite alone as she had all week long. He had thought it self-sacrificing of her at first, for surely she had burned for him in his absence as he had burned for her. But in the last few days it was apparent that she was not so aware of him as, at some other time, he might have wished.

Then roses had come for her yesterday, and he had seen boxes of sweets about, fancily wrapped. But when Christophe told him Augustin Dumanoir *père,* the colored planter, was now visiting her, Marcel had merely smiled. So that, too, is over, he had thought dryly.

Well, perhaps it's time. And he felt no guilt then for the violent and beautiful night with Anna Bella, when at last possessing that young and resilient flesh he had possessed *her,* Anna Bella, bittersweet in his grief. It had been as barbarous and tender as anything he might ever have dreamed. She smelt of flowers and springtime while death lay all around.

And what had happened afterwards? He had come back

those long wet miles from the Metairie Oaks, having watched those tiny figures from the concealing dark, to find Dazincourt there! He pushed it down, unexamined, to the deepest dungeon of his conscious thoughts.

But now as he watched his former mistress mount the stairs, as he saw her smile, one eye closing in a languid wink, he had a strange sweet feeling that unlike so many things in this world she was not quite gone forever, not lost with all the other exquisite and pure things of childhood, beyond his reach. However, he had the distinct impression, tinged with foreboding actually, that he would not of his own will reach out for her again.

He waited until he could no longer see the hem of her dress or her tiny ankle, and then he walked back the hall.

A blast of comfortable warmth greeted him as he opened the reading room door.

But in the shadows near the window beyond the illumination of the fire, there stood a tall figure that Marcel knew for certain was Richard, could be none other than Richard though the figure had its back to the door. He was unprepared for the sudden anxiety Richard's presence aroused in him, the bitter and destructive emotion not unlike that which had prompted him to break the Lermontant window in plain view of an uncomprehending crowd. He threw one desperate and weary glance at Christophe as he moved on into the room.

"He wants to see your sister," Christophe said.

Richard turned slowly, the high collar of his cape half concealing his face.

"Why?" Marcel asked.

"I've explained to him that she won't see anyone, that she will not even see you," Christophe said. And then with a pointed glance at Marcel, he produced a letter from his breast pocket. And seeing the expression on Christophe's face, Marcel's lips pressed into an involuntary and bitter smile.

That morning Marcel had outlined a brief but detailed plan to Christophe of how he might take Marie away. He proposed to sell the cottage and its furnishings, taking her abroad were the funds sufficient, or at least to Boston or New York. Christophe had immediately added his small fortune to this, two hundred dollars remaining of the money left him by the Englishman, and a small amount received for the right to adapt *Nuits de Charlotte* for the Paris stage. It would be a difficult life, steerage, scant meals, rented rooms. And then subsistence on a clerk's wages when Marcel secured a position in time. But it was the only hope Marcel had. And Christophe had gone to Dolly's this afternoon with the proposal, and to assure Marie that her mother was on her way upriver, Marie need never see her mother again.

But now Christophe's face gave Marcel the answer, and here it was written in Marie's own hand:

> I shall always love you, however, nothing is required of you except that you forget your sister so that she may cease to worry about her brother. I am content where I am.

> Marie

Marcel reflected for a moment, absorbing what he had sensed to be inevitable and then he passed this note to the tall figure in the corner of the room. Richard merely stared at it, and then appeared to take it with reluctance, eyes averted slightly, as if afraid. In fact, his face was rigid with fear. The paper quavered slightly, and then he returned the note to Marcel.

"I want to see her," he said.

"Why!" Marcel demanded again.

"She won't see you, *mon fils*," Christophe said. "And if you were to see her, you would find her much changed." He glanced at Marcel, his face mildly agitated with concern.

"Then you have seen her yourself," Marcel whispered.

"She's much recovered," Christophe sighed. "Last night she appeared in the parlor of Dolly's house for the first time. Only for a short while, however, and she returned alone to Dolly's room. But she did appear there, causing a mild sensation as one might imagine, and she was very much admired."

Marcel couldn't conceal his reaction. He swallowed with effort and sitting at the round table, ran his hands back slowly through his hair.

"She means to stay with Dolly from now on," Christophe said. "I've heard this from her myself."

"I want to hear it from her!" Richard whispered.

"You do?" Marcel threw him a venomous glance. "And suppose she didn't want to stay there, suppose you didn't hear it from her yourself? What would you do? Take her out of there and announce the banns? Marry her at High Mass at the Cathedral and have all the Charleston cousins, and the

Villier cousins and the Vacquerie cousins and all the *Famille Lermontant!*"

"Marcel!" Christophe whispered with an emphatic shake of his head.

"I'm sorry," Marcel sighed. "If there is anyone who is blameless in this affair; it's you...But we cannot help each other now, you must spare me your presence, and I shall spare you mine."

Richard's only answer was silence. For a long moment he stood at the window, his eyes on the steamy panes. The rain had stopped, and the night and the room were perfectly still. And then slowly he crossed the room, his heavy boots making the faintest sound, and without a word he left.

Christophe was watching the fire.

"I was cruel to him, wasn't I?" Marcel said.

Christophe made a small gesture, Let it be.

"But did she...did she go into the parlor of Dolly's house?..." Marcel's voice faltered. He was going to cry again like a child if he went on, and seeing Christophe's nod, he turned away.

"Marcel, I don't expect you to understand this," Christophe murmured, "but this is not the worst fate that could have been visited on Marie. I think you remember the bitter and destructive human being that Dolly was before she chose her path. And in some very real way, that path for Dolly was a choice of life over death. Now she is offering that to your sister, and she will care for your sister, and again it just may be a choice of life over death."

It was more than Marcel could bear. He rose to go.

"But sooner or later, Marcel," Christophe said gently, "you must begin to think of yourself."

"Christophe, I cannot think of anything now, I cannot breathe."

"I understand that," Christophe answered, "but this situation with Marie is not likely to change. I don't know what could save Marie at this point, I don't know that anything will. But I do know that you must go on living, you cannot spend your life mourning her as if she were buried alive."

He urged Marcel to be seated at the table again and he commenced to speak to him steadily, calmly, in a low voice.

"Now you planned to sell the cottage," he said, "you planned to sell the furnishings, get what you could. And as you know, I have some two hundred dollars here of my own...."

"If Marie would have gone with me!" Marcel said, "I would have accepted then for her."

"I realize that. But I am asking you now to accept it for me! I am asking you to take this money and whatever you can get for your property and go on to Paris on your own. As soon as you arrive there I can send you money, each month I can send you money, I can send you enough that you could enter the university..."

"Christophe you are torturing me," Marcel said, "I cannot accept this and I will not."

However, Christophe was adamant. "But you do this for me, don't you understand?" he pleaded. "I've had my chance, Marcel, I know what it's like to live where I am not a man of color but simply a man. Now I want *you* to have that chance. Don't look away, Marcel, you must let me do it—for my sake as much as yours....I know this can be done if you only let me..."

Marcel rose abruptly as if again he meant to go.

"All my life," he said, looking down at Christophe, "I was taught that someone was going to give me my future, that Monsieur Philippe would provide me with my inheritance, send me to Paris in style. I heard it so often I came to believe I was entitled to it, that I was born to be a gentleman of means. Well, it was an illusion, and my expectation, my conviction that I could never be happy anywhere but in Paris has caused too much misery to me, it has caused too much misery to those I love.

"If I hadn't wandered off to *Bontemps* that day enraged because of Monsieur Philippe's broken promises, I wouldn't have been sent away to *Sans Souci*. I would have been here when Marie needed me, when my mother tried to get that dream for me again by using her. I would have been here to look out for her, I should have been looking out for her all along."

"If you blame yourself for this," Christophe said, "you are making a dreadful mistake."

"I don't blame myself. I know the world isn't that simple, that good and evil—as you once explained to me—are not that neat. What I'm saying is that I have pursued a certain path in vain. And it's time for me to change. It is time for me to make something of myself on my own. And when I do make that voyage to France, and I will make it, I will have earned it myself as well as the means to sustain myself when I am there.

(599)

"So you see no matter what happens to Marie, I can't accept your offer. And as long as Marie is with Dolly Rose, I must remain here."

IV

THERE WAS ALWAYS an excitement in the house at this hour, an excitement that you could feel. Even in the quarters you could feel it, the rushing steps along the galleries, the piano music echoing down the long hall so that when the back door opened, you could hear it in the yard. And under a clearing sky, the yard had been strung with lanterns so that the gentlemen could wander there, for the fresh air, in spite of the cold.

Dolly was dressed and beautifully dressed, in her favorite black velvet, placing the white camellias, with her own careful hands, in her hair. She had laced Marie, put two silver rings on Marie's fingers, and chosen the sprigged lavender silk dress at first, only to put this aside. "Royal blue," she said, "you must wear a strong color, a passionate color." Royal blue silk, the hem scalloped and studded with clusters of pearls. Bits of green ribbon flared from the clusters as if they were tiny leaves. Dolly pulled the small puffed sleeves down low from Marie's shoulders and turned Marie to the mirror so that she might approve. A deep cleft showed the fullness of Marie's breasts.

And when Dolly went off to the parlor of the big house for her *de rigueur* appearance—never very long—she left Marie alone in the blazing room. And then Marie went out quietly to walk under the stars.

It was a delicious coldness, the winter air. The bare limbs of the crepe myrtles glistened white under the moon while all about the ivy, still wet from the earlier rain, shivered on the high brick walls. It wound its way along the banisters of the big house, hanging down in drifts over the entrance of the carriageway, where it swayed lightly in the breeze as it scraped the ground. A man had come out on the porch above and seeing Marie below tipped his hat. She had watched him pass along the shuttered doors of the long rear wing that ran like an arm against one side of the darkened court; she knew his eyes were fixed on her, she could see the trace of a smile beneath his mustache. Again he tipped his hat before he disappeared into one of those long narrow rooms.

The music was fast. It seemed, even where she stood among the bare trees and the glimmering lanterns, she could hear the reverberations of the dancers on the boards. Horses clopped on the distant cobblestone street and the stars were dim behind the ghostly shapes of the drifting clouds. She wished now she had brought her glass with her. It would have been nice to feel the warmth of the wine. But she walked round and round, enjoying the sound of her heels on the flags, knowing she might go into the house tonight, that she might bring herself to do it, even though she had been so frightened the first time.

This was a new life, a new life, she said this to herself over and over. She had no history, no existence beyond this place. She would not even say the name Richard in her mind, she would not even picture him. All that was gone now, along with its miseries and its betrayals, its half-understood ecstasy, its love, this was a new life and—her mind went blank!

She wished suddenly that Dolly was with her.

If Dolly were with her, just for a few moments, then maybe, just maybe she could go into the parlor again. But at this moment, it seemed quite impossible that she had gone, on her own, the night before. What vague excitement had led her there, unannounced, as Dolly was waltzing wildly in a flurry of velvet with an old white man, his hair silver, his gestures graceful but self-satirical as he attempted to appear spry. The room had been a flicker of shadowy faces, dim candles, and ripping music. Women smiled at her from the dark edges of the carpet and men bowed their heads. She had slipped away to the corner of the dining room from which she might survey all unseen, but then that old man, having kissed Dolly's hand, had come toward her and she had felt herself stiffen as he sat by her side. There was something tender, doting, in his manner, but then she heard his breathing, too rapid beneath those enormous white whiskers, and there was the insistent pressure of his hand. She had felt panic then, *what am I doing here, Marie Ste. Marie in this room!* She didn't remember rushing out, she didn't remember crossing the yard.

But when Dolly had come to her, she had said, "Time is not important, you are safe with me here, but you will do it someday. You will do it because it's there waiting for you, and there will come that moment when you are bored and unhappy here, when you are restless, and you yourself want to leave this room." And Marie, strangely reassured, had fallen asleep in Dolly's arms.

Was she bored tonight? Was she restless? Was that why Marie had been so eager to dress, to wander out here alone in the yard? No, it was something else, something which Dolly had not yet begun to understand. Because Dolly didn't know that no one had ever loved Marie as Dolly loved her, nor how extraordinary was the warmth of that bed, the two of them together, those soft maternal touches, that candor, that delicacy, that trust. And revealing to Marie purely and so honestly the secrets of a woman's body, the passions to which all women were subject, be they sheltered or experienced, innocent or skilled, Dolly had led her farther and farther away from the voices of the past which had only deceived, distorted, betrayed. Marie wanted to please Dolly more than she had ever wanted to please anyone, and it was for this that she had come out tonight, for this reason that she wanted to go into the parlor again.

For though Dolly spoke of time and patience, Dolly really wanted this: that Marie be alive and happy, that Marie be born again with Dolly's freedom and Dolly's curiously guarded heart.

Yes, Marie was here for Dolly. But she could not do it suddenly. She could not move toward the big house. Not just now.

She bowed her head, and made a silent little promenade about the fountain until out of the corner of her eyes she saw in the carriageway, behind those drifts of ivy, the unmistakable figure of a tall man.

She turned away at once. She walked quickly towards the quarters. For one second she thought she imagined the boots thudding fast across the courtyard, but then she realized the man was after her, he had even come up behind her on the stairs. She ought to shout for Dolly's maid, Sanitte, she ought to shout for Dolly. But perhaps she was being foolish, and this was some regular visitor on business of his own. She rushed along the gallery, her cheeks burning, and just as she reached the door of her sanctuary, she felt his hand on her bare arm.

"Marie!" he whispered.

She gasped, shutting her eyes, "Let me go!" she said.

"Marie, it's me, Richard, please!" He stepped in front of her.

"Richard, go away from here," she whispered. "I'll scream if you don't go away, I'll scream now." She reached past him pushing open the bedroom doors. He followed her, letting them bang shut behind him, and when he saw where he was...the cluttered dresser, the huge unmade bed, he was obviously at a loss.

It seemed a hundred years since she had laid eyes on him. In all this time, she had not allowed herself even once to visualize him, and there he was, the majestic height, the dark hair curling over the heavy collar of his winter cape, his large brown eyes, tinged with sadness, surveying this garishly lighted room. He looked at the lamps atop the armoire, he looked at the lamps beside the settee, and as Marie settled in front of the dresser on the long padded bench, he looked at her. And then away.

"Why did you come?" she asked bitterly. "You cannot even look at me, so why did you come?"

His heavy lids lifted slowly and she could see the confusion in his face. But she did not know what he saw in hers. "Greatly changed," Christophe had told him. The words were pathetically inadequate, for sitting there with her long hair undone down her back, her bosom and arms bare in the glare of these lamps, she was as always perfectly beautiful. But the veil of serenity was gone from her eyes. Some new fire radiated from within. It was as if the young girl he'd known had been an unstamped coin, and here was the woman, eyes ablaze with some new passion infecting all of her features, and all of her manner, even to her posture on the bench, her elbow on the dresser, and head turned toward him almost arrogantly, her finger to her cheek. And all about her were the sumptuous trappings of Dolly's world, so like he had seen them in the big house the first time he had entered it when Dolly's little girl was dead.

"Richard," she said. "Go!"

"I had to see for myself," he said, meeting her gaze though it took all his strength not to pull himself away. "I had to know that it's your decision to stay here. I had to hear it from you." His face convulsed. Some awful sadness had come over him, looking at her.

"There's got to be someplace else for you," he stammered, "there are other places. Marcel has the cottage, you could go home..."

But this was nonsense. Her live in that cottage now? With people stopping as they passed to try to get a glimpse of her

(603)

from the gate? There would be the whispering and turning of heads every time she set her foot out the door. And what else? The inevitable familiarities from the rough men of the neighborhood who believed her tarnished and fair game? Why had he spoken such nonsense to her, what had he meant to say? That surely there was some answer, some way?

"Your aunt, Marie, in the country, the Cane River," he whispered desperately, shocked, as he gazed at her, by the incandescence of her wide black eyes.

"And what makes you think that she would have me, Richard? My mother and my aunts have disowned me and my mother and my aunt Louisa have gone to *Sans Souci*. I would die first before I'd live with them, and I assure you, they would never consent to live with me..."

"The nuns, then, Marie, the nuns..."

"Why, Richard, to make it easier for you?"

He had never heard such a voice from her, such a rapid and searing tone, quicker than his thoughts. Her voice had always been so tentative, so soft. He could not endure this much longer. He had not cried since he was twelve years old. But he was on the edge of it now.

And he turned his back. It was simply more than he could bear.

"Nuns, aunts...the country..." she said in that same quick voice. "Did you come here to let me know yourself that my life is finished in your eyes? That I am dead to you, so you wish that I would entomb myself? You're grieving for me, Richard, as if I had already passed from this earth, and indeed it would be easier for you, and for Marcel, were I to bury myself alive. Well, I have no such intention. You've done your duty, Richard. Go home."

He couldn't answer her now. He couldn't move. He stood there struggling against his tears as a much older man might who did not know how to give vent to tears at all.

"You know," she said softly behind him, "I have known love only twice in my life. Once with you...and then again here in this room. I never thought I'd find it here, I was crazy when I came here, but I found it nevertheless. And I have come to an appalling conclusion, Richard, that this love, this powerful sweet love, is something that others know in varied ways all their lives. They know it from mother and father and sisters and brothers, they feel it even from friends. My brother has basked in it ever since he was born. But I've never really known it except for those few moments when I was with you. And now I have it here with Dolly, day-to-day love, and affection, and care. Well, I'm through with the world of cruel and unfeeling women, their virtue or discretion does not impress me. I am not leaving here. You have it from me now, in my own words. So spare me your grief, take it away."

He was grieving for her, it was true. He was grieving for her and for himself, He was grieving for the Marie that had been and the Richard who had loved her, both of whom were now lost. But as he stood there staring at the wall before him, he was wishing desperately that the world were a place he could shape to his own choosing, that he could make his father and mother such that they would have to accept her were he to bring her home, and he could make himself such that he could stand up to them and to everyone around them and say she is going to be my wife. He wished that he could make himself the man who could take her out of here, and stand them off, all of them, no matter what were their proscriptions and their declarations.

But suppose he was that man and they were such malleable creatures that that great fortress of respectability, the Lermontant house, could be stormed? Could he do it? Could he love her again? Want to touch her? The very thought of it filled him with violent confusion, a violent revulsion for what had happened to her, and a longing for her at the same time so that he felt he was literally coming apart. Love her, he loved her more than ever, but it was over, finished, and he could not save her. Another man, another time in history, another family, perhaps...

He turned to face her. His eyes were fixed on her, and then gazing past her and beyond her so that he didn't see her at all. Rather he saw the frightening fire that emanated from her like the heat deep within a dark sealed stove, and he was not conscious of her rising or of her coming toward him. All the mingled sensations of a vast and endless funeral rite invaded his mind, with that awful sense of finality, the sheer futility of weeping, or making one's hand into a fist in the face of God.

Then clearly, completely, she came into view. She was standing in front of him. The arrogant posture had broken away because it had only been a guise and she was moving toward him as if some supernatural force moved her limbs.

He could not know what she was thinking; he couldn't know the terror that gripped her at the thought of touching any human being except Dolly, the fear in which she lived, slipping night after night in and out of nightmare, as those fragmented sensations from that long night of rape and cruelty came back to her unbidden, on their own. He couldn't know that she was thinking wildly, desperately, of how much she loved him, and that if she could just cross this space that separated them, if she could just touch him and feel his arms again, then maybe she could love again, live again, maybe even get out of this crazy world where she had become a child clinging to Dolly Rose.

"Richard," she whispered suddenly. "It's Marie. It's the same Marie! Nothing's changed in me, Richard," she said. "Don't you understand? They did this to me! I did not do it to myself. I am the same in my heart, and I love you..."

He stood rigid, his eyes closed. He could feel her hands on his arms, and feel her soft bosom pressed to his chest. But he couldn't move, he couldn't feel. And then suddenly, he held her. He almost crushed her against him. His lips pressed her eyelids, her cheek, her mouth. He was trembling violently as he lifted her off the ground and kissed her over and over again, and there came that old shock, that powerful vibrant shock radiating from her body through his so that he could see and feel nothing around him except Marie, Marie in his arms.

"O God..." he whispered suddenly. "God!" He had set her down, roughly. He had backed away from her, and he turned, opening the doors so that the night air hit him, cold and bracing, and he stumbled down the porch. He could hear her crying behind him, a bitter despairing crying. And the doors banged shut, the latch sliding into place. He was standing at the head of the stairs above the empty courtyard, the music of the big house distant, the lanterns below him a series of scattered beacons in the dark. He touched the rail. He willed himself to go down.

But something struck him then. All his life he would remain unable to explain it. He would never fully understand the wealth of sensation that overcame him and the clarity of the wordless vision that appeared before his eyes. It was as if when his fingers curled on that banister he knew that he was privy to a rare secret: that the move he would make now would fix the course of his life. And he knew, without pride or guilt, that it would fix the course of Marie's life too.

A great mingling of impressions visited him. He saw himself in the small dim parlor of his Vacquerie cousins, those sweet-faced girls his mother had so recently taken him to visit, and he heard his cousin Isabella singing softly as her fingers touched the keys, the dull afternoon light glinting on the lacquered portraits of men and women who had been dead for one hundred years. And even as he sat in that dusty, stifling, room, his spirit caught in his throat, he was in another place, alone with his father and he was telling him in an animated voice, reserved only for his rare and precious secrets, of that dark force that he could feel as it menaced Marie, that dark force that seemed always to surround Marie, that dark force which he drove back when he held her in his arms. And he knew now in this instant what that dark force had been; it had been the lovelessness of her world, it had been all the powers that had sought to destroy her in that lovelessness, and now those powers had done their damndest to force him away from her forever. They had dragged her down, abused her, and even Dolly had become part of them. Dolly with her sheltering affection and her perverse and vengeful brothel world. But just now, just for an instant, he'd been able to drive that force back again when he held Marie in his arms. He had felt that exquisite love between them, pure and untouched by all that had menaced it, and he was turning his back on it now! For what? A lackluster void that stretched before him like the dusty parlor of those Vacquerie cousins, an eternity of decorum and mellow rooms, a life sentence of mourning for the one real passion his life had ever known? Was the peace of his house worth that? Was his family worth that? Was the world worth that, jeer as it might, ostracize as it would? Why didn't he take Grandpère's pistol off the wall, if he was going to leave her, and just put it right to his head?

He went down the length of the porch. He pushed at the doors. They had been latched, but it was easy enough to break them in. And instantly, with the hard thrust of his shoulders, he sent them caving backward, the latch tearing loose from the wood.

She was standing there, stark still in front of the dresser, and in her hand was a raw piece of glass. He could see the broken hand mirror amid the powder and combs, and he could see that pure jagged piece of it in her hand. He took it quickly and threw it aside.

"You are coming with me," he said. "Now."

V

RICHARD DROPPED HIS CAPE on the hat rack without so much
as stopping so that before the heavy front door had closed he
had crossed the parlor, careless of the mud on his boots, and
was standing before the ancient portrait of Jean Baptiste,
and the guns that were affixed to the wall beneath it, the
long shotguns, and the pistols with their pearl handles that
Grandpère polished twice a year. He was reaching for the
first of these pistols when Rudolphe's voice cracked from the
deep shadows.

"Have you given up the custom of dining with this family?
We waited for you, one half hour at your mother's request,
and it is nine o'clock."

The voice lacked its usual edge of exasperation. A gloom
hung over the family just as if Marie had recently died and
been buried, and no one would touch the piano for days, nor
laugh too loudly, nor think of any light entertainments out
of deference for Richard and for the girl herself whom they
had in their own way loved.

"What is the matter with you?" Rudolphe leaned forward,
from behind the heavy leather wing of his chair.

Richard had the pistol in his hands and was trying the
triggers. It was not loaded. But he knew how to load it, and
he knew where the bullets were kept. He moved to the sideboard and opened the first of three very tiny top drawers.
There were the bullets. He proceeded to load the gun. "What
has come over you!" Rudolphe demanded. And Richard could
understand why. It was seldom that he didn't crumple politely at the sound of his father's voice, and his own movements felt marvelously light to him. All the world was clearly
delineated and devoid of shadowy margins. It was just that
simple when you had made up your mind. "What are you
doing with that gun!"

"I am loading it, that's what I'm doing with it. Where's
Maman, is she in bed?"

"Loading it, why? Yes, she's in bed."

"Grandpère?"

"In bed." For days they had all gone up to their rooms
early, having no desire to share the feeling of depression that
lingered in the house.

"All right, then," Richard said. He could see the shape of

his father's head clearly in the light from the grate but not the features of his face. Better that way, he calculated. "Now you see I am placing the gun to my head."

"Stop that!" his father's voice was a resentful growl. "Stop that this instant, put that gun down!"

"No, look at it, I have it against my temple," Richard answered. "And if I pull the trigger..."

Rudolphe was afraid. Afraid even to move from the chair. He was bent forward, afraid even to rise and try to snatch the gun. He sighed audibly as Richard put the gun down and let it hang at his side.

"If I had pulled the trigger," Richard said coldly, "I would be dead. I am your only son, and I would be dead."

"Keep this up and I'll shoot you!" Rudolphe said furiously.

"No, you won't," Richard said, but he couldn't repress a smile. It was perfectly fine this little touch of humor because he had made his point. He came forward to the fire, but he did not sit down. Rudolphe glowered at him, the brown leather behind him gleaming faintly with the reflection of the flames. "But you might as well do it," Richard said. "That is, one of us might as well pull the trigger if I do not marry Marie."

Rudolphe was visibly startled. But his eyes never left Richard for a second. "Don't torment yourself," he said in a low voice.

"I mean it, *mon Père,* if you do not consent you might as well put the gun to my head. You know what it would do to me if I left this house and married without your consent. And frankly, you know what it would do to Maman, and you know what it would do to you."

"Don't threaten me, Richard," Rudolphe's voice was low. He was straining to perceive if Richard were serious.

"Mon Père, I want to marry her now, tonight, and bring her home."

"O my God," Rudolphe gasped. He placed his elbow on the arm of the chair and ran his fingers across his forehead. *"Mon fils,"* he said softly, "you cannot turn back the calendar or the clock."

"Mon Père, you misunderstand me. My mind is made up. I love you and I love Maman, Grandpère, all of you. But I am going to marry Marie with or without your consent. If I cannot find a priest in the Quarter who doesn't know you, I will go out of the Quarter. I will do what I can to obtain witnesses, and I will marry her just as soon as I can. It will

(609)

kill me to go against you, kill me to leave this house, but I have no choice."

The voice was cool, respectful, but utterly confident. Richard had no idea himself of how resolute his tone was. He was thinking only of what he had to do, and feeling again that clarity, that simplicity of one who has made up his mind. The impression of the future which he had seen from the top of the stairs only an hour before hadn't left him, not for a moment, and he knew that once he went back into the bedroom for Marie the path was irrevocable.

And Rudolphe was just beginning to understand. He was regarding his son with a peculiar expression almost as if the two had just met.

"So that's it, is it?" Rudolphe sighed. "If I do not bend to the will of my eldest son, my eldest son leaves this house."

"Mon Père, I am devoted to you. I have always been devoted to you. But in this matter I must do what my conscience tells me and my heart tells me."

"And that is to destroy what this family has labored to build over four generations?" Rudolphe asked. "That's what you will do, you know. You will destroy it if you attempt to bring that girl into this house as your wife."

Richard felt a surprising calm as he stood there. He had not been aware of any tension in himself, that up until this very second, he had been poised as a soldier in battle. Rudolphe had never spoken to him with this seriousness before. Rudolphe had never spoken to him as if he were a man. And the relaxation which Richard experienced was almost delicious. Half the battle had been won.

"Because even if I accept her," Rudolphe said gravely, "and I'm not so sure I can! Even if I accept her and your mother accepts her, and somehow Grandpère could be won over, which strikes me as a sheer impossibility...the community would never accept her! The people who tip their hats to us today would turn their backs tomorrow. My clients would vanish overnight. We wouldn't be the ones whom they would call into the sanctuary of their homes to attend their dead. Everything I've worked for would be destroyed. But why must I say this to you? Don't you know it?"

"There has to be a way!" Richard said. "There has to be a way. To stand up to them all! They need us, *mon Père,* they can't turn their backs on us after years and years of our faithful service, not just like that. There has to be a way."

Rudolphe shook his head. "Richard, my heart aches for

(610)

that girl. She made a foolish mistake! She was led into it, obviously, by that miserable Lisette and never dreamed what was going to happen to her. And she compounded that mistake, in her hurt and her confusion, when she sought refuge with Dolly. But it's done, *mon fils*, it's done."

"No, *mon Père*. Now you must listen to me. I know how you've worked, I know how Jean Baptiste worked, I was that high when Grandpère told me the story of how he bought his freedom and his wife's freedom, I've heard all of my life of how Grandpère worked in the tavern in the Tchoupitoulas Road saving every dime that he made, and teaching himself to read and to write at night by the fire. I cherish this heritage, *mon Père*, I have always cherished it. But I tell you, if you do not help me find a way to make Marie my wife, then you have made me the victim of this heritage, the victim of all you've worked for, not its heir. Don't do that, *mon Père*, don't doom me to a life of lowered voices in the parlor and balancing coffee cups on my knees. If it hasn't been for me that you've done all this, me as much as Giselle, then who was it for?"

Rudolphe sat back, his sigh almost a groan.

Richard was looking at the gun, the barrel of it cradled in his left hand. "The Lermontants have always been workers, *mon Père*, fighters! They've always had the strength to beat impossible odds."

There was a soft creak beyond them then, from the darkness of the stairwell. But both men were wrapped in their thoughts, Richard staring at the gun, and his father's eyes on the flames.

"There has to be a way for that strength to prevail in this affair, now!" Richard whispered.

Rudolphe shook his head.

But from the darkness of the hallway there came another voice which said calmly.

"There is a way. It might be done."

Richard started. Rudolphe sat forward peering at the open doors.

It was Grandpère. He came slowly into the room, his slippers scraping with every step. His long wool scarf was wound twice around his neck and his small spectacles became brilliant and opaque with the reflected fire. "There just might be a way..." he said. He waved Richard out of his path as he approached the chair. Richard took his arm as he seated himself slowly and with obvious pain.

Rudolphe was staring at his father, amazed.

"I always swore..." Grandpère commenced now that he was settled, "that I would never consent to this boy going to France, not after what happened with his brothers. That I would never give my blessing to such a voyage until he was married, settled, with children in the house. Well, I am ready for a change of mind. He and the Ste. Marie girl should go together, just as soon as the ceremony can be performed, and they should stay abroad until all the tongues of the Quarter cease their wagging. A year, I should think, and then they will come home. Marie Ste. Marie will be the wife of a Lermontant, and I should like to hear anyone dare to insult her then!" He stopped and held up his hand. "Come here, Richard, so that I can see you," he said.

Richard clasped the hand tightly. His heart was pounding. "Yes, Grandpère."

"After that year..." Grandpère said, "you come home!"

"Grandpère, I will live all my life in this house, my children will be born in this house, I will live here until I die."

But Grandpère held tight to his hand as if he did not quite believe this. And then he said. *"Mon fils..."* then he stopped.

Rudolphe motioned for Richard to be silent. Richard thought Grandpère was thinking of those brothers of his that he'd never seen, those grandsons sent off with such high hopes for the education abroad.

"Grandpère," he whispered, "you've done the Lord's work."

"And the girl?" the old man asked. "How do you propose..."

"I took her out of Dolly Rose's house two hours ago," Richard said. "She's at home now with Marcel."

Both grandfather and father stared at Richard in amazement.

"Well," Rudolphe began angrily.

But this time Grandpère motioned for quiet. "Go bring her here," he said. "We won't assemble the family, it will be too hard on her. I'll tell your mother, go on."

But as soon as Richard had left, he sat back in his chair morosely and seemed almost to have fallen asleep. Rudolphe was studying him, aware that it was time to wake Suzette, to prepare a room, but some vague anxiety kept him there near his father, something greater it seemed than the sum total of all the difficulties they now faced.

"Mon Père," he said finally, leaning forward and touching

Grandpère lightly on the knee, "if you believe it can be done, I know it can be done."

The old man did not stir. His eyelids fluttered for an instant behind his spectacles.

"And Richard will be in this house at the end of that year, *mon Père*, nothing will prevent that." Rudolphe said.

"I know," Grandpère sighed, his voice barely audible, "I never doubted that. It's I who might not be here." But abruptly he rose, shaking his head, and started slowly toward the door.

Rudolphe wanted to speak to him, he wanted to tell him not to talk of such things, but he felt a fear like a spasm of pain. He was still sitting in the chair when Richard and Marie came through the front door. In fact, he was somewhat confused as it seemed only an instant had passed, and taken by surprise he found himself staring up at the girl, who clung to Richard, her eyes like those of a wounded animal, her hair free and tousled by the wind. In an instant he was on his feet without thinking, and much to his own surprise he'd taken this girl in his arms. A wild flowery fragrance rose from her hair as he kissed her, and he realized that some powerful protective instinct had infected him. He drew back holding her at arm's length, as was perhaps a father-in-law's prerogative and realized that she had already become one of them in his mind. She was shy, miserable, but when she looked up at his son, her eyes were filled with dazzling love.

VI

CHRISTOPHE DID NOT GO TO Dolly directly after the wedding as he had promised. He knew that he ought to do this, however, because Dolly was not in a good frame of mind. She declared herself quite happy for Marie and Richard, but some well of buried emotion had been stirred in her by Marie's coming and going and she had in the last few days exhibited those very characteristics of debilitating grief that she had shown after the death of her own child. She did not dress or comb her hair, and keeping to her room, left her girls on their own. When no orders came from her for cook, maid, or valet, the house ceased to run itself, quarrels broke out, and all realized soon enough that she was quite willing to tell every-

(613)

one and anyone to leave if they chose, and go their own way. The door in the Rue Dumaine was now locked.

But Marie's sojourn had brought Christophe and Dolly together again, just as the grief for little Lisa Rose had once brought them together, and Christophe knew as he left the Cathedral that indeed he would go to see her, confirm for her that the wedding had in fact taken place (she had her doubts, *eh bien,* the proper Lermontants) but he could not go just now.

And why he was not sure. Except that the quiet afternoon ceremony in the sacristy of the church had affected him profoundly in ways that he did not anticipate. And as he wandered off along the waterfront, engulfed by the eternal crowds, he felt something of the desperation he had known during his last days in Paris, and recognizing this for what it was, he felt fear. Before five o'clock, he had stopped in half a dozen dram shops, and as the early winter dusk came on fast, with a heavy shrouding fog, he had the sense that he might be in any one of the vast cities he had once visited—the winding dirty alleyways of Cairo, the majestic and wildly beautiful squalor of Rome. All was alien to him, and the feeling of being home and where he belonged left him, so that he was disconnected and he did not understand why.

The school went well, better than ever, he was writing steadily, though nothing of real consequence, and a Paris journal had just written to him asking for more of his recent poems. Yet this harrowing feeling had mounted ever since he left the Cathedral and his mind would grant him no reprieve from some ruthless self-examination as he wandered about, feet often slipping on the wet cobblestones, terrified that were he to encounter anyone he knew at this moment, even his own mother, he would be visited by a sensation he had once experienced in Paris with Michael of simply not knowing who the person was, why he was with that person, why they were on that very spot.

Of course he was happy for Richard and Marie, supremely happy.

In general, respectable people had never interested him very much; and seldom had he invested any emotion in what seemed the most inevitable course of their lives. Among his students, he had loved most the wild, the unpredictable, and often the poor rather than those stalwart sons of the good families who in truth tended to grate on his nerves. He had never for a moment entertained the notion, even in childhood, that Juliet was respectable, and she herself had repeatedly throughout her life chosen the more rash and flamboyant of men. It seemed, in fact, that she invariably demanded some monstrous breach of decorum as the price of her favors. She had demanded this of Marcel, surely. And she was demanding it now of Augustin Dumanoir *père* who came to see her much too often for the good of his plantation and was even murmuring to Christophe something about marriage as if it were entirely possible to make Juliet the mistress of his house. Juliet managing a plantation household, kitchen, scores of slave women and children, the eternal round of sewing, entertaining—someone was losing his or her mind.

But the great exception to this quiet disdain for the respectable had always been the *Famille Lermontant* who struck Christophe not so much as desperately conforming bourgeoisie but rather the genuine article of middle-class gentility possessed of whatever nobility that hard-won position might allow. And Rudolphe's conviction that the family could absorb the tragedy and scandal which had all but destroyed Marie Ste. Marie, as well as Richard's courage in marrying her, had gone to Christophe's heart. Of course his love and relief for Marie and for Marcel knew no bounds.

So why then had an excess of emotion at the wedding caught him so off guard?

Had he not expected the current of shared feeling in that crowded sacristy, the bride's uncommon radiance, the raw and innocent love in the eyes of the tall groom? When Marie had spoken her vows in a halting and vibrant voice, Christophe's eyes had misted over, and it seemed to him, though he had scorned all things romantic since his exile from Paris, that the immense structure of the Cathedral itself veritably trembled when the bride and the groom embraced.

Reasonably enough, he could tell himself now that it had been a rare moment when the very concept of marriage had been exalted, and that the collective act of faith in that room had transcended the sum of all the individual hopes. Marry they had, in spite of everything. And even Richard's wan little cousins come so valiantly from far and wide to peer fearfully at the resplendent bride had been affected by it as well as the more worldly Anna Bella, Marcel, and Juliet.

So why this unhappiness, why as darkness fell completely over the struggling gas lamps, and the burnished light of the open taverns spilled into the fog, was Christophe on the verge of panic, trudging through these streets? Was it a sense of exclusion, no, that could not be, he told himself. And muscling to a crowded bar, he drank down another shot of cheap rum.

And yet summoned back and back to the sacristy door in his imagination, he was confronted by a bewildering sight, that of Marcel turning from the young couple, and smiling almost sadly at Christophe as he went off down the alley beside the Cathedral alone. Christophe's eyes followed that retreating figure unwilling now as they had been then to let the figure go. And he realized with a stultifying amazement that all this long dreary afternoon he'd been thinking of that moment, weaving it in and out of his more lofty considerations of the wedding, his more conscientious considerations of Dolly Rose. Marcel. And what was so remarkable about his leaving that sacristy, about his evanescent and melancholy smile? What was so remarkable about that figure moving on through Pirate's Alley, tall, blond-haired, indifferent, moving steadily away from the Cathedral and steadily away from him!

Images came back to him, images alien to these waterfront streets, images so old that their freshness startled him, shook him in their clarity, images of a mountainside at Sounion, the tip of Greece, below the Temple of Neptune where Lord Byron had carved his name. And Christophe was thinking of the low peasant's hut where he had first made love to Michael, after a year's wandering from Paris during which Michael had never once touched him, leaving it to Christophe to make the first move. No, Christophe wasn't thinking of it now, he was there!

And stumbling suddenly on the gunwale sidewalk, the crowd jostling him, he looked up with an exquisite relief to realize that he had found the familiar door to Madame Lelaud's.

In a moment he had pushed through the knot of white men blocking the entrance, and that relief still coursing through him, relaxing him, quieting him, he rested his back for a moment against a heavy rough-hewn wooden beam. Not ten yards from him was his regular table, the table where he and Marcel had talked when he had first come home. And the feeling of Sounion descended on him again, wouldn't leave him, and he was seeing in disconnected blasts those rocky cliffs, the sea itself stretching out forever and those few columns piercing the sky. Not this crowded bar, not the sweetly shabby figure of Madame Lelaud with skin the color of a walnut shell, who very obligingly left the bar to put the usual mug of beer in his hand. He was feeling, smelling that Greek countryside, and he could hear the tinkle of the bell about the neck of the Judas goat, see the shepherd climbing the steep cliff. He had to rest his back against the rough post to drink the beer. Where was Marcel now, at this moment? The smoke of this crowded place burned his eyes.

"And where's my blue-eyed *bébé?*" Madame Lelaud smiled at him, flecking the smallest bit of dust from his lapel. He laughed. She wore a dark rouge on her lips that was dried and powdery, "Hmmm, I haven't seen my blued-eyed *bébé* in ever so long, he stayed here for three days, right at that table, and then he was gone." Gone, gone, gone, gone. "Hmmm, you give him a kiss for me, hmmmmmmm?"

"Certainly!" Christophe winked as he blew the foam off the beer. And then on tiptoe Madame Lelaud kissed him, a worn working mouth but gentle, and resisting the urge to wipe the bit of moisture left on his lip, he smiled at her, beamed at her in fact. He and Marcel together at that table which he could no longer see for the crowd, "Monsieur, you don't know how I admire you, if you would only give me a chance..."

"I'll kiss you again if you don't watch out," she winked, but the man behind the bar was shouting at her, taunting her, they teased her about Christophe as they always did when he came in.

"Billiards, Madame, billiards," he said to her in English, quite unaware of the crisp British sound of it, a white man in a broad-brimmed hat looking up suddenly from the billiard table, his mouth a moist smile beneath the shadow of the brim. "It's time to play some serious billiards," and pushing toward the brightly illuminated felt as the white man was chalking his cue Christophe surveyed the scattered ivory balls. There was the black man who was always there, the one with the two camellias in his lapel, the silk vest and the frock coat with its velvet collar, his skin so black it reflected the light all over it, the lips almost purple.

"Aaaah, Monsieur le Schoolteacher," he said, he spoke English also, elegant British English with just the hint of Jamaica, and saluted Christophe with his cue. He was running the balls, had shot the last three in while Christophe was downing the beer. And now he moved around the table for his fourth. Christophe slapped a five-dollar gold piece on the rail of the table, and the black man smiled, nodding. "Yes sir, Monsieur le Schoolteacher." He bent over the table, made

(617)

a high bridge with his very long fingers, and banked the red ball before it went in.

Sounion in this place, it was enough to drive a man mad! Some sudden irrelevant flash of sitting in his room drunk after Michael's death, on the very same bed in which Michael died, explaining something to Marcel about Sounion and telling him only some vaguely metaphorical image for the real truth, the raw and passionate truth in the hut. "Not very high stakes," said the black man driving in the eight ball.

The white man with the broad-brimmed hat threw up his hands. The cue was standing against the table for Christophe to take it. The man wore fancy river gambler clothes, and rested his back with a feline movement on the rough-hewn support, crossing his ankles in pale immaculate buckskin pants that were tight over the bulge between his legs, the shimmer of his gray vest making Christophe grit his teeth suddenly at the thought of a fingernail running across the silk. The chest beneath it was solid, broad.

"Ten dollars, Monsieur," said the black man chalking the cue, "and you break."

"Generous, generous, let's lag for break," Christophe fished in his pocket, put the ten-dollar piece on the rail. "That's fifteen, sir." He liked the feel of this cue because it was heavy and short. "Eight ball," he said. The Jamaican nodded. Marcel had listened so patiently, the blue eyes so intense, the face exactly the color of honey poured from a glass pitcher in the sunlight. The same Marcel who did not seek my company today after the wedding, who turned and gave me that affectionate, almost intimate smile, easy, touched my arm and then walked out of the church precisely when I had expected, expected what, that we would go on together???

"You break, Monsieur," a smile on the sculpted black face, the high sloping forehead, prominent nose, white teeth.

"So I do." There were several ways to approaach it, take a risk, he felt the thrust perfect and then the balls went everywhere. Or so it seemed. He had sunk three.

A cluster of men pushed suddenly against the head of the table, and the usual din was underscored by the hard heavy sounds of a scuffle, shouts. And passing then was the spectacle of a man hoisted in the air, brogans dangling above a score of rising, shoving hands. Into the street, the fog curling just for an instant as those who blocked the door gave way, and then closed again against the cold.

There was thirty dollars in gold gleaming on the rail, Christophe took his time, knowing now that he was at that perfect stage of drunkenness when this would be easy, this would go well. An hour from now, maybe less, get out of the game. "You have another one of those, cold and foaming?" he whispered to Madame Lelaud. Her apron was filthy, her thin rippling hair reminded him of his mother who said of Marcel so indifferently last night, "But he's no longer a boy, he's a man now," as if that made all the difference in the world to her passion.

"But Dumanoir is no boy, what is that to you!"

"Ah, yes!" she'd answered with remarkable candor. "But he is a very old man!" Nothing like you, Maman, since ancient Rome, he had thought.

"Watch out for these boys, darling!" Madame Lelaud said to him in English. "You know what I mean?"

"Seven ball, far right pocket," he said and with a quick and somewhat reckless thrust sent it in.

"Hmmmm," he took the beer from her, drank a mouthful and giving it back, wiped his hand on his pants.

"They let you win a little at first, hmmmm? Watch out."

"Five ball, side pocket," he tapped the leather edge with the tip of the cue, then banked the ball at the perfect angle so that the black man smiled. He wore pomade on his tightly waving hair. It gleamed like his face under the low-hanging lamp, the little camellias in his lapel browning at the edges, but otherwise he was perfect, the coat tapering at his narrow waist, his nails shining as if they'd been buffed. A rough-bearded Dutchman appraised him slowly as he passed, thudding up the wooden stairs to the rooms above. Men in the corner suddenly roared with laughter, heads bowing, rising, at some perfect exchange.

"Three ball, far left pocket," Christophe said, but he had been thinking this was the time to try to get both of them in, the three and the two, the two chasing the three perfectly, very tricky. And as they sank, he heard the murmur around him like applause, the riverboat gambler in his green coat shifting his weight from one foot to the other with that moist smile and only shadows for eyes. "Very good, Monsieur le Schoolteacher," said the black man.

"Now this is your Waterloo!" Madame Lelaud's hair brushed his ear. "This is where you always go crazy, with the eight ball."

(619)

"Madame, for the love of heaven," he rubbed the chalk on the cue, "have a little faith."

He was sizing it up, why not make it a beauty? And calling the farthest pocket, he heard them gasp.

"But on second thought," he said suddenly with a slight mocking lilt to his voice, and a touch of the fop to his gestures, "I think that ball looks just fine right where it is."

The black man was laughing, the riverboat gambler let out a low rumble as he smiled. Adjusting the brim of his hat he showed for one instant the gleam of a clear hazel eye.

"You are a witty man, Monsieur le Schoolteacher," said the black man. Christophe tapped the pocket again. Marcel had just left the church as though that smile were enough.

"Did you think he was going to be a boy forever?" his mother had turned the questioning around the night before, pulling the hair from her brush, "And you, Christophe, are you going to be a boy forever?"

"Stop, Maman, enjoy your old man."

"And suppose I go to the country with him..."

"But you won't!"

"I don't know," she had shrugged, flicking the long hair over her shoulder again, "I was born in the country, maybe I want to go back to the country, and you, Christophe, you?"

He drew in his breath and shot, hard, fast, the ball crashing against the right bank, left bank, right bank again and straight into the wrong pocket!

The black man had thrown back his head to laugh, his long concave fingers sliding the thirty dollars off the rail. "You should teach the art of billiards, Monsieur le Schoolteacher."

"The *art* of billiards, the *art?*" Christophe surrendered the cue to an anonymous hand. It seemed the black man's pocket jingled with coins. "Billiards is not an art, Monsieur," Christophe smiled as he turned to push his way toward the bar. "You wouldn't think of marrying," he had said to Juliet, and she with that wan smile, "Ah, but what you mean to say is I wouldn't think of leaving you!"

He was staring at himself in the filthy mirror beyond the row of bottles. All the shades on the oil lamps that hung from the ceiling were completely black. "And I would think of it," she had touched him lightly with the handle of the brush. There loomed suddenly behind his own reflected image the broad-brimmed hat of the river gambler, the light skittering again on his gray silk vest.

(620)

"Kentucky sipping whiskey!" the barkeep stared into the river gambler's face, the glinting shadows that were the man's eyes. "*Sipping* whiskey, *sipping* whiskey!"

"I know you have it," came the velvet whisper, a shoulder nudging Christophe.

What had he expected, that Marcel would come to him then after the wedding, alone, and vulnerable, what are you going to do now with your life, which direction, and they would sit again in his room always talking, sharing all of it, the wine, the relief, the despair? Marcel didn't need him anymore, Marcel had not needed him for some time, the young man who returned from the Cane River was without that certain yearning, it was simply absent, replaced by that confident and remote smile. A hand was squeezing his arm.

He felt a pain in his temples as if the skin were tightening and the veins were protruding, veins that were always there, a small expressionless and completely unremarkable brown face confronting him in the splotched mirror, and the panic rising again which he had left, somehow or other, by magic at the door. This isn't the component of a great emotion, Christophe, this is petty, the thinking of a child. How to live without it, that's the question, without the cool Englishman sitting in the door of the hut at Sounion waiting, waiting, knowing precisely what was going to happen through all the confusion, the exposure, the pain. And the boy with the blue eyes, "But I don't know how to be your lover, you have to show me, be my teacher!" "No, the answer is now and forever no." Yes, love and pain, that's exquisite, but how to make life worthwhile even when they aren't there, how to be sustained by what you do, what you want, what you are yourself! "But you can't marry Dumanoir!" he had said to her, and she, "Ten long years I kept my vigil for you, Chris, I tell you I will marry him, I will leave this house." He shuddered. And in the dim mirror saw again the ruddy square face of the riverboat gambler, light glinting on the fine bones of his cheeks, his jaw. The lips spread in that moist, easy smile. The editor from Paris had written just months ago. "This novel has your old brilliance, but not your narrative strength. Send more, we want to see more, can't you recapture your old narrative strength?" One had somehow to feel one's own powers, one's own skill coursing through one's veins!

"I know you have good sipping whiskey, I've seen it!" said the river gambler.

"Ah, darling, you lost your money, I told you to be careful."

(621)

Madame Lelaud leaned on Christophe's shoulder like a child going to sleep. I feel empty, empty! And over all is laid a layer of ash so that nothing has its former brilliance, all is indistinct. "Give them the good Kentucky bourbon," she winked her eye. "You don't play any more billiards tonight." She brushed Christophe's hair back from his temples which was perfectly absurd because his hair was so wiry and close-cut it never actually moved. "You watch out for these boys!" she smiled at the gambler.

"I always watch out for the boys, Madame," Christophe beamed down at her. And he heard the river gambler's soft American laugh. The man had placed his elbow on the bar beside Christophe, one foot on the brass rail so the buckskin pants pulled over the bulge between his legs.

"And this house is going to be empty, empty," she had warned him with another long swipe at her dark hair. "You grow up, hmmmmm?"

"You want to find a little amusement?" the gambler whispered in French.

Of course it will all come back to you! Christophe drank the mellow expensive bourbon, soothing the rawness of his tongue. In the classroom tomorrow it will come back to you when you see their faces, when you see young Gaston with those poems he won't dare to show to anyone but you, and Frederick, that brilliant Jean Louis, Paul. This deadening cloud will lift when you hear their voices, there will be a flavor to things, color, you were living with some foolish notion while Marcel was gone, or were you merely living with the notion that he would come back? "He's not a boy anymore," flick of the hairbrush, "and that's why I didn't wait for him. And you, *mon cher,* when I'm gone, what will you do?" Go to hell, Maman, go to hell for all I care, go to the country, go to hell.

"Amusement?" he whispered to the mirror. The buckskin leg nudged him gently. "Women?"

"Is *that* what amuses you?" asked the unobtrusive American voice.

"*Mon Dieu,*" Christophe smiled.

"I have a room just down the street, nothing fancy, just clean," the gambler pushed the gold coin at the barkeep, the sleeve of his green coat resting against Christophe's arm. "I want the bottle," he said. His lean smooth face wrinkled softly again in a smile.

"Kiss that boy for me," Madame Lelaud sang out as they moved toward the door.

"Most definitely, Madame," Christophe made her a quick bow as, laughing softly, the gambler stepped into the dirt street.

Christophe stood on the gunwale banquette, staring up at the sky. Wisps of dark cloud obliterated the stars and there was a ring around the moon now that the rain had stopped. The panic was gone again as if it had never come, and the street was a riot of lighted windows, racket, the scream of the whistle of the gendarmes. In this very spot he had stood with Marcel that first night, and from this very spot he had watched Marcel walk away, and then gazed up at this sky.

The gambler was walking up and down slowly, that feline form flowing beautifully under the gray vest, the taut pants, that smile a permanent fixture beneath the shadow of the hat.

"I just had the most reassuring sensation," Christophe murmured. And here we stood in this very spot that first night and you were that tall. "The most revealing sensation," he whispered, *"that this is all there will ever be."*

"Come on, Mister Schoolteacher," said the low American voice, as for the first time the gambler removed the wide-brimmed hat revealing his golden hair and the full invitation in his brilliant deepset hazel eyes.

VII

IT WAS BARELY LIGHT, and the market was awakening with a clatter. The Lermontants had urged Marcel to come back with them for breakfast, but he had refused. Madame Suzette was crying bitterly, once the ship had moved far enough downstream so that she could no longer see the bride and the groom, and the bride and the groom could no longer see her. And Rudolphe, very quiet now that there was no more opportunity for giving Richard advice, stood still on the levee for a long moment, seemingly unaware that the ship was no longer in sight. Christophe was the first to leave. He had to be in the classroom in an hour. And Marcel excused himself quickly saying that he wanted to be alone. He had tried then to catch up with Christophe, but Christophe was already gone.

It had been a grueling week, filled with a scintillating

(623)

excitement and recurrent pain. There had been the inevitable
offer from Rudolphe to lend Marcel the money to join Richard
and Marie on the trip. But Rudolphe had taken out a note
on the stables and sold two lots in the Faubourg Marigny
just to meet the immediate expenses of the couple's journey,
and it was quite out of the question that Marcel would go
traipsing about Europe, while at home Rudolphe worked
night and day with Antoine and his nephew Pierre, as was
usual, the family shorthanded now besides. The conversation
had been humiliating for Marcel.

In fact, as the day of departure grew closer and closer, he
found himself experiencing very intense pain, sometimes so intense that he could not hide it from others. He would shun the
Lermontant house at such moments, and go on those long walks
which had so often soothed him in the past, seeking any distraction from the desperation that was crippling his heart.

And over and over, he ached for Christophe, ached simply
to sit with Chris by the fire, or more truly, to seek Chris's
quiet guidance as he wandered through the broken glass of
his old world. But he could not turn to Chris now. Marie was
safe with Richard, the entire course of her life altered, and
Marcel could not, would not, let Chris see the smallness, the
weakness of his soul. He would rather die than disappoint
Chris. He would struggle through this alone.

As for Anna Bella, he could neither think of her, nor put
her out of his mind. He felt rage against Dazincourt, and this
was a man who had faced death for him on the field of honor,
it was insupportable, and yet it seemed a devastating cruelty
that Marcel had ever possessed Anna Bella, ever tasted what
life might have been with her day-to-day love. And in the
days that followed their lone night together, he saw again
and again the image of Dazincourt's barouche beside her
cottage, and praying for some note from her, some sign as to
how things stood with her, he was answered with silence
which told him all.

Of course the wedding had lifted his spirits. Until the
priest said the final words he did not, in fact, believe that it
would happen. Some calamity must prevent it. But at last
came that moment when his sister, a stranger to him now
in light of all that had bruised and almost destroyed her, was
lifted on tiptoe into her husband's arms. The world was shut
out then, and it seemed the very air of the sacristy was suffused with love as they all left it afterwards, and he had
hoped that he would not have to see Richard alone again.

But Richard wanted it otherwise. And this morning he had come down to the cottage and caught Marcel unawares. Of course Marcel knew what Richard had to say, but he had never expected the simple and direct expression of it which followed.

"I never wanted this trip," Richard had begun at once, "I never planned for it, prepared for it as you did. As a matter of fact, were the truth to be known, I wish that Marie and I could stay right here. But I know what this means to you, the irony of it is not lost for me. I know the disappointment you are feeling. I am going and you are not going. I will be on the deck of that ship waving good-bye and you will be the one on the shore. Now, I don't want you to come to the dock. I want for you to say good-bye here; then you come to the house and be alone for a moment with Marie."

It was strange the effect of those words. They tested Marcel to the limit, he wasn't even sure at one point whether or not he could hear Richard out. But this was unthinkable really. He knew what he must say to put Richard at ease and he said it at once, "Do you think I'm not happy for you and Marie! Do you think my heart's not with both of you? I've a lifetime to think of myself, and nothing could keep me from coming with you to the dock. I want you to write to me, to describe everything you see from Notre Dame to the Grand Canal, I want to hear about Florence, about Rome...every place that you go."

But then, as they walked through the early morning together toward the Lermontant house, that pain had welled up in Marcel again, and just before the front door, he had stopped Richard and drawn him aside at the carriageway, and for a tense moment been quite unable to speak.

"Look," he said finally, "it's not over for me. It will just take time. I'm going to do things in my life, important things, it will just take time. It will be harder, and...and... it will just take time." Then he realized that his lips were moving but the words were not coming out. He drew himself up, swallowing slowly, and then shook his head as if to clear it, as if to see sharply and distinctly what it was he was trying to say. "Look at Monsieur Philippe," he whispered, "all that money and what did he ever do? I think he would have been happy in the cottage all his life with some good bourbon and my mother, and a deck of cards. And Christophe, he turned his back on Paris and came home to start a school. People make their own lives, Richard, and I'll make mine."

Richard had nodded. His large drowsy brown eyes watered

slowly and he started as if he wanted to say something, but then he merely nodded emphatically again.

That had been the end of it.

And that was going to be the end of it.

But as he wound his way back from the dock toward the Rue Ste. Anne, the sun just breaking through the gray clouds, the last of an earlier rain still shining on the banquettes, he realized he could not endure the cottage just now. He did not wish to see the bare shelves, the latched doors of the kitchen, and frankly, the small pile of bills accumulating on the table by his chair.

Of course Dazincourt had wiped the slate clean of Monsieur Philippe's debts with the notary Jacquemine, and had even left instructions that if Marcel required assistance in finding some means of livelihood, he was to be contacted at once. But Marcel could not endure the thought of further "assistance" from this man. And neither Jacquemine or Dazincourt would ever know of these bills. They were from tradesmen who had known nothing of the notary, people whom over the years Marcel had always paid on the first of every month himself. And in the time Marcel had spent on the Cane River they had not been paid at all. Now their bills were trickling in, $150 from the tailor, $75 from the seamstress who had made Marcel's shirts, $85 owing the shoemaker, and then there was the coal man, the fish man and the poultry man who had always been paid at the back door. Let it wait, and let the whole dusty unkempt atmosphere of the cottage wait until later, perhaps, when this warm sun that had just come out as he walked through the streets, was gone again.

So as he approached the corner of the Rue Dauphine and found himself within sight of home, he dragged his feet, and went out of his way as a child might to kick a lump of coal that had just fallen from a cart.

A score of voices startled him. It was the children gathered on the corner, and for a rare moment, he stared at these children, all of them boys, and wondered what they were doing here now in this place. It was almost with a laugh that he realized they were Christophe's students, some twenty or more, many of them only eleven or twelve, clamoring for Christophe to open the school. There were the older boys that he knew, of course, but many of them were strange faces, and as usual, there was a wild assortment of color from the very fair to the very dark. Christophe didn't see Marcel as he unlocked the door. He was dressed as always in one of his old but serviceable Parisian coats, quite clean and well-cared-

(626)

for, but much worn. And there was in his face the usual brightness as he clasped the shoulders of the boys who passed into the house. His keen brown eyes warmed as he exchanged a few words here, there, and then without seeing Marcel even yet, he disappeared inside.

Marcel experienced a sinking feeling. He stood for a while, his back to the lamp post merely looking at the façade of the house. Suddenly a wild impulse gripped him to go in. To sit in the back reading room for a while with the papers, perhaps drink some very strong coffee, talk with Juliet. But he did not do this, he did not move.

"And why are you moping about?" he asked himself frankly. With all of New Orleans before you, mud streaming in the streets, the slops reeking in the alleys, and a thousand billiard parlors and confectioners and restaurants and cabarets that you cannot enter unless you want to be pitched on your face in the street.

He began to laugh suddenly at the irony of his thoughts, the little games of bitterness he had been playing with himself. It wasn't very much like him, after all. To be walking casually past the shops as they opened their doors, calculating that at best he might make a dollar and a half a day as a clerk somewhere, and that he had never bought a coat in his life that didn't cost fifty dollars, or a pair of pants that was less than twenty, or a shirt that was less than three. And he was growing still, which meant that he would be naked by summer when it was too late to use the old clothes to burn for warmth. Maybe he should burn all those outstanding bills now. But passing one small shop with very dark dormer windows, he positively laughed aloud. For there he was reflected in the glass in all his gentlemanly splendor, the perfect picture of a young man of means.

The laughter was exhilarating though people were staring at him. And he realized that in a way, all this ironical foolishness was a good sign. It was lighter. It was not so bad. And a small plan leapt into his mind as amusing as everything else. Why not go on down toward the Rue Canal and see Picard and Duval, and have one last Daguerreotype made, one final relic, a memento of the gentleman he had been, a memento of this peculiar day? After all, he had a spare ten dollars, did he not, he had fifteen times that amount to be exact, and none of it likely to make or break his fortune since it constituted less than one-fourth of his debts, and was the sum total that he possessed. And he wanted this little picture, it would be the last for his collection, he would take it home at once and hang it on the wall.

It was eight thirty when he arrived and Picard was just opening the door. "Ah, Marcel," said the old man, adjusting his spectacles, "haven't seen you in months, thought you'd left these parts."

"Oh, no, Monsieur," Marcel followed him up the dusty stairway, the old man's steps slow, his hand hoisting his weight as it clutched the rail "Only in the country for a little while. And Monsieur Duval?" he asked quickly. "Is Monsieur Duval here?"

"Aaaah, Duval!" the old man said over his shoulder as he entered the studio. The typical exasperation made Marcel smile. He did not realize until that moment how much he wanted to talk to Duval, how much he wanted to tell him of his discoveries on the Cane River, of the adventurous Daguerrean who had taken pictures of Niagara Falls, and the talk among the itinerants of a new buffing wheel.

As a matter of fact, all of Marcel's old enthusiasm for the invention was kindled again as he smelt the familiar chemicals, and saw Picard throw back the flap of his shabby little tent.

"Don't you mention that name to me," the old man had been murmuring, and now some low invective escaped under his breath. "What would you like today, Marcel, as a matter of fact I'll make you an offer, whole plate, whole plate for half price, five dollars, just for you."

"Monsieur Duval is not here?" Marcel asked, attempting to sound casual. The little platform creaked dangerously as ever, there was dust on the velvet prop behind it, dust on the ornately carved chair. But the sun, the sun was a miracle.

"No, Duval's not here! And I wouldn't make that offer for just anyone, whole plate, five dollars, what do you say?"

"Aah...yes, of course," Marcel shrugged. He had always preferred the smaller quarter plates, actually, because it was easier for him to see patterns in them, appealing masses of black and white, but a whole plate for half price—And what did it matter now, if he had missed Duval, Duval who could have taken a perfect picture. "But do you expect him, Monsieur?" he asked.

"Expect him, I expect him to fall on his face, that's what I expect," came the angry voice from beneath the muslin. "Set up his own studio, that's what he's gone and done, with

(628)

everything I taught him, the years of patience, training, and he ups and goes into business for himself!"

Marcel's lips pressed together into a bitter but patient smile. And if I had only known that five minutes ago, he thought wearily. But how could he leave now with the old man already at work on the plate, and the old man would guess the reason for his departure, the old man would be hurt.

"And two dollars a day I was paying him at the end," Picard's voice continued, high-pitched with habitual outrage, "and he ups and sets up on his own. Damn fool if you ask me, but there's always a damn fool ready to set up in this business, thinks he can make a fortune with the camera, well let's just see how Duval can manage on his own! What with an endless procession of women who want to look ten years younger, and children who won't sit still. What with the chemicals twelve hours a day, and no one to lend him a helping hand, advance him a little salary, or send him on home early when business is slow. Monsieur Duval, the artist! Well, we shall see what we shall see."

And where, Marcel was wondering, where was Duval's studio, and if only he were there instead of here. It was more than a blight on his spirits, the room about him appeared intolerably shabby, and his thoughts were wandering slowly, away from this entire venture, to times when he had been here before. The afternoon when he had first brought Marie, or that Saturday morning when he'd stolen Lisette out of the kitchen in her new calico dress. Lisette had refused to sit in this chair, rather she stood behind it, her *tignon* tied like a gypsy's scarf at the nape of her neck. "I always thought Monsieur Duval would set up on his own," he murmured. "He has such a talent, such an eye." And he would do so marvelously no matter what the old man said.

"Well, a talent for conniving and ingratitude if you ask me," Picard threw back the flap as he slid the plate into the camera case. "And that last one, a perfect idiot, demanding two days wages in advance and me fool enough to give it to him, never saw him again!" He threw up his hand, turned as if on an axis to consult his thermometer, the sun glinting on the pink flesh of his bald head. "And without another pair of hands in this business a man can't even leave his establishment long enough to go to the...to go to the...bank!" He gazed at the freshly washed windows, he waved his hand before the hot stove.

A curious rigidity had invaded Marcel. He was staring at the old man dimly, watching him adjust the camera's height. The warm air was unpleasant, the chemicals noxious, so that he wondered why he had ever come. The days were past for this extravagance and he was wasting time here as well. "What do you pay your assistants?" he asked, but the voice was low, spiritless as was the light in his eyes. Duval had always been the rarity in this business, and Picard was run of the mill. Why had he risked encountering Picard here alone?

"One dollar a day!" the old man trumpeted. "And that's one dollar too much! The one after Duval, he couldn't take a picture with me standing over his shoulder, that one, and the next was a thief!" His heavy florid brow puckered, the white eyebrows closing on the fine gold frame of the spectacles. "And with all I have to teach," he muttered, "why the excellent training and . . ."

"And the chemicals twelve hours a day," Marcel murmured, "the endless procession of women who want to look ten years younger, and the children who won't sit still."

"Oh, now it's not that bad!" the old man put his knuckles on his hip. "You're the one who used to tell me it was an art, young man! One dollar a day for the privilege of learning an art? What do you think they pay a clerk in a shop!" The old man's gray eyes widened. He drew his handkerchief out and wiped the sweat from his upper lip. "Starvation wages, that's what they pay. As a matter of fact, you wouldn't know anyone who wanted such an opportunity, would you? Oh, not you, of course, not you, I can see you're well fixed. But your people do quite well in this business, look at Jules Lion. No, I wouldn't be opposed to hiring some honest, hardworking man of color, no, indeed."

"For a dollar a day?" Marcel uttered a slight, dry laugh. He had lost all appetite for this venture, he wished flatly that he had not come.

"All right, young man," Picard drew himself up. "Forty seconds when you are quite ready . . ."

"No!" Marcel roused himself as if from some unpleasant dream. "Thirty, Monsieur," he insisted gently. It was the final irritation that the old man had never really understood the importance of the time of day, the light, the dampness, conditions subject moment by moment to change. Enough times Marcel had calculated, watched, he knew. "Thirty seconds, Monsieur, and not a moment longer and I assure you I'll pay for the result."

"Eh bien," Picard shook his head. "Pity you don't want to make your fortune with the Daguerreotype, Marcel."

It was noon when Anna Bella left her house, entrusting little Martin to Idabel so that she had to carry the small kettle of soup herself. But she had sealed its lid with a bit of moist dough and nothing would spill as she carried the iron handle easily at her side.

There was no answer when she knocked at the cottage in the Rue Ste. Anne and this produced in her neither disappointment nor surpirse. She entered quietly and surveyed with an impassive face the dirty plates here and there, boots in the middle of the rug, a shirt dangling from the back of a chair. And as there was only enough coal to last a few more nights at best, she lit a very small fire, setting the kettle over it in the little parlor grate, and went to work slowly but steadily with a dust rag and a broom.

And as she moved about the small rooms, she made little discoveries that stopped her, so that she would stand for long periods transfixed, the dust swirling about her in the pale rays of the winter sun. A stack of bills lay on a chair-side table which at a reserved glance indicated an enormous debt. And Cecile had taken her mahogany bed with her to the Cane River along with the carpet from the back room. But in the middle bedroom, where Marcel was now sleeping, little had changed. Marie's clothes were still in the armoire, and on the dresser lay her hairbrush and mirror as if the girl she had been had died as surely as Lisette.

But it was another aspect of the cottage which caused Anna Bella finally to give up her small tasks and to sit oddly stranded at Marie's dresser staring at the reflection of the unmade bed. For everywhere—in the handkerchiefs strewn about, the brass ashtrays, the cluttered desk moved down from the *garçonnière*—everywhere she felt the presence of Marcel. And for a protracted moment she looked at a black silk tie that lay on the floor, then gathered it up, and catching a breath of the masculine cologne that permeated the cloth, she felt the chills rise on her neck. What would it be like to live in this little house, to see through these windows the sky and the trees? To hear the sounds of the block on which she'd grown up, to be at home with these frock coats bulging from the armoire door, this particular white washbasin, pitcher, marble stand? But a numbness overcame her when there might have been a longing, and she pondered that Michie

Vince had never left his imprint on her own house. He had come and gone repeatedly without a trace. No matter, her thoughts now had nothing to do with him, and she felt powerless to move, powerless even to raise her eyes when she heard a step at the front door.

A moment later, Marcel was standing on the threshold of the room. And again she felt that chill on her neck. She didn't rise to greet him, she said nothing, she merely watched him come near.

His arms were full of bundles, one hand clasping a bottle of wine, and he had a large Daguerrotype in its pressed paper case which he laid on the dresser in front of her. Her head was bowed. "It isn't often that I find a beautiful woman in my boudoir," he whispered. "And what of 'Michie Vince,' Madame, how is it he let you slip away?"

She didn't answer for a moment. She was deep in thought. It was almost as if his words didn't make any particular difference. And chilled again, she rubbed the backs of her arms. She saw him very distinctly as she raised her eyes.

"There isn't any more Michie Vince," she whispered. "Had you come an hour after, you would have known." But this was not a recrimination, it was merely a fact.

She studied him, thinking how his face had changed. How the roundness of the cherub was quite entirely gone, he was a tall, lean young man, and in some particular way his expression was softer for all its sobriety, its reflectiveness, as if suffering could soften, not just twist and destroy.

"But you love that man, don't you?" he whispered, the lips barely moving, the flesh as smooth as wax. And the eyes alone radiated feeling, brilliant as blue eyes so often are, brilliant as two lights.

"I've never in my life stopped loving anyone once I started," she answered. She lowered her lids and raised them again slowly, oddly aware of their effect. "I don't guess I ever will stop loving...once I've started...whether it was yesterday or a long time ago." And she felt keenly the house around her, the unmade bed with its velvet curtains, the peculiar stillness of noon, the secluded and sunny little room. It seemed he had stepped closer to her, that his shadow fell over her face. She felt such an overwhelming desire to touch his hand then that she shut her eyes as she rose and feeling him enfold her, she listened to the beat of his heart. It was suddenly just as it had been so long ago in Christophe's house when the Englishman lay dead, and just as it had been after they had taken Lisette away, that they were alive and in one another's arms, and though some sorrow threatened them, surrounded them, they were touching each other, and the hunger, the waiting so terrible for so long, made it less pleasure than pain.

An hour later, it was Marcel who, throwing back the cover gently, rose first.

He put on his clothes quickly and then bending over her as she lay still in a torpor, whispered, "Come into the parlor, there is something I must say to you, and it can't wait."

For a long time she didn't move. She lay staring at the tester, that same quietness which had been in her all day, all the days since Michie Vince had left, in fact, that wordless wondering, holding her there. Then she dressed without the slightest indication of anxiety and for want of anything else drew Marie's silver-handled brush through her hair.

He was standing by the fire, having built it up and he had put the Daguerrotype on the mantel, and had set out the food he had brought home with him, and the wine. The glasses had been filled, and he himself was dressed again even to his silk tie. A ruthless and irrelevant thought came to her as she seated herself and lifted the glass. Had it been a pleasure to him, with the women he had known, that beautiful Juliet Mercier? For her it had been a surrender of the body and the heart. She had devoured him utterly, his honey-brown skin, his clumsy passion, his feline grace, and it had cast into dim light forever those many nights with Michie Vince when, so eager to please, she had never once thought of herself. It wasn't her custom to drink wine in the day, in fact, it wasn't her custom to drink it at all, but she drank this wine now.

Marcel was staring at her with that remarkably intense expression that so often came over him, and she thought, either he is going to kill me or say that he loves me. She filled the empty glass again.

"I'm going to say something to you right now," he began. "I am going to ask you a certain question. And I'm afraid that you won't believe how much I want you to say yes. You'll only remember the way I let you go before, you'll think of the boy I was then and not the one who loves you now. Loves you and wants you." He stopped. "The fact that I've got nothing to offer you, nothing but faith in myself and some indistinct future which has never done anything but disappoint me, well, that makes it harder, because I am keenly aware that you just may be better off by yourself."

"Don't ask it," she said.

He was stunned. His eyebrows came together, the blue eyes firing slowly as the mouth went slack.

"Because," she said looking up at him, "the answer is no."

The pain in his face was more than she could bear. It was as if she'd slapped him, hard, and he was nothing but a child and he stared at her, uncomprehending, wounded to the soul.

"Well," he whispered, "no one can blame you for that." But he was brutally hurt, and his posture, his expression, everything about him belied the resignation in his voice. "I suppose I deserve it."

She watched him retreat to the mantel. His back was to her and he put his foot on the brass fender, and she could see the flicker of the fire on the edges of his yellow hair. He didn't know that she was trembling, he couldn't see it, he couldn't see the breaking of that numbness which had gripped her since Michie Vince had left.

"What you don't deserve," she said, "is to reach out blindly right now and take that millstone you once told me about and put it around your neck. What you don't deserve is a wife and a child to worry about—a passel of screaming children, matter of fact—and a stack of bills three times the size of that one over there, and problems you can't even imagine becoming so regular that they're like supper on the table every night and the wrinkles in your brow. That's what you don't deserve, and that's what you're asking for, along with the love and the comfort you need right now."

He didn't answer her.

"Don't think it wouldn't be easy to say yes to you, don't think I haven't been thinking of it night and day for six months. God, I can remember times when if you had only said those words to me...but best not to think of that now, best not to think about how if we were married I could help you, I could give you what income I've got and..."

"Never!" he whispered. He turned to her, the smooth face convulsed with rage.

"Shush, I know all about pride," she shook her head. "Just because I don't have much of it doesn't mean I don't know about it, I've lived around it all my life. And I'm not talking about your intentions, or your honor, I'm talking about what would be so easy for me to do! But the fact is, I don't want to talk about that either, I don't want to talk about me at all, I want to talk about you. You've got to make something of yourself, by yourself, and while you're still young and still free. You take this step now and you'll despise me in the years to come. I'll be all mixed up with your broken dreams and the terrible things that happened to you and your sister at this time. You'll wonder, as the years pass, how come you ever got entangled with me, with the children we'll have, with us! No. I won't have it happen. Not for your sake, and frankly not for mine. And you know why? Because I love you, and I know if you don't use the talent God gave you, if you don't do something with that talent then I'll never have you. But when you have done that, well, then, I'll be here."

"Talent? What talent?" he whispered softly, incredulously. But he was not asking her. He wondered did she know the deep wound that she touched. Talent! There had never been any talent, any talent to draw or paint or to make music or to write or to make any of the wonderful and beautiful things he'd loved. There was only the keen eye to appreciate it, the heartbreaking capacity to perceive talent in others all around. No, she couldn't know because he'd never told her, never told anyone, not even Christophe. And only a gentleman's prerogatives, only a gentleman's means could have kept him close to the talents of others, kept him close to all that was fine and enduring and filled life with daily grace. What do you pay your assistants, he had asked that irascible old Picard, the Daguerreotypist, the answer had been a dollar a day, and his mind worked with the precision of a clock measuring that against the common expenses of ordinary life, not the luxuries but the commodities, coal, food, clothing, and then the cost of a seat at the opera, the philharmonic, an afternoon of Shakespeare, the cost of books. The cost of some small statue or engraving glimpsed day after day in a shopwindow until it became a beacon in a dreary regimen and was then suddenly snatched from view by those who could afford to purchase it, to have it forever. He turned away from her. He couldn't answer her. He couldn't even shake his head.

"Do you remember," she asked quietly, "what you said to me the night that Jean Jacques died?"

"God knows and you know," he whispered, "but I do not."

"Well, I'll tell you what you said. You said, 'Anna Bella, if I hadn't been born rich I could have learned the cabinet-maker's trade from that man and been happy making fine things till the end of my days.'"

It was a torture to him to hear this, it was a torture to remember the fervor and waste of that time. "Well, *ma chère*," he said softly, "Jean Jacques is dead, and I never learned the cabinetmaker's trade."

"But don't you understand, Marcel," she went on, "you had an eye to see the greatness in that old man, when others just saw a workman on his knees. You had an eye to see the difference between an ordinary task and something beautiful, something fine."

"An eye to see, yes!" he whispered. "I've always seen!" The proper little gentleman on that stool in Jean Jacques' shop, the young man who had hovered over the country painters in Tante Josette's house watching the colors form the life on the canvas, the young man who had pestered the Daguerreotypists relentlessly, arguing the time of the exposure, the importance of the preparations, the optimum light. Hadn't he argued with Picard this very day, and hadn't he seen as soon as the picture was in his hands that Picard had not...

She was watching him. She saw the subtle change in his posture, saw him turn slowly, saw the change in his face. It was struggle she witnessed, struggle and a slow, violent awakening which he appeared bitterly, obdurately to resist.

"Remember the first night you came to me at my house," she went on gently, not sure of her timing now, the expression on his face so fierce. "The first time, when you knew Lisette was your sister and all, and we sat talking about Michie Vince. I told you Michie Vince reminded me of my Daddy, remember that, I told you how those two men were alike. They were men who worked, they loved their work, it took everything out of them, and there was one of them a fine gentleman with twenty thousand arpents of sugar cane, and the other a country barber in a dirt-road town..."

He was not looking at her. She wasn't sure that he had heard. He was battling something deep in himself, the pupils of his eyes moving back and forth, his mouth frozen on the verge of speech. *As a matter of fact, you wouldn't know anyone who wanted such an opportunity, would you? Oh, not you, of course, I can see you're well fixed.* His eyes clouded suddenly, misted over, and it was almost with an anguished expression that he shook his head. What had stopped him then, what, Anna Bella was talking to him and he couldn't hear. Why had he stiffened when Picard had asked him, why had he felt the stamina drain from his body while his hand clutched the back of that carved chair? He turned to the picture on the mantel, the perfect little gentleman staring back at him, against that flowered paper, that velvet drape. It was pride that had stopped him, pride as he stood on that ornate little stage.

Pride bred into him by that bleary-eyed drunken planter who had ended his life under this very roof turning over one shiny playing card after another, and a mother who said to him all his life you must leave here to be a man, you must leave here, because she herself had loathed every man of color on whom she had ever set eyes. A groan escaped his lips. *Endless procession of women who want to look ten years younger, children who will not sit still*, and the stench of the chemicals twelve hours a day, the heat, the dampness, the haggling over prices, his head literally swam.

"And what you loved about that old man," Anna Bella ventured softly, "was that he got his hands dirty with what he loved, he got down in the dirt with his chisels, his hammer and his nails..."

He put his hands to the side of his head. He stared still at the little picture, could see all the flaws in it, the fading at the edges, the face that had not been turned properly to the light. "But it could be more than that," he whispered. "Much, much more!" Good Lord, what awaited him if he did *not* take this step, some abyss of meaningless labor separating him inevitably from all that made life bearable, when this, this, the making of these pictures had always been what he loved, loved it as much as he loved to draw, to read, to walk about Christophe's yard at twilight listening to Bubbles's haunting and exquisite songs. His mind was on fire suddenly, all the mundane details which a moment ago had struck him as mean and debilitating were yielded up to him slowly in a new light. Work for Picard, he didn't have to work for Picard, sell the cottage, no, he didn't have to sell the cottage, the title to his property was his collateral, and there was money in his clip, that small fortune right here in his hands.

But fear gripped him, slowly, overtaking him it seemed even as he stood there on the verge of this decision, his hand out for that little picture which in a shift of the sun had become a mirror so that he wanted to set it right. It was that same fear which had overcome him in Picard's studio, and it was working its way again stealthily to his heart. He reached for his winter cape, he stared numbly at Anna Bella, he bent to kiss her warmly on the cheek. And he did not know that her heart was breaking for him as she watched him, so mournful was his expression; or that after he left her, the door shutting behind him as he stepped into the sun, she put her head down to cry against her folded arms.

*　*　*

All the long afternoon he walked. Through the rain and
the sun, and the rain and sun together, and the occasional
thunder rumbling over the low wet roofs and the golden windows, round and back and through all the familiar and favorite streets he walked. He passed the studios of the Daguerreotypists with their oval specimens shining silver in
the dormers, and discovering Duval in the Rue Chartres stood
for an hour before his small display, entranced with the perfection of a family portrait, each face molded magnificently
by the light, figures exquisitely grouped even to the turn of
each head. But he did not go up the stairs. And passing the
hock shops with their old cameras, battered flotsam and jet-
sam of others' dreams which he had often handled in the
past, he did not open the doors. And his feet even carried him
across the Rue Canal into the American city to view the plate
glass show windows of the dealers in chemicals, cases, and
plates for the Daguerreotype, but again, he did not turn the
knob, he did not go in. And at twilight, though he stood for
some quarter of an hour in his beloved waterfront street
watching Christophe at billiards under the warm lamps of
Madame Lelaud's, he did not approach the open door.

It was midnight as he roamed the Place d'Armes, early morning when he prowled the deserted market, and dawn at last
when he stood over the river where he could glance back at the
twin towers of the Cathedral shining wet under the lightening
sky or out over the immense swell of brown water which ran on
to the darkness as though it were the open sea. He was not tired.
He was no longer restless, rather his mind had that razor clarity
with which he could best perceive. The masts of the ships made
a forest under the fading stars, the glitter of a drifting steamboat played like candles on the faceted current, while on the
wind there came in snatches the last melancholy and discordant music of a late night Negro band.

The fear was melting in him. Melting gradually as he
weighed all about him, saw the world in which he lived, not
the world he would some day escape, but the world to which
he'd been born. And the desperation of his early years was
mellowing into something somber and no longer important
as he considered the choice at hand.

He knew the camera, knew the alchemy of vision, patience
and precision it had always required. And though the years
stretched before him in a heavy sentence of trial and error,
he knew without doubt that he could use it well! He would

risk all for it, and it would yield to him a treasure of those stunning and complex icons he had always cherished, just as the wood under Jean Jacques' chisel had yielded to him again and again the perfect line.

And the small universe around him was his to capture, his to fix and frame at the perfect instant in light and shadow exactly as he perceived: the shabby grandeur of the old city, faces of all nations, ragged trees, the ever-drifting clouds—this time and this place as it had shaped his childhood and the man he had become—from the melancholy spectacle of the barefoot *vendeuse* who passed him now on her way to market, to the majesty of the mourners on the Feast of All Saints.

Time stopped in one sterling moment after another, time defeated in the little miracle of the Daguerreotype, time that was the destroyer of young men's dreams.

He turned his back to the river. He felt the vibrant hum of the awakening port. The streets were silver in the morning damp, and a lone *marchande* in the Place d'Armes with her steaming cakes wound her way towards him, saluting him in a high-pitched song. The decision had been made, really; it had been lifted from him some time long before this moment, and he knew now what he must do.

But as he commenced the long walk uptown, toward the bankers and the shopkeepers and the landlords and the dust and the ink and the tinkle of brass, an even greater perception was breaking from the shell of his soul. A future lay before him, a future beyond the rosy image of the planter's son roaming the capitals of Europe forever outside the things he loved. For this was something he himself could really do, something he himself could really be! And whatever happened, be it failure or the art in which he had always believed, no one could take it away from him, no one could nullify it, no one could ever wake him rudely to say it had all been a dream.

He felt close to Jean Jacques. He felt the fragrances of that small shop. He felt near to Christophe at the lectern, or bent over the lamplit desk the pen in hand.

And as his steps quickened, as the sun leaked down over the gabled roofs and through the rusted gates, he gazed in wonder at the streets about him, at the same old splendor and ruin he had known all his life, and for the first time, he felt, perhaps the world in all its unspeakable beauty could really belong to him.

AFTERWORD

The Feast of All Saints *is a work of fiction, but certain real people are mentioned in the book, among them the quadroon fencing master, Basile Crockere; the mulatto Daguerreotypist, Jules Lion; the colored inventor, Norbert Rillieux; and the Metoyer Family of the Cane River, including "Grandpère Augustin" who built the church of St. Augustine which exists on Isle Brevelle today. The "African house" described in the novel stands on the* Melrose *Plantation which was called Yucca at the time this story takes place.*

L'Album Littéraire, *the quarterly of prose and poetry by men of color, probably commenced publication in 1843, not 1842 as the novel suggests.*

But aside from a few liberties with dates, every effort has been made to render the world of New Orleans' Free People of Color accurately. And the occupations of real men and women of color provided the inspiration for the purely fictional characters in the book.

Therefore, I am deeply indebted to many who have written about New Orleans and the Free People of Color in the antebellum South, from the popular writers who have kept alive the romance and richness of those days to the scholars whose books, articles, theses and dissertations continue to swell the growing body of work on the free Afro-American before the Civil War.

But above all, I am indebted to the gens de couleur *themselves who left us painting, sculpture, music and literature— to Armand Lanusse, poet, editor and teacher, for his work with* L'Album Littéraire *and the later anthology,* Les Cenelles; *and to R. L. Desdunes, whose unique and priceless* Our People and Our History *remains the cornerstone of research in this field.*

ANNE RICE